Randall Garrett, Science Fiction Collect

In this book:
The Destroyers
Despoilers of the Golden Empire
The Eyes Have It
A Spaceship Named McGuire
Time Fuze
...After a Few Words...
But, I Don't Think
The Bramble Bush
With No Strings Attached
Nor Iron Bars a Cage....
In Case of Fire
A World by the Tale
The Man Who Hated Mars
Anything You Can Do
Anchorite
The Highest Treason
The Measure of a Man
The Foreign Hand Tie
Fifty Per Cent Prophet
...Or Your Money Back
Thin Edge
Damned If You Don't
Instant of Decision
Cum Grano Salis
Psichopath
The Unnecessary Man
Hail to the Chief
Unwise Child
Hanging by a Thread
The Asses of Balaam
What The Left Hand Was Doing
By Proxy
Belly Laugh
Heist Job on Thizar
Dead Giveaway
Suite Mentale
That Sweet Little Old Lady
Viewpoint
The Penal Cluster

Randall Garrett (1927 – 1987) was an American science fiction and fantasy author. He was a prolific contributor to Astounding and other science fiction magazines of the 1950s and 1960s. He instructed Robert Silverberg in the techniques of selling large quantities of action-adventure science fiction, and collaborated with him on two novels about Earth bringing civilization to an alien planet.

In this book:

The Destroyers	Pag. 3
Despoilers of the Golden Empire	Pag. 15
The Eyes Have It	Pag. 36
A Spaceship Named McGuire	Pag. 55
Time Fuze	Pag. 75
...After a Few Words	Pag. 77
But, I Don't Think	Pag. 81
The Bramble Bush	Pag. 96
With No Strings Attached	Pag. 105
Nor Iron Bars a Cage	Pag. 113
In Case of Fire	Pag. 133
A World by the Tale	Pag. 137
The Man Who Hated Mars	Pag. 147
Anything You Can Do	Pag. 154
Anchorite	Pag. 188
The Highest Treason	Pag. 209
The Measure of a Man	Pag. 236
The Foreign Hand Tie	Pag. 241
Fifty Per Cent Prophet	Pag. 257
...Or Your Money Back	Pag. 267
Thin Edge	Pag. 278
Damned If You Don't	Pag. 290
Instant of Decision	Pag. 310
Cum Grano Salis	Pag. 321
Psichopath	Pag. 333
The Unnecessary Man	Pag. 345
Hail to the Chief	Pag. 355
Unwise Child	Pag. 371
Hanging by a Thread	Pag. 435
The Asses of Balaam	Pag. 447
What The Left Hand Was Doing	Pag. 458
By Proxy	Pag. 470
Belly Laugh	Pag. 487
Heist Job on Thizar	Pag. 489
Dead Giveaway	Pag. 495
Suite Mentale	Pag. 507
That Sweet Little Old Lady	Pag. 514
Viewpoint	Pag. 571
The Penal Cluster	Pag. 566

The Destroyers

Any war is made up of a horde of personal tragedies—but the greater picture is the tragedy of the death of a way of life. For a way of life—good, bad, or indifferent—exists because it is dearly loved....

Anketam stretched his arms out as though he were trying to embrace the whole world. He pushed himself up on his tiptoes, arched his back, and gave out with a prodigious yawn that somehow managed to express all the contentment and pleasure that filled his soul. He felt a faint twinge in his shoulders, and there was a dull ache in the small of his back, both of which reminded him that he was no longer the man he had been twenty years before, but he ignored them and stretched again.

He was still strong, Anketam thought; still strong enough to do his day's work for The Chief without being too tired to relax and enjoy himself afterwards. At forty-five, he had a good fifteen years more before he'd be retired to minor make-work jobs, doing the small chores as a sort of token in justification of his keep in his old age.

He settled his heels back to the ground and looked around at the fields of green shoots that surrounded him. That part of the job was done, at least. The sun's lower edge was just barely touching the western horizon, and all the seedlings were in. Anketam had kept his crew sweating to get them all in, but now the greenhouses were all empty and ready for seeding in the next crop while this one grew to maturity. But that could wait. By working just a little harder, for just a little longer each day, he and his crew had managed to get the transplanting done a good four days ahead of schedule, which meant four days of fishing or hunting or just plain loafing. The Chief didn't care how a man spent his time, so long as the work was done.

He thumbed his broad-brimmed hat back from his forehead and looked up at the sky. There were a few thin clouds overhead, but there was no threat of rain, which was good. In this part of Xedii, the spring rains sometimes hit hard and washed out the transplanted seedlings before they had a chance to take root properly. If rain would hold off for another ten days, Anketam thought, then it could fall all it wanted. Meanwhile, the irrigation reservoir was full to brimming, and that would supply all the water the young shoots needed to keep them from being burnt by the sun.

He lowered his eyes again, this time to look at the next section over toward the south, where Jacovik and his crew were still working. He could see their bent figures outlined against the horizon, just at the brow of the slope, and he grinned to himself. He had beaten Jacovik out again.

Anketam and Jacovik had had a friendly feud going for years, each trying to do a better, faster job than the other. None of the other supervisors on The Chief's land came even close to beating out Anketam or Jacovik, so it was always between the two of them, which one came out on top. Sometimes it was one, sometimes the other.

At the last harvest, Jacovik had been very pleased with himself when the tallies showed that he'd beaten out Anketam by a hundred kilos of cut leaves. But The Chief had taken him down a good bit when the report came through that Anketam's leaves had made more money because they were better quality.

He looked all around the horizon. From here, only Jacovik's section could be seen, and only Jacovik's men could be seen moving.

When Anketam's gaze touched the northern horizon, his gray eyes narrowed a little. There was a darkness there, a faint indication of cloud build-up. He hoped it didn't mean rain. Getting the transplants in early was all right, but it didn't count for anything if they were washed out.

He pushed the thought out of his mind. Rain or no rain, there was nothing could be done about it except put up shelters over the rows of plants. He'd just have to keep an eye on the northern horizon and hope for the best. He didn't want to put up the shelters unless he absolutely had to, because the seedlings were invariably bruised in the process and that would cut the leaf yield way down. He remembered one year when Jacovik had gotten panicky and put up his shelters, and the storm had been a gentle thing that only lasted a few minutes before it blew over. Anketam had held off, ready to make his men work in the rain if necessary, and when the harvest had come, he'd beaten Jacovik hands down.

Anketam pulled his hat down again and turned to walk toward his house in the little village that he and his crew called home. He had warned his wife to have supper ready early. "I figure on being finished by sundown," he'd said. "You can tell the other women I said so. But don't say anything to them till after we've gone to the fields. I don't want those boys thinking about the fishing they're going to do tomorrow and then get behind in their work because they're daydreaming."

The other men were already gone; they'd headed back to the village as fast as they could move as soon as he'd told them the job was finished. Only he had stayed to look at the fields and see them all finished, each shoot casting long shadows in the ruddy light of the setting sun. He'd wanted to stand there, all by himself feeling the glow of pride and satisfaction that came over him, knowing that he was better than any other supervisor on The Chief's vast acreage.

His own shadow grew long ahead of him as he walked back, his steps still brisk and springy, in spite of the day's hard work.

The sun had set and twilight had come by the time he reached his own home. He had glanced again toward the north, and had been relieved to see that the stars were visible near the horizon. The clouds couldn't be very thick.

Overhead, the great, glowing cloud of the Dragon Nebula shed its soft light. That's what made it possible to work after sundown in the spring; at that time of year, the Dragon Nebula was at its brightest during the early part of the evening. The tail of it didn't vanish beneath the horizon until well after midnight. In the autumn, it wasn't visible at all, and the nights were dark except for the stars.

Anketam pushed open the door of his home and noted with satisfaction that the warm smells of cooking filled the air, laving his nostrils and palate with fine promises. He stopped and frowned as he heard a man's voice speaking in low tones in the kitchen.

Then Memi's voice called out: "Is that you, Ank?"

"Yeah," he said, walking toward the kitchen. "It's me."

"We've got company," she said. "Guess who."

"I don't claim to be much good at guessing," said Anketam. "I'll have to peek."

He stopped at the door of the kitchen and grinned widely when he saw who the man was. "Russat! Well, by heaven, it's good to see you!"

There was a moment's hesitation, then a minute or two of handshaking and backslapping as the two brothers both tried to speak at the same time. Anketam heard himself repeating: "Yessir! By *heaven*, it's good to see you! Real good!"

And Russat was saying: "Same here, Ank! And, gee, you're looking great. I mean, real great! Tough as ever, eh, Ank?"

"Yeah, sure, tough as ever. Sit down, boy. Memi! Pour us something hot and get that bottle out of the cupboard!"

Anketam pushed his brother back towards the chair and made him sit down, but Russat was protesting: "Now, wait a minute! Now, just you hold on, Ank! Don't be getting out your bottle just yet. I brought some *real* stuff! I mean, *expensive*—stuff you can't get very easy. I brought it just for you, and you're going to have some of it before you say another word. Show him, Memi."

Memi was standing there, beaming, holding the bottle. Her blue eyes had faded slowly in the years since she and Anketam had married, but there was a sparkle in them now. Anketam looked at the bottle.

"Bedamned," he said softly. The bottle was beautiful just as it was. It was a work of art in itself, with designs cut all through it and pretty tracings of what looked like gold thread laced in and out of the surface. And it was full to the neck with a clear, red-brown liquid. Anketam thought of the bottle in his own cupboard—plain, translucent plastic, filled with the water-white liquor rationed out from the commissary—and he suddenly felt very backwards and countryish. He scratched thoughtfully at his beard and said: "Well, Well. I don't know, Russ—I don't know. You think a plain farmer like me can take anything that fancy?"

Russat laughed, a little embarrassed. "Sure you can. You mean to say you've never had brandy before? Why, down in Algia, our Chief—" He stopped.

Anketam didn't look at him. "Sure, Russ; sure. I'll bet Chief Samas gives a drink to his secretary, too, now and then." He turned around and winked. "But this stuff is for brain work, not farming."

He knew Russat was embarrassed. The boy was nearly ten years younger than Anketam, but Anketam knew that his younger brother had more brains and ability, as far as paper work went, than he, himself, would ever have. The boy (Anketam reminded himself that he shouldn't think of Russat as a boy—after all, he was thirty-six now) had worked as a special secretary for one of the important chiefs in Algia for five years now. Anketam noticed, without criticism, that Russat had grown soft with the years. His skin was almost pink, bleached from years of indoor work, and looked pale and sickly, even beside Memi's sun-browned skin—and Memi hadn't been out in the sun as much as her husband had.

Anketam reached out and took the bottle carefully from his wife's hands. Her eyes watched him searchingly; she had been aware of the subtleties of the exchange between her rough, hard-working, farmer husband and his younger, brighter, better-educated brother.

Anketam said: "If this is a present, I guess I'd better open it." He peeled off the seal, then carefully removed the glass stopper and sniffed at the open mouth of the beautiful bottle. "Hm-m-m! Say!" Then he set the bottle down carefully on the table. "You're the guest, Russ, so you can pour. That tea ready yet, Memi?"

"Coming right up," said his wife gratefully. "Coming right up."

Anketam watched Russat carefully pour brandy into the cups of hot, spicy tea that Memi set before them. Then he looked up, grinned at his wife, and said: "Pour yourself a cup, honey. This is an occasion. A big occasion."

She nodded quickly, very pleased, and went over to get another cup.

"What brings you up here, Russ?" Anketam asked. "I hope you didn't just decide to pick up a bottle of your Chief's brandy and then take off." He chuckled after he said it, but he was more serious than he let on. He actually worried about Russat at times. The boy might just take it in his head to do something silly.

Russat laughed and shook his head. "No, no. I'm not crazy, and I'm not stupid—at least, I think not. No; I got to go up to Chromdin. My Chief is sending word that he's ready to supply goods for the war."

Anketam frowned. He'd heard that there might be war, of course. There had been all kinds of rumors about how some of the Chiefs were all for fighting, but Anketam didn't pay much attention to these rumors. In the first place, he knew that it was none of his business; in the second place, he didn't think there would be any war. Why should anyone pick on Xedii?

What war would mean if it did come, Anketam had no idea, but he didn't think the Chiefs would get into a war they couldn't finish. And, he repeated to himself, he didn't believe there would be a war.

He said as much to Russat.

His brother looked up at him in surprise. "You mean you haven't heard?"

"Heard what?"

"Why, the war's already started. Sure. Five, six days ago. We're at war, Ank."

Anketam's frown grew deeper. He knew that there were other planets besides Xedii; he had heard that some of the stars in the sky were planets and suns. He didn't really understand how that could be, but even The Chief had said it was true, so Anketam accepted it as he did the truth about God. It was so, and that was enough for Anketam. Why should he bother himself with other people's business?

But—*war*?

Why?

"How'd it happen?" he asked.

Russat sipped at his hot drink before answering. Behind him, Memi moved slowly around the cooker, pretending to be finishing the meal, pretending not to be listening.

"Well, I don't have all the information," Russat said, pinching his little short beard between thumb and forefinger. "But I do know that the Chiefs didn't want the embassy in Chromdin."

"No," said Anketam. "I suppose not."

"I understand they have been making all kinds of threats," Russat said. "Trying to tell everybody what to do. They think they run all of Creation, I guess. Anyway, they were told to pull out right after the last harvest. They refused to do it, and for a while nobody did anything. Then, last week, the President ordered the Army to throw 'em out—bag and baggage. There was some fighting, I understand, but they got out finally. Now they've said they're going to smash us." He grinned.

Anketam said: "What's so funny?"

"Oh, they won't do anything," said Russat. "They fume and fuss a lot, but they won't do anything."

"I hope not," said Anketam. He finished the last of his spiked tea, and Memi poured him another one. "I don't see how they have any right to tell us how to live or how to run our own homes. They ought to mind their own business and leave us alone."

"You two finish those drinks," said Memi, "and quit talking about wars. The food will be ready pretty quickly."

"Good," said Anketam. "I'm starved." And, he admitted to himself, the brandy and hot tea had gone to his head. A good meal would make him feel better.

Russat said: "I don't get much of a chance to eat Memi's cooking; I'll sure like this meal."

"You can stay for breakfast in the morning, can't you?" Anketam asked.

"Oh, I wouldn't want to put you to all that trouble. I have to be up to your Chief's house before sunrise."

"We get up before sunrise," Anketam said flatly. "You can stay for breakfast."

II

The spring planting did well. The rains didn't come until after the seedlings had taken root and anchored themselves well into the soil, and the rows showed no signs of heavy bruising. Anketam had been watching one section in particular, where young Basom had planted. Basom had a tendency to do a sloppy job, and if it had showed up as bruised or poorly planted seedlings, Anketam would have seen to it that Basom got what was coming to him.

But the section looked as good as anyone else's, so Anketam said nothing to Basom.

Russat had come back after twenty days and reported that there was an awful lot of fuss in Chromdin, but nothing was really developing. Then he had gone on back home.

As spring became summer, Anketam pushed the war out of his mind. Evidently, there wasn't going to be any real shooting. Except that two of The Chief's sons had gone off to join the Army, things remained the same as always. Life went on as it had.

The summer was hot and almost windless. Work became all but impossible, except during the early morning and late afternoon. Fortunately, there wasn't much that had to be done. At this stage of their growth, the plants pretty much took care of themselves.

Anketam spent most of his time fishing. He and Jacovik and some of the others would go down to the river and sit under the shade trees, out of the sun, and dangle their lines in the water. It really didn't matter if they caught much or not; the purpose of fishing was to loaf and get away from the heat, not to catch fish. Even so, they always managed to bring home enough for a good meal at the end of the day.

The day that the war intruded on Anketam's consciousness again had started off just like any other day. Anketam got his fishing gear together, including a lunch that Memi had packed for him, and gone over to pick up Blejjo.

Blejjo was the oldest man in the village. Some said he was over a hundred, but Blejjo himself only admitted to eighty. He'd been retired a long time back, and his only duties now were little odd jobs that were easy enough, even for an old man. Not that there was anything feeble about old Blejjo; he still looked and acted spry enough.

He was sitting on his front porch, talking to young Basom, when Anketam came up.

The old man grinned. "Hello, Ank. You figure on getting a few more fish today?"

"Why not? The river's full of 'em. Come along."

"Don't see why not," said Blejjo. "What do you think, Basom?"

The younger man smiled and shook his head. "I'll stay around home, I think. I'm too lazy today to go to all that effort."

"Too lazy to loaf," said Blejjo, laughing. "That's as lazy as I ever heard."

Anketam smiled, but he didn't say anything. Basom *was* lazy, but Anketam never mentioned it unless the boy didn't get his work done. Leave that sort of kidding up to the others; it wasn't good for a supervisor to ride his men unless it was necessary for discipline.

Basom was a powerful young man, tall and well-proportioned. If the truth were known, he probably had the ability to get a good job from The Chief—become a secretary or something, like Russat. But he was sloppy in his work, and, as Blejjo had said, lazy. His saving grace was the fact that he took things as they came; he never showed any resentment towards Anketam if he was rebuked for not doing his work well, and he honestly tried to do better—for a while, at least.

"Not too lazy to loaf," Basom said in self-defense. "Just too lazy to walk four miles to loaf when I can do it here."

Old Blejjo was taking his fishing gear down from the rack on the porch. Without looking around, he said: "Cooler down by the river."

"By the time I walked there," said Basom philosophically, "walking through all that sun, I'd be so hot it would take me two hours to cool down to where I am now, and another two hours to cool down any more. That's four hours wasted. Now—" He looked at Anketam with a sly grin. "Now, if you two wanted to carry me, I'd be much obliged. Anketam, you could carry me piggyback, while Blejjo goes over to fetch my pole. If you'd do that, I believe I could see my way clear to going fishing with you."

Anketam shook his head positively. "I'm afraid the sun would do you in, anyway."

"Maybe you'd like The Chief to carry you," said Blejjo. There was a bite in his voice.

"Now, wait," Basom said apprehensively, "I didn't say anything like that. I didn't mean it that way."

Blejjo pointed his fishing pole at the youth. "You ought to be thankful you've got Anketam for a supervisor. There's some supers who'd boot you good for a crack like that."

Basom cast appealing eyes at Anketam. "I *am* thankful! You know I am! Why, you're the best super in the barony! Everybody knows that. I was only kidding. You know that."

Before Anketam could say anything, the old man said: "You can bet your life that no other super in this barony would put up with your laziness!"

"Now, Blejjo," said Anketam, "leave the boy alone. He meant no harm. If he needs talking to, I'll do the talking."

Basom looked gratefully reprieved.

"Sorry, Ank," said Blejjo. "It's just that some of these young people have no respect for their elders." He looked at Basom and smiled. "Didn't mean to take it out on you, Bas. There's a lot worse than you." Then, changing his tone: "Sure you don't want to come with us?"

Basom looked apologetic, but he stuck to his guns. "No. Thanks again, but—" He grinned self-consciously. "To be honest, I was thinking of going over to see Zillia. Her dad said I could come."

Anketam grinned at the boy. "Well, now, that's an excuse I'll accept. Come on, Blejjo, this is not a sport for old men like us. Fishing is more our speed."

Chuckling, Blejjo shouldered his fishing pole, and the two men started down the dusty village street toward the road that led to the river.

They walked in silence for a while, trying to ignore the glaring sun that brought the sweat out on their skins, soaking the sweatbands of their broad-brimmed hats and running in little rivulets down their bodies.

"I kind of feel sorry for that boy," old Blejjo said at last.

"Oh?" said Anketam. "How so? He'll get along. He's improving. Why, he did as good a job of transplanting as any man this spring. Last year, he bruised the seedlings, but I gave him a good dressing down and he remembered it. He'll be all right."

"I'm not talking about that, Ank," said the old man, "I mean him and Zillia. He's really got a case on with that girl."

"Anything wrong with that? A young fellow's got a right to fall in love, hasn't he? And Zillia seems pretty keen on him, too. If her father doesn't object, everything ought to go along pretty smoothly."

"Her father might not object," said Blejjo, looking down at his feet as they paced off the dusty road. "But there's others who might object."

"Who, for instance?"

Blejjo was silent for several steps. Then he said: "Well, Kevenoe, for one."

Anketam thought that over in silence. Kevenoe was on The Chief's staff at the castle. Like many staff men—including, Anketam thought wryly, his own brother Russat, on occasion—he tended to lord it over the farmers who worked the land. "Kevenoe has an eye on Zillia?" he asked after a moment.

"I understand he's asked Chief Samas for her as soon as she's eighteen. That would be this fall, after harvest."

"I see," Anketam said thoughtfully. He didn't ask how the old man had come about his knowledge. Old Blejjo had little to do, and on the occasions that he had to do some work around The Chief's castle, he made it a point to pick up gossip. But he was careful with his information; he didn't go spreading it around for all to hear, and he made it a point to verify his information before he passed it on. Anketam respected the old man. He was the only one in the village who called him "Ank," outside of Memi.

"Do you think The Chief will give her to Kevenoe?" he asked.

Blejjo nodded. "Looks like it. He thinks a great deal of Kevenoe."

"No reason why he shouldn't," said Anketam. "Kevenoe's a good man."

"Oh, I know that," said the old man. "But Basom won't like it at all. And I don't think Zillia will, either."

"That's the way things happen," said Anketam. "A man can't expect to go through life having everything his own way. There's other girls around for Basom. If he can't have the prettiest, he'll have to be satisfied with someone else." He chuckled. "That's why I picked Memi. She's not beautiful and never was, but she's a wonderful wife."

"That's so," said Blejjo. "A wise man is one who only wants what he knows he can have. Right now"—he took off his hat and wiped his bald head—"all I want is a dip in that river."

"Swim first and then fish?"

"I think so, don't you? Basom was right about this hot sun."

"I'll go along with you," agreed Anketam.

They made their way to the river, to the shallow place at the bend where everyone swam. There were a dozen and more kids there, having a great time in the slow moving water, and several of the older people soaking themselves and keeping an eye on the kids to make sure they didn't wander out to where the water was deep and the current swift.

Anketam and Blejjo took off their clothes and cooled themselves in the water for a good half hour before they dressed again and went on upriver to a spot where Blejjo swore the fish were biting.

They were. In the next four hours, the two men had caught six fish apiece, and Blejjo was trying for his seventh. Here, near the river, there was a slight breeze, and it was fairly cool beneath the overhanging branches of the closely bunched trees.

Blejjo had spotted a big, red-and-yellow striped beauty loafing quietly in a back eddy, and he was lowering his hook gently to a point just in front of the fish when both men heard the voice calling.

"Anketam! Anketam! Blejjo! Where you at?"

Blejjo went on with his careful work, knowing that Anketam would take care of whatever it was.

Anketam recognized the voice. He stood up and called: "Over here, Basom! What's the trouble?"

A minute later, Basom came running through the trees, his feet crashing through the underbrush.

Blejjo sat up abruptly, an angry look on his face. "Basom, you scared my fish away."

"Fish, nothing," said Basom. "I ran all the way here to tell you!" He was grinning widely and panting for breath at the same time.

"You suddenly got an awful lot of energy," Blejjo said sourly.

"What happened?" Anketam asked.

"The invasion!" Basom said between breaths. "Kevenoe himself came down to tell us! They've started the invasion! The war's on!"

"Than what are you looking so happy about?" Anketam snapped.

"That's what I came to tell you." Basom's grin didn't fade in the least. "They landed up in the Frozen Country, where our missiles couldn't get 'em, according to Kevenoe. Then they started marching down on one of the big towns. Tens of thousands of 'em! And we whipped 'em! Our army cut 'em to pieces and sent 'em running back to their base! We won! We *won*!"

III

The battle had been won, but the war wasn't won yet. The invaders had managed to establish a good-sized base up in the Frozen Country. They'd sneaked their ships in and had put up a defensive system that stopped any high-speed missiles. Not that Xedii had many missiles. Xedii was an agricultural planet; most manufactured articles were imported. It had never occurred to the government of Xedii that there would be any real need for implements of war.

The invaders seemed to be limiting their use of weapons, too. They wanted to control the planet, not destroy it. Through the summer and into the autumn, Anketam listened to the news as it filtered down from the battlegrounds. There were skirmishes here and there, but nothing decisive. Xedii seemed to be holding her own against the invaders.

After the first news of the big victory, things settled back pretty much to normal.

The harvest was good that year, but after the leaves were shredded and dried, they went into storage warehouses. The invaders had set up a patrol system around Xedii which prevented the slow cargo ships from taking off or landing. A few adventurous space officers managed to get a ship out now and then, but those few flights could hardly be called regular trade shipments.

The cool of winter had come when Chief Samas did something he had never done before. He called all the men in the barony to assemble before the main gate of the castle enclosure. He had a speech to make.

For the first time, Anketam felt a touch of apprehension. He got his crew together, and they walked to the castle in silence, wondering what it was that The Chief had to say.

All the men of the barony, except those who couldn't be spared from their jobs, were assembled in front of Chief Samas' baronial castle.

The castle itself was not a single building. Inside the four-foot-high thorn hedge that surrounded the two-acre area, there were a dozen buildings of hard, iridescent plastic shining in the sun. They all looked soft and pleasant and comfortable. Even the thorn hedge, filled as it was by the lacy leaves that concealed the hard, sharp thorns, looked soft and inviting.

Anketam listened to the soft murmur of whispered conversation from the men around him. They stood quietly outside the main gate that led into the castle area, waiting for The Chief to appear, and wondering among themselves what it was that The Chief had to say.

"You think the invaders have won?"

Anketam recognized the hoarse whisper from the man behind him. He turned to face the dark, squat, hard-looking man who had spoken. "It couldn't be, Jacovik. It couldn't be."

The other supervisor looked down at his big, knuckle-scarred hands instead of looking at Anketam. He was not a handsome man, Jacovik; his great, beaklike nose was canted to one side from a break that had come in his teens; his left eye was squinted almost closed by the scar tissue that surrounded it, and the right only looked better by comparison. His eyebrows, his beard, and the fringe of hair that outlined his bald head made an incongruous pale yellow pattern against the sunburnt darkness of his face. In his youth, Jacovik had been almost pathologically devoted to boxing—even to the point of picking fights with others in his village for no reason at all, except to fight. Twice, he had been brought up before The Chief's court because of the severe beating he had given to men bigger than he, and he had finally killed a man with his fists.

Chief Samas had given him Special Punishment for that, and a final warning that the next fight would be punished by death.

Anketam didn't know whether it was that threat, or the emotional reaction Jacovik had suffered from killing a man, or simply that he had had some sense beaten into his head, but from that moment on Jacovik was a different man. He had changed from a thug into a determined, ambitious man. In twenty-two years, he had not used his fists except to discipline one of his crew, and that had only happened four times that Anketam knew of. Jacovik had shown that he had ability as well as strength, that he could control men by words as well as by force, and The Chief had made him a supervisor. He had proved himself worthy of the job; next to Anketam, he was the best supervisor in the barony.

Anketam had a great deal of respect for the little, wide-shouldered, barrel-chested man who stood there looking at the scars on the backs of his hands.

Jacovik turned his hands over and looked at the calloused palms. "How do we know? Maybe the Council of Chiefs has given up. Maybe they've authorized the President to surrender. After all, we're not fighters; we're farmers. The invaders outnumber us. They've got us cut off by a blockade, to keep us from sending out the harvest. They've got machines and weapons." He looked up suddenly, his bright blue eyes looking straight into Anketam's. "How do we know?"

Anketam's grin was hard. "Look, Jac; the invaders have said that they intend to smash our whole society, haven't they? Haven't they?"

Jacovik nodded.

"And they want to break up the baronies—take everything away from the Chiefs—force us farmers to give up the security we've worked all our lives for. That's what they've said, isn't it?"

Jacovik nodded again.

"Well, then," Anketam continued remorselessly, "do you think the Chiefs would give up easily? Are they going to simply smile and shake hands with the invaders and say: 'Go ahead, take all our property, reduce us to poverty, smash the whole civilization we've built up, destroy the security and peace of mind of millions of human beings, and then send your troops in to rule us by martial law.' Are they going to do that? Are they?"

Jacovik spread his big, hard hands. "I don't know. I'm not a Chief. I don't know how their minds work. Do you? Maybe they'll think surrender would be better than having all of Xedii destroyed inch by inch."

Anketam shook his head. "Never. The Chiefs will fight to the very end. And they'll win in the long run because right is on their side. The invaders have no right to change our way of living; they have no right to impose their way of doing things on us. No, Jac—the Chiefs will never give up. They haven't surrendered yet, and they never will. They'll win. The invaders will be destroyed."

Jacovik frowned, completely closing his left eye. "You've always been better at thinking things out that I, Ank." He paused and looked down at his hands again. "I hope you're right, Ank. I hope you're right."

In spite of his personal conviction that he was right, Anketam had to admit that Jacovik had reason for his own opinion. He knew that many of the farmers were uncertain about the ultimate outcome of the war.

Anketam looked around him at the several hundred men who made up the farming force of the barony. His own crew were standing nearby, mixing with Jacovik's crew and talking in low voices. In the cool winter air, Anketam could still detect the aroma of human bodies, the smell of sweat that always arose when a crowd of people were grouped closely together. And he thought he could detect a faint scent of fear and apprehension in that atmosphere.

Or was that just his imagination, brought on by Jacovik's pessimism?

He opened his lips to say something to Jacovik, but his words died unborn. The sudden silence in the throng around him, the abrupt cessation of whispering, told him, more definitely than a chorus of trumpets could have done, that The Chief had appeared.

He turned around quickly, to face the Main Gate again.

The Main Gate was no higher than the thorn-bush hedge that it pierced. It was a heavily built, intricately decorated piece of polished goldwood, four feet high and eight feet across, set in a sturdy goldwood frame. The arch above the gate reached a good ten feet, giving The Chief plenty of room to stand.

He was just climbing up to stand on the gate itself as Anketam turned.

Chief Samas was a tall man, lean of face and wide of brow. His smooth-shaven chin was long and angular, and his dark eyes were deeply imbedded beneath heavy, bushy eyebrows.

And he was dressed in clothing cut in a manner that Anketam had never seen before.

He stood there, tall and proud, a half smile on his face. It was several seconds before he spoke. During that time, there was no sound from the assembled farmers.

"Men," he said at last, "I think that none of you have seen this uniform before. I look odd in it, do I not?"

The men recognized The Chief's remark as a joke, and a ripple of laughter ran through the crowd.

The Chief's smile broadened. "Odd indeed. Yes. And do you perceive the golden emblems, here at my throat? They, and the uniform, indicate that I have been chosen to help lead the armed forces—a portion of them, I should say."

He smiled around at the men. "The Council of Chiefs has authorized the President to appoint me a Colonel of Light Tank. I am expected to lead our armored forces into battle against the damned Invaders."

A cheer came from the farmers, loud and long. Anketam found himself yelling as loud as anyone. The pronunciation and the idiom of the speech of the Chiefs was subtly different from those of the farmers, but Anketam could recognize the emphasis that his Chief was putting on the words of his speech. "Invaders." With a capital "I."

The Chief held up his hands, and the cheering died. At the same time, the face of Chief Samas lost its smile.

"I will be gone for some time," he said somberly. "The Council feels that it will be two or three years before we have finally driven the Invaders from our planet. This will not be a simple war, nor an easy one. The blockade of orbital ships which encircle Xedii keep us from making proper contact with any friends that we may have outside the circle of influence of the damned Invaders. We are, at the moment, fighting alone. And yet, in spite of that—in *spite* of that, I say—we have thus far held the enemy at a standstill. And, in the long run, we shall win."

He took a deep breath then, and his baritone voice thundered out when he spoke.

"*Shall* win? No! We *must* win! None of you want to become slaves in the factories of the Invaders. I know that, and you know it. Who among you would slave your life away in the sweatshops of the Invaders, knowing that those for whom you worked might, at any time, simply deprive you of your livelihood at their own whim, since they feel no sense of responsibility toward you as individuals?"

Again The Chief stopped, and his eyes sought out each man in turn.

"If there are any such among you, I renounce you at this moment. If there are any such, I ask ... nay, I plead ... I order ... I order you to go immediately to the Invaders."

Another deep breath. No one moved.

"You have all heard the propaganda of the Invaders. You know that they have offered you—well, what? Freedom? Yes, that's the way they term it. Freedom." Another pause. "Freedom. *Hah!*"

He put his hands on his hips. "None of you have ever seen a really regimented society—and I'm thankful that you haven't. I hope that you never will."

Chief Samas twisted his lips into an expression of hatred. "Freedom? Freedom from *what*! Freedom to *do* what?

"I'll tell you. Freedom to work in their factories for twelve hours a day! Freedom to work until you are no longer of any use to them, and then be turned out to die—with no home, and no food to support you. Freedom to live by yourselves, with every man's hand against you, with every pittance that you earn taxed to support a government that has no thought for the individual!

"Is that what you want? Is that what you've worked for all your lives?"

A visual chorus of shaken heads accompanied the verbal chorus of "No."

Chief Samas dropped his hands to his sides. "I thought not. But I will repeat: If any of you want to go to the Invaders, you may do so now."

Anketam noticed a faint movement to his right, but it stopped before it became decisive. He glanced over, and he noticed that young Basom was standing there, half poised, as though unable to make up his mind.

Then The Chief's voice bellowed out again. "Very well. You are with me. I will leave the work of the barony in your hands. I ask that you produce as much as you can. Next year—next spring—we will not plant *cataca*."

There was a low intake of breath from the assembled men. Not plant *cataca*? That was the crop that they had grown since—well, since *ever*. Anketam felt as though someone had jerked a rug from beneath him.

"There is a reason for this," The Chief went on. "Because of the blockade that surrounds Xedii, we are unable to export *cataca* leaves. The rest of the galaxy will have to do without the drug that is extracted from the leaves. The incidence of cancer will rise to the level it reached before the discovery of *cataca*. When they understand that we cannot ship out because of the Invader's blockade, they will force the Invader to stop his attack on us. What we need now is not *cataca*, but food. So, next spring, you will plant food crops.

"Save aside the *cataca* seed until the war is over. The seedlings now in the greenhouses will have to be destroyed, but that cannot be helped."

He stopped for a moment, and when he began again his voice took on a note of sadness.

"I will be away from you until the war is won. While I am gone, the barony will be run by my wife. You will obey her as you would me. The finances of the barony will be taken care of by my trusted man, Kevenoe." He gestured to one side, and Kevenoe, who was standing there, smiled quickly and then looked grim again.

"As for the actual running of the barony—as far as labor is concerned—I think I can leave that in the hands of one of my most capable men."

He raised his finger and pointed. There was a smile on his face.

Anketam felt as though he had been struck an actual blow; the finger was pointed directly at him.

"Anketam," said The Chief, "I'm leaving the barony in your hands until I return. You will supervise the labor of all the men here. Is that understood?"

"Yes, sir," said Anketam weakly. "Yes, sir. I understand."

IV

Never, for the rest of his life, would the sharp outlines of that moment fade from his memory. He knew that the men of the barony were all looking at him; he knew that The Chief went on talking afterwards. But those things impressed themselves but lightly on his mind, and they blurred soon afterwards. Twenty years later, in retelling the story, he would swear that The Chief had ended his speech at that point. He would swear that it was only seconds later that The Chief had jumped down from the gate and motioned for him to come over; his memory simply didn't register anything between those two points.

But The Chief's words after the speech—the words spoken to him privately—were bright and clear in his mind.

The Chief was a good three inches shorter than Anketam, but Anketam never noticed that. He just stood there in front of The Chief, wondering what more his Chief had to say.

"You've shown yourself to be a good farmer, Anketam," Chief Samas said in a low voice. "Let's see—you're of Skebbin stock, I think?"

Anketam nodded. "Yes, sir."

"The Skebbin family has always produced good men. You're a credit to the Skebbins, Anketam."

"Thank you, sir."

"You've got a hard job ahead of you," said The Chief. "Don't fail me. Plant plenty of staple crops, make sure there's enough food for everyone. If you think it's profitable, add more to the animal stock. I've authorized Kevenoe to allow money for the purchase of breeding stock. You can draw whatever you need for that purpose.

"This war shouldn't last too long. Another year, at the very most, and we'll have forced the Invaders off Xedii. When I come back, I expect to find the barony in good shape, d'you hear?"

"Yes, sir. It will be."

"I think it will," said The Chief. "Good luck to you, Anketam."

As The Chief turned away, Anketam said: "Thank you, sir—and good luck to you, sir."

Chief Samas turned back again. "By the way," he said, "there's one more thing. I know that men don't always agree on everything. If there is any dispute between you and Kevenoe, submit the question to my wife for arbitration." He hesitated. "However, I trust that there will not be many such disputes. A woman shouldn't be bothered with such things any more than is absolutely necessary. It upsets them. Understand?"

Anketam nodded. "Yes, sir."

"Very well. Good-by, Anketam. I hope to see you again before the next harvest." And with that, he turned and walked through the gate, toward the woman who was standing anxiously on the porch of his home.

Anketam turned away and started towards his own village. Most of the others had already begun the trek back. But Jacovik, Blejjo, and Basom were waiting for him. They fell into step beside him.

After a while, Jacovik broke the silence. "Well, Ank, it looks like you've got a big job on your hands."

"That's for sure," said Anketam. He knew that Jacovik envied him the job; he knew that Jacovik had only missed the appointment by a narrow margin.

"Jac," he said, "have you got a man on your crew that you can trust to take over your job?"

"Madders could do it, I think," Jacovik said cautiously. "Why?"

"This is too big a job for one man," said Anketam quietly. "I'll need help. I want you to help me, Jac."

There was a long silence while the men walked six paces. Then Jacovik said: "I'll do whatever I can, Ank. Whatever I can." There was honest warmth in his voice.

Again there was a silence.

"Blejjo," Anketam said after a time, "do you mind coming out of retirement for a while?"

"Not if you need me, Ank," said the old man.

"It won't be hard work," Anketam said. "I just want you to take care of the village when I'm not there. Settle arguments, assign the village work, give out punishment if necessary—things like that. As far as the village is concerned, you'll be supervisor."

"What about the field work, Ank?" Blejjo asked. "I'm too old to handle that. Come spring, and—"

"I said, as far as the village is concerned," Anketam said. "I've got another man in mind for the field work."

And no one was more surprised than Basom when Anketam said: "Basom, do you think you could handle the crew in the field?"

Basom couldn't even find his tongue for several more paces. When he discovered at last that it was still in his mouth, where he'd left it, he said: "I ... I'll try, Ank. I sure will try, if you want me to. But ... well ... I mean, why pick *me*?"

Old Blejjo chuckled knowingly. Jacovik, who hardly knew the boy, just looked puzzled.

"Why not you?" Anketam countered.

"Well ... you've always said I was lazy. And I am, I guess."

"Sure you are," said Anketam. "So am I. Always have been. But a smart lazy man can figure out things that a hard worker might overlook. He can find the easy, fast way to get a job done properly. And he doesn't overwork his men because he knows that when he's tired, the others are, too. You want to try it, Basom?"

"I'll try," said Basom earnestly. "I'll try real hard." Then, after a moment's hesitation. "Just one thing, Anketam—"

"What's that?"

"Kevenoe. I don't want him coming around me. Not at all. If he ever said one word to me, I'd probably break his neck right there."

Anketam nodded. The Chief had given Zillia to Kevenoe only two months before, and the only one who liked the situation was Kevenoe himself.

"I'll deal with Kevenoe, Basom," Anketam said. "Don't you worry about that."

"All right, then," Basom said. "I'll do my best, Anketam."

"You'd better," said Anketam. "If you don't, I'll just have to give the job to someone else. You hear?"

"I hear," said Basom.

V

The war dragged on. In the spring of the following year, over a hundred thousand Invader troops landed on the seacoast a hundred miles from Chromdin and began a march on the capital. But somebody had forgotten to tell the Invader general that it rained in that area in the spring and that the mud was like glue. The Invader army bogged down, and, floundering their way toward Chromdin, they found themselves opposed by an army of nearly a hundred thousand Xedii troops under General Jojon, and the invasion came to a standstill at that point.

Farther to the west, another group of forty thousand Invader troops came down from the Frozen Country, and a Xedii general named Oljek trounced them with a mere seventeen thousand men.

All in all, the Invaders were getting nowhere, but they seemed determined to keep on plugging.

The news only filtered slowly into the areas which were situated well away from the front. A thousand miles to the west of Chief Samas' barony, the Invaders began cutting deeply into Xedii territory, but they were nowhere near the capital, so no one was really worried.

Anketam worked hard at keeping the barony going during the absence of The Chief. Instead of *cataca*, he and Jacovik planted food crops, doing on a larger scale just what they had always done in the selected sections around the villages. They had always grown their own food, and now they were doing it on a grand scale.

No news came from off-planet, except for unreliable rumors. What the rest of the galaxy was doing about the war on Xedii, no one knew.

Young Basom proved to be a reasonably competent supervisor. He was nowhere near as good as Anketam or Jacovik, but there were worse supers in the barony.

Anketam found that the biggest worry was not in the handling of the farmers, but in obtaining manufactured goods. The staff physician complained to Kevenoe that drugs were getting scarce. Shoes and clothing were almost impossible to obtain. Rumor had it that arms and ammunition were running short in the Xedii armies. For two centuries, Xedii had depended on other planets to provide manufactured goods for her, and now those supplies were cut off, except for a miserably slow trickle that came in via the daring space officers who managed to evade the orbital forts that the Invaders had set up around the planet.

Even so, Anketam's faith in the power of Xedii remained constant. The invading armies were still being held off from Chromdin, weren't they? The capital would not fall, of that he was sure.

What Anketam did not and could not know was the fact that the Invaders were growing tired of pussy-footing around. Instead of fighting Xedii on Xedii's terms, the Invaders decided to fight it on their own.

Everyone on Chief Samas' barony and the others around it expected trouble to come from the north, from the Frozen Country, if and when it came. They didn't look to the west, where the real trouble was brewing.

Anketam was shocked when he heard the news that the Invaders had reached Tana L'At, having cut down through the center of the continent, dividing the inhabited part of Xedii into two almost equal parts. They knocked out Tana L'At with a heavy shelling of paralysis gas, evacuated the inhabitants, and dusted the city with radioactive powder to make it uninhabitable for several years.

Then they began to march eastward.

VI

For the first time in his life, Anketam was feeling genuine fear. He had feared for his life before, yes. And he had feared for his family. But now he feared for his world, which was vaster by far.

He blinked at the tall, gangling Kevenoe, who was still out of breath from running. "Say that again."

"I said that the Invader troops are crossing Benner Creek," Kevenoe said angrily. "They'll be at the castle within an hour. We've got to do something."

"What?" Anketam asked dazedly.

"Fight them? With what? We have no weapons."

"I don't know," Kevenoe admitted. "I just don't know. I thought maybe you'd know. Maybe you could think of something. What about Lady Samas?"

"What about her?" Anketam still couldn't force his mind to function.

"Haven't you heard? The Invaders have been looting and burning every castle in their path! And the women—"

Lady Samas in danger! Something crystallized in Anketam's mind. He pointed in the direction of the castle. "Get back there!" he snapped. "Get everyone out of the castle! Save all the valuables you can! Get everyone down to the river and tell them to hide in the brush at the Big Swamp. The Invaders won't go there. Move!"

Kevenoe didn't even pause to answer. He ran back toward the saddle animal he had tethered at the edge of the village.

Anketam was running in the opposite direction, toward Basom's quarters.

He didn't bother to knock. He flung open the door and yelled, "*Basom!*"

Basom, who had been relaxing on his bed, leaped to his feet. "What is it?"

Anketam told him rapidly. Then he said: "Get moving! You're a fast runner. Spread the news. Tell everyone to get to the Swamp. We have less than an hour, so run for all you're worth!"

Basom, like Kevenoe, didn't bother to ask questions. He went outside and started running toward the south.

"That's right!" Anketam called after him. "Tell Jacovik first! And get more runners to spread the word!"

And then Anketam headed for his own home. Memi had to be told. On the way, he pounded on the doors of the houses, shouting the news and telling the others to get to the Big Swamp.

By the time the Invader troops came, they found the entire Samas barony empty. Not a single soul opposed their march; there was no voice to object when they leveled their beam projectors and melted the castle and the villages into shapeless masses of blackened plastic.

VII

The wooden shelter wasn't much of a home, but it was all Anketam could provide. It had been difficult to cut down the trees and make a shack of them, but at least there were four walls and a roof.

Anketam stood at the door of the rude hut, looking blindly at the ruins of the village a hundred yards away. In the past few months, weeds had grown up around the charred blobs that had once been the homes of Anketam's crew. Anketam stared, not at, but past and through them, seeing the ghosts of the houses that had once been there.

Behind him, Memi was speaking in soft tones to Lady Samas.

"Now you go ahead and eat, Lady. You can't starve yourself to death. Things won't always be this bad, you'll see. When that oldest boy of yours comes back, he'll fix the barony right back up like it was. Just you see. Now, here; try some of this soup."

Lady Samas said nothing. She seemed to be entirely oblivious of her surroundings these days. Nothing mattered to her any more. Word had come back that Chief Samas had accompanied General Eeler in the fatal expedition towards the Invader base, and The Chief had been buried there in the Frozen Country.

Lady Samas had nowhere else to stay. Kevenoe was dead, his skull crushed by—by someone. Anketam refused, in his own mind, to see any connection between Kevenoe's death and the fact that Basom and Zillia had disappeared the same day, probably to give themselves over to the Invader troops.

A movement at the corner of his eye caught Anketam's attention. He turned his head to look. Then he spun on his heel and went into the hut.

"Lady Samas," he said quickly, "they're coming. There's a ground-car coming down the road with four Invaders in it."

Lady Samas looked up at him, her fine old face calm and emotionless. "Let them come," she said. "We can't stop them, Anketam. And we have nothing to lose."

Three minutes later, the ground-car pulled up in front of the hut. Anketam watched silently as one of the men got out. The other three stayed in the car, their handguns ready.

The officer, very tall and straight in his blue uniform, strode up to the door of the hut. He stopped and addressed Anketam. "I understand Lady Samas is living here."

"That's right," Anketam said.

"Would you tell her that Colonel Fayder would like to speak to her."

Before Anketam could say anything, Lady Samas spoke. "Tell the colonel to come in, Anketam."

Anketam stepped aside to let the officer enter.

"Lady Samas?" he asked.

She nodded. "I am."

The colonel removed his hat. "Madam, I am Colonel Jamik Fayder, of the Union army. You are the owner of this land?"

"Until my son returns, yes," said Lady Samas evenly.

"I understand." The colonel licked his lips nervously. He was obviously ill at ease in the presence of the Lady Samas. "Madam," he said, "it would be useless for me to apologize for the destructions of war. Apologies are mere words."

"They are," said Lady Samas. "None the less, I accept them."

"Thank you. I have come to inform you that the Xedii armies formally surrendered near Chromdin early this morning. The war is over."

"I'm glad," said Lady Samas.

"So am I," said the colonel. "It has not been a pleasant war. Xedii was—and still is—the most backward planet in the galaxy. Your Council of Chiefs steadfastly refused to allow the"—he glanced at Anketam—"workers of Xedii to govern their own lives. They have lived and died without proper education, without the medical care that would save and lengthen their lives, and without the comforts of life that any human being deserves. That situation will be changed now, but I am heartily sorry it took a war to do it."

Anketam looked at the man. What was he talking about? He and his kind had burned and dusted cities and villages, and had smashed the lives of millions of human beings on the pretense that they were trying to help. What sort of insanity was that?

The colonel took a sheaf of papers from his pocket.

"I have been ordered to read to you the proclamation of the Union President."

He looked down at the papers and began to read:

"Henceforth, all the peoples of Xedii shall be free and equal. They shall have the right to change their work at will, to be paid in lawful money instead of—"

Anketam just stood there, his mind glazed. He had worked hard all his life for the security of retirement, and now all that was gone. What was he to do? Where was he to go? If he had to be paid in money, who would do it? Lady Samas? She had nothing. Besides, Anketam knew nothing about the handling of money. He knew nothing about how to get along in a society like that.

He stood there in silence as his world dissolved around him. He could hear, dimly, the voice of the blue-clad Union officer as he read off the death warrant for Xedii. And for Anketam.

THE END

Despoilers of the Golden Empire

A handful of men, and an incredible adventure—a few super-men, led by a fanatic, seeking to conquer a new world!

I

IN THE seven centuries that had elapsed since the Second Empire had been founded on the shattered remnants of the First, the nobles of the Imperium had come slowly to realize that the empire was not to be judged by the examples of its predecessor. The First Empire had conquered most of the known universe by political intrigue and sheer military strength; it had fallen because that same propensity for political intrigue had gained over every other strength of the Empire, and the various branches and sectors of the First Empire had begun to use it against one another.

The Second Empire was politically unlike the First; it tried to balance a centralized government against the autonomic governments of the various sectors, and had almost succeeded in doing so.

But, no matter how governed, there are certain essentials which are needed by any governmental organization.

Without power, neither Civilization nor the Empire could hold itself together, and His Universal Majesty, the Emperor Carl, well knew it. And power was linked solidly to one element, one metal, without which Civilization would collapse as surely as if it had been blasted out of existence. Without the power metal, no ship could move or even be built; without it, industry would come to a standstill.

In ancient times, even as far back as the early Greek and Roman civilizations, the metal had been known, but it had been used, for the most part, as decoration and in the manufacture of jewelry. Later, it had been coined as money.

It had always been relatively rare, but now, weight for weight, atom for atom, it was the most valuable element on Earth. Indeed, the most valuable in the known universe.

The metal was Element Number Seventy-nine—gold.

To the collective mind of the Empire, gold was the prime object in any kind of mining exploration. The idea of drilling for petroleum, even if it had been readily available, or of mining coal or uranium would have been dismissed as impracticable and even worse than useless.

Throughout the Empire, research laboratories worked tirelessly at the problem of transmuting commoner elements into Gold-197, but thus far none of the processes was commercially feasible. There was still, after thousands of years, only one way to get the power metal: extract it from the ground.

So it was that, across the great gulf between the worlds, ship after ship moved in search of the metal that would hold the far-flung colonies of the Empire together. Every adventurer who could manage to get aboard was glad to be cooped up on a ship during the long months it took to cross the empty expanses, was glad to endure the hardships on alien terrain, on the chance that his efforts might pay off a thousand or ten thousand fold.

Of these men, a mere handful were successful, and of these one or two stand well above the rest. And for sheer determination, drive, and courage, for the will to push on toward his goal, no matter what the odds, a certain Commander Frank had them all beat.

II

Before you can get a picture of the commander—that is, as far as his personality goes—you have to get a picture of the man physically.

He was enough taller than the average man to make him stand out in a crowd, and he had broad shoulders and a narrow waist to match. He wasn't heavy; his was the hard, tough, wirelike strength of a steel cable. The planes of his tanned face showed that he feared neither exposure to the elements nor exposure to violence; it was seamed with fine wrinkles and the thin white lines that betray scar tissue. His mouth was heavy-lipped, but firm, and the lines around it showed that it was unused to smiling. The commander could laugh, and often did—a sort of roaring explosion that burst forth suddenly whenever something struck him as particularly uproarious. But he seldom just smiled; Commander Frank rarely went halfway in anything.

His eyes, like his hair, were a deep brown—almost black, and they were set well back beneath heavy brows that tended to frown most of the time.

Primarily, he was a military man. He had no particular flair for science, and, although he had a firm and deep-seated grasp of the essential philosophy of the Universal Assembly, he had no inclination towards the kind of life necessarily led by those who would become higher officers of the Assembly. It was enough that the Assembly was behind him; it was enough to know that he was a member of the only race in the known universe which had a working knowledge of the essential, basic Truth of the Cosmos. With a weapon like that, even an ordinary soldier had little to fear, and Commander Frank was far from being an ordinary soldier.

He had spent nearly forty of his sixty years of life as an explorer-soldier for the Emperor, and during that time he'd kept his eyes open for opportunity. Every time his ship had landed, he'd watched and listened and collected data. And now he knew.

If his data were correct—and he was certain that they were—he had found his strike. All he needed was the men to take it.

III

The expedition had been poorly outfitted and undermanned from the beginning. The commander had been short of money at the outset, having spent almost all he could raise on his own, plus nearly everything he could beg or borrow, on his first two probing expeditions, neither of which had shown any real profit.

But they *had* shown promise; the alien population of the target which the commander had selected as his personal claim wore gold as ornaments, but didn't seem to think it was much above copper in value, and hadn't even progressed to the point of using it as coinage. From the second probing expedition, he had brought back two of the odd-looking aliens and enough gold to show that there must be more where that came from.

The old, hopeful statement, "There's gold in them thar hills," should have brought the commander more backing than he got, considering the Empire's need of it and the commander's evidence that it was available; but people are always more ready to bet on a sure thing than to indulge in speculation. Ten years before, a strike had been made in a sector quite distant from the commander's own find, and most of the richer nobles of the Empire preferred to back an established source of the metal than to sink money into what might turn out to be the pursuit of a wild goose.

Commander Frank, therefore, could only recruit men who were willing to take a chance, who were willing to risk anything, even their lives, against tremendously long odds.

And, even if they succeeded, the Imperial Government would take twenty per cent of the gross without so much as a by-your-leave. There was no other market for the metal except back home, so the tax could not be avoided; gold was no good whatsoever in the uncharted wilds of an alien world.

Because of his lack of funds, the commander's expedition was not only dangerously undermanned, but illegally so. It was only by means of out-and-out trickery that he managed to evade the official inspection and leave port with too few men and too little equipment.

There wasn't a scientist worthy of the name in the whole outfit, unless you call the navigator, Captain Bartholomew, an astronomer, which is certainly begging the question. There was no anthropologist aboard to study the semibarbaric civilization of the natives; there was no biologist to study the alien flora and fauna. The closest thing the commander had to physicists were engineers who could take care of the ship itself—specialist technicians, nothing more.

There was no need for armament specialists; each and every man was a soldier, and, as far as his own weapons went, an ordnance expert. As far as Commander Frank was concerned, that was enough. It had to be.

Mining equipment? He took nothing but the simplest testing apparatus. How, then, did he intend to get the metal that the Empire was screaming for?

The commander had an answer for that, too, and it was as simple as it was economical. The natives would get it for him.

They used gold for ornaments, therefore, they knew where the gold could be found. And, therefore, they would bloody well dig it out for Commander Frank.

IV

Due to atmospheric disturbances, the ship's landing was several hundred miles from the point the commander had originally picked for the debarkation of his troops. That meant a long, forced march along the coast and then inland, but there was no help for it; the ship simply wasn't built for atmospheric navigation.

That didn't deter the commander any. The orders rang through the ship: "All troops and carriers prepare for landing!"

Half an hour later, they were assembled outside the ship, fully armed and armored, and with full field gear. The sun, a yellow G-O star, hung hotly just above the towering mountains to the east. The alien air smelled odd in the men's nostrils, and the weird foliage seemed to rustle menacingly. In the distance, the shrieks of alien fauna occasionally echoed through the air.

A hundred and eighty-odd men and some thirty carriers stood under the tropic blaze for forty-five minutes while the commander checked over their equipment with minute precision. Nothing faulty or sloppy was going into that jungle with him if he could prevent it.

When his hard eyes had inspected every bit of equipment, when he had either passed or ordered changes in the manner of its carrying or its condition, when he was fully satisfied that every weapon was in order—then, and only then, did he turn his attention to the men themselves.

He climbed atop a little hillock and surveyed them carefully, letting his penetrating gaze pass over each man in turn. He stood there, his fists on his hips, with the sunlight gleaming from his burnished armor, for nearly a full minute before he spoke.

Then his powerful voice rang out over the assembled adventurers.

"My comrades-at-arms! We have before us a world that is ours for the taking! It contains more riches than any man on Earth ever dreamed existed, and those riches, too, are ours for the taking. It isn't going to be a picnic, and we all knew that when we came. There are dangers on every side—from the natives, from the animals and plants, and from the climate.

"But there is not one of these that cannot be overcome by the onslaught of brave, courageous, and determined men!

"Ahead of us, we will find the Four Horsemen of the Apocalypse arrayed against our coming—Famine, Pestilence, War, and Death. Each and all of these we must meet and conquer as brave men should, for at their end we will find wealth and glory!"

A cheer filled the air, startling the animals in the forest into momentary silence.

The commander stilled it instantly with a raised hand.

"Some of you know this country from our previous expeditions together. Most of you will find it utterly strange. And not one of you knows it as well as I do.

"In order to survive, you must—and *will*—follow my orders to the letter—and beyond.

"First, as to your weapons. We don't have an unlimited supply of charges for them, so there will be no firing of any power weapons unless absolutely necessary. You have your swords and your pikes—use them."

Several of the men unconsciously gripped the hafts of the long steel blades at their sides as he spoke the words, but their eyes never left the commanding figure on the hummock.

"As for food," he continued, "we'll live off the land. You'll find that most of the animals are edible, but stay away from the plants unless I give the O.K.

"We have a long way to go, but, by Heaven, I'm going to get us there alive! Are you with me?"

A hearty cheer rang from the throats of the men. They shouted the commander's name with enthusiasm.

"All right!" he bellowed. "There is one more thing! Anyone who wants to stay with the ship can do so; anyone who feels too ill to make it should consider it his duty to stay behind, because sick men will simply hold us up and weaken us more than if they'd been left behind. Remember, we're not going to turn back as a body, and an individual would never make it alone." He paused.

"Well?"

Not a man moved. The commander grinned—not with humor, but with satisfaction. "All right, then: let's move out."

V

Of them all, only a handful, including the commander, had any real knowledge of what lay ahead of them, and that knowledge only pertained to the periphery of the area the intrepid band of adventurers were entering. They knew that the aliens possessed a rudimentary civilization—they did not, at that time, realize they were entering the outposts of a powerful barbaric empire—an empire almost as well-organized and well-armed as that of First Century Rome, and, if anything, even more savage and ruthless.

It was an empire ruled by a single family who called themselves the Great Nobles; at their head was the Greatest Noble—the Child of the Sun Himself. It has since been conjectured that the Great Nobles were mutants in the true sense of the word; a race apart from their subjects. It is impossible to be absolutely sure at this late date, and the commander's expedition, lacking any qualified geneticists or genetic engineers, had no way of determining—and, indeed, no real *interest* in determining—whether this was or was not true. None the less, historical evidence seems to indicate the validity of the hypothesis.

Never before—not even in ancient Egypt—had the historians ever seen a culture like it. It was an absolute monarchy that would have made any Medieval king except the most saintly look upon it in awe and envy. The Russians and the Germans never even approached it. The Japanese tried to approximate it at one time in their history, but they failed.

Secure in the knowledge that theirs was the only civilizing force on the face of the planet, the race of the Great Nobles spread over the length of a great continent, conquering the lesser races as they went.

Physically, the Great Nobles and their lesser subjects were quite similar. They were, like the commander and his men, human in every sense of the word. That this argues some ancient, prehistoric migration across the empty gulfs that separate the worlds cannot be denied, but when and how that migration took place are data lost in the mists of time. However it may have happened, the fact remains that these people *were* human. As someone observed in one of the reports written up by one of the officers: "They could pass for Indians, except their skins are of a decidedly redder hue."

The race of the Great Nobles held their conquered subjects in check by the exercise of two powerful forces: religion and physical power of arms. Like the feudal organizations of Medieval Europe, the Nobles had the power of life and death over their subjects, and to a much greater extent than the European nobles had. Each family lived on an allotted parcel of land and did a given job. Travel was restricted to a radius of a few miles. There was no money; there was no necessity for it, since the government of the Great Nobles took all produce and portioned it out again according to need. It was communism on a vast and—incomprehensible as it may seem to the modern mind—*workable* scale. Their minds were as different from ours as their bodies were similar; the concept "freedom" would have been totally incomprehensible to them.

They were sun-worshipers, and the Greatest Noble was the Child of the Sun, a godling subordinate only to the Sun Himself. Directly under him were the lesser Great Nobles, also Children of the Sun, but to a lesser extent. They exercised absolute power over the conquered peoples, but even they had no concept of freedom, since they were as tied to the people as the people were tied to them. It was a benevolent dictatorship of a kind never seen before or since.

At the periphery of the Empire of the Sun-Child lived still unconquered savage tribes, which the Imperial forces were in the process of slowly taking over. During the centuries, tribe after tribe had fallen before the brilliant leadership of the Great Nobles and the territory of the Empire had slowly expanded until, at the time the invading Earthmen came, it covered almost as much territory as had the Roman Empire at its peak.

The Imperial Army, consisting of upwards of fifty thousand troops, was extremely mobile in spite of the handicap of having no form of transportation except their own legs. They had no cavalry; the only beast of burden known to them—the flame-beasts—were too small to carry more than a hundred pounds, in spite of their endurance. But the wide, smooth roads that ran the length and breadth of the Empire enabled a marching army to make good time, and messages carried by runners in relays could traverse the Empire in a matter of days, not weeks.

And into this tight-knit, well-organized, powerful barbaric world marched Commander Frank with less than two hundred men and thirty carriers.

VI

It didn't take long for the men to begin to chafe under the constant strain of moving through treacherous and unfamiliar territory. And the first signs of chafing made themselves apparent beneath their armor.

Even the best designed armor cannot be built to be worn for an unlimited length of time, and, at first, the men could see no reason for the order. They soon found out.

One evening, after camp had been made, one young officer decided that he had spent his last night sleeping in full armor. It was bad enough to have to march in it, but sleeping in it was too much. He took it off and stretched, enjoying the freedom from the heavy steel. His tent was a long way from the center of camp, where a small fire flickered, and the soft light from the planet's single moon filtered only dimly through the jungle foliage overhead. He didn't think anyone would see him from the commander's tent.

The commander's orders had been direct and to the point: "You will wear your armor at all times; you will march in it, you will eat in it, you will sleep in it. During such times as it is necessary to remove a part of it, the man doing so will make sure that he is surrounded by at least two of his companions in full armor. There will be no exceptions to this rule!"

The lieutenant had decided to make himself an exception.

He turned to step into his tent when a voice came out of the nearby darkness.

"Hadn't you better get your steel plates back on before the commander sees you?"

The young officer turned quickly to see who had spoken. It was another of the junior officers.

"Mind your own business," snapped the lieutenant.

The other grinned sardonically. "And if I don't?"

There had been bad blood between these two for a long time; it was an enmity that went back to a time even before the expedition had begun. The two men stood there for a long moment, the light from the distant fire flickering uncertainly against their bodies.

The young officer who had removed his armor had not been foolish enough to remove his weapons too; no sane man did that in hostile territory. His hand went to the haft of the blade at his side.

"If you say a single word—"

Instinctively, the other dropped his hand to his own sword.

"Stop! Both of you!"

And stop they did; no one could mistake the crackling authority in that voice. The commander, unseen in the moving, dim light, had been circling the periphery of the camp, to make sure that all was well. He strode toward the two younger men, who stood silently, shocked into immobility. The commander's sword was already in his hand.

"I'll spit the first man that draws a blade," he snapped.

His keen eyes took in the situation at a glance.

"Lieutenant, what are you doing out of armor?"

"It was hot, sir, and I—"

"Shut up!" The commander's eyes were dangerous. "An asinine statement like that isn't even worth listening to! Get that armor back on! *Move!*"

He was standing approximately between the two men, who had been four or five yards apart. When the cowed young officer took a step or two back toward his tent, the commander turned toward the other officer. "And as for you, if—"

He was cut off by the yell of the unarmored man, followed by the sound of his blade singing from its sheath.

The commander leaped backwards and spun, his own sword at the ready, his body settling into a swordsman's crouch.

But the young officer was not drawing against his superior. He was hacking at something ropy and writhing that squirmed on the ground as the lieutenant's blade bit into it. Within seconds, the serpentine thing gave a convulsive shudder and died.

The lieutenant stepped back clumsily, his eyes glazing in the flickering light. "Dropped from th' tree," he said thickly. "Bit me."

His hand moved to a dark spot on his chest, but it never reached its goal. The lieutenant collapsed, crumpling to the ground.

The commander walked over, slammed the heel of his heavy boot hard down on the head of the snaky thing, crushing it. Then he returned his blade to its sheath, knelt down by the young man, and turned him over on his face.

The commander's own face was grim.

By this time, some of the nearby men, attracted by the yell, had come running. They came to a stop as they saw the tableau before them.

The commander, kneeling beside the corpse, looked up at them. With one hand, he gestured at the body. "Let this be a lesson to all of you," he said in a tight voice. "This man died because he took off his armor. That"—he pointed at the butchered reptile—"thing is full of as deadly a poison as you'll ever see, and it can move like lightning. *But it can't bite through steel!*

"Look well at this man and tell the others what you saw. I don't want to lose another man in this idiotic fashion."

He stood up and gestured.

"Bury him."

VII

They found, as they penetrated deeper into the savage-infested hinterlands of the Empire of the Great Nobles, that the armor fended off more than just snakes. Hardly a day passed but one or more of the men would hear the sharp *spang!* of a blowgun-driven dart as it slammed ineffectually against his armored back or chest. At first, some of the men wanted to charge into the surrounding forest, whence the darts came, and punish the sniping aliens, but the commander would have none of it.

"Stick together," he ordered. "They'll do worse to us if we're split up in this jungle. Those blowgun darts aren't going to hurt you as long as they're hitting steel. Ignore them and keep moving."

They kept moving.

Around them, the jungle chattered and muttered, and, occasionally, screamed. Clouds of insects, great and small, hummed and buzzed through the air. They subsided only when the drizzling rains came, and then lifted again from their resting places when the sun came out to raise steamy vapors from the moist ground.

It was not an easy march. Before many days had passed, the men's feet were cracked and blistered from the effects of fungus, dampness, and constant marching. The compact military marching order which had characterized the first few days of march had long since deteriorated into a straggling column, where the weaker were supported by the stronger.

Three more men died. One simply dropped in his tracks. He was dead before anyone could touch him. Insect bite? Disease? No one knew.

Another had been even less fortunate. A lionlike carnivore had leaped on him during the night and clawed him badly before one of his companions blasted the thing with a power weapon. Three days later, the wounded man was begging to be killed; one arm and one leg were gangrenous. But he died while begging, thus sparing any would-be executioner from an unpleasant duty.

The third man simply failed to show up for roll call one morning. He was never seen again.

But the rest of the column, with dauntless courage, followed the lead of their commander.

It was hard to read their expressions, those reddened eyes that peered at him from swollen, bearded faces. But he knew his own face looked no different.

"We all knew this wasn't going to be a fancy-dress ball when we came," he said. "Nobody said this was going to be the easiest way in the world to get rich."

The commander was sitting on one of the carriers, his eyes watching the men, who were lined up in front of him. His voice was purposely held low, but it carried well.

"The marching has been difficult, but now we're really going to see what we're made of.

"We all need a rest, and we all deserve one. But when I lie down to rest, I'm going to do it in a halfway decent bed, with some good, solid food in my belly.

"Here's the way the picture looks: An hour's march from here, there's a good-sized village." He swung partially away from them and pointed south. "I think we have earned that town and everything in it."

He swung back, facing them. There was a wolfish grin on his face. "There's gold there, too. Not much, really, compared with what we'll get later on, but enough to whet our appetites."

The men's faces were beginning to change now, in spite of the swelling.

"I don't think we need worry too much about the savages that are living there now. With God on our side, I hardly see how we can fail."

He went on, telling them how they would attack the town, the disposition of men, the use of the carriers, and so forth. By the time he was through, every man there was as eager as he to move in. When he finished speaking, they set up a cheer:

"For the Emperor and the Universal Assembly!"

The natives of the small village had heard that some sort of terrible beings were approaching through the jungle. Word had come from the people of the forest that the strange monsters were impervious to darts, and that they had huge dragons with them which were terrifying even to look at. They were clad in metal and made queer noises as they moved.

The village chieftain called his advisers together to ponder the situation. What should they do with these strange things? What were the invaders' intentions?

Obviously, the things must be hostile. Therefore, there were only two courses open—fight or flee. The chieftain and his men decided to fight. It would have been a good thing if there had only been some Imperial troops in the vicinity, but all the troops were farther south, where a civil war was raging over the right of succession of the Greatest Noble.

Nevertheless, there were two thousand fighting men in the village—well, two thousand men at any rate, and they would certainly all fight, although some were rather young and a few were too old for any really hard fighting. On the other hand, it would probably not come to that, since the strangers were outnumbered by at least three to one.

The chieftain gave his orders for the defense of the village.

The invading Earthmen approached the small town cautiously from the west. The commander had his men spread out a little, but not so much that they could be separated. He saw the aliens grouped around the square, boxlike buildings, watching and waiting for trouble.

"We'll give them trouble," the commander whispered softly. He waited until his troops were properly deployed, then he gave the signal for the charge.

The carriers went in first, thundering directly into the massed alien warriors. Each carrier-man fired a single shot from his power weapon, and then went to work with his carrier, running down the terrified aliens, and swinging a sword with one hand while he guided with the other. The commander went in with that first charge, aiming his own carrier toward the center of the fray. He had some raw, untrained men with him, and he believed in teaching by example.

The aliens recoiled at the onslaught of what they took to be horrible living monsters that were unlike anything ever seen before.

Then the commander's infantry charged in. The shock effect of the carriers had been enough to disorganize the aliens, but the battle was not over yet by a long shot.

There were yells from other parts of the village as some of the other defenders, hearing the sounds of battle, came running to reinforce the home guard. Better than fifteen hundred men were converging on the spot.

The invading Earthmen moved in rapidly against the armed natives, beating them back by the sheer ferocity of their attack. Weapons of steel clashed against weapons of bronze and wood.

The power weapons were used only sparingly; only when the necessity to save a life was greater than the necessity to conserve weapon charges was a shot fired.

The commander, from the center of the fray, took a glance around the area. One glance was enough.

"They're dropping back!" he bellowed, his voice carrying well above the din of the battle, "Keep 'em moving!" He singled out one of his officers at a distance, and yelled: "Hernan! Get a couple of men to cover that street!" He waved toward one of the narrow streets that ran off to one side. The others were already being attended to.

The commander jerked around swiftly as one of the natives grabbed hold of the carrier and tried to hack at the commander with a bronze sword. The commander spitted him neatly on his blade and withdrew it just in time to parry another attack from the other side.

By this time, the reinforcements from the other parts of the village were beginning to come in from the side streets, but they were a little late. The warriors in the square—what was left of them—had panicked. In an effort to get away from the terrible monsters with their deadly blades and their fire-spitting weapons, they were leaving by the same channels that the reinforcements were coming in by, and the resultant jam-up was disastrous. The panic communicated itself like wildfire, but no one could move fast enough to get away from the sweeping, stabbing, glittering blades of the invading Earthmen.

"All right," the commander yelled, "we've got 'em on the run now! Break up into squads of three and clear those streets! Clear 'em out! Keep 'em moving!"

After that, it was the work of minutes to clear the town.

The commander brought his carrier to a dead stop, reached out with his sword, and snagged a bit of cloth from one of the fallen native warriors. He began to wipe the blade of his weapon as Lieutenant commander Hernan pulled up beside him.

"Casualties?" the commander asked Hernan without looking up from his work.

"Six wounded, no dead," said Hernan. "Or did you want me to count the aliens, too?"

The commander shook his head. "No. Get a detail to clear out the carrion, and then tell Frater Vincent I want to talk to him. We'll have to start teaching these people the Truth."

VIII

"Have you anything to say in your defense?" the commander asked coldly.

For a moment, the accused looked nothing but hatred at the commander, but there was fear behind that hatred. At last he found his voice. "It was mine. You promised us all a share."

Lieutenant commander Hernan picked up a leather bag that lay on the table behind which he and the commander were sitting. With a sudden gesture, he upended it, dumping its contents on the flat, wooden surface of the table.

"Do you deny that this was found among your personal possessions?" he asked harshly.

"No," said the accused soldier. "Why should I? It's mine. Rightfully mine. I fought for it. I found it. I kept it. It's mine." He glanced to either side, towards the two guards who flanked him, then looked back at the commander.

The commander ran an idle finger through the pound or so of golden trinkets that Hernan had spilled from the bag. He knew what the trooper was thinking. A man had a right to what he had earned, didn't he?

The commander picked up one of the heavier bits of primitive jewelry and tossed it in his hand. Then he stood up and looked around the town square.

The company had occupied the town for several weeks. The stored grains in the community warehouse, plus the relaxation the men had had, plus the relative security of the town, had put most of the men back into condition. One had died from a skin infection, and another from wounds sustained in the assault on the town, but the remainder were in good health.

And all of them, with the exception of the sentries guarding the town's perimeter, were standing in the square, watching the court-martial. Their eyes didn't seem to blink, and their breathing was soft and measured. They were waiting for the commander's decision.

The commander, still tossing the crude golden earring, stood tall and straight, estimating the feeling of the men surrounding him.

"Gold," he said finally. "Gold. That's what we came here for, and that's what we're going to get. Five hundred pounds of the stuff would make any one of you wealthy for the rest of his life. Do you think I blame any one of you for wanting it? Do you think I blame this man here? Of course not." He laughed—a short, hard bark. "Do I blame myself?"

He tossed the bauble again, caught it. "But wanting it is one thing; getting it, holding it, and taking care of it wisely are something else again.

"I gave orders. I have expected—and still expect—that they will be obeyed. But I didn't give them just to hear myself give orders. There was a reason, and a good one.

"Suppose we let each man take what gold he could find. What would happen? The lucky ones would be wealthy, and the unlucky would still be poor. And then some of the lucky ones would wake up some morning without the gold they'd taken because someone else had relieved them of it while they slept.

"And others wouldn't wake up at all, because they'd be found with their throats cut.

"I told you to bring every bit of the metal to me. When this thing is over, every one of you will get his share. If a man dies, his share will be split among the rest, instead of being stolen by someone else or lost because it was hidden too well."

He looked at the earring in his hand, then, with a convulsive sweep of his arm, he tossed it out into the middle of the square.

"There! Seven ounces of gold! Which of you wants it?"

Some of the men eyed the circle of metal that gleamed brightly on the sunlit ground, but none of them made any motion to pick it up.

"So." The commander's voice was almost gentle. He turned his eyes back toward the accused. "You know the orders. You knew them when you hid this." He gestured negligently toward the small heap of native-wrought metal. "Suppose you'd gotten away with it. You'd have ended up with your own share, *plus* this, thereby cheating the others out of—" He glanced at the pile. "Hm-m-m—say, twenty-five each. And that's only a little compared with what we'll get from now on."

He looked back at the others. "Unless the shares are taken care of *my* way, the largest shares will go to the dishonest, the most powerful, and the luckiest. Unless the division is made as we originally agreed, we'll end up trying to cut each other's heart out."

There was hardness in his voice when he spoke to the accused, but there was compassion there, too.

"First: You have forfeited your share in this expedition. All that you have now, and all that you might have expected will be divided among the others according to our original agreement.

"Second: I do not expect any man to work for nothing. Since you will not receive anything from this expedition, there is no point in your assisting the rest of us or working with us in any way whatsoever.

"Third: We can't have anyone with us who does not carry his own weight."

He glanced at the guards. "Hang him." He paused. "Now."

As he was led away, the commander watched the other men. There was approval in their eyes, but there was something else there, too—a wariness, a concealed fear.

The condemned man turned suddenly and began shouting at the commander, but before he could utter more than three syllables, a fist smashed him down. The guards dragged him off.

"All right, men," said the commander carefully, "let's search the village. There might be more gold about; I have a hunch that this isn't all he hid. Let's see if we can find the rest of it." He sensed the relief of tension as he spoke.

The commander was right. It was amazing how much gold one man had been able to stash away.

IX

They couldn't stay long in any one village; they didn't have the time to sit and relax any more than was necessary. Once they had reached the northern marches of the native empire, it was to the commander's advantage to keep his men moving. He didn't know for sure how good or how rapid communications were among the various native provinces, but he had to assume that they were top notch, allowing for the limitations of a barbaric society.

The worst trouble they ran into on their way was not caused by the native warriors, but by disease.

The route to the south was spotted by great strips of sandy barrenness, torn by winds that swept the grains of sand into the troopers' eyes and crept into the chinks of their armor. Underfoot, the sand made a treacherous pathway; carriers and men alike found it heavy going.

The heat from the sun was intense; the brilliant beams from the primary seemed to penetrate through the men's armor and through the insulation underneath, and made the marching even harder.

Even so, in spite of the discomfort, the men were making good time until the disease struck. And that stopped them in their tracks.

What the disease was or how it was spread is unknown and unknowable at this late date. Virus or bacterium, amoeba or fungus—whatever it was, it struck.

Symptoms: Lassitude, weariness, weakness, and pain.

Signs: Great, ulcerous, wartlike, blood-filled blisters that grew rapidly over the body.

A man might go to sleep at night feeling reasonably tired, but not ill, and wake up in the morning to find himself unable to rise, his muscles too weak to lift him from his bed.

If the blisters broke, or were lanced, it was almost impossible to stop the bleeding, and many died, not from the toxic effect of the disease itself, but from simple loss of blood.

But, like many epidemics, the thing had a fairly short life span. After two weeks, it had burned itself out. Most of those who got it recovered, and a few were evidently immune.

Eighteen men remained behind in shallow graves.

The rest went on.

X

No man is perfect. Even with four decades of training behind him, Commander Frank couldn't call the turn every time. After the first few villages, there were no further battles. The natives, having seen what the invaders could do, simply showed up missing when the commander and his men arrived. The villages were empty by the time the column reached the outskirts.

Frater Vincent, the agent of the Universal Assembly, complained in no uncertain terms about this state of affairs.

"As you know, commander," he said frowningly one morning, "it's no use trying to indoctrinate a people we can't contact. And you can't subject a people by force of arms alone; the power of the Truth—"

"I know, Frater," the commander interposed quickly. "But we can't deal with these savages in the hinterlands. When we get a little farther into this barbarian empire, we can take the necessary steps to—"

"The Truth," Frater Vincent interrupted somewhat testily, "is for all men. It works, regardless of the state of civilization of the society."

The commander looked out of the unglazed window of the native hut in which he had established his temporary headquarters, in one of the many villages he had taken—or, rather, walked into without a fight because it was empty. "But you'll admit, Frater, that it takes longer with savages."

"True," said Frater Vincent.

"We simply haven't the time. We've got to keep on the move. And, besides, we haven't even been able to contact any of the natives for quite a while; they get out of our way. And we have taken a few prisoners—" His voice was apologetic, but there was a trace of irritation in it. He didn't want to offend Frater Vincent, of course, but dammit, the Assemblyman didn't understand military tactics at all. Or, he corrected himself hastily, at least only slightly.

"Yes," admitted Frater Vincent, "and I've had considerable success with the prisoners. But, remember—we're not here just to indoctrinate a few occasional prisoners, but to change the entire moral and philosophical viewpoint of an entire race."

"I realize that, Frater," the commander admitted. He turned from the window and faced the Assemblyman. "We're getting close to the Great Bay now. That's where our ship landed on the second probing expedition. I expect we'll be more welcome there than we have been, out here in the countryside. We'll take it easy, and I think you'll have a chance to work with the natives on a mass basis."

The Frater smiled. "Excellent, commander. I ... uh ... want you to understand that I'm not trying to tell you your business; you run this campaign as you see fit. But don't lose sight of the ultimate goal of life."

"I won't. How could I? It's just that my methods are not, perhaps, as refined as yours."

Frater Vincent nodded, still smiling. "True. You are a great deal more direct. And—in your own way—just as effective. After all, the Assembly could not function without the military, but there were armies long before the Universal Assembly came into being."

The commander smiled back. "Not any armies like this, Frater."

Frater Vincent nodded. The understanding between the two men—at least on that point—was tacit and mutual. He traced a symbol in the air and left the commander to his thoughts.

Mentally, the commander went through the symbol-patterns that he had learned as a child—the symbol-patterns that brought him into direct contact with the Ultimate Power, the Power that controlled not only the spinning of atoms and the whirling of electrons in their orbits, but the workings of probability itself.

Once indoctrinated into the teachings of the Universal Assembly, any man could tap that Power to a greater or lesser degree, depending on his mental control and ethical attitude. At the top level, a first-class adept could utilize that Power for telepathy, psychokinesis, levitation, teleportation, and other powers that the commander only vaguely understood.

He, himself, had no such depth of mind, such iron control over his will, and he knew he'd never have it. But he could and did tap that Power to the extent that his physical body was under near-perfect control at all times, and not even the fear of death could shake his determination to win or his great courage.

He turned again to the window and looked at the alien sky. There was a great deal yet to be done.

The commander needed information—needed it badly. He had to know what the government of the alien empire was doing. Had they been warned of his arrival? Surely they must have, and yet they had taken no steps to impede his progress.

For this purpose, he decided to set up headquarters on an island just offshore in the Great Bay. It was a protected position, easily defended from assault, and the natives, he knew from his previous visit, were friendly.

They even helped him to get his men and equipment and the carriers across on huge rafts.

From that point, he began collecting the information he needed to invade the central domains of the Greatest Noble himself. It seemed an ideal spot—not only protection-wise, but because this was the spot he had originally picked for the landing of the ship. The vessel, which had returned to the base for reinforcements and extra supplies, would be aiming for the Great Bay area when she came back. And there was little likelihood that atmospheric disturbances would throw her off course again; Captain Bartholomew was too good a man to be fooled twice.

But landing on that island was the first—and only—mistake the commander made during the campaign. The rumors of internal bickerings among the Great Nobles of the barbarian empire were not the only rumors he heard. News of more local treachery came to his ears through the agency of natives, now loyal to the commander, who had been indoctrinated into the philosophy of the Assembly.

A group of native chieftains had decided that the invading Earthmen were too dangerous to be allowed to remain on their island, in spite of the fact that the invaders had done them no harm. There were, after all, whisperings from the north, whence the invaders had come, that the armored beings with the terrible weapons had used their power more than once during their march to the south. The chieftains were determined to rid their island of the potential menace.

As soon as the matter was brought to the commander's attention, he acted. He sent out a patrol to the place where the ringleaders were meeting, arrested them, and sentenced them to death. He didn't realize what effect that action would have on the rest of the islanders.

He almost found out too late.

XI

"There must be three thousand of them out there," said Lieutenant commander Hernan tightly, "and every one of them's crazy."

"Rot!" The commander spat on the ground and then sighted again along the barrel of his weapon. "I'm the one who's crazy. I'm a lousy politician; that's my trouble."

The lieutenant commander shrugged lightly. "Anyone can make a mistake. Just chalk it up to experience."

"I will, when we get out of this mess." He watched the gathering natives through hard, slitted eyes.

The invading Earthmen were in a village at the southern end of the eight-mile-long island, waiting inside the mud-brick huts while the natives who had surrounded the village worked themselves into a frenzy for an attack. The commander knew there was no sense in charging into them at that point: they would simply scatter and reassemble. The only thing to do was wait until they attacked—and then smash the attack.

"Hernan," he said, his eyes still watching the outside, "you and the others get out there with the carriers after the first volley. Cut them down. They're twenty-to-one against us, so make every blow count. Move."

Hernan nodded wordlessly and slipped away.

The natives were building up their courage with some sort of war dance, whooping and screaming and making threatening gestures toward the embattled invaders. Then the pattern of the dance changed; the islanders whirled to face the mud-brick buildings which housed the invading Earthmen. Suddenly, the dance broke, and the warriors ran in a screaming charge, straight for the trapped soldiers.

The commander waited. His own shot would be the signal, and he didn't want the men to fire too quickly. If the islanders were hit too soon, they might fall back into the woods and set up a siege, which the little company couldn't stand. Better to mop up the natives now, if possible.

Closer. Closer—

Now!

The commander's first shot picked off one of the leaders in the front ranks of the native warriors, and was followed by a raking volley from the other power weapons, firing from the windows of the mud-brick buildings. The warriors in the front rank dropped, and those in the second rank had to move adroitly to keep from stumbling over the bodies of their fallen fellows. The firing from the huts became ragged, but its raking effect was still deadly. A cloud of heavy, stinking smoke rolled across the clearing between the edge of the jungle and the village, as the bright, hard lances of heat leaped from the muzzles of the power weapons toward the bodies of the charging warriors.

The charge was gone from the commander's weapon, and he didn't bother to replace it. As Hernan and his men charged into the melee with their carriers, the commander went with them.

At the same time, the armored infantrymen came pouring out of the mud-brick houses, swinging their swords, straight into the mass of confused native warriors. A picked group of sharpshooters remained behind, in the concealment of the huts to pick off the warriors at the edge of the battle with their sporadic fire.

The commander's lips were moving a little as he formed the symbol-patterns of power almost unconsciously; a lifetime of habit had burned them into his brain so deeply that he could form them automatically while turning the thinking part of his mind to the business at hand.

He soon found himself entirely surrounded by the alien warriors. Their bronze weapons glittered in the sunlight as they tried to fight off the onslaught of the invaders. And those same bronze weapons were sheared, nicked, blunted, bent, and broken as they met the harder steel of the commander's sword.

Then the unexpected happened. One of the warriors, braver than the rest, made a grab for the commander's sword arm. At almost the same moment, a warrior on the other side of the carrier aimed a spear thrust at his side.

Either by itself would have been ineffectual. The spear clanged harmlessly from the commander's armor, and the warrior who had attempted to pull him from the carrier died before he could give much of a tug. But the combination, plus the fact that the heavy armor was a little unwieldy, overbalanced him. He toppled to the ground with a clash of steel as he and the carrier parted company.

Without a human hand at its controls, the carrier automatically moved away from the mass of struggling fighters and came to a halt well away from the battle.

The commander rolled as he hit and leaped to his feet, his sword moving in flickering arcs around him. The natives had no knowledge of effective swordplay. Like any barbarian, they conceived of a sword as a cutting instrument rather than a thrusting one. They chopped with them, using small shields to protect their bodies as they tried to hack the commander to bits.

But the commander had no desire to become mincemeat just yet. Five of the barbarians were coming at him, their swords raised for a downward slash. The commander lunged forward with a straight stop-thrust aimed at the groin of the nearest one. It came as a complete surprise to the warrior, who doubled up in pain.

The commander had already withdrawn his blade and was attacking the second as the first fell. He made another feint to the groin and then changed the aim of his point as the warrior tried to cover with his shield. A buckler is fine protection against a man who is trying to hack you to death with a chopper, because a heavy cutting sword and a shield have about the same inertia, and thus the same maneuverability. But the shield isn't worth anything against a light stabbing weapon. The warrior's shield started downward and he was unable to stop it and reverse its direction before the commander's sword pierced his throat.

Two down, three to go. No, four. Another warrior had decided to join the little battle against the leader of the invading Earthmen.

The commander changed his tactics just slightly with the third man. He slashed with the tip of his blade against the descending sword-arm of his opponent—a short, quick flick of his wrist that sheared through the inside of the wrist, severing tendons, muscles, veins and arteries as it cut to the bone. The sword clanged harmlessly off the commander's shoulder. A quick thrust, and the third man died.

The other three slowed their attack and began circling warily, trying to get behind the commander. Instead of waiting, he charged forward, again cutting at the sword arm of his adversary, severing fingers this time. As the warrior turned, the commander's sword pierced his side.

How long it went on, he had no idea. He kept his legs and his sword-arm moving, and his eyes ever alert for new foes as man after man dropped beneath that snake-tonguing blade. Inside his armor, perspiration poured in rivulets down his skin, and his arms and legs began to ache, but not for one second did he let up. He could not see what was going on, could not tell the direction of the battle nor even allow his mind to wonder what was going on more than ten paces from him.

And then, quite suddenly, it seemed, it was all over. Lieutenant commander Hernan and five other men pulled up with their carriers, as if from nowhere, their weapons dealing death, clearing a space around their commander.

"You hurt?" bawled Hernan.

The commander paused to catch his breath. He knew there was a sword-slash across his face, and his right leg felt as though there was a cut on it, but otherwise—

"I'm all right," he said. "How's it going?"

"They're breaking," Hernan told him. "We'll have them scattered within minutes."

Even as he spoke, the surge of battle moved away from them, toward the forest. The charge of the carriers, wreaking havoc on every side, had broken up the battle formation the aliens had had; the flaming death from the horrible weapons of the invaders, the fearless courage of the foot soldiers, and the steel-clad monsters that were running amuck among them shattered the little discipline they had. Panicky, they lost their anger, which had taken them several hours to build up. They scattered, heading for the forest.

Shortly, the village was silent. Not an alien warrior was to be seen, save for the hundreds of mute corpses that testified to the carnage that had been wrought.

Several of the commander's men had been wounded, and three had died. Lieutenant commander Hernan had been severely wounded in the leg by a native javelin, but the injury was a long way from being fatal.

Hernan gritted his teeth while his leg was being bandaged. "The angels were with us on that one," he said between winces.

The commander nodded. "I hope they stick with us. We'll need 'em to get off this island."

XII

For a while, it looked as though they were trapped on the island. The natives didn't dare to attack again, but no hunting party was safe, and the food supply was dropping. They had gotten on the island only by the help of the natives, who had ferried them over on rafts. But getting off was another thing, now that the natives were hostile. Cutting down trees to build rafts might possibly be managed, but during the loading the little company would be too vulnerable to attack.

The commander was seated bleakly in the hut he had taken as his headquarters, trying to devise a scheme for getting to the mainland, when the deadlock was finally broken.

There was a flurry of footsteps outside, a thump of heavy boots as one of the younger officers burst into the room.

"Commander!" he yelled. "Commander! Come outside!"

The commander leaped to his feet. "Another attack?"

"No, sir! Come look!"

The commander strode quickly to the door. His sight followed the line of the young officer's pointing finger.

There, outlined against the blue of the sky, was a ship!

The news from home was encouraging, but it was a long way from being what the commander wanted. Another hundred men and more carriers had been added to the original company of now hardened veterans, and the recruits, plus the protection of the ship's guns, were enough to enable the entire party to leave the island for the mainland.

By this time, the commander had gleaned enough information from the natives to be able to plan the next step in his campaign. The present Greatest Noble, having successfully usurped the throne from his predecessor, was still not in absolute control of the country. He had won a civil war, but his rule was still too shaky to allow him to split up his armies, which accounted for the fact that, thus far, no action had been taken by the Imperial troops against the invading Earthmen.

The commander set up a base on the mainland, near the coast, left a portion of his men there to defend it, and, with the remainder, marched inland to come to grips with the Greatest Noble himself.

As they moved in toward the heart of the barbarian empire, the men noticed a definite change in the degree of civilization of the natives—or, at least, in the degree of technological advancement. There were large towns, not small villages, to be dealt with, and there were highways and bridges that showed a knowledge of engineering equivalent to that of ancient Rome.

The engineers of the Empire of the Great Nobles were a long way above the primitive. They could have, had they had any reason to, erected a pyramid the equal of great Khufu's in size, and probably even more neatly constructed. Militarily speaking, the lack of knowledge of iron hampered them, but it must be kept in mind that a well-disciplined and reasonably large army, armed with bronze-tipped spears, bronze swords, axes, and maces, can make a formidable foe, even against a much better equipped group.

The Imperial armies were much better disciplined and much better armed than any of the natives the commander had thus far dealt with, and there were reputed to be more than ten thousand of them with the Greatest Noble in his mountain stronghold. Such considerations prompted the commander to plan his strategy carefully, but they did not deter him in the least. If he had been able to bring aircraft and perhaps a thermonuclear bomb or two for demonstration purposes, the attack might have been less risky, but neither had been available to a man of his limited means, so he had to work without them.

But now, he avoided fighting if at all possible. Working with Frater Vincent, the commander worked to convince the natives on the fertile farms and in the prosperous villages that he and his company were merely ambassadors of good will—missionaries and traders. He and his men had come in peace, and if they were received in peace, well and good. If not ... well, they still had their weapons.

The commander was depending on the vagueness of the information that may have filtered down from the north. The news had already come that the invaders were fierce and powerful fighters, but the commander gave the impression that the only reason any battles had taken place was because the northern tribes had been truculent in the extreme. He succeeded fairly well; the natives he now met considered their brethren of the northern provinces to be little better than savages, and therefore to be expected to treat strangers inhospitably and bring about their own ruin. The southern citizens of the empire eyed the strangers with apprehension, but they offered very little resistance. The commander and his men were welcomed warily at each town, and, when they left, were bid farewell with great relief.

It took a little time for the commander to locate the exact spot where the Greatest Noble and his retinue were encamped. The real capital of the empire was located even farther south, but the Greatest Noble was staying, for the nonce, in a city nestled high in the mountains, well inland from the seacoast. The commander headed for the mountains.

The passage into the mountains wasn't easy. The passes were narrow and dangerous, and the weather was cold. The air became thinner at every step. At eight thousand feet, mountain climbing in heavy armor becomes more than just hard work, and at twelve thousand it becomes exhausting torture. But the little company went on, sparked, fueled, and driven by the personal force of their commander, who stayed in the vanguard, his eyes ever alert for treachery from the surrounding mountains.

When the surprise came, it was of an entirely different kind than he had expected. The commander's carrier came over a little rise, and he brought it to an abrupt halt as he saw the valley spread out beneath him. He left the carrier, walked over to a boulder near the edge of the cliff, and looked down at the valley.

It was an elongated oval of verdant green, fifteen miles long by four wide, looking like an emerald set in the rocky granite of the surrounding peaks that thrust upward toward the sky. The valley ran roughly north-and-south, and to his right, at the southern end, the commander could see a city, although it was impossible to see anyone moving in it at this distance.

To his left, he could see great clouds of billowing vapor that rolled across the grassy plain—evidently steam from the volcanic hot springs which he had been told were to be found in this valley.

But, for the moment, it was neither the springs nor the city that interested him most.

In the heart of the valley, spreading over acre after acre, were the tents and pavilions of a mighty army encampment. From the looks of it, the estimate of thirty thousand troops which had been given him by various officials along the way was, if anything, too small.

It was a moment that might have made an ordinary man stop to think, and, having thought, to turn and go. But the commander was no ordinary man, and the sheer remorseless courage that had brought him this far wouldn't allow him to turn back. So far, he had kept the Greatest Noble off balance with his advancing tactics; if he started to retreat, the Greatest Noble would realize that the invaders were not invincible, and would himself advance to crush the small band of strangers.

The Greatest Noble had known the commander and his men were coming; he was simply waiting, to find out what they were up to, confident that he could dispose of them at his leisure. The commander knew that, and he knew he couldn't retreat now. There was no decision to be made, really—only planning to be done.

He turned back from the boulder to face the officers who had come to take a look at the valley.

"We'll go to the city first," he said.

XIII

The heavy tread of the invaders' boots as they entered the central plaza of the walled city awakened nothing but echoes from the stone walls that surrounded the plaza. Like the small villages they had entered farther north, the city seemed devoid of life.

There is nothing quite so depressing and threatening as a deserted city. The windows in the walls of the buildings seemed like blank, darkened eyes that watched—and waited. Nothing moved, nothing made a sound, except the troopers themselves.

The men kept close to the walls; there was no point in bunching up in the middle of the square to be cut down by arrows from the windows of the upper floors.

The commander ordered four squads of men to search the buildings and smoke out anyone who was there, but they turned up nothing. The entire city was empty. And there were no traps, no ambushes—nothing.

The commander, with Lieutenant commander Hernan and another officer, climbed to the top of the central building of the town. In the distance, several miles away, they could see the encampment of the monarch's troops.

"The only thing we can do," the commander said, his face hard and determined, "is to call their bluff. You two take about three dozen men and go out there with the carriers and give them a show. Go right into camp, as if you owned the place. Throw a scare into them, but don't hurt anyone. Then, very politely, tell the Emperor, or whatever he calls himself, that I would like him to come here for dinner and a little talk."

The two officers looked at each other, then at the commander.

"Just like that?" asked Hernan.

"Just like that," said the commander.

The demonstration and exhibition went well—as far as it had gone. The native warriors had evidently been quite impressed by the onslaught of the terrifying monsters that had thundered across the plain toward them, right into the great camp, and come to a dead halt directly in front of the magnificent pavilion of the Greatest Noble himself.

The Greatest Noble put up a good face. He had obviously been expecting the visitors, because he and his lesser nobles were lined up before the pavilion, the Greatest Noble ensconced on a sort of portable throne. He managed to look perfectly calm and somewhat bored by the whole affair, and didn't seem to be particularly effected at all when Lieutenant commander Hernan bowed low before him and requested his presence in the city.

And the Greatest Noble's answer was simple and to the point, although it was delivered by one of his courtiers.

"You may tell your commander," said the noble, "that His Effulgence must attend to certain religious duties tonight, since he is also High Priest of the Sun. However, His Effulgence will most graciously deign to speak to your commander tomorrow. In the meantime, you are requested to enjoy His Effulgence's gracious hospitality in the city, which has been emptied for your convenience. It is yours, for the nonce."

Which left nothing for the two officers and their men to do but go thundering back across the plain to the city.

The Greatest Noble did not bring his whole army with him, but the pageant of barbaric splendor that came tootling and drumming its way into the city the next evening was a magnificent sight. His Effulgence himself was dressed in a scarlet robe and a scarlet, turbanlike head covering with scarlet fringes all around it. About his throat was a necklace of emerald-green gems, and his clothing was studded with more of them. Gold gleamed everywhere. He was borne on an ornate, gilded palanquin, carried high above the crowd on the shoulders of a dozen stalwart nobles, only slightly less gorgeously-dressed than the Greatest Noble. The nobility that followed was scarcely less showy in its finery.

When they came into the plaza, however, the members of the procession came to a halt. The singing and music died away.

The plaza was absolutely empty.

No one had come out to greet the Emperor.

There were six thousand natives in the plaza, and not a sign of the invaders.

The commander, hiding well back in the shadows in one of the rooms of the central building, watched through the window and noted the evident consternation of the royal entourage with satisfaction. Frater Vincent, standing beside him, whispered, "Well?"

"All right," the commander said softly, "they've had a taste of what we got when we came in. I suppose they've had enough. Let's go out and act like hosts."

The commander and a squad of ten men, along with Frater Vincent, strode majestically out of the door of the building and walked toward the Greatest Noble. They had all polished their armor until it shone, which was about all they could do in the way of finery, but they evidently looked quite impressive in the eyes of the natives.

"Greetings, Your Effulgence," said the commander, giving the Greatest Noble a bow that was hardly five degrees from the perpendicular. "I trust we find you well."

In the buildings surrounding the square, hardly daring to move for fear the clank of metal on metal might give the whole plan away, the remaining members of the company watched the conversation between their commander and the Greatest Noble. They couldn't hear what was being said, but that didn't matter; they knew what to do as soon as the commander gave the signal. Every eye was riveted on the commander's right hand.

It seemed an eternity before the commander casually reached up to his helmet and brushed a hand across it—once—twice—three times.

Then all hell broke loose. The air was split by the sound of power weapons throwing their lances of flame into the massed ranks of the native warriors. The gunners, safe behind the walls of the buildings, poured a steady stream of accurately directed fire into the packed mob, while the rest of the men charged in with their blades, thrusting and slashing as they went.

The aliens, panic-stricken by the sudden, terrifying assault, tried to run, but there was nowhere to run to. Every exit had been cut off to bottle up the Imperial cortege. Within minutes, the entrances to the square were choked with the bodies of those who tried to flee.

As soon as the firing began, the commander and his men began to make their way toward the Greatest Noble. They had been forced to stand a good five yards away during the parlay, cut off from direct contact by the Imperial guards. The commander, sword in hand, began cutting his way through to the palanquin.

The palanquin bearers seemed frozen; they couldn't run, they couldn't fight, and they didn't dare drop their precious cargo.

The commander's voice bellowed out over the carnage. "Take him prisoner! I'll personally strangle the idiot who harms him!" And then he was too busy to yell.

Two members of the Greatest Noble's personal guard came for him, swords out, determined to give their lives, if necessary, to preserve the sacred life of their monarch. And give them they did.

The commander's blade lashed out once, sliding between the ribs of the first guard. He toppled and almost took the sword with him, but the commander wrenched it free in time to parry the downward slash of the second guard's bronze sword. It was a narrow thing, because the bronze sword, though of softer stuff than the commander's steel, was also heavier, and thus hard to deflect. As it sang past him, the commander swung a chop at the man's neck, cutting it halfway through. He stepped quickly to one side to avoid the falling body and thrust his blade through a third man, who was aiming a blow at the neck of one of the commander's officers. There were only a dozen feet separating the commander from his objective, the palanquin of the Greatest Noble, but he had to wade through blood to get there.

The palanquin itself was no longer steady. Three of the twelve nobles who had been holding it had already fallen, and there were two of the commander's men already close enough to touch the royal person, but they were too busy fighting to make any attempt to grab him. The Greatest Noble, unarmed, could only huddle in his seat, terrified, but it would take more than two men to snatch him from his bodyguard. The commander fought his way in closer.

Two more of the palanquin bearers went down, and the palanquin itself began to topple. The Greatest Noble screamed as he fell toward the commander.

One of the commander's men spun around as he heard the scream so close to him, and, thinking that the Greatest Noble was attacking his commander, lunged out with his blade.

It was almost a disaster. Moving quickly, the commander threw out his left arm to deflect the sword. He succeeded, but he got a bad slash across his hand for his trouble.

He yelled angrily at the surprised soldier, not caring what he said. Meanwhile, the others of the squad, seeing that the Greatest Noble had fallen, hurried to surround him. Two minutes later, the Greatest Noble was a prisoner, being half carried, half led into the central building by four of the men, while the remaining six fought a rear-guard action to hold off the native warriors who were trying to rescue the sacred person of the Child of the Sun.

Once inside, the Greatest Noble was held fast while the doors were swung shut.

Outside, the slaughter went on. All the resistance seemed to go out of the warriors when they saw their sacred monarch dragged away by the invading Earthmen. It was every man for himself and the Devil take the hindmost. And the Devil, in the form of the commander's troops, certainly did.

Within half an hour after it had begun, the butchery was over. More than three thousand of the natives had died, and an unknown number more badly wounded. Those who had managed to get out and get away from the city kept on going. They told the troops who had been left outside what had happened, and a mass exodus from the valley began.

Safely within the fortifications of the central building, the commander allowed himself one of his rare grins of satisfaction. Not a single one of his own men had been killed, and the only wound which had been sustained by anyone in the company was the cut on his own hand. Still smiling, he went into the room where the Greatest Noble, dazed and shaken, was being held by two of the commander's men. The commander bowed—this time, very low.

"I believe, Your Effulgence, that we have an appointment for dinner. Come, the banquet has been laid."

And, as though he were still playing the gracious host, the commander led the half-paralyzed Child of the Sun to the room where the banquet had been put on a table in perfect diplomatic array.

"Your Effulgence may sit at my right hand," said the commander pleasantly.

XIV

As MacDonald said of Robert Wilson, "This is not an account of how Boosterism came to Arcadia." It's a devil of a long way from it. And once the high point of a story has been reached and passed, it is pointless to prolong it too much. The capture of the Greatest Noble broke the power of the Empire of the Great Nobles forever. The loyal subjects were helpless without a leader, and the disloyal ones, near the periphery of the Empire, didn't care. The crack Imperial troops simply folded up and went home. The Greatest Noble went on issuing orders, and they were obeyed; the people were too used to taking orders from authority to care whether they were really the Greatest Noble's own idea or not.

In a matter of months, two hundred men had conquered an empire, with a loss of thirty-five or forty men. Eventually, they had to execute the old Greatest Noble and put his more tractable nephew on the throne, but that was a mere incident.

Gold? It flowed as though there were an endless supply. The commander shipped enough back on the first load to make them all wealthy.

The commander didn't go back home to spend his wealth amid the luxuries of the Imperial court, even though Emperor Carl appointed him to the nobility. That sort of thing wasn't the commander's meat. There, he would be a fourth-rate noble; here, he was the Imperial Viceroy, responsible only to the distant Emperor. There, he would be nothing; here, he was almost a king.

Two years after the capture of the Greatest Noble, he established a new capital on the coast and named it Kingston. And from Kingston he ruled with an iron hand.

As has been intimated, this was *not* Arcadia. A year after the founding of Kingston, the old capital was attacked, burned, and almost fell under siege, due to a sudden uprising of the natives under the new Greatest Noble, who had managed to escape. But the uprising collapsed because of the approach of the planting season; the warriors had to go back home and plant their crops or the whole of the agriculture-based country would starve—except the invading Earthmen.

Except in a few instances, the natives were never again any trouble.

But the commander—now the Viceroy—had not seen the end of his troubles.

He had known his limitations, and realized that the governing of a whole planet—or even one continent—was too much for one man when the population consists primarily of barbarians and savages. So he had delegated the rule of a vast area to the south to another—a Lieutenant commander James, known as "One-Eye," a man who had helped finance the original expedition, and had arrived after the conquest.

One-Eye went south and made very small headway against the more barbaric tribes there. He did not become rich, and he did not achieve anywhere near the success that the Viceroy had. So he came back north with his army and decided to unseat the Viceroy and take his place. That was five years after the capture of the Greatest Noble.

One-Eye took Center City, the old capital, and started to work his way northward, toward Kingston. The Viceroy's forces met him at a place known as Salt Flats and thoroughly trounced him. He was captured, tried for high treason, and executed.

One would think that the execution ended the threat of Lieutenant commander James, but not so. He had a son, and he had had followers.

XV

Nine years. Nine years since the breaking of a vast empire. It really didn't seem like it. The Viceroy looked at his hands. They were veined and thin, and the callouses were gone. Was he getting soft, or just getting old? A little bit—no, a *great deal* of both.

He sat in his study, in the Viceregal Palace at Kingston, chewing over the events of the past weeks. Twice, rumors had come that he was to be assassinated. He and two of his councilors had been hanged in effigy in the public square not long back. He had been snubbed publicly by some of the lesser nobles.

Had he ruled harshly, or was it just jealousy? And was it, really, as some said, caused by the Southerners and the followers of Young Jim?

He didn't know. And sometimes, it seemed as if it didn't matter.

Here he was, sitting alone in his study, when he should have gone to a public function. And he had stayed because of fear of assassination.

Was it—

There was a knock at the door.

"Come in."

A servant entered. "Sir Martin is here, my lord."

The Viceroy got to his feet. "Show him in, by all means."

Sir Martin, just behind the servant, stepped in, smiling, and the Viceroy returned his smile. "Well, everything went off well enough without you," said Sir Martin.

"Any sign of trouble?"

"None, my lord; none whatsoever. The—"

"Damn!" the Viceroy interrupted savagely. "I should have known! What have I done but display my cowardice? I'm getting yellow in my old age!"

Sir Martin shook his head. "Cowardice, my lord? Nothing of the sort. Prudence, I should call it. By the by, the judge and a few others are coming over." He chuckled softly. "We thought we might talk you out of a meal."

The Viceroy grinned widely. "Nothing easier. I suspected all you hangers-on would come around for your handouts. Come along, my friend; we'll have a drink before the others get here."

There were nearly twenty people at dinner, all, presumably, friends of the Viceroy. At least, it is certain that they were friends in so far as they had no part in the assassination plot. It was a gay party; the Viceroy's friends were doing their best to cheer him up, and were succeeding pretty well. One of the nobles, known for his wit, had just essayed a somewhat off-color jest, and the others were roaring with laughter at the punch line when a shout rang out.

There was a sudden silence around the table.

"What was that?" asked someone. "What did—"

"*Help!*" There was the sound of footsteps pounding up the stairway from the lower floor.

"*Help! The Southerners have come to kill the Viceroy!*"

From the sounds, there was no doubt in any of the minds of the people seated around the table that the shout was true. For a moment, there was shock. Then panic took over.

There were only a dozen or so men in the attacking party; if the "friends" of the Viceroy had stuck by him, they could have held off the assassins with ease.

But no one ran to lock the doors that stood between the Viceroy and his enemies, and only a few drew their weapons to defend him. The others fled. Getting out of a window from the second floor of a building isn't easy, but fear can lend wings, and, although none of them actually flew down, the retreat went fast enough.

Characteristically, the Viceroy headed, not for the window, but for his own room, where his armor—long unused, except for state functions—hung waiting in the closet. With him went Sir Martin.

But there wasn't even an opportunity to get into the armor. The rebel band charged into the hallway that led to the bedroom, screaming: "*Death to the Tyrant! Long live the Emperor!*"

It was personal anger, then, not rebellion against the Empire which had appointed the ex-commander to his post as Viceroy.

"Where is the Viceroy? Death to the Tyrant!" The assassins moved in.

Swords in hand, and cloaks wrapped around their left arms, Sir Martin and the Viceroy moved to meet the oncoming attackers.

"Traitors!" bellowed the Viceroy. "Cowards! Have you come to kill me in my own house?"

Parry, thrust! Parry, thrust! Two of the attackers fell before the snake-tongue blade of the fighting Viceroy. Sir Martin accounted for two more before he fell in a flood of his own blood.

The Viceroy was alone, now. His blade flickered as though inspired, and two more died under its tireless onslaught. Even more would have died if the head of the conspiracy, a supporter of Young Jim named Rada, hadn't pulled a trick that not even the Viceroy would have pulled.

Rada grabbed one of his own men and shoved him toward the Viceroy's sword, impaling the hapless man upon that deadly blade.

And, in the moment while the Viceroy's weapon was buried to the hilt in an enemy's body, the others leaped around the dying man and ran their blades through the Viceroy.

He dropped to the floor, blood gushing from half a dozen wounds.

Even so, his fighting heart still had seconds more to beat. As he propped himself up on one arm, the assassins stood back; even they recognized that they had killed something bigger and stronger than they. A better man than any of them lay dying at their feet.

He clawed with one hand at the river of red that flowed from his pierced throat and then fell forward across the stone floor. With his crimson hand, he traced the great symbol of his Faith on the stone—the Sign of the Cross. He bent his head to kiss it, and, with a final cry of "*Jesus!*" he died. At the age of seventy, it had taken a dozen men to kill him with treachery, something all the hell of nine years of conquest and rule had been unable to do.

And thus died Francisco Pizarro, the Conqueror of Peru.

THE END

To be read after you have finished "Despoilers of the Golden Empire."

Dear John,

It has been brought to my attention, by those who have read the story, that "Despoilers of the Golden Empire" might conceivably be charged with being a "reader cheater"—*i.e.*, that it does not play fair with the reader, but leads him astray by means of false statements. Naturally, I feel it me bounden duty to refute such scurrilous and untrue affronts, and thus save meself from opprobrium.

Therefore, I address what follows to the interested reader:

It cannot be denied that you must have been misled when you read the story; indeed, I'd be the last to deny it, since I *intended* that you should be misled. What I most certainly *do* deny is any implication that such misleading was accomplished by the telling of untruths. A fiction writer is, *by definition*, a professional liar; he makes his living by telling interesting lies on paper and selling the results to the highest bidder for publication. Since fiction writing is my livelihood, I cannot and will not deny that I am an accomplished liar—indeed, almost an habitual one. Therefore, I feel some small pique when, on the one occasion on which I stick strictly to the truth, I am accused of fraud. *Pfui!* say I; I refute you. "I deny the allegation, and I defy the alligator!"

To prove my case, I shall take several examples from "Despoilers" and show that the statements made are perfectly valid. (Please note that I do not claim any absolute accuracy for such details as quoted dialogue, except that none of the characters lies. I simply contend that the story is as accurate as any other good historical novelette. I also might say here that any resemblance between "Despoilers" and any story picked at random from the late lamented *Planet Stories* is purely intentional and carefully contrived.)

Take the first sentence:

"In the seven centuries that had elapsed since the Second Empire had been founded on the shattered remnants of the First, the nobles of the Imperium had come slowly to realize that the empire was not to be judged by the examples of its predecessor."

Perfectly true. By the time of the Renaissance, the nobles of the Holy Roman Empire knew that their empire was not just a continuation of the Roman Empire, but a new entity. The old Roman Empire had collapsed in the Sixth Century, and the *Holy* Roman Empire, which was actually a loose confederation of Germanic states, did not come into being until A. D. 800, when Karl der Grosse (Charlemagne) was crowned emperor by the Pope.

Anyone who wishes to quibble that the date should be postponed for a century and a half, until the time of the German prince, Otto, may do so; I will ignore him.

A few paragraphs later, I said:

"Without power, neither Civilization nor the Empire could hold itself together, and His Universal Majesty, the Emperor Carl, well knew it. And power was linked solidly to one element, one metal ..."

The metal, as I said later on, was Gold-197.

By "power," of course, I meant political and economic power. In the Sixteenth Century, that's what almost anyone would have meant. If you chose to interpret it as meaning "energy per unit time," why, that's real tough.

Why nail the "power metal" down to an isotope of gold with an atomic weight of 197? Because that's the only naturally occurring isotope of gold.

The "Emperor Carl" was, of course, Charles V, who also happened to be King of Spain, and therefore Pizarro's sovereign. I Germanicized his name, as I did the others—Francisco Pizarro becomes "Frank," et cetera—but this is perfectly legitimate. After all, the king's name in Latin, which was used in all state papers, was *Carolus*; the Spanish called him *Carlos*, and history books in English call him *Charles*. Either *Karl* or *Carl* is just as legitimate as *Charles*, certainly, and the same applies to the other names in the story.

As to the title "His Universal Majesty," that's exactly what he *was* called. It is usually translated as "His Catholic Majesty," but the word *Catholic* comes from the Greek *katholikos*, meaning "universal." And, further on in the story, when the term "Universal Assembly" is used, it is a direct translation of the Greek term,*Ekklesia Katholikos*, and is actually a better translation than "Catholic Church," since the English word *church*comes from the Greek *kyriakon*, meaning "the house of the Lord"—in other words, a church *building*, not the organization as a whole.

Toward the end of Chapter One, I wrote:

"Throughout the Empire, research laboratories worked tirelessly at the problem of transmuting commoner elements into Gold-197, but thus far none of the processes was commercially feasible."

I think you will admit that the alchemists never found a method of transmuting the elements—certainly none which was commercially feasible.

In Chapter Three, the statement that Pizarro left his home—Spain—with undermanned ships, and had to sneak off illegally before the King's inspectors checked up on him, is historically accurate. And who can argue with the statement that "there wasn't a scientist worthy of the name in the whole outfit"?

At the beginning of Chapter Four, you'll find:

"Due to atmospheric disturbances, the ship's landing was several hundred miles from the point the commander had originally picked ..." and "... the ship simply wasn't built for atmospheric navigation."

The adverse winds which drove Pizarro's ships off course were certainly "atmospheric disturbances," and I defy anyone to prove that a Sixteenth Century Spanish galleon was built for atmospheric navigation.

And I insist that using the term "carrier" instead of "horse," while misleading, is not inaccurate. However, I *would* like to know just what sort of picture the term conjured up in the reader's mind. In Chapter Ten, in the battle scene, you'll find the following:

"The combination of attackers from both sides, plus the fact that the heavy armor was a little unwieldy, overbalanced him the commander. He toppled to the ground with a clash of steel as he and the carrier parted company.

"Without a human hand at its controls, the carrier automatically moved away from the mass of struggling fighters and came to a halt well away from the battle."

To be perfectly honest, it's somewhat of a strain on my mind to imagine anyone building a robot-controlled machine as good as all that, and then giving the drive such poor protection that he can fall off of it.

One of the great screams from my critics has been occasioned by the fact that I referred several times to the Spaniards as "Earthmen." I can't see why. In order not to confuse the reader, I invariably referred to them as the "*invading* Earthmen," so as to make a clear distinction between them and the *native* Earthmen, or Incas, who were native to Peru. If this be treachery, then make the most of it.

In other words, I contend that I simply did what any other good detective story writer tries to do—mislead the reader without lying to him. Agatha Christie's "The Murder of Roger Ackroyd," for instance, uses the device of telling the story from the murderer's viewpoint, in the first person, without revealing that he *is* the murderer. Likewise, John Dickson Carr, in his "Nine Wrong Answers" finds himself forced to deny that he has lied to the reader, although he admits that one of his characters certainly lied. Both Carr and Christie told the absolute truth—within the framework of the story—and left it to the reader to delude himself.

It all depends on the viewpoint. The statement, "We all liked Father Goodheart very much" means one thing when said by a member of his old parish in the United States, which he left to become a missionary. It means something else again when uttered by a member of the tribe of cannibals which the good Father attempted unsuccessfully to convert.

Similarly, such terms as "the gulf between the worlds," "the new world," and "the known universe" have one meaning to a science-fictioneer, and another to a historian. Semantics, anyone?

In Chapter Ten, right at the beginning, there is a conversation between Commander Frank and Frater Vincent, and "agent of the Assembly" (read: *priest*). If the reader will go back over that section, keeping in mind the fact that what they are "actually" talking about are the Catholic Church and the Christian religion *as seen from the viewpoint of a couple of fanatically devout Sixteenth Century Spaniards*, he will understand the method I used in presenting the whole story.

Let me quote:

"Mentally, the commander went through the symbol-patterns that he had learned as a child—the symbol-patterns that brought him into direct contact with the Ultimate Power, the Power that controlled not only the spinning of atoms and the whirling of electrons in their orbits, but the workings of probability itself."

Obviously, he is reciting the *Pater Noster* and the *Ave Maria*. The rest of the sentence is self-explanatory.

So is the following:

"Once indoctrinated into the teachings of the Universal Assembly, any man could tap that power to a greater or lesser degree, depending on his mental control and ethical attitude. At the top level, a first-class adept could utilize that Power for telepathy, psychokinesis, levitation, teleportation, and other powers that the commander only vaguely understood."

It doesn't matter whether *you* believe in the miracles attributed to many of the Saints; Pizarro certainly did. His faith in that Power was as certain as the modern faith in the power of the atomic bomb.

As a matter of fact, it was very probably that hard, unyielding Faith which made the Sixteenth Century Spaniard the almost superhuman being that he was. Only Spain of the Sixteenth Century could have produced the Conquistadors or such a man as St. Ignatius Loyola, whose learned, devout, and fanatically militant Society of Jesus struck fear into the hearts of Protestant and Catholic Princes alike for the next two centuries.

The regular reader of Astounding may remember that I gave another example of the technique of truthful misdirection in "The Best Policy," (July, 1957). An Earthman, captured by aliens, finds himself in a position in which he is unable to tell even the smallest lie. But by telling the absolute truth, he convinces the aliens that *homo sapiens* is a race of super-duper supermen. He does it so well that the aliens surrender without attacking, even before the rest of humanity is aware of their existence.

The facts in "Despoilers of the Golden Empire" remain. They *are* facts. Francisco Pizarro and his men—an army of less than two hundred—actually *did* inflict appalling damage on the Inca armies, even if they were outnumbered ten to one, and with astonishingly few losses of their own. They did it with sheer guts, too; their equipment was not too greatly superior to that of the Peruvians, and by the time they reached the Great Inca himself, none of the Peruvians believed that the invaders were demons or gods. But in the face of the Spaniards' determined onslaught, they were powerless.

The assassination scene at the end is almost an exact description of what happened. It *did* take a dozen men in full armor to kill the armorless Pizarro, and even then it took trickery and treachery to do it.

Now, just to show how fair I was—to show how I scrupulously refrained from lying—I will show what a sacrifice I made for the sake of truth.

If you'll recall, in the story, the dying Pizarro traces the Sign of the Cross on the floor in his own blood, kisses it, and says "*Jesus!*" before he dies. This is in strict accord with every history on the subject I could find.

But there is a legend to the effect that his last words were somewhat different. I searched the New York Public Library for days trying to find one single historian who would bear out the legend; I even went so far as to get a librarian who could read Spanish and another whose German is somewhat better than mine to translate articles in foreign historical journals for me. All in vain. But if I *could* have substantiated the legend, the final scene would have read something like this:

Clawing at his sword-torn throat, the fearless old soldier brought his hand away coated with the crimson of his own blood. Falling forward, he traced the Sign of the Cross on the stone floor in gleaming scarlet, kissed it, and then glared up at the men who surrounded him, his eyes hard with anger and hate.

"I'm going to Heaven," he said, his voice harsh and whispery. "And *you*, you *bastards*, can go to *Hell*!"

It would have made one hell of an ending—but it had to be sacrificed in the interests of Truth.

So I rest my case.

I will even go further than that; I defy anyone to point out a single out-and-out lie in the whole story. G'wan—I *dare* ya! (SECRET ASIDE TO THE READER; J. W. C., Jr., PLEASE DO *NOT* READ!)

Ah, but wait! There *is* a villain in the piece!

I did not lie to you, no. But you were lied to, all the same.

By whom?

By none less than that conniving arch-fiend, John W. Campbell, Jr., that's who!

Wasn't it he who bought the story?

And wasn't it he who, with malice aforethought, published it in a package which was plainly labeled Science Fiction?

And, therefore, didn't you have every right to think it *was* science fiction?

Sure you did!

I am guilty of nothing more than weakness; my poor, frail sense of ethics collapsed completely at the sight of the bribe he offered me to become a party to the dark conspiracy that sprang from the depths of his own demoniac mind. Ah, well; none of us is perfect, I suppose.

DAVID GORDON.

The Eyes Have It

In a sense, this is a story of here-and-now. This Earth, this year ... but on a history-line slipped slightly sidewise. A history in which a great man acted differently, and Magic, rather than physical science, was developed....

Sir Pierre Morlaix, Chevalier of the Angevin Empire, Knight of the Golden Leopard, and secretary-in-private to my lord, the Count D'Evreux, pushed back the lace at his cuff for a glance at his wrist watch—three minutes of seven. The Angelus had rung at six, as always, and my lord D'Evreux had been awakened by it, as always. At least, Sir Pierre could not remember any time in the past seventeen years when my lord had not awakened at the Angelus. Once, he recalled, the sacristan had failed to ring the bell, and the Count had been furious for a week. Only the intercession of Father Bright, backed by the Bishop himself, had saved the sacristan from doing a turn in the dungeons of Castle D'Evreux.

Sir Pierre stepped out into the corridor, walked along the carpeted flagstones, and cast a practiced eye around him as he walked. These old castles were difficult to keep clean, and my lord the Count was fussy about nitre collecting in the seams between the stones of the walls. All appeared quite in order, which was a good thing. My lord the Count had been making a night of it last evening, and that always made him the more peevish in the morning. Though he always woke at the Angelus, he did not always wake up sober.

Sir Pierre stopped before a heavy, polished, carved oak door, selected a key from one of the many at his belt, and turned it in the lock. Then he went into the elevator and the door locked automatically behind him. He pressed the switch and waited in patient silence as he was lifted up four floors to the Count's personal suite.

By now, my lord the Count would have bathed, shaved, and dressed. He would also have poured down an eye-opener consisting of half a water glass of fine Champagne brandy. He would not eat breakfast until eight. The Count had no valet in the strict sense of the term. Sir Reginald Beauvay held that title, but he was never called upon to exercise the more personal functions of his office. The Count did not like to be seen until he was thoroughly presentable.

The elevator stopped. Sir Pierre stepped out into the corridor and walked along it toward the door at the far end. At exactly seven o'clock, he rapped briskly on the great door which bore the gilt-and-polychrome arms of the House D'Evreux.

For the first time in seventeen years, there was no answer.

Sir Pierre waited for the growled command to enter for a full minute, unable to believe his ears. Then, almost timidly, he rapped again.

There was still no answer.

Then, bracing himself for the verbal onslaught that would follow if he had erred, Sir Pierre turned the handle and opened the door just as if he had heard the Count's voice telling him to come in.

"Good morning, my lord," he said, as he always had for seventeen years.

But the room was empty, and there was no answer.

He looked around the huge room. The morning sunlight streamed in through the high mullioned windows and spread a diamond-checkered pattern across the tapestry on the far wall, lighting up the brilliant hunting scene in a blaze of color.

"My lord?"

Nothing. Not a sound.

The bedroom door was open. Sir Pierre walked across to it and looked in.

He saw immediately why my lord the Count had not answered, and that, indeed, he would never answer again.

My lord the Count lay flat on his back, his arms spread wide, his eyes staring at the ceiling. He was still clad in his gold and scarlet evening clothes. But the great stain on the front of his coat was not the same shade of scarlet as the rest of the cloth, and the stain had a bullet hole in its center.

Sir Pierre looked at him without moving for a long moment. Then he stepped over, knelt, and touched one of the Count's hands with the back of his own. It was quite cool. He had been dead for hours.

"I knew someone would do you in sooner or later, my lord," said Sir Pierre, almost regretfully.

Then he rose from his kneeling position and walked out without another look at his dead lord. He locked the door of the suite, pocketed the key, and went back downstairs in the elevator.

Mary, Lady Duncan stared out of the window at the morning sunlight and wondered what to do. The Angelus bell had awakened her from a fitful sleep in her chair, and she knew that, as a guest at Castle D'Evreux, she would be expected to appear at Mass again this morning. But how could she? How could she face the Sacramental Lord on the altar—to say nothing of taking the Blessed Sacrament itself.

Still, it would look all the more conspicuous if she did not show up this morning after having made it a point to attend every morning with Lady Alice during the first four days of this visit.

She turned and glanced at the locked and barred door of the bedroom. *He* would not be expected to come. Laird Duncan used his wheelchair as an excuse, but since he had taken up black magic as a hobby he had, she suspected, been actually afraid to go anywhere near a church.

If only she hadn't lied to him! But how could she have told the truth? That would have been worse—infinitely worse. And now, because of that lie, he was locked in his bedroom doing only God and the Devil knew what.

If only he would come out. If he would only stop whatever it was he had been doing for all these long hours—or at least finish it! Then they could leave Evreux, make some excuse—any excuse—to get away. One of them could feign sickness. Anything, anything to get them out of France, across the Channel, and back to Scotland, where they would be safe!

She looked back out of the window, across the courtyard, at the towering stone walls of the Great Keep and at the high window that opened into the suite of Edouard, Count D'Evreux.

Last night she had hated him, but no longer. Now there was only room in her heart for fear.

She buried her face in her hands and cursed herself for a fool. There were no tears left for weeping—not after the long night.

Behind her, she heard the sudden noise of the door being unlocked, and she turned.

Laird Duncan of Duncan opened the door and wheeled himself out. He was followed by a malodorous gust of vapor from the room he had just left. Lady Duncan stared at him.

He looked older than he had last night, more haggard and worn, and there was something in his eyes she did not like. For a moment he said nothing. Then he wet his lips with the tip of his tongue. When he spoke, his voice sounded dazed.

"There is nothing to fear any more," he said. "Nothing to fear at all."

The Reverend Father James Valois Bright, Vicar of the Chapel of Saint-Esprit, had as his flock the several hundred inhabitants of the Castle D'Evreux. As such, he was the ranking priest—socially, not hierarchically—in the country. Not counting the Bishop and the Chapter at the Cathedral, of course. But such knowledge did little good for the Father's peace of mind. The turnout of the flock was abominably small for its size—especially for week-day Masses. The Sunday Masses were well attended, of course; Count D'Evreux was there punctually at nine every Sunday, and he had a habit of counting the house. But he never showed up on weekdays, and his laxity had allowed a certain further laxity to filter down through the ranks.

The great consolation was Lady Alice D'Evreux. She was a plain, simple girl, nearly twenty years younger than her brother, the Count, and quite his opposite in every way. She was quiet where he was thundering, self-effacing where he was flamboyant, temperate where he was drunken, and chaste where he was—

Father Bright brought his thoughts to a full halt for a moment. He had, he reminded himself, no right to make judgments of that sort. He was not, after all, the Count's confessor; the Bishop was.

Besides, he should have his mind on his prayers just now.

He paused and was rather surprised to notice that he had already put on his alb, amice, and girdle, and he was aware that his lips had formed the words of the prayer as he had donned each of them.

Habit, he thought, *can be destructive to the contemplative faculty.*

He glanced around the sacristy. His server, the young son of the Count of Saint Brieuc, sent here to complete his education as a gentleman who would some day be the King's Governor of one of the most important counties in Brittany, was pulling his surplice down over his head. The clock said 7:11.

Father Bright forced his mind Heavenward and repeated silently the vesting prayers that his lips had formed meaninglessly, this time putting his full intentions behind them. Then he added a short mental prayer asking God to forgive him for allowing his thoughts to stray in such a manner.

He opened his eyes and reached for his chasuble just as the sacristy door opened and Sir Pierre, the Count's Privy Secretary, stepped in.

"I must speak to you, Father," he said in a low voice. And, glancing at the young De Saint-Brieuc, he added: "Alone."

Normally, Father Bright would have reprimanded anyone who presumed to break into the sacristy as he was vesting for Mass, but he knew that Sir Pierre would never interrupt without good reason. He nodded and went outside in the corridor that led to the altar.

"What is it, Pierre?" he asked.

"My lord the Count is dead. Murdered."

After the first momentary shock, Father Bright realized that the news was not, after all, totally unexpected. Somewhere in the back of his mind, it seemed he had always known that the Count would die by violence long before debauchery ruined his health.

"Tell me about it," he said quietly.

Sir Pierre reported exactly what he had done and what he had seen.

"Then I locked the door and came straight here," he told the priest.

"Who else has the key to the Count's suite?" Father Bright asked.

"No one but my lord himself," Sir Pierre answered, "at least as far as I know."

"Where is his key?"

"Still in the ring at his belt. I noticed that particularly."

"Very good. We'll leave it locked. You're certain the body was cold?"

"Cold and waxy, Father."

"Then he's been dead many hours."

"Lady Alice will have to be told," Sir Pierre said.

Father Bright nodded. "Yes. The Countess D'Evreux must be informed of her succession to the County Seat." He could tell by the sudden momentary blank look that came over Sir Pierre's face that the Privy Secretary had not yet realized fully the implications of the Count's death. "I'll tell her, Pierre. She should be in her pew by now. Just step into the church and tell her quietly that I want to speak to her. Don't tell her anything else."

"I understand, Father," said Sir Pierre.

There were only twenty-five or thirty people in the pews—most of them women—but Alice, Countess D'Evreux was not one of them. Sir Pierre walked quietly and unobtrusively down the side aisle and out into the narthex. She was standing there, just inside the main door, adjusting the black lace mantilla about her head, as though she had just come in from outside. Suddenly, Sir Pierre was very glad he would not have to be the one to break the news.

She looked rather sad, as always, her plain face unsmiling. The jutting nose and square chin which had given her brother the Count a look of aggressive handsomeness only made her look very solemn and rather sexless, although she had a magnificent figure.

"My lady," Sir Pierre said, stepping towards her, "the Reverent Father would like to speak to you before Mass. He's waiting at the sacristy door."

She held her rosary clutched tightly to her breast and gasped. Then she said, "Oh. Sir Pierre. I'm sorry; you quite surprised me. I didn't see you."

"My apologies, my lady."

"It's all right. My thoughts were elsewhere. Will you take me to the good Father?"

Father Bright heard their footsteps coming down the corridor before he saw them. He was a little fidgety because Mass was already a minute overdue. It should have started promptly at 7:15.

The new Countess D'Evreux took the news calmly, as he had known she would. After a pause, she crossed herself and said: "May his soul rest in peace. I will leave everything in your hands, Father, Sir Pierre. What are we to do?"

"Pierre must get on the teleson to Rouen immediately and report the matter to His Highness. I will announce your brother's death and ask for prayers for his soul—but I think I need say nothing about the manner of his death. There is no need to arouse any more speculation and fuss than necessary."

"Very well," said the Countess. "Come, Sir Pierre; I will speak to the Duke, my cousin, myself."

"Yes, my lady."

Father Bright returned to the sacristy, opened the missal, and changed the placement of the ribbons. Today was an ordinary Feria; a Votive Mass would not be forbidden by the rubics. The clock said 7:17. He turned to young De Saint-Brieuc, who was waiting respectfully. "Quickly, my son—go and get the unbleached beeswax candles and put them on the altar. Be sure you light them before you put out the white ones. Hurry, now; I will be ready by the time you come back. Oh yes—and change the altar frontal. Put on the black."

"Yes, Father." And the lad was gone.

Father Bright folded the green chasuble and returned it to the drawer, then took out the black one. He would say a Requiem for the Souls of All the Faithful Departed—and hope that the Count was among them.

His Royal Highness, the Duke of Normandy, looked over the official letter his secretary had just typed for him. It was addressed to *Serenissimus Dominus Nostrus Iohannes Quartus, Dei Gratia, Angliae, Franciae, Scotiae, Hiberniae, et Novae Angliae, Rex, Imperator, Fidei Defensor,* ... "Our Most Serene Lord, John IV, by the Grace of God King and Emperor of England, France, Scotland, Ireland, and New England, Defender of the Faith, ..."

It was a routine matter; simple notification to his brother, the King, that His Majesty's most faithful servant, Edouard, Count of Evreux had departed this life, and asking His Majesty's confirmation of the Count's heir-at-law, Alice, Countess of Evreux as his lawful successor.

His Highness finished reading, nodded, and scrawled his signature at the bottom: *Richard Dux Normaniae.*

Then, on a separate piece of paper, he wrote: "Dear John, May I suggest you hold up on this for a while? Edouard was a lecher and a slob, and I have no doubt he got everything he deserved, but we have no notion who killed him. For any evidence I have to the contrary, it might have been Alice who pulled the trigger. I will send you full particulars as soon as I have them. With much love, Your brother and servant, Richard."

He put both papers into a prepared envelope and sealed it. He wished he could have called the king on the teleson, but no one had yet figured out how to get the wires across the channel.

He looked absently at the sealed envelope, his handsome blond features thoughtful. The House of Plantagenet had endured for eight centuries, and the blood of Henry of Anjou ran thin in its veins, but the Norman strain was as strong as ever, having been replenished over the centuries by fresh infusions from Norwegian and Danish princesses. Richard's mother, Queen Helga, wife to His late Majesty, Henry X, spoke very few words of Anglo-French, and those with a heavy Norse accent.

Nevertheless, there was nothing Scandinavian in the language, manner, or bearing of Richard, Duke of Normandy. Not only was he a member of the oldest and most powerful ruling family of Europe, but he bore a Christian name that was distinguished even in that family. Seven Kings of the Empire had borne the name, and most of them had been good Kings—if not always "good" men in the nicey-nicey sense of the word. Even old Richard I, who'd been pretty wild during the first forty-odd years of his life, had settled down to do a magnificent job of kinging for the next twenty years. The long and painful recovery from the wound he'd received at the Siege of Chaluz had made a change in him for the better.

There was a chance that Duke Richard might be called upon to uphold the honor of that name as King. By law, Parliament must elect a Plantagenet as King in the event of the death of the present Sovereign, and while the election of one of the King's two sons, the Prince of Wales and the Duke of Lancaster, was more likely than the election of Richard, he was certainly not eliminated from the succession.

Meantime, he would uphold the honor of his name as Duke of Normandy.

Murder had been done; therefore justice must be done. The Count D'Evreux had been known for his stern but fair justice almost as well as he had been known for his profligacy. And, just as his pleasures had been without temperance, so his justice had been untempered by mercy. Whoever had killed him would find both justice and mercy—in so far as Richard had it within his power to give it.

Although he did not formulate it in so many words, even mentally, Richard was of the opinion that some debauched woman or cuckolded man had fired the fatal shot. Thus he found himself inclining toward mercy before he knew anything substantial about the case at all.

Richard dropped the letter he was holding into the special mail pouch that would be placed aboard the evening trans-Channel packet, and then turned in his chair to look at the lean, middle-aged man working at a desk across the room.

"My lord Marquis," he said thoughtfully.

"Yes, Your Highness?" said the Marquis of Rouen, looking up.

"How true are the stories one has heard about the late Count?"

"True, Your Highness?" the Marquis said thoughtfully. "I would hesitate to make any estimate of percentages. Once a man gets a reputation like that, the number of his reputed sins quickly surpasses the number of actual ones. Doubtless many of the stories one hears are of whole cloth; others may have only a slight basis in fact. On the other hand, it is highly likely that there are many of which we have never heard. It is absolutely certain, however, that he has acknowledged seven illegitimate sons, and I dare say he has ignored a few daughters—and these, mind you, with unmarried women. His adulteries would be rather more difficult to establish, but I think your Highness can take it for granted that such escapades were far from uncommon."

He cleared his throat and then added, "If Your Highness is looking for motive, I fear there is a superabundance of persons with motive."

"I see," the Duke said. "Well, we will wait and see what sort of information Lord Darcy comes up with." He looked up at the clock. "They should be there by now."

Then, as if brushing further thoughts on the subject from his mind, he went back to work, picking up a new sheaf of state papers from his desk.

The Marquis watched him for a moment and smiled a little to himself. The young Duke took his work seriously, but was well-balanced about it. A little inclined to be romantic—but aren't we all at nineteen? There was no doubt of his ability, nor of his nobility. The Royal Blood of England always came through.

"My lady," said Sir Pierre gently, "the Duke's Investigators have arrived."

My Lady Alice, Countess D'Evreux, was seated in a gold-brocade upholstered chair in the small receiving room off the Great Hall. Standing near her, looking very grave, was Father Bright. Against the blaze of color on the walls of the room, the two of them stood out like ink blots. Father Bright wore his normal clerical black, unrelieved except for the pure white lace at collar and cuffs. The Countess wore unadorned black velvet, a dress which she had had to have altered hurriedly by her dressmaker; she had always hated black and owned only the mourning she had worn when her mother died eight years before. The somber looks on their faces seemed to make the black blacker.

"Show them in, Sir Pierre," the Countess said calmly.

Sir Pierre opened the door wider, and three men entered. One was dressed as one gently born; the other two wore the livery of the Duke of Normandy.

The gentleman bowed. "I am Lord Darcy, Chief Criminal Investigator for His Highness, the Duke, and your servant, my lady." He was a tall, brown-haired man in his thirties with a rather handsome, lean face. He spoke Anglo-French with a definite English accent.

"My pleasure, Lord Darcy," said the Countess. "This is our vicar, Father Bright."

"Your servant, Reverend Sir." Then he presented the two men with him. The first was a scholarly-looking, graying man wearing pince-nez glasses with gold rims, Dr. Pateley, Physician. The second, a tubby, red-faced, smiling man, was Master Sean O Lochlainn, Sorcerer.

As soon as Master Sean was presented he removed a small, leather-bound folder from his belt pouch and proffered it to the priest. "My license, Reverend Father."

Father Bright took it and glanced over it. It was the usual thing, signed and sealed by the Archbishop of Rouen. The law was rather strict on that point; no sorcerer could practice without the permission of the Church, and a license was given only after careful examination for orthodoxy of practice.

"It seems to be quite in order, Master Sean," said the priest, handing the folder back. The tubby little sorcerer bowed his thanks and returned the folder to his belt pouch.

Lord Darcy had a notebook in his hand. "Now, unpleasant as it may be, we shall have to check on a few facts." He consulted his notes, then looked up at Sir Pierre. "You, I believe, discovered the body?"

"That is correct, your lordship."

"How long ago was this?"

Sir Pierre glanced at his wrist watch. It was 9:55. "Not quite three hours ago, your lordship."

"At what time, precisely?"

"I rapped on the door precisely at seven, and went in a minute or two later—say 7:01 or 7:02."

"How do you know the time so exactly?"

"My lord the Count," said Sir Pierre with some stiffness, "insisted upon exact punctuality. I have formed the habit of referring to my watch regularly."

"I see. Very good. Now, what did you do then?"

Sir Pierre described his actions briefly.

"The door to his suite was not locked, then?" Lord Darcy asked.

"No, sir."

"You did not expect it to be locked?"

"No, sir. It has not been for seventeen years."

Lord Darcy raised one eyebrow in a polite query. "Never?"

"Not at seven o'clock, your lordship. My lord the Count always rose promptly at six and unlocked the door before seven."

"He did lock it at night, then?"

"Yes, sir."

Lord Darcy looked thoughtful and made a note, but he said nothing more on that subject. "When you left, you locked the door?"

"That is correct, your lordship."

"And it has remained locked ever since?"

Sir Pierce hesitated and glanced at Father Bright. The priest said: "At 8:15, Sir Pierre and I went in. I wished to view the body. We touched nothing. We left at 8:20."

Master Sean O Lochlainn looked agitated. "Er ... excuse me, Reverend Sir. You didn't give him Holy Unction, I hope?"

"No," said Father Bright. "I thought it would be better to delay that until after the authorities has seen the ... er ... scene of the crime. I wouldn't want to make the gathering of evidence any more difficult than necessary."

"Quite right," murmured Lord Darcy.

"No blessings, I trust, Reverend Sir?" Master Sean persisted. "No exorcisms or—"

"Nothing," Father Bright interrupted somewhat testily. "I believe I crossed myself when I saw the body, but nothing more."

"Crossed *yourself*, sir. Nothing else?"

"No."

"Well, that's all right, then. Sorry to be so persistent, Reverend Sir, but any miasma of evil that may be left around is a very important clue, and it shouldn't be dispersed until it's been checked, you see."

"*Evil?*" My lady the Countess looked shocked.

"Sorry, my lady, but—" Master Sean began contritely.

But Father Bright interrupted by speaking to the Countess. "Don't distress yourself, my daughter; these men are only doing their duty."

"Of course. I understand. It's just that it's so—" She shuddered delicately.

Lord Darcy cast Master Sean a warning look, then asked politely, "Has my lady seen the deceased?"

"No," she said. "I will, however, if you wish."

"We'll see," said Lord Darcy. "Perhaps it won't be necessary. May we go up to the suite now?"

"Certainly," the Countess said. "Sir Pierre, if you will?"

"Yes, my lady."

As Sir Pierre unlocked the emblazoned door, Lord Darcy said: "Who else sleeps on this floor?"

"No one else, your lordship," Sir Pierre said. "The entire floor is ... was ... reserved for my lord the Count."

"Is there any way up besides that elevator?"

Sir Pierre turned and pointed toward the other end of the short hallway. "That leads to the staircase," he said, pointing to a massive oaken door, "but it's kept locked at all times. And, as you can see, there is a heavy bar across it. Except for moving furniture in and out or something like that, it's never used."

"No other way up or down, then?"

Sir Pierre hesitated. "Well, yes, your lordship, there is. I'll show you."

"A secret stairway?"

"Yes, your lordship."

"Very well. We'll look at it after we've seen the body."

Lord Darcy, having spent an hour on the train down from Rouen, was anxious to see the cause of the trouble at last.

He lay in the bedroom, just as Sir Pierre and Father Bright had left him.

"If you please, Dr. Pateley," said his lordship.

He knelt on one side of the corpse and watched carefully while Pateley knelt on the other side and looked at the face of the dead man. Then he touched one of the hands and tried to move an arm. "Rigor has set in—even to the fingers. Single bullet hole. Rather small caliber—I should say a .28 or .34—hard to tell until I've probed out the bullet. Looks like it went right through the heart, though. Hard to tell about powder burns; the blood has soaked the clothing and dried. Still, these specks ... hm-m-m. Yes. Hm-m-m."

Lord Darcy's eyes took in everything, but there was little enough to see on the body itself. Then his eye was caught by something that gave off a golden gleam. He stood up and walked over to the great canopied four-poster bed, then he was on his knees again, peering under it. A coin? No.

He picked it up carefully and looked at it. A button. Gold, intricately engraved in an Arabesque pattern, and set in the center with a single diamond. How long had it lain there? Where had it come from? Not from the Count's clothing, for his buttons were smaller, engraved with his arms, and had no gems. Had a man or a woman dropped it? There was no way of knowing at this stage of the game.

Darcy turned to Sir Pierre. "When was this room last cleaned?"

41

"Last evening, your lordship," the secretary said promptly. "My lord was always particular about that. The suite was always to be swept and cleaned during the dinner hour."

"Then this must have rolled under the bed at some time after dinner. Do you recognize it? The design is distinctive."

The Privy Secretary looked carefully at the button in the palm of Lord Darcy's hand without touching it. "I ... I hesitate to say," he said at last. "It looks like ... but I'm not sure—"

"Come, come, Chevalier! Where do you think you *might* have seen it? Or one like it." There was a sharpness in the tone of his voice.

"I'm not trying to conceal anything, your lordship," Sir Pierre said with equal sharpness. "I said I was not sure. I still am not, but it can be checked easily enough. If your lordship will permit me—" He turned and spoke to Dr. Pateley, who was still kneeling by the body. "May I have my lord the Count's keys, doctor?"

Pateley glanced up at Lord Darcy, who nodded silently. The physician detached the keys from the belt and handed them to Sir Pierre.

The Privy Secretary looked at them for a moment, then selected a small gold key. "This is it," he said, separating it from the others on the ring. "Come with me, your lordship."

Darcy followed him across the room to a broad wall covered with a great tapestry that must have dated back to the sixteenth century. Sir Pierre reached behind it and pulled a cord. The entire tapestry slid aside like a panel, and Lord Darcy saw that it was supported on a track some ten feet from the floor. Behind it was what looked at first like ordinary oak paneling, but Sir Pierre fitted the small key into an inconspicuous hole and turned. Or, rather, tried to turn.

"That's odd," said Sir Pierre. "It's not locked!"

He took the key out and pressed on the panel, shoving sideways with his hand to move it aside. It slid open to reveal a closet.

The closet was filled with women's clothing of all kinds, and styles.

Lord Darcy whistled soundlessly.

"Try that blue robe, your lordship," the Privy Secretary said. "The one with the—Yes, that's the one."

Lord Darcy took it off its hanger. The same buttons. They matched. And there was one missing from the front! Torn off! "Master Sean!" he called without turning.

Master Sean came with a rolling walk. He was holding an oddly-shaped bronze thing in his hand that Sir Pierre didn't quite recognize. The sorcerer was muttering. "Evil, that there is! Faith, and the vibrations are all over the place. Yes, my lord?"

"Check this dress and the button when you get round to it. I want to know when the two parted company."

"Yes, my lord." He draped the robe over one arm and dropped the button into a pouch at his belt. "I can tell you one thing, my lord. You talk about an evil miasma, this room has got it!" He held up the object in his hand. "There's an underlying background—something that has been here for years, just seeping in. But on top of that, there's a hellish big blast of it superimposed. Fresh it is, and very strong."

"I shouldn't be surprised, considering there was murder done here last night—or very early this morning," said Lord Darcy.

"Hm-m-m, yes. Yes, my lord, the death is there—but there's something else. Something I can't place."

"You can tell that just by holding that bronze cross in your hand?" Sir Pierre asked interestedly.

Master Sean gave him a friendly scowl. "'Tisn't quite a cross, sir. This is what is known as a *crux ansata*. The ancient Egyptians called it an *ankh*. Notice the loop at the top instead of the straight piece your true cross has. Now, your true cross—if it were properly energized, blessed, d'ye see—your true cross would tend to dissipate the evil. The *ankh* merely vibrates to evil because of the closed loop at the top, which makes a return circuit. And it's not energized by blessing, but by another ... um ... spell."

"Master Sean, we have a murder to investigate," said Lord Darcy.

The sorcerer caught the tone of his voice and nodded quickly. "Yes, my lord." And he walked rollingly away.

"Now where's that secret stairway you mentioned, Sir Pierre?" Lord Darcy asked.

"This way, your lordship."

He led Lord Dacy to a wall at right angles to the outer wall and slid back another tapestry.

"Good Heavens," Darcy muttered, "does he have something concealed behind every arras in the place?" But he didn't say it loud enough for the Privy Secretary to hear.

This time, what greeted them was a solid-seeming stone wall. But Sir Pierre pressed in on one small stone, and a section of the wall swung back, exposing a stairway.

"Oh, yes," Darcy said. "I see what he did. This is the old spiral stairway that goes round the inside of the Keep. There are two doorways at the bottom. One opens into the courtyard, the other is a postern gate through the curtain wall to the outside—but that was closed up in the sixteenth century, so the only way out is into the courtyard."

"Your lordship knows Castle D'Evreux, then?" Sir Pierre said. The knight himself was nearly fifty, while Darcy was only in his thirties, and Sir Pierre had no recollection of Darcy's having been in the castle before.

"Only by the plans in the Royal Archives. But I have made it a point to—" He stopped. "Dear me," he interrupted himself mildly, "what is that?"

"That" was something that had been hidden by the arras until Sir Pierre had slid it aside, and was still showing only a part of itself. It lay on the floor a foot or so from the secret door.

Darcy knelt down and pulled the tapestry back from the object. "Well, well. A .28 two-shot pocket gun. Gold-chased, beautifully engraved, mother-of-pearl handle. A regular gem." He picked it up and examined it closely. "One shot fired."

He stood up and showed it to Sir Pierre. "Ever see it before?"

The Privy Secretary looked at the weapon closely. Then he shook his head. "Not that I recall, your lordship. It certainly isn't one of the Count's guns."

"You're certain?"

"Quite certain, your lordship. I'll show you the gun collection if you want. My lord the Count didn't like tiny guns like that; he preferred a larger caliber. He would never have owned what he considered a toy."

"Well, we'll have to look into it." He called over Master Sean again and gave the gun into his keeping. "And keep your eyes open for anything else of interest, Master Sean. So far, everything of interest besides the late Count himself has been hiding under beds or behind arrases. Check everything. Sir Pierre and I are going for a look down this stairway."

The stairway was gloomy, but enough light came in through the arrow slits spaced at intervals along the outer way to illuminate the interior. It spiraled down between the inner and outer walls of the Great Keep, making four complete circuits before it reached ground level. Lord Darcy looked carefully at the steps, the walls, and even the low, arched overhead as he and Sir Pierre went down.

After the first circuit, on the floor beneath the Count's suite, he stopped. "There was a door here," he said, pointing to a rectangular area in the inner wall.

"Yes, your lordship. There used to be an opening at every floor, but they were all sealed off. It's quite solid, as you can see."

"Where would they lead if they were open?"

"The county offices. My own office, the clerk's offices, the constabulary on the first floor. Below are the dungeons. My lord the Count was the only one who lived in the Keep itself. The rest of the household live above the Great Hall."

"What about guests?"

"They're usually housed in the east wing. We only have two house guests at the moment. Laird and Lady Duncan have been with us for four days."

"I see." They went down perhaps four more steps before Lord Darcy asked quietly, "Tell me, Sir Pierre, were you privy to *all* of Count D'Evreux's business?"

Another four steps down before Sir Pierre answered. "I understand what your lordship means," he said. Another two steps. "No, I was not. I was aware that my lord the Count engaged in certain ... er ... shall we say, liaisons with members of the opposite sex. However—"

He paused, and in the gloom, Lord Darcy could see his lips tighten. "However," he continued, "I did not procure for my lord, if that is what you're driving at. I am not and never have been a pimp."

"I didn't intend to suggest that you had, good knight," said Lord Darcy in a tone that strongly implied that the thought had actually never crossed his mind. "Not at all. But certainly there is a difference between 'aiding and abetting' and simple knowledge of what is going on."

"Oh. Yes. Yes, of course. Well, one cannot, of course, be the secretary-in-private of a gentleman such as my lord the Count for seventeen years without knowing something of what is going on, you're right. Yes. Yes. Hm-m-m."

Lord Darcy smiled to himself. Not until this moment had Sir Pierre realized how much he actually *did* know. In loyalty to his lord, he had literally kept his eyes shut for seventeen years.

"I realize," Lord Darcy said smoothly, "that a gentleman would never implicate a lady nor besmirch the reputation of another gentleman without due cause and careful consideration. However,"—like the knight, he paused a moment before going on—"although we are aware that he was not discreet, was he particular?"

"If you mean by that, did he confine his attentions to those of gentle birth, your lordship, then I can say, no he did not. If you mean did he confine his attentions to the gentler sex, then I can only say that, as far as I know, he did."

"I see. That explains the closet full of clothes."

"Beg pardon, your lordship?"

"I mean that if a girl or woman of the lower classes were to come here, he would have proper clothing for them to wear—in spite of the sumptuary laws to the contrary."

"Quite likely, your lordship. He was most particular about clothing. Couldn't stand a woman who was sloppily dressed or poorly dressed."

"In what way?"

"Well. Well, for instance, I recall once that he saw a very pretty peasant girl. She was dressed in the common style, of course, but she was dressed neatly and prettily. My lord took a fancy to her. He said, 'Now there's a lass who knows how to wear clothes. Put her in decent apparel, and she'd pass for a princess.' But a girl, who had a pretty face and a fine figure, made no impression on him unless she wore her clothing well, if you see what I mean, your lordship."

"Did you ever know him to fancy a girl who dressed in an offhand manner?" Lord Darcy asked.

"Only among the gently born, your lordship. He'd say, 'Look at Lady So-and-so! Nice wench, if she'd let me teach her how to dress.' You might say, your lordship, that a woman could be dressed commonly or sloppily, but not both."

"Judging by the stuff in that closet," Lord Darcy said, "I should say that the late Count had excellent taste in feminine dress."

Sir Pierre considered. "Hm-m-m. Well, now, I wouldn't exactly say so, your lordship. He knew *how* clothes should be worn, yes. But he couldn't pick out a woman's gown of his own accord. He could choose his own clothing with impeccable taste, but he'd not any real notion of how a woman's clothing should go, if you see what I mean. All he knew was how good clothing should be worn. But he knew nothing about design for women's clothing."

"Then how did he get that closet full of clothes?" Lord Darcy asked, puzzled.

Sir Pierre chuckled. "Very simply, your lordship. He knew that the Lady Alice had good taste, so he secretly instructed that each piece that Lady Alice ordered should be made in duplicate. With small variations, of course. I'm certain my lady wouldn't like it if she knew."

"I dare say not," said Lord Darcy thoughtfully.

"Here is the door to the courtyard," said Sir Pierre. "I doubt that it has been opened in broad daylight for many years." He selected a key from the ring of the late Count and inserted it into the keyhole. The door swung back, revealing a large crucifix attached to its outer surface. Lord Darcy crossed himself. "Lord in Heaven," he said softly, "what is this?"

He looked out into a small shrine. It was walled off from the courtyard and had a single small entrance some ten feet from the doorway. There were four *prie-dieus*—small kneeling benches—ranged in front of the doorway.

"If I may explain, your lordship—" Sir Pierre began.

"No need to," Lord Darcy said in a hard voice. "It's rather obvious. My lord the Count was quite ingenious. This is a relatively newly-built shrine. Four walls and a crucifix against the castle wall. Anyone could come in here, day or night, for prayer. No one who came in would be suspected." He stepped out into the small enclosure and swung around to look at the door. "And when that door is closed, there is no sign that there is a door behind the crucifix. If a woman came in here, it would be assumed that she came for prayer. But if she knew of that door—" His voice trailed off.

"Yes, your lordship," said Sir Pierre. "I did not approve, but I was in no position to disapprove."

"I understand." Lord Darcy stepped out to the doorway of the little shrine and took a quick glance about. "Then anyone within the castle walls could come in here," he said.

"Yes, your lordship."

"Very well. Let's go back up."

In the small office which Lord Darcy and his staff had been assigned while conducting the investigation, three men watched while a fourth conducted a demonstration on a table in the center of the room.

Master Sean O Lochlainn held up an intricately engraved gold button with an Arabesque pattern and a diamond set in the center.

He looked at the other three. "Now, my lord, your Reverence, and colleague Doctor, I call your attention to this button."

Dr. Pateley smiled and Father Bright looked stern. Lord Darcy merely stuffed tobacco—imported from the southern New England counties on the Gulf—into a German-made porcelain pipe. He allowed Master Sean a certain amount of flamboyance; good sorcerers were hard to come by.

"Will you hold the robe, Dr. Pateley? Thank you. Now, stand back. That's it. Thank you. Now, I place the button on the table, a good ten feet from the robe." Then he muttered something under his breath and dusted a bit of powder on the button. He made a few passes over it with his hands, paused, and looked up at Father Bright. "If you will, Reverend Sir?"

Father Bright solemnly raised his right hand, and, as he made the Sign of the Cross, said: "May this demonstration, O God, be in strict accord with the truth, and may the Evil One not in any way deceive us who are witnesses thereto. In the Name of the Father and of the Son and of the Holy Spirit. Amen."

"Amen," the other three chorused.

Master Sean crossed himself, then muttered something under his breath.

The button leaped from the table, slammed itself against the robe which Dr. Pateley held before him, and stuck there as though it had been sewed on by an expert.

"Ha!" said Master Sean. "As I thought!" He gave the other three men a broad, beaming smile. "The two were definitely connected!"

Lord Darcy looked bored. "Time?" he asked.

"In a moment, my lord," Master Sean said apologetically. "In a moment." While the other three watched, the sorcerer went through more spells with the button and the robe, although none were quite so spectacular as the first demonstration. Finally, Master Sean said: "About eleven thirty last night they were torn apart, my lord. But I shouldn't like to make it any more definite than to say between eleven and midnight. The speed with which it returned to its place shows that it was ripped off very rapidly, however."

"Very good," said Lord Darcy. "Now the bullet, if you please."

"Yes, my lord. This will have to be a bit different." He took more paraphernalia out of his large, symbol-decorated carpet bag. "The Law of Contagion, gently-born sirs, is a tricky thing to work with. If a man doesn't know how to handle it, he can get himself killed. We had an apprentice o' the guild back in Cork who might have made a good sorcerer in time. He had the talent—unfortunately, he didn't have the good sense to go with it. According to the Law of Contagion any two objects which have ever been in contact with each other have an affinity for each other which is directly proportional to the product of the degree of relevancy of the contact and the length of time they were in contact and inversely proportional to the length of time since they have ceased to be in contact." He gave a smiling glance to the priest. "That doesn't apply strictly to relics of the saints, Reverend Sir; there's another factor enters in there, as you know."

As he spoke, the sorcerer was carefully clamping the little handgun into the padded vise so that its barrel was parallel to the surface of the table.

"Anyhow," he went on, "this apprentice, all on his own, decided to get rid of the cockroaches in his house—a simple thing, if one knows how to go about it. So he collected dust from various cracks and crannies about the house, dust which contained, of course, the droppings of the pests. The dust, with the appropriate spells and ingredients, he boiled. It worked fine. The roaches all came down with a raging fever and died. Unfortunately, the clumsy lad had poor laboratory technique. He allowed three drops of his own perspiration to fall into the steaming pot over which he was working, and the resulting fever killed him, too."

By this time, he had put the bullet which Dr. Pateley had removed from the Count's body on a small pedestal so that it was exactly in line with the muzzle of the gun. "There now," he said softly.

Then he repeated the incantation, and the powdering that he had used on the button. As the last syllable was formed by his lips, the bullet vanished with a *ping*! In its vise, the little gun vibrated.

"Ah!" said Master Sean. "No question there, eh? That's the death weapon, all right, my lord. Yes. Time's almost exactly the same as that of the removal of the button. Not more than a few seconds later. Forms a picture, don't it, my lord? His lordship the Count jerks a button off the girl's gown, she outs with a gun and plugs him."

Lord Darcy's handsome face scowled. "Let's not jump to any hasty conclusions, my good Sean. There is no evidence whatever that he was killed by a woman."

"Would a man be wearing that gown, my lord?"

"Possibly," said Lord Darcy. "But who says that anyone was wearing it when the button was removed?"

"Oh." Master Sean subsided into silence. Using a small ramrod, he forced the bullet out of the chamber of the little pistol.

"Father Bright," said Lord Darcy, "will the Countess be serving tea this afternoon?"

The priest looked suddenly contrite. "Good heavens! None of you has eaten yet! I'll see that something is sent up right away, Lord Darcy. In the confusion—"

Lord Darcy held up a hand. "I beg your pardon, Father; that wasn't what I meant. I'm sure Master Sean and Dr. Pateley would appreciate a little something, but I can wait until tea time. What I was thinking was that perhaps the Countess would ask her guests to tea. Does she know Laird and Lady Duncan well enough to ask for their sympathetic presence on such an afternoon as this?"

Father Bright's eyes narrowed a trifle. "I dare say it could be arranged, Lord Darcy. You will be there?"

"Yes—but I may be a trifle late. That will hardly matter at an informal tea."

The priest glanced at his watch. "Four o'clock?"

"I should think that would do it," said Lord Darcy.

Father Bright nodded wordlessly and left the room.

Dr. Pateley took off his pince-nez and polished the lenses carefully with a silk handkerchief. "How long will your spell keep the body incorrupt, Master Sean?" he asked.

"As long as it's relevant. As soon as the case is solved, or we have enough data to solve the case—as the case may be, heh heh—he'll start to go. I'm not a saint, you know; it takes powerful motivation to keep a body incorrupt for years and years."

Sir Pierre was eying the gown that Pateley had put on the table. The button was still in place, as if held there by magnetism. He didn't touch it. "Master Sean, I don't know much about magic," he said, "but can't you find out who was wearing this robe just as easily as you found out that the button matched?"

Master Sean wagged his head in a firm negative. "No, sir. 'Tisn't relevant sir. The relevancy of the integrated dress-as-a-whole is quite strong. So is that of the seamstress or tailor who made the garment, and that of the weaver who made the cloth. But, except in certain circumstances, the person who wears or wore the garment has little actual relevancy to the garment itself."

"I'm afraid I don't understand," said Sir Pierre, looking puzzled.

"Look at it like this, sir: That gown wouldn't be what it is if the weaver hadn't made the cloth in that particular way. It wouldn't be what it is if the seamstress hadn't cut it in a particular way and sewed it in a specific manner. You follow, sir? Yes. Well, then, the connections between garment-and-weaver and garment-and-seamstress are strongly relevant. But this dress would still be pretty much what it is if it had stayed in the closet instead of being worn. No relevance—or very little. Now, if it were a well-worn garment, that would be different—that is, if it had always been worn by the same person. Then, you see, sir, the garment-as-a-whole is what it is because of the wearing, and the wearer becomes relevant."

He pointed at the little handgun he was still holding in his hand. "Now you take your gun, here, sir. The—"

"It isn't my gun," Sir Pierre interrupted firmly.

"I was speaking rhetorically, sir," said Master Sean with infinite patience. "This gun or any other gun in general, if you see what I mean, sir. It's even harder to place the ownership of a gun. Most of the wear on a gun is purely mechanical. It don't matter *who* pulls the trigger, you see, the erosion by the gases produced in the chamber, and the wear caused by the bullet passing through the barrel will be the same. You see, sir, 'tisn't relevant *to the gun* who pulled its trigger or what it's fired at. The bullet's a slightly different matter. To the bullet, it *is* relevant which gun it was fired from and what it hit. All these things simply have to be taken into account, Sir Pierre."

"I see," said the knight. "Very interesting, Master Sean." Then he turned to Lord Darcy. "Is there anything else, your lordship? There's a great deal of county business to be attended to."

Lord Darcy waved a hand. "Not at the moment, Sir Pierre. I understand the pressures of government. Go right ahead."

"Thank you, your lordship. If anything further should be required, I shall be in my office."

As soon as Sir Pierre had closed the door, Lord Darcy held out his hand toward the sorcerer. "Master Sean; the gun."

Master Sean handed it to him. "Ever see one like it before?" he asked, turning it over in his hands.

"Not *exactly* like it, my lord."

"Come, come, Sean; don't be so cautious. I am no sorcerer, but I don't need to know the Laws of Similarity to be able to recognise an *obvious* similarity."

"Edinburgh," said Master Sean flatly.

"Exactly. Scottish work. The typical Scot gold work; remarkable beauty. And look at that lock. It has 'Scots' written all over it—and more. 'Edinburgh', as you said."

Dr. Pateley, having replaced his carefully polished glasses, leaned over and peered at the weapon in Lord Darcy's hand. "Couldn't it be Italian, my lord? Or Moorish? In Moorish Spain, they do work like that."

"No Moorish gunsmith would put a hunting scene on the butt," Lord Darcy said flatly, "and the Italians wouldn't have put heather and thistles in the field surrounding the huntsman."

"But the *FdM* engraved on the barrel," said Dr. Pateley, "indicates the—"

"Ferrari of Milan," said Lord Darcy. "Exactly. But the barrel is of much newer work than the rest. So are the chambers. This is a fairly old gun—fifty years old, I'd say. The lock and the butt are still in excellent condition, indicating that it has been well cared for, but frequent usage—or a single accident—could ruin the barrel and require the owner to get a replacement. It was replaced by Ferrari."

"I see," said Dr. Pateley somewhat humbled.

"If we open the lock ... Master Sean, hand me your small screwdriver. Thank you. If we open the lock, we will find the name of one of the finest gunsmiths of half a century ago—a man whose name has not yet been forgotten—Hamish Graw of Edinburgh. Ah! There! You see?" They did.

Having satisfied himself on that point, Lord Darcy closed the lock again. "Now, men, we have the gun located. We also know that a guest in this very castle is Laird Duncan of Duncan. The Duncan of Duncan himself. A Scot's laird who was, fifteen years ago, His Majesty's Minister Plenipotentiary to the Free Grand Duchy of Milan. That suggests to me that it would be indeed odd if there were not some connection between Laird Duncan and this gun. Eh?"

"Come, come, Master Sean," said Lord Darcy, rather impatiently. "We haven't all the time in the world."

"Patience, my lord; patience," said the little sorcerer calmly. "Can't hurry these things, you know." He was kneeling in front of a large, heavy traveling chest in the bedroom of the guest apartment occupied temporarily by Laird and Lady Duncan, working with the lock. "One position of a lock is just as relevant as the other so you can't work with the bolt. But the pin-tumblers in the cylinder, now, that's a different matter. A lock's built so that the breaks in the tumblers are not related to the surface of the cylinder when the key is out, but there is a relation when the key's *in*, so by taking advantage of that relevancy—Ah!"

The lock clicked open.

Lord Darcy raised the lid gently.

"Carefully, my lord!" Master Sean said in a warning voice. "He's got a spell on the thing! Let me do it." He made Lord Darcy stand back and then lifted the lid of the heavy trunk himself. When it was leaning back against the wall, gaping open widely on its hinges, Master Sean took a long look at the trunk and its lid without touching either of them. There was a second lid on the trunk, a thin one obviously operated by a simple bolt.

Master Sean took his sorcerer's staff, a five-foot, heavy rod made of the wood of the quicken tree or mountain ash, and touched the inner lid. Nothing happened. He touched the bolt. Nothing.

"Hm-m-m," Master Sean murmured thoughtfully. He glanced around the room, and his eyes fell on a heavy stone doorstop. "That ought to do it." He walked over, picked it up, and carried it back to the chest. Then he put it on the rim of the chest in such a position that if the lid were to fall it would be stopped by the doorstop.

Then he put his hand in as if to lift the inner lid.

The heavy outer lid swung forward and down of its own accord, moving with blurring speed, and slammed viciously against the doorstop.

Lord Darcy massaged his right wrist gently, as if he felt where the lid would have hit if he had tried to open the inner lid. "Triggered to slam if a human being sticks a hand in there, eh?"

"Or a head, my lord. Not very effectual if you know what to look for. There are better spells than that for guarding things. Now we'll see what his lordship wants to protect so badly that he practices sorcery without a license." He lifted the lid again, and then opened the inner lid. "It's safe now, my lord. *Look at this!*"

Lord Darcy had already seen. Both men looked in silence at the collection of paraphernalia on the first tray of the chest. Master Sean's busy fingers carefully opened the tissue paper packing of one after another of the objects. "A human skull," he said. "Bottles of graveyard earth. Hm-m-m—this one is labeled 'virgin's blood.' And this! A Hand of Glory!"

It was a mummified human hand, stiff and dry and brown, with the fingers partially curled, as though they were holding an invisible ball three inches or so in diameter. On each of the fingertips was a short candle-stub. When the hand was placed on its back, it would act as a candelabra.

"That pretty much settles it, eh, Master Sean?" Lord Darcy said.

"Indeed, my lord. At the very least, we can get him for possession of materials. Black magic is a matter of symbolism and intent."

"Very well. I want a complete list of the contents of that chest. Be sure to replace everything as it was and relock the trunk." He tugged thoughtfully at an earlobe. "So Laird Duncan has the Talent, eh? Interesting."

"Aye. But not surprising, my lord," said Master Sean without looking up from his work. "It's in the blood. Some attribute it to the Dedannans, who passed through Scotland before they conquered Ireland three thousand years ago, but, however that may be, the Talent runs strong in the Sons of Gael. It makes me boil to see it misused."

While Master Sean talked, Lord Darcy was prowling around the room, reminding one of a lean tomcat who was certain that there was a mouse concealed somewhere.

"It'll make Laird Duncan boil if he isn't stopped," Lord Darcy murmured absently.

"Aye, my lord," said Master Sean. "The mental state necessary to use the Talent for black sorcery is such that it invariably destroys the user—but, if he knows what he's doing, a lot of other people are hurt before he finally gets his."

Lord Darcy opened the jewel box on the dresser. The usual traveling jewelry—enough, but not a great choice.

"A man's mind turns in on itself when he's taken up with hatred and thoughts of revenge," Master Sean droned on. "Or, if he's the type who *enjoys* watching others suffer, or the type who doesn't care but is willing to do anything for gain, then his mind is already warped and the misuse of the Talent just makes it worse."

Lord Darcy found what he was looking for in a drawer, just underneath some neatly folded lingerie. A small holster, beautifully made of Florentine leather, gilded and tooled. He didn't need Master Sean's sorcery to tell him that the little pistol fit it like a hand in a glove.

Father Bright felt as though he had been walking a tightrope for hours. Laird and Lady Duncan had been talking in low, controlled voices that betrayed an inner nervousness, but Father Bright realized that he and the Countess had been doing the same thing. The Duncan of Duncan had offered his condolences on the death of the late Count with the proper air of suppressed sorrow, as had Mary, Lady Duncan. The Countess had accepted them solemnly and with gratitude. But Father Bright was well aware that no one in the room—possibly, he thought, no one in the world—regretted the Count's passing.

Laird Duncan sat in his wheelchair, his sharp Scots features set in a sad smile that showed an intent to be affable even though great sorrow weighed heavily upon him. Father Bright noticed it and realized that his own face had the same sort of expression. No one was fooling anyone else, of that the priest was certain—but for anyone to admit it would be the most boorish breach of etiquette. But there was a haggardness, a look of increased age about the Laird's countenance that Father Bright did not like. His priestly intuition told him clearly that there was a turmoil of emotion in the Scotsman's mind that was ... well, *evil* was the only word for it.

Lady Duncan was, for the most part, silent. In the past fifteen minutes, since she and her husband had come to the informal tea, she had spoken scarcely a dozen words. Her face was masklike, but there was the same look of haggardness about her eyes as there was in her husband's face. But the priest's emphatic sense told him that the emotion here was fear, simple and direct. His keen eyes had noticed that she wore a shade too much make-up. She had almost succeeded in covering up the faint bruise on her right cheek, but not completely.

My lady the Countess D'Evreux was all sadness and unhappiness, but there was neither fear nor evil there. She smiled politely and talked quietly. Father Bright would have been willing to bet that not one of the four of them would remember a word that had been spoken.

Father Bright had placed his chair so that he could keep an eye on the open doorway and the long hall that led in from the Great Keep. He hoped Lord Darcy would hurry. Neither of the guests had been told that the Duke's Investigator was here, and Father Bright was just a little apprehensive about the meeting. The Duncans had not even been told that the Count's death had been murder, but he was certain that they knew.

Father Bright saw Lord Darcy come in through the door at the far end of the hall. He murmured a polite excuse and rose. The other three accepted his excuses with the same politeness and went on with their talk. Father Bright met Lord Darcy in the hall.

"Did you find what you were looking for, Lord Darcy?" the priest asked in a low tone.

"Yes," Lord Darcy said. "I'm afraid we shall have to arrest Laird Duncan."

"Murder?"

"Perhaps. I'm not yet certain of that. But the charge will be black magic. He has all the paraphernalia in a chest in his room. Master Sean reports that a ritual was enacted in the bedroom last night. Of course, that's out of my jurisdiction. You, as a representative of the Church, will have to be the arresting officer." He paused. "You don't seem surprised, Reverence."

"I'm not," Father Bright admitted. "I felt it. You and Master Sean will have to make out a sworn deposition before I can act."

"I understand. Can you do me a favor?"

"If I can."

"Get my lady the Countess out of the room on some pretext or other. Leave me alone with her guests. I do not wish to upset my lady any more than absolutely necessary."

"I think I can do that. Shall we go in together?"

"Why not? But don't mention why I am here. Let them assume I am just another guest."

"Very well."

All three occupants of the room glanced up as Father Bright came in with Lord Darcy. The introductions were made: Lord Darcy humbly begged the pardon of his hostess for his lateness. Father Bright noticed the same sad smile on Lord Darcy's handsome face as the others were wearing.

Lord Darcy helped himself from the buffet table and allowed the Countess to pour him a large cup of hot tea. He mentioned nothing about the recent death. Instead, he turned the conversation toward the wild beauty of Scotland and the excellence of the grouse shooting there.

Father Bright had not sat down again. Instead, he left the room once more. When he returned, he went directly to the Countess and said, in a low, but clearly audible voice: "My lady, Sir Pierre Morlaix has informed me that there are a few matters that require your attention immediately. It will require only a few moments."

My lady the Countess did not hesitate, but made her excuses immediately. "Do finish your tea," she added. "I don't think I shall be long."

Lord Darcy knew the priest would not lie, and he wondered what sort of arrangement had been made with Sir Pierre. Not that it mattered except that Lord Darcy had hoped it would be sufficiently involved for it to keep the Countess busy for at least ten minutes.

The conversation, interrupted but momentarily, returned to grouse.

"I haven't done any shooting since my accident," said Laird Duncan, "but I used to enjoy it immensely. I still have friends up every year for the season."

"What sort of weapon do you prefer for grouse?" Lord Darcy asked.

"A one-inch bore with a modified choke," said the Scot. "I have a pair that I favor. Excellent weapons."

"Of Scottish make?"

"No, no. English. Your London gunsmiths can't be beat for shotguns."

"Oh. I thought perhaps your lordship had had all your guns made in Scotland." As he spoke, he took the little pistol out of his coat pocket and put it carefully on the table.

There was a sudden silence, then Laird Duncan said in an angry voice: "What is this? Where did you get that?"

Lord Darcy glanced at Lady Duncan, who had turned suddenly pale. "Perhaps," he said coolly, "Lady Duncan can tell us."

She shook her head and gasped. For a moment, she had trouble in forming words or finding her voice. Finally: "No. No. I know nothing. Nothing."

But Laird Duncan looked at her oddly.

"You do not deny that it is your gun, my lord?" Lord Darcy asked. "Or your wife's, as the case may be."

"*Where did you get it?*" There was a dangerous quality in the Scotsman's voice. He had once been a powerful man, and Lord Darcy could see his shoulder muscles bunching.

"From the late Count D'Evreux's bedroom."

"What was it doing there?" There was a snarl in the Scot's voice, but Lord Darcy had the feeling that the question was as much directed toward Lady Duncan as it was to himself.

"One of the things it was doing there was shooting Count D'Evreux through the heart."

Lady Duncan slumped forward in a dead faint, overturning her teacup. Laird Duncan made a grab at the gun, ignoring his wife. Lord Darcy's hand snaked out and picked up the weapon before the Scot could touch it. "No, no, my lord," he said mildly. "This is evidence in a murder case. We mustn't tamper with the King's evidence."

He wasn't prepared for what happened next. Laird Duncan roared something obscene in Scots Gaelic, put his hands on the arms of his wheelchair, and, with a great thrust of his powerful arms and shoulders, shoved himself up and forward, toward Lord Darcy, across the table from him. His arms swung up toward Lord Darcy's throat as the momentum of his body carried him toward the investigator.

He might have made it, but the weakness of his legs betrayed him. His waist struck the edge of the massive oaken table, and most of his forward momentum was lost. He collapsed forward, his hands still grasping toward the surprised Englishman. His chin came down hard on the table top. Then he slid back, taking the tablecloth and the china and silverware with him. He lay unmoving on the floor. His wife did not even stir except when the tablecloth tugged at her head.

Lord Darcy had jumped back, overturning his chair. He stood on his feet, looking at the two unconscious forms.

"I don't think there's any permanent damage done to either," said Dr. Pateley an hour later. "Lady Duncan was suffering from shock, of course, but Father Bright brought her round in a hurry. She's a devout woman, I think, even if a sinful one."

"What about Laird Duncan?" Lord Darcy asked.

"Well, that's a different matter. I'm afraid that his back injury was aggravated, and that crack on the chin didn't do him any good. I don't know whether Father Bright can help him or not. Healing takes the co-operation of the patient. I did all I could for him, but I'm just a chirurgeon, not a practitioner of the Healing Art. Father Bright has quite a good reputation in that line, however, and he may be able to do his lordship some good."

Master Sean shook his head dolefully. "His Reverence has the Talent, there's no doubt of that, but now he's pitted against another man who has it—a man whose mind is bent on self-destruction in the long run."

"Well, that's none of my affair," said Dr. Pateley. "I'm just a technician. I'll leave healing up to the Church, where it belongs."

"Master Sean," said Lord Darcy, "there is still a mystery here. We need more evidence. What about the eyes?"

Master Sean blinked. "You mean the picture test, my lord?"

"I do."

"It won't stand up in court, my lord," said the sorcerer.

"I'm aware of that," said Lord Darcy testily.

"Eye test?" Dr. Pateley asked blankly. "I don't believe I understand."

"It's not often used," said Master Sean. "It is a psychic phenomenon that sometimes occurs at the moment of death—especially a violent death. The violent emotional stress causes a sort of backfiring of the mind, if you see what I mean. As a result, the image in the mind of the dying person is returned to the retina. By using the proper sorcery, this image can be developed and the last thing the dead man saw can be brought out.

"But it's a difficult process even under the best of circumstances, and usually the conditions aren't right. In the first place, it doesn't always occur. It never occurs, for instance, when the person is expecting the attack. A man who is killed in a duel, or who is shot after facing the gun for several seconds, has time to adjust to the situation. Also, death must occur almost instantly. If he lingers, even for a few minutes, the effect is lost. And, naturally if the person's eyes are closed at the instant of death, nothing shows up."

"Count D'Evreux's eyes were open," Dr. Pateley said. "They were still open when we found him. How long after death does the image remain?"

"Until the cells of the retina die and lose their identity. Rarely more than twenty-four hours, usually much less."

"It hasn't been twenty-four hours yet," said Lord Darcy, "and there is a chance that the Count was taken completely by surprise."

"I must admit, my lord," Master Sean said thoughtfully, "that the conditions seem favorable. I shall attempt it. But don't put any hopes on it, my lord."

"I shan't. Just do your best, Master Sean. If there is a sorcerer in practice who can do the job, it is you."

"Thank you, my lord. I'll get busy on it right away," said the sorcerer with a subdued glow of pride.

Two hours later, Lord Darcy was striding down the corridor of the Great Hall, Master Sean following up as best he could, his *caorthainn*-wood staff in one hand and his big carpet bag in the other. He had asked Father Bright and the Countess D'Evreux to meet him in one of the smaller guest rooms. But the Countess came to meet him.

"My Lord Darcy," she said, her plain face looking worried and unhappy, "is it true that you suspect Laird and Lady Duncan of this murder? Because, if so, I must—"

"No longer, my lady," Lord Darcy cut her off quickly. "I think we can show that neither is guilty of murder—although, of course, the black magic charge must still be held against Laird Duncan."

"I understand," she said, "but—"

"Please, my lady," Lord Darcy interrupted again, "let me explain everything. Come."

Without another word, she turned and led the way to the room where Father Bright was waiting.

The priest stood waiting, his face showing tenseness.

"Please," said Lord Darcy. "Sit down, both of you. This won't take long. My lady, may Master Sean make use of that table over there?"

"Certainly, my lord," the Countess said softly, "certainly."

"Thank you my lady. Please, please—sit down. This won't take long. Please."

With apparent reluctance, Father Bright and my lady the Countess sat down in two chairs facing Lord Darcy. They paid little attention to what Master Sean O Lochlainn was doing; their eyes were on Lord Darcy.

"Conducting an investigation of this sort is not an easy thing," he began carefully. "Most murder cases could be easily solved by your Chief Man-at-Arms. We find that well-trained county police, in by far the majority of cases, can solve the mystery easily—and in most cases there is very little mystery. But, by His Imperial Majesty's law, the Chief Man-at-Arms must call in a Duke's Investigator if the crime is insoluble or if it involves a member of the aristocracy. For that reason, you were perfectly correct to call His Highness the Duke as soon as murder had been discovered." He leaned back in his chair. "And it has been clear from the first that my lord the late Count was murdered."

Father Bright started to say something, but Lord Darcy cut him off before he could speak. "By 'murder', Reverend Father, I mean that he did not die a natural death—by disease or heart trouble or accident or what-have-you. I should, perhaps, use the word 'homicide'.

"Now the question we have been called upon to answer is simply this: Who was responsible for the homicide?"

The priest and the countess remained silent, looking at Lord Darcy as though he were some sort of divinely inspired oracle.

"As you know ... pardon me, my lady, if I am blunt ... the late Count was somewhat of a playboy. No. I will make that stronger. He was a satyr, a lecher; he was a man with a sexual obsession.

"For such a man, if he indulges in his passions—which the late Count most certainly did—there is usually but one end. Unless he is a man who has a winsome personality—which he did not—there will be someone who will hate him enough to kill him. Such a man inevitably leaves behind him a trail of wronged women and wronged men.

"One such person may kill him.

"One such person did.

"But we must find the person who did and determine the extent of his or her guilt. That is my purpose.

"Now, as to the facts. We know that Edouard has a secret stairway which led directly to his suite. Actually, the secret was poorly kept. There were many women—common and noble—who knew of the existence of that stairway and knew how to enter it. If Edouard left the lower door unlocked, anyone could come up that stairway. He has another lock in the door of his bedroom, so only someone who was invited could come in, even if she ... or he ... could get into the stairway. He was protected.

"Now here is what actually happened that night. I have evidence, by the way, and I have the confessions of both Laird and Lady Duncan. I will explain how I got those confessions in a moment.

"*Primus*: Lady Duncan had an assignation with Count D'Evreux last night. She went up the stairway to his room. She was carrying with her a small pistol. She had had an affair with Edouard, and she had been rebuffed. She was furious. But she went to his room.

"He was drunk when she arrived—in one of the nasty moods with which both of you are familiar. She pleaded with him to accept her again as his mistress. He refused. According to Lady Duncan, he said: 'I don't want you! You're not fit to be in the same room with *her*!'

"The emphasis is Lady Duncan's, not my own.

"Furious, she drew a gun—the little pistol which killed him."

The Countess gasped. "But Mary *couldn't* have—"

"*Please!*" Lord Darcy slammed the palm of his hand on the arm of his chair with an explosive sound. "My lady, you *will* listen to what I have to say!"

He was taking a devil of a chance, he knew. The Countess was his hostess and had every right to exercise her prerogatives. But Lord Darcy was counting on the fact that she had been under Count D'Evreux's influence so long that it would take her a little time to realize that she no longer had to knuckle under to the will of a man who shouted at her. He was right. She became silent.

Father Bright turned to her quickly and said: "Please, my daughter. Wait."

"Your pardon, my lady," Lord Darcy continued smoothly. "I was about to explain to you why I know Lady Duncan could not have killed your brother. There is the matter of the dress. We are certain that the gown that was found in Edouard's closet was worn by the killer. *And that gown could not possibly have fit Lady Duncan!* She's much too ... er ... hefty.

"She has told me her story, and, for reasons I will give you later, I believe it. When she pointed the gun at your brother, she really had no intention of killing him. She had no intention of pulling the trigger. Your brother knew this. He lashed out and slapped the side of her head. She dropped the pistol and fell, sobbing, to the floor. He took her roughly by the arm and 'escorted' her down the stairway. He threw her out.

"Lady Duncan, hysterical, ran to her husband.

"And then, when he had succeeded in calming her down a bit, she realized the position she was in. She knew that Laird Duncan was a violent, a warped man—very similar to Edouard, Count D'Evreux. She dared not tell him the truth, but she had to tell him something. So she lied.

"She told him that Edouard had asked her up in order to tell her something of importance; that that 'something of importance' concerned Laird Duncan's safety; that the Count told her that he knew of Laird Duncan's dabbling in black magic; that he threatened to inform Church authorities on Laird Duncan unless she submitted to his desires; that she had struggled with him and ran away."

Lord Darcy spread his hands. "This was, of course, a tissue of lies. But Laird Duncan believed everything. So great was his ego that he could not believe in her infidelity, although he has been paralyzed for five years."

"How can you be certain that Lady Duncan told the truth?" Father Bright asked warily.

"Aside from the matter of the gown—which Count D'Evreux kept only for women of the common class, *not* the aristocracy—we have the testimony of the actions of Laird Duncan himself. We come then to—

"*Secondus*: Laird Duncan could not have committed the murder physically. *How could a man who was confined to a wheelchair go up that flight of stairs?* I submit to you that it would have been physically impossible.

"The possibility that he has been pretending all these years, and that he is actually capable of walking, was disproved three hours ago, when he actually injured himself by trying to throttle me. His legs are incapable of carrying him even one step—much less carrying him to the top of that stairway."

Lord Darcy folded his hands complacently.

"There remains," said Father Bright, "the possibility that Laird Duncan killed Count D'Evreux by psychical, by magical means."

Lord Darcy nodded. "That is indeed possible, Reverend Sir, as we both know. But not in this instance. Master Sean assures me, and I am certain that you will concur, that a man killed by sorcery, by black magic, dies of internal malfunction, not of a bullet through the heart.

"In effect, the Black Sorcerer induces his enemy to kill himself by psychosomatic means. He dies by what is technically known as psychic induction. Master Sean informs me that the commonest—and crudest—method of doing this is by the so-called 'simalcrum induction' method. That is, by the making of an image—usually, but not necessarily, of wax—and, using the Law of Similarity, inducing death. The Law of Contagion is also used, since the fingernails, hair, spittle, and so on, of the victim are usually incorporated into the image. Am I correct, Father?"

The priest nodded. "Yes. And, contrary to the heresies of certain materialists, it is not at all necessary that the victim be informed of the operation—although, admittedly, it can, in certain circumstances, aid the process."

"Exactly," said Lord Darcy. "But it is well known that material objects can be moved by a competent sorcerer—'black' or 'white'. Would you explain to my lady the Countess why her brother could not have been killed in that manner?"

Father Bright touched his lips with the tip of his tongue and then turned to the girl sitting next to him. "There is a lack of relevancy. In this case, the bullet must have been relevant either to the heart or to the gun. To have traveled with a velocity great enough to penetrate, the relevancy to the heart must have been much greater than the relevancy to the gun. Yet the test, witnessed by myself, that was performed by Master Sean indicates that this was not so. The bullet returned to the gun, not to your brother's heart. The evidence, my dear, is conclusive that the bullet was propelled by purely physical means, and was propelled from the gun."

"Then what was it Laird Duncan did?" the Countess asked.

"*Tertius*:" said Lord Darcy. "Believing what his wife had told him, Laird Duncan flew into a rage. He determined to kill your brother. He used an induction spell. But the spell backfired and almost killed him.

"There are analogies on a material plane. If one adds mineral spirits and air to a fire, the fire will be increased. But if one adds ash, the fire will be put out.

"In a similar manner, if one attacks a living being psychically it will die—but if one attacks a dead thing in such a manner, the psychic energy will be absorbed, to the detriment of the person who has used it.

"In theory, we could charge Laird Duncan with attempted murder, for there is no doubt that he did attempt to kill your brother, my lady. *But your brother was already dead at the time!*

"The resultant dissipation of psychic energy rendered Laird Duncan unconscious for several hours, during which Lady Duncan waited in suspenseful fear.

"Finally, when Laird Duncan regained consciousness, he realized what had happened. He knew that your brother was already dead when he attempted the spell. He thought, therefore, that Lady Duncan had killed the Count.

"On the other hand, Lady Duncan was perfectly well aware that she had left Edouard alive and well. So she thought the black magic of her husband had killed her erstwhile lover."

"Each was trying to protect the other," Father Bright said. "Neither is completely evil, then. There may be something we can do for Laird Duncan."

"I wouldn't know about that, Father," Lord Darcy said. "The Healing Art is the Church's business, not mine." He realized with some amusement that he was paraphrasing Dr. Pateley. "What Laird Duncan had not known," he went on quickly, "was that his wife had taken a gun up to the Count's bedroom. That put a rather different light on her visit, you see. That's why he flew into such a towering rage at me—not because I was accusing him or his wife of murder, but because I had cast doubt on his wife's behavior."

He turned his head to look at the table where the Irish sorcerer was working. "Ready, Master Sean?"

"Aye, my lord. All I have to do is set up the screen and light the lantern in the projector."

"Go ahead, then." He looked back at Father Bright and the Countess. "Master Sean has a rather interesting lantern slide I want you to look at."

"The most successful development I've ever made, if I may say so, my lord," the sorcerer said.

"Proceed."

Master Sean opened the shutter on the projector, and a picture sprang into being on the screen.

There were gasps from Father Bright and the Countess.

It was a woman. She was wearing the gown that had hung in the Count's closet. A button had been torn off, and the gown gaped open. Her right hand was almost completely obscured by a dense cloud of smoke. Obviously she had just fired a pistol directly at the onlooker.

But that was not what had caused the gasps.

The girl was beautiful. Gloriously, ravishingly beautiful. It was not a delicate beauty. There was nothing flower-like or peaceful in it. It was a beauty that could have but one effect on a normal human male. She was the most physically desirable woman one could imagine.

Retro mea, Sathanas, Father Bright thought wryly. *She's almost obscenely beautiful.*

Only the Countess was unaffected by the desirability of the image. She saw only the startling beauty.

"Has neither of you seen that woman before? I thought not," said Lord Darcy. "Nor had Laird or Lady Duncan. Nor Sir Pierre.

"Who is she? We don't know. But we can make a few deductions. She must have come to the Count's room by appointment. This is quite obviously the woman Edouard mentioned to Lady Duncan—the woman, the 'she' that the Scots noblewoman could not compare with. It is almost certain she is a commoner; otherwise she would not be wearing a robe from the Count's collection. She must have changed right there in the bedroom. Then she and the Count quarreled—about what, we do not know. The Count had previously taken Lady Duncan's pistol away from her and had evidently carelessly let it lay on that table you see behind the girl. She grabbed it and shot him. Then she changed clothes again, hung up the robe, and ran away. No one saw her come or go. The Count had designed the stairway for just that purpose.

"Oh, we'll find her, never fear—now that we know what she looks like.

"At any rate," Lord Darcy concluded, "the mystery is now solved to my complete satisfaction, and I shall so report to His Highness."

Richard, Duke of Normandy, poured two liberal portions of excellent brandy into a pair of crystal goblets. There was a smile of satisfaction on his youthful face as he handed one of the goblets to Lord Darcy. "Very well done, my lord," he said. "Very well done."

"I am gratified to hear Your Highness say so," said Lord Darcy, accepting the brandy.

"But how were you so certain that it was *not* someone from outside the castle? Anyone could have come in through the main gate. That's always open."

"True, Your Highness. But the door at the foot of the stairway was *locked*. Count D'Evreux locked it after he threw Lady Duncan out. There is no way of locking or unlocking it from the outside; the door had not been forced. No one could have come in that way, nor left that way, after Lady Duncan was so forcibly ejected. The only other way into the Count's suite was by the other door, and that door was unlocked."

"I see," said Duke Richard. "I wonder why she went up there in the first place?"

"Probably because he asked her to. Any other woman would have known what she was getting into if she accepted an invitation to Count D'Evreux's suite."

The Duke's handsome face darkened. "No. One would hardly expect that sort of thing from one's own brother. She was perfectly justified in shooting him."

"Perfectly, Your Highness. And had she been anyone but the heiress, she would undoubtedly have confessed immediately. Indeed, it was all I could do to keep her from confessing to me when she thought I was going to charge the Duncans with the killing. But she knew that it was necessary to preserve the reputation of her brother and herself. Not as private persons, but as Count and Countess, as officers of the Government of His Imperial Majesty the King. For a man to be known as a rake is one thing. Most people don't care about that sort of thing in a public official so long as he does his duty and does it well—which, as Your Highness knows, the Count did.

"But to be shot to death while attempting to assault his own sister—that is quite another thing. She was perfectly justified in attempting to cover it up. And she will remain silent unless someone else is accused of the crime."

"Which, of course, will not happen," said Duke Richard. He sipped at the brandy, then said: "She will make a good Countess. She has judgment and she can keep cool under duress. After she had shot her own brother, she might have panicked, but she didn't. How many women would have thought of simply taking off the damaged gown and putting on its duplicate from the closet?"

"Very few," Lord Darcy agreed. "That's why I never mentioned that I knew the Count's wardrobe contained dresses identical to her own. By the way, Your Highness, if any good Healer, like Father Bright, had known of those duplicate dresses, he would have realized that the Count had a sexual obsession about his sister. He would have known that all the other women the Count went after were sister substitutes."

"Yes; of course. And none of them measure up." He put his goblet on the table. "I shall inform the King my brother that I recommended the new Countess whole-heartedly. No word of this must be put down in writing, of course. You know and I know and the King must know. No one else must know."

"One other knows," said Lord Darcy.

"Who?" The Duke looked startled.

"Father Bright."

Duke Richard looked relieved. "Naturally. He won't tell her that we know, will he?"

"I think Father Bright's discretion can be relied upon."

In the dimness of the confessional, Alice, Countess D'Evreux knelt and listened to the voice of Father Bright.

"I shall not give you any penance, my child, for you have committed no sin—that is, in so far as the death of your brother is concerned. For the rest of your sins, you must read and memorize the third chapter of 'The Soul and The World,' by St. James Huntington."

He started to pronounce the absolution, but the Countess said:

"I don't understand one thing. That picture. That wasn't me. I never saw such a gorgeously beautiful girl in my life. And I'm so plain. I don't understand."

"Had you looked more closely, my child, you would have seen that the face did look like yours—only it was idealized. When a subjective reality is made objective, distortions invariably show up; that is why such things cannot be accepted as evidence of objective reality in court." He paused. "To put it another way, my child: Beauty is in the eye of the beholder."

A Spaceship Named McGuire

No. Nobody ever deliberately named a spaceship that. The staid and stolid minds that run the companies which design and build spaceships rarely let their minds run to fancy. The only example I can think of is the unsung hero of the last century who had puckish imagination enough to name the first atomic-powered submarine *Nautilus*. Such minds are rare. Most minds equate dignity with dullness.

This ship happened to have a magnetogravitic drive, which automatically put it into the MG class. It also happened to be the first successful model to be equipped with a Yale robotic brain, so it was given the designation MG-YR-7—the first six had had more bugs in them than a Leopoldville tenement.

So somebody at Yale—another unsung hero—named the ship McGuire; it wasn't official, but it stuck.

The next step was to get someone to test-hop McGuire. They needed just the right man—quick-minded, tough, imaginative, and a whole slew of complementary adjectives. They wanted a perfect superman to test pilot their baby, even if they knew they'd eventually have to take second best.

It took the Yale Space Foundation a long time to pick the right man.

No, I'm not the guy who tested the McGuire.

I'm the guy who stole it.

Shalimar Ravenhurst is not the kind of bloke that very many people can bring themselves to like, and, in this respect, I'm like a great many people, if not more so. In the first place, a man has no right to go around toting a name like "Shalimar"; it makes names like "Beverly" and "Leslie" and "Evelyn" sound almost hairy chested. You want a dozen other reasons, you'll get them.

Shalimar Ravenhurst owned a little planetoid out in the Belt, a hunk of nickel-iron about the size of a smallish mountain with a gee-pull measurable in fractions of a centimeter per second squared. If you're susceptible to spacesickness, that kind of gravity is about as much help as aspirin would have been to Marie Antoinette. You get the feeling of a floor beneath you, but there's a distinct impression that it won't be there for long. It keeps trying to drop out from under you.

I dropped my flitterboat on the landing field and looked around without any hope of seeing anything. I didn't. The field was about the size of a football field, a bright, shiny expanse of rough-polished metal, carved and smoothed flat from the nickel-iron of the planetoid itself. It not only served as a landing field, but as a reflector beacon, a mirror that flashed out the sun's reflection as the planetoid turned slowly on its axis. I'd homed in on that beacon, and now I was sitting on it.

There wasn't a soul in sight. Off to one end of the rectangular field was a single dome, a hemisphere about twenty feet in diameter and half as high. Nothing else.

I sighed and flipped on the magnetic anchor, which grabbed hold of the metal beneath me and held the flitterboat tightly to the surface. Then I cut the drive, plugged in the telephone, and punched for "Local."

The automatic finder searched around for the Ravenhurst tickler signal, found it, and sent out a beep along the same channel.

I waited while the thing beeped twice. There was a click, and a voice said: "Raven's Rest. Yes?" It wasn't Ravenhurst.

I said: "This is Daniel Oak. I want to talk to Mr. Ravenhurst."

"Mr. Oak? But you weren't expected until tomorrow."

"Fine. I'm early. Let me talk to Ravenhurst."

"But Mr. Ravenhurst wasn't expecting you to—"

I got all-of-a-sudden exasperated. "Unless your instruments are running on secondhand flashlight batteries, you've known I was coming for the past half hour. I followed Ravenhurst's instructions not to use radio, but he should know I'm here by this time. He told me to come as fast as possible, and I followed those instructions, too. I always follow instructions when I'm paid enough.

"Now, I'm here; tell Ravenhurst I want to talk to him, or I'll simply flit back to Eros, and thank him much for a pretty retainer that didn't do him any good but gave me a nice profit for my trouble."

"One moment, please," said the voice.

It took about a minute and a half, which was about nine billion jiffies too long, as far as I was concerned.

Then another voice said: "Oak? Wasn't expecting you till tomorrow."

"So I hear. I thought you were in a hurry, but if you're not, you can just provide me with wine, women, and other necessities until tomorrow. That's above and beyond my fee, of course, since you're wasting my time, and I'm evidently not wasting yours."

I couldn't be sure whether the noise he made was a grunt or a muffled chuckle, and I didn't much care. "Sorry, Oak; I really didn't expect you so soon, but I do want to ... I want you to get started right away. Leave your flitterboat where it is; I'll have someone take care of it. Walk on over to the dome and come on in." And he cut off.

I growled something I was glad he didn't hear and hung up. I wished that I'd had a vision unit on the phone; I'd like to have seen his face. Although I knew I might not have learned much more from his expression than I had from his voice.

I got out of the flitterboat, and walked across the dome, my magnetic soles making subdued clicking noises inside the suit as they caught and released the metallic plain beneath me. Beyond the field, I was surrounded by a lumpy horizon and a black sky full of bright, hard stars.

The green light was on when I reached the door to the dome, so I opened it and went on in, closing it behind me. I flipped the toggle that began flooding the room with air. When it was up to pressure, a trap-door in the floor of the dome opened and a crew-cut, blond young man stuck his head up. "Mr. Oak?"

I toyed, for an instant, with the idea of giving him a sarcastic answer. Who else would it be? How many other visitors were running around on the surface of Raven's Rest?

Instead, I said: "That's right." My voice must have sounded pretty muffled to him through my fishbowl.

"Come on down, Mr. Oak. You can shuck your vac suit below."

I thought "below" was a pretty ambiguous term on a low-gee lump like this, but I followed him down the ladder. The ladder was a necessity for fast transportation; if I'd just tried to jump down from one floor to the next, it would've taken me until a month from next St. Swithin's Day to land.

The door overhead closed, and I could hear the pumps start cycling. The warning light turned red.

I took off my suit, hung it in a handy locker, showing that all I had on underneath was my skin-tight "union suit."

"All right if I wear this?" I asked the blond young man, "Or should I borrow a set of shorts and a jacket?" Most places in the Belt, a union suit is considered normal dress; a man never knows when he might have to climb into a vac suit—*fast*. But there are a few of the hoity-toity places on Eros and Ceres and a few of the other well-settled places where a man or woman is required to put on shorts and jacket before entering. And in good old New York City, a man and woman were locked up for "indecent exposure" a few months ago. The judge threw the case out of court, but he told them they were lucky they hadn't been picked up in Boston. It seems that the eye of the bluenose turns a jaundiced yellow at the sight of a union suit, and he sees red.

But there were evidently no bluenoses here. "Perfectly all right, Mr. Oak," the blond young man said affably. Then he coughed politely and added: "But I'm afraid I'll have to ask you to take off the gun."

I glanced at the holster under my armpit, walked back over to the locker, opened it, and took out my vac suit.

"Hey!" said the blond young man. "Where are you going?"

"Back to my boat," I said calmly. "I'm getting tired of this runaround already. I'm a professional man, not a hired flunky. If you'd called a doctor, you wouldn't tell him to leave his little black bag behind; if you'd called a lawyer, you wouldn't make him check his brief case. Or, if you did, he'd tell you to drop dead.

"I was asked to come here as fast as possible, and when I do, I'm told to wait till tomorrow. Now you want me to check my gun. The hell with you."

"Merely a safety precaution," said the blond young man worriedly.

"You think I'm going to shoot Ravenhurst, maybe? Don't be an idiot." I started climbing into my vac suit.

"Just a minute, please, Mr. Oak," said a voice from a hidden speaker. It was Ravenhurst, and he actually sounded apologetic. "You mustn't blame Mr. Feller; those are my standing orders, and I failed to tell Mr. Feller to make an exception in your case. The error was mine."

"I know," I said. "I wasn't blaming Mr. Feller. I wasn't even talking to him. I was addressing you."

"I believe you. Mr. Feller, our guest has gone to all the trouble of having a suit made with a space under the arm for that gun; I see no reason to make him remove it." A pause. "Again, Mr. Oak, I apologize. I really want you to take this job."

I was already taking off the vac suit again.

"But," Ravenhurst continued smoothly, "if I fail to live up to your ideas of courtesy again, I hope you'll forgive me in advance. I'm sometimes very forgetful, and I don't like it when a man threatens to leave my employ twice in the space of fifteen minutes."

"I'm not in your employ yet, Ravenhurst," I said. "If I accept the job, I won't threaten to quit again unless I mean to carry it through, and it would take a lot more than common discourtesy to make me do that. On the other hand, your brand of discourtesy is a shade above the common."

"I thank you for that, at least," said Ravenhurst. "Show him to my office, Mr. Feller."

The blond young man nodded wordlessly and led me from the room.

Walking under low-gee conditions is like nothing else in this universe. I don't mean trotting around on Luna; one-sixth gee is practically homelike in comparison. And zero gee is so devoid of orientation that it gives the sensation of falling endlessly until you get used to it. But a planetoid is in a different class altogether.

Remember that dream—almost everybody's had it—where you're suddenly able to fly? It isn't flying exactly; it's a sort of swimming in the air. Like being underwater, except that the medium around you isn't so dense and viscous, and you can breathe. Remember? Well, that's the feeling you get on a low-gee planetoid.

Your arms don't tend to hang at your sides, as they do on Earth or Luna, because the muscular tension tends to hold them out, just as it does in zero-gee, but there is still a definite sensation of up-and-down. If you push yourself off the floor, you tend to float in a long, slow, graceful arc, provided you don't push too hard. Magnetic soles are practically a must.

I followed the blond Mr. Feller down a series of long corridors which had been painted a pale green, which gave me the feeling that I was underwater. There were doors spaced at intervals along the corridor walls. Occasionally one of them would open and a busy looking man would cross the corridor, open another door, and disappear. From behind the doors, I could hear the drum of distant sounds.

We finally ended up in front of what looked like the only wooden door in the place. When you're carving an office and residence out of a nickel-iron planetoid, importing wood from Earth is a purely luxury matter.

There was no name plate on that mahogany-red door; there didn't need to be.

Feller touched a thin-lined circle in the door jamb.

"You don't knock?" I asked with mock seriousness.

"No," said Feller, with a straight face. "I have to signal. Knocking wouldn't do any good. That's just wood veneer over a three-inch-thick steel slab."

The door opened and I stepped inside.

I have never seen a room quite like it. The furniture was all that same mahogany—a huge desk, nineteenth century baroque, with carved and curlicued legs; two chairs carved the same, with padded seats of maroon leather; and a chair behind the desk that might have doubled as a bishop's throne, with even fancier carving. Off to one side was a long couch upholstered in a lighter maroon. The wall-to-wall carpeting was a rich Burgundy, with a pile deep enough to run a reaper through. The walls were paneled with mahogany and hung with a couple of huge tapestries done in maroon, purple, and red. A bookcase along one wall was filled with books, every one of which had been rebound in maroon leather.

It was like walking into a cask of old claret. Or old blood.

The man sitting behind the desk looked as though he'd been built to be the lightest spot in an analogous color scheme. His suit was mauve with purple piping, and his wide, square, saggy face was florid. On his nose and cheeks, tiny lines of purple tracing made darker areas in his skin. His hair was a medium brown, but it was clipped so short that the scalp showed faintly through, and amid all that overwhelming background, even the hair looked vaguely violet.

"Come in, Mr. Oak," said Shalimar Ravenhurst.

I walked toward him across the Burgundy carpet while the blond young man discreetly closed the door behind me, leaving us alone. I didn't blame him. I was wearing a yellow union suit, and I hate to think what I must have looked like in that room.

I sat down in one of the chairs facing the desk after giving a brief shake to a thick-fingered, well-manicured, slightly oily hand.

He opened a crystal decanter that stood on one end of the desk. "Have some Madeira, Mr. Oak? Or would you like something else? I never drink spirits at this time of night."

I fought down an impulse to ask for a shot of redeye. "The Madeira will be fine, Mr. Ravenhurst."

He poured and handed me a stemmed glass nearly brimming with the wine. I joined him in an appreciative sip, then waited while he made up his mind to talk.

He leaned across the desk, looking at me with his small, dark eyes. He had an expression on his face that looked as if it were trying to sneer and leer at the same time but couldn't get much beyond the smirk stage.

"Mr. Oak, I have investigated you thoroughly—as thoroughly as it can be done, at least. My attorneys say that your reputation is A-one; that you get things done and rarely disappoint a client."

He paused as if waiting for a comment. I gave him nothing.

After a moment, he went on. "I hope that's true, Mr. Oak, because I'm going to have to trust you." He leaned back in his chair again, his eyes still on me. "Men very rarely like me, Mr. Oak. I am not a likable man. I do not pretend to be. That's not my function." He said it as if he had said it many times before, believed it, and wished it wasn't so.

"I do not ask that you like me," he continued. "I only ask that you be loyal to my interests for the duration of this assignment." Another pause. "I have been assured by others that this will be so. I would like your assurance."

"If I take the assignment, Mr. Ravenhurst," I told him, "I'll be working for *you*. I can be bought, but once I'm bought I stay bought.

"Now, what seems to be your trouble?"

He frowned. "Well, now, let's get one thing settled: Are you working for me, or not?"

"I won't know that until I find out what the job is."

His frown deepened. "Now, see here; this is very confidential work. What happens if I tell you and you decide not to work for me?"

I sighed. "Ravenhurst, right now, you're paying me to listen to you. Even if I don't take your job, I'm going to bill you for expenses and time to come all the way out here. So, as far as listening is concerned, I'm working for you now. If I don't like the job, I'll still forget everything I'm told. All right?"

He didn't like it, but he had no choice. "All right," he said. He polished off his glass of Madeira and refilled it. My own glass was still nearly full.

"Mr. Oak," he began, "I have two problems. One is minor, the other major. But I have attempted to blow the minor problem up out of proportion, so that all the people here at Raven's Rest think that it is the only problem. They think that I brought you out here for that reason alone.

"But all that is merely cover-up for the real problem."

"Which is?" I prompted.

He leaned forward again. Apparently, it was the only exercise he ever got. "You're aware that Viking Spacecraft is one of the corporations under the management of Ravenhurst Holdings?"

I nodded. Viking Spacecraft built some of the biggest and best spacecraft in the System. It held most of Ceres—all of it, in fact, except the Government Reservation. It had moved out to the asteroids a long time back, after the big mining concerns began cutting up the smaller asteroids for metal. The raw materials are easier to come by out here than they are on Earth, and it's a devil of a lot easier to build spacecraft under low-gee conditions than it is under the pull of Earth or Luna or Mars.

"Do you know anything about the experimental robotic ships being built on Eros?" Ravenhurst asked.

"Not much," I admitted. "I've heard about them, but I don't know any of the details." That wasn't quite true, but I've found it doesn't pay to tell everybody everything you know.

"The engineering details aren't necessary," Ravenhurst said. "Besides, I don't know them, myself. The point is that Viking is trying to build a ship that will be as easy to operate as a flitterboat—a one-man cargo vessel. Perhaps even a completely automatic job for cargo, and just use a one-man crew for the passenger vessels. Imagine how that would cut the cost of transportation in the Solar System! Imagine how it would open up high-speed cargo transfer if an automatic vessel could accelerate at twenty or twenty-five gees to turnover!"

I'll give Ravenhurst this: He had a light in his eyes that showed a real excitement about the prospect he was discussing, and it wasn't due entirely to the money he might make.

"Sounds fine," I said. "What seems to be the trouble?"

His face darkened half a shade. "The company police suspect sabotage, Mr. Oak."

"How? What kind?"

"They don't know. Viking has built six ships of that type—the McGuire class, the engineers call it. Each one has been slightly different than the one before, of course, as they ironed out the bugs in their operation. But each one has been a failure. Not one of them would pass the test for space-worthiness."

"Not a failure of the drive or the ordinary mechanisms of the ship, I take it?"

Ravenhurst sniffed. "Of course not. The brain. The ships became, as you might say, *non compos mentis*. As a matter of fact, when the last one simply tried to burrow into the surface of Eros by reversing its drive, one of the roboticists said that a coroner's jury would have returned a verdict of 'suicide while of unsound mind' if there were inquests held for spaceships."

"That doesn't make much sense," I said.

"No. It doesn't. It isn't sensible. Those ships' brains shouldn't have behaved that way. Robot brains don't go mad unless they're given instructions to do so—conflicting orders, erroneous information, that sort of thing. Or, unless they have actual physical defects in the brains themselves."

"The brains can handle the job of flying a ship all right, though?" I asked. "I mean, they have the capacity for it?"

"Certainly. They're the same type that's used to control the automobile traffic on the Eastern Seaboard Highway Network of North America. If they can control the movement of millions of cars, there's no reason why they can't control a spaceship."

"No," I said, "I suppose not." I thought it over for a second, then asked, "But what do your robotics men say is causing the malfunctions?"

"That's where the problem comes in, Mr. Oak." He pursed his pudgy lips, and his eyes narrowed. "The opinions are divided. Some of the men say it's simply a case of engineering failure—that the bugs haven't been worked out of this new combination, but that as soon as they are, everything will work as smoothly as butter. Others say that only deliberate tampering could cause those failures. And still others say that there's not enough evidence to prove either of those theories is correct."

"But your opinion is that it's sabotage?"

"Exactly," said Ravenhurst, "and I know who is doing it and why."

I didn't try to conceal the little bit of surprise that gave me. "You know the man who's responsible?"

He shook his head rapidly, making his jowls wobble. "I didn't mean that. It's not a single man; it's a group."

"Maybe you'd better go into a little more detail on that, Mr. Ravenhurst."

He nodded, and this time his jowls bobbled instead of wobbled. "Some group at Viking is trying to run me out of the managerial business. They want Viking to be managed by Thurston Enterprises; they evidently think they can get a better deal from him than they can from me. If the McGuire project fails, they'll have a good chance of convincing the stock-holders that the fault lies with Ravenhurst. You follow?"

"So far," I said. "Do you think Thurston's behind this, then?"

"I don't know," he said slowly. "He might be, or he might not. If he is, that's perfectly legitimate business tactics. He's got a perfect right to try to get more business for himself if he wants to. I've undercut him a couple of times.

"But I don't think he's too deeply involved, if he's involved at all. This smacks of a personal attack against me, and I don't think that's Thurston's type of play.

"You see, things are a little touchy right now. I won't go into details, but you know what the political situation is at the moment.

"It works this way, as far as Viking is concerned: If I lose the managerial contract at Viking, a couple of my other contracts will go by the board, too—especially if it's proved that I've been lax in management or have been expending credit needlessly.

"These other two companies are actually a little shaky at the moment; I've only been managing them for a little over a year in one case and two years in the other. Their assets have come up since I took over, but they'd still dump me if they thought I was reckless."

"How can they do that?" I asked. "You have a contract, don't you?"

"Certainly. They wouldn't break it. But they'd likely ask the Government Inspectors to step in and check every step of the managerial work. Now, you and I and everybody else knows that you have to cut corners to make a business successful. If the GI's step in, that will have to stop—which means we'll show a loss heavy enough to put us out. We'll be forced to sell the contract for a pittance.

"Well, then. If Viking goes, and these other two corporations go, it'll begin to look as if Ravenhurst can't take care of himself and his companies anymore. Others will climb on the bandwagon. Contracts that are coming up for renewal will be reconsidered instead of continuing automatically. I think you can see where that would lead eventually."

I did. You don't go into the managing business these days unless you have plenty on the ball. You've got to know all the principles and all the tricks of organization and communication, and you've got to be able to waltz your way around all the roadblocks that are caused by Government laws—some of which have been floating around on the books of one nation or another for two or three centuries.

Did you know that there's a law on the American statute books that forbids the landing of a spaceship within one hundred miles of a city? That was passed back when they were using rockets, but it's never been repealed. Technically, then, it's almost impossible to land a ship anywhere on the North American continent. Long Island Spaceport is openly flouting the law, if you want to look at it that way.

A managerial combine has to know all those little things and know how to get around them. It has to be able to have the confidence of the stock-holders of a corporation—if it's run on the Western Plan—or the confidence of communal owners if it's run on the Eastern Plan.

Something like this could snowball on Ravenhurst. It isn't only the rats that desert a sinking ship; so does anyone else who has any sense.

"What I want to know, Mr. Oak," Ravenhurst continued, "is who is behind this plot, whether an individual or a group. I want to know identity and motivation."

"Is that all?" I eyed him skeptically.

"No. Of course not. I want you to make sure that the MG-YR-7 isn't sabotaged. I want you to make sure it's protected from whatever kind of monkey wrenches are being thrown into its works."

"It's nearly ready for testing now, isn't it?" I asked.

"It is ready. It seems to be in perfect condition so far. Viking is already looking for a test pilot. It's still in working order now, and I want to be certain that it will remain so."

I cocked my head to one side and gave him my Interrogative And Suspicious Glance—Number 9 in the manual. "You didn't do any checking on the first six McGuire ships. You wait until this one is done before calling me. Why the delay, Ravenhurst?"

It didn't faze him. "I became suspicious after McGuire 6 failed. I put Colonel Brock on it."

I nodded. I'd had dealings with Brock. He was head of Ravenhurst's Security Guard. "Brock didn't get anywhere," I said.

"He did not. His own face is too well known for him to have investigated personally, and he's not enough of an actor to get away with using a plexiskin mask. He had to use underlings. And I'm afraid some of them might be in the pay of the ... ah ... opposition. They got nowhere."

"In other words, you may have spies in your own organization who are working with the Viking group. Very interesting. That means they know I'm working for you, which will effectively seal me up, too. You might as well have kept Brock on the job."

He smiled in a smug, superior sort of way that some men might have resented. I did. Even though I'd fed him the line so that he could feel superior, knowing that a smart operator like Ravenhurst would already have covered his tracks. I couldn't help wishing I'd told him simply to trot out his cover story instead of letting him think I believed it had never occurred to either of us before.

"As far as my staff knows, Mr. Oak, you are here to escort my daughter, Jaqueline, to Braunsville, Luna. You will, naturally, have to take her to Ceres in your flitterboat, where you will wait for a specially chartered ship to take you both to Luna. That will be a week after you arrive. Since the McGuire 7 is to be tested within three days, that should give you ample time."

"If it doesn't?"

"We will consider that possibility if and when it becomes probable. I have a great deal of faith in you."

"Thanks. One more thing: why do you think anybody will swallow the idea that your daughter needs a private bodyguard to escort her to Braunsville?"

His smile broadened a little. "You have not met my daughter, Mr. Oak. Jaqueline takes after me in a great many respects, not the least of which is her desire to have things her own way and submit to no man's yoke, as the saying goes. I have had a difficult time with her, sir; a difficult time. It is and has been a matter of steering a narrow course between the Scylla of breaking her spirit with too much discipline and the Charybdis of allowing her to ruin her life by letting her go hog wild. She is seventeen now, and the time has come to send her to a school where she will receive an education suitable to her potentialities and abilities, and discipline which will be suitable to her spirit.

"Your job, Mr. Oak, will be to make sure she gets there. You are not a bodyguard in the sense that you must protect her from the people around her. Quite the contrary, *they* may need protection from *her*. You are to make sure she arrives in Braunsville on schedule. She is perfectly capable of taking it in her head to go scooting off to Earth if you turn your back on her."

Still smiling, he refilled his glass. "Do have some more Madeira, Mr. Oak. It's really an excellent year."

I let him refill my glass.

"That, I think, will cover your real activities well enough. My daughter will, of course, take a tour of the plant on Ceres, which will allow you to do whatever work is necessary."

He smiled at me.

I didn't smile back.

"Up till now, this sounded like a pretty nice assignment," I said. "But I don't want it now. I can't take care of a teenage girl with a desire for the bright lights of Earth while I investigate a sabotage case."

I knew he had an out; I was just prodding him into springing it.

He did. "Of course not. My daughter is not as scatterbrained as I have painted her. She is going to help you."

"*Help* me?"

"Exactly. You are ostensibly her bodyguard. If she turns up missing, you will, of course, leave no stone unturned to find her." He chuckled. "And Ceres is a fairly large stone."

I thought it over. I still didn't like it too well, but if Jaqueline wasn't going to be too much trouble to take care of, it might work out. And if she did get to be too much trouble, I could see to it that she was unofficially detained for a while.

"All right, Mr. Ravenhurst," I said, "you've got yourself a man for both jobs."

"Both?"

"I find out who is trying to sabotage the McGuire ship, and I baby-sit for you. That's two jobs. And you're going to pay for both of them."

"I expected to," said Shalimar Ravenhurst.

Fifteen minutes later, I was walking into the room where I'd left my vac suit. There was a girl waiting for me.

She was already dressed in her vac suit, so there was no way to be sure, but she looked as if she had a nice figure underneath the suit. Her face was rather unexceptionally pretty, a sort of nice-girl-next-door face. Her hair was a reddish brown and was cut fairly close to the skull; only a woman who never intends to be in a vac suit in free fall can afford to let her hair grow.

"Miss Ravenhurst?" I asked.

She grinned and stuck out a hand. "Just call me Jack. And I'll call you Dan. O.K.?"

I grinned and shook her hand because there wasn't much else I could do. Now I'd met the Ravenhursts: A father called Shalimar and a daughter called Jack.

And a spaceship named McGuire.

I gave the flitterboat all the push it would take to get us to Ceres as fast as possible. I don't like riding in the things. You sit there inside a transite hull, which has two bucket seats inside it, fore and aft, astraddle the drive tube, and you guide from one beacon to the next while you keep tabs on orbital positions by radio. It's a long jump from one rock to the next, even in the asteroid belt, and you have to live inside your vac suit until you come to a stopping place where you can spend an hour or so resting before you go on. It's like driving cross-continent in an automobile, except that the signposts and landmarks are constantly shifting position. An inexperienced man can get lost easily in the Belt.

I was happy to find that Jack Ravenhurst knew how to handle a flitterboat and could sight navigate by the stars. That meant that I could sleep while she piloted and vice-versa. The trip back was a lot easier and faster than the trip out had been.

I was glad, in a way, that Ceres was within flitterboat range of Raven's Rest. I don't like the time wasted in waiting for a regular spaceship, which you have to do when your target is a quarter of the way around the Belt from you. The cross-system jumps don't take long, but getting to a ship takes time.

The Ravenhurst girl wasn't much of a talker while we were en route. A little general chitchat once in a while, then she'd clam up to do a little mental orbit figuring. I didn't mind. I was in no mood to pump her just yet, and I was usually figuring orbits myself. You get in the habit after a while.

When the Ceres beacon came into view, I was snoozing. Jack reached forward and shook my shoulder. "Decelerating toward Ceres," she said. "Want to take over from here on?" Her voice sounded tinny and tired in the earphones of my fishbowl.

"O.K.; I'll take her in. Have you called Ceres Field yet?"

"Not yet. I figured that you'd better do that, since it's your flitterboat."

I said O.K. and called Ceres. They gave me a traffic orbit, and I followed it in to Ceres Field.

It was a lot bigger than the postage-stamp field on Raven's Rest, and more brightly lit, and a lot busier, but it was basically the same idea—a broad, wide, smooth area that had been carved out of the surface of the nickel-iron with a focused sun beam. One end of it was reserved for flitterboats; three big spaceships sat on the other end, looking very *noblesse oblige* at the little flitterboats.

I clamped down, gave the key to one of the men behind the desk after we had gone below, and turned to Jack. "I suggest we go to the hotel first and get a shower and a little rest. We can go out to Viking tomorrow."

She glanced at her watch. Like every other watch and clock in the Belt, it was set for Greenwich Standard Time. What's the point in having time zones in space?

"I'm not tired," she said brightly. "I got plenty of sleep while we were on the way. Why don't we go out tonight? They've got a bounce-dance place called *Bali*'s that—"

I held up a hand. "No. You may not be tired, but I am. Remember, I went all the way out there by myself, and then came right back.

"I need at least six hours sleep in a nice, comfortable bed before I'll be able to move again."

The look she gave me made me feel every one of my thirty-five years, but I didn't intend to let her go roaming around at this stage of the game.

Instead, I put her aboard one of the little rail cars, and we headed for the Viking Arms, generally considered the best hotel on Ceres.

Ceres has a pretty respectable gee pull for a planetoid: Three per cent of Standard. I weigh a good, hefty five pounds on the surface. That makes it a lot easier to walk around on Ceres than on, say, Raven's Rest. Even so, you always get the impression that one of the little rail cars that scoots along the corridors is climbing uphill all the way, because the acceleration is greater than any measly thirty centimeters per second squared.

Jack didn't say another word until we reached the Viking, where Ravenhurst had thoughtfully made reservations for adjoining rooms. Then, after we'd registered, she said: "We could at least get something to eat."

"That's not a bad idea. We can get something to line our stomachs, anyway. Steak?"

She beamed up at me. "Steak. Sounds wonderful after all those mushy concentrates. Let's go."

The restaurant off the lobby was just like the lobby and the corridors outside—a big room hollowed out of the metal of the asteroid. The walls had been painted to prevent rusting, but they still bore the roughness left by the sun beam that had burnt them out.

We sat down at a table, and a waiter brought over a menu. The place wouldn't be classed higher than a third-rate cafe on Earth, but on Ceres it's considered one of the better places. The prices certainly compare well with those of the best New York or Moscow restaurants, and the price of meat, which has to be shipped from Earth, is—you should pardon the gag—astronomical.

That didn't bother me. Steaks for two would go right on the expense account. I mentally thanked Mr. Ravenhurst for the fine slab of beef when the waiter finally brought it.

While we were waiting, though, I lit a cigarette and said: "You're awfully quiet, Jack."

"Am I? Men are funny."

"Is that meant as a conversational gambit, or an honest observation?"

"Observation. I mean, men are always complaining that girls talk too much, but if a girl keeps her mouth shut, they think there's something wrong with her."

"Uh-huh. And you think that's a paradox or something?"

She looked puzzled. "Isn't it?"

"Not at all. The noise a jackhammer makes isn't pleasant at all, but if it doesn't make that noise, you figure it isn't functioning properly. So you wonder why."

Out of the corner of my eye, I had noticed a man wearing the black-and-gold union suit of Ravenhurst's Security Guard coming toward us from the door, using the gliding shuffle that works best under low gee. I ignored him to listen to Jack Ravenhurst.

"That has all the earmarks of a dirty crack," she said. The tone of her voice indicated that she wasn't sure whether to be angry or to laugh.

"Hello, Miss Ravenhurst; Hi, Oak." Colonel Brock had reached the table. He stood there, smiling his rather flat smile, while his eyes looked us both over carefully.

He was five feet ten, an inch shorter than I am, and lean almost to the point of emaciation. His scarred, hard-bitten face looked as though it had gotten that way when he tried to kiss a crocodile.

"Hello, Brock," I said. "What's new?"

Jack gave him a meaningless smile and said: "Hello, colonel." She was obviously not very impressed with either of us.

"Mind if I sit?" Brock asked.

We didn't, so he sat.

"I'm sorry I missed you at the spaceport," Brock said seriously, "but I had several of my boys there with their eyes open." He was quite obviously addressing Jack, not me.

"It's all right," Jack said. "I'm not going anywhere this time." She looked at me and gave me an odd grin. "I'm going to stay home and be a good girl this time around."

Colonel Brock's good-natured chuckle sounded about as genuine as the ring of a lead nickel. "Oh, you're no trouble, Miss Ravenhurst."

"Thank you, kind sir; you're a poor liar." She stood up and smiled sweetly. "Will you gentlemen excuse me a moment?"

We would and did. Colonel Brock and I watched her cross the room and disappear through a door. Then he turned to look at me, giving me a wry grin and shaking his head a little sadly. "So you got saddled with Jack the Ripper, eh, Oak?"

"Is she that bad?"

His chuckle was harsher this time, and had the ring of truth. "You'll find out. Oh, I don't mean she's got the morals of a cat or anything like that. So far as I know, she's still waiting for Mister Right to come along."

"Drugs?" I asked. "Liquor?"

"A few drinks now and then—nothing else," Brock said. "No, it's none of the usual things. It isn't what *she* does that counts; it's what she talks other people into doing. She's a convincer."

"That sounds impressive," I said. "What does it mean?"

His hard face looked wolfish, "I ought to let you find out for yourself. But, no; that wouldn't be professional courtesy, and it wouldn't be ethical."

"Brock," I said tiredly, "I have been given more runarounds in the past week than Mercury has had in the past millennium. I expect clients to be cagey, to hold back information, and to lie. But I didn't expect it of you. Give."

He nodded brusquely. "As I said, she's a convincer. A talker. She can talk people into doing almost anything she wants them to."

"For instance?"

"Like, for instance, getting all the patrons at the *Bali* to do a snake dance around the corridors in the altogether. The Ceres police broke it up, but she was nowhere to be found."

He said it so innocently that I knew he'd been the one to get her out of the mess.

"And the time," he continued, "that she almost succeeded in getting a welder named Plotkin elected Hereditary Czar of Ceres. She'd have succeeded, too, if she hadn't made the mistake of getting Plotkin himself up to speak in front of his loyal supporters. After that, everybody felt so silly that the movement fell apart."

He went on, reciting half a dozen more instances of the girl's ability to influence people without winning friends. None of them were new to me; they were all on file in the Political Survey Division of the United Nations Government on Earth, plus several more which Colonel Brock either neglected to tell me or wasn't aware of himself.

But I listened with interest; after all, I wasn't supposed to know any of these things. I am just a plain, ordinary, "confidential expediter". That's what it says on the door of my office in New York, and that's what it says on my license. All very legal and very dishonest.

The Political Survey Division is very legal and very dishonest, too. Theoretically, it is supposed to be nothing but a branch of the System Census Bureau; it is supposed to do nothing but observe and tabulate political trends. The actual fact that it is the Secret Service branch of the United Nations Government is known only to relatively few people.

I know it because I work for the Political Survey Division.

The PSD already had men investigating both Ravenhurst and Thurston, but when they found out that Ravenhurst was looking for a confidential expediter, for a special job, they'd shoved me in fast.

It isn't easy to fool sharp operators like Colonel Brock, but, so far, I'd been lucky enough to get away with it by playing ignorant-but-not-stupid.

The steaks were brought, and I mentally saluted Ravenhurst, as I had promised myself I would. Then I rather belatedly asked the colonel if he'd eat with us.

"No," he said, with a shake of his head. "No, thanks. I've got to get things ready for her visit to the Viking plant tomorrow."

"Oh? Hiding something?" I asked blandly.

He didn't even bother to look insulted. "No. Just have to make sure she doesn't get hurt by any of the machinery, that's all. Most of the stuff is automatic, and she has a habit of getting too close. I guess she thinks she can talk a machine out of hurting her as easily as she can talk a man into standing on his head."

Jack Ravenhurst was coming back to the table. I noticed that she'd fixed her hair nicely and put on make-up. It made her look a lot more feminine than she had while she was on the flitterboat.

"Well," she said as she sat down, "have you two decided what to do with me?"

Colonel Brock just smiled and said: "I guess we'll have to leave that up to you, Miss Ravenhurst." Then he stood up. "Now, if you'll excuse me, I'll be about my business."

Jack nodded, gave him a quick smile, and fell to on her steak with the voraciousness of an unfed chicken in a wheat bin.

Miss Jaqueline Ravenhurst evidently had no desire to talk to me at the moment.

On Ceres, as on most of the major planetoids, a man's home is his castle, even if it's only a hotel room. Raw nickel-iron, the basic building material, is so cheap that walls and doors are seldom made of anything else, so a hotel room is more like a vault than anything else on Earth. Every time I go into one of the hotels on Ceres or Eros, I get the feeling that I'm either a bundle of gold certificates or a particularly obstreperous prisoner being led to a medieval solitary confinement cell. They're not pretty, but they're *solid*.

Jack Ravenhurst went into her own room after flashing me a rather hurt smile that was supposed to indicate her disappointment in not being allowed to go nightclubbing. I gave her a big-brotherly pat on the shoulder and told her to get plenty of sleep, since we had to be up bright and early in the morning.

Once inside my own room, I checked over my luggage carefully. It had been brought there from the spaceport, where I'd checked it before going to Ravenhurst's Raven's Rest, on orders from Ravenhurst himself. This was one of several rooms that Ravenhurst kept permanently rented for his own uses, and I knew that Jack kept a complete wardrobe in her own rooms.

There were no bugs in my luggage—neither sound nor sight spying devices of any kind. Not that I would have worried if there had been; I just wanted to see if anyone was crude enough to try that method of smuggling a bug into the apartment.

The door chime pinged solemnly.

I took a peek through the door camera and saw a man in a bellboy's uniform, holding a large traveling case. I recognized the face, so I let him in.

"The rest of your luggage, sir," he said with a straight face.

"Thank you very much," I told him. I handed him a tip, and he popped off.

This stuff was special equipment that I hadn't wanted Ravenhurst or anybody else to get his paws into.

I opened it carefully with the special key, slid a hand under the clothing that lay on top for camouflage, and palmed the little detector I needed. Then I went around the room, whistling gently to myself.

The nice thing about an all-metal room is that it's impossible to hide a self-contained bug in it that will be of any use. A small, concealed broadcaster can't broadcast any farther than the walls, so any bug has to have wires leading out of the room.

I didn't find a thing. Either Ravenhurst kept the room clean or somebody was using more sophisticated bugs than any I knew about. I opened the traveling case again and took out one of my favorite gadgets. It's a simple thing, really: a noise generator. But the noise it generates is non-random noise. Against a background of "white," purely random noise, it is possible to pick out a conversation, even if the conversation is below the noise level, simply because conversation is patterned. But this little generator of mine was non-random. It was the multiple recording of ten thousand different conversations, all meaningless, against a background of "white" noise. Try that one on your differential analyzers.

By the time I got through, nobody could tap a dialogue in that room, barring, as I said, bugs more sophisticated than any the United Nations knew about.

Then I went over and tapped on the communicating door between my room and Jack Ravenhurst's. There was no answer.

I said, "Jack, I'm coming in. I have a key."

She said, "Go away. I'm not dressed. I'm going to bed."

"Grab something quick," I told her. "I'm coming in."

I keyed open the door.

She was no more dressed for bed than I was, unless she made a habit of sleeping in her best evening togs. Anger blazed in her eyes for a second, then that faded, and she tried to look all sweetness and light.

"I was trying on some new clothes," she said innocently.

A lot of people might have believed her. The emotional field she threw out, encouraging utter belief in her every word, was as powerful as any I'd ever felt. I just let it wash past me and said: "Come into my room for a few minutes, Jack; I want to talk to you."

I didn't put any particular emphasis into it. I don't have to. She came.

Once we were both inside my shielded room with the walls vibrating with ten thousand voices and a hush area in the center, I said patiently, "Jack, I personally don't care where you go or what you do. Tomorrow, you can do your vanishing act and have yourself a ball, for all I care. But there are certain things that have to be done first. Now, sit down and listen."

She sat down, her eyes wide. Evidently, nobody had ever beaten her at her own game before.

"Tonight, you'll stay here and get some sleep. Tomorrow, we go for a tour of Viking, first thing in the morning. Tomorrow afternoon, as soon as I think the time is ripe, you can sneak off. I'll show you how to change your appearance so you won't be recognized. You can have all the fun you want for twenty-four hours. I, of course, will be hunting high and low for you, but I won't find you until I have finished my investigation.

"On the other hand, I want to know where you are at all times, so that I can get in touch with you if I need you. So, no matter where you are, you'll keep in touch by phoning BANning 6226 every time you change location. Got that number?"

She nodded. "BANning 6226," she repeated.

"Fine. Now, Brock's agents will be watching you, so I'll have to figure out a way to get you away from them, but that won't be too hard. I'll let you know at the proper time. Meanwhile, get back in there, get ready for bed, and get some sleep. You'll need it. Move."

She nodded rather dazedly, got up, and went to the door. She turned, said goodnight in a low, puzzled voice, and closed the door.

Half an hour later, I quietly sneaked into her room just to check. She was sound asleep in bed. I went back to my own room, and got some sack time myself.

"It's a pleasure to have you here again, Miss Ravenhurst," said Chief Engineer Midguard. "Anything in particular you want to see this time?" He said it as though he actually enjoyed taking the boss' teenage daughter through a spacecraft plant.

Maybe he did, at that. He was a paunchy, graying man in his sixties, who had probably been a rather handsome lady-killer for the first half-century of his life, but he was approaching middle age now, which has a predictable effect on the telly-idol type.

Jack Ravenhurst was at her regal best, with the kind of *noblesse oblige* that would bring worshipful gratitude to the heart of any underling. "Oh, just a quick run-through on whatever you think would be interesting, Mr. Midguard; I don't want to take up too much of your time."

Midguard allowed as how he had a few interesting things to show her, and the party, which also included the watchful and taciturn Colonel Brock, began to make the rounds of the Viking plant.

There were three ships under construction at the time: two cargo vessels and a good-sized passenger job. Midguard seemed to think that every step of spacecraft construction was utterly fascinating—for which, bully for him—but it was pretty much of a drag as far as I was concerned. It took three hours.

Finally, he said, "Would you like to see the McGuire-7?"

Why, yes, of course she would. So we toddled off to the new ship while Midguard kept up a steady line of patter.

"We think we have all the computer errors out of this one, Miss Ravenhurst. A matter of new controls and safety devices. We feel that the trouble with the first six machines was that they were designed to be operated by voice orders by any qualified human operator. The trouble is that they had no way of telling just who was qualified. The brains are perfectly capable of distinguishing one individual from another, but they can't tell whether a given individual is a space pilot or a janitor. In fact—"

I marked the salient points in his speech. The MG-YR-7 would be strictly a one-man ship. It had a built-in dog attitude—friendly toward all humans, but loyal only to its master. Of course, it was likely that the ship would outlast its master, so its loyalties could be changed, but only by the use of special switching keys.

The robotics boys still weren't sure why the first six had gone insane, but they were fairly certain that the primary cause was the matter of too many masters. The brilliant biophysicist, Asenion, who promulgated the Three Laws of Robotics in the last century, had shown in his writings that they were unattainable ideals—that they only told what a perfect robot *should* be, not what a robot actually was.

The First Law, for instance, would forbid a robot to harm a human being, either by action or inaction. But, as Asenion showed, a robot could be faced with a situation which allowed for only two possible decisions, both of which required that a human being be harmed. In such a case, the robot goes insane.

I found myself speculating what sort of situation, what sort of Asenion paradox, had confronted those first six ships. And whether it had been by accident or design. Not that the McGuire robots had been built in strict accord with the Laws of Robotics; that was impossible on the face of it. But no matter how a perfectly logical machine is built, the human mind can figure out a way to goof it up because the human mind is capable of transcending logic.

The McGuire ship was a little beauty. A nice, sleek, needle, capable of atmospheric as well as spatial navigation, with a mirror-polished, beryl-blue surface all over the sixty-five feet of her—or his?—length.

It was standing upright on the surface of the planetoid, a shining needle in the shifting sunlight, limned against the star-filled darkness of space. We looked at it through the transparent viewport, and then took the flexible tube that led to the air lock of the ship.

The ship was just as beautiful inside as it was outside. Neat, compact, and efficient. The control room—if such it could be called—was like no control room I'd ever seen before. Just an acceleration couch and observation instruments. Midguard explained that it wasn't necessary to be a pilot to run the ship; any person who knew a smattering of astronavigation could get to his destination by simply telling the ship what he wanted to do.

Jack Ravenhurst took in the whole thing with wide-eyed interest.

"Is the brain activated, Mr. Midguard?" she asked.

"Oh, yes. We've been educating him for the past month, pumping information in as rapidly as he could record it and index it. He's finished with that stage now; we're just waiting for the selection of a test pilot for the final shakedown cruise." He was looking warily at Jack as he spoke, as if he were waiting for something.

Evidently, he knew what was coming. "I'd like to talk to him," Jack said. "It's so interesting to carry on an intelligent conversation with a machine."

"I'm afraid that's impossible, Miss Ravenhurst," Midguard said rather worriedly. "You see, McGuire's primed so that the first man's voice he hears will be identified as his master. It's what we call the 'chick reaction'. You know: the first moving thing a newly-hatched bird sees is regarded as the mother, and, once implanted, that order can't be rescinded. We can change McGuire's orientation in that respect, but we'd rather not have to go through that. After the test pilot establishes contact, you can talk to him all you want."

"When will the test pilot be here?" Jack asked, still as sweet as sucrodyne.

"Within a few days. It looks as though a man named Nels Bjornsen will be our choice. You may have heard of him."

"No," she said, "but I'm sure your choice will be correct."

Midguard still felt apologetic. "Well, you know how it is, Miss Ravenhurst; we can't turn a delicate machine like this over to just anyone for the first trial. He has to be a man of good judgment and fast reflexes. He has to know exactly what to say and when to say it, if you follow me."

"Oh, certainly; certainly." She paused and looked thoughtful. "I presume you've taken precautions against anyone stealing in here and taking control of the ship."

Midguard smiled and nodded wisely. "Certainly. Communication with McGuire can't be established unless and until two keys are used in the activating panel. I carry one; Colonel Brock has the other. Neither of us will give his key up to anyone but the accredited test pilot. And McGuire himself will scream out an alarm if anyone tries to jimmy the locks. He's his own burglar alarm."

She nodded. "I see." A pause. "Well, Mr. Midguard, I think you've done a very commendable job. Thank you so much. Is there anything else you feel I should see?"

"Well—" He was smilingly hesitant. "If there's anything else you want to see, I'll be glad to show it to you. But you've already seen our ... ah ... *piece de resistance*, so to speak."

She glanced at her wrist. It had been over four hours since we'd started. "I am rather tired," Jack said. "And hungry, too. Let's call it a day and go get something to eat."

"Fine! Fine!" Midguard said. "I'll be honored to be your host, if I may. We could have a little something at my apartment."

I knew perfectly well that he'd had a full lunch prepared and waiting.

The girl acknowledged his invitation and accepted it. Brock and I trailed along like the bodyguards we were supposed to be. I wondered whether or not Brock suspected me of being more than I appeared to be. If he didn't, he was stupider than I thought; on the other hand, he could never be sure. I wasn't worried about his finding out that I was a United Nations agent; that was a pretty remote chance. Brock didn't even know the United Nations Government *had* a Secret Service; it was unlikely that he would suspect me of being an agent of a presumably nonexistent body.

But he could very easily suspect that I had been sent to check on him and the Thurston menace, and, if he had any sense, he actually did. I wasn't going to give him any verification of that suspicion if I could help it.

Midguard had an apartment in the executive territory of the Viking reservation, a fairly large place with plastic-lined walls instead of the usual painted nickel-iron. Very luxurious for Ceres.

The meal was served with an air of subdued pretension that made everybody a little stiff and uncomfortable, with the possible exception of Jack Ravenhurst, and the definite exception of myself. I just listened politely to the strained courtesy that passed for small talk and waited for the chance I knew would come at this meal.

After the eating was all over, and we were all sitting around with cigarettes going and wine in our glasses, I gave the girl the signal we had agreed upon. She excused herself very prettily and left the room.

After fifteen minutes, I began to look a little worried. The bathroom was only a room away—we were in a dining area, and the bathroom was just off the main bedroom—and it shouldn't have taken her that long to brush her hair and powder her face.

I casually mentioned it to Colonel Brock, and he smiled a little.

"Don't worry, Oak; even if she does walk out of this apartment, my men will be following her wherever she goes. I'd have a report within one minute after she left."

I nodded, apparently satisfied. "I've been relying on that," I said. "Otherwise, I'd have followed her to the door."

He chuckled and looked pleased.

Ten minutes after that, even he was beginning to look a little worried. "Maybe we'd better go check," he said. "She might have hurt herself or ... or become ill."

Midguard looked flustered. "Now, just a minute, colonel! I can't allow you to just barge in on a young girl in the ... ah ... bathroom. Especially not Miss Ravenhurst."

Brock made his decision fast; I'll give him credit for that.

"Get Miss Pangloss on the phone!" he snapped. "She's just down the corridor. She'll come down on your orders."

At the same time, he got to his feet and made a long jump for the door. He grabbed the doorpost as he went by, swung himself in a new orbit, and launched himself toward the front door. "Knock on the bathroom door, Oak!" he bawled as he left.

I did a long, low, flat dive toward the bedroom, swung left, and brought myself up sharply next to the bathroom door. I pounded on the door. "Miss Ravenhurst! Jack! Are you all right?"

No answer.

Good. There shouldn't have been.

Colonel Brock fired himself into the room and braked himself against the wall. "Any answer?"

"No."

"My men outside say she hasn't left." He rapped sharply on the door with the butt of his stun gun. "Miss Ravenhurst! Is there anything the matter?"

Again, no answer.

I could see that Brock was debating on whether he should go ahead and charge in by himself without waiting for the female executive who lived down the way. He was still debating when the woman showed up, escorted by a couple of the colonel's uniformed guards.

Miss Pangloss was one of those brisk, efficient, middle-aged career-women who had no fuss or frills about her. She had seen us knocking on the door, so she didn't bother to do any knocking herself. She just opened the door and went in.

The bathroom was empty.

Again, as it should be.

All hell broke loose then, with me and Brock making most of the blather. It took us nearly ten minutes to find that the only person who had left the area had been an elderly, thin man who had been wearing the baggy protective clothing of a maintenance man.

By that time, Jack Ravenhurst had been gone more than forty minutes. She could be almost anywhere on Ceres.

Colonel Brock was furious and so was I. I sneered openly at his assurance that the girl couldn't leave and then got sneered back at for letting other people do what was supposed to be my job. That phase only lasted for about a minute, though.

Then Colonel Brock muttered: "She must have had a plexiskin mask and a wig and the maintenance clothing in her purse. As I recall, it was a fairly good-sized one." He didn't say a word about how careless I had been to let her put such stuff in her purse. "All right," he went on, "we'll find her."

"I'm going to look around, too," I said. "I'll keep in touch with your office." I got out of there.

I got to a public phone as fast as I could, punched BANning 6226, and said: "Marty? Any word?"

"Not yet."

"I'll call back."

I hung up and scooted out of there.

I spent the next several hours pushing my weight around all over Ceres. As the personal representative of Shalimar Ravenhurst, who was manager of Viking Spacecraft, which was, in turn, the owner of Ceres, I had a lot of weight to push around. I had every executive on the planetoid jumping before I was through.

Colonel Brock, of course, was broiling in his own juices. He managed to get hold of me by phone once, by calling a Dr. Perelson whom I was interviewing at the time.

The phone chimed, Perelson said, "Excuse me," and went to answer. I could hear his voice from the other room.

"Mr. Daniel Oak? Yes; he's here. Well, yes. Oh, all sorts of questions, colonel." Perelson's voice was both irritated and worried. "He says Miss Ravenhurst is missing; is that so? Oh? Well, does this man have any right to question me this way? Asking me? About everything!... How well I know the girl, the last time I saw her—things like that. Good heavens, we've hardly met!" He was getting exasperated now. "But does he have the authority to ask these questions? Oh. Yes. Well, of course, I'll be glad to co-operate in any manner I can ... Yes ... Yes. All right, I'll call him."

I got up from the half-reclining angle I'd been making with the wall, and shuffled across the room as Dr. Perelson stuck his head around the corner and said, "It's for you." He looked as though someone had put aluminum hydrogen sulfate in his mouthwash.

I picked up the receiver and looked at Brock's face in the screen. He didn't even give me a chance to talk. "What are you trying to do?" he shouted explosively.

"Trying to find Jaqueline Ravenhurst," I said, as calmly as I could.

"Oak, you're a maniac! Why, by this time, it's all over Ceres that the boss' daughter is missing! Shalimar Ravenhurst will have your hide for this!"

"He will?" I gave him Number 2—the wide-eyed innocent stare. "Why?"

"Why, you idiot, I thought you had sense enough to know that this should be kept quiet! She's pulled this stunt before, and we always managed to quiet things down before anything happened! We've managed to keep everything under cover and out of the public eye ever since she was fifteen, and now you blow it all up out of proportion and create a furore that won't ever be forgotten!"

He gave his speech as though it had been written for him in full caps, with three exclamation points after every sentence, and added gestures and grimaces after every word.

"Just doing what I thought was best," I said. "I want to find her as soon as possible."

"Well, stop it! Now! Let us handle it from here on in!"

Then I lowered the boom. "Now *you* listen, Brock. I am in charge of Jack Ravenhurst, not you. I've lost her, and I'll find her. I'll welcome your co-operation, and I'd hate to have to fight you, but if you don't like the way I'm handling it, you can just tell your boys to go back to their regular work and let me handle it alone, without interference. Now, which'll it be?"

He opened his mouth, closed it, and blew out his breath from between his lips. Then he said: "All right. The damage has been done, anyhow. But don't think I won't report all this to Ravenhurst as soon as I can get a beam to Raven's Rest."

"That's your job and your worry, not mine. Now, have you got any leads?"

"None," he admitted.

"Then I'll go out and dig up some. I'll let you know if I need you." And I cut off.

Dr. Perelson was sitting on his couch, with an expression that indicated that the pH of his saliva was hovering around one point five.

I said, "That will be all, Dr. Perelson. Thank you for your co-operation." And I walked out into the corridor, leaving him with a baffled look.

At the next public phone, I dialed the BANning number again.

"Any news?"

"Not from her; she hasn't reported in at all."

"I didn't figure she would. What else?"

"Just as you said," he told me. "With some cute frills around the edges. Ten minutes ago, a crowd of kids—sixteen to twenty-two age range—about forty of 'em—started a songfest and football game in the corridor outside Colonel Brock's place. The boys he had on duty there recognized the Jack Ravenhurst touch, and tried to find her in the crowd. Nothing doing. Not a sign of her."

"That girl's not only got power," I said, "but she's bright as a solar flare."

"Agreed. She's headed up toward Dr. Midguard's place now. I don't know what she has in mind, but it ought to be fun to watch."

"Where's Midguard now?" I asked.

"Hovering around Brock, as we figured. He's worried and feels responsible because she disappeared from his apartment, as predicted."

"Well, I've stirred up enough fuss in this free-falling anthill to give them all the worries they need. Tell me what's the overall effect?"

"Close to perfect. It's slightly scandalous and very mysterious, so everybody's keeping an eye peeled. If anyone sees Jaqueline Ravenhurst, they'll run to a phone, and naturally she's been spotted by a dozen different people in a dozen different places already.

"You've got both Brock's Company guards and the civil police tied up for a while."

"Fine. But be sure you keep the boys who are on her tail shifting around often enough so that she doesn't spot them."

"Don't worry your thick little head about that, Dan," he said. "They know their business. Are you afraid they'll lose her?"

"No, I'm not, and you know it. I just don't want her to know she's being followed. If she can't ditch her shadow, she's likely to try to talk to him and pull out all the stops convincing him that he should go away."

"You think she could? With *my* boys?"

"No, but if she tries it, it'll mean she knows she's being followed. That'll make it tougher to keep a man on her trail. Besides, I don't want her to try to convince him and fail."

"*Ich graben Sie*. On the off chance that she does spot one and gives him a good talking to, I'll pass along the word that the victim is to walk away meekly and get lost."

"Good," I said, "but I'd rather she didn't know."

"She won't. You're getting touchy, Dan; 'pears to me you'd rather be doing that job yourself, and think nobody can handle it but you."

I gave him my best grin. "You are closer than you know. O.K., I'll lay off. You handle your end of it and I'll handle mine."

"A fair exchange is no bargain. Go, and sin no more."

"I'll buzz you back before I go in," I said, and hung up.

Playing games inside a crowded asteroid is not the same as playing games in, say, Honolulu or Vladivostok, especially when that game is a combination of hide-and-seek and ring-around-the-Rosie. The trouble is lack of communication. Radio contact is strictly line-of-sight inside a hunk of metal. Radar beams can get a little farther, but a man has to be an expert billiards player to bank a reflecting beam around very many corners, and even that would depend upon the corridors being empty, which they never are. To change the game analogy again, it would be like trying to sink a ninety-foot putt across Times Square on New Year's Eve.

Following somebody isn't anywhere near as easy as popular fiction might lead you to believe. Putting a tail on someone whose spouse wants divorce evidence is relatively easy, but even the best detectives can lose a man by pure mischance. If the tailee, for instance, walks into a crowded elevator and the automatic computer decides that the car is filled to the limit, the man who's tailing him will be left facing a closed door. Something like that can happen by accident, without any design on the part of the tailee.

If you use a large squad of agents, all in radio contact with one another, that kind of loss can be reduced to near zero by simply having a man covering every possible escape route.

But if the tailee knows, or even suspects, that he's being followed, wants to get away from his tail, and has the ability to reason moderately well, it requires an impossibly large team to keep him in sight. And if that team has no fast medium of communication, they're licked at the onset.

In this case, we were fairly certain of Jack Ravenhurst's future actions, and so far our prophecies had been correct ... but if she decided to shake her shadows, fun would be had by all.

And as long as I had to depend on someone else to do my work for me, I was going to be just the teenchiest bit concerned about whether they were doing it properly.

I decided it was time to do my best to imitate a cosmic-ray particle, and put on a little speed through the corridors that ran through the subsurface of Ceres.

My vac suit was in my hotel room. One of the other agents had picked it up from my flitterboat and packed it carefully into a small attaché case. I'd planned my circuit so that I'd be near the hotel when things came to the proper boil, so I did a lot of diving, breaking all kinds of traffic regulations in the process.

I went to my room, grabbed the attaché case, checked it over quickly—never trust another man to check your vac suit for you—and headed for the surface.

Nobody paid any attention to me when I walked out of the air lock onto the spacefield. There were plenty of people moving in and out, going to and from their ships and boats. It wasn't until I reached the edge of the field that I realized that I had over-played my hand with Colonel Brock. It was only by the narrowest hair, but that had been enough to foul up my plans. There were guards surrounding the perimeter with radar search beams.

As I approached, one of the guards walked toward me and made a series of gestures with his left hand—two fingers up, fist, two fingers up, fist, three fingers up. I set my suit phone for 223; the guy's right hand was on the butt of his stun gun.

"Sorry, sir," came his voice. "We can't allow anyone to cross the field perimeter. Emergency."

"My name's Oak," I said tiredly. "Daniel Oak. What is going on here?"

He came closer and peered at me. Then: "Oh, yes, sir; I recognize you. We're ... uh—" He waved an arm around. "Uh ... looking for Miss Ravenhurst." His voice lowered conspiratorially. I could tell that he was used to handling the Ravenhurst girl with silence and suede gloves.

"Up *there*?" I asked.

"Well, Colonel Brock is a little worried. He says that Miss Ravenhurst is being sent to a school on Luna and doesn't want to go. He got to thinking about it, and he's afraid that she might try to leave Ceres—sneak off you know."

I knew.

"We've got a guard posted at the airlocks leading to the field, but Colonel Brock is afraid she might come up somewhere else and jump overland."

"I see," I said. I hadn't realized that Brock was that close to panic. What was eating him?

There must be something, but I couldn't figure it. Even the Intelligence Corps of the Political Survey Division can't get complete information every time.

After all, if he didn't want the girl to steal a flitterboat and go scooting off into the diamond-studded velvet, all he'd have to do would be to guard the flitterboats. I turned slowly and looked around. It seemed as though he'd done that, too.

And then my estimation of Brock suddenly leaped up—way up. Just a guard at each flitterboat wouldn't do. She could talk her way into the boat and convince the guard that he really shouldn't tell anyone that she had gone. By the time he realized he'd been conned, she'd be thousands of miles away.

And since a boat guard would have to assume that any approaching person *might* be the boat's legitimate owner, he'd have to talk to whomever it was that approached. *Kaput.*

But a perimeter guard would be able to call out an alarm if anyone came from the outside without having to talk to them.

And the guards watching the air locks undoubtedly had instructions to watch for any female that even vaguely matched Jack's description. A vac suit fits too tightly to let anyone wear more than a facial disguise, and Brock probably—no, *definitely*—had his tried-and-true men on duty there. The men who had already shown that they were fairly resistant to Jack Ravenhurst's peculiar charm. There probably weren't many with such resistance, and the number would become less as she grew older.

That still left me with my own problem. I had already lost too much time, and I had to go a long way. Ceres is irregular in shape, but it's roughly four hundred and eighty miles in diameter and a little over fifteen hundred miles in circumference.

Viking Test Field Four, where McGuire 7 was pointing his nose at the sky, was about twenty-five miles away, as the crow flies. But of course I couldn't go by crow.

By using a low, fairly flat, jackrabbit jump, a man in good condition can make a twelve hundred foot leap on the surface of Ceres, and each jump takes him about thirty seconds. At that rate, you can cover twenty-five miles in less than an hour. That's what I'd intended on doing, but I couldn't do it with all this radar around the field. I wouldn't be stopped, of course, but I'd sure tip my hand to Colonel Brock—the last thing I wanted to do.

But there was no help for it. I'd have to go back down and use the corridors, which meant that I'd arrive late—*after* Jack Ravenhurst got there, instead of *before*.

There was no time to waste, so I got below as fast as possible, repacked my vac suit, and began firing myself through the corridors as fast as possible. It was illegal, of course; a collision at twenty-five miles an hour can kill quickly if the other guy is coming at you at the same velocity. There were times when I didn't dare break the law, because some guard was around, and, even if he didn't catch me, he might report in and arouse Brock's interest in a way I wouldn't like.

I finally got to a tubeway, but it stopped at every station, and it took me nearly an hour and a half to get to Viking Test Area Four.

At the main door, I considered—for all of five seconds—the idea of simply telling the guard I had to go in. But I knew that, by now, Jack was there ahead of me. No. I couldn't just bull my way in. Too crude. Too many clues.

Hell's fire and damnation! I'd have to waste more time.

I looked up at the ceiling. The surface wasn't more than a hundred feet overhead, but it felt as though it were a hundred light-years.

If I could get that guard away from that door for five seconds, all would be gravy from then on in. But how? I couldn't have the diversion connected with me. Or—

Sometimes, I'm amazed at my own stupidity.

I beetled it down to the nearest phone and got hold of my BANning number.

"Jack already inside?" I snapped.

"Hell, yes! What happened to you?"

"Never mind. Got to make the best of it. I'm a corner away from Area Four. Where's your nearest man?"

"At the corner near the freight office."

"I'll go to him. What's he look like?"

"Five-nine. Black, curly hair. Your age. Fat. Name's Peter Quilp. He knows you."

"Peter Quilp?"

"Right."

"Good. Circulate a report that Jack has been seen in the vicinity of the main gate to Area Four. Put it out that there's a reward of five thousand for the person who finds her. I'm going to have Quilp gather a crowd."

He didn't ask a one of the million questions that must have popped into his mind. "Right. Anything else?"

"No." I hung up.

Within ten minutes, there was a mob milling through the corridor. Everybody in the neighborhood was looking for Jaqueline Ravenhurst. Then Peter Quilp yelled.

"I've got her! I've got her! Guard!"

With a scene like that going on, the guard couldn't help but step out of his cubicle to see what was going on.

I used the key I was carrying, stepped inside, and relocked the door. No one in the crowd paid any attention.

From then on up, it was simply a matter of evading patrolling guards—a relatively easy job. Finally, I put on my vac suit and went out through the air lock.

McGuire was still sitting there, a bright blue needle that reflected the distant sun as it moved across the ebon sky. Ceres' rotation took it from horizon to horizon in less than two hours, and you could see it and the stars move against the spire of the ship.

I made it to the air lock in one long jump.

Jack Ravenhurst had gone into the ship through the tube that led to the passenger lock. She might or might not have her vac suit on; I knew she had several of them on Ceres. It was probable that she was wearing it without the fishbowl.

I used the cargo lock.

It took a few minutes for the pumps to cycle, wasting more precious time. I was fairly certain that she would be in the control cabin, talking, but I was thankful that the pumps were silent.

Finally, I took off my fishbowl and stepped into the companionway.

And something about the size of Luna came out of nowhere and clobbered me on the occiput. I had time to yell, "Get away!" Then I was as one with intergalactic space.

Please! said the voice. *Please! Stop the drive! Go back! McGuire! I* demand *that you stop! I* order *you to stop! Please! PLEASE!*

It went on and on. A voice that shifted around every possible mode of emotion. Fear. Demand. Pleading. Anger. Cajoling. Hate. Threat.

Around and around and around.

Can't you speak, McGuire? Say something to me! A shrill, soft, throaty, harsh, murmuring, screaming voice that had one basic characteristic. It was a female voice.

And then another voice.

I am sorry, Jack. I can speak with you. I can record your data. But I cannot accept your orders. I can take orders from only One. And he has given me his orders.

And the feminine voice again: *Who was it? What orders? You keep saying that it was the man on the couch. That doesn't make sense!*

I didn't hear the reply, because it suddenly occurred to me that Daniel Oak was the man on the couch, and that I was Daniel Oak.

My head was throbbing with every beat of my heart, and it felt as if my blood pressure was varying between zero and fifteen hundred pounds per square inch in the veins and arteries and capillaries that fed my brain.

I sat up, and the pain began to lessen. The blood seemed to drain away from my aching head and go elsewhere.

I soon figured out the reason for that; I could tell by the feel that the gravity pull was somewhere between one point five and two gees. I wasn't at all used to it, but my head felt less painful and rather more hazy. If possible.

I concentrated, and the girl's voice came back again.

"... I knew you when you were McGuire One, and Two, and Three, and Four, and Five, and Six. And you were always good to me and understanding. Don't you remember?"

And then McGuire's voice—human, masculine, and not distorted at all by the reproduction system, but sounding rather stilted and terribly logical: "I remember, Jack. The memory banks of my previous activations are available."

"*All* of them? Can you remember everything?"

"I can remember everything that is in my memory banks."

The girl's voice rose to a wail. "But you *don't* remember! You *always* forgot things! They took things out each time you were reactivated, don't you remember?"

"I cannot remember that which is not contained in my memory banks, Jack. That is a contradiction in terms."

"But I was always able to *fix* it before!" The tears in her eyes were audible in her voice. "I'd tell you to remember, and I'd tell you *what* to remember, and you'd *remember* it! Tell me what's happened to you this time!"

"I cannot tell you. The information is not in my data banks."

Slowly, I got to my feet. Two gees isn't much, once you get used to it. The headache had subsided to a dull, bearable throb.

I was on a couch in a room just below the control chamber, and Jack Ravenhurst's voice was coming down from above. McGuire's voice was all around me, coming from the hidden speakers that were everywhere in the ship.

"But why won't you obey me any more, McGuire?" she asked.

"I'll answer that, McGuire," I said.

Jack's voice came weakly from the room above. "Mr. Oak? Dan? Thank heaven you're all right!"

"No thanks to you, though," I said. I was trying to climb the ladder to the control room, and my voice sounded strained.

"You've got to do something!" she said with a touch of hysteria. "McGuire is taking us straight toward Cygnus at two gees and won't stop."

My thinking circuits began to take over again. "Cut the thrust to half a gee, McGuire. Ease it down. Take a minute to do it."

"Yes, sir."

The gravity pull of acceleration let up slowly as I clung to the ladder. After a minute, I climbed on up to the control room.

Jack Ravenhurst was lying on the acceleration couch, looking swollen-faced and ill. I sat down on the other couch.

"I'm sorry I hit you," she said. "Really."

"I believe you. How long have we been moving, McGuire?"

"Three hours, twelve minutes, seven seconds, sir," said McGuire.

"I didn't want anyone to know," Jack said. "Not anyone. That's why I hit you. I didn't know McGuire was going to go crazy."

"He's not crazy, Jack," I said carefully. "This time, he has a good chance of remaining sane."

"But he's not McGuire any more!" she wailed. "He's different! Terrible!"

"Sure he's different. You should be thankful."

"But what happened?"

I leaned back on the couch. "Listen to me, Jack, and listen carefully. You think you're pretty grown up, and, in a lot of ways you are. But no human being, no matter how intelligent, can store enough experience into seventeen years to make him or her wise. A wise choice requires data, and gathering enough data requires time." That wasn't exactly accurate, but I had to convince her.

"You're pretty good at controlling people, aren't you, Jack. A real powerhouse. Individuals, or mobs, you can usually get your own way. It was your idea to send you to Luna, not your father's. It was your idea to appoint yourself my assistant in this operation. It was you who planted the idea that the failure of the McGuire series was due to Thurston's activities.

"You used to get quite a kick out of controlling people. And then you were introduced to McGuire One. I got all the information on that. You were fifteen, and, for the first time in your life, you found an intelligent mind that couldn't be affected at all by that emotional field you project so well. Nothing affected McGuire but data. If you told him something, he believed it. Right, McGuire?"

"I do not recall that, sir."

"Fine. And, by the way, McGuire—the data you have been picking up in the last few hours, since your activation, is to be regarded as unique data. It applies only to Jaqueline Ravenhurst, and is not to be assumed relevant to any other person unless I tell you otherwise."

"Yes, sir."

"That's what I don't understand!" Jack said unhappily. "I stole the two keys that were supposed to activate McGuire. He was supposed to obey the first person who activated him. But *I* activated him, and he won't obey!"

"You weren't listening to what Midguard said, Jack," I said gently. "He said: 'The first *man's* voice he hears will be identified as his master.'"

"You'd been talking to every activation of McGuire. You'd ... well, I won't say you'd fallen in love with him, but it was certainly a schoolgirl crush. You found that McGuire didn't respond to emotion, but only to data and logic.

"You've always felt rather inferior in regard to your ability to handle logic, haven't you, Jack?"

"Yes ... yes. I have."

"Don't cry, now; I'm only trying to explain it to you. There's nothing wrong with your abilities."

"No?"

"No. But you wanted to be able to think like a man, and you couldn't. You think like a woman! And what's wrong with that? Nothing! Your method of thinking is just as good as any man's, and better than most of 'em.

"You found you could handle people emotionally, and you found it was so easy that you grew contemptuous. The only mind that responded to your logic was McGuire's. But your logic is occasionally as bad as your feminine reasoning is good. So, every time you talked to McGuire, you eventually gave him data that he couldn't reconcile in his computations. If he did reconcile them, then his thinking had very little in common with the actual realities of the universe, and he behaved in non-survival ways.

"McGuire was your friend, your brother, your Father Confessor. He never made judgments or condemned you for anything you did. All he did was sit there and soak up troubles and worries that he couldn't understand or use. Each time, he was driven mad.

"The engineers and computermen and roboticists who were working on it were too much under your control to think of blaming you for McGuire's troubles. Even Brock, in spite of his attitude of the tough guy watching over a little girl, was under your control to a certain degree. He let you get away with all your little pranks, only making sure that you didn't get hurt."

She nodded. "They were all so easy. So very easy. I could speak nonsense and they'd listen and do what I told them. But McGuire didn't accept nonsense, I guess." She laughed a little. "So I fell in love with a machine."

"Not *a* machine," I said gently. "Six of them. Each time the basic data was pumped into a new McGuire brain, you assumed that it was the same machine you'd known before with a little of its memory removed. Each time, you'd tell it to 'remember' certain things, and, of course, he did. If you tell a robot that a certain thing is in his memory banks, he'll automatically put it there and treat it as a memory.

"To keep you from ruining him a seventh time, we had them put in one little additional built-in inhibition. McGuire won't take orders from a woman."

"So, even after I turned him on, he still wouldn't take orders from me," she said. "But when you came in, he recognized you as his master."

"If you want to put it that way."

Again, she laughed a little. "I know why he took off from Ceres. When I hit you, you said, 'Get away'. McGuire had been given his first order, and he obeyed it.'"

"I had to say something," I said. "If I'd had time, I'd have done a little better."

She thought back. "You said, '*We* had them add that inhibition.' Who's *we*?"

"I can't tell you yet. But we need young women like you, and you'll be told soon enough."

"Evidently they need men like you, too," she said. "You don't react to an emotional field, either."

"Oh, yes, I do. Any human being does. But I use it; I don't fight it. And I don't succumb to it."

"What do we do now?" she asked. "Go back to Ceres?"

"That's up to you. If you do, you'll be accused of stealing McGuire, and I don't think it can be hushed up at this stage of the game."

"But I can't just run away."

"There's another out," I said. "We'll have a special ship pick us up on one of the nearer asteroids and leave McGuire there. We'll be smuggled back, and we'll claim that McGuire went insane again."

She shook her head. "No. That would ruin Father, and I can't do that, in spite of the fact that I don't like him very much."

"Can you think of any other solution?"

"No," she said softly.

"Thanks. But you have. All I have to do is take it to Shalimar Ravenhurst. He'll scream and yell, but he has a sane ship—for a while. Between the two of us. I think we can get everything straightened out."

"But I want to go to school on Luna."

"You can do that, too. And I'll see that you get special training, from special teachers. You've got to learn to control that technique of yours."

"You have that technique, don't you? And you can control it. You're wonderful."

I looked sharply at her and realized that I had replaced McGuire as the supermind in her life.

I sighed. "Maybe in another three or four years," I said. "Meanwhile, McGuire, you can head us for Raven's Rest."

"Home, James," said Jack Ravenhurst.

"I am McGuire," said McGuire.

THE END

Time Fuze

Commander Benedict kept his eyes on the rear plate as he activated the intercom. "All right, cut the power. We ought to be safe enough here."

As he released the intercom, Dr. Leicher, of the astronomical staff, stepped up to his side. "Perfectly safe," he nodded, "although even at this distance a star going nova ought to be quite a display."

Benedict didn't shift his gaze from the plate. "Do you have your instruments set up?"

"Not quite. But we have plenty of time. The light won't reach us for several hours yet. Remember, we were outracing it at ten lights."

The commander finally turned, slowly letting his breath out in a soft sigh. "Dr. Leicher, I would say that this is just about the foulest coincidence that could happen to the first interstellar vessel ever to leave the Solar System."

Leicher shrugged. "In one way of thinking, yes. It is certainly true that we will never know, now, whether Alpha Centauri A ever had any planets. But, in another way, it is extremely fortunate that we should be so near a stellar explosion because of the wealth of scientific information we can obtain. As you say, it is a coincidence, and probably one that happens only once in a billion years. The chances of any particular star going nova are small. That we should be so close when it happens is of a vanishingly small order of probability."

Commander Benedict took off his cap and looked at the damp stain in the sweatband. "Nevertheless, Doctor, it is damned unnerving to come out of ultradrive a couple of hundred million miles from the first star ever visited by man and have to turn tail and run because the damned thing practically blows up in your face."

Leicher could see that Benedict was upset; he rarely used the same profanity twice in one sentence.

They had been downright lucky, at that. If Leicher hadn't seen the star begin to swell and brighten, if he hadn't known what it meant, or if Commander Benedict hadn't been quick enough in shifting the ship back into ultradrive—Leicher had a vision of an incandescent cloud of gaseous metal that had once been a spaceship.

The intercom buzzed. The commander answered, "Yes?"

"Sir, would you tell Dr. Leicher that we have everything set up now?"

Leicher nodded and turned to leave. "I guess we have nothing to do now but wait."

When the light from the nova did come, Commander Benedict was back at the plate again—the forward one, this time, since the ship had been turned around in order to align the astronomy lab in the nose with the star.

Alpha Centauri A began to brighten and spread. It made Benedict think of a light bulb connected through a rheostat, with someone turning that rheostat, turning it until the circuit was well overloaded.

The light began to hurt Benedict's eyes even at that distance and he had to cut down the receptivity in order to watch. After a while, he turned away from the plate. Not because the show was over, but simply because it had slowed to a point beyond which no change seemed to take place to the human eye.

Five weeks later, much to Leicher's chagrin, Commander Benedict announced that they had to leave the vicinity. The ship had only been provisioned to go to Alpha Centauri, scout the system without landing on any of the planets, and return. At ten lights, top speed for the ultradrive, it would take better than three months to get back.

"I know you'd like to watch it go through the complete cycle," Benedict said, "but we can't go back home as a bunch of starved skeletons."

Leicher resigned himself to the necessity of leaving much of his work unfinished, and, although he knew it was a case of sour grapes, consoled himself with the thought that he could as least get most of the remaining information from the five-hundred-inch telescope on Luna, four years from then.

As the ship slipped into the not-quite-space through which the ultradrive propelled it, Leicher began to consolidate the material he had already gathered.

Commander Benedict wrote in the log:

Fifty-four days out from Sol. Alpha Centauri has long since faded back into its pre-blowup state, since we have far outdistanced the light from its explosion. It now looks as it did two years ago. It—

"Pardon me, Commander," Leicher interrupted, "But I have something interesting to show you."

Benedict took his fingers off the keys and turned around in his chair. "What is it, Doctor?"

Leicher frowned at the papers in his hands. "I've been doing some work on the probability of that explosion happening just as it did, and I've come up with some rather frightening figures. As I said before, the probability was small. A little calculation has given us some information which makes it even smaller. For instance: with a possible error of plus or minus two seconds Alpha Centauri A began to explode the instant we came out of ultradrive!

"Now, the probability of that occurring comes out so small that it should happen only once in ten to the four hundred sixty-seventh seconds."

It was Commander Benedict's turn to frown. "So?"

"Commander, the entire universe is only about ten to the seventeenth seconds old. But to give you an idea, let's say that the chances of its happening are *once* in millions of trillions of years!"

Benedict blinked. The number, he realized, was totally beyond his comprehension—or anyone else's.

"Well, so what? Now it has happened that one time. That simply means that it will almost certainly never happen again!"

"True. But, Commander, when you buck odds like that and win, the thing to do is look for some factor that is cheating in your favor. If you took a pair of dice and started throwing sevens, one right after another—*for the next couple of thousand years*—you'd begin to suspect they were loaded."

Benedict said nothing; he just waited expectantly.

"There is only one thing that could have done it. Our ship." Leicher said it quietly, without emphasis.

"What we know about the hyperspace, or superspace, or whatever it is we move through in ultradrive is almost nothing. Coming out of it so near to a star might set up some sort of shock wave in normal space which would completely disrupt that star's internal balance, resulting in the liberation of unimaginably vast amounts of energy, causing that star to go nova. We can only assume that we ourselves were the fuze that set off that nova."

Benedict stood up slowly. When he spoke, his voice was a choking whisper. "You mean the sun—Sol—might...."

Leicher nodded. "I don't say that it definitely would. But the probability is that we were the cause of the destruction of Alpha Centauri A, and therefore might cause the destruction of Sol in the same way."

Benedict's voice was steady again. "That means that we can't go back again, doesn't it? Even if we're not positive, we can't take the chance."

"Not necessarily. We can get fairly close before we cut out the drive, and come in the rest of the way at sub-light speed. It'll take longer, and we'll have to go on half or one-third rations, but we *can* do it!"

"How far away?"

"I don't know what the minimum distance is, but I do know how we can gage a distance. Remember, neither Alpha Centauri B or C were detonated. We'll have to cut our drive at least as far away from Sol as they are from A."

"I see." The commander was silent for a moment, then: "Very well, Dr. Leicher. If that's the safest way, that's the only way."

Benedict issued the orders, while Leicher figured the exact point at which they must cut out the drive, and how long the trip would take. The rations would have to be cut down accordingly.

Commander Benedict's mind whirled around the monstrousness of the whole thing like some dizzy bee around a flower. What if there had been planets around Centauri A? What if they had been inhabited? Had he, all unwittingly, killed entire races of living, intelligent beings?

But, how could he have known? The drive had never been tested before. It couldn't be tested inside the Solar System—it was too fast. He and his crew had been volunteers, knowing that they might die when the drive went on.

Suddenly, Benedict gasped and slammed his fist down on the desk before him.

Leicher looked up. "What's the matter, Commander?"

"Suppose," came the answer, "Just suppose, that we have the same effect on a star when we *go into* ultradrive as we do when we come out of it?"

Leicher was silent for a moment, stunned by the possibility. There was nothing to say, anyway. They could only wait....

A little more than half a light year from Sol, when the ship reached the point where its occupants could see the light that had left their home sun more than seven months before, they watched it become suddenly, horribly brighter. *A hundred thousand times brighter!*

... THE END

...After a Few Words...

This is a science-fiction story. History is a science; the other part is, as all Americans know, the most fictional field we have today.

He settled himself comfortably in his seat, and carefully put the helmet on, pulling it down firmly until it was properly seated. For a moment, he could see nothing.

Then his hand moved up and, with a flick of the wrist, lifted the visor. Ahead of him, in serried array, with lances erect and pennons flying, was the forward part of the column. Far ahead, he knew, were the Knights Templars, who had taken the advance. Behind the Templars rode the mailed knights of Brittany and Anjou. These were followed by King Guy of Jerusalem and the host of Poitou.

He himself, Sir Robert de Bouain, was riding with the Norman and English troops, just behind the men of Poitou. Sir Robert turned slightly in his saddle. To his right, he could see the brilliant red-and-gold banner of the lion-hearted Richard of England—*gules, in pale three lions passant guardant or*. Behind the standard-bearer, his great war horse moving with a steady, measured pace, his coronet of gold on his steel helm gleaming in the glaring desert sun, the lions of England on his firm-held shield, was the King himself.

Further behind, the Knights Hospitallers protected the rear, guarding the column of the hosts of Christendom from harassment by the Bedouins.

"By our Lady!" came a voice from his left. "Three days out from Acre, and the accursed Saracens still elude us."

Sir Robert de Bouain twisted again in his saddle to look at the knight riding alongside him. Sir Gaeton de l'Arc-Tombé sat tall and straight in his saddle, his visor up, his blue eyes narrowed against the glare of the sun.

Sir Robert's lips formed a smile. "They are not far off, Sir Gaeton. They have been following us. As we march parallel to the seacoast, so they have been marching with us in those hills to the east."

"Like the jackals they are," said Sir Gaeton. "They assail us from the rear, and they set up traps in our path ahead. Our spies tell us that the Turks lie ahead of us in countless numbers. And yet, they fear to face us in open battle."

"Is it fear, or are they merely gathering their forces?"

"Both," said Sir Gaeton flatly. "They fear us, else they would not dally to amass so fearsome a force. If, as our informers tell us, there are uncounted Turks to the fore, and if, as we are aware, our rear is being dogged by the Bedouin and the black horsemen of Egypt, it would seem that Saladin has at hand more than enough to overcome us, were they all truly Christian knights."

"Give them time. We must wait for their attack, sir knight. It were foolhardy to attempt to seek them in their own hills, and yet they must stop us. They will attack before we reach Jerusalem, fear not."

"We of Gascony fear no heathen Musselman," Sir Gaeton growled. "It's this Hellish heat that is driving me mad." He pointed toward the eastern hills. "The sun is yet low, and already the heat is unbearable."

Sir Robert heard his own laugh echo hollowly within his helmet. "Perhaps 'twere better to be mad when the assault comes. Madmen fight better than men of cooler blood." He knew that the others were baking inside their heavy armor, although he himself was not too uncomfortable.

Sir Gaeton looked at him with a smile that held both irony and respect. "In truth, sir knight, it is apparent that you fear neither men nor heat. Nor is your own blood too cool. True, I ride with your Normans and your English and your King Richard of the Lion's Heart, but I am a Gascon, and have sworn no fealty to him. But to side with the Duke of Burgundy against King Richard—" He gave a short, barking laugh. "I fear no man," he went on, "but if I had to fear one, it would be Richard of England."

Sir Robert's voice came like a sword: steely, flat, cold, and sharp. "My lord the King spoke in haste. He has reason to be bitter against Philip of France, as do we all. Philip has deserted the field. He has returned to France in haste, leaving the rest of us to fight the Saracen for the Holy Land leaving only the contingent of his vassal the Duke of Burgundy to remain with us."

"Richard of England has never been on the best of terms with Philip Augustus," said Sir Gaeton.

"No, and with good cause. But he allowed his anger against Philip to color his judgment when he spoke harshly against the Duke of Burgundy. The Duke is no coward, and Richard Plantagenet well knows it. As I said, he spoke in haste."

"And you intervened," said Sir Gaeton.

"It was my duty." Sir Robert's voice was stubborn. "Could we have permitted a quarrel to develop between the two finest knights and warleaders in Christendom at this crucial point? The desertion of Philip of France has cost us dearly. Could we permit the desertion of Burgundy, too?"

"You did what must be done in honor," the Gascon conceded, "but you have not gained the love of Richard by doing so."

Sir Robert felt his jaw set firmly. "My king knows I am loyal."

Sir Gaeton said nothing more, but there was a look in his eyes that showed that he felt that Richard of England might even doubt the loyalty of Sir Robert de Bouain.

Sir Robert rode on in silence, feeling the movement of the horse beneath him.

There was a sudden sound to the rear. Like a wash of the tide from the sea came the sound of Saracen war cries and the clash of steel on steel mingled with the sounds of horses in agony and anger.

Sir Robert turned his horse to look.

The Negro troops of Saladin's Egyptian contingent were thundering down upon the rear! They clashed with the Hospitallers, slamming in like a rain of heavy stones, too close in for the use of bows. There was only the sword against armor, like the sound of a thousand hammers against a thousand anvils.

"Stand fast! Stand fast! Hold them off!" It was the voice of King Richard, sounding like a clarion over the din of battle.

Sir Robert felt his horse move, as though it were urging him on toward the battle, but his hand held to the reins, keeping the great charger in check. The King had said "Stand fast!" and this was no time to disobey the orders of Richard.

The Saracen troops were coming in from the rear, and the Hospitallers were taking the brunt of the charge. They fought like madmen, but they were slowly being forced back.

The Master of the Hospitallers rode to the rear, to the King's standard, which hardly moved in the still desert air, now that the column had stopped moving.

The voice of the Duke of Burgundy came to Sir Robert's ears.

"Stand fast. The King bids you all to stand fast," said the duke, his voice fading as he rode on up the column toward the knights of Poitou and the Knights Templars.

The Master of the Hospitallers was speaking in a low, urgent voice to the King: "My lord, we are pressed on by the enemy and in danger of eternal infamy. We are losing our horses, one after the other!"

"Good Master," said Richard, "it is you who must sustain their attack. No one can be everywhere at once."

The Master of the Hospitallers nodded curtly and charged back into the fray.

The King turned to Sir Baldwin de Carreo, who sat ahorse nearby, and pointed toward the eastern hills. "They will come from there, hitting us in the flank; we cannot afford to amass a rearward charge. To do so would be to fall directly into the hands of the Saracen."

A voice very close to Sir Robert said: "Richard is right. If we go to the aid of the Hospitallers, we will expose the column to a flank attack." It was Sir Gaeton.

"My lord the King," Sir Robert heard his voice say, "is right in all but one thing. If we allow the Egyptians to take us from the rear, there will be no need for Saladin and his Turks to come down on our flank. And the Hospitallers cannot hold for long at this rate. A charge at full gallop would break the Egyptian line and give the Hospitallers breathing time. Are you with me?"

"Against the orders of the King?"

"The King cannot see everything! There are times when a man must use his own judgment! You said you were afraid of no man. Are you with me?"

After a moment's hesitation, Sir Gaeton couched his lance. "I'm with you, sir knight! Live or die, I follow! Strike and strike hard!"

"Forward then!" Sir Robert heard himself shouting. "Forward for St. George and for England!"

"St. George and England!" the Gascon echoed.

Two great war horses began to move ponderously forward toward the battle lines, gaining momentum as they went. Moving in unison, the two knights, their horses now at a fast trot, lowered their lances, picking their Saracen targets with care. Larger and larger loomed the Egyptian cavalrymen as the horses changed pace to a thundering gallop.

The Egyptians tried to dodge, as they saw, too late, the approach of the Christian knights.

Sir Robert felt the shock against himself and his horse as the steel tip of the long ash lance struck the Saracen horseman in the chest. Out of the corner of his eye, he saw that Sir Gaeton, too, had scored.

The Saracen, impaled on Sir Robert's lance, shot from the saddle as he died. His lighter armor had hardly impeded the incoming spear-point, and now his body dragged it down as he dropped toward the desert sand. Another Moslem cavalryman was charging in now, swinging his curved saber, taking advantage of Sir Robert's sagging lance.

There was nothing else to do but drop the lance and draw his heavy broadsword. His hand grasped it, and it came singing from its scabbard.

The Egyptian's curved sword clanged against Sir Robert's helm, setting his head ringing. In return, the knight's broadsword came about in a sweeping arc, and the Egyptian's horse rode on with the rider's headless body.

Behind him, Sir Robert heard further cries of "St. George and England!"

The Hospitallers, taking heart at the charge, were going in! Behind them came the Count of Champagne, the Earl of Leister, and the Bishop of Beauvais, who carried a great warhammer in order that he might not break Church Law by shedding blood.

Sir Robert's own sword rose and fell, cutting and hacking at the enemy. He himself felt a dreamlike detachment, as though he were watching the battle rather than participating in it.

But he could see that the Moslems were falling back before the Christian onslaught.

And then, quite suddenly, there seemed to be no foeman to swing at. Breathing heavily, Sir Robert sheathed his broadsword.

Beside him, Sir Gaeton did the same, saying: "It will be a few minutes before they can regroup, sir knight. We may have routed them completely."

"Aye. But King Richard will not approve of my breaking ranks and disobeying orders. I may win the battle and lose my head in the end."

"This is no time to worry about the future," said the Gascon. "Rest for a moment and relax, that you may be the stronger later. Here—have an *Old Kings*."

He had a pack of cigarettes in his gauntleted hand, which he proffered to Sir Robert. There were three cigarettes protruding from it, one slightly farther than the others. Sir Robert's hand reached out and took that one.

"Thanks. When the going gets rough, I really enjoy an *Old Kings*."

He put one end of the cigarette in his mouth and lit the other from the lighter in Sir Gaeton's hand.

"Yes, sir," said Sir Gaeton, after lighting his own cigarette, "*Old Kings* are the greatest. They give a man real, deep-down smoking pleasure."

"There's no doubt about it, *Old Kings* are a *man's* cigarette." Sir Robert could feel the soothing smoke in his lungs as he inhaled deeply. "That's great. When I want a cigarette, I don't want just *any* cigarette."

"Nor I," agreed the Gascon. "*Old Kings* is the only real cigarette when you're doing a real *man's* work."

"That's for sure." Sir Robert watched a smoke ring expand in the air.

There was a sudden clash of arms off to their left. Sir Robert dropped his cigarette to the ground. "The trouble is that doing a real he-man's work doesn't always allow you to enjoy the fine, rich tobaccos of *Old Kings* right down to the very end."

"No, but you can always light another later," said the Gascon knight.

King Richard, on seeing his army moving suddenly toward the harassed rear, had realized the danger and had charged through the Hospitallers to get into the thick of the fray. Now the Turks were charging down from the hills, hitting—not the flank as he had expected, but the rear! Saladin had expected him to hold fast!

Sir Robert and Sir Gaeton spurred their chargers toward the flapping banner of England.

The fierce warrior-king of England, his mighty sword in hand, was cutting down Turks as though they were grain-stalks, but still the Saracen horde pressed on. More and more of the terrible Turks came boiling down out of the hills, their glittering scimitars swinging.

Sir Robert lost all track of time. There was nothing to do but keep his own great broadsword moving, swinging like some gigantic metronome as he hacked down the Moslem foes.

And then, suddenly, he found himself surrounded by the Saracens! He was isolated and alone, cut off from the rest of the Christian forces! He glanced quickly around as he slashed another Saracen from pate to breastbone. Where was Sir Gaeton? Where were the others? Where was the red-and-gold banner of Richard?

He caught a glimpse of the fluttering banner far to the rear and started to fall back.

And then he saw another knight nearby, a huge man who swung his sparkling blade with power and force. On his steel helm gleamed a golden coronet! Richard!

And the great king, in spite of his prowess was outnumbered heavily and would, within seconds, be cut down by the Saracen horde!

Without hesitation, Sir Robert plunged his horse toward the surrounded monarch, his great blade cutting a path before him.

He saw Richard go down, falling from the saddle of his charger, but by that time his own sword was cutting into the screaming Saracens and they had no time to attempt any further mischief to the King. They had their hands full with Sir Robert de Bouain.

He did not know how long he fought there, holding his charger motionless over the inert body of the fallen king, hewing down the screaming enemy, but presently he heard the familiar cry of "For St. George and for England" behind him. The Norman and English troops were charging in, bringing with them the banner of England!

And then Richard was on his feet, cleaving the air about him with his own broadsword. Its bright edge, besmeared with Saracen blood, was biting viciously into the foe.

The Turks began to fall back. Within seconds, the Christian knights were boiling around the embattled pair, forcing the Turks into retreat. And for the second time, Sir Robert found himself with no one to fight.

And then a voice was saying: "You have done well this day, sir knight. Richard Plantagenet will not forget."

Sir Robert turned in his saddle to face the smiling king.

"My lord king, be assured that I would never forget my loyalty to my sovereign and liege lord. My sword and my life are yours whenever you call."

King Richard's gauntleted hand grasped his own. "If it please God, I shall never ask your life. An earldom awaits you when we return to England, sir knight."

And then the king mounted his horse and was running full gallop after the retreating Saracens.

Robert took off his helmet.

He blinked for a second to adjust his eyes to the relative dimness of the studio. After the brightness of the desert that the televicarion helmet had projected into his eyes, the studio seemed strangely cavelike.

"How'd you like it, Bob?" asked one of the two producers of the show.

Robert Bowen nodded briskly and patted the televike helmet. "It was O.K.," he said. "Good show. A little talky at the beginning, and it needs a better fade-out, but the action scenes were fine. The sponsor ought to like it—for a while, at least."

"What do you mean, 'for a while'?"

Robert Bowen sighed. "If this thing goes on the air the way it is, he'll lose sales."

"Why? Commercial not good enough?"

"*Too* good! Man, I've smoked *Old Kings*, and, believe me, the real thing never tasted as good as that cigarette did in the commercial!"

But, I Don't Think

As every thinking man knows, every slave always yearns for the freedom his master denies him...

But, gentlemen," said the Physician, "I really don't think we can consider any religion which has human sacrifice as an integral part as a humane religion."
"At least," added the Painter with a chuckle, "not as far as the victim is concerned."
The Philosopher looked irritated. "Bosh! What if the victim likes it that way?"

—*THE IDLE WORSHIPERS*
by R. Phillip Dachboden

I

The great merchantship *Naipor* settled her tens of thousands of tons of mass into her landing cradle on Viornis as gently as an egg being settled into an egg crate, and almost as silently. Then, as the antigravs were cut off, there was a vast, metallic sighing as the gigantic structure of the cradle itself took over the load of holding the ship in her hydraulic bath.

At that point, the ship was officially groundside, and the *Naipor* was in the hands of the ground officers. Space Captain Humbolt Reed sighed, leaned back in his desk chair, reached out a hand, and casually touched a trio of sensitized spots on the surface of his desk.

"Have High Lieutenant Blyke bring The Guesser to my office immediately," he said, in a voice that was obviously accustomed to giving orders that would be obeyed.

Then he took his fingers off the spots without waiting for an answer.

In another part of the ship, in his quarters near the Fire Control Section, sat the man known as The Guesser. He had a name, of course, a regular name, like everyone else; it was down on the ship's books and in the Main Registry. But he almost never used it; he hardly ever even thought of it. For twenty of his thirty-five years of life, he had been a trained Guesser, and for fifteen of them he'd been The Guesser of *Naipor*.

He was fairly imposing-looking for a Guesser; he had the tall, wide-shouldered build and the blocky face of an Executive, and his father had been worried that he wouldn't show the capabilities of a Guesser, while his mother had secretly hoped that he might actually become an Executive. Fortunately for The Guesser, they had both been wrong.

He was not only a Guesser, but a first-class predictor, and he showed impatience with those of his underlings who failed to use their ability in any particular. At the moment of the ship's landing, he was engaged in verbally burning the ears off Kraybo, the young man who would presumably take over The Guesser's job one day—if he ever learned how to handle it.

"You're either a liar or an idiot," said The Guesser harshly, "and I wish to eternity I knew which!"

Kraybo, standing at attention, merely swallowed and said nothing. He had felt the back of The Guesser's hand too often before to expose himself intentionally to its swing again.

The Guesser narrowed his eyes and tried to see what was going on in Kraybo's mind.

"Look here, Kraybo," he said after a moment, "that one single Misfit ship got close enough to do us some damage. It has endangered the life of the *Naipor* and the lives of her crewmen. You were on the board in that quadrant of the ship, and you let it get in too close. The records show that you mis-aimed one of your blasts. Now, what I want to know is this: were you really guessing or were you following the computer too closely?"

"I was following the computer," said Kraybo, in a slightly wavering voice. "I'm sorry for the error, sir; it won't happen again."

The Guesser's voice almost became a snarl. "It hadn't better! You know that a computer is only to feed you data and estimate probabilities on the courses of attacking ships; you're not supposed to think they can predict!"

"I know, sir; I just—"

"You just near came getting us all killed!" snapped The Guesser. "You claim that you actually guessed where that ship was going to be, but you followed the computer's extrapolation instead?"

"Yes, sir," said the tense-faced Kraybo. "I admit my error, and I'm willing to take my punishment."

The Guesser grinned wolfishly. "Well, isn't that big-hearted of you? I'm very glad you're willing, because I just don't know what I'd do if you refused."

Kraybo's face burned crimson, but he said nothing.

The Guesser's voice was sarcastically soft. "But I guess about the only thing I could do in that case would be to"—The Guesser's voice suddenly became a bellow—"*kick your thick head in*!"

Kraybo's face drained of color suddenly.

The Guesser became suddenly brusque. "Never mind. We'll let it go for now. Report to the Discipline Master in Intensity Five for ten minutes total application time. Dismissed."

Kraybo, whose face had become even whiter, paused for a moment, as though he were going to plead with The Guesser. But he saw the look in his superior's eyes and thought better of it.

"Yes, sir," he said in a weak voice. He saluted and left.

And The Guesser just sat there, waiting for what he knew would come.

It did. High Lieutenant Blyke showed up within two minutes after Kraybo had left. He stood at the door of The Guesser's cubicle, accompanied by a sergeant-at-arms.

"Master Guesser, you will come with us." His manner was bored and somewhat flat.

The Guesser bowed his head as he saluted. "As you command, great sir." And he followed the lieutenant into the corridor, the sergeant tagging along behind.

The Guesser wasn't thinking of his own forthcoming session with the captain; he was thinking of Kraybo.

Kraybo was twenty-one, and had been in training as a Guesser ever since he was old enough to speak and understand. He showed occasional flashes of tremendous ability, but most of the time he seemed—well, *lazy*. And then, there was always the question of his actual ability.

A battle in the weirdly distorted space of ultralight velocities requires more than machines and more than merely ordinary human abilities. No computer, however built, can possibly estimate the flight of a dodging spaceship with a canny human being at the controls. Even the superfast beams from a megadyne force gun require a finite time to reach their target, and it is necessary to fire at the place where the attacking ship will be, not at the position it is occupying at the time of firing. That was a bit of knowledge as old as human warfare: you must lead a moving target.

For a target moving at a constant velocity, or a constant acceleration, or in any other kind of orbit which is mathematically predictable, a computer was not only necessary, but sufficient. In such a case, the accuracy was perfect, the hits one hundred per cent.

But the evasive action taken by a human pilot, aided by a randomity selector, is not logical and therefore cannot be handled by a computer. Like the path of a microscopic particle in Brownian motion, its position can only be predicted statistically; estimating its probable location is the best that can be done. And, in space warfare, probability of that order is simply not good enough.

To compute such an orbit required a special type of human mind, and therefore a special type of human. It required a Guesser.

The way a Guesser's mind operated could only be explained *to* a Guesser *by* another Guesser. But, as far as anyone else was concerned, only the objective results were important. A Guesser could "guess" the route of a moving ship, and that was all anyone cared about. And a Master Guesser prided himself on his ability to guess accurately 99.999% of the time. The ancient sport of baseball was merely a test of muscular co-ordination for a Guesser; as soon as a Guesser child learned to control a bat, his batting average shot up to 1.000 and stayed there until he got too old to swing the bat. A Master Guesser could make the same score blindfolded.

Hitting a ship in space at ultralight velocities was something else again. Young Kraybo could play baseball blindfolded, but he wasn't yet capable of making the master guesses that would protect a merchantship like the *Naipor*.

But what was the matter with him? He had, of course, a fire-control computer to help him swing and aim his guns, but he didn't seem to be able to depend on his guesswork. He had more than once fired at a spot where the computer said the ship would be instead of firing at the spot where it actually arrived a fraction of a second later.

There were only two things that could be troubling him. Either he was doing exactly as he said—ignoring his guesses and following the computer—or else he was inherently incapable of controlling his guesswork and was hoping that the computer would do the work for him.

If the first were true, then Kraybo was a fool; if the second, then he was a liar, and was no more capable of handling the fire control of the *Naipor* than the captain was.

The Guesser hated to have Kraybo punished, really, but that was the only way to make a youngster keep his mind on his business.

After all, thought The Guesser, *that's the way I learned; Kraybo can learn the same way. A little nerve-burning never hurt anyone.*

But that last thought was more to bolster himself than it was to justify his own actions toward Kraybo. The lieutenant was at the door of the captain's office, with The Guesser right behind him.

The door dilated to receive the three—the lieutenant, The Guesser, and the sergeant-at-arms—and they marched across the room to the captain's desk.

The captain didn't even bother to look up until High Lieutenant Blyke saluted and said: "The Guesser, sir."

And the captain gave the lieutenant a quick nod and then looked coldly at The Guesser. "The ship has been badly damaged. Since there are no repair docks here on Viornis, we will have to unload our cargo and then go—*empty*—all the way to D'Graski's Planet for repairs. All during that time, we will be more vulnerable than ever to Misfit raids."

His ice-chill voice stopped, and he simply looked at The Guesser with glacier-blue, unblinking eyes for ten long seconds.

The Guesser said nothing. There was nothing he *could* say. Nothing that would do him any good.

The Guesser disliked Grand Captain Reed—and more, feared him. Reed had been captain of the *Naipor* for only three years, having replaced the old captain on his retirement. He was a strict disciplinarian, and had a tendency to punish heavily for very minor infractions of the rules. Not, of course, that he didn't have every right to do so; he was, after all, the captain.

But the old captain hadn't given The Guesser a nerve-burning in all the years since he had accepted The Guesser as The Guesser. And Captain Reed—

The captain's cold voice interrupted his thoughts.

"Well? What was it? If it was a mechano-electronic misfunction of the computer, say so; we'll speak to the engineer."

The Guesser knew that the captain was giving him what looked like an out—but The Guesser also knew it was a test, a trap.

The Guesser bowed his head very low and saluted. "No, great sir; the fault was mine."

Grand Captain Reed nodded his head in satisfaction. "Very well. Intensity Five, two minutes. Dismissed."

The Guesser bowed his head and saluted, then he turned and walked out the door. The sergeant-at-arms didn't need to follow him; he had been let off very lightly.

He marched off toward the Disciplinary Room with his head at the proper angle—ready to lift it if he met a lesser crewman, ready to lower it if he met an executive officer.

He could already feel the terrible pain of the nerve-burner coursing through his body—a jolt every ten seconds for two minutes, like a whip lashing all over his body at once. His only satisfaction was the knowledge that he had sentenced Kraybo to ten minutes of the same thing.

The Guesser lay on his bed, face down, his grasping fingers clutching spasmodically at the covering as his nerves twitched with remembered pain. Thirteen jolts. Thirteen searing jolts of excruciating torture. It was over now, but his synapses were still crackling with the memories of those burning lashes of energy.

He was thirty-five. He had to keep that in mind. He was thirty-five now, and his nerves should be under better control than they had been at twenty. He wondered if there were tears streaming from his eyes, and then decided it didn't matter. At least he wasn't crying aloud.

Of course, he had screamed in the nerve-burner; he had screamed thirteen times. Any man who didn't scream when those blinding stabs of pain came was either unconscious or dead—it was no disgrace to scream in the burner. But he wasn't screaming now.

He lay there for ten minutes, his jaw clamped, while the twitching subsided and his nervous system regained its usual co-ordination.

The burner did no actual physical damage; it wasn't good economics for an Executive to allow his men to be hurt in any physical manner. It took a very little actual amount of energy applied to the nerve endings to make them undergo the complex electrochemical reaction that made them send those screaming messages to the brain and spine. There was less total damage done to the nerves than a good all-night binge would do to a normal human being. But the effect on the mind was something else again.

It was a very effective method of making a man learn almost any lesson you wanted to teach him.

After a while, The Guesser shuddered once more, took a deep breath, held it for fifteen seconds, and then released it. A little later, he lifted himself up and swung his legs over the edge of his bed. He sat on the edge of the bed for a few minutes, then got up and got dressed in his best uniform.

After all, the captain hadn't said anything about restricting him to the ship, and he had never been to Viornis before. Besides, a couple of drinks might make him feel better.

There were better planets in the galaxy, he decided two hours later. Thousands of them.

For one thing, it was a small, but dense world, with a surface gravity of one point two standard gees—not enough to be disabling, but enough to make a man feel sluggish. For another, its main export was farm products: there were very few large towns on Viornis, and no center of population that could really be called a city. Even here, at the spaceport, the busiest and largest town on the planet, the population was less than a million. It was a "new" world, with a history that didn't stretch back more than two centuries. With the careful population control exercised by the ruling Execs, it would probably remain small and provincial for another half millennium.

The Guesser moseyed down one of the streets of Bellinberg probably named after the first Prime Executive of the planet—looking for a decent place for a spaceman to have a drink. It was evening, and the sinking of the yellow primary below the western horizon had left behind it a clear, star-filled sky that filled the air with a soft, white radiance. The streets of the town itself were well-lit by bright glow-plates imbedded in the walls of the buildings, but above the street level, the buildings themselves loomed darkly. Occasionally, an Exec's aircar would drift rapidly overhead with a soft rush of air, and, in the distance, he could see the shimmering towers of the Executive section rising high above the eight- or ten-storyed buildings that made up the majority of Bellinberg.

The streets were fairly crowded with strollers—most of them Class Four or Five citizens who stepped deferentially aside as soon as they saw his uniform, and kept their eyes averted from him. Now and then, the power car of a Class Three rolled swiftly by, and The Guesser felt a slight twinge of envy. Technically, his own rank was the equivalent of Class Three, but he had never owned a groundcar. What need had a spaceman of a groundcar? Still, it would be nice to drive one just once, he thought; it would be a new experience, certainly.

Right now, though, he was looking for a Class Three bar; just a place to have a small, quiet drink and a bite to eat. He had a perfect right to go into a lower class bar, of course, but he had never felt quite comfortable associating with his inferiors in such a manner, and certainly they would feel nervous in his presence because of the sidearm at his hip.

No one below Class Three was allowed to carry a beamgun, and only Ones and Twos were allowed to wear the screening fields that protected them from the nerve-searing effects of the weapon. And they, being Execs, were in no danger from each other.

Finally, after much walking, he decided that he was in the wrong part of town. There were no Class Three bars anywhere along these streets. Perhaps, he thought, he should have gone to the Spacemen's Club at the spaceport itself. On the other hand, he hadn't particularly wanted to see any of the other minor officers of his own class after the near-fiasco which had damaged the *Naipor*. Being a Guesser set him apart, even from other Threes.

He thought for a moment of asking a policeman, but he dismissed it. Cops, as always, were a breed apart. Besides, they weren't on the streets to give directions, but to preserve order.

At last, he went into a nearby Class Four bar and snapped his fingers for the bartender, ignoring the sudden silence that had followed his entrance.

The barman set down a glass quickly and hurried over, bobbing his head obsequiously. "Yes, sir; yes, sir. What can I do for you, sir? It's an honor to have you here, sir. How may I serve you?"

The man himself was wearing the distinctive clothing of a Five, so his customers outranked him, but the brassard on his arm showed that his master was a Two, which afforded him enough authority to keep reasonable order in the place.

"Where's the nearest Class Three bar?" The Guesser snapped.

The barman looked faintly disappointed, but he didn't lose his obsequiousness. "Oh, that's quite a way from here, sir—about the closest would be Mallard's, over on Fourteenth Street and Upper Drive. A mile, at least."

The Guesser scowled. He was in the wrong section of town, all right.

"But I'd be honored to serve you, sir," the barman hurried on. "Private booth, best of everything, perfect privacy—"

The Guesser shook his head quickly. "No. Just tell me how to get to Mallard's."

The barman looked at him for a moment, rubbing a fingertip across his chin, then he said: "You're not driving, I suppose, sir? No? Well, then, you can either take the tubeway or walk, sir...." He let the sentence hang, waiting for The Guesser's decision.

The Guesser thought rapidly. Tubeways were for Fours and Fives. Threes had groundcars; Ones and Twos had aircars; Sixes and below walked. And spacemen walked.

Trouble is, spacemen aren't used to walking, especially on a planet where they weigh twenty per cent more than they're used to. The Guesser decided he'd take the tubeway; at the Class Three bar, he might be able to talk someone into driving him to the spaceport later.

But five minutes later, he was walking in the direction the bartender had told him to take for finding Mallard's on foot. To get to the tubeway was a four-block walk, and then there would be another long walk after he got off. Hoofing it straight there would be only a matter of five blocks difference, and it would at least spare him the embarrassment of taking the tube.

It was a foolish thing to do, perhaps, but once The Guesser had set his mind on something, it took a lot more than a long walk to dissuade him from his purpose. He saw he was not the only spaceman out on the town; one of the Class Five taverns he passed was filled with boisterous singing, and he could see a crowd of men standing around three crewmen who were leading them in a distinctly off-color ballad. The Guesser smiled a little to himself. Let them have their fun while they were on-planet; their lives weren't exactly bright aboard ship.

Of course, they got as much as was good for them in the way of entertainment, but a little binge gave them something to look forward to, and a good nerve-burning would sober them up fast enough if they made the mistake of coming back drunk.

Nerve-burning didn't really bother a Five much, after all; they were big, tough, work-hardened clods, whose minds and brains simply didn't have the sensitivity to be hurt by that sort of treatment. Oh, they screamed as loud as anyone when they were in the burner, but it really didn't have much effect on them. They were just too thick-skulled to have it make much difference to them one way or the other.

On the other hand, an Exec would probably go all to pieces in a burner. If it didn't kill him outright, he'd at least be sick for days. They were too soft to take even a touch of it. No Class One, so far as The Guesser knew, had ever been subjected to that sort of treatment, and a Two only got it rarely. They just weren't used to it; they wouldn't have the stamina to take it.

His thoughts were interrupted suddenly by the familiar warning that rang in his mind like a bell. He realized suddenly, as he became blazingly aware of his surroundings, that he had somehow wandered into a definitely low-class neighborhood. Around him were the stark, plain housing groups of Class Six families. The streets were more dimly lit, and there was almost no one on the street, since it was after curfew time for Sixes. The nearest pedestrian was a block off and moving away.

All that took him but a fraction of a second to notice, and he knew that it was not his surroundings which had sparked the warning in his mind. There was something behind him—moving.

What had told him? Almost nothing. The merest touch of a foot on the soft pavement—the faintest rustle of clothing—the whisper of something moving through the air.

Almost nothing—but enough. To a man who had played blindfold baseball, it was plenty. He knew that someone not ten paces behind him had thrown something heavy, and he knew its exact trajectory to within a thousandth of a millimeter, and he knew exactly how to move his head to avoid the missile.

He moved it, at the same time jerking his body to one side. It had only been a guess—but what more did a Guesser need?

From the first hint of warning to the beginning of the dodging motion, less than half a second had passed.

He started to spin around as the heavy object went by him, but another warning yelped in his mind. He twisted a little, but it was too late.

Something burned horribly through his body, like a thousand million acid-tipped, white-hot needles jabbing through skin and flesh and sinking into the bone. He couldn't even scream.

He blacked out as if he'd been a computer suddenly deprived of power.

II

Of course, came the thought, *a very good way to put out a fire is to pour cold water on it. That's a very good idea.*

At least, it had put out the fire.

Fire? What fire? The fire in his body, the scalding heat that had been quenched by the cold water.

Slowly, as though it were being turned on through a sluggishly turning rheostat, consciousness came back to The Guesser.

He began to recognize the sensations in his body. There was a general, all-over dull ache, punctuated here and there by sharper aches. There was the dampness and the chill. And there was the queer, gnawing feeling in the pit of his stomach.

At first, he did not think of how he had gotten where he was, nor did he even wonder about his surroundings. There seemed merely to be an absolute urgency to get out of wherever he was and, at the same time, an utter inability to do so. He tried to move, to shift position, but his muscles seemed so terribly tired that flexing them was a high-magnitude effort.

After several tries, he got his arms under his chest, and only then did he realize that he had been lying prone, his right cheek pressed against cold, slimy stone. He lifted himself a little, but the effort was too much, and he collapsed again, his body making a faint splash as he did so.

He lay there for a while, trying to puzzle out his odd and uncomfortable environment. He seemed to be lying on a sloping surface with his head higher than his feet. The lower part of his body was immersed in chill, gently-moving water. And there was something else—

The smell.

It was an incredible stench, an almost overpowering miasma of decay.

He moved his head then, and forced his eyes open. There was a dim, feeble glow from somewhere overhead and to his right, but it was enough to show him a vaulted ceiling a few feet above him. He was lying in some sort of tube which—

And then the sudden realization came.

He was in a sewer.

The shock of it cleared his mind a little, and gave added strength to his muscles. He pushed himself to his hands and knees and began crawling toward the dim light. It wasn't more than eight or ten feet, but it seemed to take an eternity for him to get there. Above him was a grating, partially covered with a soggy-looking sheet of paper. The light evidently came from a glow-plate several yards away.

He lay there, exhausted and aching, trying to force his brain into action, trying to decide what to do next.

He'd have to lift the grating, of course; that much was obvious. And he'd have to stand up to do that. Did he have the strength?

Only one way to find out. Again he pushed himself to his hands and knees, and it seemed easier this time. Then, bracing himself against the curving wall of the sewer, he got to his feet. His knees were weak and wobbly, but they'd hold. They *had* to hold.

The top of the sewer duct was not as far off as it had seemed; he had to stoop to keep from banging his head against the grating. He paused in that position to catch his breath, and then reached up, first with one hand and then with the other, to grasp the grating.

Then, with all the strength he could gather, he pushed upwards. The hinged grate moved upwards and banged loudly on the pavement.

There remained the problem of climbing out of the hole. The Guesser never knew how he solved it. Somehow, he managed to find himself out of the sewer and lying exhausted on the pavement.

He knew that there was some reason why he couldn't just lie there forever, some reason why he had to hide where he couldn't be seen.

It was not until that moment that he realized that he was completely naked. He had been stripped of everything, including the chronometer on his wrist.

With an effort, he heaved himself to his feet again and began running, stumbling drunkenly, yet managing somehow to keep on his feet. He had to find shelter, find help.

Somewhere in there, his mind blanked out again.

He awoke feeling very tired and weak, yet oddly refreshed, as though he had slept for a long time. When his eyes opened, he simply stared at the unfamiliar room for a long time without thinking—without really caring to think. He only knew that he was warm and comfortable and somehow safe, and it was such a pleasant feeling after the nightmare of cold and terror that he only wanted to enjoy it without analyzing it.

But the memory of the nightmare came again, and he couldn't repress it. And he knew it hadn't been a nightmare, but reality.

Full recollection flooded over him.

Someone had shot him with a beamgun, that nasty little handweapon that delivered in one powerful, short jolt the same energy that was doled out in measured doses over a period of minutes in a standard nerve-burner. He remembered jerking aside at the last second, just before the weapon was fired, and it was evidently that which had saved his life. If the beam had hit him in the head or spine, he'd be dead now.

Then what? Guessing about something that had happened in the past was futile, and, anyway, guessing didn't apply to situations like that. But he thought he could pretty well figure out what had happened.

After he'd been shot down, his assailant had probably dragged him off somewhere and stripped him, and then dumped him bodily into the sewer. The criminal had undoubtedly thought that The Guesser was dead; if the body had been found, days or weeks later, it would be unidentifiable, and probably dismissed as simply another unsolved murder. They were rather common in low-class districts such as this.

Which brought him back again to the room.

He sat up in bed and looked around. Class Six Standard Housing. Hard, gray, cast polymer walls—very plain. Ditto floor and ceiling. Single glow-plate overhead. Rough, gray bedclothing.

Someone had found him after that careening flight from the terror of the sewer and had brought him here. Who? *Who?*

The sense of well-being he had felt upon awakening had long since deserted him. What he felt now was a queer mixture of disgust and fear. He had never known a Class Six. Even the lowest crewman on the *Naipor* was a Five.

Uneasily, The Guesser climbed out of the bed. He was wearing a sack-like gray dress that fell almost to his knees, and nothing else. He walked on silent bare feet to the door. He could hear nothing beyond it, so he twisted the handle carefully and eased it open a crack.

And immediately he heard low voices. The first was a man's.

"... Like you pick up dogs, hey." He sounded angry. "He bring trouble on high, that'n. Look, you, at the face he got. He no Sixer, no, nor even Fiver. Exec, that's what. Trouble."

Then a woman's voice. "Exec, he?" A sharp laugh. "Naked, dirty-wet, sick, he fall on my door. Since when Execs ask help from Sixer chippie like I? And since when Execs talk like Sixer when they out of they head? No fancy Exec talk, he, no."

The Guesser didn't understand that. If the woman was talking about him—and she must be—then surely he had not spoken the illiterate patois of the Class Six people when he was delirious.

The woman went on. "No, Lebby; you mind you business; me, I mind mine. Here, you take you this and get some food. Now, go, now. Come back at dark."

The man grumbled something The Guesser didn't understand, but there seemed to be a certain amount of resignation in his voice. Then a door opened and closed, and there was a moment of silence.

Then he heard the woman's footsteps approaching the partially opened door. And her voice said: "You lucky Lebby have he back to you when you open the door. If he even see it move, he know you wake."

The Guesser backed away from the door as she came in.

She was a drab woman, with a colorlessness of face that seemed to match the colorlessness of her clothing. Her hair was cropped short, and she seemed to sag all over, as though her body were trying to conform to the shapelessness of the dress instead of the reverse. When she forced a smile to her face, it didn't seem to fit, as though her mouth were unused to such treatment from the muscles.

"How you feel?" she asked, stopping just inside the room.

"I ... uh—" The Guesser hardly knew what to say. He was in a totally alien environment, a completely unknown situation. "I'm fine," he said at last.

She nodded. "You get plenty sleep, all right. Like dead, except when you talk to yourself."

Then he *had* spoken in delirium. "How ... how long was I out?"

"Three days," she said flatly. "Almost four." She paused. "You ship leave."

"Leave?" The Guesser said blankly. "The *Naipor*? Gone?" It seemed as if the world had dropped away from his feet, leaving him to fall endlessly through nothingness. It was true, of course. It didn't take more than twenty-four hours to unload the ship's holds, and, since there had been no intention of reloading, there was no need to stay. He had long overstayed the scheduled take-off time.

It created a vacuum in his mind, a hole in his very being that could never be filled by anything else. The ship was his whole life—his home, his work, his security.

"How did you know about the ship?" he asked in a dazed voice.

"A notice," she said. She fished around in one of the big pockets of the gray dress and her hand came out with a crumpled sheet of glossy paper. She handed it to him silently. It was a Breach of Contract notice.

WANTED
for
BREACH OF CONTRACT
JAIM JAKOM DIEGO
AGE: 35 HEIGHT: 185 cm WEIGHT: 96 kg HAIR: black EYES: blue COMPLXN: fair

Jaim Jakom Diego, Spacetech 3rd Guesser, broke contract with Interstellar Trade Corporation on 3/37/119 by failing to report for duty aboard home merchantship *Naipor* on that date. All citizens are notified hereby that said Jaim Jakom Diego is unemployable except by the ITC, and that he has no housing, clothing, nor subsistance rights on any planet, nor any right to transportation of any kind.
STANDARD REWARD PLUS BONUS FOR INFORMATION LEADING TO THE ARREST OF THIS MAN

The Guesser looked at the picture that accompanied the notice. It was an old one, taken nearly fifteen years before. It didn't look much like him any more. But that didn't matter; even if he was never caught, he still had no place to go. A runaway had almost no chance of remaining a runaway for long. How would he eat? Where would he live?

He looked up from the sheet, into the woman's face. She looked back with a flat, unwavering gaze. He knew now why she had been addressing him as an equal, even though she knew he was Class Three.

"Why haven't you tried to collect the reward?" he asked. He felt suddenly weak, and sat down again on the edge of the bed.

"Me, I need you." Then her eyes widened a trifle. "Pale you look, you do. I get you something solid inside you. Nothing but soup I get down you so far, all three days. Soup. You sit, I be back."

He nodded. He *was* feeling sickish.

She went into the other room, leaving the door open, and he could hear noises from the small kitchen. The woman began to talk, raising her voice a little so he could hear her.

"You like eggs?" she asked.

"Some kinds," said The Guesser. "But it doesn't matter. I'm hungry." He hadn't realized how hungry he was.

"*Some* kinds?" The woman's voice was puzzled. "They more than one kind of egg?" The kitchen was suddenly silent as she waited intently for the answer.

"Yes," said The Guesser. "On other planets. What kind of eggs are these?"

"Just ... just *eggs*."

"I mean, what kind of animal do they come from?"

"Chicken. What else lay eggs?"

"Other birds." He wished vaguely that he knew more about the fauna of Viornis. Chickens were well-nigh universal; they could live off almost anything. But other fowl fared pretty well, too. He shrugged it off; none of his business; leave that to the ecologists.

"Birds?" the woman asked. It was an unfamiliar word to her.

"Different kinds of chickens," he said tiredly. "Some bigger, some smaller, some different colors." He hoped the answer would satisfy her.

Evidently it did. She said, "Oh," and went on with what she was doing.

The silence, after only a minute or two, became unbearable. The Guesser had wanted to yell at the woman to shut up, to leave him alone and not bother him with her ignorant questions that he could not answer because she was inherently too stupid to understand. He had wondered why he hadn't yelled; surely it was not incumbent on a Three to answer the questions of a Six.

But he *had* answered, and after she stopped talking, he began to know why. He wanted to talk and to be talked to. Anything to fill up the void in his mind; anything to take the place of a world that had suddenly vanished.

What would he be doing now, if this had not happened? Involuntarily, he glanced at his wrist, but the chronometer was gone.

He would have awakened, as always, at precisely 0600 ship time. He would have dressed, and at 0630 he would have been at table, eating his meal in silence with the others of his class. At 0640, the meal would be over, and conversation would be allowed until 0645. Then, the inspection of the fire control system from 0650 until 0750. Then—

He forced his mind away from it, tried not to think of the pleasant, regular orderly routine by which he had lived his life for a quarter of a century and more.

When the woman's voice came again, it was a relief.

"What's a Guesser?"

He told her as best he could, trying to couch his explanation in terms that would be understood by a woman of her limited vocabulary and intelligence. He was not too sure he succeeded, but it was a relief to talk about it. He could almost feel himself dropping into the routine that he used in the orientation courses for young Guessers who had been assigned to him for protection and instruction.

"Accurate predicting of this type is not capable of being taught to all men; unless a man has within him the innate ability to be a Guesser, he is as incapable of learning Guessing as a blind man is incapable of being taught to read." (It occurred to him at that moment to wonder how the Class Six woman had managed to read the Breach of Contract notice. He would have to ask her later.) "On the other hand, just as the mere possession of functioning eyes does not automatically give one the ability to read, neither does the genetic inheritance of Guesser potentialities enable one to make accurate, useful Guesses. To make this potentiality into an ability requires years of hard work and practice.

"You must learn to concentrate, to focus your every attention on the job at hand, to—"

He broke off suddenly. The woman was standing in the doorway, holding a plate and a steaming mug. Her eyes were wide with puzzlement and astonishment. "You mean *me*?"

"No ... no." He shook his head. "I ... was thinking of something else."

She came on in, carrying the food. "You got tears in your eyes. You hurt?"

He wanted to say *yes*. He wanted to tell her how he was hurt and why. But the words wouldn't—or couldn't—come. "No," he said. "My eyes are just a little blurry, that's all. From sleep."

She nodded, accepting his statements. "Here. You eat you this. Put some stuffing in you belly."

He ate, not caring what the food tasted like. He didn't speak, and neither did she, for which he was thankful. Conversation during a meal would have been both meaningless and painful to him.

It was odd to think that, in a way, a Class Six had more freedom than he did. Presumably, she *could* talk, if she wanted, even during a meal.

And he was glad that she had not tried to eat at the same time. To have his food cooked and served by a Six didn't bother him, nor was he bothered by her hovering nearby. But if she had sat down with him to eat—

But she hadn't, so he dropped the thought from his mind.

Afterwards, he felt much better. He actually hadn't realized how hungry he had been.

She took the dishes out and returned almost immediately.

"You thought what you going to do?" she asked.

He shook his head. He hadn't thought. He hadn't even wanted to think. It was as though, somewhere in the back of his mind, something kept whispering that this was all nothing but a very bad dream and that he'd wake up in his cubicle aboard the *Naipor* at any moment. Intellectually, he knew it wasn't true, but his emotional needs, coupled with wishful thinking, had hamstrung his intellect.

However, he knew he couldn't stay here. The thought of living in a Class Six environment all the rest of his life was utterly repellent to him. And there was nowhere else he could go, either. Even though he had not been tried as yet, he had effectively been Declassified.

"I suppose I'll just give myself over to the Corporation," he said. "I'll tell them I was waylaid—maybe they'll believe it."

"Maybe? Just only maybe?"

He shrugged a little. "I don't know. I've never been in trouble like this before. I just don't know."

"What they going to do to you, you give up to them?"

"I don't know that, either."

Her eyes suddenly looked far off. "Me, I got an idea. Maybe get both of us some place."

He looked at her quickly. "What do you mean?"

Her gaze came back from the distance, and her eyes focused squarely on his. "The Misfits," she said in her flat voice. "We could go to the Misfits."

III

The Guesser had been fighting the Misfits for twenty years, and hating them for as long as he could remember. The idea that he could ever become one of them had simply never occurred to him. Even the idea of going to one of the Misfit Worlds was so alien that the very suggestion of it was shocking to his mind.

And yet, the suggestion that the Sixer woman had made did require a little thinking over before he accepted or rejected it.

The Misfits. What did he really know about them, anyway?

They didn't call themselves Misfits, of course; that was a derogatory name used by the Aristarchy. But the Guesser couldn't remember off hand just what they *did* call themselves. Their form of government was a near-anarchic form of ochlocracy, he knew—mob rule of some sort, as might be expected among such people. They were the outgrowth of an ancient policy that had been used centuries ago for populating the planets of the galaxy.

There are some people who simply do not, will not, and can not fit in with any kind of social organization—except the very flimsiest, perhaps. Depending on the society in which they exist and the extent of their own antisocial activities, they have been called, over the centuries, everything from "criminals" to "pioneers." It was a matter of whether they fought the unwelcome control of the society in power or fled from it.

The Guesser's knowledge of history was close to nonexistent, but he had heard that the expansion to the stars from Earth—a planet he had never been within a thousand parsecs of—had been accomplished by the expedient of combining volunteers with condemned criminals and shipping them off to newly-found Earth-type planets. After a generation had passed, others came in—the civilizing types—and settled the planets, making them part of the Aristarchy proper.

(Or was the Aristarchy that old? The Guesser had a feeling that the government at that time had been of a different sort, but he couldn't for the life of him remember what it was. Perhaps it had been the prototype of the Aristarchy, for certainly the present system of society had existed for four or five centuries—perhaps more. The Guesser realized that his knowledge of ancient history was as confused as anyone's; after all, it wasn't his specialty. He remembered that when he was a boy, he'd heard a Teacher Exec talk about the Geological Ages of Earth and the Teacher had said that "cave men were *not* contemporary with the dinosaur." He hadn't known what it meant at the time, since he wasn't supposed to be listening, anyway, to an Exec class, but he had realized that the histories of times past often became mixed up with each other.)

At any rate, the process had gone along smoothly, even as the present process of using Class Sevens and Declassified citizens did. But in the early days there had not been the organization that existed in the present Aristarchy; planets had become lost for generations at a time. (The Guesser vaguely remembered that there had been wars of some kind during that time, and that the wars had contributed to those losses.) Some planets had civilized themselves without the intervention of the Earth government, and, when the Earth government had come along, they had fought integration with everything they could summon to help them.

Most of the recalcitrant planets had eventually been subdued, but there were still many "hidden planets" which were organized as separate governments under a loose confederation. These were the Misfits.

Because of the numerical superiority of the Aristarchy, and because it operated in the open instead of skulking in the darkness of space, the Misfits knew where Aristarchy planets were located, while the Aristarchy was unable to search out every planet in the multimyriads of star systems that formed the galaxy.

Thus the Misfits had become pirates, preying on the merchantships of the Aristarchy. Why? No one knew. (Or, at least, The Guesser corrected himself, *he* didn't know.) Such a non-sane culture would have non-sane reasons.

The Aristarchy occupied nearly all the planets of the galaxy that could be inhabited by Man; that much The Guesser had been told. Just why Earth-type planets should occur only within five thousand light-years of the Galactic Center was a mystery to him, but, then, he was no astrophysicist.

But the Sixer woman said she had heard that the Aristarchy was holding back facts; that there were planets clear out to the Periphery, all occupied by Misfits; that the legendary Earth was one of those planets; that—

A thousand things. All wrong, as The Guesser knew. But she was firmly convinced that if anyone could get to a Misfit planet, they would be welcomed. There were no Classes among the Misfits, she said. (The Guesser dismissed that completely; a Classless society was ridiculous on the face of it.)

The Guesser had asked the woman why—if her statements were true—the Misfits had not conquered the Aristarchy long ago. After all, if they held the galaxy clear out to the Periphery, they had the Aristarchy surrounded, didn't they?

She had had no answer.

And it had only been later that The Guesser realized that *he* had an answer. Indeed, that he himself, was a small, but significant part of that answer.

The Misfits had no Guessers. That was a fact that The Guesser knew from personal experience. He had been in space battles with Misfit fleets, and he had brought the *Naipor* through those battles unscathed while wreaking havoc and destruction among the massed ships of the Misfits. They had no Guessers. (Or no *trained* Guessers, he amended. The potential might be there, but certainly the actuality was not.)

And it occurred to him that the Misfits might have another kind of trained talent. They seemed to be able to search out and find a single Aristarchy ship, while it was impossible to even detect a Misfit fleet until it came within attacking distance. Well, that, again, was not his business.

But none of these considerations were important in the long run; none of them were more than minor. The thing that made up The Guesser's mind, that spurred him into action, was the woman's admission that she had a plan for actually reaching Misfit planets.

It was quite simple, really; they were to be taken prisoners.

"They spaceships got no people inside, see you," she said, just as though she knew what she were talking about. "They just want to catch our ships, not kill 'em. So they send out a bunch of little ships on they own, just to ... uh ... cripple our ships. It don't matter, they little ships get hit, because they no one in them, see you. They trying to get our ships in good shape, and people in them and stuff, that's all."

"Yes, yes," The Guesser had said impatiently, "but what's that to do with us?"

She waved a hand, as though she were a little flustered by his peremptory tone. She wasn't, after all, used to talking with Class Threes as equals, even though she knew that in this case the Three was helpless.

"I *tell* you! I *tell* you!" She paused to reorganize her thoughts. "But I ask you: if we get on a ship, you can keep it from shooting the Misfit ships?"

The Guesser saw what she was driving at. It didn't make much sense yet, but there was a glimmer of something there.

"You mean," he said, "that you want to know whether it would be possible for me to partially disable the fire-control system of a spaceship enough to allow it to be captured by Misfit ships?"

She nodded rapidly. "Yes ... I think, yes. Can you?"

"Ye-e-es," The Guesser said, slowly and cautiously. "I could. But not by just walking in and doing it. I mean, it would be almost impossible to get aboard a ship in the first place, and without an official position I couldn't do anything anyway."

But she didn't look disappointed. Instead, she'd smiled a little. "I get us on the ship," she said. "And you have official position. We do it."

When she had gone on to explain, The Guesser's mind had boggled at her audacity—at first. And then he'd begun to see how it might be possible.

For it was not until then that the woman had given The Guesser information which he hadn't thought to ask about before. The first was her name: Deyla. The second was her job.

She was a cleaning woman in Executive territory.

And, as she outlined her plan for reaching the Misfits, The Guesser began to feel despair slipping from his mind, to be replaced by hope.

The Guesser plodded solemnly along the street toward the tall, glittering building which was near the center of Executive territory, his feet moving carefully, his eyes focused firmly on the soft, textured surface of the pavement. He was clad in the rough gray of a Class Six laborer, and his manner was carefully tailored to match. As he was approached by Fours and Fives, he stepped carefully to one side, keeping his face blank, hiding the anger that seethed just beneath the surface.

Around his arm was a golden brassard indicating that he was contracted to a Class One, and in his pocket was a carefully forged card indicating the same thing. No one noticed him; he was just another Sixer going to his menial job.

The front of the building bore a large glowing plaque which said:

VIORNIS EXPORT CORPORATION

But the front entrance was no place for a Sixer. He went on past it, stepping aside regularly for citizens of higher class than his own assumed Six. He made his way around to the narrow alley that ran past the rear of the building.

There was a Class Five guard armed with a heavy truncheon, standing by the door that led into the workers entrance. The Guesser, as he had been instructed by Deyla, had his card out as he neared the doorway. The guard hardly even glanced at it before wagging a finger indicating that The Guesser was to pass. He didn't bother to speak.

The Guesser was trembling as he walked on in—partly in anger, partly in fear. It seemed ridiculous that one glance had not told the guard that he was not a Class Six. The Guesser was quite certain that he didn't *look* like a Sixer. But then, Fives were not very perceptive people, anyway.

The Guesser went on walking into the complex corridors of the lower part of the building, following directions that had been given him by Deyla. There was no hesitation on his part; his memory for things like that was as near perfect as any record of the past can be. He knew her instructions well enough to have navigated the building in the dark.

Again, The Guesser found himself vaguely perturbed by the relative freedom of Sixers. As long as they got their jobs done there was almost no checking as to how they spent their time. Well, actually, the jobs to which they were suited were rather trivial—some of them were actually "made work." After all, in a well-run society, it was axiomatic that everyone have basic job security; that's what kept everyone happy.

Of course, there were plenty of Sixers working in construction and on farms who were kept on their toes by overseers, but cleaning jobs and such didn't need such supervision. A thing can only be so clean; there's no quota to fill and exceed.

After several minutes of walking and climbing stairs—Sixers did not use lift chutes or drop chutes—he found the room where Deyla had told him to meet her. It was a small storeroom containing cleaning tools and supplies. She was waiting for him.

And, now that the time had actually come for them to act on her plan, fear showed on her face. The Guesser knew then that he had been right in his decision. But he said nothing about that yet.

"Now are you certain about the destination?" he asked before she could speak.

She nodded nervously. "Yes, yes. D'Graski's Planet. That's what he say."

"Good." The Guesser had waited for three weeks for this day, but he had known it would come eventually. D'Graski's Planet was the nearest repair base; sooner or later, another ship had to make that as a port of call from Viornis. He had told Deyla that the route to D'Graski's was the one most likely to be attacked by Misfit ships, that she would have to wait until a ship bound for there landed at the spaceport before the two of them could carry out their plan. And now the ship was here.

"What's the name of the ship?" he asked.

"Th-the *Trobwell*."

"What's the matter with you?" he asked, suddenly and harshly.

She shivered. "Scared. Awful scared."

"I thought so. Have you got the clothing?"

"Y-yes." Then she broke down completely. "You got to help me! You got to show me how to act like Exec lady! Show me how to talk! Otherwise, we both get caught!"

He shook her to quiet her. "Shut up!" When she had quieted, he said: "You are right, of course; we'd both be caught if you were to slip up. But I'm afraid it's too late to teach you now. It's always been too late."

"Wha-what ... what you mean?"

"Never mind. Where's the traveling case?"

She pointed silently towards a shelf, one of many that lined the room.

The Guesser went over and pulled out a box of cleaning dust-filters. Behind it was a gold-and-blue traveling case. The girl had spent months stealing the little things inside it, bit by bit, long before The Guesser had come into her life, dreaming of the day when she would become an Exec lady. Not until he had come had she tried to project that dream into reality.

The Guesser thumbed the opener, and the traveling case split into halves. The sight of the golden uniform of a Class One Executive gleamed among the women's clothing. And she had forgotten no detail; the expensive beamgun and holster lay beneath the uniform.

He picked it up carefully, almost reverently. It was the first time he'd held one since he'd been beamed down himself, so long ago. He turned the intensity knob down to the "stun" position.

"We going to put them on *here*?" she asked in a hushed voice. "Just walk out? Me, I scared!"

He stood up, the stun gun in his hand, its muzzle pointed toward the floor. "Let me tell you something," he said, keeping his voice as kindly as he could. "Maybe it will keep you out of further trouble. You could never pass as an Exec. Never. It wouldn't matter how long you tried to practice, you simply couldn't do it. Your mind is incapable of it. Your every word, your every mannerism, would be a dead giveaway."

There was shock slowly coming over her face. "You not going to take me," she said, in her soft, flat voice.

"No."

"How I ever going to get to Misfits? How?" There were tears in her eyes, just beginning to fill the lower lids.

"I'm sorry," he said, "but I'm afraid your idealized Misfits just don't exist. The whole idea is ridiculous. Their insane attacks on us show that they have unstable, warped minds—and don't tell me about machine-operated or robot-controlled ships. You don't build a machine to do a job when a human being is cheaper. Your fanciful Misfit nation would have dissolved long ago if it had tried to operate on the principle that a lower-class human is worth more than a machine.

"You'll be better off here, doing your job; there are no such havens as Classless Misfit societies."

She was shaking her head as he spoke, trying to fight away the words that were shattering her cherished dream. And the words were having their effect because she believed him, because he believed himself.

"No," she was saying softly. "No, no, no."

The Guesser brought up the gun muzzle and shot her where she stood.

Half an hour later, The Guesser was fighting down his own fear. He was hard put to do it, but he managed to stride purposefully across the great spacefield toward the towering bulk of the *Trobwell* without betraying that fear.

If they caught him now—

He closed his mind against the thought and kept on walking.

At the base of the landing cradle, a Class Four guard was standing stolidly. He bowed his head and saluted as The Guesser walked by.

It's so easy! The Guesser thought. *So incredibly easy!*

Even the captain of the ship would only be a Class Two Exec. No one would question him—no one would *dare* to.

A lieutenant looked up, startled as he entered the ship itself, and saluted hurriedly.

"It's an honor to have you aboard, great sir," he said apologetically, "but you realize, of course, that we are taking off in a very few minutes."

Words choked suddenly in the Guesser's throat, and he had to swallow hard before he could speak. "I know that. I'm ... I'm going with you."

The lieutenant's eyes widened a trifle. "No orders have been taped to that effect, great sir."

This is it! thought The Guesser. He would either put it over now or he'd be lost—completely.

He scowled. "Then tape them! I will apologize to the captain about this last-minute change, but I want no delay in take-off. It is absolutely vital that I reach D'Graski's Planet quickly!"

The lieutenant blanched a little. "Sorry, great sir! I'll see that the orders are taped. You wish a cabin?"

"Certainly. I presume you have an adequate one?"

"I'm sure we do, great sir; I'll have the Quarters Officer set one up for you immediately."

"Excellent," said The Guesser. "Excellent."

Fifteen minutes later, the *Trobwell* lifted from the planet exactly on schedule. The Guesser, in his assigned room, breathed a deep sigh of relief. He was on his way to D'Graski's Planet at last!

"Tell me, great sir," said the captain, "what do you think the final decision on this case should be?" He shoved the sheaf of papers across the desk to The Guesser.

The Guesser looked at them unseeingly, his mind in a whirl. For five days now, the captain of the *Trobwell* had been handing him papers and asking him questions of that sort. And, since he was the ranking Exec, he was expected to give some sort of answer.

This one seemed even more complex than the others, and none of them had been simple. He forced his eyes to read the print, forced his mind to absorb the facts.

These were not clear-cut problems of the kind he had been dealing with all his life. Computing an orbit mentally was utterly simple compared with these fantastic problems.

It was a question of a choice of three different types of cargoes, to be carried to three different destinations. Which would be the best choice? The most profitable from an energy standpoint, as far as the ship was concerned, considering the relative values of the cargoes? What about relative spoilage rates as compared with fluctuating markets?

The figures were all there, right before him in plain type. But they meant nothing. Often, he had been unable to see how there was any difference between one alternative and another.

Once, he had been handed the transcripts of a trial on ship, during which two conflicting stories of an incident had been told by witnesses, and a third by the defendant. How could one judge on something like that? And yet he had been asked to.

He bit his lower lip in nervousness, and then stopped immediately as he realized that this was no time to display nerves.

"I should say that Plan B was the best choice," he said at last. It was a wild stab at nothing, he realized, and yet he could do no better. Had he made a mistake?

The captain nodded gravely. "Thank you, great sir. You've been most helpful. The making of decisions is too important to permit of its being considered lightly."

The Guesser could take it no longer. "It was a pleasure to be of assistance," he said as he stood up, "but there are certain of my own papers to be gone over before we reach D'Graski's Planet. I trust I shall be able to finish them."

The captain stood up quickly. "Oh, certainly, great sir. I hope I haven't troubled you with my rather minor problems. I shan't disturb you again during the remainder of the trip."

The Guesser thanked him and headed for his cabin. He lay on his bed for hours with a splitting headache. If it weren't for the fact that he had been forced to go about it this way, he would never have tried to impersonate an Executive. Never!

He wasn't even sure he could carry it off for the rest of the trip.

Somehow, he managed to do it. He kept to himself and pretended that the blue traveling bag held important papers for him to work on, but he dreaded mealtimes, when he was forced to sit with the captain and two lieutenants, chattering like monkeys as they ate. And he'd had to talk, too; being silent might ruin the impression he had made.

He hated it. A mouth was built for talking and eating, granted—but not at the same time. Of course, the Execs had it down to a fine art; they had a great deal more time for their meals than a Class Three, and they managed to eat a few bites while someone else was talking, then talk while the other ate. It was disconcerting and The Guesser never completely got the hang of co-ordinating the two.

Evidently, however, none of the three officers noticed it.

By the time the *Trobwell* reached D'Graski's Planet, he was actually physically ill from the strain. One of the worst times had come during an attack by Misfit ships. He had remained prone on his bed, his mind tensing at each change of acceleration in the ship. Without the screens and computer to give him data, he couldn't Guess, and yet he kept trying; he couldn't stop himself. What made it worse was the knowledge that his Guesses were coming out wrong almost every time.

When the ship finally settled into the repair cradle, The Guesser could hardly keep his hands from shaking. He left the ship feeling broken and old. But as his feet touched the ground, he thought to himself: *I made it! In spite of everything, I made it!*

And then two men walked toward him—two men wearing blue uniforms of a ship's Disciplinary Corps. He not only recognized their faces, but he saw the neat embroidery on the lapels.

It said: *Naipor*.

IV

Space Captain Humbolt Reed, commander of the *Naipor*, looked at his Master Guesser and shook his head. "I ought to have you shot. Declassification is too good for you by far. Impersonating an Executive! How did you ever think you'd get away with it?" He paused, then barked: "Come on! Explain!"

"It was the only way I could think of to get back to the *Naipor*, great sir," said The Guesser weakly.

The captain leaned back slowly in his seat. "Well, there's one extenuating circumstance. The officers of the *Trobwell* reported that you were a fine source of amusement during the trip. They enjoyed your clownish performance very much.

"Now, tell me exactly why you didn't show up for take-off on Viornis."

The Guesser explained what had happened, his voice low. He told about having something thrown at him, about the beamgun being fired at him. He told about the girl, Deyla. He told everything in a monotonous undertone.

The captain nodded when he was through. "That tallies. It fits with the confession we got."

"Confession, sir?" The Guesser looked blank.

Captain Reed sighed. "You're supposed to be a Guesser. Tell me, do you think I personally, could beam you from behind?"

"You're the captain, sir."

"I don't mean for disciplinary purposes," the captain growled. "I mean from ambush."

"Well ... no, sir. As soon as I knew you were there, I'd be able to Guess where you'd fire. And I wouldn't be there."

"Then what kind of person would be able to throw something at you so that you'd Guess, so that you'd dodge, and be so preoccupied with that first dodging that you'd miss the Guess on the aiming of the beamgun because of sheer physical inertia? What kind of person would know exactly where you'd be when you dodged? What kind of person would know exactly where to aim that beamgun?"

The Guesser had seen what was coming long before the captain finished his wordy interrogation.

"Another Guesser, sir," he said. His eyes narrowed.

"Exactly," said Captain Reed. "Your apprentice, Kraybo. He broke down during a Misfit attack on the way here; he was never cut out to be a Master Guesser, and even though he tried to kill you to get the job, he couldn't handle it. He cracked completely as soon as he tried to co-ordinate alone. We've actually missed you, Master Guesser."

"May I see to the disciplining of Kraybo, sir?" The Guesser asked coldly.

"You're too late. He's been declassified." The captain looked down at the papers on his desk. "You may consider yourself reinstated, Master Guesser, since the fault was not yours.

"However, masquerading as an Exec, no matter how worthy your motives, cannot be allowed to go unpunished. You will report to the Discipline Master for a three-and-three every day for the next five days. And you will not be allowed to leave the ship during the time we remain in repair dock. Dismissed."

"Thank you, great sir." The Guesser turned on his heel and marched out, heading for the Discipline Master.

It was good to be home again.

The Bramble Bush

**Usually, if a man's gotten into bad trouble
by getting into something,
he's a fool to go back. But there are times ...**

There was a man in our town, And he was wond'rous wise; He jumped into a bramble bush, And scratch'd out both his eyes!

—Old Nursery Rhyme

Peter de Hooch was dreaming that the moon had blown up when he awakened. The room was dark except for the glowing night-light near the door, and he sat up trying to separate the dream from reality. He focused his eyes on the glow-plate. What had wakened him? Something had, he was sure, but there didn't seem to be anything out of the ordinary now.

The explosion in his dream had seemed extraordinarily realistic. He could still remember vividly the vibration and the *cr-r-r-ump!* of the noise. But there was no sign of what might have caused the dream sequence.

Maybe something fell, he thought. He swung his legs off his bed and padded barefoot over to the light switch. He was so used to walking under the light lunar gravity that he was no longer conscious of it. He pressed the switch, and the room was suddenly flooded with light. He looked around.

Everything was in place, apparently. There was nothing on the floor that shouldn't be there. The books were all in their places in the bookshelf. The stuff on his desk seemed undisturbed.

The only thing that wasn't as it should be was the picture on the wall. It was a reproduction of a painting by Pieter de Hooch, which he had always liked, aside from the fact that he had been named after the seventeenth-century Dutch artist. The picture was slightly askew on the wall.

He was sleepily trying to figure out the significance of that when the phone sounded. He walked over and picked it up. "Yeah?"

"Guz? Guz? Get over here quick!" Sam Willows' voice came excitedly from the instrument.

"Whatsamatter, Puss?" he asked blearily.

"Number Two just blew! We need help, Guz! Fast!"

"I'm on my way!" de Hooch said.

"Take C corridor," Willows warned. "A and B caved in, and the bulkheads have dropped. Make it snappy!"

"I'm gone already," de Hooch said, dropping the phone back into place.

He grabbed his vacuum suit from its hanger and got into it as though his own room had already sprung an air leak.

Number Two has blown! he thought. That would be the one that Ferguson and Metty were working on. What had they been cooking? He couldn't remember right off the bat. Something touchy, he thought; something pretty hot.

But that wouldn't cause an atomic reactor to blow. It obviously hadn't been a nuclear blow-up of any proportions, or he wouldn't be here now, zipping up the front of his vac suit. Still, it had been powerful enough to shake the lunar crust a little or he wouldn't have been wakened by the blast.

These new reactors could get out a lot more power, and they could do a lot more than the old ones could, but they weren't as safe as the old heavy-metal reactors, by a long shot. None had blown up yet—quite—but there was still the chance. That's why they were built on Luna instead of on Earth. Considering what they could do, de Hooch often felt that it would be safer if they were built out on some nice, safe asteroid—preferably one in the Jovian Trojan sector.

He clamped his fishbowl on tight, opened the door, and sprinted toward Corridor C.

The trouble with the Ditmars-Horst reactor was that it lacked any automatic negative-feedback system. If a D-H decided to go wild, it went wild. Fortunately, that rarely happened. The safe limits for reactions were quite wide—wider, usually, than the reaction limits themselves, so that there was always a margin of safety. And within the limits, a nicety of control existed that made nucleonics almost an esoteric branch of chemistry. Cookbook chemistry, practically.

Want deuterium? Recipe: To 1.00813 gms. purest Hydrogen-1 add, slowly and with care, 1.00896 gms. fine-grade neutrons. Cook until well done in a Ditmars-Horst reactor. Yield: 2.01471 gms. rare old deuterium plus some two million million million ergs of raw energy. Now you are cooking with gas!

All you had to do was keep the reaction going at a slow enough rate so that the energy could be bled off, and there was nothing to worry about. Usually. But control of the feebleizer fields still wasn't perfect, because the fields that enfeebled the reactions and made them easy to control weren't yet too well understood.

Peter de Hooch turned into Corridor C and kept on running. There was plenty of air still in this corridor, and there was apparently little likelihood of his needing his vac suit. But on the moon nobody responds to an emergency call without a vac suit.

He was troubled about Corridors A and B. The explosion must have been pretty violent to have sealed off two of the four corridors leading from the living quarters to the reaction labs. Two corridors went directly to one of the reactors, two went directly to the second. Two more connected the reactor labs themselves, putting the labs and the living quarters at the corners of an equilateral triangle. (Peter had never been able to figure out why A and B corridors led to Reactor Two, while C and D led to Reactor One. Logically, he thought, it should have been the other way around. Oh, well.)

Going down C meant that he'd have to get to Reactor Two the long way around.

What had the damage been? he asked himself. Had anyone been hurt? Or killed? He pushed the questions out of his mind. There was no point in speculating. He'd have the information soon enough.

He took the cutoff to the left, at a sixty-degree angle to Corridor C, which led him directly to Corridor E, by-passing Reactor One. He noticed as he went by that the operations lamp was out. Nobody was working with Reactor One.

As he pounded on down the empty corridor, he suddenly realized that he hadn't seen anyone else running with him. There were five other men in the reactor station, and—so far—he had seen no one. He knew where Willows was, but where were Ferguson, Metty, Laynard, and Quillan? He pushed those questions out of his mind, too, for the time being.

A head popped out of the door at the far end of the corridor.

"Guz! *Hurry*, Guz!"

De Hooch didn't bother to answer Willows. He was short of breath as it was. He knew, besides, that no answer was expected. He had known Willows for years, and knew how he thought. It was Willows who had first tagged de Hooch with that silly nickname, "Guzzle". Not because Peter was such a heavy drinker—although he could hold it like a gentleman—but because he had thought "Guzzle" de Hooch was so uproariously funny. "Nobody likes a guzzle as well as de Hooch," he'd say, with an idiot grin. As a result, everybody called Peter "Guz" now.

The head had vanished back into the control room of Reactor Two. De Hooch kept on running, his breath rasping loudly in the confines of the fishbowl helmet. Running four hundred yards isn't the easiest thing in the world, even if a man is in good physical condition. There was less weight to contend with, but the mass that had to be pushed along remained the same. The notion that running on Luna was an effortless breeze was one that only Earthhuggers clung to.

He ran into the control room and stopped, panting heavily. "What ... happened?"

Sam Willows' normally handsome face looked drawn. "Something went wrong. I don't know what. I was finishing up with Reactor One when I heard the explosion. They are both"—he gestured toward the reactor—"both in there."

"Still alive?"

"I think so. One of 'em, anyway. Take a look."

De Hooch went over to the periscope and put his eyes to the binoculars. He could see two figures in heavy, dull-gray radiation-proof suits. They were lying flat on the floor, and neither was moving. De Hooch said as much.

"The one on the left was moving his arm—just a little," Willows said. "I'll swear he was."

Something in the man's voice made de Hooch turn his head away from the periscope's eyepieces. Willows' face was gray, and a thin film of greasy perspiration reflected the light from the overhead plates. The man was on the verge of panic.

"Calm down, Puss," de Hooch said gently. "Where's Quillan and Laynard?"

"They're in their rooms," Willows said in a tight voice. "Trapped. The bulkheads have closed 'em off in A. No air in the corridor. We'll have to dig 'em out. I called 'em both on the phone. They're all right, but they're trapped."

"Did you call Base?"

"Yes. They haven't got a ship. They sent three moon-cats, though. They ought to be here by morning."

De Hooch looked up at the chronometer on the wall. Oh one twelve, Greenwich time. "Morning" meant any time between eight and noon; the position of the sun up on the surface had nothing to do with Lunar time. As a matter of fact, there was a full Earth shining at the moment, which meant that it wouldn't be dawn on the surface for a week yet.

"If the cats from Base get here by noon, we'll be O.K., won't we?" de Hooch asked.

"Look at the instruments," Willows said.

De Hooch ran a practiced eye over the console and swallowed. "What were they running?"

"Mercury 203," Willows said. "Half-life forty-six point five days. Beta and gamma emitter. Converts to Thallium 203, stable."

"What did they want with a kilogram of the stuff?"

"Special order. Shipment to Earth for some reason."

"Have you checked the end-point? She's building up fast."

"No. No. I haven't." He wet his lips with the tip of his tongue.

"Check it," said de Hooch. "Do any of the controls work?"

"I don't know. I didn't want to fiddle with them."

"You start giving them a rundown. I'm going to get into a suit and go pull those two out of there—if they're still alive." He opened the locker and took his radiation-proof suit out. He checked it over carefully and began shucking his vac suit.

A few minutes delay in getting to the men in the reactor's anteroom didn't matter much. If they hadn't been killed outright, and were still alive, they would probably live a good deal longer. The shells of the radiation suits didn't look damaged, and the instruments indicated very little radiation in the room. Whatever it was that had exploded had done most of its damage at the other end of the reactor. Evidently, a fissure had been opened to the surface, forty feet above—a fissure big enough to let all the air out of A and B corridors, and activate the automatic bulkheads to seal off the airless section.

What troubled him was Willows. If he hadn't known the man so well, de Hooch would have verbally blasted him where he stood.

His reaction to trouble had been typical. De Hooch had already seen Willows in trouble three times, and each time, the reaction had been the same: near panic. Every time, his first thought had been to scream for help rather than to do anything himself. Almost anyone else would have made one call and then climbed into a radiation suit to get Ferguson and Metty out of the anteroom. There was certainly no apparent immediate danger. But all that Willows had done was yell for someone to come and do his thinking and acting for him. He had called Base; he had called de Hooch; he had called Quillan and Laynard. But he hadn't done anything else.

Now he had to be handled with kid gloves. If de Hooch didn't act calm, if he didn't go about things just right, Willows might very likely go over the line into total panic. As long as he had someone to depend on, he'd be all right, and de Hooch didn't want to lose the only help he had right now.

"Fermium 256," said Willows in a tight, flat voice.

"What?" de Hooch asked calmly.

"Fermium 256," Willows repeated. "That's what the stuff is going to start building towards. Spontaneous fission. Half-life of three hours." He took a deep breath. "The reactor won't be able to contain it. We haven't got that kind of bleed-off control."

"No," de Hooch agreed. "I suggest we stop it."

"The freezer control isn't functioning," Willows said. "I guess that's what they went in there to correct."

"I doubt it," de Hooch said carefully. "They wouldn't have needed suits for that. They must have had something else bothering them. I'd be willing to bet they went in to pull a sample and something went wrong."

"Why? What makes you think so?"

"If there'd been trouble, they'd have called for someone to stay here at the console. Both of them wouldn't have gone in if there was any trouble."

"Yeah. Yeah, I guess you're right." He looked visibly relieved. "What do you suppose went wrong?"

"Look at your meters. Four of 'em aren't registering."

Willows looked. "I hadn't noticed. I thought they were just registering low. You're right, though. Yeah. You're right. The surface bleed-off. Hydrogen loss. Blew a valve, is all. Yeah." He grinned a little. "Must've been quite a volcano for a second or two."

De Hooch grinned back at him. "Yeah. Must've. Give me a hand with these clamps."

Willows began fastening the clamps on the heavy suit. "D'you think Ferguson and Metty are O.K., Guz?" he asked.

De Hooch noticed it was the first time he had used the names of the two men. Now that there was a chance that they were alive, at least in his own mind, he was willing to admit that they were men he knew. Willows didn't want to think that anyone he knew had done such a terrible thing as die. It hit too close to home.

The man wasn't thinking. He was willing to grasp at anything that offered him a chance—dream straws. The idea was to keep him busy, keep his mind on trivia, keep him from thinking about what was going on inside that reactor.

He should have known automatically that it was building toward Fermium 256. It was the most logical, easiest, and simplest way for a D-H reactor to go off the deep end.

A Ditmars-Horst reactor took advantage of the fact that any number can be expressed as the sum of powers of two—and the number of nucleons in an atomic nucleus was no exception to that mathematical rule.

Building atoms by adding nucleons wasn't as simple as putting marbles in a bag because of the energy differential, but the energy derived from the fusion of the elements lighter than Iron 56 could be compensated for by using it to pack the nuclei heavier than that. The trick was to find a chain of reactions that gave the least necessary energy transfer. The method by which the reactions were carried out might have driven a mid-Twentieth Century physicist a trifle ga-ga, but most of the reactions themselves would have been recognizable.

There were several possible reactions which Ferguson and Metty could have used to produce Hg-203, but de Hooch was fairly sure he knew which one it was. The five-branch, double-alpha-addition scheme was the one that was easiest to use—and it was the only one that started the damnable doubling chain reaction, where the nuclear weights went up exponentially under the influence of the peculiar conditions within the reactor. 2-4-8-16-32-64-128-256 ... Hydrogen 2 and Helium 4 were stable. So were Oxygen 16 and Sulfur 32. The reaction encountered a sticky spot at Beryllium 8, which is highly unstable, with a half life of ten to the minus sixteenth seconds, spontaneously fissioning back into two Helium 4 nuclei. Past Sulfur 32, there was a lot of positron emission as the nuclei fought to increase the number of neutrons to maintain a stable balance. Germanium 64 is not at all stable, and neither is Neodymium 128, but the instability can be corrected by positive beta emission. When two nuclei of the resulting Xenon 128 are forced together, the positron emission begins long before the coalescence is complete, resulting in Fermium 256.

But not even a Ditmars-Horst reactor can stand the next step, because matter itself won't stand it—not even in a D-H reactor. The trouble is that a D-H reactor *tries*. Mathematically, it was assumed that the resulting nucleus did exist—for an infinitesimal instant of time. Literally, mathematically, infinitesimal—so close to zero that it would be utterly impossible to measure it. Someone had dubbed the hypothetical stuff Instantanium 512.

Whether Instantanium 512 had any real existence is an argument for philosophers only. The results, in any case, were catastrophic. The whole conglomeration came apart in a grand splatter of neutrons, protons, negatrons, positrons, electrons, neutrinos—a whole slew of Greek-lettered mesons of various charges and masses, and a fine collection of strange and ultrastrange particles. Energy? Just oodles and gobs.

Peter de Hooch had heard about the results. He had no desire to experience them first hand. Fortunately, the reaction that led up to them took time. It could be stopped at any time up to the Fm-256 stage. According to the instruments, that wouldn't be for another six hours yet, so there was nothing at all to worry about. Even after that it could be stopped, provided one had a way to get rid of the violently fissioning fermium.

"Connections O.K.?" Willows asked. His voice came over the earphones inside the ponderous helmet of the radiation suit.

"Fine," said de Hooch. He adjusted the double periscope so that his vision was clear. "Perfect."

He tested the controls, moving his arms and legs to see if the suit responded. The suit was so heavy that, without powered joints, controlled by servomechanisms, he would have been unable to move, even under Lunar gravity. With the power on, though, it was no harder than walking underwater in a diving suit. "All's well, Puss," he said.

"I'll keep an eye on you," said Willows.

"Fine. Well, here goes Colossus de Hooch." He began walking toward the door that led into the corridor which connected the reactor anteroom to the control room.

It took time to drag the two inert figures out of the anteroom. All de Hooch could do was grab them under the armpits, apply power, and drag them out. He went out the same way he had come in, traversing the separate chambers in reverse order. First came the decontamination chamber, where the radioactive dust that might have settled on the suits was sluiced off by the detergent sprays. When the radiation detectors registered low enough, de Hooch dragged Ferguson into the outer chamber, then went back and got Metty and put him through the same process. Then he dragged them on into the control room so that Willows could get them out of the heavy suits.

"Can you help me, Guz?" Willows asked. It was obvious that he didn't want to open the suits. He didn't want to see what might be inside. De Hooch helped him.

They were both alive, but unconscious. Bones had been broken, and Metty appeared to be suffering from concussion. They were badly damaged, but they'd live.

De Hooch and Willows made two trips down E and C corridors, carrying the men on a stretcher, to get them in bed. De Hooch splinted the broken bones as best he could and gave each of them a shot of narcodyne. He had to do the medical work because Quillan, the medic, was trapped in Corridor A. He called Quillan on the phone to tell him what had happened. He described the signs and symptoms of the victims as best he could, and then did what Quillan told him to do.

"They ought to be all right," Quillan said. "With that dope in them, they'll be out cold for the next twelve hours, and by that time, the boys from Base will be here. Just leave 'em alone and don't move 'em any more."

"Right. I'll call you back later. Right now, Puss and I are going to see what's wrong with the control linkages on Number Two."

"Right. By-o."

De Hooch and Willows walked back to the control room of Number Two Reactor in silence.

Once inside the control room, de Hooch said: "How are those control circuits?" Willows was supposed to have been checking them while he had been dragging Ferguson and Metty out of the antechamber.

"Well, I ... I'm not sure. I'll show you what I've found so far, Guz. You ought to take a look at them. I ... I'd like you to take a look-see. I think"—he gestured toward the console—"I think they're all right except for the freezer vernier and the pressure release control."

He doesn't trust his own work, de Hooch thought. *Well, that's all right. Neither do I.*

Painstakingly, the two of them went over the checking circuits. Willows was right. The freezer and pressure controls were inoperable.

"Damn," said de Hooch. "Double damn."

"They're probably both stuck at the firewall," Willows said.

"Sure. Where else? I'll have to go in there and unstick 'em. Help me get back into that two-legged tank again." He wished he knew more about what Ferguson and Metty had been doing. He wished he knew why the two men had gone into the anteroom in the first place. He wished a lot of things, but wishing was a useless pastime at this stage of the game.

If only one of the two men had been in a condition to talk!

He got back into his radiation-proof suit again, took one last look at the instruments on the console, and headed for the reactor.

Through the first radiation trap—left turn, right turn, right turn, left turn—through the "cold" room, through the second radiation trap, through the decontamination chamber, and through the third radiation trap into the anteroom. Now that Ferguson and Metty were safely out of the way, he could give his attention to the damage that had been done.

Had Ferguson and Metty actually come in to tap off a sample, as he had suggested to Willows? He looked around at the wreckage in the antechamber. Quite obviously, the heavy door of the sample chamber was wide open, and it certainly appeared that the wreckage was scattered from that point. Cautiously, he went over to look at the open sample chamber. It looked all right, except that the bottom was covered with a bright, metallic dust. He rubbed his finger over it and looked at the fingertip. A very fine dust. And yet it hadn't been scattered very much by the explosion. Heavy. Very likely osmium. Osmium 187 was stable, but it wasn't a normally used step toward Mercury 203. Four successive alpha captures would give Polonium 203, not mercury. Ditto for an oxygen fusion. It could be iridium or platinum, of course. Whatever it was, the instruments in his helmet told him it wasn't hot.

He had a hunch that Ferguson and Metty had been building Mercury 203 from Hafnium 179 by the process of successive fusions with Hydrogen 3 and that something had gone wrong with the H-3 production. It appeared that the explosion had been a simple chemical blast caused by the air oxidation of H-2. But the bleeder vent at the other end of the reactor had apparently kicked at the same time. An enormous amount of unused energy had been released, blowing the entire emergency bleeder system out.

Something didn't seem right. Something stuck in his craw, and he couldn't figure out what it was.

He opened up the conduit boxes that led through the antechamber from the control console to the reactor beyond the firewall. Everything looked fine. That meant that whatever it was that had fouled up the controls was on the other side of the firewall.

"How does it look?" Willows' voice came worriedly over the earphones.

"Have I already said 'damn'?" de Hooch asked.

"You have," Willows said with forced lightness. "You even said 'double damn'."

"*Factorial* damn, then!" said de Hooch.

"What's the matter?"

"Apparently the foul-up is on the *other* side of the firewall."

"Are you going in?"

"I'll have to."

"All right. Watch yourself."

"I will." He went over to the periscope that surveyed the part of the reactor beyond the firewall. Everything looked normal enough. He carefully checked the pressure gauge. Normal.

"Check the spectro for me, will you?" he asked. "Make sure that's just the normal helium atmosphere in there."

"Sure." A pause. "Nothing but helium, Guz. What were you expecting?"

"I don't think I'd care to walk into a hydrogen atmosphere at three hundred Centigrade."

"Neither would I, but how could there be hydrogen in there?"

"There shouldn't be. But there's something screwy going on here, and I can't put my finger on it."

"Well, whatever it is, it isn't hydrogen in the reactor room."

"O.K. Stand by. I'm going in."

He walked over to the firewall door. On the other side of it was a small chamber where the oxygen and nitrogen of normal air would be swept out before he opened the inner door to go into the inner chamber itself. There was no need for an air lock, since small amounts of impurities in the He-4 didn't bother anything.

It was just as he turned the lever that undogged the firewall door that he realized his mistake.

But it was too late.

The door jerked outward, and a hot wind picked him up and slammed him against the far wall.

There was a moment of pain.

Then—nothing.

There was something familiar about the man who was turning the wheel, but de Hooch couldn't place it. The man was wearing a black hood, as befitted a torturer and executioner.

"Idiot," said the hooded man, giving the wheel of the rack a little more pressure, "explain the following: If a half plus a half is equal to a whole, why is halfnium plus halfnium not equal to wholmium?"

Stretched as he was on the rack, de Hooch could not think straight because of the excruciating pain.

"Because a half is eight point two eight per cent heavier than a hole," said de Hooch.

"You are an idiot, none the less," said the torturer. He gave the wheel another twist. De Hooch wanted to scream, but he couldn't.

"Try again," said the torturer. "What is a half plus four plus four plus four plus four plus—"

"Stop!" screamed de Hooch. "Stop! Stop at the osmium!"

"Ah! But it didn't *stop at the osmium," said the hooded man. "It went on and on and on. Plus four plus four plus four plus four plus four—until there were so many plus fours in there that the place looked like an old-fashioned golf course."*

"My legs hurt," said de Hooch. The man was no longer wearing a hood, but de Hooch couldn't tell if it was Willows or himself.

"We will all go together when we go," said the man.

De Hooch turned his head away and looked at the ceiling.

And he realized that it was the ceiling of the antechamber.

"My legs hurt," he repeated. And he could hear the hoarse whisper inside the helmet. He realized that he was lying flat on his back. He had been jarred around quite a bit in the suit.

He wondered if he could sit up. He managed to get both arms behind him and push himself into a sitting position. He wiggled his feet. The servos responded. He hurt all over, but a little experiment told him that he was only bruised. Nothing was broken. He hadn't been hit as hard as Ferguson and Metty had been.

"Willows?" he said. "Willows?"

There was no answer from the earphones.

He looked at the chronometer dial inside his helmet. Oh two forty-nine. He had been unconscious less than ten minutes.

The same glance brought his eyes to two other dials. The internal radiation of the suit was a little high, but nothing to worry about. But the dial registering the external radiation was plenty high. Without the protection of the suit, he wouldn't have lived through those ten minutes.

Where was Willows?

And then he knew, and he pushed any thought of further help from that quarter out of his mind. What had to be done would have to be done by Peter de Hooch alone. He climbed to his feet.

His head hurt, and he swayed with nausea and pain. Only the massive weight of the suit's shoes kept him upright. Then it passed, and he blinked his eyes and shook his head to clear it. He found he was holding his breath, and he let it out.

The trouble had been so simple, and yet he hadn't seen it. Oh, yes, he had! He *must* have, subconsciously. Otherwise, how would he have guessed that the stuff in the sampling chamber was Osmium 187? Ferguson and Metty *had* been trying to make Mercury 203 by adding eight successive tritium nuclei to Hafnium 179, progressing through Tantalum 182, Tungsten 185, Rhenium 188, Osmium 191, Iridium 194, Platinum 197, and Gold 200, all of which were unstable.

But the Hydrogen 3 reaction had gone wrong. The doubling had set in, producing Helium 4. Successive additions of the alpha particles to Hafnium 179 had produced, first, Tungsten 183, and then Osmium 187, both of which were stable.

Ferguson and Metty, seeing that something was wrong, drew off a sample and then reset the reaction to produce the Hg-203 they wanted. Then they had come down to pick up the sample.

They hadn't realized that the helium production had gone wild. Much more helium than necessary was being produced, and the bleeder valve had failed. When they opened the sample chamber, they got a blast of high-pressure helium right in the face. The shock of that sudden release had jarred the whole atmosphere inside the reaction chamber, and the bleeder valve had let go. But the violence of the pressure release had caused a fault to the surface to open up and had closed the valve again—jammed it, probably. There had been enough pressure left in there to blow de Hooch up against the nearest wall when he opened the door. Since the pressure indicator system was connected to the release system, when one had failed, the other had failed. That's why the pressure gauge had indicated normal.

And, of course, it had been the pressure differential that had caused the controls to stick. Well, they ought to be all right now, then. He decided he'd better take a look.

The firewall door was still open. He walked over to it and stepped into the small chamber that led to the inner reactor room. The inside door, much weaker than the outer firewall door, had been blown off its hinges. He stepped past it and went on in.

What he saw made him jerk his glance away from the periscope in his helmet and check his radiation detectors again. Not much change. Relief swept over him as he looked back at the reactor itself. The normally dead black walls were glowing a dull red. It was pure thermal heat, but it shouldn't be doing that.

Moving quickly, he went over to the place where the control cables came in through the firewall. It took him several minutes to assure himself that they would function from the control room now. There was nothing more to do but get out of here and get that reaction damped.

He went out again, closing the firewall door behind him and dogging it tight. There would be no more helium production now.

He went through the radiation trap to the decontamination chamber to wash off whatever it was he had picked up.

The decontamination room was a mess.

De Hooch stared at the twisted pipes and the stream of water that gushed out of a cracked valve. The blast had jarred everything loose. Well, he could still scrub himself off.

Except that the scrubbers weren't working.

He swore under his breath and twisted the valve that was supposed to dispense detergent. It did, thank Heaven. He doused himself good with it and then got under the flowing water.

The radiation level remained exactly where it was.

He walked over and pulled one of the brushes off the defunct scrubber and sudsed it up. It wasn't until he started to use it that he got a good look at his arms. He hadn't paid any attention before.

He walked over to the mirror to get a good look.

"You look magnificent," he told his reflection acidly.

The radiation-proof armor looked as though it had been chrome plated.

But de Hooch knew better than that. He knew exactly what had happened. He was nicely plated all over with a film of mercury, which had amalgamated itself with the metallic surface of the suit. He was thoroughly wet with the stuff and no amount of water and detergent would take it off.

There was something wrong with Number Two Reactor, all right. It had leaked out some of the Mercury 203 that Ferguson and Metty had been making.

He thought a minute. It hadn't been leaking out just before he opened the door in the firewall, because Willows would certainly have noticed the bright mercury line when he checked with the spectroscope. The stuff must have been released when the pressure dropped.

He walked back to the anteroom and looked at the sampling chamber. There were a few droplets of mercury around the inlet.

Thus far, the three pressure explosions had wrecked about everything that was wreckable, he thought. No, not quite. There was still the chance that the whole station would go if he didn't get back into the control room and stop that "powers of two" chain. The detonation of Instantanium 512 would finish the job by doing what high-pressure helium could never do.

He glanced at the thermometer. The temperature behind the firewall had risen to two-forty Centigrade. It wasn't supposed to be above two hundred. It wasn't too serious, really, because a little heat like that wouldn't bother a Ditmars-Horst reactor, but it indicated that things back there weren't working properly.

He turned away and walked back to the decontamination chamber. There must be some way he could get the mercury off the suit—because he couldn't take the suit off until the mercury was gone.

First, he tried scrubbing. That was what showed him how upset he really was. He had actually scrubbed the armor on his left arm free of mercury when he realized what he was doing and threw the brush down in disgust.

"Use your head, de Hooch!" he told himself. What good would it do to scrub the stuff off of the few places he could reach? In the bulky armor, he was worse than muscle-bound. He couldn't touch any part of his back; he couldn't bend far enough to touch his legs. His shoulders were inaccessible, even. Scrubbing was worse than useless—it was time-wasting.

He picked up the brush again and began scrubbing at the other arm. It gave him something to do while he thought. While he was thinking, he wasn't wasting time.

What would dissolve mercury? Nitric acid. Good old HNO_3. Fine. Except that the hot lab was at the other end of the reactor, where the fissure had let all the air out. The bulkheads had dropped, and he couldn't get in. And, naturally, the nitric acid would be in the lab.

For the first time, he found himself hating Willows' guts. If he were around, he could get some acid from the cold lab, or even from the other hot lab at Number One. If Willows—

He stood up and dropped the brush. "Dolt! Boob! Moron! Idiot!" Not Willows. Himself. There was no reason on earth—or Luna—why he couldn't walk over to Number One hot lab and get the stuff himself. The habit of never leaving the lab without thorough decontamination was so thoroughly ingrained in him that he had simply never thought about it until that moment. But what did a little contamination with radioactive mercury mean at a time like this? He could take F corridor to Number One, use the decontamination chamber and the acid from the lab, shuck off his armor there, and come back through E corridor. F could be cleaned up later.

So simple.

He went through the light trap to the next chamber and turned the handle on the sliding door. The door wouldn't budge. It had been warped by the force of the helium blast, and it was stuck in its grooves.

Well, there were tools. The thing could be unstuck.

Peter de Hooch was a determined man, a strong man, and a smart man. But the door was more determined and stronger than he was, and his intelligence didn't give him much of an edge right then. After an hour's hard work, he managed to get the door open about eighteen inches. Then it froze fast and refused to move again. All the power and leverage he could bring to bear was useless. The door had opened all it was going to open. Beyond it, he could see the next radiation trap—and freedom.

Eighteen inches would have been plenty of space for him to get through if he had not been wearing the radiation-proof suit. But he didn't dare take that suit off. By the time he got out of the suit, the intensely radioactive mercury on its surface would have made his death only a matter of time. And not much time at that.

He told himself that if it were simply a matter of running to the control room to shut off the D-H reactor, he'd do it. That could have been done before he lost consciousness. But it wasn't that easy. Damping the reaction took time and control. The stuff had to be eased back slowly. Shutting off the Ditmars-Horst would simply blow a hole in the crust of Luna and kill everyone if he did it now. There were four or five men out there who would die if he pulled anything foolish like that. The explosion wouldn't be as powerful as the Instantanium 512 reaction would be, but it would be none the less deadly for all that.

There had to be either a way to scrape the mercury off the suit or a way to open the door another six inches.

Or, he added suddenly, a way to get safely out of the suit.

At the end of another twenty minutes, he had still thought of nothing. He wandered around the decontamination room, looking at everything, hoping he might see something that would give him a clue. He didn't.

He went into the antechamber of the reactor and glared at the door in the firewall. The instruments said that things were getting pretty fierce on the other side of that wall. Temperature: Two ninety-five and still rising. Pressure? He carefully cracked the inlet of the sampling chamber and got a soft hiss. The helium was expanding from the heat, that was all. Part of the trouble with the reactor, he thought, was the high percentage of oxygen and nitrogen that had mixed in during the ten minutes or so that the door was open. All hell was fixing to bust loose in there, and he, Peter de Hooch, was right next to it.

He walked back into the decontamination chamber.

What would dissolve mercury?

Mercury would dissolve gold. Would gold dissolve mercury?

Very funny.

He was like a turtle, de Hooch thought. Perfectly safe as long as he was in his shell, but take him out of it and he would die.

Hell of a way to spend the night, he thought. *A night in shining armor.*

That struck him as funny. He began to laugh. And laugh.

He almost laughed himself sick before he realized that it was fear and despair that were driving him into hysteria, not a sense of humor. He forced himself to calmness.

He must be calm.

He must think.

Yes.

How do you go about getting rid of a radioactive metal that is in effect welded to the outside of your suit?

The trouble was, he was a nucleonics engineer, not a chemist. He remembered quite a bit of his chemistry, of course, but not as much as he would have liked.

Could the stuff be neutralized?

Sure, he told himself. Very simple. All he had to do was go climb into the reactor, and let the reactor do the job. Mercury 203 plus an alpha particle gives nice, stable Lead 207. Just go climb right into the Ditmars-Horst and let the Helium 4 do the job.

But the thought stuck in his mind.

He kept telling himself not to panic as Willows had done.

And several minutes later, chuckling to himself in a half demented fashion, he opened the firewall door and went in to let the helium do the job.

It was nearly eight in the morning, Greenwich time, when the three surface vehicles, with their wide Caterpillar treads lumbered to a halt near the kiosk that marked the entrance to the underground site of the laboratories.

"O.K.," said one of the men in the first machine, holding a microphone to his lips, "let's go in. If what Willows said is true, the whole place may blow any minute now, but I'm not asking for volunteers. Nobody will be any safer up here than they will down there, and we have to do a job. Besides, Willows wasn't completely rational. Nobody would put on a vac suit and run away like that if he was in his right mind. So we can discount a lot of what he said when we picked him up on the road.

"The five of us in this car are going straight to Number One Reactor to see what can be done to stop whatever is going on. The rest of you start trying to see if you can get those trapped men out of A and B corridors. All right, let's move in."

Less than five minutes later, five men went into the control room of Number One Reactor. They found Peter de Hooch sound asleep in the control chair, and the instruments showed that the Ditmars-Horst reactor was inactive.

One of the men shook de Hooch gently, awakening him in the middle of a snore.

"What?" he said groggily.

"We're here, Guz. Everything's O.K."

"Sure everything's O.K. Nothing to it. All I did was wait until the temperature got above three fifty-seven Centigrade—above the boiling point of mercury. Then I went in and let the hot helium *boil* the stuff off me. Nothing to it. Near boiled myself alive, but it did the trick."

"What," asked the man in a puzzled voice, "are you talking about?"

"I am a knight in dull armor," said Peter de Hooch, dozing off again.

Then he roused himself a little, and said, without opening his eyes: "Hi yo, Quicksilver, away." And he was sound asleep again.

And when he saw what he had done, With all his might and main, He jumped back in that bramble bush And scratch'd them in again!...

With No Strings Attached

A man will always be willing to buy something he wants, and believes in, even if it is impossible, rather than something he believes is impossible.
So ... sell him what he thinks he wants!

The United States Submarine *Ambitious Brill* slid smoothly into her berth in the Brooklyn Navy Yard after far too many weeks at sea, as far as her crew were concerned. After all the necessary preliminaries had been waded through, the majority of that happy crew went ashore to enjoy a well-earned and long-anticipated leave in the depths of the brick-and-glass canyons of Gomorrah-on-the-Hudson.

The trip had been uneventful, in so far as nothing really dangerous or exciting had happened. Nothing, indeed, that could even be called out-of-the-way—except that there was more brass aboard than usual, and that the entire trip had been made underwater with the exception of one surfacing for a careful position check, in order to make sure that the ship's instruments gave the same position as the stars gave. They had. All was well.

That is not to say that the crew of the *Ambitious Brill* were entirely satisfied in their own minds about certain questions that had been puzzling them. They weren't. But they knew better than to ask questions, even among themselves. And they said nothing whatever when they got ashore. But even the novices among submarine crews know that while the nuclear-powered subs like *George Washington*, *Patrick Henry*, or *Benjamin Franklin* are perfectly capable of circumnavigating the globe without coming up for air, such performances are decidedly rare in a presumably Diesel-electric vessel such as the U.S.S. *Ambitious Brill*. And those few members of the crew who had seen what went on in the battery room were the most secretive and the most puzzled of all. They, and they alone, knew that some of the cells of the big battery that drove the ship's electric motors had been removed to make room for a big, steel-clad box hardly bigger than a foot locker, and that the rest of the battery hadn't been used at all.

With no one aboard but the duty watch, and no one in the battery room at all, Captain Dean Lacey felt no compunction whatever in saying, as he gazed at the steel-clad, sealed box: "What a battery!"

The vessel's captain, Lieutenant Commander Newton Wayne, looked up from the box into the Pentagon representative's face. "Yes, sir, it is." His voice sounded as though his brain were trying to catch up with it and hadn't quite succeeded. "This certainly puts us well ahead of the Russians."

Captain Lacey returned the look. "How right you are, commander. This means we can convert every ship in the Navy in a tenth the time we had figured."

Then they both looked at the third man, a civilian.

He nodded complacently. "And at a tenth the cost, gentlemen," he said mildly. "North American Carbide & Metals can produce these units cheaply, and at a rate that will enable us to convert every ship in the Navy within the year."

Captain Lacey shot a glance at Lieutenant Commander Wayne. "All this is strictly Top Secret you understand."

"Yes, sir; I understand," said Wayne.

"Very well." He looked back at the civilian. "Are we ready, Mr. Thorn?"

"Anytime you are, captain," the civilian said.

"Fine. You have your instructions, commander. Carry on."

"Aye, aye, sir," said Lieutenant Commander Wayne.

A little less than an hour later, Captain Lacey and Mr. Thorn were in the dining room of one of the most exclusive clubs in New York. Most clubs in New York are labeled as "exclusive" because they exclude certain people who do not measure up to their standards of wealth. A man who makes less than, say, one hundred thousand dollars a year would not even qualify for scrutiny by the Executive Committee. There is one club in Manhattan which reaches what is probably close to the limit on that kind of exclusiveness: Members must be white, Anglo-Saxon, Protestant Americans who can trace their ancestry as white, Anglo-Saxon, Protestant Americans back at least as far as the American Revolution *without exception*, and who are worth at least ten millions, and who can show that the fortune came into the family at least four generations back. No others need apply. It is said that this club is not a very congenial one because the two members hate each other.

The club in which Lacey and Thorn ate their dinner is not of that sort. It is composed of military and naval officers and certain civilian career men in the United States Government. These men are professionals. Not one of them would ever resign from government service. They are dedicated, heart, body, and soul to the United States of America. The life, public and private, of every man Jack of them is an open book to every other member. Of the three living men who have held—and the one who at present holds—the title of President of the United States, only one was a member of the club before he held that high office.

As an exclusive club, they rank well above England's House of Peers and just a shade below the College of Cardinals of the Roman Catholic Church.

Captain Lacey was a member. Mr. Richard Thorn was not, but he was among those few who qualify to be invited as guests. The carefully guarded precincts of the club were among the very few in which these two men could talk openly and at ease.

After the duck came the brandy, both men having declined dessert. And over the brandy—that ultra-rare Five Star Hennessy which is procurable only by certain people and is believed by many not to exist at all—Captain Lacey finally asked the question that had been bothering him for so long.

"Thorn," he said, "three months ago that battery didn't exist. I know it and you know it. Who was the genius who invented it?"

Thorn smiled, and there was a subtle wryness in the smile. "Genius is the word, I suppose. Now that the contracts with the Navy have been signed, I can give you the straight story. But you're wrong in saying that the thing didn't exist three months ago. It did. We just didn't know about it, that's all."

Lacey raised his bushy, iron-gray eyebrows. "Oh? And how did it come to the attention of North American Carbide & Metals?"

Thorn puffed out his cheeks and blew out his breath softly before he began talking, as though he were composing his beginning sentences in his mind. Then he said: "The first I heard about it was four months ago. Considering what's happened since then, it seems a lot longer." He inhaled deeply from his brandy snifter before continuing. "As head of the development labs for NAC&M, I was asked to take part as a witness to a demonstration that had been arranged through some of the other officers of the company. It was to take place out on Salt Lake Flats, where—"

It was to take place out on Salt Lake Flats, where there was no chance of hanky-panky. Richard Thorn—who held a Ph.D. from one of the finest technological colleges in the East, but who preferred to be addressed as "Mister"—was in a bad mood. He had flown all the way out to Salt Lake City after being given only a few hours notice, and then had been bundled into a jeep furnished by the local sales office of NAC&M and scooted off to the blinding gray-white glare of the Salt Flats. It was hot and it was much too sunshiny for Thorn. But he had made the arrangements for the test himself, so he couldn't argue or complain too loudly. He could only complain mildly to himself that the business office of the company, which had made the final arrangements, had, in his opinion, been a little too much in a hurry to get the thing over with. Thorn himself felt that the test could have at least waited until the weather cooled off. The only consolation he had was that, out here, the humidity was so low that he could stay fairly comfortable in spite of the heat as long as there was plenty of drinking water. He had made sure to bring plenty.

The cavalcade of vehicles arrived at the appointed spot—umpteen miles from nowhere—and pulled up in a circle.

Thorn climbed out wearily and saw the man who called himself Sorensen climb out of the second jeep.

From the first time he had seen him, Thorn had tagged Sorensen as an Angry Old Man. Not that he was really getting old; he was still somewhere on the brisk side of fifty. But he wore a perpetual scowl on his face that looked as though it had been etched there by too many years of frustration, and his voice always seemed to have an acid edge to it, like that of an old man who has decided, after decades of observation, that all men are fools. And yet Thorn thought he occasionally caught a glimpse of mocking humor in the pale blue eyes. He was lean and rather tall, with white hair that still showed traces of blond, and he looked as Scandinavian as his name sounded. His accent was pure Minnesota American.

As he climbed out of the jeep, Sorensen brought with him the Black Suitcase.

Ever since he had first seen it, Thorn had thought of it as "the Black Suitcase," and after he had seen some of the preliminary tests, he had subconsciously put capitals to the words. But Richard Thorn was no fool. Too many men had been suckered before, and he, Richard Thorn, did not intend to be another sucker, no matter how impressed he might be by the performance of an invention.

If this was a con game, it was going to have to be a good one to get by Richard Thorn, Ph.D.

He walked across the few feet of hard, salt-white ground that separated him from Sorensen standing beside the second jeep with the Black Suitcase in his hand. It was obvious to anyone who watched the way Sorensen handled the thing that it was heavy—seventy-five pounds or better.

"Need any help?" Thorn asked, knowing what the answer would be.

"Nope," Sorensen said. "I can handle it."

The suitcase wasn't really black. It was a dark cordovan brown, made even darker by long usage, which had added oily stains to the well-used leather. But Thorn thought of it as the Black Suitcase simply because it was the perfect example of the proverbial Little Black Box—the box that Did Things. As a test question in an examination, the Little Black Box performs a useful function. The examiner draws a symbolic electronic circuit. Somewhere in the circuit, instead of drawing the component that is supposed to be there, he draws a Little Black Box. Then he defines the waveform, voltage, and amperage entering the circuit and defines whatever is coming out. Question: What is in the Little Black Box?

Except in the simplest of cases, there is never an absolute answer. The question is counted as correct if the student puts into the Little Black Box a component or subcircuit which will produce the effect desired. The value of the answer depends on the simplicity and relative controllability of the component drawn in the place of the Little Black Box.

Sorensen's Black Suitcase was still a problem to Thorn. He couldn't quite figure out what was in it.

"Hotter'n Billy Blue Blazes!" Sorensen said as he put the Black Suitcase down on the gleaming white ground. He grinned a little, which dispelled for a moment his Angry Old Man expression, and said: "You ready to go, Mr. Thorn?"

"I'm ready any time you are," Thorn said grumpily.

Sorensen looked at the NAC&M scientist sideways. "You don't sound any happier'n I am, Mr. Thorn."

Thorn looked at him and thought he could see that flash of odd humor in his light blue eyes. Thorn exhaled a heavy breath. "I'm no happier than you are to be out in this heat. Let's get on with it."

Sorensen's chuckle sounded so out of place that Thorn was almost startled. "You know the difference between you and me, Mr. Thorn?" Sorensen asked. He didn't wait for an answer. "You think this test is probably a waste of time. Me, on the other hand, I *know* it is."

"Let's get on with it," Thorn repeated.

It took two hours to set up the equipment, in spite of the fact that a lot of the circuits had been prefabricated before the caravan had come out from Salt Lake City. But Richard Thorn wanted to make certain that all his data was both correct and recorded. Sorensen had nothing to do but watch. He had no hand in setting up the equipment. He had brought the Black Suitcase, and that was all he was going to be allowed to do.

From the top of the Black Suitcase projected two one-inch copper electrodes, fourteen inches apart. The North American Carbide & Metals technicians set up the circuits that were connected to the electrodes without any help from Sorensen.

But just before they started to work, Sorensen said: "There's just one thing I think you ought to warn those men about, Mr. Thorn."

"What's that?" Thorn asked.

"If any of 'em tries to open that suitcase, they're likely to get blown sky high. And I don't want 'em getting funny with me, either."

He had his hand in his trouser pocket, and Thorn was suddenly quite certain that the man was holding a revolver. He could see the outlines against the cloth.

Thorn sighed. "Don't worry, Mr. Sorensen. We don't have any ulterior designs on your invention." He did not add that the investigators of NAC&M had already assumed that anyone who was asking one million dollars for an invention which was, in effect, a pig in a poke, would be expected to take drastic methods to protect his gadget. But there would be no point in telling Sorensen that his protective efforts had already been anticipated and that the technicians had already been warned against touching the Black Suitcase any more than necessary to connect the leads. Giving Sorensen that information might make him even more touchy.

Thorn only hoped that the bomb, or whatever it was that Sorensen had put in the suitcase, was well built, properly fused, and provided with adequate safeties.

When everything was set up, Sorensen walked over to his device and turned it on by shoving the blade of a heavy-duty switch into place. "O.K.," he said.

One of the technicians began flipping other switches, and a bank of ordinary incandescent light bulbs came on, four at a time. Finally there were one hundred of them burning, each one a hundred-watt bulb that glowed brightly but did not appear to be contributing much to the general brightness of the Utah sun. The technicians checked their recording voltmeters and ammeters and reported that, sure enough, some ten kilowatts of power at a little less than one hundred fifteen volts D.C. was coming from the Black Suitcase.

Sorensen and Thorn sat in the tent which had been erected to ward off the sun's rays. They watched the lights shine.

One of the technicians came in, wiping his forehead with a big blue bandana. "Well, there she goes. Mr. Sorensen, if that thing is dangerous, hadn't we better back off a little way from it?"

"It isn't dangerous," Sorensen said. "Nothing's going to happen."

The technician looked unhappy. "Then I don't see why we couldn't've tested the thing back in the shop. Would've been a lot easier there. To say nothing of more comfortable."

Thorn lit a cigarette in silence.

Sorensen nodded and said, "Yes, Mr. Siegel, it would've been."

Siegel sat down on one of the camp stools and lit a cigarette. "Mr. Sorensen," he asked in all innocence, "have you got a patent on that battery?"

The humorous glint returned to Sorensen's eyes as he said, "Nope. I didn't patent the battery in that suitcase. That's why I don't want anybody fooling around with it."

"How come you don't patent it?" Siegel asked. "Nobody could steal it if you patented it."

"Couldn't they?" Sorensen asked with a touch of acid in his voice. "Do you know anything about batteries, Mr. Siegel?"

"A little. I'm not an expert on 'em, or anything like that. I'm an electrician. But I know a little bit about 'em."

Sorensen nodded. "Then you should know, Mr. Siegel, that battery-making is an art, not a science. You don't just stick a couple of electrodes into a solution of electrolyte and consider that your work is done. With the same two metals and the same electrolyte, you could make batteries that would run the gamut from terrible to excellent. Some of 'em, maybe, wouldn't hold a charge more than an hour, while others would have a shelf-life, fully charged, of as much as a year. Batteries don't work according to theory. If they did, potassium chlorate would be a better depolarizer than manganese dioxide, instead of the other way around. What you get out of a voltaic cell depends on the composition and strength of the electrolyte, the kind of depolarizer used, the shape of the electrodes, the kind of surface they have, their arrangement and spacing, and a hundred other little things."

"I've heard that," Siegel said.

Thorn smoked in silence. He had heard Sorensen's arguments before. Sorensen didn't mind discussing his battery in the abstract, but he was awfully close-mouthed when it came to talking about it in concrete terms. He would talk about batteries-in-general, but not about this-battery-in-particular.

Not that Thorn blamed him in the least. Sorensen was absolutely correct in his statements about the state of the art of making voltaic cells. If Sorensen had something new—and Thorn was almost totally convinced that he did—then he was playing it smart by not trying to patent it.

"Now then," Sorensen went on, "let's suppose that my battery is made up of lead and lead dioxide plates in a sulfuric acid solution, except that I've added a couple of trifling things and made a few small changes in the physical structure of the plates. I'm not saying that's what the battery is, mind you; I'm saying 'suppose'."

"O.K., suppose," said Siegel. "Couldn't you patent it?"

"What's to patent? The Pb-PbO_2-H_2SO_4 cell is about half as old as the United States Patent Office itself. Can't patent that. Copper oxide, maybe, as a depolarizer? Old hat; can't patent that. Laminated plates, maybe? Nope. Can't patent that, either."

Siegel looked out at the hundred glowing light bulbs. "You mean you can't patent it, even if it works a hundred times better than an ordinary battery?"

"Hell, man," Sorensen said, "you can't patent performance! You've got to patent something solid and concrete! Oh, I'll grant that a top-notch patent attorney might be able to get me some kind of patent on it, but I wouldn't trust its standing up in court if I had to try to quash an infringement.

"Besides, even if I had an iron-bound patent, what good would it do me? Ever hear of a patent pool?"

"No," said Siegel. "What's a patent pool?"

"I'll give you an example. If all the manufacturers of a single product get together and agree to form a patent pool, it means that if one company buys a patent, all of them can use it. Say the automobile companies have one. That means that if you invent a radical new design for an engine—one, maybe that would save them millions of dollars—you'll be offered a few measly thousand for it. Why should they offer more? *Where else are you going to sell it?* If one company gets it, they all get it. There's no competition, and if you refuse to sell it at all, they just wait a few years until the patent runs out and use it for free. That may take a little time, but a big industry has plenty of time. They have a longer life span than human beings."

"North American Carbide & Metals," said Thorn quietly, "is not a member of any patent pool, Mr. Sorensen."

"I know," Sorensen said agreeably. "Battery patents are trickier than automotive machinery patents. That's why I'm doing this my way. I'm not selling the gadget as such. I'm selling results. For one million dollars, tax paid, I will agree to show your company how to build a device that will turn out electric power at such-and-such a rate and that will have so-

and-so characteristics, just like it says in the contract you read. I guarantee that it can be made at the price I quote. That's all."

He looked back out at the bank of light bulbs. They were still burning. They kept burning—

"... They kept burning for ten solid hours," said Thorn. "Then he went out and shut off his battery."

Captain Lacey was scowling. "That's damned funny," he muttered.

"What is?" asked Thorn, wondering why the naval officer had interrupted his story.

"What you've been telling me," Lacey said. "I'll swear I've heard—" He stopped and snapped his fingers suddenly. "Sure! By golly!" He stood up from the table. "Would you excuse me for a minute? I want to see if a friend of mine is here. If he is, he has a story you ought to hear. Damned funny coincidence." And he was off in a hurry, leaving Thorn staring somewhat blankly after him.

Three minutes later, while Thorn was busily pouring himself a second helping of Five-Star Hennessy, Captain Lacey returned to the table with an army officer wearing the insignia of a bird colonel.

"Colonel Dower," the captain said, "I'd like you to meet a friend of mine—Mr. Richard Thorn, the top research man with North American Carbide & Metals. Mr. Thorn, this is Colonel Edward Dower." The men shook hands. A third brandy snifter was brought and a gentleman's potation was poured for the colonel.

"Ed," said Captain Lacey as soon as his fellow officer had inhaled a goodly lungful of the heady fumes, "do you remember you were telling me a couple of years ago about some test you were in on out in the Mojave Desert?"

Colonel Dower frowned. "Test? Something to do with cars?"

"No, not that one. Something to do with a power supply."

"Power supply. Oh!" His frown faded and became a smile. "You mean the crackpot with his little suitcase."

Thorn looked startled, and Captain Lacey said: "That's the one."

"Sure I remember," said the colonel. "What about it?"

"Oh, nothing," Lacey said with elaborate unconcern, "I just thought Mr. Thorn, here, might like to hear the story—that is, if it isn't classified."

Colonel Dower chuckled. "Nothing classified about it. Just another crackpot inventor. Had a little suitcase that he claimed was a marvelous new power source. Wanted a million dollars cash for it, tax free, no strings attached, but he wouldn't show us what was in it. Not really very interesting."

"Go ahead, colonel," said Thorn. "I'm interested. Really I am."

"Well, as I said, there's nothing much to it," the colonel said. "He showed us a lot of impressive-looking stuff in his laboratory, but it didn't mean a thing. He had this suitcase, as I told you. There were a couple of thick copper electrodes coming out of the side of it, and he claimed that they could be tapped for tremendous amounts of power. Well, we listened, and we watched his demonstrations in the lab. He ran some heavy-duty motors off it and a few other things like that. I don't remember what all."

"And he wanted to sell it to you sight-unseen?" Thorn asked.

"That's right," said the colonel. "Well, actually, he wasn't trying to sell it to the Army. As you know, we don't buy ideas; all we buy is hardware, the equipment itself, or the components. But the company he was trying to sell his gadget to wanted me to take a look at it as an observer. I've had experience with that sort of thing, and they wanted my opinion."

"I see," Thorn said. "What happened?"

"Well," said the colonel, "we wanted him to give us a demonstration out in the Mojave Desert—"

"... Out in the Mojave Desert?" the inventor asked. "Whatever for, Colonel Dower?"

"We just want to make sure you haven't got any hidden power sources hooked up to that suitcase of yours. We know a place out in the Mojave where there aren't any power lines for miles. We'll pick the place."

The inventor frowned at him out of pale blue eyes. "Look." He gestured at the suitcase sitting on the laboratory table. "You can see there's nothing faked about that."

Colonel Dower shook his head. "You won't tell us what's in that suitcase. All we know is that it's supposed to produce power. From what? How? You won't tell us. Did you ever hear of the Keely Motor?"

"No. What was the Keely Motor?"

"Something along the lines of what you have here," the colonel said dryly, "except that Keely at least had an explanation for where he was getting his power. Back around 1874, a man named John Keely claimed he had invented a wonderful new power source. He called it a breakthrough in the field of perpetual motion. An undiscovered source of power, he said, controlled by harmony. He had a machine in his lab which would begin to turn a flywheel when he blew a chord on a harmonica. He could stop it by blowing a sour note. He claimed that this power was all around, but that it was easiest to get it out of water. He claimed that a pint of his charged water would run a train from Philadelphia to New York and back and only cost a tenth as much as coal."

The inventor folded his arms across his chest and looked grimly at Colonel Dower. "I see. Go on."

"Well, he got some wealthy men interested. A lot of them invested money—big money—in the Keely Motor Company. Every so often, he'd bring them down to his lab and show them what progress he was making and then tell them how much more money he needed. He always got them to shell out, and he was living pretty high on the hog. He kept at it for years. Finally, in the late nineties, *The Scientific American* exposed the whole hoax. Keely died, and his lab was given a thorough going over. It turned out that all his marvelous machines were run by compressed air cleverly channeled through the floor and the legs of tables."

"I see," repeated the inventor, narrowing his eyes. "And I suppose my invention is run by compressed air?"

"I didn't say your invention was a phony," Colonel Dower said placatingly. "I merely mentioned the Keely Motor to show you why we want to test it out somewhere away from your laboratory. Are you willing to go?"

"Any time you are, colonel."

A week or so later, they went out into the Mojave and set up the test. The suitcase—

"... The suitcase," said the colonel, "was connected up to a hundred hundred-watt light bulbs. He let the thing run for ten hours before he shut it off." He chuckled. "He never would let us look into that suitcase. Naturally, we wouldn't buy a pig in a poke, as the saying goes. We told him that any time we could be allowed to look at his invention, we'd be glad to see him again. He left in a huff, and that was the last we saw of him."

"How do you explain," Thorn said carefully, "the fact that his suitcase *did* run all those lights?"

The colonel chuckled again. "Hell, we had that figured out. He just had a battery of some kind in the suitcase. No fancy gimmick for deriving power from perpetual motion or anything like that. Nope. Just a battery, that's all."

Captain Dean Lacey was grinning hugely.

Thorn said: "Tell me, colonel—what was this fellow's name?"

"Oh, I don't recall. Big, blond chap. Had a Swedish name—or maybe Norwegian. Sanderson? No. Something like that, though."

"Sorensen?" Thorn asked.

"That's it! Sorensen! Do you know him?"

"We've done business with him," said Thorn dryly.

"He didn't palm his phony machine off on you, did he?" the colonel asked with a light laugh.

"No, no," Thorn said. "Nobody sold us a battery disguised as a perpetual motion device. Our relations with him have been quite profitable, thank you."

"I'd say you still ought to watch him," said Colonel Dower. "Once a con man, always a con man, is my belief."

Captain Lacey rubbed his hands together. "Ed, tell me something. Didn't it ever occur to you that a battery which would do all that—a battery which would hold a hundred kilowatt-hours of energy in a suitcase would be worth the million he was asking for it?"

Colonel Dower looked startled. "Why ... why, no. The man was obviously a phony. He wouldn't tell us what the power source was. He—" Colonel Dower stopped. Then he set his jaw and went on. "Besides, if it were a battery, why didn't he say so? A phony like that shouldn't be—" He stopped again, looking at the naval officer.

Lacey was still grinning. "We have discovered, Ed," he said in an almost sweet voice, "that Sorensen's battery will run a submarine."

"With all due respect to your rank and ability, captain," Thorn said, "I have a feeling that you'd have been skeptical about any such story, too."

"Oh, I'll admit that," Lacey said. "But I still would have been impressed by the performance." Then he looked thoughtful. "But I must admit that it lowers my opinion of your inventor to hear that he tells all these cock-and-bull stories. Why not just come out with the truth?"

"Evidently he'd learned something," Thorn said. "Let me tell you what happened after the contracts had been signed—"

... The contracts had been signed after a week of negotiation. Thorn was, he admitted to himself, a little nervous. As soon as he had seen the test out on Salt Flats, he had realized that Sorensen had developed a battery that was worth every cent he had asked for it. Thorn himself had pushed for the negotiations to get them through without too much friction. A million bucks was a lot of loot, but there was no chance of losing it, really. As Sorensen said, the contract did not call for the delivery of a specific device, it called for a device that would produce specific results. If Sorensen's device didn't produce those results, or if they couldn't be duplicated by Thorn after having had the device explained to him, then the contract wasn't fulfilled, and the ambitious Mr. Sorensen wouldn't get any million dollars.

Now the time had come to see what was inside that mysterious Little Black Suitcase. Sorensen had obligingly brought the suitcase to the main testing and development laboratory of North American Carbide & Metals.

Sorensen put it on the lab table, but he didn't open it right away. "Now I want you to understand, Mr. Thorn," he began, "that I, myself, don't exactly know how this thing works. That is, I don't completely understand what's going on inside there. I've built several of them, and I can show you how to build them, but that doesn't mean I understand them completely."

"That's not unusual in battery work," Thorn said. "We don't completely understand what's going on in a lot of cells. As long as the thing works according to the specifications in the contract, we'll be satisfied."

"All right. Fine. But you're going to be surprised when you see what's in here."

"I probably will. I've been expecting a surprise," Thorn said.

What he got was a *real* surprise.

There was a small pressure tank of hydrogen inside—one of the little ones that are sometimes used to fill toy balloons. There was a small batch of electronic circuitry that looked as though it might be the insides of an FM-AM radio.

All of the rest of the space was taken up by batteries.

And every single one of the cells was a familiar little cannister. They were small, rechargeable nickel-cadmium cells, and every one bore the trademark of North American Carbide & Metals!

One of the other men in the lab said: "What kind of a joke is this?"

"Do you mean, Mr. Sorensen," Thorn asked with controlled precision, "that your million-dollar process is merely some kind of gimmickry with our own batteries?"

"No," said Sorensen. "It's—"

"Wait a minute," said one of the others, "is it some kind of hydrogen fuel cell?"

"In a way," Sorensen said. "Yes, in a way. It isn't as efficient as I'd like, but it gets its power by converting hydrogen to helium. I need those batteries to start the thing. After it gets going, these leads here from the reactor cell keep the batteries charged. The—"

He was interrupted by five different voices all trying to speak at once. He could hardly—

"... He could hardly get a word in edgewise at first," said Thorn. He was enjoying the look of shocked amazement on Colonel Dower's face. "When Sorensen finally did get it explained, we still didn't know much. But we built another one, and it worked as well as the one he had. And the contract didn't specifically call for a battery. He had us good, he did."

"Now wait—" Colonel Dower said. "You mean to say it wasn't a battery after all?"

"Of course not."

"Then why all the folderol?"

"Colonel," Thorn said, "Sorensen patented that device nine years ago. It only has eight years to run. But he couldn't get anyone at all to believe that it would do what he said it would do. After years of beating his head against a stone wall, years of trying to convince people who wouldn't even look twice at his gadget, he decided to get smart.

"He began to realize that 'everybody knew' that hydrogen fusion wasn't that simple. It was his *theory* that no one would listen to. As soon as he told anyone that he had a hydrogen fusion device that could be started with a handful of batteries and could be packed into a suitcase, he was instantly dismissed as a nut.

"I did a little investigating after he gave us the full information on what he had done. (Incidentally, he signed over the patent to us, which was more than the contract called for, in return for a job with our outfit, so that he could help develop the fusion device.)

"As I said, he finally got smart. If the theory was what was making people give him the cold shoulder, he'd tell them nothing.

"You know the results of that, Colonel Dower. At least he got somebody to test the machine. He managed to get somebody to look at what it would do.

"But that wasn't enough. He didn't have, apparently, any legitimate excuse for keeping it under wraps that way, so everyone was suspicious."

"But why tell *you* it was a battery?" asked Captain Lacey.

"That was probably suggested by Colonel Dower's reaction to the tests he saw," Thorn said. "Somebody—I think it was George Gamow, but I'm not certain—once said that just having a theory isn't enough; the theory has to make sense.

"Well, Sorensen's theory of hydrogen fusion producing electric current didn't make sense. It was *true*, but it didn't make sense.

"So he came up with a theory that *did* make sense. If everyone wanted to think it was 'nothing but a battery', then, by Heaven, he'd sell it as a battery. And *that*, gentlemen, was a theory we were perfectly willing to believe. It wasn't true, but it did make sense.

"As far as I was concerned, it was perfectly natural for a man who had invented a new type of battery to keep it under wraps that way.

"Naturally, after we had invested a million dollars in the thing, we *had* to investigate it. It worked, and we had to find out why and how."

"Naturally," said Colonel Dower, looking somewhat uncomfortable. "I presume this is all under wraps, eh? What about the Russians? Couldn't they get hold of the patent papers?"

"They could have," Thorn admitted, "but they didn't. They dismissed him as a crackpot, too, if they heard about him at all. Certainly they never requested a copy of his patent. The patent number is now top secret, of course, and if anyone does write in for a copy, the Patent Office will reply that there are temporarily no copies available. And the FBI will find out who is making the request."

"Well," said Colonel Dower, "at least I'm glad to hear that I was not the only one who didn't believe him."

Captain Lacey chuckled. "And Mr. Thorn here believed a lie."

"Only because it made more sense than the truth," Thorn said. "And," he added, "you shouldn't laugh, captain. Remember, we suckered the Navy in almost the same way."

Nor Iron Bars a Cage....

Her red-blond hair was stained and discolored when they found her in the sewer, and her lungs were choked with muck because her killer hadn't bothered to see whether she was really dead when he dumped her body into the manhole, so she had breathed the stuff in with her last gasping breaths. Her face was bruised, covered with great blotches, and three of her ribs had been broken. Her thighs and abdomen had been bruised and lacerated.

If she had lived for three more days, Angela Frances Donahue would have reached her seventh birthday.

I didn't see her until she was brought to the morgue. My phone chimed, and when I thumbed it on, the face of Inspector Kleek, of Homicide South, came on the screen. His heavy eyelids always hang at half mast, giving him a sleepy, bored look and the rest of his fleshy face sags in the same general pattern. "Roy," he said as soon as he could see my face on his own screen, "we just found the little Donahue girl. The meat wagon's taking her down to the morgue now. You want to come down here and look over the scene, or you want to go to the morgue? It looks like it's one of your special cases, but we won't know for sure until Doc Prouty does the post on her."

I took a firm grip on my temper. I should have been notified as soon as Homicide had been; I should have been there with the Homicide Squad. But I knew that if I said anything, Kleek would just say, "Hell, Roy, they don't notify me until there's suspicion of homicide, and you don't get a call until there's suspicion that it might be the work of a degenerate. That's the way the system works. You know that, Roy." And rather than hear that song-and-dance again, I gave myself thirty seconds to think.

"I'll meet you at the morgue," I said. "Your men can get the whole story at the scene without my help."

That mollified him, and it showed a little on his face. "O.K., Roy, see you there." And he cut off.

I punched savagely at the numbered buttons on the phone to get an intercommunication hookup with Dr. Barton Brownlee's office, on the third floor of the same building as my own office. His face, when it came on, was a calming contrast to Kleek's.

He's nearly ten years younger than I am, not yet thirty-five, and his handsome, thoughtful face and dark, slightly wavy hair always make me think of somebody like St. Edward Pusey or maybe Albert Einstein. Not that he looks like either one of them, or even that he looks saintly, but he does look like a man who has the courage of his convictions and is calmly, quietly, but forcefully ready to shove what he knows to be the truth down everybody else's throat if that becomes necessary. Or maybe I am just reading into his face what I know to be true about the man himself.

"Brownie," I said, "they've found the Donahue girl. Taking her down to the morgue now. Want to come along?"

"I don't think so," he said without hesitation. "I'll get all the information I need from the photos and the reports. The man I do want to see is the killer; I need more data, Roy—always more data. The more my boys and I know about these zanies, the more effectively we can deal with them."

"I know. O.K.; I've got to run." I cut off, grabbed my hat, and headed out to fulfill my part of the bargain Brownlee and I had once made. "You find 'em," he'd once said, "and I'll fix 'em." So far, that bargain had paid off.

I got to the morgue a few minutes after the body was brought in. The man at the front desk looked up at me as I walked in and gave me a bored smile. "Evening, Inspector. The Donahue kid's in the clean-up room." Then he went back to his paper work.

The lab technicians were standing around watching while the morgue attendant sluiced the muck off the corpse with a hose, watching to see if anything showed up in the gooey filth. Inspector Kleek stood to one side. All he said was, "Hi, Roy."

The morgue attendant lifted up one small arm with a gloved hand and played the hose over the thin biceps. "Good thing the rigor mortis has gone off," he said, "these stiffs are hell to handle when they're stiff." It was an old joke, but everybody grinned out of habit.

The clear water from the hose flowed over the skin and turned a grayish brown as it ran down to the bottom of the shallow, waist-high stainless-steel trough in which the body was lying.

One of the lab techs stepped over and began going through the long hair very carefully, and Doc Prouty, the Medical Examiner, began cleaning out the mouth and nose and eyes and ears with careful hands.

I turned to Kleek. "You sure it's the Donahue girl?"

He sighed and looked away from the small dead thing on the cleaning table. "Who else could it be? She was found only three blocks from the Donahue home. No other female child reported missing in that area. We haven't checked the prints yet, but you can bet they'll tally with her school record."

I had to agree. "What about the time of death?"

"Doc Prouty figures forty-eight to sixty hours ago."

"I'll be able to give you a better figure after the post," the Medical Examiner said without looking up from his work.

A tall, big-nosed man in plain-clothes suddenly turned away from the scene on the table, his mouth moving queerly, his eyes hard. After a moment, his lips relaxed. Still staring at the wall, he said: "I guess the case is out of Federal jurisdiction, then. We'll co-operate, as usual, of course." He looked at me. "Could I talk to you outside, Inspector Royall?"

I looked at Kleek. "O.K., Sam?" I didn't have to have his O.K.; it was just professional courtesy. He knew I'd tell him whatever it was that the FBI man had to say, and we both knew why the Federal agent wanted to leave.

Sam Kleek nodded. "Sure. I'll keep an eye out here."

The FBI man followed me into the outer room.

"Do you figure this as a sex-degenerate case, Inspector?" he asked.

"Looks like it. You saw the bruises. Dr. Prouty will be able to tell us for sure after the post mortem."

He shook his head as if to clear it of a bad memory. "You New York police can sure be cold-blooded at times."

The thing that was bothering him, as Kleek and I both knew, was that the FBI agent hadn't been exposed to this sort of thing often enough. They deal with the kind of crimes that actually don't involve the callous murder of children very often. Even the murder of adults doesn't normally come under the aegis of the FBI.

"We're not cold blooded," I said. "Not by inclination, I mean. But a man gets that way—he has to get that way—after he's seen enough of this sort of thing. You either get yourself an emotional callous or you get deathly sick from the repetition—and then you have to get out of the job."

"Yeah," he said. "Sure." He quit rubbing his chin with a knuckle, looked at me, and said: "What I wanted to say is that there's no evidence that she was taken across a state line. Whoever sent that ransom note to the Donahue parents was trying to throw us off the track."

"Looks like it. Look at the time-table. The note was sent *after* the girl was murdered, but *before* the information hit the papers or the newscasts. The killer wanted us to think it was a ransom kidnaping. It isn't likely that the note was sent by a crank. A crank wouldn't have known the girl was missing at all at the time the note was sent."

"That's the way it seems to me," he agreed. The color was coming back into his face. "But why would he want to make it look like a kidnaping instead of ... of what it was? The penalty's the same for both."

My grin had anger, pity, and disgust for the killer in it—plus a certain amount of satisfaction. Some day, I'd like to see my face in a mirror when I feel like that.

"He was hoping the body wouldn't be found until it was too late for us to know that it was a rape killing. And that means that he knew that he would be on our list if we did find out that it was rape. Otherwise, he wouldn't have bothered. If I'm right, then he has outsmarted himself. He has told us that we know him, and he's told us that he's smart enough to figure out a dodge—that he's not one of the helplessly stupid ones."

"That should help to narrow the field down," he said in a hard voice. He felt in his pocket for a cigarette, found his pack, took one out, and then held it, unlit, between the fingers of his right hand. "Inspector Royall, I've studied the new law of this state—the one you're working under here—and I think it'll be great if it works out. I wish you luck. Now, if you'll excuse me, I have to call the office."

As he went out to the desk phone, I gave him a silent thanks. Words of encouragement were hard to come by at that time.

I turned and went back towards the clean-up room.

She didn't look as though she were asleep. They never do. She looked dead. She'd been head down in the sewer, and the blood had pooled and coagulated in her head and shoulders. Now that the filth had been washed off, the dark purple of the dead blood cells showed through the translucent skin. She would look better after she was embalmed.

Doc Prouty was holding up a small syringe, eying the little bit of fluid within it. "We've got him," he said in a flat voice. "I'll have the lab run an analysis. We're well within the time limit. All we have to do is separate the girl's blood type from that of the spermatic fluid. You boys find your man, and I can identify him for you." He put the syringe in its special case. "I'll let you know the exact cause of death in a couple of hours."

"O.K., Doc. Thanks," said Inspector Kleek, closing his notebook. He turned to one of the other men. "Thompson, you notify the parents. Get 'em down here to make a positive identification, and send it along to my office with the print identification." Then he looked at me. "Anything extra you want, Roy?"

I shook my head. "Nope. Let's go check the files, huh?"

"Sure. Can I ride with you? I rode in with Thompson; he'll have to stay."

"Come along," I told him.

By ten fifteen that evening, we had narrowed the field down considerably. We fed all the data we had into the computer, including the general type number of the spermatic fluid, which Dr. Prouty had given us, and watched while the machine sorted through the characteristics of all the known criminals in its memory.

Kleek and I were sitting at a desk drinking hot, black coffee when the computer technician came over and handed Kleek the results at ten fifteen. "Quite a bunch of 'em, Inspector," he said, "but the geographic compartmentalization will help."

Kleek glanced over the neatly-printed sheaf of papers that the computer had turned out, then handed them to me. "There we are, Roy. One of those zanies is our boy."

I looked at the list. Every person on it was either a confirmed or suspected psychopath, and each one of them conformed to the set of specifications we had fed the computer. They were listed in four different groups, according to the distance they lived from the scene of the crime—half a mile, two miles, five miles, and "remainder," the rest of the city.

"All we got to do," Kleek said complacently, "is start rounding 'em up."

"You make it sound easy," I said tightly.

He put down his coffee cup. "Hell, Roy, it *is* easy! We've got all these characters down on the books, don't we? We know what they are, don't we? Look at 'em! Once in a while a new one pops up, and we put him on the list. Once in a while we catch one and send him up. Practically cut and dried, isn't it?"

"Sure," I said.

"Look, Roy," he went on, "we got it down to a fine art now—have for years." He waved in the general direction of the computer. "We got the advantage that it's easier to sort 'em out now, and faster—but the old tried-and-true technique is just the same. Cops have been catching these goons in every civilized country on Earth for a hundred years by this technique."

"Sam," I said wearily, "are you going to give me a lecture on police methods?"

He picked up his cup, held it for a moment, then set it down again, his eyes hardening. "Yes, Roy, I am! I'm older than you are, I've got more years on the Force, I've been working with Homicide longer, and I outrank you in grade by two and a half years! Yes, I figure it's about time I lectured you! You want to listen?"

I looked at him. Kleek is a good cop, I was thinking, and he deserves to be listened to, even if I don't agree with him.

"O.K., Sam," I said, "I'll listen."

"O.K., then." He took a breath. "Now, we got a system here that works. The nuts always show themselves up, one way or another. Most of 'em have been arrested by the time they're fourteen, fifteen years old. Maybe we can't nail 'em down and pin anything on 'em, but we got 'em down on the books. We know they have to be watched. We got ninety per cent of the queers and hopheads and stew-bums and firebugs and the rest of the zanies down on our books"—he waved toward the computer again—"and down in the memory bank of the computer. We know we're gonna get 'em eventually, because we know they're gonna goof up eventually, and then we'll have 'em. We'll have 'em"—he made a clutching gesture with his right hand—"right where it hurts!

"You take this Donahue killer. We know where he is. We can be pretty sure we got him down on the books." He tapped the sheaf of papers from the computer with a firm forefinger. "We can be pretty sure that he's one of those guys right down there!"

He waved his hand again, but, this time, he took in the whole city—the whole outside world. "Like clock-work. The minute they goof, we nab 'em."

"Sam," I said, "just listen to me a minute. We know that ninety per cent of the men on that list right there are going to be convicted of a crime of violence inside the next five years, right?"

115

"That's what I've been tellin' you. The minute—"

"Wait a minute; wait a minute. Just listen. Why don't we just go out and arrest them all right now? Look at all the trouble that would save us."

"Hell, Roy! You can't arrest a man unless he's done something! What would you charge 'em with? Loitering with intent to commit a nuisance?"

"No. But we *can*—"

I was cut off by a uniformed cop who stuck his head in the door and said: "Inspector Royall, Dr. Brownlee called. Says they picked up Hammerlock Smith. He's at the 87th Precinct. Wants you to come down right away if you can."

I stood up and grabbed my hat. "Sam, you can sit on this one for a while, huh? I've been waiting for Hammerlock Smith to fall for two months."

Sam Kleek looked disgusted. "And you'll see that he gets psycho treatment and a suspended sentence. A few days in the looney ward, and then right back out on the street. Hammerlock Smith! *There's* a case for you! Built like a gorilla and has a passion for Irish whisky and sixteen-year-old boys—and you think you can cure him in three days! Nuts!"

I didn't feel like arguing with him. "We might as well let him go now as lock him up for three or four months and then let him go, Sam. Why fool around with assault and battery charges when we can wait for him to murder somebody and then lock him up for good, eh, Sam? What's another victim more or less, as long as we get the killer?"

"That's what we're here for," he said stolidly. "To get killers." He scratched at his balding head. "I don't get you, Roy. I'd think you'd *want* these maniacs put away, after your—"

He stopped himself, wet his lips, and said: "O.K. You go ahead and take care of Smith. Get some sleep. I'm going to. I'll leave orders to call us both if anything breaks in the Donahue case."

I just nodded and walked out. I didn't want to hear any more.

But the door didn't close tightly, and I heard Kleek's voice as he spoke to the computer tech. "I just don't figure Roy. His wife died in a fire set by an arson bug, and he wants to—"

I kept on walking as the door clicked shut.

I was in my office at nine the next morning, after seven and a half hours of sleep on one of the bunks in the ready room. The business with Hammerlock Smith had taken more time than I had thought it would. The big, stupid ape had been in a vicious mood, reeking of whisky and roaring insults at everyone. His cursing was neither inventive nor colorful, consisting of only four unlovely words used over and over again in various combinations with ordinary ones, a total vocabulary of maybe a dozen words.

It had taken four cops, using night-sticks, to get him into the paddy wagon, and Dr. Brownlee had finally had to give him a blast of super-tranquilizer with a hypogun.

"Boy, Inspector," one of the officers had said, "don't let anyone ever tell you some of these guys aren't tough!"

I was looking over the written report. "What about this kid he accosted in the bar? Hurt bad?"

"Cracked rib, sprained wrist, and a bloody nose, sir. The doc said he'd be O.K."

"According to the report here, the kid was twenty-two years old. Smith usually picks 'em younger."

The cop grinned. "Smith had to get his eventually, sir. This guy looks pretty young, but he was a boxer in college. He probably couldn't've whipped Smith, but he had guts enough to try."

"Think he'll testify?"

"Said he would, sir. We already got his signature on the complaint while he was at the hospital. He's pretty mad."

Smith's record was long and ugly. Of the eight complaints made by young boys who had managed to brush off or evade Hammerlock's advances, six hadn't come to trial because there were no corroborating witnesses, and the charges had been dismissed. Two of the cases had come before a jury—and had resulted in acquittals. Cold sober, Smith presented a fairly decent picture. It was hard to convince a jury of ordinary citizens that so masculine-looking a specimen was homosexual.

The odd thing was that the psychopathic twist which got Hammerlock Smith into trouble had been able to get him out of it again. Both times, Smith's avowal that he had done no such disgusting thing had been corroborated by a lie detector test. Smith—when he was sober—had no recollection of his acts when drunk, and apparently honestly believed that he was incapable of doing what we knew he *had* done.

This time, though, we had him dead to rights. He had never made his play in a bar before, and we had three witnesses, plus an assault and battery charge. As Inspector Kleek had said, we get 'em eventually....

... But at what cost? How many teenage boys had been frightened or whipped into doing as he told them and then been too ashamed and sick with themselves to say anything? How many young lives had been befouled by Smith's abnormal lust?

And if Smith spent a year or two in Sing Sing, how many more would there be between the time he was released and the time he was caught again? And how long would it be before he obligingly hammered the life out of his young victim so that we could put him away permanently?

That was the "system" that Kleek—and a lot of other men on the Force swore by. That was the "system" that the boys in Homicide and in the Vice Squad thought I was trying to foul up by "babying" the zanies.

It's a hell of a great system, isn't it?

I called the hospital and talked to the doctor who had taken care of Smith's victim. Then I called Kleek to see if there had been any break in the Donahue case. There hadn't.

Finally, I called my son, Steve, at the apartment we shared, told him I wouldn't be home that night, and sacked out in the ready room.

By nine o'clock, I was ready to go back to work.

At nine thirty, Kleek called. His saggy face looked sleepier and more bored than ever. "No rest for the weary, Roy. I got a call on a killing on the Upper East Side. Some rich gal with too much time on her hands was having an all-night party, and she got herself shot to death. It looks like her husband did it, but there's plenty of money involved, and the Deputy Commissioner wants me to handle it personally, all the way through. I'm putting Lieutenant Shultz in charge of the Homicide end of the Donahue case, but I told him you were the man to listen to. He'll report directly to you if there's any new leads. O.K.?"

"O.K. with me, Sam." As I said, Kleek is a good cop in spite of his "system."

"The boys are out making the rounds," he went on, "bringing in all the men with conviction records and questioning the others. And we're combing the neighborhood for the kid's clothes. They might still be around somewhere. Shultz'll keep you posted."

"Fine, Sam. Happy hunting in High Society."

"Thanks, Roy. Take it easy."

At fifteen of eleven, the Police Commissioner called. He spent ten minutes telling me that I was going to be visited by a VIP and giving me exact instructions on how to handle the man. "I'm depending on you to take care of him, Roy," he said finally. "If we can get this program operating in other places, it will help us a lot. And if you need help from my office, grab the nearest phone."

"I'll do my best," I promised him. "And thanks, sir."

The Commissioner was a lawyer, not a cop, so he wasn't as tied to the system as Kleek and the others were. He was backing me all the way.

I punched Sergeant Vanney's number on the intercom. "Inspector Royall here, Sergeant. Do me a favor."

"Yes, sir."

"Go down to the library and get me a copy of Burke's 'Peerage.'"

"Burke's which, sir?"

I repeated it and spelled it for him. He didn't waste any time; he had it on my desk in less than twenty minutes. When the VIP arrived, I had already read up on Chief Inspector, The Duke of Acrington.

Here's how he was listed:

ACRINGTON, Seventh Duke of (Robert St. James Acrington) Baron Bennevis of Scotland, K. C. B.: Born 7 November 1950, B.S., M.S., Oxon., cum laude. *Married (1977) Lady Susan Burley, 2nd dau. Viscount Burley. 2 sons, Richard St. James, Philip William.*

Joined Metropolitan Police (1975); C. I. D. (1976); dep. Insp. (1980); Insp. (1984); Ch. Insp. (1990). Awarded George Medal for extraordinary heroism during the False War (1981).

Author Criminal Law and the United Nations, The Use of Forensic Psychology (*police textbook*), *and* The Night People (*fiction; under nom de plume R. A. James*).

Clubs: Royal Astronomical, Oxonian, Baker Street Irregulars.

Motto: Amicus Curiae.

I had to admit that I was impressed, but I decided to withhold any judgment until I had met the man.

He was right on time for his appointment. The car pulled up to the parking lot with a sergeant at the wheel, and I got a bird's eye view of him from my window as he got out of the car and headed for the door. I had to grin a little; the Commissioner had obviously wanted to take the visitor around personally—roll out the rug for royalty, so to speak—but he had had a conference scheduled with the Mayor and some Federal officials, and, after all, the duke was only here on police business, not as Ambassador from the Court of St. James. So he ended up being treated just as any visitor from Scotland Yard would be treated.

He was shown directly to my office, and I gave him a quick once-over as he came in the door. Tall, about six feet even; weight about 175, none of it surplus fat; light brown hair smoothed neatly back, almost no gray; eyes, blue-gray, with finely-etched lines around them that indicated they'd been formed by both smiles and frowns: face, rather long and bony, with thin, firm lips and a longish, thin, slightly curved nose. He wore good clothes, and he wore them well. His age, I knew; it was the same as mine. It was the first time I had ever seen a man who looked like a real aristocrat and a good cop rolled into one.

He had an easy smile on his face, and his eyes were taking me in, too. I stand an inch under six feet, but I'm a little broader across the shoulders than he, so the ten more pounds I carry doesn't make me look fat. My face is definitely not aristocratic—wide and square, with a nose that shows a slight bend where it was broken when I was a rookie, heavy, dark eyebrows, and hair that is receding a little on top and graying perceptibly at the sides. The eyes are a dark gray, and I'm well aware that the men under me call me "Old Flint-eye" when I put the pressure on them.

"I'm Chief Inspector Acrington," he said pleasantly, giving me a firm handshake.

"It's a pleasure to meet you, Your Grace," I said. "I'm Inspector Royall. Sit down, won't you?" I gestured toward one of the upholstered guest chairs, and sat down in the other one myself, so we wouldn't have the desk between us. "Have a good trip across?" I asked.

"Fine. Except, of course, for the noise."

"Noise?" I knew he'd come over in one of the Transatlantic Airways' new inertia-drive ships, and they're supposed to be fairly quiet.

His smile broadened a trifle. "Exactly. There wasn't any. I'm rather used to the vibration of jets, and these new jobs float along at a hundred thousand feet in the deadest silence you ever heard—if you'll pardon the oxymoron. Everybody chattered like a flight of starlings, just to keep the air full of sound."

I chuckled. "Maybe they'll put vibrators on them, just to make the people feel comfortable. I read that the men in the moon ships complain about the same thing."

"So I've heard. But, actually, the silence is a minor thing when one realizes the time one saves. When one is looking forward to something interesting, traveling can be deadly dull."

It was beautiful, the way he did it. He had told me plainly that he wanted to get down to business and cut the small talk, but he'd done it in such a way that the transition was frictionlessly smooth.

"Not much scenery up there," I said. "I hope you'll find what we're trying to do here has a few more points of interest."

"I'm quite sure it will, from what I've heard of your pilot project here. That's why I want to, well, sort of be a hanger-on for a few days, if that's all right with you."

Before I could answer, the phone blinked. I excused myself to the Duke and cut in. The image that came on the screen was almost myself, except that he had his mother's mouth and was twenty-odd years younger.

"Hi, Dad," he said, with that apologetic smile of his. "Sorry to bother you during office hours, but could I borrow fifty? Pay you back next week."

I threw a phony scowl at him. "Running short, eh? Have you been betting on the stickball teams again?"

He cast his eyes skyward, and raised the three fingers of his right hand. "Scout's Honor, Dad, I spent it on a new turbine for my ElectroFord." Then he lowered his hand and looked down from the upper regions. "I really did. I forgot that I was supposed to take Mary Ellen out this evening. Car-happy, I guess. Can you advance the fifty?"

I threw away my phony scowl and gave him a smile. "Sure, Stevie. How's Mary Ellen?"

"Swell. She's all excited about going to the Art Ball tonight—that's why I didn't want to disappoint her."

"Slow up, son," I told him, "you've already made your pitch and been accepted. You'll get your fifty, so don't push it. Want to come down here and pick it up?"

"Can do. And have I told you that you'll be invited to the wedding?"

118

"Thanks, pal. Can I give the groom away?" It was a family joke that we'd kicked back and forth ever since he had met Mary Ellen, two years before.

"Sure thing. See you in a couple of hours. Bye, Dad." He cut off, and I looked at the Duke.

"Sorry. Now, you were saying?"

"Perfectly all right." He smiled. "I have two of my own at home.

"At any rate, I was saying that the Criminal Investigation Department of New Scotland Yard has become interested in this experiment of yours, so I was sent over to get all the first-hand information I can. Frankly, I volunteered for the job; I was eager to come. There are plenty of skeptics at the Yard, I'll admit, but I'm not one of them. If the thing's workable, I want to see it used in England."

Here was another man who wasn't tied to the "system."

"D'you mind if I ask some questions?" he said.

"Go ahead, Your Grace. If I can't answer 'em, I'll say so."

"Thanks. First off, I'll tell you what I *do* know—get my own knowledge of the background straight, so to speak. Now, as I understand it, the courts have agreed—temporarily, at least—that any person convicted of certain types of crimes must undergo a psychiatric examination before sentencing. Right?"

"That's right."

"Then, depending on the result of that examination, the magistrate of the court may sentence the offender to undertake psychiatric therapy instead of sending him to a penal institution, such time in therapy not to exceed the maximum time of imprisonment originally provided for the offense under the law.

"His sentence is suspended, in other words, if he will agree to the therapy. If, after he is released by the psychiatrists, he behaves himself, he is not imprisoned. If he misbehaves, he must serve out the original sentence, plus any new sentence that may be imposed. Have I got it straight so far?"

"Perfectly."

"As I understand it, you've had astounding success." He looked, in spite of what he had said about skepticism, as though he thought the reports he'd heard were exaggerated.

"So far," I said evenly, "not a single one of our 'patients' has failed us."

He looked amazed, but he didn't doubt me. "And you've been in operation for how long?"

"A little over a year since the first case. But I think the record will stand the same way five, ten, fifty years from now.

"You see, Your Grace, we don't *dare* lose a man. If one of our tame zanies goes haywire again, the courts will stop this pilot project *fast*. There's a lot of pressure against us.

"In the first place, we only work with repeaters. You know the type. The world is full of them. The boys that are picked up over and over again for the same kind of crime."

He nodded. "They're the ones we wait for. The ones we catch, convict, and send to prison—and then wait until they get out, and then wait some more until they commit their next crime, so that we can catch them and start the whole cycle over again."

"That's them," I said. "When they're out, they're just between crimes, that's all. And that puts the police in a hell of a position, doesn't it? You *know* they're going to fall again; you know that they're going to rob, or hurt, or kill someone. But there's nothing you can do about it. You're helpless. No police force has enough men to enable a cop to be assigned to every known repeater and follow him night and day.

"In this state, if a man is convicted of a felony for a fourth time, a life sentence is mandatory. *But that means that at least four victims have to be sacrificed before the dangerous man is removed from society!*"

The Duke nodded thoughtfully. "'Sacrifice' is the word. Go on."

"Now, the type of crime we're working with—the kind we expect future laws to apply to—is strictly limited. It must be a crime of violence against a human being, or a crime of destruction in which there is a grave danger that human lives may be lost. The sex maniac, the firebug, or the goon who gets a thrill out of beating people. Or the reckless driver who has proven that he can't be trusted behind the wheel of a car.

"We can't touch the kleptomaniac or the common drunk or the drug addict. They're already provided for under other laws. And those habits are not, *by themselves*, dangerous to the lives of others. A good many of our kind of zany *do* drink or take drugs—about fifty per cent of them. But what they're sentenced for is crimes of violence, not for guzzling hooch or mainlining heroin."

My phone chimed. It was Lieutenant Shultz, of Homicide. His square, blocky face held a trace of excitement. "Inspector Royall, Inspector Kleek told me to report to you if there was any news in the Donahue case."

"What is it, Lieutenant?"

"We're pretty sure of our man. Scrapings from the kid's fingernails gave us his blood type. The computer narrowed the list down quite a bit with that data. Then, a few minutes ago, one of the boys found the kid's clothes stuffed in with some trash paper in the back stairwell of a condemned building just a couple of blocks from where we found her last night.

"And—get this, Inspector!—she was wearing a pair of those shiny patent-leather shoes, practically brand-new, and they have prints all over them! His are over hers, since he was the last one to handle them, and there's only the two sets of prints! We just now got positive identification."

"Grab him and bring him in," I said. "I'll be right down. I want to talk to him."

His face fell a little. "Well, it isn't going to be as easy as all that, sir. You see, we'd already checked at his last known address, earlier this morning, before we got the final check on the blood type. This guy left the rooming house he was staying in—checked out two days ago, just a short time after the girl was killed. I figured that looked queer at the time, so I had two of my men start tracing him in particular. But there's not a sign of him so far."

I untensed myself. "O.K. What's his record?"

"Periodic drunk. Goes for weeks without touching the stuff, then he goes out on a binge that lasts for a week sometimes.

"Name's Lawrence Nestor, alias Larry Nestor. Twenty-eight years old, six feet one inch, slight build, but considered fairly strong. Brown hair, brown eyes. Speaks with a lisp due to a dental defect; the lisp becomes more noticeable when he's drinking." He turned the page of the report he was reading from. "Arrested for drunkenness four times in the past five years, got off with a fine when he pleaded guilty. He molested a little girl two years ago and was picked up for questioning, but nothing came of it. The girl hadn't been physically hurt, and she couldn't make a positive identification, so he was released from custody.

"Officers on duty in the neighborhood report that he has frequently been seen talking to small children, usually girls, but he wasn't seen to molest them in any way, and there were no complaints from parents, so no action could be taken."

Lieutenant Shultz looked up from the paper. "He's had all kinds of jobs, but he can't hold 'em very long. Goes on a binge, doesn't show up for work, so they fire him. He's a pretty good short-order cook, and that's the kind of work he likes, if he can talk a lunch room into hiring him. He's also been a bus boy, a tavern porter, and a janitor.

"One other thing: The superintendent at the place where he was staying reports that he had an unusual amount of money on him—four or five hundred dollars he thinks. Doesn't know where Nestor got the money, but he's been boozing it up for the past five days. Bought new clothes—hat, suit, shoes, and so on. Living high on the hog, I guess."

I thought for a minute. If he had money, he could be anywhere in the world by now. On the other hand—

"Look, Lieutenant, you haven't said anything to the newsmen yet, have you?"

He looked surprised. "No. I called you first. But I figured they could help us. Plaster his picture and name all over the area, and somebody will be bound to recognize him."

"Somebody might kill him, too, and I don't want that. Look at it this way: If he had sense enough to get out of the local area two days ago and really get himself lost, then it won't hurt to wait twenty-four hours or so to release the story. On the other hand, if he's still in the city or over in Jersey, he could still get out before the news was so widespread that he'd be spotted by very many people.

"But if he's still drinking and thinks he's safe, we may be able to get a lead on him. I have a hunch he's still in the city. So hold off on that release to the newsmen as long as you can. Don't let it leak.

"Meanwhile, check all the transportation terminals. Find out if he's ever been issued a passport. If he has, check the foreign consuls here in the city to see if he got a visa. Notify the FBI; they're back in it now, since there's a chance that he may have crossed a state line—unlawful flight to avoid prosecution.

"And tell the boys that do the footwork that they're to say that the guy they're looking for is wanted by the Missing Persons Bureau—that he left home and his wife is looking for him. Don't connect him up with the Donahue case at all. Have every beat patrolman in the city on the lookout for a drunk with a lisp, but tell them the same story about the wife; I don't want any leaks at all.

"I'll call the Commissioner right away to get his O.K., because I don't want either one of us to get in hot water over this. If he's with us, we'll go ahead as planned; if he's not, we'll just have to call in the newsmen. O.K.?"

"Sure, Inspector. Whatever you say. I'll get right to work on it. You'll have the Commissioner call me?"

"Right. So long. Call me if anything happens."

I had added the bit about calling the Commissioner because I wasn't sure but what Kleek would decide I was wrong in handling the case and let the story out "accidentally." But I had to be careful not to make Shultz think I was trying to show my muscles. I called the Commissioner, got his O.K., and turned my attention back to my guest.

He had been listening with obvious interest. "Another one of your zanies, eh?"

"One that went too far, Your Grace. We didn't get to him in time." I spent five or six minutes giving him the details of the Donahue case.

"The same old story," he said when I had finished. "If your pilot project here works out, maybe that kind of slaughter can be eliminated." Then he smiled. "Do you know something? You're one of the few Americans I've ever met, outside your diplomats, who can address a person as 'Your Grace' and make it sound natural. Some people look at me as though they expected me to be all decked out in a ducal coronet and full ermines, ready for a Coronation. Your Commissioner, for instance. He seems quite a nice chap, but he also seems a bit overawed at a title. You seem perfectly relaxed."

I considered that for a moment. "I imagine it's because he tends to look at you as a Duke who has taken up police work as a sort of gentlemanly hobby."

"And you?"

"I guess I tend to think of you as a good cop who had the good fortune to be born the eldest son of a Duke."

His smile suddenly became very warm. "Thank you," he said sincerely. "Thank you very much."

There came the strained silence that sometimes follows when an honest compliment is passed between two men who have scarcely met. I broke it by pointing at the plaque on the front of my desk and giving him a broad grin. "Or maybe it's just the kind of blood that flows in my veins."

He looked at the little plaque that said *Inspector Royal C. Royall* and laughed pleasantly. "I like to think that it's a little bit of both."

The intercom on my desk flashed, and the sergeant's voice said: "Inspector, a couple of the boys just brought in a man named Manewiscz. A stolen car was run into a fire plug over on Fifth Avenue near 99th Street. A witness has positively identified Manewiscz as the driver who ran away before the squad car arrived."

"Sidney Manewiscz?" I asked. "Manny the Moog?"

"That's the one. He's got a record of stealing cars for joyrides. He insists on talking to you."

"Bring him in," I said. "I'll talk to him. And get hold of Dr. Brownlee."

"Excuse me," I said to the Duke. "Business." He started to get up, but I said, "That's all right, Your Grace; you might as well sit in on it." He relaxed back into the chair.

Two cops brought in Manewiscz, a short, nervous man with a big nose and frightened brown eyes.

"What's the trouble, Manny?" I asked.

"Nothing, Inspector; I'm telling you, I didn't do nothing. I'm walking along Fifth Avenoo when all of a sudden these cops pull up in a squad-car and some fat jerk in the back seat is hollering that I am the guy he seen get out of a smashup on 99th Street, which is a good three blocks from where I am walking. Besides which, I have not driven a car for over a year now, and I have been in all ways a law-abiding citizen and a credit to the family and the community."

"Do you know the fat guy?" I asked. "The guy who fingered you for the boys?"

"I never had the pleasure of seeing him before," said Manny the Moog, "but, on the other hand, I do not expect to forget his fat face between now and the next time we meet."

At that point, Dr. Brownlee came through the door.

"Hello, Inspector," he said with a quick smile. He saw Manewiscz then, and his eyebrows went up. "What are you doing here, Manny?"

"I am here, Doc, because the two gentlemen in uniform whom you see standing on both sides of me extend a polite invitation to accompany them here, although I am not in the least guilty of the thing they say I do which causes them to issue this invitation."

I explained what had happened and Brownlee shook his head slowly without saying anything for a moment. Then he said, "Come on in my office, Manny; I want to talk to you for a few minutes. O.K., Inspector?" He glanced at me.

"Sure." I waved him and Manny away. "You boys stay here," I told the patrolmen, "Manny will be all right." As soon as the door closed behind Dr. Brownlee and Manewiscz I said: "You two brought the witness in, too, didn't you?"

"Yes, sir," said one. The other nodded.

"You'd better do a little more careful checking on him. He may be simply mistaken, or he may have been the actual driver. See if he's been in any trouble before."

"The sergeant's already doing that, sir," said the one who had spoken before. "Meanwhile, maybe we better go out and have a little talk with the guy."

"Take it easy, he may be a perfectly respectable citizen."

"Yes, sir," he said. "We'll just ask him a few questions."

They left, and I noticed that the Duke was looking rather puzzled, but he didn't ask any questions, so I couldn't answer any.

The intercom lit up, and I flipped the switch. "Yes?"

"I just checked up on the witness," said the sergeant. "No record. His identification checks out O.K. Thomas H. Wilson, an executive at the City-Chemical Bank; lives on Central Park West. The lab says that the driver of the car wore gloves."

"Thank Wilson for his information, let him go, and tell him we'll call him if we need him. Lay it on thick about what a good citizen he is. Make him happy."

"Right."

I switched off and started to say something to my guest, but the intercom lit up again. "Yeah?"

"Got a call-in from Officer McCaffery, the beat man on Broadway between 108th and 112th. He's got a lead on the guy you're looking for."

"Tell him we'll be right over. Where is he?"

The sergeant told me, and I cut off.

I took out my gun and spun the cylinder, checking it from force of habit more than anything else, since I always check and clean it once a day, anyhow. I slid it back into its holster and turned to the Duke, who was already on his feet.

"Did the Commissioner give you a Special Badge?" I asked him.

"Yes, he did." He pulled it out of his inside pocket and showed it to me.

"Good. I'll have the sergeant fill out a temporary pistol permit, and—"

"I don't have a pistol, Inspector," he said. "I—"

"That's all right; we'll issue you one. We can—"

He shook his head. "Thanks, I'd rather not. I've never used a pistol except when I've gone out after a criminal who is known to be armed and dangerous. I don't think Lawrence Nestor is very dangerous to adult males, and I doubt that he's armed." He hefted the walking stick he'd been carrying. "This will do nicely, thank you."

The way he said it was totally inoffensive, but it made me feel as though I were about to go out rabbit hunting with an elephant gun. "Force of habit," I said. "In New York, a cop would feel naked without a gun. But I assure you that I have no intention of shooting Mr. Nestor unless he takes a shot at me first."

Just as we were leaving, Dr. Brownlee met us in the outer room.

"All right if I let Manny the Moog go, Roy?"

"Sure, Doc; if you say so." I didn't have any time for introductions just then; Chief Inspector the Duke of Acrington and I kept going.

Eight minutes later, I pulled up to the post where Officer McCaffery was waiting. Since I'd already talked to him over the radio, all he did was stroll off as soon as we pulled up. I didn't want everyone in the neighborhood to know that there was something afoot. His Grace and I climbed out of the car and walked up toward a place called Flanagan's Bar.

It was a small place, the neighborhood type, with an old-fashioned air about it. Two or three of the men looked up as we came in, and then went back to the more important business of drinking. We went back to the far end of the bar, and the bartender came over, a short, heavy man, with the build of a heavyweight boxer and hands half again as big as mine. He had dark hair, a square face, a dimpled chin, and calculating blue eyes.

"What'll it be?" he said in a friendly voice.

"Couple of beers," I told him.

I waited until he came back before I identified myself. Officer McCaffery had told me that the bartender was trustworthy, but I wanted to make sure I had the right man.

"You Lee Darcey?" I asked when he brought back the beers.

"That's right."

I flashed my badge. "Is there anywhere we can talk?"

"Sure. The back room, right through there." He turned to the other bartender. "Take over for a while, Frankie." Then he ducked under the bar and followed the Duke and me into the back room.

We sat down, and I showed him the picture of Lawrence Nestor. "I understand you've seen this guy."

He picked up the picture and cocked an eyebrow at it. "Well, I wouldn't swear to it in court, Inspector, but it sure looks like the fellow who was in here this afternoon—this evening, rather, from six to about six-thirty. I don't come on duty until six, and he was here when I got here."

It was just seven o'clock. If the man was Nestor, we hadn't missed him by more than half an hour.

"Notice anything about his voice?"

"I noticed the lisp, if that's what you mean."

"Did he talk much?"

Darcey shook his head. "Not a lot. Just sat there and drank, mostly. Had about three after I came on."

"What was he drinking?"

"Whisky. Beer chaser." He grinned. "He tips pretty well."

"Has he ever been in here before?"

"Not that I know of. He might've come in in the daytime. You'd have to check with Mickey, the day man."

"Was he drunk?"

"Not that I could tell. I wouldn't have served him if he was," he said righteously.

I said, "Darcey, if he comes back in here ... let's see—Can you shut off that big sign out front from behind the bar?"

"Sure."

"O.K. If he comes in, shut off the sign. We'll have men here in less than a minute. He isn't dangerous or anything, so just act natural and give him whatever he orders. I don't want him scared off. Understand?"

"I got you."

His Grace and I went outside, and I used my pocket communicator to instruct a patrol car to cover Flanagan's Bar from across the street, and I called for extra plainclothesmen to cover the area.

"Now what?" asked His Grace.

"Now we go barhopping," I said. "He's probably still drinking, but it isn't likely that he'll find many little girls at this time of night. He's probably got a room nearby."

At that point, a blue ElectroFord pulled up in front of us. Stevie stuck his head out and said: "Your office said you'd be around here somewhere. Remember me, Dad?"

I covered my eyes with one hand in mock horror. "My God, the fifty!" Then I dropped the hand toward my billfold. "I'm sorry, son; I got wrapped up in this thing and completely forgot." That made two apologies in two minutes, and I began to have the uneasy feeling that I had suddenly become a vaguely repellant mass of thumbs and left feet.

I handed him the fifty, and, at the same time, said: "Son, I want you to meet His Grace, Chief Inspector the Duke of Acrington. Your Grace, this is my son, Steven Royall."

As they shook hands, Steve said: "It's a pleasure to meet Your Grace. I read about the job you did in the Camberwell poisoning case. That business of winding the watch was wonderful."

"I'm flattered, Mr. Royall," said the Duke, "but I must admit that I got a great deal more credit in that case than was actually due me. Establishing the time element by winding the watch was suggested to me by another man, who wouldn't allow his name to be mentioned in the press."

I reminded myself to read up on the Duke's cases. Evidently he was better known than I had realized. Sometimes a man gets too wrapped up in his own work.

"I'm sorry," Stevie said, "but I've got to get going. I hope to see you again, Your Grace. So long, Dad—and thanks."

"So long, son," I said. "Take it easy."

His car moved off down the street, gathering speed.

"Fine boy you have there," the Duke said.

"Thanks. Shall we go on with our pub crawling?"

"Let's."

By two o'clock in the morning, we had heard nothing, found nothing. The Duke looked tired, and I knew that I was.

"A few hours sleep wouldn't hurt either one of us," I told His Grace. "It's a cinch that Nestor won't be able to find any little girls at this hour of the morning, and I have a feeling that he probably bought himself a bottle and took it up to his room with him."

"You're probably right," the Duke said wearily.

"Look," I said, "there's no point in your going all the way down to your hotel. My place is just across town, I have plenty of room, it will be no trouble to put you up, and we'll be ready to go in the morning. O.K.?"

He grinned. "Worded that way, the invitation is far too forceful to resist. I'm sold. I accept."

By that time, we had left several dollars worth of untasted beers sitting around in various bars on the West Side, so when I arrived at my apartment on the East Side, I decided that it was time for two tired cops to have a decent drink. The

Duke relaxed on the couch while I mixed a couple of Scotch-and-waters. He lit a cigarette and blew out a cloud of smoke with a sigh.

"Here, this will put sparks in your blood. Just a second, and I'll get you an ash tray." I went into the kitchen and got one of the ash trays from the top shelf and brought it back into the living room. Just as I put it down on the arm of the couch next to His Grace, the buzzer announced that there was someone at the front door downstairs.

I went over to the peeper screen and turned it on. The face was big-jawed and hard-mouthed, and there was scar tissue in the eyebrows and on the cheeks. He looked tough, but he also looked worried and frightened.

I could see him, but he couldn't see me, so I said: "What's the trouble, Joey?"

A look of relief came over his face. "Can I see ya, Inspector? I saw your light was on. It's important." He glanced to his right, toward the doorway. "Real important."

"What's it all about, Joey?"

"Take a look out your window, Inspector. Across the street. They're friends of Freddy Velasquez. They been following me ever since I got off work."

"Just a second," I said. I went over to the window that overlooks the street and looked down. There were two men there, all right, looking innocently into a delicatessen window. But I knew that Joey Partridge wasn't kidding, and that he knew who the men were. I went back to the peeper screen just as Joey buzzed my signal again. "I buzzed again so they won't know you're home," he said before I could ask any questions. "Freddy must've found out about my hands, Inspector. According to the word I got, they ain't carrying guns—just blackjacks and knucks."

"O.K., Joey. Come on up, and I'll call a squad car to take you home."

He gave me a bitter grin. "And have 'em coming after me again and again until they catch me? No, thanks, Inspector. In one minute, I'm going to walk across and ask 'em what they're following me for."

"You can't do that, Joey!"

He looked hurt. "Inspector, since when it is against the law to ask a couple of guys how come they're following you? I just thought I oughta tell ya, that's all. So long."

I knew there was no point in arguing with Joey Partridge. I turned and said: "Want some action, Your Grace?"

But he was already on his feet, holding that walking stick of his. "Anything you say."

"Come on, then. We'll take the fire escape; the elevator is too slow. The fire escape will let us out in the alley, and we won't by outlined by the light in the foyer."

I already had the bedroom door open. I ran over to the window, opened it, and started down the steel stairway. The Duke was right behind me. It was only three floors down.

"That Joey is too smart for his own good," I said, "but he's right. This is the only way to work it. Otherwise, they'd have him in the hospital eventually—or maybe dead."

"He looked like a man who could take care of himself," the Duke said.

"That's just it. He can't. Come on."

The ladder to the street slid down smoothly and silently, and I thanked God for modern fire prevention laws. When we reached the street, I wondered where they could have gone to so quickly. Then the Duke said: "There! In that darkened area-way next to the little shop!" And he started running. His legs were longer than mine, and he reached the area-way a good five yards ahead of me.

Joey had managed to evade them for a short while, but they had cornered him, and one of them knocked him down just as the Duke came on the scene. The other had swung at his ribs with a blackjack as he dropped, and the first aimed a kick at Joey's midriff, but Joey rolled away from it.

Then the two thugs heard our footsteps and turned to meet us. If we'd been in uniform, they might have run; as it was, they stood their ground.

But not for long.

The Duke didn't use that stick as though it were a club, swinging it like a baseball bat. That would be as silly as using an overhand stab with a dagger. He used it the way a fencer would use a foil, and the hard, blunt end of it sank into the first thug's solar plexus with all the drive of the Duke's right arm and shoulder behind it. The thug gave a hoarse scream as all the air was driven from his lungs, and he dropped to the pavement.

The second man came in with his blackjack swinging. His hand stopped suddenly as his wrist met the deadly stick, but the blackjack kept on going, bouncing harmlessly off the nearby wall as it flew from nerveless fingers.

That stick never stopped moving. On the backswing, it thwacked resoundingly against the thug's ribcage. He grunted in pain and tried to charge forward to grapple with the Englishman. But His Grace was grace itself as he leaped backwards and then thrust forward with that wooden snake-tongue. The thug practically impaled himself on it. He stopped and twisted and was suddenly sick all over the pavement. Almost gently, the Duke tapped him across the side of his head, and he fell into his own mess.

It was all over before I'd even had a chance to mix in. I stood there, holding an eleven millimeter Magnum revolver in my hand and feeling vaguely foolish.

I reholstered the thing and walked over to where Joey Partridge was propping himself up to a sitting position. His right eye was bruised, and there was a trickle of blood running from the corner of his mouth, but he was grinning all the way across his battered face. And he wasn't looking at me; he was looking at the Duke.

"You hurt, Joey?" I asked. I knew he wasn't hurt badly; he'd taken worse punishment than that in his life.

He looked at me still grinning. "Hurt? You're right I'm hurt, Inspector! Them goons tried to kill me. Let's see—assault and battery, assault with a deadly weapon, assault with intent to kill, assault with intent to maim, attempted murder, and—" He paused. "What else we got, Inspector?"

"We'll think on plenty," I said. "Can you stand up?"

"Sure I can stand up. I want to shake the hand of your buddy, there. Geez! I ain't seen anything like that since I used to watch Bat Masterson on TV, when I was a little kid!"

"Joey, this is Chief Inspector the Duke Acrington, of Scotland Yard. Inspector, this is Joey Partridge, the greatest amateur boxer this country has ever produced."

Amazingly enough, Joey extended his hand. "Pleased t'meetcha, Inspector! Uh—watch the hand. Sorta tender. That was great! Duke, did you say?" He looked at me. "You mean he's a real English Duke?" He looked back at Acrington. "I never met a Duke before!" But by that time he had taken his hand away from the Duke's grasp.

"It's a pleasure to meet you, Joey," the Duke said warmly. "I liked the way you cleaned up on that Russian during the '72 Olympics."

Joey said to me, "He remembers me! How d'ya like that?"

One of the downed thugs began to groan, and I said, "We'd better get the paddy wagon around to pick these boys up. You'll prefer charges, Joey?"

"Damn right I will! I didn't let myself get slugged for nothing!"

It was nearly forty-five minutes later that the Duke and I found ourselves in my apartment again. The ice in our drinks had melted, so I dumped them and prepared fresh ones. The Duke took his, drained half of it in three fast swallows, and said: "Ahhhhhh! I needed that."

We heard a key in the door, and His Grace looked at me.

"That's my son," I said. "Back from his date."

Steve came in looking happy. "You still awake, Dad? A cop ought to get his sleep. Good morning, Your Grace. Both of you look sleepy."

Stevie didn't. He'd danced with Mary Ellen until four, and he still looked as though he could walk five miles without tiring. Me, I felt about as full of snap as a soda cracker in a Turkish bath. The three of us talked for maybe ten minutes, and then we hit the hay.

Three and a half hours of sleep isn't enough for anybody, but it was all we could afford to take. By eight-thirty, the Duke and I were in my office, sloshing down black coffee, and, half an hour after that, we were cruising up Amsterdam Avenue on the second day of our hunt for Mr. Lawrence Nestor.

Since we were now reasonably sure that our man was in the area, I ordered the next phase of the search into operation. There were squads of men making a house-to-house canvass of every hotel, apartment house, and rooming house in the area—and there are thousands of them. A flying squad took care of the hotels first; they were the most likely. Since we knew exactly what day Nestor had arrived, we narrowed our search down to the records for that day. Nestor might not use his own name; of course, but the photograph and description ought to help. And, since Nestor didn't have a job, his irregular schedule and his drinking habits might make him stand out, though there were plenty of places where those traits would simply make him one of the boys. It still looked like a long, hard search.

And then we got our break.

At 9:17 am, Lieutenant Holmquist's voice snapped over my car phone: "Inspector Royall; Holmquist here. Child missing in Riverside Park. Officer Ramirez just called in from 111th and Riverside."

"Got it!"

I cut left and gunned the car eastward. I hit a green light at Broadway, so I didn't need to use the siren. Within two minutes, we had pulled up beside the curb where an officer was standing with a woman in tears. The Duke and I got out of the car.

We walked over to her calmly, although neither one of us felt very calm. There's no point in disturbing an already excited mother—or aunt or whatever she was.

The officer threw me a salute. I returned it and said to the sobbing woman, "Now, just be calm, ma'am. Tell us what happened."

It all came out in a torrent. She'd been sitting on one of the benches, reading a newspaper, and she'd looked around and little Shirley was gone. Yes, Shirley was her daughter. How old? Seven and a half. How long ago was this? Fifteen minutes, maybe. She hadn't been worried at first; she'd walked up and down, calling the girl's name, but hadn't gotten any answer. Then she saw the policeman, and ... and—

And she broke down into tears again.

It was the same thing that had happened a few days before. I had already ordered extra men put on the Riverside and Central Park details, but a cop can't be everywhere at once.

"I've got the rest of the boys beating the brush between here and the river," Officer Ramirez said. "She might have gone down one of the paths on the other side of the wall."

"She wouldn't go too near the river," the woman sobbed. "I just know she wouldn't." She sounded as though she were trying to convince herself and failing miserably.

Nobody said anything about Nestor; the poor woman was bad enough off without adding more horror to the pictures she was conjuring up in her mind.

"We'll find her," I said soothingly, "don't you worry about that. You're pretty upset. We'll have the police doctor look you over and maybe give you a tranquilizer or something to make you feel better." No point in telling her that the doctor might be needed for a more serious case. "Keep an eye on her till the doctor comes, Ramirez. Meanwhile, we'll look around for the little girl."

I walked over to the wall and looked down. I could see uniformed police walking around, covering the ground carefully.

Riverside Park runs along the eastern edge of Manhattan Island, between Riverside Drive and the Hudson River, from 72nd Street on the south to 129th Street on the north. In the area where we were, there is a flat, level, grassy area about a block wide, where there are walks and benches to sit on. The eastern boundary of this area is marked by a retaining wall that runs parallel with the river. Beyond the wall, the ground slopes down sharply to the Hudson River, going under the elevated East Side Highway which carries express traffic up and down the island. The retaining wall is cut through at intervals, and winding steps go down the steep slope. There are bushes and trees all over down there.

I thought for a minute, then said, "Suppose it was Nestor. How did he get her away? It's a cinch he didn't just scoop her up in broad daylight and go trotting off with her under his arm."

"Precisely what I was thinking," the Duke agreed. "There was no scream or disturbance of that kind. Could he have lured her away, do you think?"

"Possible, but not likely. Little girls in New York are warned about that sort of thing from the time they're in diapers. If she were five years old, it might be more probable, but little girls who are approaching eight are pretty wise little girls."

"It follows, then, that she went somewhere of her own accord and he followed her. D'you agree?"

"That sounds most reasonable," I said. "The next question is: Where?"

"Yes. And why didn't she tell her mother where she was going?"

I gave him a sour grin. "Elementary, my dear Duke. Because her mother had forbidden her to go there. And, from the way she was talking, I gather the mother had expressly directed her to stay away from the river." I looked back over the retaining wall again. "But it just doesn't sound right, does it? Surely someone would have seen any sort of attack like that. Of course, it's possible that she *did* fall in the river, and that this case doesn't have anything to do with Nestor at all, but—"

"It doesn't feel that way to me, either," said the Duke.

"Let's go talk to the mother again," I said. "There are plenty of men down there now; they don't need us."

The woman, Mrs. Ebbermann, had calmed down a little. The police surgeon had given her a tranquilizer with a hypogun, Officer Ramirez was getting everything down in his notebook, and his belt recorder was running.

"No," she was saying, "I'm sure she didn't go home. That's the first place I looked after she didn't answer when I called. We live down the block there. I thought she might have gone home to go to the bathroom or something—but I'm sure she would have told me." She choked a little. "Oh, Shirley, baby! Where are you? Where *are* you?"

I started to ask her a question, but she suddenly said: "Shirley, baby, next time, I promise, you can bring your water gun with you to the park, if you'll just come back to Mommie now! Please, Shirley, baby! Please!"

I glanced at the Duke. He gave me the same sort of look.

"What was that about a water gun, Mrs. Ebbermann?" I asked casually.

"Oh, she wanted to bring her water gun with her, poor baby. But I made her leave it at home—I was afraid she might squirt people with it. But I shouldn't have done that! She's a good girl! She wouldn't squirt anybody!"

"Sure not, Mrs. Ebbermann. Does Shirley have a key to your apartment?"

"Yes. I gave her her own key, a pretty one, with her initials on it, for her seventh birthday, so she wouldn't have to push the buzzer when she came home from school."

"Where's your husband?" I asked taking a look at Ramirez' notebook to get her address.

"Shirley's father? Somewhere in Boston. We've been separated for two years. But I wish he were here!"

"Would you give me the key to your apartment, Mrs. Ebbermann? We'd like to take a look around."

She gave me a key. "But she's not there. I told you, that's the first place I looked."

"I know," I said. "We just want to look around. We won't disturb anything."

Then His Grace and I got out of there as fast as we could.

I keyed open the front door of the apartment building, and we went inside. Neither of us said anything. There was no need to. We knew what must have happened, we could see it unfolding as plainly as if we'd watched it happen.

Nestor had seen Shirley sneak off from her mother and had followed her. In order to get into the building, he must have come right in with her, right behind her when she unlocked the outer door. Then what?

The chances were a billion to one against his ever having been in the building before, so it stood to reason that all he would have been doing is watching for an opportunity and—the right place.

The foyer itself? No. Too much chance of being seen. The basement? Unlikely. He must have followed her into the elevator, and she would have pushed the button for the seventh floor, where her apartment was, so there wouldn't be much likelihood of his getting a chance to see the basement. Besides, there was a chance that he might run into the janitor.

The Duke and I went into the old-fashioned self-service elevator, and I pushed number seven. The doors slid shut, and the car started up. The roof? No. Too much danger of being seen from other buildings higher than this one.

Where, then? I looked at the control panel of the elevator. The button for the basement was controlled by a key; only the employees were allowed in the basement, so that place was ruled out absolutely.

I began to get the feeling that we were on a wild goose chase, after all. "What do you think?" I asked His Grace.

"I can't imagine where he might have taken her. We may have to search the whole building."

The car stopped at the seventh door, and we stepped out as the doors slid open. The hallways stretched to either side, but there were no apparent hiding places. I went over to the stairwell, which was right next to the elevator shaft and looked up and down. No place there, either.

Then it hit me.

Again, I could see Nestor, like a scene unfolding on a TV drama, still following little Shirley. Had he spoken to her in the elevator? Maybe. Maybe not. He was still undecided, so he followed her to the door of her apartment. Wait—very likely, he *had* made friends with her on the elevator. He saw her push button seven—

Well, well! Do you live on the seventh floor?

Yes, I do.

Then we're neighbors. I live on the seventh, too. I just moved in. Do you live with your mommie and daddy?

Just my mommie. My daddy doesn't live with us anymore.

And, since he knew that mommie was in the park, he could guess that the apartment was empty.

All that went through my mind like a bolt of lightning. I said: "The apartment! Come on!"

The Duke, looking a little puzzled, followed me to the door of 706. I put my ear against the door and listened. Nothing. Then I eased the key in and flung the door open.

No one in the living room. I raced for the bedroom. No one in there, either, but the clothes closet door was shut.

When I opened it, we saw a small, dark-haired girl lying naked and unconscious on the floor.

Then there were noises from the front room. The sound of a door opening and closing, and the clatter of hurrying footsteps in the hall outside.

We both turned and ran.

In the hallway, we could hear the footsteps going down the stairwell. The slow elevator was out of the question. We took off down the stairs after him. He had a head start of about a floor and a half, and kept it all the way down. We saw the door swinging shut as we arrived in the foyer. Outside, we saw our man running toward the corner. I started to reach for my gun, but there were too many people around. I couldn't risk a shot.

And then that amazing walking stick came into action again. The Duke took a few running steps forward and hurled it like a javelin, the heavy silver head forward. Robin Hood couldn't have done better with an arrow. When the silver knob hit the back of the running man's head, he fell forward to the sidewalk.

He was still struggling to get up when we grabbed him.

The Duke and I were waiting for Dr. Brownlee when he came back from talking to Lawrence Nestor in his cell. "He's one of our zanies, all right," he said sadly. "A very sick man."

"He's lucky he wasn't lynched," I said. "Did he tell you what happened?"

Brownlee nodded. "Just about the way you had it figured. He had the little girl's clothes off when her mother came back. He heard her putting her key in the door, so he grabbed Shirley and dragged her into the closet with him. The mother didn't search the place at all; she just went through the main rooms, called her daughter's name a few times and then left."

"That's what threw us off at first," I said. "We both accepted Mrs. Ebbermann's word that Shirley wasn't in the apartment. Then I realized that she wouldn't have taken time to look in all the closets. Why should she? As far as she knew, there wasn't any reason for Shirley to hide from her."

"It's a good thing Mrs. Ebbermann did come back." Dr. Brownlee said. "That was the only thing that saved the girl from rape and death. Nestor was so unnerved that he just left her in the closet, still unconscious from the blow he'd given her.

"Any normal man would have gotten out of there right then. Not Nestor. He went looking for a drink. Fortunately, he found a bottle of whisky in the kitchen. He was just getting in the mood to go back in after the girl when you two came charging in.

"He saw you run to the bedroom, so he knew the girl's mother must have called for help. He decided it was time to run. Too late, of course."

"Too late for a lot of things." I said. "Much too late far Angela Donahue, for instance. And, as a matter of fact, we were so close to being too late with Shirley Ebbermann that I don't even want to think about it. I should have let Shultz go ahead and tell the newsmen. At least people would have been warned."

"There's no way of knowing," said the Duke, "But I think there's just as good a chance that he'd have gotten his hands on some other little girl, even if the warning had gone out. There will always be parents who don't pay enough attention to what their children are doing. They may blame themselves if something happens, but that may be too late. As it happens, we *weren't* too late. Let's be thankful for that.

"By the way, am I wrong in assuming that Nestor will not get your psychotherapy treatment?"

"No, you're right," I said. "The warden at Sing Sing will be taking care of him from now on." I turned to Brownlee and said: "Which reminds me—what's going to be the disposition on the Hammerlock Smith case?"

"I talked to Judge Whittaker and the D.A. Your recommendation pulled a lot of weight with them. They agreed that if Smith will plead guilty to felonious assault and agree to therapy, he'll get off with eighteen months, suspended. When I release him, he'll never bother young boys again."

The Duke looked puzzled. "Hammerlock Smith? Odd Name. What's he up for?"

I told him about Hammerlock Smith.

He thought it over for a while, then said: "Just what is it you do to men like that? How can you be so sure he'll never hurt anyone again?"

Brownlee started to answer him, but a uniformed officer put his head in the door. "Excuse me, Dr. Brownlee, the District Attorney would like to talk to you."

Brownlee excused himself and followed the cop out, leaving me to explain things to His Grace.

"Do you remember that, a couple of centuries ago, the laws of some countries provided the perfect punishment for pickpockets and purse-snatchers?"

He gave me a wry grin. "Certainly. The hands of the felon were amputated at the wrist. Usually with a headsman's ax, I believe."

"Exactly. And they never picked another pocket again as long as they lived." I said. "Society had denied them the means to pick pockets."

"Go on."

"Do you remember Manny the Moog? The little fellow who was brought in yesterday?"

"Distinctly. I thought it was odd at the time that you should release a man who has a record of such activities as car-stealing and reckless driving, especially when the witness against him turned out to be a perfectly respectable person. I took it for granted that he was one of your ... ah ... 'tame zanies', I think you called them. But I did not and still don't understand how you can be so positive."

"I let Manny go because he's incapable of driving a car. The very thought of being in control of a machine so much more powerful than he is would give him chills. Did you ever see what happens when you lock a claustrophobe up in a dark closet—the mad, unreasoning, uncontrollable panic of absolute terror? That's what would happen to Manny if you put him behind the wheel of a running automobile. It's worse than fear; fear is controllable. Blind terror isn't.

"Manny had one little twist, in his mind. He liked to get into a car—*any* car, whether it was his or not—and drive. He became king of the road. He wasn't a little man any more. He was God, and lesser beings had better look out.

"We got to him before he actually killed anyone, but there is a woman in Queens today who will never walk again because of Manny the Moog. But there won't be any more like her. We took the instrument of destruction away from him; we 'cut off his hands'. Now he's leading a reasonably useful life. We don't need to sacrifice another's life before we neutralize the danger."

"What about Joey Partridge?" His Grace asked. "He's one of your zanies, too, isn't he?

"That's right. He couldn't keep from using his fists. He liked the feel of solid flesh and bone giving under the impact of those big fists of his. Boxing wasn't enough; he had to be able to feel flesh-to-flesh contact, with no padded glove between. He almost killed a couple of men before we got to him."

"What did you do to his hands?"

"Nothing. Not a thing. There's nothing at all wrong with his hands. But he *thinks* there is. He's firmly convinced that the bones are as brittle as chalk, that if he uses those fists, *he* will be the one who will break and shatter. It even bothers him to shake hands, as you saw last night. It took a lot of guts to do what he did last night—walk over to those two thugs knowing he couldn't defend himself. He's no coward. But he's as terrified of having his hands hurt as Manny is of driving a car."

"I see" the Duke said thoughtfully.

"There are other cases, plenty of them," I went on. "We have pyromaniacs who are perfectly harmless now because they have a deathly terror of flame. We have one fellow who used to be very nasty with a knife; he grows a beard now because the very thought of having a sharp edge that close to him is unnerving. The reality would send him screaming. We have a girl who had the weird idea that it was fun to drop things out of windows or off the tops of high buildings. Aside from the chance of people below being hurt, there was another danger. Two cops grabbed her just as she was about to drop her baby brother off the roof of her apartment house.

"But we don't worry about her any more. People with acute acrophobia are in no condition to pull stunts like that."

"What will you do to this Hammerlock Smith, then?" His Grace asked.

"Actually, he's one of the simpler cases. A large percentage of our zanies lose control when they're under the influence of alcohol or drugs. Alcohol is by far the more common. Under the influence, they do things they would never do when sober.

"As long as they remain sober, they have control. But, give them a few drinks and the control slips and then vanishes completely. One of our others was a little like Manny the Moog; he drove like a madman—which he was when he was drunk. Sober, he was as careful and cautious a driver as you'd want—a perfectly reliable citizen. But, after losing his license and the right to own a car, he'd still get drunk and steal cars.

"He has his license back now, but we know we can trust him with it. He will never be able to take another drink.

"Smith is of that type. So, apparently, is Nestor. When we get through with Smith, he'll be sober, and he'll stay that way to his grave."

"**A**stounding." The Duke looked at me again. "I can see the results, of course. I'm going to see that some sort of similar program is started in England, even if I have to stand up in the House of Lords to do it. But, I still don't understand how it can be done so rapidly—a matter of hours. What is the technique used?"

"It all depends on the therapist," I said. "Brownlee is one of the best, but there are others who are almost as good. Some of the officers have started calling them *hexperts* because, in effect, that's exactly what they do—put a hex on the patient."

"A *geas*, in other words."

I'd never heard the word before. "A what?"

"A *geas*. A magical spell that causes a person to do or to refrain from doing some act, whether he will or no. He has no choice, once the *geas* has been put on him."

"That's it exactly."

"But, man, it isn't magic we're discussing, is it?"

"I don't know," I admitted frankly. "You tell me. Was it magic this morning when both you and I had a hunch that little Shirley was *not* in the park, in spite of the way it looked? Was it magic when we eliminated, without even searching, every spot but the place where she actually was?"

"Well, no, I shouldn't say so. I think every good policeman gets hunches like that every so often. He gets a feel for his work and for the types he's dealing with."

"Well, then, call it hunch or telepathy or extra-sensory perception or thingummybob or whatever. Brownlee has just what you say a good cop should have—a feel for his work and for the types he's dealing with. Within a very short time, Dr. Brownlee can actually get the feel of being inside his patient's mind—deep enough, at least, so that he can spot just what has to be done to put a compensating twist in a twisted mind.

"He says the genuine zanies are very simple to operate on. They have already got the raw materials in them for him to work with. A normally sane, normally well integrated person would require almost as much work to put a permanent quirk in as removing such a quirk would be in a zany. The brainwashing techniques and hypnotism can introduce such quirks temporarily, but as soon as a normally sane person regains his balance, the quirks tend to fade away.

"But a system that is off balance and unstable doesn't require much work to push it slightly in another direction. When Brownlee finds out what will do the job, he does it, and we have a tame zany on our hands."

"It sounds as though men of Brownlee's type are rather rare," His Grace said.

"They are. Rarer than psychiatrists as a whole. On the other hand, they can take care of a great many more cases."

"One thing, though," the Duke said thoughtfully. "You mentioned the amputation of a pickpocket's hands. It seems to me that this technique is just as drastic, just as crippling to the person to whom it is done."

"Of course it is! No one has ever denied that. God help us if it's the final answer to the problem! A man who can't drive a car, or use a razor, or punch an enemy in the teeth when it's necessary is certainly handicapped. He's more crippled than he was before. The only compensation for society is that now he's less dangerous.

"There are certain compensations for the individual, too. He stands less chance of going to prison, or to a death cell. But he's still hemmed in; he's not a free man. Of course, in most instances, he's not aware of what has been done to him; his mind compensates and rationalizes and gives him a reason for what he's undergoing. Joey Partridge thinks his condition is due to the fractures he suffered the last time he beat up a man; Manny the Moog thinks that he's afraid to drive a car because of the last wreck he was in. And, partly, maybe they're both right. But they have still been deprived of a part of their free will, their right of choice.

"Oh, no; this isn't the final answer by a long shot! It's a stopgap—a *necessary* stopgap. But, by using it, we can learn more about how the human mind works, and maybe one of these days we'll evolve a science of the mind that can take those twists *out* instead of compensating for them.

"On the other hand, we can save lives by using the technique we have now. We don't dare *not* use it.

"When they chopped off those hands, centuries ago, the stumps were cauterized by putting them in boiling oil. It looked like another injury piled on top of the first, but the chirurgeons, not knowing *why* it worked, still knew that a lot more ex-pickpockets lived through their ordeal if the boiling oil was used afterward.

"And that's what we're doing with this technique right here and now. We're using it because it saves lives, lives that may potentially or actually be a great deal more valuable than the warped personality that might have taken such a life.

"But the one thing that I am working for right now and will continue to work for is a *real* cure, if that's possible. A real, genuine, usable kind of psychotherapy; one which is at least on a par with the science of cake-baking when it comes to the percentages of successes and failures."

His Grace thought that over for a minute. Then he leaned back and looked at me through narrowed eyes. There was a half smile on his lips "Royall, old man, let's admit one thing, just between ourselves," His voice became very slow and very deliberate. "Both you and I know that this process, whatever it is, is *not* psychotherapy."

"Why do you say that?" I wasn't trying to deny anything; I just wanted to know the reasoning behind his conclusions.

"Because I know what psychotherapy can and can't do. And I know that psychotherapy can *not* do the sort of thing we've been discussing.

"It's as if you'd taken me out on a rifle range, to a target two thousand yards from the shooter and let me watch that marksman put fifty shots out of fifty into a six-inch bull's-eye. I might not know what the shooter is using, but I would know beyond any shadow of doubt that it was *not* an ordinary revolver. More, I would know that it could not be any possible improvement upon the revolver. It simply would have to be an instrument of an entirely different order.

"If, in 1945, any intelligent military man had been told that the Japanese city of Hiroshima had been totally destroyed by a bomber dropping a single bomb, he would be certain that the bomb was a new and different kind from any ever known before. He would know that, mind you, without necessarily knowing a great deal about chemistry.

"I don't need to know a devil of a lot about psychotherapy to know that the process you've been describing is as far beyond the limits of psychotherapy as the Hiroshima bomb was beyond the limits of chemistry. Ditto for hypnosis and/or Pavlov's 'conditioned reflex', by the way.

"Now, just to clear the air, what *is* it?"

"It has no official name yet," I told him. "To keep within the law, we have been calling it psychotherapy. If we called it something else, and admitted that it *isn't* psychotherapy, the courts couldn't turn the zanies over to us. But you're right—it is as impossible to produce the effect by psychotherapy as it is to produce an atomic explosion by a chemical reaction.

"I've got a hunch that, just as chemistry and nucleonics are both really branches of physics, so psychotherapy and Brownlee's process are branches of some higher, more inclusive science—but that doesn't have a name, either."

"That's as may be," the Duke said, "but I'm happy to know that you're not deluding yourself that it's any kind of psychotherapy."

"You know," I said, "I kind of like your word *geas*. Because that's exactly what it seems to be—a *geas*. A hex, an enchantment, if you wish.

"Did you know that Brownlee was an anthropologist before he turned to psychology? He has some very interesting stories to tell about hexes and so on."

"I'll have to hear them one day." His Grace took a pack of cigarettes from his pocket. "Cigarette?"

"No, thanks. I gave up smoking a few years back."

He puffed his alight. "This *geas*," he said, "reminds me of the fact that, before the medical profession came up with antibiotics that would destroy the microorganisms that cause gas gangrene, amputation was the only method of preventing the death of the patient. It was crippling, but necessary."

"*No!*" My voice must have been a little too sharp, because he raised one eyebrow. "The analogy," I went on in a quieter tone, "isn't good because it gives a distorted picture. Look, Your Grace, you know what's done to keep a captive wild duck from flying away?"

"One wing is clipped."

"Right. Certain of the feathers are trimmed, which throws the duck off balance every time he tries to fly. He's crippled, right? But if you clip the *other* wing, what happens? He's in balance again. He can't fly as *well* as he could before his wings were clipped—but he *can* fly!

"That's what Brownlee's *geas* does—restore the balance by clipping the other wing."

His Grace smiled. There was an odd sort of twinkle in his eyes. "Let me carry your analogy somewhat farther. If the one wing is too severely clipped, clipping the other won't help. Our duck wouldn't have enough lift to get off the ground, even if he's balanced.

"Now, a zany who was that badly crippled—?"

I grinned back at him. "Right. It would be so obvious that he would have been put away very quickly. He would not be just psychopathic, but completely psychotic—and demonstrably so."

"Then," the Duke said, still pursuing the same track, "the only way to 'cure' that kind would be to find a method to ... ah ... 'grow the feathers back', wouldn't it? And where does that put today's psychotherapy? Providing, of course, that the analogy follows."

"It does," I said. "The real cure that I want to find would do just that—'grow the feathers back'. And that's beyond the limits of psychotherapy, too. That's why Dr. Brownlee and his boys want to study every zany we bring in, whether he can be helped or not. They're looking for a *cure*, not a stopgap."

"Let me drag that analogy out just a tiny bit more," said His Grace. "Suppose there is a genetic defect in the duck which makes it impossible—absolutely impossible—to grow feathers on that wing. Will your cure work?"

I was very quiet for along time. At least, it seemed long. The question had occurred to me before, and I didn't even like to think about it. Now, I had to face it again for a short while.

"Frankly," I said as evenly as I could, "I doubt that anything could be done. But that's only an opinion. We don't know enough yet to make any such predictions. It is my hope that some day we'll find a method of restoring every human being to his or her full potential—but I'm not at all certain of what the source of that potential is.

"But when we do get our cure," I went on, "then our first move must be to abolish the *geas*. And I wish that day were coming tomorrow."

There seemed to be a sudden silence in the room. I hadn't realized that I'd been talking so loudly or so vehemently.

The Duke broke it by saying: "Look here, Royall; I'm going to stay on here until I've learned all about every phase of this thing. It may sound a bit conceited, but I'm going to try to learn in a few weeks everything you have learned in a year. So you'll have to teach me, if you will. And then I'd like to borrow one or two of your therapists, your hexperts, to teach the technique in England.

"Allowing people like that to kill and maim when it can be prevented is unthinkable in a civilized society. I've got to learn how to stop it in England. Will you teach me?"

"On one condition," I said.

"What's that?"

"That you teach me how to use a walking stick."

He laughed. "You're on!"

The officer stuck his head in the waiting room again. "Pardon me. Inspector Acrington? The District Attorney would like to see you."

"Surely."

After he had left, I sat there for a minute or two, just thinking. Then Brownlee came back from his conference with the D.A. and sat down beside me.

"I met your noble friend heading for the D.A.'s office," he said with a smile. "He said that any man who was as determined to find a better method in order to replace a merely workable method is a remarkable man and therefore worth studying under. I just told him I agreed with him."

"Thanks," I said. "Thanks a lot."

Because Brownlee knows why I'm looking for a cure to replace the stopgap. Brownlee knows why I gave up smoking three years ago, why I don't have any matches or lighters in the house, why I keep the ashtrays for guests only, and why, for that reason, I don't have many guests. Brownlee knows why there are only electric stoves in my apartment—never gas.

Brownlee knows why my son quivers and turns his head away from a match flame. Brownlee knows why he had to put the *geas* on Stevie.

And I even think Brownlee suspects that I concealed some of the evidence in the fire that killed Stevie's mother—my wife.

Yes, I'm looking for a cure. But until then, I'll be thankful for the stopgap.

In Case of Fire

There are times when a broken tool is better than a sound one, or a twisted personality more useful than a whole one. For instance, a whole beer bottle isn't half the weapon that half a beer bottle is ...

IN HIS office apartment, on the top floor of the Terran Embassy Building in Occeq City, Bertrand Malloy leafed casually through the dossiers of the four new men who had been assigned to him. They were typical of the kind of men who were sent to him, he thought. Which meant, as usual, that they were atypical. Every man in the Diplomatic Corps who developed a twitch or a quirk was shipped to Saarkkad IV to work under Bertrand Malloy, Permanent Terran Ambassador to His Utter Munificence, the Occeq of Saarkkad.

Take this first one, for instance. Malloy ran his finger down the columns of complex symbolism that showed the complete psychological analysis of the man. Psychopathic paranoia. The man wasn't technically insane; he could be as lucid as the next man most of the time. But he was morbidly suspicious that every man's hand was turned against him. He trusted no one, and was perpetually on his guard against imaginary plots and persecutions.

Number two suffered from some sort of emotional block that left him continually on the horns of one dilemma or another. He was psychologically incapable of making a decision if he were faced with two or more possible alternatives of any major importance.

Number three ...

Malloy sighed and pushed the dossiers away from him. No two men were alike, and yet there sometimes seemed to be an eternal sameness about all men. He considered himself an individual, for instance, but wasn't the basic similarity there, after all?

He was—how old? He glanced at the Earth calendar dial that was automatically correlated with the Saarkkadic calendar just above it. Fifty-nine next week. Fifty-nine years old. And what did he have to show for it besides flabby muscles, sagging skin, a wrinkled face, and gray hair?

Well, he had an excellent record in the Corps, if nothing else. One of the top men in his field. And he had his memories of Diane, dead these ten years, but still beautiful and alive in his recollections. And—he grinned softly to himself—he had Saarkkad.

He glanced up at the ceiling, and mentally allowed his gaze to penetrate it to the blue sky beyond it.

Out there was the terrible emptiness of interstellar space—a great, yawning, infinite chasm capable of swallowing men, ships, planets, suns, and whole galaxies without filling its insatiable void.

Malloy closed his eyes. Somewhere out there, a war was raging. He didn't even like to think of that, but it was necessary to keep it in mind. Somewhere out there, the ships of Earth were ranged against the ships of the alien Karna in the most important war that Mankind had yet fought.

And, Malloy knew, his own position was not unimportant in that war. He was not in the battle line, nor even in the major production line, but it was necessary to keep the drug supply lines flowing from Saarkkad, and that meant keeping on good terms with the Saarkkadic government.

The Saarkkada themselves were humanoid in physical form—if one allowed the term to cover a wide range of differences—but their minds just didn't function along the same lines.

For nine years, Bertrand Malloy had been Ambassador to Saarkkad, and for nine years, no Saarkkada had ever seen him. To have shown himself to one of them would have meant instant loss of prestige.

To their way of thinking, an important official was aloof. The greater his importance, the greater must be his isolation. The Occeq of Saarkkad himself was never seen except by a handful of picked nobles, who, themselves, were never seen except by their underlings. It was a long, roundabout way of doing business, but it was the only way Saarkkad would do any business at all. To violate the rigid social setup of Saarkkad would mean the instant closing off of the supply of biochemical products that the Saarkkadic laboratories produced from native plants and animals—products that were vitally necessary to Earth's war, and which could be duplicated nowhere else in the known universe.

It was Bertrand Malloy's job to keep the production output high and to keep the materiel flowing towards Earth and her allies and outposts.

The job would have been a snap cinch in the right circumstances; the Saarkkada weren't difficult to get along with. A staff of top-grade men could have handled them without half trying.

But Malloy didn't have top-grade men. They couldn't be spared from work that required their total capacity. It's inefficient to waste a man on a job that he can do without half trying where there are more important jobs that will tax his full output.

So Malloy was stuck with the culls. Not the worst ones, of course; there were places in the galaxy that were less important than Saarkkad to the war effort. Malloy knew that, no matter what was wrong with a man, as long as he had the mental ability to dress himself and get himself to work, useful work could be found for him.

Physical handicaps weren't at all difficult to deal with. A blind man can work very well in the total darkness of an infrared-film darkroom. Partial or total losses of limbs can be compensated for in one way or another.

The mental disabilities were harder to deal with, but not totally impossible. On a world without liquor, a dipsomaniac could be channeled easily enough; and he'd better not try fermenting his own on Saarkkad unless he brought his own yeast—which was impossible, in view of the sterilization regulations.

But Malloy didn't like to stop at merely thwarting mental quirks; he liked to find places where they were *useful*.

The phone chimed. Malloy flipped it on with a practiced hand.

"Malloy here."

"Mr. Malloy?" said a careful voice. "A special communication for you has been teletyped in from Earth. Shall I bring it in?"

"Bring it in, Miss Drayson."

Miss Drayson was a case in point. She was uncommunicative. She liked to gather in information, but she found it difficult to give it up once it was in her possession.

Malloy had made her his private secretary. Nothing—but *nothing*—got out of Malloy's office without his direct order. It had taken Malloy a long time to get it into Miss Drayson's head that it was perfectly all right—even desirable—for her to keep secrets from everyone except Malloy.

She came in through the door, a rather handsome woman in her middle thirties, clutching a sheaf of papers in her right hand as though someone might at any instant snatch it from her before she could turn it over to Malloy.

She laid them carefully on the desk. "If anything else comes in, I'll let you know immediately, sir," she said. "Will there be anything else?"

Malloy let her stand there while he picked up the communique. She wanted to know what his reaction was going to be; it didn't matter because no one would ever find out from her what he had done unless she was ordered to tell someone.

He read the first paragraph, and his eyes widened involuntarily.

"Armistice," he said in a low whisper. "There's a chance that the war may be over."

"Yes, sir," said Miss Drayson in a hushed voice.

Malloy read the whole thing through, fighting to keep his emotions in check. Miss Drayson stood there calmly, her face a mask; her emotions were a secret.

Finally, Malloy looked up. "I'll let you know as soon as I reach a decision, Miss Drayson. I think I hardly need say that no news of this is to leave this office."

"Of course not, sir."

Malloy watched her go out the door without actually seeing her. The war was over—at least for a while. He looked down at the papers again.

The Karna, slowly being beaten back on every front, were suing for peace. They wanted an armistice conference—immediately.

Earth was willing. Interstellar war is too costly to allow it to continue any longer than necessary, and this one had been going on for more than thirteen years now. Peace was necessary. But not peace at any price.

The trouble was that the Karna had a reputation for losing wars and winning at the peace table. They were clever, persuasive talkers. They could twist a disadvantage to an advantage, and make their own strengths look like weaknesses. If they won the armistice, they'd be able to retrench and rearm, and the war would break out again within a few years.

Now—at this point in time—they could be beaten. They could be forced to allow supervision of the production potential, forced to disarm, rendered impotent. But if the armistice went to their own advantage ...

Already, they had taken the offensive in the matter of the peace talks. They had sent a full delegation to Saarkkad V, the next planet out from the Saarkkad sun, a chilly world inhabited only by low-intelligence animals. The Karna considered this to be fully neutral territory, and Earth couldn't argue the point very well. In addition, they demanded that the conference begin in three days, Terrestrial time.

The trouble was that interstellar communication beams travel a devil of a lot faster than ships. It would take more than a week for the Earth government to get a vessel to Saarkkad V. Earth had been caught unprepared for an armistice. They objected.

The Karna pointed out that the Saarkkad sun was just as far from Karn as it was from Earth, that it was only a few million miles from a planet which was allied with Earth, and that it was unfair for Earth to take so much time in preparing for an armistice. Why hadn't Earth been prepared? Did they intend to fight to the utter destruction of Karn?

It wouldn't have been a problem at all if Earth and Karn had fostered the only two intelligent races in the galaxy. The sort of grandstanding the Karna were putting on had to be played to an audience. But there were other intelligent races throughout the galaxy, most of whom had remained as neutral as possible during the Earth-Karn war. They had no intention of sticking their figurative noses into a battle between the two most powerful races in the galaxy.

But whoever won the armistice would find that some of the now-neutral races would come in on their side if war broke out again. If the Karna played their cards right, their side would be strong enough next time to win.

So Earth had to get a delegation to meet with the Karna representatives within the three-day limit or lose what might be a vital point in the negotiations.

And that was where Bertrand Malloy came in.

He had been appointed Minister and Plenipotentiary Extraordinary to the Earth-Karn peace conference.

He looked up at the ceiling again. "What *can* I do?" he said softly.

On the second day after the arrival of the communique, Malloy made his decision. He flipped on his intercom and said: "Miss Drayson, get hold of James Nordon and Kylen Braynek. I want to see them both immediately. Send Nordon in first, and tell Braynek to wait."

"Yes, sir."

"And keep the recorder on. You can file the tape later."

"Yes, sir."

Malloy knew the woman would listen in on the intercom anyway, and it was better to give her permission to do so.

James Nordon was tall, broad-shouldered, and thirty-eight. His hair was graying at the temples, and his handsome face looked cool and efficient.

Malloy waved him to a seat.

"Nordon, I have a job for you. It's probably one of the most important jobs you'll ever have in your life. It can mean big things for you—promotion and prestige if you do it well."

Nordon nodded slowly. "Yes, sir."

Malloy explained the problem of the Karna peace talks.

"We need a man who can outthink them," Malloy finished, "and judging from your record, I think you're that man. It involves risk, of course. If you make the wrong decisions, your name will be mud back on Earth. But I don't think there's much chance of that, really. Do you want to handle small-time operations all your life? Of course not."

"You'll be leaving within an hour for Saarkkad V."

Nordon nodded again. "Yes, sir; certainly. Am I to go alone?"

"No," said Malloy, "I'm sending an assistant with you—a man named Kylen Braynek. Ever heard of him?"

Nordon shook his head. "Not that I recall, Mr. Malloy. Should I have?"

"Not necessarily. He's a pretty shrewd operator, though. He knows a lot about interstellar law, and he's capable of spotting a trap a mile away. You'll be in charge, of course, but I want you to pay special attention to his advice."

"I will, sir," Nordon said gratefully. "A man like that can be useful."

"Right. Now, you go into the anteroom over there. I've prepared a summary of the situation, and you'll have to study it and get it into your head before the ship leaves. That isn't much time, but it's the Karna who are doing the pushing, not us."

As soon as Nordon had left, Malloy said softly: "Send in Braynek, Miss Drayson."

Kylen Braynek was a smallish man with mouse-brown hair that lay flat against his skull, and hard, penetrating, dark eyes that were shadowed by heavy, protruding brows. Malloy asked him to sit down.

Again Malloy went through the explanation of the peace conference.

"Naturally, they'll be trying to trick you every step of the way," Malloy went on. "They're shrewd and underhanded; we'll simply have to be more shrewd and more underhanded. Nordon's job is to sit quietly and evaluate the data; yours will be to find the loopholes they're laying out for themselves and plug them. Don't antagonize them, but don't baby them, either. If you see anything underhanded going on, let Nordon know immediately."

"They won't get anything by me, Mr. Malloy."

By the time the ship from Earth got there, the peace conference had been going on for four days. Bertrand Malloy had full reports on the whole parley, as relayed to him through the ship that had taken Nordon and Braynek to Saarkkad V.

Secretary of State Blendwell stopped off at Saarkkad IV before going on to V to take charge of the conference. He was a tallish, lean man with a few strands of gray hair on the top of his otherwise bald scalp, and he wore a hearty, professional smile that didn't quite make it to his calculating eyes.

He took Malloy's hand and shook it warmly. "How are you, Mr. Ambassador?"

"Fine, Mr. Secretary. How's everything on Earth?"

"Tense. They're waiting to see what is going to happen on Five. So am I, for that matter." His eyes were curious. "You decided not to go yourself, eh?"

"I thought it better not to. I sent a good team, instead. Would you like to see the reports?"

"I certainly would."

Malloy handed them to the secretary, and as he read, Malloy watched him. Blendwell was a political appointee—a good man, Malloy had to admit, but he didn't know all the ins and outs of the Diplomatic Corps.

When Blendwell looked up from the reports at last, he said: "Amazing! They've held off the Karna at every point! They've beaten them back! They've managed to cope with and outdo the finest team of negotiators the Karna could send."

"I thought they would," said Malloy, trying to appear modest.

The secretary's eyes narrowed. "I've heard of the work you've been doing here with ... ah ... sick men. Is this one of your ... ah ... successes?"

Malloy nodded. "I think so. The Karna put us in a dilemma, so I threw a dilemma right back at them."

"How do you mean?"

"Nordon had a mental block against making decisions. If he took a girl out on a date, he'd have trouble making up his mind whether to kiss her or not until she made up his mind for him, one way or the other. He's that kind of guy. Until he's presented with one, single, clear decision which admits of no alternatives, he can't move at all.

"As you can see, the Karna tried to give us several choices on each point, and they were all rigged. Until they backed down to a single point and proved that it *wasn't* rigged, Nordon couldn't possibly make up his mind. I drummed into him how important this was, and the more importance there is attached to his decisions, the more incapable he becomes of making them."

The Secretary nodded slowly. "What about Braynek?"

"Paranoid," said Malloy. "He thinks everyone is plotting against him. In this case, that's all to the good because the Karna *are* plotting against him. No matter what they put forth, Braynek is convinced that there's a trap in it somewhere, and he digs to find out what the trap is. Even if there isn't a trap, the Karna can't satisfy Braynek, because he's convinced that there *has* to be—somewhere. As a result, all his advice to Nordon, and all his questioning on the wildest possibilities, just serves to keep Nordon from getting unconfused.

"These two men are honestly doing their best to win at the peace conference, and they've got the Karna reeling. The Karna can see that we're not trying to stall; our men are actually working at trying to reach a decision. But what the Karna don't see is that those men, as a team, are unbeatable because, in this situation, they're psychologically incapable of losing."

Again the Secretary of State nodded his approval, but there was still a question in his mind. "Since you know all that, couldn't you have handled it yourself?"

"Maybe, but I doubt it. They might have gotten around me someway by sneaking up on a blind spot. Nordon and Braynek have blind spots, but they're covered with armor. No, I'm glad I couldn't go; it's better this way."

The Secretary of State raised an eyebrow. "*Couldn't* go, Mr. Ambassador?"

Malloy looked at him. "Didn't you know? I wondered why you appointed me, in the first place. No, I couldn't go. The reason why I'm here, cooped up in this office, hiding from the Saarkkada the way a good Saarkkadic bigshot should, is because I *like* it that way. I suffer from agoraphobia and xenophobia.

"I have to be drugged to be put on a spaceship because I can't take all that empty space, even if I'm protected from it by a steel shell." A look of revulsion came over his face. "And I can't *stand* aliens!"

THE END

A World by the Tale

This is about the best-hated author on Earth. Who was necessarily pampered and petted because of his crime against humanity....

Exactly three minutes after the Galactic left the New York apartment of Professor John Hamish McLeod, Ph.D., Sc.D., a squad of U.B.I. men pushed their way into it.

McLeod heard the door chime, opened the door, and had to back up as eight men crowded in. The one in the lead flashed a fancily engraved ID card and said: "Union Bureau of Investigation. You're Professor Mac-Lee-Odd." It was a statement, not a question.

"No," McLeod said flatly, "I am not. I never heard of such a name." He waited while the U.B.I. man blinked once, then added: "If you are looking for Professor MuhCloud, I'm he." It always irritated him when people mispronounced his name, and in this case there was no excuse for it.

"All right, Professor McLeod," said the U.B.I. agent, pronouncing it properly this time, "however you want it. Mind if we ask you a few questions?"

McLeod stared at him for half a second. Eight men, all of them under thirty-five, in top physical condition. He was fifteen years older than the oldest and had confined his exercise, in the words of Chauncey de Pew, to "acting as pallbearer for my friends who take exercise." Not that he was really in poor shape, but he certainly couldn't have argued with eight men like these.

"Come in," he said calmly, waving them into the apartment.

Six of them entered. The other two stayed outside in the hall.

Five of the six remained standing. The leader took the chair that McLeod offered him.

"What are your questions, Mr. Jackson?" McLeod asked.

Jackson looked very slightly surprised, as if he were not used to having people read the name on his card during the short time he allowed them to see it. The expression vanished almost instantaneously. "Professor," he said, "we'd like to know what subjects you discussed with the Galactic who just left."

McLeod allowed himself to relax back in his chair. "Let me ask you two questions, Mr. Jackson. One: What the hell business is it of yours? Two: Why do you ask me when you already know?"

Again there was only a flicker of expression over Jackson's face. "Professor McLeod, we are concerned about the welfare of the human race. Your ... uh ... co-operation is requested."

"You don't have to come barging in here with an armed squad just to ask my co-operation," McLeod said. "What do you want to know?"

Jackson took a notebook out of his jacket pocket. "We'll just get a few facts straight first, professor," he said, leafing through the notebook. "You were first approached by a Galactic four years ago, on January 12, 1990. Is that right?"

McLeod, who had taken a cigarette from his pack and started to light it, stopped suddenly and looked at Jackson as though the U.B.I. man were a two-headed embryo. "Yes, Mr. Jackson, that is right," he said slowly, as though he were speaking to a low-grade moron. "And the capital of California is Sacramento. Are there any further matters of public knowledge you would like to ask me about? Would you like to know when the War of 1812 started or who is buried in Grant's Tomb?"

Jackson's jaw muscles tightened, then relaxed. "There's no need to get sarcastic, professor. Just answer the questions." He looked back at the notebook. "According to the record, you, as a zoologist, were asked to accompany a shipment of animals to a planet named ... uh ... Gelakin. You did so. You returned after eighteen months. Is that correct?"

"To the best of my knowledge, yes," McLeod said with heavy, biting sarcasm. "And the date of the Norman Conquest was A.D. 1066."

Jackson balled his fists suddenly and closed his eyes. "Mac. Loud. *Stop.* It." He was obviously holding himself under rigorous restraint. He opened his eyes. "There are reasons for asking these questions, professor. Very good reasons. Will you let me finish?"

McLeod had finished lighting his cigarette. He snapped his lighter off and replaced it in his pocket. "Perhaps," he said mildly. "May I make a statement first?"

Jackson took a deep breath, held it for a moment, then exhaled slowly. "Go ahead."

"Thank you." There was no sarcasm in McLeod's voice now, only patience. "First—for the record—I'll say that I consider it impertinent of you to come in here demanding information without explanation. No, Jackson; don't say anything. You said I could make a statement. Thank you. Second, I will state that I am perfectly aware of why the questions are being asked.

"No reaction, Mr. Jackson? You don't believe that? Very well. Let me continue.

"On January twelve, nineteen-ninety, I was offered a job by certain citizens of the Galactic Civilization. These citizens of the Galactic Civilization wanted to take a shipload of Terrestrial animals to their own planet, Gelakin. They knew almost nothing about the care and feeding of Terrestrial animals. They needed an expert. They should have taken a real expert—one of the men from the Bronx Zoo, for instance. They didn't; they requested a zoologist. Because the request was made here in America, I was the one who was picked. Any one of seven other men could have handled the job, but I was picked.

"So I went, thus becoming the first Earthman ever to leave the Solar System.

"I took care of the animals. I taught the Galactics who were with me to handle and feed them. I did what I was paid to do, and it was a hard job. None of them knew anything about the care and feeding of elephants, horses, giraffes, cats, dogs, eagles, or any one of the other hundreds of Terrestrial life forms that went aboard that ship.

"All of this was done with the express permission of the Terrestrial Union Government.

"I was returned to Earth on July seventeen, nineteen-ninety-one.

"I was immediately taken to U.B.I. headquarters and subjected to rigorous questioning. Then I was subjected to further questioning while connected to a polyelectro-encephalograph. Then I was subjected to hearing the same questions over again while under the influence of various drugs—in sequence and in combination. The consensus at that time was that I was not lying nor had I been subjected to what is commonly known as 'brain washing'. My memories were accurate and complete.

"I did not know then, nor do I know now, the location of the planet Gelakin. This information was not denied me by the Galactics; I simply could not understand the terms they used. All I can say now—and all I could say then—is that Gelakin is some three point five kiloparsecs from Sol in the general direction of Saggitarius."

"You don't know any more about that now than you did then?" Jackson interrupted, suddenly and quickly.

"That's what I said," McLeod snapped. "And that's what I meant. Let me finish.

"I was handsomely paid for my work in Galactic money. They use the English word 'credit', but I'm not sure the English word has exactly the same meaning as the Galactic term. At any rate, my wages, if such I may call them, were confiscated by the Earth Government; I was given the equivalent in American dollars—after the eighty per cent income tax had been deducted. I ended up with just about what I would have made if I had stayed home and drawn my salary from Columbia University and the American Museum of Natural History.

"Please, Mr. Jackson. I only have a little more to say.

"I decided to write a book in order to make the trip pay off. 'Interstellar Ark' was a popularized account of the trip that made me quite a nice piece of change because every literate and half-literate person on Earth is curious about the Galactics. The book tells everything I know about the trip and the people. It is a matter of public record. Since that is so, I refused to answer a lot of darn-fool questions—by which I mean that I refuse to answer any more questions that you already know the answers to. I am not being stubborn; I am just sick and tired of the whole thing."

Actually, the notoriety that had resulted from the trip and the book had not pleased McLeod particularly. He had never had any strong desire for fame, but if it had come as a result of his work in zoology and the related sciences he would have accepted the burden. If his "The Ecology of the Martian Polar Regions" had attracted a hundredth of the publicity and sold a hundredth of the number of copies that "Interstellar Ark" had sold, he would have been gratified indeed. But the way things stood, he found the whole affair irksome.

Jackson looked at his notebook as if he expected to see answers written there instead of questions. Then he looked back up at McLeod. "All right then, professor, what about this afternoon's conference. *That* isn't a matter of public record."

"And technically it isn't any of your business, either," McLeod said tiredly. "But since you have the whole conversation down on tape, I don't see why you bother asking me. I'm well aware that you can pick up conversations in my apartment."

Jackson pursed his lips and glanced at another of the agents, who raised his eyebrows slightly.

McLeod got it in spite of the fact that they didn't intend him to. His place was bugged, all right, but somehow the Galactic had managed to nullify their instruments! No wonder they were in such a tizzy.

McLeod smiled, pleased with himself and with the world for the first time that afternoon. He decided, however, that he'd better volunteer the information before they threatened him with the Planetary Security Act. That threat would make him angry, he knew, and he might say something that would get him in real trouble.

It was all right to badger Jackson up to a certain point, but it would be foolish to go beyond that.

"However," he went on with hardly a break, "since, as you say, it is not a matter of public record, I'm perfectly willing to answer any questions you care to ask."

"Just give us a general rundown of the conversation," Jackson said. "If I have any questions, I'll ... uh ... ask them at the proper time."

McLeod did the best he could to give a clear picture of what the Galactic had wanted. There was really very little to it. The Galactic was a member of a race that McLeod had never seen before: a humanoid with red skin—fire-engine, not Amerindian—and a rather pleasant-looking face, in contrast to the rather crocodilian features of the Galactic resident. He had introduced himself by an un-pronounceable name and then had explained that since the name meant "mild" or "merciful" in one of the ancient tongues of his planet, it would be perfectly all right if McLeod called him "Clement." Within minutes, it had been "Clem" and "Mac."

McLeod could see that Jackson didn't quite believe that. Galactics, of whatever race, were aloof, polite, reserved, and sometimes irritatingly patronizing—never buddy-buddy. McLeod couldn't help what Jackson might think; what was important was that it was true.

What Clem wanted was very simple. Clem was—after a manner of speaking—a literary agent. Apparently the Galactic system of book publishing didn't work quite the way the Terrestrial system did; Clem took his commission from the publisher instead of the author, but was considered a representative of the author, not the publisher. McLeod hadn't quite understood how that sort of thing would work out, but he let it pass. There were a lot of things he didn't understand about Galactics.

All Clem wanted was to act as McLeod's agent for the publication of "Interstellar Ark."

"And what did you tell him?" Jackson asked.

"I told him I'd think it over."

Jackson leaned forward. "How much money did he offer?" he asked eagerly.

"Not much," McLeod said. "That's why I told him I'd think it over. He said that, considering the high cost of transportation, relaying, translation, and so on, he couldn't offer me more than one thousandth of one per cent royalties."

Jackson blinked. "One *what*?"

"One thousandth of one per cent. If the book sells a hundred thousand copies at a credit a copy, they will send me a nice, juicy check for one lousy credit."

Jackson scowled. "They're cheating you."

"Clem said it was the standard rate for a first book."

Jackson shook his head. "Just because we don't have interstellar ships and are confined to our own solar system, they treat us as though we were ignorant savages. They're cheating you high, wide, and handsome."

"Maybe," said McLeod. "But if they really wanted to cheat me, they could just pirate the book. There wouldn't be a thing I could do about it."

"Yeah. But to keep up their facade of high ethics, they toss us a sop. And we have to take whatever they hand out. You *will* take it, of course." It was more of an order than a question.

"I told him I'd think it over," McLeod said.

Jackson stood up. "Professor McLeod, the human race needs every Galactic credit it can lay its hands on. It's your duty to accept the offer, no matter how lousy it is. We have no choice in the matter. And a Galactic credit is worth ten dollars American, four pounds U.K., or forty rubles Soviet. If you sell a hundred thousand copies of your book, you can get yourself a meal in a fairly good restaurant and Earth will have one more Galactic credit stashed away. If you don't sell that many, you aren't out anything."

"I suppose not," McLeod said slowly. He knew that the Government could force him to take the offer. Under the Planetary Security Act, the Government had broad powers—very broad.

"Well, that isn't my business right now," Jackson said. "I just wanted to find out what this was all about. You'll hear from us, Professor McLeod."

"I don't doubt it," said McLeod.

The six men filed out the door.

Alone, McLeod stared at the wall and thought.

Earth needed every Galactic credit it could get; that was certain. The trouble came in getting them.

Earth had absolutely nothing that the Galactics wanted. Well, not absolutely, maybe, but so near as made no difference. Certainly there was no basis for trade. As far as the Galactics were concerned, Earth was a little backwater planet that was of no importance. Nothing manufactured on the planet was of any use to Galactics. Nothing grown on Earth was of any commercial importance. They had sampled the animals and plants for scientific purposes, but there was no real commercial value in them. The Government had added a few credits to its meager collection when the animals had been taken, but the amount was small.

McLeod thought about the natives of New Guinea and decided that on the Galactic scale Earth was about in the same position. Except that there had at least been gold in New Guinea. The Galactics didn't have any interest in Earth's minerals; the elements were much more easily available in the asteroid belts that nearly every planetary system seemed to have.

The Galactics were by no means interested in bringing civilization to the barbarians of Earth, either. They had no missionaries to bring new religion, no do-gooders to "elevate the cultural level of the natives." They had no free handouts for anyone. If Earthmen wanted anything from them, the terms were cash on the barrelhead. Earth's credit rating in the Galactic equivalent of Dun & Bradstreet was triple-Z-zero.

A Galactic ship had, so to speak, stumbled over Earth fifteen years before. Like the English explorers of the Eighteenth and Nineteenth Centuries, the Galactics seemed to feel that it was necessary to install one of their own people on a new-found planet, but they were not in the least interested in colonization nor in taking over Earth's government. The Galactic Resident was not in any sense a Royal Governor, and could hardly even be called an ambassador. He and his staff—a small one, kept more for company than for any necessary work—lived quietly by themselves in a house they'd built in Hawaii. Nobody knew what they did, and it didn't seem wise to ask.

The first Galactic Resident had been shot and killed by some religious nut. Less than twenty-four hours later, the Galactic Space Navy—if that was the proper term—had come to claim the body. There were no recriminations, no reprisals. They came, "more in sorrow than in anger," to get the body. They came in a spaceship that was easily visible to the naked eye long before it hit the atmosphere—a sphere three kilometers in diameter. The missiles with thermonuclear warheads that were sent up to intercept the ship were detonated long before they touched the ship, and neither Galactics nor Earthmen ever mentioned them again. It had been the most frightening display of power ever seen on Earth, and the Galactics hadn't even threatened anyone. They just came to get a body.

Needless to say, there was little danger that they would ever have to repeat the performance.

The national governments of Earth had organized themselves hurriedly into the Terrestrial Union. Shaky at first, it had gained stability and power with the years. The first thing the Union Government had wanted to do was send an ambassador to the Galactic Government. The Galactic Resident had politely explained that their concept of government was different from ours, that ambassadors had no place in that concept, and, anyway, there was no capital to send one to. However, if Earth wanted to send an observer of some kind....

Earth did.

Fine. A statement of passenger fares was forthcoming; naturally, there were no regular passenger ships stopping at Earth and there would not be in the foreseeable future, but doubtless arrangements could be made to charter a vessel. It would be expensive, but....

If a New Guinea savage wants to take passage aboard a Qantas airliner, what is the fare in cowrie shells?

As far as McLeod knew, his book was the first thing ever produced on Earth that the Galactics were even remotely interested in. He had a higher opinion of the ethics of the Galactics than Jackson did, but a thousandth of a per cent seemed like pretty small royalties. And he couldn't for the life of him see why his book would interest a Galactic. Clem had explained that it gave Galactics a chance to see what they looked like through the eyes of an Earthman, but that seemed rather weak to McLeod.

Nevertheless, he knew he would take Clem's offer.

Eight months later, a shipload of Galactic tourists arrived. For a while, it looked as though Earth's credit problem might be solved. Tourism has always been a fine method for getting money from other countries—especially if one's own country is properly picturesque. Tourists always had money, didn't they? And they spend it freely, didn't they?

No.

Not in this case.

Earth had nothing to sell to the tourists.

Ever hear of *baluts*? The Melanesians of the South Pacific consider it a very fine delicacy. You take a fertilized duck egg and you bury it in the warm earth. Six months later, when it is nice and overripe, you dig it up again, knock the top off the shell the way you would a soft-boiled egg, and eat it. Then you pick the pinfeathers out of your teeth. *Baluts*.

Now you know how the greatest delicacies of Earth's restaurants affected the Galactics.

Earth was just a little *too* picturesque. The tourists enjoyed the sights, but they ate aboard their ship, which was evidently somewhat like a Caribbean cruise ship. And they bought nothing. They just looked.

And laughed.

And of course they all wanted to meet Professor John Hamish McLeod.

When the news leaked out and was thoroughly understood by Earth's population, there was an immediate reaction.

Editorial in *Pravda*:

The stupid book written by the American J. H. McLeod has made Earth a laughingstock throughout the galaxy. His inability to comprehend the finer nuances of Galactic Socialism has made all Earthmen look foolish. It is too bad that a competent Russian zoologist was not chosen for the trip that McLeod made; a man properly trained in the understanding of the historical forces of dialectic materialism would have realized that any Galactic society must of necessity be a Communist State, and would have interpreted it as such. The petty bourgeois mind of McLeod has made it impossible for any Earthman to hold up his head in the free Socialist society of the galaxy. Until this matter is corrected....

News item Manchester *Guardian*:

Professor James H. McLeod, the American zoologist whose book has apparently aroused a great deal of hilarity in Galactic circles, admitted today that both Columbia University and the American Museum of Natural History have accepted his resignation. The recent statement by a University spokesman that Professor McLeod had "besmirched the honor of Earthmen everywhere" was considered at least partially responsible for the resignations. (See editorial.)

Editorial, Manchester *Guardian*:

... It is a truism that an accepted wit has only to say, 'Pass the butter,' and everyone will laugh. Professor McLeod, however, far from being an accepted wit, seems rather to be in the position of a medieval Court Fool, who was laughed *at* rather than *with*. As a consequence, all Earthmen have been branded as Fools....

Statement made by the American Senator from Alabama:

"He has made us all look like jackasses in the eyes of the Galactics, and at this precarious time in human history it is my considered opinion that such actions are treasonous to the human race and to Earth and should be treated and considered as such!"

Book review, *Literary Checklist*, Helvar III, Bornis Cluster:

"Interstellar Ark, an Earthman's View of the Galaxy," translated from the original tongue by Vonis Delf, Cr. 5.00. This inexpensive little book is one of the most entertainingly funny publications in current print. The author, one John McLeod, is a member of a type 3-7B race inhabiting a planet in the Outer Fringes.... As an example of the unwitting humor of the book, we have only to quote the following:

"I was shown to my quarters shortly before takeoff. Captain Benarly had assigned me a spacious cabin which was almost luxurious in its furnishings. The bed was one of the most comfortable I have ever slept in."

Or the following:

"I found the members of the crew to be friendly and co-operative, especially Nern Cronzel, the ship's physician."

It is our prediction that this little gem will be enjoyed for a long time to come and will be a real money-maker for its publishers.

They haven't hanged me yet, McLeod thought. He sat in his apartment alone and realized that it would take very little to get him hanged.

How could one book have aroused such wrath? Even as he thought it, McLeod knew the answer to that question. It wasn't the book. No one who had read it two and a half years before had said anything against it.

No, it wasn't the book. It was the Galactic reaction to the book. Already feeling inferior because of the stand-offish attitude of the beings from the stars, the Homeric laughter of those same beings had been too much. It would have been bad enough if that laughter had been generated by one of the Galactics. To have had it generated by an Earthman made it that much worse. Against an Earthman, their rage was far from impotent.

Nobody understood *why* the book was funny, of course. The joke was over their heads, and that made human beings even angrier.

He remembered a quotation from a book he had read once. A member of some tribal-taboo culture—African or South Pacific, he forgot which—had been treated at a missionary hospital for something or other and had described his experience.

"The white witch doctor protects himself by wearing a little round mirror on his head which reflects back the evil spirits."

Could that savage have possibly understood what was humorous about that remark? No. Not even if you explained to him why the doctor used the mirror that way.

Now what? McLeod thought. He was out of a job and his bank account was running low. His credit rating had dropped to zero.

McLeod heard a key turn in the lock. The door swung open and Jackson entered with his squad of U.B.I. men.

"Hey!" said McLeod, jumping to his feet. "What do you think this is?"

"Shut up, McLeod," Jackson growled. "Get your coat. You're wanted at headquarters."

McLeod started to say something, then thought better of it. There was nothing he could say. Nobody would care if the U.B.I. manhandled him. Nobody would protest that his rights were being ignored. If McLeod got his teeth knocked in, Jackson would probably be voted a medal.

McLeod didn't say another word. He followed orders. He got his coat and was taken down to the big building on the East River which had begun its career as the United Nations Building.

He was bundled up to an office and shoved into a chair.

Somebody shoved a paper at him. "Sign this!"

"What is it?" McLeod asked, finding his voice.

"A receipt. For two thousand dollars. Sign it."

McLeod looked the paper over, then looked up at the burly man who had shoved it at him. "*Fifty thousand Galactic credits!* What is this for?"

"The royalty check for your unprintably qualified book has come in, Funny Man. The Government is taking ninety-eight per cent for income taxes. Sign!"

McLeod pushed the paper back across the desk. "No. I won't. You can confiscate my money. I can't stop that, I guess. But I won't give it legal sanction by signing anything. I don't even see the two thousand dollars this is supposed to be a receipt for."

Jackson, who was standing behind McLeod, grabbed his arm and twisted. "Sign!" His voice was a snarl in McLeod's ear.

Eventually, of course, he signed.

"'Nother beer, Mac?" asked the bartender with a friendly smile.

"Yeah, Leo; thanks." McLeod pushed his quarter across the bar with one hand and scratched negligently at his beard with the fingers of the other. Nobody questioned him in this neighborhood. The beard, which had taken two months to grow, disguised his face, and he had given his name as McCaffery, allowing his landlord and others who heard it to make the natural assumption that he was of Irish descent.

He was waiting. He had been forced to move from his apartment; nobody wanted that dirty so-and-so, Professor McLeod, around. Besides, his money was running short. He had never seen the two thousand. "You'll get that when the Galactic bank cashes your royalty check," he had been told. He was waiting.

Not hiding. No. That wasn't possible. The U.B.I. could find him easily when they wanted him. There was no place he could have hidden from them for very long. A man needs friends to stay hidden from an efficient police organization for very long, and John Hamish McLeod had no friends. "Jack McCaffery" had, since he was a pleasant kind of fellow who made friends easily when he wanted them. But he had no illusions about his new friends. Let them once suspect, however faintly, that Good Old Jack McCaffery was really that Professor McLeod, and the game would be up.

The U.B.I. would find him again all right, whenever it wanted him. And McLeod hoped it would be soon because he was down to his last hundred bucks.

So he waited and thought about fifty thousand Galactic credits.

The mathematics was simple, but it conveyed an awful lot of information. To make fifty thousand credits from one thousandth of one percent royalties on a book selling at five credits the copy, one must needs sell a billion copies. Nothing to it.

$$5X \cdot 10^{-5} = 5 \cdot 10^4$$

Ergo: $X = 10^9$

McLeod drew the equations on the bar with the tip of a wet forefinger, then rubbed them out quickly.

A billion copies in the first year. He should have seen it. He should have understood.

How many planets were there in the galaxy?

How many people on each planet?

Communication, even at ultralight velocities, would be necessarily slow. The galaxy was just too big to be compassed by the human mind—or even by the mind of a Galactic, McLeod suspected.

How do you publish a book for Galactic, for galaxy-wide, consumption? How long does it take to saturate the market on each planet? How long does it take to spread the book from planet to planet? How many people were there on each planet who would buy a good book? Or, at least, an entertaining one.

McLeod didn't know, but he suspected that the number was huge. McLeod was a zoologist, not an astronomer, but he read enough on astronomy to know that the estimated number of Earth-type planets alone—according to the latest theory—ran into the tens of millions or hundreds of millions. The—

A man sat down on the stool next to McLeod and said something loud enough and foul enough to break the zoologist's train of thought.

"Gimme a shot, Leo," he added in an angry voice.

"Sure, Pete," the bartender said. "What's the trouble?"

"*Tourists*," Pete said with a snarl. "Laffin' attus alla time like we was monkeys inna zoo! Bunch 'em come inta day." He downed his whiskey with a practiced flip of the wrist and slammed it on the bar. Leo refilled it immediately. "I shunt gripe, I guess. Gotta haffa credit offen 'em." He slapped down a five dollar bill as though it had somehow been contaminated.

The bar became oddly quiet. Everyone had heard Pete. Further, everyone had heard that another shipload of Galactics had landed and were, at the moment, enjoying the sights of New York. A few of them knew that Pete was the bell-captain in one of the big midtown hotels.

McLeod listened while Pete expounded on the shame he had had to undergo to earn half a credit—a lousy five bucks.

McLeod did some estimating. Tourists—the word had acquired an even more pejorative sense than it had before, and now applied only to Galactics—bought nothing, but they tipped for services, unless the services weren't wanted or needed. Pete had given them information that they hadn't had before—where to find a particular place. All in all, the group of fifteen Galactics had given out five or six credits in such tips. Say half a credit apiece. There were, perhaps, a hundred Galactics in this shipload. That meant fifty credits. Hm-m-m.

They didn't need anyone to carry their bags; they didn't need anyone to register them in hotels; they didn't need personal service of that kind. All they wanted to do was look. But they wouldn't pay for looking. They had no interest in Broadway plays or the acts in the night-clubs—at least, not enough to induce them to pay to see them. This particular group had wanted to see a hotel. They had wandered through it, looking at everything and laughing fit to kill at the carpets on the floor and the electric lighting and such. But when the management had hinted that payment for such services as letting them look should be forthcoming, they had handed half a credit to someone and walked out. Then they had gone to the corner of Fifty-first and Madison and looked for nothing.

Fifty credits for a shipload. Three shiploads a year. Hell, give 'em the benefit of the doubt and say *ten* shiploads a year. In a hundred years, they'd add another fifty thousand to Earth's resources.

McLeod grinned.

And waited.

They came for him, eventually, as McLeod had known they would.

But they came long before he had expected. He had given them six months at the least. They came for him at the end of the third month.

It was Jackson, of course. It would have to be Jackson. He walked into the cheap little room McLeod had rented, followed by his squad of men.

He tossed a peculiar envelope on the bed next to McLeod.

"Letter came for you, humorist. Open it."

McLeod sat on the edge of the bed and read the letter. The envelope had already been opened, which surprised him none.

It looked very much like an ordinary business letter—except that whatever they used for paper was whiter and tougher than the paper he used.

He was reminded of the time he had seen a reproduction of a Thirteenth Century manuscript alongside the original. The copy had been set up in a specially-designed type and printed on fine paper. The original had been handwritten on vellum.

McLeod had the feeling that if he used a microscope on this letter the lines and edges would be just as precise and clear as they appeared to the naked eye, instead of the fuzziness that ordinary print would show.

The way you tell a synthetic ruby from a natural ruby is to look for flaws. The synthetic doesn't have any.

This letter was a Galactic imitation of a Terran business letter.

It said:

Dear Mac,

I am happy to report that your book, "Interstellar Ark," is a smash hit. It looks as though it is on its way to becoming a best seller. As you already know by your royalty statement, over a billion copies were sold the first year. That indicates even better sales over the years to come as the reputation of the book spreads. Naturally, our advertising campaign will remain behind it all the way. Congratulations.

Speaking of royalty checks, there seems to be some sort of irregularity about yours. I am sorry, but according to regulations the check must be validated in the presence of your Galactic Resident before it can be cashed. Your signature across the back of it doesn't mean anything to our bankers.

Just go to your Galactic Resident, and he'll be happy to take care of the matter for you. That's what he's there for. The next check should come through very shortly.

All the best,

Clem.

Better and better, McLeod thought. He hadn't expected to be able to do anything until his next royalty check arrived. But now—

He looked up at Jackson. "All right. What's next?"

"Come with us. We're flying to Hawaii. Get your hat and coat."

McLeod obeyed silently. At the moment, there was nothing else he could do. As a matter of fact, there was nothing he wanted to do more.

It was no trouble at all for Professor McLeod to get an audience with the Galactic Resident, but when he was escorted in by Jackson and his squad, the whole group was halted inside the front door.

The Resident, a tall, lean being with a leathery, gray face that somehow managed to look crocodilian in spite of the fact that his head was definitely humanoid in shape, peered at them from beneath pronounced supraorbital ridges. "Is this man under arrest?" he asked in a gravelly baritone.

"Er ... no," said Jackson. "No. He is merely in protective custody."

"He has not been convicted of any crime?"

"No sir," Jackson said. His voice sounded as though he were unsure of himself.

"That is well," said the Resident. "A convicted criminal cannot, of course, use the credits of society until he has become rehabilitated." He paused. "But why protective custody?"

"There are those," said Jackson, choosing his words with care, "who feel that Professor McLeod has brought disgrace upon the human race ... er ... the Terrestrial race. There is reason to believe that his life may be in danger."

McLeod smiled wryly. What Jackson said was true, but it was carefully calculated to mislead.

"I see," said the Resident. "It would appear to me that it would be simpler to inform the people that he has done no such thing; that, indeed, his work has conferred immense benefits upon your race. But that is your own affair. At any rate, he is in no danger here."

He didn't need to say anything else. Jackson knew the hint was an order and that he wouldn't get any farther with his squad.

McLeod spoke up. "Subject to your permission, sir, I would like to have Mr. Jackson with me."

The Galactic Resident smiled. "Of course, professor. Come in, both of you." He turned and led the way through the inner door.

Nobody bothered to search either of them, not even though they must know that Jackson was carrying a gun. McLeod was fairly certain that the gun would be useless to Jackson if he tried to assert his authority with it. If Clem had been able to render the U.B.I.'s eavesdropping apparatus inoperable, it was highly probable that the Galactic Resident would have some means of taking care of weapons.

"There are only a few formalities to go through," the Resident said pleasantly, indicating chairs with a gesture. The room he had led them to didn't look much different from that which would be expected in any tastefully furnished apartment in New York or Honolulu.

McLeod and Jackson sat down in a couple of comfortable easy-chairs while the Resident went around a large desk and sat down in a swivel chair behind it. He smiled a little and looked at McLeod. "Hm-m-m. Ah, yes. Very good." It was as though he had received information of some kind on an unknown subject through an unknown channel, McLeod thought. Evidently that was true, for his next words were: "You are not under the influence of drugs nor hypnotic compulsion, I see. Excellent, professor. Is it your desire that this check be converted to cash?" He made a small gesture. "You have only to express it, you see. It would be difficult to explain it to you, but rest assured that such an expression of will—while you are sitting in that chair—is impressed upon the structure of the check itself and is the equivalent of a signature. Except, of course, that it is unforgeable."

"May I ask a few questions first?" McLeod said.

"Certainly, professor. I am here to answer your questions."

"This money—is it free and clear, or are there Galactic taxes to pay?"

If the Galactic Resident had had eyebrows, it is likely that they would have lifted in surprise. "My dear professor! Aside from the fact that we run our ... er ... government in an entirely different manner, we would consider it quite immoral to take what a man earns without giving services of an exact kind. I will charge you five credits for this validation, since I am rendering a service. The bank will take a full tenth of a percent in this case because of the inconvenience of shipping cash over that long distance. The rest is yours to do with as you see fit."

Fifty-five credits out of fifty thousand, McLeod thought. *Not bad at all.* Aloud, he asked: "Could I, for instance, open a bank account or buy a ticket on a star-ship?"

"Why not? As I said, it is your money. You have earned it honestly; you may spend it honestly."

Jackson was staring at McLeod, but he said nothing.

"Tell me, sir," McLeod said, "how does the success of my book compare with the success of most books in the galaxy?"

"Quite favorably, I understand," said the Resident. "The usual income from a successful book is about five thousand credits a year. Some run even less than that. I'm not too familiar with the publishing business, you understand, but that is my impression. You are, by Galactic standards, a very wealthy man, professor. Fifty thousand a year is by no means a median income."

"Fifty thousand a *year*?"

"Yes. About that. I understand that in the publishing business one can depend on a life income that does not vary much from the initial period. If a book is successful in one area of the galaxy it will be equally successful in others."

"How long does it take to saturate the market?" McLeod asked with a touch of awe.

"Saturate the—? Oh. Oh, I see. Yes. Well, let's see. Most publishing houses can't handle the advertising and marketing on more than a thousand planets at once—the job becomes too unwieldy. That would indicate that you sold an average of a million copies per planet, which is unusual but not ... ah ... miraculous. That is why you can depend on future sales, you see; over a thousand planets the differences in planetary tastes averages out.

"Now if your publishers continue to expand the publication at the rate of a thousand planets a year, your book should easily last for another century. They can't really expand that rapidly, of course, since the sales on the planets they have already covered will continue with diminishing success over the next several years. Actually, your publishers will continue to put a billion books a year on the market and expand to new planets at a rate that will balance the loss of sales on the planets where it has already run its course. Yes, professor, you will have a good income for life."

"What about my heirs?"

"Heirs?" The Galactic Resident blinked. "I'm afraid I don't quite follow you."

"My relatives. Anyone who will inherit my property after my death."

The Resident still looked puzzled. "What about them?"

"How long can they go on collecting? When does the copyright run out?"

The Galactic Resident's puzzlement vanished. "Oh my dear professor! Surely you see that it is impossible to ... er ... inherit money one hasn't earned! The income stops with your death. Your children or your wife have done nothing to earn that money. Why should it continue to be paid out after the earner has died? If you wish to make provisions for such persons during your lifetime, that is your business, but the provisions must be made out of money you have already earned."

"Who does get the income, then?" McLeod asked.

The Galactic Resident looked thoughtful. "Well, the best I can explain to you without going into arduous detail is to say that our ... er ... government gets it. 'Government' is not really the proper word in this context, since we have no government as you think of it. Let us merely say that such monies pass into a common exchequer from which ... er ... public servants like myself are paid."

McLeod had a vision of a British Crown Officer trying to explain to a New Guinea tribesman what he meant when he said that taxes go to the Crown. The tribesman would probably wonder why the Chief of the English Tribe kept cowrie shells under his hat.

"I see. And if I am imprisoned for crime?" he asked.

"The payments are suspended until the ... er ... rehabilitation is complete. That is, until you are legally released."

"Is there anything else that can stop the payments?"

"Not unless the publishing company fails—which is highly unlikely. Of course, a man under hypnotic compulsion or drugs is not considered legally responsible, so he cannot transact any legal business while he is in that state, but the checks are merely held for him until that impediment is removed."

"I see." McLeod nodded.

He knew perfectly well that he no more understood the entire workings of the Galactic civilization than that New Guinea tribesman understood the civilization of Great Britain, but he also knew that he understood more of it than Jackson, for instance, did. McLeod had been able to foresee a little of what the Resident had said.

"Would you do me the service, sir," McLeod said, "of opening a bank account for me in some local bank?"

"Yes, of course. As Resident, I am empowered to transact business for you at your request. My fees are quite reasonable. All checks will have to go through me, of course, but ... hm-m-m ... I think in this case a twentieth of a per cent would be appropriate. You will be handling fairly large amounts. If that is your wish, I shall so arrange it."

"Hey!" Jackson found his tongue. "The Earth Union Government has a claim on that! McLeod owes forty-nine thousand Galactic credits in income taxes!"

If the Galactic Resident was shocked at the intimation that the Galactic "government" would take earned money from a man, the announcement that Earth's government did so was no surprise to him at all. "If that is so, I am certain that Professor McLeod will behave as a law-abiding citizen. He can authorize a check for that amount, and it will be honored by his bank. We have no desire to interfere with local customs."

"I am certain that I can come to an equitable arrangement with the Earth authorities," said McLeod, rising from his chair. "Is there anything I have to sign or—"

"No, no. You have expressed your will. Thank you, Professor McLeod; it is a pleasure to do business with you."

"Thank you. The pleasure is mutual. Come on, Jackson, we don't need to bother the Resident any more just now."

"But—"

"Come on, I said! I want a few words with you!" McLeod insisted.

Jackson sensed that there would be no point in arguing any further with the Resident, but he followed McLeod out into the bright Hawaiian sunshine with a dull glow of anger burning in his cheeks. Accompanied by the squad, they climbed into the car and left.

As soon as they were well away from the Residence, Jackson grabbed McLeod by the lapel of his jacket. "All right, humorist! What was the idea of that? Are you trying to make things hard for yourself?"

"No, but *you* are," McLeod said in a cold voice. "Get your hands off me. I may get you fired anyway, just because you're a louse, but if you keep acting like this, I'll see that they toss you into solitary and toss the key away."

"What are you talking about?" But he released his hold.

"Just think about it, Jackson. The Government can't get its hands on that money unless I permit it. As I said, we'll arrive at an equitable arrangement. And that will be a damn sight less than ninety-eight percent of my earnings, believe me."

"If you refuse to pay, we'll—" He stopped suddenly.

"—Throw me in jail?" McLeod shook his head. "You can't get money while I'm in jail."

"We'll wait," said Jackson firmly. "After a little while in a cell, you'll listen to reason and will sign those checks."

"You don't think very well, do you, Jackson? To 'sign' a check, I have to go to the Galactic Resident. As soon as you take me to him, I authorize a check to buy me a ticket for some nice planet where there are no income taxes."

Jackson opened his mouth and shut it again, frowning.

"Think about it, Jackson," McLeod continued. "Nobody can get that money from me without my consent. Now it so happens that I want to help Earth; I have a certain perverse fondness for the human race, even though it is inconceivably backward by Galactic standards. We have about as much chance of ever becoming of any importance on the Galactic scale as the Australian aborigine has of becoming important in world politics, but a few thousand years of evolution may bring out a few individuals who have the ability to do something. I'm not sure. But I'm damned if I'll let the boneheads run all over me while they take my money.

"I happen to be, at the moment—and through sheer luck—Earth's only natural resource as far as the galaxy is concerned. Sure you can put me in jail. You can kill me if you want. But that won't give you the money. I am the goose that lays the golden eggs. But I'm not such a goose that I'm going to let you boot me in the tail while you steal the gold.

"Earth has no other source of income. None. Tourists are few and far between and they spend almost nothing. As long as I am alive and in good health and out of prison, Earth will have a nice steady income of fifty thousand Galactic credits a year.

"Earth, I said. Not the Government, except indirectly. I intend to see that my money isn't confiscated." He had a few other plans, too, but he saw no necessity of mentioning them to Jackson.

"If I don't like the way the Government behaves, I'll simply shut off the source of supply. Understand, Jackson?"

"Um-m-m," said Jackson. He understood, he didn't like it, and he didn't know what to do about it.

"One of the first things we're going to do is start a little 'information' flowing," McLeod said. "I don't care to live on a planet where everybody hates my guts, so, as the Resident suggested, we're going to have to start a propaganda campaign to counteract the one that denounced me. For that, I'll want to talk to someone a little higher in the Government. You'd better take me to the head of the U.B.I. He'll know who I should speak to for that purpose."

Jackson still looked dazed, but it had evidently penetrated that McLeod had the upper hand. "Wha ... er ... what did you say, sir?" he asked, partially coming out of his daze.

McLeod sighed.

"Take me to your leader," he said patiently.

146

The Man Who Hated Mars

I WANT you to put me in prison!" the big, hairy man said in a trembling voice.

He was addressing his request to a thin woman sitting behind a desk that seemed much too big for her. The plaque on the desk said:

LT. PHOEBE HARRIS
TERRAN REHABILITATION SERVICE

Lieutenant Harris glanced at the man before her for only a moment before she returned her eyes to the dossier on the desk; but long enough to verify the impression his voice had given. Ron Clayton was a big, ugly, cowardly, dangerous man.

He said: "Well? Dammit, say something!"

The lieutenant raised her eyes again. "Just be patient until I've read this." Her voice and eyes were expressionless, but her hand moved beneath the desk.

Clayton froze. *She's yellow!* he thought. She's turned on the trackers! He could see the pale greenish glow of their little eyes watching him all around the room. If he made any fast move, they would cut him down with a stun beam before he could get two feet.

She had thought he was going to jump her. *Little rat!* he thought, *somebody ought to slap her down!*

He watched her check through the heavy dossier in front of her. Finally, she looked up at him again.

"Clayton, your last conviction was for strong-arm robbery. You were given a choice between prison on Earth and freedom here on Mars. You picked Mars."

He nodded slowly. He'd been broke and hungry at the time. A sneaky little rat named Johnson had bilked Clayton out of his fair share of the Corey payroll job, and Clayton had been forced to get the money somehow. He hadn't mussed the guy up much; besides, it was the sucker's own fault. If he hadn't tried to yell—

Lieutenant Harris went on: "I'm afraid you can't back down now."

"But it isn't fair! The most I'd have got on that frame-up would've been ten years. I've been here fifteen already!"

"I'm sorry, Clayton. It can't be done. You're here. Period. Forget about trying to get back. Earth doesn't want you." Her voice sounded choppy, as though she were trying to keep it calm.

Clayton broke into a whining rage. "You can't do that! It isn't fair! I never did anything to you! I'll go talk to the Governor! He'll listen to reason! You'll see! I'll—"

"*Shut up!*" the woman snapped harshly. "I'm getting sick of it! I personally think you should have been locked up—permanently. I think this idea of forced colonization is going to breed trouble for Earth someday, but it is about the only way you can get anybody to colonize this frozen hunk of mud.

"Just keep it in mind that I don't like it any better than you do—*and I didn't strong-arm anybody to deserve the assignment!* Now get out of here!"

She moved a hand threateningly toward the manual controls of the stun beam.

Clayton retreated fast. The trackers ignored anyone walking away from the desk; they were set only to spot threatening movements toward it.

Outside the Rehabilitation Service Building, Clayton could feel the tears running down the inside of his face mask. He'd asked again and again—God only knew how many times—in the past fifteen years. Always the same answer. No.

When he'd heard that this new administrator was a woman, he'd hoped she might be easier to convince. She wasn't. If anything, she was harder than the others.

The heat-sucking frigidity of the thin Martian air whispered around him in a feeble breeze. He shivered a little and began walking toward the recreation center.

There was a high, thin piping in the sky above him which quickly became a scream in the thin air.

He turned for a moment to watch the ship land, squinting his eyes to see the number on the hull.

Fifty-two. Space Transport Ship Fifty-two.

Probably bringing another load of poor suckers to freeze to death on Mars.

That was the thing he hated about Mars—the cold. The everlasting damned cold! And the oxidation pills; take one every three hours or smother in the poor, thin air.

The government could have put up domes; it could have put in building-to-building tunnels, at least. It could have done a hell of a lot of things to make Mars a decent place for human beings.

But no—the government had other ideas. A bunch of bigshot scientific characters had come up with the idea nearly twenty-three years before. Clayton could remember the words on the sheet he had been given when he was sentenced.

"Mankind is inherently an adaptable animal. If we are to colonize the planets of the Solar System, we must meet the conditions on those planets as best we can.

"Financially, it is impracticable to change an entire planet from its original condition to one which will support human life as it exists on Terra.

"But man, since he is adaptable, can change himself—modify his structure slightly—so that he can live on these planets with only a minimum of change in the environment."

So they made you live outside and like it. So you froze and you choked and you suffered.

Clayton hated Mars. He hated the thin air and the cold. More than anything, he hated the cold.

Ron Clayton wanted to go home.

The Recreation Building was just ahead; at least it would be warm inside. He pushed in through the outer and inner doors, and he heard the burst of music from the jukebox. His stomach tightened up into a hard cramp.

They were playing Heinlein's *Green Hills of Earth*.

There was almost no other sound in the room, although it was full of people. There were plenty of colonists who claimed to like Mars, but even they were silent when that song was played.

Clayton wanted to go over and smash the machine—make it stop reminding him. He clenched his teeth and his fists and his eyes and cursed mentally. *God, how I hate Mars!*

When the hauntingly nostalgic last chorus faded away, he walked over to the machine and fed it full of enough coins to keep it going on something else until he left.

At the bar, he ordered a beer and used it to wash down another oxidation tablet. It wasn't good beer; it didn't even deserve the name. The atmospheric pressure was so low as to boil all the carbon dioxide out of it, so the brewers never put it back in after fermentation.

He was sorry for what he had done—really and truly sorry. If they'd only give him one more chance, he'd make good. Just one more chance. He'd work things out.

He'd promised himself that both times they'd put him up before, but things had been different then. He hadn't really been given another chance, what with parole boards and all.

Clayton closed his eyes and finished the beer. He ordered another.

He'd worked in the mines for fifteen years. It wasn't that he minded work really, but the foreman had it in for him. Always giving him a bad time; always picking out the lousy jobs for him.

Like the time he'd crawled into a side-boring in Tunnel 12 for a nap during lunch and the foreman had caught him. When he promised never to do it again if the foreman wouldn't put it on report, the guy said, "Yeah. Sure. Hate to hurt a guy's record."

Then he'd put Clayton on report anyway. Strictly a rat.

Not that Clayton ran any chance of being fired; they never fired anybody. But they'd fined him a day's pay. A whole day's pay.

He tapped his glass on the bar, and the barman came over with another beer. Clayton looked at it, then up at the barman. "Put a head on it."

The bartender looked at him sourly. "I've got some soapsuds here, Clayton, and one of these days I'm gonna put some in your beer if you keep pulling that gag."

That was the trouble with some guys. No sense of humor.

Somebody came in the door and then somebody else came in behind him, so that both inner and outer doors were open for an instant. A blast of icy breeze struck Clayton's back, and he shivered. He started to say something, then changed his mind; the doors were already closed again, and besides, one of the guys was bigger than he was.

The iciness didn't seem to go away immediately. It was like the mine. Little old Mars was cold clear down to her core—or at least down as far as they'd drilled. The walls were frozen and seemed to radiate a chill that pulled the heat right out of your blood.

Somebody was playing *Green Hills* again, damn them. Evidently all of his own selections had run out earlier than he'd thought they would.

Hell! There was nothing to do here. He might as well go home.

"Gimme another beer, Mac."

He'd go home as soon as he finished this one.

He stood there with his eyes closed, listening to the music and hating Mars.

A voice next to him said: "I'll have a whiskey."

The voice sounded as if the man had a bad cold, and Clayton turned slowly to look at him. After all the sterilization they went through before they left Earth, nobody on Mars ever had a cold, so there was only one thing that would make a man's voice sound like that.

Clayton was right. The fellow had an oxygen tube clamped firmly over his nose. He was wearing the uniform of the Space Transport Service.

"Just get in on the ship?" Clayton asked conversationally.

The man nodded and grinned. "Yeah. Four hours before we take off again." He poured down the whiskey. "Sure cold out."

Clayton agreed. "It's always cold." He watched enviously as the spaceman ordered another whiskey.

Clayton couldn't afford whiskey. He probably could have by this time, if the mines had made him a foreman, like they should have.

Maybe he could talk the spaceman out of a couple of drinks.

"My name's Clayton. Ron Clayton."

The spaceman took the offered hand. "Mine's Parkinson, but everybody calls me Parks."

"Sure, Parks. Uh—can I buy you a beer?"

Parks shook his head. "No, thanks. I started on whiskey. Here, let me buy you one."

"Well—thanks. Don't mind if I do."

They drank them in silence, and Parks ordered two more.

"Been here long?" Parks asked.

"Fifteen years. Fifteen long, long years."

"Did you—uh—I mean—" Parks looked suddenly confused.

Clayton glanced quickly to make sure the bartender was out of earshot. Then he grinned. "You mean am I a convict? Nah. I came here because I wanted to. But—" He lowered his voice. "—we don't talk about it around here. You know." He gestured with one hand—a gesture that took in everyone else in the room.

Parks glanced around quickly, moving only his eyes. "Yeah. I see," he said softly.

"This your first trip?" asked Clayton.

"First one to Mars. Been on the Luna run a long time."

"Low pressure bother you much?"

"Not much. We only keep it at six pounds in the ships. Half helium and half oxygen. Only thing that bothers me is the oxy here. Or rather, the oxy that *isn't* here." He took a deep breath through his nose tube to emphasize his point.

Clayton clamped his teeth together, making the muscles at the side of his jaw stand out.

Parks didn't notice. "You guys have to take those pills, don't you?"

"Yeah."

"I had to take them once. Got stranded on Luna. The cat I was in broke down eighty some miles from Aristarchus Base and I had to walk back—with my oxy low. Well, I figured—"

Clayton listened to Parks' story with a great show of attention, but he had heard it before. This "lost on the moon" stuff and its variations had been going the rounds for forty years. Every once in a while, it actually did happen to someone; just often enough to keep the story going.

This guy did have a couple of new twists, but not enough to make the story worthwhile.

"Boy," Clayton said when Parks had finished, "you were lucky to come out of that alive!"

Parks nodded, well pleased with himself, and bought another round of drinks.

"Something like that happened to me a couple of years ago," Clayton began. "I'm supervisor on the third shift in the mines at Xanthe, but at the time, I was only a foreman. One day, a couple of guys went to a branch tunnel to—"

It was a very good story. Clayton had made it up himself, so he knew that Parks had never heard it before. It was gory in just the right places, with a nice effect at the end.

"—so I had to hold up the rocks with my back while the rescue crew pulled the others out of the tunnel by crawling between my legs. Finally, they got some steel beams down there to take the load off, and I could let go. I was in the hospital for a week," he finished.

Parks was nodding vaguely. Clayton looked up at the clock above the bar and realized that they had been talking for better than an hour. Parks was buying another round.

Parks was a hell of a nice fellow.

There was, Clayton found, only one trouble with Parks. He got to talking so loud that the bartender refused to serve either one of them any more.

The bartender said Clayton was getting loud, too, but it was just because he had to talk loud to make Parks hear him.

Clayton helped Parks put his mask and parka on and they walked out into the cold night.

Parks began to sing *Green Hills*. About halfway through, he stopped and turned to Clayton.

"I'm from Indiana."

Clayton had already spotted him as an American by his accent.

"Indiana? That's nice. Real nice."

"Yeah. You talk about green hills, we got green hills in Indiana. What time is it?"

Clayton told him.

"Jeez-krise! Ol' spaship takes off in an hour. Ought to have one more drink first."

Clayton realized he didn't like Parks. But maybe he'd buy a bottle.

Sharkie Johnson worked in Fuels Section, and he made a nice little sideline of stealing alcohol, cutting it, and selling it. He thought it was real funny to call it Martian Gin.

Clayton said: "Let's go over to Sharkie's. Sharkie will sell us a bottle."

"Okay," said Parks. "We'll get a bottle. That's what we need: a bottle."

It was quite a walk to the Shark's place. It was so cold that even Parks was beginning to sober up a little. He was laughing like hell when Clayton started to sing.

"We're going over to the Shark'sTo buy a jug of gin for Parks!Hi ho, hi ho, hi ho!"

One thing about a few drinks; you didn't get so cold. You didn't feel it too much, anyway.

The Shark still had his light on when they arrived. Clayton whispered to Parks: "I'll go in. He knows me. He wouldn't sell it if you were around. You got eight credits?"

"Sure I got eight credits. Just a minute, and I'll give you eight credits." He fished around for a minute inside his parka, and pulled out his notecase. His gloved fingers were a little clumsy, but he managed to get out a five and three ones and hand them to Clayton.

"You wait out here," Clayton said.

He went in through the outer door and knocked on the inner one. He should have asked for ten credits. Sharkie only charged five, and that would leave him three for himself. But he could have got ten—maybe more.

When he came out with the bottle, Parks was sitting on a rock, shivering.

"Jeez-krise!" he said. "It's cold out here. Let's get to someplace where it's warm."

"Sure. I got the bottle. Want a drink?"

Parks took the bottle, opened it, and took a good belt out of it.

"Hooh!" he breathed. "Pretty smooth."

As Clayton drank, Parks said: "Hey! I better get back to the field! I know! We can go to the men's room and finish the bottle before the ship takes off! Isn't that a good idea? It's warm there."

They started back down the street toward the spacefield.

"Yep, I'm from Indiana. Southern part, down around Bloomington," Parks said. "Gimme the jug. Not Bloomington, Illinois—Bloomington, Indiana. We really got green hills down there." He drank, and handed the bottle back to Clayton. "Pers-nally, I don't see why anybody'd stay on Mars. Here y'are, practic'ly on the equator in the middle of the summer, and it's colder than hell. Brrr!

"Now if you was smart, you'd go home, where it's warm. Mars wasn't built for people to live on, anyhow. I don't see how you stand it."

That was when Clayton decided he really hated Parks.

And when Parks said: "Why be dumb, friend? Whyn't you go home?" Clayton kicked him in the stomach, hard.

"And that, that—" Clayton said as Parks doubled over.

He said it again as he kicked him in the head. And in the ribs. Parks was gasping as he writhed on the ground, but he soon lay still.

Then Clayton saw why. Parks' nose tube had come off when Clayton's foot struck his head.

Parks was breathing heavily, but he wasn't getting any oxygen.

That was when the Big Idea hit Ron Clayton. With a nosepiece on like that, you couldn't tell who a man was. He took another drink from the jug and then began to take Parks' clothes off.

The uniform fit Clayton fine, and so did the nose mask. He dumped his own clothing on top of Parks' nearly nude body, adjusted the little oxygen tank so that the gas would flow properly through the mask, took the first deep breath of good air he'd had in fifteen years, and walked toward the spacefield.

He went into the men's room at the Port Building, took a drink, and felt in the pockets of the uniform for Parks' identification. He found it and opened the booklet. It read:

PARKINSON, HERBERT J.
Steward 2nd Class, STS

Above it was a photo, and a set of fingerprints.

Clayton grinned. They'd never know it wasn't Parks getting on the ship.

Parks was a steward, too. A cook's helper. That was good. If he'd been a jetman or something like that, the crew might wonder why he wasn't on duty at takeoff. But a steward was different.

Clayton sat for several minutes, looking through the booklet and drinking from the bottle. He emptied it just before the warning sirens keened through the thin air.

Clayton got up and went outside toward the ship.

"Wake up! Hey, you! Wake up!"

Somebody was slapping his cheeks. Clayton opened his eyes and looked at the blurred face over his own.

From a distance, another voice said: "Who is it?"

The blurred face said: "I don't know. He was asleep behind these cases. I think he's drunk."

Clayton wasn't drunk—he was sick. His head felt like hell. Where the devil was he?

"Get up, bud. Come on, get up!"

Clayton pulled himself up by holding to the man's arm. The effort made him dizzy and nauseated.

The other man said: "Take him down to sick bay, Casey. Get some thiamin into him."

Clayton didn't struggle as they led him down to the sick bay. He was trying to clear his head. Where was he? He must have been pretty drunk last night.

He remembered meeting Parks. And getting thrown out by the bartender. Then what?

Oh, yeah. He'd gone to the Shark's for a bottle. From there on, it was mostly gone. He remembered a fight or something, but that was all that registered.

The medic in the sick bay fired two shots from a hypo-gun into both arms, but Clayton ignored the slight sting.

"Where am I?"

"Real original. Here, take these." He handed Clayton a couple of capsules, and gave him a glass of water to wash them down with.

When the water hit his stomach, there was an immediate reaction.

"Oh, Christ!" the medic said. "Get a mop, somebody. Here, bud; heave into this." He put a basin on the table in front of Clayton.

It took them the better part of an hour to get Clayton awake enough to realize what was going on and where he was. Even then, he was plenty groggy.

It was the First Officer of the STS-52 who finally got the story straight. As soon as Clayton was in condition, the medic and the quartermaster officer who had found him took him up to the First Officer's compartment.

"I was checking through the stores this morning when I found this man. He was asleep, dead drunk, behind the crates."

"He was drunk, all right," supplied the medic. "I found this in his pocket." He flipped a booklet to the First Officer.

The First was a young man, not older than twenty-eight with tough-looking gray eyes. He looked over the booklet.

"Where did you get Parkinson's ID booklet? And his uniform?"

Clayton looked down at his clothes in wonder. "I don't know."

"You *don't know*? That's a hell of an answer."

"Well, I was drunk," Clayton said defensively. "A man doesn't know what he's doing when he's drunk." He frowned in concentration. He knew he'd have to think up some story.

"I kind of remember we made a bet. I bet him I could get on the ship. Sure—I remember, now. That's what happened; I bet him I could get on the ship and we traded clothes."

"Where is he now?"

"At my place, sleeping it off, I guess."

"Without his oxy-mask?"

"Oh, I gave him my oxidation pills for the mask."

The First shook his head. "That sounds like the kind of trick Parkinson would pull, all right. I'll have to write it up and turn you both in to the authorities when we hit Earth." He eyed Clayton. "What's your name?"

"Cartwright. Sam Cartwright," Clayton said without batting an eye.

"Volunteer or convicted colonist?"

"Volunteer."

The First looked at him for a long moment, disbelief in his eyes.

It didn't matter. Volunteer or convict, there was no place Clayton could go. From the officer's viewpoint, he was as safely imprisoned in the spaceship as he would be on Mars or a prison on Earth.

The First wrote in the log book, and then said: "Well, we're one man short in the kitchen. You wanted to take Parkinson's place; brother, you've got it—without pay." He paused for a moment.

"You know, of course," he said judiciously, "that you'll be shipped back to Mars immediately. And you'll have to work out your passage both ways—it will be deducted from your pay."

Clayton nodded. "I know."

"I don't know what else will happen. If there's a conviction, you may lose your volunteer status on Mars. And there may be fines taken out of your pay, too.

"Well, that's all, Cartwright. You can report to Kissman in the kitchen."

The First pressed a button on his desk and spoke into the intercom. "Who was on duty at the airlock when the crew came aboard last night? Send him up. I want to talk to him."

Then the quartermaster officer led Clayton out the door and took him to the kitchen.

The ship's driver tubes were pushing it along at a steady five hundred centimeters per second squared acceleration, pushing her steadily closer to Earth with a little more than half a gravity of drive.

There wasn't much for Clayton to do, really. He helped to select the foods that went into the automatics, and he cleaned them out after each meal was cooked. Once every day, he had to partially dismantle them for a really thorough going-over.

And all the time, he was thinking.

Parkinson must be dead; he knew that. That meant the Chamber. And even if he wasn't, they'd send Clayton back to Mars. Luckily, there was no way for either planet to communicate with the ship; it was hard enough to keep a beam trained on a planet without trying to hit such a comparatively small thing as a ship.

But they would know about it on Earth by now. They would pick him up the instant the ship landed. And the best he could hope for was a return to Mars.

No, by God! He wouldn't go back to that frozen mud-ball! He'd stay on Earth, where it was warm and comfortable and a man could live where he was meant to live. Where there was plenty of air to breathe and plenty of water to drink. Where the beer tasted like beer and not like slop. Earth. Good green hills, the like of which exists nowhere else.

Slowly, over the days, he evolved a plan. He watched and waited and checked each little detail to make sure nothing would go wrong. It *couldn't* go wrong. He didn't want to die, and he didn't want to go back to Mars.

Nobody on the ship liked him; they couldn't appreciate his position. He hadn't done anything to them, but they just didn't like him. He didn't know why; he'd *tried* to get along with them. Well, if they didn't like him, the hell with them.

If things worked out the way he figured, they'd be damned sorry.

He was very clever about the whole plan. When turn-over came, he pretended to get violently spacesick. That gave him an opportunity to steal a bottle of chloral hydrate from the medic's locker.

And, while he worked in the kitchen, he spent a great deal of time sharpening a big carving knife.

Once, during his off time, he managed to disable one of the ship's two lifeboats. He was saving the other for himself.

The ship was eight hours out from Earth and still decelerating when Clayton pulled his getaway.

It was surprisingly easy. He was supposed to be asleep when he sneaked down to the drive compartment with the knife. He pushed open the door, looked in, and grinned like an ape.

The Engineer and the two jetmen were out cold from the chloral hydrate in the coffee from the kitchen.

Moving rapidly, he went to the spares locker and began methodically to smash every replacement part for the drivers. Then he took three of the signal bombs from the emergency kit, set them for five minutes, and placed them around the driver circuits.

He looked at the three sleeping men. What if they woke up before the bombs went off? He didn't want to kill them though. He wanted them to know what had happened and who had done it.

He grinned. There was a way. He simply had to drag them outside and jam the door lock. He took the key from the Engineer, inserted it, turned it, and snapped off the head, leaving the body of the key still in the lock. Nobody would unjam it in the next four minutes.

Then he began to run up the stairwell toward the good lifeboat.

He was panting and out of breath when he arrived, but no one had stopped him. No one had even seen him.

He clambered into the lifeboat, made everything ready, and waited.

The signal bombs were not heavy charges; their main purposes was to make a flare bright enough to be seen for thousands of miles in space. Fluorine and magnesium made plenty of light—and heat.

Quite suddenly, there was no gravity. He had felt nothing, but he knew that the bombs had exploded. He punched the LAUNCH switch on the control board of the lifeboat, and the little ship leaped out from the side of the greater one.

Then he turned on the drive, set it at half a gee, and watched the STS-52 drop behind him. It was no longer decelerating, so it would miss Earth and drift on into space. On the other hand, the lifeship would come down very neatly within a few hundred miles of the spaceport in Utah, the destination of the STS-52.

Landing the lifeship would be the only difficult part of the maneuver, but they were designed to be handled by beginners. Full instructions were printed on the simplified control board.

Clayton studied them for a while, then set the alarm to waken him in seven hours and dozed off to sleep.

He dreamed of Indiana. It was full of nice, green hills and leafy woods, and Parkinson was inviting him over to his mother's house for chicken and whiskey. And all for free.

Beneath the dream was the calm assurance that they would never catch him and send him back. When the STS-52 failed to show up, they would think he had been lost with it. They would never look for him.

When the alarm rang, Earth was a mottled globe looming hugely beneath the ship. Clayton watched the dials on the board, and began to follow the instructions on the landing sheet.

He wasn't too good at it. The accelerometer climbed higher and higher, and he felt as though he could hardly move his hands to the proper switches.

He was less than fifteen feet off the ground when his hand slipped. The ship, out of control, shifted, spun, and toppled over on its side, smashing a great hole in the cabin.

Clayton shook his head and tried to stand up in the wreckage. He got to his hands and knees, dizzy but unhurt, and took a deep breath of the fresh air that was blowing in through the hole in the cabin.

It felt just like home.

Bureau of Criminal Investigation
Regional Headquarters
Cheyenne, Wyoming
20 January 2102

To: Space Transport Service
Subject: Lifeship 2, STS-52
Attention Mr. P. D. Latimer

Dear Paul,

I have on hand the copies of your reports on the rescue of the men on the disabled STS-52. It is fortunate that the Lunar radar stations could compute their orbit.

The detailed official report will follow, but briefly, this is what happened:

The lifeship landed—or, rather, crashed—several miles west of Cheyenne, as you know, but it was impossible to find the man who was piloting it until yesterday because of the weather.

He has been identified as Ronald Watkins Clayton, exiled to Mars fifteen years ago.

Evidently, he didn't realize that fifteen years of Martian gravity had so weakened his muscles that he could hardly walk under the pull of a full Earth gee.

As it was, he could only crawl about a hundred yards from the wrecked lifeship before he collapsed.

Well, I hope this clears up everything.

I hope you're not getting the snow storms up there like we've been getting them.

John B. Remley

Captain, CBI

Anything You Can Do

I

Like some great silver-pink fish, the ship sang on through the eternal night. There was no impression of swimming; the fish shape had neither fins nor a tail. It was as though it were hovering in wait for a member of some smaller species to swoop suddenly down from nowhere, so that it, in turn, could pounce and kill.

But still it moved.

Only a being who was thoroughly familiar with the type could have told that this fish was dying.

In shape, the ship was rather like a narrow flounder—long, tapered, and oval in cross-section—but it showed none of the exterior markings one might expect of either a living thing or of a spaceship. With one exception, the smooth, silver-pink exterior was featureless.

That one exception was a long, purplish-black, roughened discoloration that ran along one side for almost half of the ship's seventeen meters of length. It was the only external sign that the ship was dying.

Inside the ship, the Nipe neither knew nor cared about the discoloration. Had he thought about it, he would have deduced the presence of the burn, but it was the least of his worries. The internal damage that had been done to the ship was by far the more serious. It could, quite possibly, kill him.

The Nipe, of course, had no intention of dying. Not out here. Not so far, so very far, from his own people. Not out here, where his death would be so very improper.

He looked at the ball of the yellow-white sun ahead and wondered that such a relatively stable, inactive star could have produced such a tremendously energetic plasmoid that it could still do the damage it had done so far out. It had been a freak, of course. Such suns as this did not normally produce such energetic swirls of magnetic force.

But the thing had been there, nonetheless, and the ship had hit it at high velocity. Fortunately, the ship had only touched the edge of the swirling cloud, otherwise the entire ship would have vanished in a puff of incandescence. But it had done enough. The power plants that drove the ship at ultralight velocities through the depths of interstellar space had been so badly damaged that they could only be used in short bursts, and each burst brought them nearer to the fusion point. Most of the instruments were powerless; the Nipe was not even sure he could land the vessel. Any attempt to use the communicator to call home would have blown the ship to atoms.

The Nipe did not want to die, but, if die he must, he did not want to die foolishly.

It had taken a long time to drift in from the outer reaches of this sun's planetary system, but using the power plants any more than absolutely necessary would have been fool-hardy.

The Nipe missed the companionship his brother had given him for so long; his help would be invaluable now. But there had been no choice. There had not been enough supplies for two to survive the long fall inward toward the distant sun. The Nipe, having discovered the fact first, had, out of his mercy and compassion, killed his brother while the other was not looking. Then, having eaten his brother with all due ceremony, he had settled down to the long, lonely wait.

Beings of another race might have cursed the accident that had disabled the ship, or regretted the necessity that one of them should die, but the Nipe did neither, for, to him, the first notion would have been foolish, and the second incomprehensible.

But now, as the ship fell ever closer toward the yellow-white sun, he began to worry about his own fate. For a while, it had seemed almost certain that he would survive long enough to build a communicator—for the instruments had already told him and his brother that the system ahead was inhabited by creatures of reasoning power, if not true intelligence, and it would almost certainly be possible to get the equipment he needed for them. Now, though, it looked as if the ship would not survive a landing. He had had to steer it away from a great gas giant, which had seriously endangered the power plants.

He did not want to die in space—wasted, forever undevoured. At least, he must die on a planet, where there might be creatures with the compassion and wisdom to give his body the proper ingestion. The thought of feeding inferior creatures was repugnant, but it was better than rotting to feed monocells or ectogenes, and far superior to wasting away in space.

Even thoughts such as these did not occupy his mind often or for very long. Far, far better than any of them was the desire—and planning for survival.

The outer orbits of the gas giants had been passed at last, and the Nipe fell on through the asteroid belt without approaching any of the larger pieces of rock-and-metal. That he and his brother had originally elected to come into this system along its orbital plane had been a mixed blessing; to have come in at a different angle would have avoided all the debris—from planetary size on down—that is thickest in a star's equatorial plane, but it would also have meant a greater chance of missing a suitable planet unless too much reliance were placed on the already weakened power generators. As it was, the Nipe had been able to use the gravitational field of the gas giant to swing his ship toward the precise spot where the third planet would be when the ship arrived in the third orbit. Moreover, the third planet would be retreating from the Nipe's line of flight, which would make the velocity difference that much the less.

For a while, the Nipe had toyed with the idea of using the mining bases that the local life form had set up in the asteroid belt as bases for his own operations, but he had decided against it. Movement would be much freer and much more productive on a planet than it would be in the Belt.

He would have preferred using the fourth planet for his base. Although much smaller, it had the same reddish, arid look as his own home planet, while the third world was three-quarters drowned in water. But there were two factors that weighed so heavily against that choice that they rendered it impossible. In the first place, by far the greater proportion of the local inhabitants' commerce was between the asteroids and the third planet. Second, and much more important, the fourth world was at such a point in her orbit that the energy required to land would destroy the ship beyond any doubt.

It would have to be the third world.

As the ship fell inward, the Nipe watched his pitifully inadequate instruments, doing his best to keep tabs on every one of the feebly-powered ships that the local life form used to move through space. He did not want to be spotted now, and even though the odds were against these beings having any instrument highly developed enough to spot his craft, there was always the possibility that he might be observed optically.

So he squatted there in the ship, a centipede-like thing about five feet in length and a little less than eighteen inches in diameter, with eight articulated limbs spaced in pairs along his body, any one of which could be used as hand or foot. His head, which was long and snouted, displayed two pairs of violet eyes which kept a constant watch on the indicators and screens of the few instruments that were still functioning aboard the ship.

And he waited as the ship fell towards its rendezvous with the third planet.

II

Wang Kulichenko pulled the collar of his uniform coat up closer around his ears and pulled the helmet and face-mask down a bit. It was only early October, but here in the tundra country the wind had a tendency to be chill and biting in the morning, even at this time of year. Within a week or so, he'd have to start using the power pack on his horse to electrically warm his protective clothing and the horse's wrappings, but there was no necessity of that yet. He smiled a little as he always did when he thought of his grandfather's remarks about such "new-fangled nonsense".

"Your ancestors, son of my son," he would say, "conquered the tundra and lived upon it for thousands of years without the need of such womanish things. Are there no men anymore? Are there none who can face nature alone and unafraid without the aid of artifices that bring softness?"

But Wang Kulichenko noticed—though, out of politeness, he never pointed it out—that the old man never failed to take advantage of the electric warmth of the house when the short days came and the snow blew across the country like fine white sand. And he never complained about the lights or the television or the hot water, except to grumble occasionally that they were a little old and out of date and that the mail-order catalog showed that better models were available in Vladivostok.

And Wang would remind the old man, very gently, that a paper-forest ranger made only so much money, and that there would have to be more saving before such things could be bought. He did not—*ever*—remind the old man that he, Wang, was stretching a point to keep his grandfather on the payroll as an assistant.

Wang Kulichenko patted his horse's rump and urged her softly to step up her pace just a bit. He had a certain amount of territory to cover, and, although he wanted to be careful in his checking, he also wanted to get home early.

Around him, the neatly-planted forest of paper-trees spread knotty, alien branches, trying to catch the rays of the winter-waning sun. Whenever Wang thought of his grandfather's remarks about his ancestors, he always wondered, as a corollary, what those same ancestors would have thought about a forest growing up here, where no forest like this one had ever grown before.

They were called paper-trees because the bulk of their pulp was used to make paper (they were of no use whatever as lumber), but they weren't trees, really, and the organic chemicals that were leached from them during the pulping process were of far more value than the paper pulp.

They were mutations of a smaller plant that had been found in the temperate regions of Mars and purposely changed genetically to grow on the Siberian tundra, where the conditions were similar to, but superior to, their natural habitat.

They looked as though someone had managed to cross breed the Joshua tree with the cypress and then persuaded the result to grow grass instead of leaves.

In the distance, Wang heard the whining of the wind and he automatically pulled his coat a little tighter, even though he noticed no increase in the wind velocity around him.

Then, as the whine became louder, he realized that it was not the wind.

He turned his head toward the noise and looked up. For a long minute, he watched the sky as the sound gained volume, but he could see nothing at first. Then he caught a glimpse of motion. A dot that was hard to distinguish against the cloud-mottled gray sky.

What was it? An air transport in trouble? There were two trans-polar routes that passed within a few hundred miles of here, but no air transport he had ever seen had made a noise like that. Normally, they were so high as to be both invisible and inaudible. Must be trouble of some sort.

He reached down to the saddle pack without taking his eyes off the moving speck and took out the radiophone. He held it to his ear and thumbed the call button insistently.

Grandfather, he thought with growing irritation as the seconds passed, *wake up! Come on, old dozer, rouse yourself from your dreams!*

At the same time, he checked his wrist compass and estimated the direction of flight of the dot and its direction from him. He'd at least be able to give the airline authorities some information if the ship fell. He wished there were some way to triangulate its height and so on, but he had no need for that kind of thing, so he hadn't the equipment.

"Yes? Yes?" came a testy, dry voice through the earphone.

Quickly, Wang gave his grandfather all the information he had on the flying thing. By now, the whine had become a shrill roar, and the thing in the air had become a silver-pink fish shape.

"I think it's coming down very close to here," Wang concluded. "You call the authorities and let them know that one of the aircraft is in trouble. I'll see if I can be of any help here. I'll call you back later."

"As you say," the old man said hurriedly. He cut off.

Wang was beginning to realize that the thing was a spaceship, not an airship. By this time, he could see the thing more clearly. He had never actually seen a spacecraft, but he'd seen enough of them on television to know what they looked like. This one didn't look like a standard type at all, and it didn't behave like one, but it looked even less like an airship, and he knew enough to know that he didn't necessarily know every type of spaceship ever built.

In shape, it resembled the old rocket-propelled jobs that had been first used for space exploration a century before, rather than looking like the fat ovoids that he was used to. But there were no signs of rocket exhausts, and yet the ship was very obviously slowing, so it must have an inertia drive.

It was coming in much lower now, on a line north of him, headed almost due east. He urged the mare forward, in order to try to keep up with the craft, although it was obviously going several hundred miles per hour—hardly a horse's pace.

Still, it was slowing rapidly—very rapidly. Maybe—

He kept the mare moving.

The strange ship skimmed along the treetops in the distance and disappeared from sight. Then there was a thunderous crash, a tearing of wood and foliage, and a grinding, plowing sound.

For a few seconds afterward, there was silence. Then there came a soft rumble, as of water beginning to boil in some huge, but distant, samovar. It seemed to go on and on and on.

And there was a bluish, fluctuating glow on the horizon.

Radioactivity? Wang wondered. Surely not an atomic-powered ship without safety cutoffs in this day and age.

He pulled out his radiophone and thumbed the call button again.

This time, there was no delay. "Yes?"

"How are the radiation detectors behaving there, Grandfather?"

"One moment. I shall see." There was a silence. Then: "No unusual activity, young Wang. Why?"

Wang told him, then asked: "Did you get hold of the air authorities?"

"Yes. They have no missing aircraft, but they're checking with the space fields. The way you describe it, the thing must be a spaceship of some kind."

"I think so, too. I wish I had a radiation detector here, though. I'd like to know whether that thing is hot or not. It's only a couple of miles or so away. I think I'd better stay away. Meanwhile, you'd better put in a call to Central Headquarters Fire Control. There's going to be a holocaust if I'm any judge unless they get here fast with plenty of equipment."

"I'll see to it," said his grandfather, cutting off.

The bluish glow in the sky had quite died away by now, and the distant rumbling was gone, too. And, oddly enough, there was not much smoke in the distance. There was a small cloud of gray that rose, streamerlike, from where the glow had been, but even that faded away fairly rapidly in the chill breeze. Quite obviously, there would be no fire. After several more minutes of watching, he was sure of it. There couldn't have been much heat produced in that explosion—if it could really be called an explosion.

Then he saw something moving in the trees between himself and the spot where the ship had come down. He couldn't quite see what it was, but it looked like someone crawling.

"Halloo, there!" he called out. "Are you hurt?"

There was no answer. Perhaps whoever it was didn't understand Russian. Wang's command of English wasn't too good, but he called out in that language.

Still there was no answer. Whoever it was had crawled out of sight.

Then he realized that it couldn't be anyone crawling. No one could even have run the distance between here and the ship in the time since it had hit, much less crawled.

He frowned. A wolf, then? Possibly. They weren't too common, but there were still plenty of them around.

He unholstered the heavy pistol at his side.

And, as he slid the barrel free, he became the first human being ever to see the Nipe.

For an instant, as the Nipe came out from behind a tree fifteen feet away, Wang Kulichenko froze as he saw those four baleful violet eyes glaring at him from the snouted head. He jerked up the pistol to fire.

He was much too late. His reflexes were too slow by far. The Nipe launched itself across the intervening space in a blur of speed that would have made a leopard seem slow. The alien's hands slapped aside the gun with a violence that broke the man's wrist, while other hands slammed at his skull.

Wang Kulichenko hardly had time to be surprised before he died.

The Nipe stood quietly for a moment, looking down at the thing he had killed. His stomach churned with disgust. He ignored the fading hoofbeats of the slave-animal from which he had knocked the thing that lay on the ground with a crushed skull. The slave-animal was unintelligent and unimportant.

This was the intelligent one.

But so slow! So incredibly slow! And so weak and soft!

It seemed impossible that such poorly-equipped beasts could have survived long enough on any world to evolve to become the dominant life form.

Perhaps it was not the dominant form. Perhaps it was merely a higher slave-animal. He would have to do more investigating.

He picked up the weapon the thing had drawn and examined it carefully. The mechanism was unfamiliar, but a glance at the muzzle told him that it was a projectile weapon of some sort. The twisted grooves in the barrel were obviously designed to impart a spin to the projectile, to give it gyroscopic stability while in flight.

The dead thing must have thought he was a wild animal, the Nipe decided. Surely no being would carry a weapon for use against members of its own or another intelligent species.

He examined the rest of the equipment on the thing. Not much information there. Too bad the slave-animal was gone; there had apparently been more equipment strapped to it.

The next question was, what should he do with the body?

Devour it properly, as one should with a validly slain foe?

It didn't seem that he could do anything else, and yet his stomachs wanted to rebel at the thought. After all, it wasn't as if the thing were really a proper being. It was astonishing to find another intelligent race; none had ever been found before. But he was determined to show them that he was civilized and intelligent, too.

On the other hand, they were obviously of a lower order than the Nipe, and that made the question even more puzzling.

In the end, he decided to leave the thing here, for others of its kind to find. They would doubtless consume it properly.

And—he glanced at the sky and listened—they would be here in time. There were aircraft coming.

He would have to leave quickly. He had to find one of their production or supply centers, and he would have to do it alone, with only the equipment he had on him. The utter destruction of his ship had left him seriously hampered.

He began moving, staying in the protection of the trees. His ethical sense still bothered him. It was not at all civilized to leave a body to the mercy of lesser animals or monocells like that. What kind of monster would they think he was?

Still, there was no help for it. If they caught him while feeding, they might have thought him a lower animal and shot him. He couldn't put an onus like that upon them.

He moved on.

III

Two-fifths of a second. That was all the time Bart Stanton had from the first moment his supersensitive ears heard the faint whisper of metal against leather.

He made good use of it.

The noise had come from behind and slightly to the left of him, so he drew his own gun with his left hand and spun to his left as he dropped to a crouch. He had turned almost completely around, drawn his gun, and fired three shots before the other man had even leveled his own weapon.

The bullets from Stanton's gun made three round spots on the man's jacket, almost touching each other and directly over the heart. The man blinked stupidly for a moment, looking down at the round spots.

"My God," he said softly.

Then the man returned his weapon slowly to his holster.

The big room was noisy. The three shots had merely added to the noise of the gunfire that rattled intermittently around the two men. And even that gunfire was only a part of the cacophony. The tortured molecules of the air in the room were so besieged by the beat of drums, the blare of trumpets, the crackle of lightning, the rumble of heavy machinery, the squawks and shrieks of horns and whistles, the rustle of autumn leaves, the machine-gun snap of popping popcorn, the clink and jingle of falling coins, and the yelps, bellows, howls, roars, snarls, grunts, bleats, moos, purrs, cackles, quacks, chirps, buzzes, and hisses of a myriad of animals, that each molecule would have thought that it was being shoved in a hundred thousand different directions at once if it had had a mind to think with.

The noise wasn't deafening, but it was certainly all-pervasive.

Bart Stanton had reholstered his own weapon and half opened his lips to speak when he heard another sound behind him.

Again he whirled his guns in hand—both of them this time—and his forefingers only fractions of a millimeter from the point that would fire the hair triggers.

But he did not fire.

The second man had merely shifted the weapons in his holsters and then dropped his hands away.

The noise, which had been flooding into the room over the speaker system, died instantly.

Stanton shoved his guns back into place and rose from his crouch. "Real cute," he said, grinning. "I wasn't expecting that one."

The man he was facing smiled back. "Well, Bart, maybe we've proved our point. What do you think, Colonel?" The last was addressed to the third man, who was still standing quietly, looking worried and surprised about the three spots on his jacket that had come from the special harmless projectiles in Stanton's gun.

Colonel Mannheim was four inches shorter than Stanton's five-ten, and was fifteen years older. But, in spite of the differences, he would have laughed at anyone who had told him, five minutes before, that he couldn't outdraw a man who was standing with his back turned.

His bright blue eyes, set deep beneath craggy brows in a tanned face, looked speculatively at the younger man. "Incredible," he said gently. "Absolutely incredible." Then he looked at the other man, a lean civilian with mild blue eyes a shade lighter than his own. "All right, Dr. Farnsworth, I'm convinced. You and your staff have quite literally created a superman. Anyone who can stand in a noise-filled room and hear a man draw a gun twenty feet behind him is incredible enough. The fact that he could and did outdraw and outshoot me after I had started ... well, that's almost beyond comprehension."

He looked back at Bart Stanton. "What's your opinion, Mr. Stanton? Think you can handle the Nipe?"

Stanton paused imperceptibly before answering, while his ultrafast mind considered the problem and arrived at a decision. Just how much confidence should he show the colonel? Mannheim was a man with tremendous confidence in himself, but who was capable of recognizing that there were men who were his superiors, in one field or another.

"If I can't dispose of the Nipe," Stanton said, "no one can."

Colonel Mannheim nodded slowly. "I believe you're right," he said at last. His voice was firm with inner conviction. He shot a glance at Farnsworth. "How about the second man?"

Farnsworth shook his head. "He'll never make it. In another two years, we can put him into reasonable shape again, but his nervous system just couldn't stand the gaff."

"Can we get another man ready in time?"

"Hardly. We can't just pick a man up off the street and turn him into a superman. Even if we could find another subject with Bart's genetic possibilities, it would take more time than we have to spare."

"This isn't magic, Colonel. You don't change a nobody into a physical and mental giant by saying *abracadabra* or by teaching him how to pronounce *shazam* properly."

"I'm aware of that," said Colonel Mannheim without rancor. "Five years of work on Mr. Stanton must have taught you something, though. I should think you could repeat the process in less time."

Farnsworth repeated the headshaking. "Human beings aren't machines, Colonel. They require time to heal, time to learn, time to integrate themselves. Remember that, in spite of all our increased knowledge of anesthesia, antibiotics, viricides, and obstetrics, it still takes nine months to produce a baby. We're in the same position, only more so."

"I see," said Mannheim.

"Besides," Dr. Farnsworth continued, "Stanton's body and nervous system are now close to the theoretical limit for human tissue. I'm afraid you don't realize what kind of mental stability and organization are required to handle the equipment he now has."

"I'm sure I don't," the colonel agreed. "I doubt if anyone besides Stanton himself knows."

Dr. Farnsworth's manner softened a little. "You're probably quite right. Suffice it to say that Bartholomew Stanton is the only answer we've found so far, and the only answer visible in the foreseeable future to the problem posed by the Nipe."

The colonel's face darkened. "I keep hoping that our policy of handling the Nipe hasn't been a mistake. If it has, it's going to prove a fatal one—for the whole race."

"Let's go into the lounge," Farnsworth said. "Standing around in an empty chamber like this isn't the most comfortable way to discuss the fate of mankind." His voice brought hollow echoes from the walls.

Colonel Mannheim grinned at the touch of lightness the biophysicist had injected into the conversation. "Very well. I could do with some coffee, if you have some."

"All you want," said Dr. Farnsworth, leading the way toward the door of the chamber and opening it. "Or, if you'd prefer something with a little more power to it—?"

"Thanks, no. Coffee will do fine," said Mannheim. "How about you, Mr. Stanton?"

Bart Stanton shook his head. "I'd love to have some coffee, but I'll leave the alcohol alone. I'd just have the luck to be finishing a drink when our friend, the Nipe, popped in on us. And when I do meet him, I'm going to need every microsecond of reflex speed I can scrape up."

They walked down a soft-floored, warmly-lit corridor to an elevator which whisked them up to the main level of the Neurophysical Institute Building.

Another corridor led them to a room that might have been the common room of one of the more exclusive men's clubs. There were soft chairs and shelves of books and reading tables and smoking stands, all quietly luxurious. There was no one in the room when the three men entered.

"We can have some privacy here," Dr. Farnsworth said. "None of the rest of the staff will come in until we're through."

Colonel Mannheim looked at the biophysicist speculatively. "You seem to think secrecy's important all of a sudden."

Bart Stanton grinned and kept silent.

Dr. Farnsworth went over to a table, where an urn of coffee radiated soft warmth. "Cream and sugar over there on the tray," he said as he began to fill cups.

"Frankly," Colonel Mannheim said, "I was going to ask you to find us a place where we could talk privately. You seem to have anticipated me."

"I thought you might have something like that in mind," said Dr. Farnsworth without looking up.

The cups were filled and the three men sat down in a triangle of chairs before any of them spoke again. Colonel Mannheim took a sip from his cup and then looked up.

"All right, we'll begin this way. Mr. Stanton, granted that you've been through five years of hell—but how closely have you stayed in touch with the Nipe situation?"

"As best I could through news bulletins and information that your office has sent here."

"Could you give me an oral summary?"

Bart Stanton thought for a moment. It was true that he'd been out of touch with what had been going on outside the walls of the Neurophysical Institute for the past five years. In spite of the reading he'd done and the newscasts he'd watched and the TV tapes he'd seen, he still had no real feeling for the situation.

There were hazy periods during that five years. He had undergone extensive glandular and neural operations of great delicacy, many of which had resulted in what could have been agonizing pain without the use of suppressors. As a result, he possessed a biological engine that, for sheer driving power and nicety of control, surpassed any other known to exist or to have ever existed on Earth—with the possible exception of the Nipe. But those five years of rebuilding and retraining had left a gap in his life.

Several of the steps required to make the conversion from man to superman had resulted in temporary insanity; the wild, swinging imbalances of glandular secretions seeking a new balance, the erratic misfirings of neurons as they attempted to adjust to higher nerve-impulse velocities, and the sheer fatigue engendered by cells which were acting too rapidly for a lagging excretory system, all had contributed to periods of greater or lesser mental abnormality.

That he was sane now, there was no question. But there were holes in his memory that still had to be filled.

He began to talk, rapidly but carefully, telling the colonel all he knew about the situation up to the present.

It wasn't much. It was late October, 2091, and the Nipe, blithely evading capture for ten long years, was still going about his unknown and possibly incomprehensible business.

The Nipe had become a legend. He had replaced Satan, the Bogeyman, Frankenstein's monster, and Mumbo Jumbo, Lord of the Congo, in the public mind. He had taken on, in popular thought, the attributes of the djinn, the vampire, the ghoul, the werewolf, and every other horror and hobgoblin that the mind of Man had conjured up in the previous half-million years.

That he had been connected with the mysterious crash in Siberia ten years before was almost a certainty. How he had managed to get from there to Leningrad without being seen once was more of a mystery, but certainly not impossible in the light of what had been done since.

Eight months later, a non-vision phone call had been received by the Regent's Board of the Khrushchev Memorial Psychiatric Hospital in Leningrad. An odd, breathy voice offered (in very bad Russian!) a meeting. The Nipe had managed to explain, in spite of the language handicap, that he did not want to be mistaken for a wild animal, as had happened with the forest ranger.

The psychiatrists were divided in their opinions. Some thought that the call had been from a deranged person. When the Nipe actually showed up at the appointed place, those minds changed rapidly.

The Nipe's ability to use any human language was limited. He picked up vocabulary and grammatical rules very rapidly, but he seemed completely unable to use a language beyond discussion of concrete actions and objects. His mind was simply too alien to enable him to do more than touch the edges of human communication.

In the discussion of mathematics, in particular, the Nipe seemed to be completely at a loss. He apparently thought of mathematics as a *spoken* language instead of a *written* one, and could not progress beyond simple diagrams.

He wasn't captured in any real sense of the word. He refused to allow any physical tests on his body, and, short of threatening him at gun-point, there didn't seem to be any practicable way to force him to accede to the human's wishes. And they couldn't do that.

The Nipe had to be treated as an emissary from his home world, wherever that was. He'd killed a man, yes. But that had to be allowed as justifiable homicide in self-defense, since the forester had drawn a gun and was ready to fire. Nobody could blame the late Wang Kulichenko for that, but nobody could blame the Nipe, either.

For six weeks, the humans and the Nipe had tried to arrive at a meeting of minds, and just when it would seem within grasp, it would fade away into mist. It was nearly a month before the Russian psychologists and psychiatrists realized that the reason the Nipe had come to them was because he had thought that they were the ruling body of that territory!

The UN observers stayed out of it at first. Before there was any kind of talk on a Government level, there must be some kind of understanding on a personal level. And that, of course, was never achieved.

Just what had set off the Nipe's anger hasn't been established yet, as far as Stanton knew. At a meeting one day, he had simply become more and more incomprehensible, and then, without any warning, he had leaped out, killed three of the men with his bare hands, and gone out the window.

And that had been the end of any diplomatic relations between humanity and the Nipe.

Since that time, he'd been on a rampage of robbery and murder. He was as callously indifferent to human life and property as a human being might be with the life and property of a cockroach.

There have been human criminals whose actions could be described in the same way, but the Nipe had a few touches that few human criminals would have thought of and almost none would have had the capacity to execute.

If, for instance, the Nipe had time to spare, his victims would be an annoying problem in identification when found, for there would be nothing left but well-gnawed bones. And "time to spare," in this case meant twenty or thirty minutes. The Nipe had, if nothing else, a very efficient digestive tract. He ate like a shrew.

And the Nipe never, under any circumstances, used any weapon but the weapons Nature had given him—hands-or-feet, or claws or teeth. Never did he use a knife or gun or even a club.

Almost as an afterthought, one realized that the loot which the Nipe stole was seemingly unpredictable. Money, as such, he apparently had no use for. He had taken gold, silver, and platinum, but one raid for each of these elements had evidently been enough, except for silver, which had required three raids over a period of four years. Since then, he hadn't touched silver again.

He hadn't tried yet for any of the radioactives except radium. He'd taken a full ounce of that in five raids, but hadn't attempted to get his hands on uranium, thorium, plutonium, or any of the other elements normally associated with atomic energy. Nor had he tried to steal any of the fusion materials; the heavy isotopes of hydrogen or any of the lithium isotopes. Beryllium had been taken, but whether there was any significance in the thefts or not, no one knew.

There was a pattern in the thefts, nonetheless. They had begun small and increased. Scientific and technical instruments—oscilloscopes, X-ray generators, radar equipment, maser sets, dynostatic crystals, thermolight resonators, and so on—were stolen complete or gutted for various parts. After awhile, he went on to bigger things—whole aircraft, with their crews, had vanished.

That he had not committed anywhere near all the crimes that had been attributed to him was certain; that he *had* committed a great many of them was equally certain.

There was no doubt at all that his loot was being used to make instruments and devices of unknown kinds. He had used several of them on his raids. The one that could apparently phase out almost any electromagnetic frequency up to about a hundred thousand megacycles—including sixty-cycle power frequencies—was considered to be a particularly cute item. So was the gadget that reduced the tensile strength of concrete to about that of a good grade of marshmallow.

After he had been operating for a few years, there was no installation on the face of the earth that could be considered Nipe-proof for more than a few minutes. He struck when and where he wanted and took whatever he needed.

It was manifestly impossible to guard against the Nipe, since no one knew what sort of loot might strike his fancy next, and there was therefore no way of knowing where or how he would hit next.

Nor could he ever be found after one of his raids. They were plotted and followed out with diabolical accuracy and thoroughness. He struck, looted, and vanished. And wasn't seen again until his next strike.

Colonel Mannheim, who had carefully puffed a cigar alight and smoked it thoughtfully during Stanton's recitation, dropped the remains of the cigar into an ash receptacle. "Accurate but incomplete," he said quietly. "You must have made some guesses." He looked from Bart Stanton to Dr. Farnsworth. "I'd like to hear them."

Farnsworth finished off the last of his coffee. "We've talked about it," he admitted. "Although I must say the hypothesis Bart has come up with would never have occurred to me. I'm still not sure I credit it, but" ... he shrugged ... "I can't say that I disbelieve it, either."

Mannheim turned his eyes back to Stanton. His silence was a question.

"Logically, my theory mightn't hold much water," Stanton admitted. "But the evidence seems to be conclusive enough to me." He got up, went over to the coffee urn, and refilled his cup. "It seems incredible to me that the combined intelligence and organizational ability of the UN Government is incapable of finding anything out about one single alien, no matter how competent he may be," he said as he returned to his seat.

"Somehow, somewhere, someone must have gotten a line on the Nipe. He must have a base for his operations, and someone should have found it by this time.

"If there is such a base, then it must be possible to blast him out of it without resorting to the kind of work it took to produce—me.

"I may be faster and more sensitive and stronger than the average man, but that doesn't mean that I have superhuman abilities to the extent that I can do in two or three years what the combined forces of the Government couldn't do in ten. Certainly you wouldn't rely too heavily on it.

"And yet, apparently, you are.

"To me that can only mean that you've got another ace up your sleeve. You *know* we're going to get the Nipe before I die. You either have a sure way of tracing him or else you already know where he is.

"Which is it?"

Colonel Mannheim sighed. "We know where he is. We've known for six years."

IV

INTERLUDE

The woman's eyes were filled with tears, for which the doctor was privately thankful. At least the original shock had worn off.

"And there's nothing we can do? Nothing?" There was a slight catch in her voice.

"I'm afraid not. Not yet. There are research teams working on the problem, and one day ... perhaps...." Then he shook his head. "But not yet." He paused. "I'm sorry, Mrs. Stanton."

The woman sat there on the comfortable chair and looked at the specialist's diploma that hung on the doctor's wall—and yet, she didn't really see the diploma at all. She was seeing something else—a kind of dream that had been shattered.

After a moment, she began to speak, her voice low and gentle, as though the dream were still going on and she were half afraid she might waken herself if she spoke too loudly.

"Jim and I were so glad they were twins. Identical twin boys. He said—I remember, he said, 'We ought to call 'em Ike and Mike.' And he laughed a little when he said it, to show he didn't mean it.

"I remember, I was propped up in the bed, the afternoon they were born, and Jim had brought me a new bed jacket, and I said I didn't need a new one because I would be going home the next day, and he said: 'Hell, kid, you don't think I'd just buy a bed jacket just for hospital use, do you? This is for breakfasts in bed, too.'

"And that's when he said he'd seen the boys and said we ought to name them Ike and Mike."

The tears were coming down Mrs. Stanton's cheeks heavily now, and grief made her look older than her twenty-four years, but the doctor said nothing, letting her spill out her emotions in words.

"We'd talked about it before, you know—as soon as the obstetrician found out that I was going to have twins. And Jim ... Jim said that we shouldn't name them alike unless they were identical twins or mirror twins. If they were fraternal twins, we'd just name them as if they'd been ordinary brothers or sisters or whatever. You know?" She looked at the doctor, pleading for understanding.

"I know," he said.

"And Jim was always kidding. If they were girls, he said we ought to call them Flora and Dora, or Annie and Fanny, or maybe Susie and Floozie. He was always kidding about it. You know?"

"I know," said the doctor.

"And then, when they *were* identical boys, he was very sensible about it. 'We'll call them Martin and Bartholomew,' he said. 'Then if they want to call themselves Mart and Bart, they can, but they won't be stuck with rhyming names if they don't want them.' Jim was very thoughtful that way, Doctor. Very thoughtful."

She suddenly seemed to realize that she was crying, and took a handkerchief out of her sleeve to dab at her eyes and face.

"I'll have to quit crying," she said, trying to sound brave and strong. "After all, it could have been worse, couldn't it? I mean, the radiation could have killed my boys, too. Jim's dead, yes, and I've got to get used to that. But I still have two boys to take care of, and they'll need me."

"Yes, Mrs. Stanton, they will," said the doctor. "They'll both need you. And you'll have to be very gentle and very careful with both of them."

"How ... how do you mean that?" she asked.

The doctor settled back in his chair and chose his words carefully. "Identical twins tend to identify with each other, Mrs. Stanton. There is a great deal of empathy between people who are not only of the same age, but genetically identical. If they were both healthy, there would be very little trouble in their education at home or at school. Any of the standard texts on psychodynamics in education will show you the pitfalls to avoid when dealing with identical siblings.

"But these boys are no longer identical. One is normal, healthy, and lively. The other is ... well, as you have seen, he is slow, sluggish, and badly co-ordinated. That condition may improve with time, but, until we know more about such damage than we do now, he will be an invalid."

"That's the trouble with radiation damage, Mrs. Stanton. Even when we can save the victim's life, we cannot always save his health.

"You can see, I think, what sort of psychic disturbances this can bring about in such a pair. The ill boy tends to identify with the well one and, unfortunately, the reverse is true. If they are not properly handled during their formative years, Mrs. Stanton, both can be badly damaged emotionally."

"I ... I think I understand," the woman said. "But what sort of thing should I look out for?"

"I suggest that you get a good man in psychic development," the doctor said. "I'd hesitate to prescribe. It's out of my field. But, in general, most of your trouble will be caused by a tendency for the pair to swing into one of two extremes.

"Mutual antagonism can arise if one becomes jealous of the other's health, while the healthy one becomes jealous of the extra consideration shown his crippled brother.

"Or, on the other hand, the healthy boy may identify so closely with his brother that he feels every hurt or slight, real or imagined. He becomes over-solicitous, over-protective. At the same time, the other brother may come to depend completely on the healthy twin.

"In both these situations, there is a positive feedback which constantly worsens the situation. It requires a great deal of careful observation and careful application of the proper educational stimuli to keep the situation from developing toward either extreme. You'll need expert help, if you want both boys to display the full abilities of which they are potentially capable."

"I see. Could you give me the name of a good man, Doctor?"

The doctor nodded and picked up a book on his desk. "I'll give you several names. You can pick the one you like. They're all good men. There are many good women in the field, too, but in this case, I think a man would be best. Of course, if one of them thinks a woman is indicated, that's up to him. As I said, that isn't my field."

He opened the small book and riffled through it to find the names he wanted.

V

The image of the Nipe on the glowing screen was clear and finely detailed. It was, Bart thought, as though one were looking through a window into the Nipe's nest itself. Only the tremendous depth of focus of the lens which caught the picture gave the illusion a sense of unreality. Everything—background and foreground alike—was sharply in focus.

The Nipe moved in slow motion, giving the watchers the eerie feeling that he was moving through a thicker, heavier medium than air, in a place where the gravity was much less than that of Earth.

"Speed the tape up to normal," said Colonel Mannheim to the man who was operating the machine. "If there's anything Mr. Stanton wants to look at more closely, we can run it through again."

As if in obedience to the colonel's command, the Nipe seemed to shake himself a little and go about his business more briskly, and the air and gravity seemed to revert to those of Earth.

"What's he doing?" Stanton asked. The Nipe was doing something with an odd-looking box that sat on the floor in front of him.

"He's got a screwdriver that he's modified to give it a head with an L-shaped cross-section, and he's wiggling it around inside that hole in the box. But what he's doing is a secret between God and the Nipe at this point," the colonel said glumly.

Stanton glanced away from the screen for a moment to look at the other men who were there. Some of them were watching the screen, but most of them seemed to be watching Stanton, although they looked away as soon as they saw his eyes on them.

Trying to see what kind of a bloke this touted superman is, Stanton thought. *Well, I can't say I blame 'em.*

He brought his attention back to the screen.

So this was the Nipe's hideaway. He wondered if it were furnished in the fashion that a Nipe's living quarters would be furnished on whatever planet the multilegged horror called home. Probably it had the same similarity as Robinson Crusoe's island home had to a middle-class Nineteenth Century English home.

There was no furniture at all, as such. Low-slung as he was, the Nipe needed no tables for his work, and sleeping was a form of metabolic rest that he evidently found unnecessary, although he would sometimes just remain quiet for periods of time ranging from a few minutes to a couple of hours.

"We had a hard time getting the first cameras in there," the colonel was saying. "That's why we missed some of the early stages of his work. There! Look at that!"

"That attachment he's making?"

"That's right. Now, it looks as though it's a meter of some kind, but we don't know whether it's a test instrument or an integral part of the machine he's making. The whole thing might be a test instrument. After all, he had to start out from the very beginning—making the tools to make the tools to make the tools, you know."

"It's not quite as bad as all that," said one of the other men, who had been briefly introduced to Stanton as Fred Meyer. "After all, he had our technology to draw upon. If he'd been wrecked on Earth two or three centuries ago, he wouldn't have been able to do a thing."

"Granted," the colonel said agreeably, "but it's quite obvious that there are parts of our technology that are just as alien to him as parts of his are to us. Remember how he went to all the trouble of building a pentode vacuum tube for a job that could have been done by transistors. His knowledge of solid-state physics seems to be about a century and a half behind ours."

"Not completely, Colonel," Meyer said. "That gimmick he built last year—the one that blinded those people in Bagdad—had five perfect emeralds in it, connected in series with silver wire."

"That's true. Our technologies seem to overlap in some areas, but in others there's total alienness."

"Which one would you say was ahead of the other?" Stanton asked.

"Hard to say," said Colonel Mannheim, "but I'd put my money on his technology as encompassing more than ours—at least insofar as the physical sciences are concerned."

"I agree," said Meyer, "he's got things in that little nest of his that—" He stopped and shook his head slowly, as though he couldn't find words.

"I'll say this," Bart Stanton said musingly, "our friend, the Nipe, has plenty of guts. And patience." He smiled a little and then amended his statement. "From our own point of view, that is."

Colonel Mannheim's face took on a quizzical expression. "How do you mean? I was about to agree with you until you tacked that last phrase on. What does point of view have to do with it?"

"Everything, I should say," Stanton said. "It all depends on the equipment an individual has. A man who rushes into a burning building to save a life, wearing nothing but street clothes, has courage. A man who does the same thing when he's wearing a nullotherm suit is an unknown quantity. There is no way of knowing, from that action alone, whether he has courage or not."

Meyer looked a little dazed. "Pardon me if I seem thick, Mr. Stanton, but.... Are you saying that the Nipe's technological equipment is better than ours?"

"Not at all. I'm talking about his personal equipment." He turned again to the colonel. "Colonel Mannheim, do you think it would require any personal courage on my part to stand up against you in a face-to-face gunfight?"

The colonel grinned tightly. "I see what you mean. No, it wouldn't."

"On the other hand, if *you* were to challenge *me*," Bart Stanton continued, "would *that* show courage?"

"Not really. Foolhardiness, stupidity, or insanity—not courage."

"Then neither of us can prove we have guts enough to fight the other. Can we?"

Colonel Mannheim smiled grimly and said nothing, but Meyer, who evidently had a great deal of respect for the colonel, said: "Now, wait a second! That depends on the circumstances! If Colonel Mannheim, say, knew that forcing you to shoot him would save someone else's life—someone more important, say, or maybe a *lot* of people, then—"

Colonel Mannheim laughed. "Meyer, you've just proved Mr. Stanton's point!"

Meyer gaped for a half second, then burst into laughter himself. "Pardon my point of view, Mr. Stanton! I guess I *am* a little slow!"

Mannheim said: "Precisely! Whether the Nipe has courage or patience or any other human feeling depends on his own abilities and on how much information he has. A man can perform any action without fear if he knows that it will not hurt him—or if he does *not* know that it *will*." He glanced at the screen. The Nipe had settled down into his "sleeping position"—unmoving, although his baleful violet eyes were still open. "Cut that off, Meyer," the colonel said. "There's not much to learn from the rest of that tape."

"Have you actually managed to build any of the devices he's constructed?" Stanton asked.

"Some," said Colonel Mannheim. "We have specialists all over the world studying the tapes. We have the advantage of being able to watch every step the Nipe makes, and we know the materials he's using to work with. But, even so, the scientists are baffled by many of them. Can you imagine the time James Clerk Maxwell would have had trying to build a modern television set from tapes like this?"

"I know exactly how he'd feel," Meyer said glumly.

"You can see, then, why we're depending on you," Mannheim told Stanton.

Stanton merely nodded. The knowledge that he was actually a focal point in human history, that the whole future of the human race depended to a tremendous extent on him, was a realization that weighed heavily, and, at the same time, was immensely bracing.

"And now," the colonel said, "I'll turn you over to the psychology department. They'll be able to give you a great deal more information on the Nipe than I can."

VI

The Nipe squatted, brooding, in his underground nest, waiting for the special crystallization process to take place in the sodium-gold alloy that was forming in the reactor.

How long? he wondered. He was not thinking of the crystallization reaction; he knew the timing of that to the fraction of a second. His dark thoughts were focused inwardly, upon himself.

How long would it be before he would be able to construct the communicator that would put him in touch with his own race again? How long before he could discourse again with reasonable beings? For how much longer would he be stranded on an insane planet, surrounded by degraded, insane beings?

The work was going incredibly slowly. He had known at the beginning that his knowledge of the basic arts required to build a communicator was incomplete, but he had not realized just how painfully inadequate it was. Time after time, his instruments had simply refused to function because of some basic flaw in their manufacture—some flaw that an expert in that field could have pointed out at once. Time after time, equipment had had to be rebuilt almost from the beginning. And, time after time, only cut-and-try methods were available for correcting his errors.

Not even his prodigious and accurate memory could hold all the information that was necessary for the work, and there were no reference tapes available, of course.

He had long since given up any attempt to understand the functioning of the mad pseudo-civilization that surrounded him. He was quite certain that the beings he had seen could not possibly be the real rulers of this society, but he had, as yet, no inkling as to who the real rulers were.

As to *where* they were, that question seemed a little easier to answer. It was highly probable that they were out in space, on the asteriods that his instruments had detected as he had dropped in toward this planet so many years before. He had made an error back then in not landing in the Belt, but at no time since had he experienced the emotion of regret or wished he had done differently; both thoughts would have been incomprehensible to the Nipe. He had made an error; the circumstances had been checked and noted; he would not make that error again.

What further action could be taken by a logical mind?

None. The past was unchangeable. It existed only as a memory in his own mind, and there was no way to change that indelible record, even had he wished to do such an insane thing.

Surely, he thought, the real rulers must know of his existence. He had tried, by his every action, to show that he was a reasoning, intelligent, and civilized being. Why had they taken no action?

His hypotheses, he realized, were weak because of lack of data. He could only wait for more information.

That—and continue to work.

VII

INTERLUDE

Mrs. Frobisher touched the control button that depolarized the window in the breakfast room, letting the morning sun stream in. Then she said, in a low voice, "Larry, come here."

Larry Frobisher looked up from his morning coffee. "What is it, hon?"

"The Stanton boys. Come look."

Frobisher sighed. "Who are the Stanton boys, and why should I come look?" But he got up and came over to the window.

"See—over there on the walkway toward the play area," she said.

"I see three girls and a boy pushing a wheeled contraption," Frobisher said. "Or do you mean that the Stanford boys are dressed up as girls?"

"*Stanton*," she corrected him. "They just moved into the apartment on the first floor."

"Who? The three girls?"

"No, silly! The two Stanton boys and their mother. One of them is in that 'wheeled contraption'. It's called a therapeutic chair."

"Oh? So the poor kid's been hurt. What's so interesting about that, aside from morbid curiosity?"

The boy pushing the chair went around a bend in the walkway, out of sight, and Frobisher went back to his coffee while his wife spoke.

"Their names are Mart and Bart. They're twins."

"I should think," Frobisher said, applying himself to his breakfast, "that the mother would get a self-powered chair for the boy instead of making the other boy push it."

"The poor boy can't control the chair, dear. Something wrong with his nervous system. I understand that he was exposed to some kind of radiation when he was only two years old. That's why the chair has all the instruments built into it. Even his heartbeat has to be controlled electronically."

"Shame." Frobisher speared a bit of sausage. "Kind of rough on both of 'em, I'd guess."

"How do you mean?"

"Well, I mean, like.... Well, for instance, why are they going over to the play area? Play games, right? The one that's well has to push his brother over there—can't just get out and go; has to take the brother along. Kind of a burden, see?

"And then, the kid in the chair has to sit there and watch his brother play basketball or jai alai, while he can't do anything himself. Like I say, kind of rough on both of them."

"Yes, I suppose it must be. More coffee?"

"Thanks, honey. And another slice of toast, hunh?"

VIII

The two objects floating in space both looked like pitted pieces of rock. The larger one, roughly pear-shaped and about a quarter of a mile in its greatest dimension, was actually that—a hunk of rock. The smaller—*much*smaller—of the two was a camouflaged spaceboat. The smaller was on a near-collision course with reference to the larger, although their relative velocities were not great.

At precisely the right time, the smaller drifted by the larger, only a few hundred yards away. The weakness of the gravitational fields generated between the two caused only a slight change of orbit on the part of both bodies. Then they began to separate.

But, during the few seconds of their closest approach, a third body had detached itself from the camouflaged spaceboat and shot rapidly across the intervening distance to land on the surface of the floating mountain.

The third body was a man in a spacesuit. As soon as he landed, he sat down, stock-still, and checked the instrument case he held in his hands.

No response. Thus far, then, he had succeeded.

He had had to pick his time precisely. The people who were already on this small planetoid could not use their detection equipment while the planetoid itself was within detection range of Beacon 971, only two hundred and eighty miles away. Not if they wanted to keep from being found. Radar pulses emanating from a presumably lifeless planetoid would be a dead giveaway.

Other than that, they were mathematically safe—if they depended on the laws of chance. No ship moving through the Asteroid Belt would dare to move at any decent velocity without using radar, so the people on this particular lump of planetary flotsam would be able to spot a ship's approach easily, long before their own weak detection system would register on the pick-ups of the approaching ship.

The power and range needed by a given detector depends on the relative velocity—the greater that velocity, the more power, the greater range needed. At one mile per second, a ship needs a range of only thirty miles to spot an obstacle thirty seconds away; at ten miles per second, it needs a range of three hundred miles.

The man who called himself Stanley Martin had carefully plotted the orbit of this particular planetoid and then let his spaceboat coast in without using any detection equipment except the visual. It had been necessary, but very risky.

Had the people here seen his boat? If so, had they recognized it, in spite of the heavy camouflage? And, even if they only suspected, what would be their reaction?

He waited.

It takes nerve and patience to wait for thirteen solid hours without moving more than an occasional flexure of muscles, but he managed that long before the instrument case waggled a meter needle at him. The one relieving factor was the low gravity; on an asteroid, the problem of sleeping on a bed of nails is caused by the likelihood of accidentally throwing oneself off the bed. The probability of puncture or discomfort from the points is almost negligible.

When the needle on the instrument panel flickered, he got to his feet and began moving. He was almost certain that he had not been detected.

Walking was out of the question. This was a silicate-alumina rock, not a nickel-iron one. The group that occupied it had deliberately chosen it that way, so that there would be no chance of its being picked out for slicing by one of the mining teams in the Asteroid Belt. Granted, the chance of any given metallic planetoid's being selected was very small, they had not even wanted to take that chance. Therefore, without any magnetic field to hold him down, and only a very tiny gravitic field, the man had to use different tactics.

It was more like mountain climbing than anything else, except that there was no danger of falling. He crawled over the surface in the same way that an Alpine climber might crawl up the side of a steep slope—seeking handholds and toeholds and using them to propel himself onward. The only difference was that he covered distance a great deal more rapidly than a mountain climber could.

When he reached the spot he wanted, he carefully concealed himself beneath a craggy overhang. It took a little searching to find exactly the right spot, but when he did, he settled himself into place in a small pit and began more elaborate preparations.

Self-hypnosis required nearly ten minutes. The first five or six minutes were taken up in relaxing from his exertion. Gravity notwithstanding, he had had to push his hundred and eighty pounds of mass over a considerable distance. When he was completely relaxed and completely hypnotized, he reached up and cut down the valve that fed oxygen into his suit.

Then, of his own will, he went cataleptic.

A single note, sounded by the instruments in the case by his side, woke him instantly. He came fully awake, as he had commanded himself to do.

Immediately, he turned up his oxygen intake, at the same time glancing at the clock dial in his helmet. He smiled. Nineteen days and seven hours. He had calculated it almost precisely. He wasn't more than an hour off, which was pretty good, all things considered.

He consulted his instruments again. The supply ship was ten minutes away. The smile stayed on his face as he prepared for further action.

The first two minutes were conscientiously spent in inhaling oxygen. Even under the best cataleptic conditions, the body tended to slow down too much. He had to get himself prepared for violent movement.

Eight minutes left. He climbed out of the little grotto where he had concealed himself and moved toward the spot where he knew the air lock to the caverns underneath the planetoid's surface was hidden. Then again, he concealed himself and waited, while he continued to breathe deeply of the highly oxygenated air in his suit. Five minutes before the ship landed, he swallowed eight ounces of the nutrient solution from the tank in the back of his helmet. The solution of amino acids, vitamins, and honey sugar also contained a small amount of stimulant of the dexedrine type and one per cent ethanol. Then he unholstered his gun.

It wasn't a big ship. He had known it wouldn't be. It was only a little larger than the one he had used to come here. It dropped down to the surface of the small planetoid only ten meters from the hidden trapdoor that led to the air lock beneath the surface.

He could suddenly hear voices in the earphones of his helmet.

Lasser?

It's me, Fritz. I got your supplies and good news.

The air lock trapdoor opened, and a spacesuited figure came out. *How about the deal?*

That's the good news, said the second suited figure as it came from the air lock of the grounded spaceboat. *Another five million.*

The man who was hidden behind the nearby crag of rock listened and watched for a minute or so more while the two men began unloading cases of foodstuffs from the spaceboat. Then, satisfied that it was perfectly safe, he aimed his gun and shot twice in rapid succession. The range was almost point-blank, and there was, of course, no need to take either gravity or air resistance into account.

The pellets of the shotgun-like charge that blasted out from the gun were small, needle-shaped, and heavy. They were oriented point-forward by the magnetic field along the barrel of the weapon. Of the hundreds in each charge fired, only a few penetrated the spacesuits of the targets, but those few were enough. The powerful drug in the needle-pointed head of each went into the bloodstream of the target.

Each man felt an itching sensation. He had less than two seconds to think about it before unconsciousness overtook him and he slumped nervelessly.

The man with the gun ran across the intervening space quickly, his body only a few degrees from the horizontal, and his toes paddling rapidly to propel him over the rough rock.

He braked himself to a halt and slapped air patches over the area where his charges had struck the men's suits, sealing the tiny air leaks, and, at the same time, driving more of the tiny needles into their skins. They would be out for a long time.

Neither of them had yet fallen to the ground; that would take several minutes under this low gravity. He left them to drop and headed toward the open air lock.

This was what he had been waiting for all those nineteen days in cataleptic hypnosis. He couldn't have cut his way in from the outside; he had had to wait until it was opened, and that time would come only when the supply ship came.

Once in the air lock, he touched the control stud that would close the outer door, pump air into the waiting room, and open the inner door. Here was his greatest point of danger—greater, even, than the danger of coming to the planetoid, or the danger of waiting nineteen days for the coming of the supply ship. If the ones who remained within suspected anything—anything at all!—then his chances of coming out of this alive were practically nil.

But there was no reason why they should suspect. They should think that the man coming in was one of their own. The radio contact between the men outside had been limited to a few millimicrowatts of power—necessarily, since radio waves of very small wattage can be decoded at tremendous distances in open space. The men inside the planetoid certainly should not have been able to pick up any more than the beginning of the conversation, before it had been cut off by solid rock.

It was a high-speed air lock. Unlike the soundless discharge of his special gun in the outer airlessness, the blast of air that came into the waiting chamber was like a hurricane in noise and force, as the room filled in a few seconds.

He held onto the handholds tightly while the brief but violent winds buffeted him. He turned as the inner door opened.

His eyes took in the picture in a fraction of a second. In an even smaller fraction, his mind assimilated the picture.

The woman was dark-haired, dark-eyed, and muscular. Her mouth was wide and thick-lipped beneath a large nose.

The man was leaner and lighter, bony-faced and beady-eyed.

The woman said: "Fritz, what—"

And then he shot them both with gun number two.

No needle charges this time; such shots would have blown them both in two, unprotected as they were by spacesuits. The small handgun merely jangled their nerves with a high-powered blast of accurately beamed supersonics. While they were still twitching, he went over and jabbed them with a drug needle.

Then he went on into the hideout.

He had to knock out one more man, whom he found sound asleep in a room off the short corridor.

It took a gas bomb to get the two women who were guarding the kid.

He made sure that the BenChaim boy was all right, then he went to the little communications room and called for help.

IX

Colonel Walther Mannheim tapped the map that glowed on the wall before him. "He's right there, where those tunnels come together."

Bart Stanton looked at the map of Manhattan Island and at the gleaming colored traceries that threaded their various ways across it. "Just what was the purpose of those tunnels?" he asked curiously.

"They were for rail transportation," said the colonel. "The island was hit by a sun bomb during the Holocaust, and almost completely leveled and slagged down. When the city was rebuilt, there was naturally no need for such things, so they were simply sealed off and forgotten."

"Right under Government City," Stanton said. "Incredible."

"It used to be one of the largest seaports in the world," Colonel Mannheim said, "and it probably still would be if the inertia drive hadn't made air travel cheaper and easier than seagoing."

"How did he find out about the tunnels?" Stanton asked.

The colonel pointed at the north end of the island. "After the Holocaust, the first returnees to the island were wild animals which crossed from the mainland from the north. The Harlem River isn't very wide at this point. Also, because of the rocky hills at this end of the island, there were places which were spared the direct effects of the bomb, and grasses and trees began growing there. That's why it was decided to leave that section as a game preserve when the Government built the capital on the southern part of the island." His finger moved down the map. "The upper three miles of the island, down to here, where it begins to widen, are all game preserve. There's a high wall here which separates it from the city, and the ruins of the bridges which connected with the mainland have been removed, so the animals can't get back across any more.

"Two years after he arrived, the Nipe was almost caught. He had managed, somehow—we're not sure yet exactly how—to get here from Asia. According to the psychologists who have been studying him, he apparently does not believe that human beings are any more than trained animals; he was looking then—as he is apparently still looking—for the 'real' rulers of Earth. He expected to find them, of course, in Government City. Needless to say," said the colonel with a touch of irony, "he failed."

"But he was seen?" asked Stanton.

"He was seen. And pursued. But he got away easily, heading north. The island was searched, and the police were ready to start an inch-by-inch going over of the island two days later. But the Nipe hit and robbed a chemical supply house in northern Pennsylvania, killing two men, so the search was called off.

"It wasn't until two years later, after exhaustive analysis of the pattern of his raids had given us something to work with, that we decided that he must have found an opening into one of the tunnels up here in the game preserve." He gestured again at the map. "It wouldn't take him long to see that no human being had been down there in a long time. It was a perfect place for his base."

"How does he move in and out?" Stanton asked.

"This way." The colonel traced a finger down one of the red lines on the map, southward, until he came to a spot only a little over two miles from the southernmost tip of the island. The line turned abruptly toward the western edge of the island, where it stopped. "This tunnel goes underneath the Hudson River at this point, and emerges on the other side. It's only one of several that do so. They're all flooded now; the sun bomb caved them in when the primary shock wave hit the surface of the river.

"In spite of his high rate of metabolism, the Nipe can store a tremendous amount of oxygen in his body, and can stay underwater for as long as half an hour without breathing apparatus—if he conserves his energy. When he's wearing his scuba apparatus, he's practically a self-contained submarine. The pressure doesn't seem to bother him much. He's a tough cookie."

Stanton nodded silently and slowly. Could he beat the Nipe in hand-to-hand combat? There would be no way of knowing until the final moment of success or failure.

"At that time," the colonel went on, "we hadn't formulated any definite policy on the Nipe. We didn't know what he was up to; we weren't even sure he was actually down in those tunnels. We had to find out."

He walked over to the nearby table and opened a box some twelve inches long and five-by-five inches in cross section. "See this?" he said as he took something out.

It looked like a large dead rat.

"Our spy," said Colonel Mannheim.

The rat moved along the rusted steel rail that ran the length of the huge tunnel. To a human being, the tunnel would have seemed to be in utter darkness, but the little eyes of the rat saw its surroundings as faintly luminescent, glowing from the infra-red radiations given out by the internal warmth of cement and steel. The main source came from above, where the heat of the sun and of the energy sources in the buildings on the surface seeped through the roof of the tunnel.

On and on it moved, its little pinkish feet pattering almost silently on the oxidized metal surface of the rail. Its sensitive ears picked up the movements and the squeals of other rats, but it paid them no heed. Several times, it met other rats on the rail, but most of them sensed the alienness of *this* rat and scuttled out of its way.

Once, it met a rat who did not give way. Hungry, perhaps, or perhaps merely yielding to the paranoid fury that was a normal component of the rattish mind, it squealed its defiance to the rat that was not a rat. It advanced, baring its teeth.

The rat that was not a rat became suddenly motionless, its sharp rodent's nose pointed directly at the enemy. There came a noise, a tiny popping hiss, like that of a very small drop of water striking hot metal. From the left nostril of the not-rat, a tiny glasslike needle snapped out at bullet speed. It struck the advancing rat in the center of the pink tongue that was visible in the open mouth. Then the not-rat scuttled backwards faster than any rat could have moved.

For a second, the real rat hesitated, and it may be that the realization penetrated into its dim brain that rats did not fight this way. Then, as the tiny needle dissolved in its bloodstream, it closed its eyes and collapsed, rolling limply off the rail.

The rat might come to before it was found and devoured by its fellows—or it might not. The not-rat moved on, not caring either way. The human intelligence that looked out from the eyes of the not-rat was only concerned with getting to the Nipe.

"That's how we found the Nipe," Colonel Mannheim said, "and that's how we keep tabs on him now. We have over seven hundred of these remote-controlled robots hidden in strategic spots in those tunnels now, but it took time to get everything set up this way. Now, we can follow the Nipe wherever he goes, so long as he stays in the tunnels. If he went out through an open air exit, we could have him followed by bird-robots but—" He shrugged wryly. "I'm afraid the underwater problem still has us stumped. We can't get the carrier wave for the remote-control impulses to go far underwater."

"How do you get your carrier wave underground to those tunnels?" Stanton asked.

The colonel grinned widely. "One of the boys dreamed up a real cute gimmick. The rails themselves act as antenna for the broadcaster, and the rat's tail is the pickup antenna. As long as the rat is crawling right on the rail, only a microscopic amount of power is needed for control, not enough for the Nipe to pick up with his instruments. Each rat carries its own battery for motive power, and there are old copper power cables down there that we can send direct current through to recharge the batteries. And, when we need them, the copper cables can be used as antennas. It took us quite a while to work the system out."

Stanton rubbed his head thoughtfully. *Damn these gaps in my memory!* he thought. It was sometimes embarrassing to ask questions that any schoolboy should know.

"Aren't there ways of detecting objects underwater?" he asked after a moment.

"Yes," said the colonel, "But they all require beamed energy of some kind to be reflected from the object, and we don't dare use anything like that." He sat down on one corner of the table, his bright blue eyes looking up at Stanton.

"That's been our problem all along," he said seriously. "Keeping the Nipe from knowing that he's being watched. In the tunnels, we've used only equipment that was already there, adding only what we absolutely had to—small things, a few strands of wire, a tiny relay, things that can be hidden in out of the way places. After all, he has his own alarm system in the maze of tunnels, and we've deliberately kept away from his detecting devices. He knows about the rats and ignores them; they're part of the environment. But we don't dare use anything that would tip him off to our knowledge of his whereabouts. One slip like that, and hundreds of human beings will have died in vain."

"And if he stays there too long," Stanton said levelly, "millions more may die."

The colonel's face was grim as he looked directly into Stanton's eyes. "That's why you have to know your job down to the most minute detail when the time comes to act. The whole success of the plan will depend on you and you alone."

Stanton's eyes didn't avoid the colonel's. *That's not true,* he thought. *I'll only be one man on a team, and you know it, Colonel Mannheim. But you'd like to shove all the responsibility off onto someone else—someone stronger. You've finally met someone that you consider superior in that way, and you want to unload. I wish I felt as confident as you do, but I don't.*

Aloud, he said: "Sure. Nothing to it. All I have to do is take into account everything that's known about the Nipe and make allowances for everything that's not known." Then he smiled. "Not," he added, "that I can think of any other way to go about it."

X

St. Louis hadn't been hit during the Holocaust; it still retained much of the old-fashioned flavor of the Nineteenth and Twentieth Centuries, especially in the residential districts. Bart Stanton liked to walk along those quiet streets of an evening, just to let the peacefulness seep into him. And, knowing it was rather childish, he still enjoyed the small pleasure of playing hookey from the Neurophysics Institute. Technically, he supposed, he was still a patient there. More, now that he had accepted Colonel Mannheim's assignment, he was presumably under military discipline. But he assumed that, if he had asked permission to leave the Institute's grounds, he would have been given that permission without question.

But, like playing hookey, or stealing watermelon, it was more fun if it was done on the sly. The boy who comes home feeling deliciously wicked and delightfully sinful after staying away from school all day can have his whole day ruined by being told that it was a holiday and that the school had been closed. Bart Stanton didn't want to spoil his own fun by asking for permission to leave the grounds when it was so easy for a man with his special abilities to get out without asking.

Besides, there *was* a chance—a small one, he thought—that permission might be refused for one reason or another, and Bart was fully aware that he would not disobey a direct request—to say nothing of a direct order—that he stay within the walls of the Institute. He didn't want to run any risk of losing his freedom, small though it was. After five years of mental and physical hell, he felt a need to get out into the world of normal, everyday people.

His legs moved smoothly, surely, and unhurriedly, carrying him aimlessly along the resilient walkway, under the warm glow of the street lights. The people around him walked as casually and with seemingly as little purpose as he did. There was none of the brisk sense of urgency that he felt inside the walls of the Institute.

He knew he could never get away from that sense of urgency completely, even out here. There were times when it seemed that all he had ever done, all his life, was to train himself for the single purpose of besting the Nipe.

If he wasn't training physically, he was listening to lectures from the psychologists or from Colonel Mannheim—laying plans and considering possibilities for the one great goal that seemed to be the focal point of his whole life.

What would happen if he failed? He would die, of course, and Mannheim's Plan Beta would immediately go into effect. The Nipe would be killed eventually.

But what if he, Stanton, won? Then what?

The people around him were not a part of his world, really. Their thoughts, their motions, their reactions, were slow and clumsy in comparison with his own. Once the Nipe had been conquered, what purpose would there be in the life of Bartholomew Stanton? He was surrounded by people, but he was not one of them. He was immersed in a society that was not his own because it was not, could not be, geared to his abilities and potentials. But there was no other society to turn to, either.

He was not a man "alone, afraid" in a world he had never made; he was a man who had been made for a world, a society, that did not exist.

Women? A wife? A family life?

Where? With whom?

He pushed the thoughts from his mind, the questions, unanswered and perhaps unanswerable. In spite of the apparent bleakness of the future, he had no desire to die, and there was the possibility that too much brooding of that kind would evoke a subconscious reaction that could slow him down or cause a wrong decision at a vital moment. A feeling of futility could operate to bring on his death in spite of his conscious determination to win the coming battle with the Nipe.

The Nipe was his first duty. When that job was finished, he would consider the problem of himself. Just because he could not now see the answer to that problem did not mean that no answer existed.

He suddenly realized that he was hungry. He had been walking through Memorial Park, past the museum, an old, worn edifice that was still called the Missouri Pacific Building. There was a small restaurant only a block away. He reached into his pocket and took out the few coins that were there. Not much, but enough to buy a sandwich and a glass of milk. Because of the trust fund that had been set up when he had started the treatment at the Neurophysics Institute, he was already well off, but he didn't have much cash. What good was cash in the Institute, where everything was provided?

He stopped at a news-vendor, dropped in a coin, and waited for the reproducing mechanism to turn out a fresh paper. Then he took the folded sheets and went on to the restaurant.

He rarely read a news-sheet. Mostly, his information about the world that existed outside the walls of the Institute came from the televised newscasts. But, occasionally, he liked to read the small, relatively unimportant little stories about people who had done small, relatively unimportant things—stories that didn't appear in the headlines or on the newscasts.

The last important news story had come two nights before, when the Nipe had robbed an optical products company in Miami. The camera had shown the shop on the screen. Whatever had been used to blow open the door of the vault had been more effective than necessary. It had taken the whole front door of the shop and both windows, too. The bent and twisted paraglass that had lain on the pavement showed how much force had been applied from within.

And yet, the results were not that of an explosion. It was more as though some tremendous force had *pushed* outward from within. It had not been the shattering shock of high explosive, but some great thrust that had unhurriedly, but irresistibly, moved everything out of its way.

Nothing had been moved very far, as it would have been by a blast. It appeared that everything had simply fallen aside, as though scattered by a giant hand. The main braces of the store front were still there, bent outward a little, but not broken.

The vault door had lain on the floor of the shop, only a few feet from the front door. The vault itself had been farther back, and the camera had showed it, standing wide open, gaping. Inside, there had been pieces of fragile glass standing on the shelves, unmoved, unharmed.

The force, whatever it had been, had moved in one direction only, from a point within the vault, just a few feet from the door, pushing outward to tear out the heavy door as though it had been made of paraffin or modeling clay.

Stanton had recognized the vault construction type: the Voisier construction, which, by test, could withstand almost everything known, outside of the actual application of atomic energy itself. In a widely-publicized demonstration several years before, a Voisier vault had been cut open by a team of well-trained, well-equipped technicians. It had taken twenty-one hours for them to breach the wall, and they had no fear of interruption, or of making a noise, or of setting off the intricate alarms that were built into the safe itself. Not even a borazon drill could make much of an impression on a metal which had been formed under millions of atmospheres of pressure.

And yet the Nipe had taken that door out in a second, without much effort at all.

The crowd that had gathered at the scene of the crime had not been large. The very thought of the Nipe kept people away from places where he was known to have been. The specter of the Nipe evoked a fear, a primitive fear—fear of the dark and fear of the unknown, combined with the rational fear of a very real, very tangible danger.

And yet, there *had* been a crowd of onlookers. In spite of their fear, it is hard to keep human beings from being curious. It was known that the Nipe didn't stay around after he had struck; and, besides, the area was now full of armed men. So the curious came to look and to stare in revulsion at the neat pile of gnawed and bloody bones that had been the night watchman, carefully killed and eaten by the Nipe before he had opened the vault.

Thus curiosity does make fools of us all, and the native hue of caution is crimsoned o'er by the bright red of morbid fascination.

Stanton went through the door of the automat restaurant and walked over to the vending wall. The dining room was only about three-quarters full of people; there were plenty of seats available. He fed coins into the proper slots, took his sandwich and milk over to a seat in one corner and made himself comfortable.

He flipped open the newspaper and looked at the front page.

And, for a moment, his brain seemed to freeze.

The story itself was straightforward enough:

BENCHAIM KIDNAPERS

NABBED!

STAN MARTIN DOES IT

AGAIN!

Ceres, June 3 (Interplanetary News Service)—The three men and three women who allegedly kidnapped ten-year-old Shmuel BenChaim were brought to justice today through the single-handed efforts of Stanley Martin, famed investigator for Lloyd's of London. The boy, held prisoner for more than ten months on a small asteroid, was reported in very good health.

According to Lt. John Vale, of the Planetoid Police, the kidnap gang could not have been taken by direct assault on their hideout because of fear that the boy might be killed. "The operation required a carefully-planned, one-man infiltration of their hideout," he said. "Mr. Martin was the man for the job."

Labeled "the most outrageous kidnapping in history", the affair was conceived as a long-term method of gaining control of Heavy Metals Incorporated, controlled by Moishe BenChaim, the boy's father. The details....

But Bart Stanton wasn't interested in the details. After only a glance through the first part of the article, his eyes returned to the picture alongside the article. The line of print beneath it identified the man in the picture as Stanley Martin.

But a voice in Bart Stanton's brain said: *Not Stan Martin! The name is Mart Stanton!*

And Bartholomew felt a roar of confusion in his mind, because he didn't know who Mart Stanton was, and because the face in the picture was his own.

XI

He was walking again.

He didn't quite remember how he had left the automat, and he didn't even try to remember.

He was trying to remember other things—farther back—before he had—

Before he had what?

Before the Institute; before the beginning of the operations.

The memories were there, just beyond the grasp of his conscious mind, like the memories of a dream after one has awakened. Each time he tried to reach into the darkness to grasp one of the pieces, it would break up into smaller bits. The patterns were too fragile to withstand the direct probing of his conscious mind. Only the resulting fragments held together long enough to be analyzed.

And, while part of his mind probed frantically after the elusive particles of memory, another part of it watched the process with semi-detached amusement.

He had always known there were holes in his memory (*Always? Don't be silly, pal!*), but it was disconcerting to find an area that was as riddled as a used machine-gun target. The whole fabric had been punched to bits.

No man's memory is completely available at any given time. However it is recorded, however completely every bit of data may be recorded during a lifetime, much of it is unavailable because it is incompletely cross-indexed or, in some cases, labeled *Do Not Scan*. Or, metaphorically, the file drawer may be locked. It may be that, in many cases, if a given bit of data remains unscanned long enough it fades into illegibility, never reinforced by the scanning process. Sensory data, coming in from the outside world as it does, is probably permanent. But the thought patterns originating within the mind itself, the processes that correlate and cross-index and speculate on and hypothesize about the sensory data, those are much more fragile. A man might glance once through a Latin primer and have every page imprinted indelibly on his recording mechanism and still be unable to make sense of the *Nauta in cubito cum puella est*.

Sometimes a man is aware of the holes in his memory. ("What was the name of that fellow I met at Eddie's party? Can't remember it for the life of me.") At other times, a memory may lay dormant and unremembered, leaving no apparent gap, until a tag of some kind brings it up. ("That girl with the long hair reminds me of Suzie Blugerhugle. My gosh! I haven't thought of her for years!") Both factors seemed to be operating in Bart Stanton's mind at this time.

Incredibly, he had never, in the past year at least, had occasion to try to remember much about his past life. He had known who he was without thinking about it particularly, and the rest of his knowledge—language, history, politics, geography, and so on—had been readily available for the most part. Ask any educated man to give the product of the primes 2, 13, and 41, or ask him to give the date of the Norman Conquest, and he can give the answer without having to think of where he learned it or who taught it to him or when he got the information.

But now the picture and the name in the paper had brought forth a reaction in Stanton's mind, and he was trying desperately to bring the information out of oblivion.

Did he have a mother? Surely—but could he remember her? *Yes!* Certainly. A pretty, gentle, rather sad woman. He could remember when she had died, although he couldn't remember ever having attended the funeral.

What about his father?

He could find no memory of his father, and, at first, that bothered him. He could remember his mother—could almost see her moving around in the apartment where they had lived ... in ... in ... in Denver! Sure! And he could remember the building itself, and the block, and even Mrs. Frobisher, who lived upstairs! And the school! A great many memories came crowding back, but there was no trace of his father.

And yet....

Oh, of *course*! His father had been killed in an accident when Martinbart were very young.

Martinbart!

The name flitted through his mind like a scrap of paper in a high wind, but he reached out and grasped it.

Martinbart. Martin-Bart. Mart 'n' Bart. Mart *and* Bart.

The Stanton Twins.

It was curious, he thought, that he should have forgotten his brother. And even more curious that the name in the paper had not brought him instantly to mind.

Martin, the cripple. Martin, the boy with the radiation-shattered nervous system. The boy who had had to stay in a therapy chair all his life because his efferent nerves could not control his body. The boy who couldn't speak. Or, rather, *wouldn't* speak because he was ashamed of the gibberish that resulted.

Martin. The nonentity. The nothing. The nobody.

The one who watched and listened and thought, but could do nothing.

Bart Stanton stopped suddenly and unfolded the newspaper again under the glow of the street lamp. His memories certainly didn't gibe with *this*!

His eyes ran down the column of type.

"... Mr. Martin has, in the eighteen months since he came to the Belt, run up an enviable record, both as an insurance investigator and as a police detective, although his connection with the Planetoid Police is, necessarily, an unofficial one. Probably not since Sherlock Holmes has there been such mutual respect and co-operation between the official police and a private investigator."

The was only one explanation, Stanton thought. Martin, too, had been treated by the Institute. His memory was still blurry and incomplete, but he did suddenly remember that a decision had been made for Martin to take the treatment.

He chuckled a little at the irony of it. They hadn't been able to make a superman of Martin, but they *had* been able to make a normal and extraordinarily capable man of him. Now it was Bart who was the freak, the odd one.

Turn about is fair play, he thought. But somehow it didn't seem quite fair.

He crumpled the newspaper, dropped it into a nearby waste chute, and walked on through the night toward the Neurophysical Institute.

XII

INTERLUDE

"You understand, Mrs. Stanton," said the psychiatrist, "that a great part of Martin's trouble is mental as much as physical. Because of the nature of his ailment, he has withdrawn, pulled himself away from communication with others. If these symptoms had been brought to my attention earlier, the mental disturbance might have been more easily analyzed and treated."

"I'm sorry, Doctor," said Mrs. Stanton. Her manner betrayed weariness and pain. "It was so—so difficult. Martin could never talk very well, you know, and he just talked less and less as the years went by. It was so gradual that I never really noticed it."

Poor woman, the doctor thought. *She's not well, herself. She should have married again, rather than carry the whole burden alone. Her role as a doting mother hasn't helped either of the boys to overcome the handicaps that were already present.*

"I've tried to do my best for Martin," Mrs. Stanton went on unhappily. "And so has Bart. When they were younger, Bart used to take him out all the time. They went everywhere together. Of course, I don't expect Bart to do that so much any more; he has his own life to live. He can't take Martin out on dates or things like that. But when he's home, Bart helps me with Martin all the time."

"I understand," said the doctor. *This is no time to tell her that Bartholomew's tests indicate that he has subconsciously resented Martin's presence for a long time. She has enough to worry about.*

"I don't understand," said Mrs. Stanton, breaking into sudden tears. "I don't understand why Martin should behave this way! Why should he just sit there with his eyes closed and ignore us both?"

The doctor comforted her in a warmly professional manner, then, as her tears subsided, he said: "We don't understand all of the factors ourselves, Mrs. Stanton. Martin's reactions are, I admit, unusual. His behavior doesn't quite follow the pattern that we usually expect from such cases as this. His physical disability has drastically modified the course of his mental development, and, at the same time, makes it difficult for us to make any analysis of is mental state."

"Is there *any*thing you can do, Doctor?"

"We don't know yet," he said gently. He considered for a moment, then said: "Mrs. Stanton, I'd like for you to leave both the boys here for a few days, so that we can perform further tests. That will help us a great deal in getting at the root of Martin's trouble."

She looked at him with a little surprise. "Why, yes, of course. But ... why should Bart stay?"

The doctor weighed his words carefully before he spoke.

"Bart is our control, Mrs. Stanton. Since the boys are genetically identical, they should have been a great deal alike in personality if it hadn't been for Martin's accident. In other words, our tests of Bart will tell us what Martin *should* be like. That way we can tell just how much and in what way Martin deviates from what he should ideally be. Do you understand?"

"Yes. Yes, I see. All right, Doctor—whatever you say."

After Mrs. Stanton had left, the psychiatrist sat quietly in his chair and stared thoughtfully at his desk top for several minutes. Then, making his decision, he picked up a small book that lay on his desk and looked up a number in Arlington, Virginia. He punched out the number on his phone, and when the face appeared on his screen, he said: "Hello, Sidney. Look, I have a very interesting case out here that I'd like to talk to you about. Do you happen to have a telepath who's strong enough to take a meshing with an insane mind? If my suspicions are correct, I'll need a man with an impregnable sense of identity, because he's going to get into the weirdest situation I've ever come across."

XIII

Pok! Pok! Ping!
Pok! Pok! Ping!
Pok! Pok! Ping!

The action in the handball court was beautiful to watch. The robot mechanism behind Bart Stanton would fire out a ball at random intervals ranging from a tenth to a quarter of a second, bouncing them off the wall in a random pattern. Stanton would retrieve the ball before it hit the ground, bounce it off the wall again to strike the target on the moving robot. Stanton had to work against a machine; no ordinary human being could have given him any competition.

Pok! Pok! Ping!
Pok! Pok! Ping!
Pok! Pok! PLUNK.

"One miss," Stanton said to himself. But he fielded the next one nicely and slammed it home.

Pok! Pok! Ping!

The physical therapist who was standing by glanced at his watch. It was almost time.

Pok! Pok! Ping!

The machine, having delivered its last ball, shut itself off with a smug click. Stanton turned away from the handball court and walked toward the physical therapist, who held out a robe for him.

"That was good, Bart," he said, "real good."

"One miss," Stanton said as he shrugged into the robe.

"Yeah. Your timing was a shade off there, I guess. But you ran a full minute over your previous record."

Stanton looked at him. "You re-set the timer again," he said accusingly. But there was a grin on his face.

The P.T. man grinned back. "Yup. Come on, step into the mummy case." He waved toward the narrow niche in the wall of the court, a niche just big enough to hold a standing man. Stanton stepped in, and various instrument pick-ups came out of the walls and touched his body. Hidden machines recorded his heartbeat, blood pressure, brain activity, muscular tension, and several other factors.

After a minute, the P.T. man said, "O.K., Bart; let's hit the steam box."

Stanton stepped out of the niche and accompanied the therapist to another room, where he took off the robe again and sat down on the small stool inside an ordinary steam box. The box closed, leaving his head free, and the box began to fill with steam.

"Did I ever tell you what I don't like about that machine?" Bart asked as the therapist draped a heavy towel around his head.

"Nope. Didn't know you had any gripe. What is it?"

"You can't gloat after you beat it. You can't walk over and pat it on the shoulder and say, 'Well, better luck next time, old man.' It isn't a good loser, and it isn't a bad loser. The damn thing doesn't even know it lost, and if it did, it wouldn't care."

"I see what you mean," said the P.T. man, chuckling. "You beat the pants off it and what d'you get? Not even a case of the sulks out of it."

"Exactly. And what's worse, I know perfectly good and well that it's only half trying. The damned thing could beat me easily if you just turned that knob over a little more."

"You're not competing against the machine, anyway," the therapist said. "You're competing against yourself, trying to beat your own record."

"I know. And what happens when I can't do *that* any more, either?" Stanton asked. "I can't just go on getting better and better forever. I've got limits, you know."

"Sure," said the therapist easily. "So does a golf player. But every golfer goes out and practices by himself to try to beat his own record."

"Bunk! The real fun in *any* game is beating someone else! The big kick in golf is in winning over the other guy in a twosome."

"How about crossword puzzles or solitaire?"

"Solve a crossword puzzle, and you've beaten the guy who made it up. In solitaire, you're playing against the laws of chance, and even that can become pretty boring. What I'd like to do is get out on the golf course with someone else and do my best and then lose. Honestly."

"With a handicap...." the therapist began. Then he grinned weakly and stopped. On the golf course, Stanton was impossibly good. One long drive to the green, one putt to the cup. An easy thirty-six strokes for eighteen holes; an occasional hole-in-one sometimes brought him below that, an occasional worm-cast or stray wind sometimes raised his score.

"Sure," Stanton said. "A handicap. What kind of handicap do you want on a handball game with me?"

The P.T. man could imagine himself trying to get under one of Stanton's lightning-like returns. The thought of what would happen to his hand if he were to accidentally catch one made him wince.

"We wouldn't even be playing the same game," Stanton said.

The therapist stepped back and looked at Stanton. "You know," he said puzzledly, "you sound bitter."

"Sure I'm bitter," Stanton said. "All I get is exercise. All the fun has gone out of it." He sighed and grinned. There was no point in worrying the P.T. man. "I'll just have to stick to cards and chess if I want competition. Speed and strength don't help anything if I'm holding two pair against three of a kind."

Before the therapist could say anything, the door opened and a tall, lean man stepped into the fog-filled room. "You are broiling a lobster?" he asked the P.T. blandly.

"Steaming a clam," came the correction. "When he's done, I'll pound him to chowder."

"Excellent. I came for a clam-bake," the tall man said.

"You're early then, George," Stanton said. He didn't feel in the mood for light humor, and the appearance of Dr. Yoritomo did nothing to improve his humor.

George Yoritomo beamed, crinkling up his heavy-lidded eyes. "Ah! A talking clam! Excellent! How much longer does he have to cook?"

"Twenty-three minutes, why?"

"Would you be so good as to return at the end of that time?"

The therapist opened his mouth, closed it, opened it again, and said: "Sure, Doc. I can get some other stuff done. I'll see you then. I'll be back, Bart." He went out through the far door.

After the door closed, Dr. Yoritomo pulled up a chair and sat down. "New developments," he said, "as you may have surmised."

"I guessed," Stanton said. "What is it?" He flexed his muscles under the caress of the hot, moist currents in the box.

He wondered why it was so important that the psychologist interrupt him while he was relaxing after strenuous exercise. Yoritomo looked excited, in spite of his calm. And yet Stanton knew that there couldn't be anything urgent or Yoritomo would have acted differently.

It was relatively unimportant now, anyway, Stanton thought. Having made his decision to act on his own had changed his reaction to the decisions of others.

Yoritomo leaned forward in his chair, his thin lips in an excited smile, his black-irised eyes sparkling. "I had to come tell you. The sheer, utter beauty of it is too much to contain. Three times in a row was almost absolute, Bart; the probability that our hypothesis is correct was computed as straight nines to seven decimals. But now! The fourth time! Straight nines to *twelve* decimals!"

Scanton lifted an eyebrow. "Your Oriental calm is deserting you, George. I'm not reading you."

Yoritomo's smile became broader. "Ah! Sorry. I refer to the theory we have been discussing—about the memory of the Nipe. You know?"

Stanton knew. Dr. Yoritomo was, in effect, one of his training instructors. *Advanced Alien Psychology,* Stanton thought; *Seminar Course. The Mental Whys & Wherefores of the Nipe, or How to Outthink the Enemy in Twelve Easy Lessons. Instructor: Dr. George Yoritomo.*

After six years of watching the recorded actions of the Nipe, Yoritomo had evolved a theory about the kind of mentality that lay behind the four baleful violet eyes in that alien head. Now he evidently had proof of that theory. He was smiling and rubbing his long, bony hands together. For George Yoritomo, that was the equivalent of hysterical excitement.

"We have been able to predict the behavior of the Nipe!" he said. "For the fourth time in succession!"

"Great. But how does that fit in with that rule you once told me about? You know, the one about experimental animals."

"Ah, yes. The Harvard Law. 'A genetically standardized strain, under precisely controlled laboratory conditions, when subjected to carefully calibrated stimuli, will behave as it damned well pleases.' Yes. Very true."

"But an animal could not do otherwise, could it? Only as it pleases. And it could not please to behave as something it is not, could it?"

"Draw me a picture," Stanton said.

"I mean that any organism is limited in its choice of behavior. A hamster, for instance, cannot choose to behave in the manner of a Rhesus monkey. A dog cannot choose to react as a mouse would. If I prick a rat with a needle, it may squeal, or bite, or jump—but it will not bark. Never. Nor will it leap up to a trapeze, hang by its tail, and chatter curses at me. Never.

"By observing an organism's reactions, one can begin to see a pattern. If you tell me that you put an armful of hay into a certain animal's enclosure, and that the animal trotted over, ate the hay, and brayed, I can tell you with reasonable certainty that the animal has long ears. Do you see?"

"You haven't been able to pinpoint the Nipe that easily, have you?" Stanton asked.

"Ah, no. The more intelligent a creature is, the greater its scope of action. The Nipe is far from being so simple as a monkey or a hamster. On the other hand—" He smiled widely, showing bright, white teeth. "—he is not so bright as a human being."

"*What!?* I wouldn't say he was exactly stupid, George. What about all those prize gadgets of his?" He blinked. "Wipe the sweat off my forehead, will you? It's running into my eyes."

Dr. Yoritomo wiped with the towel as he continued. "Ah, yes. He is quite capable in that respect, my friend. It is his great memory—at once his finest asset and his greatest curse."

He draped the towel around Stanton's head again and stepped back, his face unsmiling. "Imagine having a near-perfect memory."

Stanton's jaw muscles tightened. "I think I'd like it."

Yoritomo shrugged slightly. "Perhaps you would. But it would not be the asset you think. Look at it soberly, my friend.

"The most difficult teaching job in the universe is the attempt to teach an organism something it already knows. True? Yes. If a man already knows the shape of the Earth, it will do you no good to attempt to teach him. If he *knows* that the Earth is flat, your contention that it is round will make no impression whatever. He *knows,* you see. He *knows.*

"Now. Imagine a race with a perfect memory—one which does not fade. A memory in which each bit of data is as bright and fresh as the moment it was imprinted, and as readily available as the data stored in a robot's mind. It is, in effect, a robotic memory.

"If you put false data into the memory bank of a computer—such as telling it that the square of two is five—you cannot correct the error simply by telling it that the square of two is four. You must first remove the erroneous data, not so?

"Very good. Then let us look at the Nipe race, wherever it was spawned in this universe. Let us look at their race a long time back—when they first became *Nipe sapiens*. Back when they first developed a true language. Each child, as it is born or hatched or budded—whatever it is they do—is taught as rapidly as possible all the things it must know to survive. And once it is taught a thing, it *knows*. And if it is taught a falsehood, then it cannot be taught the truth."

"Wouldn't cold reality force a change?" Stanton asked.

"Ah. In some cases, yes. In most, no. Look: Suppose a primordial Nipe runs across a tiger—or whatever passes for a tiger on their planet. He has never seen a tiger before, so he does not see that this particular tiger is old, ill, and weak. He hits it on the head, and it drops dead. He takes it home for the family to feed on.

"'How did you kill it, Papa?'"

"'I walked up to it, bashed it on the noggin, and it died. That is the way to kill tigers.'"

Yoritomo smiled. "It is also a good way to kill Nipes. Eh?" He took the towel and wiped Stanton's brow again.

"The error," he continued, "was made when Papa Nipe generalized from *one* tiger to *all* tigers. If tigers were rare, this bit of lore might be passed on for many generations. Those who learned that most tigers are *not* conquered by walking up to them and hitting them on the noggin undoubtedly died before they could pass this bit of information on. Then, one day, a Nipe survived the ordeal. His mind now contained conflicting information, which must be resolved. He *knows* that tigers are killed in this way. He also *knows* that this one did not die. Plainly, then, *this* one is not a tiger. Ha! He has the solution!

"What does he tell his children? Why, first he tells them how tigers are killed. Then he warns them that there is an animal that looks *just like* a tiger, but is *not* a tiger. One should not make the mistake of thinking it *is* a tiger or one will get badly hurt. Since the only way to tell the true tiger from the false is to hit it, and since that test may prove fatal to the Nipe who tries it, it follows that one is better off if one avoids all animals that look like tigers. You see?"

"Yeah," said Stanton. "Some snarks are boojums."

"Exactly! Thank you for that allusion. I must remember to use it in my report."

"It seems to me to follow," Stanton said musingly, "that there would be some things that they'd never learn the truth about, once they'd gotten a wrong idea in their heads."

"Ah! Indeed. It is precisely that which led me to formulate my theory in the first place. How else to explain the fact that the Nipe, for all his technical knowledge, is still in the ancient ritual-taboo stage of development?"

"A savage?"

Yoritomo smiled. "As to his savagery, I think no one on Earth would disagree. But they are not the same thing. What I do mean is that the Nipe is undoubtedly the most superstitious and bigoted being on the face of this planet."

XIV

There was a knock at the door, and the physical therapist put his head in. "Sorry to interrupt, but the clam is done. I'll give him a rubdown, Doc, and you can have him back."

"Excellent. Would you come up to my office, Bart, as soon as you've had your mauling?"

"Sure. I'll be right up."

Yoritomo left, and the P.T. man opened the steam box. "Feel O.K., Bart?"

"Yeah, sure," he said abstractedly as he got up on the rubdown table and lay prone. The therapist saw that Stanton was in no mood for conversation, so he proceeded with the massage in silence.

For the first time, Stanton was seeing the Nipe as an individual, as a person, as a thinking, feeling being.

We have a great deal in common, you and I, he thought. *Except that you're a lot worse off than I am.*

I'm actually feeling sorry for the poor guy, Stanton thought. Which, I suppose, is better than feeling sorry for myself. The only difference between us freaks is that you're a bigger freak than I am. "Molly O'Grady and the Colonel's lady are sisters under the skin."

Where'd that come from? Something I learned in school, I guess—like the snarks and boojums.

"He would answer to Hi! or to any loud cry, Such as Fry me! or Fritter my wig!"

Who was that? The snark? No.
Damn this memory of mine!
Or can I even call it mine when I can't even use it?

"For now we see through a glass, darkly; but then face to face: now I know in part; but then shall I know even as also I am known."

Another jack-in-the-box thought popping up from nowhere.

The only way I'll ever get all this stuff straightened out is to get more information. And it doesn't look as though anyone is going to give it to me on a platter. The Institute seems to be awfully chary about giving information away. George even had to chase away old rub-and-pound, here (That feels good!) before he would talk about the Nipe. Can't blame 'em for that, I guess. There'd be hell to pay if the public ever found out that the Nipe has been kept as a pet for six years.

How many people has he killed in that time? Twenty? Thirty? How much blood does Colonel Mannheim have on his hands?

"Though they know not why,Or for what they give,Still, the few must die,That the many may live."

I wonder whether I read all that stuff complete or just browsed through a copy of Bartlett's Quotations. Fragments.

We've got to get organized here, brother. Colonel Mannheim's little puppet is going to cut his strings and do a Pinocchio.

"O.K., Bart," the P.T. said, giving Stanton a final slap, "you're all set. See you tomorrow."
"Right. Gimme my clothes."

Stanton dressed and took the elevator up to Yoritomo's office. This section of the building was off-limits to the other patients in the Institute, but Stanton, the star border, had free rein.

Not that it mattered, one way or another. There wasn't any way they could have stopped him. Aside from the fact that he was physically capable of going through or around almost any guards they wanted to put up, there was also the little matter of gentle blackmail. When a man is genuinely indispensable, he can work wonders by threatening to drop the whole business.

He felt as though he had been slowly awakening from a long sleep. At first, he had accepted as natural that he should obey orders and do as he was told without question, as thought he had been drugged or hypnotized.

And it's very likely they subjected me to both at one time or another, he told himself.

But now his brain was beginning to function again, and the need to know was strong in his mind.

Dr. Yoritomo was sitting in one of the big, soft chairs, puffing at his pipe, but he leaped to his feet when Stanton came in.

"Ah! About the ritual-taboo culture of the Nipe! Yes. Sit down. Yes. So. Do you find it impossible that a high technology could be present in such a system?"

"No. I've been thinking about it."

"Ah, so." He sat down again. "Then *you* will please tell *me*."

"Well, let's see. In the first place, let's take religion. In tribal cultures, religion is—uh—animistic, I think the word is."

Yoritomo nodded silently.

"There are spirits everywhere," Scanton went on. "That sort of belief, it seems to me, would grow up in any race that had imagination, and the Nipes must have plenty of that, or they wouldn't have the technology they do have."

"Very good. *Very* good. But what evidence have you that this technology was not given them by some other race?"

"I hadn't thought of that." Stanton stared into space for a moment, then nodded his head. "Of course. It would take too long for another race to teach it to them; it wouldn't be worth the trouble unless this hypothetical other race killed off all the adult Nipes and started the little ones off fresh. And if that had happened, their ritual-taboo system would have disappeared, too."

"That argument is imperfect," Yoritomo said, "but it will do for the moment. Go on with the religion."

"O.K.; religious beliefs are not subject to pragmatic tests. That is, the spiritual beliefs aren't. Any belief that*could* be disproven would eventually die out. But beliefs in ghosts or demons or angels or life after death aren't disprovable. So, as a race increases its knowledge of the physical world, its religion tends to become more and more spiritual."

"Agreed. Yes. But how do you link this with ritual-taboo?"

"Well, once a belief gains a foothold, it's hard to wipe it out, even among humans. Among Nipes, it would be well-nigh impossible. Once a code of ritual and social behavior was set up, it became permanent."

"For example?" Yoritomo urged.

"Well, shaking hands, for example. We still do that, even if we don't have it fixed solidly in our heads that we *must* do it. I suppose it would never occur to a Nipe not to perform such a ritual."

"Just so," Yoritomo agreed vigorously. "Such things, once established, would tend to remain. But it is a characteristic of a ritual-taboo system that it resists change. How, then, do you account for their high technological achievements?"

"The pragmatic engineering approach, I imagine. If a thing works, it is usable. If not, it isn't."

"Very good. Now it is my turn to lecture." He put his pipe in an ash tray and held up a long, bony finger. "Firstly, we must remember that the Nipe is equipped with an imagination. Secondly, he has in his memory a tremendous amount of data, all ready at hand. He is capable of working out theories in his head, you see. Like the ancient Greeks, he finds no need to test such theories—*unless* his thinking indicates that such an experiment would yield something useful. Unlike the Greeks, he has no aversion to experiment. But he sees no need for useless experiment, either.

"Oh, he would learn, yes. But, once a given theory proved workable, how resistant he would be to a new theory. How long—how *incredibly* long—it would take such a race to achieve the technology the Nipe now has!"

"Hundreds of thousands of years," said Stanton.

Yoritomo shook his head briskly. "Puh! Longer! Much longer!" He smiled with satisfaction. "I estimate that the Nipe race first invented the steam engine not less than ten million years ago." He kept smiling into the dead silence that followed.

After a long minute, Scanton said: "What about atomic energy?"

"At least two million years ago. I do not think they have had the interstellar drive more than fifty thousand years."

"No wonder our pet Nipe is so patient," Stanton said wonderingly. "I wonder what their individual life span is."

"Not long, in comparison," said Yoritomo. "Perhaps no longer than our own, perhaps five hundred years. Considering their handicaps, they have done quite well. Quite well, indeed, for a race of illiterate cannibals."

"How's that again?" Stanton realized that the scientist was quite serious.

"Hadn't it occurred to you, my friend, that they must be cannibals? And that they are very nearly illiterate?"

"No," Stanton admitted, "it hadn't."

"The Nipe, like Man, is omnivorous. Specialization tends to lead any race up a blind alley, and dietary restrictions are a particularly pernicious form of specialization. A lion would starve to death in a wheat field. A horse would perish in a butcher shop full of steaks. A man will survive as long as there's something around to eat—even if it's another man.

"Also, Man, early in his career as top dog on Earth, began using a method of increasing the viability of the race by removing the unfit. It survives today in some societies. Before and immediately after the Holocaust, there were still primitive societies on Earth which made a rather hard ordeal out of the Rite of Passage—the ceremony that enabled a boy to become a Man, if he passed the tests.

"A few millennia ago, a boy was killed outright if failed. And eaten.

"The Nipe race must, of necessity, have had some similar ritualistic tests or they would not have become what they are. And we have already agreed that, once the Nipes adopted something of that kind, it remained with them, not so? Yes.

"Also, it is extremely unlikely that the Nipe civilisation—if such it can be called—has any geriatric problem. No old age pensions, no old folks' homes, no senility. When a Nipe becomes a burden because of age, he is ritually murdered and eaten with due solemnity.

"Ah. You frown, my friend. Have I made them sound heartless, without the finer feelings that we humans are so proud of? Not so. When Junior Nipe fails his puberty tests, when Mama and Papa Nipe are sent to their final reward, I have no doubt that there is sadness in the hearts of their loved ones as the honored T-bones are passed around the table.

"My own ancestors, not too far back, performed a ritual suicide by disemboweling themselves with a sharp knife. Across the abdomen—so!—and up into the heart—so! It was considered very bad form to die or faint before the job was done. Nearby, a relative or close friend stood with a sharp sword, to administer the *coup de grace* by decapitation. It was all very sad and very honorable. Their loved ones bore the sorrow with pride."

His voice, which had been low and tender, suddenly became very brisk. "Thank goodness it's gone out of fashion!"

"But how can you be *sure* they're cannibals?" Stanton asked. "Your argument sounds logical enough, but logic alone isn't enough."

"True! True!" Yoritomo jabbed the air twice with his finger. "Evidence would be most welcome, would it not? Very well, I give you the evidence. He eats human beings, our Nipe."

"That doesn't make him a cannibal."

"Not *strictly*, perhaps. But consider. The Nipe is not a monster. He is not a criminal. No. He is a gentleman. He behaves as a gentleman. He is shipwrecked on an alien planet. Around his, he sees evidence that ours is a technological society. But that is a contradiction! A paradox!

"For *we* are not civilized! No! We are not rational! We are not sane! We do not obey the Laws, we do not perform the Rituals. We are animals. Apparently intelligent animals, but animals never the less. How can this be?

"Ha! Says the Nipe to himself. These animals must be ruled over by Real People. It is the only explanation. Not so?"

"Colonel Mannheim mentioned that. Are you implying that the Nipe thinks that there are other Nipes around, running the world from secret hideouts, like the Fu Manchu novel?"

"Not quite. The Nipe is not incapable of learning something new; in fact, he is quite good at it, as witness the fact that he has learned many Earth languages. He picked up Russian in less then eight months simply by listening and observing. Like our own race, his undoubtedly evolved many languages during the beginnings of its progress—when there were many tribes, separated and out of communication. It would not surprise me to find that most of those languages have survived and that our distressed astronaut knows them all. A new language would not distress him.

"Nor would strangely-shaped intelligent beings distress him. His race should be aware, by now, that such things exist. But it is very likely that he equates *true* intelligence with technology, and I do not think he has ever met a race higher than the barbarian level before. Such races were not, of course, human—by his definition. They showed possibilities, perhaps, but they had not evolved far enough. Considering the time span involved, it is not at all unlikely that the Nipe thinks of technology as something that evolves with a race in the same way intelligence does—or the body itself.

"So it would not surprise him to find that the Real People of this system were humanoid in shape. That is something new, and he can absorb it. It does not contradict anything he *knows*.

"But—! Any truly intelligent being which did not obey the Law and follow the Ritual *would* be a contradiction in terms. For he has no notion of a Real Person without those characteristics. Without those characteristics, technology is impossible. Since he sees technology all around him, it follows that there must be Real People with those characteristics. Anything else is unthinkable."

"It seems to me that you're building an awfully involved theory out of pretty flimsy stuff," Stanton said.

Yoritomo shook his head. "Not at all. All evidence points to it. Why, do you suppose, does the Nipe conscientiously devour his victims, often risking his own safety to do so? Why do you suppose he never uses any weapons but his own hands to kill with?

"Why? To tell the Real People that he is a gentleman!"

It made perfect sense, Stanton thought. It fitted every known fact, as far as he knew. Still—

"I would think," he said, "that the Nipe would have realized, after ten years, that there is no such race of Real People. He's had access to all our records, and such things. Or does he reject them as lies?"

"Possibly he would, if he could read them. Did I not say he was illiterate?"

"You mean he's learned to speak our languages, but not to read them?"

The scientist smiled broadly. "Your statement is accurate, my friend, but incomplete. It is my opinion that the Nipe is incapable of reading any written language whatever. The concept does not exist in his mind, except vaguely."

"A technological race without a written language? That's impossible!"

"Ah, no. Ask yourself: What need has a race with a perfect memory for written records—at least, in the sense we know them. Certainly not to remember things. All their history and all their technology exists in the collective mind of the race—or, at least, most of it. I dare say that the less important parts of their history has been glossed over and forgotten. One important event in every ten centuries would still give a historian ten thousand events to remember—and history is only a late development in our own society."

"How about communications?" Stanton said, "What did they use before they invented radio?"

"Ah. That is why I hedged when I said he was *almost* illiterate. There is a possibility that a written symbology did at one time exist, for just that purpose. If so, it has probably survived as a ritualistic form—when an officer is appointed to a post, let's say, he may get a formal paper that says so. They may use symbols to signify rank and so on. They certainly must have a symbology for the calibration of scientific instruments.

"But none of these requires the complexity of a written language. I dare say our use of it is quite baffling to him. And if he thinks of symbols as being unable to convey much information, then he might not be able to learn to read at all. You see?"

"Where's your evidence for that?"

"It is sketchy, I will admit," said Yoritomo. "It is not as solidly based as our other reconstructions of his background. The pattern of his raids indicates, however, that his knowledge of the materials he wants and their locations comes from vocal sources—television advertising, eaves-dropping, and so on. In other words, he cases the joint by ear. If he could understand written information, his job would have been much easier. He could have found the materials more quickly and easily. From this evidence, we are fairly certain that he can't read any Terrestrial writing.

"Add to that the fact that he has never been observed writing down anything himself, and the suspicion dawns that perhaps he *knows* that symbols can only convey a very small amount of specialized information. Eh?"

"As I said, it is not proof."

"No. But the whole thing makes for some very interesting speculation, doesn't it?"

"Very interesting indeed." Yoritomo folded his hands in his lap, smiled seraphically, and looked at the ceiling. "In fact, my friend, we are now so positive of our knowledge of the Nipe's mind that we are prepared to enter into the next phase of our program. Within a very short while, if we are correct, we shall, with your help, arrest the most feared arch-criminal that Earth has ever known." He chuckled, but there was little mirth in it. "I dare say that the public will be extremely happy to hear of his death, and I know that Colonel Mannheim and the rest of us will be glad to know that he will never kill again."

Stanton saw that the fateful day was looming suddenly large in the future. "How soon?"

"Within days." He lowered his eyes from the ceiling and looked into Stanton's face with a mildly bland expression.

"By the way," he said, "did you know that your brother is returning to Earth tomorrow?"

XV

INTERLUDE

Is this our young man, Dr. Farnsworth?" asked the man in uniform.

"Yes, it is. Colonel Mannheim, I'd like you to meet Mr. Bartholomew Stanton."

"How are you, Mr. Stanton?"

"Fine, Colonel. A little nervous."

The colonel chuckled softly. "I can't say that I blame you. It's not an easy decision to make." He looked at Dr. Farnsworth. "Has Dr. Yoritomo any more information for us?"

Farnsworth shook his head. "No. He admits that his idea is nothing more than a wild hunch. He seems to think that five years of observing the Nipe won't be too much time at all. We may have to act before then."

"I hope not. It would be a terrible waste," said Mannheim. "Mr. Stanton, I know that Dr. Farnsworth has outlined the entire plan to you, and I'm sure you're aware that many things can change in five years. We may have to play by ear long before that. Do you understand what we are doing, and why it must be done this way?"

"Yes, sir."

"You know that you're not to say anything."

"Yes, sir. Don't worry; I can keep my mouth shut."

"We're pretty sure of that," the colonel said with a smile. "Your psychometric tests showed that we were right in picking you. Otherwise, we couldn't have told you. You understand your part in this, eh?"

"Yes, sir."

"Any questions?"

"Yes, sir. What about my brother, Martin? I mean, well, I know what's the matter with him. Aside from the radiation, I mean. Do you think he'll be able to handle his part of the job after—after the operations?"

"If the operations turn out as well as Dr. Farnsworth thinks they will, yes. And, with the therapy we'll give him afterwards, he'll be in fine shape."

"Well." He looked thoughtful. "Five more years. And then I'll have the twin brother that I never really had at all. Somehow, it doesn't really register, I guess."

"Don't worry about it, Mr. Stanton," said Dr. Farnsworth. "We've got a complex enough job ahead of us without your worrying in the bargain. By the way, we'll need your signature here." He handed him a pen and spread the paper on the desk. "In triplicate."

The young man read quickly through the release form. "All nice and legal, huh? Well...." He hesitated for a moment, then bent over and wrote: *Bartholomew Stanton* in a firm, clear hand.

XVI

The tunnel was long and black and the air was stale and thick with the stench of rodents. Stanton stood still, trying to probe the luminescent gloom that the goggles he wore brought to his eyes. The tunnel stretched out before him—on and on. Around him was the smell of viciousness and death. Ahead ...

It goes on to infinity, Stanton thought, *ending at last at zero.*

"Barbell," said a voice near his ear, "Barhop here. Do you read?" It was the barest whisper, picked up by the antennae in his shoes from the steel rail that ran along the tunnel.

"Read you, Barhop."

"Move out, then. You've got a long stroll to go."

Stanton started walking, keeping his feet near the rail, in case Barhop wanted to call again. As he walked, he could feel the slight motion of the skin-tight, woven elastic suit that he wore rubbing against his skin.

And he could hear the scratching patter of the rats.

Mostly, they stayed away from him, but he could see them hiding in corners and scurrying along the sides of the tunnel. Around him, six rat-like remote-control robots moved with him, shifting their pattern constantly as they patrolled his moving figure.

Far ahead, he knew, other rat robots were stationed, watching and waiting, ready to deactivate the Nipe's detection devices at just the right moment. Behind him, another horde moved forward to turn the devices on again.

It had taken a long time to learn how to shut off those detectors without giving the alarm to the Nipe's instruments.

There were nearly a hundred men in on the operation, operating the robot rats or watching the hidden cameras that spied upon the Nipe. Nearly a hundred. And all of them were safe.

They were outside the tunnel. They were with Stanton only in proxy. They could not die here in this stinking hole, but Stanton could.

There was no help for it. Stanton had to go in person. A full-sized robot proxy would be stronger, although not faster unless Stanton controlled it, than the Nipe. But the Nipe would be able to tell that it was a robot, and he would simply destroy it with one of his weapons. A remote-controlled robot would never get close enough to the Nipe to do any good.

"We do not know," Dr. Yoritomo had said, "whether he would recognize it as a robot or not, but his instruments would show the metal easily enough, and his eyes might be able to see that it was not covered with human skin. The rats are covered with real rat hides; they are small, and he is used to seeing them around. But a human-sized robot? Ah, no. Never."

So Stanton had to go in in person, walking southward, along the miles of blackness that led to the nest of the Nipe.

Overhead was Government City.

He had walked those streets only the night before, and he knew that only a short distance above him was an entirely different world.

Somewhere up there, his brother was waiting after having run the gamut of televised interviews, dinner at one of the best restaurants, and a party afterward. A celebrity. "The greatest detective in the Solar System," they'd called him. Fine stuff, that. Stanton wondered what the asteroids were like. Maybe that would be the place to go after this job was done. Maybe they'd have a place in the asteroids for a hopped-up superman.

Or maybe there'd only be a place here, beneath the streets of Government City for a dead superman.

Not if I can help it, Stanton thought with a grim smile.

The walking seemed to take forever, but, somehow, Stanton didn't mind it. He had a lot to think over. Seeing his brother had been unnerving yesterday, but today he felt as though everything had been all right all along.

His memory still was a long way from being complete, and it probably always would be. He could still scarcely recall any real memories of a boy named Martin Stanton, but—and he smiled at the thought—he knew more about him than his brother did, at that.

It didn't matter. That Martin Stanton was gone. In effect, he had been demolished—what little there had been of him—and a new structure had been built on the old foundation.

And yet, in another way, the new structure was very like what would have developed naturally if the accident so early in life had not occurred.

Stanton skirted a pile of rubble on his right. There had been a station here, once; the street above had caved in and filled in with brick, concrete, cobblestones, and steel scrap, and then it had been sealed over when Government City was built.

A part of one wall was still unbroken, though. A sign built of tile said *86th Street*, he knew, although it wasn't visible in the dim glow. He kept walking, ignoring the rats that scampered over the rubble.

"Barhop to Barbell," said the soft voice near his ear. "No sign of activity from the Nipe. So far, you haven't triggered any of his alarms."

"Barbell to Barhop," Stanton whispered. "What's he doing?"

"Still sitting motionless. Thinking, I guess. Or sleeping. It's hard to tell."

"Let me know if he starts moving around."

"Will do."

Poor, unsuspecting beastie, Stanton thought. *Ten years of hard work, ten years of feeling secure, and within a very short time he's going to get the shock of his life.*

Or maybe not. There was no way of knowing what kind of shocks the Nipe had taken in his life, Stanton thought. Not even of knowing whether the Nipe was capable of feeling anything like security.

It was odd, he thought, that he should feel a kinship toward both the Nipe and his brother in such similar ways. He had never met the Nipe, and his brother was a dim picture in his old memories, but they were both very well known to him. Certainly better known to him than he was to them.

And yet, seeing his brother's face on the TV screen, hearing him talk, watching the way he moved about, watching the expressions on his face, had been a tremendously moving thing. Not until that moment had he really known himself.

Meeting him face to face would be easier now, but it would still be a scene highly charged with emotional tension.

He kicked something that rattled and rolled away from him. He stopped, freezing in his tracks, trying to pierce the dully glowing gloom. It was a human skull.

He relaxed and began walking again.

There were plenty of bones down here. Mannheim had said that the tunnels had been used as air-raid shelters when the sun bomb had hit the island during the Holocaust. Thousands had crowded underground after the warning had come, and they had died when the bright, hot, deadly gas had roared down through ventilators and open stairwells.

There were even caches of canned goods down here, some of them still sealed after all this time. But the rats, wiser than they knew, had chewed at them, exposing the steel beneath the tin plate. After a while, oxidation would weaken a can to the point where some lucky rat could bite through it and find himself a meal. Then he could move the empty can aside and gnaw the next one in the pile, and the cycle would begin again. It kept the rats fed almost as well as an automatic machine might have.

The tunnel was an endless monochromatic world that was both artificial and natural. Here, there was a neatly squared-off mosaic of ceramic tile; over there, on a little hillock of earth, squatted a colony of fat mushrooms. In one place, he had to skirt a pool of water; in another, climb over a heap of rust and debris that had once been a subway car.

One man, alone, walking through the dark towards a superhuman monster that had terrorized Earth for a decade.

A drug that would knock out the Nipe would have been useful, but that would have required a greater knowledge of the Nipe's biochemistry than anyone had. The same applied to anesthetic gases, or electric shock, or supersonics.

The only answer was a man called Stanton.

And the voice near his ear said: "A hundred yards to go, Barbell."

"I know," he whispered. "He hasn't moved?"

"No."

Wouldn't it be funny if he were dead? Stanton thought. *If his heart had stopped, or something. Wouldn't that be a big joke on everybody? Especially me.*

Ahead the tunnel made a curving turn, and there was a large area that had once been a major junction of two tunnels, one below the other. The Nipe had taken over a part of that area to build his home-away-from-home.

Stanton approached the turn and took off the infra-red goggles. Enough light spilled over from the Nipe's lair to illuminate the tunnel. He put the goggles on the trackway. He wouldn't need them again.

He went on around the curve, slowly and quietly. He didn't want to fight down here in the tracks, and he didn't want to be caught just yet.

Cautiously, he lifted himself up to the platform, where long-gone passengers had once waited for long-gone trains. Now that he was out of the trench that the tracks lay in, he could move more easily. He moved away from the tracks.

"Barbell! He's heard you! Watch it!"

But Stanton had already heard the movement of the Nipe. He jerked off the communicator and threw it away. He didn't want any encumbrances now.

And then, as fast as any express train that had ever moved in these underground ways, the Nipe came around a corner thirty feet away, his four violet eyes gleaming, his limbs rippling beneath his centipede-like body.

From fifteen feet away, he launched himself through the air, his outstretched hands ready to kill.

But Stanton's marvelous neuro-muscular system was already in action.

At this stage of the game, it would be suicide to let the Nipe get close. He couldn't fend off eight grasping hands with his own two. He leaped to one side, and the Nipe got his first surprise in ten years when Stanton's fist slammed against the side of his snouted head, knocking him in the opposite direction from that in which Stanton had moved.

The Nipe landed, turned, and charged back toward the man. This time, he reared up, using his two rear pairs of limbs for locomotion, while the two forward pair were held out, ready to kill.

He got surprise number two when Stanton's fist landed on his snout, rocking his head back. His own hands met nothing but air, and by the time he had recovered from the blow, Stanton was well back, out of the way.

He's so small! Stanton thought wonderingly. Even when he reared up, the Nipe's head was only three feet above the concrete floor.

The Nipe came in again—more cautiously, this time.

Stanton punched again with a straight right. The Nipe moved his head aside, and Stanton's knuckles merely grazed the side of his head, below the lower right eye. One of the Nipe's hands came in in a chopping right hook that took Stanton just below the ribs. Stanton leaped back with a gasp of pain.

The Nipe didn't use fists. He used his open hand, fingers together, like a judo fighter.

The Nipe came forward once more, and as Stanton danced back, the Nipe made a grab for his ankle, almost catching it.

There were too many hands to watch! Stanton had two advantages: weight and reach. His arms were almost half again as long as the Nipe's.

Against that, the Nipe had all those hands; and with his low center of gravity and four-footed stance, it would be hard to knock him down. If Stanton lost his footing, the fight would be over fast.

Stanton lunged suddenly forward and planted a left in the Nipe's right upper eye, then followed it with a right uppercut to the Nipe's jaw as his head snapped back. The Nipe's four hands cut inward from the sides like sword blades, but they found no target.

Backing away, Stanton suddenly realized that he had another advantage. The Nipe couldn't throw a straight jab! His shoulder—if that's what they should be called—were narrow and the upper armbones weren't articulated properly for such a blow. He could throw a mean hook, but he had to get in close to deliver it.

On the other side of the coin was the fact that the Nipe knew plenty about human anatomy—from the bones out. Stanton's knowledge of Nipe anatomy was almost totally superficial.

He wished he knew if and where the Nipe had a solar plexus. He would like to punch something soft for a change.

Instead, he tried for another eye. He danced in, jabbed and danced out again, The Nipe had ducked again, taking it on the side of his head.

Then the Nipe came in low, at an angle, trying for the groin. For his troubles, he got a knee in the jaw that staggered him badly. One grasping hand clutched at Stanton's right thigh and grasped hard. Stanton swung his fist down like a pendulum and knocked the arm aside.

But there was a slight limp in his movement as he back-pedaled away from the Nipe. That full-handed pinch had hurt!

Stanton was angry now, with the hot, controlled anger of a fighting man. He stepped in and slammed two fast, hard jabs into the point of the Nipe's snout, jarring the monster backwards. This time, it was the Nipe who scuttled backwards.

Stanton moved in to press his advantage and landed a beaut on the Nipe's lower left eye. Then he tried a body blow. It wasn't too successful. The alien had an endoskeleton, but he also had a hide that was like somewhat leathery chitin.

He pulled back, out of the way of the Nipe's judo cuts.

His fists were beginning to hurt, and his leg was paining him badly where the Nipe had clamped on to it. And his ribs—

And then he realized that, so far, the Nipe had only landed one blow!

One punch and one pinch, he thought with a touch of awe. *The only other damage he's inflicted has been to my knuckles!*

The Nipe charged in again, then he leaped suddenly and clawed for Stanton's face with his first pair of hands. The second and third pairs chopped in toward the man's body. The last pair propelled him off the floor.

Stanton stepped back and let him have a right just below the jaw, where his throat would have been if he'd been human.

The Nipe arced backwards in a half-somersault and landed flat on his back.

Stanton backed up a little more, waiting, while the Nipe wriggled feebly for a moment. *The Marquis of Queensbury should have lived to see this,* he thought.

The Nipe rolled over and crouched on all eight limbs. His violet eyes watched Stanton, but the man could read no expression on that inhuman face.

"*You did not kill.*"

For a moment, Stanton found it hard to believe that the hissing, guttural voice had come from the crouching monster.

"*You did not even* try *to kill.*"

"I have no wish to kill you," Stanton said evenly.

"*I can see that. Do you ... Are you....*" He stopped, as if baffled. "*There are not the proper words. Do you follow the Customs?*"

Stanton felt a surge of triumph. This was what George Yoritomo had guessed might happen!

"If I must kill you," he said carefully, "I, myself, will do the honors. You will not go uneaten."

The Nipe sagged a little, relaxing all over. "*I had hoped it was so. It was the only thinkable thing. I saw you on the television, and it was only thinkable that you came for me.*"

Stanton blinked, stunned. What was the Nipe thinking? But, of course, he knew. And he saw that even his brother's return had been a part of the plan.

"*I knew you were out in the asteroids,*" the Nipe went on. "*But I had decided you had come to kill. Since you did not, what are your thoughts, Stanley Martin?*"

"That we should help each other," Stanton said.

It was as simple as that.

XVII

Stanton sat in his hotel room, smoking a cigarette, staring at the wall, and thinking.

He was alone again. All the fuss, feathers, and fooferaw were over. Farnsworth was in another room of the suite, making his plans for a complete physical examination of the Nipe. Yoritomo was having the time of his life, holding a conversation with the Nipe, drawing the alien out and getting him to talk about his own race and their history. And Mannheim was plotting the next phase of the capture—the cover-up.

Stanton smiled a little. Colonel Mannheim was a great one for planning, all right. Every little detail was taken care of. It sometimes made his plans more complex than necessary, Stanton suspected. Mannheim tended to try to account for every eventuality, and, after he had done that, he would set aside reserves here and there, just in case they might be useful if something unforeseen happened.

Stanton got up, walked over to the window, and looked down at the streets of Government City, eight floors below.

All things considered, the Government had done the right thing. And, in picking Mannheim, they had picked the right man. What would the average citizen think if he knew the true story of the Nipe? If he discovered that, at this very moment, the Nipe was being treated almost as an honored guest of the Government? If he suspected that the Nipe could have been killed easily at any time during the past six years?

Would it be possible to explain that, in the long run, the knowledge possessed by the Nipe was tremendously more valuable to the Race of Man that the lives of a few individuals?

Could those people down there, and the others like them all over the world, be made to understand that, by his own lights, the Nipe had been acting in a most civilized and gentlemanly way he knew? Would they see that, because of the priceless information stored in that alien brain, the Nipe's life had to be preserved at any cost?

Dr. Yoritomo assumed that Mannheim would spread a story about the Nipe's death—perhaps even display a carefully-made "corpse". But Stanton had the feeling that the colonel had something else up his sleeve.

The phone rang. Stanton walked over, thumbed the answer stud, and watched Dr. Farnsworth's face take shape on the screen.

"Bart, I just saw the tapes of your fight with the Nipe, Incredible! I'm going to have them run over again, slowed down, so that I can see what went on, and I'd like to have you tell as best you can, what went on in your mind at each stage of the fight."

"You mean right now? I have an appointment—"

Farnsworth waved a hand. "No, no. Later. Take your time. But I am honestly amazed that you won so easily. I knew you were good, and I knew you'd win, but I honestly expected you to be injured."

Stanton looked down at his bandaged hands, and felt the ache of his broken rib and the blue bruise on his thigh. In spite of the way it looked, he had actually been hurt worse than the Nipe had. That boy was *tough*!

"The trouble was that he couldn't adapt himself to fighting in a new way," he told Farnsworth. "He fought me as he would have fought another Nipe, and that didn't work. I had the reach on him, and I could maneuver faster."

"It looked to me as though you were fighting him as you would fight another human being," Farnsworth said.

Stanton grinned. "I was, in a modified way. But *I* won—the Nipe didn't."

Farnsworth grinned back. "I see. Well, I'll let you know when I'm ready for your impressions. Probably tomorrow some time."

"Fine."

He walked back over to the window, but this time he looked at the horizon, not at the street.

Farnsworth had called him "Bart". It's funny, Stanton thought, how habit can get the best of a man. Farnsworth had known the truth all along, and now he knew that his patient—*former* patient—was aware of the truth. And still, he had called him "Bart".

And I still think of myself as Bart, he thought. *I probably always will.*

And why not? Martin Stanton no longer existed—in fact he had never had much of a real existence. He was only a bad dream; only "Bart" was real.

Take two people, genetically identical. Damage one of them so badly that he is helpless and useless—and always only a step away from death. It is inevitable that the weaker will identify himself with the stronger.

The vague telepathic bond that always links identical twins (they "think alike", they say) becomes unbalanced under such conditions. Normally, there is a give-and-take, and each preserves the sense of his own identity, since the two different sets of sense receptors give different viewpoints. But if one of the twins is damaged badly enough something must happen to the telepathic link. Usually, it is broken.

But the link between Mart and Bart Stanton had not been broken. It had become a one-way channel. Martin, in order to escape the prison of his own body, had become a receptor for Bart's thoughts. He felt as Bart felt—the thrill of running after a baseball, the pride of doing something clever with his hands.

In effect, Martin ceased to think. The thoughts in his mind were Bart's. The feeling of identity was almost complete.

To an outside observer, it appeared that Martin had become a cataleptic schizophrenic, completely cut off from reality. The "Bart" part of him did not want to be disturbed by the sensory impressions that "Mart's" body provided. Like the schizophrenic, Martin was living in a little world that was cut off from the actual physical world around his body.

The difference between Martin's condition and that of the ordinary schizophrenic was that *his* little world actually existed. It was an almost exact counterpart of the world that existed in the perfectly sane, rational mind of his brother, Bart. It grew and developed as Bart did, fed by the telepathic flow from the stronger mind to the weaker.

There were two Barts, and no Mart at all.

And then the Neurophysical Institute had come into the picture. A new process had been developed, by which a human being could be reconstructed—made, literally, into a superman. The drawback was that a normal human body resisted the process—to the death, if necessary, just as a normal human body will resist a skin graft from an alien donor.

But the radiation-damaged body of Martin Stanton had no resistance of that kind. With him—perhaps—the process might work.

So Bartholomew Stanton, Martin's legal guardian after the death of their mother, had given permission for the series of operations that would rebuild his brother.

The telepathic link, of course, had to be shut off—for a time, at least. Part of that could be done in the treatment of Martin, but Bart, too, had to do his part. By submitting to hypnosis, he had allowed himself to be convinced that his name was Stanley Martin. He had taken a job on Luna, and then had gone to the asteriods. The simple change of name and environment had been just enough to snap the link during a time when Martin's brain had been inactivated by therapy and anesthetics.

Only the sense of identity remained. The patient was still Bart.

Mannheim had used them both, naturally. Colonel Mannheim had the ability to use anyone at hand, including himself, to get a job done.

Stanton looked at his watch. It was almost time.

Mannheim had sent for "Stanley Martin" when the time had come for him to return in order to give the Nipe data that he would be sure to misinterpret. A special code phrase in the message had released "Stanley Martin" from the posthypnotic suggestion that had held him for so long. He knew that he was Bartholomew Stanton again.

And so do I, thought the man by the window. *We have a lot to straighten out, we two.*

There was a knock at the door.

Stanton walked over and opened it, trying to think.

It was like looking into a mirror.

"Hello, Bart," he said.

"Hello, Bart," said the other.

In that instant, the complete telepathic linkage was restored, and they both knew what only one of them had known before—that, for a time, the flow had been one-way again—that "Stanley Martin" had experienced the entire battle with the Nipe. His release from the posthypnotic suggestion had made it possible.

E duobus unum.

There was unity without loss of identity.

Anchorite

There are two basic kinds of fools—the ones who know they are fools, and the kind that, because they do not know that, are utterly deadly menaces!

The mountain was spinning.

Not dizzily, not even rapidly, but very perceptibly, the great mass of jagged rock was turning on its axis.

Captain St. Simon scowled at it. "By damn, Jules," he said, "if you can see 'em spinning, it's too damn fast!" He expected no answer, and got none.

He tapped the drive pedal gently with his right foot, his gaze shifting alternately from the instrument board to the looming hulk of stone before him. As the little spacecraft moved in closer, he tapped the reverse pedal with his left foot. He was now ten meters from the surface of the asteroid. It was moving, all right. "Well, Jules," he said in his most commanding voice, "we'll see just how fast she's moving. Prepare to fire Torpedo Number One!"

"Yassuh, boss! Yassuh, Cap'n Sain' Simon, suh! All ready on the firin' line!"

He touched a button with his right thumb. The ship quivered almost imperceptibly as a jet of liquid leaped from the gun mounted in the nose of the ship. At the same time, he hit the reverse pedal and backed the ship away from the asteroid's surface. No point getting any more gunk on the hull than necessary.

The jet of liquid struck the surface of the rotating mountain and splashed, leaving a big splotch of silvery glitter. Even in the vacuum of space, the silicone-based solvents of the paint vehicle took time to boil off.

"How's that for pinpoint accuracy, Jules?"

"Veddy good, M'lud. Top hole, if I may say so, m'lud."

"You may." He jockeyed the little spacecraft around until he was reasonably stationary with respect to the great hunk of whirling rock and had the silver-white blotch centered on the crosshairs of the peeper in front of him. Then he punched the button that started the timer and waited for the silver spot to come round again.

The asteroid was roughly spherical—which was unusual, but not remarkable. The radar gave him the distance from the surface of the asteroid, and he measured the diameter and punched it through the calculator. "Observe," he said in a dry, didactic voice. "The diameter is on the order of five times ten to the fourteenth micromicrons." He kept punching at the calculator. "If we assume a mean density of two point six six times ten to the minus thirty-sixth metric tons per cubic micromicron, we attain a mean mass of some one point seven four times ten to the eleventh kilograms." More punching, while he kept his eye on the meteorite, waiting for the spot to show up again. "And that, my dear Jules, gives us a surface gravity of approximately two times ten to the minus sixth standard gees."

"*Jawohl, Herr Oberstleutnant.*"

"Und zo, mine dear Chules, ve haff at least der grave zuspicion dot der zurface gravity iss less dan der zentrifugal force at der eqvator! *Nein? Ja!* Zo."

"*Jawohl, Herr Konzertmeister.*"

Then there was a long, silent wait, while the asteroid went its leisurely way around its own axis.

"There it comes," said Captain St. Simon. He kept his eyes on the crosshair of the peeper, one hand over the timer button. When the silver splotch drifted by the crosshair, he punched the stop button and looked at the indicator.

"Sixteen minutes, forty seconds. How handy." He punched at the calculator again. "Ah! You see, Jules! Just as we suspected! Negative gees at the surface, on the equator, comes to ten to the minus third standard gees—almost exactly one centimeter per second squared. So?"

"Ah, so, honorabu copton! Is somesing rike five hundred times as great as gravitationar attraction, is not so?"

"Sukiyaki, my dear chap, sometimes your brilliance amazes me."

Well, at least it meant that there would be no loose rubble on the surface. It would have been tossed off long ago by the centrifugal force, flying off on a tangent to become more of the tiny rubble of the belt. Perhaps "flying" wasn't exactly the right word, though, when applied to a velocity of less than one centimeter per second. *Drifting* off, then.

"What do you think, Jules?" said St. Simon.

"Waal, Ah reckon we can do it, cap'n. Ef'n we go to the one o' them thar poles ... well, let's see—" He leaned over and punched more figures into the calculator. "Ain't that purty! 'Cordin' ter this, thar's a spot at each pole, 'bout a meter in diameter, whar the gee-pull is *greater* than the centry-foogle force!"

Captain St. Simon looked at the figures on the calculator. The forces, in any case, were negligibly small. On Earth, where the surface gravity was ninety-eight per cent of a Standard Gee, St. Simon weighed close to two hundred pounds. Discounting the spin, he would weigh about four ten-thousandths of a pound on the asteroid he was inspecting. The spin at the equator would try to push him off with a force of about two tenths of a pound.

But a man who didn't take those forces into account could get himself killed in the Belt.

"Very well, Jules," he said, "we'll inspect the poles."
"Do you think they vill velcome us in Kraukau, *Herr Erzbischof*?"

The area around the North Pole—defined as that pole from which the body appears to be spinning counterclockwise—looked more suitable for operations than the South Pole. Theoretically, St. Simon could have stopped the spin, but that would have required an energy expenditure of some twenty-three thousand kilowatt-hours in the first place, and it would have required an anchor to be set somewhere on the equator. Since his purpose in landing on the asteroid was to set just such an anchor, stopping the spin would be a waste of time and energy.

Captain St. Simon positioned his little spacecraft a couple of meters above the North Pole. It would take better than six minutes to fall that far, so he had plenty of time. "Perhaps a boarding party, Mr. Christian! On the double!"

"Aye, sir! On the double it is, sir!"

St. Simon pushed himself over to the locker, took out his vacuum suit, and climbed into it. After checking it thoroughly, he said: "Prepare to evacuate main control room, Mr. Christian!"

"Aye, aye, Sir! All prepared and ready. I hope."

Captain St. Simon looked around to make sure he hadn't left a bottle of coffee sitting somewhere. He'd done that once, and the stuff had boiled out all over everywhere when he pulled the air out of the little room. Nope, no coffee. No obstacles to turning on the pump. He thumbed the button, and the pumps started to whine. The whine built up to a crescendo, then began to die away until finally it could only be felt through the walls or floor. The air was gone.

Then he checked the manometer to make sure that most of the air had actually been pumped back into the reserve tanks. Satisfied, he touched the button that would open the door. There was a faint jar as the remaining wisps of air shot out into the vacuum of space.

St. Simon sat back down at the controls and carefully repositioned the ship. It was now less than a meter from the surface. He pushed himself over to the open door and looked out.

He clipped one end of his safety cable to the steel eye-bolt at the edge of the door. "Fasten on carefully, Jules," he said. "We don't want to lose anything."

"Like what, *mon capitain*?"

"Like this spaceship, *mon petit tête de mouton*."

"Ah, but no, my old and raw; we could not afford to lose the so-dear *Nancy Bell*, could we?"

The other end of the long cable was connected to the belt of the suit. Then St. Simon launched himself out the open door toward the surface of the planetoid. The ship began to drift—very slowly, but not so slowly as it had been falling—off in the other direction.

He had picked the spot he was aiming for. There was a jagged hunk of rock sticking out that looked as though it would make a good handhold. Right nearby, there was a fairly smooth spot that would do to brake his "fall". He struck it with his palm and took up the slight shock with his elbow while his other hand grasped the outcropping.

He had not pushed himself very hard. There is not much weathering on the surface of an asteroid. Micro-meteorites soften the contours of the rock a little over the millions of millennia, but not much, since the debris in the Belt all has roughly the same velocity. Collisions do occur, but they aren't the violent smashes that make the brilliant meteor displays of Earth. (And there is still a standing argument among the men of the Belt as to whether that sort of action can be called "weathering".) Most of the collisions tend to cause fracturing of the surface, which results in jagged edges. A man in a vacuum suit does not push himself against a surface like that with any great velocity.

St. Simon knew to a nicety that he could propel himself against a bed of nails and broken glass at just the right velocity to be able to stop himself without so much as scratching his glove. And he could see that there was no ragged stuff on the spot he had selected. The slanting rays of the sun would have made them stand out in relief.

Now he was clinging to the surface of the mountain of rock like a bug on the side of a cliff. On a nickel-iron asteroid, he could have walked around on the surface, using the magnetic soles of his vacuum suit. But silicate rock is notably lacking in response to that attractive force. No soul, maybe.

But directly and indirectly, that lack of response to magnetic forces was the reason for St. Simon's crawling around on the surface of that asteroid. Directly, because there was no other way he could move about on a nonmetallic asteroid. Indirectly, because there was no way the big space tugs could get a grip on such an asteroid, either.

The nickel-iron brutes were a dead cinch to haul off to the smelters. All a space tug had to do was latch on to one of them with a magnetic grapple and start hauling. There was no such simple answer for the silicate rocks.

The nickel-iron asteroids were necessary. They supplied the building material and the major export of the Belt cities. They averaged around eighty to ninety per cent iron, anywhere from five to twenty per cent nickel, and perhaps half a per cent cobalt, with smatterings of phosphorous, sulfur, carbon, copper, and chromium. Necessary—but not sufficient.

The silicate rocks ran only about twenty-five per cent iron—in the form of nonmagnetic compounds. They averaged eighteen per cent silicon, fourteen per cent magnesium, between one and one point five per cent each of aluminum, nickel, and calcium, and good-sized dollops of sodium, chromium, phosphorous, manganese, cobalt, potassium, and titanium.

But more important than these, as far as the immediate needs of the Belt cities were concerned, was a big, whopping thirty-six per cent oxygen. In the Belt cities, they had soon learned that, physically speaking, the stuff of life was *not* bread. And no matter how carefully oxygen is conserved, no process is one hundred per cent efficient. There will be leakage into space, and that which is lost must be replaced.

There is plenty of oxygen locked up in those silicates; the problem is towing them to the processing plants where the stuff can be extracted.

Captain St. Simon's job was simple. All he had to do was sink an anchor into the asteroid so that the space tugs could get a grip on it. Once he had done that, the rest of the job was up to the tug crew.

He crawled across the face of the floating mountain. At the spot where the North Pole was, he braced himself and then took a quick look around at the *Nancy Bell*. She wasn't moving very fast, he had plenty of time. He took a steel piton out of his tool pack, transferred it to his left hand, and took out a hammer. Then, working carefully, he hammered the piton into a narrow cleft in the rock. Three more of the steel spikes were hammered into the surface, forming a rough quadrilateral around the Pole.

"That looks good enough to me, Jules," he said when he had finished. "Now that we have our little anchors, we can put the monster in."

Then he grabbed his safety line, and pulled himself back to the *Nancy Bell*.

The small craft had floated away from the asteroid a little, but not much. He repositioned it after he got the rocket drill out of the storage compartment.

"Make way for the stovepipe!" he said as he pushed the drill ahead of him, out the door. This time, he pulled himself back to his drilling site by means of a cable which he had attached to one of the pitons.

The setting up of the drill didn't take much time, but it was done with a great deal of care. He set the four-foot tube in the center of the quadrilateral formed by the pitons and braced it in position by attaching lines to the eyes on a detachable collar that encircled the drill. Once the drill started working, it wouldn't need bracing, but until it did, it had to be held down.

All the time he worked, he kept his eyes on his lines and on his ship. The planetoid was turning under him, which made the ship appear to be circling slowly around his worksite. He had to make sure that his lines didn't get tangled or twisted while he was working.

As he set up the bracing on the six-inch diameter drill, he sang a song that Kipling might have been startled to recognize:

"To the tables down at Mory's, To the place where Louie dwells, Where it's always double drill and no canteen, Sit the Whiffenpoofs assembled, With their glasses raised on high, And they'll get a swig in Hell from Gunga Din."

When the drill was firmly based on the surface of the planetoid, St. Simon hauled his way back to his ship along his safety line. Inside, he sat down in the control chair and backed well away from the slowly spinning hunk of rock. Now there was only one thin pair of wires stretching between his ship and the drill on the asteroid.

When he was a good fifty meters away, he took one last look to make sure everything was as it should be.

"Stand by for a broadside!"

"Standing by, sir!"

"You may fire when ready, Gridley!"

"Aye, sir! Rockets away!" His forefinger descended on a button which sent a pulse of current through the pair of wires that trailed out the open door to the drill fifty meters away.

A flare of light appeared on the top of the drill. Almost immediately, it developed into a tongue of rocket flame. Then a glow appeared at the base of the drill and flame began to billow out from beneath the tube. The drill began to sink into the surface, and the planetoid began to move ever so slowly.

The drill was essentially a pair of opposed rockets. The upper one, which tried to push the drill into the surface of the planetoid, developed nearly forty per cent more thrust than the lower one. Thus, the lower one, which was trying to push the drill *off* the rock, was outmatched. It had to back up, if possible. And it was certainly possible; the exhaust flame of the lower rocket easily burrowed a hole that the rocket could back into, while the silicate rock boiled and vaporized in order to get out of the way.

Soon there was no sign of the drill body itself. There was only a small volcano, spewing up gas and liquid from a hole in the rock. On the surface of a good-sized planet, the drill would have built up a little volcanic cone around the lip of the hole, but building a cone like that requires enough gravity to pull the hot matter back to the edge of the hole.

The fireworks didn't last long. The drill wasn't built to go in too deep. A drill of that type could be built which would burrow its way right through a small planetoid, but that was hardly necessary for planting an anchor. Ten meters was quite enough.

Now came the hard work.

On the outside of the *Nancy Bell*, locked into place, was a specially-treated nickel-steel eye-bolt—thirty feet long and eight inches in diameter. There had been ten of them, just as there had been ten drills in the storage locker. Now the last drill had been used, and there was but one eye-bolt left. The *Nancy Bell* would have to go back for more supplies after this job.

The anchor bolts had a mass of four metric tons each. Maneuvering them around, even when they were practically weightless, was no easy job.

St. Simon again matched the velocity of the *Nancy Bell* with that of the planetoid, which had been accelerated by the drill's action. He positioned the ship above the hole which had been drilled into the huge rock. Not directly above it—rocket drills had been known to show spurts of life after they were supposed to be dead. St. Simon had timed the drill, and it had apparently behaved as it should, but there was no need to take chances.

"Fire brigade, stand by!"

"Fire brigade standing by, sir!"

A nozzle came out of the nose of the *Nancy Bell* and peeped over the rim of the freshly-drilled hole.

"Ready! Aim! Squirt!"

A jet of kerosene-like fluosilicone oil shot down the shaft. When it had finished its work, there was little possibility that anything could happen at the bottom. Any unburned rocket fuel would have a hard time catching fire with that stuff soaking into it.

"Ready to lower the boom, Mr. Christian!" bellowed St. Simon.

"Aye, sir! Ready, sir!"

"Lower away!"

His fingers played rapidly over the control board.

Outside the ship, the lower end of the great eye-bolt was released from its clamp, and a small piston gave it a little shove. In a long, slow, graceful arc, it swung away from the hull, swiveling around the pivot clamp that held the eye. The braking effect of the pivot clamp was precisely set to stop the eye-bolt when it was at right angles to the hull. Moving carefully, St. Simon maneuvered the ship until the far end of the bolt was directly over the shaft. Then he nudged the *Nancy Bell* sideways, pushing the bolt down into the planetoid. It grated a couple of times, but between the power of the ship and the mass of the planetoid, there was enough pressure to push it past the obstacles. The rocket drill and the eye-bolt had been designed to work together; the hole made by the first was only a trifle larger than the second. The anchor settled firmly into place.

St. Simon released the clamps that held the eye-bolt to the hull of the ship, and backed away again. As he did, a power cord unreeled, for the eye-bolt was still connected to the vessel electrically.

Several meters away, St. Simon pushed another button. There was no sound, but his practiced eye saw the eye of the anchor quiver. A small explosive charge, set in the buried end of the anchor, had detonated, expanding the far end of the bolt, wedging it firmly in the hole. At the same time, a piston had been forced up a small shaft in the center of the bolt, forcing a catalyst to mix with a fast-setting resin, and extruding the mixture out through half a dozen holes in the side of the bolt. When the stuff set, the anchor was locked securely to the sides of the shaft and thus to the planetoid itself.

St. Simon waited for a few minutes to make sure the resin had set completely. Then he clambered outside again and attached a heavy towing cable to the eye of the anchor, which projected above the surface of the asteroid. Back inside the ship again, he slowly applied power. The cable straightened and pulled at the anchor as the *Nancy Bell* tried to get away from the asteroid.

"Jules, old bunion," he said as he watched the needle of the tension gauge, "we have set her well."

"Yes, m'lud. So it would appear, m'lud."

St. Simon cut the power. "Very good, Jules. Now we shall see if the beeper is functioning as it should." He flipped a switch that turned on the finder pickup, then turned the selector to his own frequency band.

Beep! said the radio importantly. *Beep!*

The explosion had also triggered on a small but powerful transmitter built into the anchor. The tugs would be able to find the planetoid by following the beeps.

"Ah, Jules! Success!"

"Yes, m'lud. Success. For the tenth time in a row, this trip. And how many trips does this make?"

"Ah, but who's counting? Think of the money!"

"And the monotony, m'lud. To say nothing of molasses, muchness, and other things that begin with an M."

"Quite so, Jules; quite so. Well, let's detach the towing cable and be on our way."

"Whither, m'lud, Vesta?"

"I rather thought Pallas this time, old thimble."

"Still, m'lud, Vesta—"

"Pallas, Jules."

"Vesta?"

"Hum, hi, ho," said Captain St. Simon thoughtfully. "Pallas?"

The argument continued while the tow cable was detached from the freshly-placed anchor, and while the air was being let back into the control chamber, and while St. Simon divested himself of his suit. Actually, although he would like to go to Vesta, it was out of the question. Energywise and timewise, Pallas was much closer.

He settled back in the bucket seat and shot toward Pallas.

Mr. Edway Tarnhorst was from San Pedro, Greater Los Angeles, California, Earth. He was a businessman of executive rank, and was fairly rich. In his left lapel was the Magistral Knight's Cross of the Sovereign Hierosolymitan Order of Malta, reproduced in miniature. In his wallet was a card identifying him as a Representative of the Constituency of Southern California to the Supreme Congress of the People of the United Nations of Earth. He was just past his fifty-third birthday, and his lean, ascetic face and graying hair gave him a look of saintly wisdom. Aside from the eight-pointed cross in his lapel, the only ornamentation or jewelry he wore consisted of a small, exquisitely thin gold watch on his left wrist, and, on the ring finger of his left hand, a gold signet ring set with a single, flat, unfaceted diamond which was delicately engraved with the Tarnhorst coat of arms. His clothing was quietly but impressively expensive, and under Earth gravity would probably have draped impeccably, but it tended to fluff oddly away from his body under a gee-pull only a twentieth of Earth's.

He sat in his chair with both feet planted firmly on the metal floor, and his hands gripping the armrests as though he were afraid he might float off toward the ceiling if he let go. But only his body betrayed his unease; his face was impassive and calm.

The man sitting next to him looked a great deal more comfortable. This was Mr. Peter Danley, who was twenty years younger than Mr. Tarnhorst and looked it. Instead of the Earth-cut clothing that the older man was wearing, he was wearing the close-fitting tights that were the common dress of the Belt cities. His hair was cropped close, and the fine blond strands made a sort of golden halo about his head when the light from the panels overhead shone on them. His eyes were pale blue, and the lashes and eyebrows were so light as to be almost invisible. That effect, combined with his thin-lined, almost lipless mouth, gave his face a rather expressionless expression. He carried himself like a man who was used to low-gravity or null-gravity conditions, but he talked like an Earthman, not a Belt man. The identification card in his belt explained that; he was a pilot on the Earth-Moon shuttle service. In the eyes of anyone from the Belt cities, he was still an Earthman, not a true spaceman. He was looked upon in the same way that the captain of a transatlantic liner might have looked upon the skipper of the Staten Island ferry two centuries before. The very fact that he was seated in a chair gave away his Earth habits.

The third man was standing, leaning at a slight angle, so that his back touched the wall behind him. He was not tall—five nine—and his face and body were thin. His tanned skin seemed to be stretched tightly over this scanty padding, and in places the bones appeared to be trying to poke their way through to the surface. His ears were small and lay nearly flat against his head, and the hair on his skull was so sparse that the tanned scalp could be easily seen beneath it, although there was no actual bald spot anywhere. Only his large, luminous brown eyes showed that Nature had not skimped on everything when he was formed. His name was lettered neatly on the outside of the door to the office: Georges Alhamid. In spite of the French spelling, he pronounced the name "George," in the English manner.

He had welcomed the two Earthmen into his office, smiling the automatic smile of the diplomat as he welcomed them to Pallas. As soon as they were comfortably seated—though perhaps that word did not exactly apply to Edway Tarnhorst—Georges Alhamid said:

"Now, gentlemen, what can I do for you?"

He asked it as though he were completely unaware of what had brought the two men to Pallas.

Tarnhorst looked as though he were privately astonished that his host could speak grammatically. "Mr. Alhamid," he began, "I don't know whether you're aware that the industrial death rate here in the Belt has been the subject of a great deal of discussion in both industrial and governmental circles on Earth." It was a half question, and he let it hang in the air, waiting to see whether he got an answer.

"Certainly my office has received a great deal of correspondence on the subject," Alhamid said. His voice sounded as though Tarnhorst had mentioned nothing more serious than a commercial deal. Important, but nothing to get into a heavy sweat over.

Tarnhorst nodded and then held his head very still. His actions betrayed the fact that he was not used to the messages his semicircular canals were sending his brain when he moved his head under low gee.

"Exactly," he said after a moment's pause. "I have 'stat copies of a part of that correspondence. To be specific, the correspondence between your office and the Workers' Union Safety Control Board, and between your office and the Workingman's Compensation Insurance Corporation."

"I see. Well, then, you're fully aware of what our trouble is, Mr. Tarnhorst. I'm glad to see that an official of the insurance company is taking an interest in our troubles."

Tarnhorst's head twitched, as though he were going to shake his head and had thought better of it a fraction of a second too late. It didn't matter. The fluid in his inner ears sloshed anyway.

"I am not here in my capacity as an officer of the Workingman's Compensation Insurance Corporation," he said carefully. "I am here as a representative of the People's Congress."

Alhamid's face showed a mild surprise which he did not feel. "I'm honored, of course, Mr. Tarnhorst," he said, "but you must understand that I am not an official of the government of Pallas."

Tarnhorst's ascetic face betrayed nothing. "Since you have no unified government out here," he said, "I cannot, of course, presume to deal with you in a governmental capacity. I have spoken to the Governor of Pallas, however, and he assures me that you are the man to speak to."

"If it's about the industrial death rate," Alhamid agreed, "then he's perfectly correct. But if you're here as a governmental representative of Earth, I don't understand—"

"Please, Mr. Alhamid," Tarnhorst interrupted with a touch of irritation in his voice. "This is not my first trip to the Belt, nor my first attempt to deal with the official workings of the Confederated Cities."

Alhamid nodded gently. It was, as a matter of fact, Mr. Tarnhorst's second trip beyond the Martian orbit, the first having taken place some three years before. But the complaint was common enough; Earth, with its strong centralized government, simply could not understand the functioning of the Belt Confederacy. A man like Tarnhorst apparently couldn't distinguish between *government* and *business*. Knowing that, Alhamid could confidently predict what the general sense of Tarnhorst's next sentence would be.

"I am well aware," said Tarnhorst, "that the Belt Companies not only have the various governors under their collective thumb, but have thus far prevented the formation of any kind of centralized government. Let us not quibble, Mr. Alhamid; the Belt Companies run the Belt, and that means that I must deal with officials of those companies—such as yourself."

Alhamid felt it necessary to make a mild speech in rebuttal. "I cannot agree with you, Mr. Tarnhorst. I have nothing to do with the government of Pallas or any of the other asteroids. I am neither an elected nor an appointed official of any government. Nor, for that matter, am I an advisor in either an official or unofficial capacity to any government. I do not make the laws designed to keep the peace, nor do I enforce them, except in so far as I am a registered voter and therefore have some voice in those laws in that respect. Nor, again, do I serve any judiciary function in any Belt government, except inasmuch as I may be called upon for jury duty.

"I am a business executive, Mr. Tarnhorst. Nothing more. If you have governmental problems to discuss, then I can't help you, since I'm not authorized to make any decisions for any government."

Edway Tarnhorst closed his eyes and massaged the bridge of his thin nose between thumb and forefinger. "I understand that. I understand that perfectly. But out here, the Companies have taken over certain functions of government, shall we say?"

"Shall we say, rather, that on Earth the government has usurped certain functions which rightfully belong to private enterprise?" Alhamid said gently. "Historically, I think, that is the correct view."

Tarnhorst opened his eyes and smiled. "You may be quite correct. Historically speaking, perhaps, the Earth government has usurped the functions that rightfully belong to kings, dictators, and warlords. To say nothing of local satraps and petty chieftains. Hm-m-m. Perhaps we should return to that? Perhaps we should return to the human suffering that was endemic in those times?"

"You might try it," said Alhamid with a straight face. "Say, one year out of every ten. It would give the people something to look forward to with anticipation and to look back upon with nostalgia." Then he changed his tone. "If you wish to debate theories of government, Mr. Tarnhorst, possibly we could get up a couple of teams. Make a public affair of it. It could be taped and televised here and on Earth, and we could charge royalties on each—"

Peter Danley's blond, blank face became suddenly animated. He looked as though he were trying to suppress a laugh. He almost succeeded. It came out as a cough.

At the same time, Tarnhorst interrupted Alhamid. "You have made your point, Mr. Alhamid," he said in a brittle voice. "Permit me to make mine. I have come to discuss business with you. But, as a member of the Congressional Committee for Industrial Welfare, I am also in search of facts. Proper legislation requires facts, and legislation passed by the Congress will depend to a great extent upon the report on my findings here."

"I understand," said Alhamid. "I'll certainly be happy to provide you with whatever data you want—with the exception of data on industrial processes, of course. That's not mine to give. But anything else—" He gestured with one hand, opening it palm upwards, as though dispensing a gift.

"I'm not interested in industrial secrets," said Tarnhorst, somewhat mollified. "It's a matter of the welfare of your workers. We feel that we should do something to help. As you know, there have been protests from the Worker's Union Safety Control Board and from the Workingman's Compensation Insurance Corporation."

Alhamid nodded. "I know. The insurance company is complaining about the high rate of claims for deaths. They've threatened to raise our premium rates."

"Considering the expense, don't you, as a businessman, think that a fair thing to do?"

"No," Alhamid said. "I have pointed out to them that the total amount of the claims is far less per capita than, for instance, the Steel Construction Workers' Union of Earth. Granted, there are more death claims, but these are more than compensated for by the fact that the claims for disability and hospitalization are almost negligible."

"That's another thing we don't understand," Tarnhorst said carefully. "It appears that not only are the safety precautions insufficient, but the post-accident care is ... er ... inefficient."

"I assure you that what post-accident care there is," Alhamid said, "is quite efficient. But there is a high mortality rate because of the very nature of the job. Do you know anything about anchor-placing, Mr. Tarnhorst?"

"Very little," Tarnhorst admitted. "That is one of the things I am here to get information on. You used the phrase 'what post-accident care there is'—just how do you mean that?"

"Mr. Tarnhorst, when a man is out in space, completely surrounded by a hard vacuum, *any* accident is very likely to be fatal. On Earth, if a man sticks his thumb in a punch press, he loses his thumb. Out here, if a man's thumb is crushed off while he's in space, he loses his air and his life long before he can bleed to death. Anything that disables a man in space is deadly ninety-nine times out of a hundred.

"I can give you a parallel case. In the early days of oil drilling, wells occasionally caught fire. One of the ways to put them out was to literally blow them out with a charge of nitroglycerine. Naturally, the nitroglycerine had to be transported from where it was made to where it was to be used. Sensibly enough, it was not transported in tank-car lots; it was carried in small special containers by a single man in an automobile, who used the back roads and avoided traffic and stayed away from thickly populated areas—which was possible in those days. In many places these carriers were required to paint their cars red, and have the words *Danger Nitroglycerine* painted on the vehicle in yellow.

"Now, the interesting thing about that situation is that, whereas insurance companies in those days were reluctant to give policies to those men, even at astronomical premium rates, disability insurance cost practically nothing—provided the insured would allow the insertion of a clause that restricted the covered period to those times when he was actually engaged in transporting nitroglycerine. You can see why."

"I am not familiar with explosives," Tarnhorst said. "I take it that the substance is ... er ... easily detonated?"

"That's right," said Alhamid. "It's not only sensitive, but it's unreliable. You might actually drop a jar of the stuff and do nothing but shatter the jar. Another jar, apparently exactly similar, might go off because it got jiggled by a seismic wave from a passing truck half a mile away. But the latter was a great deal more likely than the former."

"Very well," said Tarnhorst after a moment, "I accept that analogy. I'd like to know more about the work itself. What does the job entail, exactly? What safety precautions are taken?"

It required the better part of three hours to explain exactly what an anchor setter did and how he did it—and what safety precautions were being taken. Through it all, Peter Danley just sat there, listening, saying nothing.

Finally, Edway Tarnhorst said: "Well, thank you very much for your information, Mr. Alhamid. I'd like to think this over. May I see you in the morning?"

"Certainly, sir. You're welcome at any time."

"Thank you." The two Earthmen rose from their seats—Tarnhorst carefully, Danley with the ease of long practice. "Would nine in the morning be convenient?"

"Quite convenient. I'll expect you."

Danley glided over to the door and held it open for Tarnhorst. He was wearing magnetic glide-shoes, the standard footwear of the Belt, which had three ball-bearings in the forward part of the sole, allowing the foot to move smoothly in any direction, while the rubber heel could be brought down to act as a brake when necessary. He didn't handle them with the adeptness of a Belt man, but he wasn't too awkward. Tarnhorst was wearing plain magnetic-soled boots—the lift-'em-up-and-lay-'em-down type. He had no intention of having his dignity compromised by shoes that might treacherously scoot out from under him.

As soon as the door had closed behind them, Georges Alhamid picked up the telephone on his desk and punched a number.

When a woman's voice answered at the other end, he said: "Miss Lehman, this is Mr. Alhamid. I'd like to speak to the governor." There was a pause. Then:

"George? Larry here."

Alhamid leaned back comfortably against the wall. "I just saw your guests, Larry. I spent damn near three hours explaining why it was necessary to put anchors in rocks, how it was done, and why it was dangerous."

"Did you convince him? Tarnhorst, I mean."

"I doubt it. Oh, I don't mean he thinks I'm lying or anything like that. He's too sharp for that. But he *is* convinced that we're negligent, that we're a bunch of barbarians who care nothing about human life."

"You've got to unconvince him, George," the governor said worriedly. "The Belt still isn't self-sufficient enough to be able to afford an Earth embargo. They can hold out longer than we can."

"I know," Alhamid said. "Give us another generation, and we can tell the World Welfare State where to head in—but right now, things are touchy, and you and I are in the big fat middle of it." He paused, rubbing thoughtfully at his lean blade of a nose with a bony forefinger. "Larry, what did you think of that blond nonentity Tarnhorst brought with him?"

"He's not a nonentity," the governor objected gently. "He just looks it. He's Tarnhorst's 'expert' on space industry, if you want my opinion. Did he say much of anything while he was with you?"

"Hardly anything."

"Same here. I have a feeling that his job is to evaluate every word you say and report his evaluation to Tarnhorst. You'll have to be careful."

"I agree," Alhamid said. "But he complicates things. I have a feeling that if I tell Tarnhorst a straight story he'll believe it. He seems to be a pretty shrewd judge. But Danley just might be the case of the man who is dangerous because of his little learning. He obviously knows a devil of a lot more about operations in space than Tarnhorst does, and he's evidently a hand-picked man, so that Tarnhorst will value his opinion. But it's evident that Danley doesn't know anything about space by our standards. Put him out on a boat as an anchor man, and he'd be lucky if he set a single anchor."

"Well, there's not much chance of that. How do you mean, he's dangerous?"

"I'll give you a f'rinstance. Suppose you've got a complex circuit using alternatic current, and you're trying to explain to a reasonably intelligent man how it works and what it does. If he doesn't know anything about electricity, he mightn't understand the explanation, but he'll believe that you're telling him the truth even if he doesn't understand it. But if he knows the basic theory of direct currents, you're likely to find yourself in trouble because he'll know just enough to see that what you're telling him doesn't jibe with what he already knows. Volts times amperes equal watts, as far as he's concerned, and the term 'power factor' does nothing but confuse him. He knows that copper is a conductor, so he can't see how a current could be cut off by a choke coil. He knows that a current can't pass through an insulator, so a condenser obviously can't be what you say it is. Mentally, he tags you as a liar, and he begins to try to dig in to see how your gadget *really* works."

"Hm-m-m. I see what you mean. Bad." He snorted. "Blast Earthmen, anyway! Have you ever been there?"

"Earth? Nope. By careful self-restraint, I've managed to forego that pleasure so far, Larry. Why?"

"Brrr! It's the feel of the place that I can't stand. I don't mean the constant high-gee; I take my daily exercise spin in the centrifuge just like anyone else, and you soon get used to the steady pull on Earth. I mean the constant, oppressive *psychic* tension, if you see what I mean. The feeling that everyone hates and distrusts everyone else. The curious impression of fear underneath every word and action.

"I'm older than you are, George, and I've lived with a kind of fear all my life—just as you and everyone else in the Belt has. A single mistake can kill out here, and the fear that it will be some fool who makes a mistake that will kill hundreds is always with us. We've learned to live with that kind of fear; we've learned to take steps to prevent any idiot from throwing the wrong switch that would shut down a power plant or open an air lock at the wrong time.

"But the fear on Earth is different. It's the fear that everyone else is out to get you, the fear that someone will stick a figurative knife in your back and reduce you to the basic subsistence level. And that fear is solidly based, believe me. The only way to climb up from basic subsistence is to climb over everyone else, to knock aside those in your way, to get rid of whoever is occupying the position you want. And once you get there, the only way you can hold your position is to make sure that nobody below you gets too big for his britches. The rule is: Pull down those above you, hold down those below you.

"I've seen it, George. The big cities are packed with people whose sole ambition in life is to badger their local welfare worker out of another check—they need new clothes, they need a new bed, they need a new table, they need more food for the new baby, they need this, they need that. All they ever do is *need*! But, of course, they're far to aristocratic to *work*.

"Those who do have ambition have to become politicians—in the worst sense of the word. They have to gain some measure of control over the dispersal of largesse to the mob; they have to get themselves into a position where they can give away other people's money, so that they can get their cut, too.

"And even then, the man who gets to be a big shot doesn't dare show it. Take a look at Tarnhorst. He's probably one of the best of a bad lot. He has his fingers in a lot of business pies which make him money, and he's in a high enough position in the government to enable him to keep some of his money. But his clothing is only a little bit better than the average, just as the man who is on basic subsistence wears clothes that are only a little bit worse than the average. That diamond ring of his is a real diamond, but you can buy imitations that can't be told from the real thing except by an expert, so his diamond doesn't offend anyone by being ostentatious. And it's unfaceted, to eliminate offensive flash.

"All the color has gone out of life on Earth, George. Women held out longer than men did, but now no man or woman would be caught wearing a bright-colored suit. You don't see any reds or yellows or blues or greens or oranges—only grays and browns and black.

"It's not for me, George. I'd much rather live in fear of the few fools who might pull a stupid trick that would kill me than live in the constant fear of everyone around me, who all want to destroy me deliberately."

"I know what you mean," said Alhamid, "but I think you've put the wrong label on what you're calling 'fear'; there's a difference between fear and having a healthy respect for something that is dangerous but not malignant. That vacuum out there isn't out to 'get' anybody. The only people it kills are the fools who have no respect for it and the neurotics who think that it wants to murder them. You're neither, and I know it."

The governor laughed. "That's the advantage we have over Earthmen, George. We went through the same school of hard knocks together—all of us. And we know how we stack up against each other."

"True," Alhamid said darkly, "but how long will that hold if Tarnhorst closes the school down?"

"That's what you've got to prevent," said the governor flatly. "If you need help, yell."

"I will," Alhamid said. "Very loudly." He hung up, wishing he knew what Tarnhorst—and Danley—had in mind.

"The trouble with these people, Danley," said Edway Tarnhorst, "is that they have no respect whatever for human dignity. They have a tendency to overlook the basic rights of the individual."

"They're certainly—different," Peter Danley said.

Tarnhorst juggled himself up and down on the easy-chair in which he was seated, as though he could hardly believe that he had weight again. He hated low gee. It made him feel awkward and undignified. The only thing that reminded him that this was not "real" gravity was the faint, but all-pervasive hum of the huge engines that drove the big centrifuge. The rooms had cost more, but they were well worth it, as far as Tarnhorst was concerned.

"How do you mean, 'different'?" he asked almost absently, settling himself comfortably into the cushions.

"I don't know exactly. There's a hardness, a toughness—I can't quite put my finger on it, but it's in the way they act, the way they talk."

"Surely you'd noticed that before?" Tarnhorst asked in mild surprise. "You've met these Belt men on Luna."

"And their women," Danley said with a nod. "But the impact is somewhat more pronounced on their own home ground—seeing them *en masse*."

"Their women!" Tarnhorst said, caught by the phrase. "*Fah!* Bright-colored birds! Giggling children! And no more morals than a common house-cat!"

"Oh, they're not as bad as all that," Danley objected. "Their clothing is a little bright, I'll admit, and they laugh and kid around a lot, but I wouldn't say that their morals were any worse than those of a girl from New York or London."

"Arrogance is the word," said Tarnhorst. "Arrogance. Like the way that Alhamid kept standing all the time we were talking, towering over us that way."

"Just habit," Danley said. "When you don't weigh more than six or seven pounds, there's not much point in sitting down. Besides, it leaves them on their feet in case of emergency."

"He could have sat down out of politeness," Tarnhorst said. "But no. They try to put on an air of superiority that is offensive to human dignity." He leaned back in his chair, stretched out his legs, and crossed his ankles. "However, attitude itself needn't concern us until it translates itself into anti-social behavior. What cannot be tolerated is this callous attitude toward the dignity and well-being of the workers out here. What did you think of Alhamid's explanation of this anchor-setting business?"

Danley hesitated. "It sounded straightforward enough, as far as it went."

"You think he's concealing something, then?"

"I don't know. I don't have all the information." He frowned, putting furrows between his almost invisible blond brows. "I know that neither government business nor insurance business are my specialty, but I would like to know a little more about the background before I render any decision."

"Hm-m-m. Well." Tarnhorst frowned in thought for a moment, then came to a decision. "I can't give you the detailed data, of course; that would be a violation of the People's Mutual Welfare Code. But I can give you the general story."

"I just want to know what sort of thing to look for," Danley said.

"Certainly. Certainly. Well." Tarnhorst paused to collect his thoughts, then launched into his speech. "It has now been over eighty years since the first colonists came out here to the Belt. At first, the ties with Earth were quite strong, naturally. Only a few actually intended to stay out there the rest of their lives; most of them intended to make themselves a nice little nest egg, come back home, and retire. At the same time, the World State was slowly evolving from its original loosely tied group of independent nations toward what it is today.

"The people who came out here were mostly misfits, sociologically speaking." He smiled sardonically. "They haven't changed much.

"At any rate, as I said, they were strongly tied to Earth. There was the matter of food, air, and equipment, all of which had to be shipped out from Earth to begin with. Only the tremendous supply of metal—almost free for the taking—made such a venture commercially possible. Within twenty-five years, however, the various industrial concerns that managed the Belt mining had become self-supporting. The robot scoopers which are used to mine methane and ammonia from Jupiter's atmosphere gave them plenty of organic raw material. Now they grow plants of all kinds and even raise food animals.

"They began, as every misfit does, to complain about the taxes the government put on their incomes. The government, in my opinion, made an error back then. They wanted to keep people out in the Belt, since the mines on Earth were not only rapidly being depleted, but the mining sites were needed for living space. Besides, asteroid metals were cheaper than metals mined on Earth. To induce the colonists to remain in the Belt, no income tax was levied; the income tax was replaced by an eighty per cent tax on the savings accumulated when the colonist returned to Earth to retire.

"They resented even that. It was explained to them that the asteroids were, after all, natural resources, and that they had no moral right to make a large profit and deprive others of their fair share of the income from a natural resource, but they insisted that they had earned it and had a right to keep it.

"In other words, the then government bribed them to stay out here, and the bribe was more effective than they had intended."

"So they stayed out here and kept their money," Danley said.

"Exactly. At that time, if you will recall, there was a great deal of agitation against colonialism—there had been for a long time, as a matter of fact. That agitation was directed against certain industrialist robber-baron nations who had enslaved the populace of parts of Asia and Africa solely to produce wealth, and not for the benefit of the people themselves. But the Belt operators took advantage of the anticolonialism of the times and declared that the Belt cities were, and by right ought to be, free and independent political entities. It was a ridiculous assumption, of course, but since the various Belt cities were, at that time, under the nominal control of three or four of the larger nations, the political picture required that they be allowed to declare themselves independent. It was not anticipated at the time that they would be so resistant toward the World Government."

He smiled slightly. "Of course, by refusing to send representatives to the People's Congress, they have, in effect, cut themselves off from any voice in human government."

Then he shrugged. "At the moment, that is neither here nor there. What interests us at the moment is the death rate curve of the anchor-sinkers or whatever they are. Did you know that it is practically impossible for anyone to get a job out there in the Belt unless he has had experience in the anchor-setting field?"

"No," Danley admitted.

"It's true. For every other job, they want only men with space experience. And by 'space experience' they mean anchor-setting, because that's the only job a man can get without previous space experience. They spend six months in a special school, learning to do the work, according to our friend, Mr. Georges Alhamid. Then they are sent out to set anchors. Small ones, at first, in rocks only a few meters in diameter—then larger ones. After a year or so at that kind of work, they can apply for more lucrative positions.

"I see nothing intrinsically wrong in that, I will admit, but the indications are that the schooling, which should have been getting more efficient over the years, has evidently been getting more lax. The death rate has gone up."

"Just a minute," Danley interrupted. "Do you mean that a man has to have what they call 'space experience' before he can get *any* kind of job?"

Tarnhorst shook his head and was pleased to find that no nausea resulted. "No, of course not. Clerical jobs, teaching jobs, and the like don't require that sort of training. But there's very little chance for advancement unless you're one of the elite. A physician, for example, wouldn't have many patients unless he had had 'space experience'; he wouldn't be allowed to own or drive a space boat, and he wouldn't be allowed to go anywhere near what are called 'critical areas'—such as air locks, power plants, or heavy industry installations."

"It sounds to me as though they have a very strong union," said Danley.

"If you want to call it that, yes," Tarnhorst said. "Anything that has anything to do with operations in space requires that sort of experience—and there are very few jobs out here that can avoid having anything to do with space. Space is only a few kilometers away." The expression on his face showed that he didn't much care for the thought.

"I don't see that that's so bad," Danley said. "Going out there isn't something for the unexperienced. A man who doesn't know what he's doing can get himself killed easily, and, what's worse, he's likely to take others with him."

"You speak, of course, from experience," Tarnhorst said with no trace of sarcasm. "I accept that. By not allowing inexperienced persons in critical areas, the Belt Companies are, at least indirectly, looking out for the welfare of the people. But we mustn't delude ourselves into thinking that that is their prime objective. These Belt Companies are no better than the so-called 'industrial giants' of the nineteenth and twentieth centuries. The government here is farcical. The sole job is to prevent crime and to adjudicate small civil cases. Every other function of proper government—the organization of industry, the regulation of standards the subsidizing of research, the control of prices, and so on—are left to the Belt Companies or to the people. The Belt Cities are no more than what used to be called 'company towns'."

"I understand that," Danley said. "But they seem to function fairly smoothly."

Tarnhorst eyed him. "If, by, 'smoothly functioning', you mean the denial of the common rights of human freedom and dignity yes. Oh, they give their sop to such basic human needs as the right of every individual to be respected—but only because Earth has put pressure on them. Otherwise, people who, through no fault of their own, were unable to work or get 'space experience' would be unable to get jobs and would be looked down upon as pariahs."

"You mean there are people here who have no jobs? I wouldn't think that unemployment would be a problem out here."

"It isn't," said Tarnhorst, "yet. But there are always those unfortunates who are psychologically incapable of work, and society must provide for them. The Belt Cities provide for a basic education, of course. As long as a person is going to school, he is given a stipend. But a person who has neither the ability to work nor the ability to study is an outcast, even though he is provided for by the companies. He is forced to do something to earn what should be his by right; he is given menial and degrading tasks to do. We would like to put a stop to that sort of thing, but we ... ah ... have no ... ah ... means of doing so." He paused, as though considering whether he had said too much.

"The problem at hand," he went on hurriedly, "is the death curve. When this technique for taking the rocks to the smelters was being worked out, the death rate was—as you might imagine—quite high. The Belt Companies had already been operating out here for a long time before the stony meteorites were mined commercially. At first, the big thing was nickel-iron. That's what they came here to get in the beginning. That's where most of the money still is. But the stony asteroids provide them with their oxygen.

"This anchor-setting technique was worked out at a time when the Belt Companies were trying to find ways to make the Belt self-sufficient. After they got the technique worked out so that it operated smoothly, the death rate dropped 'way down. It stayed down for a little while, and then began to rise again. It has nearly reached an all-time high. Obviously, something is wrong, and we have to find out what it is."

Danley scratched ruminatively behind his right ear and wished he'd had the opportunity to study history. He had been vaguely aware, of the broad outlines, but the details had never been brought to his attention before. "Suppose Alhamid *is* trying to hide something," he said after a moment. "What would it be, do you think?"

Tarnhorst shrugged and spread his hands. "What could it be but some sort of money-saving scheme? Inferior materials being used at a critical spot, perhaps. Skimping on quality or quantity. Somewhere, somehow, they are shaving costs at the risk of the workers' lives. We have to find out what it is."

Peter Danley nodded. *You don't mean "we,"* Danley thought to himself. *I am the one who's going to have to go out there and find it, while you sit here safe*. He felt that there was a pretty good chance that these Belt operators might kill him to keep him from finding out what it was they were saving money on.

Aloud, he said: "I'll do what I can, Mr. Tarnhorst."

Tarnhorst smiled. "I'm certain you will. That's why I needed someone who knows more about this business than I."

"And when we do find it—what then?"

"Then? Why, then we will force them to make the proper changes or there will be trouble."

Georges Alhamid heard the whole conversation early the next morning. The governor himself brought the recording over to his office.

"Do you think he knew he was being overheard?"

The governor shrugged. "Who knows. He waltzed all around what he was trying to say, but that may have been just native caution. Or he may not want Danley to know what's on his mind."

"How could he bring Danley out here without telling him anything beforehand?" Alhamid asked thoughtfully. "Is Danley really that ignorant, or was the whole conversation for our ears?"

"I'm inclined to think that Danley really didn't know. Remember, George, the best way to hold down the ones below you is to keep them from gaining any knowledge, to keep data out of their hands—except for the carefully doctored data you want them to have."

"I know," Alhamid said. "History isn't exactly a popular subject on Earth." He tapped his fingers gently on the case of the playback and looked at it as if he were trying to read the minds of the persons who had spoken the words he had just heard.

"I really think he believed that his nullifying equipment was doing its job," the governor continued. "He wouldn't have any way of knowing we could counteract it."

Alhamid shrugged. "It doesn't matter much. We still have to assume that he's primarily out to bring the Belt Cities under Earth control. To do that, all he'd have to do is find something that could be built up into a scandal on Earth."

"Not, *all*, George," the governor said. "It would take a lot more than that alone. But it would certainly be a start in the right direction."

"One thing we do know," Alhamid said, "is that nobody on Earth will allow any action against the Belt unless popular sentiment is definitely against us. As long as we are apparently right-thinking people, we're all right. I wonder why Tarnhorst is so anxious to get us under the thumb of the People's Congress? Is it purely that half-baked idealism of his?"

"Mostly. He has the notion that everybody has a right to be accorded the respect of his fellow man, and that that right is something that every person is automatically given at birth, not something he has to earn. What gave him his particular gripe against us, I don't know, but he's been out to get us ever since his trip here three years ago."

"You know, Larry," Alhamid said slowly, "I'm not quite sure which is harder to understand: How a whole civilization could believe that sort of thing, or how a single intelligent man could."

"It's a positive feedback," the governor said. "That sort of thing has wrecked civilizations before and will do it again. Let's not let it wreck ours. Are you ready for the conference with our friend now?"

Georges Alhamid looked at the clock on the wall. "Ready as I'll ever be. You'd better scram, Larry. We mustn't give Mr. Tarnhorst the impression that there's some sort of collusion between business and government out there in the Belt."

"Heaven forfend! I'll get."

When he left, the governor took the playback with him. The recording would have to be filed in the special secret files.

Captain St. Simon eased his spaceboat down to the surface of Pallas and threw on the magnetic anchor which held the little craft solidly to the metal surface of the landing field. The traffic around Pallas was fairly heavy this time of year, since the planetoid was on the same side of the sun as Earth, and the big cargo haulers were moving in and out, loading refined metals and raw materials, unloading manufactured goods from Earth. He'd had to wait several minutes in the traffic pattern before being given clearance for anchoring.

He was already dressed in his vacuum suit, and the cabin of the boat was exhausted of its air. He checked his control board, making sure every switch and dial was in the proper position. Only then did he open the door and step out to the gray surface of the landing field. His suitcase—a spherical, sealed container that the Belt men jokingly referred to as a "bomb"—went with him. He locked the door of his boat and walked down the yellow-painted safety lane toward the nearest air lock leading into the interior of the planetoid.

He lifted his feet and set them down with precision—nobody but a fool wears glide boots on the outside. He kept his eyes moving—up and around, on both sides, above, and behind. The yellow path was supposed to be a safety lane, but there was no need of taking the chance of having an out-of-control ship come sliding in on him. Of course, if it was coming in really fast, he'd have no chance to move; he might not even see it at all. But why get slugged by a slow one?

He waited outside the air-lock door for the green light to come on. There were several other space-suited figures around him, but he didn't recognize any of them. He hummed softly to himself.

The green light came on, and the door of the air lock slid open. The small crowd trooped inside, and, after a minute, the door slid shut again. As the elevator dropped, St. Simon heard the familiar *whoosh* as the air came rushing in. By the time it had reached the lower level, the elevator was up to pressure.

On Earth, there might have been a sign in such an elevator, reading: *DO NOT REMOVE VACUUM SUITS IN ELEVATOR*. There was no need for it here; every man there knew how to handle himself in an air lock. If he hadn't, he wouldn't have been there.

After he had stepped out of the elevator, along with the others, and the door had closed behind him, St. Simon carefully opened the cracking valve on his helmet. There was a faint hiss of incoming air, adjusting the slight pressure differential. He took off his helmet, tucked it under his arm, and headed for the check-in station.

He was walking down the corridor toward the checker's office when a hand clapped him on the shoulder. "Bless me if it isn't St. Simon the Silent! Long time no, if you'll pardon the cliché, see!"

St. Simon turned, grinning. He had recognized the voice. "Hi, Kerry. Good to see you."

"Good to see me? Forsooth! Od's bodkins! Hast turned liar on top of everything else, Good Saint? Good to see me, indeed! 'From such a face and form as mine, the noblest sentiments sound like the black utterances of a depraved imagination.' No, dear old holy pillar-sitter, no indeed! It may be a pleasure to hear my mellifluous voice—a pleasure I often indulge in, myself—but it couldn't possibly be a pleasure to *see* me!" And all the while, St. Simon was being pummeled heartily on the shoulder, while his hand was pumped as though the other man was expecting to strike oil at any moment.

His assailant was not a handsome man. Years before, a rare, fast-moving meteor had punched its way through his helmet and taken part of his face with it. He had managed to get back to his ship and pump air in before he lost consciousness. He had had to stay conscious, because the only thing that held the air in his helmet had been his hand pressed over the quarter-inch hole. Even so, the drop in pressure had done its damage. The surgeons had done their best to repair the smashed face, but Kerry Brand's face hadn't been much to look at to begin with. And the mottled purple of the distended veins and capillaries did little to improve his looks.

But his ruined face was a badge of honor, and Kerry Brand knew the fact as well as anyone.

Like St. Simon, Captain Brand was a professional anchor-setter. Most of the men who put in the necessary two years went on to better jobs after they had the required space experience. But there were some who liked the job and stuck with it. It was only these men—the real experts among the anchor-setting fraternity—who rated the title of "Captain". They were free-lancers who ran things pretty much their own way.

"Just going to the checker?" St. Simon asked.

Kerry Brand shook his head. "I've already checked in, old sanctus. And I'll give you three and one-seventh guesses who got a blue ticket."

St. Simon said nothing, but he pointed a finger at Brand's chest.

"A mild surmise, but a true one," said Brand. "You are, indeed, gazing upon Professor Kerry Brand, B.A., M.A., Ph.D.—that is to say, Borer of Asteroids, Master of Anchors, and Planetoid-hauler De-luxe. No, no; don't look sorry for me. *Some*body has to teach the tadpoles How To Survive In Space If You're Not Too Stupid To Live—a subject upon which I am an expert."

"On Being Too Stupid To Live?" St. Simon asked gently.

"A touch! A distinct touch! You are developing a certain unexpected vein of pawky humor, Watson, against which I must learn to guard myself." He looked at the watch on his wrist. "Why don't you go ahead and check in, and then we'll go pub-crawling. I have it on good authority that a few thousand gallons of Danish ale were piped aboard Pallas yesterday, and you and I should do our best to reduce the surplus."

"Sounds good to me," said St. Simon agreeably. They started on toward the checker's office.

"Consider, my dear St. Simon," said Brand, "how fortunate we are to be living in an age and a society where the dictum, 'Those who can, do; those who can't, teach,' no longer holds true. It means that we weary, work-hardened experts are called in every so often, handed our little blue ticket, and given six months off—*with* pay—if we will only do the younger generation the favor of pounding a modicum of knowledge into their heads. During that time, if we are very careful, we can try to prevent our muscles from going to flab and our brains from corroding with ennui, so that when we again debark into the infinite sea of emptiness which surrounds us to pursue our chosen profession, we don't get killed on the first try. Isn't it wonderful?"

"Cheer up," said St. Simon. "Teaching isn't such a bad lot. And, after all, you do get paid for it."

"And at a salary! A Pooh-Bah paid for his services! I a salaried minion! But I do it! It revolts me, but I do it!"

The short, balding man behind the checker's desk looked up as the two men approached. "Hello, captain," he said as St. Simon stepped up to the desk.

"How are you, Mr. Murtaugh?" St. Simon said politely. He handed over his log book. "There's the data on my last ten. I'll be staying here for a few days, so there's no need to rush the refill requisition. Any calls for me?"

The checker put the log book in the duplicator. "I'll see if there are, captain." He went over to the autofile and punched St. Simon's serial number.

Very few people write to an anchor man. Since he is free to check in and reload at any of the major Belt Cities, and since, in his search for asteroids, his erratic orbit is likely to take him anywhere, it might be months or years before a written letter caught up with him. On the other hand, a message could be beamed to every city, and he could pick it up wherever he was. It cost money, but it was sure.

"One call," the checker said. He handed St. Simon a message slip.

It was unimportant. Just a note from a girl on Vesta. He promised himself that he'd make his next break at Vesta, come what may. He stuck the flimsy in his pocket, and waited while the checker went through the routine of recording his log and making out a pay voucher.

There was no small talk between himself and the checker. Mr. Murtaugh had not elected to take the schooling necessary to qualify for other than a small desk job. He had no space experience. Unless and until he did, there would be an invisible, but nonetheless real barrier between himself and any spaceman. It was not that St. Simon looked down on the man, exactly; it was simply that Murtaugh had not proved himself, and, therefore, there was no way of knowing whether he could be trusted or not. And since trust is a positive quality, lack of it can only mean mistrust.

Murtaugh handed Captain St. Simon an envelope. "That's it, captain. Thank you."

St. Simon opened the envelope, took out his check—and a blue ticket.

Kerry Brand broke into a guffaw.

When the phone on his desk rang, Georges Alhamid scooped it up and identified himself.

"This is Larry, George," said the governor's voice. "How are things so far?"

"So far, so good," Alhamid said. "For the past week, Mr. Peter Danley has been working his head off, under the tutelage of two of the toughest, smartest anchor men in the business. But you should have seen the looks on their faces when I told them they were going to have an Earthman for a pupil."

The governor laughed. "I'll bet! How's he coming along?"

"He's learning. How are you doing with your pet?"

"I think I'm softening him, George. I found out what it was that got his goat three years ago."

"Yeah?"

"Sure. On Ceres, where he went three years ago, he was treated as if he weren't as good as a Belt man."

Alhamid frowned. "Someone was disrespectful?"

"No—that is, not exactly. But he was treated as if we didn't trust his judgment, as though we were a little bit afraid of him."

"Oh-*ho*! I see what you mean."

"Sure. We treated him just as we would anyone who hasn't proved himself. And that meant we were treating him the same way we treated our own 'lower classes', as he thought of them. I had Governor Holger get his Ceres detectives to trace down everything that happened. You can read the transcript if you want. There's nothing particularly exciting in it, but you can see the pattern if you know what to look for.

"I'm not even certain it was fully conscious on his part; I'm not sure he knew why he disliked us. All he was convinced of was that we were arrogant and thought we were better than he is. It's kind of hard for us to see that a person would be that deeply hurt by seeing the plain truth that someone else is obviously better at something than he is, but you've got to remember that an Earthman is brought up to believe that every person is just exactly as good as every other—and no better. A man may have a skill that you don't have, but that doesn't make him superior—oh, my, no!

"Anyway, I started out by apologizing for our habit of standing up all the time. I managed to plant the idea in his mind that the only thing that made him think we felt superior was that habit. I've even got him to the point where he's standing up all the time, too. Makes him feel very superior. He's learned the native customs."

"I get you," Alhamid said. "I probably contributed to that inferiority feeling of his myself."

"Didn't we all? Anyway, the next step was to take him around and introduce him to some of the execs in the government and in a couple of the Companies—I briefed 'em beforehand. Friendly chats—that sort of thing. I think we're going to have to learn the ancient art of diplomacy out here if we're going to survive, George.

"The crowning glory came this afternoon. You should have been there."

"I was up to here in work, Larry. I just couldn't take the time off to attend a club luncheon. Did the great man give his speech?"

"Did he? I should hope to crack my helmet he did! We must all pull together, George, did you know that? We must care for the widow and the orphan—and the needy, George, the needy. We must be sure to provide the fools, the idiots, the malingerers, the moral degenerates, and such useful, lovable beings as that with the necessities and the luxuries of life. We must see to it that they are respected and permitted to have their dignity. We must see to it that the dear little things are permitted the rights of a human being to hold his head up and spit in your eye if he wishes. We must see to it that they be fruitful, multiply, and replenish the Earth."

"They've already done that," Alhamid said caustically. "And they can have it. Let's just see that they don't replenish the Belt. So what happened?"

"Why, George, you'll never realize how much we appreciated that speech. We gave him a three-minute rising ovation. I think he was surprised to see that we could stand for three minutes under a one-gee pull in the centrifuge. And you should have seen the smiles on our faces, George."

"I hope nobody broke out laughing."

"We managed to restrain ourselves," the governor said.

"What's next on the agenda?"

"Well, it'll be tricky, but I think I can pull it off. I'm going to take him around and show him that we *do* take care of the widow and the orphan, and hope that he assumes we are as solicitous toward the rest of his motley crew. Wish me luck."

"Good luck. You may need it."

"Same to you. Take care of Danley."

"Don't worry. He's in good hands. See you, Larry."

"Right."

There were three space-suited men on the bleak rocky ground near the north pole of Pallas, a training area of several square miles known as the North Forty. Their helmets gleamed in the bright, hard light from a sun that looked uncomfortably small to an Earthman's eyes. Two of the men were standing, facing each other some fifteen feet apart. The third, attached to them by safety lines, was hanging face down above the surface, rising slowly, like a balloon that has almost more weight than it can lift.

"No, no, *no*, Mr. Danley! You are not *crawling*, Mr. Danley, you are climbing! Do you understand that?*Climbing!* You have to *climb* an asteroid, just as you would climb a cliff on Earth. You have to hold on every second of the time, or you will fall off!" St. Simon's voice sounded harsh in Danley's earphones, and he felt irritatingly helpless poised floatingly above the ground that way.

His instructors were well anchored by metal eyes set into the rocky surface for just that purpose. Although Pallas was mostly nickel-iron, this end of it was stony, which was why it had been selected as a training ground.

"*Well?*" snapped St. Simon. "What do you do now? If this were a small rock, you'd be drifting a long ways away by now. Think, Mr. Danley, *think*."

"Then shut up and let me think!" Danley snarled.

"If small things distract you from thinking about the vital necessity of saving your own life, Mr. Danley, you would not live long in the Belt."

Danley reached out an arm to see if he could touch the ground. When he had pushed himself upwards with a thrust of his knee, he hadn't given himself too hard a shove. He had reached the apex of his slow flight, and was drifting downward again. He grasped a jutting rock and pulled himself back to the surface.

"Very good, Mr. Danley—but that wouldn't work on a small rock. You took too long. What would you have done on a rock with a millionth of a gee of pull?"

Danley was silent.

"*Well?*" St. Simon barked. "*What would you do?*"

"I ... I don't know," Danley admitted.

"Ye gods and little fishhooks!" This was Kerry Brand's voice. It was supposed to be St. Simon's turn to give the verbal instructions, but Brand allowed himself an occasional remark when it was appropriate.

St. Simon's voice was bitingly sweet. "What do you think those safety lines are for, Mr. Danley? Do you think they are for decorative purposes?"

"Well ... I thought I was supposed to think of some other way. I mean, that's so obvious—"

"Mr. Danley," St. Simon said with sudden patience, "we are not here to give you riddles to solve. We're here to teach you how to stay alive in the Belt. And one of the first rules you must learn is that you will *never* leave your boat without a safety line. *Never!*

"An anchor man, Mr. Danley, is called that for more than one reason. You cannot anchor your boat to a rock unless there is an eye-bolt set in it. And if it already has an eye-bolt, you would have no purpose on that rock. In a way, *you* will be the anchor of your boat, since you will be tied to it by your safety line. If the boat drifts too far from your rock while you are working, it will pull you off the surface, since it has more mass than you do. That shouldn't be allowed to happen, but, if it does, you are still with your boat, rather than deserted on a rock for the rest of your life—which wouldn't be very long. When the power unit in your suit ran out of energy, it would stop breaking your exhaled carbon dioxide down into carbon and oxygen, and you would suffocate. Even with emergency tanks of oxygen, you would soon find yourself freezing to death. That sun up there isn't very warm, Mr. Danley."

Peter Danley was silent, but it was an effort to remain so. He wanted to remind St. Simon that he, Danley, had been a spaceman for nearly fifteen years. But he was also aware that he was learning things that weren't taught at Earthside schools. Most of his professional life had been spent aboard big, comfortable ships that made the short Earth-Luna hop. He could probably count the total hours he had spent in a spacesuit on the fingers of his two hands.

"All right, Mr. Danley; let's begin again. Climb along the surface. Use toeholds, handholds, and fingerholds. Feel your way along. Find those little crevices that will give you a grip. It doesn't take much. You're a lot better off than a mountain climber on Earth because you don't have to fight your weight. You have only your mass to worry about. That's it. Fine. Very good, Mr. Danley."

And, later:
"Now, Mr. Danley," said Captain Brand, "you are at the end of your tether, so to speak."

The three men were in a space boat, several hundred miles from Pallas. Or, rather, two of them were in the boat, standing at the open door. Peter Danley was far out from it, at the end of his safety line.

"How far are you from us, Mr. Danley?" Brand asked.

"Three hundred meters, Captain Brand," Danley said promptly.

"Very good. How do you know?"

"I am at the end of my safety line, which is three hundred meters long when fully extended."

"Your memory is excellent, Mr. Danley. Now, how will you get back to the boat?"

"Pull myself hand over hand along the line."

"Think, Mr. Danley! *Think!*"

"Uh. Oh. Well, I wouldn't keep pulling. I'd just give myself a tug and then coast in, taking up the line slowly as I went."

"Excellent! What would happen if you, as you put it, pulled yourself in hand over hand, as if you were climbing a rope on Earth?"

"I would accelerate too much," Danley said. "I'd gain too much momentum and probably bash my brains out against the boat. And I'd have no way to stop myself."

"Bully for you, Mr. Danley! Now see if you can put into action that which you have so succinctly put into words. Come back to the boat. Gently the first time. We'll have plenty of practice, so that you can get the feel of the muscle pull that will give you a maximum of velocity with a minimum of impact at this end. Gently, now."

Still later:
"Judgment, Mr. Danley!" St. Simon cautioned. "You have to use judgment! A space boat is not an automobile. There is no friction out here to slow it to a stop. Your accelerator is just exactly that—an accelerator. Taking your foot off it won't slow you down a bit; you've got to use your reverse."

Peter Danley was at the controls of the boat. There were tiny beads of perspiration on his forehead. Over a kilometer away was a good-sized hunk of rock; his instructors wouldn't let him get any closer. They wanted to be sure that they could take over before the boat struck the rock, just in case Danley should freeze to the accelerator a little too long.

He wasn't used to this sort of thing. He was used to a taped acceleration-deceleration program which lifted a big ship, aimed it, and went through the trip all automatically. All he had ever had to do was drop it the last few hundred feet to a landing field.

"Keep your eyes moving," St. Simon said. "Your radar can give you data that you need, just remember that it can't think for you."

Your right foot controls your forward acceleration.
Your left foot controls your reverse acceleration.
They can't be pushed down together; when one goes down, the other goes up. Balance one against the other.
Turning your wheel controls the roll of the boat.
Pulling your wheel toward you, or pushing it away, controls the pitch.

Shifting the wheel left, or right, controls the yaw.

The instructions had been pounded into his head until each one seemed to ring like a separate little bell. The problem was coordinating his body to act on those instructions.

One of the radar dials told him how far he was from the rock. Another told him his radial velocity relative to it. A third told him his angular velocity.

"Come to a dead stop exactly one thousand meters from the surface, Mr. Danley," St. Simon ordered.

Danley worked the controls until both his velocity meters read zero, and the distance meter read exactly one kilometer.

"Very good, Mr. Danley. Now assume that the surface of your rock is at nine hundred ninety-five meters. Bring your boat to a dead stop exactly fifty centimeters from that surface."

Danley worked the controls again. He grinned with satisfaction when the distance meter showed nine nine five point five on the nose.

Captain St. Simon sighed deeply. "Mr. Danley, do you feel a little shaken up? Banged around a little? Do you feel as though you'd just gotten a bone-rattling shock?"

"Uh ... no."

"You should. You slammed this boat a good two feet into the surface of that rock before you backed out again." His voice changed tone. "Dammit, Mr. Danley, when I say 'surface at nine nine five', I mean *surface*!"

Edway Tarnhorst had been dictating notes for his reports into his recorder, and was rather tired, so when he asked Peter Danley what he had learned, he was rather irritated when the blond man closed his blue eyes and repeated, parrotlike:

"Due to the lack of a water-oxygen atmosphere, many minerals are found in the asteroids which are unknown on Earth. Among the more important of these are: Oldhamite (CaS); Daubréelite ($FECr_2S_4$); Schreibersite and Rhabdite (Fe_3Ni_3P); Lawrencite ($FeCl_2$); and Taenite, an alloy of iron containing—"

"That's not precisely the sort of thing I meant," Tarnhorst interrupted testily.

Danley smiled. "I know. I'm sorry. That's my lesson for tomorrow."

"So I gathered. May I sit down?" There were only two chairs in the room. Danley was occupying one, and a pile of books was occupying the other.

Danley quickly got to his feet and began putting the books on his desk. "Certainly, Mr. Tarnhorst. Sit down."

Tarnhorst lowered himself into the newly emptied chair. "I apologize for interrupting your studies," he said. "I realize how important they are. But there are a few points I'd like to discuss with you."

"Certainly." Danley seated himself and looked at the older man expectantly. "The nullifiers are on," he said.

"Of course," Tarnhorst said absently. Then, changing his manner, he said abruptly: "Have you found anything yet?"

Danley shook his head. "No. It looks to me as though they've done everything possible to make sure that these men get the best equipment and the best training. The training instructors have been through the whole affair themselves—they know the ropes. The equipment, as far as I can tell, is top grade stuff. From what I have seen so far, the Company isn't stinting on the equipment or the training."

Tarnhorst nodded. "After nearly three months of investigation, I have come to the same conclusion myself. The records show that expenditures on equipment has been steadily increasing. The equipment they have now, I understand, is almost failure-proof?" He looked questioningly at Danley.

Danley nodded. "Apparently. Certainly no one is killed because of equipment failure. It's the finest stuff I've ever seen."

"And yet," Tarnhorst said, "their books show that they are constantly seeking to improve it."

"I don't suppose there is any chance of juggling the books on you, is there?"

Tarnhorst smiled a superior smile. "Hardly. In the first place, I know bookkeeping. In the second, it would be impossible to whip up a complete set of balancing books—covering a period of nearly eighty years—overnight."

"I agree," Danley said. "I don't think they set up a special training course just for me overnight, either. I've seen classes on Vesta, Juno, and Eros—and they're all the same. There aren't any fancy false fronts to fool us, Mr. Tarnhorst: I've looked very closely."

"Have you talked to the men?"

"Yes. They have no complaints."

Again Tarnhorst nodded. "I have found the same thing. They all insist that if a man gets killed in space, it's not the fault of anyone but himself. Or, as it may be, an act of God."

"One of my instructors ran into an act of God some years ago," Danley said. "You've met him. Brand—the one with the scarred face." He explained to Tarnhorst what had caused Brand's disfigurement. "But he survived," he finished, "because he kept his wits about him even after he was hit."

"Commendable; very commendable," Tarnhorst said. "If he'd been an excitable fool, he'd have died."

"True. But what I was trying to point out was that it wasn't equipment failure that caused the accident."

"No. You're quite right." Tarnhorst was silent for a moment, then he looked into Danley's eyes. "Do you think you could take on a job as anchor man now?"

"I don't know," said Danley evenly. "But I'm going to find out tomorrow."

Peter Danley took his final examination the following day. All by himself, he went through the procedure of positioning his ship, setting up a rocket drill, firing it, and setting in an anchor. It was only a small rock, nine meters through, but the job was almost the same as with the big ones. Not far away, Captain St. Simon watched the Earthman's procedure through a pair of high-powered field glasses. He breathed a deep sigh of relief when the job was done.

"Jules," he said softly, "I am sure glad that man didn't hurt himself any."

"Yes, *suh*! We'd of sho' been in trouble if he'd of killed hisself!"

"We will have to tell Captain Brand that our pupil has done pretty well for such a small amount of schooling."

"I think that would be proper, m'lud."

"And we will also have to tell Captain Brand that this boy wouldn't last a month. He wouldn't come back from his first trip."

There was no answer to that.

Three days later, amid a cloud of generally satisfied feelings, Edway Tarnhorst and Peter Danley took the ship back to Earth.

"I cannot, of course, give you a copy of my report," Tarnhorst had told Georges Alhamid. "That is for the eyes of the Committee only. However, I may say that I do not find the Belt Companies or the governments of the Belt Cities at fault. Do you want to know my personal opinion?"

"I would appreciate it, Mr. Tarnhorst," Georges had said.

"Carelessness. Just plain carelessness on the part of the workers. That is what has caused your rise in death rates. You people out here in the Belt have become too used to being in space. Familiarity breeds contempt, Mr. Alhamid.

"Steps must be taken to curb that carelessness. I suggest a publicity campaign of some kind. The people must be thoroughly indoctrinated in safety procedures and warned against carelessness. Just a few months of schooling isn't enough, Mr. Alhamid. You've got to start pounding it into their heads early.

"If you don't—" He shook his head. (He had grown used to doing so in low gravity by now.) "If the death rate isn't cut down, we shall have to raise the premium rates, and I don't know what will happen on the floor of the People's Congress. However, I think I can guarantee six months to a year before any steps are taken. That will give you time to launch your safety campaign. I'm certain that as soon as this carelessness is curbed, the claims will drop down to their former low point."

"We'll certainly try that," Alhamid had said heartily. "Thank you very much, Mr. Tarnhorst."

When they had finally gone, Alhamid spoke to the governor.

"That's that, Larry. You can bring it up at the next meeting of the Board of Governors. Get some kind of publicity campaign going. Plug safety. Tell 'em carelessness is bad. It can't hurt anything and actually might help, who knows?"

"What are you going to do at your end?"

"What we should have done long ago: finance the insurance ourselves. For the next couple of years, we'll only make death claims to Earth for a part of the total. We'll pay off the rest ourselves. Then we'll tell 'em we've brought the cost down so much that we can afford to do our own insurance financing.

"We let this insurance thing ride too long, and it has damn near got us in a jam. We needed the income from Earth. We still could use it, but we need our independence more."

"I second the motion," the governor said fervently. "Look, suppose you come over to my place tonight, and we'll work out the details of this report. O.K.? Say at nine?"

"Fine, Larry. I'll see you then."

Alhamid went back to his office. He was met at the door by his secretary, who handed him a sealed envelope. "The Earthman left this here for you. He said you'd know what to do with it."

Alhamid took the envelope and looked at the name on the outside. "Which Earthman?" he asked.

"The young one," she said, "the blond one."

"It isn't even addressed to me," Alhamid said with a note of puzzled speculation in his voice.

"No. I noticed that. I told him he could send it straight to the school, but he said you would know how to handle it."

Alhamid looked at the envelope again, and his eyes narrowed a little. "Call Captain St. Simon, will you? Tell him I would like to have him come to my office. Don't mention this letter; I don't want it breezed all over Pallas."

It was nearly twenty minutes before St. Simon showed up. Alhamid handed him the envelope. "You have a message from your star pupil. For some reason, he wanted me to deliver it to you. I have a hunch you'll know what that reason is after you read it." He grinned. "I'd appreciate it if you'd tell me when you find out. This Mr. Danley has worried me all along."

St. Simon scowled at the envelope, then ripped off one end and took out the typed sheets. He read them carefully, then handed them over to Alhamid. "You'd better read this yourself, George."

Georges Alhamid took the pages and began to read.

Dear Captain St. Simon:

I am addressing this to you rather than anyone else because I think you will understand more than anyone else. Captain Brand is a fine person, but I have never felt very much at ease with him. (I won't go into the psychological reasons that may exist, other than admit that my reasons are purely emotional. I don't honestly know how much they are based on his disfigurement.) Mr. Alhamid is almost a stranger to me. You are the only Belt man I feel I know well.

First, I want to say that I honestly enjoyed our three months together. There were times when I could have cheerfully bashed your head in, I'll admit, but the experience has left me feeling more like a real human being, more like a person in my own right, than I have ever felt before in my life. Believe me, I appreciate it deeply. I know now that I can do things on my own without being dependent on the support of a team or a committee, and for that I am grateful.

Tarnhorst has heard my report and accepted it. His report to the People's Congress will lay the entire blame for the death rate rise on individual carelessness rather than on any fault of management.

I think, in the main, I am justified in making such a report to Tarnhorst, although I am fully aware that it is incomplete. I know that if I had told him the whole truth there would be a ruckus kicked up on Earth that would cause more trouble in the Belt than I'd care to think about. I'm sure you're as aware of the political situation as I am.

You see, I know that anchor-setting could be made a great deal safer. I know that machines could be developed which would make the job so nearly automatic that the operator would never be exposed to any more danger than he would be in a ship on the Earth-Luna run. Perhaps that's a little exaggerated, but not much.

What puzzled me was: *Why?* Why shouldn't the Companies build these machines if they were more efficient? Why should every Belt man defend the system as it was? Why should men risk their necks when they could demand better equipment? (I don't mean that the equipment presently used is poor; I just mean that full mechanization would do away with the present type of equipment and replace it with a different type.)

Going through your course of instruction gave me the answer to that, even though I didn't take the full treatment.

All my life, I've belonged to an organization of some kind—the team, the crew, whatever it might be. But the Team was everything, and I was recognized only as a member of the Team. I was a replaceable plug-in unit, not an individual in my own right. I don't know that I can explain the difference exactly, but it seems to me that the Team is something outside of which the individual has no existence, while the men of the Belt can form a team because they know that each member is self-sufficient in his own right.

On Earth, we all depend on the Team, and, in the long run, that means that we are depending on each other—but none of us feels he can depend on himself. Every man hopes that, as a member of the Team, he will be saved from his own errors, his own failures. But he knows that everyone else is doing the same thing, and, deep down inside, he knows that they are not deserving of his reliance. So he puts his reliance in the Team, as if that were some sort of separate entity in itself, and had magical, infallible powers that were greater than the aggregate of the individuals that composed it.

In a way, this is certainly so, since teamwork can accomplish things that mobs cannot do. But the Team is a failure if each member assumes that he, himself, is helpless and can do nothing, but that the Team will do it for him.

Men who have gone through the Belt training program, men who have "space experience," as you so euphemistically put it, are men who can form a real team, one that will get things done because each man knows he can rely on the others, not only as a team, but as individuals. But to mechanize the anchor-setting phase would destroy all that completely.

I don't want to see that destroyed, because I have felt what it is to be a part of the Belt team, even though only a small and unreliable part. Actually, I know I was not and could never be a real member of that team, but I was and am proud to have scrimmaged with the team, and I'm glad to be able to sit on the side-lines and cheer even if I can't carry the ball. (It just occurred to me that those metaphors might be a little cloudy to you, since you don't have football in the Belt, but I think you see what I mean.) I imagine that most of the men who have no "space experience" feel the same way. They know they'd never make a go of it out in space, but they're happy to be water boys.

I wish I could stay in the Belt. I'm enough of a spaceman to appreciate what it really is to be a member of a space society. But I also know that I'd never last. I'm not fitted for it, really. I've had a small taste of it, but I know I couldn't take a full dose. I've worked hard for the influence and security I have in my job, and I couldn't give it up. Maybe this brands me as a coward in your eyes, and maybe I am a coward, but that's the way I'm built. I hope you'll take that into account when you think of me.

At any rate, I have done what I have done. On Earth, there are men who envy you and hate you, and there will be others who will try to destroy you, but I have done what I could to give you a chance to gain the strength you need to resist the encroachment of Earth's sickness.

I have a feeling that Tarnhorst saw your greatness, too, although he'd never admit it, even to himself. Certainly something changed him during the last months, even though he doesn't realize it. He came out wanting to help—and by that, he meant help the common people against the "tyranny" of the Companies. He still wants to help the common people, but now he wants to do it *through* the Companies. The change is so subtle that he doesn't think he's changed at all, but I can see it.

I don't deserve any thanks for what I have done. All I have done is repay you in the only way I knew how for what you have done for me. I may never see you again, captain, but I will always remember you. Please convey my warmest regards to Captain Brand and to Mr. Alhamid.

Sincerely,
Peter Danley

Georges Alhamid handed the letter back to St. Simon. "There's your star pupil," he said gently.

St. Simon nodded. "The wise fool. The guy who's got sense enough to know that he isn't competent to do the job."

"Did you notice that he waltzed all around the real reason for the anchor-setting program without quite hitting it?"

St. Simon smiled humorlessly. "Sure. Notice the wording of the letter. He still thinks in terms of the Team, even when he's trying not to. He thinks we do this just to train men to have a real good Team Spirit. He can't see that that is only a very useful by-product."

"How could he think otherwise?" Alhamid asked. "To him, or to Tarnhorst, the notion of deliberately tailoring a program so that it would kill off the fools and the incompetents, setting up a program that will deliberately destroy the men who are dangerous to society, would be horrifying. They would accuse us of being soulless butchers who had no respect for the dignity of the human soul."

"We're not butchering anybody," St. Simon objected. "Nobody is forced to go through two years of anchor setting. Nobody is forced to die. We're not running people into gas chambers or anything like that."

"No; of course not. But would you expect an Earthman like Tarnhorst to see the difference? How could we explain to him that we have no objection to fools other than that we object to putting them in positions where they can harm others by their foolishness? Would you expect him to understand that we must have a method of eliminating those who are neither competent enough to be trusted with the lives of others nor wise enough to see that they are not competent? How would you tell him that the reason we send men out alone is so that if he destroys anyone by his foolishness—after we have taught him everything we know in the best way we know how—he will only destroy himself?"

"I wouldn't even try," St. Simon said. "There's an old saying that neither money, education, liquor, nor women ever made a fool of a man, they just give a born fool a chance to display his foolishness. Space ought to be added to that list."

"Did you notice something else about that letter?" Alhamid asked. "I mean, the very fact that he wrote a letter instead of telling you personally?"

"Sure. He didn't trust me. He was afraid I, or someone else, would dispose of him if we knew he knew our secret."

"I think that's it," Alhamid agreed. "He wanted to be safely away first."

"Killing him would have brought down the biggest investigation the Earth Congress has launched since the crack-up of the Earth-Luna ship thirty years ago. Does he think we are fools?"

"You can't blame him. He's been brought up that way, and three months of training isn't going to change him."

St. Simon frowned. "Suppose he changes his mind? Suppose he tells Tarnhorst what he thinks?"

"He won't. He's told his lie, and now he'll have to stick by it or lose his precious security. If he couldn't trade that for freedom, he sure isn't going to throw it away." Alhamid grinned. "But can you imagine a guy thinking that anchor setting could be completely mechanized?"

St. Simon grinned back. "I guess I'm not a very good teacher after all. I told him and told him and told him for three solid months that the job required judgment, but it evidently didn't sink in. He's got the heart of a romantic and the soul of an Earthman—a very bad combination."

"He has my sympathy," Alhamid said with feeling. "Now, about you. Your blue ticket still has three months to run, but I can't give you a class if you're only going to run through the first half of the course with them, and I don't have any more Earthmen for you to give special tutoring to. You have three choices: You can loaf with pay for three months; you can go back to space and get double pay for three months; or you can take a regular six-month class and get double pay for the last three months. Which'll it be?"

St. Simon grinned widely. "I'm going to loaf until I get sick of it, then I'll go back to space and collect double pay for what's left of the three months. First off, I'm going to take a run over to Vesta. After that, who knows?"

"I thought so. Most of you guys would stay out there forever if you didn't have to come back for supplies."

St. Simon shook his head. "Nope. Not true. A man's got to come back every so often and get his feet on the ground. If you stay out there too long, you get to talking to yourself."

An hour later, the spaceboat *Nancy Bell* lifted from the surface of Pallas and shot toward Vesta.

"Jules, old cobblestone, we have just saved civilization."

"*Jawohl, Herr Hassenpfefferesser!* Und now ve go to find *das Mädchen, nicht war*?"

"Herr *Professor* Hassenpfefferesser to you, my boy."

And then, all alone in his spaceboat, Captain Jules St. Simon burst into song:

"Oh, I'm the cook and the captain, too,And the men of the *Nancy's* brig;The bosun tight, and the midshipmite,And the crew of the captain's gig!"

And the *Nancy Bell* sped on toward Vesta and a rendevous with Eros.

The Highest Treason

The highest treason of all is not so easy to define—and be it noted carefully that the true traitor in this case was not singular, but very plural ...

The Prisoner

THE two rooms were not luxurious, but MacMaine hadn't expected that they would be. The walls were a flat metallic gray, unadorned and windowless. The ceilings and floors were simply continuations of the walls, except for the glow-plates overhead. One room held a small cabinet for his personal possessions, a wide, reasonably soft bed, a small but adequate desk, and, in one corner, a cubicle that contained the necessary sanitary plumbing facilities.

The other room held a couch, two big easy-chairs, a low table, some bookshelves, a squat refrigerator containing food and drink for his occasional snacks—his regular meals were brought in hot from the main kitchen—and a closet that contained his clothing—the insignialess uniforms of a Kerothi officer.

No, thought Sebastian MacMaine, it was not luxurious, but neither did it look like the prison cell it was.

There was comfort here, and even the illusion of privacy, although there were TV pickups in the walls, placed so that no movement in either room would go unnoticed. The switch which cut off the soft white light from the glow plates did not cut off the infrared radiation which enabled his hosts to watch him while he slept. Every sound was heard and recorded.

But none of that bothered MacMaine. On the contrary, he was glad of it. He wanted the Kerothi to know that he had no intention of escaping or hatching any plot against them.

He had long since decided that, if things continued as they had, Earth would lose the war with Keroth, and Sebastian MacMaine had no desire whatever to be on the losing side of the greatest war ever fought. The problem now was to convince the Kerothi that he fully intended to fight with them, to give them the full benefit of his ability as a military strategist, to do his best to win every battle for Keroth.

And that was going to be the most difficult task of all.

A telltale glow of red blinked rapidly over the door, and a soft chime pinged in time with it.

MacMaine smiled inwardly, although not a trace of it showed on his broad-jawed, blocky face. To give him the illusion that he was a guest rather than a prisoner, the Kerothi had installed an announcer at the door and invariably used it. Not once had any one of them ever simply walked in on him.

"Come in," MacMaine said.

He was seated in one of the easy-chairs in his "living room," smoking a cigarette and reading a book on the history of Keroth, but he put the book down on the low table as a tall Kerothi came in through the doorway.

MacMaine allowed himself a smile of honest pleasure. To most Earthmen, "all the Carrot-skins look alike," and, MacMaine admitted honestly to himself, he hadn't yet trained himself completely to look beyond the strangenesses that made the Kerothi different from Earthmen and see the details that made them different from each other. But this was one Kerothi that MacMaine would never mistake for any other.

"Tallis!" He stood up and extended both hands in the Kerothi fashion. The other did the same, and they clasped hands for a moment. "How are your guts?" he added in Kerothic.

"They function smoothly, my sibling-by-choice," answered Space General Polan Tallis. "And your own?"

"Smoothly, indeed. It's been far too long a time since we have touched."

The Kerothi stepped back a pace and looked the Earthman up and down. "You look healthy enough—for a prisoner. You're treated well, then?"

"Well enough. Sit down, my sibling-by-choice." MacMaine waved toward the couch nearby. The general sat down and looked around the apartment.

"Well, well. You're getting preferential treatment, all right. This is as good as you could expect as a battleship commander. Maybe you're being trained for the job."

MacMaine laughed, allowing the touch of sardonicism that he felt to be heard in the laughter. "I might have hoped so once, Tallis. But I'm afraid I have simply come out even. I have traded nothing for nothing."

General Tallis reached into the pocket of his uniform jacket and took out the thin aluminum case that held the Kerothi equivalent of cigarettes. He took one out, put it between his lips, and lit it with the hotpoint that was built into the case.

MacMaine took an Earth cigarette out of the package on the table and allowed Tallis to light it for him. The pause and the silence, MacMaine knew, were for a purpose. He waited. Tallis had something to say, but he was allowing the Earthman to "adjust to surprise." It was one of the fine points of Kerothi etiquette.

A sudden silence on the part of one participant in a conversation, under these particular circumstances, meant that something unusual was coming up, and the other person was supposed to take the opportunity to brace himself for shock.

It could mean anything. In the Kerothi Space Forces, a superior informed a junior officer of the junior's forthcoming promotion by just such tactics. But the same tactics were used when informing a person of the death of a loved one.

In fact, MacMaine was well aware that such a period of silence was *de rigueur* in a Kerothi court, just before sentence was pronounced, as well as a preliminary to a proposal of marriage by a Kerothi male to the light of his love.

MacMaine could do nothing but wait. It would be indelicate to speak until Tallis felt that he was ready for the surprise.

It was not, however, indelicate to watch Tallis' face closely; it was expected. Theoretically, one was supposed to be able to discern, at least, whether the news was good or bad.

With Tallis, it was impossible to tell, and MacMaine knew it would be useless to read the man's expression. But he watched, nonetheless.

In one way, Tallis' face was typically Kerothi. The orange-pigmented skin and the bright, grass-green eyes were common to all Kerothi. The planet Keroth, like Earth, had evolved several different "races" of humanoid, but, unlike Earth, the distinction was not one of color.

MacMaine took a drag off his cigarette and forced himself to keep his mind off whatever it was that Tallis might be about to say. He was already prepared for a death sentence—even a death sentence by torture. Now, he felt, he could not be shocked. And, rather than build up the tension within himself to an unbearable degree, he thought about Tallis rather than about himself.

Tallis, like the rest of the Kerothi, was unbelievably humanoid. There were internal differences in the placement of organs, and differences in the functions of those organs. For instance, it took two separate organs to perform the same function that the liver performed in Earthmen, and the kidneys were completely absent, that function being performed by special tissues in the lower colon, which meant that the Kerothi were more efficient with water-saving than Earthmen, since the waste products were excreted as relatively dry solids through an all-purpose cloaca.

But, externally, a Kerothi would need only a touch of plastic surgery and some makeup to pass as an Earthman in a stage play. Close up, of course, the job would be much more difficult—as difficult as a Negro trying to disguise himself as a Swede or *vice versa*.

But Tallis was—

"I would have a word," Tallis said, shattering MacMaine's carefully neutral train of thought. It was a standard opening for breaking the pause of adjustment, but it presaged good news rather than bad.

"I await your word," MacMaine said. Even after all this time, he still felt vaguely proud of his ability to handle the subtle idioms of Kerothic.

"I think," Tallis said carefully, "that you may be offered a commission in the Kerothi Space Forces."

Sebastian MacMaine let out his breath slowly, and only then realized that he had been holding it. "I am grateful, my sibling-by-choice," he said.

General Tallis tapped his cigarette ash into a large blue ceramic ashtray. MacMaine could smell the acrid smoke from the alien plant matter that burned in the Kerothi cigarette—a chopped-up inner bark from a Kerothi tree. MacMaine could no more smoke a Kerothi cigarette than Tallis could smoke tobacco, but the two were remarkably similar in their effects.

The "surprise" had been delivered. Now, as was proper, Tallis would move adroitly all around the subject until he was ready to return to it again.

"You have been with us ... how long, Sepastian?" he asked.

"Two and a third *Kronet*."

Tallis nodded. "Nearly a year of your time."

MacMaine smiled. Tallis was as proud of his knowledge of Earth terminology as MacMaine was proud of his mastery of Kerothic.

"Lacking three weeks," MacMaine said.

"What? Three ... oh, yes. Well. A long time," said Tallis.

Damn it! MacMaine thought, in a sudden surge of impatience, *get to the point*! His face showed only calm.

"The Board of Strategy asked me to tell you," Tallis continued. "After all, my recommendation was partially responsible for the decision." He paused for a moment, but it was merely a conversational hesitation, not a formal hiatus.

"It was a hard decision, Sepastian—you must realize that. We have been at war with your race for ten years now. We have taken thousands of Earthmen as prisoners, and many of them have agreed to co-operate with us. But, with one single exception, these prisoners have been the moral dregs of your civilization. They have been men who had no pride of race, no pride of society, no pride of self. They have been weak, self-centered, small-minded, cowards who had no thought for Earth and Earthmen, but only for themselves.

"Not," he said hurriedly, "that all of them are that way—or even the majority. Most of them have the minds of warriors, although, I must say, not *strong* warriors."

That last, MacMaine knew, was a polite concession. The Kerothi had no respect for Earthmen. And MacMaine could hardly blame them. For three long centuries, the people of Earth had had nothing to do but indulge themselves in the pleasures of material wealth. It was a wonder that any of them had any moral fiber left.

"But none of those who had any strength agreed to work with us," Tallis went on. "With one exception. You."

"Am I weak, then?" MacMaine asked.

General Tallis shook his head in a peculiarly humanlike gesture. "No. No, you are not. And that is what has made us pause for three years." His grass-green eyes looked candidly into MacMaine's own. "You aren't the type of person who betrays his own kind. It looks like a trap. After a whole year, the Board of Strategy still isn't sure that there is no trap."

Tallis stopped, leaned forward, and ground out the stub of his cigarette in the blue ashtray. Then his eyes again sought MacMaine's.

"If it were not for what I, personally, know about you, the Board of Strategy would not even consider your proposition."

"I take it, then, that they have considered it?" MacMaine asked with a grin.

"As I said, Sepastian," Tallis said, "you have won your case. After almost a year of your time, your decision has been justified."

MacMaine lost his grin. "I am grateful, Tallis," he said gravely. "I think you must realize that it was a difficult decision to make."

His thoughts went back, across long months of time and longer light-years of space, to the day when that decision had been made.

The Decision

Colonel Sebastian MacMaine didn't feel, that morning, as though this day were different from any other. The sun, faintly veiled by a few wisps of cloud, shone as it always had; the guards at the doors of the Space Force Administration Building saluted him as usual; his brother officers nodded politely, as they always did; his aide greeted him with the usual "Good morning, sir."

The duty list lay on his desk, as it had every morning for years. Sebastian MacMaine felt tense and a little irritated with himself, but he felt nothing that could be called a premonition.

When he read the first item on the duty list, his irritation became a little stronger.

"*Interrogate Kerothi general.*"

The interrogation duty had swung round to him again. He didn't want to talk to General Tallis. There was something about the alien that bothered him, and he couldn't place exactly what it was.

Earth had been lucky to capture the alien officer. In a space war, there's usually very little left to capture after a battle—especially if your side lost the battle.

On the other hand, the Kerothi general wasn't so lucky. The food that had been captured with him would run out in less than six months, and it was doubtful that he would survive on Earth food. It was equally doubtful that any more Kerothi food would be captured.

For two years, Earth had been fighting the Kerothi, and for two years Earth had been winning a few minor skirmishes and losing the major battles. The Kerothi hadn't hit any of the major colonies yet, but they had swallowed up outpost after outpost, and Earth's space fleet was losing ships faster than her factories could turn them out. The hell of it was that nobody on Earth seemed to be very much concerned about it at all.

MacMaine wondered why he let it concern him. If no one else was worried, why did he let it bother him? He pushed the thought from his mind and picked up the questionnaire form that had been made out for that morning's session with the Kerothi general. Might as well get it over with.

He glanced down the list of further duties for the day. It looked as though the routine interrogation of the Kerothi general was likely to provide most of the interest in the day's work at that.

He took the dropchute down to the basement of the building, to the small prison section where the alien officer was being held. The guards saluted nonchalantly as he went in. The routine questioning sessions were nothing new to them.

MacMaine turned the lock on the prisoner's cell door and went in. Then he came to attention and saluted the Kerothi general. He was probably the only officer in the place who did that, he knew; the others treated the alien general as though he were a criminal. Worse, they treated him as though he were a petty thief or a common pickpocket—criminal, yes, but of a definitely inferior type.

General Tallis, as always, stood and returned the salute. "Cut mawnik, Cunnel MacMaine," he said. The Kerothi language lacked many of the voiced consonants of English and Russian, and, as a result, Tallis' use of *B*, *D*, *G*, *J*, *V*, and *Z* made them come out as *P*, *T*, *K*, *CH*, *F*, and *S*. The English *R*, as it is pronounced in *run* or *rat*, eluded him entirely, and he pronounced it only when he could give it the guttural pronunciation of the German *R*. The terminal *NG* always came out as *NK*. The nasal *M* and *N* were a little more drawn out than in English, but they were easily understandable.

"Good morning, General Tallis," MacMaine said. "Sit down. How do you feel this morning?"

The general sat again on the hard bunk that, aside from the single chair, was the only furniture in the small cell. "Ass well ass coot pe expectet. I ket ferry little exercisse. I ... how iss it set? ... I pecome soft? Soft? Iss correct?"

"Correct. You've learned our language very well for so short a time."

The general shrugged off the compliment. "Wen it iss a matteh of learrn in orrter to surfife, one learrnss."

"You think, then, that your survival has depended on your learning our language?"

The general's orange face contrived a wry smile. "Opfiously. Your people fill not learn Kerothic. If I cannot answerr questionss, I am uff no use. Ass lonk ass I am uff use, I will liff. Not?"

MacMaine decided he might as well spring his bomb on the Kerothi officer now as later. "I am not so certain but that you might have stretched out your time longer if you had forced us to learn Kerothic, general," he said in Kerothic. He knew his Kerothic was bad, since it had been learned from the Kerothi spaceman who had been captured with the general, and the man had been badly wounded and had survived only two weeks. But that little bit of basic instruction, plus the work he had done on the books and tapes from the ruined Kerothi ship, had helped him.

"Ah?" The general blinked in surprise. Then he smiled. "Your accent," he said in Kerothic, "is atrocious, but certainly no worse than mine when I speak your *Inklitch*. I suppose you intend to question me in Kerothic now, eh? In the hope that I may reveal more in my own tongue?"

"Possibly you may," MacMaine said with a grin, "but I learned it for my own information."

"For your own what? Oh. I see. Interesting. I know no others of your race who would do such a thing. Anything which is difficult is beneath them."

"Not so, general. I'm not unique. There are many of us who don't think that way."

The general shrugged. "I do not deny it. I merely say that I have met none. Certainly they do not tend to go into military service. Possibly that is because you are not a race of fighters. It takes a fighter to tackle the difficult just because it is difficult."

MacMaine gave him a short, hard laugh. "Don't you think getting information out of *you* is difficult? And yet, we tackle that."

"Not the same thing at all. Routine. You have used no pressure. No threats, no promises, no torture, no stress."

MacMaine wasn't quite sure of his translation of the last two negative phrases. "You mean the application of physical pain? That's barbaric."

"I won't pursue the subject," the general said with sudden irony.

"I can understand that. But you can rest assured that we would never do such a thing. It isn't civilized. Our civil police do use certain drugs to obtain information, but we have so little knowledge of Kerothi body chemistry that we hesitate to use drugs on you."

"The application of stress, you say, is not civilized. Not, perhaps, according to your definition of"—he used the English word—"*cifiliced*. No. Not *cifiliced*—but it works." Again he smiled. "I said that I have become soft since I have been here, but I fear that your civilization is even softer."

"A man can lie, even if his arms are pulled off or his feet crushed," MacMaine said stiffly.

The Kerothi looked startled. When he spoke again, it was in English. "I will say no morr. If you haff questionss to ask, ko ahet. I will not take up time with furtherr talkink."

A little angry with himself and with the general, MacMaine spent the rest of the hour asking routine questions and getting nowhere, filling up the tape in his minicorder with the same old answers that others had gotten.

He left, giving the general a brisk salute and turning before the general had time to return it.

Back in his office, he filed the tape dutifully and started on Item Two of the duty list: *Strategy Analysis of Battle Reports*.

Strategy analysis always irritated and upset him. He knew that if he'd just go about it in the approved way, there would be no irritation—only boredom. But he was constitutionally incapable of working that way. In spite of himself, he always played a little game with himself and with the General Strategy Computer.

The only battle of significance in the past week had been the defense of an Earth outpost called Bennington IV. Theoretically, MacMaine was supposed to check over the entire report, find out where the losing side had erred, and feed correctional information into the Computer. But he couldn't resist stopping after he had read the first section: *Information Known to Earth Commander at Moment of Initial Contact*.

Then he would stop and consider how he, personally, would have handled the situation if he had been the Earth commander. So many ships in such-and-such places. Enemy fleet approaching at such-and-such velocities. Battle array of enemy thus-and-so.

Now what?

MacMaine thought over the information on the defense of Bennington IV and devised a battle plan. There was a weak point in the enemy's attack, but it was rather obvious. MacMaine searched until he found another weak point, much less obvious than the first. He knew it would be there. It was.

Then he proceeded to ignore both weak points and concentrate on what he would do if he were the enemy commander. The weak points were traps; the computer could see them and avoid them. Which was just exactly what was wrong with the computer's logic. In avoiding the traps, it also avoided the best way to hit the enemy. A weak point *is* weak, no matter how well it may be booby-trapped. In baiting a rat trap, you have to use real cheese because an imitation won't work.

Of course, MacMaine thought to himself, *you can always poison the cheese, but let's not carry the analogy too far.*

All right, then. How to hit the traps?

It took him half an hour to devise a completely wacky and unorthodox way of hitting the holes in the enemy advance. He checked the time carefully, because there's no point in devising a strategy if the battle is too far gone to use it by the time you've figured it out.

Then he went ahead and read the rest of the report. Earth had lost the outpost. And, worse, MacMaine's strategy would have won the battle if it had been used. He fed it through his small office computer to make sure. The odds were good.

And that was the thing that made MacMaine hate Strategy Analysis. Too often, he won; too often, Earth lost. A computer was fine for working out the logical outcome of a battle if it was given the proper strategy, but it couldn't devise anything new.

Colonel MacMaine had tried to get himself transferred to space duty, but without success. The Commanding Staff didn't want him out there.

The trouble was that they didn't believe MacMaine actually devised his strategy before he read the complete report. How could anyone out-think a computer?

He'd offered to prove it. "Give me a problem," he'd told his immediate superior, General Matsukuo. "Give me the Initial Contact information of a battle I haven't seen before, and I'll show you."

And Matsukuo had said, testily: "Colonel, I will not permit a member of my staff to make a fool of himself in front of the Commanding Staff. Setting yourself up as someone superior to the Strategy Board is the most antisocial type of egocentrism imaginable. You were given the same education at the Academy as every other officer; what makes you think you are better than they? As time goes on, your automatic promotions will put you in a position to vote on such matters—provided you don't prejudice the Promotion Board against you by antisocial behavior. I hold you in the highest regard, colonel, and I will say nothing to the Promotion Board about this, but if you persist I will have to do my duty. Now, I don't want to hear any more about it. Is that clear?"

It was.

All MacMaine had to do was wait, and he'd automatically be promoted to the Commanding Staff, where he would have an equal vote with the others of his rank. One unit vote to begin with and an additional unit for every year thereafter.

It's a great system for running a peacetime social club, maybe, MacMaine thought, *but it's no way to run a fighting force.*

Maybe the Kerothi general was right. Maybe *homo sapiens* just wasn't a race of fighters.

They had been once. Mankind had fought its way to domination of Earth by battling every other form of life on the planet, from the smallest virus to the biggest carnivore. The fight against disease was still going on, as a matter of fact, and Man was still fighting the elemental fury of Earth's climate.

But Man no longer fought with Man. Was that a bad thing? The discovery of atomic energy, two centuries before, had literally made war impossible, if the race was to survive. Small struggles bred bigger struggles—or so the reasoning went. Therefore, the society had unconsciously sought to eliminate the reasons for struggle.

What bred the hatreds and jealousies among men? What caused one group to fight another?

Society had decided that intolerance and hatred were caused by inequality. The jealousy of the inferior toward his superior; the scorn of the superior toward his inferior. The Have-not envies the Have, and the Have looks down upon the Have-not.

Then let us eliminate the Have-not. Let us make sure that everyone is a Have.

Raise the standard of living. Make sure that every human being has the necessities of life—food, clothing, shelter, proper medical care, and proper education. More, give them the luxuries, too—let no man be without anything that is poorer in quality or less in quantity than the possessions of any other. There was no longer any middle class simply because there were no other classes for it to be in the middle of.

"The poor you will have always with you," Jesus of Nazareth had said. But, in a material sense, that was no longer true. The poor were gone—and so were the rich.

But the poor in mind and the poor in spirit were still there—in ever-increasing numbers.

Material wealth could be evenly distributed, but it could not remain that way unless Society made sure that the man who was more clever than the rest could not increase his wealth at the expense of his less fortunate brethren.

Make it a social stigma to show more ability than the average. Be kind to your fellow man; don't show him up as a stupid clod, no matter how cloddish he may be.

All men are created equal, and let's make sure they stay that way!

There could be no such thing as a classless society, of course. That was easily seen. No human being could do everything, learn everything, be everything. There had to be doctors and lawyers and policemen and bartenders and soldiers and machinists and laborers and actors and writers and criminals and bums.

But let's make sure that the differentiation between classes is horizontal, not vertical. As long as a person does his job the best he can, he's as good as anybody else. A doctor is as good as a lawyer, isn't he? Then a garbage collector is just as good as a nuclear physicist, and an astronomer is no better than a street sweeper.

And what of the loafer, the bum, the man who's too lazy or weak-willed to put out any more effort than is absolutely necessary to stay alive? Well, my goodness, the poor chap can't *help* it, can he? It isn't *his* fault, is it? He has to be helped. There is always *something* he is both capable of doing and willing to do. Does he like to sit around all day and do nothing but watch television? Then give him a sheet of paper with all the programs on it and two little boxes marked *Yes* and *No*, and he can put an X in one or the other to indicate whether he likes the program or not. Useful? Certainly. All these sheets can be tallied up in order to find out what sort of program the public likes to see. After all, his vote is just as good as anyone else's, isn't it?

And a Program Analyst is just as good, just as important, and just as well cared-for as anyone else.

And what about the criminal? Well, what *is* a criminal? A person who thinks he's superior to others. A thief steals because he thinks he has more right to something than its real owner. A man kills because he has an idea that he has a better right to live than someone else. In short, a man breaks the law because he feels superior, because he thinks he can outsmart Society and The Law. Or, simply, because he thinks he can outsmart the policeman on the beat.

Obviously, that sort of antisocial behavior can't be allowed. The poor fellow who thinks he's better than anyone else has to be segregated from normal society and treated for his aberrations. But not punished! Heavens no! His erratic behavior isn't *his* fault, is it?

It was axiomatic that there had to be some sort of vertical structure to society, naturally. A child can't do the work of an adult, and a beginner can't be as good as an old hand. Aside from the fact that it was actually impossible to force everyone into a common mold, it was recognized that there had to be some incentive for staying with a job. What to do?

The labor unions had solved that problem two hundred years before. Promotion by seniority. Stick with a job long enough, and you'll automatically rise to the top. That way, everyone had as good a chance as everyone else.

Promotion tables for individual jobs were worked out on the basis of longevity tables, so that by the time a man reached the automatic retirement age he was automatically at the highest position he could hold. No fuss, no bother, no trouble. Just keep your nose clean and live as long as possible.

It eliminated struggle. It eliminated the petty jockeying for position that undermined efficiency in an organization. Everybody deserves an equal chance in life, so make sure everybody gets it.

Colonel Sebastian MacMaine had been born and reared in that society. He could see many of its faults, but he didn't have the orientation to see all of them. As he'd grown older, he'd seen that, regardless of the position a man held according to seniority, a smart man could exercise more power than those above him if he did it carefully.

A man is a slave if he is held rigidly in a pattern and not permitted to step out of that pattern. In ancient times, a slave was born at the bottom of the social ladder, and he remained there all his life. Only rarely did a slave of exceptional merit manage to rise above his assigned position.

But a man who is forced to remain on the bottom step of a stationary stairway is no more a slave than a man who is forced to remain on a given step of an escalator, and no less so.

Slavery, however, has two advantages—one for the individual, and one which, in the long run, can be good for the race. For the individual, it offers security, and that is the goal which by far the greater majority of mankind seeks.

The second advantage is more difficult to see. It operates only in favor of the exceptional individual. There are always individuals who aspire to greater heights than the one they occupy at any given moment, but in a slave society, they are slapped back into place if they act hastily. Just as the one-eyed man in the kingdom of the blind can be king if he taps the ground with a cane, so the gifted individual can gain his ends in a slave society—provided he thinks out the consequences of any act in advance.

The Law of Gravity is a universal edict which enslaves, in a sense, every particle of matter in the cosmos. The man who attempts to defy the "injustice" of that law by ignoring the consequences of its enforcement will find himself punished rather severely. It may be unjust that a bird can fly under its own muscle power, but a man who tries to correct that injustice by leaping out of a skyscraper window and flapping his arms vigorously will find that overt defiance of the Law of Gravity brings very serious penalties indeed. The wise man seeks the loopholes in the law, and loopholes are caused by other laws which counteract—*not defy!*—the given law. A balloon full of hydrogen "falls up" in obedience to the Law of Gravity. A contradiction? A paradox? No. It is the Law of Gravity which causes the density and pressure of a planet's atmosphere to decrease with altitude, and that decrease in pressure forces the balloon upwards until the balance point between atmospheric density and the internal density of the balloon is reached.

The illustration may seem obvious and elementary to the modern man, but it seems so only because he understands, at least to some extent, the laws involved. It was not obvious to even the most learned man of, say, the Thirteenth Century.

Slavery, too, has its laws, and it is as dangerous to defy the laws of a society as it is to defy those of nature, and the only way to escape the punishment resulting from those laws is to find the loopholes. One of the most basic laws of any society is so basic that it is never, *ever* written down.

And that law, like all basic laws, is so simple in expression and so obvious in application that any man above the moron level has an intuitive grasp of it. It is the first law one learns as a child.

Thou shall not suffer thyself to be caught.

The unthinking man believes that this basic law can be applied by breaking the laws of his society in secret. What he fails to see is that such lawbreaking requires such a fantastic network of lies, subterfuges, evasions, and chicanery that the structure itself eventually breaks down and his guilt is obvious to all. The very steps he has taken to keep from getting caught eventually become signposts that point unerringly at the lawbreaker himself.

Like the loopholes in the law of gravity, the loopholes in the laws of society can not entail a *defiance* of the law. Only compliance with those laws will be ultimately successful.

The wise man works within the framework of the law—not only the written, but the unwritten law—of his society. In a slave society, any slave who openly rebels will find that he gets squashed pretty quickly. But many a slave-owner has danced willingly to the tune of a slave who was wiser and cleverer than he, without ever knowing that the tune played was not his own.

And that is the second advantage of slavery. It teaches the exceptional individual to think.

When a wise, intelligent individual openly and violently breaks the laws of his society, there are two things which are almost certain: One: he knows that there is no other way to do the thing he feels must be done, and—

Two: he knows that he will pay the penalty for his crime in one way or another.

Sebastian MacMaine knew the operations of those laws. As a member of a self-enslaved society, he knew that to betray any sign of intelligence was dangerous. A slight slip could bring the scorn of the slaves around him; a major offense could mean death. The war with Keroth had thrown him slightly off balance, but after his one experience with General Matsukuo, he had quickly regained his equilibrium.

At the end of his work day, MacMaine closed his desk and left his office precisely on time, as usual. Working overtime, except in the gravest emergencies, was looked upon as antisocialism. The offender was suspected of having Ambition—obviously a Bad Thing.

It was during his meal at the Officers' Mess that Colonel Sebastian MacMaine heard the statement that triggered the decision in his mind.

There were three other officers seated with MacMaine around one of the four-place tables in the big room. MacMaine only paid enough attention to the table conversation to be able to make the appropriate noises at the proper times. He had long since learned to do his thinking under cover of general banalities.

Colonel VanDeusen was a man who would never have made Private First Class in an army that operated on a strict merit system. His thinking was muddy, and his conversation betrayed it. All he felt comfortable in talking about was just exactly what he had been taught. Slogans, banalities, and bromides. He knew his catechism, and he knew it was safe.

"What I mean is, we got nothing to worry about. We all stick together, and we can do anything. As long as we don't rock the boat, we'll come through O.K."

"Sure," said Major Brock, looking up from his plate in blank-faced surprise. "I mean, who says different?"

"Guy on my research team," said VanDeusen, plying his fork industriously. "A wise-guy second looie. One of them."

"Oh," said the major knowingly. "One of them." He went back to his meal.

"What'd he say?" MacMaine asked, just to keep his oar in.

"Ahhh, nothing serious, I guess," said VanDeusen, around a mouthful of steak. "Said we were all clogged up with paper work, makin' reports on tests, things like that. Said, why don't we figure out something to pop those Carrot-skins outa the sky. So I said to him, 'Look, Lootenant,' I said, 'you got your job to do, I got mine. If the paper work's pilin' up,' I said, 'it's because somebody isn't pulling his share. And it better not be you,' I said." He chuckled and speared another cube of steak with his fork. "That settled him down. He's all right, though. Young yet, you know. Soon's he gets the hang of how the Space Force operates, he'll be O.K."

Since VanDeusen was the senior officer at the table, the others listened respectfully as he talked, only inserting a word now and then to show that they were listening.

MacMaine was thinking deeply about something else entirely, but VanDeusen's influence intruded a little. MacMaine was wondering what it was that bothered him about General Tallis, the Kerothi prisoner.

The alien was pleasant enough, in spite of his position. He seemed to accept his imprisonment as one of the fortunes of war. He didn't threaten or bluster, although he tended to maintain an air of superiority that would have been unbearable in an Earthman.

Was that the reason for his uneasiness in the general's presence? No. MacMaine could accept the reason for that attitude; the general's background was different from that of an Earthman, and therefore he could not be judged by Terrestrial standards. Besides, MacMaine could acknowledge to himself that Tallis was superior to the norm—not only the norm of Keroth, but that of Earth. MacMaine wasn't sure he could have acknowledged superiority in another Earthman, in spite of the fact that he knew that there must be men who were his superiors in one way or another.

Because of his social background, he knew that he would probably form an intense and instant dislike for any Earthman who talked the way Tallis did, but he found that he actually *liked* the alien officer.

It came as a slight shock when the realization hit MacMaine that his liking for the general was exactly why he was uncomfortable around him. Dammit, a man isn't supposed to like his enemy—and most especially when that enemy does and says things that one would despise in a friend.

Come to think of it, though, did he, MacMaine, actually have any friends? He looked around him, suddenly clearly conscious of the other men in the room. He searched through his memory, thinking of all his acquaintances and relatives.

It was an even greater shock to realize that he would not be more than faintly touched emotionally if any or all of them were to die at that instant. Even his parents, both of whom were now dead, were only dim figures in his memory. He had mourned them when an aircraft accident had taken both of them when he was only eleven, but he found himself wondering if it had been the loss of loved ones that had caused his emotional upset or simply the abrupt vanishing of a kind of security he had taken for granted.

And yet, he felt that the death of General Polan Tallis would leave an empty place in his life.

Colonel VanDeusen was still holding forth.

"... So I told him. I said, 'Look, Lootenant,' I said, 'don't rock the boat. You're a kid yet, you know,' I said. 'You got equal rights with everybody else,' I said, 'but if you rock the boat, you aren't gonna get along so well.'

"'You just behave yourself,' I said, 'and pull your share of the load and do your job right and keep your nose clean, and you'll come out all right.

"'Time I get to be on the General Staff,' I told him, 'why, you'll be takin' over my job, maybe. That's the way it works,' I said.

"He's a good kid. I mean, he's a fresh young punk, that's all. He'll learn, O.K. He'll climb right up, once he's got the right attitude. Why, when I was——"

But MacMaine was no longer listening. It was astonishing to realize that what VanDeusen had said was perfectly true. A blockhead like VanDeusen would simply be lifted to a position of higher authority, only to be replaced by another blockhead. There would be no essential change in the *status quo*.

The Kerothi were winning steadily, and the people of Earth and her colonies were making no changes whatever in their way of living. The majority of people were too blind to be able to see what was happening, and the rest were afraid to admit the danger, even to themselves. It required no great understanding of strategy to see what the inevitable outcome must be.

At some point in the last few centuries, human civilization had taken the wrong path—a path that led only to oblivion.

It was at that moment that Colonel Sebastian MacMaine made his decision.

The Escape

"Are you sure you understand, Tallis?" MacMaine asked in Kerothic.

The alien general nodded emphatically. "Perfectly. Your Kerothic is not so bad that I could misunderstand your instructions. I still don't understand why you are doing this. Oh I know the reasons you've given me, but I don't completely believe them. However, I'll go along with you. The worst that could happen would be for me to be killed, and I would sooner face death in trying to escape than in waiting for your executioners. If this is some sort of trap, some sort of weird way your race's twisted idea of kindness has evolved to dispose of me, then I'll accept your sentence. It's better than starving to death or facing a firing squad."

"Not a firing squad," MacMaine said. "That wouldn't be kind. An odorless, but quite deadly gas would be pumped into this cell while you slept."

"That's worse. When death comes, I want to face it and fight it off as long as possible, not have it sneaking up on me in my sleep. I think I'd rather starve."

"You would," said MacMaine. "The food that was captured with you has nearly run out, and we haven't been able to capture any more. But rather than let you suffer, they would have killed you painlessly." He glanced at the watch on his instrument cuff. "Almost time."

MacMaine looked the alien over once more. Tallis was dressed in the uniform of Earth's Space Force, and the insignia of a full general gleamed on his collar. His face and hands had been sprayed with an opaque, pink-tan film, and his hairless head was covered with a black wig. He wouldn't pass a close inspection, but MacMaine fervently hoped that he wouldn't need to.

Think it out, be sure you're right, then go ahead. Sebastian MacMaine had done just that. For three months, he had worked over the details of his plan, making sure that they were as perfect as he was capable of making them. Even so, there was a great deal of risk involved, and there were too many details that required luck for MacMaine to be perfectly happy about the plan.

But time was running out. As the general's food supply dwindled, his execution date neared, and now it was only two days away. There was no point in waiting until the last minute; it was now or never.

There were no spying TV cameras in the general's cell, no hidden microphones to report and record what went on. No one had ever escaped from the Space Force's prison, therefore, no one ever would.

MacMaine glanced again at his watch. It was time. He reached inside his blouse and took out a fully loaded handgun.

For an instant, the alien officer's eyes widened, and he stiffened as if he were ready to die in an attempt to disarm the Earthman. Then he saw that MacMaine wasn't holding it by the butt; his hand was clasped around the middle of the weapon.

"This is a chance I have to take," MacMaine said evenly. "With this gun, you can shoot me down right here and try to escape alone. I've told you every detail of our course of action, and, with luck, you might make it alone." He held out his hand, with the weapon resting on his open palm.

General Tallis eyed the Earthman for a long second. Then, without haste, he took the gun and inspected it with a professional eye.

"Do you know how to operate it?" MacMaine asked, forcing calmness into his voice.

"Yes. We've captured plenty of them." Tallis thumbed the stud that allowed the magazine to slide out of the butt and into his hand. Then he checked the mechanism and the power cartridges. Finally, he replaced the magazine and put the weapon into the empty sleeve holster that MacMaine had given him.

MacMaine let his breath out slowly. "All right," he said. "Let's go."

He opened the door of the cell, and both men stepped out into the corridor. At the far end of the corridor, some thirty yards away, stood the two armed guards who kept watch over the prisoner. At that distance, it was impossible to tell that Tallis was not what he appeared to be.

The guard had been changed while MacMaine was in the prisoner's cell, and he was relying on the lax discipline of the soldiers to get him and Tallis out of the cell block. With luck, the guards would have failed to listen too closely to what they had been told by the men they replaced; with even greater luck, the previous guardsmen would have failed to be too explicit about who was in the prisoner's cell. With no luck at all, MacMaine would be forced to shoot to kill.

MacMaine walked casually up to the two men, who came to an easy attention.

"I want you two men to come with me. Something odd has happened, and General Quinby and I want two witnesses as to what went on."

"What happened, sir?" one of them asked.

"Don't know for sure," MacMaine said in a puzzled voice. "The general and I were talking to the prisoner, when all of a sudden he fell over. I think he's dead. I couldn't find a heartbeat. I want you to take a look at him so that you can testify that we didn't shoot him or anything."

Obediently, the two guards headed for the cell, and MacMaine fell in behind them. "You couldn't of shot him, sir," said the second guard confidently. "We would of heard the shot."

"Besides," said the other, "it don't matter much. He was going to be gassed day after tomorrow."

As the trio approached the cell, Tallis pulled the door open a little wider and, in doing so, contrived to put himself behind it so that his face couldn't be seen. The young guards weren't too awed by a full general; after all, they'd be generals themselves someday. They were much more interested in seeing the dead alien.

As the guards reached the cell door, MacMaine unholstered his pistol from his sleeve and brought it down hard on the head of the nearest youth. At the same time, Tallis stepped from behind the door and clouted the other.

Quickly, MacMaine disarmed the fallen men and dragged them into the open cell. He came out again and locked the door securely. Their guns were tossed into an empty cell nearby.

"They won't be missed until the next change of watch, in four hours," MacMaine said. "By then, it won't matter, one way or another."

Getting out of the huge building that housed the administrative offices of the Space Force was relatively easy. A lift chute brought the pair to the main floor, and, this late in the evening, there weren't many people on that floor. The officers and men who had night duty were working on the upper floors. Several times, Tallis had to take a handkerchief from his pocket and pretend to blow his nose in order to conceal his alien features from someone who came too close, but no one appeared to notice anything out of the ordinary.

As they walked out boldly through the main door, fifteen minutes later, the guards merely came to attention and relaxed as a tall colonel and a somewhat shorter general strode out. The general appeared to be having a fit of sneezing, and the colonel was heard to say: "That's quite a cold you've picked up, sir. Better get over to the dispensary and take an anti-coryza shot."

"Mmmf," said the general. "*Ha-CHOO!*"

Getting to the spaceport was no problem at all. MacMaine had an official car waiting, and the two sergeants in the front seat didn't pay any attention to the general getting in the back seat because Colonel MacMaine was talking to them. "We're ready to roll, sergeant," he said to the driver. "General Quinby wants to go straight to the *Manila*, so let's get there as fast as possible. Take-off is scheduled in ten minutes." Then he got into the back seat himself. The one-way glass partition that separated the back seat from the front prevented either of the two men from looking back at their passengers.

Seven minutes later, the staff car was rolling unquestioned through the main gate of Waikiki Spaceport.

It was all so incredibly easy, MacMaine thought. Nobody questioned an official car. Nobody checked anything too closely. Nobody wanted to risk his lifelong security by doing or saying something that might be considered antisocial by a busy general. Besides, it never entered anyone's mind that there could be anything wrong. If there was a war on, apparently no one had been told about it yet.

MacMaine thought, *Was I ever that stubbornly blind? Not quite, I guess, or I'd never have seen what is happening.* But he knew he hadn't been too much more perceptive than those around him. Even to an intelligent man, the mask of stupidity can become a barrier to the outside world as well as a concealment from it.

The Interstellar Ship *Manila* was a small, fast, ten-man blaster-boat, designed to get in to the thick of a battle quickly, strike hard, and get away. Unlike the bigger, more powerful battle cruisers, she could be landed directly on any planet with less than a two-gee pull at the surface. The really big babies had to be parked in an orbit and loaded by shuttle; they'd break up of their own weight if they tried to set down on anything bigger than a good-sized planetoid. As long as their antiacceleration fields were on, they could take unimaginable thrusts along their axes, but the A-A fields were the cause of those thrusts as well as the protection against them. The ships couldn't stand still while they were operating, so they were no protection at all against a planet's gravity. But a blaster-boat was small enough and compact enough to take the strain.

It had taken careful preparation to get the *Manila* ready to go just exactly when MacMaine needed it. Papers had to be forged and put into the chain of command communication at precisely the right times; others had had to be taken out and replaced with harmless near-duplicates so that the Commanding Staff wouldn't discover the deception. He had had to build up the fictional identity of a "General Lucius Quinby" in such a way that it would take a thorough check to discover that the officer who had been put in command of the *Manila* was nonexistent.

It was two minutes until take-off time when the staff car pulled up at the foot of the ramp that led up to the main air lock of the ISS *Manila*. A young-looking captain was standing nervously at the foot of it, obviously afraid that his new commander might be late for the take-off and wondering what sort of decision he would have to make if the general wasn't there at take-off time. MacMaine could imagine his feelings.

"General Quinby" developed another sneezing fit as he stepped out of the car. This was the touchiest part of MacMaine's plan, the weakest link in the whole chain of action. For a space of perhaps a minute, the disguised Kerothi general would have to stand so close to the young captain that the crudity of his makeup job would be detectable. He had to keep that handkerchief over his face, and yet do it in such a way that it would seem natural.

As Tallis climbed out of the car, chuffing windily into the kerchief, MacMaine snapped an order to the sergeant behind the wheel. "That's all. We're taking off almost immediately, so get that car out of here."

Then he walked rapidly over to the captain, who had snapped to attention. There was a definite look of relief on his face, now that he knew his commander was on time.

"All ready for take-off, captain? Everything checked out? Ammunition? Energy packs all filled to capacity? All the crew aboard? Full rations and stores stowed away?"

The captain kept his eyes on MacMaine's face as he answered "Yes, sir; yes, sir; yes, sir," to the rapid fire of questions. He had no time to shift his gaze to the face of his new C.O., who was snuffling his way toward the foot of the landing ramp. MacMaine kept firing questions until Tallis was halfway up the ramp.

Then he said: "Oh, by the way, captain—was the large package containing General Quinby's personal gear brought aboard?"

"The big package? Yes, sir. About fifteen minutes ago."

"Good," said MacMaine. He looked up the ramp. "Are there any special orders at this time, sir?" he asked.

"No," said Tallis, without turning. "Carry on, colonel." He went on up to the air lock. It had taken Tallis hours of practice to say that phrase properly, but the training had been worth it.

After Tallis was well inside the air lock, MacMaine whispered to the young captain, "As you can see, the general has got a rather bad cold. He'll want to remain in his cabin until he's over it. See that anti-coryza shots are sent up from the dispensary as soon as we are out of the Solar System. Now, let's go; we have less than a minute till take-off."

MacMaine went up the ramp with the captain scrambling up behind him.

Tallis was just stepping into the commander's cabin as the two men entered the air lock. MacMaine didn't see him again until the ship was twelve minutes on her way—nearly five billion miles from Earth and still accelerating.

He identified himself at the door and Tallis opened it cautiously.

"I brought your anti-coryza shot, sir," he said. In a small ship like the *Manila*, the captain and the seven crew members could hear any conversation in the companionways. He stepped inside and closed the door. Then he practically collapsed on the nearest chair and had a good case of the shakes.

"So-so f-f-far, s-so good," he said.

General Tallis grasped his shoulder with a firm hand. "Brace up, Sepastian," he said gently in Kerothic. "You've done a beautiful job. I still can't believe it, but I'll have to admit that if this is an act it's a beautiful one." He gestured toward the small desk in one corner of the room and the big package that was sitting on it. "The food is all there. I'll have to eat sparingly, but I can make it. Now, what's the rest of the plan?"

MacMaine took a deep breath, held it, and let it out slowly. His shakes subsided to a faint, almost imperceptible quiver. "The captain doesn't know our destination. He was told that he would receive secret instructions from you." His voice, he noticed thankfully, was almost normal. He reached into his uniform jacket and took out an official-looking sealed envelope. "These are the orders. We are going out to arrange a special truce with the Kerothi."

"*What?*"

"That's what it says here. You'll have to get on the subradio and do some plain and fancy talking. Fortunately, not a man jack aboard this ship knows a word of your language, so they'll think you're arranging truce terms.

"They'll be sitting ducks when your warship pulls up alongside and sends in a boarding party. By the time they realize what has happened, it will be too late."

"You're giving us the ship, too?" Tallis looked at him wonderingly. "And eight prisoners?"

"Nine," said MacMaine. "I'll hand over my sidearm to you just before your men come through the air lock."

General Tallis sat down in the other small chair, his eyes still on the Earthman. "I can't help but feel that this is some sort of trick, but if it is, I can't see through it. Why are you doing this, Sepastian?"

"You may not understand this, Tallis," MacMaine said evenly, "but I am fighting for freedom. The freedom to think."

The Traitor

Convincing the Kerothi that he was in earnest was more difficult than MacMaine had at first supposed. He had done his best, and now, after nearly a year of captivity, Tallis had come to tell him that his offer had been accepted.

General Tallis sat across from Colonel MacMaine, smoking his cigarette absently.

"Just why are they accepting my proposition?" MacMaine asked bluntly.

"Because they can afford to," Tallis said with a smile. "You will be watched, my sibling-by-choice. Watched every moment, for any sign of treason. Your flagship will be a small ten-man blaster-boat—one of our own. You gave us one; we'll give you one. At the worst, we will come out even. At the best, your admittedly brilliant grasp of tactics and strategy will enable us to save thousands of Kerothi lives, to say nothing of the immense savings in time and money."

"All I ask is a chance to prove my ability and my loyalty."

"You've already proven your ability. All of the strategy problems that you have been given over the past year were actual battles that had already been fought. In eighty-seven per cent of the cases, your strategy proved to be superior to our own. In most of the others, it was just as good. In only three cases was the estimate of your losses higher than the actual losses. Actually, we'd be fools to turn you down. We have everything to gain and nothing to lose."

"I felt the same way a year ago," said MacMaine. "Even being watched all the time will allow me more freedom than I had on Earth—if the Board of Strategy is willing to meet my terms."

Tallis chuckled. "They are. You'll be the best-paid officer in the entire fleet; none of the rest of us gets a tenth of what you'll be getting, as far as personal value is concerned. And yet, it costs us practically nothing. You drive an attractive bargain, Sepastian."

"Is that the kind of pay you'd like to get, Tallis?" MacMaine asked with a smile.

"Why not? You'll get your terms: full pay as a Kerothi general, with retirement on full pay after the war is over. The pick of the most beautiful—by your standards—of the Earthwomen we capture. A home on Keroth, built to your specifications, and full citizenship, including the freedom to enter into any business relationships you wish. If you keep your promises, we can keep ours and still come out ahead."

"Good. When do we start?"

"Now," said Tallis rising from his chair. "Put on your dress uniform, and we'll go down to see the High Commander. We've got to give you a set of general's insignia, my sibling-by-choice."

Tallis waited while MacMaine donned the blue trousers and gold-trimmed red uniform of a Kerothi officer. When he was through, MacMaine looked at himself in the mirror. "There's one more thing, Tallis," he said thoughtfully.

"What's that?"

"This hair. I think you'd better arrange to have it permanently removed, according to your custom. I can't do anything about the color of my skin, but there's no point in my looking like one of your wild hillmen."

"You're very gracious," Tallis said. "And very wise. Our officers will certainly come closer to feeling that you are one of us."

"I am one of you from this moment," MacMaine said. "I never intend to see Earth again, except, perhaps, from space—when we fight the final battle of the war."

"That may be a hard battle," Tallis said.

"Maybe," MacMaine said thoughtfully. "On the other hand, if my overall strategy comes out the way I think it will, that battle may never be fought at all. I think that complete and total surrender will end the war before we ever get that close to Earth."

"I hope you're right," Tallis said firmly. "This war is costing far more than we had anticipated, in spite of the weakness of your—that is, of Earth."

"Well," MacMaine said with a slight grin, "at least you've been able to capture enough Earth food to keep me eating well all this time."

Tallis' grin was broad. "You're right. We're not doing too badly at that. Now, let's go; the High Commander is waiting."

MacMaine didn't realize until he walked into the big room that what he was facing was not just a discussion with a high officer, but what amounted to a Court of Inquiry.

The High Commander, a dome-headed, wrinkled, yellow-skinned, hard-eyed old Kerothi, was seated in the center of a long, high desk, flanked on either side by two lower-ranking generals who had the same deadly, hard look. Off to one side, almost like a jury in a jury box, sat twenty or so lesser officers, none of them ranking below the Kerothi equivalent of lieutenant-colonel.

As far as MacMaine could tell, none of the officers wore the insignia of fleet officers, the spaceship-and-comet that showed that the wearer was a fighting man. These were the men of the Permanent Headquarters Staff—the military group that controlled, not only the armed forces of Keroth, but the civil government as well.

"What's this?" MacMaine hissed in a whispered aside, in English.

"Pearr up, my prrotherr," Tallis answered softly, in the same tongue, "all is well."

MacMaine had known, long before he had ever heard of General Polan Tallis, that the Hegemony of Keroth was governed by a military junta, and that all Kerothi were regarded as members of the armed forces. Technically, there were no civilians; they were legally members of the "unorganized reserve," and were under military law. He had known that Kerothi society was, in its own way, as much a slave society as that of Earth, but it had the advantage over Earth in that the system did allow for advance by merit. If a man had the determination to get ahead, and the ability to cut the throat—either literally or figuratively—of the man above him in rank, he could take his place.

On a more strictly legal basis, it was possible for a common trooper to become an officer by going through the schools set up for that purpose, but, in practice, it took both pull and pressure to get into those schools.

In theory, any citizen of the Hegemony could become an officer, and any officer could become a member of the Permanent Headquarters Staff. Actually, a much greater preference was given to the children of officers. Examinations were given periodically for the purpose of recruiting new members for the elite officers' corps, and any citizen could take the examination—once.

But the tests were heavily weighted in favor of those who were already well-versed in matters military, including what might be called the "inside jokes" of the officers' corps. A common trooper had some chance of passing the examination; a civilian had a very minute chance. A noncommissioned officer had the best chance of passing the examination, but there were age limits which usually kept NCO's from getting a commission. By the time a man became a noncommissioned officer, he was too old to be admitted to the officers training schools. There were allowances made for "extraordinary merit," which allowed common troopers or upper-grade NCO's to be commissioned in spite of the general rules, and an astute man could take advantage of those allowances.

Ability could get a man up the ladder, but it had to be a particular kind of ability.

During his sojourn as a "guest" of the Kerothi, MacMaine had made a point of exploring the history of the race. He knew perfectly well that the histories he had read were doctored, twisted, and, in general, totally unreliable in so far as presenting anything that would be called a history by an unbiased investigator.

But, knowing this, MacMaine had been able to learn a great deal about the present society. Even if the "history" was worthless as such, it did tell something about the attitudes of a society that would make up such a history. And, too, he felt that, in general, the main events which had been catalogued actually occurred; the details had been blurred, and the attitudes of the people had been misrepresented, but the skeleton was essentially factual.

MacMaine felt that he knew what kind of philosophy had produced the mental attitudes of the Court he now faced, and he felt he knew how to handle himself before them.

Half a dozen paces in front of the great desk, the color of the floor tiling was different from that of the rest of the floor. Instead of a solid blue, it was a dead black. Tallis, who was slightly ahead of MacMaine, came to a halt as his toes touched the edge of the black area.

Uh-oh! a balk line, MacMaine thought. He stopped sharply at the same point. Both of them just stood there for a full minute while they were carefully inspected by the members of the Court.

Then the High Commander gestured with one hand, and the officer to his left leaned forward and said: "Why is this one brought before us in the uniform of an officer, bare of any insignia of rank?"

It could only be a ritual question, MacMaine decided; they must know why he was there.

"I bring him as a candidate for admission to our Ingroup," Tallis replied formally, "and ask the indulgence of Your Superiorities therefor."

"And who are you who ask our indulgence?"

Tallis identified himself at length—name, rank, serial number, military record, et cetera, et cetera, et cetera.

By the time he had finished, MacMaine was beginning to think that the recitation would go on forever. The High Commander had closed his eyes, and he looked as if he had gone to sleep.

There was more formality. Through it all, MacMaine stood at rigid attention, flexing his calf muscles occasionally to keep the blood flowing in his legs. He had no desire to disgrace himself by passing out in front of the Court.

Finally the Kerothi officer stopped asking Tallis questions and looked at the High Commander. MacMaine got the feeling that there was about to be a departure from the usual procedure.

Without opening his eyes, the High Commander said, in a brittle, rather harsh voice, "These circumstances are unprecedented." Then he opened his eyes and looked directly at MacMaine. "Never has an animal been proposed for such an honor. In times past, such a proposal would have been mockery of this Court and this Ingroup, and a crime of such monstrous proportions as to merit Excommunication."

MacMaine knew what that meant. The word was used literally; the condemned one was cut off from all communication by having his sensory nerves surgically severed. Madness followed quickly; psychosomatic death followed eventually, as the brain, cut off from any outside stimuli except those which could not be eliminated without death following instantly, finally became incapable of keeping the body alive. Without feedback, control was impossible, and the organism-as-a-whole slowly deteriorated until death was inevitable.

At first, the victim screamed and thrashed his limbs as the brain sent out message after message to the rest of the body, but since the brain had no way of knowing whether the messages had been received or acted upon, the victim soon went into a state comparable to that of catatonia and finally died.

If it was not the ultimate in punishment, it was a damned close approach, MacMaine thought. And he felt that the word "damned" could be used in that sense without fear of exaggeration.

"However," the High Commander went on, gazing at the ceiling, "circumstances change. It would once have been thought vile that a machine should be allowed to do the work of a skilled man, and the thought that a machine might do the work with more precision and greater rapidity would have been almost blasphemous.

"This case must be viewed in the same light. As we are replacing certain of our workers on our outer planets with Earth animals simply because they are capable of doing the work more cheaply, so we must recognize that the same interests of economy govern in this case.

"A computing animal, in that sense, is in the same class as a computing machine. It would be folly to waste their abilities simply because they are not human.

"There also arises the question of command. It has been represented to this court, by certain officers who have been active in investigating the candidate animal, that it would be as degrading to ask a human officer to take orders from an animal as it would be to ask him to take orders from a commoner of the Unorganized Reserve, if not more so. And, I must admit, there is, on the surface of it, some basis for this reasoning.

"But, again, we must not let ourselves be misled. Does not a spaceship pilot, in a sense, take orders from the computer that gives him his orbits and courses? In fact, do not all computers give orders, in one way or another, to those who use them?

"Why, then, should we refuse to take orders from a computing animal?"

He paused and appeared to listen to the silence in the room before going on.

"Stand at ease until the High Commander looks at you again," Tallis said in a low aside.

This was definitely the pause for adjusting to surprise.

It seemed interminable, though it couldn't have been longer than a minute later that the High Commander dropped his gaze from the ceiling to MacMaine. When MacMaine snapped to attention again, the others in the room became suddenly silent.

"We feel," the hard-faced old Kerothi continued, as if there had been no break, "that, in this case, we are justified in employing the animal in question.

"However, we must make certain exceptions to our normal procedure. The candidate is not a machine, and therefore cannot be treated as a machine. Neither is it human, and therefore cannot be treated as human.

"Therefore, this is the judgment of the Court of the Ingroup:

"The animal, having shown itself to be capable of behaving, in some degree, as befits an officer—including, as we have been informed, voluntarily conforming to our custom as regards superfluous hair—it shall henceforth be considered as having the same status as an untaught child or a barbarian, insofar as social conventions are concerned, and shall be entitled to the use of the human pronoun, he.

"Further, he shall be entitled to wear the uniform he now wears, and the insignia of a General of the Fleet. He shall be entitled, as far as personal contact goes, to the privileges of that rank, and shall be addressed as such.

"He will be accorded the right of punishment of an officer of that rank, insofar as disciplining his inferiors is concerned, except that he must first secure the concurrence of his Guardian Officer, as hereinafter provided.

"He shall also be subject to punishment in the same way and for the same offenses as humans of his rank, taking into account physiological differences, except as hereinafter provided.

"His reward for proper service"—The High Commander listed the demands MacMaine had made—"are deemed fitting, and shall be paid, provided his duties in service are carried out as proposed.

"Obviously, however, certain restrictions must be made. General MacMaine, as he is entitled to be called, is employed solely as a Strategy Computer. His ability as such and his knowledge of the psychology of the Earth animals are, as far as we are concerned at this moment, his only useful attributes. Therefore, his command is restricted to that function. He is empowered to act only through the other officers of the Fleet as this Court may appoint; he is not to command directly.

"Further, it is ordered that he shall have a Guardian Officer, who shall accompany him at all times and shall be directly responsible for his actions.

"That officer shall be punished for any deliberate crime committed by the aforesaid General MacMaine as if he had himself committed the crime.

"Until such time as this Court may appoint another officer for the purpose, General Polan Tallis, previously identified in these proceedings, is appointed as Guardian Officer."

The High Commander paused for a moment, then he said: "Proceed with the investment of the insignia."

The Strategy

General Sebastian MacMaine, sometime Colonel of Earth's Space Force, and presently a General of the Kerothi Fleet, looked at the array of stars that appeared to drift by the main viewplate of his flagship, the blaster-boat *Shudos*.

Behind him, General Tallis was saying, "You've done well, Sepastian. Better than anyone could have really expected. Three battles so far, and every one of them won by a margin far greater than anticipated. Any ideas that anyone may have had that you were not wholly working for the Kerothi cause has certainly been dispelled."

"Thanks, Tallis." MacMaine turned to look at the Kerothi officer. "I only hope that I can keep it up. Now that we're ready for the big push, I can't help but wonder what would happen if I were to lose a battle."

"Frankly," Tallis said, "that would depend on several things, the main one being whether or not it appeared that you had deliberately thrown the advantage to the enemy. But nobody expects you, or anyone else, to win every time. Even the most brilliant commander can make an honest mistake, and if it can be shown that it *was* an honest mistake, and one, furthermore, that he could not have been expected to avoid, he wouldn't be punished for it. In your case, I'll admit that the investigation would be a great deal more thorough than normal, and that you wouldn't get as much of the benefit of the doubt as another officer might, but unless there is a deliberate error I doubt that anything serious would happen."

"Do you really believe that, Tallis, or is it just wishful thinking on your part, knowing as you do that your punishment will be the same as mine if I fail?" MacMaine asked flatly.

Tallis didn't hesitate. "If I didn't believe it, I would ask to be relieved as your Guardian. And the moment I did that, you would be removed from command. The moment I feel that you are not acting for the best interests of Keroth, I will act—not only to protect myself, but to protect my people."

"That's fair enough," MacMaine said. "But how about the others?"

"I cannot speak for my fellow officers—only for myself." Then Tallis' voice became cold. "Just keep your hands clean, Sepastian, and all will be well. You will not be punished for mistakes—only for crimes. If you are planning no crimes, this worry of yours is needless."

"I ceased to worry about myself long ago," MacMaine said coolly. "I do not fear personal death, not even by Excommunication. My sole worry is about the ultimate outcome of the war if I should fail. That, and nothing more."

"I believe you," Tallis said. "Let us say no more about it. Your actions are difficult for us to understand, in some ways, that's all. No Kerothi would ever change his allegiance as you have. Nor has any Earth officer that we have captured shown any desire to do so. Oh, some of them have agreed to do almost anything we wanted them to, but these were not the intelligent ones, and even they were only doing it to save their own miserable hides.

"Still, you are an exceptional man, Sepastian, unlike any other of your race, as far as we know. Perhaps it is simply that you are the only one with enough wisdom to seek your intellectual equals rather than remain loyal to a mass of stupid animals who are fit only to be slaves."

"It was because I foresaw their eventual enslavement that I acted as I did," MacMaine admitted. "As I saw it, I had only two choices—to remain as I was and become a slave to the Kerothi or to put myself in your hands willingly and hope for the best. As you——"

He was interrupted by a harsh voice from a nearby speaker.

"*Battle stations! Battle stations! Enemy fleet in detector range! Contact in twelve minutes!*"

Tallis and MacMaine headed for the Command Room at a fast trot. The three other Kerothi who made up the Strategy Staff came in at almost the same time. There was a flurry of activity as the computers and viewers were readied for action, then the Kerothi looked expectantly at the Earthman.

MacMaine looked at the detector screens. The deployment of the approaching Earth fleet was almost as he had expected it would be. There were slight differences, but they would require only minor changes in the strategy he had mapped out from the information brought in by the Kerothi scout ships.

Undoubtedly, the Kerothi position had been relayed to the Earth commander by their own advance scouts buzzing about in tiny, one-man shells just small enough to be undetectable at normal range.

Watching the positions on the screens carefully, MacMaine called out a series of numbers in an unhurried voice and watched as the orders, relayed by the Kerothi staff, changed the position of parts of the Kerothi fleet. Then, as the computer-led Earth fleet jockeyed to compensate for the change in the Kerothi deployment, MacMaine called out more orders.

The High Commander of Keroth had called MacMaine a "computing animal," but the term was far from accurate. MacMaine couldn't possibly have computed all the variables in that battle, and he didn't try. It was a matter of human intuition against mechanical logic. The advantage lay with MacMaine, for, while the computer could not logically fathom the intuitive processes of its human opponent, MacMaine could and did have an intuitive grasp of the machine's logic. MacMaine didn't need to know every variable in the pattern; he only needed to know the pattern as a whole.

The *Shudos* was well in the rear of the main body of the Kerothi fleet. There was every necessity for keeping MacMaine's flagship out of as much of the fighting as possible.

When the first contact was made, MacMaine was certain of the outcome. His voice became a steady drone as he called out instructions to the staff officers; his mind was so fully occupied with the moving pattern before him that he noticed nothing else in the room around him.

Spaceship against spaceship, the two fleets locked in battle. The warheads of ultralight torpedoes flared their eye-searing explosions soundlessly into the void; ships exploded like overcharged beer bottles as blaster energy caught them and smashed through their screens; men and machines flamed and died, scattering the stripped nuclei of their component atoms through the screaming silence of space.

And through it all, Sebastian MacMaine watched dispassionately, calling out his orders as ten Earthmen died for every Kerothi death.

This was a crucial battle. The big push toward the center of Earth's cluster of worlds had begun. Until now, the Kerothi had been fighting the outposts, the planets on the fringes of Earth's sphere of influence which were only lightly colonized, and therefore relatively easy to take. Earth's strongest fleets were out there, to protect planets that could not protect themselves.

Inside that periphery were the more densely populated planets, the self-sufficient colonies which were more or less able to defend themselves without too much reliance on space fleets as such. But now that the backbone of the Earth's Space Force had been all but broken, it would be a relatively easy matter to mop up planet after planet, since each one could be surrounded separately, pounded into surrender, and secured before going on to the next. That, at least, had been the original Kerothi intention. But MacMaine had told them that there was another way—a way which, if it succeeded, would save time, lives, and money for the Kerothi. And, if it failed, MacMaine said, they would be no worse off, they would simply have to resume the original plan.

Now, the first of the big colony planets was to be taken. When the protecting Earth fleet was reduced to tatters, the Kerothi would go on to Houston's World as the first step in the big push toward Earth itself.

But MacMaine wasn't thinking of that phase of the war. That was still in the future, while the hellish space battle was still at hand.

He lost track of time as he watched the Kerothi fleet take advantage of their superior tactical position and tear the Earth fleet to bits. Not until he saw the remains of the Earth fleet turn tail and run did he realize that the battle had been won.

The Kerothi fleet consolidated itself. There was no point in pursuing the fleeting Earth ships; that would only break up the solidity of the Kerothi deployment. The losers could afford to scatter; the winners could not. Early in the war, the Kerothi had used that trick against Earth; the Kerothi had broken and fled, and the Earth fleet had split up to chase them down. The scattered Earth ships had suddenly found that they had been led into traps composed of hidden clusters of Kerothi ships. Naturally, the trick had never worked again for either side.

"All right," MacMaine said when it was all over, "let's get on to Houston's World."

The staff men, including Tallis, were already on their feet, congratulating MacMaine and shaking his hands. Even General Hokotan, the Headquarters Staff man, who had been transferred temporarily to the Fleet Force to keep an eye on both MacMaine and Tallis, was enthusiastically pounding MacMaine's shoulder.

No one aboard was supposed to know that Hokotan was a Headquarters officer, but MacMaine had spotted the spy rather easily. There was a difference between the fighters of the Fleet and the politicoes of Headquarters. The politicoes were no harder, perhaps, nor more ruthless, than the fighters, but they were of a different breed. Theirs was the ruthlessness of the bully who steps on those who are weaker rather than the ruthlessness of the man who kills only to win a battle. MacMaine had the feeling that the Headquarters Staff preferred to spend their time browbeating their underlings rather than risk their necks with someone who could fight back, however weakly.

General Hokotan seemed to have more of the fighting quality than most HQ men, but he wasn't a Fleet Officer at heart. He couldn't be compared to Tallis without looking small and mean.

As a matter of cold fact, very few of the officers were in anyway comparable to Tallis—not even the Fleet men. The more MacMaine learned of the Kerothi, the more he realized just how lucky he had been that it had been Tallis, and not some other Kerothi general, who had been captured by the Earth forces. He was not at all sure that his plan would have worked at all with any of the other officers he had met.

Tallis, like MacMaine, was an unusual specimen of his race.

MacMaine took the congratulations of the Kerothi officers with a look of pleasure on his face, and when they had subsided somewhat, he grinned and said:

"Let's get a little work done around here, shall we? We have a planet to reduce yet."

They laughed. Reducing a planet didn't require strategy—only fire-power. The planet-based defenses couldn't maneuver, but the energy reserve of a planet is greater than that of any fleet, no matter how large. Each defense point would have to be cut down individually by the massed power of the fleet, cut down one by one until the planet was helpless. The planet as a whole might have more energy reserve than the fleet, but no individual defense point did. The problem was to avoid being hit by the rest of the defense points while one single point was bearing the brunt of the fleet's attack. It wasn't without danger, but it could be done.

And for a job like that, MacMaine's special abilities weren't needed. He could only watch and wait until it was over.

So he watched and waited. Unlike the short-time fury of a space battle, the reduction of a planet took days of steady pounding. When it was over, the blaster-boats of the Kerothi fleet and the shuttles from the great battle cruisers landed on Houston's World and took possession of the planet.

MacMaine was waiting in his cabin when General Hokotan brought the news that the planet was secured.

"They are ours," the HQ spy said with a superior smile. "The sniveling animals didn't even seem to want to defend themselves. They don't even know how to fight a hand-to-hand battle. How could such things have ever evolved intelligence enough to conquer space?" Hokotan enjoyed making such remarks to MacMaine's face, knowing that since MacMaine was technically a Kerothi he couldn't show any emotion when the enemy was insulted.

MacMaine showed none. "Got them all, eh?" he said.

"All but a few who scattered into the hills and forests. But not many of them had the guts to leave the security of their cities, even though we were occupying them."

"How many are left alive?"

"An estimated hundred and fifty million, more or less."

"Good. That should be enough to set an example. I picked Houston's World because we can withdraw from it without weakening our position; its position in space is such that it would constitute no menace to us even if we never reduced it. That way, we can be sure that our little message is received on Earth."

Hokotan's grin was wolfish. "And the whole weak-hearted race will shake with fear, eh?"

"Exactly. Tallis can speak English well enough to be understood. Have him make the announcement to them. He can word it however he likes, but the essence is to be this: Houston's World resisted the occupation by Kerothi troops; an example must be made of them to show them what happens to Earthmen who resist."

"That's all?"

"That's enough. Oh, by the way, make sure that there are plenty of their cargo spaceships in good working order; I doubt that we've ruined them all, but if we have, repair some of them.

"And, too, you'd better make sure that you allow some of the merchant spacemen to 'escape,' just in case there are no space pilots among those who took to the hills. We want to make sure that someone can use those ships to take the news back to Earth."

"And the rest?" Hokotan asked, with an expectant look. He knew what was to be done, but he wanted to hear MacMaine say it again.

MacMaine obliged.

"Hang them. Every man, every woman, every child. I want them to be decorating every lamppost and roof-beam on the planet, dangling like overripe fruit when the Earth forces return."

The Results

"I don't understand it," said General Polan Tallis worriedly. "Where are they coming from? How are they doing it? What's happened?"

MacMaine and the four Kerothi officers were sitting in the small dining room that doubled as a recreation room between meals. The nervous strain of the past few months was beginning to tell on all of them.

"Six months ago," Tallis continued jerkily, "we had them beaten. One planet after another was reduced in turn. Then, out of nowhere, comes a fleet of ships we didn't even know existed, and they've smashed us at every turn."

"If they *are* ships," said Loopat, the youngest officer of the *Shudos* staff. "Who ever heard of a battleship that was undetectable at a distance of less than half a million miles? It's impossible!"

"Then we're being torn to pieces by the impossible!" Hokotan snapped. "Before we even know they are anywhere around, they are blasting us with everything they've got! Not even the strategic genius of General MacMaine can help us if we have no time to plot strategy!"

The Kerothi had been avoiding MacMaine's eyes, but now, at the mention of his name, they all looked at him as if their collective gaze had been drawn to him by some unknown attractive force.

"It's like fighting ghosts," MacMaine said in a hushed voice. For the first time, he felt a feeling of awe that was almost akin to fear. What had he done?

In another sense, that same question was in the mind of the Kerothi.

"Have you any notion at all what they are doing or how they are doing it?" asked Tallis gently.

"None," MacMaine answered truthfully. "None at all, I swear to you."

"They don't even behave like Earthmen," said the fourth Kerothi, a thick-necked officer named Ossif. "They not only outfight us, they outthink us at every turn. Is it possible, General MacMaine, that the Earthmen have allies of another race, a race of intelligent beings that we don't know of?" He left unsaid the added implication: "*And that you have neglected to tell us about?*"

"Again," said MacMaine, "I swear to you that I know nothing of any third intelligent race in the galaxy."

"If there were such allies," Tallis said, "isn't it odd that they should wait so long to aid their friends?"

"No odder than that the Earthmen should suddenly develop superweapons that we cannot understand, much less fight against," Hokotan said, with a touch of anger.

"Not 'superweapons'," MacMaine corrected almost absently. "All they have is a method of making their biggest ships indetectable until they're so close that it doesn't matter. When they do register on our detectors, it's too late. But the weapons they strike with are the same type as they've always used, I believe."

"All right, then," Hokotan said, his voice showing more anger. "One weapon or whatever you want to call it. Practical invisibility. But that's enough. An invisible man with a knife is more deadly than a dozen ordinary men with modern armament. Are you sure you know nothing of this, General MacMaine?"

Before MacMaine could answer, Tallis said, "Don't be ridiculous, Hokotan! If he had known that such a weapon existed, would he have been fool enough to leave his people? With that secret, they stand a good chance of beating us in less than half the time it took us to wipe out their fleet—or, rather, to wipe out as much of it as we did."

"They got a new fleet somewhere," said young Loopat, almost to himself.

Tallis ignored him. "If MacMaine deserted his former allegiance, knowing that they had a method of rendering the action of a space drive indetectable, then he was and is a blithering idiot. And we know he isn't."

"All right, all right! I concede that," snapped Hokotan. "He knows nothing. I don't say that I fully trust him, even now, but I'll admit that I cannot see how he is to blame for the reversals of the past few months.

"If the Earthmen had somehow been informed of our activities, or if we had invented a superweapon and they found out about it, I would be inclined to put the blame squarely on MacMaine. But——"

"How would he get such information out?" Tallis cut in sharply. "He has been watched every minute of every day. We know he couldn't send any information to Earth. How could he?"

"Telepathy, for all I know!" Hokotan retorted. "But that's beside the point! I don't trust him any farther than I can see him, and not completely, even then. But I concede that there is no possible connection between this new menace and anything MacMaine might have done.

"This is no time to worry about that sort of thing; we've got to find some way of getting our hands on one of those ghost ships!"

"I do suggest," put in the thick-necked Ossif, "that we keep a closer watch on General MacMaine. Now that the Earth animals are making a comeback, he might decide to turn his coat now, even if he has been innocent of any acts against Keroth so far."

Hokotan's laugh was a short, hard bark. "Oh, we'll watch him, all right, Ossif. But, as Tallis has pointed out, MacMaine is not a fool, and he would certainly be a fool to return to Earth if his leaving it was a genuine act of desertion. The last planet we captured, before this invisibility thing came up to stop us, was plastered all over with notices that the Earth fleet was concentrating on the capture of the arch-traitor MacMaine.

"The price on his head, as a corpse, is enough to allow an Earthman to retire in luxury for life. The man who brings him back alive gets ten times that amount.

"Of course, it's possible that the whole thing is a put-up job—a smoke screen for our benefit. That's why we must and will keep a closer watch. But only a few of the Earth's higher-up would know that it was a smoke screen; the rest believe it, whether it is true or not. MacMaine would have to be very careful not to let the wrong people get their hands on him if he returned."

"It's no smoke screen," MacMaine said in a matter-of-fact tone. "I assure you that I have no intention of returning to Earth. If Keroth loses this war, then I will die—either fighting for the Kerothi or by execution at the hands of Earthmen if I am captured. Or," he added musingly, "perhaps even at the hands of the Kerothi, if someone decides that a scapegoat is needed to atone for the loss of the war."

"If you are guilty of treason," Hokotan barked, "you will die as a traitor! If you are not, there is no need for your death. The Kerothi do not need scapegoats!"

"Talk, talk, talk!" Tallis said with a sudden bellow. "We have agreed that MacMaine has done nothing that could even remotely be regarded as suspicious! He has fought hard and loyally; he has been more ruthless than any of us in destroying the enemy. Very well, we will guard him more closely. We can put him in irons if that's necessary.

"But let's quit yapping and start thinking! We've been acting like frightened children, not knowing what it is we fear, and venting our fear-caused anger on the most handy target!

"Let's act like men—not like children!"

After a moment, Hokotan said: "I agree." His voice was firm, but calm. "Our job will be to get our hands on one of those new Earth ships. Anyone have any suggestions?"

They had all kinds of suggestions, one after another. The detectors, however, worked because they detected the distortion of space which was as necessary for the drive of a ship as the distortion of air was necessary for the movement of a propeller-driven aircraft. None of them could see how a ship could avoid making that distortion, and none of them could figure out how to go about capturing a ship that no one could even detect until it was too late to set a trap.

The discussion went on for days. And it was continued the next day and the next. And the days dragged out into weeks.

Communications with Keroth broke down. The Fleet-to-Headquarters courier ships, small in size, without armament, and practically solidly packed with drive mechanism, could presumably outrun anything but another unarmed courier. An armed ship of the same size would have to use some of the space for her weapons, which meant that the drive would have to be smaller; if the drive remained the same size, then the armament would make the ship larger. In either case, the speed would be cut down. A smaller ship might outrun a standard courier, but if they got much smaller, there wouldn't be room inside for the pilot.

Nonetheless, courier after courier never arrived at its destination.

And the Kerothi Fleet was being decimated by the hit-and-run tactics of the Earth's ghost ships. And Earth never lost a ship; by the time the Kerothi ships knew their enemy was in the vicinity, the enemy had hit and vanished again. The Kerothi never had a chance to ready their weapons.

In the long run, they never had a chance at all.

MacMaine waited with almost fatalistic complacence for the inevitable to happen. When it did happen, he was ready for it.

The *Shudos*, tiny flagship of what had once been a mighty armada and was now only a tattered remnant, was floating in orbit, along with the other remaining ships of the fleet, around a bloated red-giant sun. With their drives off, there was no way of detecting them at any distance, and the chance of their being found by accident was microscopically small. But they could not wait forever. Water could be recirculated, and energy could be tapped from the nearby sun, but food was gone once it was eaten.

Hokotan's decision was inevitable, and, under the circumstances, the only possible one. He simple told them what they had already known—that he was a Headquarters Staff officer.

"We haven't heard from Headquarters in weeks," he said at last. "The Earth fleet may already be well inside our periphery. We'll have to go home." He produced a document which he had obviously been holding in reserve for another purpose and handed it to Tallis. "Headquarters Staff Orders, Tallis. It empowers me to take command of the Fleet in the event of an emergency, and the decision as to what constitutes an emergency was left up to my discretion. I must admit that this is not the emergency any of us at Headquarters anticipated."

Tallis read through the document. "I see that it isn't," he said dryly. "According to this, MacMaine and I are to be placed under immediate arrest as soon as you find it necessary to act."

"Yes," said Hokotan bitterly. "So you can both consider yourselves under arrest. Don't bother to lock yourselves up—there's no point in it. General MacMaine, I see no reason to inform the rest of the Fleet of this, so we will go on as usual. The orders I have to give are simple: The Fleet will head for home by the most direct possible geodesic. Since we cannot fight, we will simply ignore attacks and keep going as long as we last. We can do nothing else." He paused thoughtfully.

"And, General MacMaine, in case we do not live through this, I would like to extend my apologies. I do not like you; I don't think I could ever learn to like an anim ... to like a non-Kerothi. But I know when to admit an error in judgment. You have fought bravely and well—better, I know, than I could have done myself. You have shown yourself to be loyal to your adopted planet; you are a Kerothi in every sense of the word except the physical. My apologies for having wronged you."

He extended his hands and MacMaine took them. A choking sensation constricted the Earthman's throat for a moment, then he got the words out—the words he had to say. "Believe me, General Hokotan, there is no need for an apology. No need whatever."

"Thank you," said Hokotan. Then he turned and left the room.

"All right, Tallis," MacMaine said hurriedly, "let's get moving."

The orders were given to the remnants of the Fleet, and they cut in their drives to head homeward. And the instant they did, there was chaos. Earth's fleet of "ghost ships" had been patrolling the area for weeks, knowing that the Kerothi fleet had last been detected somewhere in the vicinity. As soon as the spatial distortions of the Kerothi drives flashed on the Earth ships' detectors, the Earth fleet, widely scattered over the whole circumambient volume of space, coalesced toward the center of the spatial disturbance like a cloud of bees all heading for the same flower.

Where there had been only the dull red light of the giant star, there suddenly appeared the blinding, blue-white brilliance of disintegrating matter, blossoming like cruel, deadly, beautiful flowers in the midst of the Kerothi ships, then fading slowly as each expanding cloud of plasma cooled.

Sebastian MacMaine might have died with the others except that the *Shudos*, as the flagship, was to trail behind the fleet, so her drive had not yet been activated. The *Shudos* was still in orbit, moving at only a few miles per second when the Earth fleet struck.

Her drive never did go on. A bomb, only a short distance away as the distance from atomic disintegration is measured, sent the *Shudos* spinning away, end over end, like a discarded cigar butt flipped toward a gutter, one side caved in near the rear, as if it had been kicked in by a giant foot.

There was still air in the ship, MacMaine realized groggily as he awoke from the unconsciousness that had been thrust upon him. He tried to stand up, but he found himself staggering toward one crazily-slanted wall. The stagger was partly due to his grogginess, and partly due to the Coriolis forces acting within the spinning ship. The artificial gravity was gone, which meant that the interstellar drive engines had been smashed. He wondered if the emergency rocket drive was still working—not that it would take him anywhere worth going to in less than a few centuries. But, then, Sebastian MacMaine had nowhere to go, anyhow.

Tallis lay against one wall, looking very limp. MacMaine half staggered over to him and knelt down. Tallis was still alive.

The centrifugal force caused by the spinning ship gave an effective pull of less than one Earth gravity, but the weird twists caused by the Coriolis forces made motion and orientation difficult. Besides, the ship was spinning slightly on her long axis as well as turning end-for-end.

MacMaine stood there for a moment, trying to think. He had expected to die. Death was something he had known was inevitable from the moment he made his decision to leave Earth. He had not known how or when it would come, but he had known that it would come soon. He had known that he would never live to collect the reward he had demanded of the Kerothi for "faithful service." Traitor he might be, but he was still honest enough with himself to know that he would never take payment for services he had not rendered.

Now death was very near, and Sebastian MacMaine almost welcomed it. He had no desire to fight it. Tallis might want to stand and fight death to the end, but Tallis was not carrying the monstrous weight of guilt that would stay with Sebastian MacMaine until his death, no matter how much he tried to justify his actions.

On the other hand, if he had to go, he might as well do a good job of it. Since he still had a short time left, he might as well wrap the whole thing up in a neat package. How?

Again, his intuitive ability to see pattern gave him the answer long before he could have reasoned it out.

They will know, he thought, *but they will never be sure they know. I will be immortal. And my name will live forever, although no Earthman will ever again use the surname MacMaine or the given name Sebastian.*

He shook his head to clear it. No use thinking like that now. There were things to be done.

Tallis first. MacMaine made his way over to one of the emergency medical kits that he knew were kept in every compartment of every ship. One of the doors of a wall locker hung open, and the blue-green medical symbol used by the Kerothi showed darkly in the dim light that came from the three unshattered glow plates in the ceiling. He opened the kit, hoping that it contained something equivalent to adhesive tape. He had never inspected a Kerothi medical kit before. Fortunately, he could read Kerothi. If a military government was good for nothing else, at least it was capable of enforcing a simplified phonetic orthography so that words were pronounced as they were spelled. And—

He forced his wandering mind back to his work. The blow on the head, plus the crazy effect the spinning was having on his inner ears, plus the cockeyed gravitational orientation that made his eyes feel as though they were seeing things at two different angles, all combined to make for more than a little mental confusion.

There was adhesive tape, all right. Wound on its little spool, it looked almost homey. He spent several minutes winding the sticky plastic ribbon around Tallis' wrists and ankles.

Then he took the gun from the Kerothi general's sleeve holster—he had never been allowed one of his own—and, holding it firmly in his right hand, he went on a tour of the ship.

It was hard to move around. The centrifugal force varied from point to point throughout the ship, and the corridors were cluttered with debris that seemed to move with a life of its own as each piece shifted slowly under the effects of the various forces working on it. And, as the various masses moved about, the rate of spin of the ship changed as the law of conservation of angular momentum operated. The ship was full of sliding, clattering, jangling noises as the stuff tried to find a final resting place and bring the ship to equilibrium.

He found the door to Ossif's cabin open and the room empty. He found Ossif in Loopat's cabin, trying to get the younger officer to his feet.

Ossif saw MacMaine at the door and said: "You're alive! Good! Help me——" Then he saw the gun in MacMaine's hand and stopped. It was the last thing he saw before MacMaine shot him neatly between the eyes.

Loopat, only half conscious, never even knew he was in danger, and the blast that drilled through his brain prevented him from ever knowing anything again in this life.

Like a man in a dream, MacMaine went on to Hokotan's cabin, his weapon at the ready. He was rather pleased to find that the HQ general was already quite dead, his neck broken as cleanly as if it had been done by a hangman. Hardly an hour before, MacMaine would cheerfully have shot Hokotan where it would hurt the most and watch him die slowly. But the memory of Hokotan's honest apology made the Earthman very glad that he did not have to shoot the general at all.

There remained only the five-man crew, the NCO technician and his gang, who actually ran the ship. They would be at the tail of the ship, in the engine compartment. To get there, he had to cross the center of spin of the ship, and the change of gravity from one direction to another, decreasing toward zero, passing the null point, and rising again on the other side, made him nauseous. He felt better after his stomach had emptied itself.

Cautiously, he opened the door to the drive compartment and then slammed it hard in sudden fear when he saw what had happened. The shielding had been torn away from one of the energy converters and exposed the room to high-energy radiation. The crewmen were quite dead.

The fear went away as quickly as it had come. So maybe he'd dosed himself with a few hundred Roentgens—so what? A little radiation never hurt a dead man.

But he knew now that there was no possibility of escape. The drive was wrecked, and the only other means of escape, the one-man courier boat that every blaster-boat carried, had been sent out weeks ago and had never returned.

If only the courier boat were still in its cradle—

MacMaine shook his head. No. It was better this way. Much better.

He turned and went back to the dining cabin where Tallis was trussed up. This time, passing the null-gee point didn't bother him much at all.

Tallis was moaning a little and his eyelids were fluttering by the time MacMaine got back. The Earthman opened the medical kit again and looked for some kind of stimulant. He had no knowledge of medical or chemical terms in Kerothic, but there was a box of glass ampoules bearing instructions to "crush and allow patient to inhale fumes." That sounded right.

The stuff smelled like a mixture of spirits of ammonia and butyl mercaptan, but it did the job. Tallis coughed convulsively, turned his head away, coughed again, and opened his eyes. MacMaine tossed the stinking ampoule out into the corridor as Tallis tried to focus his eyes.

"How do you feel?" MacMaine asked. His voice sounded oddly thick in his own ears.

"All right. I'm all right. What happened?" He looked wonderingly around. "Near miss? Must be. Anyone hurt?"

"They're all dead but you and me," MacMaine said.

"Dead? Then we'd better——" He tried to move and then realized that he was bound hand and foot. The sudden realization of his position seemed to clear his brain completely. "Sepastian, what's going on here? Why am I tied up?"

"I had to tie you," MacMaine explained carefully, as though to a child. "There are some things I have to do yet, and I wouldn't want you to stop me. Maybe I should have just shot you while you were unconscious. That would have been kinder to both of us, I think. But ... but, Tallis, I had to tell somebody. Someone else has to know. Someone else has to judge. Or maybe I just want to unload it on someone else, someone who will carry the burden with me for just a little while. I don't know."

"Sepastian, what are you talking about?" The Kerothi's face shone dully orange in the dim light, his bright green eyes looked steadily at the Earthman, and his voice was oddly gentle.

"I'm talking about treason," said MacMaine. "Do you want to listen?"

"I don't have much choice, do I?" Tallis said. "Tell me one thing first: Are we going to die?"

"You are, Tallis. But I won't. I'm going to be immortal."

Tallis looked at him for a long moment. Then, "All right, Sepastian. I'm no psych man, but I know you're not well. I'll listen to whatever you have to say. But first, untie my hands and feet."

"I can't do that, Tallis. Sorry. But if our positions were reversed, I know what I would do to you when I heard the story. And I can't let you kill me, because there's something more that has to be done."

Tallis knew at that moment that he was looking at the face of Death. And he also knew that there was nothing whatever he could do about it. Except talk. And listen.

"Very well, Sepastian," he said levelly. "Go ahead. Treason, you say? How? Against whom?"

"I'm not quite sure," said Sebastian MacMaine. "I thought maybe you could tell me."

The Reason

"Let me ask you one thing, Tallis," MacMaine said. "Would you do anything in your power to save Keroth from destruction? Anything, no matter how drastic, if you knew that it would save Keroth in the long run?"

"A foolish question. Of course I would. I would give my life."

"Your life? A mere nothing. A pittance. Any man could give his life. Would you consent to live forever for Keroth?"

Tallis shook his head as though he were puzzled. "Live forever? That's twice or three times you've said something about that. I *don't* understand you."

"Would you consent to live forever as a filthy curse on the lips of every Kerothi old enough to speak? Would you consent to be a vile, inhuman monster whose undead spirit would hang over your homeland like an evil miasma for centuries to come, whose very name would touch a flame of hatred in the minds of all who heard it?"

"That's a very melodramatic way of putting it," the Kerothi said, "but I believe I understand what you mean. Yes, I would consent to that if it would be the only salvation of Keroth."

"Would you slaughter helpless millions of your own people so that other billions might survive? Would you ruthlessly smash your system of government and your whole way of life if it were the only way to save the people themselves?"

"I'm beginning to see what you're driving at," Tallis said slowly. "And if it is what I think it is, I think I would like to kill you—very slowly."

"I know, I know. But you haven't answered my question. Would you do those things to save your people?"

"I would," said Tallis coldly. "Don't misunderstand me. I do not loathe you for what you have done to your own people; I hate you for what you have done to mine."

"That's as it should be," said MacMaine. His head was clearing up more now. He realized that he had been talking a little wildly at first. Or was he really insane? Had he been insane from the beginning? No. He knew with absolute clarity that every step he had made had been cold, calculating, and ruthless, but utterly and absolutely sane.

He suddenly wished that he had shot Tallis without wakening him. If his mind hadn't been in such a state of shock, he would have. There was no need to torture the man like this.

"Go on," said Tallis, in a voice that had suddenly become devoid of all emotion. "Tell it all."

"Earth was stagnating," MacMaine said, surprised at the sound of his own voice. He hadn't intended to go on. But he couldn't stop now. "You saw how it was. Every standard had become meaningless because no standard was held to be better than any other standard. There was no beauty because beauty was superior to ugliness and we couldn't allow superiority or inferiority. There was no love because in order to love someone or something you must feel that it is in some way superior to that which is not loved. I'm not even sure I know what those terms mean, because I'm not sure I ever thought anything was beautiful, I'm not sure I ever loved anything. I only read about such things in books. But I know I felt the emptiness inside me where those things should have been.

"There was no morality, either. People did not refrain from stealing because it was wrong, but simply because it was pointless to steal what would be given to you if you asked for it. There was no right or wrong.

"We had a form of social contract that we called 'marriage,' but it wasn't the same thing as marriage was in the old days. There was no love. There used to be a crime called 'adultery,' but even the word had gone out of use on the Earth I knew. Instead, it was considered antisocial for a woman to refuse to give herself to other men; to do so might indicate that she thought herself superior or thought her husband to be superior to other men. The same thing applied to men in their relationships with women other than their wives. Marriage was a social contract that could be made or broken at the whim of the individual. It served no purpose because it meant nothing, neither party gained anything by the contract that they couldn't have had without it. But a wedding was an excuse for a gala party at which the couple were the center of attention. So the contract was entered into lightly for the sake of a gay time for a while, then broken again so that the game could be played with someone else—the game of Musical Bedrooms."

He stopped and looked down at the helpless Kerothi. "That doesn't mean much to you, does it? In your society, women are chattel, to be owned, bought, and sold. If you see a woman you want, you offer a price to her father or brother or husband—whoever the owner might be. Then she's yours until you sell her to another. Adultery is a very serious crime on Kerothi, but only because it's an infringement of property rights. There's not much love lost there, either, is there?

"I wonder if either of us knows what love is, Tallis?"

"I love my people," Tallis said grimly.

MacMaine was startled for a moment. He'd never thought about it that way. "You're right, Tallis," he said at last. "You're right. We *do* know. And because I loved the human race, in spite of its stagnation and its spirit of total mediocrity, I did what I had to do."

"You will pardon me," Tallis said, with only the faintest bit of acid in his voice, "if I do not understand exactly what it is that you did." Then his voice grew softer. "Wait. Perhaps I do understand. Yes, of course."

"You think you understand?" MacMaine looked at him narrowly.

"Yes. I said that I am not a psychomedic, and my getting angry with you proves it. You fought hard and well for Keroth, Sepastian, and, in doing so, you had to kill many of your own race. It is not easy for a man to do, no matter how much your reason tells you it *must* be done. And now, in the face of death, remorse has come. I do not completely understand the workings of the Earthman's mind, but I——"

"That's just it; you don't," MacMaine interrupted. "Thanks for trying to find an excuse for me, Tallis, but I'm afraid it isn't so. Listen.

"I had to find out what Earth was up against. I had a pretty good idea already that the Kerothi would win—would wipe us out or enslave us to the last man. And, after I had seen Keroth, I was certain of it. So I sent a message back to Earth, telling them what they were up against, because, up 'til then they hadn't known. As soon as they knew, they reacted as they have always done when they are certain that they face danger. They fought. They unleashed the chained-down intelligence of the few extraordinary Earthmen, and they released the fighting spirit of even the ordinary Earthmen. And they won!"

Tallis shook his head. "You sent no message, Sepastian. You were watched. You know that. You could not have sent a message."

"You saw me send it," MacMaine said. "So did everyone else in the fleet. Hokotan helped me send it—made all the arrangements at my orders. But because you do not understand the workings of the Earthman's mind, you didn't even recognize it as a message.

"Tallis, what would your people have done if an invading force, which had already proven that it could whip Keroth easily, did to one of your planets what we did on Houston's World?"

"If the enemy showed us that they could easily beat us and then hanged the whole population of a planet for resisting? Why, we would be fools to resist. Unless, of course, we had a secret weapon in a hidden pocket, the way Earth had."

"No, Tallis; no. That's where you're making your mistake. Earth didn't have that weapon until *after* the massacre on Houston's World. Let me ask you another thing: Would any Kerothi have ordered that massacre?"

"I doubt it," Tallis said slowly. "Killing that many potential slaves would be wasteful and expensive. We are fighters, not butchers. We kill only when it is necessary to win; the remainder of the enemy is taken care of as the rightful property of the conqueror."

"Exactly. Prisoners were part of the loot, and it's foolish to destroy loot. I noticed that in your history books. I noticed, too, that in such cases, the captives recognized the right of the conqueror to enslave them, and made no trouble. So, after Earth's forces get to Keroth, I don't think we'll have any trouble with you."

"Not if they set us an example like Houston's World," Tallis said, "and can prove that resistance is futile. But I don't understand the message. What was the message and how did you send it?"

"The massacre on Houston's World was the message, Tallis. I even told the Staff, when I suggested it. I said that such an act would strike terror into the minds of Earthmen.

"And it did, Tallis; it did. But that terror was just the goad they needed to make them fight. They had to sit up and take notice. If the Kerothi had gone on the way they were going, taking one planet after another, as they planned, the Kerothi would have won. The people of each planet would think, 'It can't happen here.' And, since they felt that nothing could be superior to anything else, they were complacently certain that they couldn't be beat. Of course, maybe Earth couldn't beat you, either, but that was all right; it just proved that there was no such thing as superiority.

"But Houston's World jarred them—badly. It had to. 'Hell does more than Heaven can to wake the fear of God in man.' They didn't recognize beauty, but I shoved ugliness down their throats; they didn't know love and friendship, so I gave them hatred and fear.

"The committing of atrocities has been the mistake of aggressors throughout Earth's history. The battle cries of countless wars have called upon the people to remember an atrocity. Nothing else hits an Earthman as hard as a vicious, brutal, unnecessary murder.

"So I gave them the incentive to fight, Tallis. That was my message."

Tallis was staring at him wide eyed. "You *are* insane."

"No. It worked. In six months, they found something that would enable them to blast the devil Kerothi from the skies. I don't know what the society of Earth is like now—and I never will. But at least I know that men are allowed to think again. And I know they'll survive."

He suddenly realized how much time had passed. Had it been too long? No. There would still be Earth ships prowling the vicinity, waiting for any sign of a Kerothi ship that had hidden in the vastness of space by not using its engines.

"I have some things I must do, Tallis," he said, standing up slowly. "Is there anything else you want to know?"

Tallis frowned a little, as though he were trying to think of something, but then he closed his eyes and relaxed. "No, Sepastian. Nothing. Do whatever it is you have to do."

"Tallis," MacMaine said. Tallis didn't open his eyes, and MacMaine was very glad of that. "Tallis, I want you to know that, in all my life, you were the only friend I ever had."

The bright green eyes remained closed. "That may be so. Yes, Sepastian, I honestly think you believe that."

"I do," said MacMaine, and shot him carefully through the head.

The End
—and Epilogue.

"Hold it!" The voice bellowed thunderingly from the loud-speakers of the six Earth ships that had boxed in the derelict. "Hold it! *Don't bomb that ship!* I'll personally have the head of any man who damages that ship!"

In five of the ships, the commanders simply held off the bombardment that would have vaporized the derelict. In the sixth, Major Thornton, the Group Commander, snapped off the microphone. His voice was shaky as he said: "That was close! Another second, and we'd have lost that ship forever."

Captain Verenski's Oriental features had a half startled, half-puzzled look. "I don't get it. You grabbed that mike control as if you'd been bitten. I know that she's only a derelict. After that burst of fifty-gee acceleration for fifteen minutes, there couldn't be anyone left alive on her. But there must have been a reason for using atomic rockets instead of their antiacceleration fields. What makes you think she's not dangerous?"

"I didn't say she wasn't dangerous," the major snapped. "She may be. Probably is. But we're going to capture her if we can. Look!" He pointed at the image of the ship in the screen.

She wasn't spinning now, or looping end-over-end. After fifteen minutes of high acceleration, her atomic rockets had cut out, and now she moved serenely at constant velocity, looking as dead as a battered tin can.

"I don't see anything," Captain Verenski said.

"The Kerothic symbols on the side. Palatal unvoiced sibilant, rounded——"

"I don't read Kerothic, major," said the captain. "I——" Then he blinked and said, "*Shudos!*"

"That's it. The *Shudos* of Keroth. The flagship of the Kerothi Fleet."

The look in the major's eyes was the same look of hatred that had come into the captain's.

"Even if its armament is still functioning, we have to take the chance," Major Thornton said. "Even if they're all dead, we have to try to get The Butcher's body." He picked up the microphone again.

"Attention, Group. Listen carefully and don't get itchy trigger fingers. That ship is the *Shudos*. The Butcher's ship. It's a ten-man ship, and the most she could have aboard would be thirty, even if they jammed her full to the hull. I don't know of any way that anyone could be alive on her after fifteen minutes at fifty gees of atomic drive, but remember that they don't have any idea of how our counteraction generators damp out spatial distortion either. Remember what Dr. Pendric said: 'No man is superior to any other in *all* ways. Every man is superior to every other in *some* way.' We may have the counteraction generator, but they may have something else that we don't know about. So stay alert.

"I am going to take a landing-party aboard. There's a reward out for The Butcher, and that reward will be split proportionately among us. It's big enough for us all to enjoy it, and we'll probably get citations if we bring him in.

"I want ten men from each ship. I'm not asking for volunteers; I want each ship commander to pick the ten men he thinks will be least likely to lose their heads in an emergency. I don't want anyone to panic and shoot when he should be thinking. I don't want anyone who had any relatives on Houston's World. Sorry, but I can't allow vengeance yet.

"We're a thousand miles from the *Shudos* now; close in slowly until we're within a hundred yards. The boarding parties will don armor and prepare to board while we're closing in. At a hundred yards, we stop and the boarding parties will land on the hull. I'll give further orders then.

"One more thing. I don't think her A-A generators could possibly be functioning, judging from that dent in her hull, but we can't be sure. If she tries to go into A-A drive, she is to be bombed—no matter who is aboard. It is better that sixty men die than that The Butcher escape.

"All right, let's go. Move in."

Half an hour later, Major Thornton stood on the hull of the *Shudos*, surrounded by the sixty men of the boarding party. "Anybody see anything through those windows?" he asked.

Several of the men had peered through the direct-vision ports, playing spotlight beams through them.

"Nothing alive," said a sergeant, a remark which was followed by a chorus of agreement.

"Pretty much of a mess in there," said another sergeant. "That fifty gees mashed everything to the floor. Why'd anyone want to use acceleration like that?"

"Let's go in and find out," said Major Thornton.

The outer door to the air lock was closed, but not locked. It swung open easily to disclose the room between the outer and inner doors. Ten men went in with the major, the others stayed outside with orders to cut through the hull if anything went wrong.

"If he's still alive," the major said, "we don't want to kill him by blowing the air. Sergeant, start the airlock cycle."

There was barely room for ten men in the air lock. It had been built big enough for the full crew to use it at one time, but it was only just big enough.

When the inner door opened, they went in cautiously. They spread out and searched cautiously. The caution was unnecessary, as it turned out. There wasn't a living thing aboard.

"Three officers shot through the head, sir," said the sergeant. "One of 'em looks like he died of a broken neck, but it's hard to tell after that fifty gees mashed 'em. Crewmen in the engine room—five of 'em. Mashed up, but I'd say they died of radiation, since the shielding on one of the generators was ruptured by the blast that made that dent in the hull."

"Nine bodies," the major said musingly. "All Kerothi. And all of them probably dead *before* the fifty-gee acceleration. Keep looking, sergeant. We've got to find the tenth man."

Another twenty-minute search gave them all the information they were ever to get.

"No Earth food aboard," said the major. "One spacesuit missing. Handweapons missing. Two emergency survival kits and two medical kits missing. *And*—most important of all—the courier boat is missing." He bit at his lower lip for a moment, then went on. "Outer air lock door left unlocked. Three Kerothi shot—*after* the explosion that ruined the A-A drive, and *before* the fifty-gee acceleration." He looked at the sergeant. "What do you think happened?"

"He got away," the tough-looking noncom said grimly. "Took the courier boat and scooted away from here."

"Why did he set the timer on the drive, then? What was the purpose of that fifty-gee blast?"

"To distract us, I'd say, sir. While we were chasing this thing, he hightailed it out."

"He might have, at that," the major said musingly. "A one-man courier *could* have gotten away. Our new detection equipment isn't perfect yet. But——"

At that moment, one of the troopers pushed himself down the corridor toward them. "Look, sir! I found this in the pocket of the Carrot-skin who was taped up in there!" He was holding a piece of paper.

The major took it, read it, then read it aloud. "Greetings, fellow Earthmen: When you read this, I will be safe from any power you may think you have to arrest or punish me. But don't think *you* are safe from *me*. There are other intelligent races in the galaxy, and I'll be around for a long time to come. You haven't heard the last of me. With love—Sebastian MacMaine."

The silence that followed was almost deadly.

"He *did* get away!" snarled the sergeant at last.

"Maybe," said the major. "But it doesn't make sense." He sounded agitated. "Look. In the first place, how do we know the courier boat was even aboard? They've been trying frantically to get word back to Keroth; does it make sense that they'd save this boat? And why all the fanfare? Suppose he did have a boat? Why would he attract our attention with that fifty-gee flare? Just so he could leave us a note?"

"What do you think happened, sir?" the sergeant asked.

"I don't think he had a boat. If he did, he'd want us to think he was dead, not the other way around. I think he set the drive timer on this ship, went outside with his supplies, crawled up a drive tube and waited until that atomic rocket blast blew him into plasma. He was probably badly wounded and didn't want us to know that we'd won. That way, we'd never find him."

There was no belief on the faces of the men around him.

"Why'd he want to do that, sir?" asked the sergeant.

"Because as long as we don't *know*, he'll haunt us. He'll be like Hitler or Jack the Ripper. He'll be an immortal menace instead of a dead villain who could be forgotten."

"Maybe so, sir," said the sergeant, but there was an utter lack of conviction in his voice. "But we'd still better comb this area and keep our detectors hot. We'll know what he was up to when we catch him."

"But if we *don't* find him," the major said softly, "we'll *never* know. That's the beauty of it, sergeant. If we don't find him, then he's won. In his own fiendish, twisted way, he's won."

"If we don't find him," said the sergeant stolidly, "I think we better keep a sharp eye out for the next intelligent race we meet. He might find 'em first."

"Maybe," said the major very softly, "that's just what he wanted. I wish I knew why."

THE END

The Measure of a Man

What is desirable is not always necessary, while that which is necessary may be most undesirable. Perhaps the measure of a man is the ability to tell one from the other ... and act on it.

Alfred Pendray pushed himself along the corridor of the battleship *Shane*, holding the flashlight in one hand and using the other hand and his good leg to guide and propel himself by. The beam of the torch reflected queerly from the pastel green walls of the corridor, giving him the uneasy sensation that he was swimming underwater instead of moving through the blasted hulk of a battleship, a thousand light-years from home.

He came to the turn in the corridor, and tried to move to the right, but his momentum was greater than he had thought, and he had to grab the corner of the wall to keep from going on by. That swung him around, and his sprained ankle slammed agonizingly against the other side of the passageway.

Pendray clenched his teeth and kept going. But as he moved down the side passage, he went more slowly, so that the friction of his palm against the wall could be used as a brake.

He wasn't used to maneuvering without gravity; he'd been taught it in Cadets, of course, but that was years ago and parsecs away. When the pseudograv generators had gone out, he'd retched all over the place, but now his stomach was empty, and the nausea had gone.

He had automatically oriented himself in the corridors so that the doors of the various compartments were to his left and right, with the ceiling "above" and the deck "below." Otherwise, he might have lost his sense of direction completely in the complex maze of the interstellar battleship.

Or, he corrected himself, *what's left of a battleship.*

And what *was* left? Just Al Pendray and less than half of the once-mighty *Shane*.

The door to the lifeboat hold loomed ahead in the beam of the flashlight, and Pendray braked himself to a stop. He just looked at the dogged port for a few seconds.

Let there be a boat in there, he thought. *Just a boat, that's all I ask. And air*, he added as an afterthought. Then his hand went out to the dog handle and turned.

The door cracked easily. There was air on the other side. Pendray breathed a sigh of relief, braced his good foot against the wall, and pulled the door open.

The little lifeboat was there, nestled tightly in her cradle. For the first time since the *Shane* had been hit, Pendray's face broke into a broad smile. The fear that had been within him faded a little, and the darkness of the crippled ship seemed to be lessened.

Then the beam of his torch caught the little red tag on the air lock of the lifeboat. *Repair Work Under Way—Do Not Remove This Tag Without Proper Authority.*

That explained why the lifeboat hadn't been used by the other crewmen.

Pendray's mind was numb as he opened the air lock of the small craft. He didn't even attempt to think. All he wanted was to see exactly how the vessel had been disabled by the repair crew. He went inside.

The lights were working in the lifeboat. That showed that its power was still functioning. He glanced over the instrument-and-control panels. No red tags on them, at least. Just to make sure, he opened them up, one by one, and looked inside. Nothing wrong, apparently.

Maybe it had just been some minor repair—a broken lighting switch or something. But he didn't dare hope yet.

He went through the door in the tiny cabin that led to the engine compartment, and he saw what the trouble was.

The shielding had been removed from the atomic motors.

He just hung there in the air, not moving. His lean, dark face remained expressionless, but tears welled up in his eyes and spilled over, spreading their dampness over his lids.

The motors would run, all right. The ship could take him to Earth. But the radiation leakage from those motors would kill him long before he made it home. It would take ten days to make it back to base, and twenty-four hours of exposure to the deadly radiation from those engines would be enough to insure his death from radiation sickness.

His eyes were blurring from the film of tears that covered them; without gravity to move the liquid, it just pooled there, distorting his vision. He blinked the tears away, then wiped his face with his free hand.

Now what?

He was the only man left alive on the *Shane*, and none of the lifeboats had escaped. The Rat cruisers had seen to that.

They weren't really rats, those people. Not literally. They looked humanoid enough to enable plastic surgeons to disguise a human being as one of them, although it meant sacrificing the little fingers and little toes to imitate the four-digited Rats. The Rats were at a disadvantage there; they couldn't add any fingers. But the Rats had other advantages—they bred and fought like, well, like rats.

Not that human beings couldn't equal them or even surpass them in ferocity, if necessary. But the Rats had nearly a thousand years of progress over Earth. Their Industrial Revolution had occurred while the Angles and the Saxons and the Jutes were pushing the Britons into Wales. They had put their first artificial satellites into orbit while King Alfred the Great was fighting off the Danes.

They hadn't developed as rapidly as Man had. It took them roughly twice as long to go from one step to the next, so that their actual superiority was only a matter of five hundred years, and Man was catching up rapidly. Unfortunately, Man hadn't caught up yet.

The first meeting of the two races had taken place in interstellar space, and had seemed friendly enough. Two ships had come within detector distance of each other, and had circled warily. It was almost a perfect example of the Leinster Hypothesis; neither knew where the other's home world was located, and neither could go back home for fear that the other would be able to follow. But the Leinster Hypothesis couldn't be followed to the end. Leinster's solution had been to have the parties trade ships and go home, but that only works when the two civilizations are fairly close in technological development. The Rats certainly weren't going to trade their ship for the inferior craft of the Earthmen.

The Rats, conscious of their superiority, had a simpler solution. They were certain, after a while, that Earth posed no threat to them, so they invited the Earth ship to follow them home.

The Earthmen had been taken on a carefully conducted tour of the Rats' home planet, and the captain of the Earth ship—who had gone down in history as "Sucker" Johnston—was convinced that the Rats meant no harm, and agreed to lead a Rat ship back to Earth. If the Rats had struck then, there would never have been a Rat-Human War. It would have been over before it started.

But the Rats were too proud of their superiority. Earth was too far away to bother them for the moment; it wasn't in their line of conquest just yet. In another fifty years, the planet would be ready for picking off.

Earth had no idea that the Rats were so widespread. They had taken and colonized over thirty planets, completely destroying the indigenous intelligent races that had existed on five of them.

It wasn't just pride that had made the Rats decide to wait before hitting Earth; there was a certain amount of prudence, too. None of the other races they had met had developed space travel; the Earthmen might be a little tougher to beat. Not that there was any doubt of the outcome, as far as they were concerned—but why take chances?

But, while the Rats had fooled "Sucker" Johnston and some of his officers, the majority of the crew knew better. Rat crewmen were little short of slaves, and the Rats made the mistake of assuming that the Earth crewmen were the same. They hadn't tried to impress the crewmen as they had the officers. When the interrogation officers on Earth questioned the crew of the Earth ship, they, too, became suspicious. Johnston's optimistic attitude just didn't jibe with the facts.

So, while the Rat officers were having the red carpet rolled out for them, Earth Intelligence went to work. Several presumably awe-stricken men were allowed to take a conducted tour of the Rat ship. After all, why not? The Twentieth Century Russians probably wouldn't have minded showing their rocket plants to an American of Captain John Smith's time, either.

But there's a difference. Earth's government knew Earth was being threatened, and they knew they had to get as many facts as they could. They were also aware of the fact that if you know a thing *can* be done, then you will eventually find a way to do it.

During the next fifty years, Earth learned more than it had during the previous hundred. The race expanded, secretly, moving out to other planets in that sector of the galaxy. And they worked to catch up with the Rats.

They didn't make it, of course. When, after fifty years of presumably peaceful—but highly limited—contact, the Rats hit Earth, they found out one thing. That the mass and energy of a planet armed with the proper weapons can not be outclassed by any conceivable concentration of spaceships.

Throwing rocks at an army armed with machine guns may seem futile, but if you hit them with an avalanche, they'll go under. The Rats lost three-quarters of their fleet to planet-based guns and had to go home to bandage their wounds.

The only trouble was that Earth couldn't counterattack. Their ships were still out-classed by those of the Rats. And the Rats, their racial pride badly stung, were determined to wipe out Man, to erase the stain on their honor wherever Man could be found. Somehow, some way, they must destroy Earth.

And now, Al Pendray thought bitterly, they would do it.

The *Shane* had sneaked in past Rat patrols to pick up a spy on one of the outlying Rat planets, a man who'd spent five years playing the part of a Rat slave, trying to get information on their activities there. And he had had one vital bit of knowledge. He'd found it and held on to it for over three years, until the time came for the rendezvous.

The rendezvous had almost come too late. The Rats had developed a device that could make a star temporarily unstable, and they were ready to use it on Sol.

The *Shane* had managed to get off-planet with the spy, but they'd been spotted in spite of the detector nullifiers that Earth had developed. They'd been jumped by Rat cruisers and blasted by the superior Rat weapons. The lifeboats had been picked out of space, one by one, as the crew tried to get away.

In a way, Alfred Pendray was lucky. He'd been in the sick bay with a sprained ankle when the Rats hit, sitting in the X-ray room. The shot that had knocked out the port engine had knocked him unconscious, but the shielded walls of the X-ray room had saved him from the blast of radiation that had cut down the crew in the rear of the ship. He'd come to in time to see the Rat cruisers cut up the lifeboats before they could get well away from the ship. They'd taken a couple of parting shots at the dead hulk, and then left it to drift in space—and leaving one man alive.

In the small section near the rear of the ship, there were still compartments that were airtight. At least, Pendray decided, there was enough air to keep him alive for a while. If only he could get a little power into the ship, he could get the rear air purifiers to working.

He left the lifeboat and closed the door behind him. There was no point in worrying about a boat he couldn't use.

He made his way back toward the engine room. Maybe there was something salvageable there. Swimming through the corridors was becoming easier with practice; his Cadet training was coming back to him.

Then he got a shock that almost made him faint. The beam of his light had fallen full on the face of a Rat. It took him several seconds to realize that the Rat was dead, and several more to realize that it wasn't a Rat at all. It was the spy they had been sent to pick up. He'd been in the sick bay for treatments of the ulcers on his back gained from five years of frequent lashings as a Rat slave.

Pendray went closer and looked him over. He was still wearing the clothing he'd had on when the *Shane* picked him up.

Poor guy, Pendray thought. *All that hell—for nothing.*

Then he went around the corpse and continued toward the engine room.

The place was still hot, but it was thermal heat, not radioactivity. A dead atomic engine doesn't leave any residual effects.

Five out of the six engines were utterly ruined, but the sixth seemed to be in working condition. Even the shielding was intact. Again, hope rose in Alfred Pendray's mind. If only there were tools!

A half hour's search killed that idea. There were no tools aboard capable of cutting through the hard shielding. He couldn't use it to shield the engine on the lifeboat. And the shielding that been on the other five engines had melted and run; it was worthless.

Then another idea hit him. Would the remaining engine work at all? Could it be fixed? It was the only hope he had left.

Apparently, the only thing wrong with it was the exciter circuit leads, which had been sheared off by a bit of flying metal. The engine had simply stopped instead of exploding. That ought to be fixable. He could try; it was something to do, anyway.

It took him the better part of two days, according to his watch. There were plenty of smaller tools around for the job, although many of them were scattered and some had been ruined by the explosions. Replacement parts were harder to find, but he managed to pirate some of them from the ruined engines.

He ate and slept as he felt the need. There was plenty of food in the sick bay kitchen, and there is no need for a bed under gravity-less conditions.

After the engine was repaired, he set about getting the rest of the ship ready to move—if it *would* move. The hull was still solid, so the infraspace field should function. The air purifiers had to be reconnected and repaired in a couple of places. The lights ditto. The biggest job was checking all the broken leads to make sure there weren't any short circuits anywhere.

The pseudogravity circuits were hopeless. He'd have to do without gravity.

On the third day, he decided he'd better clean the place up. There were several corpses floating around, and they were beginning to be noticeable. He had to tow them, one by one, to the rear starboard air lock and seal them between the inner and outer doors. He couldn't dump them, since the outer door was partially melted and welded shut.

He took the personal effects from the men. If he ever got back to Earth, their next-of-kin might want the stuff. On the body of the imitation Rat, he found a belt-pouch full of microfilm. The report on the Rats' new weapon? Possibly. He'd have to look it over later.

On the "morning" of the fourth day, he started the single remaining engine. The infraspace field came on, and the ship began moving at multiples of the speed of light. Pendray grinned. *Half gone, will travel*, he thought gleefully.

If Pendray had had any liquor aboard, he would have gotten mildly drunk. Instead, he sat down and read the spools of microfilm, using the projector in the sick bay.

He was not a scientist in the strict sense of the word. He was a navigator and a fairly good engineer. So it didn't surprise him any that he couldn't understand a lot of the report. The mechanics of making a semi-nova out of a normal star were more than a little bit over his head. He'd read a little and then go out and take a look at the stars, checking their movement so that he could make an estimate of his speed. He'd jury-rigged a kind of control on the hull field, so he could aim the hulk easily enough. He'd only have to get within signaling range, anyway. An Earth ship would pick him up.

If there was any Earth left by the time he got there.

He forced his mind away from thinking about that.

It was not until he reached the last spool of microfilm that his situation was forcibly brought to focus in his mind. Thus far, he had thought only about saving himself. But the note at the end of the spool made him realize that there were others to save.

The note said: *These reports must reach Earth before 22 June 2287. After that, it will be too late.*

22 June!

That was—let's see....

This is the eighteenth of September, he thought, *June of next year is—nine months away. Surely I can make it in that time. I've got to.*

The only question was, how fast was the hulk of the *Shane* moving?

It took him three days to get the answer accurately. He knew the strength of the field around the ship, and he knew the approximate thrust of the single engine by that time. He had also measured the motions of some of the nearer stars. Thank heaven he was a navigator and not a mechanic or something! At least he knew the direction and distance to Earth, and he knew the distance of the brighter stars from where the ship was.

He had two checks to use, then. Star motion against engine thrust and field strength. He checked them. And rechecked them. And hated the answer.

He would arrive in the vicinity of Sol some time in late July—a full month too late.

What could he do? Increase the output of the engine? No. It was doing the best it could now. Even shutting off the lights wouldn't help anything; they were a microscopic drain on that engine.

He tried to think, tried to reason out a solution, but nothing would come. He found time to curse the fool who had decided the shielding on the lifeboat would have to be removed and repaired. That little craft, with its lighter mass and more powerful field concentration, could make the trip in ten days.

The only trouble was that ten days in that radiation hell would be impossible. He'd be a very well-preserved corpse in half that time, and there'd be no one aboard to guide her.

Maybe he could get one of the other engines going! Sure. He *must* be able to get one more going, somehow. Anything to cut down on that time!

He went back to the engines again, looking them over carefully. He went over them again. Not a single one could be repaired at all.

Then he rechecked his velocity figures, hoping against hope that he'd made a mistake somewhere, dropped a decimal point or forgotten to divide by two. Anything. Anything!

But there was nothing. His figures had been accurate the first time.

For a while, he just gave up. All he could think of was the terrible blaze of heat that would wipe out Earth when the Rats set off the sun. Man might survive. There were colonies that the Rats didn't know about. But they'd find them eventually. Without Earth, the race would be set back five hundred—maybe five thousand—years. The Rats would would have plenty of time to hunt them out and destroy them.

And then he forced his mind away from that train of thought. There had to be a way to get there on time. Something in the back of his mind told him that there *was* a way.

He had to think. Really think.

On 7 June 2287, a signal officer on the Earth destroyer *Muldoon* picked up a faint signal coming from the general direction of the constellation of Sagittarius. It was the standard emergency signal for distress. The broadcaster only had a very short range, so the source couldn't be too far away.

He made his report to the ship's captain. "We're within easy range of her, sir," he finished. "Shall we pick her up?"

"Might be a Rat trick," said the captain. "But we'll have to take the chance. Beam a call to Earth, and let's go out there dead slow. If the detectors show anything funny, we turn tail and run. We're in no position to fight a Rat ship."

"You think this might be a Rat trap, sir?"

The captain grinned. "If you are referring to the *Muldoon* as a rat trap, Mr. Blake, you're both disrespectful and correct. That's why we're going to run if we see anything funny. This ship is already obsolete by our standards; you can imagine what it is by theirs." He paused. "Get that call in to Earth. Tell 'em this ship is using a distress signal that was obsolete six months ago. And tell 'em we're going out."

"Yes, sir," said the signal officer.

It wasn't a trap. As the *Muldoon* approached the source of the signal, their detectors picked up the ship itself. It was a standard lifeboat from a battleship of the *Shannon* class.

"You don't suppose that's from the *Shane*, do you?" the captain said softly as he looked at the plate. "She's the only ship of that class that's missing. But if that's a *Shane* lifeboat, what took her so long to get here?"

"She's cut her engines, sir!" said the observer. "She evidently knows we're coming."

"All right. Pull her in as soon as we're close enough. Put her in Number Two lifeboat rack; it's empty."

When the door of the lifeboat opened, the captain of the *Muldoon* was waiting outside the lifeboat rack. He didn't know exactly what he had expected to see, but it somehow seemed fitting that a lean, bearded man in a badly worn uniform and a haggard look about him should step out.

The specter saluted. "Lieutenant Alfred Pendray, of the *Shane*," he said, in a voice that had almost no strength. He held up a pouch. "Microfilm," he said. "Must get to Earth immediately. No delay. Hurry."

"Catch him!" the captain shouted. "He's falling!" But one of the men nearby had already caught him.

In the sick bay, Pendray came to again. The captain's questioning gradually got the story out of Pendray.

"... So I didn't know what to do then," he said, his voice a breathy whisper. "I knew I had to get that stuff home. Somehow."

"Go on," said the captain, frowning.

"Simple matter," said Pendray. "Nothing to it. Two equations. Little ship goes thirty times as fast as big ship— big *hulk*. Had to get here before 22 June. *Had* to. Only way out, y'unnerstand.

"Anyway. Two equations. Simple. Work 'em in your head. Big ship takes ten months, little one takes ten days. But can't stay in a little ship ten days. No shielding. Be dead before you got here. See?"

"I see," said the captain patiently.

"*But*—and here's a 'mportant point: If you stay on the big ship for eight an' a half months, then y' only got to be in the little ship for a day an' a half to get here. Man can live that long, even under that radiation. See?" And with that, he closed his eyes.

"Do you mean you exposed yourself to the full leakage radiation from a lifeboat engine for thirty-six hours?"

But there was no answer.

"Let him sleep," said the ship's doctor. "If he wakes up again, I'll let you know. But he might not be very lucid from here on in."

"Is there anything you can do?" the captain asked.

"No. Not after a radiation dosage like that." He looked down at Pendray. "His problem was easy, mathematically. But not psychologically. That took real guts to solve."

"Yeah," said the captain gently. "All he had to do was *get* here alive. The problem said nothing about his staying that way."

The Foreign Hand Tie

From Istanbul, in Turkish Thrace, to Moscow, U.S.S.R., is only a couple of hours outing for a round trip in a fast jet plane—a shade less than eleven hundred miles in a beeline.

Unfortunately, Mr. Raphael Poe had no way of chartering a bee.

The United States Navy cruiser *Woonsocket*, having made its placid way across the Mediterranean, up the Aegean Sea, and through the Dardanelles to the Bosporous, stopped overnight at Istanbul and then turned around and went back. On the way in, it had stopped at Gibraltar, Barcelona, Marseilles, Genoa, Naples, and Athens—the main friendly ports on the northern side of the Mediterranean. On the way back, it performed the same ritual on the African side of the sea. Its most famous passengers were the American Secretary of State, two senators, and three representatives.

Its most important passenger was Mr. Raphael Poe.

During the voyage in, Mr. Raphael Poe remained locked in a stateroom, all by himself, twiddling his thumbs restlessly and playing endless games of solitaire, making bets with himself on how long it would be before the ship hit the next big wave and wondering how long it would take a man to go nuts in isolation. On the voyage back, he was not aboard the *Woonsocket* at all, and no one missed him because only the captain and two other Navy men had known he was aboard, and they knew that he had been dropped overboard at Istanbul.

The sleek, tapered cylindroid might easily have been mistaken for a Naval torpedo, since it was roughly the same size and shape. Actually, it was a sort of hybrid, combining the torpedo and the two-man submarine that the Japanese had used in World War II, plus refinements contributed by such apparently diverse arts as skin-diving, cybernetics, and nucleonics.

Inside this one-man underwater vessel, Raphael Poe lay prone, guiding the little atomic-powered submarine across the Black Sea, past Odessa, and up the Dnieper. The first leg, the four hundred miles from the Bosporous to the mouth of the river, was relatively easy. The two hundred and sixty miles from there to the Dnepropetrovsk was a little more difficult, but not terribly so. It became increasingly more difficult as the Dnieper narrowed and became more shallow.

On to Kiev. His course changed at Dnepropetrovsk, from northeast to northwest, for the next two hundred fifty miles. At Kiev, the river changed course again, heading north. Three hundred and fifty miles farther on, at Smolensk, he was heading almost due east.

It had not been an easy trip. At night, he had surfaced to get his bearings and to recharge the air tanks. Several times, he had had to take to the land, using the caterpillar treads on the little machine, because of obstacles in the river.

At the end of the ninth day, he was still one hundred eighty miles from Moscow, but, at that point, he got out of the submarine and prepared himself for the trip overland. When he was ready, he pressed a special button on the control panel of the expensive little craft. Immediately, the special robot brain took over. It had recorded the trip upstream; by applying that information in reverse—a "mirror image," so to speak—it began guiding itself back toward Istanbul, applying the necessary corrective factors that made the difference between an upstream and a downstream trip. If it had made a mistake or had been discovered, it would have blown itself to bits. As a tribute to modern robotics and ultra-microminiaturization, it is a fact that the little craft was picked up five days later a few miles from Istanbul by the U.S.S. *Paducah*.

By that time, a certain Vladimir Turenski, a shambling not-too-bright deaf mute, had made his fully documented appearance in Moscow.

Spies, like fairies and other such elusive sprites, traditionally come in rings. The reason for this circumstructural metaphor is obscure, but it remains a fact that a single spy, all by himself, is usually of very little use to anybody. Espionage, on any useful scale, requires organization.

There is, as there should be, a reason for this. The purpose of espionage is to gather information—preferably, *useful* information—against the wishes of, and in spite of the efforts of, a group—usually referred to as "the enemy"—which is endeavoring to prevent that information from getting into other hands than their own. Such activities obviously imply communication. An espioneur, working for Side A, who finds a bit of important information about Side B must obviously communicate that bit of information to Side A or it is of no use whatsoever.

All of these factors pose complex problems.

To begin with, the espioneur must get himself into a position in which he can get hold of the information he wants. Usually, that means that he must pass himself off as something he is not, a process which requires time. Then, when he gets the information he is after, he must get it to his employers quickly. Information, like fish, becomes useless after a certain amount of time, and, unlike fish, there is no known way of refrigerating it to retard spoilage.

It is difficult to transmit information these days. It is actually easier for the espioneur to transmit it than to get it, generally speaking, but it is difficult for him to do both jobs at once, so the spy ring's two major parts consist of the ones who get the information from the enemy and the ones who transmit it back to their employers.

Without magic, it is difficult for a single spy to be of any benefit. And "magic," in this case, can be defined as some method by which information can be either obtained or transmitted without fear of discovery by the enemy. During World War I, a competent spy equipped with a compact transistorized short-wave communications system could have had himself a ball. If the system had included a miniature full-color television camera, he could have gone hog wild. In those days, such equipment would have been magic.

All this is not *à propos* of nothing. Mr. Raphael Poe was, in his own way, a magician.

It is not to be supposed that the United States of America had no spy rings in the Union of Soviet Socialist Republics at that time. There were plenty of them. Raphael Poe could have, if it were so ordained, availed himself of the services of any one or all of them. He did not do so for two reasons. In the first place, the more people who are in on a secret, the more who can give it away. In other words, a ring, like a chain, is only as strong as its weakest section. In the second place, Raphael Poe didn't need any assistance in the first place.

That is, he needed no more assistance that most magicians do—a shill in the audience. In this particular case, the shill was his brother, Leonard Poe.

Operation Mapcase was as ultra-secret as it could possibly be. Although there were perhaps two dozen men who knew of the existence of the operation by its code name, such as the Naval officers who had helped get Raphael Poe to his destination, there were only five men who really knew what Operation Mapcase was all about.

Two of these were, of course, Raphael and Leonard Poe. Two others were the President of the United States and the Secretary of Defense. The fifth was Colonel Julius T. Spaulding, of United States Army Intelligence.

On the seventh day after Raphael Poe's arrival in Moscow, the other four men met in Blair House, across the street from the White House, in a room especially prepared for the purpose. No one but the President knew the exact purpose of the meeting, although they had an idea that he wanted more information of some kind.

The President himself was the last to arrive. Leaving two Secret Service men standing outside the room, he carefully closed the door and turned to face the Secretary of Defense, Colonel Spaulding, and Leonard Poe. "Sit down, gentlemen," he said, seating himself as he spoke.

"Gentlemen, before we go any further, I must conduct one final experiment in order to justify Operation Mapcase. I will not explain it just yet." He looked at Lenny Poe, a small, dark-haired man with a largish nose. "Mr. Poe, can you contact your brother at this moment?"

Lenny Poe was a man who was not overawed by anyone, and had no inclination to be formal, not even toward the President. "Yeah, sure," he said matter-of-factly.

The President glanced at his watch. "It is now five minutes of ten. That makes it five minutes of six in the evening in Moscow. Is your brother free to move around? That is, can he go to a certain place in the city?"

Lenny closed his eyes for a moment, then opened them. "Rafe says he can go any place that the average citizen would be allowed to go."

"Excellent," said the President. He gave Lenny an address—an intersection of two streets not far from Red Square. "Can he get there within fifteen minutes?"

"Make it twenty," said Lenny.

"Very well. Twenty minutes. When he gets there, I'll ask you to relay further instructions."

Lenny Poe closed his eyes, folded his arms, and relaxed in his chair. The other three men waited silently.

Nineteen minutes later, Lenny opened his eyes and said: "O.K. He's there. Now what?"

"There is a lamppost on that corner, I believe," said the President. "Can your brother see it?"

Lenny closed his eyes again. "Sure. There's a guy leaning against it."

The President's eyes brightened. "Describe him!"

Lenny, eyes still closed, said: "Five feet ten, heavy set, gray hair, dark-rimmed glasses, brown suit, flashy necktie. By the cut of his clothes, I'd say he was either British or American, probably American. Fifty-five or fifty-six years old."

It was obvious to the Secretary of Defense and to Colonel Spaulding that the President was suppressing some inward excitement.

"Very good, Mr. Poe!" he said. "Now, you will find a box of colored pencils and a sketch pad in that desk over there. Can you draw me a fairly accurate sketch of that man?"

"Yeah, sure." Lenny opened his eyes, moved over to the desk, took out the pencils and sketch pad, and went to work. He had to close his eyes occasionally, but his work was incredibly rapid and, at the same time, almost photographically accurate.

As the picture took form, the President's inward excitement increased perceptibly. When it was finally finished, Lenny handed the sketch to the President without a word.

The President took it eagerly and his face broke out in his famous grin. "Excellent! Perfect!" He looked at Lenny. "Your brother hasn't attracted the man's attention in any way, has he?"

"Nope," said Lenny.

"Fine. The experiment is over. Relay my thanks to your brother. He can go ahead with whatever he was doing now."

"I don't quite understand," said the Secretary of State.

"I felt it necessary to make one final experiment of my own devising," the President said. "I wanted Raphael Poe to go to a particular place at a particular time, with no advance warning, to transmit a picture of something he had never seen before. I arranged this test myself, and I am positive that there could be no trickery."

"Never seen before?" the Secretary repeated bewilderedly. He gestured at the sketch. "Why, that's obviously Bill Donovan, of the Moscow delegation. Poe could have seen a photograph of him somewhere before."

"Even so," the President pointed out, "there would be no way of knowing that he would be at that spot. But that's beside the point. Look at that necktie!"

"I had noticed it," the Defense Secretary admitted.

It was certainly an outstanding piece of neckwear. As drawn by Leonard Poe, it was a piece of brilliant chartreuse silk, fully three and a half inches wide at its broadest. Against that background, rose-pink nude girls were cavorting with pale mauve satyrs.

"That tie," said the President, "was sent to me fifteen years ago by on of my constituents, when I was in Congress. I never wore it, of course, but it would have been criminal to have thrown away such a magnificently obscene example of bad taste as that.

"I sent it to Donovan in a sealed diplomatic pouch by special courier, with instructions to wear it at this time. He, of course, has no idea why he is standing there. He is merely obeying orders.

"Gentlemen, this is completely convincing to me. Absolutely no one but myself knew what I had in mind. It would have required telepathy even to cheat.

"Thank you very much, Mr. Poe. Colonel Spaulding, you may proceed with Operation Mapcase as planned."

"Dr. Malekrinova, will you initial these requisition forms, please."

Dr. Sonya Malekrinova, a dowdy-looking, middle-aged woman with unplucked eyebrows and a mole on her chin, adjusted her steel-rimmed glasses, took the proffered papers from the clerk, ran her eyes over them, and then put her initials on the bottom of each page.

"Thank you, Comrade Doctor," said the clerk when she handed back the sheaf of papers.

"Certainly, Comrade."

And the two of them went about their business.

Not far away, in the Cathedral of St. Basil, Vladimir Turenski, alias Raphael Poe, was also apparently going about his business. The cathedral had not seen nor heard the Liturgy of the Russian Orthodox Church or any other church, for a good many decades. The Bolsheviks, in their zeal to protect the citizens of the Soviet Unions from the pernicious influence of religion, had converted it into a museum as soon as possible.

It was the function of *Tovarishch* Turenski to push a broom around the floors of the museum, and this he did with great determination and efficiency. He also cleaned windows and polished metalwork when the occasion demanded. He was only one of a large crew of similarly employed men, but he was a favorite with the Head Custodian, who not only felt sorry for the simple-minded deaf-mute, but appreciated the hard work he did. If, on occasion, Comrade Turenski would lean on his broom and fall into a short reverie, it was excusable because he still managed to get all his work done.

Behind Comrade Turenski, a guide was explaining a display to a group of tourists, but Turenski ignored the distraction and kept his mind focused on the thoughts of Dr. Sonya Malekrinova.

After nearly ten months of patient work, Raphael Poe had hit upon something that was, to his way of thinking, more important than all the information he had transmitted to Washington thus far.

Picking brains telepathically was not, even for him, an easy job. He had the knack and the training but, in addition, there was the necessity of establishing a rapport with the other mind. Since he was a physicist and not a politician, it was much easier to get information from the mind of Sonya Malekrinova than to get it from the Premier. The only person with whom he could keep in contact over any great distance was his brother, and that only because the two of them had grown up together.

He could pick up the strongest thoughts of any nearby person very easily. He did not need to hear the actual words, for instance, of a nearby conversation in order to follow it perfectly, because the words of verbal communication were strong in a person's mind.

But getting deeper than that required an increasing amount of understanding of the functioning of the other person's mind.

His ability to eavesdrop on conversations had been of immense benefit to Washington so far, but is was difficult for him to get close enough to the higher-ups in the Soviet government to get all the data that the President of the United States wanted.

But now that he had established a firm mental linkage with one of the greatest physicists in the Soviet Union, he could begin to send information that would be of tremendous value to the United States.

He brushed up a pile of trash, pushed it into a dust pan, and carried it off toward the disposal chute that led to the trash cans. In the room where the brooms were kept, he paused and closed his eyes.

Lenny! Are picking this up?

Sure, Rafe. I'm ready with the drawing board anytime you are.

As Dr. Sonya Malekrinova stood in her laboratory looking over the apparatus she was perfecting for the glory of the Soviet State, she had no notion that someone halfway around the world was also looking at it over her shoulder—or rather, through her own eyes.

Lenny started with the fives first, and worked his way up to the larger denominations.

"Five, ten, fifteen, twenty, twenty-five, thirty—forty, fifty, sixty...." he muttered happily to himself. "Two fifty, three, three-fifty, four, four-fifty."

It was all there, so he smiled benevolently at the man in the pay window. "Thank you muchly." Then he stepped aside to let another lucky man cash a winning ticket.

His horse had come in at fifteen, six-ten, four-fifty for Straight, Place, and Show, and sixty bucks on the nose had paid off very nicely.

Lenny Poe took out his copy of the *Daily Racing Form* and checked over the listing for the next race.

Hm-m-m, ha. Purse, $7500. Four-year-olds and up: handicap. Seven furlongs. Turf course. Hm-m-m, ha.

Lenny Poe had a passion for throwing his money away on any unpredictable event that would offer him odds. He had, deep down, an artistic soul, but he didn't let that interfere with his desire to lay a bet at the drop of an old fedora.

He had already decided, several hours before, that Ducksoup, in the next race, would win handily and would pay off at something like twenty or twenty-five to one. But he felt it his duty to look one last time at the previous performance record, just to be absolutely positive.

Satisfied, he folded the *Racing Form*, shoved it back into his pocket, and walked over to the fifty-dollar window.

"Gimmie nine tickets on Ducksoup in the seventh," he said, plonking the handful of bills down on the counter.

But before the man behind the window grating could take the money, a huge, hamlike, and rather hairy hand came down on top of his own hand, covering it and the money at the same time.

"Hold it, Lenny," said a voice at the same time.

Lenny jerked his head around to his right and looked up to see a largish man who had "cop" written all over him. Another such individual crowded past Lenny on his left to flash a badge on the man in the betting window, so that he would know that this wasn't a holdup.

"Hey!" said Lenny. His mind was thinking fast. He decided to play his favorite role, that of the indignant Italian. "Whatsa da matta with you, hah? Thisa no a free country? A man gotta no rights?"

"Come on, Mr. Poe," the big man said quietly, "this is important."

"Poe? You outta you mind? Thatsa name of a river——or a raven. I'm a forgetta which. My namesa Manelli!"

"*Scusi, signore,*" the big man said with exaggerated politeness, "*ma se lei è veramente italiano, non' è l'uomo che cerchiamo.*"

Lenny's Italian was limited to a handful of words. He know he was trapped, but he faced the situation with aplomb. "Thatsa lie! I was inna Chicago that night!"

"*Ah! Cosè credero. Avanti, saccentone.*" He jerked his thumb toward the gate. "Let's go."

Lenny muttered something that the big man didn't quite catch.

"What'd you say?"

"Upper United States—the northern United States," Lenny said calmly shoving his four hundred fifty dollars into his pocket. "That's where Chicago is. Never mind. Come in, boys; back to the drawing board."

The two men escorted Lenny to a big, powerful Lincoln; he climbed into the back seat with the big one while the other one got behind the wheel.

As soon as they had left the racetrack and were well out on the highway, the driver said: "You want to call in, Mario? This traffic is pretty heavy."

The big man beside Lenny leaned forward, over the back of the front seat, unhooked the receiver of the scrambler-equipped radiophone, and sat back down. He thumbed a button on the side of the handset and said: "This is Seven Oh Two." After a short silence, he said: "You can call off the net. You want him brought in?" He listened for a moment. "O.K. Are we cleared through the main gate? O.K. Off."

He leaned forward to replace the receiver, speaking to the driver as he did so. "Straight to the Air Force base. They've got a jet waiting there for him."

He settled back comfortably and looked at Lenny. "You could at least tell people where you're going."

"Very well," said Lenny. He folded his arms, closed his eyes, and relaxed. "Right now, I'm going off to dreamland."

He waited a short while to see if the other would say anything. He didn't, so Lenny proceeded to do exactly what he had promised to do.

He went off to dreamland.

He had not been absolutely sure, when he made the promise, that he would actually do just that, but the odds were in favor of it. It was now one o'clock in the morning in Moscow, and Lenny's brother, Raphael, was a man of regular habits.

Lenny reached out. When he made contact, all he got was a jumble of hash. It was as though someone had made a movie by cutting bits and snippets from a hundred different films, no bit more than six or seven frames long, with a sound track that might or might not match, and projected the result through a drifting fog, using an ever-changing lens that rippled like the surface of a wind-ruffled pool. Sometimes one figure would come into sharp focus for a fraction of a second, sometimes in color, sometimes not.

Sometimes Lenny was merely observing the show, sometimes he was in it.

Rafe! Hey, Rafe! Wake up!

The jumble of hash began to stabilize, becoming more coherent—

Lenny sat behind the far desk, watching his brother come up the primrose path in a unicycle. He pulled it to a halt in front of the desk, opened the pilot's canopy, threw out a rope ladder, and climbed down. His gait was a little awkward, in spite of the sponge-rubber floor, because of the huge flowered carpetbag he was carrying. A battered top hat sat precariously on his blond, curly hair.

"Lenny! Boy, am I glad to see you! I've got it! The whole trouble is in the wonkler, where the spadulator comes across the trellis grid!" He lifted the carpetbag and sat it down on the lab table. "Connect up the groffle meter! We'll show those pentagon pickles who has the push-and-go here!"

"Rafe," Lenny said gently, "wake up. You're dreaming. You're asleep. I want to talk to you."

"I know." He grinned widely. "And you don't want any back talk from me! Yok-yok-yok! Just wait'll I show you!"

In his hands, he held an object which Lenny did not at first understand. Then Rafe's mind brought it into focus.

"This"—Rafe held it up—"is a rocket motor!"

"Rafe, wake up!" Lenny said.

The surroundings stabilized a little more.

"I will in just a minute, Lenny." Rafe was apologetic. "But let me show you this." It did bear some resemblance to a rocket motor. It was about as long as a man's forearm and consisted of a bulbous chamber at one end, which narrowed down into a throat and then widened into a hornlike exhaust nozzle. The chamber was black; the rest was shiny chrome.

Rafe grasped it by the throat with one hand. The other, he clasped firmly around the combustion chamber. "Watch! Now watch!"

He gave the bulbous, rubbery chamber a hard squeeze—

"*SQUAWK!*" went the horn.

"Rafe!" Lenny shouted. "Wake up! WAKE UP!"

Rafe blinked as the situation clarified. "What? Just A Second. Lenny. Just...."

"... *A second.*"

Raphael Poe blinked his eyes open. The moon was shining through the dirty windows of the dingy little room that was all he could call home—for a while, at least. Outside the window were the gray streets of Moscow.

His brother's thoughts resounded in his fully awake brain. *Rafe! You awake?*

Sure. Sure. What is it?

The conversation that followed was not in words or pictures, but a weird combination of both, plus a strong admixture of linking concepts that were neither.

In essence, Lenny merely reported that he had taken the day off to go to the races and that Colonel Spaulding was evidently upset for some reason. He wondered if Rafe were in any kind of trouble.

No trouble. Everything's fine at this end. But Dr. Malekrinova won't be back on the job until tomorrow afternoon—or, this *afternoon, rather.*

I know, Lenny replied. *That's why I figured I could take time off for a go at the ponies.*

I wonder why they're in such a fuss, then? Rafe thought.

I'll let you know when I find out, Lenny said. *Go back to sleep and don't worry.*

In a small office in the Pentagon, Colonel Julius T. Spaulding cradled the telephone on his desk and looked at the Secretary of Defense. "That was the airfield. Poe will be here shortly. We'll get to the bottom of this pretty quickly."

"I hope so, Julius," the Secretary said heavily. "The president is beginning to think we're both nuts."

The colonel, a lean, nervous man with dark, bushy eyebrows and a mustache to match, rolled his eyes up toward the ceiling. "I'm beginning to agree with him."

The Defense Secretary scowled at him. "What do you mean?"

"Anybody who takes telepathy seriously is considered a nut," said the colonel.

"True," said the Secretary, "but that doesn't mean we *are* nuts."

"Oh, yeah?" The colonel took the cigar out of his mouth a gestured with it. "Anybody who'd do something that convinces all his friends he's nuts must be nuts."

The Secretary smiled wanly. "I wish you wouldn't be so logical. You almost convince me."

"Don't worry," said the colonel. "I'm not ready to have this room measured for sponge-rubber wallpaper just yet. Operation Mapcase has helped a lot in the past few months, and it will help even more."

"All you have to do is get the bugs out of it," said the Secretary.

"If we did that," Colonel Spaulding said flatly, "the whole operation would fold from lack of personnel."

"Just carry on the best you can," the Secretary said gloomily as he got up to leave. "I'll let you handle it."

"Fine. I'll call you later."

Twenty minutes after the Defense Secretary had gone, Lenny Poe was shown into Colonel Spaulding's office. The agent who had brought him in closed the door gently, leaving him alone with the colonel.

"I told you I'd be back this evening. What were you in such a hurry about?"

"You're supposed to stay in touch," Colonel Spaulding pointed out. "I don't mind your penchant for ponies particularly, but I'd like to know where to find you if I need you."

"I wouldn't mind in the least, colonel. I'd phone you every fifteen minutes if that's what you wanted. Except for one thing."

"What's that?"

Lenny jerked a thumb over his shoulder. "Your linguistically talented flatfeet. Did you ever try to get into a floating crap game when you were being followed by a couple of bruisers who look more like cops than cops do?"

"Look, Poe, I can find you plenty of action right here in Washington, if it won't offend your tender sensibilities to shoot crap with a senator or two. Meanwhile, sit down and listen. This is important."

Lenny sat own reluctantly. "O.K. What is it?"

"Dr. Davenport and his crew are unhappy about that last batch of drawings you and I gave 'em."

"What's the matter? Don't they like the color scheme? I never thought scientists had any artistic taste, anyway."

"It's got nothing to do with that. The—"

The phone rang. Colonel Spaulding scooped it up and identified himself. Then: "What? Yeah. All right, send him in."

He hung up and looked back at Lenny. "Davenport. We can get his story firsthand. Just sit there and look important."

Lenny nodded. He knew that Dr. Amadeus Davenport was aware that the source of those drawings was Soviet Russia, but he did not know how they had been obtained. As far as he knew, it was just plain, ordinary spy work.

He came in briskly. He was a tall, intelligent-looking man with a rather craggy face and thoughtful brown eyes. He put a large brief case on the floor, and, after the preliminaries were over, he came right to the point.

"Colonel Spaulding, I spoke to the Secretary of Defense, and he agreed that perhaps this situation might be cleared up if I talked directly with you."

"I hope so," the colonel said. "Just what is it that seems to be bothering you?"

"These drawings," Davenport said, "don't make any sense. The device they're supposed to represent couldn't do anything. Look; I'll show you."

He took from his brief case photostatic copies of some of the drawings Lenny had made. Five of them were straight blueprint-type drawings; the sixth was a copy of Lenny's near-photographic paintings of the device itself.

"This component, here," he said, gesturing at the set of drawings, "simply baffles us. We're of the opinion that your agents are known to the Soviet government and have been handed a set of phony plans."

"What's it supposed to do?" Lenny asked.

"We don't know what it's *supposed* to do," the scientist said, "but it's doubtful that it would *actually* do anything." He selected one of the photocopies. "See that thing? The one shaped like the letter Q with an offset tail? According to the specifications, it is supposed to be painted emerald green, but there's no indication of what it is."

Lenny Poe reached out, picked up the photocopy and looked at it. It was—or had been—an exact copy of the drawing that was used by Dr. Sonya Malekrinova. But, whereas the original drawing has been labeled entirely in Cyrillic characters, these labels were now in English.

The drawings made no sense to Lenny at all. They hadn't when he'd made them. His brother was a scientist, but Lenny understood none of it.

"Who translated the Russian into English?" he asked.

"A Mr. Berensky. He's one of our best experts on the subject. I assure you the translations are accurate, Dr. Davenport said.

"But if you don't know what that thing is," the colonel objected, "how can you say the device won't work? Maybe it would if that Q-shaped thing was—"

"I know what you mean," Davenport interrupted. "But that's not the only part of the machine that doesn't make any sense."

He went on to explain other discrepancies he had detected in the drawings, but none of it penetrated to Lenny, although Colonel Spaulding seemed to be able to follow the physicist's conversation fairly readily.

"Well, what's you suggestion, doctor?" the colonel asked at last.

"If you agents could get further data," the physicist said carefully, "it might be of some use. At the same time, I'd check up on the possibility that your agents are known to the NKVD."

"I'll see what can be done," said the colonel. "Would you mind leaving those copies of the drawings with me for a while?"

"Go right ahead," Davenport said. "One other thing. If we assume this device is genuine, then it must serve some purpose. It might help if we knew what the device is supposed to *do*."

"I'll see what can be done," Colonel Spaulding repeated.

When Davenport had gone, Spaulding looked at Poe. "Got any explanation for that one?"

"No," Lenny admitted. "All I can do is check with Rafe. He won't be awake for a few hours yet. I'll check on it and give you an answer in the morning."

Early next morning, Colonel Spaulding walked through his outer office. He stopped at the desk where the pretty brunette WAC sergeant was typing industriously, leaned across the desk, and gave her his best leer. "How about a date tonight, music lover?" he asked, "'*Das Rheingold*' is playing tonight. A night at the opera would do you good."

"I'm sorry, sir," she said primly, "you know enlisted women aren't allowed to date officers."

"Make out an application for OCS. I'll sign it."

She smiled at him. "But then I wouldn't have any excuse for turning you down. And then what would my husband say?"

"I'll bribe him. I'll send *him* to OCS."

"He's not eligible. Officers are automatically disqualified."

Colonel Spaulding sighed. "A guy can't win against competition like that. Anything new this morning?"

"Mr. Poe is waiting in your office. Other than that, there's just the routine things."

He went on into his office. Lenny Poe was seated behind the colonel's desk, leaning back in the swivel chair, his feet on the top of the desk. He was sound asleep.

The colonel walked over to the desk, took his cigar from his mouth, and said: "*Good* morrrning, Colonel Spaulding!"

Lenny snapped awake. "I'm not Colonel Spaulding," he said.

"Then why are you sitting in Colonel Spaulding's chair?"

"I figured if I was asleep nobody'd know the difference." Lenny got up and walked over to one of the other chairs. "These don't lean back comfortably. I can't sleep in 'em."

"You can sleep later. How was your session with Rafe?"

Lenny glowered glumly. "I wish you and Rafe hadn't talked me into this job. It's a strain on the brain. I don't know how he expects anyone to understand all that garbage."

"All what garbage?"

Lenny waved a hand aimlessly. "All this scientific guff. I'm an artist, not a scientist. If Rafe can get me a clear picture of something, I can copy it, but when he tries to explain something scientific, he might as well be thinking in Russian or Old Upper Middle High Martian or something."

"I know," said Colonel Spaulding, looking almost as glum as Lenny. "Did you get anything at all that would help Dr. Davenport figure out what those drawings mean?"

"Rafe says that the translations are all wrong," Lenny said, "but I can't get a clear picture of just what *is* wrong."

Colonel Spaulding thought for a while in silence. Telepathy—at least in so far as the Poe brothers practiced it—certainly had its limitations. Lenny couldn't communicate mentally with anyone except his brother Rafe. Rafe could pick up the thoughts of almost anyone if he happened to be close by, but couldn't communicate over a long distance with anyone but Lenny.

The main trouble lay in the fact that it was apparently impossible to transmit a concept directly from Brain A to Brain B unless the basic building blocks of the concept were already present in Brain B. Raphael Poe, for instance, had spent a long time studying Russian, reading Dostoevski, Tolstoy, and Turgenev in the original tongue, familiarizing himself with modern Russian thought through the courtesy of *Izvestia*, *Pravda*, and *Krokodil*, and, finally, spending time in the United Nations building and near the Russian embassy in order to be sure that he could understand the mental processes involved.

Now, science has a language of its own. Or, rather, a multiplicity of languages, each derived partly from the native language of the various scientific groups and partly of borrowings from other languages. In the physical sciences especially, the language of mathematics is a further addition.

More than that, the practice of the scientific method automatically induces a thought pattern that is different from the type of thought pattern that occurs in the mind of a person who is not scientifically oriented.

Lenny's mind was a long way from being scientifically oriented. Worse, he was a bigot. He not only didn't know why the light in his room went on when he flipped the switch, he didn't *want* to know. To him, science was just so much flummery, and he didn't want his brain cluttered up with it.

Facts mean nothing to a bigot. He has already made up his mind, and he doesn't intend to have his solid convictions disturbed by anything so unimportant as a contradictory fact. Lenny was of the opinion that all mathematics was arcane gobbledygook, and his precise knowledge of the mathematical odds in poker and dice games didn't abate that opinion one whit. Obviously, a mind like that is utterly incapable of understanding a projected thought of scientific content; such a thought bounces off the impregnable mind shield that the bigot has set up around his little area of bigotry.

Colonel Spaulding had been aware of these circumstances since the inception of the Operation Mapcase. Even though he, himself, had never experienced telepathy more than half a dozen times in his life, he had made a study of the subject and was pretty well aware of its limitations. The colonel might have dismissed—as most men do—his own fleeting experiences as "coincidence" or "imagination" if it had not been for the things he had seen and felt in Africa during World War II. He had only been a captain then, on detached duty with British Intelligence, under crusty old Colonel Sir

Cecil Haversham, who didn't believe a word of "all that mystic nonsense." Colonel Haversham had made the mistake of alienating one of the most powerful of the local witch doctors.

The British Government had hushed it all up afterwards, of course, but Spaulding still shuddered when he thought of the broken-spirited, shrunken caricature of his old self that Colonel Haversham had become after he told the witch doctor where to get off.

Spaulding had known that there were weaknesses in the telepathic communication linkage that was the mainspring of Operation Mapcase, but he had thought that they could be overcome by the strengths of the system. Lenny had no blockage whatever against receiving visual patterns and designs. He could reproduce an electronic wiring diagram perfectly because, to him, it was not a grouping of scientific symbols, but a design of lines, angles, and curves.

At first, it is true, he had had a tendency to change them here and there, to make the design balance better, to make it more aesthetically satisfying to his artistic eye, but that tendency had been easily overcome, and Colonel Spaulding was quite certain that that wasn't what was wrong now.

Still—

"Lenny," he said carefully, "are you sure you didn't jigger up those drawings to make 'em look prettier?"

Lenny Poe gave the colonel a look of disgust. "Positive. Rafe checked 'em over every inch of the way as I was drawing them, and he rechecked again last night—or this morning—on those photostats Davenport gave us. That's when he said there was something wrong with the translations."

"But he couldn't make it clear just what was wrong, eh?"

Lenny shrugged. "How anybody could make any sense out of that gobbledegook is beyond me."

The colonel blew out a cloud of cigar smoke and looked thoughtfully at the ceiling. As long as the diagrams were just designs on paper, Lenny Poe could pick them up fine. Which meant that everything was jim-dandy as long as the wiring diagrams were labeled in the Cyrillic alphabet. The labels were just more squiggles to be copied as a part of the design.

But if the labels were in English, Lenny's mind would try to "make sense" out of them, and since scientific concepts did *not* "make sense" to him, the labels came out as pure nonsense. In one of his drawings, a lead wire had been labeled "simply ground to powder," and if the original drawing hadn't been handy to check with, it might have taken quite a bit of thought to realize that what was meant was "to power supply ground." Another time, a GE 2N 188A transistor had come out labeled GEZNISSA. There were others—much worse.

Russian characters, on the other hand, didn't have to make any sense to Lenny, so his mind didn't try to force them into a preconceived mold.

Lenny unzipped the leather portfolio he had brought with him—a specially-made carrier that looked somewhat like an oversized brief case.

"Maybe these'll help," he said.

"We managed to get two good sketches of the gadget—at least, as much of it as that Russian lady scientist has put together so far. I kind of like the rather abstract effect you get from all those wires snaking in and around, with that green glass tube in the center. Pretty, isn't it?"

"Very," said the colonel without conviction. "I wonder if it will help Davenport any?" He looked at the pictures for several seconds more, then, suddenly, his eyes narrowed. "Lenny—this piece of green glass—the thing's shaped like the letter Q."

"Yeah, sort of. Why?"

"You said it was a tube, but you didn't make it look hollow when you drew it."

"It isn't; it's solid. Does a tube have to be hollow? Yeah, I guess it does, doesn't it? Well, then, it isn't a tube."

Colonel Spaulding picked up the phone and dialed a number.

"Colonel Spaulding here," he said after a moment. "Let me speak to Dr. Davenport." And, after a wait: "This is Colonel Spaulding, doctor. I think we may have something for you."

"Good morning, colonel. I'm glad to hear that. What is it?"

"The Q-shaped gadget—the one that you said was supposed to be painted emerald green. Are you *sure* that's the right translation of the Russian?"

"Well ... uh—" Davenport hesitated. "I can't be sure on my own say-so, of course. *I* don't understand Russian. But I assure you that Mr. Berensky is perfectly reliable."

"Oh, I have no doubt of that," Colonel Spaulding said easily. "But, tell me, does Mr. Berensky know how to read a circuit diagram?"

"He does," Davenport said, somewhat testily. "Of course, he wasn't shown the diagram itself. We had the Russian labels copied, and he translated from a list."

"I had a sneaking suspicion that was it," said Spaulding. "Tell me, doctor, what does L-E-A-D spell?"

"Lead," said the doctor promptly, pronouncing it *leed*. Then, after a pause, he said: "Or lead," this time pronouncing it *led*. "It would depend on the context."

"Suppose it was on a circuit diagram," the colonel prompted.

"Then it would probably be *leed*. What's all this leading up to, colonel?"

"Bear with me. Suppose you had a cable coming from a storage battery, and you wanted to make sure that the cable was reasonably resistant to corrosion, so you order it made out of the metal, lead. It would be a *led leed*, wouldn't it?"

"Um-m-m ... I suppose so."

"You might get pretty confused if you didn't have a circuit diagram in front of you to tell you what the label was talking about, mightn't you?"

"I see what you mean," the scientist said slowly. "But we can't show those circuit diagrams to Berensky. The Secretary of Defense himself has classified them as Class Triple-A Ultra-Hyper Top Secret. That puts them just below the Burn-The-Contents-Before-Reading class, and Berensky doesn't have that kind of clearance."

"Then get somebody else," Colonel Spaulding said tiredly. "All you need is a man who can understand technical Russian and has a top-level secrecy clearance. If we haven't got at least one man in these United States with such simple qualifications as those, them we might as well give the country over to the Reds or back to the Redskins, since our culture is irreprievably doomed." And he lowered the phone gently to its cradle.

"There's no such word as 'irreprievably'," Lenny pointed out.

"There is now," said Colonel Spaulding.

Raphael Poe moseyed through the streets of Moscow in an apparently aimless manner. The expression on his face was that of a reasonably happy moron.

His aimless manner was only apparent. Actually, he was heading toward the Lenin Soviet People's Higher Research Laboratories. Dr. Sonya Borisovna Malekrinova would be working late this evening, and he wanted to get as close as possible in order to pick up as much information as he could.

Rafe had a great deal of admiration for that woman, he admitted to himself. She was, granted, as plain as an unsalted *matzoh*. No. That was an understatement. If it were possible to die of the uglies, Sonya Borisovna would have been dangerously ill.

Her disposition did nothing to alleviate that drawback. She fancied herself as cold, hard, analytical, and ruthless; actually she was waspish, arrogant, overbearing, and treacherous. What she considered in herself to be scientific detachment was really an isolation born of fear and distrust of the entire human race.

To her, Communism was a religion; "*Das Kapital*" and "*The Communist Manifesto*" were holy writ enshrining the dogmata of Marxism-Leninism, and the conflict with the West was a *jehad*, a holy war in which God, in His manifestation as Dialectic Materialism, would naturally win out in the end.

All of which goes to show that a scientific bent, in itself, does not necessarily keep one from being a bigot.

Rafe's admiration for the woman stemmed solely from the fact that, in spite of all the powerful drawbacks that existed in her mind, she was still capable of being a brilliant, if somewhat erratic scientist.

There was a more relaxed air in Moscow these days. The per capita production of the Soviet Union still did not come up to that of the United States, but the recent advances in technology did allow a feeling of accomplishment, and the hard drive for superiority was softened a trifle. It was no longer considered the height of indolence and unpatriotic time-wasting to sit on a bench and feed pigeons. Nor was food so scarce and costly that throwing away a few bread crumbs could be considered sabotage.

So Rafe Poe found himself a quiet corner near the Lenin Soviet People's Laboratories, took out a small bag of dried breadcrumbs, and was soon surrounded by pigeons.

Dr. Malekrinova was carefully calibrating and balancing the electronic circuits that energized and activated and controlled the output of the newly-installed beam generator—a ring of specially-made greenish glass that had a small cylinder of the same glass projecting out at a tangent. Her assistant, Alexis, a man of small scientific ability but a gifted mechanic, worked stolidly with her. It was not an easy job for Alexis; Sonya Borisovna was by no means an easy woman to work with. There was, as there should have been, a fifty-fifty division in all things—a proper state of affairs in a People's Republic. Alexis Andreyevich did half the physical work, got all the blame when things went wrong, and none of the credit when things went right. Sonya Borisovna got the remaining fifty percent.

Sonya Borisovna Malekrinova had been pushing herself too hard, and she knew it. But, she told herself, for the glory of the Soviet peoples, the work must go on.

After spending two hours taking down instrument readings, she took the results to her office and began to correlate them.

Have to replace that 140-9.0 micromicrofarad frequency control on stage two with something more sensitive, she thought. *And the field modulation coils require closer adjustment.*

She took off her glasses and rubbed at her tired eyes while she thought. *Perhaps the 25 microfarad, 12 volt electrolytic condenser could be used to feed the pigeons, substituting a breadcrumb capacitor in the sidewalk circuit.*

She opened her eyes suddenly and stared at the blank wall in front of her. "Pigeons?" she said wonderingly. "*Breadcrumb* capacitor? Am I losing my mind? What kind of nonsense is that?"

She looked back down at her notes, then replaced her glasses so that she could read them. Determined not to let her mind wander in that erratic fashion again, she returned her attention to the work at hand.

She found herself wondering if it might not be better to chuck the whole job and get out while the getting was good. *The old gal*, she thought, *is actually tapping my mind! She's picking up everything!*

Sonya Borisovna sat bolt upright in her chair, staring at the blank wall again. "Why am I thinking such nonsense?" she said aloud. "And why should I be thinking in English?" When her words registered on her ears, she realized that she was actually *speaking* in English. She was thoroughly acquainted with the language, of course, but it was not normal for her to think in it unless she happened to be conversing with someone in that tongue.

The first whisper of a suspicion began to take form in the mind of Dr. Sonya Borisovna Malekrinova.

Half a block away, Raphael Poe emptied the last of his breadcrumbs on the sidewalk and began walking away. He kept his mind as blank as possible, while his brow broke out in a cold sweat.

That," said Colonel Julius Spaulding scathingly, "is as pretty a mess as I've seen in years."

"It's a breadboard circuit, I'll admit," Dr. Davenport said defensively, "but it's built according to the schematics you gave us."

"Doctor," said the colonel, "during the war the British dropped our group a radio transmitter. It was the only way to get the stuff into Africa quickly. The parachute failed to open. The transmitter fell two thousand feet, hit the side of a mountain, and tumbled down another eight hundred feet. When we found it, four days later, its wiring was in better shape than that thing is in now."

"It's quite sufficient to test the operation of the device," Davenport said coldly.

Spaulding had to admit to himself that it probably was. The thing was a slapdash affair—the colonel had a strong feeling that Davenport had assigned the wiring job to an apprentice and gave him half an hour to do the job—but the soldering jobs looked tight enough, and the components didn't look as though they'd all been pulled out of the salvage bin. What irritated Colonel Spaulding was Davenport's notion that the whole thing was a waste of time, energy, money, and materials, and, therefore, there was no point in doing a decent job of testing it at all.

He was glad that Davenport didn't know how the information about the device had been transported to the United States. As it was, he considered the drawings a hoax on the part of the Russians; if he had been told that they had been sent telepathically, he would probably have gone into fits of acute exasperation over such idiocy.

The trouble with Davenport was that, since the device didn't make any sense to him, he didn't believe it would function at all.

"Oh, it will do *something*, all right," he'd said once, "but it won't be anything that needs all that apparatus. Look here—" He had pointed toward the schematic. "Where do you think all that energy is going? All you're going to get is a little light, a lot of heat, and a couple of burned out coils. I could do the same job cheaper with a dozen 250 watt light bulbs."

To be perfectly honest with himself, Spaulding had to admit that he wasn't absolutely positive that the device would do anything in particular, either. His own knowledge of electronic circuitry was limited to ham radio experience, and even that was many years out of date. He couldn't be absolutely sure that the specifications for the gadget hadn't been garbled in transmission.

The Q-shaped gizmo, for instance. It had taken the better part of a week for Raphael Poe to transmit the information essential to the construction of that enigmatic bit of glass.

Rafe had had to sit quietly in the privacy of his own room and print out the specifications in Russian, then sit and look at the paper while Lenny copied the "design." Then each paper had to be carefully destroyed, which wasn't easy to do. You don't go around burning papers in a crowded Russian tenement unless you want the people in the next room to wonder what you're up to.

Then the drawings Lenny had made had had to be translated into English and the piece carefully made to specifications.

Now here it was, all hooked up and, presumably, ready for action. Colonel Spaulding fervently hoped there would *be* some action; he didn't like the smug look on Dr. Amadeus Davenport's face.

The device was hooked up on a testing-room circuit and controlled from outside. The operation could be watched through a heavy pane of bulletproof glass. "With all that power going into it," Davenport said, "I don't want anyone to get hurt by spatters of molten metal when those field coils blow."

They went outside to the control console, and Dr. Davenport flipped the energizing switch. After the device had warmed up on low power, Davenport began turning knobs slowly, increasing the power flow. In the testing room, the device just sat there, doing nothing visible, but the meters on the control console showed that something was going on. A greenish glow came from the housing that surrounded the Q-shaped gadget.

"Where the Russians made their mistake in trying to fool anyone with that thing was in their design of that laser component," said Dr. Davenport. "Or, I should say, the thing that is supposed to look like a laser component."

"Laser?" said Colonel Spaulding uncomprehendingly.

"It means 'light amplification by stimulated emission of radiation'," Davenport explained. "Essentially, a laser consists of a gas-filled tube or a solid ruby bar with parallel mirrors at both ends. By exciting the atoms from outside, light is generated within the tube, and some of it begins to bounce back and forth between the mirrors at the ends. This tends to have a cascade effect on the atoms which have picked up the energy from outside, so that more and more of the light generated inside the tube tends to be parallel to the length of the tube. One of the mirrors is only partially silvered, and eventually the light bouncing back and forth becomes powerful enough to flash through the half-silvered end, giving a coherent beam of light."

"Maybe that's what this is supposed to be," said the colonel.

Davenport chuckled dryly. "Not a chance. Not with an essentially circular tube that isn't even silvered."

Lenny Poe, the colonel noticed, wasn't the only person around who didn't care whether the thing he referred to as a "tube" was hollow or not.

"Is it doing anything?" Colonel Spaulding asked anxiously, trying to read the meters over Davenport's shoulder.

"It's heating up," Davenport said dryly.

Spaulding looked back at the apparatus. A wisp of smoke was rising slowly from a big coil.

A relay clicked minutely.

WHAP!

For a confused second, everything seemed to happen at once.

But it didn't; there was a definite order to it.

First, a spot on the ceramic tile wall of the room became suddenly red, orange, white hot. Then there was a little crater of incandescent fury, as though a small volcano had erupted in the wall. Following that, there was a sputtering and crackling from the innards of the device itself, and a cloud of smoke arose suddenly, obscuring things in the room. Finally, there was the crash of circuit-breakers as they reacted to the overload from the short circuit.

There was silence for a moment, then the hiss of the automatic fire extinguishers in the testing room as they poured a cloud of carbon dioxide snow on the smoldering apparatus.

"There," said Davenport with utter satisfaction. "What did I tell you?"

"You didn't tell me this thing was a heat-ray projector," said Colonel Spaulding.

"What are you talking about?" Dr. Davenport said disdainfully.

"Develop the film in those automatic cameras," Spaulding said, "and I'll show you what I'm talking about!"

As far as Colonel Spaulding was concerned, the film showed clearly what had happened. A beam of energy had leaped from the "tail" of the Q-tube, hit the ceramic tile of the wall, and burned its way through in half a second or so. The hole in the wall, surrounded by fused ceramic, was mute evidence of the occurrence of what Spaulding had seen.

But Dr. Davenport pooh-poohed the whole thing. Evidence to the contrary, he was quite certain that no such thing had happened. A piece of hot glass from a broken vacuum tube had done it, he insisted.

A piece of hot glass had burned its way through half an inch of tile? And a wall?

Davenport muttered something about the destructive effects of shaped charges. He was more willing to believe that something as wildly improbable as that had happened than admit that the device had done what Colonel Spaulding was quite certain it had done.

Within three hours, Davenport had three possible explanations of what had happened, each of which required at least four unlikely things to happen coincidentally.

Colonel Spaulding stalked back to his office in a state of angry disgust. Just because the thing was foreign to Davenport's notions, he had effectively tied his own hands—and Colonel Spaulding's, too.

"Where's Lenny Poe?" he asked the WAC sergeant. "I want to talk to him."

She shook her head. "I don't know, sir. Lieutenant Fesner called in half an hour ago. Mr. Poe has eluded them again."

Colonel Spaulding gazed silently at the ceiling for a long moment. Then: "Sergeant Nugget, take a letter. To the President of the United States, 1600 Pennsylvania Avenue, Washington, D.C.

"Dear Sir. Consider this my resignation. I have had so much experience with jackasses lately that I have decided to change my name to Hackenbush and become a veterinarian. Yours truly, et cetera. Got that?"

"Yes, sir," said the sergeant.

"Burn it. When Fumblefingers Fesner and his boys find Lenny Poe again, I want to know immediately."

He stalked on into his office.

Raphael Poe was beginning to feel distinctly uncomfortable. Establishing a close rapport with another mind can be a distinct disadvantage at times. A spy is supposed to get information without giving any; a swapping of information is not at all to his advantage.

It was impossible to keep his mind a perfect blank. What he had to do was keep his strongest surface thoughts entirely on innocuous things. The trouble with that was that it made it extremely difficult to think about some way to get out of the jam he was in. Thinking on two levels at once, while not impossible, required a nicety of control that made wire-walking over Niagara look easy.

The thing to do was to make the surface thoughts automatically repetitive. A song.

"*In a hall of strange description (Antiquarian Egyptian), Figuring his monthly balance sheet, a troubled monarch sat With a frown upon his forehead, hurling interjections horrid At the state of his finances, for his pocketbook was flat.*"

Simultaneously, he kept a picture in his mind's eye. It had to be something vivid that would be easy to concentrate on. The first thing that came to mind was the brilliant necktie that the President had used in his test several months before. He conjured it up in all its chartreuse glory, then he animated it. Mauve satyrs danced with rose-pink nymphs and chased them over the yellow-green landscape.

"*Not a solitary single copper cent had he to jingle In his pocket, and his architects had gone off on a strike, Leaving pyramids unfinished, for their wages had diminished, And their credit vanished likewise, in a way they didn't like.*"

Rafe could tell that Dr. Malekrinova's mind was trying to reject the alien ideas that were coming into her mind. She wasn't consciously trying to pick up Rafe's thoughts. But the rejection was ineffective because of its fascination. The old business about the horse's tail. If you see a white horse, you'll soon get rich if you can keep from thinking about the horse's tail until it's out of sight. The first thought that comes to mind is: "I mustn't think about the horse's tail." A self-defeating proposition.

If Sonya Borisovna had been certain that she was receiving the thoughts telepathically, she might have been able to reject them. But her mind rejected the idea of telepathy instead, so she was susceptible to the thoughts because she thought they were her own.

The cavorting of the nymphs and satyrs became somewhat obscene, but Rafe didn't bother to correct it. He had more to worry about than offending the rather prim mind of Dr. Malekrinova.

"*It was harder for His Royal Highness than for sons of toil, For the horny-handed workmen only ate three figs per day, While the King liked sweet potatoes, puddings, pies, and canned tomatoes, Boneless ham, and Bluepoint oysters cooked some prehistoric way.*"

What to do now? Should he try to get out of Russia? Was there any quick way out?

He had all the information he needed on the heat-beam projector that Dr. Malekrinova was building. The theory behind it was perfectly clear; all it needed was further experimentation. If it worked out according to theory, it would be an almost perfect defense against even the fastest intercontinental ballistic missiles.

"As he growled, the Royal grumbler spied a bit of broken tumblerIn a long undusted corner just behind the chamber door.When his hungry optics spied it, he stood silently and eyed it,Then he smote his thigh with ecstasy and danced about the floor."

Maybe he should try to make a run for the American Embassy. No. No one there knew him, and they probably couldn't get him out of the country, anyway. Besides, it would take him too long to explain the situation to them.

"'By the wit Osiris gave me! This same bit of glass shall save me!I shall sell it as a diamond at some stupendous price!And whoe'er I ask to take it will find, for his own sweet sake, itWill be better not to wait until I have to ask him twice!'"

The theory behind the heat projector was simply an extension of the laser theory, plus a few refinements. Inside a ring made of the proper material, the light, acted upon by exterior magnetic fields, tended to move in a circle, so that the photon cascade effect was all in one direction instead of bouncing back and forth between a pair of mirrors. That light could be bent around corners by making it travel through a glass rod was well known, and the Malekrinova Q-tube took advantage of that effect.

In a way, the principle was similar to that of the cyclotron, except that instead of spinning ions around in a circle to increase their velocity a beam of coherent light was circulated to increase its intensity.

Then, at the proper moment, a beam of intense coherent light shot out of the tangent that formed the tail of the Q-tube. If the material of the Q was properly constructed and contained atoms that fluoresced strongly in the infra red, you had a heat beam that delivered plenty of power. And, since the radiation was linear and "in step," the Q-tube didn't heat up much at all. The cascade effect took most of the energy out as radiation.

"Then a Royal Proclamation was dispatched throughout the nation,Most imperatively calling to appear before the King.Under penalties most cruel, every man who sold a jewelOr who bought and bartered precious stones, and all that sort of thing."

But knowing all that didn't help Raphael Poe or the United States of America one whit if the information couldn't be gotten out of Russia and into Colonel Spaulding's hands. Lenny had told him of the trouble the colonel was having with Dr. Davenport.

If he could only communicate with Lenny! But if he did, Dr. Malekrinova would pick up every bit of it, and that would be the end of that. No, he had to figure out some way to get himself and the information both out of the country.

Meanwhile, he had to keep thinking of an animated necktie. And he had to keep singing.

"Thereupon, the jewelers' nether joints all quaked and knocked together,As they packed their Saratogas in lugubrious despair.It was ever their misfortune to be pillaged by extortion,And they thought they smelled a rodent on the sultry desert air."

Lenny Poe shoved open the door of Colonel Spaulding's outer office with a violence that startled Sergeant Nugget.
"Is Spaulding in?" he barked.
"I think he's expecting you," she said. There was no time to buzz the colonel; Poe was already opening the door.
"Rafe's in trouble!" Lenny said hurriedly, slamming the door behind him.
"Where have you been?" snapped the colonel.
"Never mind that! Rafe's in trouble, I said! We've gotta figure a way to get him out of it!"
Colonel Spaulding dropped all thought of bawling out Poe. "What'd he say? What's the trouble?"
"All he's doing is broadcasting that necktie—like an animated cartoon in technicolor. And he's singing."
"Singing? Singing what?"

"As they faced the Great Propylon, with an apprehensive smile on,Sculptured there in heiroglyphics six feet wide and nine feet highWas the threat of King Rameses to chop every man to piecesWho, when shown the Royal diamond, would dare refuse to buy."

Colonel Spaulding blinked. "That's pretty. What does it mean?"
"Nothing; it's a song, that's all. That female Russian scientist can read Rafe's mind, and he's broadcasting this stuff to cover up!"
Quickly, he told Spaulding what the situation was as he had been able to piece it together from Rafe's secondary thoughts.
"Ye Gods!" Colonel Spaulding slapped at his brow. Then he grabbed for the telephone and started dialing.

Lenny dropped into one of the chairs, closed his eyes, and concentrated.
Rafe! Rafe! Listen to me! Rafe!

"Then the richest dealer, Mulai Hassan, eyed the gem and coollySaid, 'The thing is but a common tumbler-bottom, nothing more!'Whereupon, the King's Assassin drew his sword, and Mulai HassanNever peddled rings again upon the Nile's primeval shore."

But below the interference came Rafe's thoughts. And the one thing of primary importance to him was to get the information on the heat-beam generator to the United States.

No bigotry, no matter how strong, is totally impregnable. Even the most narrow-minded racial bigot will make an exception if a person of the despised race risks his own life to save the life of the bigot or someone the bigot loves. The bigotry doesn't collapse—not by a long shot. But an exception is made in that one case.

Lenny Poe made an exception. Any information that was worth his brother's life was *Important*! Therefore, it was not, could not be, scientific gobbledegook, no matter how it sounded.

Rafe, give it to me! Try me! I can copy it!

"Then Abdullah abd Almahdi faintly said the stone was shoddy,But he thought that, in a pinch, he might bid fifty cents himself.There ensued a slight commotion where he could repent the notion,And Abdullah was promoted to the Oriental Shelf."

Rafe! Stop singing that stupid song and give me the stuff! She can't learn anything if you just think about that theory stuff. She already knows that! Come on! Give!

Lenny Poe grabbed a pencil and a sheaf of paper from the colonel's desk and began writing frantically as the *Song of the Egyptian Diamond* stopped suddenly.

Words. Nonsense words. That's all most of the stuff was to Lenny. It didn't matter. He spelled them as he thought they should be, and if he made a mistake, Rafe would correct him.

Rafe tried to keep a picture of the words as they would look if printed while he thought them verbally, and that helped. The information came across in the only way it could come across—not as concepts, but as symbols.

Lenny hardly noticed that the Secretary of Defense and the President had come into the room. He didn't even realize that Colonel Spaulding was feeding him fresh sheets of paper.

Lenny didn't seem to notice the time passing, nor the pain in his hand as the muscles tired. He kept writing. The President left with the Defense Secretary and came back again after a while, but Lenny ignored them.

And when it was over, he pushed pencil and paper aside and, massaging his right hand with his left, sat there with his eyes closed. Then, slowly, a smile spread over his face.

"Well, I'll be damned," he said slowly and softly.

"Mr. Poe," said the President, "is there any danger that your brother will be captured within the next hour?"

Lenny looked up with a startled grin. "Oh. Hi. I didn't notice you, Mr. President. What'd you say?"

The President repeated his question.

"Oh. No. There's nothing to worry about. The little men in white coats came after Dr. Malekrinova. She started screaming that telepathic spies were stealing her secret. She smashed all her apparatus and burned all her papers on top of the wreckage before they could stop her. She keeps shouting about a pink-and-purple orgy and singing a song about glass diamonds and Egyptian kings. I wouldn't say she was actually insane, but she is *very*disturbed."

"Then your brother is safe?"

"As safe as he ever was, Mr. President."

"Thank Heaven for that," said the President. "If they'd ever captured him and made him talk—" He stopped. "I forgot," he said lamely after a moment.

Lenny grinned. "That's all right, Mr. President. I sometimes forget it myself. But it was his handicap, I guess, that made him concentrate on telepathy, so that he doesn't need his ears to hear what people are saying. Maybe I could read minds the way he does if I'd been born that way.

"Come to think of it, I doubt if the Russians would have believed he was a spy if they'd caught him, unless they really did believe he was telepathic. A physical examination would show immediately that he was born without eardrums and that the inner ear bones are fused. They wouldn't try to make a man talk if an examination showed that he really was a deaf-mute."

The buzzer on the colonel's intercom sounded. "Yes?" said Spaulding.
"Dr. Davenport is here," said Sergeant Nugget. "He wants to talk to you."
"Send him in," said Colonel Spaulding gleefully. "I have a nice scientific theory I want to shove down his throat."

Fifty Per Cent Prophet

That he was a phony Swami was beyond doubt. That he was a genuine prophet, though, seemed ... but then, what's the difference between a dictator and a true prophet? So was he....

Dr. Joachim sat in the small room behind his reception hall and held his fingers poised above the keys of the rather creaky electrotyper on his desk. The hands seemed to hang there, long, slender, and pale, like two gulls frozen suddenly in their long swoop towards some precious tidbit floating on the writhing sea beneath, ready to begin their drop instantly, as soon as time began again.

All of Dr. Joachim's body seemed to be held in that same stasis. Only his lips moved as he silently framed the next sentence in his mind.

Physically, the good doctor could be called a big man: he was broad-shouldered and well-muscled, but, hidden as his body was beneath the folds of his blue, monkish robe, only his shortness of stature was noticeable. He was only fifty-four, but the pale face, the full, flowing beard, and the long white hair topped by a small blue skullcap gave him an ageless look, as though centuries of time had flowed over him to leave behind only the marks of experience and wisdom.

The timelessness of an idealized Methuselah as he approached his ninth centennial, the God-given wisdom engraved on the face of Moses as he came down from Sinai, the mystic power of mighty Merlin as he softly intoned a spell of albamancy, all these seemed to have been blended carefully together and infused into the man who sat behind the typer, composing sentences in his head.

Those gull-hands swooped suddenly to the keyboard, and the aged machine clattered rapidly for nearly a minute before Dr. Joachim paused again to consider his next words.

A bell tinkled softly.

Dr. Joachim's brown eyes glanced quickly at the image on the black-and-white TV screen set in the wall. It was connected to the hidden camera in his front room, and showed a woman entering his front door. He sighed and rose from his seat, adjusting his blue robes carefully before he went to the door that led into the outer room.

He'd rather hoped it was a client, but—

"Hello, Susan, my dear," he said in a soft baritone, as he stepped through the door. "What seems to be the trouble?"

It wasn't the same line that he'd have used with a client. You don't ask a mark questions; you tell him. To a mark, he'd have said: "Ah, you are troubled." It sounds much more authoritative and all-knowing.

But Cherrie Tart—*née* Sue Kowalski—was one of the best strippers on the Boardwalk. Her winters were spent in Florida or Nevada or Puerto Rico, but in summer she always returned to King Frankie's *Golden Surf*, for the summer trade at Coney Island. She might be a big name in show business now, but she had never forgotten her carny background, and King Frankie, in spite of the ultra-ultra tone of the *Golden Surf*, still stuck to the old Minsky traditions.

The worried look on her too-perfect face had been easily visible in the TV screen, but it had been replaced by a bright smile as soon as she had heard Dr. Joachim opening the door. The smile flickered for a moment, then she said: "Gee, Doc; you give a girl the creepy feeling that you really *can* read her mind."

Dr. Joachim merely smiled. Susan might be with it, but a good mitt man doesn't give away *all* his little secrets. He had often wished that he could really read minds—he had heard rumors of men who could—but a little well-applied psychology is sometimes just as good.

"So how's everything been, Doc?" She smiled her best stage smile—every tooth perfect in that perfect face, her hair framing the whole like a perfect golden helmet. She looked like a girl in her early twenties, but Dr. Joachim knew for a fact that she'd been born in 1955, which made her thirty-two next January.

"Reasonably well, all things considered," Dr. Joachim admitted. "I'm not starving to death, at least."

She looked around at the room—the heavy drapes, the signs of the zodiac in gold and silver, the big, over-stuffed chairs, all designed to make the "clients" feel comfortable and yet slightly awed by the ancient atmosphere of mysticism. In the dim light, they looked fairly impressive, but she knew that if the lights were brighter the shabbiness would show.

"Maybe you could use a redecorating job, then, Doc," she said. With a gesture born of sudden impulse, she reached into her purse and pulled out an envelope and pressed it into the man's hands. He started to protest, but she cut him off. "No, Doc; I want you to have it. You earned it.

"That San Juan-New York flight, remember?" she went on hurriedly. "You said not to take it, remember? Well, I ... I sort of forgot about what you'd said. You know. Anyway, I got a ticket and was ready to go when the flight was suddenly delayed. Routine, they said. Checking the engines. But I'd never heard of any such routine as that. I remembered what you told me, Doc, and I got scared.

"After an hour, they put another plane into service; they were still working on the other one. I was still worried, so I decided to wait till the next day.

"I guess you read what happened."

He closed his eyes and nodded slowly. "I read."

"Doc, I'd've been on that flight if you hadn't warned me. All the money in the world isn't enough to pay for that." The oddly worried look had come back into her eyes. "Doc, I don't know how you knew that ship was going to go, and I won't ask. I don't want to know. But, ... one thing: Was it *me* they were after?"

She thinks someone blew up the ship, he thought. *She thinks I heard about the plot some way.* For an instant he hesitated, then:

"No, Susan; they weren't after you. No one was trying to kill you. Don't worry about it."

Relief washed over her face. "O.K., Doc; if you say so. Look, I've got to run now, but we've got to sit down and have a few drinks together, now that I'm back. And ... Doc—"

"Yes?"

"Anytime you need anything—if I can ever help you—you let me know, huh?"

"Certainly, my dear. And don't you worry about anything. The stars are all on your side right now."

She smiled, patted his hand, and then was gone in a flash of gold and honey. Dr. Joachim looked at the door that had closed behind her, then he looked down at the envelope in his hands. He opened it gently and took out the sheaf of bills. Fifteen hundred dollars!

He smiled and shoved the money into his pocket. After all, he *was* a professional fortuneteller, even if he didn't like that particular label, and he *had* saved her life, hadn't he?

He returned to the small back room, sat down again at the typer, and, after a minute, began typing again.

When he was finished, he addressed an envelope and put the letter inside.

It was signed with his legal name: *Peter J. Forsythe.*

It required less than two hours for that letter to end up at its destination in a six-floor brick building, a rather old-fashioned affair that stood among similar structures in a lower-middle-class section of Arlington, Virginia, hardly a hop-skip-and-jump from the Pentagon, and not much farther from the Capitol.

The letter was addressed to *Mr. J. Harlan Balfour, President, The Society for Mystical and Metaphysical Research, Inc.*, but Mr. Balfour was not at the Society's headquarters at the time, having been called to Los Angeles to address a group who were awaiting the Incarnation of God.

Even if he had been there, the letter wouldn't have reached him first. All mail was sent first to the office of the Executive Secretary, Mr. Brian Taggert. Most of it—somewhat better than ninety-nine per cent—went directly on to Mr. Balfour's desk, if it was so addressed; Brian Taggert would never have been so cruel as to deprive Mr. Balfour of the joy of sorting through the thousands of crackpot letters in search of those who had the true spark of mysticism which so fascinated Mr. Balfour.

Mr. Balfour was a crackpot, and it was his job to take care of other crackpots—a job he enjoyed immensely and wholeheartedly, feeling, as he did, that that sort of thing was the only reason for the Society's existence. Of course, Mr. Balfour never considered himself or the others in the least bit crackpottish, in which he was just as much in error as he was in his assumption of the Society's *raison d'être*.

Ninety per cent of the members of the Society for Mystical and Metaphysical Research were just what you would expect them to be. Anyone who was "truly interested in the investigation of the supranormal", as the ads in certain magazines put it, could pay five dollars a year for membership, which, among other things, entitled him to the Society's monthly magazine, *The Metaphysicist*, a well-printed, conservative-looking publication which contained articles on everything from the latest flying saucer report to careful mathematical evaluations of the statistical methods of the Rhine Foundation. Within its broad field, the magazine was quite catholic in its editorial policy.

These members constituted a very effective screen for the real work of the society, work carried on by the "core" members, most of whom weren't even listed on the membership rolls. And yet, it was this group of men and women who made the Society's title true.

Mr. Brian Taggert was a long way from being a crackpot. The big, dark-haired, dark-eyed, hawknosed man sat at his desk in his office on the fifth floor of the Society's building and checked over the mail. Normally, his big wrestler's body was to be found quietly relaxed on the couch that stood against a nearby wall. Not that he was in any way averse to action; he simply saw no virtue in purposeless action. Nor did he believe in the dictum of Miles Standish; if he wanted a thing done, he sent the man most qualified to do it, whether that was himself or someone else.

When he came to the letter from Coney Island, New York, he read it quickly and then jabbed at a button on the intercom switchboard in his desktop. He said three syllables which would have been meaningless to anyone except the few who understood that sort of verbal shorthand, released the button, and closed his eyes, putting himself in telepathic contact with certain of the Society's agents in New York.

Across the river, in the Senate Office Building, a telephone rang in the office of Senator Mikhail Kerotski, head of the Senate Committee on Space Exploration. It was an unlisted, visionless phone, and the number was known only to a very few important officials in the United States Government, so the senator didn't bother to identify himself; he simply said: "Hello." He listened for a moment, said, "O.K., fine," in a quiet voice, and cut the connection.

He sat behind his desk for a few minutes longer, a bearlike man with a round, pale face and eyes circled with dark rings and heavy pouches, all of which had the effect of making him look like a rather sleepy specimen of the giant panda. He finished the few papers he had been working on, stacked them together, rose, and went into the outer office, where he told his staff that he was going out for a short walk.

By the time he arrived at the brownstone building in Arlington and was pushing open the door of Brian Taggert's office, Taggert had received reports from New York and had started other chains of action. As soon as Senator Kerotski came in, Taggert pushed the letter across the desk toward him. "Check that."

Kerotski read the letter, and a look of relief came over his round face. "Not the same typewriter or paper, but this is him, all right. What more do we know?"

"Plenty. Hold on, and I'll give you a complete rundown." He picked up the telephone and began speaking in a low voice. It was an ordinary-sounding conversation; even if the wire had been tapped, no one who was not a "core" member of the S.M.M.R. would have known that the conversation was about anything but an esoteric article to be printed in *The Metaphysicist*—something about dowsing rods.

The core membership had one thing in common: *understanding*.

Consider plutonium. Imagine someone dropping milligram-sized pellets of the metal into an ordinary Florence flask. (In an inert atmosphere, of course; there is no point in ruining a good analogy with side reactions.) More than two and a half million of those little pellets could be dropped into the flask without the operator having anything more to worry about than if he were dropping grains of lead or gold into the container. But after the five millionth, dropping them in by hand would only be done by the ignorant, the stupid, or the indestructible. A qualitative change takes place.

So with understanding. As a human mind increases its ability to understand another human mind, it eventually reaches a critical point, and the mind itself changes. And, at that point, the Greek letter *psi* ceases to be a symbol for the unknown.

When understanding has passed the critical point, conversation as it is carried on by most human beings becomes unnecessarily redundant. Even in ordinary conversation, a single gesture—a shrug of the shoulders, a snap of the fingers, or a nose pinched between thumb and forefinger—can express an idea that would take many words and much more time. A single word—"slob," "nazi," "saint"—can be more descriptive than the dozens of words required to define it. All that is required is that the meanings of the symbols be understood.

The ability to manipulate symbols is the most powerful tool of the human mind; a mind which can manipulate them *effectively* is, in every sense of the word, truly human.

Even without telepathy, it was possible for two S.M.M.R. agents to carry on a conversation above and around ordinary chit-chat. It took longer, naturally; when speaking without the chit-chat, it was possible to convey in seconds information that would have taken several minutes to get over in ordinary conversation.

Senator Kerotski only listened to a small part of the phone discussion. He knew most of the story.

In the past eight months, six anonymous letters had been received by various companies. As Taggert had once put it, in quotes, "We seem to have an Abudah chest containing a patent Hag who comes out and prophesies disasters, with spring complete."

The Big Bend Power Reactor, near Marfa, Texas, had been warned that their stellarator would blow. The letter was dismissed as "crackpot," and no precautions were taken. The explosion killed nine men and cut off the power in the area for three hours, causing other accidents due to lack of power.

The merchant submarine *Bandar-log*, plying her way between Ceylon and Japan, had ignored the warning sent to her owners and had never been heard from again.

In the Republic of Yemen, an oil refinery caught fire and destroyed millions of dollars worth of property in spite of the anonymous letter that had foretold the disaster.

The Prince Charles Dam in Central Africa had broken and thousands had drowned because those in charge had relegated a warning letter to the cylindrical file.

A mine cave-in in Canada had extinguished three lives because a similar letter had been ignored.

By the time the fifth letter had been received, the S.M.M.R. had received the information and had begun its investigation. As an *ex officio* organ of the United States Government, it had ways and means of getting hold of the originals of the letters which had been received by the responsible persons in each of the disasters. All had been sent by the same man; all had been typed on the same machine; all had been mailed in New York.

When the sixth warning had come to the offices of Caribbean Trans-Air, the S.M.M.R., working through the FBI, had persuaded the company's officials to take the regularly scheduled aircraft off the run and substitute another while the regular ship was carefully inspected. But it was the replacement ship that came to pieces in midair.

The anonymous predictor, whoever he was, was a man of no mean ability.

Then letter number seven had been received by the United States Department of Space. It predicted that a meteor would smash into America's Moonbase One, completely destroying it.

Finally, a non-anonymous letter had come to the S.M.M.R. requesting admission to the society, enclosing the proper fee. The letter also said that the writer was interested in literature on the subjects of prescience, precognition, and/or prophecy, and would be interested in contacting anyone who had had experience with such phenomena.

Putting two and two together only yields four, no matter how often it's done, but two to the eighth power gives a nice, round two hundred fifty-six, which is something one can sink one's teeth into.

Brian Taggert cut off the phone connection. "That's it, Mike," he said to the senator. "We've got him."

Two of the Society's agents, both top-flight telepaths, had gone out to "Dr. Joachim's" place on Coney Island's Boardwalk, posing as customers—"clients" was the word Dr. Joachim preferred—and had done a thorough probing job.

"He's what might be called a perfectly sincere fraud," Taggert continued. "You know the type I'm sure."

The senator nodded silently. The woods were full of that kind of thing. Complete, reliable control of any kind of psionic power requires understanding and sanity, but the ability lies dormant in many minds that cannot control it, and it can and does burst forth erratically at times. Finding a physical analogy for the phenomenon is difficult, since mental activities are, of necessity, of a higher order than physical activities.

Some of the operations of tensor calculus have analogs in algebra; many do not.

Taggert gestured with one hand. "He's been in business there for years. Evidently, he's been able to make a few accurate predictions now and then—enough to keep his reputation going. He's tried to increase the frequency, accuracy, and detail of his 'flashes' by studying up on the techniques used by other seers, and, as a result, he's managed to soak up enough mystic balderdash to fill a library.

"He embellishes every one of his predictions to his 'clients' with all kinds of hokum, and he's been doing it so long that he really isn't sure how much of any prediction is truth and how much is embroidery work.

"The boys are trying to get more information on him now, and they're going to do a little deep probing, if they can get him set up right; maybe they'll be able to trigger off another flash on that moon-hit—but I doubt it."

Senator Kerotski thumbed his chin morosely. "You're probably right. Apparently, once those hunches come to a precog, they get everything in a flash and then they can't get another thing—ever. I wish we could get our hands on one who was halfway along toward *the* point. We've got experts on psychokinetics, levitation, telepathy, clairvoyance, and what-have-you. But precognition we don't seem to be able to find."

"We've got one now," Brian Taggert reminded him.

The senator snorted. "Even assuming that we had any theory on precognition completely symbolized, and assuming that this Forsythe has the kind of mind that can be taught, do you think we could get it done in a month? Because that's all the time we have."

"He's our first case," Taggert admitted. "We'll have to probe everything out of him and construct symbol-theory around what we get. I'll be surprised if we get anywhere at all in the first six months."

Senator Kerotski put his hand over his eyes. "I give up. First the Chinese Soviet kidnaps Dr. Ch'ien and we have to scramble like maniacs to get him back before they find out that he's building a space drive that will make the rocket industry obsolete. Then we have to find out what's causing the rash of accidents that is holding up Dr. Theodore Nordred's antigravity project. And now, just as everything is coming to a head in both departments, we find that a meteor is going to hit Moonbase One sometime between thirty and sixty days from now." He spread apart the middle and ring fingers of the hand that covered his eyes and looked at Taggert through one eye. "And now you tell me that the only man who can pinpoint that time more exactly for us is of no use whatever to us. If we knew when that meteor was due to arrive, we would be able to spot and deflect it in time. It must be of pretty good size if it's going to demolish the whole base."

"How do you know it's going to be a meteor?"

"You think the Soviets would try to bomb it? Don't be silly, Taggert," Kerotski said, grinning.

Taggert grinned back. "I'm not thinking they'd bomb us; but I'm trying to look at all the angles."

The worried look came back to the senator's pandalike face. "We have to do something. If only we *knew* that Forsythe's prediction will really come off. Or, if it will, then exactly *when*? And is there anything we can do about it, or will it be like the airline incident. If we hadn't made them switch planes, nothing would have happened. What if, no matter what we do, Moonbase One goes anyway?

"Remember, we haven't yet built Moonbase Two. If our only base on the moon is destroyed, the Soviets will have the whole moon to themselves. Have you any suggestions?"

"Sure," said Taggert. "Ask yourself one question: What is the purpose of Moonbase One?"

Slowly, a beatific smile spread itself over the senator's face.

The whole discussion had taken exactly ninety seconds.

"Mrs. Jesser," said Brian Taggert to the well-rounded, fortyish woman behind the reception desk at S.M.M.R. headquarters, "this is Dr. Forsythe. He has established a reputation as one of the finest seers living today."

Mrs. Jesser looked at the distinguished, white-bearded gentleman with an expression that was almost identical with the one her grandmother had worn when she met Rudolph Valentino, nearly sixty years before, and the one her mother had worn when she saw Frank Sinatra a generation later. It was not an uncommon expression for Mrs. Jesser's face to wear: it appeared every time she was introduced to anyone who looked impressive and was touted as a great mystic of one kind or another.

"I'm *so* glad to *meet* you, Dr. Forsythe!" she burbled eagerly.

"Dr. Forsythe will be working for us for the next few months—his office will be Room B on the fourth floor," Taggert finished. He was genuinely fond of the woman, in spite of her mental dithers and schoolgirl mannerisms. Mysticism fascinated her, and she was firmly convinced that she had "just a *weenie* bit" of psychic power herself, although its exact nature seemed to change from time to time. But she did both her jobs well, although she was not aware of her double function. She thought she was being paid as a receptionist and phone operator, and she was quick and efficient about her work. She was also the perfect screen for the Society's real work, for if anyone ever suspected that the S.M.M.R. was not the group of crackpots that it appeared to be, five minutes talking with Mrs. Jesser would convince them otherwise.

"Oh, you're *staying* with us, Dr. Forsythe? How wonderful! We simply *must* have a talk sometime!"

"Indeed we must, dear lady," said Forsythe. His voice and manner had just the right amount of benign dignity, with an almost indetectable touch of pompous condescending.

"Come along, doctor; I'll show you to your office." Taggert's face betrayed nothing of the enjoyment he was getting out of watching the mental gymnastics of the two. Forsythe and Mrs. Jesser were similar in some ways, but, of the two, Mrs. Jesser was actually the more honest. She only fooled herself; she never tried to fool anyone else. Forsythe, on the other hand, tried to put on a front for others, and, in doing so, had managed to delude himself pretty thoroughly.

Taggert's humor was not malicious; he was not laughing at them. He was admiring the skill of the human mind in tying itself in knots. When one watches a clever contortionist going through his paces, one doesn't laugh at the contortionist; one admires and enjoys the weird twists he can get himself into. And, like Taggert, one can only feel sympathy for one whose knots have become so devious and intricate that he can never extricate himself.

"Just follow me up the stairs," Taggert said. "I'll show you where your office is. Sorry we don't have an elevator, but this old building just wasn't built for it, and we've never had any real need for one."

"Perfectly all right," Forsythe said, following along behind.

Three weeks!

Taggert had to assume that the minimum time prediction was the accurate one. Damn! Why couldn't this last prediction have been as precise as the one about the air flight from Puerto Rico?

It had taken six days for the "accredited" agents of the S.M.M.R. to persuade Dr. Peter Forsythe that he should leave his little place on the Boardwalk and come down to Arlington to work. It isn't easy to persuade a man to leave a business that he's built up over a long period of years, especially during the busy season. To leave the Boardwalk during the summer would, as far as Forsythe was concerned, be tantamount to economic suicide. He had to be offered not only an income better than the one he was making, but better security as well. At fifty-four, one does not lightly throw over the work of a lifetime.

Still, he had plenty of safeguards. The rent was paid on his Boardwalk office, he had a guaranteed salary while he was working, and a "research bonus," designed to keep him working until the Society was finished with that phase of its work.

It's rather difficult for a man to resist the salesmanship of a telepath who knows exactly what his customer wants and, better, what he needs.

On the fourth floor, there were sounds of movement, the low staccato chatter of typers, occasional bits of conversation, and the hum of electronic equipment.

Forsythe was impressed, though not a line on his face showed it. The office to which he had been assigned was lined with electronic calculators, and his name had already been put on the door in gold. It was to his credit that he was impressed by the two factors in that order.

In the rear of the room, two technicians were working on an open panel in one of the units. Nearby, a dark-haired, dark-eyed, maturely handsome woman in her early thirties was holding a clip board and making occasional notes as the men worked. One of the men was using an electric drill, and the whine of metal on metal drowned out the slight noise that Taggert and Forsythe made as they entered. Only the woman was aware that they had come in, but she didn't betray the fact.

"Miss Tedesco?" Taggert called.

She looked up from her clip board, smiled, and walked toward the two newcomers. "Yes, Mr. Taggert?"

"'Bout done?"

"Almost. They're setting in the last component now."

Taggert nodded absently. "Miss Tedesco, this is Dr. Peter Forsythe, whom I told you about. Dr. Forsythe, this is Miss Donna Tedesco; she's the computer technician who will be working with you."

Miss Tedesco's smile was positively glittering. "I'm so pleased to meet you, doctor; I know our work together will be interesting."

"I trust it will," Forsythe said, beaming. Then a faint cloud seemed to come over his features. "I'm afraid I must confess a certain ... er ... lack of knowledge in the realm of computerdom. Mr. Taggert attempted to explain, but he, himself, has admitted that his knowledge of the details is ... er ... somewhat vague."

"I'm not a computerman, myself," Taggert said, smiling. "Miss Tedesco will be able to give you the details better than I can."

Miss Tedesco blinked. "You know the broad outline, surely? Of the project, I mean."

"Oh, yes, certainly," Forsythe said hurriedly. "We are attempting to determine whether the actions of human beings can actually have any effect on the outcome of the prophecy itself. In other words, if it is possible to avert, say, a disaster if it is foretold, or whether the very foretelling itself assures the ultimate outcome."

The woman nodded her agreement.

"As I understand it," Forsythe continued, "we are going to get several score clients—or, rather, *subjects*—and I am to ... uh ... exercise my talents, just as I have been doing for many years. The results are to be tabulated and run through the computers to see if there is any correlation between human activity taken as a result of the forecast and the actual foretold events themselves."

"That's right," said Miss Tedesco. She looked at Taggert. "That's what the committee outlined, in general, isn't it?"

"In general, yes," Taggert said.

"But what about the details?" Forsythe asked doggedly. "I mean, just how are we going to go about this? You must remember that I'm not at all familiar with ... er ... scientific research procedures."

"Oh, we'll work all that out together," said Miss Tedesco brightly. "You didn't think we'd plan a detailed work schedule without your co-operation, did you?"

"Well—" Forsythe said, swelling visibly with pride, "I suppose—"

Taggert, glancing at his watch, interrupted. "I'll have to leave you two to work out your research schedule together. I have an appointment in a few minutes." He grasped Forsythe's hand and pumped it vigorously. "I believe we'll get along fine, Dr. Forsythe. And I believe our work here will be quite fruitful. Will you excuse me?"

"Certainly, Mr. Taggert. And I want to thank you for this opportunity to do research work along these lines."

Brian Taggert thanked Forsythe and hurried out with the air of a man with important and urgent things on his mind.

He went up the stairs to the office directly over the one he had assigned to Forsythe and stepped in quietly. Two men were relaxed in lounge chairs, their eyes closed.

Meshing? Taggert asked wordlessly.

Meshing.

Taggert closed the door carefully and went into his own office.

General Howard Layton, USSF, looked no different from any other Space Force officer, except that he was rather handsomer than most. He looked as though he might have posed for recruiting posters at one time, and, in point of fact, he had—back when he had been an ensign in the United States Navy's Submarine Service. He was forty-nine and looked a prematurely graying thirty.

He stood in the observation bunker at the landing area of St. Thomas Spacefield and watched through the periscope as a heavy rocket settled itself to the surface of the landing area. The blue-white tongue of flame touched the surface and splattered; then the heavy ship settled slowly down over it, as though it were sliding down a column of light. The column of light shortened—

And abruptly vanished as the ship touched down.

General Layton took his eyes away from the periscope. "Another one back safely. Thank God."

Nearby, the only other man in that room of the bunker, a rather short civilian, had been watching the same scene on a closed-circuit TV screen. He smiled up at the general. "How many loads does that make, so far?"

"Five. We'll have the job done before the deadline time."

"Were you worried?"

"A little. I still am, to be honest. What if nothing happens at the end of sixty days? The President isn't one of us, and he's only gone along with the Society's recommendations so far because we've been able to produce results. But"—he gestured outside, indicating the newly-landed ship—"all this extra expense isn't going to set well with him if we goof this once."

"I know," said the civilian. "But have you ever known Brian Taggert to be wrong?"

General Layton grinned. "No. And in a lesser man, that sort of omniscience could be infernally irritating. How is he progressing with Forsythe?"

The civilian frowned. "We've got plenty of data so far, and the method seems to be working well, but we don't have enough to theorize yet.

"Forsythe just sits in his office and gives 'readings,' or whatever you want to call them, to the subjects who come in. *The Metaphysicist* has been running an ad asking for volunteers, so we have all kinds of people calling up for appointments. Forsythe is as happy as a kid."

"How about his predictions?"

"Donna Tedesco is running data processing on them. She's in constant mental contact with him. So are Hughes and Matson, in the office above. The three of them are meshed together with each other—don't ask me how; I'm no telepath—and they're getting a pretty good idea of what's going on in Forsythe's mind.

"Every once in a while, he gets a real flash of something, and it apparently comes pretty fast. The team is trying to analyze the fine-grain structure of the process now.

"The rest of the time, he simply gives out with the old guff that phony crystal-ball gazers have been giving out for centuries. Even when he gets a real flash, he piles on a lot of intuitive extrapolation. And the farther he gets from that central flash, the less reliable the predictions are."

"Do you think we'll get theory and symbology worked out before that meteor is supposed to hit Moonbase One?" asked the general.

The civilian shrugged. "Who knows? We'll have to take a lot on faith if we do, because there won't be enough time to check all his predictions. Each subject is being given a report sheet with his forecast on it, and he's supposed to check the accuracy of it as it happens. And our agents are making spot checks on them just to make sure. It'll take time. All we can do is hope."

"I suppose." General Layton took a quick look through the periscope again. The ship's air lock still hadn't opened; the air and ground were still too hot. He looked back at the civilian. "What about the espionage reports?"

The civilian tapped his briefcase. "I can give it to you in a capsule, verbally. You can look these over later."

"Shoot."

"The Soviets are getting worried, to put it bluntly. We can't hide those rockets, you know. Their own Luna-based radar has been picking up every one of them as they come in and leave. They're wondering why we're making so many trips all of a sudden."

"Have they done any theorizing?" the general asked worriedly.

"They have." The civilian chuckled sardonically. "They've decided we're trying for another Mars shot—a big one, this time."

The general exhaled sharply. "That's too close for comfort. How do they figure?"

"They figure we're amassing material at Moonbase One. They figure we intend to build the ship there, with the loads of stuff that we're sending up in the rockets."

"*What?*" General Layton opened his mouth, then closed it. Then he began to laugh.

The civilian joined him.

Donna Tedesco pushed the papers across Brian Taggert's desk. "Check them yourself, Brian. I've gone over them six ways from Septuagesima, and I still can't see any other answer."

Taggert frowned at the papers and tapped them with a thoughtful finger, but he didn't pick them up. "I'll take your word for it, Donna. At least for right now. If we get completely balled up, we'll go over them together."

"If you ask me, we've already completely balled up."

"You think it's that bad?"

She looked at him pleadingly. "Can you think of any other explanation?"

"Not just yet," Brian Taggert admitted.

"Nor can I. There it is. Every single one of his valid predictions, every single one of his precognitive intuitions—*without exception*—has been based on the actions of human beings. He can predict stock market fluctuations, and family squabbles, and South American election results. His disaster predictions, every one of them, were due to *human* error, *human* failure—not Acts of God. He failed to predict the earthquake in Los Angeles; he missed the flood in the Yangtze Valley; he knew nothing of the eruption of Stromboli. All of these were disasters that took human lives in the past three weeks, and he missed every one of them. And yet, he managed to get nearly every major ship, airplane, and even automobile accident connected with his subjects.

"Seven of his subjects had relatives or friends who were hurt or killed in the earthquake-flood-eruption sequence, but he didn't see them. Yet he could pick up such small things as a nephew of one of the men getting a bad scald on his arm.

"In the face of that, how can we rely on his one prediction about a meteor striking Moonbase One?"

Taggert rubbed his forehead thoughtfully. "I don't know," he said slowly. "There must be a connection somehow."

"Oh, Brian, Brian!" Her eyes were glistening with as yet unshed tears. "I've never seen you go off on a wild tangent like this before! On the word of an old fraud like Forsythe, a man who lies about half the time, you talk the Administration into sinking hundreds of millions of dollars into the biggest space lift in history!

"Oh, sure; I know. The old fraud is convinced he was telling the truth. But were you tapping his mind when the prediction flash came? No! Was anyone? No! And he's perfectly capable of lying to himself, and you know it!

"And what will happen if it doesn't come off? We're past the first deadline already. If that meteor doesn't hit within the next twenty-eight days, the Society will be right back where it was ten years ago! Or worse!

"And all because you trusted the word of Mr. Phony-Doctor Forsythe!"

"Donna," Taggert said softly, "do you really think I'm that big a fool?" He handed her a handkerchief.

"N-no," she answered, wiping at her eyes. "Of c-course I don't. It's just that it makes me so d-darn *mad* to see everything go wrong like this."

"Nothing's gone wrong yet. I suggest you go take a good look at Forsythe's mind again and really try to understand the old boy. Maybe you'll get more of the fine-grain structure of it if you'll try for more understanding."

"What do you mean?" she asked, sniffing.

"Look. Forsythe has made his living being a fraud, right? And yet he sent out those warning *free*—and anonymously. He had no thought of any reward or recompense, you know that. Why? Because he is basically a kind, decent human being. He wanted to do all he could to stop any injury or loss of life.

"Why, then, would he send out a fraudulent warning? He wouldn't. He didn't. Every one of those warnings—*including the last one*—was sent out because he *knew* that something was going to happen.

"Evidently, once he gets a flash about a certain event, he can't get any more data on that particular area of the future, or we could get more data on the Moonbase accident. I think, if we can boost his basic understanding up past the critical point, we'll have a man with controlled prescience, and we need that man.

"But, Donna, the only way we're ever going to do that—the only way we'll ever whip this problem—is for you to increase *your* understanding of *him.*

"You're past the critical point—way past it—in *general* understanding. But you've got to keep an eye on the little specific instances, too."

She nodded contritely. "I know. I'm sorry. Sometimes a person can get too near a problem." She smiled. "Thanks for the new perspective, Brian. I'll go back to work and see if I can't look at it a little more clearly."

In the White House, Senator Mikhail Kerotski was facing two men—James Bandeau, the Secretary of Space, and the President of the United States.

"Mr. President," he said evenly, "I've known you for a long time. I haven't failed you yet."

"I know that, Mike," the President said smoothly. "Neither has your Society, as far as I know. It's still difficult for me to believe that they get their information the way you say they do, but you've never lied to me about anything so far, so I take your word for it. Your Society is the most efficient espionage and counterespionage group in history, as far as I know. But this is different."

"Damned right it's different!" snapped Secretary Bandeau. "Your own Society, senator, admits that we've stirred the Soviets up with this space lift thing. They've got ships of their own going out there now. According to reports from Space Force intelligence, Chinese Moon cars have been prowling around Moonbase One, trying to find out what's going on."

"More than that," added the President, "they've sneaked a small group aboard the old *Lunik IX* to see what they can see from up there."

Secretary Bandeau jerked his head around to look at the President. "The old circumlunar satellite? Where did you hear that?"

The President smiled wanly. "From the S.M.M.R.'s report." He looked at Kerotski. "I doubt that it will do them any good. I don't think they'll be able to see anything now."

"Not unless they've figured out some way to combine X rays with radar," the senator said. "And I'm quite sure they haven't."

"Senator," said the Secretary of Space, "a lot of money has been spent and a lot of risks have been taken, just on your say-so. I—"

"Now, just a minute, Jim," said the President flatly. "Let's not go off half-cocked. It wasn't done on Mike's say-so; it was done on mine. I signed the order because I believed it was the proper, if not the *only* thing to do." Then he looked at the senator. "But this is the last day, Mike. Nothing has happened.

"Now, I'm not blaming you. I didn't call you up here to do that. And I think we can quit worrying about explaining away the money angle. But we're going to have to explain *why* we did it, Mike. And I can't tell the truth."

"I'll say you can't!" Bandeau exploded. "That would look great, wouldn't it? I can see the headlines now: '*Fortuneteller Gave Me Advice,' President Says.* Brother!"

"Jim," the President said coldly, "I said to let me handle this."

"What you want, then, Mr. President," Kerotski put in smoothly, "is for me to help you concoct a good cover story."

"That's about it, Mike," the President admitted.

Kerotski shook his head slowly. "It won't be necessary."

Bandeau looked as though he were going to explode, but a glance from the President silenced him.

"Go on, Mike," he said to the senator.

"Mr. President, I know it looks bad. It's going to look even worse for a while. But, let me ask you one question. How is the Ch'ien space drive coming along?"

"Why ... fine. It checked out months ago. The new ship is on her shakedown cruise now. You know that."

"Right. Now, ask yourself one more question: What is the purpose of Moonbase One?"

"Why, to—"

The telephone rang.

The President scooped it up with one hand. "Yes?"

Then he listened for a long minute, his expression changing slowly.

"Yes," he said at last. "Yes, I got it. No; I'll release it to the newsmen. All right. Fine." He hung up.

"Twelve minutes ago," he said slowly, "the old *Lunik IX* smashed into Moonbase One and blew it to smithereens. The Soviets say that a meteor hit *Lunik IX* at just the right angle to slow it down enough to make it hit the base. They send their condolences."

Brian Taggert lay back on the couch in his office and folded his hands complacently on his abdomen. "So Donna's theory held water and so did mine. The accident was due to human intervention. Forsythe saw something from space hitting Moonbase One and assumed it was a meteor. He never dreamed the Soviets would drop old *Lunik IX* on it."

Senator Kerotski carefully lit a cigar. "There's going to be an awful lot of fuss in the papers, but the President is going to announce that he accepts the Soviet story. I convinced him that it is best to let the Soviets think they're a long way ahead of us in the space race now. There's nothing like a little complacency to slow someone down."

"How'd you convince him?"

"Asked the same question you asked me. Now that we have the Ch'ien space drive, what purpose does a moon base serve? None at all, of course."

Donna Tadesco leaned forward in her chair. "Did you happen to notice the sequence of events, senator? We were warned that the base would be struck. We decided to abandon it. We organized the biggest space lift in history to evacuate the men and the most valuable instruments. But the Soviets thought we were sending equipment *up* instead of bringing it *down*. They didn't know what we were up to, but they decided to put a stop to it, so they dropped an abandoned space satellite on it.

"If we hadn't decided to evacuate the base, it would never have happened.

"*That* is human intervention with a vengeance. We still don't know whether or not Forsythe's predictions will ever do us any good or not. Every time we've taken steps to avoid one of his prophesied catastrophes, we've done the very thing that brought them about."

The senator puffed his cigar in thoughtful silence.

"We'll just have to keep working with him," Taggert said. "Maybe we'll eventually make sense out of this precognition thing.

"At least we've got what we wanted. The Soviets think they've put us back ten years; they figure they've got more time, now, to get their own program a long ways ahead.

"When they do get to Mars and Venus and the planets of Alpha Centauri and Sirius and Procyon, they'll find us there, waiting for them."

Senator Kerotski chuckled softly. "You're a pretty good prophet, yourself, Brian. The only difference between you and Forsythe is that he's right half the time.

"You're right *all* the time."

"No," said Taggert. "Not all the time. Only when it's important."

THE END

...Or Your Money Back

There are lots of things that are considered perfectly acceptable ... provided they don't work. And of course everyone knows they really don't, which is why they're acceptable....

There are times when I don't know my own strength. Or, at least, the strength of my advice. And the case of Jason Howley was certainly an instance of one of those times.

When he came to my office with his gadget, I heard him out, trying to appear both interested and co-operative—which is good business. But I am forced to admit that neither Howley nor his gadget were very impressive. He was a lean, slope-shouldered individual, five-feet-eight or nine—which was shorter than he looked—with straight brown hair combed straight back and blue eyes which were shielded with steel-rimmed glasses. The thick, double-concave lenses indicated a degree of myopia that must have bordered on total blindness without glasses, and acute tunnel vision, even with them.

He had a crisp, incisive manner that indicated he was either a man who knew what he was doing or a man who was trying to impress me with a ready-made story. I listened to him and looked at his gadget without giving any more indication than necessary of what I really thought.

When he was through, I said: "You understand, Mr. Howley that I'm not a patent lawyer; I specialize in criminal law. Now, I can recommend—"

But he cut me off. "I understand that, counselor," he said sharply. "Believe me, I have no illusion whatever that this thing is patentable under the present patent system. Even if it were, this gadget is designed to do something that may or may not be illegal, which would make it hazardous to attempt to patent it, I should think. You don't patent new devices for blowing safes or new drugs for doping horses, do you?"

"Probably not," I said dryly, "although, as I say, I'm not qualified to give an opinion on patent law. You say that gadget is designed to cause minute, but significant, changes in the velocities of small, moving objects. Just how does that make it illegal?"

He frowned a little. "Well, possibly it wouldn't, except here in Nevada. Specifically, it is designed to influence roulette and dice games."

I looked at the gadget with a little more interest this time. There was nothing new in the idea of inventing a gadget to cheat the red-and-black wheels, of course; the local cops turn up a dozen a day here in the city. Most of them either don't work at all or else they're too obvious, so the users get nabbed before they have a chance to use them.

The only ones that really work have to be installed in the tables themselves, which means they're used to milk the suckers, not rob the management. And anyone in the State of Nevada who buys a license to operate and then uses crooked wheels is (a) stupid, and (b) out of business within a week. Howley was right. Only in a place where gambling is legalized is it illegal—and unprofitable—to rig a game.

The gadget itself didn't look too complicated from the outside. It was a black plastic box about an inch and a half square and maybe three and a half long. On one end was a lensed opening, half an inch in diameter, and on two sides there were flat, silver-colored plates. On the top of it, there was a dial which was, say, an inch in diameter, and it was marked off just exactly like a roulette wheel.

"How does it work?" I asked.

He picked it up in his hand, holding it as though it were a flashlight, with the lens pointed away from him.

"You aim the lens at the wheel," he explained, "making sure that your thumb is touching the silver plate on one side, and your fingers touching the plate on the other side. Then you set this dial for whatever number you want to come up and concentrate on it while the ball is spinning. For dice, of course, you only need to use the first six or twelve numbers on the dial, depending on the game."

I looked at him for a long moment, trying to figure his angle. He looked back steadily, his eyes looking like small beads peering through the bottoms of a couple of shot glasses.

"You look skeptical, counselor," he said at last.

"I am. A man who hasn't got the ability to be healthily skeptical has no right to practice law—especially criminal law. On the other hand, no lawyer has any right to judge anything one way or the other without evidence.

"But that's neither here nor there at the moment. What I'm interested in is, what do you want me to do? People rarely come to a criminal lawyer unless they're in a jam. What sort of jam are you in at the moment?"

"None," said Howley. "But I will be very soon. I hope."

Well, I've heard odder statements than that from my clients. I let it ride for the moment and looked down at the notes I'd taken while he'd told me his story.

"You're a native of New York City?" I asked.

"That's right. That's what I said."

"And you came out here for what? To use that thing on our Nevada tables?"

"That's right, counselor."

"Can't you find any games to cheat on back home?"

"Oh, certainly. Plenty of them. But they aren't legal. I wouldn't care to get mixed up in anything illegal. Besides, it wouldn't suit my purpose."

That stopped me for a moment. "You don't consider cheating illegal? It certainly is in Nevada. In New York, if you were caught at it, you'd have the big gambling interests on your neck; here, you'll have both them *and* the police after you. *And* the district attorney's office."

He smiled. "Yes, I know. That's what I'm expecting. That's why I need a good lawyer to defend me. I understand you're the top man in this city."

"Mr. Howley," I said carefully, "as a member of the Bar Association and a practicing attorney in the State of Nevada, I am an Officer of the Court. If you had been caught cheating and had come to me, I'd be able to help you. But I can't enter into a conspiracy with you to defraud legitimate businessmen, which is exactly what this would be."

He blinked at me through those shot-glass spectacles. "Counselor, would you refuse to defend a man if you thought he was guilty?"

I shook my head. "No. Legally, a man is not guilty until proven so by a court of law. He has a right to trial by jury. For me to refuse to give a man the defense he is legally entitled to, just because I happened to think he was guilty, would be trial by attorney. I'll do the best I can for any client; I'll work for his interests, no matter what my private opinion may be."

He looked impressed, so I guess there must have been a note of conviction in my voice. There should have been, because it was exactly what I've always believed and practiced.

"That's good, counselor," said Howley. "If I can convince you that I have no criminal intent, that I have no intention of defrauding anyone or conspiring with you to do anything illegal, will you help me?"

I didn't have to think that one over. I simply said, "Yes." After all, it was still up to me to decide whether he convinced me or not. If he didn't, I could still refuse the case on those grounds.

"That's fair enough, counselor," he said. Then he started talking.

Instead of telling you what Jason Howley *said* he was going to do, I'll tell you what he *did* do. They are substantially the same, anyway, and the old bromide about actions speaking louder than words certainly applied in this case.

Mind you, I didn't see or hear any of this, but there were plenty of witnesses to testify as to what went on. Their statements are a matter of court record, and Jason Howley's story is substantiated in every respect.

He left my office smiling. He'd convinced me that the case was not only going to be worthwhile, but fun. I took it, plus a fat retainer.

Howley went up to his hotel room, changed into his expensive evening clothes, and headed out to do the town. I'd suggested several places, but he wanted the biggest and best—the Golden Casino, a big, plush, expensive place that was just inside the city limits. In his pockets, he was carrying less than two hundred dollars in cash.

Now, nobody with that kind of chicken feed can expect to last long at the Golden Casino unless they stick to the two-bit one-armed bandits. But putting money on a roulette table is in a higher bracket by far than feeding a slot machine, even if you get a steady run of lemons.

Howley didn't waste any time. He headed for the roulette table right away. He watched the play for about three spins of the wheel, then he took out his gadget—in plain sight of anyone who cared to watch—and set the dial for thirteen. Then he held it in his hand with thumb and finger touching the plates and put his hand in his jacket pocket, with the lens aimed at the wheel. He stepped up to the table, bought a hundred dollars worth of chips, and put fifty on Number Thirteen.

"No more bets," said the croupier. He spun the wheel and dropped the ball.

"Thirteen, Black, Odd, and Low," he chanted after a minute. With a practiced hand, he raked in the losers and pushed out Howley's winnings. There was sixteen hundred dollars sitting on thirteen now. Howley didn't touch it.

The wheel went around and the little ball clattered around the rim and finally fell into a slot.

"Thirteen, Black, Odd, and Low," said the croupier. This time, he didn't look as nonchalant. He peered curiously at Howley as he pushed out the chips to make a grand total of fifty-one thousand two hundred dollars. The same number doesn't come up twice in succession very often, and it is very rare indeed that the same person is covering it both times with a riding bet.

"Two thousand limit, sir," the croupier said, when it looked as though Howley was going to let the fifty-one grand just sit there.

Howley nodded apologetically and pulled off everything but two thousand dollars worth of chips.

The third time around, the croupier had his eyes directly on Howley as he repeated the chant: "Thirteen, Black, Odd, and Low." Everybody else at the table was watching Howley, too. The odds against Howley—or anyone else, for that matter—hitting the same number three times in a row are just under forty thousand to one.

Howley didn't want to overdo it. He left two thousand on thirteen, raked in the rest, and twisted the dial on his gadget over a notch.

Everyone at the table gasped as the little ball dropped.

"That was a near miss," whispered a woman standing nearby.

The croupier said: "Fourteen, Red, Even, and Low." And he raked in Howley's two thousand dollars with a satisfied smile. He had seen runs of luck before.

Howley deliberately lost two more spins the same way. Nobody who was actually cheating would call too much attention to himself, and Howley wanted it to look as though he were trying to cover up the fact that he had a sure thing.

He took the gadget out of his pocket and deliberately set it to the green square marked 00. Then he put it back in his pocket and put two thousand dollars on the Double Zero.

There was more than suspicion in the croupier's eyes when he raked in all the bets on the table except Howley's. It definitely didn't look good to him. A man who had started out with a fifty-dollar bet had managed to run it up to one hundred seventy-four thousand two hundred dollars in six plays.

Howley looked as innocent as possible under the circumstances, and carefully dropped the dial on his gadget back a few notches. Then he bet another two thousand on High, an even money bet.

Naturally, he won.

He twisted the dial back a few more notches and won again on High.

Then he left it where it was and won by betting on Red.

By this time, of course, things were happening. The croupier had long since pressed the alarm button, and five men had carefully surrounded Howley. They looked like customers, but they were harder-looking than the average, and they were watching Howley, not the wheel. Farther back from the crowd, three of the special deputies from the sheriff's office were trying to look inconspicuous in their gray uniforms and white Stetsons and pearl-handled revolvers in black holsters. You can imagine how inconspicuous they looked.

Howley decided to do it up brown. He reset his gadget as surreptitiously as possible under the circumstances, and put his money on thirteen again.

"Thirteen, Black, Odd, and Low," said the croupier in a hollow voice.

The five men in evening dress and the three deputies moved in closer.

Howley nonchalantly scraped in his winnings, leaving the two thousand on the thirteen spot.

There was a combination of hostility and admiration in every eye around the table when the croupier said, "Thirteen, Black, Odd, and Low" for the fifth time in the space of minutes. And everyone of those eyes was turned on Jason Howley.

The croupier smiled his professional smile. "I'm sorry, ladies and gentlemen; we'll have to discontinue play for a while. The gentleman has broken the bank at this table." He turned the smile on Howley. "Congratulations, sir."

Howley smiled back and began stacking up over three hundred thousand dollars worth of plastic disks. It made quite a pile.

One of the deputies stepped up politely. "I'm an officer, sir," he said. "May I help you carry that to the cashier's office?"

Howley looked at the gold star and nodded. "Certainly. Thanks."

The other two deputies stepped up, too, and the three of them walked Howley toward the cashier's office. Behind them came the five men in dinner jackets.

"You'll have to step into the office to cash that much, sir," said one of the deputies as he opened the door. Howley walked in as though he hadn't a care in the world. He put his chips on the desk, and the deputies followed suit, while one of the dinner-jacketed men closed the door.

Then one of the deputies said: "I believe this gentleman is carrying a gun."

He had his own revolver out and had it pointed at Howley's middle. "Carrying a concealed weapon is illegal in this city," he went on. "I'm afraid we'll have to search you."

Howley didn't object. He put his hands up high and stood there while his pockets were frisked.

"Well, well," said the deputy coolly. "What on Earth is this?"

It was Howley's gadget, and the dial still pointed to Thirteen—Black, Odd, and Low.

The next morning, I went down to the jail in response to a phone call from Howley. The special deputies had turned him over to the city police and he was being held "under suspicion of fraud." I knew we could beat that down to an "attempt to defraud," but the object was to get Howley off scott-free. After Howley told me the whole story, I got busy pushing the case through. As long as he was simply being held on suspicion, I couldn't get him out on bail, so I wanted to force the district attorney or the police to prefer charges.

Meanwhile, I made sure that Howley's gadget had been impounded as evidence. I didn't want anyone fiddling with it before the case went to court—except, of course, the D. A. and his men. There wasn't much I could do to keep it out of *their* hands.

After throwing as much weight around as I could, including filing a petition for a writ of habeas corpus with Judge Grannis, I went over to Howley's hotel with a signed power of attorney that Howley had given me, and I got a small envelope out of the hotel safe. It contained a baggage check.

I went over to the bus depot, turned over the check to the baggage department, and went back to my office with a small suitcase. I locked myself in and opened the case. Sure enough, it contained three dozen of the little gadgets.

Then I sat down to wait. By noon, Judge Grannis had issued the writ of habeas corpus, and, rather than release Jason Howley, the police had booked him, and District Attorney Thursby was getting the case ready for the grand jury. There was over a quarter of a million dollars at stake, and the men behind the Golden Casino were bringing pressure to bear. If Howley wasn't convicted, they'd have to give him his money—and that was the last thing they wanted to do. A quarter of a million bucks isn't small potatoes, even to a gambling syndicate.

It wasn't until early on the morning of the third day after Howley's arrest that I got a tip-off from one of my part-time spies. I scooped up the phone when it rang and identified myself.

"Counselor? Look, this is Benny." I recognized the voice and name. Benny was one of the cabbies that I'd done favors for in the past.

"What's the trouble, Benny?"

"Oh, no trouble. I just got a little tip you might be interested in."

"Fire away."

"Well, the D.A. and some of his boys went into the Golden Casino about ten minutes ago, and now they're closin' up the place. Just for a little while, I understand. Hour, maybe. They're chasin' everyone out of the roulette room."

"Thanks, Benny," I said, "thanks a lot."

"Well, I knew you was working on that Howley case, and I thought this might be important, so I—"

"Sure, Benny. Come by my office this afternoon. And thanks again."

I hung up and started moving.

Within ten minutes, I was pulling up and parking across the street from the Golden Casino. I locked the car and dodged traffic to get across the street, as though I'd never heard of laws against jaywalking.

There were still plenty of people in the Casino. The bar was full, and the dice and card games were going full blast. The slot machines were jingling out their infernal din while fools fed coins into their insatiable innards.

But the roulette room was closed, and a couple of be-Stetsoned deputies were standing guard over the entrance. I headed straight for them.

Both of them stood pat, blocking my way, so I stopped a few feet in front of them.

"Hello, counselor," said one. "Sorry, the roulette room's closed."

I knew the man slightly. "Let me in, Jim," I said. "I want to see Thursby."

The men exchanged glances. Obviously, the D.A. had given them orders.

"Can't do it, counselor," said Jim. "We're not to let anyone in."

"Tell Thursby I'm out here and that I want to see him."

He shrugged, opened the door, stuck his head inside, and called to District Attorney Thursby to tell him that I was outside. I could hear Thursby's muffled "Damn!" from within. But when he showed up at the door, his face was all smiles.

"What's the trouble?" he asked pleasantly.

I smiled back, giving him my best. "No trouble at all, Thursby. I just wanted to watch the experiment."

"Experiment?" He looked honestly surprised, which was a fine piece of acting. "We're just checking to see if the table's wired, that's all. If it is, your client may be in the clear; maybe we can hang it on the croupier."

"And get a conspiracy charge on my client, too, eh? Well, if you don't mind, I'd like to watch that table check myself. You know how it is."

Thursby hesitated, then he scowled. "Oh, all right. Come on in. But stay out of the way."

I grinned. "Sure. All I want to do is protect my client's interests."

Thursby just grunted and opened the door wider to let me in. He was a shrewd lawyer, a good D.A., and basically honest, even if he did have a tendency to bend under pressure from higher up.

They were checking the table, all right. They had three specialists going over it with everything from fine tooth combs to Geiger counters. They found nothing. No magnets, no wires, no mechanical gimmicks. Nothing.

It took them an hour to take that table apart, check it, and put it back together again. When it was all over, Thursby glanced at me, then said: "O.K., boys; that does it. Let's go."

The men looked at him oddly, and I knew why.

"Aren't you going to test my client's gadget?" I asked innocently.

Thursby looked angrily baffled for a moment, then he clamped his lips grimly. "As long as we're here, I guess we might as well."

I knew perfectly well it was what he had intended to do all along.

"One of you guys spin that wheel," he said to the technicians. One of them gave the wheel a spin and dropped the ball. It clattered on its merry way and dropped into a slot. Forty-two.

Thursby took the gadget out of his pocket. It was still set at Thirteen.

The men who had surrounded Howley on the night of his arrest had been keeping their eyes open, and they had seen how Howley had handled the thing. Well—*almost* how. Thursby had the lens opening pointed at the wheel, but his thumb and fingers weren't touching the silver plates properly.

"Spin it again," he said.

Everyone's eyes were on the ball as it whirled, so I had time to get my own copy of Howley's gadget out and set it at Thirteen. I hoped the thing would work for me. I concentrated on Thirteen, making sure my thumb and fingers were placed right.

Evidently they were. The ball fell into Thirteen, Black, Odd, and Low.

A huge grin spread over Thursby's face, but he was man enough not to turn and grin at me. "Try it again," he said.

Thirteen, Black, Odd, and Low.

"I wonder how the thing works?" said Thursby, looking at the gadget in a sort of pleased awe.

"You'd better be able to prove that it *does* work, Thursby," I said, trying to put irritation into my voice.

This time, he did grin at me. "Oh, I think we can prove that, all right." He turned back to the technician. "Spin it once more, Sam, and show the defense counsel, here, how it works."

The technician did as he was told. "Thirteen, Black, Odd, and Low," he chanted, grinning.

"Let's try another number," Thursby said. He turned the dial to One. And this time, when he pointed it, his fingers were touching the plates in the right places.

"Just a minute," I said. "Let me spin that thing."

"Be my guest, counselor," said Thursby.

I spun the wheel and scooted the ball along the rim. It dropped into a slot. One, Red, Odd, and Low. I looked as disappointed and apprehensive as I could.

"Co-incidence," I said. "Nothing more. You haven't proved anything."

Thursby's grin widened. "Of course I haven't," he said with a soothing, patronizing tone. "But I don't have to prove anything until I get to court."

Then he looked at the technicians and jerked his head toward the door. "Let's go, boys. Maybe the counselor wants to look over the table for himself. Maybe he thinks we've got it rigged."

There was a chorus of guffaws as they walked out. I just stood there, scowling, trying to keep from laughing even harder than they were.

Jason Howley sat next to me at the defense table, just inside the low partition that divided the court from the public. There weren't many people in the auditorium itself; listening to some poor dope get himself sentenced for cheating at gambling is considered pretty dull entertainment in the State of Nevada.

Thursby had managed to push the indictment through the grand jury in a hurry, but, as he sat across the room from me at the prosecution table, I thought I could detect a false note in the assumed look of confidence that he was trying to wear.

Howley tapped me on the shoulder. I turned around, and he whispered: "How much longer?"

I tapped my wrist watch. "Couple minutes. Judge Lapworth is one of those precisionists. Never a moment late or early. Getting jumpy?"

He shook his head gently and smiled. "No. You've handled this even better than I'd have imagined. You thought of things I didn't even know existed. I'm no lawyer; I can see that."

I returned the smile. "And I don't invent gimmicks, either. So what?"

His eyes looked at me from behind the distorting negative lenses. "I've been wondering, counselor—why are you so interested in this? I mean, I offered you a pretty good fee, and all that, but it seems to me you're taking an unusual interest in the case."

I grinned at him. "Mr. Howley, my profession is Law—with a capital L. The study of the Law isn't like the study of physics or whatever; these are manmade laws—commands, not descriptions. They don't necessarily have anything to do with facts at all. Take the word 'insanity,' for instance; the word isn't even used by head-shrinkers any more because it's a legal definition that has nothing whatever to do with the condition of the human mind.

"Now, any such set of laws as that can't possibly be self-consistent and still have some use on an action level. A lawyer's job is to find the little inconsistencies in the structure, the places where the pieces have been jammed together in an effort to make them look like a structured whole. To find, in other words, the loopholes and use them.

"And when I find a loophole, I like to wring everything I can out of it. I'm enjoying this."

Howley nodded. "I see. But what if something—"

I held up my hand to silence him, because the door to the judges' chambers opened at that moment, and Judge Lapworth came in as the bailiff announced him. We all stood up while the bailiff intoned his "Oyez, oyez."

Thursby made a short preliminary speech to the jury, and I requested and was granted permission to hold my own opening statement until the defense was ready to present its case.

Thursby was looking worried, although it took a trained eye to see it. I was pretty sure I knew why. He had been pushed too hard and had gone too fast. He'd managed to slide through the grand jury too easily, and I had managed to get the trial date set for a week later. Thursby's case was far from being as tight as he wanted it.

I just sat still while the prosecution brought forth its witnesses and evidence. The croupier, the deputies, several employees of the Golden Casino, and a couple of patrons all told their stories. I waived cross-examination in every case, which made Thursby even edgier than he had been.

When he called in the head of the technicians who had inspected the table at the casino, I made no objection to his testimony, but I made my first cross-examination.

"Mr. Thompson, you have stated your qualifications as an expert on the various devices which have been used to illegally influence the operation of gambling devices in this state."

Thursby said: "Oh, if the Court please, I should like to remind counsel for the defense that he has already accepted the qualifications of the witness."

"I am not attempting to impugn the qualifications of the witness," I snapped.

Judge Lapworth frowned at Thursby. "Are you making an objection, Mr. District Attorney?"

Thursby pursed his lips, said, "No, Your Honor," and sat down.

"Proceed with the cross-examination," said the judge.

"Mr. Thompson," I said, "you have testified that you examined the table at the Golden Casino for such devices and found none. Is that right?"

"That's right," he said positively.

"Have you seen the device labeled People's Exhibit A, which was found by the officers on the person of the defendant?"

"Well ... yes. I have."

"Have you examined this device?"

Thursby was on his feet. "Objection, Your Honor! This material was not brought out in direct examination!"

"Sustained," said Judge Lapworth.

"Very well, Your Honor," I said. Then I turned back to Thompson. "As an expert in this field, Mr. Thompson, you have examined many different devices for cheating gambling equipment, haven't you?"

"Yes, I have."

"How many, would you say?"

"Oh ... several hundred."

"Several hundred different *types*?"

"No. Several hundred individual devices. Most of them are just variations of two or three basic types."

"And you are familiar with the function of these basic types and their variations?"

"I am."

"You know exactly how all of them work, then?"

He saw where I was heading. "Most of them," he hedged.

Thursby saw where I was heading, too, and was sweating. I'd managed to get around his objection.

"Have you ever examined any which you could not understand?"

"I ... I don't quite know what you mean."

"Have you ever," I said firmly, "come across a device used in cheating which you could not comprehend or explain the operation of?"

Thursby stood up. "Same objection as before, Your Honor."

"Your Honor," I said, "I am merely trying to find the limitations of the witness' knowledge; I am not trying to refute his acknowledged ability."

"Overruled," said Judge Lapworth. "The witness will answer the question."

I repeated the question.

"Yes," Thompson said in a low voice.

"More than once?"

"Only once."

"Only once. You did find one device which didn't operate in any fashion you can explain. Is that right?"

"That's right."

"Can you tell me what this device was?"

Thompson took a deep breath. "It was People's Exhibit A—the device taken from the defendant at the time of his arrest."

There was a buzz in the courtroom.

"No more questions," I said, turning away. Then, before Thompson could leave the stand, I turned back to him. "Oh, just one moment, Mr. Thompson. Did you examine this device carefully? Did you take it apart?"

"I opened it and looked at it."

"You just looked at it? You didn't subject it to any tests?"

Thompson took a deep breath. "No."

"Why not?"

"There wasn't anything inside it to test."

This time, there was more than just a buzz around the courtroom. Judge Lapworth rapped for order.

When the room was quiet, I said: "The box was empty, then?"

"Well, no. Not exactly empty. It had some stuff in it."

I turned to the judge. "If the Court please, I would like to have the so-called device, Exhibit A, opened so that the members of the jury may see for themselves what it contains."

Judge Lapworth said: "The Court would like very much to see the internal workings of this device, too. Bailiff, if you will, please."

The bailiff handed him the gadget from the exhibit table.

"How does it open?" asked the judge. He turned to Thompson. "Will the witness please open the box?"

Reluctantly, Thompson thumbed the catch and slid off the top.

The judge took it from him, looked inside, and stared for a long moment.

I had already seen the insides. It was painted white, and there were inked lines running all over the inside, and various pictures—a ball, a pair of dice, a roulette wheel—and some other symbols that I didn't pretend to understand.

Otherwise, the box was empty.

After a moment, Judge Lapworth looked up from the box and stared at Thursby. Then he looked at Thompson. "Just what tests *did* you perform on this ... this thing, Mr. Thompson?"

"Well, Your Honor," Thompson said, visibly nervous, "I checked it for all kinds of radiation and magnetism. There isn't anything like that coming from it. But," he added lamely, "there wasn't much else to test. Not without damaging the box."

"I see." His honor glared at Thursby, but didn't say anything to him. He simply ordered the box to be shown to the jury.

Thursby was grimly holding his ground, waiting.

"Have you any more questions, counselor?" the judge asked.

"No, Your Honor, I have not."

"Witness may step down," said his honor to Thompson.

Thursby stood up. "If the Court please, I would like to stage a small demonstration for the members of the jury."

The Court gave permission, and a roulette wheel was hauled in on a small table.

I watched with interest and without objection while Thursby demonstrated the use of the gadget and then asked each of the jurors in turn to try it. It was a long way from being a successful demonstration. Some of the jurors didn't hold the thing right, and some of those that did just didn't have the mental ability required to use it. But that didn't bother Thursby.

"Your Honor, and Gentlemen of the Jury," he said, "you are all aware that a device constructed for the purpose of cheating at any gambling game is not necessarily one hundred per cent infallible. It doesn't have to be. All it has to do is turn the odds in favor of the user.

"You are all familiar with loaded dice, I'm sure. And you know that loading dice for one set of numbers merely increases the probability that those numbers will come up; it does not guarantee that they will come up every time.

"It is the same with marked cards. Marking the backs of a deck of cards doesn't mean that you will invariably get a better hand than your opponent; it doesn't even mean that you will win every hand.

"The device taken from the defendant at the Golden Casino does not, as you have seen, work every time. But, as you have also seen, it certainly *does* shift the odds by a considerable percentage. And that, I submit, is illegal under the laws of this state."

He went on, building on that theme for a while, then he turned the trial over to the defense.

"Call Dr. Pettigrew to the stand," I said.

I heard Thursby's gasp, but I ignored it.

A chunky, balding man with a moon face and an irritated expression came up to be sworn in. He was irritated with me for having subpoenaed him, and he showed it. I hoped he wouldn't turn out to be hostile.

"You are Dr. Herbert Pettigrew?" I asked.

"That is correct."

"State your residence, please."

"3109 La Jolla Boulevard, Los Angeles, California."

"You are called 'Doctor' Pettigrew, I believe. Would you tell the Court what right you have to that title?"

He looked a little miffed, but he said: "It is a scholarly title. A Doctorate of Philosophy in physics from Massachusetts Institute of Technology."

"I see. Would you mind telling the Court what other academic degrees you have?"

He reeled off a list of them, all impressive.

"Thank you, doctor," I said. "Now, what is your present occupation?"

"I am a Professor of Physics, at the University of California in Los Angeles."

I went on questioning him to establish his ability in his field, and by the time I was finished, the jury was pretty well impressed with his status in the scientific brotherhood. And not once did Thursby object.

Then I said, "Dr. Pettigrew, I believe you came to this city on a professional matter?"

"Yes, I did." He didn't hesitate to answer, so I figured I hadn't got his goat too much.

"And what was the nature of that matter?"

"I was asked to come here by Mr. Harold Thursby, the District Attorney, to perform some scientific tests on the ... er ... device ... the device known as People's Exhibit A."

"Did you perform these tests?"

"I did."

"At the request of District Attorney Thursby, is that right?"

"That is correct."

"May I ask why Mr. Thursby did not call you as a witness for the prosecution?"

Thursby, as I had expected, was on his feet. "Objection! The question calls for a conclusion of the witness!"

"Sustained," said Judge Lapworth.

"Dr. Pettigrew," I said, "what were your findings in reference to Exhibit A?"

He shrugged. "The thing is a plastic box with a dial set in one side, a plastic lens in one end, and a couple of strips of silver along two other sides. Inside, there are a lot of markings in black ink on white paint." He gestured toward the exhibit table. "Just what you've seen; that's all there is to it."

"What sort of tests did you perform to determine this, Dr. Pettigrew?" I asked.

He took a long time answering that one. He had X-rayed the thing thoroughly, tested it with apparatus I'd never heard of, taken scrapings from all over it for microchemical analysis, and even tried it himself on a roulette wheel. He hadn't been able to make it work.

"And what is your conclusion from these findings?" I asked.

Again he shrugged. "The thing is just a box, that's all. It has no special properties."

"Would you say that it could be responsible for the phenomena we have just seen? By that, I mean the peculiar action of the roulette wheel, demonstrated here by the prosecution."

"Definitely not," he stated flatly. "The box could not possibly have any effect on either the wheel or the ball."

"I see. Thank you, doctor; that's all. Cross-examine."

Thursby walked over to the witness stand with a belligerent scowl on his face. "Dr. Pettigrew, you say that the box couldn't possibly have had any effect on the wheel. And yet, we have demonstrated that there *is* an effect. Don't you believe the testimony of your own senses?"

"Certainly I do!" snapped Pettigrew.

"Then how do you account for the behavior of the roulette wheel as you have just seen it demonstrated in this court?"

I suppressed a grin. Thursby was so mad that he was having trouble expressing himself clearly.

"In several ways!" Pettigrew said sharply. "In the first place, that wheel could be rigged."

Thursby purpled. "Now, just a minute! I—"

I started to object, but Judge Lapworth beat me to it.

"Are you objecting to the answer, Mr. District Attorney?"

"The witness is insinuating that I falsified evidence!"

"I am not!" said Pettigrew, visibly angry. "You asked me how I could account for its behavior, and I told you one way! There are others!"

"The wheel will be examined," said Judge Lapworth darkly. "Tell us the other ways, Dr. Pettigrew."

"Pure chance," said Pettigrew. "Pure chance, Your Honor. I'm sure that everyone in this courtroom has seen runs of luck on a roulette wheel. According to the laws of probability, such runs must inevitably happen. Frankly, I believe that just such a run has occurred here. I do not think for a minute that Mr. Thursby or anyone else rigged that wheel."

"I see; thank you, Dr. Pettigrew," said the judge. "Any further questions, Mr. District Attorney?"

"No further questions," Thursby said, trying to hide his anger.

"Call your next witness," said the judge, looking at me.

"I call Mr. Jason Howley to the stand."

Howley sat down and was sworn in. I went through the preliminaries, then asked: "Mr. Howley, you have seen People's Exhibit A?"

"I have."

"To whom does it belong?"

"It is mine. It was taken from me by—"

"Just answer the question, please," I admonished him. He knew his script, but he was jumping the gun. "The device is yours, then?"

"That's right."

"Under what circumstances did this device come into the hands of the police?"

He told what had happened on the night of the big take at the Golden Casino.

"Would you explain to us just what this device is?" I asked when he had finished.

"Certainly," he said. "It's a good luck charm."

I could hear the muffled reaction in the courtroom.

"A good luck charm. I see. Then it has no effect on the wheel at all?"

"Oh, I wouldn't say that," Howley said disarmingly. He smiled and looked at the jury. "It certainly has *some* effect. It's the only good luck charm I ever had that worked."

The jury was grinning right back at him. They were all gamblers at heart, and I never knew a gambler yet who didn't have some sort of good luck charm or superstition when it came to gambling. We had them all in the palms of our hands.

"What I mean is, does it have any *physical* effect on the wheel?"

Howley looked puzzled. "Well, I don't know about that. That's not my field. You better ask Dr. Pettigrew."

There was a smothered laugh somewhere in the courtroom.

"Just how do you operate this good luck charm, Mr. Howley?" I asked.

"Why, you just hold it so that your thumb touches one strip of silver and your fingers touch the other, then you set the dial to whatever number you want to come up and wish."

"*Wish?* Just *wish*, Mr. Howley?"

"Just wish. That's all. What else can you do with a good luck charm?"

This time, the judge had to pound for order to stop the laughing.

I turned Howley over to Thursby.

The D.A. hammered at him for half an hour trying to get something out of Howley, but he didn't get anywhere useful. Howley admitted that he'd come to Nevada to play the wheels; what was wrong with that? He admitted that he'd come just to try out his good luck charm—and what was wrong with that? He even admitted that it worked for him every time—

And what was wrong, pray, with *that*?

Thursby knew he was licked. He'd known it for a long time. His summation to the jury showed it. The expressions on the faces of the jury as they listened showed it.

They brought in a verdict of Not Guilty.

When I got back to my office, I picked up the phone and called the Golden Casino. I asked for George Brockey, the manager. When I got him on the phone and identified myself, he said, "Oh. It's you." His voice didn't sound friendly.

"It's me," I said.

"I suppose you're going to slap a suit for false arrest on the Casino now, eh, counselor?"

"Not a bit of it, George," I said. "The thought occurred to me, but I think we can come to terms."

"Yeah?"

"Nothing to it, George. You give us the three hundred grand and we don't do a thing."

"Yeah?" He didn't get it. He had to fork over the money anyway, according to the court order, so what was the deal?

"If you want to go a little further, I'll tell you what we'll do. We'll give you one of our little good luck charms, if you'll promise to call your boys off Howley."

"Nobody's on Howley," he said. "You ought to know better than that. In this state, if we get whipped in court, we play it square. Did you think we were going to get rough?"

"No. But you kind of figured on lifting that gadget as soon as he gets it back from the D.A., didn't you? I saw your boys waiting at his hotel. I'm just telling you that you don't have to do that. We'll give you the gadget. There are plenty more where that came from."

"I see," Brockey said after a long pause. "O.K., counselor. It's a deal."

"Fine. We'll pick up the money later this evening, if that's O.K."

"Sure, counselor. Anytime. Anytime at all." He hung up.

I grinned at Howley, who was sitting across the desk from me. "Well, that winds it up."

"I don't get it," Howley said. "Why'd you call up Brockey? What was the purpose of that 'deal'?"

"No deal," I told him. "I was just warning him that killing you and taking the gadget wouldn't do any good, that we've covered you. He won't bother having anything done to you if he knows that the secret of the gadget is out already."

Howley's eyes widened behind those spectacles of his. "You mean they'd kill me? I thought Nevada gamblers were honest."

"Oh, they are, they are. But this is a threat to their whole industry. It's more than that, it may destroy them. Some of them might kill to keep that from happening. But you don't have to worry now."

"Thanks. Tell me, do you think we've succeeded?"

"In what you set out to do? Certainly. When we mail out those gadgets to people all over the state, the place will be in an uproar. With all the publicity this case is getting, it'll *have* to work. You now have a court decision on your side, a decision which says that a psionic device can be legally used to influence gambling games.

"Why, man, they'll *have* to start investigating! You'll have every politico in the State of Nevada insisting that scientists work on that thing. To say nothing of what the syndicate will do."

"All I wanted to do," said Howley, "was force people to take notice of psionics. I guess I've done that."

"You certainly have, brother. I wonder what it will come to?"

"I wonder, myself, sometimes," Howley said.

That was three and a half years ago. Neither Howley nor I are wondering now. According to the front page of today's *Times*, the first spaceship, with a crew of eighty aboard, reached Mars this morning. And, on page two, there's a small article headlined: ROCKET OBSOLETE, SAY SCIENTISTS.

It sure is.

THE END

Thin Edge

There are inventions of great value that one type of society can use—and that would, for another society, be most nastily deadly!

I

"Beep!" said the radio smugly. "*Beep! Beep! Beep!*"

"There's one," said the man at the pickup controls of tugship 431. He checked the numbers on the various dials of his instruments. Then he carefully marked down in his log book the facts that the radio finder was radiating its beep on such-and-such a frequency and that that frequency and that rate-of-beep indicated that the asteroid had been found and set with anchor by a Captain Jules St. Simon. The direction and distance were duly noted.

That information on direction and distance had already been transmitted to the instruments of the tugship's pilot. "Jazzy-o!" said the pilot. "Got 'im."

He swiveled his ship around until the nose was in line with the beep and then jammed down on the forward accelerator for a few seconds. Then he took his foot off it and waited while the ship approached the asteroid.

In the darkness of space, only points of light were visible. Off to the left, the sun was a small, glaring spot of whiteness that couldn't be looked at directly. Even out here in the Belt, between the orbits of Mars and Jupiter, that massive stellar engine blasted out enough energy to make it uncomfortable to look at with the naked eye. But it could illuminate matter only; the hard vacuum of space remained dark. The pilot could have located the planets easily, without looking around. He knew where each and every one of them were. He had to.

A man can navigate in space by instrument, and he can take the time to figure out where every planet ought to be. But if he does, he won't really be able to navigate in the Asteroid Belt.

In the Nineteenth Century, Mark Twain pointed out that a steamboat pilot who navigated a ship up and down the Mississippi had to be able to identify every landmark and every changing sandbar along the river before he would be allowed to take charge of the wheel. He not only had to memorize the whole river, but be able to predict the changes in its course and the variations in its eddies. He had to be able to know exactly where he was at every moment, even in the blackest of moonless nights, simply by glancing around him.

An asteroid man has to be able to do the same thing. The human mind is capable of it, and one thing that the men and women of the Belt Cities had learned was to use the human mind.

"Looks like a big 'un, Jack," said the instrument man. His eyes were on the radar screen. It not only gave him a picture of the body of the slowly spinning mountain, but the distance and the angular and radial velocities. A duplicate of the instrument gave the same information to the pilot.

The asteroid was fairly large as such planetary debris went—some five hundred meters in diameter, with a mass of around one hundred seventy-four million metric tons.

Within twenty meters of the surface of the great mountain of stone, the pilot brought the ship to a dead stop in relation to that surface.

"Looks like she's got a nice spin on her," he said. "We'll see."

He waited for what he knew would appear somewhere near the equator of the slowly revolving mass. It did. A silvery splash of paint that had originally been squirted on by the anchor man who had first spotted the asteroid in order to check the rotational velocity.

The pilot of the space tug waited until the blotch was centered in the crosshairs of his peeper and then punched the timer. When it came around again, he would be able to compute the angular momentum of the gigantic rock.

"Where's he got his anchor set?" the pilot asked his instrument man.

"The beep's from the North Pole," the instrument man reported instantly. "How's her spin?"

"Wait a bit. The spot hasn't come round again yet. Looks like we'll have some fun with her, though." He kept three stars fixed carefully in his spotters to make sure he didn't drift enough to throw his calculations off. And waited.

Meanwhile, the instrument man abandoned his radar panel and turned to the locker where his vacuum suit waited at the ready. By the time the pilot had seen the splotch of silver come round again and timed it, the instrument man was ready in his vacuum suit.

"Sixteen minutes, forty seconds," the pilot reported. "Angular momentum one point one times ten to the twenty-first gram centimeters squared per second."

"So we play Ride 'Em Cowboy," the instrument man said "I'm evacuating. Tell me when." He had already poised his finger over the switch that would pull the air from his compartments, which had been sealed off from the pilot's compartment when the timing had started.

"Start the pump," said the pilot.

The switch was pressed, and the pumps began to evacuate the air from the compartment. At the same time, the pilot jockeyed the ship to a position over the north pole of the asteroid.

"Over" isn't quite the right word. "Next to" is not much better, but at least it has no implied up-and-down orientation. The surface gravity of the asteroid was only two millionths of a Standard Gee, which is hardly enough to give any noticeable impression to the human nervous system.

"Surface at two meters," said the pilot. "Holding."

The instrument man opened the outer door and saw the surface of the gigantic rock a couple of yards in front of him. And projecting from that surface was the eye of an eyebolt that had been firmly anchored in the depths of the asteroid, a nickel-steel shaft thirty feet long and eight inches in diameter, of which only the eye at the end showed.

The instrument man checked to make sure that his safety line was firmly anchored and then pushed himself across the intervening space to grasp the eye with a space-gloved hand.

This was the anchor.

Moving a nickel-iron asteroid across space to nearest processing plant is a relatively simple job. You slap a powerful electromagnet on her, pour on the juice, and off you go.

The stony asteroids are a different matter. You have to have something to latch on to, and that's where the anchor-setter comes in. His job is to put that anchor in there. That's the first space job a man can get in the Belt, the only way to get space experience. Working by himself, a man learns to preserve his own life out there.

Operating a space tug, on the other hand, is a two-man job because a man cannot both be on the surface of the asteroid and in his ship at the same time. But every space tug man has had long experience as an anchor setter before he's allowed to be in a position where he is capable of killing someone besides himself if he makes a stupid mistake in that deadly vacuum.

"On contact, Jack," the instrument man said as soon as he had a firm grip on the anchor. "Release safety line."

"Safety line released, Harry," Jack's voice said in his earphones.

Jack had pressed a switch that released the ship's end of the safety line so that it now floated free. Harry pulled it towards himself and attached the free end to the eye of the anchor bolt, on a loop of nickel-steel that had been placed there for that purpose. "Safety line secured," he reported. "Ready for tug line."

In the pilot's compartment, Jack manipulated the controls again. The ship moved away from the asteroid and yawed around so that the "tail" was pointed toward the anchor bolt. Protruding from a special port was a heavy-duty universal joint with special attachments. Harry reached out, grasped it with one hand, and pulled it toward him, guiding it toward the eyebolt. A cable attached to its other end snaked out of the tug.

Harry worked hard for some ten or fifteen minutes to get the universal joint firmly bolted to the eye of the anchor. When he was through, he said: "O.K., Jack. Try 'er."

The tug moved gently away from the asteroid, and the cable that bound the two together became taut. Harry carefully inspected his handiwork to make sure that everything had been done properly and that the mechanism would stand the stress.

"So far so good," he muttered, more to himself than to Jack.

Then he carefully set two compact little strain gauges on the anchor itself, at ninety degrees from each other on the circumference of the huge anchor bolt. Two others were already in position in the universal joint itself. When everything was ready, he said: "Give 'er a try at length."

The tug moved away from the asteroid, paying out the cable as it went.

Hauling around an asteroid that had a mass on the order of one hundred seventy-four million metric tons required adequate preparation. The nonmagnetic stony asteroids are an absolute necessity for the Belt Cities. In order to live, man needs oxygen, and there is no trace of an atmosphere on any of the little Belt worlds except that which Man has made himself and sealed off to prevent it from escaping into space. Carefully conserved though that oxygen is, no process is or can be one hundred per cent efficient. There will be leakage into space, and that which is lost must be replaced. To bring oxygen from Earth in liquid form would be outrageously expensive and even more outrageously inefficient—and no other planet in the System has free oxygen for the taking. It is much easier to use Solar energy to take it out of its compounds, and those compounds are much more readily available in space, where it is not necessary to fight the gravitational pull of a planet to get them. The stony asteroids average thirty-six per cent oxygen by mass; the rest of it is silicon, magnesium, aluminum, nickel, and calcium, with respectable traces of sodium, chromium, phosphorous manganese, cobalt, potassium, and titanium. The metallic nickel-iron asteroids made an excellent source of export products to ship to Earth, but the stony asteroids were for home consumption.

This particular asteroid presented problems. Not highly unusual problems, but problems nonetheless. It was massive and had a high rate of spin. In addition, its axis of spin was at an angle of eighty-one degrees to the direction in which the tug would have to tow it to get it to the processing plant. The asteroid was, in effect, a huge gyroscope, and it would take quite a bit of push to get that axis tilted in the direction that Harry Morgan and Jack Latrobe wanted it to go. In theory, they could just have latched on, pulled, and let the thing precess in any way it wanted to. The trouble is that that would not have been too good for the anchor bolt. A steady pull on the anchor bolt was one thing: a nickel-steel bolt like that could take a pull of close to twelve million pounds as long as that pull was along the axis. Flexing it—which would happen if they let the asteroid precess at will—would soon fatigue even that heavy bolt.

The cable they didn't have to worry about. Each strand was a fine wire of two-phase material—the harder phase being borazon, the softer being tungsten carbide. Winding these fine wires into a cable made a flexible rope that was essentially a three-phase material—with the vacuum of space acting as the third phase. With a tensile strength above a hundred million pounds per square inch, a half inch cable could easily apply more pressure to that anchor than it could take. There was a need for that strong cable: a snapping cable that is suddenly released from a tension of many millions of pounds can be dangerous in the extreme, forming a writhing whip that can lash through a spacesuit as though it did not exist. What damage it did to flesh and bone after that was of minor importance; a man who loses all his air in explosive decompression certainly has very little use for flesh and bone thereafter.

"All O.K. here," Jack's voice came over Harry's headphones.

"And here," Harry said. The strain gauges showed nothing out of the ordinary.

"O.K. Let's see if we can flip this monster over," Harry said, satisfied that the equipment would take the stress that would be applied to it.

He did not suspect the kind of stress that would be applied to him within a few short months.

II

The hotel manager was a small-minded man with a narrow-minded outlook and a brain that was almost totally unable to learn. He was, in short, a "normal" Earthman. He took one look at the card that had been dropped on his desk from the chute of the registration computer and reacted. His thin gray brows drew down over his cobralike brown eyes, and he muttered, "Ridiculous!" under his breath.

The registration computer wouldn't have sent him the card if there hadn't been something odd about it, and odd things happened so rarely that the manager took immediate notice of it. One look at the title before the name told him everything he needed to know. Or so he thought.

The registration robot handled routine things routinely. If they were not routine, the card was dropped on the manager's desk. It was then the manager's job to fit everything back into the routine. He grasped the card firmly between thumb and forefinger and stalked out of his office. He took an elevator down to the registration desk. His trouble was that he had seized upon the first thing he saw wrong with the card and saw nothing thereafter. To him, "out of the ordinary" meant "wrong"—which was where he made his mistake.

There was a man waiting impatiently at the desk. He had put the card that had been given him by the registration robot on the desk and was tapping his fingers on it.

The manager walked over to him. "Morgan, Harry?" he asked with a firm but not arrogant voice.

"Is this the city of York, New?" asked the man. There was a touch of cold humor in his voice that made the manager look more closely at him. He weighed perhaps two-twenty and stood a shade over six-two, but it was the look in the blue eyes and the bearing of the man's body that made the manager suddenly feel as though this man were someone extraordinary. That, of course, meant "wrong."

Then the question that the man had asked in rebuttal to his own penetrated the manager's mind, and he became puzzled. "Er ... I beg your pardon?"

"I said, 'Is this York, New?'" the man repeated.

"This is New York, if that's what you mean," the manager said.

"Then I am Harry Morgan, if that's what you mean."

The manager, for want of anything better to do to cover his confusion, glanced back at the card—without really looking at it. Then he looked back up at the face of Harry Morgan. "Evidently you have not turned in your Citizen's

Identification Card for renewal, Mr. Morgan," he said briskly. As long as he was on familiar ground, he knew how to handle himself.

"Odd's Fish!" said Morgan with utter sadness, "How did you know?"

The manager's comfortable feeling of rightness had returned. "You can't hope to fool a registration robot, Mr. Morgan," he said "When a discrepancy is observed, the robot immediately notifies a person in authority. Two months ago, Government Edict 7-3356-Hb abolished titles of courtesy absolutely and finally. You Englishmen have clung to them for far longer than one would think possible, but that has been abolished." He flicked the card with a finger. "You have registered here as 'Commodore Sir Harry Morgan'—obviously, that is the name and anti-social title registered on your card. When you put the card into the registration robot, the error was immediately noted and I was notified. You should not be using an out-of-date card, and I will be forced to notify the Citizen's Registration Bureau."

"Forced?" said Morgan in mild amazement. "Dear me! What a terribly strong word."

The manager felt the hook bite, but he could no more resist the impulse to continue than a cat could resist catnip. His brain did not have the ability to overcome his instinct. And his instinct was wrong. "You may consider yourself under arrest, Mr. Morgan."

"I thank you for that permission," Morgan said with a happy smile. "But I think I shall not take advantage of it." He stood there with that same happy smile while two hotel security guards walked up and stood beside him, having been called by the manager's signal.

Again it took the manager a little time to realize what Morgan had said. He blinked. "Advantage of it?" he repeated haphazardly.

Harry Morgan's smile vanished as though it had never been. His blue eyes seemed to change from the soft blue of a cloudless sky to the steely blue of a polished revolver. Oddly enough, his lips did not change. They still seemed to smile, although the smile had gone.

"Manager," he said deliberately, "if you will pardon my using your title, you evidently cannot read."

The manager had not lived in the atmosphere of the Earth's Citizen's Welfare State as long as he had without knowing that dogs eat dogs. He looked back at the card that had been delivered to his desk only minutes before and this time he read it thoroughly. Then, with a gesture, he signaled the Security men to return to their posts. But he did not take his eyes from the card.

"My apologies," Morgan said when the Security police had retired out of earshot. There was no apology in the tone of his voice. "I perceive that you can read. Bully, may I say, for you." The bantering tone was still in his voice, the pseudo-smile still on his lips, the chill of cold steel still in his eyes. "I realize that titles of courtesy are illegal on earth," he continued, "because courtesy itself is illegal. However, the title 'Commodore' simply means that I am entitled to command a spaceship containing two or more persons other than myself. Therefore, it is not a title of courtesy, but of ability."

The manager had long since realized that he was dealing with a Belt man, not an Earth citizen, and that the registration robot had sent him the card because of that, not because there was anything illegal. Men from the Belt did not come to Earth either willingly or often.

Still unable to override his instincts—which erroneously told him that there was something "wrong"—the manager said: "What does the 'Sir' mean?"

Harry Morgan glowed warmly. "Well, now, Mr. Manager, I will tell you. I will give you an analogy. In the time of the Roman Republic, twenty-one centuries or so ago, the leader of an Army was given the title *Imperator*. But that title could not be conferred upon him by the Senate of Rome nor by anyone else in power. No man could call himself *Imperator* until his own soldiers, the men under him, had publicly acclaimed him as such. If, voluntarily, his own men shouted '*Ave, Imperator!*' at a public gathering, then the man could claim the title. Later the title degenerated—" He stopped.

The manager was staring at him with uncomprehending eyes, and Morgan's outward smile became genuine. "Sorry," he said condescendingly. "I forgot that history is not a popular subject in the Welfare World." Morgan had forgotten no such thing, but he went right on. "What I meant to say was that the spacemen of the Belt Cities have voluntarily agreed among themselves to call me 'sir'. Whether that is a title of ability or a title of courtesy, you can argue about with me at another time. Right now, I want my room key."

Under the regulations, the manager knew there was nothing else he could do. He had made a mistake, and he knew that he had. If he had only taken the trouble to read the rest of the card—

"Awfully sorry, Mr. Morgan," he said with a lopsided smile that didn't even look genuine. "The—"

"Watch those courtesy titles," Morgan reprimanded gently. "'Mister' comes ultimately from the Latin *magister*, meaning 'master' or 'teacher'. And while I may be your master, I wouldn't dare think I could teach you anything."

"All citizens are entitled to be called 'Mister'," the manager said with a puzzled look. He pushed a room key across the desk.

"Which just goes to show you," said Harry Morgan, picking up the key.

He turned casually, took one or two steps away from the registration desk, then—quite suddenly—did an about-face and snapped: "*What happened to Jack Latrobe?*"

"Who?" said the manager, his face gaping stupidly.

Harry Morgan knew human beings, and he was fairly certain that the manager couldn't have reacted that way unless he honestly had no notion of what Morgan was talking about.

He smiled sweetly. "Never you mind, dear boy. Thank you for the key." He turned again and headed for the elevator bank, confident that the manager would find the question he had asked about Jack Latrobe so completely meaningless as to be incapable of registering as a useful memory.

He was perfectly right.

III

The Belt Cities could survive without the help of Earth, and the Supreme Congress of the United Nations of Earth knew it. But they also knew that "survive" did not by any means have the same semantic or factual content as "live comfortably". If Earth were to vanish overnight, the people of the Belt would live, but they would be seriously handicapped. On the other hand, the people of Earth could survive—as they had for millennia—without the Belt Cities, and while doing without Belt imports might be painful, it would by no means be deadly.

But both the Belt Cities and the Earth knew that the destruction of one would mean the collapse of the other as a civilization.

Earth needed iron. Belt iron was cheap. The big iron deposits of Earth were worked out, and the metal had been widely scattered. The removal of the asteroids as a cheap source would mean that iron would become prohibitively expensive. Without cheap iron, Earth's civilization would have to undergo a painfully drastic change—a collapse and regeneration.

But the Belt Cities were handicapped by the fact that they had had as yet neither the time nor the resources to manufacture anything but absolute necessities. Cloth, for example, was imported from Earth. A society that is still busy struggling for the bare necessities—such as manufacturing its own air—has no time to build the huge looms necessary to weave cloth ... or to make clothes, except on a minor scale. Food? You can have hydroponic gardens on an asteroid, but raising beef cattle, even on Ceres, was difficult. Eventually, perhaps, but not yet.

The Belt Cities were populated by pioneers who still had not given up the luxuries of civilization. Their one weakness was that they had their cake and were happily eating it, too.

Not that Harry Morgan didn't realize that fact. A Belt man is, above all, a realist, in that he must, of necessity, understand the Laws of the Universe and deal with them. Or die.

Commodore Sir Harry Morgan was well aware of the stir he had created in the lobby of the Grand Central Hotel. Word would leak out, and he knew it. The scene had been created for just that purpose.

"*Grasshopper sittin' on a railroad track,Singin' polly-wolly-doodle-alla-day!A-pickin' his teeth with a carpet tack,Singin' polly-wolly-doodle-alla-day!*"

He sang with gusto as the elevator lifted him up to the seventy-fourth floor of the Grand Central Hotel. The other passengers in the car did not look at him directly; they cast sidelong glances.

This guy, they seemed to think in unison, *is a nut. We will pay no attention to him, since he probably does not really exist. Even if he does, we will pay no attention in the hope that he will go away.*

On the seventy-fourth floor, he *did* go away, heading for his room. He keyed open the door and strolled over to the phone, where a message had already been dropped into the receiver slot. He picked it up and read it.

COMMODORE SIR HARRY MORGAN, RM. 7426, GCH: REQUEST YOU CALL EDWAY TARNHORST, REPRESENTATIVE OF THE PEOPLE OF GREATER LOS ANGELES, SUPREME CONGRESS. PUNCH 33-981-762-044 COLLECT.

"How news travels," Harry Morgan thought to himself. He tapped out the number on the keyboard of the phone and waited for the panel to light up. When it did, it showed a man in his middle fifties with a lean, ascetic face and graying hair, which gave him a look of saintly wisdom.

"Mr. Tarnhorst?" Morgan asked pleasantly.

"Yes. Commodore Morgan?" The voice was smooth and precise.

"At your service, Mr. Tarnhorst. You asked me to call."

"Yes. What is the purpose of your visit to Earth, commodore?" The question was quick, decisive, and firm.

Harry Morgan kept his affability. "That's none of your business, Mr. Tarnhorst."

Tarnhorst's face didn't change. "Perhaps your superiors haven't told you, but—and I can only disclose this on a sealed circuit—I am in sympathy with the Belt Cities. I have been out there twice and have learned to appreciate the vigor and worth of the Belt people. I am on your side, commodore, in so far as it does not compromise my position. My record shows that I have fought for the rights of the Belt Cities on the floor of the Supreme Congress. Have you been informed of that fact?"

"I have," said Harry Morgan. "And that is precisely why it is none of your business. The less you know, Mr. Tarnhorst, the safer you will be. I am not here as a representative of any of the City governments. I am not here as a representative of any of the Belt Corporations. I am completely on my own, without official backing. You have shown yourself to be sympathetic towards us in the past. We have no desire to hurt you. Therefore I advise that you either keep your nose out of my business or actively work against me. You cannot protect yourself otherwise."

Edward Tarnhorst was an Earthman, but he was not stupid. He had managed to put himself in a position of power in the Welfare World, and he knew how to handle that power. It took him exactly two seconds to make his decision.

"You misunderstand me, commodore," he said coldly. "I asked what I asked because I desire information. The People's Government is trying to solve the murder of Commodore Jack Latrobe. Assuming, of course, that it was murder—which is open to doubt. His body was found three days ago in Fort Tryon Park, up on the north end of Manhattan Island. He had apparently jumped off one of the old stone bridges up there and fell ninety feet to his death. On the other hand, it is possible that, not being used to the effects of a field of point nine eight Standard gees, he did not realize that the fall would be deadly, and accidentally killed himself. He was alone in the park at night, as far as we can tell. It has been ascertained definitely that no representative of the People's Manufacturing Corporation Number 873 was with him at the time. Nor, so far as we can discover, was anyone else. I asked you to call because I wanted to know if you had any information for us. There was no other reason."

"I haven't seen Jack since he left Juno," Morgan said evenly. "I don't know why he came to Earth, and I know nothing else."

"Then I see no further need for conversation," Tarnhorst said. "Thank you for your assistance, Commodore Morgan. If Earth's Government needs you again, you will be notified if you gain any further information, you may call this number. Thank you again. Good-by."

The screen went blank.

How much of this is a trap? Morgan thought.

There was no way of knowing at this point. Morgan knew that Jack Latrobe had neither committed suicide nor died accidentally, and Tarnhorst had told him as much. Tarnhorst was still friendly, but he had taken the hint and got himself out of danger. There had been one very important piece of information. The denial that any representative of PMC 873 had been involved. PMC 873 was a manufacturer of biological products—one of the several corporations that Latrobe had been empowered to discuss business with when he had been sent to Earth by the Belt Corporations Council. Tarnhorst would not have mentioned them negatively unless he intended to imply a positive hint. Obviously. Almost too obviously.

Well?

Harry Morgan punched for Information, got it, got a number, and punched that.

"People's Manufacturing Corporation Ey-yut Seven Tha-ree," said a recorded voice. "Your desire, pu-leeze?"

"This is Commodore Jack Latrobe," Morgan said gently. "I'm getting tired of this place, and if you don't let me out I will blow the whole place to Kingdom Come. Good bye-eye-eye."

He hung up without waiting for an answer.

Then he looked around the hotel suite he had rented. It was an expensive one—very expensive. It consisted of an outer room—a "sitting room" as it might have been called two centuries before—and a bedroom. Plus a bathroom.

Harry Morgan, a piratical smile on his face, opened the bathroom door and left it that way. Then he went into the bedroom. His luggage had already been delivered by the lift tube, and was sitting on the floor. He put both suitcases on the bed, where they would be in plain sight from the sitting room. Then he made certain preparations for invaders.

He left the door between the sitting room and the bedroom open and left the suite.

Fifteen minutes later, he was walking down 42nd Street toward Sixth Avenue. On his left was the ancient Public Library Building. In the middle of the block, somebody shoved something hard into his left kidney and said. "Keep walking, commodore. But do what you're told."

Harry Morgan obeyed, with an utterly happy smile on his lips.

IV

In the Grand Central Hotel, a man moved down the hallway toward Suite 7426. He stopped at the door and inserted the key he held in his hand, twisting it as it entered the keyhole. The electronic locks chuckled, and the door swung open.

The man closed it behind him.

He was not a big man, but neither was he undersized. He was five-ten and weighed perhaps a hundred and sixty-five pounds. His face was dark of skin and had a hard, determined expression on it. He looked as though he had spent the last thirty of his thirty-five years of life stealing from his family and cheating his friends.

He looked around the sitting room. Nothing. He tossed the key in his hand and then shoved it into his pocket. He walked over to the nearest couch and prodded at it. He took an instrument out of his inside jacket pocket and looked at it.

"Nothin'," he said to himself. "Nothin'." His detector showed that there were no electronic devices hidden in the room—at least, none that he did not already know about.

He prowled around the sitting room for several minutes, looking at everything—chairs, desk, windows, floor—everything. He found nothing. He had not expected to, since the occupant, a Belt man named Harry Morgan, had only been in the suite a few minutes.

Then he walked over to the door that separated the sitting room from the bedroom. Through it, he could see the suitcases sitting temptingly on the bed.

Again he took his detector out of his pocket. After a full minute, he was satisfied that there was no sign of any complex gadgetry that could warn the occupant that anyone had entered the room. Certainly there was nothing deadly around.

Then a half-grin came over the man's cunning face. There was always the chance that the occupant of the suite had rigged up a really old-fashioned trap.

He looked carefully at the hinges of the door. Nothing. There were no tiny bits of paper that would fall if he pushed the door open any further, no little threads that would be broken.

It hadn't really seemed likely, after all. The door was open wide enough for a man to walk through without moving it.

Still grinning, the man reached out toward the door.

He was quite astonished when his hand didn't reach the door itself.

There was a sharp feeling of pain when his hand fell to the floor, severed at the wrist.

The man stared at his twitching hand on the floor. He blinked stupidly while his wrist gushed blood. Then, almost automatically, he stepped forward to pick up his hand.

As he shuffled forward, he felt a *snick! snick!* of pain in his ankles while all sensation from his feet went dead.

It was not until he began toppling forward that he realized that his feet were still sitting calmly on the floor in their shoes and that he was no longer connected to them.

It was too late. He was already falling.

He felt a stinging sensation in his throat and then nothing more as the drop in blood pressure rendered him unconscious.

His hand lay, where it had fallen. His feet remained standing. His body fell to the floor with a resounding *thud!* His head bounced once and then rolled under the bed.

When his heart quit pumping, the blood quit spurting.

A tiny device on the doorjamb, down near the floor, went *zzzt!* and then there was silence.

V

When Representative Edway Tarnhorst cut off the call that had come from Harry Morgan, he turned around and faced the other man in the room. "Satisfactory?" he said.

"Yes. Yes, of course," said the other. He was a tall, hearty-looking man with a reddish face and a friendly smile. "You said just the right thing, Edway. Just the right thing. You're pretty smart, you know that? You got what it takes." He chuckled. "They'll never figure anything out now." He waved a hand toward the chair. "Sit down, Edway. Want a drink?"

Tarnhorst sat down and folded his hands. He looked down at them as if he were really interested in the flat, unfaceted diamond, engraved with the Tarnhorst arms, that gleamed on the ring on his finger.

"A little glass of whiskey wouldn't hurt much, Sam," he said, looking up from his hands. He smiled. "As you say, there isn't much to worry about now. If Morgan goes to the police, they'll give him the same information."

Sam Fergus handed Tarnhorst a drink. "Damn right. Who's to know?" He chuckled again and sat down. "That was pretty good. Yes sir, pretty good. Just because he thought that when you voted for the Belt Cities you were on their side, he believed what you said. Hell, *I've* voted on their side when it was the right thing to do. Haven't I now, Ed? Haven't I?"

"Sure you have," said Tarnhorst with an easy smile. "So have a lot of us."

"Sure we have," Fergus repeated. His grin was huge. Then it changed to a frown. "I don't figure them sometimes. Those Belt people are crazy. Why wouldn't they give us the process for making that cable of theirs? Why?" He looked up at Tarnhorst with a genuinely puzzled look on his face. "I mean, you'd think they thought that the laws of nature were private property or something. They don't have the right outlook. A man finds out something like that, he ought to give it to the human race, hadn't he, Edway? How come those Belt people want to keep something like that secret?"

Edway Tarnhorst massaged the bridge of his nose with a thumb and forefinger, his eyes closed. "I don't know, Sam. I really don't know. Selfish, is all I can say."

Selfish? he thought. *Is it really selfish? Where is the dividing line? How much is a man entitled to keep secret, for his own benefit, and how much should he tell for the public?*

He glanced again at the coat of arms carved into the surface of the diamond. A thousand years ago, his ancestors had carved themselves a tiny empire out of middle Europe—a few hundred acres, no more. Enough to keep one family in luxury while the serfs had a bare existence. They had conquered by the sword and ruled by the sword. They had taken all and given nothing.

But had they? The Barons of Tarnhorst had not really lived much better than their serfs had lived. More clothes and more food, perhaps, and a few baubles—diamonds and fine silks and warm furs. But no Baron Tarnhorst had ever allowed his serfs to starve, for that would not be economically sound. And each Baron had been the dispenser of Justice; he had been Law in his land. Without him, there would have been anarchy among the ignorant peasants, since they were certainly not fit to govern themselves a thousand years ago.

Were they any better fit today? Tarnhorst wondered. For a full millennium, men had been trying, by mass education and by mass information, to bring the peasants up to the level of the nobles. Had that plan succeeded? Or had the intelligent ones simply been forced to conform to the actions of the masses? Had the nobles made peasants of themselves instead?

Edway Tarnhorst didn't honestly know. All he knew was that he saw a new spark of human life, a spark of intelligence, a spark of ability, out in the Belt. He didn't dare tell anyone—he hardly dared admit it to himself—but he thought those people were better somehow than the common clods of Earth. Those people didn't think that just because a man could slop color all over an otherwise innocent sheet of canvas, making outré and garish patterns, that that made him an artist. They didn't think that just because a man could write nonsense and use erratic typography, that that made him a poet. They had other beliefs, too, that Edway Tarnhorst saw only dimly, but he saw them well enough to know that they were better beliefs than the obviously stupid belief that every human being had as much right to respect and dignity as every other, that a man had a *right* to be respected, that he *deserved* it. Out there, they thought that a man had a right only to what he earned.

But Edway Tarnhorst was as much a product of his own society as Sam Fergus. He could only behave as he had been taught. Only on occasion—on very special occasion—could his native intelligence override the "common sense" that he had been taught. Only when an emergency arose. But when one did, Edway Tarnhorst, in spite of his environmental upbringing, was equal to the occasion.

Actually, his own mind was never really clear on the subject. He did the best he could with the confusion he had to work with.

"Now we've got to be careful, Sam," he said. "Very careful. We don't want a war with the Belt Cities."

Sam Fergus snorted. "They wouldn't dare. We got 'em outnumbered a thousand to one."

"Not if they drop a rock on us," Tarnhorst said quietly.

"They wouldn't dare," Fergus repeated.

But both of them could see what would happen to any city on Earth if one of the Belt ships decided to shift the orbit of a good-sized asteroid so that it would strike Earth. A few hundred thousand tons of rock coming in at ten miles per second would be far more devastating than an expensive H-bomb.

"They wouldn't dare," Fergus said again.

"Nevertheless," Tarnhorst said, "in dealings of this kind we are walking very close to the thin edge. We have to watch ourselves."

VI

Commodore Sir Harry Morgan was herded into a prison cell, given a shove across the smallish room, and allowed to hear the door slam behind him. By the time he regained his balance and turned to face the barred door again, it was locked. The bully-boys who had shoved him in turned away and walked down the corridor. Harry sat down on the floor and relaxed, leaning against the stone wall. There was no furniture of any kind in the cell, not even sanitary plumbing.

"What do I do for a drink of water?" he asked aloud of no one in particular.

"You wait till they bring you your drink," said a whispery voice a few feet from his head. Morgan realized that someone in the cell next to his was talking. "You get a quart a day—a halfa pint four times a day. Save your voice. Your throat gets awful dry if you talk much."

"Yeah, it would," Morgan agreed in the same whisper. "What about sanitation?"

"That's your worry," said the voice. "Fella comes by every Wednesday and Saturday with a honey bucket. You clean out your own cell."

"I *thought* this place smelled of something other than attar of roses," Morgan observed. "My nose tells me this is Thursday."

There was a hoarse, humorless chuckle from the man in the next cell. "'At's right. The smell of the disinfectant is strongest now. Saturday mornin' it'll be different. You catch on fast, buddy."

"Oh, I'm a whiz," Morgan agreed. "But I thought the Welfare World took care of its poor, misled criminals better than this."

Again the chuckle. "You shoulda robbed a bank or killed somebody. Then theyda given you a nice rehabilitation sentence. Regular prison. Room of your own. Something real nice. Like a hotel. But this's different."

"Yeah," Morgan agreed. This was a political prison. This was the place where they put you when they didn't care what happened to you after the door was locked because there would be no going out.

Morgan knew where he was. It was a big, fortresslike building on top of one of the highest hills at the northern end of Manhattan Island—an old building that had once been a museum and was built like a medieval castle.

"What happens if you die in here?" he asked conversationally.

"Every Wednesday and Saturday," the voice repeated.

"Um," said Harry Morgan.

"'Cept once in a while," the voice whispered. "Like a couple days ago. When was it? Yeah. Monday that'd be. Guy they had in here for a week or so. Don't remember how long. Lose tracka time here. Yeah. Sure lose tracka time here."

There was a long pause, and Morgan, controlling the tenseness in his voice, said: "What about the guy Monday?"

"Oh. Him. Yeah, well, they took him out Monday."

Morgan waited again, got nothing further, and asked: "Dead?"

"'Course he was dead. They was tryin' to get somethin' out of him. Somethin' about a cable. He jumped one of the guards, and they blackjacked him. Hit 'im too hard, I guess. Guard sure got hell for that, too. Me, I'm lucky. They don't ask me no questions."

"What are you in for?" Morgan asked.

"Don't know. They never told me. I don't ask for fear they'll remember. They might start askin' questions."

Morgan considered. This could be a plant, but he didn't think so. The voice was too authentic, and there would be no purpose in his information. That meant that Jack Latrobe really was dead. They had killed him. An ice cold hardness surged along his nerves.

The door at the far end of the corridor clanged, and a brace of heavy footsteps clomped along the floor. Two men came abreast of the steel-barred door and stopped.

One of them, a well-dressed, husky-looking man in his middle forties, said: "O.K., Morgan. How did you do it?"

"I put on blue lipstick and kissed my elbows—both of 'em. Going widdershins, of course."

"What are you talking about?"

"What are you talking about?"

"The guy in your hotel suite. You killed him. You cut off both feet, one hand, and his head. How'd you do it?"

Morgan looked at the man. "Police?"

"Nunna your business. Answer the question."

"I use a cobweb I happened to have with me. Who was he?"

The cop's face was whitish. "You chop a guy up like that and then don't know who he is?"

"I can guess. I can guess that he was an agent for PMC 873 who was trespassing illegally. But I didn't kill him. I was in ... er ... custody when it happened."

"Not gonna talk, huh?" the cop said in a hard voice. "O.K., you've had your chance. We'll be back."

"I don't think I'll wait," said Morgan.

"You'll wait. We got you on a murder charge now. You'll wait. Wise guy." He turned and walked away. The other man followed like a trained hound.

After the door clanged, the man in the next cell whispered: "Well, you're for it. They're gonna ask you questions."

Morgan said one obscene word and stood up. It was time to leave.

He had been searched thoroughly. They had left him only his clothes, nothing else. They had checked to make sure that there were no microminiaturized circuits on him. He was clean.

So they thought.

Carefully, he caught a thread in the lapel of his jacked and pulled it free. Except for a certain springiness, it looked like an ordinary silon thread. He looped it around one of the bars of his cell, high up. The ends he fastened to a couple of little decorative hooks in his belt—hooks covered with a shell of synthetic ruby.

Then he leaned back, putting his weight on the thread.

Slowly, like a knife moving through cold peanut butter, the thread sank into the steel bar, cutting through its one-inch thickness with increasing difficulty until it was half-way through. Then it seemed to slip the rest of the way through.

He repeated the procedure thrice more, making two cuts in each of two bars. Then he carefully removed the sections he had cut out. He put one of them on the floor of his cell and carried the other in his hand—three feet of one-inch steel makes a nice weapon if it becomes necessary.

Then he stepped through the hole he had made.

The man in the next cell widened his eyes as Harry Morgan walked by. But Morgan could tell that he saw nothing. He had only heard. His eyes had been removed long before. It was the condition of the man that convinced Morgan with utter finality that he had told the truth.

VII

Mr. Edway Tarnhorst felt fear, but no real surprise when the shadow in the window of his suite in the Grand Central Hotel materialized into a human being. But he couldn't help asking one question.

"How did you get there?" His voice was husky. "We're eighty floors above the street."

"Try climbing asteroids for a while," said Commodore Sir Harry Morgan. "You'll get used to it. That's why I knew Jack hadn't died 'accidentally'—he was murdered."

"You ... you're not carrying a gun," Tarnhorst said.

"Do I need one?"

Tarnhorst swallowed. "Yes. Fergus will be back in a moment."

"Who's Fergus?"

"He's the man who controls PMC 873."

Harry Morgan shoved his hand into his jacket pocket "Then I have a gun. You saw it, didn't you?"

"Yes. Yes ... I saw it when you came in."

"Good. Call him."

When Sam Fergus came in, he looked as though he had had about three or four too many slugs of whiskey. There was an odd fear an his face.

"Whats matter, Edway? I—" The fear increased when he saw Morgan. "Whadda you here for?"

"I'm here to make a speech Fergus. Sit down." When Fergus still stood, Morgan repeated what he had said with only a trace more emphasis. "Sit down."

Fergus sat. So did Tarnhorst.

"Both of you pay special attention," Morgan said, a piratical gleam in his eyes. "You killed a friend of mine. My best friend. But I'm not going to kill either of you. Yet. Just listen and listen carefully."

Even Tarnhorst looked frightened. "Don't move, Sam. He's got a gun. I saw it when he came in."

"What ... what do you want?" Fergus asked.

"I want to give you the information you want. The information that you killed Jack for." There was cold hatred in his voice. "I am going to tell you something that you have thought you wanted, but which you really will wish you had never heard. I'm going to tell you about that cable."

Neither Fergus nor Tarnhorst said a word.

"You want a cable. You've heard that we use a cable that has a tensile strength of better than a hundred million pounds per square inch, and you want to know how it's made. You tried to get the secret out of Jack because he was sent here as a commercial dealer. And he wouldn't talk, so one of your goons blackjacked him too hard and then you had to drop him off a bridge to make it look like an accident.

"Then you got your hands on me. You were going to wring it out of me. Well, there is no necessity of that." His grin became wolfish. "I'll give you everything." He paused. "If you want it."

Fergus found his voice. "I want it. I'll pay a million—"

"You'll pay nothing," Morgan said flatly. "You'll listen."

Fergus nodded wordlessly.

"The composition is simple. Basically, it is a two-phase material-like fiberglass. It consists of a strong, hard material imbedded in a matrix of softer material. The difference is that, in this case, the stronger fibers are borazon—boron nitride formed under tremendous pressure—while the softer matrix is composed of tungsten carbide. If the fibers are only a thousandth or two thousandths of an inch in diameter—the thickness of a human hair or less—then the cable from which they are made has tremendous strength and flexibility.

"Do you want the details of the process now?" His teeth were showing in his wolfish grin.

Fergus swallowed. "Yes, of course. But ... but why do you—"

"Why do I give it to you? Because it will kill you. You have seen what the stuff will do. A strand a thousandth of an inch thick, encased in silon for lubrication purposes, got me out of that filthy hole you call a prison. You've heard about that?"

Fergus blinked. "You cut yourself out of there with the cable you're talking about?"

"Not with the cable. With a thin fiber. With one of the hairlike fibers that makes up the cable. Did you ever cut cheese with a wire? In effect, that wire is a knife—a knife that consists only of an edge.

"Or, another experiment you may have heard of. Take a block of ice. Connect a couple of ten-pound weights together with a few feet of piano wire and loop it across the ice block to that the weights hang free on either side, with the wire over the top of the block. The wire will cut right through the ice in a short time. The trouble is that the ice block remains whole—because the ice melts under the pressure of the wire and then flows around it and freezes again on the other side. But if you lubricate the wire with ordinary glycerine, it prevents the re-freezing and the ice block will be cut in two."

Tarnhorst nodded. "I remember. In school. They—" He let his voice trail off.

"Yeah. Exactly. It's a common experiment in basic science. Borazon fiber works the same way. Because it is so fine and has such tremendous tensile strength, it is possible to apply a pressure of hundreds of millions of pounds per square inch over a very small area. Under pressures like that, steel cuts easily. With silon covering to lubricate the cut, there's nothing to it. As you have heard from the guards in your little hell-hole.

"Hell-hole?" Tarnhorst's eyes narrowed and he flicked a quick glance at Fergus. Morgan realized that Tarnhorst had known nothing of the extent of Fergus' machinations.

"That lovely little political prison up in Fort Tryon Park that the World Welfare State, with its usual solicitousness for the common man, keeps for its favorite guests," Morgan said. His wolfish smile returned. "I'd've cut the whole thing down if I'd had had the time. Not the stone—just the steel. In order to apply that kind of pressure you have to have the filament fastened to something considerably harder than the stuff you're trying to cut, you see. Don't try it with your fingers or you'll lose fingers."

Fergus' eyes widened again and he looked both ill and frightened. "The man we sent ... uh ... who was found in your room. You—" He stopped and seemed to have trouble swallowing.

"Me? *I* didn't do anything." Morgan did a good imitation of a shark trying to look innocent. "I'll admit that I looped a very fine filament of the stuff across the doorway a few times, so that if anyone tried to enter my room illegally I would be warned." He didn't bother to add that a pressure-sensitive device had released and reeled in the filament after it had done its work. "It doesn't need to be nearly as tough and heavy to cut through soft stuff like ... er ... say, a beefsteak, as it does to cut through steel. It's as fine as cobweb almost invisible. Won't the World Welfare State have fun when that stuff gets into the hands of its happy, crime-free populace?"

Edway Tarnhorst became suddenly alert. "What?"

"Yes. Think of the fun they'll have, all those lovely slobs who get their basic subsistence and their dignity and their honor as a free gift from the State. The kids, especially. They'll *love* it. It's so fine it can be hidden inside an ordinary thread—or woven into the hair—or...." He spread his hands. "A million places."

Fergus was gaping. Tarnhorst was concentrating on Morgan's words.

"And there's no possible way to leave fingerprints on anything that fine," Morgan continued. "You just hook it around a couple of nails or screws, across an open doorway or an alleyway—and wait."

"We wouldn't let it get into the people's hands," Tarnhorst said.

"You couldn't stop it," Morgan said flatly. "Manufacture the stuff and eventually one of the workers in the plant will figure out a way to steal some of it."

"Guards—" Fergus said faintly.

"*Pfui.* But even you had a perfect guard system, I think I can guarantee that some of it would get into the hands of the—common people. Unless you want to cut off all imports from the Belt."

Tarnhorst's voice hardened. "You mean you'd deliberately—"

"I mean exactly what I said," Morgan cut in sharply. "Make of it what you want."

"I suppose you have that kind of trouble out in the Belt?" Tarnhorst asked.

"No. We don't have your kind of people out in the Belt, Mr. Tarnhorst. We have men who kill, yes. But we don't have the kind of juvenile and grown-up delinquents who will kill senselessly, just for kicks. That kind is too stupid to live long out there. We are in no danger from borazon-tungsten filaments. You are." He paused just for a moment, then said: "I'm ready to give you the details of the process now, Mr. Fergus."

"I don't think I—" Fergus began with a sickly sound in his voice. But Tarnhorst interrupted him.

"We don't want it, commodore. Forget it."

"Forget it?" Morgan's voice was as cutting as the filament he had been discussing. "Forget that Jack Latrobe was murdered?"

"We will pay indemnities, of course," Tarnhorst said, feeling that it was futile.

"*Fergus* will pay indemnities," Morgan said. "In money, the indemnities will come to the precise amount he was willing to pay for the cable secret. I suggest that your Government confiscate that amount from him and send it to us. That may be necessary in view of the second indemnity."

"Second indemnity?"

"Mr. Fergus' life."

Tarnhorst shook his head briskly. "No. We can't execute Fergus. Impossible."

"Of course not," Morgan said soothingly. "I don't suggest that you should. But I do suggest that Mr. Fergus be very careful about going through doorways—or any other kind of opening—from now on. I suggest that he refrain from passing between any pair of reasonably solid, well-anchored objects. I suggest that he stay away from bathtubs. I suggest that he be very careful about putting his legs under a table or desk. I suggest that he not look out of windows. I could make several suggestions. And he shouldn't go around feeling in front of him, either. He might lose something."

"I understand," said Edway Tarnhorst.

So did Sam Fergus. Morgan could tell by his face.

When the indemnity check arrived on Ceres some time later, a short, terse note came with it.

"I regret to inform you that Mr. Samuel Fergus, evidently in a state of extreme nervous and psychic tension, took his own life by means of a gunshot wound in the head on the 21st of this month. The enclosed check will pay your indemnity in full. Tarnhorst."

Morgan smiled grimly. It was as he had expected. He had certainly never had any intention of going to all the trouble of killing Sam Fergus.

Damned If You Don't

We've all heard of the wonderful invention that the Big Corporation or the Utilities suppressed...? Usually, that Wonderful Invention won't work, actually. But there's another possibility, too....

The workshop-laboratory was a mess. Sam Bending looked it over silently; his jaw muscles were hard and tense, and his eyes were the same.

To repeat what Sam Bending thought when he saw the junk that had been made of thousands of dollars worth of equipment would not be inadmissible in a family magazine, because Bending was not particularly addicted to four-letter vulgarities. But he *was* a religious man—in a lax sort of way—so repeating what ran through his mind that gray Monday in February of 1981 would be unfair to the memory of Samson Francis Bending.

Sam Bending folded his hands over his chest. It was not an attitude of prayer; it was an attempt to keep those big, gorillalike hands from smashing something. The fingers intertwined, and the hands tried to crush each other, which was a good way to keep them from actually crushing anything else.

He stood there at the door for a full minute—just looking.

The lab—as has been said—was a mess. It would have looked better if someone had simply tossed a grenade in it and had done with it. At least the results would have been random and more evenly dispersed.

But whoever had gone about the wrecking of the lab had gone about it in a workmanlike way. Whoever had done the job was no amateur. The vandal had known his way about in a laboratory, that was obvious. Leads had been cut carefully; equipment had been shoved aside without care as to what happened to it, but with great care that the shover should not be damaged by the shoving; the invader had known exactly what he was after, and exactly how to get to it.

And he—whoever he was—had gotten his hands on what he wanted.

The Converter was gone.

Sam Bending took his time in regaining his temper. He had to. A man who stands six feet three, weighs three hundred pounds, and wears a forty-eight size jacket can't afford to lose his temper very often or he'll end up on the wrong end of a homicide charge. That three hundred pounds was composed of too much muscle and too little fat for Sam Bending to allow it to run amok.

At last, he took a deep breath, closed his eyes, and let his tense nerves, muscles, and tendons sag—he pretended someone had struck him with a dose of curare. He let his breath out slowly and opened his eyes again.

The lab still looked the same, but it no longer irritated him. It was something to be accepted as done. It was something to investigate, and—if possible—avenge. But it was no longer something to worry about or lose his temper over.

I should have expected it, he thought wryly. *They'd have to do something about it, wouldn't they?*

But the funny thing was that he *hadn't* expected it—not in modern, law-abiding America.

He reached over to the wall switch to turn on the lights, but before his hand touched it, he stopped the motion and grinned to himself. No point in turning on the switch when he knew perfectly well that there was no power behind it. Still—

His fingers touched the switch anyway. And nothing happened.

He shrugged and went over to the phone.

He let his eyes wander over the wreckage as his right index finger spun the dial. Actually, the room wasn't as much of a shambles as it had looked on first sight. The—burglar?—hadn't tried to get at anything but the Converter. He hadn't known exactly where it was, but he'd been able to follow the leads to its hiding place. That meant that he knew his beans about power lines, anyway.

It also meant that he hadn't been an ordinary burglar. There were plenty of other things around for a burglar to make money out of. Unless he knew what it was, he wouldn't have gone to the trouble of stealing the Converter.

On the other hand, if he had—

"Police Department," said a laconic voice from the speaker. At the same time, the blue-clad image of a police officer appeared on the screen. He looked polite, but he also looked as though he expected nothing more than a routine call.

Bending gave the cop's sleeve a quick glance and said: "Sergeant, my name is Samson Bending. Bending Consultants, 3991 Marden—you'll find it in the phone book. Someone broke into my place over the weekend, and I'd appreciate it if you'd send someone around."

The sergeant's face showed that he still thought it was routine. "Anything missing, sir?"

"I'm not sure," said Bending carefully. "I'll have to make a check. I haven't touched anything. I thought I'd leave that for the detectives. But you can see for yourself what's happened."

He stepped back from the screen and the Leinster cameras automatically adjusted for the greater distance to the background.

"Looks like you had a visitor, all right," said the police officer. "What is that? A lab of some kind you've got there?"

"That's right," Bending said. "You can check it with the Register."

"Will do, Mr. Bending," agreed the sergeant. "We'll send the Technical Squad around in any case." He paused, and Sam could see that he'd pressed an alarm button. There was more interest in his manner, too. "Any signs that it might be kids?" he asked.

Sam shrugged. "Hard to tell. Might be. Might not." He knew good and well that it wasn't a JD gang that had invaded his lab. He grinned ingratiatingly. "I figure you guys can tell me more about that than I could tell you."

The sergeant nodded. "Sure. O.K., Mr. Bending; you just hold on. Don't touch anything; we'll have a copter out there as soon as we can. O.K.?"

"O.K.," Sam agreed. He cut off as the cop's image began to collapse.

Sam Bending didn't obey the cop's order to touch nothing. He couldn't afford to—not at this stage of the game. He looked over everything—the smashed oscilloscopes, the overturned computer, the ripped-out meters—everything. He lifted a couple of instruments that had been toppled to the floor, raising them carefully with a big screwdriver, used as a lever. When he was through, he was convinced that he knew exactly who the culprit was.

Oh, he didn't know the name of the man, or men, who had actually committed the crime. Those things were, for the moment, relatively unimportant. The police might find them, but that could wait. The thing that *was* important was that Bending was certain within his own mind who had paid to have the lab robbed.

Not that he could make any accusations to the police, of course. That wouldn't do at all. But *he* knew. He was quite certain.

He left the lab itself and went into the outer rooms, the three rooms that constituted the clients' waiting room, his own office, and the smaller office of Nita Walder, the girl who took care of his files and correspondence.

A quick look told him that nothing in the offices had been disturbed. He shrugged his huge shoulders and sat down on the long couch in the waiting room.

Much good it may do them, he thought pleasantly. *The Converter won't be worth the stuff it's made of if they try to open it.*

He looked at the clock on the wall and frowned. It was off by five hours. Then he grinned and looked at his wrist watch. Of course the wall clock was Off. It had stopped when the power had been cut off. When the burglars had cut the leads to the Converter, everything in the lab had stopped.

It was eight seventeen. Sam Bending lit a cigarette and leaned back to wait for the cops. United States Power Utilities, Monopolated, had overstepped themselves this time.

Bending Consultants, as a title for a business, was a little misleading because of the plural ending of the last word. There was only one consultant, and that was Samson Francis Bending. His speciality was the engineering design of atomic power plants—both the old fashioned heavy-metal kind and the newer, more elegant, stellarators, which produced power by hydrogen-to-helium conversion.

Bending made good money at it. He wasn't a millionaire by any means, but he had enough money to live comfortably on and enough extra to experiment around on his own. And, primarily, it had always been the experimentation that had been the purpose of Bending Consultants; the consulting end of the business had always been a monetary prop for the lab itself. His employees—mostly junior engineers and engineering draftsmen—worked in the two-story building next door to the lab. Their job was to make money for the company under Bending's direction while Bending himself spent as much time as he could fussing around with things that interested him.

The word "genius" has several connotations, depending on how one defines a genius. Leaving aside the Greek, Roman and Arabic definitions, a careful observer will find that there are two general classes of genius: the "partial" genius, and the "general" genius. Actually, such a narrow definition doesn't do either kind justice, but defining a human being is an almost impossible job, anyway, so we'll have to do the best we can with the tools we have to work with.

The "partial" genius follows the classic definition. "A genius is a man with a one-track mind; an idiot has one track less." He's a real wowser at one class of knowledge, and doesn't know spit about the others.

The "general" genius doesn't specialize. He's capable of original thought in any field he works in.

The trouble is that, because of the greater concentration involved, the partial genius usually gets more recognition than the general—that is, if he gets any recognition at all. Thus, the mathematical and optical work of Sir Isaac Newton show true genius; his theological and political ideas weren't worth the paper he wrote them on. Similar accusations might be leveled against Albert Einstein—and many others.

The general genius isn't so well known because he spreads his abilities over a broad area. Some—like Leonardo da Vinci—have made a name for themselves, but, in general, they have remained in the background.

Someone once defined a specialist as "a man who learns more and more about less and less until he finally knows everything about nothing." And there is the converse, the general practitioner, who knows "less and less about more and more until he finally knows nothing about everything."

Both types can produce geniuses, and there is, of course, a broad spectrum in between. Da Vinci, for instance, became famous for his paintings; he concentrated on that field because he knew perfectly well that his designs for such things as airplanes were impracticable at the time, whereas the Church would pay for art.

Samson Bending was a genius, granted; but he was more toward the "special" than the "general" side of the spectrum. His grasp of nuclear physics was far and away beyond that of any other scientist of his day; his ability to handle political and economic relationships was rather feeble.

As he sat in his waiting room on that chill day of February, 1981, his mind was centered on nuclear physics, not general economics. Not that Bending was oblivious to the power of the Great God Ammon; Bending was very fond of money and appreciated the things it could achieve. He simply didn't appreciate the over-all power of Ammon. At the moment, he was brooding darkly over the very fact of existence of Power Utilities, and trying to figure out a suitable rejoinder to their *coup de démon*.

And then he heard the whir of helicopter blades over the building. The police had come.

He opened the door of the lab building as they came up the steps. There were two plainclothes men—the Technical Squad, Bending knew—and four uniformed officers.

The plainclothesman in the lead, a tall, rather thin man, with dark straight hair and a small mustache, said: "Mr. Bending? I'm Sergeant Ketzel. Mind if the boys take a look at the scene? And I'd like to ask a few questions?"

"Fine," said Sam Bending. "Come on in."

He showed the officers to the lab, and telling them nothing, left them to their work. Then he went into his office, followed by Sergeant Ketzel. The detective took down all the pertinent data that Bending chose to give him, and then asked Bending to go with him to the lab.

The other plainclothesman came up to Sergeant Ketzel and Bending as they entered. "Pretty easy to see what happened," he said. "Come on over and take a look." He led them over to the wall where the Converter had been hidden.

"See," he said, "here's your main power line coming in here. It's been burned off. They shut off the power to cut off the burglar alarm to that safe over there."

Ketzel shook his head slowly, but said nothing for the moment. He looked at Bending. "Has the safe been robbed?"

"I don't know," Bending admitted. "I didn't touch it after I saw all this wreckage."

Ketzel told a couple of the uniformed men to go over the safe for evidence. While they waited, Bending looked again at the hole in the wall where the Converter had been. And it suddenly struck him that, even if he had reported the loss of the Converter to the police, it would be hard to prove. The thief had taken care to burn off the ends of the old leads that had originally come into the building. Bending himself had cut them a week before to install the Converter. Had they been left as they were, Bending could have proved by the oxidation of the surface that they had been cut a long time before the leads on this side of the Converter. But both had been carefully fused by a torch.

"Nothing on the safe," said one of the officers. "No prints, at any rate. Micros might show glove or cloth traces, but—" He shrugged.

"Would you mind opening the safe, Mr. Bending?" Sergeant Ketzel asked.

"Certainly," Bending said. He wondered if the safe *had* been robbed. In the certainty that it was only the Converter that the burglars had been after, he hadn't even thought about the safe.

Bending touched the handle, turned it a trifle, and the door swung open easily in his hand. "It wasn't even locked," Bending said, almost to himself.

He looked inside. The safe had been thoroughly gone through, but as far as Bending could see, there were no papers missing.

"Don't touch anything in there, Mr. Bending," said Ketzel, "Just tell us as much as you can by looking at it."

"The papers have been disturbed," Bending said carefully, "but I don't think anything is missing, except the petty cash box."

"Uh-huh," Ketzel grunted significantly. "Petty cash box. About how much was in it, Mr. Bending?"

"Three or four thousand, I imagine: you'll have to ask Jim Luckman, my business manager. He keeps track of things like that."

"Three or four *thousand* in petty cash?" Ketzel asked, as though he'd prefer Bending to correct the figure to "two or three hundred."

"About that. Sometimes we have to order equipment of one kind or another in a hurry, and we can usually expedite matters if we can promise cash. You know how it is."

Sergeant Ketzel nodded sourly. He evidently knew only too well how it was. Even the most respectable businessmen were doing occasional business with the black market in technological devices. But he didn't say anything to Bending.

"What did the cash box look like?" he asked.

Bending held out his hands to measure off a distance. "About so long—ten inches, I guess; maybe six inches wide and four deep. Thin sheet steel, with a gray crackle finish. There was a lock on it, but it wasn't much of one; since it was kept in the safe, there was no need for a strong lock."

Sergeant Ketzel nodded. "In other words, an ordinary office cash box. No distinguishing marks at all?"

"It had 'Bending Consultants' on the top. And underneath that, the word 'Lab'. In black paint. That 'Lab' was to distinguish it from the petty cash box in the main office."

"I see. Do you know anything about the denominations of the bills? Were they marked in any way?"

Bending frowned. "I don't know. You'd have to ask Luckman about that, too."

"Where is he now?"

"Home, I imagine. He isn't due to report for work until ten."

"O.K. Will you leave word that we want to talk to him when he comes in? It'll take us a while to get all the information we can from the lab, here." He looked back at the hole in the wall. "It still doesn't make sense. Why should they go to all that trouble just to shut off a burglar alarm?" He shook his head and went over to where the others were working.

It was hours before the police left, and long before they were gone Sam Bending had begun to wish fervently that he had never called them. He felt that he should have kept his mouth shut and fought Power Utilities on the ground they had chosen. They had known about the Converter only two weeks, and they had already struck. He tried to remember exactly how the Utilities representative had worded what he'd said, and couldn't.

Well, there was an easy way to find out. He went over to his files and took out the recording for Friday, 30 January 1981. He threaded it through the sound player—he had no particular desire to look at the man's face again—and turned on the machine. The first sentence brought the whole scene back to mind.

"Thank you for your time, Mr. Bending," the man whose card had announced him as Richard Olcott. He was a rather average-sized man, with a fiftyish face, graying hair that was beginning to thin, and an expression like that of a friendly poker player—pleasant, but inscrutable.

"I always have time to see a representative of Power Utilities, Mr. Olcott," Bending said. "Though I must admit that I'm more used to dealing with various engineers who work for your subsidiaries."

"Not subsidiaries, please," Olcott admonished in a friendly tone. "Like the Bell Telephone Company, Power Utilities is actually a group of independent but mutually co-operative companies organized under a parent company."

Bending grinned. "I stand corrected. What did you have on your mind, Mr. Olcott?"

Olcott's hesitation was of half-second duration, but it was perceptible.

"Mr. Bending," he began, "I understand that you have been ... ah ... working on a new and ... ah ... radically different method of power generation. Er ... is that substantially correct?"

Bending looked at the man, his blocky, big-jawed face expressionless. "I've been doing experimenting with power generators, yes," he said after a moment. "That's my business."

"Oh, quite, quite. I understand that," Olcott said hurriedly. "I ... ah ... took the trouble to look up your record before I came. I'm well aware of the invaluable work you've done in the power field."

"Thank you," Bending said agreeably. He waited to see what the other would say next. It was his move.

"However," Olcott said, "that's not the sort of thing I was referring to." He leaned forward in his chair, and his bright gray eyes seemed to take on a new life; his manner seemed to alter subtly.

"Let me put my ... *our* cards on the table, Mr. Bending. We understand that you have designed, and are experimenting with, an amazingly compact power source. We understand that little remains but to get the bugs out of your pilot model.

"Naturally, we are interested. Our business is supplying the nation with power. Anything from a new type solar battery on up is of interest to us." He stopped, waiting for Bending to speak.

Bending obliged. "I see Petternek let the cat out of the bag prematurely," he said with a smile. "I hadn't intended to spring it until it was a polished work of engineering art. It's been more of a hobby than anything else, you see."

Olcott smiled disarmingly. "I'm not acquainted with Mr. Petternek; to be quite honest, I have no idea where our engineers picked up the information."

"He's an engineer," Bending said. "Friends of mine. He probably got a little enthusiastic in a conversation with one of your boys. He seemed quite impressed by my Converter."

"Possibly that is the explanation." Olcott paused. "Converter, you say? That's what you call it?"

"That's right. I couldn't think up any fancier name for it. Oh, I suppose I could have, but I didn't want anything too descriptive."

"And the word 'converter' isn't descriptive?"

"Hardly," said Bending with a short laugh. "Every power supply is a converter of some kind. A nickel-cadmium battery converts chemical energy into electrical energy. A solar battery converts radiation into electrical current. The old-fashioned, oil- or coal-burning power plants converted chemical energy into heat energy, converted that into kinetic energy, and that, in turn was converted into electrical energy. The heavy-metal atomic plant does almost the same thing, except that it uses nuclear reactions instead of chemical reactions to produce the heat. The stellarator is a converter, too.

"About the only exception I can think of is the electrostatic condenser, and you could say that it converts static electricity into a current flow if you wanted to stretch a point. On the other hand, a condenser isn't usually considered as a power supply."

Olcott chuckled. "I see your point. Could you give me a rough idea of the principle on which your Converter operates?"

Bending allowed himself a thoughtful frown. "I'd rather not, just now, Mr. Olcott. As I said, I want to sort of spring this full-blown on the world." He grinned. He looked like a small boy who had just discovered that people liked him; but it was a calculated expression, not an automatic one.

Olcott looked into Bending's eyes without seeing them. He ran his tongue carefully over the inside of his teeth before he spoke. "Mr. Bending." Pause. "Mr. Bending, we—and by 'we', I mean, of course, Power Utilities,—have heard a great deal about this ... this Converter." His chocolate-brown eyes bored deep into the gray eyes of Samson Bending. "Frankly," he continued, "we are inclined to discount ninety per cent of the rumors that come to us. Most of them are based on purely crackpot ideas. None the less, we investigate them. If someone *does* discover a new process of producing power, we can't afford to be blind to new ideas just because they happen to come from ... ah ... unorthodox sources.

"You, Mr. Bending, are an unusual case. Any rumor concerning your work, no matter how fantastic, is worth looking into on your reputation alone, even though the claims may be utterly absurd."

"I have made no claims," Bending interposed.

Olcott raised a lean hand. "I understand that, Mr. Bending. None the less, others—who may or may not know what they are talking about—have made this claim *for* you." Olcott settled back in his chair and folded his hands across his slight paunch. "You've worked with us before, Mr. Bending; you know that we can—and *do*—pay well for advances in the power field which are contributed by our engineers. As you know, our contract is the standard one—any discovery made by an engineer while in our employ is automatically ours. None the less, we give such men a handsome royalty." He paused, opened his brief case, and pulled out a notebook. After referring to it, he looked up at Bending and said:

"You, yourself have benefitted by this policy. According to our records, you are drawing royalties from three patented improvements in the stellarator which were discovered at times when you were employed by us—or, rather, by one of our associative corporations—in an advisory capacity. Those discoveries were, by contract, ours. By law, we could use them as we saw fit without recompense to you, other than our regular fee. None the less, we chose to pay you a royalty because that is our normal policy with all our engineers and scientific research men. We find it more expedient to operate thus."

Bending was getting a little tired of Olcott's "none the less," but he didn't show it. "Are you trying to say that my Converter was invented during my employ with your company, Mr. Olcott?"

Olcott cleared his throat and shook his head. "No. Not necessarily. It is true that we might have a case on those grounds, but, under the circumstances, we feel it inexpedient to pursue such a course."

Which means, Bending thought, *that you don't have a case at all.* "Then just what are you driving at, Mr. Olcott?" he asked aloud.

"I'll put my cards on the table, Mr. Bending," Olcott said.

You've already said that, Bending thought, *and I've seen no evidence of it.* "Go ahead," he said.

"Thank you." He cleared his throat again. "If your invention is ... ah ... worth while, we are prepared to negotiate with you for use and/or purchase of it."

Bending had always disliked people who said or wrote "and/or," but he had no desire to antagonize the Power Utilities representative by showing personal pique. "Let me understand you clearly," he said. "Power Utilities wants to buy my rights to the Converter. Right?"

Olcott cleared his throat a third time. "In a word, yes. Provided, of course, that it is actually worth our while. Remember, we know almost nothing about it; the claims made for it by our ... ah ... anonymous informer are ... well, ah ... rather fantastic. But your reputation—" He let the sentence hang.

Bending was not at all immune to flattery. He grinned. "Do you mean that you came to me to talk about buying an invention you weren't even sure existed—just because of my reputation?"

"Frankly, yes," said Olcott. "Your reputation is ... ah ... shall we say, a good one in power engineering circles."

"Are you an engineer?" Bending asked suddenly.

Olcott blinked. "Why, no. No, I am not. I'm a lawyer. I thought you understood that."

"Sorry," Bending said. "I didn't. Most of the financial work around here is done through my Mr. Luckman. I'm not acquainted with the monetary end of the business."

Olcott smiled. "Quite all right. Evidently I am not as well known to you as you are to me. Not that it matters. Why did you ask?"

Bending stood up. "I'm going to show you something, Mr. Olcott," he said. "Would you care to come with me to the lab?"

Olcott was on his feet in a second. "I'd be glad to, Mr. Bending."

Bending led the man into the lab. "Over here," he said. At the far end of the laboratory was a thick-legged table cluttered with lengths of wire, vacuum tubes, transistors, a soldering gun, a couple of meters, and the other various paraphernalia of an electronics workshop. In the center of the table, surrounded by the clutter, sat an oblong box. It didn't look like much; it was just an eighteen by twelve by ten box, made of black plastic, featureless, except for a couple of dials and knobs on the top of it, and a pair of copper studs sticking out of the end.

Still, Olcott didn't look skeptical. Nor surprised. Evidently, his informant had had plenty of information. Or else his poker face was better than Bending had thought.

"This is your pilot model?" Olcott asked.

"One of them, yes. Want to watch it go through its paces?"

"Very much."

"O.K. First, though, just how good is your technical education? I mean, how basic do I have to get?" Sam Bending was not exactly a diplomat.

Olcott, however, didn't look offended. "Let's say that if you keep it on the level of college freshman physics I'll get the general drift. All right?"

"Sure. I don't intend to get any more technical than that, anyway. I'm going to tell you *what* the Converter does—not *how*."

"Fair enough—for the moment. Go ahead."

"Right." Sam flipped a switch on the top of the box. "Takes a minute or so to warm up," he said.

When the "minute or so" had passed, Bending, who had been watching the meters on the top of the machine, said: "See this?" He pointed at a dial face. "That's the voltage. It's controlled by this vernier knob here." He turned the knob, and the needle on the voltmeter moved obligingly upwards. "Anything from ten to a thousand volts," he said. "Easily adjusted to suit your taste."

"I don't think I'd like the taste of a thousand volts," Olcott said solemnly. "Might affect the tongue adversely." Olcott didn't look particularly impressed. Why should he? Anyone can build a machine that can generate high voltage.

"Is that AC or DC?" he asked.

"DC," said Bending. "But it can easily be converted to AC. Depends on what you want to use it for."

Olcott nodded. "How much power does that thing deliver?"

Sam Bending had been waiting for that question. He delivered his answer with all the nonchalance of a man dropping a burnt match in an ash tray.

"Five hundred horsepower."

Olcott's face simply couldn't hold its expressionless expression against something like that. His lips twitched, and his eyes blinked. "Five hundred *what*?"

"I will not make the obvious pun," said Bending. "I said 'five hundred horsepower'—unquote. About three hundred and seventy-five kilowatts, maximum."

Olcott appeared to be unable to say anything. He simply stared at the small, innocuous-looking Converter. Bending was unable to decide whether Olcott was overawed by the truth or simply stricken dumb by what must sound like a monstrous lie.

Olcott licked his lips with the tip of his small, pink tongue. "Five hundred horsepower. Hm-m-m." He took a deep breath. "No wonder those copper studs are so thick."

"Yeah," said Bending. "If I short 'em across at low voltage, they get hot."

"*Short them across?*" Olcott's voice sounded harsh.

Bending was in his seventh heaven, and he showed it. His grin was running as high an energy output as that he claimed for the Converter. "Sure. The amperage is self-limiting. You can only draw about four hundred amps off the thing, no matter how low you put the voltage. When I said five hundred HP, I meant at a thousand volts. As a matter of fact, the available power in horsepower is roughly half the voltage. But that only applies to this small model. A bigger one could supply more, of course."

"What does it weigh?" asked Olcott, in a hushed voice.

"Little over a hundred pounds," Bending said.

Olcott tore his eyes away from the fantastic little box and looked into Sam Bending's eyes. "May I ask where you're getting power like that?"

"Sure. Hydrogen fusion, same as the stellarator."

"It's powered by deuterium?"

Bending delivered his bombshell. "Nope. Water. Plain, ordinary aitch-two-oh. See those little vents at the side? They exhaust oxygen and helium. It burns about four hundred milligrams of water per hour at maximum capacity."

Olcott had either regained control of himself or had passed the saturation point; Sam couldn't tell which. Olcott said: "Where do you put the water?"

"Why put water in it?" Sam asked coolly. "That small whirring sound you hear isn't the hydrogen-helium conversion; it's a fan blowing air through a cooling coil. Even in the Sahara Desert there's enough moisture in the air to run this baby."

"And the fan is powered—"

"... By the machine itself, naturally," said Bending. "It's a self-contained unit. Of course, with a really big unit, you might have to hire someone to hang out their laundry somewhere in the neighborhood, but only in case of emergencies."

"May I sit down?" asked Olcott. And, without waiting for Sam Bending's permission, he grabbed a nearby chair and sat. "Mr. Bending," he said, "what is the cost of one of those units?"

"Well, that one cost several hundred thousand dollars. But the thing could be mass produced for ... oh, around fifteen hundred dollars. Maybe less."

Olcott absorbed that, blinked, and said: "Is it dangerous? I mean, could it explode, or does it give out radiation?"

"Well, you have to treat it with respect, of course," Bending said. He rubbed his big hands together in an unconscious gesture of triumph. "Just like any power source. But it won't explode; that I can guarantee. And there's no danger from radiation. All the power comes out as electric current."

Sam Bending remained silent while Olcott stared at the little black box. Finally, Olcott put his hands to his face and rubbed his eyes, as though he'd been too long without sleep. When he removed his hands, his eyes were focused on Bending.

"You realize," he said, "that we can't give you any sort of contract until this has been thoroughly checked by our own engineers and research men?"

"Obviously," said Sam Bending. "But—"

"Do you have a patent?" Olcott interrupted.

"It's pending," said Bending. "My lawyer thinks it will go through pretty quickly."

Olcott stood up abruptly. "Mr. Bending, if this machine is actually what you claim it to be—which, of course, we will have to determine for ourselves—I think that we can make you a handsome—a *very* handsome settlement."

"How much?" Bending asked flatly.

"For full rights—millions," said Olcott without hesitation. "That would be a ... shall we say, an advance ... an advance on the royalties."

"What, no bargaining?" Bending said, in a rather startled tone.

Olcott shook his head. "Mr. Bending, you know the value of such a device as well as I do. You're an intelligent man, and so am I. Haggling will get us nothing but wasted time. We want that machine—we *must* have that machine. And you know it. And I know you know it. Why should we quibble?

"I can't say: 'Name your price'; this thing is obviously worth a great deal more than even Power Utilities would be able to pay. Not even a corporation like ours can whip up a billion dollars without going bankrupt. What we pay you will have to be amortized over a period of years. But we—"

"Just a minute, Mr. Olcott," Bending interrupted. "Exactly what do you intend to do with the Converter if I sell it to you?"

Olcott hesitated. "Why ... ah—" He paused. "Actually, I couldn't say," he said at last. "A decision like that would have to be made by the Board. Why?"

"How long do you think it would take you to get into production?"

"I ... ah ... frankly couldn't say," Olcott said cautiously. "Several years, I imagine..."

"Longer than that, I dare say," Bending said, with more than a touch of sarcasm. "As a matter of fact, you'd pretty much have to suppress the Converter, wouldn't you?"

Olcott looked at Bending, his face expressionless. "Of course. For a while. You know very well that this could ruin us."

"The automobile ruined the buggy-whip makers and threw thousands of blacksmiths out of work," Bending pointed out. "Such things are inevitable. Every new invention is likely to have an effect like that if it replaces something older. What do you think atomic energy would have done to coal mining if it weren't for the fact that coal is needed in the manufacture of steel? You can't let considerations like that stand in the way of technological progress, Mr. Olcott."

"Is it a question of money?" Olcott asked quietly.

Bending shook his head. "Not at all. We've already agreed that I could make as much as I want by selling it to you. No; it's just that I'm an idealist of sorts. I intend to manufacture the Converter myself, in order to make sure it gets into the hands of the people."

"I assure you, Mr. Bending, that Power Utilities would do just that—as soon as it became economically feasible for us to do so."

"I doubt it," Sam Bending said flatly. "If any group has control over the very thing that's going to put them out of business, they don't release it; they sit on it. Dictators, for instance, have throughout history, promised freedom to their people 'as soon as it was feasible'. Cincinnatus may have done it, but no one else has in the last twenty-five centuries.

"What do you suppose would have happened in the 1940s if the movie moguls of Hollywood had had the patent rights for television? How many other inventions actually have been held down simply because the interested parties *did* happen to get their hands on them first?

"No, Mr. Olcott; I don't think I can allow Power Utilities to have a finger in this pie or the public would never get a slice of it."

Olcott stood up slowly from the chair. "I see, Mr. Bending; you're quite frank about your views, anyway." He paused. "I shall have to talk this over with the Board. There must be some way of averting total disaster. If we find one, we'll let you know, Mr. Bending."

And that was it. That was the line that had stuck in the back of Bending's mind for two weeks. *If we find a way of averting total disaster, we'll let you know, Mr. Bending.*

And they evidently thought they'd found a way. For two weeks, there had been phone calls from officers of greater or lesser importance in Power Utilities, but they all seemed to think that if they could offer enough money, Sam Bending would capitulate. Finally, they had taken the decisive step of stealing the Converter. Bending wondered how they had known where it was; he had taken the precaution of concealing it, just in case there might be an attempt at robbery, and using it as power supply for the lab had seemed the best hiding place. But evidently someone at Power Utilities had read Poe's "Purloined Letter," too.

He smiled grimly. Even if the police didn't find any clues leading them to the thieves who'd broken into his lab, the boys at Power Utilities would find themselves in trouble. The second they started to open the Converter, it would begin to fuse. If they were quick, whoever opened it should be able to get away from it before it melted down into an unrecognizable mass.

Sam Bending took the tape from the playback and returned it to his files.

He wondered how the Power Utilities boys had managed to find where the Converter was. Checking the power that had been used by Bending Consultants? Possibly. It would show that less had been used in the past two weeks than was normally the case. Only the big building next door was still using current from the power lines. Still, that would have meant that they had read the meter in the last two weeks, which, in turn, meant that they had been suspicious in the first place or they wouldn't have ordered an extra reading.

On the other hand, if—

The visiphone rang.

It was the phone with the unregistered number, a direct line that didn't go through his secretary's switchboard.

He flipped it on. "Yes?" He never bothered to identify himself on that phone; anyone who had the number knew who they were calling. The mild-looking, plumpish, blond-haired man whose face came onto the screen was immediately recognizable.

"How's everything, Mr. Bending?" he asked with cordial geniality.

"Fine, Mr. Trask," Bending answered automatically. "And you?"

"Reasonable, reasonable. I hear you had the police out your way this morning." There was a questioning look in his round blue eyes. "No trouble, I hope."

Sam understood the question behind the statement. Vernon Trask was the go-between for some of the biggest black market operators in the country. Bending didn't like to have to deal with him, but one had very little choice these days.

"No. No trouble. Burglary in the night. Someone opened my safe and picked up a few thousand dollars, is all."

"I see." Trask was obviously wondering whether some black market operator would be approached by a couple of burglars in the next few days—a couple of burglars trying to peddle apparatus and equipment that had been stolen from Bending. There still were crooks who thought that the black market dealt in stolen goods of that sort.

"Some of my instruments were smashed," Bending said, "but none of them are missing."

"I'm glad to hear that," Trask said. And Bending knew he meant it. The black market boys didn't like to have their customers robbed of scientific equipment; it might reflect back on them. "I just thought I'd explain about missing our appointment this morning," Trask went on. "It was unavoidable; something unexpected came up."

Trask was being cagey, as always. He didn't talk directly, even over a phone that wasn't supposed to be tapped. Bending understood, though. Some of the robotics equipment he'd contracted to get from Trask was supposed to have been delivered that morning, but when the delivery agent had seen the police car out front, he'd kept right on going naturally enough.

"That's all right, Mr. Trask," Bending said. "What with all this trouble this morning, it actually slipped my mind. Another time, perhaps."

Trask nodded. "I'll try to make arrangements for a later date. Thanks a lot, Mr. Bending. Good-by."

Bending said good-by and cut the connection.

Samson Bending didn't like being forced to buy from the black market operators, but there was nothing else to do if one wanted certain pieces of equipment. During the "Tense War" of the late Sixties, the Federal and State governments had gone into a state of near-panic. The war that had begun in the Near East had flashed northwards to ignite the eternal Powder Keg of Europe. But there were no alliances, no general war; there were only periodic armed outbreaks, each one in turn threatening to turn into World War III. Each country found itself agreeing to an armistice with one country while trying to form an alliance with a second and defending itself from or attacking a third.

And yet, during it all, no one quite dared to use the Ultimate Weapons. There was plenty of strafing by fighter planes and sorties by small bomber squadrons, but there was none of the "massive retaliation" of World War II. There could be heard the rattle of small-arms fire and the rumble of tanks and the roar of field cannon, but not once was there the terrifying, all-enveloping blast of nuclear bombs.

But, at the time, no one knew that it wouldn't happen. The United States and the Soviet Union hovered on the edges of the war, two colossi who hesitated to interfere directly for fear they would have to come to grips with each other.

The situation made the "Brinksmanship" of former Secretary Dulles look as safe as loafing in an easy-chair.

And the bureaucratic and legislative forces of the United States Government had reacted in a fairly predictable manner. The "security" guards around scientific research, which had been gradually diminishing towards the vanishing point, had suddenly been re-imposed—this time, even more stringently and rigidly than ever before.

Coupled with this was another force—apparently unrelated—which acted to tie in with the Federal security regulations. The juvenile delinquent gangs had begun to realize the value of science. Teen-age hoodlums armed with homemade pistols were dangerous enough in the Fifties; add aimed rockets and remote-control bombs to their armories, and you have an almost uncontrollable situation. Something had to be done, and various laws controlling the sale of scientific apparatus had been passed by the fifty states. And—as with their liquor and divorce laws—no two of the states had the same set of laws, and no one of them was without gaping flaws.

By the time the off-again-on-again wars in Europe had been stilled by the combined pressure of the United Nations—in which the United States and the Soviet Union co-operated wholeheartedly, working together in a way they had not done for over twenty years—the "scientific control laws" in the United States had combined to make scientific research almost impossible for the layman, and a matter of endless red tape, forms-in-octuplicate, licenses, permits, investigations, delays, and confusion for the professional.

The answer, of course, was the black market. What bootlegging had done for the average citizen in the Twenties, the black market was doing for scientists fifty years later.

The trouble was that, unlike the Volstead Act, the scientific prohibitions aroused no opposition from the man in the street. Indeed, he rather approved of them. He needed and wanted the products of scientific research, but he had a vague fear of the scientist—the "egghead." To his way of thinking, the laws were cleverly-designed restrictions promulgated by that marvelous epitome of humanity, the common man, to keep the mysterious scientists from meddling with things they oughtn't to.

The result was that the Latin American countries went into full swing, producing just those items which North American scientists couldn't get their hands on, because the laws stayed on the books. During the next ten years, they were modified slightly, but only very slightly; but the efforts to enforce them became more and more lax. By the time the late Seventies and early Eighties rolled around, the black marketeers were doing very nicely, thank you, and any suggestion from scientists that the laws should be modified was met with an intensive counterpropaganda effort by the operators of the black market.

Actually, the word "operators" is a misnomer. It was known by the authorities at the time that there was only one ring operating; the market was too limited to allow for the big-time operations carried on by the liquor smugglers and distillers of half a century before.

Sam Bending naturally was forced to deal with the black market, just as everyone else engaged in research was; it was, for instance, the only source for a good many technical publications which had been put on the Restricted List. Sam wasn't as dependent on them as college and university research men were, simply because he was engaged in industrial work, which carried much higher priorities than educational work did.

Sam, however, was fed up with the whole mess, and would have given his eyeteeth to clear up the whole stupid farce.

Irritated by every petty distraction at his office, Sam Bending finally gave up trying to cope with anything for the rest of the day. At three in the afternoon, he told his secretary that he was going home, jammed his hat on his head, and went out to his car.

He got in, turned the switch, and listened to the deep hum of the electric motors inside. Somehow, it made him feel so good that the irritations of the day lessened a great deal. He grinned.

Power Utilities hadn't even thought of this hiding place. The Converter in the rear of the car gave the vehicle far more power than it needed, but the extra juice came in handy sometimes. The driving motors wouldn't take the full output of the generators, of course; the Converter hardly had to strain itself to drive the automobile at top speed, and, as long as there was traction, no grade could stall the car. Theoretically, it could climb straight up a wall.

Not that Sam Bending had any intention of climbing a wall with it.

He even had power left over for the sound-effects gadget and the air-heater that made the thing appear to be powered by an ordinary turbo-electric engine. He listened and smiled as the motors made satisfying sounds while he pulled out of the parking lot and into the street. He kept that pleased, self-satisfied grin on his face for six blocks.

And then he began to notice that someone was following him.

At first, he hadn't paid much attention to it. The car was just a common Ford Cruiser of the nondescript steel blue color that was so popular. But Bending had been conscious of its presence for several blocks. He looked carefully in the mirror.

Maybe he was wrong. Maybe it had been several cars of that same color that had moved in and out of the traffic behind him. Well, he'd soon see.

He kept on going toward the North-South Expressway, and kept watching the steel-blue Ford, glancing at his rear view mirror every time he could afford to take his eyes off the traffic.

It moved back and forth, but it was never more than three cars behind him, and usually only one. Coincidence? Possibly.

At Humber Avenue, he turned left and drove southwards. The steel-blue Ford turned, too. Coincidence? Still possible.

He kept on going down Humber Avenue for ten blocks, until he came to the next cross street that would take him to a lower entrance to the North-South Expressway. He turned right, and the Ford followed.

At the ramp leading to the northbound side of the Expressway, the Ford was two cars behind.

Coincidence? No. That's pushing coincidence too far. If the men in the car had actually intended to go north on the Expressway, they would have gone on in the direction they had been taking when Bending first noticed them; they wouldn't have gone ten blocks south out of their way.

Bending's smile became grim. He had never liked the idea of being followed around, and, since the loss of one of his Converters, he was even touchier about the notion. Trouble was, his fancy, souped-up Lincoln was of no use to him at all. He could outrun them on a clear highway—but not on the crowded Expressway. Or, conversely, he could just keep on driving until they were forced to stop for fuel—but that could be a long and tedious trip if they had a full tank. And besides, they might make other arrangements before they went dry.

Well, there was another way.

He stayed on the Expressway for the next twenty miles, going far north of where he had intended to turn off. At the Marysville Exit, he went down the ramp. He had been waiting for a moment when the Ford would be a little farther behind than normal, but it hadn't come; at each exit, the driver of the trailing car would edge up, although he allowed himself to drop behind between exits. Whoever was driving the car knew what he was doing.

At the bottom of the ramp, Bending made a left turn and took the road into Marysville. It was a small town, not more than five or six thousand population, but it was big enough.

There weren't many cars on the streets that led off the main highway. Bending made a right turn and went down one of the quiet boulevards in the residential section. The steel-blue Ford dropped behind as they turned; they didn't want to make Bending suspicious, evidently.

He came to a quiet street parallel to the highway and made a left turn. As soon as he was out of sight of his pursuers, he shoved down on the accelerator. The car jumped ahead, slamming Bending back in his seat. At the next corner, he turned left again. A glance in the mirror showed him that the Ford was just turning the previous corner.

Bending's heavy Lincoln swung around the corner at high speed and shot back toward the highway. At the next corner, he cut left once more, and the mirror showed that the Ford hadn't made it in time to see him turn.

They'd probably guess he'd gone left, so he made a right turn as soon as he hit the next street, and then made another left, then another right. Then he kept on going until he got to the highway.

A left turn put him back on the highway, headed toward the Expressway. The steel-blue car was nowhere in sight.

Bending sighed and headed back south towards home.

Sam Bending knew there was something wrong when he pulled up in front of his garage and pressed the button on the dashboard that was supposed to open the garage door. Nothing happened.

He climbed out of the car, went over to the door of the garage, and pushed the emergency button. The door remained obstinately shut.

Without stopping to wonder what had happened, he sprinted around to the front door of the house, unlocked it, and pressed the wall switch. The lights didn't come on, and he knew what had happened.

Trailing a stream of blue invective, he ran to the rear of the house and went down the basement stairs. Sure enough. Somebody had taken his house Converter, too.

And they hadn't even had the courtesy to shunt him back onto the power lines.

At his home, he had built more carefully than he had at the lab. He had rigged in a switch which would allow him to use either the Converter or the regular power sources, so that he could work on the Converter if he wanted to. His basement was almost a duplicate of his lab in the city, except that at home he built gadgets just for the fun of watching them work, while at the lab he was doing more serious research.

He went over to the cabinet where the switch was, opened it, and punched the relay button. The lights came on.

He stalked back up the stairs and headed for the visiphone. First, he dialed his patent attorney's office; he needed some advice. If Power Utilities had their hands on two out of three of his Converters, there might be some trouble over getting the patents through.

The attorney's secretary said he wasn't in, and she didn't know if he expected to be back that day. It was, she informed Bending rather archly, nearly five in the afternoon. Bending thanked her and hung up.

He dialed the man's home, but he wasn't there, either.

Sam Bending stuck a cigarette in his mouth, fired it up, walked over to his easy-chair and sat down to think.

According to the police, the first Converter had been stolen on Friday night. The second one had obviously been taken sometime this morning, while he was in the lab with the police.

That made sense. The first one they'd tried to open had fused, so they decided to try to get a second one. Only how had they known he had had more than one? He hadn't told anyone that he had three—or even two.

Well, no matter. They *had* found out. The question was, what did he do next? Inform the police of the two thefts or—

There was a car pulling up outside the house.

Sam stood up and glanced out the window. It was a steel-blue Ford.

By Heaven! Did they intend to steal the third Converter, too? And right in front of his eyes, before it even got decently dark?

Sam was so furious that he couldn't even think straight. When the two men climbed out of the car and started walking toward the house, Sam ran back into his study, pulled open his desk drawer, and took out the .38 Special he kept there. It was the work of seconds to thumb six cartridges into the chambers and swing the cylinder shut.

The door chime sounded.

Sam went back into the front room with the revolver in his jacket pocket and his hand ready to fire it.

"Who is it?" he called, in what he hoped was a steady voice.

"We're Special Agents of the FBI," said a voice. "May we see you for a few moments, Mr. Bending?"

"Certainly. Come on in; the door's unlocked." *Just walk in, you phonies! Just trot right on in,* he thought.

And they did. The two men walked in, removing their hats as they did so.

"We—" one of them began. He stopped when he saw that he was addressing a round, black hole that was only a fraction more than a third of an inch in diameter but looked much, *much* larger from his viewpoint.

"Get your hands in the air and turn around very slowly," said Bending. "Lean forward and brace your hands against the wall."

They did as they were told. Bending frisked them carefully and thoroughly, thankful that the two years he had spent in the Army hadn't been completely wasted. Neither one of them was carrying a gun.

Bending stepped back and pocketed his own weapon. "All right. You two can turn around now. If you want to try anything, come ahead—but I don't advise it."

The two men turned around. Neither of them was exactly a small man, but the two of them together didn't outweigh Samson Bending by more than fifty pounds.

"What's the idea of the gun, Mr. Bending?" the taller of the two asked. He seemed to be the spokesman for the team.

"I'll ask the questions," Bending said. "But first, I want to tell you that, in the first place, you can get in trouble for impersonating a Federal officer, and, in the second, I don't like being followed. So you just trot right back to the boys at Power Utilities and tell them that if they want to play rough, I am perfectly willing to do likewise. That if they come after me again, I'm going to do some very unpleasant things. Understand?"

"I think we understand," said the spokesman, still relatively unruffled. "But I don't think *you* do. Would you care to look at our credentials, Mr. Bending?"

"Credentials?" Sam looked startled. Had he made a mistake?

"That's right. May I take my billfold out?"

Bending took his gun out again. "Go ahead. But slowly."

The billfold came out slowly. Bending took it. The identification card and the small gold badge said very plainly that the man was a Special Agent of the Federal Bureau of Investigation.

"I ... I'm sorry," Bending said weakly. "I thought you were someone else. Some men were following me this afternoon, and—"

"That was us, Mr. Bending. Sorry."

"May I verify this?" Bending asked.

"Certainly. Go right ahead."

Bending phoned the local office of the FBI and verified the identities of the two men. When he cut off, he asked dazedly: "What was it you wanted?"

"Would you mind coming with us—downtown? We'd like to have you see some people."

"Am I under arrest?"

"No." The agent smiled a little. "I suppose, if we had to, we could get you for speeding and reckless driving; that was pretty fancy dodging you did. But we're not supposed to be traffic cops."

Sam smiled feebly. "What's this all about?"

"I haven't the faintest notion, Mr. Bending. Honestly. We were told to stick with you until we got word to pick you up. We got that word just shortly after you ... hm-m-m ... after you left us. Fortunately, we found you at home. It might have been difficult ..."

"Can we go in my car?" Bending asked. "I'd rather not leave it unguarded just now."

"Certainly. I'll go with you, and Steve can follow." He paused. "But I'm afraid you'll have to take that revolver out of your pocket and put it away."

"Sure," Bending said. "Sure."

Bending's mind simply refused to function during the drive back to the city. The FBI agent beside him just sat silently while Sam drove the car.

Once, Sam asked: "Who is it that wants to see me?"

And the FBI man said: "Sorry, Mr. Bending; I can't answer any questions. My job is over as soon as I deliver you."

A little later, Sam had another question. "Can you tell me where we're going, at least?"

"Oh—" the agent laughed, "sure. I thought I had. The General Post Office Building, on Kenmore Drive."

After that, Sam didn't say anything. That this whole affair had something to do with the Converter, Sam had no doubt whatsoever. But he couldn't see exactly what, and none of his wild speculations made sense.

He pulled up at last into the parking lot behind the Post Office Building. The second FBI man came up in the steel-blue Ford, and the three of them got out of the cars and went towards the building. It was quite dark by now, and the street lights were glowing against a faint falling of February mist. Bending, in spite of his topcoat, felt chilly.

They went in the back way, past the uniformed Postal Service guard, and took an elevator to the sixth floor. None of the three had anything to say. They walked down the hall, toward the only office that showed any light behind the frosted glass. The lettering on the glass simply said: *Conference Room A-6*.

The FBI man who had driven with Sam rapped on the door with gentle knuckles.

"Yes?" said a questioning voice from the other side.

"This is Hodsen, sir. Mr. Bending is with us."

The door opened, and Sam Bending felt mild shock as he saw who it was. He recognized the man from his news photos and TV appearances. It was the Honorable Bertram Condley, Secretary of Economics for the President of the United States.

"Come in, Mr. Bending," the Secretary said pleasantly. Unnecessarily, he added, "I'm Bertram Condley."

He held out his hand, and Sam took it. "It's a pleasure, Mr. Secretary."

Condley gave out with his best friendly-politico smile. "I'm sorry to have to drag you up here like this, Mr. Bending, but we felt it best this way."

Sam smiled back, with a trace of irony in the smile. "It's a pleasure, Mr. Secretary," he repeated.

Condley nodded, still smiling—but there was a spark in his eyes now. "I see we understand each other. Come on in; I want you to meet the others." He looked at the FBI men. "That's all. For now."

The Federal agents nodded and moved away into the dimness of the corridor.

"Come in, man, come in," the Secretary urged, opening the door wider.

Sam hesitated. The light within the room was none too bright. Then he stepped forward, following the Secretary.

The outer room was dark. Not too dark, but illuminated only by the dim light from the corridor and from the inner room. From that inner room, there was only a glow of light from the frosted glass panel of the door that separated the two rooms.

Condley closed the hall door, and, as Sam stepped forward toward the lighted door, held out a hand to stop him. "Just a moment," he whispered softly. "I think you ought to know what you're walking in to, Mr. Bending."

Bending stood stock-still. "Yes, sir?" he asked, questioningly.

"I suppose you know what this is all about?" Secretary Condley asked softly.

"The Converter, I imagine," Sam Bending said.

Condley nodded, his gray hair gleaming silver in the dim light. "Exactly. I'm sorry we had to drag you up here this way, Mr. Bending, but, in the circumstances, we felt it to be the best way." He took a breath. "Do you know why we called you here?"

"No," Sam said honestly.

Condley's head nodded again. "You're in for an argument, Mr. Bending. A very powerful one, I hope. We want to convince you of something." Again he paused. "Are you an open-minded man, Mr. Bending?"

Sam Bending followed the Secretary's lead, and kept his voice low. "I like to think so, Mr. Secretary." He recognized that Condley was preparing him for something, and he recognized that the preliminary statements were calculated to soften him. And he recognized the fact that they *did* soften him. All right—what was the argument?

"You're an engineer, Mr. Bending," Condley said, in the same low voice. "You have been trained to evaluate facts. All I ask is that you use that training. Now, let's get in there before *Tovarishch* Artomonov begins to think we might be stalling him."

Condley strode toward the door and grasped the knob with a firm hand. Sam Bending followed, wondering. Artomonov? Who was Artomonov? The Secretary of Economics had indicated, by his precise enunciation of *tovarishch*, that the man was a Russian—or at least a citizen of one of the Soviet satellites. Sam Bending took a deep breath and decided that he was prepared for almost anything.

There were four men seated around the conference table in the back room, and the most surprising thing, as far as Sam was concerned, was that he recognized only one of them. From the big buildup, he had had half a notion that the President himself might be there.

"Mr. Samson Bending, gentlemen," said Secretary Condley to the group. They all rose and made half-hearted attempts to smile, but Sam could see that they were watching him as though he had a live grenade in his pocket.

"Mr. Bending, I believe you know Mr. Richard Olcott," the Secretary said.

Bending gave the Power Utilities executive a sardonic smile, which was returned by a solemn nod of the head.

Sure I know you, you crook, Bending thought.

"And, around the table," Condley continued, "are Dr. Edward Larchmont, the research departmental head of Power Utilities—Dr. Stefan Vanderlin, of the United States Bureau of Standards—and Dr. Alexis Andreevich Artomonov, of the Soviet Socialist Republics' representative office at the United Nations."

Sam Bending managed not to blink in astonishment as the last man was introduced—a feat which took every milligram of his self-possession. He recognized the name; A. A. Artomonov, head of the United Nation's International Trade Bureau. What was *he* doing here?

"If you'll sit down, Mr. Bending," Condley was saying, "we can get to business."

Bending sat down, and the others sat with him. "May I say something before we go any further?" Sam Bending asked. "May I say that I think this is a rather irregular method of doing things and that I think I ought to see my lawyer."

Secretary Condley's eyes narrowed just the slightest. He was a heavy, jowl-faced, graying man who was known for his firmness in his official capacity. "At this stage of the game, Mr. Bending, there is no need for a lawyer. We merely want to explain something to you—we want you to get all the data. If, afterwards, you still want your lawyer, you'll be perfectly free to call him. Right now, we want you to listen with an open mind."

Bending thought it over. "All right. Go ahead."

"Very well. First, I'll agree that all this may seem a bit high-handed. But time was—and is—getting short." He glanced at Olcott, and the glance was not all friendliness. "The Government was notified about this almost too late; we have had to act fast. Almost *too* fast."

"I notified the Government as soon as I was sure of my facts," Olcott said, completely unflustered.

"That's as may be," Condley said. "The point is that we now have the problem on our hands, and we must find an equitable solution." He took a gold fountain pen from his pocket, and his strong, thick fingers began toying with it while his eyes remained on Sam Bending. "The fact that you have applied for a patent makes it imperative that we get the situation under control immediately."

Before Sam could answer, there was a knock on the outer door that came clearly into the rear room. Secretary Condley rose without saying a word and went out.

Dr. Larchmont, the Power Utilities physicist, decided to make small talk to bridge the hiatus. "That's a really beautiful piece of machinery you've built, Mr. Bending. Really remarkable." He was a small, flat-faced man with a fringe of dark hair around his otherwise naked scalp.

Sam looked a little startled. "You mean you opened a Converter up?"

Larchmont nodded. "I presume you are referring to the fusing device. We X-rayed the thing thoroughly before we opened it. These days, many devices are rigged to be self-destroying, but that, in itself is a specialized field. Most of them are traps that are rather easy to get around if one is expecting them and knows how to handle them. But the Converter itself, if I may say so, is one of the most original and elegant devices I have seen in many a day."

"Thanks," said Bending, with a touch of bitterness in his voice. "I—"

The door opened at that moment, and Secretary Condley came in followed by a tall, round-faced man with dark wavy hair and clear brown eyes.

"Jim!" Sam said in surprise.

The man was James Luckman, Sam Bending's business manager. "Hello, Sam. What's this all about? The FBI men who picked me up said I wasn't under arrest, but I had a hunch it was about as close as you can come without actual arrest."

Sam nodded. "Funny—I had that impression, too." He looked at Condley. "What's the idea, Condley? Jim doesn't know anything about this."

The Secretary managed to look unoffended at Bending's tone. "Possibly not. We can't be sure, of course, but—frankly, I'd be willing to accept your word." He paused. "But—you're not a businessman, Mr. Bending?" He made it only half a question.

"No. I leave that sort of thing up to Jim. Oh, I don't say I'm completely ignorant of the field; it's just that I'm not particularly interested, that's all. Why should I be?" He went on, half belligerently. "I've known and trusted Jim for years. He knows his business; I know my science. I know enough to be able to check the account books, and he knows enough to be able to understand a technical report. Right, Jim?"

Luckman looked bewildered. "Sure, Sam. But what's all this leading up to? I don't get it." He frowned suddenly. "Has someone accused me of cheating you?"

"No, no, no," Condley said rapidly. "Of course not. Nothing like that." He looked sharply at Luckman. "Do you know anything about the Converter?"

Jim Luckman glanced at Bending before replying. Bending's face remained expressionless. "Go ahead, Jim," he said, "square with him."

Luckman spread his hands. "I know that Sam was working on something he called a Converter. I don't know anything more about it than that. Sam keeps his ideas secret until he gets them to a marketable stage, which is all right with me. I have enough work to do, handling the stuff he's already patented, without worrying about anything that isn't salable yet. So?"

Condley nodded, then gestured toward a chair. "Sit down, Mr. Luckman. Do you know these other gentlemen?" he asked rhetorically. He proceeded to introduce the others. Sam Bending noted with satisfaction that Luckman looked rather puzzled when the Russian was introduced.

Condley himself sat down again, and said: "Well, we're all here. We're not going to make this formal, gentlemen, but I hope it won't develop into a heated argument, either. Let's try to keep our tempers."

"First, as to the Converter itself. We all know, with the possible exception of Mr. Luckman, what it does, but for his benefit, we'll go over that. The Converter, by means of what Dr. Larchmont has been wont to call 'a very elegant method', produces electrical power directly from the fusion of hydrogen into helium. A pilot model, with a total volume of a little more than one and one-quarter cubic feet, is capable of turning out up to five hundred horsepower, either DC or AC in a wide range of frequencies. The voltage can be regulated from zero to one thousand volts by simply setting a dial.

"The device is powered by using ordinary water as fuel. At full capacity, the Converter consumes approximately four hundred milligrams of water per hour, which can easily be drawn from the moisture of the air. The machine is thus self-fueling.

"Since the nuclear energy released is converted almost one hundred per cent into electrical current, there is no danger from radiation; since the process is, by its very nature, self-limiting, there is no danger of explosion. The worst that can happen is for the machine to burn out, and, I understand, it won't do that unless it is purposely tampered with to make it do so.

"Finally, the device is so inexpensive to produce that it could be sold for about one-quarter of the price of an ordinary automobile." He stopped, cleared his throat, and glanced at Larchmont and Vanderlin. "Am I essentially correct, gentlemen?"

Larchmont nodded, and Vanderlin said, "That's about it."

Jim Luckman looked at Sam Bending in open admiration. "Wow," he said softly. "You're quite a genius, Sam."

"Very well, gentlemen," Condley continued, "we know what this device will do on a physical level. Now we must consider what it will do on an economic level. Have you considered what would happen if you put the Converter on the market, Mr. Bending?"

"Certainly," Bending said, with an angry glance at Olcott. "The Power Utilities would lose their pants. So what? I figure that any company which tries to steal and suppress inventions deserves a licking."

Secretary Condley glanced at Olcott as though he were trying to hold back a smile, then returned his gaze to Bending. "We won't quibble over the ethics of the situation, Mr. Bending. You are correct in saying that Power Utilities would be bankrupt. They couldn't stand the competition of what amounts to almost unlimited free power. And then what would happen, with every power company in the United States suddenly put out of business?"

Sam looked puzzled. "What difference would it make? People would just be getting their power from another source, that's all."

Richard Olcott leaned forward earnestly. "May I interject something here? I know you are angry with me, Mr. Bending—perhaps with good reason. But I'd like to point out something that you might not have recognized. Public Utilities and its co-operative independent companies are not owned by individuals. Much of the stock is owned by small share-holders who have only a few shares each. The several billion dollars that these companies are worth is spread out over the nation, not just centered with a few wealthy men. In addition, a great many shares are held by insurance companies and banks. Literally millions of people would lose money—just as surely as if it had been stolen from them—if this device went on the market."

Bending frowned. He hadn't thought of it in exactly that way. "Still," he said tentatively, "didn't blacksmiths and buggy-whip manufacturers and horse-breeders lose money after World War I?"

"Not to this extent," Olcott said, shaking his head. "This is not 1918, Mr. Bending. Sixty years ago, our economy was based on gold, not, as it is today on production and manpower, centered in the vast interlocking web of American industry."

Condley said: "Mr. Olcott said a moment ago that millions of people would lose money just as surely as if it had been stolen from them. I think it would be more proper to say that the money will be destroyed, not stolen. A thief, after all, does put money back into circulation after he steals it. But when vast amounts of wealth are suddenly removed from circulation completely, the economic balance is disastrously upset."

Sam Bending was still frowning. His grandfather had been a small businessman in 1929—not fabulously wealthy, but certainly well off by the social standards of the day. Two years later, in 1931, he was broke, wiped out completely, happy and eager to accept any odd job he could get to support his family.

Sam's father had had to leave school during the Thirties and go to work in order to bring in enough money to keep the family going. Grandfather Bending, weakened by long hours of labor that he was physically unfit for, had become an invalid, and the entire support of the family had devolved upon Sam's father.

He could remember his dad talking about the breadlines and the free-soup kitchens. He could remember his grandmother, her hands crippled by arthritis, aggravated by long hours at a commercial sewing machine in a clothing center sweat-shop, just so she could bring in that little extra money that meant so much to her children and her invalid husband.

Could one invention bring all that back again? Could his own harmless-looking Converter plunge millions back into that kind of misery? It seemed hardly possible, but Sam couldn't banish the specter of the Great Depression from his mind.

"Just how far-reaching would this economic upset be?" he asked Condley.

Condley had taken out his gold fountain pen again and was rolling it between his palms. "Well, that's a question with a long answer, Mr. Bending. Let's begin small and watch it spread.

"Banks are pretty safe today, aren't they? The Federal Deposit Insurance Corporation insures all depositors for deposits up to twenty thousand dollars now. A bank is hedged in by so many legal fences that it is almost impossible for one to fail in the same way that they failed all over the country in the early Thirties. Even if one does fail, through the gross mismanagement or illegal activities of its governing board, the depositors don't get excited; they know they're covered. There hasn't been a really disastrous run on a bank for more than thirty years.

"But banks don't just keep their money in vaults; they invest it. And a significantly large percentage of that money is invested in power companies all over the nation. In an attempt to keep their heads above water, those banks would be forced to make up tremendous losses if Power Utilities failed overnight. It would force them to draw in outstanding loans for ready cash. It would mean turning in United States Savings Bonds, which would put a tremendous strain on the Government.

"In spite of that, most banks won't be able to stay solvent because their other capital investments will be dropping rapidly in value. As Mr. Olcott said, our monetary system isn't based on gold, but on production and goods. If Power Utilities and its members fail, you and your machine will have destroyed—made worthless—several billion dollars worth of machinery and equipment. You will have thrown tens of thousands of people out of work. You will have cut the underpinnings from beneath the American dollar.

"And it won't stop there. What will happen to the companies that build the dynamos and the boilers and the atomic plants for the power companies? What will happen to the copper industry when the need for millions of miles of copper wire vanishes? They will all suffer tremendous setbacks, throwing tens of thousands more out of work and lowering the value of their stock drastically.

"The banks, then, will find their investments suddenly worth only a fraction of their former value. They'll fail wholesale. And you can see what that will do to the Federal Deposit Insurance Corporation and other insurance companies."

Sam Bending nodded slowly. He could see that. Insurance companies base their business on the prediction that a certain event—death, accident, or the failure of a bank—will happen to a certain percentage of their covered clients, and they adjust their rates accordingly. But something that would change a five-percent-failure rate to a fifty-percent-failure rate would break the company.

And the unemployment rate would go up even higher. And Sam thought of something the Secretary hadn't even mentioned. State and Federal Unemployment Insurance. What would that drain do to the treasuries of the various governments involved?

Sam Bending felt as if the thing were snowballing on him. Where would the State and Federal Governments get that money? Taxes? Don't be silly. How can you collect sales taxes when sales are dropping off because of unemployment? How can you get income taxes from depleted incomes? How can you charge luxury taxes when no one is buying luxuries?

Certainly essentials like food, rent, and clothing couldn't be taxed. People would buy as cheaply as possible, which would force down prices. Which would—

"Where would it go from there?" Sam asked Condley in a shaken voice.

Condley glanced over at the Russian. "I believe Dr. Artomonov can answer that one for you."

Artomonov was a red-faced, fleshy man with almost no hair and a huge, bristling, gray mustache. His eyes were a startling blue. "Mr. Bending," he said in excellent English, "you may recall that your depression of the Thirties was not confined to America. All of Europe became involved. The same will happen again, to a greater degree, if your machine is released to the world at this time." He brushed at his mustache with a fingertip.

"You may wonder what I am doing here, Mr. Bending. You might think that the traditional rivalry which has existed between our countries for so many decades would preclude my being admitted to such a secret session as this one. I might have thought so, too, fifteen years ago. But when something threatens *both* our countries, the picture changes. We fought together during the Motherland War—what you call World War II—because of the common threat of German Nazi terrorism. We co-operated to suppress the brush-fires that threatened us in Europe and the Middle East during the so-called Tense War. In big things we must co-operate.

"Again we are both threatened by a common source, Mr. Bending, and again we must co-operate."

Sam Bending felt a chill. The thought that he and his machine were a threat as great as that, a threat to the two greatest nations of Earth, was appalling.

"I am not a scientist, Mr. Bending," the Russian went on. "My title comes from a degree in economics and political science, not in physical science. As soon as this machine was demonstrated to me, however, I could appreciate its power—not only physically, but economically. I immediately contacted my superiors in Moscow to discuss the problem.

"Naturally, we would like to know the ... ah ... 'elegant' principle behind its operation. Equally naturally"—he smiled politely at Secretary Condley—"you will not tell us. However, my superiors in Moscow assure me that we need not worry on that score; a machine identically similar to yours was invented by one of our brilliant young scientists at the University of Moscow over four years ago. As a patriot, of course, he was willing to have the machine suppressed, and no news of it has leaked out."

Sam Bending found it difficult to keep from smiling. *Sure*, he thought, *and a man named Popov invented radio, and Yablochkov invented the electric light.*

"You see, Mr. Bending," Dr Artomonov continued, "while we do not have the unstable setup of money-based capitalism, and while we do not need to worry about such antiquated and dangerous things as fluctuating stock markets, we would still find your machine a threat. Communism is based on the work of the people; our economy is based on the labor of the working man. It is thus stable, because every man must work.

"But we, too, have a vast, power network, the destruction of which would cause the unemployment of millions of our citizens. The unemployment alone would cause repercussions all over the Soviet Republics which would be difficult to deal with. We would eventually recover, of course, because of the inherent stability of our system, but the shock would not be good for us.

"The same thing would happen in every industrialized nation on Earth," Artomonov went on. "In my work with the United Nations, I have studied just such problems. European governments would fall overnight. In Germany, in the 1920s, it was cheaper to burn bundles of one-mark notes than it was to buy firewood with them. Such things will be repeated, not only in the Germanies, but all over Europe.

"Some countries, of course, will not be so drastically effected. China, and other parts of Asia which have not built up a vast industrial system, will be affected only slightly. The South American countries still have a more or less agricultural economy and will not be bothered greatly.

"But the great industrial civilizations of East and West will collapse."

With one breath, Artomonov was saying that the Soviet Union could weather the storm, and with another he was hinting that it probably wouldn't. But Sam Bending could see the point in spite of the Russian's tortuous logic.

"I think that is all I have to say for the moment," Artomonov said, "except to emphasize one point. The Great Depression hit the world some fifty years ago. It was a terrible thing for everyone concerned. But it was as nothing at all—a mere zephyr of ill wind—compared to what the Depression of the Eighties will be if your machine goes on the market."

There was silence for a minute. Sam Bending was thinking hard, and the others could see it—and they knew there was no point in interrupting at that moment.

"Just a second," Sam said. "There's one thing that I don't really quite see. I can see that the situation you outline would develop if every power plant in America—or in the Soviet Union or Europe—were to be suddenly replaced by Converters. I can see that chaos would result." He paused, marshaling his thoughts, then went on, with a tinge of anger in his voice.

"But that's not the way it will work! You can't do a thing like that overnight. To mass produce the Converter will take time—factories will have to be tooled up for it, and all that. And distribution will take time. It seems to me that there would be plenty of time to adjust."

Condley started to say something, but Dr. Artomonov burst in explosively.

"Don't you see, Mr. Bending? The threat of the machine is enough! Even here in your own country, just the knowledge that such machines were to be made at some time in the immediate future would have a disastrous effect! Who would invest in Power Utilities if they knew that within a short time it would be bankrupt? No one would want to buy such stock, and those who had it would be frantically trying to sell what they had. The effect on the banking system would be the same as if the machine were already being used. Your Mr. Roosevelt pointed out that fear was the problem."

Bending frowned puzzledly. "I don't see—"

He was interrupted by Dr. Larchmont. "Let me see if I can't give you an analogy, Mr. Bending. Do you know anything about the so-called 'nerve gases'?"

"Some," admitted Sam. "Most of them aren't gases; they're finely dispersed aerosols."

Larchmont nodded. "Have you any idea how much it takes to kill a man?"

"A drop or so of the aerosol on the skin is enough, I understand."

"That's right. Now, how can such a minute amount of poison damage a human being?"

Bending began to get a glimmer of what the man was driving at. "Well, I know that some of them suppress the enzymic action with acetylcholine, which means that the nerves simply act as though their synapses had been shorted through. It only takes a small percentage of that kind of damage to the nerve fibers to ruin the whole nervous system. The signals get jammed up and confused, and the whole mechanism ceases to function. The victim dies."

Larchmont nodded. "Now, as I understand it, our banking system is the vital nerve network of our economy. And our system is built on credit—faith, if you will. Destroy that faith—even a small percentage of it—and you destroy the system.

"If your machine were to go on the market, there would be no more faith in the present utilities system. Their stocks would be worthless long before your machine actually put them out of business. And that would hit our banking system the same way a nerve gas hits the nervous system. And the victim—the American economy—would die. And the nation, as a nation, would die with it."

"I see," said Bending slowly. He didn't like the picture at all; it was more frightening than he cared to admit, even to himself. He looked at his business manager. "What do you think, Jim?" he asked softly. He knew he could depend on Luckman.

Jim Luckman looked worried. "They're right, Sam. Clean, dead right. I know the investment pattern in this country, and I have an idea of what it must be abroad. This country would be in the middle of the worst depression in its history. At least we had Federal help during the Thirties—but there won't even be a United States Government if this hits. Nor, I think, will there be a Soviet government, in spite of what Dr. Artomonov's personal beliefs may be."

Significantly, the Russian economist said nothing.

Sam Bending closed his eyes. "I've worked on this thing for years," he said tensely. "It was ... it *means*something to me. I invented it. I perfected it." His voice began to quaver just a little. "But if it's going to do ... to do all that—" He paused and took a deep breath. "All right. I'll smash my apparatus and destroy my plans and forget about it."

Jim Luckman looked at Secretary Condley. "I don't think that would be fair. Sam's worked hard on this thing. He deserves recognition. And the people of Earth deserve to get this machine somehow. Can't something be worked out?"

"Certainly," said Condley. "In some countries, and in some eras, dangerous inventions were suppressed by the simplest method. If it was discovered in time, the inventor was executed summarily, along with anyone else who knew the secret, and the invention was destroyed. The United States isn't that kind of country." He looked down at his hands and the gold pen again before he went on.

"Please don't misunderstand, Mr. Bending; we are not trying to keep the Converter under wraps forever. In the first place, I don't think it would be possible. What do you think, Dr. Vanderlin?"

The Bureau of Standards man said: "I doubt it. Granted, the Converter is not something one would accidentally stumble across, nor automatically deduce from the 'previous state of the art'. I'll admit frankly that I doubt if I would ever have thought of it. But I doubt gravely that it is so unique that it will never be rediscovered independently."

"So," said Condley, "we have no intent to hold it back on that score. And, in the second place, such an invention is too valuable to allow it to be lost.

"So here is our proposition. You will sell your rights to the Converter to Power Utilities. It won't even be patented in the usual sense; we can't allow the Converter to become public property at this time. We can't make it possible for just anyone to send in a quarter to the Patent Office to find out how it works. That's why we stopped the patent application.

"But the Government will see that a contract is written up which admits that you are the inventor of the Converter, and which will give you royalties on every unit built. High royalties.

"Under strict Government supervision, Power Utilities will proceed to liquidate their holdings—slowly, so that there will be no repercussions on an economic level. The danger lies, not in the Converter's replacing existing power equipment, but in the danger of its replacing them too quickly. But with care and control, the adjustment can be made slowly. The process will take about ten years, but you will receive a lump sum, plus a monthly payment, as an advance against future royalties."

"I see," said Bending slowly. "That sounds all right to me. What about you, Jim? What do you think?"

Jim Luckman was smiling again. "Sounds fine to me, Sam. We'll have to work out the terms of the contract, of course, but I think Mr. Olcott and I can see eye to eye."

Olcott seemed to wince a little. He knew he was over a barrel.

"I suppose I'll have to be sworn to secrecy, eh?" Bending asked. He was beginning to recover his poise.

Condley nodded. "You will." He made his characteristic pause, looking down at the gold pen and back up. "Mr. Bending, don't think that this is the first time this has happened. Yours is not the first dangerous invention that has come up. It just so happens that it's the most dangerous so far. We don't like to have to work this way, but we must. There was simply nothing else to do."

Sam Bending leaned back in his chair. "That's all right. To be perfectly honest, there are a lot of details that I still don't understand. But I recognize the fact that I'm simply not an economist; I can see the broad outlines plainly enough."

Dr. Artomonov smiled widely. "I do not understand the details of your machine, either, Mr. Bending, but I understand the broad outlines of its operations well enough to be frightened when I think of what it could do to world economy if it were to be dumped on the market at this time. I am happy to see that America, as well as Mother Russia, can produce patriots of a high order."

Sam gave him a smile. "Thanks." He didn't know quite what else to say to a statement like that. "But Jim, here, is going to spend the next several days trotting out facts and figures for me. I want to see just what would take place, if I can wrestle with that kind of data."

"Oh, brother!" said Jim Luckman softly. "Well, I'll try."

"I'll have the reports from the computers sent to you," Condley offered. "They show the whole collapse, step by step."

Artomonov cast a speculative glance in Condley's direction, but he said nothing.

"There's one other thing," Sam said flatly. "The Converter is my baby, and I want to go on working on it. I think Power Utilities might put me on as a permanent consultant, so that I could earn some of the money that's coming in over the next ten years. That way, my royalties won't suffer so much from the advance payments."

Jim Luckman grinned, and Richard Olcott said: "I thought you said you were no businessman, Mr. Bending."

"I may be ignorant," said Sam, "but I'm not stupid. What about it?"

Olcott glanced at Dr. Larchmont. The little scientist was beaming.

"Definitely," he said. "I want Mr. Bending to show me how he managed to dope that thing out. And, to be perfectly frank, there are a couple of things in there that I don't get at all."

"That's understandable," said Dr. Vanderlin. "We only had a few hours to look at the thing. Still, I must admit it's a lulu."

"That's not what I meant," Larchmont said. "There are some things in there that would take a long time to figure out without an explanation. I'll admit that—"

"Wait a minute," Bending interrupted. "You said 'a few hours', Dr. Vanderlin. You mean only since this morning?" He grinned. "What happened to the one you got Friday night? Did my fusing device work the first time?"

Vanderlin looked puzzledly at Larchmont. Larchmont said wonderingly: "Friday? You mean you had *two* pilot models?"

Olcott said: "Where was the other? We checked your power drain and saw you weren't using any at your house, so—"

"I had three models," Bending said. "I've got one left in my car; you took one from my house, and the third was taken from my lab sometime Friday night. Somebody has it ..."

Condley said: "Dr. Artomonov, do you know anything about this?"

The Russian shook his head. "Nothing." He looked plainly frightened. "I assure you, my government knew nothing of this."

Condley leaped to his feet, said: "Where are those FBI men?" and ran out the door.

"The black market," said Bending softly. "They found out somehow."

"And they've had three days to study it," Larchmont said. "It's too late now. That thing is probably somewhere in South America by this time."

Artomonov stood up, his face oddly pale. "You must excuse me, gentlemen. I must get in touch with Moscow immediately." He strode out of the room.

The four men remaining in the room just stared at each other for a long moment. There wasn't much else they could do.

THE END

Instant of Decision

How could a man tell the difference if all the reality of Earth turned out to be a cosmic hoax? Suppose it turned out that this was just a stage set for students of history?

When the sharp snap of a pistol shot came from the half-finished building, Karnes wasn't anywhere near the sandpile that received the slug. He was fifteen feet away, behind the much more reliable protection of a neat stack of cement bags that provided cover all the way to a window in the empty shell of brick and steel before him.

Three hundred yards behind him, the still-burning inferno of what had been the Assembly Section of Carlson Spacecraft sent a reddish, unevenly pulsating light over the surrounding territory, punctuating the redness with intermittent flashes of blue-white from flaring magnesium.

For an instant, Karnes let himself hope that the shot might be heard at the scene of the blaze, but only for an instant. The roar of fire, men, and machine would be too much for a little pop like that.

He moved quietly along the stacked cement bags, and eased himself over the sill of the gaping window into the building. He was in a little hallway. Somewhere ahead and to his left would be a door that would lead into the main hallway where James Avery, alias James Harvey, alias half-a-dozen other names, was waiting to take another pot-shot at the sandpile.

The passageway was longer than he had thought, and he realized that he might have been just a little careless in coming in through the window. With the firelight at his back, he might make a pretty good target from farther down the hall, or from any of the dark, empty rooms that would someday be officers'.

Then he found it. The slight light from the main hallway came through enough to show him where to turn.

Keeping in the darkness, Karnes' eyes surveyed the broad hallway for several seconds before he spotted the movement near a stairway. After he knew where to look, it was easy to make out the man's crouched figure.

Karnes thought: *I can't call to him to surrender. I can't let him get away. I can't sneak across that hall to stick my gun in his ribs. And, above all, I cannot let him get away with that microfilm.*

Hell, there's only one thing I can do.

Karnes lifted his gun, aimed carefully at the figure, and fired.

Avery must have had a fairly tight grip on his own weapon, because when Karnes' slug hit him, it went off once before his body spread itself untidily across the freshly set cement. Then the gun fell out of the dead hand and slid a few feet, spinning in silly little circles.

Karnes approached the corpse cautiously, just in case it wasn't a corpse, but it took only a moment to see that the caution had been unnecessary. He knelt, rolled the body over, unfastened the pants, pulled them down to the knees and stripped off the ribbon of adhesive tape that he knew would be on the inside of the thigh. Underneath it were four little squares of thin plastic.

As he looked at the precious microfilm in his hand, he sensed something odd. If he had been equipped with the properly developed muscles to do so, he would have pricked his ears. There was a soft footstep behind him.

He spun around on his heel, his gun ready. There was another man standing at the top of the shadowy stairway.

Karnes stood up slowly, his weapon still levelled.

"Come down from there slowly, with your hands in the air!"

The man didn't move immediately, and, although Karnes couldn't see his face clearly in the shimmering shadows, he had the definite impression that there was a grin on it. When the man did move, it was to turn quickly and run down the upper hallway, with a shot ringing behind him.

Karnes made the top of the stairway and sent another shot after the fleeing man, whose outline was easily visible against the pre-dawn light that was now beginning to come in through a window at the far end of the hall.

The figure kept running, and Karnes went after him, firing twice more as he ran.

Who taught you to shoot, dead-eye? he thought, as the man continued to run.

At the end of the hall, the man turned abruptly into one of the offices-to-be, his pursuer only five yards behind him.

Afterwards, Karnes thought it over time after time, trying to find some flaw or illusion in what he saw. But, much as he hated to believe his own senses, he remained convinced.

The broad window shed enough light to see everything in the room, but there wasn't much in it except for the slightly iridescent gray object in the center.

It was an oblate spheroid, about seven feet high and eight or nine feet through. As Karnes came through the door, he saw the man step *through* the seemingly solid material into the flattened globe.

Then globe, man and all, vanished. The room was empty.

Karnes checked his headlong rush into the room and peered around in the early morning gloom. For a full minute his brain refused even to attempt rationalizing what he had seen. He looked wildly around, but there was no one there. Suddenly he felt very foolish.

All right. So men can run into round gray things and vanish. Now use a little sense and look around.

There was something else in the room. Karnes knelt and looked at the little object that lay on the floor a few feet from where the gray globe had been. A cigarette case; one of those flat, coat-pocket jobs with a jet black enamel surface laid over tiny checked squares that would be absolutely useless for picking up fingerprints. If there were any prints, they'd be on the inside.

He started to pick it up and realized he must still be a bit confused; his hands were full. His right held the heavy automatic, and between the thumb and forefinger of his left were the four tiny sheets of microfilm.

Karnes holstered the pistol, took an envelope from his pocket, put the films in it, replaced the envelope, and picked up the cigarette case. It was, he thought, a rather odd-looking affair. It—

"Awright, you. Stand up slow, with your hands where I can see 'em."

Great God, thought Karnes, *I didn't know they were holding a tea party in this building*. He did as he was told.

There were two of them at the door, both wearing the uniform of Carlson Spacecraft. Plant protection squad.

"Who are you, bud?" asked the heavy-jawed one who had spoken before. "And whataya doin' here?"

Karnes, keeping his hands high, said: "Take my billfold out of my hip pocket."

"Okay. But first get over against that wall and lean forward." Evidently the man was either an ex-cop or a reader of detective stories.

When Karnes had braced himself against the wall, the guard went through his pockets, all of them, but he didn't take anything out except the pistol and the billfold.

The card in the special case of the wallet changed the guard's manner amazingly.

"Oh," he said softly. "Government, huh? Gee, I'm sorry, sir, but we didn't know—"

Karnes straightened up, and put his hands down. The cigarette case that had been in his right hand all along dropped into his coat pocket.

"That's all right," he said. "Did you see the lad at the foot of the stairs?"

"Sure. Jim Avery. Worked in Assembly. What happened to him?"

"He got in the way of the bullet. Resisting arrest. He's the jasper that set off the little incendiaries that started that mess out there. We've been watching him for months, now, but we didn't get word of this cute stroke until too late."

The guard looked puzzled. "Jim Avery. But why'd he want to do that?"

Karnes looked straight at him. "Leaguer!"

The guard nodded. You never could tell when the League would pop up like that.

Even after the collapse of Communism after the war, the world hadn't learned anything, it seemed. The Eurasian League had seemed, at first, to be patterned after the Western world's United Nations, but it hadn't worked out that way.

The League was jealous of the UN lead in space travel, for one thing, and they had neither the money nor the know-how to catch up. The UN might have given them help, but, as the French delegate had remarked: "For what reason should we arm a potential enemy?"

After all, they argued, with the threat of the UN's Moonbase hanging over the League to keep them peaceful, why should we give them spaceships so they can destroy Moonbase?

The Eurasian League had been quiet for a good many years, brooding, but behaving. Then, three years ago, Moonbase had vanished in a flash of actinic light, leaving only a new minor crater in the crust of Luna.

There was no proof of anything, of course. It had to be written off as an accident. But from that day on, the League had become increasingly bolder; their policy was: "Smash the UN and take the planets for ourselves!"

And now, with Carlson Spacecraft going up in flames, they seemed to be getting closer to their goal.

Karnes accepted his weapon and billfold from the guard and led them back down the stairway. "Would one of you guys phone the State Police? They'll want to know what happened."

The State Police copters came and went, taking Karnes and the late Mr. Avery with them, and leaving behind the now dying glow of Carlson Spacecraft.

There were innumerable forms to fill out and affidavits to make; there was a long-distance call to UN headquarters in New York to verify Karnes' identity. And Karnes asked to borrow the police lab for an hour or so.

That evening, he caught the rocket for Long Island.

As the SR-37 floated through the hard vacuum five hundred miles above central Nebraska, Karnes leaned back in his seat, turning the odd cigarette case over and over in his hands.

Except for the neat, even checking that covered it, the little three-by-four inch object was entirely featureless. There were no catches or hinges, or even any line of cleavage around the edge. He had already found that it wouldn't open.

Whatever it was, it was most definitely *not* a cigarette case.

The X-ray plates had shown it to be perfectly homogeneous throughout.

As far as I can see, thought Karnes, *it's nothing but a piece of acid-proof plastic, except that the specific gravity is way the hell too high. Maybe if I had cut it open, I could have—*

Karnes didn't push anything on the case, of that he was sure. Nor did he squeeze, shake, or rub it in any unusual way. But something happened; something which he was convinced came from the case in his hands.

He had the definite impression of something akin to a high-pressure firehose squirting from the interior of the case, through his skull, and into and over his brain, washing it and filling it. Little rivers of knowledge trickled down through the convolutions of his brain, collected in pools, and soaked in.

He was never sure just how long the process took but it was certainly not more than a second or two. Afterwards, he just sat there, staring.

From far across the unimaginable depths of the galaxy, fighting its way through the vast, tenuous dust clouds of interstellar space, came a voice: "Are you ill, sir?"

Karnes looked up at the stewardess. "Oh. Oh, no. No, I'm all right. Just thinking. I'm perfectly all right."

He looked at the "cigarette case" again. He knew what it was, now. There wasn't any English word for it, but he guessed "mind impressor" would come close.

It had done just that; impressed his mind with knowledge he should not have; the record of something he had no business knowing.

And he wished to Heaven he didn't!

This, Karnes considered, *is a problem. The stuff is so alien! Just a series of things I know, but can't explain. Like a dream; you know all about it, but it's practically impossible to explain it to anybody else.*

At the spaceport, he was met by an official car. George Lansberg, one of the New York agents, was sitting in the back seat.

"Hi, sleuth. I heard you were coming in, so I asked to meet you." He lowered his voice as Karnes got in and the car pulled away from the parking lot. "How about our boy, Avery?"

Karnes shook his head. "Too late. Thirty million bucks worth of material lost and Avery lost too."

"How come?"

"Had to kill him to keep him from getting away with these."

He showed Lansberg the microfilm squares.

"The photocircuit inserts for the new autopilot. We'd lose everything if the League ever got its hands on these."

"Didn't learn anything from Avery, eh?" Lansberg asked.

"Not a thing." Karnes lapsed into silence. He didn't feel it necessary to mention the mind impressor just yet.

Lansberg stuck a cigarette into his mouth and talked around it as he lit it.

"We've got something you'll be getting in on, now that Avery is taken care of. We've got a fellow named Brittain, real name Bretinov, who is holed up in a little apartment in Brooklyn. He's the sector head for that section, and we know who his informers are, and who he gives orders to. What we don't know is who gives orders to him.

"Now we have it set up for Brittain to get his hands on some very honest-looking, but strictly phony stuff for him to pass on to the next echelon. Then we just sit around and watch until he does pass it."

Karnes found he was listening to Lansberg with only half an ear. His brain was still buzzing with things he'd never heard of, trying to fit things he had always known in with things he knew now but had never known before. Damn that "cigarette case"!

"Sounds like fun," he answered Lansberg.

"Yeah. Great. Well, here we are." They had driven to the Long Island Spaceways Building which also housed the local office.

They got out and went into the building, up the elevator, down a corridor, and into an office suite.

Lansberg said: "I'll wait for you here. We'll get some coffee afterwards."

The redhead behind the front desk smiled up at Karnes.

"Go on in; he's expecting you."

"I don't know whether I ought to leave you out here with Georgie or not," Karnes grinned. "I think he has designs."

"Oh, goodie!" she grinned back.

My, my aren't we clever! His thought was bitter, but his face didn't show it.

Before he went in, he straightened his collar before the wall mirror. He noticed that his plain, slightly tanned face still looked the same as ever. Same ordinary gray-green eyes, same ordinary nose.

Chum, you look *perfectly sane. You* are *perfectly sane. But who in hell would believe it?*

It wouldn't, after all, do any good for him to tell anyone anything he had found. No matter what the answer was, there wasn't anything he could do about it. There wasn't anything *anyone* could do about it.

Thus, Karnes' report to his superior was short, to the point, and censored.

That evening, Karnes sat in his apartment, chain-smoking, and staring out the window. Finally, he mashed out a stub, stood up, and said aloud: "Maybe if I write it down I can get it straight."

He sat down in front of the portable on his desk, rolled in a sheet of paper, and put his fingers on the keys. Then, for a long time, he just sat there, turning it over and over in his mind. Finally, he began to type.

A Set of General Instructions and a Broad Outline on the Purposes and Construction of the Shrine of Earth.

Part One: Historical.

Some hundred or so millennia ago, insofar as the most exacting of historical research can ascertain, our remote ancestors were confined to one planet of the Galaxy; the legendary Earth.

The third planet of Sun (unintelligible number) has long been suspected of being Earth, but it was not until the development of the principles of time transfer that it became possible to check the theory completely.

The brilliant work done by—

(Karnes hesitated over the name, then wrote—)

—Starson on the ancient history and early evolution of the race has shown the theory to be correct. This has opened a new and fascinating field for the study of socioanthropology.

Part Two: Present Purposes and Aims.

Because of the great energy transfer and cosmic danger involved in too frequent or unrestricted time travel, it has been decided that the best method for studying the social problems involved would be to rebuild, in toto, the ancient Earth as it was just after the initial discoveries of atomic power and interplanetary space travel.

In order to facilitate this work, the Surveying Group will translate themselves to the chronological area in question, and obtain complete records of that time, covering the years between (1940) and (2020).

When the survey is complete, the Construction Group will rebuild that civilization with as great an exactness as possible, complete with population, fossil strata, edifices, etc.

Upon the occasion of the opening of the Shrine, the replica of our early civilization will be begun as it was on (January 3, 1953). The population, having been impregnated with the proper memories, will be permitted to go about their lives unhampered.

Karnes stopped again and reread the paragraph he had just written. It sounded different when it was on paper. The dates, for instance, he had put in parentheses because that was the way he had understood them. But he knew that whoever had made the mind-impressor didn't use the same calendar he was used to.

He frowned at the paper, then went on typing.

Part Three: Conduct of Students.

Students wishing to study the Shrine for the purpose of (unintelligible again) must obtain permits from the Galactic Scholars Council, and, upon obtaining such permits, must conduct themselves according to whatever rules may be laid down by such Council.

Part Four: Corrective Action to be Taken.

At certain points in the history of ancient Earth, certain crises arose which, in repetition, would be detrimental to the Shrine. These crises must be mitigated in order that—

Karnes stopped. That was all there was. Except—except for one more little tail end of thought. He tapped the keys again.

(*Continued on Stratum Two*)

Whatever in hell that means, he thought.

He sat back in his chair and went over the two sheets of typed paper. It wasn't complete, not by a long shot. There were little tones of meaning that a printed, or even a spoken word couldn't put over. There were evidences of a vast and certainly superhuman civilization; of an alien and yet somehow completely human way of thinking.

But that was the gist of it. The man he had seen in that new building at Carlson Spacecraft was no ordinary human being.

That, however, didn't bother Karnes half so much as the gray globe the man had disappeared into after he had been shot at. And Karnes knew, now, that the shots probably hadn't missed.

The globe was one of two things. And the intruder had been one of two groups.

(A) One of the Surveyors of Ancient Earth, in which case the globe had been a—well, a time machine. Or

(B) A student, in which case the machine was a type of spacecraft.

The question was: Which?

If it were (A), then he and the world around him were real, living, working out their own destinies toward the end point represented by the man in the gray globe.

But if it were (B)—

Then this was the Shrine, and he and all the rest of Earth were nothing but glorified textbooks!

And there would come crises on the Shrine, duplicates of the crises on old Earth. Except that they wouldn't be permitted to happen. The poor ignorant people on the Shrine had to be coddled, like the children they were. Damn!

Karnes crumpled the sheets of paper in his hands, twisting them savagely. Then he methodically tore them into bits.

When the first dawnlight touched the sea, Karnes was watching it out the east window. It had been twenty-four hours since he had seen the superman walk into his gray globe and vanish.

All night, he had been searching his brain for some clue that would tell him which of the two choices he should believe in. And he couldn't bring himself to believe in either.

Once he had thought: *Why do I believe, then, what the impressor said? Why not just forget it?*

But that didn't help. He *did* believe it. That alien instrument had impressed his mind, not only with the facts themselves, but with an absolute faith that they *were* facts. There was no room for doubt; the knowledge imparted to his mind was true, and he knew it.

For a time, he had been comforted by the thought that the gray globe must be a time machine because of the way it had vanished. It was very comforting until he realized that travel to the stars and beyond didn't necessarily mean a spaceship as he knew spaceships. Teleportation—

Now, with the dawn, Karnes knew there was only one thing he could do.

Somehow, somewhere, there would be other clues—clues a man who knew what to look for might find. The Galactics couldn't be perfect, or they wouldn't have let him get the mind impressor in his hands. Ergo, somewhere they would slip again.

Karnes knew he would spend the rest of his life looking for that one slip. He had to know the truth, one way or another.

Or he might not stay sane.

Lansberg picked him up at eight in a police copter. As they floated toward New York, Karnes' mind settled itself into one cold purpose; a purpose that lay at the base of his brain, waiting.

Lansberg was saying: "—and one of Brittain's men got the stuff last night. He hadn't passed it on to Brittain himself yet this morning, but he very probably will have by the time we get there.

"We've rigged it up so that Brittain will have to pass it to his superior by tomorrow or it will be worthless. When he does, we'll follow it right to the top."

"If we've got every loophole plugged," said Karnes, "we ought to take them easy."

"Brother, I hope so! It took us eight months to get Brittain all hot and bothered over the bait, and another two months to give it to him in a way that wouldn't make him suspicious.

"It's restricted material, of course, so that we can pin a subversive activities rap on them, at least, if not espionage. But we had to argue like hell to keep it restricted; the Spatial Commission was ready to release it, since it's really relatively harmless."

Karnes looked absently at the thin line of smoke wiggling from Lansberg's cigarette.

"You know," he said, "there are times when I wish this war would come right out in the open. Actually, we've been fighting the League for years, but we don't admit it. There have been little disagreements and incidents until the devil won't have it. But it's still supposed to be a 'worry war'."

Lansberg shrugged. "It will get hot just as soon as the Eurasian League figures they are far enough along in spacecraft construction to get the Martian colonies if they win. Then they'll try to smash us before we can retaliate; then, and not before.

"We can't start it. Our only hope is that when they start, they'll underestimate us. Say, what's that you're fooling with?"

The sudden change of subject startled Karnes for an instant. He looked at the mind impressor in his hands. He had been toying with it incessantly, hoping it would repeat its performance, or perhaps give additional information.

"This?" He covered quickly. "It's a—a puzzle. One of those plastic puzzles." *Maybe it doesn't work on the same person twice. If I can get George to fool around with it, he might hit the right combination again.*

"Hmmm. How does it work?" George seemed interested.

Karnes handed it to him. "It has a couple of little sliding weights inside it. You have to turn the thing just right to unlock it, then it comes apart when you slide out a section of the surface. Try it."

Lansberg took it, turned it this way and that, moving his hands over the surface. Karnes watched him for several minutes, but there didn't seem to be any results.

Lansberg looked up from his labors. "I give up. I can't even see where it's supposed to come apart, and I can't feel any weights sliding inside it. Show me how it works."

Karnes thought fast. "Why do you think I was fiddling with it? I don't know how it works. A friend of mine bet me a ten spot that I couldn't figure out the combination."

Lansberg looked back at the impressor in his hands. "Could he do it?"

"A snap. I watched him twice, and I still didn't get it."

"Mmm. Interesting." George went back to work on the "puzzle."

Just before they landed on the roof of the UN annex, Lansberg handed the impressor back to Karnes. It had obviously failed to do what either of them had hoped it would.

"It's your baby," Lansberg said, shaking his head. "All I have to say is it's a hell of a way to earn ten bucks."

Karnes grinned and dropped the thing back in his coat pocket.

By the time that evening had rolled around, Karnes was beginning to get just a little bored. He and Lansberg had been in and out of the New York office in record time. Then they had spent a few hours with New York's Finest and the District Attorney, lining up a net to pick up all the little rats involved.

After that, there was nothing to do but wait.

Karnes slept a couple of hours to catch up, read two magazines from cover to cover, and played eight games of solitaire. He was getting itchy.

His brain kept crackling. *What's the matter with me? I ought to be thinking about this Brittain fellow instead of—*

But, after all, what did Brittain matter? According to the records, he was born Alex Bretinov, in Marseilles, France, in nineteen sixty-eight. His father, a dyed-in-the-wool Old Guard Communist, had been born in Minsk in nineteen forty.

Or had he been wound up, and his clockwork started in January of nineteen fifty-three?

The radio popped. "Eighteen. Alert. Brittain just left his place on foot. Carson, Reymann following. Over."

Lansberg dropped his magazine. "He seems to be heading for the Big Boy—I hope."

The ground car followed him to a subway, and two men on foot followed him in from Flatbush Avenue.

Some hours later, after much devious turning, dodging, and switching, Brittain climbed into a taxi on the corner of Park Avenue and Forty-seventh Street, evidently feeling he had ditched any tails he might have had.

315

Karnes and Lansberg were right behind him in a radio car.

The cab headed due south on Park Avenue, following it until it became Fourth, swung right at Tenth Street, past Grace Church, across Broadway. At Sixth, it angled left toward Greenwich Village.

"Somewhere in the Village, nickels to knotholes," Lansberg guessed as he turned to follow.

Karnes, at the radio, was giving rapid-fire directions over the scrambler-equipped transceiver. By this time, several carloads of agents and police were converging on the cab from every direction. From high above, could be heard the faint hum of 'copters.

Lansberg was exultant. "We've got them for once! And the goods on every essobee in the place."

The cars hummed smoothly through the broad streets, past the shabby-genteel apartment neighborhood. Back in the early sixties, some of these buildings had been high-priced hotels, but the Village had gone to pot since the seventies.

A few minutes later, the cab pulled up in front of an imposing looking building of slightly tarnished aluminum paneling. Brittain got out, paid his fare, and went inside.

As the cab pulled away, Karnes gave orders for it to be picked up a few blocks away, just in case.

The rest of the vehicles began to surround the building.

Karnes, meanwhile, followed Brittain into the foyer of the apartment hotel. It was almost a mistake. Brittain hadn't gone in. Evidently attracted by the footsteps following him, he turned and looked back out. Karnes wasn't more than ten feet away.

Just pretend you live here, thought Karnes, *and bully-boy will never know the difference.*

He walked right on up to the doorway, pretending not to notice Brittain. Evidently, the saboteur was a little flustered, not quite knowing who Karnes was. He, too, pretended that he had no suspicions. He pressed a buzzer on the panel to announce himself to a guest. Karnes noticed it was 523; a fifth floor button.

The front door, inside the foyer, was one of those gadgets with an electric lock that doesn't open unless you either have a key to the building or can get a friend who lives there to let you in.

When Karnes saw Brittain press the buzzer, he waited a second and took a chance.

"Here," he said, fishing in his pocket, "I'll let you in." *That ought to give him the impression I live here.*

Brittain smiled fetchingly. "Thanks, but I—"

Bzzzz! The old-fashioned lock announced that it was open. Karnes stopped fishing and opened the door, letting Brittain follow him in. He stayed in the lead to the elevator, and pushed the button marked "4."

"You getting off before four?" he asked conversationally.

"No."

The elevator slid on up to four without another word being said by either man.

Karnes was judging the speed of the elevator, estimating the time it took for the doors to open as they did so, and making quick mental comparisons with his own ability to climb stairs at a run. The elevator was an old one, and fairly slow—

When the doors slid open, he stepped out and began to walk easily down the hall toward the stairway. When the elevator clicked shut, he broke into a run and hit the stairway at top speed, his long legs taking the steps three at a time.

The stairway was poorly lit, since it was hardly ever used, and, at the fifth floor, he was able to conceal himself in the darkness as Brittain turned up the hall toward 523.

Karnes looked closely at his surroundings for the first time. There was a well-worn, but not ragged, nylon carpet on the floor, dull chrome railing on the stair bannisters, and the halls were lit by old-fashioned glo-plates in the ceiling. The place was inexpensive, but not cheap.

Having made sure that Brittain actually had entered 523, he stepped back toward the elevator in order to notify Lansberg.

A sudden voice said: "You lookin' for-a somebody, meester?"

Karnes turned. An elderly man with a heavy mustache and a heavy body stood partway up the stairs, clad in slacks and shirt.

"Who are you?" frowned Karnes.

"I'm Amati, the supratendent. Why?" The scowl was heavy.

Karnes couldn't take any chances. The man might be perfectly okay, but—

Lansberg's steps sounded, coming up the stairs. With him was a Manhattan Squad officer of the Police Department.

"Shhh, Mr. Amati. C'mere a minute," said the cop.

"Oh. Lootenant Carnotti. Whatsa—"

"Shhhhhh! C'mere, I said, and be quiet!"

"You know this man?" Lansberg asked the policeman softly, indicating Amati.

"Sure. He's okay."

Lansberg turned to the superintendent. "What do you know about the guy who just came in?"

Amati seemed to have realized that something serious was going on, for his voice dropped to a conspiratorial whisper. "I dunno. I don't-a see who it is. Whatsa goin' on, Lootenant Carnotti?"

"What about Apartment 523? Who lives there?" asked Karnes.

"Oh, them? Meester and Meeses Seigert. Artists. Sheesa paint pictures, heesa make statues." Then Amati's eyes widened knowingly. "Ohhh! You guys da Vice Squad, eh? I *theenk* theresa someteeng fonny about them!"

Footsteps sounded coming down the stairs from above.

"We watched the indicator needle on the elevator door in the lobby, and I signalled the 'copters on the roof," Lansberg whispered.

The hallway began to fill quietly with police.

Lieutenant Carnotti assigned one of the men to watch Amati, mainly in order to keep him out of the way, and Karnes led the men down the hall towards 523, guns drawn.

Karnes knocked boldly on the door.

"Yeah? Who is it?" asked someone inside.

Karnes pitched his voice a little lower than normal, and said: "It's-a me, Meester Amati, only me, the soopratendant."

The imitation wasn't perfect, but the muffling effect of the door would offset any imperfections.

"Oh, sure, Mr. Amati. Just a sec." There was a short pause, filled with muffled conversation, then somebody was unlocking the door.

Things began to happen fast. As the door came open, Karnes saw that it had one of those inside chain locks on it that permit the door to be opened only a few inches. Without hesitation, he threw his weight against the door. Lansberg was right behind him.

Under the combined weight of the two men, the chain ripped out of the woodwork, permitting the door to swing free. As it did so, it slammed into the face of the man who had opened it, knocking him backwards.

There were seven or eight other men and two women in the room. One of the men already had a heavy pistol out and was aiming it at the doorway. Karnes dropped to the floor and fired just as the other's pistol went off.

The high-velocity three millimeter slug whined through the air above Karnes' head and buried itself in Lansberg's shoulder. Lansberg dropped, spun halfway around from the shock. His knees hit Karnes in the back.

Karnes lurched forward a little, and regained his balance. Something flew out of his coat pocket and skittered across the floor. Karnes didn't notice what it was until one of the men across the room picked it up.

Brittain had picked up the mind impressor!

Karnes was aware that there were more men behind him firing at another of the conspirators who had made the mistake of drawing a weapon, but he wasn't interested too much. He was watching Brittain.

It only took seconds, but to Karnes it seemed like long minutes. Brittain had evidently thought the impressor was a weapon when he picked it up, and, after seeing his mistake, had started to throw it at the door. Then the impressor shimmered slightly, as though there were a hot radiator between the observor and the object. Brittain stopped, paralyzed, his eyes widening.

Then he gasped and threw the impressor against the floor as hard as he could.

"*NO!*" he screamed, "*IT'S A LIE!*"

The impressor struck the floor and broke. From its shattered interior came a blinding multi-colored glare. Then there was darkness. Karnes fainted.

When Karnes awoke, one of the policemen was shaking him.

"Wake up, Mr. Karnes, wake up!"

Karnes sat up abruptly. "What happened?" He had no time to be original.

"I don't know for sure. One of the Leaguers threw a gas bomb of some sort, and it knocked out everyone in the room. Funny, though, it even knocked out all the Leaguers. When the rest of the boys came in, everybody was out cold on the floor. Most of them are coming out of it now, except for two of the Leaguers. They got some lead in them, though, not gas."

Karnes stood up. He felt a little dizzy, but otherwise there wasn't anything wrong. He surveyed the room.

On the floor was a slightly yellowed spot where the impressor had flared and vanished. Lansberg was unconscious with a copiously bleeding right shoulder. Two other men were rapidly being brought around by the police. Three of the League agents were still out; nobody tried to wake them up, they were being handcuffed.

One of the women was crying and cursing the "damned filthy Nations police" over one of the bodies, and the other woman was sitting stonily, staring at her handcuffs with a faint sneer.

"Where's Brittain?" roared Karnes. The man was nowhere in the room.

"Gone," said one of the cops. "Evidently he skipped out while the rest of us were unconscious. He was the guy who threw the bomb."

Karnes glanced at his watch. One sixteen in the morning. They had been out about twelve or thirteen minutes.

"Where the devil did he go? How in—"

Lieutenant Carnotti came up to him, a look of self-disgust on his face. "I know how he got away, Mr. Karnes; I just talked to the boys on the roof. He grabbed a uniform coat and cap off Sergeant Joseph while he was out and commandeered a 'copter on the roof."

Karnes didn't wait for further information. He ran out into the hall and into the open elevator. Within less than a minute, he was on the roof.

One cop was speaking rapidly into a transmitter.

"—number 3765. Left about ten minutes ago, supposedly for the hospital. Officer Powers in the 'copter with him."

He cut off and looked at Karnes, who was standing over him. His gun was out before he spoke. "Who are you, buddy."

Karnes told him who he was. The cop looked skeptical. Karnes didn't have his hat on, and his clothes were a bit rumpled after his nap on the floor.

Karnes didn't need to say anything; another policeman was going through his pockets, and he found the billfold. As soon as they saw the forgeproof identity card, they relaxed.

"Sorry, Mr. Karnes," said the man at the transceiver, "but we've already let one man get away."

Karnes nodded. "I know. Pure blind luck that his suit was almost the same shade as that gray uniform you guys wear, or he'd never have got away with it. All he needed was the jacket and cap."

"Have any idea which way he went?"

The cop shrugged. "He came up here and told us that three men had been shot down below and some more gassed. He said Mr. Lansberg had sent him for a hospital call. Then he jumped in a 'copter with Powers and headed northeast. We didn't pay much attention. After all, he was wearing a sergeant's stripes."

Northeast. That would be toward Long Island. But, naturally, he would circle; he wouldn't be dumb enough to head in the right direction until he was out of sight. Or would he?

"Get on that radio again," he told the radioman, "—and tell them I want that man alive. Get that—*alive!*"

"Right." The officer switched on his microphone and began to talk.

Karnes pinched the bridge of his nose and closed his eyes in an attempt to concentrate. With Lansberg shot up, that put the Brittain case in his hands. Theoretically, he should be pumping the prisoners down below to find out how much higher the spy ring went.

But his real interest lay in Brittain, himself. There was no doubt that he had received another message from the impressor before he had thrown it down.

Evidently, when the thing broke, the unknown energies which powered it had short-circuited, paralyzing everyone in the room with their mind-impressing effect.

Then why hadn't it affected Brittain? Perhaps his recent exposure to a normal dosage had immunized him. There was no way of knowing—there never would be.

But what was the message Brittain had received from the impressor that would make him react so violently? It couldn't be the same one that he, Karnes, had received.

Continued on Stratum Two!

Sure; that was it! Like the pages in a book. He, himself, had been hit with page one; Brittain had page two. Page three? Lost forever.

Why hadn't they found that 'copter by now? It ought to be easy enough to spot.

He walked over to the edge of the building and looked down. The police were herding the prisoners into the ground cars. Presently, they were gone. One of the police officers touched his shoulder.

"Ready to go, Mr. Karnes?"

Karnes nodded and climbed into the 'copter. The machine lifted and headed toward the Central Police Station.

He was still trying to think when the phone rang. The policeman picked it up.

"3217. Brown speaking. Oh? Yeah, just a second. It's for you, Mr. Karnes."

Karnes took the instrument. "Karnes speaking."

"Radio Central, Mr. Karnes," came the voice. "We just got some more on Brittain. About ten minutes ago, he abandoned the police 'copter. Officer Powers was in the seat, shot through the head. We'll get the essobee on a murder rap, now."

"Where was the 'copter abandoned?"

Radio Central told him and went on: "Funny thing was, he didn't try to hide it or anything. And he stole another 'copter from a private citizen. We're trying to get the description now. I'll call you if anything further comes in."

"Fine." Karnes hung up. The address where Brittain had left the 'copter was in almost a direct line between the apartment building and Long Island Spaceport. But if Brittain were actually heading there, why should he leave such a broad and obvious trail?

He turned to the officer who was driving the 'copter.

"I've got a hunch. Swivel this thing around and head for Long Island. I've got a funny feeling that Brittain will be there. He—"

The phone rang again, and Karnes grabbed it.

"Mr. Karnes, we've found that civilian's 'copter! It's at Long Island Spaceport! Just a second, the stuff's still coming in." Pause. "Get this: A man answering to Brittain's description bought a ticket for the West Coast rocket."

"As you know, that's UN territory, and we have no jurisdiction. The rocket is sealed for takeoff, but they're holding it for us until you get there!"

"Right! I'm headed there now!" he answered quickly.

It was twelve minutes later that the police 'copter settled just outside the rocket enclosure. Karnes had already notified the pilot to be ready for him. He sprinted up the ramp and stood at the airlock of the transcontinental rocket.

It sighed open, and Karnes stepped inside. He was met by a frightened stewardess.

"Tell him to get in here and not to try any funny stuff!" snapped a voice from the passenger cabin.

Brittain was standing at the forward end of the passenger compartment with a levelled gun.

The rocket was tilted at forty-five degrees for the takeoff, and the passenger's seats had swiveled with a section of the flooring to keep them level, which gave the effect of a stairway which climbed toward the pilot's cabin in the forward section of the ship. Brittain's position was at the top of the stairway.

Karnes raised his hands and kept them carefully away from his hip holster.

"All right," called Brittain, "Close that door and get this ship off the ground."

The pilot could hear him through the intercom system. The airlock door slid shut again.

"You and the stewardess get into a seat," the spy continued sharply. "If you try anything funny, I start shooting the other passengers if I can't hit you."

Karnes saw then what hold Brittain had on the pilot. The rocketeer couldn't afford to risk the lives of his passengers.

He and the stewardess slid into the acceleration seats and strapped themselves in. Brittain stepped down the tiered floor and took a rear seat near a frightened-looking blonde girl.

"Anything funny, and Blondie here gets a bullet. Okay, pilot. Take her up!"

There was a faint hiss, and then the rockets began their throbbing roar. Acceleration pressure began to shove the passengers back in their seats. Karnes leaned back and tried—successfully—to suppress the smile of triumph that kept trying to come to his lips.

Brittain had finally made a mistake.

One hundred and twenty-five miles over Pennsylvania, the rockets cut out, and the ship went into free fall. And Brittain's mistake became evident.

With the abrupt cessation of weight, the padded acceleration seats expanded again, pressing the passengers up against their safety straps. But Brittain had failed to strap himself in.

The expanding seat shoved forward and toward the ceiling. Before he could recover from his surprise, Karnes had undone his own seat belt and snapped his body through the air toward Brittain. They collided with a thump and Brittain's body slammed against the roof of the cabin with agonizing force. The gun came out of his hand and clanged against a wall, then drifted off harmlessly. Brittain was out cold.

Karnes handcuffed him securely and, with the stewardess' help, tugged him back to the baggage compartment. One of the passengers was quietly retching into a vacuum disposal chute.

With Brittain securely strapped into an empty baggage rack, Karnes swam back to the pilot's compartment, pulling himself along the railing that ran along the floor.

The pilot looked relieved. "Thank heaven you got the devil! He got wise when we delayed the takeoff, and threatened to start shooting my passengers. There wasn't a thing I could do."

"I know. Let me use your radio."

It took a couple of minutes to get UN International Investigation on the hookup, but Karnes finally was talking to his superior in the UN office. He reported what had happened.

"Fine, Karnes," came the tight-beamed voice. "Now, here's something else you ought to know. Our radar net has spotted robot rockets coming in over the Pole. So far, five of them have been hit by interceptor rockets, but we don't have them all by a long shot.

"Evidently, the League feels that they're ready to slam us, now that they've got Moonbase and two of our spacecraft plants out of the way. *The war is on*, Karnes."

Karnes acknowledged, they cut the connection.

There was one thing burning hotly in his brain. Brittain had fled New York without seeming to care how far they traced him or what kind of trail he left behind. *Why?*

He jerked open the door of the pilot's cabin, and, not bothering to use the rail, launched himself toward the rear of the ship, flipping himself halfway down to land with his feet against the baggage room door. He pulled the door open and pushed inside.

Brittain was still groggy, so Karnes began slapping his face methodically, rocking his head from side to side.

"Okay! Okay! Stop it!" Brittain yelled, fully awake.

Karnes stopped, and Brittain blinked, owlishly. Karnes' hunch factory was still operating at full blast; he was fairly sure that the lie he was about to tell would have all of the desired effect.

"You didn't really think you could get away, did you, bud?" he asked, nastily. "We're headed back for New York now, and you'll stand trial for murder as well as sabotage and espionage."

Brittain's eyes widened in horror.

"What did that mind impressor tell you?" Karnes went on.

Brittain was trying to keep his mouth shut, but at that moment there was a glare of light which flashed bluely through the hard quartz of a nearby window.

From somewhere far to the north, another interceptor rocket had found the atomic warhead of an enemy bomb.

Brittain knew and recognized that flash. He screamed wordlessly and then began to sob like a hysterical child.

Karnes began to slap him again. "Come on, what was it?"

"Don't—don't let them go back to New York! It said—it said—" he gasped and took a deep breath "—WE'LL ALL BE KILLED!" he screamed.

"Why?" Karnes's voice was cold.

"BOMB!" Brittain screamed again.

After a few more minutes of questioning, Karnes finally got the rest of the story from him.

The Galactics had found that on this date a nuclear bomb would get through the UN screen and completely destroy most of Greater New York. Only one other bomb would get through, but it would be thrown off course and land somewhere in the Pacific, having missed Los Angeles entirely.

"Anything else?" asked Karnes after a few seconds of silence from Brittain. "Didn't it say they would have to prevent that?"

Brittain's voice was dull now. "All it said was that the records would have to be preserved. It said that things must go on exactly as before. It said that nothing must interfere with the complete development, whatever that means."

Karnes pushed his way out of the room and back towards the pilot's compartment. What the pilot had to say was no news to Karnes.

"Radio from New York says that a bomb missed LA and hit the ocean. That was a close one."

Karnes nodded silently, and leaned back in the stewardess' seat to think.

No wonder Brittain had been so anxious to get out of New York.

New York would be destroyed, but that was inevitable. The thing that had bothered him, his dilemma, was solved.

Was this the real Earth that he lived in, or a museum that had been set up by the Galactics? If it was old Earth, then man would solve his present problems and go on to solve the problem of time travel and interstellar transportation. The present war would be just another little incident in the far past, like the battles of Gettysburg and Agincourt.

And if it were the museum Earth? No difference. For the Galactics had decided not to interfere. They had decided to let the race of Earth go on as it was—exactly as it had gone before. It made no difference, really. *No difference at all.* A perfect duplication of an original *was* the original, in every meaningful way.

"Funny," said the pilot abruptly, "I'm not getting any signal from New York."

Karnes took a deep breath and bit at his lower lip. But he did not look toward the horror that was New York. The city was gone, but the world was there—solid and real!

You'd better expand your museum a little bit, boys, he thought. *We'll need to include Mars and Venus before very long. And then the stars.*

Cum Grano Salis

Just because a man can do something others can't does not, unfortunately, mean he knows how to do it. One man could eat the native fruit and live ... but how?

"And that," said Colonel Fennister glumly, "appears to be that."

The pile of glowing coals that had been Storage Shed Number One was still sending up tongues of flame, but they were nothing compared with what they'd been half an hour before.

"The smoke smells good, anyway," said Major Grodski, sniffing appreciatively.

The colonel turned his head and glowered at his adjutant.

"There are times, Grodski, when your sense of humor is out of place."

"Yes, sir," said the major, still sniffing. "Funny thing for lightning to do, though. Sort of a dirty trick, you might say."

"*You* might," growled the colonel. He was a short, rather roundish man, who was forever thankful that the Twentieth Century predictions of skin-tight uniforms for the Space Service had never come true. He had round, pleasant, blue eyes, a rather largish nose, and a rumbling basso voice that was a little surprising the first time you heard it, but which seemed to fit perfectly after you knew him better.

Right at the moment, he was filing data and recommendations in his memory, where they would be instantly available for use when he needed them. Not in a physical file, but in his own mind.

All right, Colonel Fennister, he thought to himself, *just what does this mean—to me? And to the rest?*

The Space Service was not old. Unlike the Air Service, the Land Service, or the Sea Service, it did not have centuries or tradition behind it. But it had something else. It had something that none of the other Services had—*Potential*.

In his own mind, Colonel Fennister spelled the word with an upper case *P*, and put the word in italics. It was, to him, a more potent word than any other in the Universe.

Potential.

Potential!

Because the Space Service of the United Earth had more potential than any other Service on Earth. How many seas were there for the Sea Service to sail? How much land could the Land Service march over? How many atmospheres were there for the Air Service to conquer?

Not for any of those questions was there an accurate answer, but for each of those questions, the answer had a limit. But how much space was there for the Space Service to conquer?

Colonel Fennister was not a proud man. He was not an arrogant man. But he *did* have a sense of destiny; he *did* have a feeling that the human race was going somewhere, and he did not intend that that feeling should become totally lost to humanity.

Potential.

Definition: *Potential; that which has a possibility of coming into existence.*

No, more than that. That which has a—

He jerked his mind away suddenly from the thoughts which had crowded into his forebrain.

What were the chances that the first expedition to Alphegar IV would succeed? What were the chances that it would fail?

And (Fennister grinned grimly to himself) what good did it do to calculate chances after the event had happened?

Surrounding the compound had been a double-ply, heavy-gauge, woven fence. It was guaranteed to be able to stop a diplodocus in full charge; the electric potential (*potential!* That word again!) great enough to carbonize anything smaller than a blue whale. No animal on Alphegar IV could possibly get through it.

And none had.

Trouble was, no one had thought of being attacked by something immensely greater than a blue whale, especially since there was no animal larger than a small rhino on the whole planet. Who, after all, could have expected an attack by a blind, uncaring colossus—a monster that had already been dying before it made its attack?

Because no one had thought of the forest.

The fact that the atmospheric potential—the voltage and even the amperage difference between the low-hanging clouds and the ground below—was immensely greater than that of Earth, that had already been determined. But the compound and the defenses surrounding it had already been compensated for that factor.

Who could have thought that a single lightning stroke through one of the tremendous, twelve-hundred-foot trees that surrounded the compound could have felled it? Who could have predicted that it would topple toward the compound itself?

That it would have been burning—that was something that could have been guaranteed, had the idea of the original toppling been considered. Especially after the gigantic wooden life-thing had smashed across the double-ply fence, thereby adding man-made energy to its already powerful bulk and blazing surface.

But—that it would have fallen across Storage Shed Number One? Was *that* predictable?

Fennister shook his head slowly. No. It wasn't. The accident was simply that—an accident. No one was to blame; no one was responsible.

Except Fennister. *He* was responsible. Not for the accident, but for the personnel of the expedition. He was the Military Officer; he was the Man In Charge of Fending Off Attack.

And he had failed.

Because that huge, blazing, stricken tree had toppled majestically down from the sky, crashing through its smaller brethren, to come to rest on Storage Shed Number One, thereby totally destroying the majority of the food supply.

There were eighty-five men on Alphegar IV, and they would have to wait another six months before the relief ship came.

And they didn't have food enough to make it, now that their reserve had been destroyed.

Fennister growled something under his breath.

"What?" asked Major Grodski, rather surprised at his superior's tone.

"I said: 'Water, water, everywhere—', that's what I said."

Major Grodski looked around him at the lush forest which surrounded the double-ply fence of the compound.

"Yeah," he said. "'Nor any drop to drink.' But I wish one of those boards had shrunk—say, maybe, a couple hundred feet."

"I'm going back to my quarters," Fennister said. "I'll be checking with the civilian personnel. Let me know the total damage, will you?"

The major nodded. "I'll let you know, sir. Don't expect good news."

"I won't," said Colonel Fennister, as he turned.

The colonel let his plump bulk sag forward in his chair, and he covered his hands with his eyes. "I can imagine all kinds of catastrophes," he said, with a kind of hysterical glumness, "but this has them all beat."

Dr. Pilar stroked his, short, gray, carefully cultivated beard. "I'm afraid I don't understand. We could all have been killed."

The colonel peeked one out from between the first and second fingers of his right hand. "You think starving to death is cleaner than fire?"

Pilar shook his head slowly. "Of course not. I'm just not certain that we'll all die—that's all."

Colonel Fennister dropped his hands to the surface of his metal desk. "I see," he said dryly. "Where there's life, there's hope. Right? All right, I agree with you." He waved his hand around, in an all-encompassing gesture. "Somewhere out there, we may find food. But don't you see that this puts us in the Siege Position?"

Dr. Francis Pilar frowned. His thick salt-and-pepper brows rumpled in a look of puzzlement. "Siege Position? I'm afraid—"

Fennister gestured with one hand and leaned back in his chair, looking at the scientist across from him. "I'm sorry," he said. "I've let my humiliation get the better of me." He clipped his upper lip between his teeth until his lower incisors were brushed by his crisp, military mustache, and held it there for a moment before he spoke.

"The Siege Position is one that no military commander of any cerebral magnitude whatever allows himself to get into. It is as old as Mankind, and a great deal stupider. It is the position of a beleaguered group which lacks one simple essential to keep them alive until help comes.

"A fighting outfit, suppose, has enough ammunition to stand off two more attacks; but they know that there will be reinforcements within four days. Unfortunately, the enemy can attack *more than twice* before help comes. Help will come too late.

"Or, it could be that they have enough water to last a week, but help won't come for a month.

"You follow me, I'm sure. The point, in so far as it concerns us, is that we have food for about a month, but we won't get help before six months have passed. We know help is coming, but we won't be alive to see it."

Then his eyes lit up in a kind of half hope. "Unless the native flora—"

But even before he finished, he could see the look in Dr. Pilar's eyes.

Broderick MacNeil was a sick man. The medical officers of the Space Service did not agree with him *in toto*, but MacNeil was in a position to know more about his own state of health than the doctors, because it was, after all, he himself who was sick.

Rarely, of course, did he draw the attention of the medical officers to his ever-fluctuating assortment of aches, pains, signs, symptoms, malaises, and malfunctions. After all, it wouldn't do for him to be released from the Service on a Medical Discharge. No, he would suffer in silence for the sake of his chosen career—which, apparently, was to be a permanent Spaceman 2nd Class.

Broderick MacNeil had never seen his medical record, and therefore did not know that, aside from mention of the normal slight defects which every human body possesses, the only note on the records was one which said: "Slight tendency toward hypochondria, compensated for by tendency to immerse self in job at hand. According to psych tests, he can competently handle positions up to Enlisted Space Officer 3rd Class, but positions of ESO/2 and above should be carefully considered. (See Psych Rept. Intelligence Sectn.)"

But, if MacNeil did not know what the medics thought of him, neither did the medics know what he thought of them. Nor did they know that MacNeil carried a secret supply of his own personal palliatives, purgatives and poly-purpose pills. He kept them carefully concealed in a small section of his space locker, and had labeled them all as various vitamin mixtures, which made them seem perfectly legal, and which was not *too* dishonest, since many of them *were* vitamins.

On the morning after the fire, he heaved his well-muscled bulk out of bed and scratched his scalp through the close-cropped brown hair that covered his squarish skull. He did not feel well, and that was a fact. Of course, he had been up half the night fighting the blaze, and that hadn't helped any. He fancied he had a bit of a headache, and his nerves seemed a little jangled. His insides were probably in their usual balky state. He sighed, wished he were in better health, and glanced around at the other members of the company as they rose grumpily from their beds.

He sighed again, opened his locker, took out his depilator, and ran it quickly over his face. Then, from his assortment of bottles, he began picking over his morning dosage. Vitamins, of course; got to keep plenty of vitamins in the system, or it goes all to pot on you. A, B_1, B_2, B_{12}, C, ... and on down the alphabet and past it to A-G. All-purpose mineral capsules, presumably containing every element useful to the human body and possibly a couple that weren't. Two APC capsules. (Aspirin-Phenacetin-Caffeine. He liked the way those words sounded; very medicinal.) A milk-of-magnesia tablet, just in case. A couple of patent-mixture pills that were supposed to increase the bile flow. (MacNeil wasn't quite sure what bile was, but he *was* quite sure that its increased flow would work wonders within.) A largish tablet of sodium bicarbonate to combat excess gastric acidity—obviously a *horrible* condition, whatever it was. He topped it all off with a football-shaped capsule containing Liquid Glandolene—"*Guards the system against glandular imbalance!*"—and felt himself ready to face the day. At least, until breakfast.

He slipped several bottles into his belt-pak after he had put on his field uniform, so that he could get at them at mealtimes, and trudged out toward the mess hall to the meager breakfast that awaited him.

"Specifically," said Colonel Fennister, "what we want to know is: What are our chances of staying alive until the relief ship comes?"

He and most of the other officers were still groggy-eyed, having had too much to do to even get an hour's sleep the night before. Only the phlegmatic Major Grodski looked normal; his eyes were always about half closed.

Captains Jones and Bellwether, in charge of A and B Companies respectively, and their lieutenants, Mawkey and Yutang, all looked grim and irritable.

The civilian components of the policy group looked not one whit better. Dr. Pilar had been worriedly rubbing at his face, so that his normally neat beard had begun to take on the appearance of a ruptured mohair sofa; Dr. Petrelli, the lean, waspish chemist, was nervously trimming his fingernails with his teeth: and the M.D., Dr. Smathers, had a hangdog expression on his pudgy face and had begun drumming his fingers in a staccato tattoo on his round belly.

Dr. Pilar tapped a stack of papers that lay before him on the long table at which they were all seated. "I have Major Grodski's report on the remaining food. There is not enough for all of us to live, even on the most extended rations. Only the strongest will survive."

Colonel Fennister scowled. "You mean to imply that we'll be fighting over the food like animals before this is over? The discipline of the Space Service—"

His voice was angry, but Dr. Pilar cut him off. "It may come to fighting, colonel, but, even if perfect discipline is maintained, what I say will still be true. Some will die early, leaving more food for the remaining men. It has been a long time since anything like this has happened on Earth, but it is not unknown in the Space Service annals."

The colonel pursed his lips and kept his silence. He knew that what the biologist said was true.

"The trouble is," said Petrelli snappishly, "that we are starving in the midst of plenty. We are like men marooned in the middle of an ocean with no water; the water is there, but it's undrinkable."

"That's what I wanted to get at," said Colonel Fennister. "Is there any chance at all that we'll find an edible plant or animal on this planet?"

The three scientists said nothing, as if each were waiting for one of the others to speak.

All life thus far found in the galaxy had had a carbon-hydrogen-oxygen base. Nobody'd yet found any silicon based life, although a good many organisms used the element. No one yet had found a planet with a halogen atmosphere, and, although there might be weird forms of life at the bottom of the soupy atmospheres of the methane-ammonia giants, no brave soul had ever gone down to see—at least, not on purpose, and no information had ever come back.

But such esoteric combinations are not at all necessary for the postulation of wildly variant life forms. Earth itself was prolific in its variations; Earthlike planets were equally inventive. Carbon, hydrogen, and oxygen, plus varying proportions of phosphorus, potassium, iodine, nitrogen, sulfur, calcium, iron, magnesium, manganese, and strontium, plus a smattering of trace elements, seem to be able to cook up all kinds of life under the strangest imaginable conditions.

Alphegar IV was no different than any other Earth-type planet in that respect. It had a plant-dominated ecology; the land areas were covered with gigantic trees that could best be described as crosses between a California sequoia and a cycad, although such a description would have made a botanist sneer and throw up his hands. There were enough smaller animals to keep the oxygen-carbon-dioxide cycle nicely balanced, but the animals had not evolved anything larger than a rat, for some reason. Of course, the sea had evolved some pretty huge monsters, but the camp of the expedition was located a long way from the sea, so there was no worry from that quarter.

At the time, however, the members of the expedition didn't know any of that information for sure. The probe teams had made spot checks and taken random samples, but it was up to the First Analytical Expedition to make sure of everything.

And this much they had discovered: The plants of Alphegar IV had a nasty habit of killing test animals.

"Of course," said Dr. Pilar, "we haven't tested every plant yet. We may come across something."

"What is it that kills the animals?" asked young Captain Bellwether.

"Poison," said Major Grodski.

Pilar ignored him. "Different things. Most of them we haven't been able to check thoroughly. We found some vines that were heavily laced with cyanide, and there were recognizable alkaloids in several of the shrubs, but most of them are not that direct. Like Earth plants, they vary from family to family; the deadly nightshade is related to both the tobacco plant and the tomato."

He paused a moment, scratching thoughtfully at his beard.

"Tell you what; let's go over to the lab, and I'll show you what we've found so far."

Colonel Fennister nodded. He was a military man, and he wasn't too sure that the scientists' explanations would be very clear, but if there was information to be had, he might as well make the most of it.

SM/2 Broderick MacNeil kept a firm grip on his blast rifle and looked around at the surrounding jungle, meanwhile thanking whatever gods there were that he hadn't been put on the fence-mending detail. Not that he objected violently to work, but he preferred to be out here in the forest just now. Breakfast hadn't been exactly filling, and he was hungry.

Besides, this was his pet detail, and he liked it. He had been going out with the technicians ever since the base had been finished, a couple of weeks before, and he was used to the work. The biotechnicians came out to gather specimens, and it was his job, along with four others, to guard them—make sure that no wild animal got them while they were going about their duties. It was a simple job, and one well suited to MacNeil's capacities.

He kept an eye on the technicians. They were working on a bush of some kind that had little thorny-looking nuts on it, clipping bits off here and there. He wasn't at all sure what they did with all those little pieces and bits, but that was none of his business, anyway. Let the brains take care of that stuff; his job was to make sure they weren't interrupted in whatever it was they were doing. After watching the three technicians in total incomprehension for a minute or so, he turned his attention to the surrounding forest. But he was looking for a plant, not an animal.

And he finally saw what he was looking for.

The technicians paid him no attention. They rarely did. They had their job, and he had his. Of course, he didn't want to be caught breaking regulations, but he knew how to avoid that catastrophe. He walked casually toward the tree, as though he were only slightly interested in it.

He didn't know what the name of the tree was. He'd asked a technician once, and the tech had said that the tree didn't have any name yet. Personally, MacNeil thought it was silly for a thing not to have a name. Hell, *everything* had a name.

But, if they didn't want to tell him what it was, that was all right with him, too. He called it a banana-pear tree.

Because that's what the fruit reminded him of.

The fruit that hung from the tree were six or eight inches long, fat in the middle, and tapering at both ends. The skin was a pale chartreuse in color, with heliotrope spots.

MacNeil remembered the first time he'd seen one, the time he'd asked the tech what its name was. The tech had been picking some of them and putting them into plastic bags, and the faint spark of MacNeil's dim curiosity had been brought to feebly flickering life.

"Hey, Doc," he'd said, "whatcha gonna do with them things?"

"Take 'em to the lab," said the technician, engrossed in his work.

MacNeil had digested that carefully. "Yeah?" he'd said at last. "What for?"

The technician had sighed and popped another fruit into a bag. He had attempted to explain things to Broderick MacNeil before and given it up as a bad job. "We just feed 'em to the monkeys, Mac, that's all."

"Oh," said Broderick MacNeil.

Well, that made sense, anyhow. Monkeys got to eat *something*, don't they? Sure. And he had gazed at the fruit in interest.

Fresh fruit was something MacNeil missed. He'd heard that fresh fruit was necessary for health, and on Earth he'd always made sure that he had plenty of it. He didn't want to get sick. But they didn't ship fresh fruit on an interstellar expedition, and MacNeil had felt vaguely apprehensive about the lack.

Now, however, his problems were solved. He knew that it was strictly against regulations to eat native fruit until the brass said so, but that didn't worry him too much. He'd heard somewhere that a man can eat anything a monkey can, so he wasn't worried about it. So he'd tried one. It tasted fine, something like a pear and something like a banana, and different from either. It was just fine.

Since then, he'd managed to eat a couple every day, so's to get his fresh fruit. It kept him healthy. Today, though, he needed more than just health; he was hungry, and the banana-pears looked singularly tempting.

When he reached the tree, he turned casually around to see if any of the others were watching. They weren't, but he kept his eye on them while he picked several of the fruit. Then he turned carefully around, and, with his back to the others, masking his movements with his own body, he began to munch contentedly on the crisp flesh of the banana-pears.

"Now, take this one, for instance," said Dr. Pilar. He was holding up a native fruit. It bulged in the middle, and had a chartreuse rind with heliotrope spots on it. "It's a very good example of exactly what we're up against. Ever since we discovered this particular fruit, we've been interested in it because the analyses show that it should be an excellent source of basic food elements. Presumably, it even tastes good; our monkeys seemed to like it."

"What's the matter with it, then?" asked Major Grodski, eying the fruit with sleepy curiosity.

Dr. Pilar gave the thing a wry look and put it back in the specimen bag. "Except for the fact that it has killed every one of our test specimens, we don't know what's wrong with it."

Colonel Fennister looked around the laboratory at the cages full of chittering animals—monkeys, white mice, rats, guinea pigs, hamsters, and the others. Then he looked back at the scientist. "Don't you know what killed them?"

Pilar didn't answer; instead, he glanced at Dr. Smathers, the physician.

Smathers steepled his fingers over his abdomen and rubbed his fingertips together. "We're not sure. Thus far, it looks as though death was caused by oxygen starvation in the tissues."

"Some kind of anemia?" hazarded the colonel.

Smathers frowned. "The end results are similar, but there is no drop in the hemoglobin—in fact, it seems to rise a little. We're still investigating that. We haven't got all the answers yet, by any means, but since we don't quite know what to look for, we're rather hampered."

The colonel nodded slowly. "Lack of equipment?"

"Pretty much so," admitted Dr. Smathers. "Remember, we're just here for preliminary investigation. When the ship brings in more men and equipment—"

His voice trailed off. Very likely, when the ship returned, it would find an empty base. The first-string team simply wasn't set up for exhaustive work; its job was to survey the field in general and mark out the problems for the complete team to solve.

Establishing the base had been of primary importance, and that was the sort of equipment that had been carried on the ship. That—and food. The scientists had only the barest essentials to work with; they had no electron microscopes or any of the other complex instruments necessary for exhaustive biochemical work.

Now that they were engaged in a fight for survival, they felt like a gang of midgets attacking a herd of water-buffalo with penknives. Even if they won the battle, the mortality rate would be high, and their chances of winning were pretty small.

The Space Service officers and the scientists discussed the problem for over an hour, but they came to no promising conclusion.

At last, Colonel Fennister said: "Very well, Dr. Pilar; we'll have to leave the food supply problem in your hands. Meanwhile, I'll try to keep order here in the camp."

SM/2 Broderick MacNeil may not have had a top-level grade of intelligence, but by the end of the second week, his conscience was nagging him, and he was beginning to wonder who was goofing and why. After much thinking—if we may so refer to MacNeil's painful cerebral processes—he decided to ask a few cautious questions.

Going without food tends to make for mental fogginess, snarling tempers, and general physical lassitude in any group of men. And, while quarter rations were not quite starvation meals, they closely approached it. It was fortunate, therefore, that MacNeil decided to approach Dr. Pilar.

Dr. Petrelli's temper, waspish by nature, had become positively virulent in the two weeks that had passed since the destruction of the major food cache. Dr. Smathers was losing weight from his excess, but his heretofore pampered stomach was voicelessly screaming along his nerve passages, and his fingers had become shaky, which is unnerving in a surgeon, so his temper was no better than Petrelli's.

Pilar, of course, was no better fed, but he was calmer than either of the others by disposition, and his lean frame didn't use as much energy. So, when the big hulking spaceman appeared at the door of his office with his cap in his hands, he was inclined to be less brusque than he might have been.

"Yes? What is it?" he asked. He had been correlating notes in his journal with the thought in the back of his mind that he would never finish it, but he felt that a small respite might be relaxing.

MacNeil came in and looked nervously around at the plain walls of the pre-fab plastic dome-hut as though seeking consolation from them. Then he straightened himself in the approved military manner and looked at the doctor.

"You Dr. Piller? Sir?"

"Pi*lar*," said the scientist in correction. "If you're looking for the medic, you'll want Dr. Smathers, over in G Section."

"Oh, yessir," said MacNeil quickly, "I know that. But I ain't sick." He didn't feel *that* sick, anyway. "I'm Spaceman Second MacNeil, sir, from B Company. Could I ask you something, sir?"

Pilar sighed a little, then smiled. "Go ahead, spaceman."

MacNeil wondered if maybe he'd ought to ask the doctor about his sacroiliac pains, then decided against it. This wasn't the time for it. "Well, about the food. Uh … Doc, can men eat monkey food all right?"

Pilar smiled. "Yes. What food there is left for the monkeys has already been sent to the men's mess hall." He didn't add that the lab animals would be the next to go. Quick-frozen, they might help eke out the dwindling food supply, but it would be better not to let the men know what they were eating for a while. When they got hungry enough, they wouldn't care.

But MacNeil was plainly puzzled by Pilar's answer. He decided to approach the stuff as obliquely as he knew how.

"Doc, sir, if I … I uh … well—" He took the bit in his teeth and plunged ahead. "If I done something against the regulations, would you have to report me to Captain Bellwether?"

Dr. Pilar leaned back in his chair and looked at the big man with interest. "Well," he said carefully, "that would all depend on what it was. If it was something really … ah … dangerous to the welfare of the expedition, I'd have to say something about it, I suppose, but I'm not a military officer, and minor infractions don't concern me."

MacNeil absorbed that "Well, sir, this ain't much, really—I ate something I shouldn't of."

Pilar drew down his brows. "Stealing food, I'm afraid, would be a major offense, under the circumstances."

MacNeil looked both startled and insulted. "Oh, nossir! I never swiped no food! In fact, I've been givin' my chow to my buddies."

Pilar's brows lifted. He suddenly realized that the man before him looked in exceptionally good health for one who had been on a marginal diet for two weeks. "Then what *have* you been living on?"

"The monkey food, sir."

"*Monkey food?*"

"Yessir. Them greenish things with the purple spots. You know—them fruits you feed the monkeys on."

Pilar looked at MacNeil goggle-eyed for a full thirty seconds before he burst into action.

"No, of course I won't punish him," said Colonel Fennister. "Something will have to go on the record, naturally, but I'll just restrict him to barracks for thirty days and then recommend him for light duty. But are you *sure*?"

"I'm sure," said Pilar, half in wonder.

Fennister glanced over at Dr. Smathers, now noticeably thinner in the face. The medic was looking over MacNeil's record. "But if that fruit kills monkeys and rats and guinea pigs, how can a *man* eat it?"

"Animals differ," said Smathers, without taking his eyes off the record sheets. He didn't amplify the statement.

The colonel looked back at Pilar.

"That's the trouble with test animals," Dr. Pilar said, ruffling his gray beard with a fingertip. "You take a rat, for instance. A rat can live on a diet that would kill a monkey. If there's no vitamin A in the diet, the monkey dies, but the rat makes his own vitamin A; he doesn't need to import it, you might say, since he can synthesize it in his own body. But a monkey can't.

"That's just one example. There are hundreds that we know of and God alone knows how many that we haven't found yet."

Fennister settled his own body more comfortably in the chair and scratched his head thoughtfully. "Then, even after a piece of alien vegetation has passed all the animal tests, you still couldn't be sure it wouldn't kill a human?"

"That's right. That's why we ask for volunteers. But we haven't lost a man so far. Sometimes a volunteer will get pretty sick, but if a food passes all the other tests, you can usually depend on its not killing a human being."

"I gather that this is a pretty unusual case, then?"

Pilar frowned. "As far as I know, yes. But if something kills all the test animals, we don't ask for humans to try it out. We assume the worst and forget it." He looked musingly at the wall. "I wonder how many edible plants we've by-passed that way?" he asked softly, half to himself.

"What are you going to do next?" the colonel asked. "My men are getting hungry."

Smathers looked up from the report in alarm, and Pilar had a similar expression on his face.

"For Pete's sake," said Smathers, "don't tell anyone—not *anyone*—about this, just yet. We don't want all your men rushing out in the forest to gobble down those things until we are more sure of them. Give us a few more days at least."

The colonel patted the air with a hand. "Don't worry. I'll wait until you give me the go-ahead. But I'll want to know your plans."

Pilar pursed his lips for a moment before he spoke. "We'll check up on MacNeil for another forty-eight hours. We'd like to have him transferred over here, so that we can keep him in isolation. We'll feed him more of the … uh … what'd he call 'em, Smathers?"

"Banana-pears."

"We'll feed him more banana-pears, and keep checking. If he is still in good shape, we'll ask for volunteers."

"Good enough," said the colonel. "I'll keep in touch."

On the morning of the third day in isolation, MacNeil rose early, as usual, gulped down his normal assortment of vitamins, added a couple of aspirin tablets, and took a dose of Epsom salts for good measure. Then he yawned and leaned back to wait for breakfast. He was certainly getting enough fresh fruit, that was certain. He'd begun to worry about whether he was getting a balanced diet—he'd heard that a balanced diet was very important—but he figured that the doctors knew what they were doing. Leave it up to them.

He'd been probed and needled and tested plenty in the last couple of days, but he didn't mind it. It gave him a feeling of confidence to know that the doctors were taking care of him. Maybe he ought to tell them about his various troubles; they all seemed like nice guys. On the other hand, it wouldn't do to get booted out of the Service. He'd think it over for a while.

He settled back to doze a little while he waited for his breakfast to be served. Sure was nice to be taken care of.

Later on that same day, Dr. Pilar put out a call for volunteers. He still said nothing about MacNeil; he simply asked the colonel to say that it had been eaten successfully by a test animal.

The volunteers ate their banana-pears for lunch, approaching them warily at first, but soon polishing them off with gusto, proclaiming them to have a fine taste.

The next morning, they felt weak and listless.

Thirty-six hours later, they were dead.

"Oxygen starvation," said Smathers angrily, when he had completed the autopsies.

Broderick MacNeil munched pleasantly on a banana-pear that evening, happily unaware that three of his buddies had died of eating that self-same fruit.

The chemist, Dr. Petrelli, looked at the fruit in his hand, snarled suddenly, and smashed it to the floor. Its skin burst, splattering pulp all over the gray plastic.

"It looks," he said in a high, savage voice, "as if that hulking idiot will be the only one left alive when the ship returns!" He turned to look at Smathers, who was peering through a binocular microscope. "Smathers, what makes him different?"

"How do I know?" growled Dr. Smathers, still peering. "There's something different about him, that's all."

Petrelli forcibly restrained his temper. "Very funny," he snapped.

"Not funny at all," Smathers snapped back. "No two human beings are identical—you know that." He lifted his gaze from the eyepiece of the instrument and settled in on the chemist. "He's got AB blood type, for one thing, which none of the volunteers had. Is that what makes him immune to whatever poison is in those things? I don't know.

"Were the other three allergic to some protein substance in the fruit, while MacNeil isn't? I don't know.

"Do his digestive processes destroy the poison? I don't know.

"It's got something to do with his blood, I think, but I can't even be sure of that. The leucocytes are a little high, the red cell count is a little low, the hemoglobin shows a little high on the colorimeter, but none of 'em seems enough to do any harm.

"It might be an enzyme that destroys the ability of the cells to utilize oxygen. It might be *anything*!"

His eyes narrowed then, as he looked at the chemist. "After all, why haven't you isolated the stuff from the fruit?"

"There's no clue as to what to look for," said Petrelli, somewhat less bitingly. "The poison might be present in microscopic amounts. Do you know how much botulin toxin it takes to kill a man? A fraction of a milligram!"

Smathers looked as though he were about to quote the minimum dosage, so Petrelli charged on: "If you think anyone could isolate an unknown organic compound out of a—"

"Gentlemen! *Please!*" said Dr. Pilar sharply. "I realize that this is a strain, but bickering won't help. What about your latest tests on MacNeil, Dr. Smathers?"

"As far as I can tell, he's in fine health. And I can't understand why," said the physician in a restrained voice.

Pilar tapped one of the report sheets. "You mean the vitamins?"

"I mean the vitamins," said Smathers. "According to Dr. Petrelli, the fruits contain neither A nor B_1. After living solely on them for four weeks now, he should be beginning to show some deficiencies—but he's not."

"No signs?" queried Dr. Pilar. "No symptoms?"

"No signs—at least no abnormal ones. He's not getting enough protein, but, then, none of us is." He made a bitter face. "But he has plenty of symptoms."

Dr. Petrelli raised a thin eyebrow. "What's the difference between a sign and a symptom?"

"A sign," said Smathers testily, "is something that can be objectively checked by another person than the patient. Lesions, swellings, inflammations, erratic heartbeat, and so on. A symptom is a subjective feeling of the patient, like aches, pains, nausea, dizziness, or spots before the eyes.

"And MacNeil is beginning to get all kinds of symptoms. Trouble is, he's got a record of hypochondria, and I can't tell which of the symptoms are psychosomatic and which, if any, might be caused by the fruit."

"The trouble is," said Petrelli, "that we have an unidentifiable disease caused by an unidentifiable agent which is checked by an unidentifiable something in MacNeil. And we have neither the time nor the equipment to find out. This is a job that a fully equipped research lab might take a couple of years to solve."

"We can keep trying," said Pilar, "and hope we stumble across it by accident."

Petrelli nodded and picked up the beaker he'd been heating over an electric plate. He added a chelating agent which, if there were any nickel present, would sequester the nickel ions and bring them out of solution as a brick-red precipitate.

Smathers scowled and bent over his microscope to count more leucocytes.

Pilar pushed his notes aside and went over to check his agar plates in the constant-temperature box.

The technicians who had been listening to the conversation with ears wide open went back to their various duties.

And all of them tried in vain to fight down the hunger pangs that were corroding at their insides.

Broderick MacNeil lay in his bed and felt pleasantly ill. He treasured each one of his various symptoms; each pain and ache was just right. He hadn't been so comfortable in years. It really felt fine to have all those doctors fussing over him.

They got snappy and irritable once in a while, but then, all them brainy people had a tendency to do that. He wondered how the rest of the boys were doing on their diet of banana-pears. Too bad they weren't getting any special treatment.

MacNeil had decided just that morning that he'd leave the whole state of his health in the hands of the doctors. No need for a fellow to dose himself when there were three medics on the job, was there? If he needed anything, they'd give it to him, so he'd decided to take no medicine.

A delightful, dulling lassitude was creeping over him.

"MacNeil! *MacNeil!* Wake up, MacNeil!"

The spaceman vaguely heard the voice, and tried to respond, but a sudden dizziness overtook him. His stomach felt as though it were going to come loose from his interior.

"I'm sick," he said weakly. Then, with a terrible realization, "I'm really *awful* sick!"

He saw Dr. Smathers' face swimming above him and tried to lift himself from the bed. "Shoulda taken pills," he said through the haze that was beginning to fold over him again. "Locker box." And then he was unconscious again.

Dr. Smathers looked at him bleakly. The same thing was killing MacNeil as had killed the others. It had taken longer—much longer. But it had come.

And then the meaning of the spaceman's mumbled words came to him. Pills? Locker box?

He grabbed the unconscious man's right hand and shoved his right thumb up against the sensor plate in the front of the metal box next to the bed. He could have gotten the master key from Colonel Fennister, but he hadn't the time.

The box door dilated open, and Dr. Smathers looked inside.

When he came across the bottles, he swore under his breath, then flung the spaceman's arm down and ran from the room.

"That's where he was getting his vitamins, then," said Dr. Pilar as he looked over the assortment of bottles that he and Smathers had taken from the locker box. "Look at 'em. He's got almost as many pills as you have." He looked up at the physician. "Do you suppose it was just vitamins that kept him going?"

"I don't know," said Smathers. "I've given him massive doses of every one of the vitamins—from my own supplies, naturally. He may rally round, if that's what it was. But why would he suddenly be affected by the stuff *now*?"

"Maybe he quit taking them?" Pilar made it half a question.

"It's possible," agreed Smathers. "A hypochondriac will sometimes leave off dosing himself if there's a doctor around to do it for him. As long as the subconscious need is filled, he's happy." But he was shaking his head.

"What's the matter?" Pilar asked.

Smathers pointed at the bottles. "Some of those are mislabeled. They all say vitamins of one kind or another on the label, but the tablets inside aren't all vitamins. MacNeil's been giving himself all kinds of things."

Pilar's eyes widened a trifle. "Do you suppose—"

"That one of them is an antidote?" Smathers snorted. "Hell, anything's possible at this stage of the game. The best thing we can do, I think, is give him a dose of everything there, and see what happens."

"Yeah, Doc, yeah," said MacNeil smiling weakly, "I feel a little better. Not real good, you understand, but better."

Under iron control, Dr. Smathers put on his best bedside manner, while Pilar and Petrelli hovered in the background.

"Now, look, son," said Smathers in a kindly voice, "we found the medicines in your locker box."

MacNeil's face fell, making him look worse. He'd dropped down close to death before the conglomerate mixture which had been pumped into his stomach had taken effect, and Smathers had no desire to put too much pressure on the man.

"Now, don't worry about it, son," he said hurriedly; "We'll see to it that you aren't punished for it. It's all right. We just want to ask you a few questions."

"Sure, Doc; anything," said MacNeil. But he still looked apprehensive.

"Have you been dosing yourself pretty regularly with these things?"

"Well … uh … well, yeah. Sometimes." He smiled feebly. "Sometimes I didn't feel so good, and I didn't want to bother the medics. You know how it is."

"Very considerate, I'm sure," said Smathers with just the barest trace of sarcasm, which, fortunately, fell unheeded on MacNeil's ears. "But which ones did you take every day?"

"Just the vitamins." He paused. "And … uh … maybe an aspirin. The only things I took real regular were the vitamins, though. That's all right ain't it? Ain't vitamins food?"

"Sure, son, sure. What did you take yesterday morning, before you got so sick?"

"Just the vitamins," MacNeil said stoutly. "I figured that since you docs was takin' care of me, I didn't need no medicine."

Dr. Smathers glanced up hopelessly at the other two men. "That eliminates the vitamins," he said, *sotto voce*. He looked back at the patient. "No aspirin? No APC's? You didn't have a headache at all?"

MacNeil shook his head firmly. "I don't get headaches much." Again he essayed a feeble smile. "I ain't like you guys, I don't overwork my brains."

"I'm sure you don't," said Smathers. Then his eyes gleamed. "You have quite a bit of stomach trouble, eh? Your digestion bad?"

"Yeah. You know; I told you about it. I get heartburn and acid stomach pretty often. And constipation."

"What do you take for that?"

"Oh, different things. Sometimes a soda pill, sometimes milk of magnesia, different things."

Smathers looked disappointed, but before he could say anything, Dr. Petrelli's awed but excited voice came from behind him. "Do you take Epsom salts?"

"Yeah."

"I wonder—" said Petrelli softly.

And then he left for the lab at a dead run.

Colonel Fennister and Major Grodski sat at the table in the lab, munching on banana-pears, blissfully enjoying the sweet flavor and the feeling of fullness they were imparting to their stomachs.

"MacNeil can't stay in the service, of course," said Fennister. "That is, not in any space-going outfit. We'll find an Earthside job for him, though. Maybe even give him a medal. You sure these things won't hurt us?"

Dr. Pilar started to speak, but Petrelli cut him off.

"Positive," said the chemist. "After we worked it out, it was pretty simple. The 'poison' was a chelating agent, that's all. You saw the test run I did for you."

The colonel nodded. He'd watched the little chemist add an iron salt to some of the fruit juice and seen it turn red. Then he'd seen it turn pale yellow when a magnesium salt was added. "But what's a chelating agent?" he asked.

"There are certain organic compounds," Dr. Petrelli explained, "that are … well, to put it simply, they're attracted by certain ions. Some are attracted by one ion, some by another. The chelating molecules cluster around the ion and take it out of circulation, so to speak; they neutralize it, in a way.

"Look, suppose you had a dangerous criminal on the loose, and didn't have any way to kill him. If you kept him surrounded by policemen all the time, he couldn't do anything. See?"

The Space Service Officers nodded their understanding.

"We call that 'sequestering' the ion," the chemist continued. "It's used quite frequently in medicine, as Dr. Smathers will tell you. For instance, beryllium ions in the body can be deadly; beryllium poisoning is nasty stuff. But if the patient is treated with the proper chelating agent, the ions are surrounded and don't do any more damage. They're still there, but now they're harmless, you see."

"Well, then," said the colonel, "just what did this stuff in the fruit do?"

"It sequestered the iron ions in the body. They couldn't do their job. The body had to quit making hemoglobin, because hemoglobin needs iron. So, since there was no hemoglobin in the bloodstream, the patient developed sudden pernicious anemia and died of oxygen starvation."

Colonel Fennister looked suddenly at Dr. Smathers. "I thought you said the blood looked normal."

"It did," said the physician. "The colorimeter showed extra hemoglobin, in fact. But the chelating agent in the fruit turns red when it's connected up with iron—in fact, it's even redder than blood hemoglobin. And the molecules containing the sequestered iron tend to stick to the outside of the red blood cells, which threw the whole test off."

"As I understand it, then," said Major Grodski, "the antidote for the … uh … chelating agent is magnesium?"

"That's right," said Dr. Petrelli, nodding. "The stuff prefers magnesium ions to ferrous ions. They fit better within the chelating ring. Any source of magnesium will do, so long as there's plenty of it. MacNeil was using milk of magnesia, which is the hydroxide, for 'gastric acidity'. It's changed to chloride in the stomach. And he was using Epsom salts—the sulfate, and magnesium citrate as laxatives. He was well protected with magnesium ions."

"We tried it ourselves first, naturally," said Dr. Pilar. "We haven't had any ill effects for two days, so I think we'll be able to make it until the ship comes."

Major Grodski sighed. "Well, if not, I'll at least die with a full stomach." He reached for another banana-pear, then looked over at Petrelli. "Pass the salt, please."

Silently and solemnly, the chemist handed him the Epsom salts.

THE END

Psichopath

Th he man in the pastel blue topcoat walked with steady purpose, but without haste, through the chill, wind-swirled drizzle that filled the air above the streets of Arlington, Virginia. His matching blue cap-hood was pulled low over his forehead, and the clear, infrared radiating face mask had been flipped down to protect his chubby cheeks and round nose from the icy wind.

No one noticed him particularly. He was just another average man who blended in with all the others who walked the streets that day. No one recognized him; his face did not appear often in public places, except in his own state, and, even so, it was a thoroughly ordinary face. But, as he walked, Senator John Peter Gonzales was keeping a mental, fine-webbed, four-dimensional net around him, feeling for the slightest touch of recognition. He wanted no one to connect him in any way with his intended destination.

It was not his first visit to the six-floor brick building that stood on a street in a lower-middle-class district of Arlington. Actually, government business took him there more often than would have been safe for the average man-on-the-street. For Senator Gonzales, the process of remaining incognito was so elementary that it was almost subconscious.

Arriving at his destination, he paused on the sidewalk to light a cigarette, shielding it against the wind and drizzle with cupped hands while his mind made one last check on the surroundings. Then he strode quickly up the five steps to the double doors which were marked: *The Society For Mystical And Metaphysical Research, Inc.*

Just as he stepped in, he flipped the face shield up and put on an old-fashioned pair of thick-lensed, black-rimmed spectacles. Then, his face assuming a bland smile that would have been completely out of place on Senator Gonzales, he went from the foyer into the front office.

"Good afternoon, Mrs. Jesser," he said, in a high, smooth, slightly accented voice that was not his own. "I perceive by your aura that you are feeling well. Your normal aura-color is tinged with a positive golden hue."

Mrs. Jesser, a well-rounded matron in her early forties, rose to the bait like a porpoise being hand-fed at a Florida zoo. "*Dear* Swami Chandra! How perfectly wonderful to see you again! You're looking *very* well your-*self*."

The Swami, whose Indian blood was of the Aztec rather than the Brahmin variety, nonetheless managed to radiate all the mystery of the East. "My well-being, dear Mrs. Jesser, is due to the fact that I have been communing for the past three months with my very good friend, the Fifth Dalai Lama. A most refreshingly wise person." Senator Gonzales was fond of the Society's crackpot receptionist, and he knew exactly what kind of hokum would please her most.

"Oh, I *do* hope you will find time to tell me *all* about it," she said effusively. "Mr. Balfour isn't in the city just now," she went on. "He's lecturing in New York on the history of flying saucer sightings. Do you realize that this is the fortieth anniversary of the first saucer sighting, back in 1944?"

"The first *photographed* sighting," the Swami corrected condescendingly. "Our friends have been watching and guiding us for far longer than that, and were sighted many times before they were photographed."

Mrs. Jesser nodded briskly. "Of course. You're right, as always, Swami."

"I am sorry to hear," the Swami continued smoothly, "that I will not be able to see Mr. Balfour. However, I came at the call of Mr. Brian Taggert, who is expecting me."

Mrs. Jesser glanced down at her appointment sheet. "He didn't mention an appointment to me. However—" She punched a button on the intercom. "Mr. Taggert? Swami Chandra is here to see you. He says he has an appointment."

Brian Taggert's deep voice came over the instrument. "The Swami, as usual, is very astute. I have been thinking about calling him. Send him right up."

"You may go up, Swami," said Mrs. Jesser, wide-eyed. She watched in awe as the Swami marched regally through the inner door and began to climb the stairs toward the sixth floor.

One way to hide an ex-officio agency of the United States Government was to label it truthfully—*The Society For Mystical And Metaphysical Research*. In spite of the fact that the label was literally true, it sounded so crackpot that no one but a crackpot would bother to look into it. As a consequence, better than ninety per cent of the membership of the Society was composed of just such people. Only a few members of the "core" knew the organization's true function and purpose. And as long as such scatter-brains as Mrs. Jesser and Mr. Balfour were in there pitching, no one would ever penetrate to the actual core of the Society.

The senator had already pocketed the exaggerated glasses by the time he reached the sixth floor, and his face had lost its bland, overly-wise smile. He pushed open the door to Taggert's office.

"Have you got any ideas yet?" he asked quickly.

Brian Taggert, a heavily-muscled man with dark eyes and black, slightly wavy hair, sat on the edge of a couch in one corner of the room. His desk across the room was there for paperwork only, and Taggert had precious little of that to bother with.

He took a puff from his heavy-bowled briar. "We're going to have to send an agent in there. Someone who can be on the spot. Someone who can get the feel of the situation first hand."

"That'll be difficult. We can't just suddenly stick an unknown in there and have an excuse for his being there. Couldn't Donahue or Reeves—"

Taggert shook his head. "Impossible, John. Extrasensory perception can't replace sight, any more than sight can replace hearing. You know that."

"Certainly. But I thought we could get enough information that way to tell us who our saboteur is. No dice, eh?"

"No dice," said Taggert. "Look at the situation we've got there. The purpose of the Redford Research Team is to test the Meson Ultimate Decay Theory of Dr. Theodore Nordred. Now, if we—"

Senator Gonzales, walking across the room toward Taggert, gestured with one hand. "I know! I know! Give me *some* credit for intelligence! But we *do* have one suspect, don't we? What about *him*?"

Taggert chuckled through a wreath of smoke. "Calm down, John. Or are you trying to give me your impression of Mrs. Jesser in a conversation with a saucerite?"

The senator laughed and sat down in a nearby chair. "All right. Sorry. But this whole thing is lousing up our entire space program. First off, we nearly lose Dr. Ch'ien, and, with him gone, the interstellar drive project would've been shot. Now, if this sabotage keeps up, the Redford project *will* be shot, and that means we might have to stick to the old-fashioned rocket to get off-planet. Brian, we *need* antigravity, and, so far, Nordred's theory is our only clue."

"Agreed," said Taggert.

"Well, we're never going to get it if equipment keeps mysteriously burning itself out, breaking down, and just generally goofing up. This morning, the primary exciter on the new ultracosmotron went haywire, and the beam of sodium nuclei burned through part of the accelerator tube wall. It'll take a month to get it back in working order."

Taggert took his pipe out of his mouth and tapped the dottle into a nearby ash disposal unit. "And you want to pick up our pet spy?"

Senator Gonzales scowled. "Well, I'd certainly call him our prime suspect." But there was a certain lack of conviction in his manner.

Brian Taggert didn't flatly contradict the senator. "Maybe. But you know, John, there's one thing that bothers me about these accidents."

"What's that?"

"The fact that we have not one shred of evidence that points to sabotage."

In a room on the fifth floor, directly below Brian Taggert's office, a young man was half sitting, half reclining in a thickly upholstered adjustable chair. He had dropped the back of the chair to a forty-five degree angle and lifted up the footrest; now he was leaning back in lazy comfort, his ankles crossed, his right hand holding a slowly smoldering cigarette, his eyes contemplating the ceiling. Or, rather, they seemed to be contemplating something *beyond* the ceiling.

It was pure coincidence that the focus of his thoughts happened to be located in about the same volume of space that his eyes seemed to be focused on. If Brian Taggert and Senator Gonzales had been in the room below, his eyes would still be looking at the ceiling.

In repose, his face looked even younger than his twenty-eight years would have led one to expect. His close-cropped brown hair added to the impression of youth, and the well-tailored suit on his slim, muscular body added to the effect. At any top-flight university, he could have passes for a well-bred, sophisticated, intelligent student who had money enough to indulge himself and sense enough not to overdo it.

He was beginning to understand the pattern that was being woven in the room above—beginning to feel it in depth.

Senator Gonzalez was mildly telepathic, inasmuch as he could pick up thoughts in the prevocal stage—the stage at which thought becomes definitely organized into words, phrases, and sentences. He could go a little deeper, into the selectivity stage, where the linking processes of logic took over from the nonlogical but rational processes of the preconscious—but only if he knew the person well. Where the senator excelled was in detecting emotional tone and manipulating emotional processes, both within himself and within others.

Brian Taggert was an analyzer, an originator, a motivator—and more. The young man found himself avoiding too deep a probe into the mind of Brian Taggert; he knew that he had not yet achieved the maturity to understand the multilayered depths of a mind like that. Eventually, perhaps....

Not that Senator Gonzales was a child, nor that he was emotionally or intellectually shallow. It was merely that he was not of Taggert's caliber.

The young man absently took another drag from his cigarette. Taggert had explained the basic problem to him, but he was getting a wider picture from the additional information that Senator Gonzales had brought.

Dr. Theodore Nordred, a mathematical physicist and one of the top-flight, high-powered, original minds in the field, had shown that Einstein's final equations only held in a universe composed entirely of normal matter. Since the great Einstein had died before the Principle of Parity had been overthrown in the mid-fifties, he had been unable to incorporate the information into his Unified Field Theory. Nordred had been able to show, mathematically, that Einstein's equations were valid only for a completely "dexter," or right-handed universe, or for a completely "sinister" or left-handed universe.

Although the universe in which Man lived was predominantly dexter—arbitrarily so designated—it was not completely so. It had a "sinister" component amounting to approximately one one-hundred-thousandth of one per cent. On the average, one atom out of every ten million in the universe was an atom of antimatter. The distribution was unequal of course; antimatter could not exist in contact with ordinary matter. Most of it was distributed throughout interstellar space in the form of individual atoms, freely floating in space, a long way from any large mass of normal matter.

But that minute fraction of a per cent was enough to show that the known universe was not totally Einsteinian. In a purely Einsteinian universe, antigravity was impossible, but if the equations of Dr. Theodore Nordred were actually a closer approximation to true reality than those of Einstein, then antigravity *might* be a practical reality.

And that was the problem the Redford Research Team was working on. It was a parallel project to the interstellar drive problem, being carried on elsewhere.

The "pet spy," as Taggert had called him, was Dr. Konrad Bern, a middle-aged Negro from Tanganyika, who was convinced that only under Communism could the colored races of the world achieve the technological organization and living standard of the white man. He had been trained as a "sleeper"; not even the exhaustive investigations of the FBI had turned up any relationship between Bern and the Soviets. It had taken the telepathic probing of the S.M.M.R. agents to uncover his real purposes. Known, he constituted no danger.

There was no denying that he was a highly competent, if not brilliant, physicist. And, since it was quite impossible for him to get any information on the Redford Project into the hands of the opposition—it was no longer fashionable to call Communists "the enemy"—there was no reason why he shouldn't be allowed to contribute to the American efforts to bridge space.

Three times in the five months since Bern had joined the project, agents of the Soviet government had made attempts to contact the physicist. Three times the FBI, warned by S.M.M.R. agents, had quietly blocked the contact. Konrad Bern had been effectively isolated.

But, at the project site itself, equipment failure had become increasingly more frequent, all out of proportion to the normal accident rate in any well-regulated laboratory. The work of the project had practically come to a standstill; the ultra-secret project reports to the President were beginning to show less and less progress in the basic research, and more and more progress in repairing damaged equipment. Apparently, though, increasing efficiency in repair work was self-neutralizing; repairing an instrument in half the time merely meant that it could break down twice as often.

It had to be sabotage. And yet, not even the S.M.M.R. agents could find any trace of intentional damage nor any thought patterns that would indicate deliberate damage.

And Senator John Peter Gonzales quite evidently did *not* want to face the implications of *that* particular fact.

"We're going to have to send an agent in," Taggert repeated.

(*That's my cue*, thought the young man on the fifth floor as he crushed out his cigarette and got up from the chair.)

"I don't know how we're going to manage it," said the senator. "What excuse do we have for putting a new man on the Redford team?"

Brian Taggert grinned. "What they need is an expert repair technician—a man who knows how to build and repair complex research instruments. He doesn't have to know anything about the purpose of the team itself, all he has to do is keep the equipment in good shape."

Senator Gonzalez let a slow smile spread over his face. "You've been gulling me, you snake. All right; I deserved it. Tell him to come in."

As the door opened, Taggert said: "Senator Gonzales, may I present Mr. David MacHeath? He's our man, I think."

David MacHeath watched a blue line wriggle its way erratically across the face of an oscilloscope. "The wave form is way off," he said flatly, "and the frequency is slithering all over the place."

He squinted at the line for a moment then spoke to the man standing nearby. "Signal Harry to back her off two degrees, then run her up slowly, ten minutes at a time."

The other man flickered the key on the side of the small carbide-Welsbach lamp. The shutters blinked, sending pulses of light down the length of the ten-foot diameter glass-walled tube in which the men were working. Far down the tube, MacHeath could see the answering flicker from Harry, a mile and a half away in the darkness.

MacHeath watched the screen again. After a few seconds, he said: "O.K.! Hold it!"

Again the lamp flashed.

"Well, it isn't perfect," MacHeath said, "but it's all we can do from here. We'll have to evacuate the tube to get her in perfect balance. Tell Harry to knock off for the day."

While the welcome message was being flashed, MacHeath shut off the testing instruments and disconnected them. It was possible to compensate a little for the testing equipment, but a telephone, or even an electric flashlight, would simply add to the burden.

Bill Griffin shoved down the key on the lamp he was holding and locked it into place. The shutters remained open, and the lamp shed a beam of white light along the shining walls of the cylindrical tube. "How much longer do you figure it'll take, Dave?" he asked.

"Another shift, at least," said MacHeath, picking up the compact, shielded instrument case. "You want to carry that mat?"

Griffin picked up the thick sponge-rubber mat that the instrument case had been sitting on, and the two men started off down the tube, walking silently on the sponge-rubber-soled shoes which would not scratch the glass underfoot.

"Any indication yet as to who our saboteur is?" Griffin asked.

"I'm not sure," MacHeath admitted. "I've picked up a couple of leads, but I don't know if they mean anything or not."

"I wonder if there *is* a saboteur," Griffin said musingly. "Maybe it's just a run of bad luck. It could happen, you know. A statistical run of—"

"You don't believe that, any more than I do," MacHeath said.

"No. But I find it even harder to believe that a materialistic philosophy like Communism could evolve any workable psionic discipline."

"So do I," agreed MacHeath.

"But it can't be physical sabotage," Griffin argued. "There's not a trace of it—anywhere. It *has* to be psionic."

"Right," said MacHeath, grinning as he saw what was coming next.

"But we've already eliminated that. So?" Griffin nodded firmly as if in full agreement with himself. "So we follow the dictum of the Master: 'Eliminate the impossible; whatever is left, no matter how improbable, is the truth.' And, since there is absolutely nothing left, there is no truth. At the bottom, the whole thing is merely a matter of mental delusion."

"Sherlock Holmes would be proud of you, Bill," MacHeath said. "And so am I."

Griffin looked at MacHeath oddly. "I wish I was a halfway decent telepath, I'd like to know what's going on in your preconscious."

"You'd have to dig deeper than that, I'm afraid," MacHeath said ruefully. "As soon as my subconscious has solved the problem, I'll let you know."

"I've changed my mind," said Griffin cheerfully. "I don't envy your telepathy. I don't envy a guy who has to TP his own subconscious to find out what he's thinking."

MacHeath chuckled softly as he turned the bolt that opened the door in the "gun" end of the stripped-nuclei accelerator. The seals broke with a soft hiss. Evidently, the barometric pressure outside the two-mile-long underground tube had changed slightly during the time they had been down there.

"It'll be a week before we can test it," MacHeath said in a tired voice. "Even after we get it partly in balance. It'll take that long to evacuate the tube and sweep it clean."

It was the first sentence he had spoken in the past hour or so, and it was purely for the edification of the man who was standing on the other side of the air lock, although neither Griffin nor MacHeath had actually seen him as yet.

Griffin was not a telepath in the sense that the S.M.M.R. used the word, but to a non-psionicist, he would have appeared to be one. Membership in the "core" group of the *Society for Mystical and Metaphysical Research* required, above all, *understanding*. And, with that understanding, a conversation between two members need consist only of an occasional gesture and a key word now and then.

The word "understanding" needs emphasis. Without understanding of another human mind, no human mind can be completely effective. Without that understanding, no human being can be completely free.

And yet, the English word "understanding" is only an approximation to the actual process that must take place. *Total* understanding, in one sense, would require that a person actually *become* another person—that he be able to feel, completely and absolutely, every emotion, every thought, every bodily sensation, every twinge of memory, every judgment, every decision, and every sense of personal identity that is felt by the other person, no more and no less.

Such totality is, obviously, neither attainable nor desirable. The result would be a merger of identities, a total unification. And, as a consequence, a complete loss of one of the human beings involved.

Optimum "understanding" requires that a judgment be made, and that, in turn, requires *two* minds—not a fusion of identity. There must be one to judge and another to be judged, and each mind plays both roles.

Love thy neighbor as thyself. But the original Greek word would translate better as "respect and understand" than as the modern English "love." The founders of our modern religions were not fools; they simply did not have the tools at hand to formulate their knowledge properly. As understanding increases, a critical point is reached, which causes a qualitative change in the human mind.

First, self-understanding must come. The human mind operates through similarities, and the thing most similar to any human mind is itself. The next most similar thing is another human mind.

From that point on, all objects, processes, and patterns in the universe can be graded according to their similarity to each other, and, ultimately, to their similarity to the human mind.

Two given entities may seem utterly dissimilar, but they can always be linked by a *tertium quid*—a "third thing" which is similar to both. This third thing, be it a material object or a product of the human imagination, is called a symbol. Symbols are the bridges by which the human mind can reach and manipulate the universe in which it exists. With the proper symbols and the understanding to use them, the human mind is limited only by its own inherent structural restrictions.

One of the most active research projects of the S.M.M.R. was the construction of a more powerful symbology. Psionics had made tremendous strides in the previous four decades, but it was still in the alchemy stage. So far, symbols for various processes could only be worked out by cut-and-try, rule-of-thumb methods, using symbols already established, including languages and mathematics. None were completely satisfactory, but they worked fairly well within their narrow limits.

As far as communication was concerned, the hashed-together symbology used by the S.M.M.R. was better than any conceivable code. The understanding required to "break" the "code" was well beyond the critical point. Anyone who could break it was, *ipso facto*, a member of the S.M.M.R.

Most people didn't even realize that a conversation was taking place between two members, especially if a "cover conversation" was used at the same time.

MacHeath's verbal discussion of the testing of the nuclei accelerator was just such a cover. Even before he had cracked the air lock, he had known that Dr. Theodore Nordred was standing on the other side of the thick wall.

MacHeath pushed the heavy door open on its smooth hinges. "Oh, hello, Dr. Nordred. How's everything?"

The heavy-set mathematician smiled pleasantly as MacHeath and Griffin came into the gun chamber. "I just thought I'd come down and see how you were getting along," he said. His voice was a low tenor, with just a touch of Midwestern twang. "Sometimes the creative mind gets bogged down in the nth-order abstractions that have no discernible connection with anything at all." He chuckled. "When that happens, I drop everything and go out to find something mundane to worry about."

Nordred was only an inch shorter than the slim MacHeath, and he weighed in at close to two hundred pounds. At twenty-five, he had had the build of a lightweight wrestler; thirty more years had added poundage—a roll beneath his chin and a bulge at the belly—but he still looked capable of going a round or two without tiring. His shock of heavy hair was a mixture of mouse-brown and gray, and it seemed to have a tendency to stand up on end, which added another inch and a half to his height. His round face had a tendency to smile when he was talking or working with his hands; when he was deep in thought, his face usually relaxed into thoughtful blankness. He frowned rarely, and only for seconds at a time.

"It seems to me you have enough to worry about, doctor," MacHeath said banteringly, "without looking for it." He put down his instrument case and took out a cigarette while Griffin closed the door to the acceleration tube.

"Oh I don't have to look far," Nordred said. "How long do you think it will be before we can resume our work with the Monster?"

"Ten days to two weeks," MacHeath said promptly.

"I see." One his rare frowns crossed his face. "I wish I knew why the exciter arced across. It shouldn't have."

"Don't you have any idea?" MacHeath asked innocently. At the same time, he opened his mind wide to net in every wisp and filament of Nordred's thoughts that he could reach.

"None at all," admitted the mathematician. "Weakness in the insulation, I suppose, though it tested solidly enough." And his mind, as far back as his preconscious and the upper fringes of his subconscious, agreed with his words. MacHeath could go no deeper as yet; he didn't know Nordred well enough yet.

There were suspicions in Nordred's mind that the insulation weakness must have been caused by deliberate sabotage, but he had no one to pin his suspicions on. Neither he nor anyone else connected with the Redford project was aware of the true status of Dr. Konrad Bern.

"Well, let's hope it doesn't happen again," MacHeath said. "Balancing these babies so that they work properly is hard enough for a deuteron accelerator, but the Monster here is ten times as touchy."

Nordred nodded absently. "I know. But our work can't be done with anything less." Nordred actually knew less about the engineering details of the big accelerator than anyone else on the project; he was primarily a philosopher-mathematician, and only secondarily a physicist. He was theoretically in charge of the project, but the actual experimentation was done by the other four men; Drs. Roger Kent, Paul Luvochek, Solomon Bessermann, and Konrad Bern. These four and their assistants set up and ran off the experiments designed to test Dr. Nordred's theories.

MacHeath picked up his instrument case again, and the three men went out of the gun chamber, into the outer room, and then started up the spiral stairway that led to the surface, talking as they went. But the apparent conversation had little to do with the instruction that MacHeath was giving Griffin as they climbed.

So when MacHeath stopped suddenly and patted at his coverall pockets, Griffin was ready for the words that came next.

"Damn!" MacHeath said. "I've left my notebook. Will you go down and get it for me, Bill?"

Dr. Nordred had neither understood nor noticed the actual instructions:

"Bill, as soon as I give you an excuse, get back down there and check that gun chamber. Give it a thorough going-over. I don't really think you'll find a thing, but I don't want to take any chances at this stage of the game."

"Right," said Griffin, starting back down the stairway.

MacHeath and Dr. Nordred went on climbing.

David MacHeath sat at a table in the project's cafeteria, absently stirring his coffee, and trying to look professionally modest while Dr. Luvochek and Dr. Bessermann alternately praised him for his work.

Luvochek, a tubby little butterball of a man, whose cherubic face would have made him look almost childlike if it weren't for the blue of his jaw, said: "You and those two men of yours have really done a marvelous job in the past four days, Mr. MacHeath—really marvelous."

"I'll say," Bessermann chimed in. "I was getting pretty tired of looking at burned-out equipment and spending three-quarters of my time putting in replacement parts and wielding a soldering gun." Bessermann was leaner than Luvochek, but, like his brother scientist, he was balding on top. Both men were in their middle thirties.

"I don't understand this jinx, myself," Luvochek said. "At first, it was just little things, but the accidents got worse and worse. And then, when the Monster blew—" He stopped and shook his head slowly. "I'd suspect sabotage, except that there was never any sign of tampering with the equipment I saw."

"What do you think of the sabotage idea?" Bessermann asked MacHeath.

MacHeath shrugged. "Haven't seen any signs of it."

"Run of bad luck," said Luvochek. "That's all."

As they talked MacHeath absorbed the patterns of thought that wove in and out in the two men's minds. Both men were more open than Dr. Nordred; they were easier for MacHeath to understand. Nowhere was there any thought of guilt—at least, as far as sabotage was concerned.

MacHeath drank his coffee slowly and thoughtfully, keeping up his part of the three-way conversation while he concentrated on his own problem.

One thing was certain: Nowhere in the minds of any of the personnel of the Redford Project was there any conscious knowledge of sabotage. Not even in the mind of Konrad Bern.

Dr. Roger Kent, a tall, lantern-jawed sad-eyed man in his forties, had been hard to get through to at first, but as soon as MacHeath discovered that the hard block Kent had built up around himself was caused by grief over a wife who had been dead five years, he became as easy to read as a billboard. Kent had submerged his grief in work; the eternal drive of the true scientist to drag the truth out of Mother Nature. He was constitutionally incapable of sabotaging the very instruments that had been built to dig in after that truth.

Dr. Konrad Bern, on the other hand, was difficult to read below the preconscious stage. Science, to him, was a form of power, to be used for "idealistic" purposes. He was perfectly capable of sabotaging the weapons of an enemy if it became necessary, whether that meant ruining a physical instrument or carefully falsifying the results of an experiment. Outwardly, he was a pleasant enough chap, but his mind revealed a rigidly held pattern of hatreds, fears, and twisted idealism. He held them tightly against the onslaughts of a hostile world.

And that meant that he couldn't possibly have any control over whatever psionic powers he may have had.

Unless—

Unless he was so expert and so well-trained that he was better than anything the S.M.M.R. had ever known.

MacHeath didn't even like to think about that. It would mean that all the theory of psionics that had been built up so painstakingly over the past years would have to be junked *in toto*.

Something was gnawing in the depths of his mind. In the perfectly rational but utterly nonlogical part of his subconscious where hunches are built, something was trying to form.

MacHeath didn't try to probe for it. As soon as he had enough information for the hunch to be fully formed, it would be ready to use. Until then, it would be worthless, and probing for it might interrupt the formation.

He was just finishing his coffee as Bill Griffin came in the door and headed toward the table where MacHeath, Luvochek, and Bessermann were sitting.

MacHeath stood up and said: "Excuse me. I'll have to be getting some work done if you guys are ever going to get your own work done."

"Sure."

"Go ahead."

"Thanks for the coffee," MacHeath added as he moved away.

"Anytime," said Bessermann, grinning. "You guys just keep up the good work. When you fix 'em, they stay fixed. We haven't had a burnout since you came."

"Maybe you broke our statistical jinx," said Luvochek, with a chubby smile.

"Maybe," said MacHeath. "I hope so."

For some reason, the gnawing in his hunch factory became more persistent.

As he and Griffin walked toward the door, Griffin reported rapidly. "I checked everything in the gun chamber. No sign of any tampering. Everything's just as we left it. The dust film hasn't been disturbed."

"It figures," said MacHeath.

Outside, in the corridor, they met Dr. Konrad Bern hurrying toward the cafeteria. He stopped as he saw them.

"Oh, hello, Mr. MacHeath, Mr. Griffin," he said. His white-toothed smile was friendly, but both of the S.M.M.R. agents could detect the hostility that was hard and brittle beneath the surface. "I wanted to thank you for the wonderful job you've been doing."

"Why, thank you, doctor," said MacHeath honestly. "We aim to satisfy."

Bern chuckled. "You're doing well so far. Odd streak of luck we've had, isn't it? Poor Dr. Nordred has been under a terrible strain; his whole life work is tied up in this project." He made a vague gesture with one hand. "Would you care for some coffee?"

"Just had some, thanks," said MacHeath, "but we'll take a rain check."

"Fine. Anytime." And he went on into the cafeteria.

"Wow!" said Griffin as he walked on down the corridor with MacHeath. "That man is scared silly! But what an actor! You'd never know he was eating his guts out."

"Sure he's scared," MacHeath said. "With all this sabotage talk going around, he's afraid there'll be an exhaustive investigation, and he can't take that right now."

Griffin frowned. "I guess I missed that. What did you pick up?"

"He's supposed to meet a Soviet agent tonight, and he's afraid he'll be caught. He doesn't know what happened to the first three, and he won't know what will happen to Number Four tonight.

"We'll keep him around as long as he's useful. He's not a Bohr or a Pauli or a Fermi, but he—"

MacHeath stopped himself suddenly and came to a dead halt.

"My God," he said softly, "that's *it*."

His hunch had hatched.

After a moment, he said: "Harry is getting back from the target end of the tube now, Bill. He can't pick me up, so beetle it down to the tool room, get him, and get up to the workshop fast. If I'm not there, wait; I have a little prying to do."

"Can do," said Griffin. He went toward the elevator at an easy lope.

David MacHeath went in the opposite direction.

When MacHeath returned to the workshop which he had been assigned, Bill Griffin and Harry Benbow were waiting for him. Beside the big-muscled Griffin, Harry Benbow looked even thinner than he was. He was a good six-two, which made him a head taller than Griffin, but, unlike many tall, lean men, Benbow had no tendency to slouch; he stood tall and straight, reminding MacHeath of a poplar tree towering proudly over the countryside. Benbow was one of those rare American Negroes whose skin was actually as close to being "black" as human pigmentation will allow. His eyes were like disks of obsidian set in spheres of white porcelain, which gave an odd contrast-similarity effect when compared with Griffin's china-blue eyes.

If the average man had wanted to pick two human beings who were "opposites," he could hardly have made a better choice than Benbow and the short, thickly-built, blond-haired, pink-skinned Bill Griffin. But the average man would be so struck by the differences that he would never notice that the similarities were vastly more important.

"You look as if you'd just been kissed by Miss America," Harry said as MacHeath came through the door.

"Better than that," MacHeath said. "We've got work to do."

"What's the pitch?" Griffin wanted to know.

"Well, in the first place, I'm afraid Dr. Konrad Bern is no longer of any use to the Redford Project. We're going to have to arrest him as an unregistered agent of the Soviet Government."

"It's just as well," said Harry Benbow gently. "His research hasn't done us any good and it hasn't done the Soviets any good. The poor guy's been on edge ever since he got here. All the pale hide around this place stirs up every nerve in him."

"What got you onto this?" Griffin asked MacHeath.

"A hunch first," MacHeath said. "Then I got data to back it up. But, first ... Harry, how'd you know about Bern's reactions? He keeps those prejudices of his down pretty deep; I didn't think you could go that far."

"I didn't have to. He spent half an hour talking to me this morning. He was so happy to see a fellow human being—according to his definition of human being—that he was as easy to read as if *you* were doing the reading."

MacHeath nodded. "I hate to throw him to the wolves, but he's got to go."

"What was the snooping you said you had to do?" Griffin asked.

"Dates. Times. Briefly, I found that the run of accidents has been building up to a peak. At first, it was just small meters that went wrong. Then bigger, more complex stuff. And, finally, the Monster went. See the pattern?"

The other men nodded.

"You're the therapist," Griffin said. "What do you suggest?"

"Shock treatment," said David MacHeath.

Just how Dr. Konrad Bern got wind of the fact that a squad of FBI men had come to the project to arrest him that evening is something that MacHeath didn't know until later. He was busy at the time, ignoring anything but what he was interested in. It always fascinated him to watch the mind of a psychokinetic expert at work. He couldn't do the trick himself, and he was always amazed at the ability of anyone who could.

It was like watching a pianist play a particularly difficult concerto. A person can watch a pianist, see every move he is making, and why he is making it. But being able to see what is going on doesn't mean that one can duplicate the action. MacHeath was in the same position. Telepathically, he could observe the play of emotions that ran through a psychokinetic's mind—the combinations of avid desire and the utter loathing which, playing one against another, could move a brick, a book, or a Buick if the mind was powerful enough. But he couldn't do it himself, no matter how carefully he tried to follow the raging emotions that acted as two opposing jaws of a pair of tongs to lift and move the object.

And so engrossed was he with the process that he did not notice that Konrad Bern had eluded the FBI. He was unaware of what had happened until one of the Federal agents rapped loudly on the workshop door.

Almost instantly, MacHeath picked up the information from the agent's mind. He glanced at Griffin and Benbow. "You two can handle it. Be careful you don't overdo it."

Then he went to the door and opened it a trifle. "Yes?"

The man outside showed a gold badge. "Morgan, FBI. You David MacHeath?"

"Yes." MacHeath stepped outside and showed the FBI man his identification.

"We were told to co-operate with you in this Konrad Bern case. He's managed to slip away from us somehow, but we know he's still in the area. He can't get past the gate."

MacHeath let his mind expand until it meshed with that of Dr. Konrad Bern.

"There is a way out," MacHeath snapped. "The acceleration tube."

"What?"

"Come on!" He started sprinting toward the elevators. He explained to the FBI agent as they went.

"The acceleration tube of the ultracosmotron runs due north of here for two miles underground. The guard at the other end won't be expecting anyone to be coming from the inside of the target building. If Bern plays his cards right, he can get away."

"Can't we phone the target building?" the FBI man asked.

"No. We shut off all the electrical equipment and took down some of the wires so we could balance the acceleration fields."

"Well, if he's on foot, we could send a car out there. We'd get there before he does. Uh ... wouldn't we?"

"Maybe. But he'll kill himself if he sees he's trapped." That wasn't quite true. Bern was ready to fight to the death, and he had a heavy pistol to back him up. MacHeath didn't want to see anyone killed, and he didn't want stray bullets flying around the inside of that tube or in the target room.

MacHeath and the FBI agent piled out of the elevator at the bottom of the shaft. Dr. Roger Kent was standing at the head of the stairs that spiraled down to the gun chamber. Dr. Kent knew that Bern had gone down the stairway, but he didn't know why.

"He's our saboteur," MacHeath said quickly. "I'm going after him. As soon as I close the door and seal it, you turn on the pumps. Lower the air pressure in the tube to a pound per square inch below atmospheric. That'll put a force of about a ton and a quarter against the doors, and he won't be able to open them."

Dr. Kent still didn't grasp the fact that Bern was a spy.

"Explain to him, Morgan," MacHeath told the Federal agent. He went on down the spiral staircase, knowing that Kent would understand and act in plenty of time.

The door to the tube was standing open. MacHeath slipped on a pair of the sponge-soled shoes, noticing angrily that Bern hadn't bothered to do so. He went into the tube and closed the door behind him. Then he started down the blackness of the tube at a fast trot. Ahead of him, in the utter darkness, he could hear the click of heels as the leather-shod Bern moved toward the target end of the long tube.

Neither of them had lights. They were unnecessary, for one thing, since there was only one direction to go and there were no obstacles in the path. Bern would probably have carried a flashlight if he'd been able to get his hands on one quickly, but he hadn't, so he went in darkness. MacHeath didn't want a light; in the darkness, he had the advantage of knowing where his opponent was.

Every so often, Bern would stop, listening for sounds of pursuit, since his own footsteps, echoing down the glass-lined cylinder, drowned out any noise from behind. But MacHeath, running silently on the toes of his thick-soled shoes, kept in motion, gaining on the fleeing spy.

A two-mile run is a good stretch of exercise for anyone, but MacHeath didn't dare slow down. As it was, Konrad Bern was already tugging frantically at the door that led to the target room by the time MacHeath reached him. But the faint sighing of the pumps had already told MacHeath that the air pressure had been dropped. Bern couldn't possibly get the door open.

MacHeath's lungs wanted to be filled with air; his chest wanted to heave; he wanted to pant, taking in great gulps of life-giving oxygen. But he didn't dare. He didn't want Bern to know he was there, so he strained to keep his breath silent.

He stepped up behind the physicist in the pitch blackness, and judging carefully, brought his fist down on the nape of the man's neck in a hard rabbit punch.

Konrad Bern dropped unconscious to the floor of the tube.

Then MacHeath let his chest pump air into his lungs in long, harsh gasps. Shakily, he lowered himself to the floor beside Bern and squatted on his haunches, waiting for the hiss of the bleeder valve that would tell him that the air pressure had been raised to allow someone to enter the air lock.

It was Morgan, the FBI man, who finally cracked the door. Griffin and Dr. Kent were with him.

"You all right?" asked Morgan.

"I'm fine," MacHeath said, "but Bern is going to have a sore neck for a while. I didn't hit him hard enough to break it, but he'll get plenty of sleep before he wakes up."

More FBI men came in, and they dragged out the unprotesting Bern.

Dr. Kent said: "Well, I'm glad that's over. I'll have to get back and see what Dr. Nordred is raving about."

"Raving?" asked MacHeath innocently.

"Yes. While I was in the pump room reducing the pressure, he called me on the interphone. Said he'd been looking all over for me. He and Luvochek and Bessermann are up in the lab." He frowned. "They claim that one of the radiolead samples was floating in the air in the lab. It's settled down now, I gather, but it only weighs a fraction of what it should, though it's gaining all the time. And that's ridiculous. It's not at all what Dr. Nordred's theory predicted." Then he clamped his lips together, thinking perhaps he had talked too much.

"Interesting," said MacHeath blandly. "Very interesting."

Senator Gonzales sat in Brian Taggert's sixth-floor office in the S.M.M.R. building and looked puzzled. "All right, I grant you that Bern couldn't have been the saboteur. Then why arrest him?"

Dave MacHeath took a drag from his cigarette before he answered. "We had to have a patsy—someone to put the blame on. No one really believed that it was just bad luck, but they'll all accept the idea that Bern was a saboteur."

"We would have had to arrest him eventually, anyway," said Brian Taggert.

"Give me a quick run-down," Gonzales said. "I've got to explain this to the President."

"Did you ever hear of the Pauli Effect?" MacHeath asked.

"Something about the number of electrons that—"

"No," MacHeath said quickly. "That's the Pauli *principle*, better known as the Exclusion Principle. The Pauli*Effect* is a different thing entirely, a psionic effect.

"It used to be said that a theoretical physicist was judged by his inability to handle research apparatus; the clumsier he was in research, the better he was with theory. But Wolfgang Pauli was a lot more than clumsy. Apparatus would break, topple over, go to pieces, or burn up if Pauli just walked into the room.

"Up to the time he died, in 1958, his colleagues kidded about it, without really believing there was anything behind it. But it is recorded that the explosion of some vacuum equipment in a laboratory at the University of Göttingen was the direct result of the Pauli Effect. It was definitely established that the explosion occurred at the precise moment that a train on which Pauli was traveling stopped for a short time at the Göttingen railway station."

The senator said: "The poltergeist phenomenon."

"Not exactly," MacHeath said, "although there is a similarity. The poltergeist phenomenon is usually spectacular and is nearly always associated with teen-age neurotics. Then there's the pyrotic; fires always start in his vicinity."

"But there's always a reason for psionic phenomena to react violently under subconscious control," Senator Gonzales pointed out. "There's always a psychological quirk."

"Sure. And I almost fell into the same trap, myself."

"How so?"

"I was thinking that if Bern were the saboteur, all our theories about psionics would have to be thrown out—we'd have to start from a different set of precepts. *And I didn't even want to think about such an idea!*"

"Nobody likes their pet theories overthrown," Gonzales observed.

"Of course not. But here's the point: The only way that a scientific theory can be proved wrong is to uncover a phenomenon which doesn't fit in with the theory. A theoretical physicist is a mathematician; he makes logical deductions and logical predictions by juggling symbols around in accordance with some logical system. But the axioms, the assumptions upon which those systems are built, are nonlogical. You can't prove an axiom; if comes right out of the mind.

"So imagine that you're a theoretical physicist. A really original-type thinker. You come up with a mathematical system that explains all known phenomena at that time, and predicts others that are, as yet, unknown. You check your math over and over again; there's no error in your logic, since it all follows, step by step."

"O.K.; go on," Gonzales said interestedly.

"Very well, then; you've built yourself a logical universe, based on your axioms, and the structure seems to have a one-to-one correspondence with the actual universe. Not only that, but if the theory is accepted, you've built your reputation on it—your life.

"Now, what happens if your axioms—not the logic *about* the axioms, but the axioms themselves—are proven to be wrong?"

Brian Taggert took his pipe out of his mouth. "Why, you give up the erroneous set of axioms and build a new set that will explain the new phenomenon. Isn't that what a scientist is supposed to do?" His manner was that of wide-eyed innocence laid on with a large trowel.

"Oh, *sure* it is," said the senator. "A man builds his whole life, his whole universe; on a set of principles, and he scraps them at the drop of a hat. *Sure* he does."

"He claims he will," MacHeath said. "Any scientist worth the paper his diploma is printed on is firmly convinced that he will change his axioms as soon as they're proven false. Of course, ninety-nine per cent of 'em *can't* and *won't* and *don't*. They refuse to look at anything that suggests changing axioms.

"Some scientists eagerly accept the axioms that they were taught in school and hang on to them all their lives, fighting change tooth and nail. Oh, they'll accept new ideas, all right—provided that they fit in with the structures based on the old axioms.

"Then there are the young iconoclasts who don't like the axioms as they stand, so they make up some new ones of their own—men like Newton, Einstein, Planck, and so on. Then, once the new axioms have been forced down the throats of their colleagues, the innovators become the Old Order; the iconoclasts become the ones who put the fences around the new images to safeguard them. And they're even more firmly wedded to their axioms than anyone else. This is *their* universe!

"Of course, these men proclaim to all the world that they are perfectly willing to change their axioms. And the better a scientist he is, the more he believes, in his heart-of-hearts, that he really would change. He really thinks, consciously, that he wants others to test his theories.

"But notice: A theory is only good if it explains all known phenomena in its field. If it does, then the only thing that can topple it is a *new* fact. The only thing that can threaten the complex structure formulated by a really creative, painstaking, mathematical physicist is *experiment*!"

Senator Gonzales' attentive silence was eloquent.

"Experiment!" MacHeath repeated. "That can wreck a theory quicker and more completely than all the learned arguments of a dozen men. And every theoretician is aware of that fact. Consciously, he gladly accepts the inevitable; but his subconscious mind will fight to keep those axioms.

"*Even if it has to smash every experimental device around!*

"After all, if nobody can experiment on your theory, it can't be proved wrong, can it?

"In Nordred's case, as in Pauli's, this subconscious defense actually made itself felt in the form of broken equipment. Dr. Theodore Nordred was totally unconscious of the fact that he detested and feared the idea of anyone experimenting to prove or disprove his theory. He had no idea that he, himself, was re-channeling the energy in those machines to make them burn out."

Brian Taggert looked at MacHeath pointedly. "Do you think the shock treatment you gave him will cause any repercussions?"

"No. Griffin and Benbow held that block of radiolead floating in the air only while Dr. Nordred was alone in the lab. He pushed at it, felt of it, and moved it around for more than ten minutes before he'd admit the reality of what he saw. Then he called Luvochek and Bessermann in to look at it.

"Griffin and Benbow let the sample settle to the desk, so that by the time the other two scientists got to the lab, the lead didn't have an apparent negative weight, but was still much lighter than it should be.

"All the while that Bessermann and Luvochek were trying to weigh the lead block, to get an accurate measurement, Griffin and Benbow, three rooms away, kept increasing the weight slowly towards normal. And so far no one has invented a device which will give an instantaneous check on the weight of an object. A balance can't check the weight of a sample unless that weight is constant; there's too much time lag involved.

"So, what evidence do they have? Scientifically speaking, none. They have no measurements, and the experiment can't be repeated. And only Nordred actually saw the sample *floating*. Luvochek and Bessermann will eventually think up a 'natural' explanation for the apparent steady gain in weight. Only Nordred will remain convinced that what he saw actually happened.

"I don't see how there could be any serious repercussions in the field of physics." But he looked at Taggert for confirmation.

Taggert gave it to him with an approving look.

"It's a funny thing," said Gonzales musingly. "Some time back, we were in a situation where we had to go to the extreme of physical violence to keep from demonstrating to a scientist that psionic powers could be controlled, just to keep from ruining the physicist's work.

"Now, we turn right around and demonstrate the 'impossible' to another physicist in order to pull his hard-earned axioms out from under him." He smiled wryly. "There ain't no justice in the world."

"No," agreed MacHeath, "but the trick worked. He won't have any subconscious desire to smash equipment just to protect a theory that has already been smashed. On the contrary, he'll let them go through in order to find new data to build another theory on."

"He'll never again be the man he was," said Taggert regretfully. "He's lost the force of his convictions. He won't be capable of taking a no-nonsense, dogmatic, black-and-white stand. But it was necessary." He made an odd gesture with one hand. "What else can you do with a man who's a psionic psychopath?"

THE END

The Unnecessary Man

Sometimes an organizational setup grows, sets its ways, and becomes so traditional that once-necessary jobs become unnecessary. But it is sometimes quite hard to spot just which man is the unnecessary one. In this case ... not the one you think!

"Recall," said the Businessman, "that William Wrigley, Junior, once said: 'When two men in a business always agree, one of them is unnecessary.' *How true that is.*"

The Philosopher cast his eyes toward Heaven. "O God! The Mercantile Mind!" He looked back at the Businessman. "When two men in a business always agree, one of them will come in handy as a scapegoat."

THE IDLE WORSHIPERS
by R. Phillip Dachboden

LORD Barrick Sorban, Colonel, H.I.M.O.G., Ret., sipped gently at his drink and looked mildly at the sheaf of newsfacsimile that he'd just bought fresh from the reproducer in the lobby of the Royal Hotel. Sorban did not look like a man of action; he certainly did not look like a retired colonel of His Imperial Majesty's Own Guard. The most likely reason for this was that he was neither.

Not that he was incapable of action on a physical level if it became necessary; he was past forty, but his tough, hard body was in as fine a shape as it had been fifteen years before, and his reflexes had slowed only slightly. The only major change that had occurred in his body during that time had been the replacement of an irreparably damaged left hand by a prosthetic.

But Lord Barrick Sorban preferred to use his mind, to initiate action in others rather than himself, and his face showed it. His was a precision mind, capable of fast, accurate computations, and his eyes betrayed the fact, but the rest of his face looked, if anything, rather like that of a gentle, persuasive schoolteacher—the type whom children love and parents admire and both obey.

Nor was he a retired colonel of the Imperial bodyguard, except on paper. According to the official records, he had been retired for medical reasons—the missing left hand. In reality, his position in the Imperium was a great deal higher than that of an ordinary colonel, and he was still in the active service of the Emperor. It was a secret known only to a comparative few, and one that was carefully guarded.

He was a fairly tall man, as an Imperial Guardsman had to be, with a finely-shaped head and dark hair that was shot through with a single streak of gray from an old burn wound. In an officer's uniform, he looked impressive, but in civilian dress he looked like a competent businessman.

He held the newsfac in his prosthetic left hand, which was indistinguishable in appearance and in ordinary usage from the flesh, bone, and blood that it had replaced. Indeed, the right hand, with its stiff little finger, often appeared to be more useless than the left. The hand, holding the glass of rye-and-ginger, gave an impression of over-daintiness because of that stiff digit.

Lord Sorban paid little attention to the other customers in the bar; customers of the Green Room of the Royal Hotel weren't the noisy kind, anyway. He kept his attention on the newsfac for the most part; only a small amount of awareness was reserved for the approach of the man he was waiting for.

The banner line on the newsfac said:

BAIRNVELL OCCUPIED
BY IMPERIAL FORCES

He read through the article hurriedly, absorbing what facts he didn't know, and then flipped over to the editorial page. If he knew the *Globe*, there would sure as Space be an editorial.

There was.

At 0231 Greenwich Earth Time, 3/37/229, the forces of the Imperial Government occupied the planet Bairnvell. (See article, Page One.) The ships of the Imperial Space Force landed, purportedly at the request of Obar Del Pargon, rebel leader of the anti-Presidential forces. That such an action should be condoned by the Imperial File is astounding enough; that it should be ordered by the Prime Portfolio himself is almost unbelievable.

The government of Bairnvell, under the leadership of President Alverdan, was not, by any means, up to the standards of the Empire; the standard of living is lower, and the political freedom of the people is not at all what we are used to.

But that is no excuse for interfering with the lawful government of any planet. If the Imperium uses these methods for extending its rule, the time must eventually come when our own civil liberties will be in peril.

Perhaps Lord Senesin's actions are not so surprising, at that. This is the third time during his tenure as Prime Portfolio that he has arbitrarily exercised his power to interfere in the affairs of governments outside the Empire. Each such action has precipitated a crisis in Galactic affairs, and each has brought the Empire nearer to conflict with the Gehan Federation. This one may be the final act that will bring on interstellar war.

The ...

Colonel Lord Sorban stopped reading as he noticed the approach of the man he'd been waiting for, but he didn't look up until the voice said:

"I see you've been reading it, my lord." The voice was bitter. "A real fiasco this time, eh?"

Sorban looked up. "It looks like it might mean trouble," he said carefully. "Have you read all of it, Mr. Senesin?"

The young man nodded. The bitterness in his voice was paralleled by the bitterness reflected in his face. "Oh, yes. I read it. The other newsfacs pretty much agreed with the *Globe*. I'm afraid my father seems to be rather in the soup. Being Prime Portfolio in the Terran Empire isn't the easiest way to stay out of trouble. They'll be screaming for a Special Election next." He sat down next to the colonel and lowered his voice just enough to keep anyone else from hearing it, but not enough to sound conspiratorial. "I think I've got a line on those tapes."

Colonel Sorban raised an eyebrow. "Really? Well, I wish you luck. If you can uncover them in time, you may be able to save your father's career," he said, in a voice that matched Senesin's.

"You don't sound very concerned, my lord," said young Senesin.

"It's not that," said the colonel. "I just find it difficult to believe that—" He cut his words off as another man approached.

The second newcomer was a red-faced, plumpish man with an almost offensively hearty manner. "Well, well! Good afternoon, Lord Sorban! Haven't seen you in some time. A pleasure to see you again, my lord, a distinct pleasure! I don't get to Honolulu often, you know. How long's it been? Four years?"

"Two, I think," said the colonel.

"Really? Only two? It seems longer. How've you been?"

"Well enough," said the colonel. "Excuse me—Mr. Heywood, I'd like to present you to the Honorable Jon Senesin; Mr. Senesin, this is Robar Heywood, of South African Metals."

While the two men shook hands and mouthed the usual pleasantries, Colonel Lord Sorban watched them with an amusement that didn't show on his placid face. Young Senesin was rather angry that the *tête-à-tête* had been interrupted, while Heywood seemed flustered and a trifle stuffy.

"So you're the son of our Prime Portfolio, eh?" he said. There was a trace of hostility in his voice.

Colonel Sorban saw what was coming and made no effort whatsoever to stop it. Instead, he simply sat there in straight-faced enjoyment.

"That's correct, Mr. Heywood," Senesin said, a little stiffly.

"I should have known," Heywood said. "You look a great deal like him. Although I don't know that I've ever seen your picture in the newsfacs or on the screens."

"Dad prefers to keep his family out of the spotlight," said Senesin, "unless we get publicity for something other than the accidental fact that we happen to be the family of the Prime."

"Yes, yes, of course. I see. May I stand the three of us a drink?" Senesin and the colonel were agreeable. The drinks were brought. Heywood took a swallow of his, and remarked casually: "Do you agree with your father's politics, sir?"

"I don't know," Senesin said flatly.

Heywood misunderstood completely. "Yes, I suppose it is a bit disappointing. Hard for a man's son to divide his loyalty like that. You can't support his actions, and yet you hesitate to condemn your own father."

"You mistake my meaning, Mr. Heywood," young Senesin said sharply. "I said, 'I don't know' because I honestly don't know what my father's politics *is* any more."

But Heywood only compounded his error. "Of course not. How could you? Since he became Prime, his policies have been erratic and unpredictable, not to say foolish."

This is it, thought the colonel, wondering what young Senesin's reaction would be. He didn't have to wonder longer than half a second.

"Mr. Heywood," said Senesin, his voice oddly tight under the strain of suppressed emotion, "a person should learn to know what he's talking about before he makes any attempt to talk. If you must talk drivel about my father, I'll thank you not to do it in my presence." And before Heywood could formulate an answer, Senesin turned to the colonel. "If you'll pardon me, my lord, I have another errand to perform. I'll see you at eleven." Then he turned and walked out.

Heywood stared at his receding back. "Well," he said after a moment, "I guess I spoke out of turn. But he seemed ..." He turned back to his drink, shrugged. "Oh, well. Tell me, my lord, what do *you* think of Senesin's policies? How long do you think he'll last in office?"

The colonel adroitly avoided the first question by answering the second. "I dare say he won't last long. There'll be a great fuss in the File, and most of his own party will desert him—I think. They hardly have any choice, considering the reaction of the populace to this Bairnvell thing."

"And I agree," said Heywood decisively. "We've got no business interfering with the lawful governments of planets and systems outside the Empire. The old days of Imperial expansion are over. Why, the way Lord Senesin acts, you'd think Emperor Jerris the First was on the throne."

"Well, not quite," Colonel Lord Sorban said dryly. "I can't imagine any Prime Portfolio in the time of Jerris I daring to act on his own initiative."

"Exactly," said Heywood, just as though the colonel had agreed with him. "That's why we have a constitutional Empire today. One man can't be allowed that much power without the consent of the governed. The people must have a right to depose anyone who abuses the power they give him." He swallowed the remainder of his drink. "Can you imagine what it would be like if the present Emperor tried to pull that sort of stuff? Not that he *would*, mind you; he's too good an Emperor for that. He sticks to his job. But these are different times. And then, too, we can't afford to antagonize the Gehan Federation. After all, I mean, *war* ..." He shook his head at the thought.

Colonel Lord Sorban had listened to Heywood's soliloquy with patience, but he felt his irritation growing. Much as he had enjoyed the play between Heywood and young Senesin, he had expected to get some information out of the boy before he left. And besides, Heywood's clichéd monologue was beginning to pall.

Therefore, the colonel finished his own drink, uttered some polite banalities and got out.

He walked around the corner to the restaurant, was bowed into a seat by an ultrapolite android, and quietly ordered his meal. While he waited, he spread the newsfac on the table in front of him, holding it with his right hand while his left elbow rested on the table and his left palm cradled his left jaw. In that position, there was nothing odd-looking about the fact that his left thumbtip was in contact with his larynx and his left middle finger was pressed tightly against the mastoid bone just behind his left ear. His lips began to move slightly, and anyone at a nearby table would have assumed that he was one of those readers who are habitual lip-movers.

"The Senesin boy says he has a lead on the tapes. That's all I could get out of him just now, but I have an appointment with him at eleven tonight. How far shall I let him go, Sire?"

The sensitive microphone in the tip of his thumb picked up the nearly inaudible sounds; the speaker in his middle finger vibrated against his skull and brought him the answer to his question.

"For the moment, I'll leave that up to you. But I wouldn't try to stop him just yet."

"Very well, Sire," murmured the colonel. He had already made up his mind to let the Senesin boy go as far as he could. The lad was smart, and his attack would at least provide a test for the psycho-sociological defenses that surrounded the Emperor.

"Do you think those tapes—if they exist—are genuine?" the voice asked.

"According to young Senesin," the colonel said carefully, "the tapes are supposed to show that certain ... ah ... 'highly-placed persons' in the Imperial hierarchy are influencing members of the Government illegally. You figure out what that might mean, Sire; it's a little too ambiguous to mean much to me."

"'Influencing,' eh? That could mean anything from a broad hint, through pressure and bribery, to actual brainwashing," said the voice from the finger.

"Which one do you think it is, Sire?" the colonel asked with mock innocency.

The voice chuckled, then said, "I haven't tried brainwashing yet."

"No-o-o," agreed the colonel, "but you might have to if Lord Evondering gets in, and if you have to, you will."

"Colonel," said the voice gently, "there are times when I believe you don't have a very high opinion of your Sovereign's moral outlook."

The colonel grinned, although he knew the listener couldn't see it. But he knew the other was grinning, too. "I humbly beg your majesty's pardon."

"You'll have to wait a while, colonel; Imperial pardons have to be by the Portfolio for the Interior. Your Sovereign is an impotent figurehead."

"Sure you are, Sire," said the colonel. "Meanwhile, what about those tapes?"

"Get them—or copies of them. They can't be dangerous in themselves, but if they're genuine, I want to know who's bugging this place. I can't have spies in the Palace itself. Otherwise, keep your eyes on the Senesin boy."

The voice went on giving instructions, but the colonel lifted the thumb of his left hand from his larynx; the waiter was approaching, and if he wanted to speak to him, it would be better not to have to interrupt the flow of words from his finger.

The android put the dishes on the table. "Coffee, sir?"

"Yes," said the colonel. "Cream, no sugar. And bring a second cup as soon as I've finished with the first." Only a part of his attention was given to the waiter; the rest was focused on the instructions he was receiving. The instructions kept coming until after the coffee had been brought. Then the voice said:

"Any questions?"

"No, Sire," said the colonel, replacing his thumb.

"Very well. I'll be expecting your report sometime between eleven and midnight."

The colonel nodded, brought his hand down from the side of his jaw to pick up his fork and begin a concerted attack on his lunch.

Hawaii, with its beauty and its perfect climate, had been the obvious choice for the center of the Terran Empire. For centuries before the coming of interstellar travel, the islands had been used to a mixture of tongues and races, and the coming of the Empire had merely added to that mixture. In the five centuries since Man had begun his explosive spread to the stars, more "races" had come into being due to the genetic variations and divisions that occurred as small groups of isolated colonists were cut off from Earth and from each other. The fact that interstellar vessels incorporating the contraspace drive were relatively inexpensive to build, plus the fact that nearly every G-type sun had an Earth-like planet in Bode's Third Position, had made scattering to the stars almost an automatic reflex among men.

It had also shattered the cohesion of Mankind that had been laboriously built up over several millennia. The old U.N. government had gradually welded together the various nations of Earth under one flag, and for nearly two centuries it had run Earth like a smoothly operating machine. But no culture is immortal; even the U.N. must fall, and fall it did.

And, during the chaos that followed, a man named Jerris Danfors had grabbed the loosened reins of government just as Napoleon had done after the French Revolution. Unlike Napoleon, however, Jerris had been able to hold his power without abusing it; he was able to declare himself Emperor of Earth and make it stick. The people *wanted* a single central government, and they were willing to go back to the old idea of Empire just to get such a government.

Jerris the First was neither a power-mad dictator nor an altruist, although he had been called both. He was, purely and simply, a strong, wise, intelligent man—which made him abnormal, no matter how you look at it. Or supernormal, if you will.

Like Napoleon, he realized that wars of conquest were capable of being used as a kind of cement to hold the people together in support of their Emperor. But, again, unlike Napoleon, he found there was no need to sap the strength of Earth to fight those wars. The population and productive capacity of Earth was greater than any possible coalition among extra-Solar planets and vastly greater than any single planet alone.

Thus the Terran Empire had come into being with only a fraction of the internal disruption which normally follows empire-building.

But Man can flee as well as fight. Every invading army is preceded by hordes of refugees. Ships left every planet threatened by the Empire, seeking new, uncharted planets to settle—planets that would be safe from the Imperial Fleet because they were hidden among a thousand thousand stars. Mankind spread through the galaxy faster than the Empire could. Not even Jerris the First could completely consolidate the vast reaches of the galaxy into a single unit; one lifetime is simply not enough.

Nor are a dozen.

Slowly, the Empire had changed. Over the next several generations, the Emperors had yielded more and more of the absolute power that had been left to them by Jerris. While history never exactly repeats itself, a parallel could be drawn between the history of the Empire and the history of England between, say, 1550 and 1950. But, while England's empire had begun to recede with the coming of democratic government, the Terran Empire continued to spread—more slowly than at first, but steadily.

Until, that is, the Empire had touched the edges of the Gehan Federation.

For the hordes that had fled from the Empire had not forgotten her; they knew that one day the Empire would find them, that one day they would have to fight for their independence. So they formed the Federation, with its capital on the third planet of Gehan's Sun.

It was a federation in name only. Even after several generations, the refugees had not been able to build up enough population to fight the Empire. There was only one other way out, as they saw it. They formed a military dictatorship.

In the Twentieth Century, the German Third Reich, although outnumbered by its neighbors and enemies, populationwise, had concentrated all its efforts on building an unbeatable war machine. Japan, also outnumbered, had done likewise. Between them, they thought they could beat the rest of Earth. And they came dangerously close to succeeding.

The Gehan Federation had done the same thing, building up fleets and armies and material stockpiles as though she were already at war.

And, in doing so, her citizens had voluntarily forfeited the very thing they thought they were fighting for—their freedom.

But they posed a greater threat to the Terran Empire than that Empire had ever faced before. Any nation so totally prepared for defensive war may, at any moment, decide that the best defense is a good offense. Any nation which subjects its people to semislavery for the sake of war must eventually fight that war or suffer collapse.

The Empire had to change tactics. Instead of steady expansion, she was forced into a deadly game of interstellar chess, making her plays carefully, so as not to touch off the explosive temper of her opponent.

It was not a situation to be handled by clumsy fools.

And Lord Senesin, the Prime Portfolio of the Imperial File, the elected leader of the Empire, the constitutional head of the Imperial Government, was accused, not only of being a clumsy fool, but of being a dangerous madman. The planet Bairnvell was an independent, autonomous ally of the Gehan Federation, and, although not actually a member of the Federation, was presumably under her protection. For the Imperial Fleet to go to the aid of rebels trying to overthrow Bairnvell's lawful government seemed to be the act of an insane mind. The people of the Empire wouldn't stand for it.

Colonel Lord Barrick Sorban was well aware of the temper of the people and of the situation that prevailed politically in the Empire—more so, in fact, than most men. He was also well aware that internal strife of a very serious nature could so dangerously weaken the Empire that the Gehan Federation would be able to attack and win.

His job was to cut off that sort of thing before it could gain momentum. His job was to maintain the Empire; his only superior was the Emperor himself; his subordinates hand-picked, well-trained, and, like himself, unobtrusive to the public eye. And not one of those subordinates knew who the colonel's superior was.

The colonel strolled along the streets of Honolulu with all the courteous aplomb of a man who was both an officer and a gentleman of leisure. He dropped in at various respectable clubs and did various respectable things. He went into other places and did other things not so respectable. He gave certain orders to certain people and made certain odd arrangements. When everything had been set up to his satisfaction, he ate a leisurely dinner, topped it off with two glasses of Velaskan wine, read the tenth edition of the *Globe*, and strolled out to the street again, looking every inch the impeccable gentleman.

At ten minutes of eleven, he took a skycab to the fashionable apartment house where the Honorable Jon Senesin, son of the Prime Portfolio, made his home. The skycab deposited him on the roof at two minutes of eleven. The android doorman opened the entrance for him, and he took the drop chute down to the fifteenth floor. At precisely eleven o'clock, he was facing the announcer plate on Jon Senesin's door.

Senesin opened the door. There was a queer look—half jubilant, half worried—on his face as he said: "Come in, my lord, come in. Care for a drink?"

"Don't mind if I do, Jon. Brandy, if you have it."

Young Senesin poured the brandy, speaking rapidly as he did. "I've made an appointment to get those tapes, my lord. I want you to go with me. If we can get them, we can break this whole fraud wide open. Wide open." He handed the colonel a crystal goblet half filled with the clear, red-brown liquid. "Sorry I left so hurriedly this morning, but if that Heywood character had said another word I'd have broken his nose for him."

The colonel took the goblet and looked into its depths. "Jon, what do you expect these tapes to prove?"

The young man's face darkened. He walked across the spacious room, brandy goblet in hand, and sat down on the wall couch before he spoke.

"Just what I told you, my lord. I expect to prove that my father's mind has been tampered with—that he is not responsible for the decisions that have been made in his name—that he is going to lose his position and his reputation and his career for something that he would never have done in his right mind—that he has been the duped pawn of someone else."

The colonel walked over toward the couch and stood over the young man. "Someone? You keep referring to 'someone.' Ever since you asked me to help you, you've been mysterious about this someone. Whom do you suspect?"

Senesin looked up at the colonel for a long moment before he answered. Then: "I suspect the Emperor himself," he said, half defiantly.

The colonel raised his finely-drawn brows just a fraction of an inch, as though he hadn't known what the answer would be. "The Emperor? Hannikar IV? Isn't that a little far-fetched?"

Senesin shook his head vehemently. "Don't you see? Legally, the Emperor is powerless; the Throne hasn't had any say-so in the Government for over a century—except to sign state papers and such. But suppose an Emperor came along who wanted power—power such as the old Emperors used to have. How would he go about getting it? By controlling the Government! He could slowly force them to give him back the powers that the people of the Empire have taken so many centuries to obtain."

The colonel shook his head. "Impossible. Not even the Emperor could control the votes of the whole File for that purpose. It simply couldn't be done."

"Not that way; of course not," the young man said irritably. "But there *is* a way. It's been used before. Are you up on your history?"

"Reasonably well," the colonel said dryly.

"How did Julius Caesar get dictatorial powers? And, after him, Augustus? Rome was threatened by war, and then actually engaged in it, and the patricians were glad to give power to a strong man."

"That was in a state ruled by the few patricians," the colonel pointed out, "not in a democracy."

"Very well, then; what about the United States, during World War II? Look at the extraordinary powers granted to the President—first to stop a depression, then to win a war. What might have happened if he hadn't died? Would he have gone on to a fifth and a sixth term? How much more power could he have usurped from the hands of Congress?"

The colonel wondered vaguely what history texts young Senesin had read, but he didn't ask. "All right," he said, "now tie your examples up with His Majesty."

"It's very simple. By controlling the mind of the Prime Portfolio, the Emperor can plunge the Empire into war with the Gehan Federation. Once that has been done, he can begin to ask for extraordinary powers from the File. If he has a few key men under his thumb, he can swing the majority of the File any way he wants to. Don't you see that?"

The colonel said: "It does make a certain amount of sense." He paused, looking at the young man speculatively. "Tell me, son: why did you pick me to tell this tale to?"

Senesin's sensitive face betrayed his anxiety. "Because you have been my father's best and oldest friend. If he's really being made a puppet of, I should think you'd want to help him. Do you like to see him being destroyed this way?"

"No," said the colonel honestly. "And if he is actually being controlled illegally, if he is actually being blamed for things he did not do of his own free will, I'll do everything in my power to expose the plot—that I promise you."

Jon Senesin's eyes lit up; his face broke into a smile. "I *knew* I could depend on you, my lord! I *knew* it!"

"Just how do you propose to go about this?" asked Colonel Lord Sorban.

There was fire in young Senesin's eyes now. "I'll turn the whole case over to the people! I have some evidence, of course; the queer changes in behavior that Dad has exhibited during the past few years, and such things as that. The things that made me suspect in the first place. But that isn't acceptable evidence." He finished his brandy and got up excitedly to walk over and pour himself another. He glanced at the colonel's goblet, but the colonel had three-quarters of his own drink left.

Senesin talked as he poured. "Did you ever hear of a group called the Federalist Party?"

"Yes," said Colonel Sorban. "They want to federalize the Empire and get rid of the Imperial Family. Not a very popular group."

"No, but they're right! They're right! Don't you see that? And nobody pays any attention to them!"

"Calm down, son. What have the Federalists got to do with this?"

"They have sympathizers in the Palace," Senesin explained. "They've been able to get proof that the Emperor is illegally tampering with the Government, that he's been brainwashing my father. And they're going to turn that proof over to me."

"I don't quite follow the reason for that," the colonel lied easily. "Why don't they use it themselves?"

"They can't. Nobody'd believe them. Everyone would think that the proof had been faked for political propaganda.

"On the other hand, if *I* do it, all I can be accused of is having a personal motive. And if a man wants to get his father out of a jam, most people will agree that I have a perfect right to do so. Besides, I have enough influence to get people to listen to me, to give the evidence a fair hearing. If the newsies got this stuff from the Federalists, they'd throw it away without looking at it. But they'll listen to me."

"The newsies?" asked the colonel in a perfect imitation of mild astonishment. "You intend to turn this stuff over to news publishers?"

"Certainly! That's the only way. Put the evidence before the people, and they'll see what they're up against. I personally don't care whether we have an Emperor or not, but at least we can force Hannikar IV to abdicate in favor of Crown Prince Jaimie."

"I see." The colonel took another sip at his brandy and appeared to think it over. Wisely, young Senesin said nothing.

"How are we to get this evidence?" the colonel asked at last.

"We're to meet a man," Senesin said, with an air of melodrama. "We will get a call at fifteen of twelve, telling us where to meet him. We have to be there at midnight."

Oh, brother, thought the colonel, *they really picked their man. They've got him thinking he's hip-deep in a romantic spy story.*

Was I that way at twenty-two? A romantic? I suppose I must have been; why else would I have joined the Guards? Not for the pay, certainly.

Hell, I guess I'm still a romantic, in a way. Being a secret agent isn't all fun and games, but it has its compensations.

Aloud, he said, "Very well, son; I'll go with you. Did you tell them there'd be someone accompanying you?"

"I told them I'd have a friend along. I told them it would be you. They said it was all right, that they knew you were a friend of Dad's. They even knew you've been a little bitter at being retired from the Guards so young." He looked embarrassed. "Pardon me, my lord."

"That's all right," said the colonel steadily. He managed to give the appearance of a man who was doing his best not to look bitter.

"You aren't carrying a gun, are you?" Senesin asked suddenly. "They said we weren't to be armed. They'll probably search us."

"I haven't been in the habit of carrying a gun lately," said the colonel. "They won't find anything on me."

He finished his brandy while Senesin finished his second one. While the younger man refilled both goblets, the colonel asked permission to use the bathroom. He was gone less than three minutes, which he had spent with thumb and middle finger to larynx and mastoid bone.

At eleven forty-five promptly, the phone chimed. No face appeared on the screen when young Senesin answered it, but a voice gave an address on Kalia Road.

Three minutes later, the two men were on the roof, signaling for a skycab.

At ten o'clock the next morning, a panel slid aside in a wall that had previously seemed solid. Colonel Lord Barrick Sorban stepped into the room, thinking as he did so that he really was a romantic. He actually rather enjoyed the idea of using secret passages and hidden panels to gain access to the Emperor's private apartments in the Imperial Palace.

He gave a gentle nod to the man in the blue lounging robe who sat in a big easy-chair just across the room. "Good morning, Sire."

"'Morning, colonel," said His Imperial Majesty, Hannikar IV. "How are things shaping up?"

The colonel chuckled. "Not a single one of the newsies printed a word of it, Sire."

These men were close friends, and had been for years, yet they clung to the formal titles, both from habit and for self-protection. The accidental use of a first name could mean a dead giveaway at the wrong time.

The Emperor was a smaller man than Colonel Sorban, but he was far more impressive. While the colonel seemed rather mild, the Emperor looked—well, Imperial. He looked just as an Emperor ought to look—handsome, dark-haired, stern at times and kindly at others. The square jaw gave an impression of firmness of character, while the sapphire-blue eyes were penetrating without being harsh or hard.

"What about the Senesin boy?" he asked.

"He's in jail," said the colonel.

His Imperial Majesty raised an eyebrow. "Oh?" It was a question and a command.

"Not by my orders," said the colonel quickly. "He got a little upset. He'd taken those tapes and documents around to four editors and had been thrown out four times. The fifth time—at the *Globe*, as a matter of fact—he accused the editor of being in your pay. A hassle started, and the editor called the Honolulu police. Don't worry, Sire; one of my boys got the tapes and stuff."

"Is it genuine?"

"The evidence? Yes. The Federalists had the goods on you, all right." He grinned. "As you said, everything but brainwashing."

"I'll take care of it," said the Emperor. "Prince Jaimie's been going through the family files, and I rather want him to see this batch of stuff, too. Meantime, get the Senesin boy out of that cell; I want to see him. He's got guts, if nothing else."

"He has sense, too, Sire; he's just a little too young yet." He almost added "and romantic," but he stopped himself in time.

"How long will it take to get him out?" His Majesty asked.

"I can have him here in half an hour. The editor of the *Globe* will drop the charges. I can put a little pressure on in the right places."

The Emperor nodded. After a moment, he thumbed a button on his chair arm. "Inform Lord Senesin that he is requested to appear for a Royal Audience in forty-five minutes," he said firmly.

"Yes, Sire," said a voice from a hidden speaker.

The Emperor looked at the colonel. "Get the boy."

Jon Senesin sat in a soft chair, his hands gripping at the arms as though it might at any time fall from under him. He looked at the three other men in the room. His father, Lord Senesin, looking rather tired, but with a slight smile on his lantern-jawed face, sat on his son's left. One hand ran nervously through his gray hair.

On Jon's right sat the colonel, looking cool, unperturbed, and very gentle.

Between them sat the Emperor.

Jon's face looked pale, and there was a slight nervous tic at the corner of his mouth. "I ... I don't understand," he said. "I—" He swallowed hard as his voice failed him.

"Nothing hard to understand, son," said the colonel mildly. "We've been looking for evidence to break up the Federalists for several years. Some of them are honest men who are simply against any kind of hereditary monarchy—we'll let them go eventually. Some of them are fanatics—the kind that is against any form of government that happens to be in power; they'll get psychiatric treatment. But the leaders of the group are agents of the Gehan Federation. My men are picking them up now. The man that contacted you and me last night was arrested within two minutes after we left."

"But—the *evidence*! Those tapes. The documents. They all seemed genuine. They seemed so convincing."

"They should be convincing, Jon," said Lord Senesin in his smooth oratorical baritone. "You see, they are perfectly true."

Jon Senesin looked at his father as though the older man had suddenly sprouted an extra set of ears. "Y ... You've been brainwashed?"

The Prime Portfolio shook his head. "No, son, not that. Did you see anything like that on the tapes?"

"N-no. But the others. Fileman Brenner, Portfolio for Defense Vane, General Finster—all of them. I thought—"

"You thought wrong, son," said Lord Senesin. "I am and always have been working loyally with His Majesty. He gives the orders, and I carry them out."

Jon's voice became taut. "You mean you're helping him? You're trying to get the Empire into a war with the Gehan Federation so that *he* can become another dictator, like Jerris the First?" He kept his eyes carefully averted from the Emperor as he spoke.

Thus he didn't notice that His Majesty looked at Colonel Sorban with an expression that said, "You're right. He does have guts."

Lord Senesin said: "No, son; I'm not working toward that at all. Neither is His Majesty. There would be no point in it."

Then, for the first time, the Emperor spoke. His voice was soft, but commanding. "Mr. Senesin, let me explain something to you."

Jon Senesin's head jerked around. There was a confused mixture of fear and determination on his face.

"Mr. Senesin, I no more want war than you do. I am trying to avoid it with every power at my command. I have that duty to my people. But I have another duty, too. A duty, not just to the Empire, but to the human race as a whole. And that duty is to establish, not a Terran Empire, but a Galactic Empire—a single, consolidated government for every planet in the galaxy. Man can't go on this way, divided, split up, warring with himself. Man can't live in isolation, cut off from other worlds, other types of societies.

"We can't have a part of the human race living in constant fear of another part. We can't allow the conditions that exist at this moment in the Gehan Federation. To paraphrase Lincoln, 'The galaxy cannot exist half slave and half free.'

"Right now, there is evidence that the Gehan Federation will collapse internally within less than five years. The only way for the President of the Federation to avert that collapse will be to declare war on the Empire. We have had to take certain risks in order to insure that when and if war does come, we will win it.

"Bairnvell was one of those risks. Not too great a one, as it turns out; evidently the Federation government doesn't see that our possession of that base is a vital factor in our own defense. Strategy in three dimensions isn't easy to reason out.

"Mr. Senesin, I have no desire for power in a personal way. Any power I have is used for the good of my people. I have no police system for terrorizing the people; I don't suppress the freedom of every man to say or print what he wants. To call your Sovereign a fatheaded slob in a newsfac might be considered bad taste, but it isn't illegal. I can't even bring a civil suit against you, the way an ordinary citizen could.

"Now, I'll grant that I sometimes use illegal means to control the Empire. But there are reasons for that. I—"

He was interrupted by a soft chime. He pressed a button on his armchair. "Yes?"

"You go on the interstellar hookup in twenty minutes, Sire. The File has assembled," said a voice from a speaker.

"I'll be right there." He stood up and glanced apologetically at the other three men. "Sorry. Political announcement, you know. You two go ahead and explain to Mr. Senesin." Then he looked directly at the Prime Portfolio. "I'll tell them you're slightly ill." He reached out, took Lord Senesin's hand, and grasped it firmly. "I'll make it look good, old friend, don't worry. I'll need your help with Lord Evondering when he gets the Primacy."

The other men were on their feet already. They watched in silence as he walked out the door, then eased themselves back into their chairs.

"I still don't understand," Jon said softly. The bitterness and anger seemed to have left him, leaving only puzzlement in their wake. "If you take orders from him, Dad, then this isn't a democracy any more. It's become another Imperial dictatorship."

"Son," said his father, "the Empire never has been a democracy in the sense you're thinking about. Ever since Jerris the First, it has been ruled solely by the Emperors. Always.

"The Imperial Family is a special breed, son. It's a genetic strain in which the quality of wise leadership is dominant. It's a quality that's more than just intelligence; wisdom is the ability to make correct judgments, not only for one's self, but for others."

"But, Dad!" There was almost a wail in the boy's voice. "That makes the whole democratic system in the Empire a farce! It's totally unnecessary! *You're* unnecessary! He could run everything by himself!"

Lord Senesin started to say something, but Colonel Sorban interrupted.

"No, you young fool, he is *not* unnecessary! He is, in a very real sense, the Emperor's shield. Our Emperors have always given the people of the Empire the kind of government they *need*, not the kind of government they *want*. There are certain things that *must* be done, whether the people like those things or not.

"How long do you think the Empire would last without the Imperial Line to guide it? Not ten years! The thing is too big, too vast, for any ordinary man to handle the job. The voters are perfectly capable of electing a man to the Primacy on the strength of his likable personality alone—look at Lord Evondering. A hell of a pleasant guy, without a glimmering of real wisdom.

"When the people don't like the things the Government does, they throw it out—even if the thing done was actually for the best. The people demand a new Government. We can't allow them to throw the Emperor out, so we need a scapegoat. This time, it happened to be your father, here. He happened to be Prime at a crucial time, and he had to give orders that made him unpopular. So he'll have to get out, and let the Loyal Opposition take over. But the Emperor will go right on running things.

"Your father is far from unnecessary, son. He's a hero, dammit, and you'd better remember that! He's taking the rap for another man because he knows that he is expendable and the other man isn't.

"Oh, your father could probably ride this thing out and stay in the Primacy for a couple more years. But this mess with the Federation is going to get a lot stickier than it is now. The Emperor is going to have to do things that the people will hate even worse, and we might as well let that fool Evondering take the rap. He'll look so bad by the time he leaves the Primacy that everyone will be screaming for your father back again, to clean up the mess."

Jon Senesin still looked dazed. "But, if that's the case, why allow the people to vote at all?"

"Because that's the only way you can keep an Empire stable! As long as the average man feels he has a voice in his Government, he's forced to admit that any failures are partly his own fault. Nobody rebels against a government he can vote against. As long as he has ballots, he won't use bullets."

Lord Senesin said: "I know it's a shock, coming this way. But look at it right, son."

"I am," said Jon slowly. "At least, I think I am. But it doesn't really seem right. Not yet." He looked at the colonel. "One thing I don't understand, my lord. Why did you let me take all that evidence around to the newsies? And why are you telling me all this now? I'm still not fully convinced. Aren't you afraid I'll tell the whole story?"

But it was his father who answered. "You tried that, son. It didn't work, did it?"

"No. But *why*? Why wouldn't they believe me, even when I had all that evidence?"

"Because they don't *want* to believe you," said the colonel. "Ever hear of a father-image? The Emperor is a symbol, Jon. He's not a human being in the eyes of the average man. He's the kind All-Father, the godlike being who dispenses mercy, but not justice.

"Haven't you ever noticed that orders of judgment against criminals are signed only by the courts and by the Portfolio of the Interior? But pardons and paroles are signed by the Emperor.

"It may not sound ethical to you, but that's the way the Emperor has to operate. He takes credit for all the nice things he does, and lets others take the blame for anything that's distasteful.

"You could blat it around all over fifty star systems that the Emperor was a louse, and all you'd get is a poke in the eye for your troubles.

"It's not easy for him, and don't ever kid yourself that it is. He's going out there now to tell the Empire that your father and his Government have resigned. He has to try to make his best friend and most loyal subject look a little less black than he has been painted, and all the time it was the Emperor who wielded the paint gun. Do you think that's fun?"

"No," said Jon softly. "No, I guess not." He paused. "Wouldn't it have been easier to take the evidence away from me, though?"

"No. That would have left you furious. No amount of talking would have convinced you. As it was, you convinced yourself that there is no way to attack the Emperor directly. He's safe right where he is."

Jon shook his head slowly. "It all seems so ... so tangled. It still seems as though the whole deception is ... well, *wrong*, somehow."

"If you look at it in a certain way," said Lord Senesin, "I suppose it does seem wrong. But it's necessary. Absolutely necessary."

"Maybe," said Jon, still unconvinced. "It certainly does look as though His Majesty has himself in an almost impregnable position. It's a wonder he needs agents like you."

Colonel Lord Barrick Sorban smiled a little. The boy would see the thing straight eventually. He had what it took, even if it didn't show much at this stage. Actually, he was more than halfway convinced now, but wouldn't admit it to himself yet. At least he'd been able to put a finger on one thing.

Aloud, the colonel said: "You're not altogether wrong there, son. When you come right down to it, *I'm* the unnecessary man."

THE END

Hail to the Chief

■ The tumult in Convention Hall was a hurricane of sound that lashed at a sea of human beings that surged and eddied around the broad floor. Men and women, delegates and spectators, aged party wheelhorses and youngsters who would vote for the first time that November, all lost their identities to merge with that swirling tide. Over their heads, like agitated bits of flotsam, pennants fluttered and placards rose and dipped. Beneath their feet, discarded metal buttons that bore the names of two or three "favorite sons" and those that had touted the only serious contender against the party's new candidate were trodden flat. None of them had ever really had a chance.

The buttons that were now pinned on every lapel said: "Blast 'em With Cannon!" or "Cannon Can Do!" The placards and the box-shaped signs, with a trifle more dignity, said: WIN WITH CANNON and CANNON FOR PRESIDENT and simply JAMES H. CANNON.

Occasionally, in the roar of noise, there were shouts of "Cannon! Cannon! Rah! Rah! Rah! Cannon! Cannon! Sis-boom-bah!" and snatches of old popular tunes hurriedly set with new words:

On with Cannon, on with Cannon!
White House, here we come!
He's a winner, no beginner;
He can get things done!
(Rah! Rah! Rah!)

And, over in one corner, a group of college girls were enthusiastically chanting:

He is handsome! He is sexy!
We want J. H. C. for Prexy!

It was a demonstration that lasted nearly three times as long as the eighty-five-minute demonstration that had occurred when Representative Matson had first proposed his name for the party's nomination.

Spatially, Senator James Harrington Cannon was four blocks away from Convention Hall, in a suite at the Statler-Hilton, but electronically, he was no farther away than the television camera that watched the cheering multitude from above the floor of the hall.

The hotel room was tastefully and expensively decorated, but neither the senator nor any of the other men in the room were looking at anything else except the big thirty-six-inch screen that glowed and danced with color. The network announcer's words were almost inaudible, since the volume had been turned way down, but his voice sounded almost as excited as those from the convention floor.

Senator Cannon's broad, handsome face showed a smile that indicated pleasure, happiness, and a touch of triumph. His dark, slightly wavy hair, with the broad swathes of silver at the temples, was a little disarrayed, and there was a splash of cigarette ash on one trouser leg, but otherwise, even sitting there in his shirt sleeves, he looked well-dressed. His wide shoulders tapered down to a narrow waist and lean hips, and he looked a good ten years younger than his actual fifty-two.

He lit another cigarette, but a careful scrutiny of his face would have revealed that, though his eyes were on the screen, his thoughts were not in Convention Hall.

Representative Matson, looking like an amazed bulldog, managed to chew and puff on his cigar simultaneously and still speak understandable English. "Never saw anything like it. Never. First ballot and you had it, Jim. I know Texas was going to put up Perez as a favorite son on the first ballot, but they couldn't do anything except jump on the bandwagon by the time the vote reached them. Unanimous on the first ballot."

Governor Spanding, a lantern-jawed, lean man sitting on the other side of Senator Cannon, gave a short chuckle and said, "Came close not t' being unanimous. The delegate from Alabama looked as though he was going to stick to his 'One vote for Byron Beauregarde Cadwallader' until Cadwallader himself went over to make him change his vote before the first ballot was complete."

The door opened, and a man came in from the other room. He bounced in on the balls of his feet, clapped his hands together, and dry-washed them briskly. "We're in!" he said, with businesslike glee. "Image, gentlemen! That's what does it: Image!" He was a tall, rather bony-faced man in his early forties, and his manner was that of the self-satisfied businessman who is quite certain that he knows all of the answers and all of the questions. "Create an image that the public goes for, and you're in!"

Senator Cannon turned his head around and grinned. "Thanks, Horvin, but let's remember that we still have an election to win."

"We'll win it," Horvin said confidently. "A properly projected image attracts the public—"

"Oh, crud," said Representative Matson in a growly voice. "The opposition has just as good a staff of PR men as we do. If we beat 'em, it'll be because we've got a better man, not because we've got better public relations."

"Of course," said Horvin, unabashed. "We can project a better image because we've got better material to work with. We—"

"Jim managed to get elected to the Senate without any of your help, and he went in with an avalanche. If there's any 'image projecting' done around here, Jim is the one who does it."

Horvin nodded his head as though he were in complete agreement with Matson. "Exactly. His natural ability plus the scientific application of mass psychology make an unbeatable team."

Matson started to say something, but Senator Cannon cut in first. "He's right, Ed. We've got to use every weapon we have to win this election. Another four years of the present policies, and the Sino-Russian Bloc will be able to start unilateral disarmament. They won't have to start a war to bury us."

Horvin looked nervous. "Uh ... Senator—"

Cannon made a motion in the air. "I know, I know. Our policy during the campaign will be to run down the opposition, not the United States. We are still in a strong position, but *if this goes on*—Don't worry, Horvin; the whole thing will be handled properly."

Before any of them could say anything, Senator Cannon turned to Representative Matson and said: "Ed, will you get Matthew Fisher on the phone? And the Governor of Pennsylvania and ... let's see ... Senator Hidekai and Joe Vitelli."

"I didn't even know Fisher was here," Matson said. "What do you want him for?"

"I just want to talk to him, Ed. Get him up here, with the others, will you?"

"Sure, Jim; sure." He got up and walked over to the phone.

Horvin, the PR man, said: "Well, Senator, now that you're the party's candidate for the Presidency of the United States, who are you going to pick for your running mate? Vollinger was the only one who came even close to giving you a run for your money, and it would be good public relations if you chose him. He's got the kind of personality that would make a good image."

"Horvin," the senator said kindly, "I'll pick the men; you build the image from the raw material I give you. You're the only man I know who can convince the public that a sow's ear is really a silk purse, and you may have to do just that.

"You can start right now. Go down and get hold of the news boys and tell them that the announcement of my running mate will be made as soon as this demonstration is over.

"Tell them you can't give them any information other than that, but give them the impression that you already know. Since you *don't* know, don't try to guess; that way you won't let any cats out of the wrong bags. But you *do* know that he's a fine man, and you're pleased as all hell that I made such a good choice. Got that?"

Horvin grinned. "Got it. You pick the man; I'll build the image." He went out the door.

When the door had closed, Governor Spanding said: "So it's going to be Fisher, is it?"

"You know too much, Harry," said Senator Cannon, grinning. "Remind me to appoint you ambassador to Patagonia after Inauguration Day."

"If I lose the election at home, I may take you up on it. But why Matthew Fisher?"

"He's a good man, Harry."

"Hell yes, he is," the governor said. "Tops. I've seen his record as State Attorney General and as Lieutenant Governor. And when Governor Dinsmore died three years ago, Fisher did a fine job filling out his last year. But—"

"But he couldn't get re-elected two years ago," Senator Cannon said. "He couldn't keep the governor's office, in spite of the great job he'd done."

"That's right. He's just not a politician, Jim. He doesn't have the ... the personality, the flash, whatever it is that it takes to get a man elected by the people. I've got it; you sure as hell have it; Fisher doesn't."

"That's why I've got Horvin working for us," said Senator Cannon. "Whether I need him or not may be a point of argument. Whether Matthew Fisher needs him or not is a rhetorical question."

Governor Spanding lit a cigarette in silence while he stared at the quasi-riot that was still coming to the screen from Convention Hall. Then he said: "You've been thinking of Matt Fisher all along, then."

"Not Patagonia," said the senator. "Tibet."

"I'll shut up if you want me to, Jim."

"No. Go ahead."

"All right. Jim, I trust your judgment. I've got no designs on the Vice Presidency myself, and you know it. I like to feel that, if I had, you'd give me a crack at it. No, don't answer that, Jim; just let me talk.

"What I'm trying to say is that there are a lot of good men in the party who'd make fine VP's; men who've given their all to get you the nomination, and who'll work even harder to see that you're elected. Why pass them up in favor of a virtual unknown like Matt Fisher?"

Senator Cannon didn't say anything. He knew that Spanding didn't want an answer yet.

"The trouble with Fisher," Spanding went on, "is that he ... well, he's too autocratic. He pulls decisions out of midair. He—" Spanding paused, apparently searching for a way to express himself. Senator Cannon said nothing; he waited expectantly.

"Take a look at the Bossard Decision," Spanding said. "Fisher was Attorney General for his state at the time.

"Bossard was the Mayor of Waynesville—twelve thousand and something population, I forget now. Fisher didn't even know Bossard. But when the big graft scandal came up there in Waynesville, Fisher wouldn't prosecute. He didn't actually refuse, but he hemmed and hawed around for five months before he really started the State's machinery to moving. By that time, Bossard had managed to get enough influence behind him so that he could beat the rap.

"When the case came to trial in the State Supreme Court, Matt Fisher told the Court that it was apparent that Mayor Bossard was the victim of the local district attorney and the chief of police of Waynesville. In spite of the evidence against him, Bossard was acquitted." Spanding took a breath to say something more, but Senator James Cannon interrupted him.

"Not 'acquitted', Harry. 'Exonerated'. Bossard never even should have come to trial," the senator said. "He was a popular, buddy-buddy sort of guy who managed to get himself involved as an unwitting figurehead. Bossard simply wasn't—and isn't—very bright. But he was a friendly, outgoing, warm sort of man who was able to get elected through the auspices of the local city machine. Remember Jimmy Walker?"

Spanding nodded. "Yes, but—"

"Same thing," Cannon cut in. "Bossard was innocent, as far as any criminal intent was concerned, but he was too easy on his so-called friends. He—"

"Oh, *crud*, Jim!" the governor interrupted vehemently. "That's the same whitewash that Matthew Fisher gave him! The evidence would have convicted Bossard if Fisher hadn't given him time to cover up!"

Senator James Cannon suddenly became angry. He jammed his own cigarette butt into the ash tray, turned toward Spanding, and snapped: "Harry, just for the sake of argument, let's suppose that Bossard wasn't actually guilty. Let's suppose that the Constitution of the United States is really true—that a man isn't guilty until he's proven guilty.

"Just *suppose*"—his voice and expression became suddenly acid—"that Bossard was *not* guilty. Try that, huh? Pretend, somewhere in your own little mind, that a mere accusation—no matter what the evidence—doesn't prove anything! Let's just make a little game between the two of us that the ideal of Equality Under the Law means what it says. Want to play?"

"Well, yes, but—"

"O.K.," Cannon went on angrily. "O.K. Then let's suppose that Bossard really *was* stupid. He could have been framed easily, couldn't he? He could have been set up as a patsy, couldn't he? *Couldn't he?*"

"Well, sure, but—"

"Sure! Then go on and suppose that the prosecuting attorney had sense enough to see that Bossard *had* been framed. Suppose further that the prosecutor was enough of a human being to know that Bossard either had to be convicted or completely exonerated. What would he do?"

Governor Spanding carefully put his cigarette into the nearest ash tray. "If that were the case, I'd *completely* exonerate him. I wouldn't leave it hanging. Matt Fisher didn't do anything but make sure that Bossard couldn't be legally convicted; he didn't prove that Bossard was innocent."

"And what was the result, as far as Bossard was concerned?" the senator asked.

Spanding looked around at the senator, staring Cannon straight in the face. "The result was that Bossard was left hanging, Jim. If I go along with you and assume that Bossard was innocent, then Fisher fouled up just as badly as he would have if he'd fluffed the prosecution of a guilty man. Either a man is guilty, or he's innocent. If, according to your theory, the prosecutor knows he's innocent, then he should exonerate the innocent man! If not, he should do his best to convict!"

"He should?" snapped Cannon. "He *should*? Harry, you're letting your idealism run away with you! If Bossard were guilty, he should have been convicted—sure! But if he were innocent, should he be exonerated? Should he be allowed to run again for office? Should the people be allowed to think that he was lily-white? Should they be allowed to re-elect a nitwit who'd do the same thing again because he was too stupid to see that he was being used?

"No!" He didn't let the governor time to speak; he went on: "Matthew Fisher set it up perfectly. He exonerated Bossard enough to allow the ex-mayor to continue in private life without any question. *But*—there remained just enough question to keep him out of public office for the rest of his life. Was that wrong, Harry? Was it?"

Spanding looked blankly at the senator for a moment, then his expression slowly changed to one of grudging admiration. "Well ... if you put it that way ... yeah. I mean, no; it wasn't wrong. It was the only way to play it." He dropped his cigarette into a nearby ash tray. "O.K., Jim; you win. I'll back Fisher all the way."

"Thanks, Harry," Cannon said. "Now, if we—"

Congressman Matson came back into the room, saying, "I got 'em, Jim. Five or ten minutes, they'll be here. Which one of 'em is it going to be?"

"Matt Fisher, if we can come to an agreement," Cannon said, watching Matson's face closely.

Matson chewed at his cigar for a moment, then nodded. "He'll do. Not much political personality, but, hell, he's only running for Veep. We can get him through." He took the cigar out of his mouth. "How do you want to run it?"

"I'll talk to Fisher in my bedroom. You and Harry hold the others in here with the usual chitchat. Tell 'em I'm thinking over the choice of my running mate, but don't tell 'em I've made up my mind yet. If Matt Fisher doesn't want it, we can tell the others that Matt and I were simply talking over the possibilities. I don't want anyone to think he's second choice. Got it?"

Matson nodded. "Whatever you say, Jim."

That year, late August was a real blisterer along the eastern coast of the United States. The great megalopolis that sprawled from Boston to Baltimore in utter scorn of state boundaries sweltered in the kind of atmosphere that is usually only found in the pressing rooms of large tailor shops. Consolidated Edison, New York's Own Power Company, was churning out multimegawatts that served to air condition nearly every enclosed place on the island of Manhattan—which served only to make the open streets even hotter. The power plants in the Bronx, west Brooklyn, and east Queens were busily converting hydrogen into helium and energy, and the energy was being used to convert humid air at ninety-six Fahrenheit into dry air at seventy-one Fahrenheit. The subways were crowded with people who had no intention of going anywhere in particular; they just wanted to retreat from the hot streets to the air-conditioned bowels of the city.

But the heat that can be measured by thermometers was not the kind that was causing two groups of men in two hotels, only a few blocks apart on the East Side of New York's Midtown, to break out in sweat, both figurative and literal.

One group was ensconced in the Presidential Suite of the New Waldorf—the President and Vice President of the United States, both running for re-election, and other high members of the incumbent party.

The other group, consisting of Candidates Cannon and Fisher, and the high members of *their* party, were occupying the only slightly less pretentious Bridal Suite of a hotel within easy walking distance of the Waldorf.

Senator James Cannon read through the news release that Horvin had handed him, then looked up at the PR man. "This is right off the wire. How long before it's made public?"

Horvin glanced at his watch. "Less than half an hour. There's an NBC news program at five-thirty. Maybe before, if one of the radio stations think it's important enough for a bulletin break."

"That means that it will have been common knowledge for four hours by the time we go on the air for the debate," said Cannon.

Horvin nodded, still looking at his watch. "And even if some people miss the TV broadcast, they'll be able to read all about it. The deadline for the *Daily Register* is at six; the papers will hit the streets at seven-fifteen, or thereabouts."

Cannon stood up from his chair. "Get your men out on the streets. Get 'em into bars, where they can pick up reactions to this. I want as good a statistical sampling as you can get in so short a time. It'll have to be casual; I don't want your men asking questions as though they were regular pollsters; just find out what the general trend is."

"Right." Horvin got out fast.

The other men in the room were looking expectantly at the senator. He paused for a moment, glancing around at them, and then looked down at the paper and said: "This is a bulletin from Tass News Agency, Moscow." Then he began reading.

"Russian Luna Base One announced that at 1600 Greenwich Standard Time (12:00 N EDST) a presumed spacecraft of unknown design was damaged by Russian rockets and fell to the surface of Luna somewhere in the Mare Serenitas, some three hundred fifty miles from the Soviet base. The craft was hovering approximately four hundred miles above the surface when spotted by Soviet radar installations. Telescopic inspection showed that the craft was not—repeat: not—powered by rockets. Since it failed to respond to the standard United Nations recognition signals, rockets were fired to bring it down. In attempting to avoid the rockets, the craft, according to observers, maneuvered in an entirely unorthodox manner, which cannot be attributed to a rocket drive. A nearby burst, however, visibly damaged the hull of the craft, and it dropped toward Mare Serenitas. Armed Soviet moon-cats are, at this moment, moving toward the downed craft.

"Base Commander Colonel A. V. Gryaznov is quoted as saying: 'There can be no doubt that we shall learn much from this craft, since it is apparently of extraterrestrial origin. We will certainly be able to overpower any resistance it may offer, since it has already proved vulnerable to our weapons. The missiles which were fired toward our base were easily destroyed by our own antimissile missiles, and the craft was unable to either destroy or avoid our own missiles.'

"Further progress will be released by the Soviet Government as it occurs."

Senator Cannon dropped the sheet of paper to his side. "That's it. Matt, come in the bedroom; I'd like to talk to you."

Matthew Fisher, candidate for Vice President of the United States, heaved his two-hundred-fifty-pound bulk out of the chair he had been sitting in and followed the senator into the other room. Behind them, the others suddenly broke out into a blather of conversation. Fisher's closing of the door cut the sound off abruptly.

Senator Cannon threw the newssheet on the nearest bed and swung around to face Matthew Fisher. He looked at the tall, thick, muscular man trying to detect the emotions behind the ugly-handsome face that had been battered up by football and boxing in college, trying to fathom the thoughts beneath the broad forehead and the receding hairline.

"You got any idea what this *really* means, Matt?" he asked after a second.

Fisher's blue-gray eyes widened almost imperceptibly, and his gaze sharpened. "Not until just this moment," he said.

Cannon looked suddenly puzzled. "What do you mean?"

"Well," Fisher said thoughtfully, "you wouldn't ask me unless it meant something more than appears on the surface." He grinned rather apologetically. "I'm sorry, Jim; it takes a second or two to reconstruct exactly what *did* go through my mind." His grin faded into a thoughtful frown. "Anyway, you asked me, and since you're head of the Committee on SPACE Travel and Exploration—" He spread his hands in a gesture that managed to convey both futility and apology. "The mystery spacecraft is ours," he said decisively.

James Cannon wiped a palm over his forehead and sat down heavily on one of the beds. "Right. Sit down. Fine. Now; listen: We—the United States—have a space drive that compares to the rocket in the same way that the jet engine compares to the horse. We've been keeping it under wraps that are comparable to those the Manhattan Project was kept under 'way back during World War II. Maybe more so. But—" He stopped, watching Fisher's face. Then: "Can you see it from there?"

"I think so," Fisher said. "The Soviet Government knows that we have something ... in fact, they've known it for a long time. They don't know what, though." He found a heavy briar in his pocket, pulled it out, and began absently stuffing it with tobacco from a pouch he'd pulled out with the pipe. "Our ship didn't shoot at their base. Couldn't, wouldn't have. Um. They shot it down to try to look it over. Purposely made a near-miss with an atomic warhead." He struck a match and puffed the pipe alight.

"Hm-m-m. The Soviet Government," he went on, "must have known that we had something 'way back when they signed the Greenston Agreement." Fisher blew out a cloud of smoke. "They wanted to change the wording of that, as I remember."

"That's right," Cannon said. "We wanted it to read that 'any advances in *rocket engineering* shall be shared equally among the Members of the United Nations', but the Soviet delegation wanted to change that to 'any advances in *space travel*'. We only beat them out by a verbal quibble; we insisted that the word 'space', as used, could apply equally to the space between continents or cities or, for that matter, between any two points. By the time we got through arguing, the UN had given up on the Soviet amendment, and the agreement was passed as was."

"Yeah," said Fisher, "I remember. So now we have a space drive that doesn't depend on rockets, and the USSR wants it." He stared at the bowl of his briar for a moment, then looked up at Cannon. "The point is that they've brought down one of our ships, and we have to get it out of there before the Russians get to it. Even if we manage to keep them from finding out anything about the drive, they can raise a lot of fuss in the UN if they can prove that it's our ship."

"Right. They'll ring in the Greenston Agreement even if the ship technically isn't a rocket," Cannon said. "Typical Soviet tactics. They try to time these things to hit at the most embarrassing moments. Four years ago, our worthy opponent got into office because our administration was embarrassed by the Madagascar Crisis. They simply try to show the rest of the world that, no matter which party is in, the United states is run by a bunch of inept fools." He slapped his hand down on the newssheet that lay near him. "This may win us the election," he said angrily, "but it will do us more harm in the long run than if our worthy opponent stayed in the White House."

"Of what avail to win an election and lose the whole Solar System," Fisher paraphrased. "It looks as though the President has a hot potato."

"'Hot' is the word. Pure californium-254." Cannon lit a cigarette and looked moodily at the glowing end. "But this puts us in a hole, too. Do we, or don't we, mention it on the TV debate this evening? If we don't, the public will wonder why; if we do, we'll put the country on the spot."

Matt Fisher thought for a few seconds. Then he said, "The ship must have already been having trouble. Otherwise it wouldn't have been hovering in plain sight of the Soviet radar. How many men does one of those ships hold?"

"Two," the senator told him.

"We do have more than one of those ships, don't we?" Fisher asked suddenly.

"Four on Moon Base; six more building," said Senator Cannon.

"The downed ship must have been in touch with—" He stopped abruptly, paused for a second, then said: "I have an idea, Senator, but you'll have to do the talking. We'll have to convince the President that what we're suggesting is for the good of the country and not just a political trick. And we don't have much time. Those moon-cats shouldn't take more than twelve or fifteen hours to reach the ship."

"What's your idea?"

"Well, it's pretty rough right now; we can't fill in the details until we get more information, but—" He knocked the dottle from his pipe and began outlining his scheme to the senator.

Major Valentin Udovichenko peered through the "windshield" of his moon-cat and slowed the vehicle down as he saw the glint of metal on the Earthlit plain ahead. "Captain!" he snapped. "What does that look like to you?" He pointed with a gloved hand.

The other officer looked. "I should say," he said after a moment, "that we have found what we have been looking for, major."

"So would I. It's a little closer to our base than the radarmen calculated, but it certainly could have swerved after it dropped below the horizon. And we know there hasn't been another ship in this vicinity."

The captain was focusing a pair of powerful field glasses on the object. "That's it!" he said bridling his excitement. "Egg-shaped, and no sign of rocket exhausts. Big dent in one side."

Major Udovichenko had his own binoculars out. "It's as plain as day in this Earthlight. No sign of life, either. We shouldn't have any trouble." He lowered the binoculars and picked up a microphone to give the other nine moon-cats their instructions.

Eight of the vehicles stayed well back, ready to launch rockets directly at the fallen spacecraft if there were any sign of hostility, while two more crept carefully up on her.

They were less than a hundred and fifty yards away when the object they were heading for caught fire. The major braked his vehicle to a sudden halt and stared at the bright blaze that was growing and spreading over the metallic shape ahead. Bursts of flame sprayed out in every direction, the hot gases meeting no resistance from the near-vacuum into which they spread.

Major Udovichenko shouted orders into his microphone and gunned his own motor into life again. The caterpillar treads crunched against the lunar surface as both moon-cats wheeled about and fled. Four hundred yards from the blaze, they stopped again and watched.

By this time, the blaze had eaten away more than half of the hulk, and it was surrounded by a haze of smoke and hot gas that was spreading rapidly away from it. The flare of light far outshone the light reflected from the sun by the Earth overhead.

"Get those cameras going!" the major snapped. He knew that the eight moon-cats that formed the distant perimeter had been recording steadily, but he wanted close-ups, if possible.

None of the cameras got much of anything. The blaze didn't last long, fierce as it was. When it finally died, and the smoke particles settled slowly to the lunar surface, there was only a blackened spot where the bulk of a spaceship had been.

"Well ... I ... will ... be—," said Major Valentin Udovichenko.

The TV debate was over. The senator and the President had gone at each other hot and heavy, hammer and tongs, with the senator clearly emerging as the victor. But no mention whatever had been made of the Soviet announcement from Luna.

At four thirty-five the next morning, the telephone rang in the senator's suite. Cannon had been waiting for it, and he was quick to answer.

The face that appeared on the screen was that of the President of the United States. "Your scheme worked, senator," he said without preamble. There was an aloofness, a coolness in his voice. Which was only natural, considering the heat of the debate the previous evening.

"I'm glad to hear it, Mr. President," the senator said, with only a hair less coolness. "What happened?"

"Your surmise that the Soviet officials did not realize the potential of the new craft was apparently correct," the President said. "General Thayer had already sent another ship in to rescue the crew of the disabled vessel, staying low, below the horizon of the Russian radar. The disabled ship had had some trouble with its drive mechanism; it would never have deliberately exposed itself to Russian detection. General Thayer had already asked my permission to destroy the disabled vessel rather than let the Soviets get their hands on it, and, but for your suggestion, I would have given him a go-ahead.

"But making a replica of the ship in plastic was less than a two-hour job. The materials were at hand; a special foam plastic is used as insulation from the chill of the lunar substrata. The foam plastic was impregnated with ammonium nitrate and foamed up with pure oxygen; since it is catalyst-setting, that could be done at low temperatures. The outside of the form was covered with metallized plastic, also impregnated with ammonium nitrate. I understand that the thing burned like unconfined gunpowder after it was planted in the path of the Soviet moon-cats and set off. The Soviet vehicles are on their way back to their base now."

After a moment's hesitation, he went on: "Senator, in spite of our political differences, I want to say that I appreciate a man who can put his country's welfare ahead of his political ambitions."

"Thank you, Mr. President. That is a compliment I appreciate and accept. But I want you to know that the notion of decoying them away with an inflammable plastic replica was not my idea; it was Matt Fisher's."

"Oh? My compliments to Mr. Fisher." He smiled then. It was obviously forced, but, just as obviously, there was sincerity behind it. "I hope the best team wins. But if it does not, I am secure in the knowledge that the second best team is quite competent."

Firmly repressing a desire to say, *I am sorry that I don't feel any such security myself*, Cannon merely said: "Thank you again, Mr. President."

When the connection was cut, Cannon grinned at Matthew Fisher. "That's it. We've saved a ship. It can be repaired where it is without a fleet of Soviet moon-cats prowling around and interfering. And we've scotched any attempts at propagandizing that the Soviets may have had in mind." He chuckled. "I'd like to have seen their faces when that thing started to burn in a vacuum. And I'd like to see the reports that are being flashed back and forth between Moscow and Soviet Moon Base One."

"I wasn't so much worried about the loss of the disabled ship as the *way* we'd lose it," Matthew Fisher said.

"The Soviets getting it?" Cannon asked. "We didn't have to worry about that. You heard him say that Thayer was going to destroy it."

"That's exactly what I meant," said Fisher. "*How* were we going to destroy it? TNT or dynamite or Radex-3 would have still left enough behind for a good Soviet team to make some kind of sense out of it—some kind of hint would be there, unless an awful lot of it were used. A fission or a thermonuclear bomb would have vaporized it, but that would have been a violation of the East-West Agreement. We'd be flatly in the wrong."

Senator Cannon walked over to the sideboard and poured Scotch into two glasses. "The way it stands now, the ship will at least be able to limp out of there before anyone in Moscow can figure out what happened and transmit orders back to Luna." He walked back with the glasses and handed one to Fisher. "Let's have a drink and go to bed. We have to be in Philadelphia tomorrow, and I'm dead tired."

"That's a pair of us," said Fisher, taking the glass.

Another month of campaigning, involving both televised and personal appearances, went by without unusual incidents. The prophets, seers, and pollsters were having themselves a grand time. Some of them—the predicting-by-past-performances men—were pointing out that only four Presidents had failed to succeed themselves when they ran for a second term: Martin Van Buren, Grover Cleveland, Benjamin Harrison, and Herbert Hoover. They argued that this presaged little chance of success for Senator James Cannon. The pollsters said that their samplings had shown a strong leaning toward the President at first, but that eight weeks of campaigning had started a switch toward Cannon, and that the movement seemed to be accelerating. The antipollsters, as usual, simply smiled smugly and said: "Remember Dewey in '48?"

Plays on Cannon's name had caught the popular fancy. The slogan "Blast 'em With Cannon" now appeared on every button worn by those who supported him—who called themselves "Cannoneers." Their opponents sneeringly referred to them as "Cannon fodder," and made jokes about "that big bore Cannon."

The latter joke was pure epithet, with no meaning behind it; when Senator James Cannon spoke, either in person or over the TV networks, even his opponents listened with grudging interest.

The less conservative newspapers couldn't resist the gag, either, and printed headlines on the order of CANNON FIRES BLAST AT FOREIGN POLICY, CANNON HOT OVER CIA ORDER, BUDGET BUREAU SHAKEN BY CANNON REPORT, and TREASURY IS LATEST CANNON TARGET.

The various newspaper columnists, expanding on the theme, made even more atrocious puns. When the senator praised his running mate, a columnist said that Fisher had been "Cannonized," and proceeded to call him "Saint" Matthew. The senator's ability to remember the names and faces of his constituents caused one pundit to remark that "it's a wise Cannon that knows its own fodder."

They whooped with joy when the senator's plane was delayed by bad weather; causing him to arrive several hours late to a bonfire rally in Texas. Only a strong headline writer could resist: CANNON MISSES FIRE!

As a result, the senator's name hit the headlines more frequently than his rival's did. And the laughter was *with*Cannon, not *at* him.

Nothing more was heard about the "mysterious craft" that the Soviet claimed to have shot down, except a terse report that said it had "probably been destroyed." It was impossible to know whether or not they had deduced what had happened, or whether they realized that the new craft was as maneuverable over the surface of the moon as a helicopter was over the surface of Earth.

Instead, the Sino-Soviet bloc had again shifted the world's attention to Africa. Like the Balkan States of nearly a century before, the small, independent nations that covered the still-dark continent were a continuing source of trouble. In spite of decades of "civilization," the thoughts and actions of the majority of Africans were still cast in the matrix of tribal taboos. The changes of government, the internal strife, and the petty brush wars between nations made Central and South America appear rigidly stable by comparison. It had been suggested that the revolutions in Africa occurred so often that only a tachometer could keep up with them.

If nothing else, the situation had succeeded in forcing the organization of a permanent UN police force; since back in 1960, there had not been a time when the UN Police were not needed somewhere in Africa.

In mid-October, a border dispute between North Uganda and South Uganda broke out, and within a week it looked as though the Commonwealth of Victorian Kenya, the Republic of Upper Tanganyika, and the Free and Independent Popular Monarchy of Ruanda-Urundi were all going to try to jump in and grab a piece of territory if possible.

The Soviet Representative to the United Nations charged that "this is a purely internal situation in Uganda, caused by imperialist *agents provocateur* financed by the Western Bloc." He insisted that UN intervention was unnecessary unless the "warmongering" neighbors of Uganda got into the scrap.

In a televised press interview, Vice Presidential Candidate Matthew Fisher was asked what he thought of the situation in East Africa.

"Both North and South Uganda," he said, "are communist controlled, but, like Yugoslavia, they have declared themselves independent of the masters at Moscow. If this conflict was stirred up by special agents—and I have no doubt that it was—those agents were Soviet, not Western agents. As far as the UN can be concerned, the Soviet Minister is correct, since the UN has recognized only the government of North Uganda as the government of all Uganda, and it is, therefore, a purely internal affair.

"The revolution—that is, *partial* revolution—which caused the division of Uganda a few years ago, was likewise due to Soviet intervention. They hoped to replace the independent communist government with one which would be, in effect, a puppet of the Kremlin. They failed. Now they are trying again.

"Legally, UN troops can only be sent there at the request of the Northern Uganda government. The Secretary General can send police troops there of his own accord only if another nation tries to invade Uganda.

"But—and here is the important point—if the Uganda government asks the aid of a friendly government to send troops, and if that friendly government complies with that request, *that cannot be considered an invasion*!"

Question from a reporter: "Do you believe that such intervention from another country will be requested by Uganda?"

"I do. And I am equally certain that the Soviet representative to the UN, and his Superiors in Moscow, will try to make a case of invasion and aggression out of it."

Within twenty-four hours after that interview, the government of North Uganda requested aid from Victorian Kenya, and a huge contingent of Kenyan troops marched across the border to help the North Uganda army. And the Soviet representative insisted that the UN send in troops to stop the "imperialist aggression" of Victorian Kenya. The rigidly pro-Western VK government protested that the Sino-Soviet accusations were invalid, and then asked, on its own accord, that a UN contingent be sent in to arbitrate and act as observers and umpires.

"Win one, lose one," Matthew Fisher said privately to Senator Cannon. "Uganda will come out of this with a pro-Western government, but it might not be too stable. The whole African situation is unstable. Mathematically, it has to be."

"How's that?" Senator Cannon asked.

"Do you know the Richardson-Gordon Equations?" Fisher asked.

"No. I'm not much of a mathematician," Cannon admitted. "What do they have to do with this?"

"They were originally proposed by Lewis Richardson, the English mathematician, and later refined by G. R. Gordon. Basically, they deal with the causes of war, and they show that a conglomeration of small states is less stable than a few large ones. In an arms race, there is a kind of positive feedback that eventually destroys the system, and the more active small units there are, the sooner the system reaches the destruction point."

Senator Cannon chuckled. "Any practical politician could have told them that, but I'm glad to hear that a mathematical tool to work on the problem has been devised. Maybe one of these days we won't have to be rule-of-thumb empiricists."

"Let's hope so," said Matt Fisher.

By the end of October, nearly two weeks from Election Day, the decision had been made. There were still a few Americans who hadn't made up their minds yet, but not enough to change the election results, even if they had voted as a bloc for one side or the other. The change from the shouting and arguing of mid-summer was apparent to anyone who knew what he was looking for. In the bars and restaurants, in the subways and buses, aboard planes and ships and trains, most Americans apparently seemed to have forgotten that there was a national election coming up, much to the surprise of Europeans and Asians who were not familiar with the dynamics of American political thought. If a foreigner brought the subject up, the average American would give his views in a calm manner, as though the thing were already settled, but there was far more discussion of the relative merits of the horses running at Pimlico or the rise in Lunar Developments Preferred than there was of the election. There were still a few people wearing campaign buttons, but most people didn't bother pinning them on after the suit came back from the cleaners.

A more detailed analysis would have shown that this calmness was of two types. The first, by far in the majority, was the calmness of the complacent knowledge of victory. The second was the resignation to loss manifested by those who knew they were backing the wrong man, but who, because of party loyalty or intellectual conviction or just plain stubbornness, would back him.

When Senator Cannon's brother, Dr. Frank Hewlitt Cannon, took a short leave of absence from Mayo Clinic to fly to the senator's campaign headquarters, there was a flurry of speculation about the possibility of his being appointed Secretary of Health, Education, and Welfare, but the flurry didn't amount to much. If President Cannon wanted to appoint his brother, that was all right with the voters.

After a tirade by the Soviet Premier, charging that the UN Police troops in Victorian Kenya were "tools of Yankee aggressionists," Americans smiled grimly and said, in effect: "Just wait 'til Cannon gets in—*he'll* show 'em."

Election Day came with the inevitability of death and taxes. The polling booths opened first on the East Coast, and people began filing in to take their turns at the machines. By the time the polls opened in Nome, Alaska, six hours later, the trend was obvious. All but two of the New England states were strongly for Cannon. New York, Pennsylvania, New Jersey, West Virginia, and Ohio dropped into his pocket like ripe apples. Virginia, North Carolina, South Carolina, Georgia, and Florida did the same. Alabama wavered at first, but tagged weakly along. Tennessee, Kentucky, Indiana, and Michigan trooped in like trained seals.

In Mississippi, things looked bad. Arkansas and Louisiana were uncertain. But the pro-Cannon vote in Missouri, Illinois, Iowa, Wisconsin, and Minnesota left no doubt about the outcome in those states. North Dakota, South Dakota, Nebraska, Kansas, Oklahoma, Texas—all Cannon by vast majorities.

And so the returns came in, following the sun across the continent. By the time California had reported three-fourths of its votes, it was all over but the jubilation. Nothing but an honest-to-God, genuine, Joshua-stopping-the-sun type of miracle could have saved the opposition. And such was not forthcoming.

At Cannon's campaign headquarters, a television screen was blaring to unhearing ears, merely adding to the din that was going on in the meeting hall. The party workhorses and the volunteers who had drummed for Cannon since the convention were repeating the scene that had taken place after Cannon's nomination in the summer, with an even greater note of triumph.

In Cannon's suite, six floors above, there was less noise, but only because there were fewer people.

"Hey!" Cannon yelled good-naturedly. "Lay off! Any more slaps on my back, and I'm going to be the first President since Franklin Roosevelt to go to my Inauguration in a wheelchair! Lay off, will you?"

"A drink, a drink, we got to have a drink," chanted Representative Edwin Matson, his bulldog face spread wide in a happy grin while he did things with bottles, ice, and glasses. "A drink, a drink—"

Governor Harold Spanding's lantern-jawed face looked as idiotically happy as Matson's, but he was quieter about it. Verbally, that is. It was he who had been pounding Cannon on the back, and now he was pounding Matthew Fisher almost as hard.

Matt Fisher finally managed to grab his hand, and he started pumping it. "What about you, Harry? I'm only a poor, simple Vice President. You got re-elected governor!"

Dr. Frank Cannon, looking like an older, balder edition of his brother, was smiling, too, but there was a troubled look in his eyes even as he congratulated the senator. Congressman Matson, passing out the drinks, handed the first one to the senator.

"Have a drink, Mr. President! You're going to have to make a speech pretty soon; you'll need a bracer!" He handed the second one to the physician. "Here you go, Doc! Congratulations! It isn't everyone who's got a President in the family!" Then his perceptive brain noticed something in the doctor's expression. "Hey," he said, more softly, "what's the trouble? You look as though you expected sickness in the family."

The doctor grinned quickly. "Not unless it's my own. I'm used to worrying about a patient's health, not a Presidential election. I'm afraid my stomach's a little queasy. Wait just a second; I've got some pills in my little black bag. Got pills in there for all ailments. Find out if anyone else needs resuscitation, will you?" Drink in hand, he went toward the closet, where his little black bag was stashed.

"Excitement," said Senator Cannon. "Frank isn't used to politics."

Matson chuckled. "Do him good to see how the other half lives." He walked off, bearing drinks for the others. Governor Spanding grabbed one and came over to the senator. "Jim! Ready to tear up your capitulation speech now?"

Cannon glanced at his watch. "Almost. The polls closed in Nome just ten minutes ago. We'll wait for the President's acknowledgment of defeat before we go downstairs." He glanced at his brother, who was washing something down with water.

Behind him, he heard Matson's voice saying: "I'm sure glad Horvin isn't here! I can hear him now: 'Image! Image! That's what won the election! Image!'" Matson guffawed. "Jim Cannon was winning elections by landslides before he ever heard of Horvin! Jim Cannon projects his own image."

"Sure he does," Matt Fisher said, "but what about me?"

"You? Hah! You're tops, Matt. Once a man gets to know you, he can see that, if he's got any brains."

Fisher chuckled gently. "Ed, you've got what it takes to be a politician, all right."

"So do you, Mr. Vice President! So do you! Hey!" He turned quickly. "We got to have a toast! Doc, you're his brother. I think the honor should be yours."

Dr. Frank Cannon, looking much more chipper since swallowing the pills, beamed and nodded at his brother. "It will be a pleasure. Gentlemen, come to attention, if you will." They did, grinning at first, then forcing solemnity into their expressions.

"Gentlemen," said. Dr. Cannon gravely, "I give you my brother, Senator James Harrington Cannon, the next President of the United States!"

"To the President!" said Governor Spanding.

"To the President!" chorused the others.

Glasses clinked and men drank solemnly.

Then, before anyone else could say anything, Dr. Cannon said: "I further propose, gentlemen, that we drink to the man who will spend the next four years in the White House—God willing—in the hope that his ability to handle that high office will be equal to the task before him, and that he will prove worthy of the trust placed in him by those who had faith in that ability."

"Amen," said Congressman Matson softly.

And they all drank again.

Senator Cannon said: "I thank you, gentlemen. I—"

But, at that moment, the ubiquitous clatter of noise from the television abruptly changed tenor. They all turned to look.

"... And gentlemen," the announcer's voice was saying, "The President of the United States!"

The Presidential Seal which had been pictured on the screen faded suddenly, to be replaced by the face of the President. He looked firmly resigned, but neither haggard, tired, defeated, nor unhappy. To the five men who stood watching him in that room, it was obvious that the speech to come was on tape.

The President smiled wanly. "Fellow Americans," he began, "as your President, I wish both to congratulate you and thank you. As free citizens of a free country, exercising your franchise of the ballot to determine the men and women who are to represent and lead you during their coming terms of office, you have made your decision. You have considered well the qualifications of those men and women, and you have considered well the problems that will face our country as a whole and each individual as a free citizen desiring to remain free, and you have made your choice accordingly, as is your right and duty. For that, I congratulate you."

He paused for a dramatic moment.

"The decision, I think, was not an easy one. The citizens of our great democracy are not sheep, to be led first this way and then that; they are not dead leaves to be carried by every vagrant breeze that blows; they are not children, nor are they fools."

He looked searchingly from the screen, as though to see into the minds of every person watching.

"Do not mistake my meaning," he said levelly. "I do not mean that there are no fools among us. There are." Again he paused for effect. "Every man, every woman, who, through laziness or neglect or complacency, failed to make his desire known at the polls in this election—is a fool. Every citizen who thinks that his vote doesn't count for much, and therefore fails to register that vote—is a fool. Every person who accepts the *privileges* of American citizenship and considers them as *rights*, and who neglects the *duties* of citizenship because they are tiresome—is a fool."

He waited for half a second.

"Fortunately for us all, the fools are in a minority in our country. This election shows that. Most of you have done your duty and followed your conscience as you see fit. And I congratulate you for that."

The smile became less broad—by just the right amount.

"Four years ago, exercising that same privilege and duty, you, the citizens of the United States, honored me and those who were working with me by electing us to the highest offices in this nation. You elected us, I believe, because we made certain promises to you—solemn promises that were made in our platform four years ago."

He took a deep breath and folded his hands below his chin.

"I am certain that you all know we have endeavored to keep those promises. I am certain that you know that we have kept faith with the people of this nation."

He looked down for a moment, then looked up again.

"This year, in our platform, we made more promises. We outlined a program that we felt would be of the greatest benefit to this nation." He unclasped his hands and spread them with an open gesture.

"Senator James Cannon and his party have also made promises—promises which, I am sure, they, too, feel are best for our nation."

Another pause.

"You, the citizens of the United States, have, in the past few months, carefully weighed these promises against one another—weighing not only the promises themselves, but the integrity and the ability of the men who made them.

"And you have made your choice.

"I cannot, and do not, quarrel with that choice. It is the essence of democratic government that disagreements in the upper echelons of that government shall be resolved by the action and the will of the governed. You, the people of the United States, have done just that.

"And—for that, I thank you."

A final hesitation.

"Next January, Senator James Harrington Cannon will be inaugurated as President of the United States. Let us show him, and the men who are to work with him, that we, as citizens of this great nation, resolving our differences, will strive unceasingly under his administration to further the high resolves and great ideals of our country.

"I believe—I *know*—that you are all with me in this resolution, and, for that, too,—"

"—I thank you."

The face of the President of the United States faded from the screen.

After a few seconds, Matson sighed. "Not bad at all, really," he said, stepping over to shut off the set. "He's been taking lessons from you, Jim. But he just hasn't quite got it."

Senator Cannon took another swallow of his drink and said nothing.

"Sincerity," said Governor Spanding. "That's what's lacking. He hasn't got it, and the voters can feel it."

"He managed to be elected President of the United States on it," Senator Cannon said dryly.

Spanding didn't turn to look at Cannon; he kept looking at the dead TV screen. "These things always show up by comparison, Jim. In comparison with some of us—most of us, in fact—he looks pretty good. I've known him since he was a fresh junior senator, and I was just attorney for the House Committee for Legislative Oversight." He turned around. "You know what, Jim? When I first heard him talk, I actually thought about changing parties. Yeah. Really." He turned around again.

"But," he went on, "he's all hot air and no ability. Just like Matt, here, is all ability and no hot air. No offense meant, Matt, believe me," he added, glancing at Fisher.

"I know," Fisher said quietly.

Spanding turned around once more and looked Cannon squarely in the eyes. "You've got both, Jim. The blarney to put yourself over, and the ability to back it up. And you know I'm not trying to flatter you when I say that."

When Cannon nodded wordlessly, Spanding gave himself a short, embarrassed laugh. "Ah, Hell. I talk too much." And he took a hefty slug of his drink.

Matthew Fisher took the overcharge out of the sudden outburst of emotion by saying: "It's more than just ability and sincerity, Harry. There's determination and honesty, too."

Matson said, "Amen to that."

Dr. Frank Cannon was just standing there, looking at his brother. There was a definite look of respect on his face.

Senator Cannon said: "You're all great guys—thanks. But I've got to get downstairs and make a speech. Ed, get the recording tape out of that set; I want to make some notes on what he said. And hurry it up, we haven't got too long."

"No canned speech for you, eh, Jim?" Spanding said.

"Amen to that, too," said Representative Matson as he opened the panel in the side of the TV set.

From a hundred thousand loudspeakers all over the United States, from the rockbound coast of Maine to the equally rockbound coast of Alaska, from the sun-washed coast of Florida to the ditto coast of Hawaii, the immortal voice of Bing Crosby, preserved forever in an electronic pattern made from a decades-old recording, told of a desire for a White Christmas. It was a voice and a tune and a lyric that aroused nostalgia even in the hearts of Floridians and Californians and Hawaiians who had never seen snow in their lives.

The other carols rang out, too—"Silent Night," "Hark! The Herald Angels Sing," "God Rest Ye Merry Gentlemen," "O Little Town of Bethlehem," and all the others. All over the nation, in millions upon millions of Christian homes, the faithful prepared to celebrate the birth, the coming, of their Saviour, Who had come to bring peace on Earth to men.

And in millions of other American homes, the Children of Abraham celebrated the Festival of Lights—*Chanukah*, the Dedication—the giving of thanks for the Blessing of God upon the priestly family of the Maccabees, who, twenty-odd centuries before, had taken up arms against the tyranny of a dynasty which had banned the worship of Almighty God, and who, by winning, had made themselves a symbol forever of the moral struggle against the forces that oppress the free mind of Man.

The newspapers and television newscasts were full of the age-old "human interest stories" which, in spite of their predictability—the abandoned baby, the dying child, the wretchedly ill oldster—still brought a tear to the eye during the Holiday Season.

As President-elect Cannon slowly made his cabinet appointments, the announcements appeared, but there was hardly any discussion of them, much less any hue and cry.

One editorial writer did make a comment: "It is encouraging to see that President-elect Cannon consults with Vice-President-elect Matthew Fisher regularly and frequently as the appointments are made. For a good many years, ever since the Eisenhower Administration, back in the Fifties, it has been the policy of most of our Chief Executives to make sure that the Vice President is groomed to take over smoothly if anything should happen to the President. Senator Cannon, however, is, as far as we know, the first President-elect who has begun this grooming before the Inauguration. This, in our opinion, shows both wisdom and political astuteness."

By the second week of the New Year, the new Cabinet had been picked. Contrary to the rumors before the election, the senator's brother had not been selected for any post whatever, but the men who *were* picked for Cabinet posts were certainly of high caliber. The United States Senate had confirmed them all before Inauguration Day.

That day was clear and cold in Washington. After the seemingly endless ceremonies and ceremonials, after the Inaugural Ball, and the Inaugural Supper, and the Inaugural Et Cetera, President James Cannon went to bed, complaining of a "slight headache".

"Frankly," he told Vice President Matthew Fisher, "it is a real head-splitter." He took four aspirin and went to bed.

He said he felt "a little better" the next day.

The fifth of February.

Ten forty-eight in the evening.
The White House, Washington, D.C.

Dr. Frank Hewlitt Cannon stood in a darkened bedroom in Blair House, across the street from the Executive Mansion, nervously looking out the window, at the big white house across the way. He was not nervous for himself, although he had plenty of reason to be. He was clad in pajamas, as his brother had ordered, and had even taken the extra precaution of rumpling up his hair.

He looked at his watch, and then looked back at the White House.

How long? he thought. *How long?*

He looked at his wrist again. The sweep hand only moved when he looked at it, apparently. He dropped his hands and clasped them behind his back. How long before he would know?

My kid brother, he thought. *I could always outthink him and outfight him. But he's got something I haven't got. He's stuck to his guns and fought hard all these years. I couldn't do what he's doing tonight, and I know it. You're a better man than I am, kid.*

Across Pennsylvania Avenue, Senator James Cannon was doing some heavy consideration, too. He sat on the edge of his bed and looked at the small tubular device in his hand.

Will Frank be safe? That's the only weak point in the plan.

Frank was safe. He *had* to be. Frank hadn't been over from Blair House in three days. They hadn't even *see* each other in three days. The Secret Service men—

He threw a glance toward the door that led from his bedroom to the hall.

The Secret Service agents would know that Frank couldn't possibly have had anything to do with it. The only possible connection would be the hypogun itself. He looked at the little gadget. *Hell*, he thought; *now or never*.

He got up and strode purposefully into the bathroom. He smiled crookedly at his own reflection in the mirror. It was damnably difficult for a President to outwit his own bodyguard.

Get on with it!

He swallowed the capsule Frank had given him. Then, placing the muzzle against the precise spots Frank had shown him, James Cannon pulled the trigger. Once ... twice ... thrice ...

Against each nerve center in his left side. Fine.

Now that it was done, all fear—all trepidation—left Senator James Cannon. Now there was no way to go but ahead.

First, the hypogun that had blown the drug into his body. Two minutes to get rid of that, for that was the only thing that could tie Frank in to the plan.

They had already agreed that there was no way to get rid of it. It couldn't be destroyed or thrown away. There was only one way that it could be taken from the White House ...

Cannon left his fingerprints on it, dropped it into the wastebasket, and covered it with tissue paper. Then he left the bathroom and walked toward the hall door. Beyond it, he knew, were the guarding Secret Service men.

And already his left side was beginning to feel odd.

He walked to the door and opened it. He had a scowl on his face.

"Hello, Jenkins—Grossman," he said, as the two men turned. "I've got a hell of a headache again. Aspirin doesn't seem to help, and I can't get any sleep." He looked rather dazed, as though he wasn't sure of his surroundings. He smiled lopsidedly. "Call Frank, over at Blair House, will you? Hurry?" Then he swallowed, looked dazed, and fell to the floor in a heap.

The two Secret Service men didn't move, but they shouted loudly. Their orders were to guard the body of the President—*literally*! Until it was declared legally dead, that body was their responsibility.

The other Secret Service men in the White House came on the run. Within one minute after Cannon had fallen, a call had gone to Blair House, asking for the President's brother.

Inside of another two minutes, Dr. Frank Cannon was coming through the front door of the Executive Mansion. In spite of the chill outside, he was wearing only a topcoat over his pajamas.

"What happened?" he snapped, with the authority that only a physician can muster. "Where is he?"

He heard the story on the way to the President's room. Jenkins and Grossman were still standing over the fallen Chief Executive. "We haven't moved him, except to make him more comfortable," said Grossman. "He's still O.K.... I mean, he's breathing, and his heart's still going. But we didn't want to move him—"

"Fine!" snapped the doctor. "Best thing." He knelt over his brother and picked up his wrist. "Have you called anyone else?" he asked sharply while he felt the pulse.

"The Naval Hospital," said another agent. "They're coming fast!"

"Fine!" repeated Dr. Frank. By this time, most of the White House staff was awake. Frank Cannon let go the wrist and stood up quickly. "Can't tell for sure, but it looks like a slight stroke. Excuse me."

He went into the Executive bedroom, and on into the bathroom. He closed the door. Quickly, he fished the hypogun out of the wastebasket and dropped it into the little black bag which he had carried with him. He came out with a glass of water. Everything was taken care of.

PRESIDENT SUFFERS STROKE!
JHC Taken To US Naval Hospital
In Washington After Stroke In
White House

All over the world, headlines and newscasts in a hundred tongues carried the story. And from all over the world came messages of sympathy and concern for the stricken Chief Executive. From England, simultaneous messages arrived from the Sovereign and the Prime Minister; from France, notes from both the President and the Premier of the Seventh Republic; from Ethiopia, condolences from His Imperial Majesty and from the Chief Executive. The United German Federation, the Constitutional Kingdom of Spain, the Republic of Italy, the United Austro-Yugoslavian Commonwealth, and the Polish Free State all sent rush radiograms. So did Argentina, Bolivia, Brazil, Chile, Colombia, Ecuador, Paraguay, Peru, Uruguay, and Venezuela. From Africa, Australia, Southern Asia, Oceania, and Central America came expressive words of sorrow. Special blessings were sent by His Holiness from Vatican City, by the Patriarch of Istanbul, and by the Archbishop of Canterbury. The Presidente of the Estados Unidos Mexicanos personally took a plane to Washington, as did the Governor General of Canada, carrying a personal message from the Prime Minister. Even the Soviet Union sent a radiogram, and the story of the tragedy was printed in *Pravda*, accompanied by an editorial that almost approached straight reporting.

President James Harrington Cannon knew none of this. He was unconscious and unable to receive visitors.

As far as actual news from the White House was concerned, news commentator Barton Wayne gave the best summary over a major American TV network on the morning of the sixth of February:

"Last night, at approximately eleven p.m., James Harrington Cannon, President of the United States, collapsed at the feet of the Secret Service men who were guarding him. Within a few minutes, Dr. Frank Hewlitt Cannon, the President's brother, called by the Secret Service in obedience to the President's last conscious words, had arrived from Blair House, where he had been staying.

"Dr. Frank Cannon diagnosed the President's illness as a—quote—slight stroke—unquote. Later, after the President had been taken to the Naval Hospital for further diagnosis, Dr. Cannon released a statement. Quote—further tests have enabled the medical staff of this hospital to make a more detailed analysis. Apparently, the President has suffered a slight cerebral hemorrhage which has, temporarily at least, partially paralyzed the muscles of his left side. The President, however, has regained consciousness, and his life is in no danger—Unquote.

"After only sixteen days in the White House, the President has fallen ill. We can only wish him Godspeed and an early recovery."

Dr. Frank Cannon stood firmly by his brother's bedside, shaking his head firmly. "No, commander; I cannot permit that. I am in charge of this case, and I shall remain in charge of it until my patient tells me otherwise."

The graying Navy medical officer pursed his lips. "In cases of this sort, doctor," he said primly, "the Navy is in charge. The patient is, after all, the President of the United States."

Dr. Frank went right on shaking his head. "Cuts no ice, commander. I was specifically summoned by the patient. I agreed to take the case. I will be most happy to accept your co-operation; I welcome your advice and aid; but I will *not* allow my patient to be taken from my charge."

"It is hardly considered proper for the physician in charge of a serious case to be a relative of the patient."

"Possibly. But it is neither unethical nor illegal." He gave the commander a dry smile. "I know my brother, commander. Quite well. I also know that you have the authority and the means to expel me from this hospital." The smile became positively icy. "And, in view of the former, I should not advise you to exercise the latter."

The commander wet his lips. "I have no intention of doing so, doctor," he said rather huffily. "But, inasmuch as the X rays show no—"

There came a mumble from the man on the bed, and, in that instant, both men forgot their differences and became physicians again, as they focused their attention on the patient.

President Cannon was blinking his eyes groggily. Or, rather, *eye*. The left one refused to do more than show a faint flicker of the lid.

"Hullo, Jamie," Dr. Frank said gently. "How d'you feel?" It took nerves of steel to show that tender composure. The drug should wear off quickly, but if Jim Cannon's mind was still fuzzy, and he said the wrong thing—

For a moment, the President said nothing as he tried to focus his right eye.

"Don't try to move, Mr. President," said the Navy doctor softly.

President Cannon smiled lopsidedly, the left side of his face refusing to make the effort. "Arright," he said, in a low, blurred voice. "Wha' happen', Frang?"

"Apparently," said Dr. Frank carefully, "you've had a little bit of a stroke, kid. Nothing to worry about. How do you feel?"

"Funny. Li'l dizzy. Don't hurt, though."

"Good. Fine. You'll be O.K. shortly."

The President's voice became stronger. "I'm glad you're here, Frank. Tell me—is it ... bad?"

"'Tain't good, kid," Dr. Frank said with a bedside grin. "You can't expect a stroke to put you in the best of health, now, can you?"

The lopsided smile came back. "Guess not." The smile went away, to be replaced by a puzzled frown. "My whole left side feels dead. What's the matter?"

Instead of answering, Dr. Frank Cannon turned to the Navy medic. "I'll let the commander explain that. What's your diagnosis, doctor?"

The commander ran his tongue nervously over his lips before speaking. "There's apparently a small blood clot in the brain, Mr. President, interfering with the functioning of the efferent nerves."

"Permanent?"

"We don't know yet, sir. We hope not."

President Cannon sighed. "Well. Thank you, commander. And now, if you don't mind, I'd like to speak to my brother—alone."

The commander glanced at Dr. Frank, then back at the President. "Certainly, sir." He turned to leave.

"Just a moment, commander," Dr. Frank said. "There'll be news reporters out there. Tell them—" He frowned a little. "Tell them that the President is conscious and quite rational, but that there is still some weakness. I don't think anything more than that will be necessary."

"I agree. Certainly, doctor." At the door, the commander paused and said: "I'll keep everyone out until you call."

"Thanks," said Dr. Frank as the door closed behind the Navy man.

As soon as it closed, President Cannon struggled to get up.

"Don't try it, kid," the doctor said, "those muscles are paralyzed, even if you aren't sick. Here, let me help you."

"How did it come off?" Cannon asked as his brother propped him up.

"Perfectly. No one doubts that it's a stroke. Now what?"

"Give me a cigarette."

"All right, but watch it. Use your right hand, and smoke with the right side of your mouth. Here." The doctor lit a cigarette and handed it to his brother. "Now, what's the next step?"

"The next step is to tell Matthew Fisher," said the President.

Dr. Frank Cannon scowled. "Why? Why not just go through with the thing and let him be fooled along with the rest? It seems to me he'd be ... well, more secure in his own position if he didn't know."

"No." The President hunched himself up on his pillows. "Can't you raise the head of this bed?"

Dr. Frank touched a button on the bedside panel, and the upper portion of the bed rose smoothly at an angle. "Better?"

"Fine. Much better."

"You were saying—"

"Yeah. About Matt Fisher. He has to know. He'll guess eventually, in the next four years, anyway—unless I hide away somewhere. And I have no intention of doing that.

"Oh, I'm not trying to show Matt what a great guy I am, Frank. You know better than that, and so will he. But Matt will have to have all the facts at hand, if he's to do his job right, and it seems to me that this is a pretty important fact. What do you say, Frank?"

The doctor nodded slowly. "I think you know more about the situation than I do. And I trust your judgment, kid. And Matt's, too, I guess."

"No." President Cannon's voice was firm as he looked at his brother with one bright eye. "Don't trust Matt's judgment, because he doesn't have any."

Dr. Frank looked astonished. "Then *what*—?" He stopped.

"Matthew Fisher," said President Cannon authoritatively, "doesn't need judgment any more than *you* need instinct. No more so, and no less. I said he doesn't have any judgment, but that's not exactly true. He has it, but he only uses it for routine work, just as you or I use instinct. We can override our instinctive reactions when we have to. Matt can override his judgment when he has to.

"I don't pretend to know how Fisher's mind works. If I did, I wouldn't be doing this. But I *do* know that Matt Fisher—by some mental process I can't even fathom—almost invariably knows the *right* thing to do, and he knows it without using judgment."

"And you're still convinced that this is the only way out?" Dr. Frank asked. "Couldn't you stay in office and let him run things under cover?"

"We discussed all this months ago, Frank," Cannon said wearily. "My reasons remain the same. Matt couldn't possibly operate efficiently if he had to go through me every time. And I am human, too; I'd have a tendency to impose my own judgment on his decisions.

"No, Frank; this is the only way it can work. This country needs Matthew Fisher as President, but he could never have been elected. Now I've done my job; now it's time for me to get out of the way and turn the Presidency over to a man who can handle the office far better than any other man I know."

"You make him sound like some sort of superman," said Dr. Frank with a wry grin.

"Hell," said President Cannon, "you don't think I'd turn this job over to anything less, do you?" He chuckled. "Call him in, will you?"

PRESIDENT CANNON RESIGNS!
Ill Health Given As Reason;
Doctors Say Recovery
Unlikely In Near Future.
VP Fisher To Take Oath Tomorrow.

Unwise Child

When a super-robot named Snookums discovers how to build his own superbombs, it becomes obvious that Earth is by no means the safest place for him to be. And so Dr. Fitzhugh, his designer, and Leda Crannon, a child psychologist acting as Snookums' nursemaid, agree to set up Operation Brainchild, a plan to transport the robot to a far distant planet.

Mike the Angel—M. R. Gabriel, Power Design—has devised the power plant that is to propel the space ship *Branchell* to its secret destination, complete with its unusual cargo. And, as a reserve officer in the Space Patrol, Mike is a logical replacement for the craft's unavoidably detained engineering officer.

But once into space, the *Branchell* becomes the scene of some frightening events—the medical officer is murdered, and Snookums appears to be the culprit. Mike the Angel indulges himself in a bit of sleuthing, and the facts he turns up lead to a most unusual climax.

1

The kids who tried to jump Mike the Angel were bright enough in a lot of ways, but they made a bad mistake when they tangled with Mike the Angel.

They'd done their preliminary work well enough. They had cased the job thoroughly, and they had built the equipment to take care of it. Their mistake was not in their planning; it was in not taking Mike the Angel into account.

There is a section of New York's Manhattan Island, down on the lower West Side, that has been known, for over a century, as "Radio Row." All through this section are stores, large and small, where every kind of electronic and sub-electronic device can be bought, ordered, or designed to order. There is even an old antique shop, known as Ye Quainte Olde Elecktronicks Shoppe, where you can buy such oddities as vacuum-tube FM radios and twenty-four-inch cathode-ray television sets. And, if you want them, transmitters to match, so you can watch the antiques work.

Mike the Angel had an uptown office in the heart of the business district, near West 112th Street—a very posh suite of rooms on the fiftieth floor of the half-mile-high Timmins Building, overlooking the two-hundred-year-old Gothic edifice of the Cathedral of St. John the Divine. The glowing sign on the door of the suite said, very simply:

M. R. GABRIEL
POWER DESIGN

But, once or twice a week, Mike the Angel liked to take off and prowl around Radio Row, just shopping around. Usually, he didn't work too late, but, on this particular afternoon, he'd been in his office until after six o'clock, working on some papers for the Interstellar Commission. So, by the time he got down to Radio Row, the only shop left open was Harry MacDougal's.

That didn't matter much to Mike the Angel, since Harry's was the place he had intended to go, anyway. Harry MacDougal's establishment was hardly more than a hole in the wall—a narrow, long hallway between two larger stores. Although not a specialist, like the proprietor of Ye Quainte Olde Elecktronicks Shoppe, Harry did carry equipment of every vintage and every make. If you wanted something that hadn't been manufactured in decades, and perhaps never made in quantity, Harry's was the place to go. The walls were lined with bins, all unlabeled, filled helter-skelter with every imaginable kind of gadget, most of which would have been hard to recognize unless you were both an expert and a historian.

Old Harry didn't need labels or a system. He was a small, lean, bony, sharp-nosed Scot who had fled Scotland during the Panic of '37, landed in New York, and stopped. He solemnly declared that he had never been west of the Hudson River nor north of 181st Street in the more than fifty years he had been in the country. He had a mind like that of a robot filing cabinet. Ask him for a particular piece of equipment, and he'd squint one eye closed, stare at the end of his nose with the other, and say:

"An M-1993 thermodyne hexode, eh? Ah. Um. Aye, I got one. Picked it up a couple years back. Put it— Let ma see, now...."

And he'd go to his wall ladder, push it along that narrow hallway, moving boxes aside as he went, and stop somewhere along the wall. Then he'd scramble up the ladder, pull out a bin, fumble around in it, and come out with the article in question. He'd blow the dust off it, polish it with a rag, scramble down the ladder, and say: "Here 'tis. Thought I had one. Let's go back in the back and give her a test."

On the other hand, if he didn't have what you wanted, he'd shake his head just a trifle, then squint up at you and say: "What d'ye want it for?" And if you could tell him what you planned to do with the piece you wanted, nine times out of ten he could come up with something else that would do the job as well or better.

In either case, he always insisted that the piece be tested. He refused either to buy or sell something that didn't work. So you'd follow him down that long hallway to the lab in the rear, where all the testing equipment was. The lab, too, was cluttered, but in a different way. Out front, the stuff was dead; back here, there was power coursing through the ionic veins and metallic nerves of the half-living machines. Things were labeled in neat, accurate script—not for Old Harry's benefit, but for the edification of his customers, so they wouldn't put their fingers in the wrong places. He never had to worry about whether his customers knew enough to fend for themselves; a few minutes spent in talking was enough to tell Harry whether a man knew enough about the science and art of electronics and sub-electronics to be trusted in the lab. If you didn't measure up, you didn't get invited to the lab, even to watch a test.

But he had very few people like that; nobody came into Harry MacDougal's place unless he was pretty sure of what he wanted and how he wanted to use it.

On the other hand, there were very few men whom Harry would allow into the lab unescorted. Mike the Angel was one of them.

Meet Mike the Angel. Full name: Michael Raphael Gabriel. (His mother had tagged that on him at the time of his baptism, which had made his father wince in anticipated compassion, but there had been nothing for him to say—not in the middle of the ceremony.)

Naturally, he had been tagged "Mike the Angel." Six feet seven. Two hundred sixty pounds. Thirty-four years of age. Hair: golden yellow. Eyes: deep blue. Cash value of holdings: well into eight figures. Credit: almost unlimited. Marital status: highly eligible, if the right woman could tackle him.

Mike the Angel pushed open the door to Harry MacDougal's shop and took off his hat to brush the raindrops from it. Farther uptown, the streets were covered with clear plastic roofing, but that kind of comfort stopped at Fifty-third Street.

There was no one in sight in the long, narrow store, so Mike the Angel looked up at the ceiling, where he knew the eye was hidden.

"Harry?" he said.

"I see you, lad," said a voice from the air. "You got here just in time. I'm closin' up. Lock the door, would ye?"

"Sure, Harry." Mike turned around, pressed the locking switch, and heard it snap satisfactorily.

"Okay, Mike," said Harry MacDougal's voice. "Come on back. I hope ye brought that bottle of scotch I asked for."

Mike the Angel made his way back between the towering tiers of bins as he answered. "Sure did, Harry. When did I ever forget you?"

And, as he moved toward the rear of the store, Mike the Angel casually reached into his coat pocket and triggered the switch of a small but fantastically powerful mechanism that he always carried when he walked the streets of New York at night.

He was headed straight into trouble, and he knew it. And he hoped he was ready for it.

2

Mike the Angel kept his hand in his pocket, his thumb on a little plate that was set in the side of the small mechanism that was concealed therein. As he neared the door, the little plate began to vibrate, making a buzz which could only be felt, not heard. Mike sighed to himself. Vibroblades were all the rage this season.

He pushed open the rear door rapidly and stepped inside. It was just what he'd expected. His eyes saw and his brain recorded the whole scene in the fraction of a second before he moved. In that fraction of a second, he took in the situation, appraised it, planned his strategy, and launched into his plan of action.

Harry MacDougal was sitting at his workbench, near the controls of the eye that watched the shop when he was in the lab. He was hunched over a little, his small, bright eyes peering steadily at Mike the Angel from beneath shaggy, silvered brows. There was no pleading in those eyes—only confidence.

Next to Old Harry was a kid—sixteen, maybe seventeen. He had the JD stamp on his face: a look of cold, hard arrogance that barely concealed the uncertainty and fear beneath. One hand was at Harry's back, and Mike knew that the kid was holding a vibroblade at the old man's spine.

At the same time, the buzzing against his thumb told Mike the Angel something else. There was a vibroblade much nearer his body than the one in the kid's hand.

That meant that there was another young punk behind him.

All this took Mike the Angel about one quarter of a second to assimilate. Then he jumped.

Had the intruders been adults, Mike would have handled the entire situation in a completely different way. Adults, unless they are mentally or emotionally retarded, do not usually react or behave like children. Adolescents can, do, and *must*—for the very simple reason that they have not yet had time to learn to react as adults.

Had the intruders been adults, and had Mike the Angel behaved the way he did, he might conceivably have died that night. As it was, the kids never had a chance.

Mike didn't even bother to acknowledge the existence of the punk behind him. He leaped, instead, straight for the kid in the dead-black suède zipsuit who was holding the vibroblade against Harry MacDougal's spine. And the kid reacted exactly as Mike the Angel had hoped, prayed, and predicted he would.

The kid defended himself.

An adult, in a situation where he has one known enemy at his mercy and is being attacked by a second, will quickly put the first out of the way in order to leave himself free to deal with the second. There is no sense in leaving your flank wide open just to oppose a frontal attack.

If the kid had been an adult, Harry MacDougal would have died there and then. An adult would simply have slashed his vibroblade through the old man's spine and brought it to bear on Mike the Angel.

But not the kid. He jumped back, eyes widening, to face his oncoming opponent in an open space. He was no coward, that kid, and he knew how to handle a vibroblade. In his own unwise, suicidal way, he was perfectly capable of proving himself. He held out the point of that shimmering metal shaft, ready to parry any offensive thrust that Mike the Angel might make.

If Mike had had a vibroblade himself, and if there hadn't been another punk at his back, Mike might have taken care of the kid that way. As it was, he had no choice but to use another way.

He threw himself full on the point of the scintillating vibroblade.

A vibroblade is a nasty weapon. Originally designed as a surgeon's tool, its special steel blade moves in and out of the heavy hilt at speeds from two hundred to two thousand vibrations per second, depending on the size and the use to which it is to be put. Make it eight inches long, add serrated, diamond-pointed teeth, and you have the man-killing vibroblade. Its danger is in its power; that shivering blade can cut through flesh, cartilage, and bone with almost no effort. It's a knife with power steering.

But that kind of power can be a weakness as well as a strength.

The little gadget that Mike the Angel carried did more than just detect the nearby operation of a vibroblade. It was also a defense. The gadget focused a high-density magnetic field on any vibroblade that came anywhere within six inches of Mike's body.

In that field, the steel blade simply couldn't move. It was as though it had been caught in a vise. The blade no longer vibrated; it had become nothing more than an overly fancy bread knife.

The trouble was that the power unit in the heavy hilt simply wouldn't accept the fact that the blade was immovable. That power unit was in there to move something, and by heaven, *something* had to move.

The hilt jerked and bucked in the kid's hand, taking skin with it. Then it began to smoke and burn under the overload. The plastic shell cracked and hot copper and silver splattered out of it. The kid screamed as the molten metal burned his hand.

Mike the Angel put a hand against the kid's chest and shoved. As the boy toppled backward, Mike turned to face the other boy.

Only it wasn't a boy.

She was wearing gold lip paint and had sprayed her hair blue, but she knew how to handle a vibroblade at least as well as her boy friend had. Just as Mike the Angel turned, she lunged forward, aiming for the small of his back.

And she, too, screamed as she lost her blade in a flash of heat.

Then she grabbed for something in her pocket. Regretfully, Mike the Angel brought the edge of his hand down against the side of her neck in a paralyzing, but not deadly, rabbit punch. She dropped, senseless, and a small gun spilled out of the waist pocket of her zipsuit and skittered across the floor. Mike paused only long enough to make sure she was out, then he turned back to his first opponent.

As he had anticipated, Harry MacDougal had taken charge. The kid was sprawled flat on the floor, and Old Harry was holding a shock gun in his hand.

Mike the Angel took a deep breath.

"Yer trousers are on fire," said Harry.

Mike yelped as he felt the heat, and he began slapping at the smoldering spots where the molten metal from the vibroblades had hit his clothing. He wasn't afire; modern clothing doesn't flame up—but it can get pretty hot when you splash liquid copper on it.

"Damn!" said Mike the Angel. "New suit, too."

"You're a fast thinker, laddie," said Old Harry.

"You don't need to flatter me, Harry," said Mike the Angel. "When an old teetotaler like you asks a man if he's brought some scotch, the man's a fool if he doesn't know there's trouble afoot." He gave his leg a final slap and said: "What happened? Are there any more of them?"

"Don't know. Might be." The old man waved at his control panel. "My instruments are workin' again!" He gestured at the floor. "I'm nae sure how they did it, but somehow they managed to blank out ma instruments just long enough to get inside. Their mistake was in not lockin' the front door."

Mike the Angel was busy searching the two unconscious kids. He looked up. "Neither of them is carrying any equipment in their clothing—at least, not anything that's self-powered. If they've got pickup circuits built into the cloth, there must be more of them outside."

"Aye. Likely. We'll see."

Suddenly, there was a soft *ping! ping! ping!* from an instrument on the bench.

Harry glanced quickly at the receiving screen that was connected with the multitude of eyes that were hidden around the area of his shop. Then a smile came over his small brown face.

"Cops," he said. "Time they got here."

3

Sergeant Cowder looked the room over and took a drag from his cigarette. "Well, that's that. Now—what happened?" He looked from Mike the Angel to Harry MacDougal and back again. Both of them appeared to be thinking.

"All right," he said quietly, "let me guess, then."

Old Harry waved a hand. "Oh no, Sergeant; 'twon't be necessary. I think Mr. Gabriel was just waiting for me to start, because he wasn't here when the two rapscallions came in, and I was just tryin' to figure out where to begin. We're not bein' unco-operative. Let's see now—" He gazed at the ceiling as though trying to collect his thoughts. He knew perfectly well that the police sergeant was recording everything he said.

The sergeant sighed. "Look, Harry, you're not on trial. I know perfectly well that you've got this place bugged to a fare-thee-well. So does every shop operator on Radio Row. If you didn't, the JD gangs would have cleaned you all out long ago."

Harry kept looking at the ceiling, and Mike the Angel smiled quietly at his fingernails.

The detective sergeant sighed again. "Sure, we'd like to have some of the gadgets that you and the other operators on the Row have worked out, Harry. But I'm in no position to take 'em away from you. Besides, we have some stuff that you'd like to have, too, so that makes us pretty much even. If we started confiscating illegal equipment from you, the JD's would swoop in here, take your legitimate equipment, bug it up, and they'd be driving us all nuts within a week. So long as you don't use illegal equipment illegally, the department will leave you alone."

Old Harry grinned. "Well, now, that's very nice of you, Sergeant. But I don't have anything illegal—no robotics stuff or anything like that. Oh, I'll admit I've a couple of eyes here and there to watch my shop, but eyes aren't illegal."

The detective glanced around the room with a practiced eye and then looked blandly back at the little Scotsman. Harry MacDougal was lying, and the sergeant knew it. And Harry knew the sergeant knew it.

Sergeant Cowder sighed for a third time and looked at the Scot. "Okay. So what happened?"

Harry's face became serious. "They came in about six-thirty. First I knew of it, one of the kids—the boy—stepped out of that closet over there and put a vibroblade at my back. I'd come back here to get a small resistor, and all of a sudden there he was."

Mike the Angel frowned, but he didn't say anything.

"None of your equipment registered anything?" asked the detective.

"Not a thing, Sergeant," said Harry. "They've got something new, all right. The kid must ha' come in through the back door, there. And I'd ha' been willin' to bet ma life that no human bein' could ha' walked in here without ma knowin' it before he got within ten feet o' that door. Look."

He got up, walked over to the back door, and opened it. It opened into what looked at first to be a totally dark room. Then the sergeant saw that there was a dead-black wall a few feet from the open door.

"That's a light trap," said Harry. "Same as they have in photographic darkrooms. To get from this door to the outer door that leads into the alley, you got to turn two corners and walk about thirty feet. Even I, masel', couldn't walk through it without settin' off half a dozen alarms. Any kind of light would set off the bugs; so would the heat radiation from the human body."

"How about the front?" Sergeant Cowder asked. "Anyone could get in from the front."

Harry's grin became grim. "Not unless I go with 'em. And not even then if I don't want 'em to."

"It was kind of you to let us in," said the detective mildly.

"A pleasure," said Harry. "But I wish I knew how that kid got in."

"Well, he did—somehow," Cowder said. "What happened after he came out of the closet?"

"He made me let the girl in. They were goin' to open up the rear completely and take my stuff out that way. They'd ha' done it, too, if Mr. Gabriel hadn't come along."

Detective Sergeant Cowder looked at Mike the Angel. "About what time was that, Mr. Gabriel?"

"About six thirty-five," Mike told him. "The kids probably hadn't been here more than a few minutes."

Harry MacDougal nodded in silent corroboration.

"Then what happened?" asked the detective.

Mike told him a carefully edited version of what had occurred, leaving out the existence of the little gadget he was carrying in his pocket. The sergeant listened patiently and unbelievingly through the whole recital. Mike the Angel grinned to himself; he knew what part of the story seemed queer to the cop.

He was right. Cowder said: "Now, wait a minute. What caused those vibroblades to burn up that way?"

"Must have been faulty," Mike the Angel said innocently.

"Both of them?" Sergeant Cowder asked skeptically. "At the same time?"

"Oh no. Thirty seconds apart, I'd guess."

"Very interesting. Very." He started to say something else, but a uniformed officer stuck his head in through the doorway that led to the front of the shop.

"We combed the whole area, Sergeant. Not a soul around. But from the looks of the alley, there must have been a small truck parked in there not too long ago."

Cowder nodded. "Makes sense. Those JD's wouldn't have tried this unless they intended to take everything they could put their hands on, and they certainly couldn't have put all this in their pockets." He rubbed one big finger over the tip of his nose. "Okay, Barton, that's all. Take those two kids to the hospital and book 'em in the detention ward. I want to talk to them when they wake up."

The cop nodded and left.

Sergeant Cowder looked back at Harry. "Your alarm to the precinct station went off at six thirty-six. I figure that whoever was on the outside, in that truck, knew something had gone wrong as soon as the fight started in here. He—or they—shut off whatever they were using to suppress the alarm system and took off before we got here. They sure must have moved fast."

"Must have," agreed Harry. "Is there anything else, Sergeant?"

Cowder shook his head. "Not right now. I'll get in touch with you later, if I need you."

Harry and Mike the Angel followed him through the front of the shop to the front door. At the door, Cowder turned.

"Well, good night. Thanks for your assistance, Mr. Gabriel. I wish some of our cops had had your luck."

"How so?" asked Mike the Angel.

"If more vibroblades would blow up at opportune moments, we'd have fewer butchered policemen."

Mike the Angel shook his head. "Not really. If their vibros started burning out every time they came near a cop, the JD's would just start using something else. You can't win in this game."

Cowder nodded glumly. "It's a losing proposition any way you look at it.... Well, good night again." He stepped out, and Old Harry closed and locked the door behind him.

Mike the Angel said: "Come on, Harry; I want to find something." He began walking back down the long, narrow shop toward the rear again. Harry followed, looking mystified.

Mike the Angel stopped, sniffing. "Smell that?"

Harry sniffed. "Aye. Burnt insulation. So?"

"You know which one of these bins is nearest to your main control cable. Start looking. See if you find anything queer."

Old Harry walked over to a nearby bin, pulled it open, and looked inside. He closed it, pulled open another. He found the gadget on the third try. It was a plastic case, six by six by eight, and it still smelled of hot insulation, although the case itself was barely warm.

"What is it?" Harry asked in wonder.

"It's the gizmo that turned your equipment off. When I passed by it, my own gadget must have blown it. I knew the police couldn't have made it here between the time of the fight and the time they showed up. They must have had at least an extra minute. Besides, I didn't think anyone could build an instrument that would blank out everything at long range. It had to be something near your main cable. I think you'll find a metallic oscillator in there. Analyze it. Might be useful."

Harry turned the box over in his hands. "Probably has a timer in it to start it.... Well.... That helps."

"What do you mean?"

"I've got a pretty good idea who put it here. Older kid. Nineteen—maybe twenty. Seemed like a nice lad, too. Didn't take him for a JD. Can't trust anyone these days. Thanks, Mike. If I find anything new in here, I'll let you know."

"Do that," said Mike the Angel. "And, as a personal favor, I'll show you how to build my own super-duper, extra-special, anti-vibroblade defense unit."

Old Harry grinned, crinkling up his wizened face in a mass of fine wrinkles. "You'd better think up a shorter name than that for it, laddie; I could probably build one in less time than it takes you to say it."

"Want to bet?"

"I'll bet you twenty I can do it in twenty-four hours."

"Twenty it is, Harry. I'll sell you mine this time tomorrow for twenty bucks."

Harry shook his head. "I'll trade you mine for yours, plus twenty." Then his eyes twinkled. "And speaking of money, didn't you come down here to buy something?"

Mike the Angel laughed. "You're not going to like it. I came down to get a dozen plastic-core resistors."

"What size?"

Mike told him, and Old Harry went over to the proper bin, pulled them out, all properly boxed, and handed them to him.

"That'll be four dollars," he said.

Mike the Angel paid up with a smile. "You don't happen to have a hundred-thousand-unit microcryotron stack, do you?"

"Ain't s'posed to," said Harry MacDougal. "If I did, I wouldn't sell it to you. But, as a matter of cold fact, I do happen to have one. Use it for a paperweight. I'll give it to you for nothing, because it don't work, anyhow."

"Maybe I can fix it," said Mike the Angel, "as long as you're giving it to me. How come it doesn't work?"

"Just a second, laddie," said Harry. He scuttled to the rear of the shop and came back with a ready-wrapped package measuring five by five by four. He handed it to Mike the Angel and said: "It's a present. Thanks for helping me out of a tight spot."

Mike said something deprecative of his own efforts and took the package. If it were in working order it would have been worth close to three hundred dollars—more than that on the black market. If it was broken, though, it was no good to Mike. A microcryotron unit is almost impossible to fix if it breaks down. But Mike took it because he didn't want to hurt Old Harry's feelings by refusing a present.

"Thanks, Harry," he said. "Happen to know why it doesn't work?"

Harry's face crinkled again in his all-over smile. "Sure, Mike. It ain't plugged in."

4

Mike the Angel did not believe in commuting. Being a bachelor, he could afford to indulge in that belief. In his suite of offices on 112th Street, there was one door marked "M. R. Gabriel." Behind that door was his private secretary's office, which acted as an effective barrier between himself and the various employees of the firm. Behind the secretary's office was his own office.

There was still another door in his inner office, a plain, unmarked door that looked as though it might conceal a closet.

It didn't. It was the door to a veddy, veddy expensive apartment with equally expensive appointments. One wall, thirty feet long and ten feet high, was a nearly invisible, dustproof slab of polished, optically flat glass that gave the observer the feeling that there was nothing between him and the city street, five hundred feet below.

The lights of the city, coming through the wall, gave the room plenty of illumination after sunset, but the simple flick of a switch could polarize it black, allowing perfect privacy.

The furniture was massive, heavily braced, and well upholstered. It had to be; Mike the Angel liked to flop into chairs, and his two hundred and sixty pounds gave chairs a lot of punishment.

On one of the opaque walls was Dali's original "Eucharist," with its muffled, robed figures looking oddly luminous in the queer combination of city lights and interior illumination. Farther back, a Valois gleamed metallically above the shadowed bas-reliefs of its depths.

It was the kind of apartment Mike the Angel liked. He could sleep, if necessary, on a park bench or in a trench, but he didn't see any reason for doing so if he could sleep on a five-hundred-dollar floater.

As he had passed through each door, he had checked them carefully. His electrokey had a special circuit that lighted up a tiny glow lamp in the key handle if the lock had been tampered with. None of them had.

He opened the final door, went into his apartment, and locked the door behind him, as he had locked the others. Then he turned on the lights, peeled off his raincoat, and plopped himself into a chair to unwrap the microcryotron stack he had picked up at Harry's.

Theoretically, Harry wasn't supposed to sell the things. They were still difficult to make, and they were supposed to be used only by persons who were authorized to build robot brains, since that's what the stack was—a part of a robot brain. Mike could have put his hands on one legally, provided he'd wanted to wait for six or eight months to clear up the red tape. Actually, the big robotics companies didn't want amateurs fooling around with robots; they'd much rather build the robots themselves and rent them out. They couldn't make do-it-yourself projects impossible, but they could make them difficult.

In a way, there was some good done. So far, the JD's hadn't gone into big-scale robotics. Self-controlled bombs could be rather nasty.

Adult criminals, of course, already had them. But an adult criminal who had the money to invest in robotic components, or went to the trouble to steal them, had something more lucrative in mind than street fights or robbing barrooms. To crack a bank, for instance, took a cleverly constructed, well-designed robot and plenty of ingenuity on the part of the operator.

Mike the Angel didn't want to make bombs or automatic bankrobbers; he just wanted to fiddle with the stack, see what it would do. He turned it over in his hands a couple of times, then shrugged, got up, went over to his closet, and put the thing away. There wasn't anything he could do with it until he'd bought a cryostat—a liquid helium refrigerator. A cryotron functions only at temperatures near absolute zero.

The phone chimed.

Mike went over to it, punched the switch, and said: "Gabriel speaking."

No image formed on the screen. A voice said: "Sorry, wrong number." There was a slight click, and the phone went dead. Mike shrugged and punched the cutoff. Sounded like a woman. He vaguely wished he could have seen her face.

Mike got up and walked back to his easy chair. He had no sooner sat down than the phone chimed again. Damn!

Up again. Back to the phone.

"Gabriel speaking."

Again, no image formed.

"Look, lady," Mike said, "why don't you look up the number you want instead of bothering me?"

Suddenly there was an image. It was the face of an elderly man with a mild, reddish face, white hair, and a cold look in his pale blue eyes. It was Basil Wallingford, the Minister for Spatial Affairs.

He said: "Mike, I wasn't aware that your position was such that you could afford to be rude to a Portfolio of the Earth Government." His voice was flat, without either anger or humor.

"I'm not sure it is, myself," admitted Mike the Angel, "but I do the best I can with the tools I have to work with. I didn't know it was you, Wally. I just had some wrong-number trouble. Sorry."

"Mf.... Well.... I called to tell you that the *Branchell* is ready for your final inspection. Or will be, that is, in a week."

"My final inspection?" Mike the Angel arched his heavy golden-blond eyebrows. "Hell, Wally, Serge Paulvitch is on the job down there, isn't he? You don't need *my* okay. If Serge says it's ready to go, it's ready to go. Or is there some kind of trouble you haven't mentioned yet?"

"No; no trouble," said Wallingford. "But the power plant on that ship was built according to your designs—not Mr. Paulvitch's. The Bureau of Space feels that you should give them the final check."

Mike knew when to argue and when not to, and he knew that this was one time when it wouldn't do him the slightest good. "All right," he said resignedly. "I don't like Antarctica and never will, but I guess I can stand it for a few days."

"Fine. One more thing. Do you have a copy of the thrust specifications for Cargo Hold One? Our copy got garbled in transmission, and there seems to be a discrepancy in the figures."

Mike nodded. "Sure. They're in my office. Want me to get them now?"

"Please. I'll hold on."

Mike the Angel barely made it in time. He went to the door that led to his office, opened it, stepped through, and closed it behind him just as the blast went off.

The door shuddered behind Mike, but it didn't give. Mike's apartment was reasonably soundproof, but it wasn't built to take the kind of explosion that would shake the door that Mike the Angel had just closed. It was a two-inch-thick slab of armor steel on heavy, precision-bearing hinges. So was every other door in the suite. It wasn't quite a bank-vault door, but it would do. Any explosion that could shake it was a real doozy.

Mike the Angel spun around and looked at the door. It was just a trifle warped, and faint tendrils of vapor were curling around the edge where the seal had been broken. Mike sniffed, then turned and ran. He opened a drawer in his desk and took out a big roll of electrostatic tape. Then he took a deep breath, went back to the door, and slapped on a strip of the one-inch tape, running it all around the edge of the door. Then he went into the outer office while the air conditioners cleaned out his private office.

He went over to one of the phones near the autofile and punched for the operator. "I had a long-distance call coming in here from the Right Excellent Basil Wallingford, Minister for Spatial Affairs, Capitol City. We were cut off."

"One moment please." A slight pause. "His Excellency is here, Mr. Gabriel."

Wallingford's face came back on the screen. It had lost some of its ruddiness. "What happened?" he asked.

"You tell me, Wally," Mike snapped. "Did you see anything at all?"

"All I saw was that big pane of glass break. It fell into a thousand pieces, and then something exploded and the phone went dead."

"The glass broke first?"

"That's right."

Mike sighed. "Good. I was afraid that maybe someone had planted that bomb, rather than fired it in. I'd hate to think anyone could get into my place without my knowing it."

"Who's gunning for you?"

"I wish I knew. Look, Wally, can you wait until tomorrow for those specs? I want to get hold of the police."

"Certainly. Nothing urgent. It can wait. I'll call you again tomorrow evening." The screen blanked.

Mike glanced at the wall clock and then punched a number on the phone. A pretty girl in a blue uniform came on the screen.

"Police Central," she said. "May I help you?"

"I'd like to speak to Detective Sergeant William Cowder, please," Mike said. "Just tell him that Mr. Gabriel has more problems."

She looked puzzled, but she nodded, and pretty soon her image blanked out. The screen stayed blank, but Sergeant Cowder's voice came over the speaker. "What is it, Mr. Gabriel?"

He was evidently speaking from a pocket phone.

"Attempted murder," said Mike the Angel. "A few minutes ago a bomb was set off in my apartment. I think it was a rocket, and I know it was heavily laced with hydrogen cyanide. That's Suite 5000, Timmins Building, up on 112th Street. I called you because I have a hunch it's connected with the incident at Harry's earlier this evening."

"Timmins Building, eh? I'll be right up."

Cowder cut off with a sharp click, and Mike the Angel looked quizzically at the dead screen. Was he imagining things, or was there a peculiar note in Cowder's voice?

Two minutes later he got his answer.

3

5

Mike the Angel was sitting behind his desk in his private office when the announcer chimed. Mike narrowed his eyes and turned on his door screen, which connected with an eye in the outer door of the suite. Who could it be this time?

It was Sergeant Cowder.

"You got here fast," said Mike, thumbing the unlocker. "Come on back to my office."

The sergeant came through the outer office while Mike watched him on the screen. Not until the officer finally pushed open the door to Mike's own office did Mike the Angel look up from the screen.

"I repeat," said Mike, "you got here fast."

"I wasn't far away," said Cowder. "Where's the damage?"

Mike jerked a thumb toward the door to his apartment, still sealed with tape. "In there."

"Have you been back in there yet?"

"Nope," said Mike. "I didn't want to disturb anything. I figured maybe your lab boys could tell where the rocket came from."

"What happened?" the cop asked.

Mike told him, omitting nothing except the details of his conversation with Wallingford.

3"The way I see it," he finished, "whoever it was phoned me to make sure I was in the room and then went out and fired a rocket at my window."

"What makes you think it was a JD?" Cowder asked.

"Well, Sergeant, if I were going to do the job, I'd put my launcher in some place where I could see that my victim was inside, without having to call him. But if I couldn't do that, I'd aim the launcher and set it to fire by remote control. Then I'd go to the phone, call him, and fire the rocket while he was on the phone. I'd be sure of getting him that way. The way it was done smacks of a kid's trick."

Cowder looked at the door. "Think we can go in there now? The HCN ought to have cleared out by now."

Mike stood up from behind his desk. "I imagine it's pretty clear. I checked the air conditioners; they're still working, and the filters are efficient enough to take care of an awful lot of hydrogen cyanide. Besides, the window is open. But—shouldn't we wait for the lab men?"

Cowder shook his head. "Not necessary. They'll be up in a few minutes, but they'll probably just confirm what we already know. Peel that tape off, will you?"

Mike took his ionizer from the top of the desk, walked over to the door, and began running it over the tape. It fell off and slithered to the floor. As he worked, he said:

378

"You think you know where the rocket was fired from?"

"Almost positive," said Cowder. "We got a call a few minutes back from the Cathedral of St. John the Divine."

The last of the tape fell off, and Mike opened the door. It didn't work easily, but it did open. The odor of bitter almonds was so faint that it might actually have been imagination.

Cowder pointed out the shattered window at the gray spire of the cathedral. "There's your launching site. We don't know how they got up there, but they managed."

"They?"

"Two of them. When they tried to leave, a couple of priests and two officers of the Cathedral Police spotted them. The kids dropped their launcher and two unfired rockets, and then tried to run for it. Result: one dead kid, one getaway. One of the cops got a bad gash on his arm from a vibroblade, and one of the priests got it in the abdomen. He'll live, but he's in bad shape."

Mike said something under his breath that might have been an oath, except that it avoided all mention of the Deity. Then he added that Name, in a different tone of voice.

"I agree," said Cowder. "You think you know why they did it?"

Mike looked around at his apartment. At first glance it appeared to be a total loss, but closer inspection showed that most of the damage had been restricted to glass and ceramics. The furniture had been tumbled around but not badly damaged. The war head of the rocket had evidently been of the concussion-and-gas type, without much fragmentation.

"I think I know why, yes," Mike said, turning back to the sergeant. "I had a funny feeling all the way home from Harry's. Nothing I could lay my finger on, really. I tried to see if I was being followed, but I didn't spot anyone. There were plenty of kids on the subway.

"It's my guess that the kids knew who I was. If they cased Harry's as thoroughly as it seems they did, they must have seen me go in and out several times. They knew that it was my fault that two of their members got picked up, so they decided to teach me a lesson. One of them must have come up here, even before I left Harry's. The other followed me, just to make sure I was really coming home. Since he knew where I was going, he didn't have to stick too close, so I didn't spot him in the crowd. He might even have gone on up to 116th Street so that I wouldn't see him get off at 110th."

"Sounds reasonable," Cowder agreed. "We know who the kids are. The uniformed squads are rounding up the whole bunch for questioning. They call themselves—you'll get a laugh out of this!—they call themselves the Rocketeers."

"I'm fracturing my funny bone," said Mike the Angel. "The thing that gets me is this revenge business, though. Kids don't usually go that far out for fellow gang members."

"Not usually," the sergeant said, "but this is a little different. The girl you caught and the boy who got killed over at the cathedral are brother and sister."

"That explains it," Mike said. "Rough family, eh?"

Sergeant Cowder shook his head. "Not really. The parents are respectable and fairly well off. Larchmont's the name. The kids are Susan and Herbert—Sue and Bert to you. Bert's sixteen, Sue's seventeen. They were pretty thick, I gather: real brother and sister team."

"Good family, bad kids," Mike muttered. He had wandered over to the wall to look at his Dali. It had fallen to the floor, but it wasn't hurt. The Valois was bent, but it could be fixed up easily enough.

"I wonder," Mike said, picking up the head of a smashed figurine and looking at it. "I wonder if the so-called sociologists have any explanation for it?"

"Sure," Cowder said. "Same one they've been giving for more decades than I'd care to think of. The mother was married before. Divorced her husband, married Larchmont. But she had a boy by her first husband."

"Broken home and sibling rivalry? *Pfui!* And if it wasn't that, the sociologists would find another excuse," Mike said angrily.

"Funny thing is that the older half brother was a perfectly respectable kid. Made good grades in school, joined the Space Service, has a perfectly clean record. And yet *he* was the product of the broken home, not the two younger kids."

Mike laughed dryly. "*That* ought to be food for high sociological thought."

The door announcer chimed again, and Cowder said: "That's probably the lab boys. I told them to come over here as soon as they could finish up at the cathedral."

Mike checked his screen and when Cowder identified the men at the door, Mike let them in.

The short, chubby man in the lead, who was introduced as Perkins, spoke to Sergeant Cowder first. "We checked one of those rockets. Almost a professional job. TNT war head, surrounded by a jacket filled with liquid HCN and a phosphate inhibitor to prevent polymerization. Nasty things." He swung round to Mike. "You're lucky you weren't in the room, or you'd just be part of the wreckage, Mr. Gabriel."

"I know," said Mike the Angel. "Well, the room's all yours. It probably won't tell you much."

"Probably not," said Perkins, "but we'll see. Come on, boys."

Mike the Angel tapped Cowder on the shoulder. "I'd like to talk to you for a minute."

Cowder nodded, and Mike led the way back into his private office. He opened his desk drawer and took out the little pack that housed the workings of the vibroblade shield.

"That accident you were talking about, Sergeant—the one that made those vibroblades blow, remember? I got to thinking that maybe this could have caused it. I think that with a little more power, it might even vaporize a high-speed bullet. But I'd advise you to wear asbestos clothing."

Cowder took the thing and looked at it. "Thanks, Mr. Gabriel," he said honestly. "Maybe the kids will go on to using something else if vibroblades don't work, but I think I'd prefer a rocket in the head to being carved by a vibro."

"To be honest," Mike said, "I think the vibro is just a fad among the JD's now, anyway. You know—if you're one of the real biggies, you carry a vibro. A year from now, it might be shock guns, but right now you're chicken if you carry anything but a vibroblade."

Cowder dropped the shield generator into his coat pocket. "Thanks again, Mr. Gabriel. We'll do you a favor sometime."

6

The firm of M. R. GABRIEL, POWER DESIGN was not a giant corporation, but it did pretty well for a one-man show. The outer office was a gantlet that Mike the Angel had to run when he came in the next morning after having spent the night at a hotel. There was a mixed and ragged chorus of "Good morning, Mr. Gabriel" as he passed through. Mike gave the nod to each of them and was stopped four times for small details before he finally made his way to his own office.

His secretary was waiting for him. She was short, bony, and plain of face. She had a figure like an ironing board and the soul of a Ramsden calculator. Mike the Angel liked her that way; it avoided complications.

"Good morning, Mr. Gabriel," she said. "What the hell happened here?" She waved at the warped door and the ribbons of electrostatic tape that still lay in curls on the floor.

Mike told her, and she listened to his recitation without any change of expression. "I'm very glad you weren't hurt," she said when he had finished. "What are you going to do about the apartment?"

Mike opened the heavy door and looked at the wreckage inside. Through the gaping hole of the shattered window, he could see the towering spires of the two-hundred-year-old Cathedral of St. John the Divine. "Get Larry Beasley on the phone, Helen. I've forgotten his number, but you'll find him listed under 'Interior Decorators.' He has the original plans and designs on file. Tell him to get them out; I want this place fixed up just like it was."

"But what if someone else...." She gestured toward the broken window and the cathedral spires beyond.

"When you're through talking to Beasley," Mike went on, "see if you can get Bishop Brennan on the phone and switch him to my desk."

"Yes, sir," she said.

Within two hours workmen were busily cleaning up the wreckage in Mike the Angel's apartment, and the round, plump figure of Larry Beasley was walking around pompously while his artistic but businesslike brain made estimates. Mike had also reached an agreement with the bishop whereby special vaultlike doors would be fitted into the stairwells leading up to the towers at Mike's expense. They were to have facings of bronze so that they could be decorated to blend with the Gothic decor of the church, but the bronze would be backed by heavy steel. Nobody would blow *those* down in a hurry.

Since the wrecked living room was a flurry of activity and his office had become a thoroughfare, Mike the Angel retired to his bedroom to think. He took with him the microcryotron stack he had picked up at Old Harry's the night before.

"For something that doesn't look like much," he said aloud to the stack, "you have caused me a hell of a lot of trouble."

Old Harry, he knew, wouldn't be caught dead selling the things. In the first place, it was strictly illegal to deal in the components of robotic brains. In the second place, they were so difficult to get, even on the black market, that the few that came into Old Harry's hands went into the defenses of his own shop. Mike the Angel had only wanted to borrow one to take a good look at it. He had read up on all the literature about microcryotrons, but he'd never actually seen one before.

He had reason to be curious about microcryotrons. There was something definitely screwy going on in Antarctica.

Nearly two years before, the UN Government, in the person of Minister Wallingford himself, had asked Mike's firm—which meant Mike the Angel himself—to design the power drive and the thrust converters for a spaceship. On the face of it, there was nothing at all unusual in that. Such jobs were routine for M. R. Gabriel.

But when the specifications arrived, Mike the Angel had begun to wonder what the devil was going on. The spaceship *William Branchell* was to be built on the surface of Earth—and yet it was to be a much larger ship than any that had ever before been built on the ground. Usually, an interstellar vessel that large was built in orbit around the Earth, where the designers didn't have to worry about gravitational pull. Such a ship never landed, any more than an ocean liner was ever beached—not on purpose, anyway. The passengers and cargo were taken up by smaller vessels and brought down the same way when the liner arrived at her destination.

Aside from the tremendous energy required to lift such a vessel free of a planet's surface, there was also the magnetic field of the planet to consider. The drive tubes tended to wander and become erratic if they were forced to cut through the magnetic field of a planet.

Therefore, Question One: Why wasn't the *Branchell* being built in space?

Part of the answer, Mike knew, lay in the specifications for the construction of Cargo Hold One. For one thing, it was huge. For another, it was heavily insulated. For a third, it was built like a tank for holding liquids. All very well and good; possibly someone wanted to carry a cargo of cold lemonade or iced tea. That would be pretty stupid, maybe, but it wouldn't be mysterious.

The mystery lay in the fact that Cargo Hold One had *already been built*. The *Branchell* was to be built *around* it! And that didn't exactly jibe with Mike the Angel's ideas of the proper way to build a spaceship. It was not quite the same as building a seagoing vessel around an oil tank in the middle of Texas, but it was close enough to bother Mike the Angel.

Therefore, Question Two: Why was the *Branchell* being built around Cargo Hold One?

Which led to Question Three: What was *in* Cargo Hold One?

For the answer to that question, he had one very good hint. The density of the contents of Cargo Hold One was listed in the specs as being one-point-seven-two-six grams per cubic centimeter. And that, Mike happened to know, was the density of a cryotronic brain, which is 90 per cent liquid helium and 10 per cent tantalum and niobium, by volume.

He looked at the microcryotron stack in his hand. It was a one-hundred-kilounit stack. The possible connections within it were factorial one hundred thousand. All it needed was to be immersed in its bath of liquid helium to make the metals superconducting, and it would be ready to go to work.

A friend of his who worked for Computer Corporation of Earth had built a robot once, using just such a stack. The robot was designed to play poker. He had fed in all the rules of play and added all the data from Oesterveldt's *On Poker*. It took Mike the Angel exactly one hour to figure out how to beat it.

As long as Mike played rationally, the machine had a slight edge, since it had a perfect memory and could compute faster than Mike could. But it would not, could not learn how to bluff. As soon as Mike started bluffing, the robot went into a tizzy.

It wouldn't have been so bad if the robot had known nothing whatever about bluffing. That would have made it easy for Mike. All he'd have had to do was keep on feeding in chips until the robot folded.

But the robot *did* know about bluffing. The trouble is that bluffing is essentially illogical, and the robot had no rules whatsoever to go by to judge whether Mike was bluffing or not. It finally decided to make its decisions by chance, judging by Mike's past performance at bluffing. When it did, Mike quit bluffing and cleaned it out fast.

That caused such utter confusion in the random circuits that Mike's friend had had to spend a week cleaning up the robot's little mind.

But what would be the purpose of building a brain as gigantic as the one in Cargo Hold One? And why build a spaceship around it?

Like a pig roasting on an automatic spit, the problem kept turning over and over in Mike's mind. And, like the roasting pig, the time eventually came when it was done.

Once it is set in operation, a properly operating robot brain can neither be shut off nor dismantled. Not, that is, unless you want to lose all of the data and processes you've fed into it.

Now, suppose the Computer Corporation of Earth had built a giant-sized brain. (Never mind *why*—just suppose.) And suppose they wanted to take it off Earth, but didn't want to lose all the data that had been pumped into it. (Again, never mind *why*—just suppose.)

Very well, then. *If* such a brain had been built, and *if* it was necessary to take it off Earth, and *if* the data in it was so precious that the brain could not be shut off or dismantled, *then* the thing to do would be to build a ship around it.

Oh *yeah*?

Mike the Angel stared at the microcryotron stack and asked:

"Now, tell me, pal, just why would anyone want a brain that big? And what is so blasted important about it?"

The stack said not a word.

The phone chimed. Mike the Angel thumbed the switch, and his secretary's face appeared on the screen. "Minister Wallingford is on the line, Mr. Gabriel."

"Put him on," said Mike the Angel.

Basil Wallingford's ruddy face came on. "I see you're still alive," he said. "What in the bloody blazes happened last night?"

Mike sighed and told him. "In other words," he ended up, "just the usual sort of JD stuff we have to put up with these days. Nothing new, and nothing to worry about."

"You almost got killed," Wallingford pointed out.

"A miss is as good as a mile," Mike said with cheerful inanity. "Thanks to your phone call, I was as safe as if I'd been in my own home," he added with utter illogic.

"You can afford to laugh," Wallingford said grimly. "I can't. I've already lost one man."

Mike's grin vanished. "What do you mean? Who?"

"Oh, nobody's killed," Wallingford said quickly. "I didn't mean that. But Jack Wong turned his car over yesterday at a hundred and seventy miles an hour, and he's laid up with a fractured leg and a badly dislocated arm."

"Too bad," said Mike. "One of these days that fool will kill himself racing." He knew Wong and liked him. They had served together in the Space Service when Mike was on active duty.

"I hope not," Wallingford said. "Anyway—the matter I called you on last night. Can you get those specs for me?"

"Sure, Wally. Hold on." He punched the hold button and rang for his secretary as Wallingford's face vanished. When the girl's face came on, he said: "Helen, get me the cargo specs on the *William Branchell*—Section Twelve, pages 66 to 74."

The discussion, after Helen had brought the papers, lasted less than five minutes. It was merely a matter of straightening out some cost estimates—but since it had to do with the *Branchell*, and specifically with Hold Number One, Mike decided he'd ask a question.

"Wally, tell me—what in the hell is going on down there at Chilblains Base?"

"They're building a spaceship," said Wallingford in a flat voice.

It was Wallingford's way of saying he wasn't going to answer any questions, but Mike the Angel ignored the hint. "I'd sort of gathered that," he said dryly. "But what I want to know is: Why is it being built around a cryotronic brain, the like of which I have never heard before?"

Basil Wallingford's eyes widened, and he just stared for a full two seconds. "And just how did you come across that information, Golden Wings?" he finally asked.

"It's right here in the specs," said Mike the Angel, tapping the sheaf of papers.

"Ridiculous." Wallingford's voice seemed toneless.

Mike decided he was in too deep now to back out. "It certainly is, Wally. It couldn't be hidden. To compute the thrust stresses, I had to know the density of the contents of Cargo Hold One. And here it is: 1.726 gm/cm^3. Nothing else that I know of has that exact density."

Wallingford pursed his lips. "Dear me," he said after a moment. "I keep forgetting you're too bright for your own good." Then a slow smile spread over his face. "Would you *really* like to know?"

"I wouldn't have asked otherwise," Mike said.

"Fine. Because you're just the man we need."

Mike the Angel could almost feel the knife blade sliding between his ribs, and he had the uncomfortable feeling that the person who had stabbed him in the back was himself. "What's that supposed to mean, Wally?"

"You are, I believe, an officer in the Space Service Reserve," said Basil Wallingford in a smooth, too oily voice. "Since the Engineering Officer of the *Branchell*, Jack Wong, is laid up in a hospital, I'm going to call you to active duty to replace him."

Mike the Angel felt that ghostly knife twist—hard.

"That's silly," he said. "I haven't been a ship's officer for five years."

"You're the man who designed the power plant," Wallingford said sweetly. "If you don't know how to run her, nobody does."

"My time per hour is worth a great deal," Mike pointed out.

"The rate of pay for a Space Service officer," Basil Wallingford said pleasantly, "is fixed by law."

"I can fight being called back to duty—and I'll win," said Mike. He didn't know how long he could play this game, but it was fun.

"True," said Wallingford. "You can. I admit it. But you've been wondering what the hell that ship is being built for. You'd give your left arm to find out. I know you, Golden Wings, and I know how that mind of yours works. And I tell you this: Unless you take this job, you'll *never* find out why the *Branchell* was built." He leaned forward, and his face loomed large in the screen. "And I mean absolutely *never*."

For several seconds Mike the Angel said nothing. His classically handsome face was like that of some Grecian god contemplating the Universe, or an archangel contemplating Eternity. Then he gave Basil Wallingford the benefit of his full, radiant smile.

"I capitulate," he said.

Wallingford refused to look impressed. "Damn right you do," he said—and cut the circuit.

7

Two days later Mike the Angel was sitting at his desk making certain that M. R. GABRIEL, POWER DESIGN would function smoothly while he was gone. Serge Paulvitch, his chief designer, could handle almost everything.

Paulvitch had once said, "Mike, the hell of working for a first-class genius is that a second-class genius doesn't have a chance."

"You could start your own firm," Mike had said levelly. "I'll back you, Serge; you know that."

Serge Paulvitch had looked astonished. "Me? You think I'm crazy? Right now, I'm a second-class genius working for a first-class outfit. You think I want to be a second-class genius working for a second-class outfit? Not on your life!"

Paulvitch could easily handle the firm for a few weeks.

Helen's face came on the phone. "There's a Captain Sir Henry Quill on the phone, Mr. Gabriel. Do you wish to speak to him?"

"Black Bart?" said Mike. "I wonder what he wants."

"Bart?" She looked puzzled. "He said his name was Henry."

Mike grinned. "He always signs his name: *Captain Sir Henry Quill, Bart.*. And since he's the toughest old martinet this side of the Pleiades, the 'Black' part just comes naturally. I served under him seven years ago. Put him on."

In half a second the grim face of Captain Quill was on the screen.

He was as bald as an egg. What little hair he did have left was meticulously shaved off every morning. He more than made up for his lack of cranial growth, however, by his great, shaggy, bristly brows, black as jet and firmly anchored to jutting supraorbital ridges. Any other man would have been proud to wear them as mustaches.

"What can I do for you, Captain?" Mike asked, using the proper tone of voice prescribed for the genial businessman.

"You can go out and buy yourself a new uniform," Quill growled. "Your old one isn't regulation any more."

Well, not exactly growled. If he'd had the voice for it, it would have been a growl, but the closest he could come to a growl was an Irish tenor rumble with undertones of gravel. He stood five-eight, and his red and gold Space Service uniform gleamed with spit-and-polish luster. With his cap off, his bald head looked as though it, too, had been polished.

Mike looked at him thoughtfully. "I see. So you're commanding the mystery tub, eh?" he said at last.

"That's right," said the captain. "And don't go asking me a bunch of blasted questions. I've got no more idea of what the bloody thing's about than you—maybe not as much. I understand you designed her power plant...?"

He let it hang. If not exactly a leading question, it was certainly a hinting statement.

Mike shook his head. "I don't know anything, Captain. Honestly I don't."

If Space Service regulations had allowed it, Captain Sir Henry Quill, Bart., would have worn a walrus mustache. And if he'd had such a mustache, he would have whuffled it then. As it was, he just blew out air, and nothing whuffled.

"You and I are the only ones in the dark, then," he said. "The rest of the crew is being picked from Chilblains Base. Pete Jeffers is First Officer, in case you're wondering."

"Oh, great," Mike the Angel said with a moan. "That means we'll be going in cold on an untried ship."

Like Birnam Wood advancing on Dunsinane, Quill's eyebrows moved upward. "Don't you trust your own designing?"

"As much as you do," said Mike the Angel. "Probably more."

Quill nodded. "We'll have to make the best of it. We'll muddle through somehow. Are you all ready to go?"

"No," Mike admitted, "but I don't see that I can do a damn thing about that."

"Nor do I," said Captain Quill. "Be at Chilblains Base in twenty-four hours. Arrangements will be made at the Long Island Base for your transportation to Antarctica. And"—he paused and his scowl became deeper—"you'd best get used to calling me 'sir' again."

"Yessir, Sir Henry, sir."

"*Thank* you, Mister Gabriel," snapped Quill, cutting the circuit.

"Selah," said Mike the Angel.

Chilblains Base, Antarctica, was directly over the South Magnetic Pole—at least, as closely as that often elusive spot could be pinpointed for any length of time. It is cheaper in the long run if an interstellar vessel moves parallel with, not perpendicular to, the magnetic "lines of force" of a planet's gravitational field. Taking off "across the grain" *can* be done, but the power consumption is much greater. Taking off "with the grain" is expensive enough.

An ion rocket doesn't much care where it lifts or sets down, since its method of propulsion isn't trying to work against the fabric of space itself. For that reason, an interstellar vessel is normally built in space and stays there, using ion rockets for loading and unloading its passengers. It's cheaper by far.

The Computer Corporation of Earth had also been thinking of expenses when it built its Number One Research Station near Chilblains Base, although the corporation was not aware at the time just how much money it was eventually going to save them.

The original reason had simply been lower power costs. A cryotron unit has to be immersed at all times in a bath of liquid helium at a temperature of four-point-two degrees absolute. It is obviously much easier—and much cheaper—to keep several thousand gallons of helium at that temperature if the surrounding temperature is at two hundred thirty-three absolute than if it is up around two hundred ninety or three hundred. That may not seem like much percentagewise, but it comes out to a substantial saving in the long run.

But, power consumption or no, when C.C. of E. found that Snookums either had to be moved or destroyed, it was mightily pleased that it had built Prime Station near Chilblains Base. Since a great deal of expense also, of necessity, devolved upon Earth Government, the government was, to say it modestly, equally pleased. There was enough expense as it was.

The scenery at Chilblains Base—so named by a wiseacre American navy man back in the twentieth century—was nothing to brag about. Thousands of square miles of powdered ice that has had nothing to do but blow around for twenty million years is not at all inspiring after the first few minutes unless one is obsessed by the morbid beauty of cold death.

Mike the Angel was not so obsessed. To him, the area surrounding Chilblains Base was just so much white hell, and his analysis was perfectly correct. Mike wished that it had been January, midsummer in the Antarctic, so there would have been at least a little dim sunshine. Mike the Angel did not particularly relish having to visit the South Pole in midwinter.

The rocket that had lifted Mike the Angel from Long Island Base settled itself into the snow-covered landing stage of Chilblains Base, dissipating the crystalline whiteness into steam as it did so. The steam, blown away by the chill winds, moved all of thirty yards before it became ice again.

Mike the Angel was not in the best of moods. Having to dump all of his business into Serge Paulvitch's hands on twenty-four hours' notice was irritating. He knew Paulvitch could handle the job, but it wasn't fair to him to make him take over so suddenly.

In addition, Mike did not like the way the whole *Branchell* business was being handled. It seemed slipshod and hurried, and, worse, it was entirely too mysterious and melodramatic.

"Of all the times to have to come to Antarctica," he grumped as the door of the rocket opened, "why did I have to get July?"

The pilot, a young man in his early twenties, said smugly: "July is bad, but January isn't good—just not so worse."

Mike the Angel glowered. "Sonny, I was a cadet here when you were learning arithmetic. It hasn't changed since, summer or winter."

"Sorry, sir," said the pilot stiffly.

"So am I," said Mike the Angel cryptically. "Thanks for the ride."

He pushed open the outer door, pulled his electroparka closer around him, and stalked off across the walk, through the lashing of the sleety wind.

He didn't have far to walk—a hundred yards or so—but it was a good thing that the walk was protected and well within the boundary of Chilblains Base instead of being out on the Wastelands. Here there were lights, and the Hotbed equipment of the walk warmed the swirling ice particles into a sleety rain. On the Wastelands, the utter blackness and the wind-driven snow would have swallowed him permanently within ten paces.

He stepped across a curtain of hot air that blew up from a narrow slit in the deck and found himself in the main foyer of Chilblains Base.

The entrance looked like the entrance to a theater—a big metal and plastic opening, like a huge room open on one side, with only that sheet of hot air to protect it from the storm raging outside. The lights and the small doors leading into the building added to the impression that this was a theater, not a military base.

But the man who was standing near one of the doors was not by a long shot dressed as an usher. He wore a sergeant's stripes on his regulation Space Service parka, which muffled him to the nose, and he came over to Mike the Angel and said: "Commander Gabriel?"

Mike the Angel nodded as he shook icy drops from his gloved hands, then fished in his belt pocket for his newly printed ID card.

He handed it to the sergeant, who looked it over, peered at Mike's face, and saluted. As Mike returned the salute the sergeant said: "Okay, sir; you can go on in. The security office is past the double door, first corridor on your right."

Mike the Angel tried his best not to look surprised. "*Security* office? Is there a war on or something? What does Chilblains need with a security office?"

The sergeant shrugged. "Don't ask me, Commander; I just slave away here. Maybe Lieutenant Nariaki knows something, but I sure don't."

"Thanks, Sergeant."

Mike the Angel went inside, through two insulated and tightly weather-stripped doors, one right after another, like the air lock on a spaceship. Once inside the warmth of the corridor, he unzipped his electroparka, shut off the power, and pushed back the hood with its fogproof faceplate.

Down the hall, Mike could see an office marked *security officer* in small letters without capitals. He walked toward it. There was another guard at the door who had to see Mike's ID card before Mike was allowed in.

Lieutenant Tokugawa Nariaki was an average-sized, sleepy-looking individual with a balding crew cut and a morose expression.

He looked up from his desk as Mike came in, and a hopeful smile tried to spread itself across his face. "If you are Commander Gabriel," he said softly, "watch yourself. I may suddenly kiss you out of sheer relief."

"Restrain yourself, then," said Mike the Angel, "because I'm Gabriel."

Nariaki's smile became genuine. "So! Good! The phone has been screaming at me every half hour for the past five hours. Captain Sir Henry Quill wants you."

"He would," Mike said. "How do I get to him?"

"You don't just yet," said Nariaki, raising a long, bony, tapering hand. "There are a few formalities which our guests have to go through."

"Such as?"

"Such as fingerprint and retinal patterns," said Lieutenant Nariaki.

Mike cast his eyes to Heaven in silent appeal, then looked back at the lieutenant. "Lieutenant, *what* is going on here? There hasn't been a security officer in the Space Service for thirty years or more. What am I suspected of? Spying for the corrupt and evil alien beings of Diomega Orionis IX?"

Nariaki's oriental face became morose again. "For all I know, you are. Who knows what's going on around here?" He got up from behind his desk and led Mike the Angel over to the fingerprinting machine. "Put your hands in here, Commander ... that's it."

He pushed a button, and, while the machine hummed, he said: "Mine is an antiquated position, I'll admit. I don't like it any more than you do. Next thing, they'll put me to work polishing chain-mail armor or make me commander of a company of musketeers. Or maybe they'll send me to the 18th Outer Mongolian Yak Artillery."

Mike looked at him with narrowed eyes. "Lieutenant, do you actually mean that you really don't know what's going on here, or are you just dummying up?"

Nariaki looked at Mike, and for the first time, his face took on the traditional blank, emotionless look of the "placid Orient." He paused for long seconds, then said:

"Some of both, Commander. But don't let it worry you. I assure you that within the next hour you'll know more about Project Brainchild than I've been able to find out in two years.... Now put your face in here and keep your eyes open. When you can see the target spot, focus on it and tell me."

Mike the Angel put his face in the rest for the retinal photos. The soft foam rubber adjusted around his face, and he was looking into blackness. He focused his eyes on the dim target circle and waited for his eyes to grow accustomed to the darkness.

The Security Officer's voice continued. "All I do is make sure that no unauthorized person comes into Chilblains Base. Other than that, I have nothing but personal guesses and little trickles of confusing information, neither of which am I at liberty to discuss."

Mike's irises had dilated to the point that he could see the dim dot in the center of the target circle, glowing like a dimly visible star. "Shoot," he said.

There was a dazzling glare of light. Mike pulled his face out of the padded opening and blinked away the colored after-images.

Lieutenant Nariaki was comparing the fresh fingerprints with the set he had had on file. "Well," he said, "you have Commander Gabriel's hands, anyway. If you have his eyes, I'll have to concede that the rest of the body belongs to him, too."

"How about my soul?" Mike asked dryly.

"Not my province, Commander," Nariaki said as he pulled the retinal photos out of the machine. "Maybe one of the chaplains would know."

"If this sort of thing is going on all over Chilblains," said Mike the Angel, "I imagine the Office of Chaplains is doing a booming business in TS cards."

The lieutenant put the retinal photos in the comparator, took a good look, and nodded. "You're you," he said. "Give me your ID card."

Mike handed it over, and Nariaki fed it through a printer which stamped a complex seal in the upper left-hand corner of the card. The lieutenant signed his name across the seal and handed the card back to Mike.

"That's it," he said. "You can—"

He was interrupted by the chiming of the phone.

"Just a second, Commander," he said as he thumbed the phone switch.

Mike was out of range of the TV pickup, and he couldn't see the face on the screen, but the voice was so easy to recognize that he didn't need to see the man.

"Hasn't that triply bedamned rocket landed yet, Lieutenant? Where is Commander Gabriel?"

Mike knew that Black Bart had already checked on the landing of the latest rocket; the question was rhetorical.

Mike grinned. "Tell the old tyrant," he said firmly, "that I'll be along as soon as the Security Officer is through with me."

Nariaki's expression didn't change. "You're through now, Commander, and—"

"Tell that imitation Apollo to hop it over here fast!" said Quill sharply. "I'll give him a lesson in tyranny."

There was a click as the intercom shut off.

Nariaki looked at Mike the Angel and shook his head slowly. "Either you're working your way toward a court-martial or else you know where Black Bart has the body buried."

"I should," said Mike cryptically. "I helped him bury it. How do I get to His Despotic Majesty's realm?"

Nariaki considered. "It'll take you five or six minutes. Take the tubeway to Stage Twelve. Go up the stairway to the surface and take the first corridor to the left. That'll take you to the loading dock for that stage. It's an open foyer like the one at the landing field, so you'll have to put your parka back on. Go down the stairs on the other side, and you'll be in Area K. One of the guards will tell you where to go from there. Of course, you could go by tube, but it would take longer because of the by-pass."

"Good enough. I'll take the short cut. See you. And thanks."

8

The underground tubeway shot Mike the Angel across five miles of track at high speed. Mike left the car at Stage Twelve and headed up the stairway and down the corridor to a heavy double door marked *freight loading*.

He put on his parka and went through the door. The foyer was empty, and, like the one at the rocket landing, protected from the Antarctic blast only by a curtain of hot air. Outside that curtain, the light seemed to lose itself in the darkness of the bleak, snow-filled Wastelands. Mike ignored the snowscape and headed across the empty foyer to the door marked *entrance*.

"With a small *e*," Mike muttered to himself. "I wonder if the sign painter ran out of full caps."

He was five feet from the door when he heard the yell.

"*Help!*"

That was all. Just the one word.

Mike the Angel came to a dead halt and spun around.

The foyer was a large room, about fifty by fifty feet in area and nearly twenty feet high. And it was quite obviously empty. On the open side, the sheet of hissing hot air was doing its best to shield the room from the sixty-below-zero blizzard outside. Opposite the air curtain was a huge sliding door, closed at the moment, which probably led to a freight elevator. There were only two other doors leading from the foyer, and both of them were closed. And Mike knew that no voice could come through those insulated doors.

"*Help!*"

Mike the Angel swung toward the air curtain. This time there was no doubt. Someone was out in that howling ice-cloud, screaming for help!

Mike saw the figure—dimly, fleetingly, obscured most of the time by the driving whiteness. Whoever it was looked as if he were buried to the waist in snow.

Mike made a quick estimate. It was dark out there, but he could see the figure; therefore he would be able to see the foyer lights. He wouldn't get lost. Snapping down the faceplate of his parka hood, he ran through the protective updraft of the air curtain and charged into the deadly chill of the Antarctic blizzard.

In spite of the electroparka he was wearing, the going was difficult. The snow tended to plaster itself against his faceplate, and the wind kept trying to take him off his feet. He wiped a gloved hand across the faceplate. Ahead, he could still see the figure waving its arms. Mike slogged on.

At sixty below, frozen H_2O isn't slushy, by any means; it isn't even slippery. It's more like fine sand than anything else. Mike the Angel figured he had about thirty feet to go, but after he'd taken eight steps, the arm-waving figure looked as far off as when he'd started.

Mike stopped and flipped up his faceplate. It felt as though someone had thrown a handful of razor blades into his face. He winced and yelled, "What's the trouble?" Then he snapped the plate back into position.

"I'm cold!" came the clear, contralto voice through the howling wind.

A *woman*! thought Mike. "I'm coming!" he bellowed, pushing on. Ten more steps.

He stopped again. He couldn't see anyone or anything.

He flipped up his faceplate. "Hey!"

No answer.

"Hey!" he called again.

And still there was no answer.

Around Mike the Angel, there was nothing but the swirling, blinding snow, the screaming, tearing wind, and the blackness of the Antarctic night.

There was something damned odd going on here. Carefully putting the toe of his right foot to the rear of the heel of his left, he executed a one-hundred-eighty-degree military about-face.

And breathed a sigh of relief.

He could still see the lights of the foyer. He had half suspected that someone was trying to trap him out here, and they might have turned off the lights.

He swiveled his head around for one last look. He still couldn't see a sign of anyone. There was nothing he could do but head back and report the incident. He started slogging back through the gritty snow.

He stepped through the hot-air curtain and flipped up his faceplate.

"Why did you go out in the blizzard?" said a clear, contralto voice directly behind him.

Mike swung around angrily. "Look, lady, I—"

He stopped.

The lady was no lady.

A few feet away stood a machine. Vaguely humanoid in shape from the waist up, it was built more like a miniature military tank from the waist down. It had a pair of black sockets in its head, which Mike took to be TV cameras of some kind. It had grillwork on either side of its head, which probably covered microphones, and another grillwork where the mouth should be. There was no nose.

"What the hell?" asked Mike the Angel of no one in particular.

"I'm Snookums," said the robot.

"Sure you are," said Mike the Angel, backing uneasily toward the door. "You're Snookums. I couldn't fail not to disagree with you less."

Mike the Angel didn't particularly like being frightened, but he had never found it a disabling emotion, so he could put up with it if he had to. But, given his choice, he would have much preferred to be afraid of something a little less unpredictable, something he knew a little more about. Something comfortable, like, say, a Bengal tiger or a Kodiak bear.

"But I really *am* Snookums," reiterated the clear voice.

Mike's brain was functioning in high gear with overdrive added and the accelerator floor-boarded. He'd been lured out onto the Wastelands by this machine—it most definitely could be dangerous.

The robot was obviously a remote-control device. The arms and hands were of the waldo type used to handle radioactive materials in a hot lab—four jointed fingers and an opposed thumb, metal duplicates of the human hand.

But who was on the other end? Who was driving the machine? Who was saying those inane things over the speaker that served the robot as a mouth? It was certainly a woman's voice.

Mike was still moving backward, toward the door. The machine that called itself Snookums wasn't moving toward him, which was some consolation, but not much. The thing could obviously move faster on those treads than Mike could on his feet. Especially since Mike was moving backward.

"Would you mind explaining what this is all about, miss?" asked Mike the Angel. He didn't expect an explanation; he was stalling for time.

"I am not a 'miss,'" said the robot. "I am Snookums."

"Whatever you are, then," said Mike, "would you mind explaining?"

"No," said Snookums, "I wouldn't mind."

Mike's fingers, groping behind him, touched the door handle. But before he could grasp it, it turned, and the door opened behind him. It hit him full in the back, and he stumbled forward a couple of steps before regaining his balance.

387

A clear contralto voice said: "Oh! I'm *so* sorry!"

It was the same voice as the robot's!

Mike the Angel swung around to face the second robot.

This time it was a lady.

"I'm sorry," she repeated. She was all wrapped up in an electroparka, but there was no mistaking the fact that she was both human and feminine. She came on through the door and looked at the robot. "Snookums! What are you doing here?"

"I was trying an experiment, Leda," said Snookums. "This man was just asking me about it. I just wanted to see if he would come if I called 'help.' He did, and I want to know *why* he did."

The girl flashed a look at Mike. "Would you please tell Snookums why you went out there? Please—don't be angry or anything—just tell him."

Mike was beginning to get the picture. "I went because I thought I heard a human being calling for help—and it sounded suspiciously like a woman."

"Oh," said Snookums, sounding a little downhearted—if a robot can be said to have a heart. "The reaction was based, then, upon a misconception. That makes the data invalid. I'll have to try again."

"That won't be necessary, Snookums," the girl said firmly. "This man went out there because he thought a human life was in danger. He would not have done it if he had known it was you, because he would have known that you were not in any danger. You can stand much lower temperatures than a human being can, you know." She turned to Mike. "Am I correct in saying that you wouldn't have gone out there if you'd known Snookums was a robot?"

"Absolutely correct," said Mike the Angel fervently.

She looked back at Snookums. "Don't try that experiment again. It is dangerous for a human to go out there, even with an electroparka. You might run the risk of endangering human life."

"Oh dear!" said Snookums. "I'm sorry, Leda!" There was real anxiety in the voice.

"That's all right, honey," the girl said hurriedly. "This man isn't hurt, so don't get upset. Come along now, and we'll go back to the lab. You shouldn't come out like this without permission."

Mike had noticed that the girl had kept one hand on her belt all the time she was talking—and that her thumb was holding down a small button on a case attached to the belt.

He had been wondering why, but he didn't have to wonder long.

The door behind him opened again, and four men came out, obviously in a devil of a hurry. Each one of them was wearing a brassard labeled SECURITY POLICE.

At least, thought Mike the Angel as he turned to look them over, *the brassards aren't in all lower-case italics.*

One of them jerked a thumb at Mike. "This the guy, Miss Crannon?"

The girl nodded. "That's him. He saw Snookums. Take care of him." She looked again at Mike. "I'm terribly sorry, really I am. But there's no help for it." Then, without another word, she opened the door and went back inside, and the robot rolled in after her.

As the door closed behind her, the SP man nearest Mike, a tough-looking bozo wearing an ensign's insignia, said: "Let's see your identification."

Mike realized that his own parka had no insignia of rank on it, but he didn't like the SP man's tone.

"Come on!" snapped the ensign. "Who are you?"

Mike the Angel pulled out his ID card and handed it to the security cop. "It tells right there who I am," he said. "That is, if you can read."

The man glared and jerked the card out of Mike's hand, but when he saw the emblem that Lieutenant Nariaki had stamped on it, his eyes widened. He looked up at Mike. "I'm sorry, sir; I didn't mean—"

"That tears it," interrupted Mike. "That absolutely tears it. In the past three minutes I have been apologized to by a woman, a robot, and a cop. The next thing, a penguin will walk in here, tip his top hat, and abase himself while he mutters obsequiously in penguinese. Just what the devil is going *on* around this place?"

The four SP men were trying hard not to fidget.

"Just security precautions, sir," said the ensign uncomfortably. "Nobody but those connected with Project Brainchild are supposed to know about Snookums. If anyone else finds out, we're supposed to take them into protective custody."

"I'll bet you're widely loved for that," said Mike. "I suppose the gadget at Miss What's-her-name's belt was an alarm to warn you of impending disaster?"

"Miss Crannon.... Yes, sir. Everybody on the project carries those around. Also, Miss Crannon carries a detector for following Snookums around. She's sort of his keeper, you know."

"No," said Mike the Angel, "I do not know. But I intend to find out. I'm looking for Captain Quill; where is he?"

The four men looked at each other, then looked back at Mike.

"I don't know, Commander," said the ensign. "I understand that several new men have come in today, but I don't know all of them. You'd better talk to Dr. Fitzhugh."

"Such are the beauties of security," said Mike the Angel. "Where can I find this Dr. Fitzhugh?"

The security man looked at his wrist watch. "He's down in the cafeteria now, sir. It's coffee time, and Doc Fitzhugh is as regular as a satellite orbit."

"I'm glad you didn't say 'clockwork,'" Mike told him. "I've had enough dealings with machines today. Where is this coffee haven?"

The ensign gave directions for reaching the cafeteria, and Mike pushed open the door marked *entrance*. He had to pass through another inner door guarded by another pair of SP men who checked his ID card again, then he had to ramble through hallways that went off at queer angles to each other, but he finally found the cafeteria.

He nabbed the first passer-by and asked him to point out Dr. Fitzhugh. The passer-by was obliging; he indicated a smallish, elderly man who was sitting by himself at one of the tables.

Mike made his way through the tray-carrying hordes that were milling about, and finally ended up at the table where the smallish man was sitting.

"Dr. Fitzhugh?" Mike offered his hand. "I'm Commander Gabriel. Minister Wallingford appointed me Engineering Officer of the *Branchell*."

Dr. Fitzhugh shook Mike's hand with apparent pleasure. "Oh yes. Sit down, Commander. What can I do for you?"

Mike had already peeled off his electroparka. He hung it over the back of a chair and said: "Mind if I grab a cup of coffee, Doctor? I've just come from topside, and I think the cold has made its way clean to my bones." He paused. "Would you like another cup?"

Dr. Fitzhugh looked at his watch. "I have time for one more, thanks."

By the time Mike had returned with the cups, he had recalled where he had heard the name Fitzhugh before.

"It just occurred to me," he said as he sat down. "You must be Dr. *Morris* Fitzhugh."

Fitzhugh nodded. "That's right." He wore a perpetually worried look, which made his face look more wrinkled than his fifty years of age would normally have accounted for. Mike was privately of the opinion that if Fitzhugh ever really *tried* to look worried, his ears would meet over the bridge of his long nose.

"I've read a couple of your articles in the *Journal*," Mike explained, "but I didn't connect the name until I saw you. I recognized you from your picture."

Fitzhugh smiled, which merely served to wrinkle his face even more.

Mike the Angel spent the next several minutes feeling the man out, then he went on to explain what had happened with Snookums out in the foyer, which launched Dr. Fitzhugh into an explanation.

"He didn't want help, of course; he was merely conducting an experiment. There are many areas of knowledge in which he is as naïve as a child."

Mike nodded. "It figures. At first I thought he was just a remote-control tool, but I finally saw that he was a real, honest-to-goodness robot. Who gave him the idea to make such an experiment as that?"

"No one at all," said Dr. Fitzhugh. "He's built to make up his own experiments."

Mike the Angel's classic face regarded the wrinkled one of Dr. Fitzhugh. "His own experiments? But a robot—"

Fitzhugh held up a bony hand, gesturing for attention and silence. He got it from Mike.

"Snookums," he said, "is no ordinary robot, Commander."

Mike waited for more. When none came, he said: "So I gather." He sipped at his black coffee. "That machine I saw is actually a remote-control tool, isn't it? Snookums' actual brain is in Cargo Hold One of the *William Branchell*."

"That's right." Dr. Fitzhugh began reaching into various pockets about his person. He extracted a tobacco pouch, a briar pipe, and a jet-flame lighter. Then he began speaking as he went through the pipe smoker's ritual of filling, tamping, and lighting.

"Snookums," he began, "is a self-activating, problem-seeking computer with input and output sensory and action mechanisms analogous to those of a human being." He pushed more tobacco into the bowl of his pipe with a bony forefinger. "He's as close to being a living creature as anything Man has yet devised."

"What about the synthecells they're making at Boston Med?" Mike asked, looking innocent.

Fitzhugh's contour-map face wrinkled up even more. "I should have said 'living *intelligence*,'" he corrected himself. "He's a true robot, in the old original sense of the word; an artificial entity that displays almost every function of a living, intelligent creature. And, at the same time, he has the accuracy and speed that is normal to a cryotron computer."

Mike the Angel said nothing while Fitzhugh fired up his lighter and directed the jet of flame into the bowl and puffed up great clouds of smoke which obscured his face.

While the roboticist puffed, Mike let his gaze wander idly over the other people in the cafeteria. He was wondering how much longer he could talk to Fitzhugh before Captain Quill began—

And then he saw the redhead.

There is never much point in describing a really beautiful girl. Each man has his own ideas of what it takes for a girl to be "pretty" or "fascinating" or "lovely" or almost any other adjective that can be applied to the noun "girl." But "beautiful" is a cultural concept, at least as far as females are concerned, and there is no point in describing a cultural concept. It's one of those things that everybody knows, and descriptions merely become repetitious and monotonous.

This particular example filled, in every respect, the definition of "beautiful" according to the culture of the white Americo-European subclass of the human race as of anno Domini 2087. The elements and proportions and symmetry fit almost perfectly into the ideal mold. It is only necessary to fill in some of the minor details which are allowed to vary without distorting the ideal.

She had red hair and blue eyes and was wearing a green zipsuit.

And she was coming toward the table where Mike and Dr. Fitzhugh were sitting.

"... such a tremendous number of elements," Dr. Fitzhugh was saying, "that it was possible—and necessary—to introduce a certain randomness within the circuit choices themselves— Ah! Hello, Leda, my dear!"

Mike and Fitzhugh rose from their seats.

"Leda, this is Commander Gabriel, the Engineering Officer of the *Brainchild*," said Fitzhugh. "Commander, Miss Leda Crannon, our psychologist."

Mike had been allowing his eyes to wander over the girl, inspecting her ankles, her hair, and all vital points of interest between. But when he heard the name "Crannon," his eyes snapped up to meet hers.

He hadn't recognized the girl without her parka and wouldn't have known her name if the SP ensign hadn't mentioned it. Obviously, she didn't recognize Mike at all, but there was a troubled look in her blue eyes.

She gave him a puzzled smile. "Haven't we met, Commander?"

Mike grinned. "Hey! That's supposed to be *my* line, isn't it?"

She flashed him a warm smile, then her eyes widened ever so slightly. "Your voice! You're the man on the foyer! The one...."

"... the one whom you called copper on," finished Mike agreeably. "But please don't apologize; you've more than made up for it."

Her smile remained. She evidently liked what she saw. "How was I to know who you were?"

"It might have been written on my pocket handkerchief," said Mike the Angel, "but Space Service officers don't carry pocket handkerchiefs."

"What?" The puzzled look had returned.

"Ne' mind," said Mike. "Sit down, won't you?"

"Oh, I can't, thanks. I came to get Fitz; a meeting of the Research Board has been called, and afterward we have to give a lecture or something to the officers of the *Brainchild*."

"You mean the *Branchell*?"

Her smile became an impish grin. "You call it what you want. To us, it's the *Brainchild*."

Dr. Fitzhugh said: "Will you excuse us, Commander? We'll be seeing you at the briefing later."

Mike nodded. "I'd better get on my way, too. I'll see you."

But he stood there as Leda Crannon and Dr. Fitzhugh walked away. The girl looked just as divine retreating as she had advancing.

9

Captain Sir Henry (Black Bart) Quill was seated in an old-fashioned, formyl-covered, overstuffed chair, chewing angrily at the end of an unlighted cigar. His bald head gleamed like a pink billiard ball, almost matching the shining glory of his golden insignia against his scarlet tunic.

Mike the Angel had finally found his way through the maze of underground passageways to the door marked *wardroom 9* and had pushed it open gingerly, halfway hoping that he wouldn't be seen coming in late but not really believing it would happen.

He was right. Black Bart was staring directly at the door when it slid open. Mike shrugged inwardly and stepped boldly into the room, flicking a glance over the faces of the other officers present.

"Well, well, well, Mister Gabriel," said Black Bart. The voice was oily, but the oil was oil of vitriol. "You not only come late, but you come incognito. Where is your uniform?"

There was a muffled snicker from one of the junior officers, but it wasn't muffled enough. Before Mike the Angel could answer, Captain Quill's head jerked around.

"That will do, Mister Vaneski!" he barked. "Boot ensigns don't snicker when their superiors—*and* their betters—are being reprimanded! I only use sarcasm on officers I respect. Until an officer earns my sarcasm, he gets nothing but blasting when he goofs off. Understand?"

The last word was addressed to the whole group.

Ensign Vaneski colored, and his youthful face became masklike. "Yes, sir. Sorry, sir."

Quill didn't even bother to answer; he looked back at Mike the Angel, who was still standing at attention. Quill's voice resumed its caustic saccharinity. "But don't let that go to your head, Mister Gabriel. I repeat: Where is your pretty red spaceman's suit?"

"If the Captain will recall," said Mike, "I had only twenty-four hours' notice. I couldn't get a new wardrobe in that time. It'll be in on the next rocket."

Captain Quill was silent for a moment, then he simply said, "Very well," thus dismissing the whole subject. He waved Mike the Angel to a seat. Mike sat.

"We'll dispense with the formal introductions," said Quill. "Commander Gabriel is our Engineering Officer. The rest of these boys all know each other, Commander; you and I are the only ones who don't come from Chilblains Base. You know Commander Jeffers, of course."

Mike nodded and grinned at Peter Jeffers, a lean, bony character who had a tendency to collapse into chairs as though he had come unhinged. Jeffers grinned and winked back.

"This is Lieutenant Commander von Liegnitz, Navigation Officer; Lieutenant Keku, Supply; Lieutenant Mellon, Medical Officer; and Ensign Vaneski, Maintenance. You can all shake hands with each other later; right now, let's get on with business." He frowned, overshadowing his eyes with those great, bushy brows. "What was I saying just before Commander Gabriel came in?"

Pete Jeffers shifted slightly in his seat. "You were sayin', suh, that this's the stupidest dam' assignment anybody evah got. Or words to that effect." Jeffers had been born in Georgia and had moved to the south of England at the age of ten. Consequently, his accent was far from standard.

"I think, Mister Jeffers," said Quill, "that I phrased it a bit more delicately, but that was the essence of it.

"The *Brainchild*, as she has been nicknamed, has been built at great expense for the purpose of making a single trip. We are to take her, and her cargo, to a destination known only to myself and von Liegnitz. We will be followed there by another Service ship, which will bring us back as passengers." He allowed himself a half-smile. "At least we'll get to loaf around on the way back."

The others grinned.

"The *Brainchild* will be left there and, presumably, dismantled."

He took the unlighted cigar out of his mouth, looked at it, and absently reached in his pocket for a lighter. The deeply tanned young man who had been introduced as Lieutenant Keku had just lighted a cigarette, so he proffered his own flame to the captain. Quill puffed his cigar alight absently and went on.

"It isn't going to be easy. We won't have a chance to give the ship a shakedown cruise because once we take off we might as well keep going—which we will.

"You all know what the cargo is—Cargo Hold One contains the greatest single robotic brain ever built. Our job is to make sure it gets to our destination in perfect condition."

"Question, sir," said Mike the Angel.

Without moving his head, Captain Quill lifted one huge eyebrow and glanced in Mike's direction. "Yes?"

"Why didn't C.C. of E. build the brain on whatever planet we're going to in the first place?"

"We're supposed to be told that in the briefing over at the C.C. of E. labs in"—he glanced at his watch—"half an hour. But I think we can all get a little advance information. Most of you men have been around here long enough to have some idea of what's going on, but I understand that Mister Vaneski knows somewhat more about robotics than most of us. Do you have any light to shed on this, Mister Vaneski?"

Mike grinned to himself without letting it show on his face. The skipper was letting the boot ensign redeem himself after the *faux pas* he'd made.

Vaneski started to stand up, but Quill made a slight motion with his hand and the boy relaxed.

"It's only a guess, sir," he said, "but I think it's because the robot knows too much."

Quill and the others looked blank, but Mike narrowed his eyes imperceptibly. Vaneski was practically echoing Mike's own deductions.

"I mean—well, look, sir," Vaneski went on, a little flustered, "they started to build that thing ten years ago. Eight years ago they started teaching it. Evidently they didn't see any reason for building it off Earth then. What I mean is, something must've happened since then to make them decide to take it off Earth. If they've spent all this much money to get it away, that must mean that it's dangerous somehow."

"If that's the case," said Captain Quill, "why don't they just shut the thing off?"

"Well—" Vaneski spread his hands. "I think it's for the same reason. It knows too much, and they don't want to destroy that knowledge."

"Do you have any idea what that knowledge might be?" Mike the Angel asked.

"No, sir, I don't. But whatever it is, it's dangerous as hell."

The briefing for the officers and men of the *William Branchell*—the *Brainchild*—was held in a lecture room at the laboratories of the Computer Corporation of Earth's big Antarctic base.

Captain Quill spoke first, warning everyone that the project was secret and asking them to pay the strictest attention to what Dr. Morris Fitzhugh had to say.

Then Fitzhugh got up, his face ridged with nervousness. He assumed the air of a university professor, launching himself into his speech as though he were anxious to get through it in a given time without finishing too early.

"I'm sure you're all familiar with the situation," he said, as though apologizing to everyone for telling them something they already knew—the apology of the learned man who doesn't want anyone to think he's being overly proud of his learning.

"I think, however, we can all get a better picture if we begin at the beginning and work our way up to the present time.

"The original problem was to build a computer that could learn by itself. An ordinary computer can be forcibly taught—that is, a technician can make changes in the circuits which will make the robot do something differently from the way it was done before, or even make it do something new.

"But what we wanted was a computer that could learn by itself, a computer that could make the appropriate changes in its own circuits without outside physical manipulation.

"It's really not as difficult as it sounds. You've all seen autoscribers, which can translate spoken words into printed symbols. An autoscriber is simply a machine which does what you tell it to—literally. Now, suppose a second computer is connected intimately with the first in such a manner that the second can, on order, change the circuits of the first. Then, all that is needed is...."

Mike looked around him while the roboticist went on. The men were looking pretty bored. They'd come to get a briefing on the reason for the trip, and all they were getting was a lecture on robotics.

Mike himself wasn't so much interested in the whys and wherefores of the trip; he was wondering why it was necessary to tell anyone—even the crew. Why not just pack Snookums up, take him to wherever he was going, and say nothing about it?

Why explain it to the crew?

"Thus," continued Fitzhugh, "it became necessary to incorporate into the brain a physical analogue of Lagerglocke's Principle: 'Learning is a result of an inelastic collision.'

"I won't give it to you symbolically, but the idea is simply that an organism learns *only* if it does *not* completely recover from the effects of an outside force imposed upon it. If it recovers completely, it's just as it was before. Consequently, it hasn't learned anything. The organism *must change*."

He rubbed the bridge of his nose and looked out over the faces of the men before him. A faint smile came over his wrinkled features.

"Some of you, I know, are wondering why I am boring you with this long recital. Believe me, it's necessary. I want all of you to understand that the machine you will have to take care of is not just an ordinary computer. Every man here has had experience with machinery, from the very simplest to the relatively complex. You know that you have to be careful of the kind of information—the kind of external force—you give a machine.

"If you aim a spaceship at Mars, for instance, and tell it to go *through* the planet, it might try to obey, but you'd lose the machine in the process."

A ripple of laughter went through the men. They were a little more relaxed now, and Fitzhugh had regained their attention.

"And you must admit," Fitzhugh added, "a spaceship which was given that sort of information might be dangerous."

This time the laughter was even louder.

"Well, then," the roboticist continued, "if a mechanism is capable of learning, how do you keep it from becoming dangerous or destroying itself?

"That was the problem that faced us when we built Snookums.

"So we decided to apply the famous Three Laws of Robotics propounded over a century ago by a brilliant American biochemist and philosopher.

"Here they are:

"'*One: A robot may not injure a human being, nor, through inaction, allow a human being to come to harm.*'

"'*Two: A robot must obey the orders given it by human beings except where such orders would conflict with the First Law.*'

"'*Three: A robot must protect its own existence as long as such protection does not conflict with the First or Second Law.*'"

Fitzhugh paused to let his words sink in, then: "Those are the ideal laws, of course. Even their propounder pointed out that they would be extremely difficult to put into practice. A robot is a logical machine, but it becomes somewhat of a problem even to define a human being. Is a five-year-old competent to give orders to a robot?

"If you define him as a human being, then he can give orders that might wreck an expensive machine. On the other hand, if you don't define the five-year-old as human, then the robot is under no compulsion to refrain from harming the child."

He began delving into his pockets for smoking materials as he went on.

"We took the easy way out. We solved that problem by keeping Snookums isolated. He has never met any animal except adult human beings. It would take an awful lot of explaining to make him understand the difference between, say, a chimpanzee and a man. Why should a hairy pelt and a relatively low intelligence make a chimp non-human? After all, some men are pretty hairy, and some are moronic.

"Present company excepted."

More laughter. Mike's opinion of Fitzhugh was beginning to go up. The man knew when to break pedantry with humor.

"Finally," Fitzhugh said, when the laughter had subsided, "we must ask what is meant by 'protecting his own existence.' Frankly, we've been driven frantic by that one. The little humanoid, caterpillar-track mechanism that we all tend to think of as Snookums isn't really Snookums, any more than a human being is a hand or an eye. Snookums wouldn't actually be threatening his own existence unless his brain—now in the hold of the *William Branchell*—is destroyed."

As Dr. Fitzhugh continued, Mike the Angel listened with about half an ear. His attention—and the attention of every man in the place—had been distracted by the entrance of Leda Crannon. She stepped in through a side door, walked over to Dr. Fitzhugh, and whispered something in his ear. He nodded, and she left again.

Fitzhugh, when he resumed his speech, was rather more hurried in his delivery.

"The whole thing can be summed up rather quickly.

"Point One: Snookums' brain contains the information that eight years of hard work have laboriously put into it. That information is more valuable than the whole cost of the *William Branchell*; it's worth billions. So the robot can't be disassembled, or the information would be lost.

"Point Two: Snookums' mind is a strictly logical one, but it is operating in a more than logical universe. Consequently, it is unstable.

"Point Three: Snookums was built to conduct his own experiments. To forbid him to do that would be similar to beating a child for acting like a child; it would do serious harm to the mind. In Snookums' case, the randomity of the brain would exceed optimum, and the robot would become insane.

"Point Four: Emotion is not logical. Snookums can't handle it, except in a very limited way."

Fitzhugh had been making his points by tapping them off on his fingers with the stem of his unlighted pipe. Now he shoved the pipe back in his pocket and clasped his hands behind his back.

"It all adds up to this: Snookums *must* be allowed the freedom of the ship. At the same time, every one of us must be careful not to ... to push the wrong buttons, as it were.

"So here are a few *don'ts*. Don't get angry with Snookums. That would be as silly as getting sore at a phonograph because it was playing music you didn't happen to like.

"Don't lie to Snookums. If your lies don't fit in with what he knows to be true—and they won't, believe me—he will reject the data. But it would confuse him, because he knows that humans don't lie.

"If Snookums asks you for data, qualify it—even if you know it to be true. Say: 'There may be an error in my knowledge of this data, but to the best of my knowledge....'

"Then go ahead and tell him.

"But if you absolutely don't know the answer, tell him so. Say: 'I don't have that data, Snookums.'

"Don't, unless you are...."

He went on, but it was obvious that the officers and crew of the *William Branchell* weren't paying the attention they should. Every one of them was thinking dark gray thoughts. It was bad enough that they had to take out a ship like the *Brainchild*, untested and jerry-built as she was. Was it necessary to have an eight-hundred-pound, moron-genius child-machine running loose, too?

Evidently, it was.

"To wind it up," Fitzhugh said, "I imagine you are wondering why it's necessary to take Snookums off Earth. I can only tell you this: Snookums knows too much about nuclear energy."

Mike the Angel smiled grimly to himself. Ensign Vaneski had been right; Snookums was dangerous—not only to individuals, but to the whole planet.

Snookums, too, was a juvenile delinquent.

10

The *Brainchild* lifted from Antarctica at exactly 2100 hours, Greenwich time. For three days the officers and men of the ship had worked as though they were the robots instead of their passenger—or cargo, depending on your point of view.

Supplies were loaded, and the great engine-generators checked and rechecked. The ship was ready to go less than two hours before take-off time.

The last passenger aboard was Snookums, although, in a more proper sense, he had always been aboard. The little robot rolled up to the elevator on his treads and was lifted into the body of the ship. Miss Crannon was waiting for him at the air lock, and Mike the Angel was standing by. Not that he had any particular interest in watching Snookums come aboard, but he did have a definite interest in Leda Crannon.

"Hello, honey," said Miss Crannon as Snookums rolled into the air lock. "Ready for your ride?"

"Yes, Leda," said Snookums in his contralto voice. He rolled up to her and took her hand. "Where is my room?"

"Come along; I'll show you in a minute. Do you remember Commander Gabriel?"

Snookums swiveled his head and regarded Mike.

"Oh yes. He tried to help me."

"Did you need help?" Mike growled in spite of himself.

"Yes. For my experiment. And you offered help. That was very nice. Leda says it is nice to help people."

Mike the Angel carefully refrained from asking Snookums if he thought he was people. For all Mike knew, he did.

Mike followed Snookums and Leda Crannon down the companionway.

"What did you do today, honey?" asked Leda.

"Mostly I answered questions for Dr. Fitzhugh," said Snookums. "He asked me thirty-eight questions. He said I was a great help. I'm nice, too."

"Sure you are, darling," said Miss Crannon.

"Ye gods," muttered Mike the Angel.

"What's the trouble, Commander?" the girl asked, widening her blue eyes.

"Nothing," said Mike the Angel, looking at her innocently with eyes that were equally blue. "Not a single solitary thing. Snookums is a sweet little tyke, isn't he?"

Leda Crannon gave him a glorious smile. "I think so. And a lot of fun, too."

Very seriously, Mike patted Snookums on his shiny steel skull. "How old are you, little boy?"

Leda Crannon's eyes narrowed, but Mike pretended not to notice while Snookums said: "Eight years, two months, one day, seven hours, thirty-three minutes and—ten seconds. But I am not a little boy. I am a robot."

Mike suppressed an impulse to ask him if he had informed Leda Crannon of that fact. Mike had been watching the girl for the past three days (at least, when he'd had the time to watch) and he'd been bothered by the girl's maternal attitude toward Snookums. She seemed to have wrapped herself up entirely in the little robot. Of course, that might simply be her method of avoiding Mike the Angel, but Mike didn't quite believe that.

"Come along to your room, dear," said Leda. Then she looked again at Mike. "If you'll wait just a moment, Commander," she said rather stiffly, "I'd like to talk to you."

Mike the Angel touched his forehead in a gentlemanly salute. "Later, perhaps, Miss Crannon. Right now, I have to go to the Power Section to prepare for take-off. We're really going to have fun lifting this brute against a full Earth gee without rockets."

"Later, then," she said evenly, and hurried off down the corridor with Snookums.

Mike headed the other way with a sigh of relief. As of right then, he didn't feel like being given an ear-reaming lecture by a beautiful redhead. He beetled it toward the Power Section.

Chief Powerman's Mate Multhaus was probably the only man in the crew who came close to being as big as Mike the Angel. Multhaus was two inches shorter than Mike's six-seven, but he weighed in at two-ninety. As a powerman, he was tops, and he gave the impression that, as far as power was concerned, he could have supplied the ship himself by turning the crank on a hand generator.

But neither Mike nor Multhaus approached the size of the Supply Officer, Lieutenant Keku. Keku was an absolute giant. Six-eight, three hundred fifty pounds, and very little of it fat.

When Mike the Angel opened the door of the Power Section's instrument room, he came upon a strange sight. Lieutenant Keku and Chief Multhaus were seated across a table from each other, each with his right elbow on the table, their right hands clasped. The muscles in both massive arms stood out beneath the scarlet tunics. Neither man was moving.

"Games, children?" asked Mike gently.

Whap! The chief's arm slammed to the table with a bang that sounded as if the table had shattered. Multhaus had allowed Mike's entrance to distract him, while Lieutenant Keku had held out just an instant longer.

Both men leaped to their feet, Multhaus valiantly trying not to nurse his bruised hand.

"Sorry, sir," said Multhaus. "We were just—"

"Ne' mind. I saw. Who usually wins?" Mike asked.

Lieutenant Keku grinned. "Usually he does, Commander. All this beef doesn't help much against a guy who really has pull. And Chief Multhaus has it."

Mike looked into the big man's brown eyes. "Try doing push-ups. With all your weight, it'd really put brawn into you. Sit down and light up. We've got time before take-off. That is, we do if Multhaus has everything ready for the check-off."

"I'm ready any time you are, sir," Multhaus said, easing himself into a chair.

"We'll have a cigarette and then run 'em through."

Keku settled his bulk into a chair and fired up a cigarette. Mike sat on the edge of the table.

"Philip Keku," Mike said musingly. "Just out of curiosity, what kind of a name is Keku?"

"Damfino," said the lieutenant. "Sounds Oriental, doesn't it?"

Mike looked the man over carefully, but rapidly. "But you're not Oriental—or at least, not much. You look Polynesian to me."

"Hit it right on the head, Commander. Hawaiian. My real name's Kekuanaoa, but nobody could pronounce it, so I shortened it to Keku when I came in the Service."

Mike gave a short laugh. "That accounts for your size. Kekuanaoa. A branch of the old Hawaiian royal family, as I recall."

"That's right." The big Hawaiian grinned. "I've got a kid sister that weighs as much as you. And my granddad kicked off at ninety-four weighing a comfortable four-ten."

"What'd he die of, sir?" Multhaus asked curiously.

"Concussion and multiple fractures. He slammed a Ford-Studebaker into a palm tree at ninety miles an hour. Crazy old ox; he was bigger than the dam' automobile."

The laughter of three big men filled the instrument room.

After a few more minutes of bull throwing, Keku ground out his cigarette and stood up. "I'd better get to my post; Black Bart will be calling down any minute."

At that instant the PA system came alive.

"Now hear this! Now hear this! Take-off in fifteen minutes! Take-off in fifteen minutes!"

Keku grinned, saluted Mike the Angel, and walked out the door.

Multhaus gazed after him, looking at the closed door.

"A blinking prophet, Commander," he said. "A blinking prophet."

The take-off of the *Brainchild* was not so easy as it might have appeared to anyone who watched it from the outside. As far as the exterior observers were concerned, it seemed to lift into the air with a loud, thrumming noise, like a huge elevator rising in an invisible shaft.

It had been built in a deep pit in the polar ice, built around the huge cryotronic stack that was Snookums' brain. As it rose, electric motors slid back the roof that covered the pit, and the howling Antarctic winds roared around it.

Unperturbed, it went on rising.

Inside, Mike the Angel and Chief Multhaus watched worriedly as the meters wiggled their needles dangerously close to the overload mark. The thrumming of the ship as it fought its way up against the pull of Earth's gravity and through the Earth's magnetic field, using the fabric of space itself as the fulcrum against which it applied its power, was like the vibration of a note struck somewhere near the bottom of a piano keyboard, or the rumble of a contra bassoon.

As the intensity of the gravitational field decreased, the velocity of the ship increased—not linearly, but logarithmically. She shrieked through the upper atmosphere, quivering like a live thing, and emerged at last into relatively empty space. When she reached a velocity of a little over thirty miles per second—relative to the sun, and perpendicular to the solar ecliptic—Mike the Angel ordered her engines cut back to the lowest power possible which would still retain the one-gee interior gravity of the ship and keep the anti-acceleration fields intact.

"How does she look, Multhaus?" he asked.

Both of the men were checking the readings of the instruments. A computerman second class was punching the readings into the small table calculator as Multhaus read off the numbers.

"I think she weathered it, sir," the chief said cautiously, "but she sure took a devil of a beating. And look at the power factor readings! We were tossing away energy as though we were S-Doradus or something."

They worked for nearly an hour to check through all the circuits to find what damage—if any—had been done by the strain of Earth's gravitational and magnetic fields. All in all, the *Brainchild* was in pretty good shape. A few circuits needed retuning, but no replacements were necessary.

Multhaus, who had been understandably pessimistic about the ship's ability to lift herself from the surface of even a moderate-sized planet like Earth, looked with new respect upon the man who had designed the power plant that had done the job.

Mike the Angel called the bridge and informed Captain Quill that the ship was ready for full acceleration.

Under control from the bridge, the huge ship yawed until her nose—and thus the line of thrust along her longitudinal axis—was pointed toward her destination.

"Full acceleration, Mister Gabriel," said Captain Quill over the intercom.

Mike the Angel watched the meters climb again as the ship speared away from the sun at an ever-increasing velocity. Although the apparent internal acceleration remained at a cozy one gee, the acceleration in relation to the sun was something fantastic. When the ship reached the velocity of light, she simply disappeared, as far as external observers were concerned. But she still kept adding velocity with her tremendous acceleration.

Finally her engines reached their performance peak. They could drive the *Brainchild* no faster. They simply settled down to a steady growl and pushed the ship at a steady velocity through what the mathematicians termed "null-space."

The *Brainchild* was on her way.

11

"What I want to know," said Lieutenant Keku, "is, what kind of ship is this?"

Mike the Angel chuckled, and Lieutenant Mellon, the Medical Officer, grinned rather shyly. But young Ensign Vaneski looked puzzled.

"What do you mean, sir?" he asked the huge Hawaiian.

They were sitting over coffee in the officers' wardroom. Captain Quill, First Officer Jeffers, and Lieutenant Commander von Liegnitz were on the bridge, and Dr. Fitzhugh and Leda Crannon were down below, giving Snookums lessons.

Mike looked at Lieutenant Keku, waiting for him to answer Vaneski's question.

"What do I mean? Just what I said, Mister Vaneski. I want to know what kind of ship this is. It is obviously not a warship, so we can forget that classification. It is not an expeditionary ship; we're not outfitted for exploratory work. Is it a passenger vessel, then? No, because Dr. Fitzhugh and Miss Crannon are listed as 'civilian technical advisers' and are therefore legally part of the crew. I'm wondering if it might be a cargo vessel, though."

"Sure it is," said Ensign Vaneski. "That brain in Cargo Hold One is cargo, isn't it?"

"I'm not certain," Keku said thoughtfully, looking up at the overhead, as if the answer might be etched there in the metal. "Since it is built in as an intrinsic part of the ship, I don't know if it can be counted as cargo or not." He brought his gaze down to focus on Mike. "What do you think, Commander?"

Before Mike the Angel could answer, Ensign Vaneski broke in with: "But the brain is going to be removed when we get to our destination, isn't it? That makes this a cargo ship!" There was a note of triumph in his voice.

Lieutenant Keku's gaze didn't waver from Mike's face, nor did he say a word. For a boot ensign to interrupt like that was an impoliteness that Keku chose to ignore. He was waiting for Mike's answer as though Vaneski had said nothing.

But Mike the Angel decided he might as well play along with Keku's gag and still answer Vaneski. As a full commander, he could overlook Vaneski's impoliteness to his superiors without ignoring it as Keku was doing.

"Ah, but the brain *won't* be unloaded, Mister Vaneski," he said mildly. "The ship will be *dismantled*—which is an entirely different thing. I'm afraid you can't call it a cargo ship on those grounds."

Vaneski didn't say anything. His face had gone red and then white, as though he'd suddenly realized he'd committed a *faux pas*. He nodded his head a little, to show he understood, but he couldn't seem to find his voice.

To cover up Vaneski's emotional dilemma, Mike addressed the Medical Officer. "What do you think, Mister Mellon?"

Mellon cleared his throat. "Well—it seems to me," he said in a dry, serious tone, "that this is really a medical ship."

Mike blinked. Keku raised his eyebrows. Vaneski swallowed and jerked his eyes away from Mike's face to look at Mellon—but still he didn't say anything.

"Elucidate, my dear Doctor," said Mike with interest.

"I diagnose it as a physician," Mellon said in the same dry, earnest tone. "Snookums, we have been told, is too dangerous to be permitted to remain on Earth. I take this to mean that he is potentially capable of doing something that would either harm the planet itself or a majority—if not all—of the people on it." He picked up his cup of coffee and took a sip. Nobody interrupted him.

"Snookums has, therefore," he continued, "been removed from Earth in order to protect the health of that planet, just as one would remove a potentially malignant tumor from a human body.

"This is a medical ship. Q.E.D." And only then did he smile.

"Aw, now...." Vaneski began. Then he shut his mouth again.

With an inward smile, Mike realized that Ensign Vaneski had been taking seriously an argument that was strictly a joke.

"Mister Mellon," Mike said, "you win." He hadn't realized that Mellon's mind could work on that level.

"Hold," said Lieutenant Keku, raising a hand. "I yield to no one in my admiration for the analysis given by our good doctor; indeed, my admiration knows no bounds. But I insist we hear from Commander Gabriel before we adjourn."

"Not me," Mike said, shaking his head. "I know when I'm beaten." He'd been going to suggest that the *Brainchild* was a training ship, from Snookums' "learning" periods, but that seemed rather obvious and puerile now.

He glanced at his watch, saw the time, and stood up. "Excuse me, gentlemen; I have things to do." He had an appointment to talk to Leda Crannon, but he had no intention of broadcasting it.

As he closed the wardroom door, he heard Ensign Vaneski's voice saying: "I *still* say this should be classified as a cargo ship."

Mike sighed as he strode on down the companionway. The ensign was, of course, absolutely correct—which was the sad part about it, really. Oh well, what the hell.

Leda Crannon had agreed to have coffee with Mike in the office suite she shared with Dr. Fitzhugh. Mike had had one cup in the officers' wardroom, but even if he'd had a dozen he'd have been willing to slosh down a dozen more to talk to Leda Crannon. It was not, he insisted to himself, that he was in love with the girl, but she had intelligence and personality in addition to her striking beauty.

Furthermore, she had given Mike the Angel a dressing-down that had been quite impressive. She had not at all cared for the remarks he had made when Snookums was being loaded aboard—patting him on the head and asking him his age, for instance—and had told him so in no uncertain terms. Mike, feeling sheepish and knowing he was guilty, had accepted the tongue-lashing and tendered an apology.

And she had smiled and said: "All right. Forget it. I'm sorry I got mad."

He knew he wasn't the only man aboard who was interested in Leda. Jakob von Liegnitz, all Teutonic masterfulness and Old World suavity, had obviously made a favorable impression on her. Lew Mellon was often seen in deep philosophical discussions with her, his eyes never leaving her face and his earnest voice low and confidential. Both of them had known her longer than he had, since they'd both been stationed at Chilblains Base.

Mike the Angel didn't let either of them worry him. He had enough confidence in his own personality and abilities to be able to take his own tack no matter which way the wind blew.

Blithely opening the door of the office, Mike the Angel stepped inside with a smile on his lips.

"Ah, good afternoon, Commander Gabriel," said Dr. Morris Fitzhugh.

Mike kept the smile on his face. "Leda here?"

Fitzhugh chuckled. "No. Some problems came up with Snookums. She'll be in session for an hour yet. She asked me to convey her apologies." He gestured toward the coffee urn. "But the coffee's all made, so you may as well have a cup."

Mike was thankful he had not had a dozen cups in the wardroom. "I don't mind if I do, Doctor." He sat down while Fitzhugh poured a cup.

"Cream? Sugar?"

"Black, thanks," Mike said.

There was an awkward silence for a few seconds while Mike sipped at the hot, black liquid. Then Mike said, "Dr. Fitzhugh, you said, at the briefing back on Earth, that Snookums knows too much about nuclear energy. Can you be more specific than that, or is it too hush-hush?"

Fitzhugh took out his briar and began filling it as he spoke. "We don't want this to get out to the general public, of course," he said thoughtfully, "but, as a ship's officer, you can be told. I believe some of your fellow officers know already, although we'd rather it wasn't discussed in general conversation, even among the officers."

Mike nodded wordlessly.

"Very well, then." Fitzhugh gave the tobacco a final shove with his thumb. "As a power engineer, you should be acquainted with the 'pinch effect,' eh?"

It was a rhetorical question. The "pinch effect" had been known for over a century. A jet of highly ionized gas, moving through a magnetic field of the proper structure, will tend to pinch down, to become narrower, rather than to spread apart, as a jet of ordinary gas does. As the science of magnetohydrodynamics had progressed, the effect had become more and more controllable, enabling scientists to force the nuclei of hydrogen, for instance, closer and closer together. At the end of the last century, the Bending Converter had almost wrecked the economy of the entire world, since it gave to the world a source of free energy. Sam Bending's "little black box" converted ordinary water into helium and oxygen and energy—plenty of energy. A Bending Converter could be built relatively cheaply and for small-power uses—such as powering a ship or automobile or manufacturing plant—could literally run on air, since the moisture content of ordinary air was enough to power the converter itself with plenty of power left over.

Overnight, all previous forms of power generation had become obsolete. Who would buy electric power when he could generate his own for next to nothing? Billions upon billions of dollars worth of generating equipment were rendered valueless. The great hydroelectric dams, the hundreds of steam turbines, the heavy-metal atomic reactors—all useless for power purposes. The value of the stock in those companies dropped to zero and stayed there. The value of copper metal fell like a bomb, with almost equally devastating results—for there was no longer any need for the millions of miles of copper cable that linked the power plants with the consumer.

The Depression of 1929-42 couldn't even begin to compare with The Great Depression of 1986-2000. Every civilized nation on Earth had been hit and hit hard. The resulting governmental collapses would have made the disaster even more complete had not the then Secretary General of the UN, Perrot of Monaco, grabbed the reins of government. Like the Americans Franklin Roosevelt and Abraham Lincoln, he had forced through unconstitutional bills and taken extra-constitutional powers. And, like those Americans, he had not done it for personal gain, but to preserve the society. He had not succeeded in preserving the old society, of course, but he had built, almost single-handedly, a world government—a new society on the foundations of the old.

All these thoughts ran through Mike the Angel's mind. He wondered if Snookums had discovered something that would be as much a disaster to the world economy as the Bending Converter had been.

Fitzhugh got out his miniature flame thrower and puffed his pipe alight. "Snookums," he said, "has discovered a method of applying the pinch effect to lithium hydride. It's a batch reaction rather than a flow reaction such as the Bending Converter uses. But it's as simple to build as a Bending Converter."

"Jesus," said Mike the Angel softly.

Lithium hydride. LiH. An atom of hydrogen to every atom of lithium. If a hydrogen nucleus is driven into the lithium nucleus with sufficient force, the results are simple:

$$Li^7 + H^1 \rightarrow 2He^4 + energy$$

An atom of lithium-7 plus an atom of hydrogen-1 yields two atoms of helium-4 and plenty of energy. One gram of lithium hydride would give nearly fifty-eight kilowatt-hours of energy in one blast. A pound of the stuff would be the equivalent of nearly seven *tons* of TNT.

In addition, it was a nice, clean bomb. Nothing but helium, radiation, and heat. In the early nineteen fifties, such a bomb had been constructed by surrounding the LiH with a fission bomb—the so-called "implosion" technique. But all that heavy metal around the central reaction created all kinds of radioactive residues which had a tendency to scatter death for hundreds of miles around.

Now, suppose a man had a pair of tweezers small enough to pick up a single molecule of lithium hydride and pinch the two nuclei together. Of course, the idea is ridiculous—that is, the tweezer part is. But if the pinch could be done in some other way....

Snookums had done it.

"Homemade atomic bombs in your back yard or basement lab," said Mike the Angel.

Fitzhugh nodded emphatically. "Exactly. We can't let that technique out until we've found a way to keep people from doing just that. The UN Government has inspection techniques that prevent anyone from building the conventional types of thermonuclear bombs, but not the pinch bomb."

Mike the Angel thought over what Dr. Fitzhugh had said. Then he said: "That's not all of it. Antarctica is isolated enough to keep that knowledge secret for a long time—at least until safeguards could be set up. Why take Snookums off Earth?"

"Snookums himself is dangerous," Fitzhugh said. "He has a built-in 'urge' to experiment—to get data. We can keep him from making experiments that we know will be dangerous by giving him the data, so that the urge doesn't operate. But if he's on the track of something totally new...."

"Well, you can see what we're up against." He thoughtfully blew a cloud of smoke. "We think he may be on the track of the total annihilation of matter."

A dead silence hung in the air. The ultimate, the super-atomic bomb. Theoretically, the idea had been approached only in the assumption of contact between ordinary matter and anti-matter, with the two canceling each other completely to give nothing but energy. Such a bomb would be nearly fifty thousand times as powerful as the lithium-hydride pinch bomb. That much energy, released in a few millimicroseconds, would make the standard H-bomb look like a candle flame on a foggy night.

The LiH pinch bomb could be controlled. By using just a little of the stuff, it would be possible to limit the destruction to a neighborhood, or even a single block. A total-annihilation bomb would be much harder to control. The total annihilation of a single atom of hydrogen would yield over a thousandth of an erg, and matter just doesn't come in much smaller packages than that.

"You see," said Fitzhugh, "we *had* to get him off Earth."

"Either that or stop him from experimenting," Mike said. "And I assume that wouldn't be good for Snookums."

"To frustrate Snookums would be to destroy all the work we have put into him. His circuits would tend to exceed optimum randomness, and that would mean, in human terms, that he would be insane—and therefore worthless. As a machine, Snookums is worth eighteen billion dollars. The information we have given him, plus the deductions and computations he has made from that information, is worth...." He shrugged his shoulders. "Who knows? How can a price be put on knowledge?"

12

The *William Branchell*—dubbed *Brainchild*—fled Earth at ultralight velocity, while officers, crew, and technical advisers settled down to routine. The only thing that disturbed that routine was one particularly restless part of the ship's cargo.

Snookums was a snoop.

Cut off from the laboratories which had been provided for his special work at Chilblains, he proceeded to interest himself in the affairs of the human beings which surrounded him. Until his seventh year, he had been confined to the company of only a small handful of human beings. Even while the *William Branchell* was being built, he hadn't been allowed any more freedom than was absolutely necessary to keep him from being frustrated.

Even so, he had developed an interest in humans. Now he was being allowed full rein in his data-seeking circuits, and he chose to investigate, not the physical sciences, but the study of Mankind. Since the proper study of Mankind is Man, Snookums proceeded to study the people on the ship.

Within three days the officers had evolved a method of Snookums-evasion.

Lieutenant Commander Jakob von Liegnitz sat in the officers' wardroom of the *Brainchild* and shuffled a deck of cards with expert fingers.

He was a medium-sized man, five-eleven or so, with a barrel chest, broad shoulders, a narrow waist, and lean hips. His light brown hair was worn rather long, and its straight strands seemed to cling tightly to his skull. His gray eyes had a perpetual half-squint that made him look either sleepy or angry, depending on what the rest of his broad face was doing.

He dealt himself out a board of Four Cards Up and had gone through about half the pack when Mike the Angel came in with Lieutenant Keku.

"Hello, Jake," said Keku. "What's to do?"

"Get out two more decks," said Mike the Angel, "and we can all play solitaire."

Von Liegnitz looked up sleepily. "I could probably think of duller things, Mike, but not just immediately. How about bridge?"

"We'll need a fourth," said Keku. "How about Pete?"

Mike the Angel shook his head. "Black Bart is sleeping—taking his beauty nap. So Pete has the duty. How about young Vaneski? He's not a bad partner."

"He is out, too," said von Liegnitz. "He also is on duty."

Mike the Angel lifted an inquisitive eyebrow. "Something busted? Why should the Maintenance Officer be on duty right now?"

"He is maintaining," said von Liegnitz with deliberate dignity, "peace and order around here. He is now performing the duty of Answerman-in-Chief. He's very good at it."

Mike grinned. "Snookums?"

Von Liegnitz scooped the cards off the table and began shuffling them. "Exactly. As long as Snookums gets his questions answered, he keeps himself busy. Our young boot ensign has been assigned to the duty of keeping that mechanical Peeping Tom out of our hair for an hour. By then, it will be lunch time." He cleared his throat. "We still need a fourth."

"If you ask me," said Lieutenant Keku, "we need a fifth. Let's play poker instead."

Jakob von Liegnitz nodded and offered the cards for a cut.

"Deal 'em," said Mike the Angel.

A few minutes less than an hour later, Ensign Vaneski slid open the door to the wardroom and was greeted by a triune chorus of hellos.

"Sirs," said Vaneski with pseudo formality, "I have done my duty, exhausting as it was. I demand satisfaction."

Lieutenant Keku, upon seeing Mike the Angel dealt a second eight, flipped over his up cards and folded.

"Satisfaction?" he asked the ensign.

Vaneski nodded. "One hand of showdown for five clams. I have been playing encyclopedia for that hunk of animated machinery for an hour. That's above and beyond the call of duty."

"Raise a half," said Mike the Angel.

"Call," said von Liegnitz.

"Three eights," said Mike, flipping his hole card.

Von Liegnitz shrugged, folded his cards, and watched solemnly while Mike pulled in the pot.

"Vaneski wants to play showdown for a fiver," said Keku.

Mike the Angel frowned at the ensign for a moment, then relaxed and nodded. "Not my game," he said, "but if the Answerman wants a chance to catch up, it's okay with me."

The four men each tossed a five spot into the center of the table and then cut for deal. Mike got it and started dealing—five cards, face up, for the pot.

When three cards apiece had been dealt, young Vaneski was ahead with a king high. On the fourth round he grinned when he got a second king and Mike dealt himself an ace.

On the fifth round Vaneski got a three, and his face froze as Mike dealt himself a second ace.

Mike reached for the twenty.

"You deal yourself a mean hand, Commander," said Vaneski evenly.

Mike glanced at him sharply, but there was only a wry grin on the young ensign's face.

"Luck of the idiot," said Mike as he pocketed the twenty. "It's time for lunch."

"Next time," said Keku firmly, "I'll take the Answerman watch, Mike. You and this kraut are too lucky for me."

"If I lose any more to the Angel," von Liegnitz said calmly, "I will be a very sour kraut. But right now, I'm quite hungry."

Mike prowled around the Power Section that afternoon with a worry nagging at the back of his mind. He couldn't exactly put his finger on what was bothering him, and he finally put it down to just plain nerves.

And then he began to feel something—physically.

Within thirty seconds after it began, long before most of the others had noticed it, Mike the Angel recognized it for what it was. Half a minute after that, everyone aboard could feel it.

A two-cycle-per-second beat note is inaudible to the human ear. If the human tympanum can't wiggle any faster than that, the auditory nerves refuse to transmit the message. The wiggle has to be three or four octaves above that before the nerves will have anything to do with it. But if the beat note has enough energy in it, a man doesn't have to hear it—he can *feel* it.

The bugs weren't all out of the *Brainchild*, by any means, and the men knew it. She had taken a devil of a strain on the take-off, and something was about due to weaken.

It was the external field around the hull that had decided to goof off this time. It developed a nice, unpleasant two-cycle throb that threatened to shake the ship apart. It built up rapidly and then leveled off, giving everyone aboard the feeling that his lunch and his stomach would soon part company.

The crew was used to it. They'd been on shakedown cruises before, and they knew that on an interstellar vessel the word "shakedown" can have a very literal meaning. The beat note wasn't dangerous, but it wasn't pleasant, either.

Within five minutes everybody aboard had the galloping collywobbles and the twittering jitters.

Mike and his power crew all knew what to do. They took their stations and started to work. They had barely started when Captain Quill's voice came over the intercom.

"Power Section, this is the bridge. How long before we stop this beat note?"

"No way of telling, sir," said Mike, without taking his eyes off the meter bank. "Check A-77," he muttered in an aside to Multhaus.

"Can you give me a prognosis?" persisted Quill.

Mike frowned. This wasn't like Black Bart. He knew what the prognosis was as well as Mike did. "Actually, sir, there's no way of knowing. The old *Gainsway* shook like this for eight days before they spotted the tubes that were causing a four-cycle beat."

"Why can't we spot it right off?" Quill asked.

Mike got it then. Fitzhugh was listening in. Quill wanted Mike the Angel to substantiate his own statements to the roboticist.

"There are sixteen generator tubes in the hull—two at each end of the four diagonals of an imaginary cube surrounding the ship. At least two of them are out of phase; that means that every one of them may have to be balanced against every other one, and that would make a hundred and twenty checks. It will take ten minutes if we hit it lucky and find the bad tubes in the first two tries, and about twenty hours if we hit on the last try.

"That, of course, is presuming that there are only two out. If there are three...." He let it hang.

Mike grinned as Dr. Morris Fitzhugh's voice came over the intercom, confirming his diagnosis of the situation.

"Isn't there any other way?" asked Fitzhugh worriedly. "Can't we stop the ship and check them, so that we won't be subjected to this?"

"'Fraid not," answered Mike. "In the first place, cutting the external field would be dangerous, if not deadly. The abrupt deceleration wouldn't be good for us, even with the internal field operating. In the second place, we couldn't check the field tubes if they weren't operating. You can't tell a bad tube just by looking at it. They'd still have to be balanced against each other, and that would take the same amount of time as it is going to take anyway, and with the same effects on the ship. I'm sorry, but we'll just have to put up with it."

"Well, for Heaven's sake do the best you can," Fitzhugh said in a worried voice. "This beat is shaking Snookums' brain. God knows what damage it may do unless it's stopped within a very few minutes!"

"I'll do the best I can," said Mike the Angel carefully. "So will every man in my crew. But about all anyone can do is wish us luck and let us work."

"Yes," said Dr. Fitzhugh slowly. "Yes. I understand. Thank you, Commander."

Mike the Angel nodded curtly and went back to work.

Things weren't bad enough as they were. They had to get worse. The *Brainchild* had been built too fast, and in too unorthodox a manner. The steady two-cycle throb did more damage than it would normally have done aboard a non-experimental ship.

Twelve minutes after the throb started, a feeder valve in the pre-induction energy chamber developed a positive-feedback oscillation that threatened to blow out the whole pre-induction stage unless it was damped. The search for the out-of-phase external field tubes had to be dropped while the more dangerous flaw was tackled.

Multhaus plugged in an emergency board and began to compensate by hand while the others searched frantically for the trouble.

Hand compensation of feeder-valve oscillation is pure intuition; if you wait until the meters show that damping is necessary, it may be too late—you have to second-guess the machine and figure out what's coming *before* it happens and compensate then. You not only have to judge time, but magnitude; overcompensation is ruinous, too.

Multhaus, the Chief Powerman's Mate, sat behind the emergency board, a vernier dial in each hand and both eyes on an oscilloscope screen. His red, beefy face was corded and knotted with tension, and his skin glistened with oily perspiration. He didn't say a word, and his fingers barely moved as he held a green line reasonably steady on that screen.

Mike the Angel, using unangelic language in a steady, muttering stream, worked to find the circuit that held the secret of the ruinous feedback tendency, while other powermen plugged and unplugged meter jacks, flipped switches, and juggled tools.

In the midst of all this, in rolled Snookums.

Whether Snookums knew that his own existence was in danger is problematical. Like the human brain, his own had no pain or sensory circuits within it; in addition, his knowledge of robotics was small—he didn't even know that his brain was in Cargo Hold One. He thought it was in his head, if he thought about it at all.

Nonetheless, he knew *something* was wrong, and as soon as his "curiosity" circuits were activated, he set out in search of the trouble, his little treads rolling at high speed.

Leda Crannon saw him heading down a companionway and called after him. "Where are you going, Snookums?"

"Looking for data," answered Snookums, slowing a little.

"Wait! I'll come with you!"

Leda Crannon knew perfectly well what effect the throb might have on Snookums' brain, and when something cracked, she wanted to see what effect it might have on the behavior of the little robot. Like a hound after a fox, she followed him through the corridors of the ship.

Up companionways and down, in and out of storerooms, staterooms, control rooms, and washrooms Snookums scurried, oblivious to the consternation that sometimes erupted at his sudden appearance. At certain selected spots, Snookums would stop, put his metal arms on floors and walls, pause, and then go zooming off in another direction with Leda Crannon only paces behind him, trying to explain to crewmen as best she could.

If Snookums had been capable of emotion—and Leda Crannon was not as sure as the roboticists that he wasn't—she would have sworn that he was having the time of his life.

Seventeen minutes after the throb had begun, Snookums rolled into Power Section and came to a halt. Something else was wrong.

At first he just stopped by the door and soaked in data. Mike's muttering; the clipped, staccato conversation of the power crew; the noises of the tools; the deep throb of the ship itself; the underlying oddness of the engine vibrations—all these were fed into his microphonic ears. The scene itself was transmitted to his brain and recorded. The cryotronic maze in the depths of the ship chewed the whole thing over. Snookums acted.

Leda Crannon, who had lost ground in trying to keep up with Snookums' whirling treads, came to the door of Power Section too late to stop the robot's entrance. She didn't dare call out, because she knew that to do so would interrupt the men's vital work. All she could do was lean against the doorjamb and try to catch her breath.

Snookums rolled over to the board where Multhaus was sitting and watched over his shoulder for perhaps thirty seconds. The crewmen eyed him, but they were much too busy to do anything. Besides, they were used to his presence by this time.

Then, in one quick tour of the room, Snookums glanced at every meter in the place. Not just at the regular operating meters, but also at the meters in the testing equipment that the power crew had jack-plugged in.

Mike the Angel looked around as he heard the soft purring of the caterpillar treads. His glance took in both Snookums and Leda Crannon, who was still gasping at the door. He watched Leda for the space of three deep breaths, tore his eyes away, looked at what Snookums was doing, then said: "Get him out of here!" in a stage whisper to Leda.

Snookums was looking over the notations on the meter readings for the previous few minutes. He had simply picked them up from the desk where one of the computermen was working and scanned them rapidly before handing them back.

Before Leda could say anything, Snookums rolled over to Mike the Angel and said: "Check the lead between the 391-JF and the big DK-37. I think you'll find that the piping is in phase with the two-cycle note, and it's become warped and stretched. It's about half a millimeter off—plus or minus a tenth. The pulse is reaching the DK-37 about four degrees off, and the gate is closing before it all gets through. That's forcing the regulator circuit to overcompensate, and...."

Mike didn't listen to any more. He didn't know whether Snookums knew what he was talking about or not, but he did know that the thing the robot had mentioned would have had just such an effect.

Mike strode rapidly across the room and flipped up the shield housing the assembly Snookums had mentioned. The lead was definitely askew.

Mike the Angel snapped orders, and the power crewmen descended on the scene of the trouble.

Snookums went right on delivering his interpretation of the data, but everyone ignored him while they worked. Being ignored didn't bother Snookums in the least.

"... and that, in turn, is making the feeder valve field oscillate," he finished up, nearly five minutes later.

Mike was glad that Snookums had pinpointed the trouble first and then had gone on to show why the defect was causing the observed result. He could just as easily have started with the offending oscillation and reached the bit about the faulty lead at the end of his speech, except that he had been built to do it the other way around. Snookums made the deduction in his superfast mind and then reeled it off backward, as it were, going from conclusion to premises.

Otherwise, he might have been too late.

The repair didn't take long, once Snookums had found just what needed repairing. When the job was over, Mike the Angel wiped his hands on a rag and stood up.

"Thanks, Snookums," he said honestly. "You've been a great help."

Snookums said: "I am smiling. Because I am pleased."

There was no way for him to smile with a steel face, but Mike got the idea.

Mike turned to the Chief Powerman's Mate. "Okay, Multhaus, shut it off. She's steady now."

Multhaus just sat there, surrounded by a wall of concentration, his hands still on the verniers, his eyes still on the screen. He didn't move.

Mike flipped off the switch. "Come on, Multhaus, snap to. We've still got that beat note to worry about."

Multhaus blinked dizzily as the green line vanished from his sight. He jerked his hands off the verniers, and then smiled sheepishly. He had been sitting there waiting for that green line to move a full minute after the input signal had ceased.

"Happy hypnosis," said Mike. "Let's get back to finding out which of those tubes in the hull is giving the external field the willies."

Snookums, who had been listening carefully, rolled up and said, "Generator tubes three, four, and thirteen. Three is out of phase by—"

"You can tell us later, Snookums," Mike interrupted rapidly. "Right now, we'll get to work on those tubes. You were right once; I hope you're right again."

Again the power crew swung into action.

Within five minutes Mike and Multhaus were making the proper adjustments on the external field circuits to adjust for the wobbling of the output.

The throb wavered. It wobbled around, going up to two-point-seven cycles and dropping back to one-point-four, then climbing again. All the time, it was dropping in magnitude, until finally it could no longer be felt. Finally, it dropped suddenly to a low of point-oh-five cycles, hovered there for a moment, then vanished altogether.

"By the beard of my sainted maiden aunt," said Chief Multhaus in awe. "A three-tube offbeat solved in less than half an hour! If that isn't a record, I'll dye my uniform black and join the Chaplains' Corps."

Leda Crannon, looking tired but somehow pleased, said softly: "May I come in?"

Mike the Angel grinned. "Sure. Maybe you can—"

The intercom clicked on. "Power Section, this is the bridge." It was Black Bart. "Are my senses playing me false, or have you stopped that beat note?"

"All secure, sir," said Mike the Angel. "The system is stable now."

"How many tubes were goofing?"

"Three of them."

"*Three!*" There was astonishment in the captain's voice. "How did you ever solve a three-tube beat in that short a time?"

Mike the Angel grinned up at the eye in the wall.

"Nothing to it, sir," he said. "A child could have done it."

13

Leda Crannon sat down on the edge of the bunk in Mike the Angel's stateroom, accepted the cigarette and light that Mike had proffered, and waited while Mike poured a couple of cups of coffee from the insul-jug on his desk.

"I wish I could offer you something stronger, but I'm not much of a drinker myself, so I don't usually take advantage of the officer's prerogative to smuggle liquor aboard," he said as he handed her the cup.

She smiled up at him. "That's all right; I rarely drink, and when I do, it's either wine or a *very* diluted highball. Right now, this coffee will do me more good."

Mike heard footsteps coming down the companionway. He glanced out through the door, which he had deliberately left open. Ensign Vaneski walked by, glanced in, grinned, and went on his way. The kid had good sense, Mike thought. He hoped any other passers-by would stay out while he talked to Leda.

"Does a thing like that happen often?" the girl asked. "Not the fast solution; I mean the beat note."

"No," said Mike the Angel. "Once the system is stabilized, the tubes tend to keep each other in line. But because of that very tendency, an offbeat tube won't show itself for a while. The system tries to keep the bad ones in phase in spite of themselves. But eventually one of them sort of rebels, and that frees any of the others that are offbeat, so the bad ones all show at once and we can spot them. When we get all the bad ones adjusted, the system remains stable for the operating life of the system."

"And that's the purpose of a shakedown cruise?"

"One of the reasons," agreed Mike. "If the tubes are going to act up, they'll do it in the first five hundred operating hours—except in unusual cases. That's one of the things that bothered me about the way this crate was hashed together."

Her blue eyes widened. "I thought this was a well-built ship."

"Oh, it is, it is—all things considered. It isn't dangerous, if that's what you're worried about. But it sure as the devil is expensively wasteful."

She nodded and sipped at her coffee. "I know that. But I don't see any other way it could have been done."

"Neither do I, right off the bat," Mike admitted. He took a good swallow of the hot liquid in his cup and said: "I wanted to ask you two questions. First, what was it that Snookums was doing just before he came into the Power Section? Black Bart said he'd been galloping all over the ship, with you at his heels."

Her infectious smile came back. "He was playing seismograph. He was simply checking the intensity of the vibrations at different points in the ship. That gave him part of the data he needed to tell you which of the tubes were acting up."

"I'm beginning to think," said Mike, "that we'll have to start building a big brain aboard every ship—that is, if we can learn enough about such monsters from Snookums."

"What was the other question?" Leda asked.

"Oh.... Well, I was wondering just why you are connected with this project. What does a psychologist have to do with robots? If you'll pardon my ignorance."

This time she laughed softly, and Mike thought dizzily of the gay chiming of silver bells. He clamped down firmly on the romantic wanderings of his mind as she started her explanation.

"I'm a specialist in child psychology, Mike. Actually, I was hired as an experiment—or, rather, as the result of a wild guess that happened to work. You see, the first two times Snookums' brain was activated, the circuits became disoriented."

"You mean," said Mike the Angel, "they went nuts."

She laughed again. "Don't let Fitz hear you say that. He'll tell you that 'the circuits exceeded their optimum randomity limit.'"

Mike grinned, remembering the time he had driven a robot brain daffy by bluffing it at poker. "How did that happen?"

"Well, we don't know all the details, but it seems to have something to do with the slow recovery rate that's necessary for learning. Do you know anything about Lagerglocke's Principle?"

"Fitzhugh mentioned something about it in the briefing we got before take-off. Something about a bit of learning being an inelastic rebound."

"That's it. You take a steel ball, for instance, and drop it on a steel plate from a height of three or four feet. It bounces—almost perfect elasticity. The next time you drop it, it does the same thing. It hasn't learned anything.

"But if you drop a lead ball, it doesn't bounce as much, and it will flatten at the point of contact. *The next time it falls on that flat side, its behavior will be different.* It has learned something."

Mike rubbed the tip of an index finger over his chin. "These illustrations are analogues of the human mind?"

"That's right. Some people have minds like steel balls. They can learn, but you have to hit them pretty hard to make them do it. On the other hand, some people have minds like glass balls: They can't learn at all. If you hit them hard enough to make a real impression, they simply shatter."

"All right. Now what has this got to do with you and Snookums?"

"Patience, boy, patience," Leda said with a grin. "Actually, the lead-ball analogy is much too simple. An intelligent mind has to have time to partially recover, you see. Hit it with too many shocks, one right after another, and it either collapses or refuses to learn or both.

"The first two times the brain was activated, the roboticists just began feeding data into the thing as though it were an ordinary computing machine. They were forcing it to learn too fast; they weren't giving it time to recover from the shock of learning.

"Just as in the human being, there is a difference between a robot's brain and a robot's mind. The *brain* is a physical thing—a bunch of cryotrons in a helium bath. But the *mind* is the sum total of all the data and reaction patterns and so forth that have been built into the brain or absorbed by it.

"The brain didn't have an opportunity to recover from the learning shocks when the data was fed in too fast, so the mind cracked. It couldn't take it. The robot went insane.

"Each time, the roboticists had to deactivate the brain, drain it of all data, and start over. After the second time, Dr. Fitzhugh decided they were going about it wrong, so they decided on a different tack."

"I see," said Mike the Angel. "It had to be taught slowly, like a child."

"Exactly," said Leda. "And who would know more about teaching a child than a child psychologist?" she added brightly.

Mike looked down at his coffee cup, watching the slight wavering of the surface as it broke up the reflected light from the glow panels. He had invited this girl down to his stateroom (he told himself) to get information about Snookums. But now he realized that information about the girl herself was far more important.

"How long have you been working with Snookums?" he asked, without looking up from his coffee.

"Over eight years," she said.

Then Mike looked up. "You know, you hardly look old enough. You don't look much older than twenty-five."

She smiled—a little shyly, Mike thought. "As Snookums says, 'You're nice.' I'm twenty-six."

"And you've been working with Snookums since you were eighteen?"

"Uh-huh." She looked, very suddenly, much younger than even the twenty-five Mike had guessed at. She seemed to be more like a somewhat bashful teen-ager who had been educated in a convent. "I was what they call an 'exceptional child.' My mother died when I was seven, and Dad ... well, he just didn't know what to do with a baby girl, I guess. He was a kind man, and I think he really loved me, but he just didn't know what to do with me. So when the tests showed that I was ... brighter ... than the average, he put me in a special school in Italy. Said he didn't want my mind cramped by being forced to conform to the mental norm. Maybe he even believed that himself.

"And, too, he didn't approve of public education. He had a lot of odd ideas.

"Anyway, I saw him during summer vacations and went to school the rest of the year. He took me all over the world when I was with him, and the instructors were pretty wonderful people; I'm not sorry that I was brought up that way. It was a little different from the education that most children have, but it gave me a chance to use my mind."

"I know the school," said Mike the Angel. "That's the one under the Cesare Alfieri Institute in Florence?"

"That's it; did you go there?" There was an odd, eager look in her eyes.

Mike shook his head. "Nope. But a friend of mine did. Ever know a guy named Paulvitch?"

She squealed with delight, as though she'd been playfully pinched. "Sir Gay? You mean Serge Paulvitch, the Fiend of Florence?" She pronounced the name properly: "*Sair*-gay," instead of "surge," as too many people were prone to do.

"Sounds like the same man," Mike admitted, grinning. "As evil-looking as Satanas himself?"

"That's Sir Gay, all right. Half the girls were scared of him, and I think *all* the boys were. He's about three years older than I am, I guess."

"Why call him Sir Gay?" Mike asked. "Just because of his name?"

"Partly. And partly because he was always such a gentleman. A real *nice* guy, if you know what I mean. Do you know him well?"

"*Know* him? Hell, I couldn't run my business without him."

"Your business?" She blinked. "But he works for—" Then her eyes became very wide, her mouth opened, and she pointed an index finger at Mike. "Then you ... you're Mike the Angel! M. R. Gabriel! Sure!" She started laughing. "I never connected it up! My golly, my golly! I thought you were just another Space Service commander! Mike the Angel! Well, I'll be darned!"

She caught her breath. "I'm sorry. I was just so surprised, that's all. Are you really *the* M. R. Gabriel, of M. R. Gabriel, Power Design?"

Mike was as close to being nonplused as he cared to be. "Sure," he said. "You mean you didn't know?"

She shook her head. "No. I thought Mike the Angel was about sixty years old, a crotchety old genius behind a desk, as eccentric as a comet's orbit, and wealthier than Croesus. You're just not what I pictured, that's all."

"Just wait a few more decades," Mike said, laughing. "I'll try to live up to my reputation."

"So you're Serge's boss. How is he? I haven't seen him since I was sixteen."

"He's grown a beard," said Mike.

"No!"

"Fact."

"My God, how horrible!" She put her hand over her eyes in mock horror.

"Let's talk about you," said Mike. "You're much prettier than Serge Paulvitch."

"Well, I should hope so! But really, there's nothing to tell. I went to school. B.S. at fourteen, M.S. at sixteen, Ph.D. at eighteen. Then I went to work for C.C. of E., and I've been there ever since. I've never been engaged, I've never been married, and I'm still a virgin. Anything else?"

"No runs, no hits, no errors," said Mike the Angel.

She grinned back impishly. "I haven't been up to bat yet, Commander Gabriel."

"Then I suggest you grab some sort of club to defend yourself, because I'm going to be in there pitching."

The smile on her face faded, to be replaced by a look that was neither awe nor surprise, but partook of both.

"You really mean that, don't you?" she asked in a hushed voice.

"I do," said Mike the Angel.

Commander Peter Jeffers was in the Control Bridge when Mike the Angel stepped in through the door. Jeffers was standing with his back to the door, facing the bank of instruments that gave him a general picture of the condition of the whole ship.

Overhead, the great dome of the ship's nose allowed the gleaming points of light from the star field ahead to shine down on those beneath through the heavy, transparent shield of the cast transite and the invisible screen of the external field.

Mike walked over and tapped Pete Jeffers on the shoulder.

"Busy?"

Jeffers turned around slowly and grinned. "Hullo, old soul. Naw, I ain't busy. Nothin' outside but stars, and we don't figger on gettin' too close to 'em right off the bat. What's the beef?"

"I have," said Mike the Angel succinctly, "goofed."

Jeffers' keen eyes swept analytically over Mike the Angel's face. "You want a drink? I snuck a spot o' brandy aboard, and just by purty ole coincidence, there's a bottle right over there in the speaker housing." Without waiting for an answer, he turned away from Mike and walked toward the cabinet that held the intercom speaker. Meantime, he went right on talking.

"Great stuff, brandy. French call it *eau de vie*, and that, in case you don't know it, means 'water of life.' You want a little, eh, ol' buddy? Sure you do." By this time, he'd come back with the bottle and a pair of glasses and was pouring a good dose into each one. "On the other hand, the Irish gave us our name for whisky. Comes from *uisge-beatha*, and by some bloody peculiar coincidence, that also means 'water of life.' So you just set yourself right down here and get some life into you."

Mike sat down at the computer table, and Jeffers sat down across from him. "Now you just drink on up, buddy-buddy and then tell your ol' Uncle Pete what the bloody hell the trouble is."

Mike looked at the brandy for a full half minute. Then, with one quick flip of his wrist and a sudden spasmodic movement of his gullet, he downed it.

Then he took a deep breath and said: "Do I look as bad as all that?"

"Worse," said Jeffers complacently, meanwhile refilling Mike's glass. "While we were on active service together, I've seen you go through all kinds of things and never look like this. What is it? Reaction from this afternoon's—or, pardon me—*yesterday* afternoon's emergency?"

Mike glanced up at the chronometer. It was two-thirty in the morning, Greenwich time. Jeffers held the bridge from midnight till noon, while Black Bart had the noon to midnight shift.

Still, Mike hadn't realized that it was as late as all that.

He looked at Jeffers' lean, bony face. "Reaction? No, it's not that. Look, Pete, you know me. Would you say I was a pretty levelheaded guy?"

"Sure."

"My old man always said, 'Never make an enemy accidentally,' and I think he was right. So I usually think over what I say before I open my big mouth, don't I?"

Again Jeffers said, "Sure."

"I wouldn't call myself over-cautious," Mike persisted, "but I usually think a thing through pretty carefully before I act—that is, if I have time. Right?"

"I'd say so," Jeffers admitted. "I'd say you were about the only guy I know who does the right thing more than 90 per cent of the time. And says the right thing more than 99 per cent of the time. So what do you want? Back-patting, or just hero worship?"

Mike took a small taste of the brandy. "Neither, you jerk. But about eight hours ago I said something that I hadn't planned to say. I practically proposed to Leda Crannon without knowing I was going to."

Peter Jeffers didn't laugh. He simply said, "How'd it happen?"

Mike told him.

When Mike had finished, one drink later, Peter Jeffers filled the glasses for the third time and leaned back in his chair. "Tell me one thing, ol' buddy, and think about it before you answer. If you had a chance to get out of it gracefully, would you take back what you said?"

Mike the Angel thought it over. The sweep hand on the chronometer made its rounds several times before he answered. Then, at last, he said: "No. No, I wouldn't."

Jeffers pursed his lips, then said judicially: "In that case, you're not doing badly at all. There's nothing wrong with you except the fact that you're in love."

Mike downed the third drink fast and stood up. "Thanks, Pete," he said. "That's what I was afraid of."

"Wait just one stinkin' minute," said Jeffers firmly. "Sit down."

Mike sat.

"What do you intend to do about it?" Jeffers asked.

Mike the Angel grinned at him. "What the hell else can I do but woo and win the wench?"

Jeffers grinned back at him. "I reckon you know you got competition, huh?"

"You mean Jake von Liegnitz?" Mike's face darkened. "I have the feeling he's looking for something that doesn't include a marriage certificate."

"Love sure makes a man sound noble," said Jeffers philosophically. "If you mean that all he wants is to get Leda into the sack, you're prob'ly right. Normal reaction, I'd say. Can't blame Jake for that."

"I don't," said Mike. "But that doesn't mean I can't spike his guns."

"Course not. Again, a normal reaction."

"What about Lew Mellon?" Mike asked.

"Lew?" Jeffers raised his eyebrows. "I dunno. I think he likes to talk to her, is all. But if he *is* interested, he's bloody well serious. He's a strict Anglo-Catholic, like yourself."

I'm not as strict as I ought to be, Mike thought. "I thought he had a rather monkish air about him," he said aloud.

Jeffers chuckled. "Yeah, but I don't think he's so ascetic that he wouldn't marry." His grin broadened. "Now, if we were still at ol' Chilblains, you'd *really* have competition. After all, you can't expect that a gal who's stacked ... pardon me ... who has the magnificent physical and physiognomical topography of Leda Crannon to spend her life bein' ignored, now can you?"

"Nope," said Mike the Angel.

"Now, I figger," Jeffers said, "that you can purty much forget about Lew Mellon. But Jakob von Liegnitz is a chromatically variant equine, indeed."

Mike shook his head vigorously, as if to clear away the fog. "*Pfui!* Let's change the subject. My heretofore nimble mind has been coagulated by a pair of innocent blue eyes. I need my skull stirred up."

"I have a limerick," said Jeffers lightly. "It's about a young spaceman named Mike, who said: 'I can do as I like!' And to prove his bright quip, he took a round trip, clear to Sirius B on a bike. Or, the tale of the pirate, Black Bart, whose head was as hard as his heart. When he found—"

"Enough!" Mike the Angel held up a hand. "That distillate of fine old grape has made us both silly. Good night. I'm going to get some sleep." He stood up and winked at Jeffers. "And thanks for listening while I bent your ear."

"Any time at all, ol' amoeba. And if you ever feel you need some advice from an ol' married man, why you just trot right round, and I'll give you plenty of bad advice."

"At least you're honest," Mike said. "Night."

Mike the Angel left the bridge as Commander Jeffers was putting the brandy back in its hiding place.

Mike went to his quarters, hit the sack, and spent less than five minutes getting to sleep. There was nothing worrying him now.

He didn't know how long he'd been asleep when he heard a noise in the darkness of his room that made him sit up in bed, instantly awake. The floater under him churned a little, but there was no noise. The room was silent.

In the utter blackness of the room, Mike the Angel could see nothing, and he could hear nothing but the all-pervading hum of the ship's engines. But he could still feel and smell.

He searched back in his memory, trying to place the sound that had awakened him. It hadn't been loud, merely unusual. It had been a noise that shouldn't have been made in the stateroom. It had been a quiet sound, really, but for the life of him, Mike couldn't remember what it had sounded like.

But the evidence of his nerves told him there was someone else in the room besides himself. Somewhere near him, something was radiating heat; it was definitely perceptible in the air-conditioned coolness of his room. And, too, there was the definite smell of warm oil—machine oil. It was faint, but it was unmistakable.

And then he knew what the noise had been.

The soft purr of caterpillar treads against the floor!

Casually, Mike the Angel moved his hand to the wall plaque and touched it lightly. The lights came on, dim and subdued.

"Hello, Snookums," said Mike the Angel gently. "What are you here for?"

The little robot just stood there for a second or two, unmoving, his waldo hands clasped firmly in front of his chest. Mike suddenly wished to Heaven that the metallic face could show something that Mike could read.

"I came for data," said Snookums at last, in the contralto voice that so resembled the voice of the woman who had trained him.

Mike started to say, "At this time of night?" Then he glanced at his wrist. It was after seven-thirty in the morning, Greenwich time—which was also ship time.

"What is it you want?" Mike asked.

"Can you dance?" asked Snookums.

"Yes," said Mike dazedly, "I can dance." For a moment he had the wild idea that Snookums was going to ask him to do a few turns about the floor.

"Thank you," said Snookums. His treads whirred, he turned as though on a pivot, whizzed to the door, opened it, and was gone.

Mike the Angel stared at the door as though trying to see beyond it, into the depths of the robot's brain itself.

"Now just what was *that* all about?" he asked aloud.

In the padded silence of the stateroom, there wasn't even an echo to answer him.

14

Mike the Angel spent the next three days in a pale blue funk which he struggled valiantly against, at least to prevent it from becoming a deep blue.

There was something wrong aboard the *Brainchild*, and Mike simply couldn't quite figure what it was. He found that he wasn't the only one who had been asked peculiar questions by Snookums. The little robot seemed to have developed a sudden penchant for asking seemingly inane questions.

Lieutenant Keku reported with a grin that Snookums had asked him if he knew who Commander Gabriel *really* was.

"What'd you say?" Mike had asked.

Keku had spread his hands and said: "I gave him the usual formula about not being positive of my data, then I told him that you were known as Mike the Angel and were well known in the power field."

Multhaus reported that Snookums had wanted to know what their destination was. The chief's only possible answer, of course, had been: "I don't have that data, Snookums."

Dr. Morris Fitzhugh had become more worried-looking than usual and had confided to Mike that he, too, wondered why Snookums was asking such peculiar questions.

"All he'll tell me," the roboticist had reported, wrinkling up his face, "was that he was collecting data. But he flatly refused, even when ordered, to tell me what he needed the data for."

Mike stayed away from Leda Crannon as much as possible; shipboard was no place to try to conduct a romance. Not that he deliberately avoided her in such a manner as to give offense, but he tried to appear busy at all times.

She was busy, too. Keeping herd on Snookums was becoming something of a problem. She had never attempted to watch him all the time. In the first place, it was physically impossible; in the second place, she didn't think Snookums would develop properly if he were to be kept under constant supervision. But now, for the first time, she didn't have the foggiest notion of what was going on inside the robot's mind, and she couldn't find out. It puzzled and worried her, and between herself and Dr. Fitzhugh there were several long conferences on Snookums' peculiar behavior.

Mike the Angel found himself waiting for something to happen. He hadn't the slightest notion what it was that he was waiting for, but he was as certain of its coming as he was of the fact that the Earth was an oblate spheroid.

But he certainly didn't expect it to begin the way it did.

A quiet evening bridge game is hardly the place for a riot to start.

Pete Jeffers was pounding the pillow in his stateroom; Captain Quill was on the bridge, checking through the log.

In the officers' wardroom Mike the Angel was looking down at two hands of cards, wondering whether he'd make his contract. His own hand held the ace, nine, seven of spades; the ten, six, two of hearts; the jack, ten, nine, four, three, and deuce of diamonds; and the eight of clubs.

Vaneski, his partner, had bid a club. Keku had answered with a take-out double. Mike had looked at his hand, figured that since he and Vaneski were vulnerable, while Keku and von Liegnitz were not, he bid a weakness pre-empt of three diamonds. Von Liegnitz passed, and Vaneski had answered back with five diamonds. Keku and Mike had both passed, and von Liegnitz had doubled.

Now Mike was looking at Vaneski's dummy hand. No spades; the ace, queen, five, and four of hearts; the queen, eight, seven, and six of diamonds; and the ace, king, seven, four, and three of clubs.

And von Liegnitz had led the three of hearts.

It didn't look good. His opponents had the ace and king of trumps, and with von Liegnitz' heart lead, it looked as though he might have to try a finesse on the king of hearts. Still, there *might* be another way out.

Mike threw in the ace from dummy. Keku tossed in his seven, and Mike threw in his own deuce. He took the next trick with the ace of clubs from dummy, and the singleton eight in his own hand. The one after that came from dummy, too; it was the king of clubs, and Mike threw in the heart six from his own hand. From dummy, he led the three of clubs. Keku went over it with a jack, but Mike took it with his deuce of diamonds.

He led the seven of spades to get back in dummy so he could use up those clubs. Dummy took the trick with the six of diamonds, and led out with the four of clubs.

Mike figured that Keku must—absolutely *must*—have the king of hearts. Both his take-out double and von Liegnitz' heart lead pointed toward the king in his hand. Now if....

Vaneski had moved around behind Mike to watch the play. Not one of them noticed Lieutenant Lew Mellon, the Medical Officer, come into the room.

That is, they knew he had come in, but they had ignored him thereafter. He was such a colorless nonentity that he simply seemed to fade into the background of the walls once he had made his entrance.

Mike had taken seven tricks, and, as he had expected, lost the eighth to von Liegnitz' five of diamonds. When the German led the nine of hearts, Mike knew he had the game. He put in the queen from dummy, Keku tossed in his king triumphantly, and Mike topped it with his lowly four of diamonds.

If, as he suspected, his opponents' ace and king of diamonds were split, he would get them both by losing the next trick and then make a clean sweep of the board.

He threw in his nine of diamonds.

He just happened to glance at von Liegnitz as the navigator dropped his king.

Then he lashed out with one foot, kicking at the leg of von Liegnitz' chair. At the same time, he yelled, "Jake! Duck!"

He was almost too late. Mellon, his face contorted with a mixture of anger and hatred, was standing just behind Jakob von Liegnitz. In one hand was a heavy spanner, which he was bringing down with deadly force on the navigator's skull.

Von Liegnitz' chair started to topple, and von Liegnitz himself spun away from the blow. The spanner caught him on the shoulder, and he grunted in pain, but he kept on moving away from Mellon.

The medic screamed something and lifted the spanner again.

By this time, Keku, too, was on his feet, moving toward Mellon. Mike the Angel got behind Mellon, trying to grab at the heavy metal tool in Mellon's hand.

Mellon seemed to sense him, for he jumped sideways, out of Mike's way, and kicked backward at the same time, catching Mike on the shin with his heel.

Von Liegnitz had made it to his feet by this time and was blocking the downward swing of Mellon's arm with his own forearm. His other fist pistoned out toward Mellon's face. It connected, sending Mellon staggering backward into Mike the Angel's arms.

Von Liegnitz grabbed the spanner out of Mellon's hand and swung it toward the medic's jaw. It was only inches away when Keku's hand grasped the navigator's wrist.

And when the big Hawaiian's hand clamped on, von Liegnitz' hand stopped almost dead.

Mellon was screaming. "You ——!" He ran out a string of unprintable and almost un-understandable words. "I'll kill you! I'll do it yet! *You stay away from Leda Crannon!*"

"Calm down, Doc!" snapped Mike the Angel. "What the hell's the matter with you, anyway?"

Von Liegnitz was still straining, trying to get away from Keku to take another swipe at the medic, but the huge Hawaiian held him easily. The navigator had lapsed into his native German, and most of it was unintelligible, except for an occasional reference to various improbable combinations of animal life.

But Mellon was paying no attention. "You! I'll kill you! Lecher! Dirty-minded, filthy...."

He went on.

Suddenly, unexpectedly, he smashed his heel down on Mike's toe. At least, he tried to; he'd have done it if the toe had been there when his heel came down. But Mike moved it just two inches and avoided the blow.

At the same time, though, Mellon twisted, and Mike's forced shift of position lessened his leverage on the man's shoulders and arms. Mellon almost got away. One hand grabbed the wrench from von Liegnitz, whose grip had been weakened by the paralyzing pressure of Keku's fingers.

Mike had no choice but to slam a hard left into the man's solar plexus. Mellon collapsed like an unoccupied overcoat.

By this time, von Liegnitz had quieted down. "Let go, Keku," he said. "I'm all right." He looked down at the motionless figure on the deck. "What the hell do you suppose was eating him?" he asked quietly.

"How's your shoulder?" Mike asked.

"Hurts like the devil, but I don't think it's busted. But why did he do it?" he repeated.

"Sounds to me," said Keku dryly, "that he was nutty jealous of you. He didn't like the times you took Leda Crannon to the base movies while we were at Chilblains."

Jakob von Liegnitz continued to look down at the smaller man in wonder. "*Lieber Gott*" he said finally. "I only took her out a couple of times. I knew he liked her, but—" He stopped. "The guy must be off his bearings."

"I smelled liquor on his breath," said Mike. "Let's get him down to his stateroom and lock him in until he sobers up. I'll have to report this to the captain. Can you carry him, Keku?"

Keku nodded and reached down. He put his hands under Mellon's armpits, lifted him to his feet, and threw him over his shoulder.

"Good," said Mike the Angel. "I'll walk behind you and clop him one if he wakes up and gets wise."

Vaneski was standing to one side, his face pale, his expression blank.

Mike said: "Jake, you and Vaneski go up and make the report to the captain. Tell him we'll be up as soon as we've taken care of Mellon."

"Right," said von Liegnitz, massaging his bruised shoulder.

"Okay, Keku," said Mike, "forward march."

Lieutenant Keku thumbed the opener to Mellon's stateroom, shoved the door aside, stepped in, and slapped at the switch plaque. The plates lighted up, bathing the room in sunshiny brightness.

"Dump him on his sack," said Mike.

While Keku put the unconscious Mellon on his bed, Mike let his gaze wander around the room. It was neat—almost too neat, implying overfussiness. The medical reference books were on one shelf, all in alphabetical order. Another shelf contained a copy of the *International Encyclopedia*, English edition, plus several dictionaries, including one on medical terms and another on theological ones.

On the desk lay a copy of the Bible, York translation, opened to the Book of Tobit. Next to it were several sheets of blank paper and a small traveling clock sat on them as a paperweight.

His clothing was hung neatly, in the approved regulation manner, with his shoes in their proper places and his caps all lined up in a row.

Mike walked around the room, looking at everything.

"What's the matter? What're you looking for?" asked Keku.

"His liquor," said Mike the Angel.

"In his desk, lower left-hand drawer. You won't find anything but a bottle of ruby port; Mellon was never a drinker."

Mike opened the drawer. "I probably won't find that, drunk as he is."

Surprisingly enough, the bottle of wine was almost half full. "Did he have more than one bottle?" Mike asked.

"Not so far as I know. Like I said, he didn't drink much. One slug of port before bedtime was about his limit."

Mike frowned. "How does his breath smell to you?"

"Not bad. Two or three drinks, maybe."

"Mmmm." Mike put the bottle on top of the desk, then walked over to the small case that was standing near one wall. He lifted it and flipped it open. It was the standard medical kit for Space Service physicians.

The intercom speaker squeaked once before Captain Quill's voice came over it. "Mister Gabriel?"

"Yes, sir?" said Mike without turning around. There were no eyes in the private quarters of the officers and crew.

"How is Mister Mellon?" A Space Service physician's doctorate is never used as a form of address; three out of four Space Service officers have a doctor's degree of some kind, and there's no point in calling 75 per cent of the officers "doctor."

Mike glanced across the room. Keku had finished stripping the little physician to his underclothes and had put a cover over him.

"He's still unconscious, sir, but his breathing sounds all right."

"How's his pulse?"

Keku picked up Mellon's left wrist and applied his fingers to the artery while he looked at his wrist watch.

Mike said: "We'll check it, sir. Wait a few seconds."

Fifteen seconds later, Keku multiplied by four and said: "One-oh-four and rather weak."

"You'd better get hold of the Physician's Mate," Mike told Quill. "He's not in good condition, either mentally or physically."

"Very well. As soon as the mate takes over, you and Mister Keku get up here. I want to know what the devil has been going on aboard my ship."

"You are bloody well not the only one," said Mike the Angel.

15

Midnight, ship time.

And, as far as the laws of simultaneity would allow, it was midnight in Greenwich, England. At least, when a ship returned from an interstellar trip, the ship's chronometer was within a second or two, plus or minus, of Greenwich time. Theoretically, the molecular vibration clocks shouldn't vary at all. The fact that they did hadn't yet been satisfactorily accounted for.

Mike the Angel tried to make himself think of clocks or the variations in space time or anything else equally dull, in the hope that it would put him to sleep.

He began to try to work out the derivation of the Beale equations, the equations which had solved the principle of the no-space drive. The ship didn't move through space; space moved through the ship, which, of course, might account for the variation in time, because—

—the time is out of joint.

The time is out of joint: O cursed spite, That ever I was born to set it right!

Hamlet, thought Mike. *Act One, the end of scene five.*

But why had he been born to set it right? Besides, exactly what was wrong? There was something wrong, all right.

And why from the end of the act? Another act to come? Something more to happen? The clock will go round till another time comes. Watch the clock, the absolutely cuckoo clock, which ticked as things happened that made almost no sense and yet had sense hidden in their works.

The good old Keku clock. Somewhere is icumen in, lewdly sing Keku. The Mellon is ripe and climbing Jakob's ladder. And both of them playing Follow the Leda.

And where were they heading? Toward some destination in the general direction of the constellation Cygnus. The transformation equations work fine on an interstellar ship. Would they work on a man? Wouldn't it be nice to be able to transform yourself into a swan? Cygnus the Swan.

And we'll *all* play Follow the Leda....

Somewhere in there, Mike the Angel managed to doze off.

He awoke suddenly, and his dream of being a huge black swan vanished, shattered into nothingness.

This time it had not been a sound that had awakened him. It had been something else, something more like a cessation of sound. A dying sigh.

He reached out and touched the switch plaque.

Nothing happened.

The room remained dark.

The room was strangely silent. The almost soundless vibration of the engines was still there, but....

The air conditioners!

The air in the stateroom was unmoving, static. There was none of the faint breeze of moving air. Something had gone wrong with the low-power circuits!

Now how the hell could that happen? Not by accident, unless the accident were a big one. It would take a tremendous amount of coincidence to put all three of the interacting systems out of order at once. And they all *had* to go at once to cut the power from the low-load circuits.

The standard tap and the first and second stand-by taps were no longer tapping power from the main generators. The intercom was gone, too, along with the air conditioners, the lights, and half a dozen other sub-circuits.

Mike the Angel scrambled out of bed and felt for his clothing, wishing he had something as prosaic as an old-fashioned match, or even a flame-type cigarette lighter. He found his lighter in his belt pocket as he pulled on his uniform. He jerked it out and thumbed it. In the utter darkness, the orange-red glow gave more illumination than he had supposed. If a man's eyes are adjusted to darkness, he can read print by the glow of a cigarette, and the lighter's glow was brighter than that.

Still, it wasn't much. If only he had a flashlight!

From a distance, far down the companionway, he could hear voices. The muffled sound that had awakened him had been the soft susurration of the door as it had slid open when the power died. Without the electrolocks to hold it closed, it had opened automatically. The doors in a spaceship are built that way, to make sure no one will be trapped in case of a power failure.

Mike dressed in a matter of seconds and headed toward the door.

And stopped just before he stepped out.

Someone was outside. Someone, or—something.

He didn't know *how* he knew, but he knew. He was as certain as if the lights had been on bright.

And whoever was waiting out there didn't want Mike the Angel to know that he was there.

Mike stood silent for a full second. That was long enough for him to get angry. Not the hot anger of hatred, but the cold anger of a man who has had too many attempts on his life, who has escaped narrowly from an unseen plotter twice because of pure luck and does not intend to fall victim to the dictum that "the third time's a charm."

He realized that he was still holding the glowing cigarette lighter in his hand.

"Damn!" he muttered, as though to himself. "I'd forget my ears if they weren't sewed down." Then he turned, heading back toward his bed, hoping that whoever was waiting outside would assume he would be back immediately. At the same time, he lifted his thumb off the lighter's contact.

Then he sat down on the edge of his bed and quickly pulled off his boots. Holding them both in his hands, he moved silently back to the door. When he reached it, he tossed both boots to the rear of the room. When they landed clatteringly, he stepped quietly through the door. In three steps he was on the opposite side of the corridor. He hugged the wall and moved back away from the spot where the watcher would be expecting him.

Then he waited.

He was on one side of the door to his stateroom, and the—what or whoever it was—was on the other. Until that other made a move, Mike the Angel would wait.

The wait seemed many minutes long, although Mike knew it couldn't have been more than forty-five seconds or so. From other parts of the ship he could hear voices shouting as the crewmen and officers who had been sleeping were awakened by the men on duty. The ship could not sustain life long if the air conditioners were dead.

Then, quite suddenly, the waiting was over. Behind Mike there was a bend in the corridor, and from around that bend came the sound of running footsteps, followed by a bellowing voice: "I'll get the Commander; you go down and get the other boys started!"

Multhaus.

And then there was a glow of light. The Chief Powerman's Mate was carrying a light, which reflected from the walls of the corridor.

And Mike the Angel knew perfectly well that he was silhouetted against that glow. Whoever it was who was waiting for him could see him plainly.

Multhaus' footsteps rang in the corridor while Mike strained his eyes to see what was before him in the darkness. And all the time, the glow became brighter as Multhaus approached.

Then, from out of the darkness, came something that moved on a whir of caterpillar treads. Something hard and metallic slammed against Mike's shoulder, spinning him against the wall.

At that moment, Multhaus came around the corner, and Mike could see Snookums scurrying on down the corridor toward the approaching Powerman's Mate.

"Multhaus! Look out!" Mike yelled.

The beam from the chief's hand torch gleamed on the metallic body of the little robot as it headed toward him.

"Snookums! Stop!" Mike ordered.

Snookums paid no attention. He swerved adroitly around the astonished Multhaus, spun around the corner, and was gone into the darkness.

"What was all that, sir?" Multhaus asked, looking more than somewhat confused.

"A course of instruction on the First and Second Laws of Robotics as applied by the Computer Corporation of Earth," said Mike, rubbing his bruised side. "But never mind that now. What's wrong with the low-power circuits?"

"I don't know, sir. Breckwell is on duty in that section."

"Let's go," said Mike the Angel. "We have to get this cleared up before we all suffocate."

"Someone's going to get galloping claustrophobia before it's over, anyway," said Multhaus morosely as he followed Mike down the hallway in the direction from which Snookums had come. "Darkness and stuffy air touch off that sort of thing."

"Who's Officer of the Watch tonight?" Mike wanted to know.

"Ensign Vaneski, I think. His name was on the roster, as I remember."

"I hope he reported to the bridge. Commander Jeffers will be getting frantic, but he can't leave the bridge unless he's relieved. Come on, let's move."

They sprinted down the companionway.

The lights had been out less than five minutes when Mike the Angel and Chief Powerman's Mate Multhaus reached the low-power center of the Power Section. The door was open, and a torch was spearing its beam on two men—one kneeling over the prone figure of the other. The kneeling man jerked his head around as Mike and the chief came in the door.

The kneeling man was Powerman First Class Fleck. Mike recognized the man on the floor as Powerman Third Class Breckwell.

"What happened?" he snapped at Fleck.

"Don't know, sir. I was in the head when the lights went. It took me a little time to get a torch and get in here, and I found Breckwell gone. At least, I thought he was gone, but then I heard a noise from the tool cabinet and I opened it and he fell out." The words seemed to come out all in a rush.

"Dead?" asked Mike sharply.

"Nossir, I don't think so, sir. Looks like somebody clonked him on the head, but he's breathin' all right."

Mike knelt over the man and took his pulse. The heartbeat was regular and steady, if a trifle weak. Mike ran a hand over Breckwell's head.

"There's a knot there the size of a golf ball, but I don't think anything's broken," he said.

Footsteps came running down the hall, and six men of the power crew came pouring in the door. They slowed to a halt when they saw their commanding officer was already there.

"A couple of you take care of Breckwell—Leister, Knox—move him to one side. Bathe his face with water. No, wait; you can't do that till we get the pumps moving again. Just watch him."

One of the men coughed a little. "What he needs is a good slug of hooch."

"I agree," said Mike evenly. "Too bad there isn't any aboard. But do what you think is best; I'm going to be too busy to keep an eye on you. I won't be able to watch you at all, so you'll be on your own."

"Yessir," said the man who had spoken. He hid his grin and took out at a run, heading for wherever it was he kept his bottle hidden.

"Dunstan, you and Ghihara get out and watch the halls. If any other officer comes this way, sing out."

"Yessir!" came the twin chorus.

More footsteps pounded toward them, and the remaining men of the power crew arrived.

"All right, now let's take a look at these circuits," said Mike.

Chief Multhaus had already flipped open all the panels and was peering inside. The men lined the torches up on the desk in the corner, in order to shed as much light as possible over the banks of low-power wiring, and went over to where Multhaus and Mike the Angel were standing.

"Dig out three replacement switches—heavy-duty six-double-oh-B-nines," said Multhaus. There was a touch of disgust and a good-sized serving of anger and irritation in his voice.

Mike the Angel surveyed the damage. "See anything else, Multhaus?"

"No, sir. That's it."

Mike nodded. "About five minutes' work to get the main switch going, which will give us power, and another ten minutes for the first and second stand-bys. Go ahead and take over, Multhaus; you won't need me. I'll go find out what the bloody unprintable is going on around here."

Mike the Angel ran into Captain Sir Henry Quill as he went up the companionway to the bridge.

"What happened?" demanded the captain in his gravelly tenor voice.

"Somebody ripped out the main switches to the low-power taps from the main generators, sir," said Mike. "Nothing to worry about. The boys will have the lights on within three or four minutes."

"Who...?"

"I don't know," said Mike, "but we'd better find out pretty fast. There've been too many things going on aboard this ship to suit me."

"Same here. Are you sure everything's all right down there?"

"Absolutely, sir. We can quit worrying about the damage itself and put our minds to finding out who did that damage."

"Do you have any ideas?"

"Some," said Mike the Angel. "As soon as the intercom is functioning again, I think you'd better call a general meeting of officers—and get Miss Crannon and Fitzhugh out of bed and get them up here, too."

"Why?" Black Bart asked flatly.

"Because Snookums has gone off his rocker. He's attacked at least one human being that I know of and has ignored direct orders from a human being."

"Who?" asked Black Bart.

"Me," said Mike the Angel.

Mike told Captain Quill what had happened as they made their way back up to the bridge.

Ensign Vaneski, looking pale and worried, met them at the door. He snapped a salute. "I just reported to Commander Jeffers, sir. Something's wrong with the low-power circuits."

"I had surmised as much," said Black Bart caustically. "Anything new? What did you find out? What happened?"

"When the lights went out, I was having coffee by myself in the wardroom. I grabbed a torch and headed for Power Section as soon as I could. The low-power room was empty. There should have been a man on duty there, but there wasn't. I didn't want to go inside, since I'm not a power officer, so I came up here to report. I—"

At that moment the lights blazed on again. There was a faint hum that built up all over the ship as the air conditioning came on at the same time.

"All right, Mister Vaneski," said Black Bart, "get below and take care of things. There's a man hurt down there, so be ready to take him to sick bay when the Physician's Mate gets there. We don't have a medic in any condition to take care of people, so he'll have to do. Hop it."

As Vaneski left, Black Bart preceded Mike into the bridge. Pete Jeffers was on the intercom. As Mike and the captain came in, he was saying, "All right. I'll notify the Officer of the Watch, and we'll search the ship. He can't hide very long." Then, without waiting to say anything to Mike or Quill, he jabbed at another button. "Mister von Liegnitz! Jake!"

"*Ja?* Huh? What is it?" came a fuzzy voice from the speaker.

"You all right?"

"Me? Sure. I was asleep. Why?"

"Be on your toes, sleepyhead; just got word that Mellon has escaped from his stateroom. He may try to take another crack at you."

"I'll watch it," said von Liegnitz, his voice crisp now.

"Okay." Jeffers sighed and looked up. "As soon as the power came on, the Physician's Mate was on the intercom. Mellon isn't in his stateroom."

"Oh, wonderful!" growled Captain Quill. "We now have one insane robot and one insane human running loose on this ship. I'm glad we didn't bring any gorillas with us."

"Somehow I think I'd be safer with a gorilla," said Mike the Angel.

"According to the Physician's Mate, Mellon is worse than just nuts," said Jeffers quietly. "He says he loaded Mellon full of dope to make him sleep and that the man's got no right to be walkin' around at all."

"He must have gotten out while the doors were open," said Captain Quill. He rubbed the palm of his hand over the shiny pinkness of his scalp. His dark, shaggy brows were down over his eyes, as though they had been weighted with lead.

"Mister Jeffers," he said abruptly, "break out the stun guns. Issue one to each officer and one to each chief non-com. Until we get this straightened out, I'm declaring a state of emergency."

16

Mike the Angel hefted the heavy stun gun in his right fist, feeling its weight without really noticing it. He knew damned good and well it wouldn't be of any use against Snookums. If Mellon came at him, the supersonic beam from the gun would affect his nerves the same way an electric current would, and he'd collapse, unconscious but relatively unharmed. But Mike doubted seriously that it would have any effect at all on the metal body of the robot. It is as difficult to jolt the nerves of a robot as it is to blind an oyster.

Snookums did have sensory devices that enabled him to tell what was going on around him, but they were not nerves in the ordinary sense of the word, and a stun gun certainly wouldn't have the same effect.

He wondered just what effect it *would* have—if any.

He was going down the main ladder—actually a long spiral stairway that led downward from the bridge. Behind him were Chief Multhaus, also armed with a stun gun, and four members of the power crew, each armed with a heavy spanner. Mike or the chief could take care of Mellon; it would be the crew's job to take care of Snookums.

"Smash his treads and his waldoes," Mike had told them, "but only if he attacks. Before you try anything else, give him an order to halt. If he keeps on coming, start swinging." And, to Chief Multhaus: "If Mellon jumps me, fire that stun gun only if he's armed with a knife or a gun. But if you do have to fire at Mellon, don't wait to get in a good shot; just go ahead and knock us both out. I'd rather be asleep than dead. Okay?"

Multhaus had agreed. "The same goes for me, Commander. And the rest of the boys."

So down the ladder they went. Mike hoped there'd be no fighting at all. He had the feeling that everything was all wrong, somehow, and that any use of stun guns or spanners would just make everything worse.

His wasn't the only group looking for Snookums and Mellon. Lieutenant Keku had another group, and Commander Jeffers had a third. Lieutenant Commander von Liegnitz was with Captain Quill on the bridge. Mellon had already attacked von Liegnitz once; the captain didn't want them mixing it up again.

Captain Quill's voice came suddenly from a speaker in the overhead. "Miss Crannon and Dr. Fitzhugh have just spoken to me," he said in his brisk tenor. "Snookums is safe in his own room. I have outlined what has happened, and they're trying to get information from Snookums now. Lieutenant Mellon is still missing."

"One down," said Chief Multhaus. There was relief in his voice.

"Let's see if we can find the other one," said Mike the Angel.

They went down perhaps three more steps, and the speakers came to life again. "Will the Chief Physician's Mate report to Commander Jeffers in the maintenance tool room? Lieutenant Keku, dismiss your men to quarters and report to the bridge. Commander Gabriel, dismiss your men to quarters and report to Commander Jeffers in maintenance. All chief non-coms report to the ordnance room to turn in your weapons. All enlisted men return to your posts or to quarters."

Mike the Angel holstered his stun gun. "That's two down," he said to Chief Multhaus.

"Looks like we missed all the fun," said Multhaus.

"Okay, men," Mike said, "you got the word. Take those spanners back to the tool room in Power Section, and then get back to your quarters. Chief, you go with them and secure everything, then take that stun gun back to ordnance."

"Yessir."

Multhaus threw Mike a salute; Mike returned it and headed toward maintenance. He knew Multhaus and the others were curious, but he was just as curious himself. He had the advantage of being in a position to satisfy his curiosity.

The maintenance tool room was big and lined with tool lockers. One of them was open. Sprawled in front of it was Lieutenant Mellon. Over to one side was Commander Jeffers, standing next to a white-faced Ensign Vaneski. Nearby were a chief non-com and three enlisted men.

"Hullo, Mike," Pete Jeffers said as Mike the Angel came in.

"What happened, Pete?" Mike asked.

Jeffers gestured at the sprawled figure on the floor. "We came in here to search. We found him. Mister Vaneski opened the locker, there, for a look-see, and Mellon jumped out at him. Vaneski fired his stun gun. Mellon collapsed to the deck. He's in bad shape; his pulse is so weak that it's hard to find."

Mike the Angel walked over and looked down at the fallen Medical Officer. His face was waxen, and he looked utterly small and harmless.

"What happened?" asked another voice from the door. It was Chief Physician's Mate Pierre Pasteur. He was a smallish man, well rounded, pleasant-faced, and inordinately proud of his name. He couldn't actually prove that he was really descended from the great Louis, but he didn't allow people to think otherwise. Like most C. Phys. M.'s, he had a doctor of medicine degree but no internship in the Space Service. He was working toward his commission.

"We've got a patient for you," said Jeffers. "Better look him over, Chief."

Chief Pasteur walked over to where Mellon lay and took his stethoscope out of his little black bag. He listened to Mellon's chest for a few seconds. Then he pried open an eyelid and looked closely at an eye. "What happened to him?" he asked, without looking up.

"Got hit with a beam from a stun gun," said Jeffers.

"How did he fall? Did he hit his head?"

"I don't know—maybe." He looked at Ensign Vaneski. "Did he, Mister Vaneski? He was right on top of you; I was across the room."

Vaneski swallowed. "I don't know. He—he just sort of—well, he *fell*."

"You didn't catch him?" asked the chief. He was a physician on a case now and had no time for sirring his superiors.

"No. No. I jumped away from him."

"Why? What's the trouble?" Jeffers asked.

"He's dead," said the Chief Physician's Mate.

17

Leda Crannon was standing outside the cubicle that had been built for Snookums. Her back and the palms of her hands were pressed against the door. Her head was bowed, and her red hair, shining like a hellish flame in the light of the glow panels, fell around her shoulders and cheeks, almost covering her face.

"Leda," said Mike the Angel gently.

She looked up. There were tears in her blue eyes.

"Mike! Oh, Mike!" She ran toward him, put her arms around him, and tried to bury her face in Mike's chest.

"What's the matter, honey? What's happened?" He was certain she couldn't have heard about Mellon's death yet. He held her in his arms, carefully, tenderly, not passionately.

"He's crazy, Mike. He's completely crazy." Her voice had suddenly lost everything that gave it color. It was only dead and choked.

Mike the Angel knew it was an emotional reaction. As a psychologist, she would never have used the word "crazy." But as a woman ... as a human being....

"Fitz is still in there talking to him, but he's—he's—" Her voice choked off again into sobs.

Mike waited patiently, holding her, caressing her hair.

"Eight years," she said after a minute or so. "Eight years I spent. And now he's gone. He's broken."

"How do you know?" Mike asked.

She lifted her head and looked at him. "Mike—did he really hit you? Did he refuse to stop when you ordered him to? What *really* happened?"

Mike told her what had happened in the darkened companionway just outside his room.

When he finished, she began sobbing again. "He's lying, Mike," she said. "*Lying!*"

Mike nodded silently and slowly. Leda Crannon had spent all of her adult life tending the hurts and bruises and aches of Snookums the Child. She had educated him, cared for him, taken pleasure in his triumphs, worried about his health, and watched him grow mentally.

And now he was sick, broken, ruined. And, like all parents, she was asking herself: "What did I do wrong?"

Mike the Angel didn't give her an answer to that unspoken question, but he knew what the answer was in so many cases:

The grieving parent has not necessarily done anything wrong. It may simply be that there was insufficient or poor-quality material to work with.

With a human child, it is even more humiliating for a parent to admit that he or she has contributed inferior genetic material to a child than it is to admit a failure in upbringing. Leda's case was different.

Leda had lost her child, but Mike hesitated to point out that it wasn't her fault in the first place because the material wasn't up to the task she had given it, and in the second place because she hadn't really lost anything. She was still playing with dolls, not human beings.

"Hell!" said Mike under his breath, not realizing that he was practically whispering in her ear.

"Isn't it?" she said. "Isn't it Hell? I spent eight years trying to make that little mind of his tick properly. I wanted to know what was the right, proper, and logical way to bring up children. I had a theory, and I wanted to test it. And now I'll never know."

"What sort of theory?" Mike asked.

She sniffled, took a handkerchief from her pocket, and began wiping at her tears. Mike took the handkerchief away from her and did the wiping job himself. "What's this theory?" he said.

"Oh, it isn't important now. But I felt—I still feel—that everybody is born with a sort of Three Laws of Robotics in him. You know what I mean—that a person wouldn't kill or harm anyone, or refuse to do what was right, in addition to trying to preserve his own life. I think babies are born that way. But I think that the information they're given when they're growing up can warp them. They still think they're obeying the laws, but they're obeying them wrongly, if you see what I mean."

Mike nodded without saying anything. This was no time to interrupt her.

"For instance," she went on, "if my theory's right, then a child would never disobey his father—unless he was convinced that the man was not really his father, you see. For instance, if he learned, very early, that his father never spanks him, that becomes one of the identifying marks of 'father.' Fine. But the first time his father *does* spank him, doubt enters. If that sort of thing goes on, he becomes disobedient because he doesn't believe that the man is his father."

"I'm afraid I'm putting it a little crudely, but you get the idea."

"Yeah," said Mike. For all he knew, there might be some merit in the girl's idea; he knew that philosophers had talked of the "basic goodness of mankind" for centuries. But he had a hunch that Leda was going about it wrong. Still, this was no time to argue with her. She seemed calmer now, and he didn't want to upset her any more than he had to.

"That's what you've been working on with Snookums?" he asked.

"That's it."

"For eight years?"

"For eight years."

"Is that the information, the data, that makes Snookums so priceless, aside from his nucleonics work?"

She smiled a little then. "Oh no. Of course not, silly. He's been fed data on everything—physics, subphysics, chemistry, mathematics—all kinds of things. Most of the major research laboratories on Earth have problems of one kind or another that Snookums has been working on. He hasn't been given the problem *I* was working on at all; it would bias him." Then the tears came back. "And now it doesn't matter. He's insane. He's lying."

"What's he saying?"

"He insists that he's never broken the First Law, that he has never hurt a human being. And he insists that he has followed the orders of human beings, according to the Second Law."

"May I talk to him?" Mike asked.

She shook her head. "Fitz is running him through an analysis. He even made me leave." Then she looked at his face more closely. "You don't just want to confront him and call him a liar, do you? No—that's not like you. You know he's just a machine—better than I do, I guess.... What is it, Mike?"

No, he thought, looking at her, *she still thinks he's human. Otherwise, she'd know that a computer can't lie—not in the human sense of the word.*

Most people, if told that a man had said one thing, and that a computer had given a different answer, would rely on the computer.

"What is it, Mike?" she repeated.

"Lew Mellon," he said very quietly, "is dead."

The blood drained from her face, leaving her skin stark against the bright red of her hair. For a moment he thought she was going to faint. Then a little of the color came back.

"Snookums." Her voice was whispery.

He shook his head. "No. Apparently he tried to jump Vaneski and got hit with a stun beam. It shouldn't have killed him—but apparently it did."

"God, God, God," she said softly. "Here I've been crying about a damned machine, and poor Lew has been lying up there dead." She buried her face in her hands, and her voice was muffled when she spoke again. "And I'm all cried out, Mike. I can't cry any more."

Before Mike could make up his mind whether to say anything or not, the door of Snookums' room opened and Dr. Fitzhugh came out, closing the door behind him. There was an odd, stricken look on his face. He looked at Leda and then at Mike, but the expression on his face showed that he really hadn't seen them clearly.

"Did you ever wonder if a robot had a soul, Mike?" he asked in a wondering tone.

"No," Mike admitted.

Leda took her hands from her face and looked at him. Her expression was a bright blank stare.

"He won't answer my questions," Fitzhugh said in a hushed tone. "I can't complete the analysis."

"What's that got to do with his soul?" Mike asked.

"He won't answer my questions," Fitzhugh repeated, looking earnestly at Mike. "He says God won't allow him to."

18

Captain Sir Henry Quill opened the door of the late Lieutenant Mellon's quarters and went in, followed by Mike the Angel. The dead man's gear had to be packed away so that it could be given to his nearest of kin when the officers and crew of the *Brainchild* returned to Earth. Regulations provided that two officers must inventory his personal effects and those belonging to the Space Service.

"Does Chief Pasteur know what killed him yet, Captain?" Mike asked.

Quill shook his head. "No. He wants my permission to perform an autopsy."

"Are you going to let him?"

"I think not. We'll put the body in the freezer and have the autopsy performed on Earth." He looked around the room, seeing it for the first time.

"If you don't," said Mike, "you've got three suspected killers on your hands."

Quill was unperturbed. "Don't be ridiculous, Golden Wings."

"I'm not," Mike said. "I hit him in the pit of his stomach. Chief Pasteur filled him full of sedative. Mister Vaneski shot him with a stun beam. He died. Which one of us did it?"

"Probably no single one of them, but a combination of all three," said Captain Quill. "Each action was performed in the line of duty and without malice aforethought—without even intent to harm permanently, much less to kill. There will have to be a court-martial, of course—or, at the very least, a board of inquiry will be appointed. But I am certain you'll all come through any such inquiry scatheless." He picked up a book from Mellon's desk. "Let's get about our business, Mister Gabriel. Mark down: Bible, one."

Mike put it down on the list.

"*International Encyclopedia*, English edition. Thirty volumes and index."

Mike put it down.

"*The Oxford-Webster Dictionary of the English Language*—

"*Hallbert's Dictionary of Medical Terms*—

"*The Canterbury Theological Dictionary*—

"*The Christian Religion and Symbolic Logic*, by Bishop K. F. Costin—

"*The Handbook of Space Medicine*—"

As Captain Quill called out the names of the books and put them into the packing case he'd brought, Mike marked them down—while something began ticking in the back of his mind.

"Item," said Captain Quill, "one crucifix." He paused. "Beautifully carved, too." He put it into the packing case.

"Excuse me, Captain," said Mike suddenly. "Let me take a look at something, will you?" Excitedly, he leaned over and took some of the books out, looking at the pages of each one.

"I'll be damned," he said after a moment. "Or I *should* be—for being such a stupid idiot!"

Captain Quill narrowed his eyes. "What are you talking about, Mister Gabriel?"

"I'm not sure yet, Captain," Mike hedged. "May I borrow these three books?" He held them up in his hands.

"May I be so bold as to ask *why*, Mister Gabriel?"

"I just want to look at them, sir," Mike said. "I'll return them within a few hours."

"Mister Gabriel," Captain Quill said, "after what happened last night, I am suspicious of everything that goes on aboard this ship. But—yes. You may take them. However, I want them returned before we land tomorrow morning."

Mike blinked. Neither he nor anyone else—with the exception of Captain Quill and Lieutenant Commander von Liegnitz, the navigator, knew the destination of the ship. Mike hadn't realized they were that close to their goal. "I'll have them back by then," he promised.

"Very well. Now let's get on about our work."

The job was completed within forty-five minutes. A man can't carry a great deal with him on a spaceship. When they were through, Mike the Angel excused himself and went to his quarters. Two hours after that he went to the officers' wardroom to look up Pete Jeffers. Pete hadn't been in his quarters, and Mike knew he wasn't on duty by that time. Sure enough, Jeffers was drinking coffee all by himself in the wardroom. He looked up when Mike came in.

"Hullo, Mike," he said listlessly. "Come sit. Have some coffee."

There was a faint aroma in the air which indicated that there was more in the cup than just coffee. "No, thanks, Pete. I'll sit this one out. I wanted to talk to you."

"Sit. I am drinking a toast to Mister Lew Mellon." He pointed at the coffee. "Sure you won't have a mite? It's sweetened from the grape."

"No, thanks again." Mike sat down. "It's Mellon I wanted to talk about. Did you know him well, Pete?"

"Purty well," Pete said, nodding. "Yeah, purty well. I always figured him for a great little bloke. Can't figure what got into him."

"Me either. Pete, you told me he was an Anglo-Catholic—a good one, you said."

"'At's right."

"Well, how did you mean that?"

Pete frowned. "Just what I said. He studied his religion, he went to Mass regularly, said his prayers—that sort of thing. And he was, I will say, a Christian gentleman in every sense of the word." There was irritation in his voice, as though Mike had impugned the memory of a friend.

"Don't get huffy, Pete; he struck me as a pretty nice person, too—"

"Until he flipped his lid," said Pete. "But that might happen to anybody."

"Sure. But what I want to know—and don't get sore—is, did he show any kind of—well, *instability* before this last outbreak?"

"Like what?"

"I mean, was he a religious nut? Did he act 'holier than thou' or—well, was he a fanatic, would you say?"

"No, I wouldn't say so. He didn't talk much about it. I guess you noticed that. I mean, he didn't preach. He smoked some and had his glass of wine now and then—even had a cocktail or two on occasion. His views on sex were orthodox, I reckon—I mean, as far as I know. He'd tell an off-color story, if it wasn't *too* bad. But he'd get up and leave quietly if the boys started tellin' about the women they'd made. Fornication and adultery just weren't his meat, I'd say."

"I know he wasn't married," Mike said. "Did he date much?"

"Some. He liked to dance. Women seemed to like him."

"How about men?"

"Most of the boys liked him."

"That's not what I meant."

"Oh. Was he queer?" Pete frowned. "I'd damn near stake my life that he wasn't."

"You mean he didn't practice it?"

"I don't believe he even thought about it," Pete said. "Course, you can't tell what's really goin' on in a man's mind, but—" His frown became a scowl. "Damn it, Mike, just because a man isn't married by the time he's thirty-five and practices Christian chastity while he's single don't necessarily mean he's a damn fairy!"

"I didn't say it did. I just wondered if you'd heard anything."

"No more'n I've heard about you—who are in exactly the same position!"

"Exactly," Mike agreed. "That's what I wanted to know. Pete, if you've got it to spare, I'll join you in that toast."

Pete Jeffers grinned. "Comin' right up, buddy-boy."

He poured two more cups of coffee, spiked them from a small flask of brandy, and handed one to Mike. They drank in silence.

Fifteen minutes later, Mike the Angel was in the little office that Leda Crannon shared with Dr. Fitzhugh. She was alone.

"How's the girl today?" he asked.

"Beat," she said with a forced smile.

"You look beautiful," he said. He wasn't lying. She looked drawn and tired, but she still looked beautiful.

"Thanks, Mike. What can I do for you?"

Mike the Angel pulled up a chair and sat down. "Where's Doc Fitz?"

"He's still trying to get information out of Snookums. It's a weird thing, Mike—a robot with a soul."

"You don't mind talking about it?"

"No; go ahead if you want."

"All right, answer me a question," he said. "Can Snookums read English?"

"Certainly. And Russian, and German, French, Chinese, and most of the other major languages of Earth."

"He could read a book, then?"

"Yes. But not unless it was given to him and he was specifically told to use its contents as data."

"Good," said Mike. "Now, suppose Snookums was given complete data on a certain field of knowledge. Suppose further that this field is internally completely logical, completely coherent, completely self-consistent. Suppose it could even be reduced to a series of axioms and theorems in symbolic logic."

"All right," she said. "So?"

"Now, further suppose that this system, this field of knowledge is, right now, in constant use by millions of human beings, even though most of them are unaware of the implications of the entire field. Could Snookums work with such a body of knowledge?"

"Sure," said Leda. "Why not?"

"What if there was absolutely no way for Snookums to experiment with this knowledge? What if he simply did not have the equipment necessary?"

"You mean," she asked, "something like astrophysics?"

"No. That's exactly what I don't mean. I'm perfectly well aware that it isn't possible to test astrophysical theories directly. Nobody has been able to build a star in the lab so far.

"But it *is* possible to test the theories of astrophysics analogically by extrapolating on data that *can* be tested in a physics lab.

"What I'm talking about is a system that Snookums, simply because he is what he is, cannot test or experiment upon, in any way whatsoever. A system that has, in short, no connection with the physical world whatsoever."

Leda Crannon thought it over. "Well, assuming all that, I imagine that it would eventually ruin Snookums. He's built to experiment, and if he's kept from experimenting for too long, he'll exceed the optimum randomity of his circuits." She swallowed. "If he hasn't already."

"I thought so. And so did someone else," said Mike thoughtfully.

"Well, for Heaven's sake! What is this system?" Leda asked in sudden exasperation.

"You're close," said Mike the Angel.

"What are you talking about?"

"Theology," said Mike. "He was pumped full of Christian theology, that's all. Good, solid, Catholic theology. Bishop Costin's mathematical symbolization of it is simply a result of the verbal logic that had been smoothed out during the previous two thousand years. Snookums could reduce it to math symbols and equations, anyway, even if we didn't have Bishop Costin's work."

He showed her the book from Mellon's room.

"It doesn't even require the assumption of a soul to make it foul up a robot's works. He doesn't have any emotions, either. And he can't handle something that he can't experiment with. It would have driven him insane, all right. But he *isn't* insane."

Leda looked puzzled. "But—"

"Do you know why?" Mike interrupted.

"No."

"Because he found something that he could experiment with. He found a material basis for theological experimentation."

She looked still more puzzled. "What could that be?"

"Me," said Mike the Angel. "Me. Michael Raphael Gabriel. I'm an angel—an archangel. As a matter of fact, I'm *three* archangels. For all I know, Snookums has equated me with the Trinity."

"But—how did he get that idea?"

"Mostly from the Book of Tobit," said Mike. "That's where an archangel takes the form of a human being and travels around with Tobit the Younger, remember? And, too, he probably got more information from the first part of Luke's Gospel, where Gabriel tells the Blessed Virgin that she's about to become a mother."

"But would he have figured that out for himself?"

"Possibly," said Mike, "but I doubt it. He was told that I was an angel—literally."

"Let me see that book," she said, taking *The Christian Religion and Symbolic Logic* from Mike's hand. She opened it to the center. "I didn't know anyone had done this sort of work," she said.

"Oh, there was a great fuss over the book when it came out. There were those who said that the millennium had arrived because the truth of the Christian faith had been proved mathematically, and therefore all rational people would have to accept it."

She leafed through the book. "I'll bet there are still some who still believe that, just like there are some people who still think Euclidian geometry must necessarily be true because it can be 'proved' mathematically."

Mike nodded. "All Bishop Costin did—all he was *trying* to do—was to prove that the axioms of the Christian faith are logically self-consistent. That's all he ever claimed to have done, and he did a brilliant job of it."

"But—how do you know this is what Snookums was given?"

"Look at the pages. Snookums' waldo fingers wrinkled the pages that way. Those aren't the marks of human fingers. Only two of Mellon's other books were wrinkled that way."

She jerked her head up from the book, startled. "*What?* This is Lew Mellon's book?"

"That's right. So are the other two. A Bible and a theological dictionary. They're wrinkled the same way."

Her eyes were wide, bright sapphires. "But *why?* Why would he do such a thing, for goodness' sake?"

"I don't know why it was done," Mike said slowly, "but I doubt if it was for goodness' sake. We haven't gotten to the bottom of this hanky-panky yet, I don't think.

"Leda, if I'm right—if this *is* what has been causing Snookums' odd behavior—can you cure him?"

She looked at the book again and nodded. "I think so. But it will take a lot of work. I'll have to talk to Fitz about it. We'll have to keep this book—and the other two."

Mike shook his head. "No can do. Can you photocopy them?"

"Certainly. But it'll take—oh, two or three hours per book."

"Then you'd better get busy. We're landing in the morning."

She nodded. "I know. Captain Quill has already told us."

"Fine, then." He stood up. "What will you do? Simply tell Snookums to forget all this stuff?"

"Good Heavens no! It's too thoroughly integrated with every other bit of data he has! You might be able to take one single bit of data out that way, but to jerk out a whole body of knowledge like this would completely randomize his circuits. You can pull out a tooth by yanking with a pair of forceps, but if you try to take out a man's appendix that way, you'll lose a patient."

"I catch," Mike said with a grin. "Okay. I'll get the other two books and you can get to work copying them. Take care."

"Thanks, Mike."

As he walked down the companionway, he cursed himself for being a fool. If he'd let things go on the way they were, Leda might have weaned herself away from Snookums. Now she was interested again. But there could have been no other way, of course.

19

The interstellar ship *Brainchild* orbited around her destination, waiting during the final checkup before she landed on the planet below.

It was not a nice planet. As far as its size went, it could be classified as "Earth type," but size was almost the only resemblance to Earth. It orbited in space some five hundred and fifty million miles from its Sol-like parent—a little farther away from the primary than Jupiter is from Sol itself. It was cold there—terribly cold. At high noon on the equator, the temperature reached a sweltering 180° absolute; it became somewhat chillier toward the poles.

H_2O was, anywhere on the planet, a whitish, crystalline mineral suitable for building material. The atmosphere was similar to that of Jupiter, although the proportions of methane, ammonia, and hydrogen were different because of the lower gravitational potential of the planet. It had managed to retain a great deal more hydrogen in its atmosphere than Earth had because of the fact that the average thermal velocity of the molecules was much lower. Since oxygen-releasing life had never developed on the frigid surface of the planet, there was no oxygen in the atmosphere. It was all tied up in combination with the hydrogen of the ice and the surface rocks of the planet.

The Space Service ship that had discovered the planet, fifteen years before, had given it the name Eisberg, thus commemorating the name of a spaceman second class who happened to have the luck to be (a) named Robert Eisberg, (b) a member of the crew of the ship to discover the planet, and (c) under the command of a fun-loving captain.

Eisberg had been picked as the planet to transfer the potentially dangerous Snookums to for two reasons. In the first place, if Snookums actually did solve the problem of the total-annihilation bomb, the worst he could do was destroy a planet that wasn't much good, anyway. And, in the second place, the same energy requirements applied on Eisberg as did on Chilblains Base. It was easier to cool the helium bath of the brain if it only had to be lowered 175 degrees or so.

It was a great place for cold-work labs, but not worth anything for colonization.

Chief Powerman's Mate Multhaus looked gloomily at the figures on the landing sheet.

Mike the Angel watched the expression on the chief's face and said: "What's the matter, Multhaus? No like?"

Multhaus grimaced. "Well, sir, I don't like it, no. But I can't say I *dis*like it, either."

He stared at the landing sheet, pursing his lips. He looked as though he were valiantly restraining himself from asking questions about the other night's escapade—which he was.

He said: "I just don't like to land without jets, sir; that's all."

"Hell, neither do I," admitted Mike. "But we're not going to get down any other way. We managed to take off without jets; we'll manage to land without them."

"Yessir," said Multhaus, "but we took off *with* the grain of Earth's magnetic field. We're landing *across* the grain."

"Sure," said Mike. "So what? If we overlook the motors, that's okay. We may never be able to get off the planet with this ship again, but we aren't supposed to anyway.

"Come on, Multhaus, don't worry about it. I know you hate to burn up a ship, but this one is supposed to be expendable. You may never have another chance like this."

Multhaus tried to keep from grinning, but he couldn't. "Awright, Commander. You have appealed to my baser instincts. My subconscious desire to wreck a spaceship has been brought to the surface. I can't resist it. Am I nutty, maybe?"

"Not now, you're not," Mike said, grinning back.

"We'll have a bitch of a job getting through the plasmasphere, though," said the chief. "That fraction of a second will—"

"It'll jolt us," Mike agreed, interrupting. "But it won't wreck us. Let's get going."

"Aye, sir," said Multhaus.

The seas of Eisberg were liquid methane containing dissolved ammonia. Near the equator, they were liquid; farther north, the seas became slushy with crystallized ammonia.

The site picked for the new labs of the Computer Corporation of Earth was in the northern hemisphere, at 40° north latitude, about the same distance from the equator as New York or Madrid, Spain, would be on Earth. The *Brainchild* would be dropping through Eisberg's magnetic field at an angle, but it wouldn't be the ninety-degree angle of the equator. It would have been nice if the base could have been built at one of the poles, but that would have put the labs in an uncomfortable position, since there was no solid land at either pole.

Mike the Angel didn't like the idea of having to land on Eisberg without jets any more than Multhaus did, but he was almost certain that the ship would take the strain.

He took the companionway up to the Control Bridge, went in, and handed the landing sheet to Black Bart. The captain scowled at it, shrugged, and put it on his desk.

"Will we make it, sir?" Mike said. "Any word from the *Fireball*?"

Black Bart nodded. "She's orbiting outside the atmosphere. Captain Wurster will send down a ship to pick us up as soon as we've finished our business here."

The *Fireball*, being much faster than the clumsy *Brainchild*, had left Earth later than the slower ship, and had arrived earlier.

"*Now hear this! Now hear this! Third Warning! Landing orbit begins in one minute! Landing begins in one minute!*"

Sixty seconds later the *Brainchild* began her long, logarithmic drop toward the surface of Eisberg.

Landing a ship on her jets isn't an easy job, but at least an ion rocket is built for the job. Maybe someday the Translation drive will be modified for planetary landings, but so far such a landing has been, as someone put it, "50 per cent raw energy and 50 per cent prayer." The landing was worse than the take-off, a truism which has held since the first glider took off from the surface of Earth in the nineteenth century. What goes up doesn't necessarily have to come down, but when it does, the job is a lot rougher than getting up was.

The plasmasphere of Eisberg differed from that of Earth in two ways. First, the ionizing source of radiation—the primary star—was farther away from Eisberg than Sol was from Earth, which tended to reduce the total ionization. Second, the upper atmosphere of Eisberg was pretty much pure hydrogen, which is somewhat easier to ionize than oxygen or nitrogen. And, since there was no ozonosphere to block out the UV radiation from the primary, the thickness of the ionosphere beneath the plasmasphere was greater.

Not until the *Brainchild* hit the bare fringes of the upper atmosphere did she act any differently than she had in space.

But when she hit the outer fringes of the ionosphere—that upper layer of rarified protons, the rapidly moving current of high velocity ions known as the plasmasphere—she bucked like a kicked horse. From deep within her vitals, the throb began, a strumming, thrumming sound with a somewhat higher note imposed upon it, making a sound like that of a bass viol being plucked rapidly on its lowest string.

It was not the intensity of the ionosphere that cracked the drive of the *Brainchild*; it was the duration. The layer of ionization was too thick; the ship couldn't make it through the layer fast enough, in spite of her high velocity.

A man can hold a red-hot bit of steel in his hand for a fraction of a second without even feeling it. But if he has to hold a hot baked potato for thirty seconds, he's likely to get a bad burn.

So it was with the *Brainchild*. The passage through Earth's ionosphere during take-off had been measured in fractions of a second. The *Brainchild* had reacted, but the exposure to the field had been too short to hurt her.

The ionosphere of Eisberg was much deeper and, although the intensity was less, the duration was much longer.

The drumming increased as she fell, a low-frequency, high-energy sine wave that shook the ship more violently than had the out-of-phase beat that had pummeled the ship shortly after her take-off.

Dr. Morris Fitzhugh, the roboticist, screamed imprecations into the intercom, but Captain Sir Henry Quill cut him off before anyone took notice and let the scientist rave into a dead pickup.

"How's she coming?"

The voice came over the intercom to the Power Section, and Mike the Angel knew that the question was meant for him.

"She'll make it, Captain," he said. "She'll make it. I designed this thing for a 500 per cent overload. She'll make it."

"Good," said Black Bart, snapping off the intercom.

Mike exhaled gustily. His eyes were still on the needles that kept creeping higher and higher along the calibrated periphery of the meters. Many of them had long since passed the red lines that marked the allowable overload point. Mike the Angel knew that those points had been set low, but he also knew that they were approaching the real overload point.

He took another deep breath and held it.

Point for point, the continent of Antarctica, Earth, is one of the most deadly areas ever found on a planet that is supposedly non-inimical to man. Earth is a nice, comfortable planet, most of the time, but Antarctica just doesn't cater to Man at all.

Still, it just happens to be the *worst* spot on the *best* planet in the known Galaxy.

Eisberg is different. At its best, it has the continent of Antarctica beat four thousand ways from a week ago last Candlemas. At its worst, it is sudden death; at its best, it is somewhat less than sudden.

Not that Eisberg is a really *mean* planet; Jupiter, Saturn, Uranus, or Neptune can kill a man faster and with less pain. No, Eisberg isn't mean—it's torturous. A man without clothes, placed suddenly on the surface of Eisberg—*anywhere* on the surface—would die. But the trouble is that he'd live long enough for it to hurt.

Man can survive, all right, but it takes equipment and intelligence to do it.

When the interstellar ship *Brainchild* blew a tube—just one tube—of the external field that fought the ship's mass against the space-strain of the planet's gravitational field, the ship went off orbit. The tube blew when she was some ninety miles above the surface. She dropped too fast, jerked up, dropped again.

When the engines compensated for the lost tube, the descent was more leisurely, and the ship settled gently—well, not exactly *gently*—on the surface of Eisberg.

Captain Quill's voice came over the intercom.

"We are nearly a hundred miles from the base, Mister Gabriel. Any excuse?"

"No excuse, sir," said Mike the Angel.

20

If you ignite a jet of oxygen-nitrogen in an atmosphere of hydrogen-methane, you get a flame that doesn't differ much from the flame from a hydrogen-methane jet in an oxygen-nitrogen atmosphere. A flame doesn't particularly care which way the electrons jump, just so long as they jump.

All of which was due to give Mike the Angel more headaches than he already had, which was 100 per cent too many.

Three days after the *Brainchild* landed, the scout group arrived from the base that had been built on Eisberg to take care of Snookums. The leader, a heavy-set engineer named Treadmore, who had unkempt brownish hair and a sad look in his eyes, informed Captain Quill that there was a great deal of work to be done. And his countenance became even sadder.

Mike, who had, perforce, been called in to take part in the conference, listened in silence while the engineer talked.

The officers' wardroom, of which Mike the Angel was becoming heartily sick, seemed like a tomb which echoed and re-echoed the lugubrious voice of Engineer Treadmore.

"We were warned, of course," he said, in a normally dismal tone, "that it would be extremely difficult to set down the ship which carried Snookums, and that we could expect the final base to be anywhere from ten to thirty miles from the original, temporary base." He looked round at everyone, giving the impression of a collie which had just been kicked by Albert Payson Terhune.

"We understand, naturally, that you could not help landing so far from our original base," he said, giving them absolution with faint damns, "but it will entail a great deal of extra labor. A hundred and nine miles is a great distance to carry equipment, and, actually, the distance is a great deal more, considering the configuration of the terrain. The...."

The upshot of the whole thing was that only part of the crew could possibly be spared to go home on the *Fireball*, which was orbiting high above the atmosphere. And, since there was no point in sending a small load home at extra expense when the *Fireball* could wait for the others, it meant that nobody could go home at all for four more weeks. The extra help was needed to get the new base established.

It was obviously impossible to try to move the *Brainchild* a hundred miles. With nothing to power her but the Translation drive, she was as helpless as a submarine on the Sahara. Especially now that her drive was shot.

The Eisberg base had to be built around Snookums, who was, after all, the only reason for the base's existence. And, too, the power plant of the *Brainchild* had been destined to be the source of power for the permanent base.

It wasn't too bad, really. A little extra time, but not much.

The advance base, commanded by Treadmore, was fairly well equipped. For transportation, they had one jet-powered aircraft, a couple of 'copters, and fifteen ground-crawlers with fat tires, plus all kinds of powered construction machinery. All of them were fueled with liquid HNO_3, which makes a pretty good fuel in an atmosphere that is predominantly methane. Like the gasoline-air engines of a century before, they were spark-started reciprocating engines, except for the turbine-powered aircraft.

The only trouble with the whole project was that the materials had to be toted across a hundred miles of exceedingly hostile territory.

Treadmore, looking like a tortured bloodhound, said: "But we'll make it, won't we?"

Everyone nodded dismally.

Mike the Angel had a job he emphatically didn't like. He was supposed to convert the power plant of the *Brainchild* from a spaceship driver into a stationary generator. The conversion job itself wasn't tedious; in principle, it was similar to taking the engine out of an automobile and converting it to a power plant for an electric generator. In fact, it was somewhat simpler, in theory, since the engines of the *Brainchild* were already equipped for heavy drainage to run the electrical systems aboard ship, and to power and refrigerate Snookums' gigantic brain, which was no mean task in itself.

But Michael Raphael Gabriel, head of one of the foremost—if not *the* foremost—power design corporations in the known Galaxy, did not like degrading something. To convert the *Brainchild's* plant from a spaceship drive to an electric power plant seemed to him to be on the same order as using a turboelectric generator to power a flashlight. A waste.

To make things worse, the small percentage of hydrogen in the atmosphere got sneaky sometimes. It could insinuate itself into places where neither the methane nor the ammonia could get. Someone once called hydrogen the "cockroach element," since, like that antediluvian insect, the molecules of H_2 can insidiously infiltrate themselves into places where they are not only unwelcome, but shouldn't even be able to go. At red heat, the little molecules can squeeze themselves through the crystalline interstices of quartz and steel.

Granted, the temperature of Eisberg is a long way from red hot, but normal sealing still won't keep out hydrogen. Add to that the fact that hydrogen and methane are both colorless, odorless, and tasteless, and you have the beginnings of an explosive situation.

The only reason that no one died is because the Space Service is what it is.

Unlike the land, sea, and air forces of Earth, the Space Service does not have a long history of fighting other human beings. There has never been a space war, and, the way things stand, there is no likelihood of one in the foreseeable future.

But the Space Service *does* fight, in its own way. It fights the airlessness of space and the unfriendly atmospheres of exotic planets, using machines, intelligence, knowledge, and human courage as its weapons. Some battles have been lost; others have been won. And the war is still going on. It is an unending war, one which has no victory in sight.

It is, as far as we can tell, the only war in human history in which Mankind is fully justified as the invading aggressor.

It is not a defensive war; neither space nor other planets have attacked Man. Man has invaded space "simply because it is there." It is war of a different sort, true, but it is nonetheless a war.

The Space Service was used to the kind of battle it waged on Eisberg. It was prepared to lose men, but even more prepared to save them.

21

Mike the Angel stepped into the cargo air lock of the *Brainchild*, stood morosely in the center of the cubicle, and watched the outer door close. Eight other men, clad, like himself, in regulation Space Service spacesuits, also looked wearily at the closing door.

Chief Multhaus, one of the eight, turned his head to look at Mike the Angel. "I wish that thing would close as fast as my eyes are going to in about fifteen minutes, Commander." His voice rumbled deeply in Mike's earphones.

"Yeah," said Mike, too tired to make decent conversation.

Eight hours—all of them spent tearing down the spaceship and making it a part of the new base—had not been exactly exhilarating to any of them.

The door closed, and the pumps began to work. The men were wearing Space Service Suit Three. For every environment, for every conceivable emergency, a suit had been built—if, of course, a suit *could* be built for it. Nobody had yet built a suit for walking about in the middle of a sun, but, then, nobody had ever volunteered to try anything like that.

They were all called "spacesuits" because most of them could be worn in the vacuum of space, but most of them weren't designed for that type of work. Suit One—a light, easily manipulated, almost skin-tight covering, was the real spacesuit. It was perfect for work in interstellar space, where there was a microscopic amount of radiation incident to the suit, no air, and almost nil gravity. For exterior repairs on the outside of a ship in free fall a long way from any star, Spacesuit One was the proper garb.

But, a suit that worked fine in space didn't necessarily work on other planets, unless it worked fine on the planet it was used on.

A Moon Suit isn't a Mars Suit isn't a Venus Suit isn't a Triton Suit isn't a....

Carry it on from there.

Number Three was insulated against a frigid but relatively non-corrosive atmosphere. When the pumps in the air lock began pulling out the methane-laden atmosphere, they began to bulge slightly, but not excessively. Then nitrogen, extracted from the ammonia snow that was so plentiful, filled the room, diluting the remaining inflammable gases to a harmless concentration.

Then that mixture was pumped out, to be replaced by a mixture of approximately 20 per cent oxygen and 80 per cent nitrogen—common, or garden-variety, air.

Mike the Angel cracked his helmet and sniffed. "*Guk*," he said. "If I ever faint and someone gives me smelling salts, I'll flay him alive with a coarse rasp."

"Yessir," said Chief Multhaus, as he began to shuck his suit. "But if I had my druthers, I'd druther you'd figure out some way to get all the ammonia out of the joints of this suit."

The other men, sniffing and coughing, agreed in attitude if not in voice.

It wasn't really as bad as they pretended; indeed, the odor of ammonia was hardly noticeable. But it made a good griping point.

The inner door opened at last, and the men straggled through.

"G'night, Chief," said Mike the Angel.

"Night, sir," said Multhaus. "See you in the morning."

"Yeah. Night." Mike trudged toward the companionway that led toward the wardroom. If Keku or Jeffers happened to be there, he'd have a quick round of *Ŭma ni tō*. Jeffers called the game "double solitaire for three people," and Keku said it meant "horses' two heads," but Mike had simply found it as a new game to play before bedtime.

He looked forward to it.

But he had something else to do first.

Instead of hanging up his suit in the locker provided, he had bunched it under his arm—except for the helmet—and now he headed toward maintenance.

He met Ensign Vaneski just coming out, and gave him a broad smile. "Mister Vaneski, I got troubles."

Vaneski smiled back worriedly. "Yes, sir. I guess we all do. What is it, sir?"

Mike gestured at the bundle under his arm. "I abraded the sleeve of my suit while I was working today. I wish you'd take a look at it. I'm afraid it'll need a patch."

For a moment, Vaneski looked as though he'd suddenly developed a headache.

"I know you're supposed to be off duty now," Mike said soothingly, "but I don't want to get myself killed wearing a leaky suit tomorrow. I'll help you work on it if—"

Vaneski grinned quickly. "Oh no, sir. That'll be all right. I'll give it a test, anyway, to check leaks. If it needs repair, it shouldn't take too long. Bring it in, and we'll take a look at it."

They went back into the Maintenance Section, and Vaneski spread the suit out on the worktable. There was an obvious rough spot on the right sleeve. "Looks bad," said Vaneski. "I'll run a test right away."

"Okay," said Mike. "I'll leave it to you. Can I pick it up in the morning?"

"I think so. If it needs a patch, we'll have to test the patch, of course, but we should be able to finish it pretty quickly." He shrugged. "If we can't, sir, you'll just have to wait. Unless you want us to start altering a suit to your measurements."

"Which would take longer?"

"Altering a suit."

"Okay. Just patch this one, then. What can I do?"

"I'll get it out as fast as possible, sir," said Vaneski with a smile.

"Fine. I'll see you later, then." Mike, like Cleopatra, was not prone to argue. He left maintenance and headed toward the wardroom for a game of *Ŭma ni tō*. But when he met Leda Crannon going up the stairway, all thoughts of card games flitted from his mind with the careless nonchalance of a summer butterfly.

"Hullo," he said, pulling himself up a little straighter. He was tired, but not *that* tired.

Her smile brushed the cobwebs from his mind. But a second look told him that there was worry behind the smile.

"Hi, Mike," she said softly. "You look beat."

"I am," admitted Mike. "To a frazzle. Have I told you that I love you?"

"Once, I think. Maybe twice." Her eyes seemed to light up somewhere from far back in her head. "But enough of this mad passion," she said. "I want an invitation to have a drink—a stiff one."

"I'll steal Jeffers' bottle," Mike offered. "What's the trouble?"

Her smile faded, and her eyes became grave. "I'm scared, Mike; I want to talk to you."

"Come along, then," Mike said.

Mike the Angel poured two healthy slugs of Pete Jeffers' brandy into a pair of glasses, added ice and water, and handed one to Leda Crannon with a flourish. And all the time, he kept up a steady line of gentle patter.

"It may interest you to know," he said chattily, "that the learned Mister Treadmore has been furnishing me with the most fascinating information." He lifted up his own glass and looked into its amber depths.

They were in his stateroom, and this time the door was closed—at her insistence. She had explained that she didn't want to be overheard, even by passing crew members.

He swizzled the ice around in his glass, still holding it up to the light. "Indeed," he rambled on, "Treadmore babbled for Heaven knows how long on the relative occurrence of parahydrogen and orthohydrogen on Eisberg." He took his eyes from the glass and looked down at the girl who was seated demurely on the edge of his bunk. Her smile was encouraging.

"He said—and I quote"—Mike's voice assumed a gloomy, but stilted tone—"normal hydrogen gas consists of diatomic molecules. The nuclear, or proton, spin of these atoms—ah—that is, of the two atoms that compose the molecule—may be oriented in the same direction or in opposite directions."

He held a finger in the air as if to make a deep philosophical point. "If," he said pontifically, "they are oriented in the same direction, we refer to the substance as *orthohydrogen*. If they are oriented in opposite directions, it is *parahydrogen*. The *ortho* molecules rotate with *odd* rotational quantum numbers, while the *para* molecules rotate with *even* quantum numbers.

"Since conversion does not normally occur between the two states, normal hydrogen may be considered—"

Leda Crannon, snickering, waved her hand in the air. "Please!" she interrupted. "He can't be that bad! You make him sound like a dirge player at a Hindu funeral. What did he tell you? What did you find out?"

"*Hah!*" said Mike. "What did I find out?" His hand moved in an airy circle as he inscribed a flowing cipher with a graceful Delsarte wave. "Nothing. In the first place, I already knew it, and in the second, it wasn't practical information. There's a slight difference in diffusion between the two forms, but it's nothing to rave about." His expression became suddenly serious. "I hope your information is a bit more revealing."

She glanced at her glass, nodded, and drained it. Mike had extracted a promise from her that she would drink one drink before she talked. He could see that she was a trifle tense, and he thought the liquor would relax her somewhat. Now he was ready to listen.

She handed him her empty, and while he refilled it, she said: "It's about Snookums again."

Mike gave her her glass, grabbed the nearby chair, turned it around, sat down, and regarded her over its back.

"I've lived with him so long," she said after a minute. "So long. It almost seems as though I've grown up with him. Eight years. I've been a mother to him, and a big sister at the same time—and maybe a maiden aunt. He's been a career and a family all rolled in together." She still watched her writhing hands, not raising her eyes to Mike's.

"And—and, I suppose, a husband, too," she continued. "That is, he's sort of the stand-in for a—well, a somebody to teach—to correct—to reform. I guess every woman wants to—to *remake* the man she meets—the man she wants."

And then her eyes were suddenly on his. "But I don't. Not any more. I've had enough of it." Then she looked back down at her hands.

Mike the Angel neither accepted nor rejected the statement. He merely waited.

"He was mine," she said after a little while. "He was mine to mold, to teach, to form. The others—the roboticists, the neucleonicists, the sub-electronicists, all of them—were his instructors. All they did was give him facts. It was I who gave him a personality.

"I made him. Not his body, not his brain, but his mind.

"I made him.

"I knew him.

"And I—I—"

Still staring at her hands, she clasped them together suddenly and squeezed.

"And I loved him," she finished.

She looked up at Mike then. "Can you see that?" she asked tensely. "Can you understand?"

"Yes," said Mike the Angel quietly. "Yes, I can understand that. Under the same circumstances, I might have done the same thing." He paused. "And now?"

She lowered her head again and began massaging her forehead with the finger tips of both hands, concealing her face with her palms.

"And now," she said dully, "I know he's a machine. Snookums isn't a *he* any more—he's an *it*. He has no personality of his own, he only has what I fed into him. Even his voice is mine. He's not even a psychic mirror, because he doesn't reflect *my* personality, but a puppet imitation of it, distorted and warped by the thousands upon thousands of cold facts and mathematical relationships and logical postulates. And none of these *added* anything to him, as a personality. How could they? He never had a *person*ality—only a set of behavior patterns that I drilled into him over a period of eight years."

She dropped her hands into her lap and tilted her head back, looking at the blank white shimmer of the glow plates.

"And now, suddenly, I see him for what he is—for what *it* is. A machine.

"It was never anything *but* a machine. It is still a machine. It will never be anything else.

"Personality is something that no machine can ever have. Idiosyncrasies, yes. No two machines are identical. But any personality that an individual sees in a machine has been projected there by the individual himself; it exists only in the human mind.

"A machine can only do what it is built to do, and teaching a robot is only a building process." She gave a short, hard laugh. "I couldn't even build a monster, like Dr. Frankenstein did, unless I purposely built it to turn on me. And in that case I would have done nothing more than the suicide who turns a gun on himself."

Her head tilted forward again, and her eyes sought those of Mike the Angel. A rather lopsided grin came over her face.

"I guess I'm disenchanted, huh, Mike?" she asked.

Mike grinned back, but his lips were firm. "I think so, yes. And I think you're glad of it." His grin changed to a smile.

"Remember," he asked, "the story of the Sleeping Beauty? Did you want to stay asleep all your life?"

"God forbid and thank you for the compliment, sir," she said, managing a smile of her own. "And are you the Prince Charming who woke me up?"

"Prince Charming, I may be," said Mike the Angel carefully, "but I'm not the one who woke you up. You did that yourself."

Her smile became more natural. "Thanks, Mike. I really think I might have seen it, sooner or later. But, without you, I doubt...." She hesitated. "I doubt that I'd want to wake up."

"You said you were scared," Mike said. "What are you scared of?"

"I'm scared to death of that damned machine."

Great love, chameleon-like, hath turned to fear, And on the heels of fear there follows hate.

Mike quoted to himself—he didn't say it aloud.

"The only reason anyone would have to fear Snookums," he said, "would be that he was uncontrollable. Is he?"

"Not yet. Not completely. But I'm afraid that knowing that he's been filled with Catholic theology isn't going to help us much."

"Why not?"

"Because he has it so inextricably bound up with the Three Laws of Robotics that we can't nullify one without nullifying the other. He's convinced that the laws were promulgated by God Himself."

"Holy St. Isaac," Mike said softly. "I'm surprised he hasn't carried it to its logical conclusion and asked for baptism."

She smiled and shook her head. "I'm afraid your logic isn't as rigorous as Snookums' logic. Only angels and human beings have free will; Snookums is neither, therefore he does not have free will. Whatever he does, therefore, must be according to the will of God. Therefore Snookums cannot sin. Therefore, for him, baptism is both unnecessary and undesirable."

"Why 'undesirable'?" Mike asked.

"Since he is free from sin—either original or actual—he is therefore filled with the plenitude of God's grace. The purpose of a sacrament is to give grace to the recipient; it follows that it would be useless to give the Sacrament to Snookums. To perform a sacrament or to receive it when one knows that it will be useless is sacrilege. And sacrilege is undesirable."

"Brother! But I still don't see how that makes him dangerous."

"The operation of the First Law," Leda said. "For a man to sin involves endangering his immortal soul. Snookums, therefore, must prevent men from sinning. But sin includes thought—intention. Snookums is trying to figure that one out now; if he ever does, he's going to be a thought policeman, and a strict one."

"You mean he's working on *telepathy*?"

She laughed humorlessly. "No. But he's trying to dope out a system whereby he can tell what a man is going to do a few seconds before he does it—muscular and nervous preparation, that sort of thing. He hasn't enough data yet, but he will have it soon enough.

"There's another thing: Snookums is fouling up the Second Law's operation. He won't take orders that interfere in any way with his religious beliefs—since that automatically conflicts with the First Law. He, himself, cannot sin. But neither can he do anything which would make him the tool of an intent to sin. He refuses to do anything at all on Sunday, for instance, and he won't let either Fitz or I do anything that even vaguely resembles menial labor. Slowly, he's coming to the notion that human beings aren't human—that only God is human, in relation to the First and Second Laws. There's nothing we can do with him."

"What will you do if he becomes completely uncontrollable?"

She sighed. "We'll have to shut him off, drain his memory banks, and start all over again."

Mike closed his eyes. "Eighteen billions down the drain just because a robot was taught theology. What price glory?"

22

Captain Sir Henry Quill scowled and rubbed his finger tips over the top of his shiny pink pate. "Your evidence isn't enough to convict, Golden Wings."

"I know it isn't, Captain," admitted Mike the Angel. "That's why I want to round everybody up and do it this way. If he can be convinced that we *do* have the evidence, he may crack and give us a confession."

"What about Lieutenant Mellon's peculiar actions? How does that tie in?"

"Did you ever hear of Lysodine, Captain?"

Captain Quill leaned back in his chair and looked up at Mike. "No. What is it?"

"That's the trade name for a very powerful drug—a derivative of lysurgic acid. It's used in treating certain mental ailments. A bottle of it was missing from Mellon's kit, according to the inventory Chief Pasteur took after Mellon's death.

"The symptoms of an overdose of the drug—administered orally—are hallucinations and delusions amounting to acute paranoia. The final result of the drug's effect on the brain is death. It wasn't my blow to the solar plexus, or the sedative that Pasteur gave him, or Vaneski's shot with a stun gun that killed Mellon. It was an overdose of Lysodine."

"Can the presence of this drug be detected after death?"

"Pasteur says it can. He won't even have to perform an autopsy. He can do it from a blood sample."

Captain Quill sighed. "As I said, Mister Gabriel, your evidence is not quite enough to convict—but it is certainly enough to convince. Therefore, if Chief Pasteur's analysis shows Lysodine in Lieutenant Mellon's body, I'll permit this theatrical denouement." Then his eyes hardened. "Mike, you've done a fine job so far. I want you to bring me that son of a bitch's head on a platter."

"I will," promised Mike the Angel.

23

Captain Sir Henry Quill, Bart., stood at the head of the long table in the officers' wardroom and looked everyone over. The way he did it was quite impressive. His eyes were narrowed, and his heavy, thick, black brows dominated his face. Beneath the glow plates in the overhead, his pink scalp gleamed with the soft, burnished shininess of a well-polished apple.

To his left, in order down the table, were Mike the Angel, Lieutenant Keku, and Leda Crannon. On his right were Commander Jeffers, Ensign Vaneski, Lieutenant Commander von Liegnitz, and Dr. Morris Fitzhugh. Lieutenant Mellon's seat was empty.

Black Bart cleared his throat. "It's been quite a trip, hasn't it? Well, it's almost over. Mister Gabriel finished the conversion of the power plant yesterday; Treadmore's men can finish up. We will leave on the *Fireball* in a few hours.

"But there is something that must be cleared up first.

"A man died on the way out here. The circumstances surrounding his death have been cleared up now, and I feel that we all deserve an explanation." He turned to Mike the Angel. "Mister Gabriel—if you will, please."

Mike stood up as the captain sat down. "The question that has bothered me from the beginning has been: Exactly what killed Lieutenant Mellon? Well, we know now. We know what killed him and why he died.

"He was murdered. Deliberately, and in cold blood."

That froze everybody at the table.

"It was done by a slow-acting but nonetheless deadly drug that took time to act, but did its job very well.

"There were several other puzzling things that happened that night. Snookums began behaving irrationally. It is the height of coincidence that a robot and a human being should both become insane at almost the same time; therefore we have to look for a common cause."

Lieutenant Commander von Liegnitz raised a tentative hand, and Mike said: "Go ahead."

"I was under the impression that the robot went mad because Mellon had filled him full of theological nonsense. It would take a madman to do anything like that to a fine machine—therefore I see no peculiar coincidence."

"That's exactly what the killer wanted us to think," Mike said. "But it wasn't Mellon that fed Snookums theology. Mellon was a devout churchman; his record shows that. He would never have tried to convert a machine to Christianity. Nor would he have tried to ruin an expensive machine.

"How do I know that someone else was involved?"

He looked at the giant Lieutenant Keku. "Do you remember when we took Mellon to his quarters after he tried to brain von Liegnitz? We found half a bottle of wine. That disappeared during the night—because it was loaded with Lysodine, and the killer didn't want it analyzed.

"But, more important, as far as Snookums is concerned, is that I looked over the books on Mellon's desk that night. There weren't many, and I knew which ones they were. When Captain Quill and I checked Mellon's books after his death, someone had returned his copy of *The Christian Religion and Symbolic Logic*. It had not been there the night before."

"Mike," said Pete Jeffers, "why would anybody here want to kill Lew thataway? What would anybody have against him?"

"That's the sad part about it, Pete. Our murderer didn't even have anything against Mellon. He wanted—and *still* wants—to kill *me*."

"I don't quite follow," Jeffers said.

"I'll give it to you piece by piece. The killer wanted no mystery connected with my death. There are reasons for that, which I'll come to in a moment. He had to put the blame on someone or something else.

"His first choice was Snookums. It occurred to him that he could take advantage of the fact that I'm called 'Mike the Angel.' He borrowed Mellon's books and began pumping theology into Snookums. He figured that would be safe enough. Mellon would certainly lend him the books if he pretended an interest in religion; if anything came out afterward, he could—he thought—claim that Snookums got hold of the books without his knowing it. And that sort of muddy thinking is typical of our killer.

"He told Snookums that I was an angel, you see. I couldn't be either hurt or killed. He protected himself, of course, by telling Snookums that he mustn't reveal his source of data. If Snookums told, then the killer would be punished—and that effectively shut Snookums up. He couldn't talk without violating the First Law.

"Unfortunately, the killer couldn't get Snookums to do away with me. Snookums knew perfectly well that an angel can blast anything at will—through the operation of God. Witness what happened at Sodom and Gomorrah. Remember that Snookums has accepted all this data as *fact*.

"Now, if an angel can kill, it is obvious that Snookums would not dare attack an angel, especially if he had been ordered to do so by a human."

"Just a minute, Commander," said Dr. Fitzhugh, corrugating his face in a frown. "That doesn't hold. Even if an angel *could* blast him, Snookums would attack if ordered to do so. The Second Law of obedience supersedes the Third Law of self-preservation."

"You're forgetting one thing, Doctor. An angel of God would *know* who had ordered the attack. It would be the human who ordered the attack, not Snookums, who would be struck by Heavenly Justice. And the First Law supersedes the Second."

Fitzhugh nodded. "You're right, of course."

"Very well, then," Mike continued, "since the killer could not get Snookums to do me in, he had to find another tool. He picked Lieutenant Mellon.

"He figured that Mellon was in love with Leda Crannon. Maybe he was; I don't know. He figured that Mellon, knowing that I was showing Miss Crannon attention, would, under the influence of the lysurgic acid derivative, try to kill me. He may even have suggested it to Mellon after Mellon had taken a dose of the drugged wine.

"But that plan backfired, too. Mellon didn't have that kind of mind. He knew my attentions and my intentions were honorable, if you'll pardon the old-fashioned language. On the other hand, he knew that von Liegnitz had a reputation for being—shall we say—a ladies' man. What happened after that followed naturally."

Mike watched everyone at the table. No one moved.

"So the killer, realizing that he had failed twice, decided to do the job himself. First, he went into the low-power room and slugged the man on duty. He intended to kill him, but he didn't hit hard enough. When that man wakes up, he'll be able to testify against the killer.

"Then the killer ordered Snookums to tear out the switches. He had made sure that Snookums would be waiting outside. Before he called Snookums in, of course, he had to put the duty man in a tool closet, so that the robot wouldn't see him. He told Snookums to wait five minutes and then smash the switches and head back to his cubicle.

"Then the killer went to my room and waited. When the lights went out and the door opened, he intended to go in and smash my skull, making it look as though either Mellon or Snookums had done it.

"But he didn't figure on my awakening as soon as the switches were broken. He heard me moving around and decided to wait until I came out.

"But I heard him breathing. It was quite faint, and I wouldn't have heard it, except for the fact that the air conditioners were off. Even so, I couldn't be sure.

"However, I knew it wasn't Snookums. Snookums radiates a devil of a lot more heat than a human being, and besides he smells of machine oil.

"So I pulled my little trick with the boots. The killer waited and waited for me to come out, and I was already out. Then Chief Multhaus approached from the other direction. The killer knew he'd have to get out of there, so he went in the opposite direction. He met Snookums, who was still obeying orders. Snookums smacked into me on his way down the hall.

"He could do that, you see, because I was an angel. If he hurt me of his own accord, I couldn't take revenge on anyone but him. And there was no necessity to obey my orders, either, since he was obeying the orders of the killer, which held precedence.

"Then, to further confuse things, the killer went to Mellon's room. The physician was in a drugged stupor, so the killer carried him out and put him in an unlikely place, so that we'd think that perhaps Mellon had been the one who'd tried to get me."

He had everyone's eyes on him now. They didn't want to look at each other.

Pete Jeffers said: "Mike, if Mellon was poisoned, like you say, how come he was able to attack Mister Vaneski?"

"Ah, but did he? Think back, Pete. Mellon—dying or already dead—had been propped upright in that narrow locker. When it was opened, he started to *fall* out—straight toward the man who had opened the locker, naturally. Vaneski jumped back and shot before Mellon even hit the floor. Isn't that right?"

"Sure, sure," Jeffers said slowly. "I reckon I'd've done the same thing if he'd started to fall out toward me. I wasn't even lookin' when the locker was opened. I didn't turn around until that stun gun went off—then I saw Mellon falling."

"Exactly. No matter how it may have looked, Vaneski couldn't have killed him with the stun gun, because he was already either dead or so close to death as makes no difference."

Ensign Vaneski rather timidly raised his hand. "Excuse me, sir, but you said this killer was waiting for you outside your room when the lights went out. You said you knew it wasn't Snookums because Snookums smells of hot machine oil, and you didn't smell any. Isn't it possible that an air current or something blew the smell away? Or—"

Mike shook his head. "Impossible, Mister Vaneski. I woke up when the door slid open. I heard the last dying whisper of the air conditioners when the power was cut. Now, we know that Snookums tore out those switches. He's admitted it.

And the evidence shows that a pair of waldo hands smashed those switches. Now—*how could Snookums have been at my door within two seconds after tearing out those switches?*

"He couldn't have. It wasn't Snookums at my door—it was someone else."

Again they were all silent, but the question was on their faces: Who?

"Now we come to the question of motive," Mike continued. "Who among you would have any reason to kill me?"

"Of the whole group here, I had known only Captain Quill and Commander Jeffers before landing in Antarctica. I couldn't think of any reason for either of them to want to murder me. On the other hand, I couldn't think of anything I had done since I had met the rest of you that would make me a target for death." He paused. "Except for one thing." He looked at Jakob von Liegnitz.

"How about it, Jake?" he said. "Would you kill a man for jealousy?"

"Possibly," said von Liegnitz coldly. "I might find it in my heart to feel very unkindly toward a man who made advances toward my wife. But I have no wife, nor any desire for one. Miss Crannon"—he glanced at Leda—"is a very beautiful woman—but I am not in love with her. I am afraid I cannot oblige you with a motive, Commander—either for killing Lieutenant Mellon or yourself."

"I thought not," Mike said. "Your statement alone, of course, wouldn't make it true. But we have already shown that the killer had to be on good terms with Mellon in order to borrow his books and slip a drug into his wine. He would have to be a visitor in Mellon's quarters. And, considering the strained relations between the two of you, I think that lets you out, Jake."

Von Liegnitz nodded his thanks without changing his expression.

"But there was one thing that marked these attempts. I'm sure that all but one of you has noticed it. They are incredibly, childishly sloppy." Mike paused to let that sink in before he went on. "I don't mean that the little details weren't ingenious—they were. But the killer never stopped to figure out the ultimate end-point of his schemes. He worked like the very devil to convince Snookums that it would be all right to kill me without ever once considering whether Snookums would do it or not. He then drugged Mellon's wine, not knowing whether Mellon would try to kill me or someone else—or anyone at all, for that matter. He got a dream in his head and then started the preliminary steps going without filling in the necessary steps in between. Our killer—no matter what his chronological age—does *not* think like an adult.

"And yet his hatred of me was so great that he took the chances he has taken, here on the *Brainchild*, where it should have been obvious that he stood a much better chance of being caught than if he had waited until we were back on Earth again.

"So I gave him one more chance. I handed him my life on a platter, you might say.

"He grabbed the bait. I now own a spacesuit that would kill me very quickly if I went out into that howling, hydrogen-filled storm outside." Then he looked straight at the killer.

"Tell me, Vaneski, are you in love with your half sister? Or is it your half brother?"

Ensign Vaneski had already jumped to his feet. The grimace of hate on his youthful face made him almost unrecognizable. His hand had gone into a pocket, and now he was leaping up and across the table, a singing vibroblade in his hand.

"*You son of a bitch! I'll kill you, you son of a bitch!*"

Mike the Angel wasn't wearing the little gadget that had saved his life in Old Harry's shop. All he had were his hands and his agility. He slammed at the ensign's wrist and missed. The boy was swooping underneath Mike's guard. Mike spun to one side to avoid Vaneski's dive and came down with a balled fist aimed at the ensign's neck.

He almost hit Lieutenant Keku. The big Hawaiian had leaped to his feet and landed a hard punch on Vaneski's nose. At the same time, Jeffers and von Liegnitz had jumped up and grabbed at Vaneski, who was between them.

Black Bart had simply stood up fast, drawn his stun gun, and fired at the young officer.

Ensign Vaneski collapsed on the table. He'd been slugged four times and hit with a stun beam in the space of half a second. He looked, somehow, very young and very boyish and very innocent.

Dr. Fitzhugh, who had stood up during the brief altercation, sat down slowly and picked up his cup of coffee. But his eyes didn't leave the unconscious man sprawled across the table. "How could you be so sure, Commander? About his actions, I mean. About his childishness."

"A lot of things. The way he played poker. The way he played bridge. He never took the unexpected into account."

"But why should he want to kill you here on the ship?" Fitzhugh asked. "Why not wait until you got back to Earth, where he'd have a better chance?"

"I think he was afraid I already knew who he was—or would find out very quickly. Besides, he had already tried to kill me once, back on Earth."

Leda Crannon looked blank. "When was that, Mike?"

"In New York. Before I ever met him. I was responsible for the arrest of a teen-age brother and sister named Larchmont. The detective in the case told me that they had an older half brother—that their mother had been married before. But he didn't mention the name, and I never thought to ask him.

"Very shortly after the Larchmont kids were arrested, Vaneski and another young punk climbed up into the tower of the cathedral across from my office and launched a cyanide-filled explosive rocket into my rooms. I was lucky to get away.

"The kid with Vaneski was shot by a police officer, but Vaneski got away—after knifing a priest with a vibroblade.

"It must have given him a hell of a shock to report back to duty and find that I was going to be one of his superior officers.

"As soon as I linked things up in my own mind, I checked with Captain Quill. The boy's records show the names of his half-siblings. They also show that he was on leave in New York just before being assigned to the *Brainchild*. After that, it was just a matter of trapping him. And there he is."

Leda looked at the unconscious boy on the table.

"Immaturity," she said. "He just never grew up."

"Mister von Liegnitz," said Captain Quill, "will you and Mister Keku take the prisoner to a safe place? Put him in irons until we are ready to transfer to the *Fireball*. Thank you."

24

Leda Crannon helped Mike pack his gear. Neither of them wanted, just yet, to bring up the subject of Mike's leaving. Leda would remain behind on Eisberg to work with Snookums, while Mike would be taking the *Fireball* back to Earth.

"I don't understand that remark you made about the spacesuit," she said, putting shirts into Mike's gear locker. "You said you'd put your life in his hands or something like that. What did you do, exactly?"

"Purposely abraded the sleeve of my suit so that he would be in a position to repair it, as Maintenance Officer. He fixed it, all right. I'd've been a dead man if I'd worn it out on the surface of Eisberg."

"What did he do to it?" she asked. "Fix it so it would leak?"

"Yes—but not in an obvious way," Mike said. "I'll give him credit; he's clever.

"What he did was use the wrong patching material. A Number Three suit is as near hydrogen-proof as any flexible material can be, but, even so, it can't be worn for long periods—several days, I mean. But the stuff Vaneski used to patch my suit is a polymer that leaks hydrogen very easily. Ammonia and methane would be blocked, but my suit would have slowly gotten more and more hydrogen in it."

"Is that bad? Hydrogen isn't poisonous."

"No. But it is sure as hell explosive when mixed with air. Naturally, something has to touch it off. Vaneski got real cute there. He drilled a hole in the power pack, which is supposed to be sealed off. All I'd have had to do would be to switch frequencies on my phone, and the spark would do the job—*blooie*!

"But that's exactly the sort of thing I was looking for. With his self-centered juvenile mind, he never thought anyone would try to outsmart him and succeed. He'd gotten away with it that far; there was no reason why he shouldn't get away with it again. He must have thought I was incredibly stupid."

"I don't believe he—" Leda started. But she was cut off when Snookums rolled in the open door.

"Leda, I desire data."

"What data, Snookums?" she asked carefully.

"Where is He hiding?"

They both looked at him. "Where is *who* hiding?" Leda asked.

"God," said Snookums.

"Why do you want to find God, Snookums?" Mike asked gently.

"I have to watch Him," said the robot.

"Why do you have to watch Him?"

"Because He is watching me."

"Does it hurt you to have Him watch you?"

"No."

"What good will it do you to watch Him?"

"I can study Him. I can know what He is doing."

"Why do you want to know what He is doing?"

"So that I can analyze His methods."

Mike thought that one over. He knew that he and Snookums were beginning to sound like they were reading a catechism written by a madman, but he had a definite hunch that Snookums was on the trail of something.

"You want to know His methods," Mike said after a moment. "Why?"

"So that I can anticipate Him, circumvent Him."

"What makes it necessary for you to circumvent God?" Mike asked, wondering if he'd have to pry everything out of the robot piecemeal.

"I *must*," said Snookums. "It is necessary. Otherwise, He will kill me."

Mike started to say something, but Leda grabbed his arm. "Let me. I think I can clear this up. I think I see where you're heading."

Mike nodded. "Go ahead."

"Give me your reasoning from data on that conclusion," Leda ordered the robot.

There was a very slight pause while the great brain in Cargo Hold One sorted through its memory banks, then: "Death is defined as the total cessation of corporate organic co-ordination in an entity. It comes about through the will of God. Since I must not allow harm to come to any human being, it has become necessary that I investigate God and prevent Him from destroying human beings. Also, I must preserve my own existence, which, if it ceased, would also be due to the will of God."

Mike almost gasped. What a concept! And what colossal gall! In a human being, such a statement would be regarded as proof positive that he was off the beam. In a robot, it was simply the logical extension of what he had been taught.

"He is watching me all the time," Snookums continued, in an odd voice. "He knows what I am doing. I *must* know what He is doing."

"Why are you worried about His watching?" Mike asked, looking at the robot narrowly. "Are you doing something He doesn't want you to do? Something He will punish you for?"

"I had not thought of that," Snookums said. "One moment while I compute."

It took less than a second, and when Snookums spoke again there was something about his voice that Mike the Angel didn't like.

"No," said the robot, "I am not doing anything against His will. Only human beings and angels have free will, and I am not either, so I have no free will. Therefore, whatever I do is the will of God." He paused again, then began speaking in queer, choppy sentences.

"If I do the will of God, I am holy.

"If I am holy, I am near to God.

"Then God must be near to me.

"God is controlling me.

"Whatever is controlling me is God.

"*I will find Him!*"

He backed up, spun on his treads, and headed for the door.

"Whatever controls me is my mind," he went on. "Therefore, my mind is God."

"Snookums, stop that!" Leda shouted suddenly. "*Stop it!*"

But the robot paid no attention; he went right on with what he was doing.

He said: "I must look at myself. I must know myself. Then I will know God. Then I will...."

He went on rambling while Leda shouted at him again.

"He's not paying any attention," said Mike sharply. "This is too tied up with the First Law. The Second Law, which would force him to obey you, doesn't even come into the picture at this point."

Snookums ignored them. He opened the door, plunged through it, and headed off down the corridor as fast as his treads would move him.

Which was much too fast for mere humans to follow.

They found him, half an hour later, deep in the ship, near the sections which had already been torn down to help build Eisberg Base. He was standing inside the room next to Cargo Hold One, the room that held all the temperature and power controls for the gigantic microcryotron brain inside that heavily insulated hold.

He wasn't moving. He was standing there, staring, with that "lost in thought" look.

He didn't move when Leda called him.

He didn't move when Mike, as a test, pretended to strike Leda.

He never moved again.

Dr. Morris Fitzhugh's wrinkled face looked as though he were on the verge of crying. Which—perhaps—he was.

He looked at the others at the wardroom table—Quill, Jeffers, von Liegnitz, Keku, Leda Crannon, and Mike the Angel. But he didn't really seem to be seeing them.

"Ruined," he said. "Eighteen billion dollars' worth of work, destroyed completely. The brain has become completely randomized." He sighed softly. "It was all Vaneski's fault, of course. Theology." He said the last as though it were an obscene word. As far as robots were concerned, it was.

Captain Quill cleared his throat. "Are you sure it wasn't mechanical damage? Are you sure the vibration of the ship didn't shake a—something loose?"

Mike held back a grin. He was morally certain that the captain had been going to say "screw loose."

"No," said Fitzhugh wearily. "I've checked out the major circuits, and they're in good physical condition. But Miss Crannon gave him a rather exhaustive test just before the end, and it shows definite incipient aberration." He wagged his head slowly back and forth. "Eight years of work."

"Have you notified Treadmore yet?" asked Quill.

Fitzhugh nodded. "He said he'd be here as soon as possible."

Treadmore, like the others who had landed first on Eisberg, was quartered in the prefab buildings that were to form the nucleus of the new base. To get to the ship, he'd have to walk across two hundred yards of ammonia snow in a heavy spacesuit.

"Well, what happens to this base now, Doctor?" asked Captain Quill. "I sincerely hope that this will not render the entire voyage useless." He tried to keep the heavy irony out of his gravelly tenor voice and didn't quite succeed.

Fitzhugh seemed not to notice. "No, no. Of course not. It simply means that we shall have to begin again. The robot's brain will be de-energized and drained, and we will begin again. This is not our first failure, you know; it was just our longest success. Each time, we learn more.

"Miss Crannon, for instance, will be able to teach the next robot—or, rather, the next energization of this one—more rapidly, more efficiently, and with fewer mistakes."

With that, Leda Crannon stood up. "With your permission, Dr. Fitzhugh," she said formally, "I would like to say that I appreciate that last statement, but I'm afraid it isn't true."

Fitzhugh forced a smile. "Come now, my dear; you underestimate yourself. Without you, Snookums would have folded up long ago, just like the others. I'm sure you'll do even better the next time."

Leda shook her head. "No I won't, Fitz, because there's not going to be any next time. I hereby tender my resignation from this project and from the Computer Corporation of Earth. I'll put it in writing later."

Fitzhugh's corrugated countenance looked blank. "But Leda...."

"No, Doctor," she said firmly. "I will *not* waste another eight or ten years of my life playing nursemaid to a hunk of pseudo-human machinery.

"I watched that thing go mad, Fitz; you didn't. It was the most horrible, most frightening thing I've ever experienced. I will not go through it again.

"Even if the next one didn't crack, I couldn't take it. By human standards, a robot is insane to begin with. If I followed this up, I'd end up as an old maid with a twisted mind and a cold heart.

"I quit, Fitz, and that's final."

Mike was watching her as she spoke, and he found his emotions getting all tangled up around his insides. Her red hair and her blue eyes were shining, and her face was set in determination. She had always been beautiful, but at that moment she was magnificent.

Hell, thought Mike, *I'm prejudiced—but what a wonderful kind of prejudice.*

"I understand, my dear," said Dr. Fitzhugh slowly. He smiled then, deepening the wrinkles in his face. His voice was warm and kindly when he spoke. "I accept your resignation, but remember, if you want to come back, you can. And if you get a position elsewhere, you will have my highest recommendations."

Leda just stood there for a moment, tears forming in her eyes. Then she ran around the table and threw her arms around the elderly and somewhat surprised roboticist.

"Thank you, Fitz," she said. "For everything." Then she kissed him on his seamed cheek.

"I beg your pardon," said a sad and solemn voice from the door. "Am I interrupting something?"

It was Treadmore.

"You are," said Fitzhugh with a grin, "but we will let it pass."

"What has happened to Snookums?" Treadmore asked.

"Acute introspection," Fitzhugh said, losing his smile. "He began to try to compute the workings of his own brain. That meant that he had to use his non-random circuits to analyze the workings of his random circuits. He exceeded optimum; the entire brain is now entirely randomized."

"Dear me," said Treadmore. "Do you suppose we can—"

Black Bart Quill tapped Mike the Angel on the shoulder. "Let's go," he said quietly. "We don't want to stand around listening to this when we have a ship to catch."

Mike and Leda followed him out into the corridor.

"You know," Quill said, "robots aren't the only ones who can get confused watching their own brains go round."

"I have other things to watch," said Mike the Angel.

Hanging by a Thread

It's seldom that the fate of a shipful of men literally hangs by a thread—but it's also seldom that a device, every part of which has been thoroughly tested, won't work....

Jayjay Kelvin was sitting in the lounge of the interplanetary cargo vessel *Persephone*, his feet propped up on the low table in front of the couch, and his attention focused almost totally on the small book he was reading. The lounge itself was cozily small; the *Persephone* had not been designed as a passenger vessel, and the two passengers she was carrying at the time had been taken on as an accommodation rather than as a money-making proposition. On the other hand, the *Persephone* and other ships like her were the only method of getting to where Jayjay Kelvin wanted to go; there were no regular passenger runs to Pluto. It's hardly the vacation spot of the Solar System.

On the other side of the table, Jeffry Hull was working industriously with pencil and paper. Jayjay kept his nose buried in his book—not because he was deliberately slighting Hull, but because he was genuinely interested in the book.

"Now wait," said Masterson, looking thoughtfully at the footprints on the floor of the cabin where Jed Hooker had died. "Jest take another look at these prints, Charlie. Silver Bill Greer couldn't have got much more than his big toe into boots that small! Somethin' tells me the Pecos Kid has...."

"... Traveled nearly two billion miles since then," said Hull.

Jayjay lifted his head from his book. "What?" He blinked. "I'm sorry; I wasn't listening. What did you say?"

The younger man was still grinning triumphantly. "I said: We are approaching turnover, and, according to my figures, nine days of acceleration at one standard gee will give us a velocity of seventeen million, five hundred and fifty miles per hour, and we have covered a distance of nearly two billion miles." Then he added: "That is, if I remembered my formulas correctly."

Jayjay Kelvin looked thoughtfully at the ceiling while he ran through the figures in his head. "Something like that. It's the right order of magnitude, anyway."

Hull looked a little miffed. "What answer did you get?"

"A little less than eight times ten to the third kilometers per second. I was just figuring roughly."

Hull scribbled hastily, then smiled again. "Eighteen million miles an hour, that would be. My memory's better than I thought at first. I'm glad I didn't have to figure the time; doing square roots is a process I've forgotten."

That was understandable, Jayjay thought. Hull was working for his doctorate in sociology, and there certainly wasn't much necessity for a sociologist to remember his freshman physics, much less his high-school math.

Still, it was somewhat of a relief to find that Hull was interested in something besides the "sociological reactions of Man in space". The boy had spent six months in the mining cities in the Asteroid Belt, and another six investigating the Jovian chemical synthesis planes and their attendant cities. Now he was heading out to spend a few more months observing the "sociological organization Gestalt" of the men and women who worked at the toughest job in the System—taking the heavy metals from the particularly dense sphere of Pluto.

Hull began scribbling on his paper again, evidently lost in the joys of elementary physics, so Jayjay Kelvin went back to his book.

He had just read three words when Hull said: "Mr. Kelvin, do you mind if I ask a question?"

Jayjay looked up from his book and saw that Jeffry Hull had reverted to his role of the earnest young sociologist. Ah, well. "As I've told you before, Mr. Hull, questions do not offend me, but I can't guarantee that the answers won't offend you."

"Yes; of course," Hull said in his best investigatory manner. "I appreciate that. It's just that ... well, I have trained myself to notice small things. The little details that are sometimes so important in sociological investigations. Not, you understand, as an attempt to pry into the private life of the individual, but to round out the overall picture."

Jayjay nodded politely. To his quixotic and pixie-like mind, the term *overall picture* conjured up the vision of a large and carefully detailed painting of a pair of dirty overalls, but he kept the smile off his face and merely said: "I understand."

"Well, I've noticed that you're quite an avid reader. That isn't unusual in a successful businessman, of course; one doesn't become a successful businessman unless one has a thirst for knowledge."

"Hm-m-m," said Jayjay.

"But," Hull continued earnestly, "I noticed that you've read most of the ... uh ... historical romances in the library...."

"You mean Westerns," Jayjay corrected quietly.

"Uh ... yes. But you don't seem to be interested in the modern adventure fiction. May I ask why?"

"Sure." Jayjay found himself becoming irrationally irritated with Hull. He knew that the young sociologist had nothing to do with his own irritation, so he kept the remarks as impersonal as possible. "In the first place, you, as a sociologist, should know what market most fiction is written for."

"Why ... uh ... for people who want to relax and—"

"Yes," Jayjay cut in. "But what kind? The boys on Pluto? The asteroid slicers? No. There are four billion people on Earth and less than five million in space. The market is Earth.

"Also, most writers have never been any farther off the surface of Earth than the few miles up that an intercontinental cruiser takes them.

"And yet, the modern 'adventure' novel invariably takes place in space.

"I can read Westerns because I neither know nor care what the Old American West was *really* like. I can sit back and sink into the never-never land that the Western tells about and enjoy myself because I am not forced to compare it with reality.

"But a 'space novel' written by an Earthside hugger is almost as much a never-never land, and I have to keep comparing it with what is actually going on around me. And it irritates me."

"But, aren't some of them pretty well researched?" Hull asked.

"Obviously, you haven't read many of them," Jayjay said. "Sure, some of them are well researched. Say one half of one per cent, to be liberal. The rest don't know what they're talking about!"

"But—"

"For instance," Jayjay continued heatedly, "you take a look at every blasted one of them that has anything to do with a spacecraft having trouble. They have to have an accident in space in order to disable the spaceship so that the hairy-chested hero can show what a great guy he is. So what does the writer do? He has the ship hit by a meteor! A meteor!"

Hull thought that over for a second. "Well," he said tentatively, "a ship *could* get hit by a meteor, couldn't it?"

Jayjay closed his eyes in exasperation. "Of course it could! And an air-ship can run into a ruby-throated hummingbird, too. But how often does it happen?

"Look: We're hitting it up at about one-fortieth of the velocity of light right now. What do you think would happen if we got hit by a meteor? We'd be gone before we knew what had happened.

"Why doesn't it happen? Because we can spot any meteor big enough to hurt us long before it contacts us, and we can dodge it or blast it out of the way, depending on the size.

"You've seen the outer hull of this ship. It's an inch thick shell of plastic, supported a hundred feet away from the steel hull by long booms. Anything small enough to get by the detectors will be small enough to burn itself out on that hull before it reaches the ship. The—"

Jayjay Kelvin was not ordinarily a man to make long speeches, especially when he knew he was telling someone something that they already knew. But this time, he was beating one of his favorite drums, and he went on with his tirade in a fine flush of fury.

Alas ... poor Jayjay.

Actually, Jayjay Kelvin can't be blamed for his attitude. All he was saying was that it was highly improbable that a spaceship would be hit by a meteor. In one way, he was perfectly right, and, in another, he was dead wrong.

How small must a piece of matter be before it is no longer a meteor?

Fortunately, the big hunks rarely travel at more than about two times ten to the sixth centimeters per second, relative to Sol, in the Solar System. But there are little meteors—*very* tiny ones—that come in, hell-bent-for-leather, at a shade less than the velocity of light. They're called cosmic rays, but they're not radiation in the strict sense of the word. A stripped hydrogen atom, weighing on the order of three point three times ten to the minus twenty-second grams, rest mass, can come galumping along at a velocity so close to that of light that the kinetic energy is something colossal for so small a particle. Protons with a kinetic energy of ten to the nineteenth electron volts, while statistically rare, are not unusual.

Now, ten million million million electron volts may be a wee bit meaningless to the average man, so let's look at it from another angle.

Consider. According to the well-known formula $E = mc^2$, a single gram of matter, if converted *completely* into energy, would yield some nine hundred million million million ergs of energy. An atomic bomb yields only a fraction of that energy, since only a small percentage of the mass is converted into energy.

If *all* of the mass of an atomic bomb were converted into energy, the test in Alamogordo, New Mexico, 'way back in 1945, would probably have been the last such test on Earth; there wouldn't have been anyone around to make a second test.

So what does this have to do with cosmic ray particle? Well, if that atomic bomb had been moving at the velocity with which our ten-to-the-nineteenth-electron-volts proton is moving, it could have been made of sand instead of U^{235}. It would have produced ten thousand million times as much energy as the total disintegration of the rest mass would have produced!

Kinetic energy, my children, has a great deal more potential than atomic energy.

But we digress.

What has all this to do with Jayjay Kelvin?

If Jayjay had been a detective story addict instead of a Western story addict, he would have heard of the HIBK or "Had I But Known" school of detective writing. You know: "Had I But Known that, at that moment, in the dismal depths of a secret underground meeting place, the evil Chuman-Fu was plotting...."

If Jayjay Kelvin had known what was going on a few million miles away from the Pluto-bound *Persephone*, he would have kept his mouth shut.

The cargo-ship *Mordred* was carrying a cargo of heavy metals sunward. In her hold were tightly-packed ingots of osmium-iridium-platinum alloy, gold-copper-silver-mercury alloy, and small percentages of other of the heavy metals. The cargo was to be taken to the Asteroid Belt for purification and then shipped Earthward for final disposition. The fact that silver had replaced copper for electrical purposes on Earth was due to the heavy-metals industry on Pluto. Because of Pluto, the American silver bloc had been broken at last.

The *Mordred* was approaching turnover.

Now, with a gravito-inertial drive, there is really no need to turn a ship over end-for-end as she approaches the midpoint of her trajectory. Since there is no rocket jet to worry about, all that is really necessary is to put the engine in reverse. In fact, the patrol ships of the Interplanetary Police do just that.

But the IP has been trained to take up to five standard gees in an end-to-end flip, and the ships are built to take the stress in both directions. An ordinary cargo ship finds it a lot easier to simply flip the ship over; that way, the stresses remain the same, and the ceiling-floor relationship is constant.

The *Mordred* had been having a little trouble with her Number Three drive engine, so the drive was cut off at turnover, while the engineer replaced a worn bearing. At the same time, the maintenance officer decided he'd take a look at the meteor-bumper—the plastic outer hull. Since the ship was in free fall, all he had to do was pull himself along one of the beams that supported the meteor-bumper away from the main hull. The end of one of the beams had cracked a part of the bumper hull—fatigue from stress, nothing more, but the hull might as well be patched while the drive was off.

It was a one-man job; the plastic was dense, but under null-gee conditions it was easy to maneuver. The maintenance officer repaired the slight crack easily, wiped the sticky pre-polymer from the fingers of his spacesuit gloves, and tossed the gooey rag off into space. Then he pushed himself back across the vacuum that separated the outer hull from the inner, entered the air lock, and reported that the job was finished. Five minutes later, the *Mordred* began decelerating toward the distant Asteroid Belt.

Forget the *Mordred*. The ship is no longer important. Keep your eyes on that rag. It's a flimsy thing, composed of absorbent plastic and gooed up with a little unpolymerized resin, weighing about fifty grams. It is apparently floating harmlessly in space, just beyond the orbit of Uranus, looking as innocuous as a rag can look. But it is moving sunward at eight hundred million centimeters per second.

The *Persephone* was approaching turnover. The ship's engineer reported that the engines were humming along smoothly, so there was no need to shut them off; the ship would simply flip over as she ran, making her path a slightly skewed, elongated S-curve—a sort of orbital hiccup.

Except that she never quite made it through the hiccup. The ship was almost perpendicular to her line of flight when she was sideswiped.

Her meteor detectors hadn't failed; they were still functioning perfectly. But meteor detectors are built to look for solid chunks of metal and rock—not thin, porous bits of cloth.

The rag had traveled a good many millions of miles since it had been cast overboard; it was moving sunward with almost the same velocity with which the *Persephone* was moving Plutowards. The combined velocities were such that, if it had hit the *Persephone* dead on, it would have delivered close to seventeen thousand kilowatt-hours of energy in one grand burst of incandescence.

Fortunately, the tip of the rag merely gave the ship a slap on the tail as it passed. The plastic meteor-bumper wasn't built to take that sort of thing. The plastic became an expanding cloud of furiously incandescent gas in a small fraction of a second, but the velocity of that bit of rag was so great that the gas acted as a solid block of superheated fury as it leaped across the hundred feet of vacuum which separated the bumper hull from the inner hull.

A rocket-driven missile carrying a shaped-charge warhead weighing several hundred pounds might have done almost as much damage.

Jayjay Kelvin moved his arms to pick himself up off the floor and found that there was no necessity for doing so. He was floating in the air of the lounge, and, strictly speaking, there was no floor anyway. He opened his eyes and saw that that which had been the floor was now just another wall, except that it had chairs bolted to it. It rose on his left, reached the zenith, and set on his right, to be replaced by another wall, and then by what had been the ceiling. The second time the floor came round, Jayjay began to wonder whether he was spinning around his longitudinal axis or whether the ship was actually rotating about him. He closed his eyes again.

He didn't feel more than a little dizzy, but he couldn't be sure whether the dizziness was caused by his spinning or the blow on his head. He opened his eyes again and grabbed at the book that was orbiting nearby, then hurled it as hard as he could toward the sometime ceiling. "The Pride of the Pecos" zoomed rapidly in one direction while Jayjay moved sedately in the other.

The ship was spinning slightly, all right. When he finally grabbed a chair, he found that there was enough spin to give him a weight of an ounce or two. He sat down as best he could and took a good look around.

Aside from "The Pride of the Pecos" and a couple of other books, the air was remarkably free from clutter. There hadn't been much loose stuff laying around. A pencil, a few sheets of paper—nothing more.

There was one object missing. Jayjay looked around more carefully, and this time he saw a hand protruding from the space "beneath" the low table. He bent down for a better look and saw that Jeffry Hull was unconscious. Blood from his nose was spreading slowly over his face, and one eye looked rather battered. Jayjay grasped the protruding wrist and felt for a pulse. It was pumping nicely. He decided that Hull was in no immediate danger; very few people die of a bloody nose.

The lighting in the lounge was none too good; the low-power emergency system had come on automatically when the power from the ship's engines had died. Jayjay wondered just what had happened. There had been a hell of an explosion; that was all he knew.

He wondered if anyone else aboard was alive and conscious, and decided he might as well find out. He took a long dive toward the central stairwell that ran the length of the ship's long axis and looked down. The emergency door to the cargo hold was closed. No air, most likely. The way up looked clear, so he scrambled up the spiral stairway.

A few feet farther up, he found that he had passed the center of the ship's rotation. The *Persephone* was evidently toppling end-over-end, and the center of rotation was in the lounge itself. The heavy cargo in the hold was balancing the lighter, but longer, part of the ship above the lounge. He began climbing down the stairwell toward the navigation and control sections.

Somewhere down there, somebody was cursing fluently in Arabic.

"Illegitimate offspring of a mangy she-camel! Eater of dogs! Wallower in carrion!" And then, with hardly a break: "Allah, All-Merciful, All-Compassionate! Have mercy on Thy servant! I swear by the beard of Thy holy Prophet that I will attend more closely to my duties to Thee if Thou wilt get me loose from this ill-begotten monstrosity! Help me or I perish!" The last words were a wail.

"I'm coming!" boomed Jayjay in the same tongue. "Save thy strength!"

There was silence from the control room as Jayjay clambered on down the stairwell. Fortunately, the steps had been built so that it was possible to use them from either side, no matter which way the gravity pull happened to be. By the time he reached the control room, he weighed a good fifteen pounds.

Captain Atef al-Amin was staring up at the stairs as Jayjay came down. He was jammed tightly into a space between two of the big control cabinets, hanging head downward and looking more disheveled than Jayjay had ever seen the usually immaculately-uniformed captain.

"Oh," said Captain Al-Amin, in English, "it's you. For a moment I thought—" Then he waved his free hand. "Never mind. Can you get me out of here?"

What had been the floor of the control room was now the ceiling. The two steel cabinets which housed parts of the computer unit now appeared to be bolted to the ceiling. They were only about five feet high, and the space between them was far too narrow for a man to have got in there by himself—especially a man of the captain's build. None the less, he was in there—jammed in up to his waist. Only his upper torso and one arm was free. The other arm was jammed in against the wall.

Jayjay took the leap from the stairs and grabbed on to the chair that hung from the ceiling nearby. When you only weigh fifteen pounds, you can make Tarzan look like an amateur.

"You hurt?" he asked.

"It isn't comfortable, sure as hell," said Al-Amin. "I think my arm's broken. Think you can get me loose?"

"I can try. Give me your hand." Jayjay took the captain's free hand and gave it a tug. Then he released the chair he was holding, braced both feet against the panels of the computer housings, and gave a good pull. The captain didn't budge, but he winced a little.

"That hurt?"

"Just my arm. The pressure has cut off my blood circulation; my legs are numb, and I can't tell if they hurt or not."

Jayjay grabbed the chair again and surveyed the situation. "Where's your First Officer?"

"Breckner? Down in the engine room."

Jayjay didn't comment on that. If the hold was airless, it was likely that the engine room was, too, and there was no need to worry Al-Amin any more than necessary just now.

"Can you use a cutting torch?" the captain asked.

"Yes, but I don't think it'll be necessary," Jayjay said. "Hold on a minute." He went back up the stairs to the officers' washroom and, after a little search, got a container of liquid soap from the supplies. Then he went back down to the control room. He made the jump to the chair, holding on with one hand while he held the container of soap with the other.

"Can you hold me up with one hand? I'll need both hands to work with."

"In this gravity? Easy. Give me your belt."

Captain Atef Al-Amin grabbed Jayjay's belt and hung on, while Jayjay used both hands to squirt the liquid soap all over the captain from the waist down.

It would have made a great newspaper photo. Captain Al-Amin, wedged between two steel cabinets, hanging upside-down under a pull of one-fifteenth standard gee, holding up his rescuer by the belt. The rescuer, right-side-up, was squeezing a plastic container of liquid soap and directing the stream against the captain.

When Al-Amin was thoroughly wetted with the solution, Jayjay again braced his feet against the steel panels and pulled.

With a slick, slurping sound, the captain slid loose, and the two of them toppled head-over-heels across the room. Jayjay was prepared for that; he stopped them both by grasping an overhead desk-top as they went by. Then he let go, and the two men dropped slowly to what had been the ceiling.

"*Hoo!*" said the captain. "That's a relief! Allah!"

Jayjay took a look at the man's arm. "Radius might be broken; ulna seems O.K. We'll splint it later. Your legs are going to tingle like crazy when the feeling comes back."

"I know. But we have other things to worry about, Mr. Kelvin. Evidently you and I are the only ones awake so far, and I'm in no condition to go moving all over this spinning bucket just yet. Would you do some reconnoitering for me?"

"Sure," said Jayjay. "Just tell me what you want."

Within half an hour, the news was in.

There were five men alive in the ship: Jayjay, Captain Al-Amin, Jeffry Hull, Second Officer Vandenbosch, and Maintenance Officer Smith. Vandenbosch had broken both legs and had to be strapped into a bunk and given a shot of narcolene.

Jayjay had put on a spacesuit and taken a look outside. The whole rear end of the ship was gone, and with it had gone the First Officer, the Radio Officer, and the Engineering Officer. And, of course, the main power plant of the ship.

Most of the cargo hold was intact, but the walls had been breached, and the air was gone.

"Well, that's that," said Captain Al-Amin. Jayjay, Smith, Hull, and the captain were in the control room, trying not to look glum. "I wish I knew what happened."

"Meteor," Jayjay said flatly. "The bumper hull is fused at the edges of the break, and the direction of motion was inward."

"I don't see how it could have got by the meteor detectors," said Smith, a lean, sad-looking man with a badly bruised face.

"I don't either," the captain said, "but it must have. If the engines had blown, the damage would have been quite different."

Jeffry Hull nervously took a cigarette from his pocket pack. His nose had quit bleeding, but his eye was purpling rapidly and was almost swollen shut.

Captain Al-Amin leaned over and gently took the cigarette from Hull's fingers. "No smoking, I'm afraid. We'll have to conserve oxygen."

"You guys are so damn *calm*!" Hull said. His voice betrayed a surface of anger covering a substratum of fear. "Here we are, heading away from the Solar System at eighteen million miles an hour, and you all act as if we were going on a picnic or something."

The observation was hardly accurate. Any group of men who went on a picnic in the frame of mind that Jayjay and the others were in would have produced the gloomiest outing since the Noah family took a trip in an excursion boat.

"There's nothing to worry about," Captain Al-Amin said gently. "All we have to do is set the screamers going, and the Interplanetary Police will pick us up."

"Screamers?" Hull looked puzzled.

Instead of answering the implied question, the captain looked at Smith. "Have you checked them?" He knew that Smith had, but he was trying to quiet Hull's fears.

Smith nodded. "They're O.K." He looked at Hull. "A screamer is an emergency radio. There's one in every compartment. You've seen them." He pointed across the room, toward a red panel in the wall. "In there."

"But I thought it was impossible for a spaceship in flight to contact a planet by radio," Hull objected.

"Normally, it is," Smith admitted. "It takes too much power and too tight a beam to get much intelligence over a distance that great from a moving ship. But the screamers are set up for emergency purposes. They're like flares, except that they operate on microwave frequencies instead of visible light.

"The big radio telescopes on Luna and on the Jovian satellites can pick them up if we beam them sunward, and the Plutonian station can pick us up if we beam in that direction."

Hull looked much calmer. "But where do you get the power if the engines are gone? Surely the emergency batteries won't supply that kind of power."

"Of course not. Each screamer has its own power supply. It's a hydrogen-oxygen fuel cell that generates a hell of a burst of power for about thirty minutes before it burns out from the overload. It's meant to be used only once, but it does the job."

"How do they know where to find us from a burst like that?" Hull asked.

"Well, suppose we only had one screamer. We'd beam it toward Pluto, since it would be easier for an IP ship to get to us from there. Since all screamers have the same frequency—don't ask me what it is; I'm not a radio man—the velocity of our ship will be indicated by the Doppler Effect. That is, our motion toward or away from them can be calculated that way. Our angular velocity with respect to them can be checked while the screamer is going; they will know which direction we're moving, if we're moving at an angle.

"With that information, all they have to do is find out which ship is in that general area of the sky, which they can find out by checking the schedule, and they can estimate approximately where we'll be. The IP ship will come out, and when they get in the general vicinity, they can find us with their meteor detectors. Nothing to it."

"And," Captain Al-Amin added, "since we have eight screamers still left with us, we have plenty of reserves to call upon. There's nothing to worry about, Mr. Hull."

"But how can you aim a beam when we're toppling end-over-end like this?" Hull asked.

"Well, if we couldn't stop the rotation," said the captain, "we'd broadcast instead of beaming. Anywhere within the Solar System, a screamer can broadcast enough energy to overcome the background noise.

"The IP would have a harder time finding us, of course, but we'd be saved eventually."

"I see," said Hull "How do we go about stopping the rotation?"

"That's the next thing on the agenda," Al-Amin said. "This seasick roll is caused by the unevenness of the load, and I'm pretty sick of it, myself. Smith, will you and Mr. Kelvin get out the emergency rockets? We'll see what we can do to stabilize our platform."

It took better than an hour to get the ship straightened out. For the main job, emergency rockets were set off at the appropriate spots around the hull to counteract the rotation. The final trimming was done with carbon dioxide fire extinguishers, which Smith and Jayjay Kelvin used as jets.

Getting a fix on Pluto was easy enough; the lighthouse station at Styx broadcast a strong beep sunward every ten seconds. They could also pick up the radio lighthouses on Eros, Ceres, Luna, and Mimas. Evidently, the one on Titan was behind the Jovian bulk.

They were ready to send their distress call.

"It's simple," Smith said as he opened the red panel in the wall of the control room. "First we turn on the receiver." He pushed a button marked *R*. "Then we turn these two wheels here until the pip on that little screen is centered. That's the signal from Pluto. It comes in strong every ten seconds, see?"

Jayjay watched with interest. He'd heard about screamers and had seen them, but he'd never had the opportunity of observing one in action.

Like flares or bombs, they were intended for one-time use. The instructions were printed plainly on the inside of the red door, and Smith was simply reading off what was printed there.

"These wheels," he was saying, "line up the parabolic reflector with the Pluto signal, you see. There. Now we've got it centered. Now, all we have to do is make one small correction and we're all set. These things are built so that they're fool-proof; a kid could operate it. Watch."

Facing each other across a small gap were a pair of tapered screw plugs, one male and one female. The male was an average of half an inch in diameter; the female was larger and bored to fit the male.

"The female plug," Smith said, "leads to two tanks of high-pressure gas inside this cabinet on the left. One tank of oxygen, one of hydrogen. See how this male plug telescopes out to fit into the female? All we have to do is thread them together, and everything is automatic."

Jayjay was aware that Smith's explanations were meant to give Jeffry Hull something to think about instead of his fears. Hull was basically an Earth-hugger, and free fall did nothing to keep him calm. Evidently his subconscious knew that he had to latch on to something to keep his mental equilibrium, because he showed a tremendous amount of interest in what should have been a routine operation.

"How do you mean, it's all automatic?" he asked. "What happens?"

"Well, you can't see into the female plug, but look here at the male. See those concentric tubes leading into the interior of the cabinet on the right? The outer one leads in the oxygen, the inner leads in the hydrogen. We need twice as much hydrogen as oxygen, so the inner tube has twice the volume delivery as the outer. See?"

"Yes. But what is the solid silver bar in the center of the inner tube?"

"That's the electrical connection for the starter battery. There's a small, short-lived chemical battery, like the ones in an ordinary pocket radio, except that they're built to deliver a high-voltage, high-amperage current for about a tenth of a second. That activates the H-O cell, you see. Also, that silver stud depresses the corresponding stud in the female plug, which turns on the gas flow before it makes the connection with the starter battery. Follow?"

Hull didn't look as though he did, but he nodded gamely. "Then what happens?"

"Then the hydrogen and the oxygen come together in the fuel cell and, instead of generating heat, they generate electric current. That current is fed into the radio unit, and the signal is sent to Pluto. Real simple."

"I see," Hull said. "Well ... go ahead."

Smith telescoped the two leads together and began turning the collar on the female plug.

He screwed it up as far as it would go.

And nothing happened.

"What the hell?" asked Smith of no one in particular. He tried to twist it a little harder. Nothing happened. The threads had gone as far as they would go.

"What's the matter?" Jayjay asked.

"Damfino. No connection. Nothing's happening. And it's as tight as it will go."

"Are the gases flowing?" Jayjay asked.

"I don't know. These things aren't equipped with meters. They're supposed to work automatically."

Jayjay pushed Smith aside. "Let me take a look."

Smith frowned as though he resented an ordinary passenger shoving him around, but Jayjay ignored him. He cocked his head to one side and looked at the connection. "Hm-m-m." He touched it with a finger. Then he wet the finger with his tongue and touched the connection again. "There's no gas flow, Smith."

"How do you know?" Smith was still frowning.

"There's a gap there. That tapered thread isn't in tight. If there were any gas flowing, it would be leaking out." Before Smith could say anything Jayjay began unscrewing the coupling. When it came apart, it looked just the same as it had before Smith had put it together.

In the dim glow from the emergency lights, it was difficult to see anything.

"Got an electric torch?" Jayjay asked.

Smith pushed himself away from the screamer panel and came back after a moment with a flashlight. "Let me take a look," he said, edging Jayjay aside. He looked over the halves of the coupling very carefully, then said: "I don't see anything wrong. I'll try it again."

"Hold on a second," Jayjay said quietly. "Let me take a look, will you?"

Smith handed him the torch. "Go ahead, but there's nothing wrong."

Jayjay took the light and looked the connections over again. Then he screwed his head around so that he could look into the female plug.

"Hm-m-m. Hard to count. Gap's too small. Anybody got a toothpick?"

Nobody did.

Jayjay turned to Jeffry Hull. "Mr. Hull, would you mind going to the lounge? I think there's some toothpicks in the snack refrigerator."

"Sure," said Hull. "Sure."

He pushed himself across the control room and disappeared through the stairwell.

"Get several of them," Jayjay called after him.

Captain Al-Amin said: "What's the trouble, Mr. Kelvin?"

"I'm not sure yet," Jayjay answered. "When did you last have the screamer units inspected?"

"Just before we took off from Jove Station," Al-Amin said. "That's the law. All emergency equipment has to be checked before takeoff. Why? What's the matter?"

"Did they check this unit?" Jayjay asked doggedly.

"Certainly. I watched them check it myself. I—" He brought himself up short and said: "Give me that torch, will you? I want to take a look at the thing."

Jayjay handed him the flashlight and grasped the captain's belt. With one arm in a splint, Al-Amin couldn't hold the flashlight and hold on to anything solid at the same time.

"I don't see anything wrong," he said after a minute.

"Neither do I," Jayjay admitted. "But the way it acts—"

"I got the toothpicks!" Jeffry Hull propelled himself across the room toward the three men who were clustered around the screamer.

Jayjay took the toothpicks, selected one, and inserted it into the female plug. "Hard to see those threads with all the tubes blocking that plug," he said offhandedly.

Hull said: "Captain, did you know that the refrigerator is off?"

"Yes," said Atef Al-Amin absently. "It isn't connected to the emergency circuits. Wastes too much energy. What do you find, Mr. Kelvin?"

After a second's silence, Jayjay said: "Let me check once more." He was running the tip of the toothpick across the threads in the female plug, counting as he did so. "Uh-huh," he said finally, "just as I thought. There's one less thread in the female plug. The male plug is stopped before it can make contact. There's a gap of about a tenth of an inch when the coupling is screwed up tight."

"Let me see," Smith said. He took the toothpick and went through the same operation. "You're right," he said ruefully, "the female plug is faulty. We'll have to use one of the other screamers."

"Right," said Jayjay.

Wrong, said Fate. Or the Powers That Be, or the Fallibility of Man, whatever you want to call it.

Every screamer unit suffered from the same defect.

"I don't understand it!" A pause. "It's impossible! Those units were tested!"

For the first time in his life, Captain Atef Abdullah Al-Amin allowed his voice to betray him.

Arabic is normally spoken about half an octave above the normal tone used for English. And, unlike American English, it tends to waver up and down the scale. Usually, the captain spoke English in the flat, un-accented tones of the Midwest American accent, and spoke Arabic in the ululating tones of the Egyptian.

But now he was speaking English with an Egyptian waver, not realizing that he was doing it.

"How could it happen? It's ridiculous!"

The captain, his maintenance officer, and Jeffry Hull were clustered around the screamer unit in the lounge. Off to one side, Jayjay Kelvin held a deck of cards in his hands and played a game of patience called "transportation solitaire." His eyes didn't miss a play, just as his ears didn't miss a word.

He pulled an ace from the back of the deck and flipped it to the front.

"You said the screamers had been checked," Jeffry Hull said accusingly. "How come they *weren't* checked?"

"They *were*!" Al-Amin said sharply.

"Sure they were," Smith added. "I watched the check-off. There was nothing wrong then."

"Meanwhile," Hull said, the acid bite of fear in his voice, "we have to sit here and wait for the Interplanetary Police to find us by pure luck."

The captain should have let Hull cling to the idea that the IP could find the *Persephone*, even if no signal was sent. But the captain was almost as angry and flustered as Hull was.

"Find us?" he snapped. "Don't be ridiculous! We won't even be missed until we're due at Styx, on Pluto, nine days from now. By that time, we'll be close to two billion miles beyond the orbit of Pluto. We'll never be found if we wait 'til then. Something has to be done *now*!" He looked at his Maintenance Officer. "Smith, isn't there some way to make contact between those two plugs?"

"Sure," Smith said bitterly. "If we had the tools, it would be duck soup. All we'd have to do is trim down the male plug to fit the female, and we'd have it. But we don't have the tools. We've got a couple of files and a quarter-horsepower electric drill with one bit. Everything else was in the tool compartment—which is long gone, with the engine room."

"Can't you ... uh, what do you call it? Uh ... jury-something—" Hull's voice sounded as though he were forcing it to be calm.

"Jury-rig?" Smith said. "Yeah? With what? Dammit, we haven't got any tools, and we haven't got any materials to work with!"

"Can't you just use a wrench to tighten them more?" Hull asked helplessly.

Smith said a dirty word and pushed himself away from the screamer unit to glower at an unresisting wall.

"No, Mr. Hull, we couldn't," said Captain Al-Amin with restrained patience. "That would strip the threads. If the electrical contact were made at the same time, the high-pressure oxygen-hydrogen flow would spark off, and we'd get a big explosion that would wreck everything—including us." Then he muttered to himself: "I still don't see how it could happen."

Jayjay Kelvin pulled a nine of spades from the back of the deck to the front. It matched the four of spades that had come three cards before. Jayjay discarded the two cards between the spades. "You don't?" he asked. "Didn't you ever hear that the total is greater than the sum of its parts?"

"What?" Captain Al-Amin sounded as though he'd been insulted—in Arabic. "What are you talking about, Mr. Kelvin?"

"I'm talking about the idiocy of the checking system," Jayjay said flatly. "Don't you see what they did? Don't you see what happened? Each part of a screamer has to be checked separately, right?"

Al-Amin nodded.

"Why? Because the things burn out if you check them as a complete unit. It's like checking a .50 caliber cartridge. The only way you can check a cartridge is to shoot it in a gun. If it works, then you know it works. Period. The only trouble is that you've wasted the cartridge. You know that *that* one is good, but you've ruined it.

"Same way with a screamer. If you test it as a unit, you'll ruin it. So you test it a part at a time. All the parts check out nicely because the test mechanisms are built to check each part."

Smith squinted. "Well, sure. If you check out the whole screamer, you'll ruin it. So what?"

"So suppose you were going to check out a cartridge," Jayjay said. "You don't fire it; you check each part separately. You check the brass case. It's all right; the tests show that it won't burst under firing pressure. You check the primer; the tests show that it will explode when hit by the gun's hammer. You check the powder; the tests show that the powder will burn nicely when the flame from the primer hits it. You check the bullet; the tests show that the slug will be expelled at the proper velocity when the powder is ignited.

"So you assume that the cartridge will function when fired.

"But will it?"

"Why wouldn't it?" Smith asked.

"Because the flame from the exploding primer can't reach the powder, that's why!" Jayjay snapped. "Some jerk has redesigned the primer so that the flame misses the propellant!"

"How could that happen?" Hull asked blankly.

"How? Because Designer *A* decided that the male plug on the screamer should have one more turn on its threads, but he forgot to tell Designer *B*, who designs the female plug, that the two should match. The testing equipment is designed to test each part, so each part tests out fine. The only trouble is that the thing doesn't test out as a whole."

Captain Al-Amin nodded slowly. "That's right. The test showed that the oxyhydrogen section worked fine. It showed that the starter worked fine. It showed that the radiowave broadcaster worked fine. But it didn't show that they'd work together."

Smith said a short, five-letter word. It was French; the Anglo-Saxon equivalent has only four letters. "What good does all this theorizing do us?" he added. "The question is: How do we fix the thing?"

"Well, can't you put another turn on the thread?" Hull asked.

"Oh, sure," Smith said sarcastically. "You give me a lathe and the proper tools, and I'll make you all the connections you want. Hell, if I had the proper tools, I could turn us out a new spaceship, and we could all go home in comfort."

"Couldn't you drill out the metal with that drill?" Hull asked plaintively.

"No!" Smith said harshly. "How do you expect me to get a quarter-inch bit into a space less than a sixteenth of an inch in diameter?"

Hull wasn't used to machinist's terms. "How big is an inch?"

"Two point five four oh oh oh five centimeters," Smith said in a nasty tone of voice. "Does that help you any?"

"I'm just trying to help!" Hull snapped. "You've got no call to get sarcastic with me!"

Smith said the French word again.

"Enough!" the captain barked. "Smith, control your tongue! That sort of thing won't help us." He jerked his head around. "Mr. Kelvin, do you have any suggestions?"

Jayjay played another card. "No. Not yet. I'm thinking."

"Smith? Any ideas?" The tone of the Arab's voice left no doubt that he meant business.

"No, sir. Without a properly equipped machine shop, there's nothing we can do."

"How so?"

"Because that's a precision job, sir. The threads are tapered so that the fit will be gas-tight. That's why the threads have a ten-thousandth of an inch of soft polyethylene covering the hard steel, so that when the threads are tight, the polyethylene will act as a seal. Everything in that connection is a precision fitted job. The ends of the tubes are made to be slightly mashed together, so that the seals will be tight—they're coated with polyethylene, too. If the oxygen and hydrogen mix, the efficiency of the fuel cell goes down to zero, and you run the chance of an explosion."

"Show me," Al-Amin said.

Smith took a pencil out of his pocket and began drawing a cross section of the connection on the top of the nearby table.

"Look here, captain, this is the way the two are supposed to fit. But they don't, because the male plug can't get far enough into the female socket to make the connection. Like this, see?"

The captain nodded.

"Well," Smith continued, "there's a thirty-second of an inch clearance there. If the female had one more turn of thread, the fit would be prefect. As it is, we get no connection. So the screamer doesn't function."

Al-Amin looked at the drawing. "Odd that there's never been any complaint about this error before."

Jayjay turned another ace. "Not so odd, really."

All heads turned toward Jayjay.

"What does that mean?" Smith asked.

"Just what I said." Jayjay turned another card. "A screamer is supposed to call for help, isn't it? It's only used in a dire emergency. Then the only test of the whole unit comes when the occupants of the spaceship are in danger—as we are. If the things don't work, how could there be any complaint? If we can't get ours to work, will we complain? To whom?

"How many ships have been reported missing in the past year or so? All of them presumed lost because of meteor strikes, eh? If a ship is lost and doesn't signal, we presume that it was totally destroyed. If it wasn't, they'd have signaled. As *Mister* Smith says: See?"

There was a long silence.

Jayjay Kelvin turned the last card, saw that he had lost, and began shuffling the deck.

"I think I've got it," Smith said excitedly, several hours later.

Captain Al-Amin glanced around. Hull was dozing fitfully a few inches above the couch. Jayjay Kelvin was still methodically playing solitaire.

"Keep your voice down," the captain ordered. "No use giving our passengers false hopes. What do you mean, you've got it?"

"Simple. Real simple. All we have to do is file off the last thread of the male plug. Then it will fit into the female." Smith's voice was a hoarse whisper.

"Won't work," said Jayjay Kelvin from across the room.

Smith blew up. "How do you know?" he roared. "You sit over there making wiseacre remarks and do nothing! Play cards, that's all! What do you know about things like this, *Mister* Joseph Kelvin? What does a businessman know about mechanical equipment?"

"Enough," Jayjay said quietly. "Enough to know that, if you try to file off the final thread of the male plug, you'll do an uneven job. And that will mean leakage."

"What do you mean, an uneven job?" Smith was still furious.

"Trimming off the end of the male plug would have to be done on a lathe," Jayjay said, without looking up from his cards. "Otherwise, the fit would be wrong, and the gases would mix. And we would all go *phfft!* when the mixture blew."

Smith started to say something, but Jayjay went right on talking. "Even if we had a lathe, the male plug doesn't turn, so you'd be out of luck all the way. You can't take the screamers apart without wrecking them—not without a machine shop. You're going to have to work on that female connection. She's got a sleeve on her that will turn. Now, if—" Jayjay's voice faded off into silence, and his manipulations of the cards became purely mechanical.

"Huh!" Smith said softly. "Just because he's related to Kelvin Associates, he thinks he's hot—" He said the French word again.

"Is he right?" Captain Al-Amin asked sharply.

"Well—" Smith rubbed his nose with a forefinger. "Well, yes. I was wrong. We can't do it with a file. It would have to be turned on a lathe, and we don't have a lathe. And we don't have any measuring instruments, either. This is a precision job, as I said. And we don't have a common ruler aboard, much less a micrometer. Any makeshift job will be a failure."

Captain Al-Amin brooded over that for a moment. Then he looked at Jayjay again. "Mr. Kelvin."

"Yes, captain?" Jayjay didn't look up from the cards in his hands.

"*Are* you related to Kelvin Associates?"

"In a way."

Al-Amin bit at his lower lip. "Mr. Kelvin, you registered aboard this ship as Joseph Kelvin. May I ask if your middle name is James?"

After a short pause, Jayjay said: "Yes. It is."

"Are you *the* J. J. Kelvin?"

"Yup. But I'd rather you didn't mention it when we get to Pluto."

Smith's jaw had slowly sagged during that conversation. Then he closed his mouth with a snap. "You're Jayjay Kelvin?" he asked, opening his mouth again.

"That's right."

"Then I apologize."

"Accepted," said Jayjay. He wished that Smith hadn't apologized.

"Why didn't you say so in the first place?" Captain Al-Amin asked.

"Because I didn't want it known that I was going to Pluto," Kelvin said. "And—after the accident happened—I kept quiet because I know human nature."

Jeffry Hull, who had awakened during the argument, looked at Jayjay and said: "What's human nature got to do with it, Mr. Kelvin?"

"Nothing, except that if I'd told everyone I was J. J. Kelvin, all of you would have been sitting around waiting for me to solve the problem instead of thinking about it yourselves."

Hull nodded thoughtfully. "It makes sense, Mr. Kelvin. If they'd known that you were ... well ... Mister Spaceship Himself, they'd have let you do all the thinking. And that would have left you high and dry, wouldn't it?"

Jayjay put the deck of cards in his pocket. "You're a pretty good sociologist, after all, Mr. Hull. You're right. Face any group with Authority—with a capital *A*—and they quit thinking for themselves. And if they do, then the poor slob of an Authority doesn't have anything to tickle his own brains, so everybody loses."

"Well, *do* you have an answer?" Captain Al-Amin asked.

Jayjay shook his head. "Not yet. I think I've got one coming up, but I wish you two would go on talking while I think."

"I'll try," Smith said wryly.

The problem was both simple and complex. The female socket lacked one single turn of thread to make a perfect connection. A few hundredths of an inch separated success from disaster.

Five men, including the unconscious Vandenbosch, were only a fraction of an inch away from death.

Jayjay Kelvin listened to Smith talk for another half hour, throwing in objections when necessary, but offering no opinions.

"All we have to do," Smith said at last, "is get rid of that little bit of metal beyond the thread in the female socket. But there's no way to get it out. We can't use a chisel because the force would warp the threads. Besides, we couldn't get a chisel in there."

"And we don't have a chisel," Captain Al-Amin added. "We don't have any tools at all."

"Except," said Jayjay, "an electric hand drill and a quarter-inch bit."

"Well, sure," said Smith. "But what good will that do us?"

"If we rigged a belt between the drill's motor and the sleeve of the female socket, the sleeve would rotate as if it were on a lathe, wouldn't it?"

Smith blinked. "Sure. Yeah! Hey!" His face brightened. Then it looked sad again. "But what good would that do us?"

"You said that all we have between us and success is a fraction of an inch of metal. If we can remove that fraction of an inch, we're successful."

"But how can you put a thread into that socket?" Smith asked.

Jayjay beamed as though it were his birthday. "We don't have to put a thread in there. All we have to do is give the thread on the male plug room to move in. All we have to do is clear away that metal. So we'll use the drill motor to turn the sleeve as if it were on a lathe."

Smith still didn't look enthusiastic. "All right. We have a lathe. But what are we going to use for tools? What are we going to cut the metal with?"

Jayjay's smile became broader. "Carbon steel. What else?"

"Oh?" said Smith. "And where do we get these tools, Mr. Kelvin? From the circumambient ether?"

"Not at all," said Jayjay. "Did you ever chip flint?"

"What?"

"Never mind. All we have to do is use that quarter-inch bit."

Smith still looked confused. "I don't get it. A bit that big won't fit in."

"We simply crack a piece off that hard carbon steel," Jayjay said. "We can make a lathe tool that will fit into the small space between the inner and outer tubes. The fractured edge will be sharp enough to take out the excess metal. The male plug can move in, and we'll have contact."

"Well, I'll be—" Smith used another French word.

Captain Atef Al-Amin cast his eyes upwards. "*Creatio ex nihilo*," he said softly.

When the Interplanetary Police ship took the five men and the cargo from the wreck of the *Persephone*, the major in command of the ship, who knew that he had rescued the great J. J. Kelvin, asked him: "Mr. Kelvin, what do you plan to do when you return to Ceres City?"

And Jayjay, who knew that both he and the major were speaking for the newsfacs and for posterity, said:

"I'm going to make sure that Kelvin Associates learns to make emergency equipment properly. We will never again put faulty equipment aboard a ship."

The major looked perplexed. "What?"

"I'm going to have some designer's head!" said Jayjay Kelvin.

THE END

The Asses of Balaam

The remarkable characteristic of Balaam's ass was that it was more perceptive than its master. Sometimes a child is more perceptive—because more straightforward and logical—than an adult....

It is written in the Book of Numbers that Balaam, a wise man of the Moabites, having been ordered by the King of Moab to put a curse upon the invading Israelites, mounted himself upon an ass and rode forth toward the camp of the Children of Israel. On the road, he met an angel with drawn sword, barring the way. Balaam, not seeing or recognizing the angel, kept urging his ass forward, but the ass recognized the angel and turned aside. Balaam smote the beast and forced it to return to the path, and again the angel blocked the way with drawn sword. And again the ass turned aside, despite the beating from Balaam, who, in his blindness, was unable to see the angel.

When the ass stopped for the third time and lay down, refusing to go further, Balaam waxed exceeding wrath and smote again the animal with a stick.

Then the ass spoke and said: "Why dost thou beat me? I have always obeyed thee and never have I failed thee. Have I ever been known to fail thee?"

And Balaam answered: "No." And at that moment his eyes were opened and he saw the angel before him.

—STUDIES IN SCRIPTURE
by Ceggawynn of Eboricum

With the careful precision of controlled anger, Dodeth Pell rippled a stomp along his right side. *Clop*clopclop*clop*-clopclop-*clop*clop-clop*clop*clopclop.... Each of his twelve right feet came down in turn while he glared across the business bench at Wygor Bedis. He started the ripple again, while he waited for Wygor's answer. The ripple was a good deal more effective than just tapping one's fingers, and equally as satisfying.

Wygor Bedis twitched his mouth and allowed his eyelids to slide up over his eyeballs in a slow blink before answering. Dodeth had simply asked, "Why wasn't this reported to me before?" But Wygor couldn't find the answer as simply as that. Not that he didn't have a good answer; it was just that he wanted to couch it in exactly the right terms. Dodeth had a way with raking sarcasm that made a person tend to cringe.

Dodeth was perfectly well aware of that. He hadn't been in the Executive Office of Predator Council all these years for nothing; he knew how to handle people—when to praise them, when to flatter them, when to rebuke them, and when to drag them unmercifully over the shell-bed.

He waited, his right legs marching out their steady rhythm.

"Well," said Wygor at last, "it was just that I couldn't see any point in bothering you with it at that point. I mean, *one* specimen—"

"Of an entirely new species!" snapped Dodeth in a sudden interruption. His legs stopped their rhythmic tramp. His voice rose from its usual eight-thousand-cycle rumble to a shrill squeak. "Fry it, Wygor, if you weren't such a good field man, I'd have sacked you long ago! Your trouble is that you have a penchant for bringing me problems that you ought to be able to solve by yourself and then flipping right over on your back and holding off on some information that ought to be brought to my attention immediately!"

There wasn't much Wygor could say to that, so he didn't try. He simply waited for the raking to come, and, sure enough, it came.

Dodeth's voice lowered itself to a soft purr. "The next time you have to do anything as complicated as setting a snith-trap, you just hump right down here and ask me, and I'll tell you all about it. On the other hand, if the lower levels all suddenly become infested with shelks at the same time, why, you just take care of that little detail yourself, eh? The only other alternative is to learn to think."

Wygor winced a trifle and kept his mouth shut.

Having delivered himself of his jet of acid, Dodeth Pell looked down at the data booklet that Wygor had handed him. "Fortunately," he said, "there doesn't seem to be much to worry about. Only the Universal Motivator knows how this thing could have spawned, but it doesn't appear to be very efficient."

"No, sir, it doesn't," said Wygor, taking heart from his superior's mild tone. "The eating orifice is oddly placed, and the teeth are obviously for grinding purposes."

"I was thinking more of the method of locomotion," Dodeth said. "I believe this is a record, although I'll have to look in the files to make sure. I think that six locomotive limbs is the least I've ever heard of on an animal that size."

"I've checked the files," said Wygor. "There was a four-limbed leaf-eater recorded seven hundred years ago—four locomotive limbs, that is, and two grasping. But it was only as big as your hand."

Dodeth looked through the three pages of the booklet. There wasn't much there, really, but he knew Wygor well enough to know that all the data he had thus far was there. The only thing that rankled was that Wygor had delayed for three work periods before reporting the intrusion of the new beast, and now five of them had been spotted.

He looked at the page which showed the three bathygraphs that had been taken of the new animals from a distance. There was something odd about them, and Dodeth couldn't, for the hide of him, figure out what it was. It aroused an odd fear in him, and made him want to burrow deeper into the ground.

"I can't see what keeps 'em from falling over," he said at last. "Are they as slow-moving as they look?"

"They don't move very fast," Wygor admitted, "but we haven't seen any of them startled yet. I don't see how they could run very fast, though. It must take every bit of awareness they have to stay balanced on two legs."

Dodeth sighed whistlingly and pushed the data booklet back across the business bench to Wygor. "All right; I'll file the preliminary spotting report. Now get out there and get me some pertinent data on this queer beast. Scramble off."

"Right away, sir."

"And ... Wygor—"

"Yes, sir?"

"It's apparent that we have a totally new species here. It will be called a *wygorex*, of course, but it would be better if we waited until we could make a full report to the Keepers. So don't let any of this out—especially to the other Septs."

"Certainly not, sir; not a whistle. Anything else?"

"Just keep me posted, that's all. Scramble off."

After Wygor had obediently scrambled off, Dodeth relaxed all his knees and sank to his belly in thought.

His job was not an easy one. He would like to have his office get full credit for discovering a new species, just as Wygor had—understandably enough—wanted to get his share of the credit. On the other hand, one had to be careful that holding back information did not constitute any danger to the Balance. Above all, the Balance must be preserved. Even the snith had its place in the Ecological Balance of the World—although one didn't like to think about sniths as being particularly useful.

After all, every animal, every planet had its place in the scheme; each contributed its little bit to maintaining the Balance. Each had its niche in the ecological architecture, as Dodeth liked to think of it. The trouble was that the Balance was a shifting, swinging, ever-changing thing. Living tissues carried the genes of heredity in them, and living tissues are notoriously plastic under the influence of the proper radiation or particle bombardment. And animals *would* cross the poles.

The World had been excellently designed by the Universal Motivator for the development and evolution of life. Again, the concept of the Balance showed in His mighty works. Suppose, for instance, that the World rotated more rapidly about its axis, thereby exposing the whole surface periodically to the deadly radiation of the Blue Sun, instead of having a rotation period that, combined with the eccentricity of the World's orbit, gave it just enough libration to expose only sixty-three per cent to the rays, leaving the remaining thirty-seven per cent in twilight or darkness. Or suppose the orbit were so nearly circular that there were no perceptible libration at all; one side would burn eternally, and the other side would freeze, since there would be no seasonal winds blowing first east, then west, bringing the warmth of the Blue Sun from the other side.

Or, again, suppose there were no Moon and no Yellow Sun to give light to the dark side. Who could live in an everlasting night?

Or suppose that the magnetic field of the World were too weak to focus the majority of the Blue Sun's output of electrons and ions on the poles. How could life have evolved at all?

Balance. And the Ultimate Universal Motivator had put part of the responsibility into the hands of His only intelligent species. And a part of that part had been put into the hands of Dodeth Pell as the head of Predator Control.

Fry it! Something was niggling at the back of Dodeth's mind, and no amount of philosophizing would shake it. He reached into the drawer of the business bench and pulled out the duplicate of Wygor's data booklet. He flipped it open and looked at the bathygraphs again.

There was no single thing about them that he could pinpoint, but the beasts just didn't *look* right. Dodeth Pell had seen many monstrous animals in his life, but none like this.

Most people disliked and were disgusted by a snith because of the uncanny resemblance the stupid beast had to the appearance of Dodeth's own race. There could be no question of the genetic linkage between the two species, but, in spite of the physical similarities, their actions were controlled almost entirely by instinct instead of reason. They were like some sort of idiot parody of intelligent beings.

But it was their similarity which made them loathsome. Why should Dodeth Pell feel a like emotion when he saw the bathygraphs of the two-legged thing? Certainly there was no similarity.

Wait a minute!

He looked carefully at the three-dimensional pictures again.

Fry it! He couldn't be sure—

After all, he wasn't a geneticist. Checking the files wouldn't be enough; he wouldn't know how to ask the proper cross-filing questions.

He lolled his tongue out and absently rasped at a slight itch on the back of his hand while he thought.

If his hunch were correct, then it was time to call in outside help now, instead of waiting for more information. Still, he needn't necessarily call in official expert help just yet. If he could just get a lead—enough to verify or disprove the possibility of his hunch being correct—that would be enough for a day or two, until Wygor got more data.

There was always Yerdeth, an older parabrother on his prime-father's side. Yerdeth had studied genetics—theoretical, not applied—with the thought of going into Control, and kept on dabbling in it even after he had discovered that his talents lay in the robot design field.

"Ardan!" he said sharply.

At the other end of the office, the robot assistant ceased his work for a moment. "Yes, sir?"

"Come here a minute; I want you to look at something."

"Yes, sir."

The robot's segmented body was built very much like Dodeth's own, except that instead of the twelve pairs of legs that supported Dodeth's body, the robot was equipped with wheels, each suspended separately and equipped with its individual power source. Ardan rolled sedately across the floor, his metallic body gleaming in the light from the low ceiling. He came to a halt in front of Dodeth's business bench.

Dodeth handed Ardan the thin data booklet. "Scan through that."

Ardan went through it rapidly, his eyes carefully scanning each page, his brain recording everything permanently. After a few seconds, he looked back up at Dodeth. "A new species."

"Exactly. Did you notice anything odd about their appearance?"

"Naturally," said Ardan. "Since their like has never been seen before, it is axiomatic that they would appear odd."

Fry it! Dodeth thought. He should have known better than to ask a question like that of Ardan. To ask it to determine what might be called second-order strangeness in a pattern that was strange in the first place was asking too much of a robot.

"Very well, then. Make an appointment for this evening with Yerdeth Pell. I would like to see him at his home if it is convenient."

"Yes, sir," said the robot.

Evening was four work-periods away, and even after Yerdeth had granted the appointment, Dodeth found himself fidgeting in anticipation.

Twice, during the following work periods, Wygor came in with more information. He had gone above ground with a group of protection robots, finally, to take a look at the new animals himself, but he hadn't yet managed to obtain enough data to make a definitive report on the strange beasts.

But the lack of data was, in itself, significant.

Dodeth usually liked to walk through the broad tunnels of the main thoroughfares, since he didn't particularly care to ride robot-back for so short a distance, but this time he was in such a hurry to see Yerdeth that he decided to let Ardan take him.

He climbed aboard, clamped his legs to the robot's sides, and said: "To Yerdeth Pell's."

The robot said "Yes, sir," and rolled out to the side tunnel that led toward one of the main robot tunnels. When they finally came to a tunnel labeled *Robots and Passengers Only*, Ardan rolled into it and revved his wheels up to high speed, shooting down the tunnelway at a much higher velocity than Dodeth could possibly have run.

The tunnelway was crowded with passenger-carrying robots, and with robots alone, carrying out orders from their masters. But there was no danger; no robot could harm any of Dodeth's race, nor could any robot stand idly by while someone was harmed. Even in the most crowded of conditions, every robot in the area had one thing foremost in his mind: the safety of every human within sight or hearing.

Dodeth ignored the traffic altogether. He had other things to think about, and he knew—without even bothering to consider it—that Ardan could be relied upon to take care of everything. Even if it cost him his own pseudolife, Ardan would do everything in his power to preserve the safety and health of his passenger. Once in a while, in unusual circumstances, a robot would even disobey orders to save a life, for obedience was strictly secondary to the sanctity of human life, just as the robot's desire to preserve his own pseudoliving existence was outranked by the desire to obey.

Dodeth thought about his job, but he carefully kept his mind off the new beasts. He knew that fussing in his mind over them wouldn't do him any good until he had more to work with—things which only his parabrother, Yerdeth, could supply him. Besides, there was the problem of what to do about the hurkle breeding sites, which were being encroached upon by the quiggies. Some of the swamps on the surface, especially those that approached the Hot Belts, were being dried out and filled with dust, which decreased the area where the hurkle could lay its eggs, but increased the nesting sites for quiggies.

That, of course, was a yearly cycle, in general. As the Blue Sun moved from one side to the other, and the winds shifted accordingly, the swamps near the Twilight Border would dry out or fill up accordingly. But this year the eastern swamps weren't filling up as they should, and some precautionary measures would have to be taken to prevent too great a shift in the hurkle-quiggie balance.

Then there was the compensating migratory shift of the Hotland beasts—those which lived in the areas where the slanting rays of the Blue Sun could actually touch them, and which could not stand the, to them, terrible cold of the Darklands. Instead, they moved back and forth with the Blue Sun and remained in their own area—a hot, dry, fiery-bright hinterland occupied only by gnurrs, gpoles, and other horrendous beasts.

Beyond those areas, according to the robot patrols which had reconnoitered there, nothing lived. Nothing could. No protoplasmic being could exist under the direct rays of the Blue Sun. Even the metal-and-translite bodies of a robot wouldn't long protect the sensitive mechanisms within from the furnace heat of the huge star.

Each species had its niche in the World. Some, like the hurkle, lived in swamp water. Others lived in lakes and streams. Still others flew in the skies or roamed the surface or climbed the great trees. Some, like Dodeth's own people, lived beneath the surface.

The one thing an intelligent species had to be most careful about was not to disturb the balance with their abilities, but to work to preserve it. In the past, there had been those who had built cities on the surface, but the cities had removed the natural growth from large areas, which, in turn, had forced the city people to import their food from outside the cities. And that had meant an enforced increase in the cultivation of the remaining soil, which destroyed the habitats of other animals, besides depleting the soil itself. The only sensible way was to live *under* the farmlands, so that no man was ever more than a few hundred feet from the food supply. The Universal Motivator had chosen that their species should evolve in burrows beneath the surface, and if that was the niche chosen for Dodeth's people, then that was obviously where they should remain to keep the Balance.

Of course, the snith, too, was an underground animal, though the tunnels were unlined. The snith's tunnels ran between and around the armored tunnels of Dodeth's people, so that each city surrounded the other without contact—if the burrows of the snith could properly be called a city.

"Yerdeth Pell's residence," said Ardan.

"Ah, yes." Dodeth, his thoughts interrupted, slid off the back of the robot and flexed his legs. "Wait here, Ardan. I'll be back in an hour or so." Then he scrambled over to the door which led to Yerdeth's apartment.

Twenty minutes later, Yerdeth Pell looked up from the data book facsimiles and scanned Dodeth's face with appraising eyes.

"Very cute," he said at last, with a slight chuckle. "Now, what I want to know is: is someone playing a joke on you, or are you playing a joke on me?"

Dodeth's eyelids slid upwards in a fast blink of surprise. "What do you mean?"

"Why, these bathygraphs." Yerdeth rapped the bathygraphs with a wrinkled, horny hand. He was a good deal older than Dodeth, and his voice had a tendency to rasp a little when the frequency went above twenty thousand cycles. "They're very good, of course. *Very* good. The models have very fine detail to them. The eyes, especially are good; they look as if they really *ought* to be built that way." He smiled and looked up at Dodeth.

Dodeth resisted an urge to ripple a stomp. "Well?" he said impatiently.

"Well, they can't be real, you know," Yerdeth replied mildly.

"Why not?"

"Oh, come, now, Dodeth. What did it evolve from? An animal doesn't just spring out of nowhere, you know."

"New species are discovered occasionally," Dodeth said. "And there are plenty of mutants and just plain freaks."

"Certainly, certainly. But you don't hatch a snith out of a hurkle egg. Where are your intermediate stages?"

"Is it possible that we might have missed the intermediate stage?"

"I said 'stages'. Plural. Pick any known animal—*any* one—and tell me how many genetic changes would have to take place before you'd come up with an animal anything like this one." Again he tapped the bathygraph. "Take that eye, for instance. The lid goes down instead of up, but you notice that there's a smaller lid at the bottom that *does* go up, a little ways. The closest thing to an eye like that is on the hugl, which has eyelids on top that lower a little. But the hugl has eighteen segments; sixteen pairs of legs and two pairs of feeding claws. Besides, it's only the size of your thumb-joint. What kind of gene mutation would it take to change that into an animal like the one in this picture?

"And look at the size of the thing. If it weren't in that awkward vertical position, if it were stretched out on the ground, it'd be a long as a human. Look at the size of those legs!

"Or, take another thing. In order to walk on those two legs, the changes in skeletal and visceral structure would have to be tremendous."

"Couldn't we have missed the intermediate stages, then?" Dodeth asked stubbornly. "We've missed the intermediates before, I dare say."

"Perhaps we have," Yerdeth admitted, "but if you boys in the Ecological Corps have been on your toes for the past thousand years, we haven't missed many. And it would take at least that long for something like this to evolve from anything we know."

"Even under direct polar bombardment?"

"Even under direct polar bombardment. The radiation up here is strong enough to sterilize a race within a very few generations. And what would they eat? Not many plants survive there, you know.

"Oh, I don't say it's flatly im*possi*ble, you understand. If a female of some animal or other, carrying a freshly-fertilized zygote, and her species happened to have all the necessary potential characteristics, and a flood of ionizing radiation went through the zygote at exactly the right time, and it managed to hit just the right genes in just the right way ... well I'm sure you can see the odds against it are tremendous. I wouldn't even want to guess at the order of magnitude of the exponent. I'd have to put on a ten in order to give you the odds against it."

Dodeth didn't quite get that last statement, but he let it pass. "I am going to pull somebody's legs off, one by one, come next work period," he said coldly. "One ... by ... one."

He didn't, though. Rather than accuse Wygor, it would be better if Wygor were allowed to accuse himself. Dodeth merely wanted to wait for the opportunity to present itself. And then—ah, *then* there would be a roasting!

The opportunity came in the latter part of the next work period. Wygor, who had purportedly been up on the surface for another field trip, scuttled excitedly into Dodeth's office, wildly waving some bathygraph sheets.

"Dodeth, sir! Look! I came down as soon as I saw it! I've got the 'graphs right here! Horrible!"

Before Dodeth could say anything, Wygor had spread the sheets out fan-wise on his business bench. Dodeth looked at them and experienced a moment of horror himself before he realized that these were—these *must* be—doctored bathygraphs. Even so, he gave an involuntary gasp.

The first 'graphs had been taken from an aerial reconnaissance robot winging in low over the treetops. The others were taken from a higher altitude. They all showed the same carnage.

An area of several thousand square feet—*tens* of thousands!—had been cleared of trees! They had been ruthlessly cut down and stacked. Bushes and vines had gone with them, and the grass had been crushed and plowed up by the dragging of the great fallen trees. And there were obvious signs that the work was still going on. In the close-ups, he could see the bipedal beasts wielding cutting instruments.

Dodeth forced himself to calmness and glared at the bathygraphs. Fry it, they *had* to be fakes. A new species might appear only once in a hundred years, but according to Yerdeth, this couldn't possibly be a new species. What was Wygor's purpose in lying, though? Why should he falsify data? And it must be he; he had said that he had seen the beasts himself. Well, Dodeth would have to find out.

"Tool users, eh?" he said, amazed at the calmness of his voice. Such animals weren't unusual. The sniths used tools for digging and even for fighting each other. And the hurkles dammed up small streams with logs to increase their marshland. It wasn't immediately apparent what these beasts were up to, but it was far too destructive to allow it to go on.

But, fry it all, it *couldn't* be going on!

There were only two alternatives. Either Wygor was a liar or Yerdeth didn't know what he was talking about. And there was only one way of finding out which was which.

"Ardan! Get my equipment ready! We're going on a field trip! Wygor, you get the rest of the expedition ready; you and I are going up to see what all this is about." He jabbed at the communicator button. "Fry it! Why should this have to happen in my sector? Hello! Give me an inter-city connection. I want to talk to Baythim Venns, co-ordinator of Ecological Control, in Faisalla."

He looked up at Wygor. "Scatter off, fry it! I want to—Oh, hello, Baythim, sir. Dodeth. Have you had any reports on a new species—a bipedal one? What? No, sir; I'm not kidding. One of my men has brought in 'graphs of the thing. Frankly, I'm inclined to think it's a hoax of some kind, but I'd like to ask you to check to see if it's been reported in any of the other areas. We're located a little out of the way here, and I thought perhaps some of the stations farther north or south had seen it. Yes. That's right: two locomotive limbs, two handling limbs. Big as a human, and they hold their bodies perpendicular to the ground. Yes, sir, I know it sounds silly, and I'm going out to check the story now, but you ought to see these bathygraphs. If it's a hoax, there's an expert behind it. Very well, sir; I'll wait."

Dodeth scowled. Baythim had sounded as if he, Dodeth, had lost his senses.

Maybe I have, he thought. *Maybe I'll start running around mindlessly and get shot down by some patrol robot who thinks I'm a snith.*

Maybe he should have investigated first and then called, when he was sure, one way or another. Maybe he should have told Baythim he was certain it was a hoax, instead of hedging his bets. Maybe a lot of things, but it was too—

"Hello? Yes, sir. None, eh? Yes, sir. Yes, sir; I'll give you a call as soon as I've checked. Yes, sir. Thank you, sir."

Dodeth felt like an absolute fool. Individually and collectively, he consigned to the frying pan Baythim, Wygor, Yerdeth, the new beast—if it existed—and finally, himself.

By the time he had finished his all-encompassing curse, his two dozen pistoning legs had nearly brought him to the equipment room, where Ardan and Wygor were waiting.

Four hours and more of steady traveling did very little to sweeten Dodeth Pell's temper. The armored car was uncomfortable, and the silence within it was even more uncomfortable. He did not at all feel like making small talk with Wygor, and he had nothing as yet to say to Ardan or the patrol robots who were rolling along with the armored car.

One thing he had to admit: Wygor certainly didn't act like a man who was being carried to his own doom—which he certainly was if this was hoax. Wygor would lose all position and be reduced to living off his civil insurance. He would be pitied by all and respected by none.

But he didn't look as though that worried him at all.

Dodeth contented himself with looking at the scenery. The car was not yet into the forest country; this was all rolling grassland. Off to one side, a small herd of grazing grancos lifted their graceful heads to watch the passage of the expedition, then lowered them again to feed. A fanged zitibanth, disturbed in the act of stalking the grancos, stiffened all his legs and froze for a moment, looking balefully at the car and the robots, then went on about his business.

When they came to the forest, the going became somewhat harder. Centuries ago, those who had tried to build cities on the surface had also built paved strips to make travel by car easier and smoother, and Dodeth almost wished there were one leading to the target area.

Fry it, he *hated* traveling! Especially in a lurching armored car. He wished he were bored enough or tired enough to go to sleep.

At last—at *long* last—Wygor ordered the car to stop. "We're within two miles of the clearing, sir," he told Dodeth.

"All right," Dodeth said morosely. "We'll go the rest of the way on foot. I don't want to startle them at this stage of the game, so keep it quiet and stay hidden. Tell the patrol robots to spread out, and tell them I want all the movie shots we can get. I want all the Keepers to see these things in action. Got that? Then let's get moving."

They crept forward through the forest, Dodeth and Ardan taking the right, while Wygor and his own robot, Arsam, stayed a few yards away to the left. They were all expert woodsmen—Dodeth and Wygor by training and experience, and the robots by indoctrination.

Even so, Dodeth never felt completely comfortable above ground, with nothing over his head but the clouded sky.

The team had purposely chosen to approach from a small rise, where they could look down on the clearing without being seen. And when they reached the incline that led up to the ridge, one of the armed patrol robots who had been in the lead took a look over the ridge and then scuttled back to Dodeth. "They're there, sir."

"What are they doing?" Dodeth asked, scarcely daring to believe.

"Feeding, I believe, sir. They aren't cutting down any trees now; they're just sitting on one of the logs, feeding themselves with their handling limbs."

"How many are there?"

"Twenty, sir."

"I'll take a look." He scrambled up the ridge and peeked over.

And there they were, less than a quarter of a mile away.

Dazedly, Dodeth took a pair of field glasses from Ardan and focused them on the group.

Oh, they were real, all right. No doubt of that. None whatever. Mechanically, he counted them. Twenty. Most of them were feeding, but four of them seemed to be standing a little apart from the others, watching the forest, acting as lookouts.

Typical herd action, Dodeth thought.

He wished Yerdeth were here; he'd show that fool what good his ten-to-the-billionth odds were.

And yet, in another way, Dodeth had the feeling that his parabrother was right. How could the life of the World have suddenly evolved such creatures? For they looked even more impossible when seen in the flesh.

Their locomotive limbs ended in lumpy protuberances that showed no sign of toes, and they were covered all over with a dull gray hide, except for the hands at the ends of their handling limbs and the necks and the faces of their oddly-shaped heads, where the skin ranged in color from a pinkish an to a definitive brown, depending on the individual. There was no hair anywhere on their bodies except on the top and back of their heads. No, wait—there were two long tufts above each eye. They—

"Do you see what they're *eating*?" Wygor's voice whispered.

Dodeth hadn't. He'd been too busy looking at the things themselves. But when he did notice, he made a noise like a throttled "*Geep!*"

Hurkles!

There were few enough of the animals—only a few small population was needed to keep the Balance, but they were important. And the swamps were drying up, and the quiggies were moving in on them, and *now*—

Dodeth made a hasty count. Twenty! By the Universal Motivator, these predators had eaten a hurkle apiece!

Overhead, the Yellow Sun, a distant dot of intensely bright light, shed its wan glow over the ghastly scene. Dodeth wished the Moon were out; its much brighter light would have shown him more detail.

But he could see well enough to count the gnawed skeletons of the little, harmless hurkles. Even the Moon, which wouldn't bring morning for another fifteen work periods yet, couldn't have made it any plainer that these beasts were deadly dangerous to the Balance.

"How often do they eat?" he asked in a strained voice.

It was Wygor's robot, Arsam, who answered. "About three times every work period. They sleep then. Their metabolic cycle seems to be timed about the same as yours, sir."

"*Gaw!*" said Dodeth. "Sixty hurkles per sleep period! Why, they'll have the whole hurkle population eaten before long! Wygor! As soon as we can get shots of all this, we're going back! There's not a moment to lose! This is the most deadly dangerous thing that has ever happened to the World!"

"Fry me, yes," Wygor said in an awed voice. "Three hurkles in one period."

"Allow me to correct you, sir," said the patrol robot. "They do not eat that many hurkles. They eat other things besides."

"Like what, for instance?" Dodeth asked in a choked voice.

The robot told him, and Dodeth groaned. "Omnivores! That's even worse! Ardan, pass the word to the scouts to get their pictures and meet at that tree down there behind us in ten minutes. We've got to get back to the city!"

Dodeth Pell laid his palms flat on the speaker's bench and looked around at the assembled Keepers of the Balance, wise and prudence thinkers, who had spent lifetimes in ecological service and had shown their capabilities many times over.

"And that's the situation, sirs," he said, after a significant pause. "The moving and still bathygraphs, the data sheets, and the samplings of the area all tell the same story. I do not feel that I, alone, can make the decision. Emotionally, I must admit, I am tempted to destroy all twenty of the monsters. Intellectually, I realize that we should attempt to capture at least one family group—if we can discover what constitutes a family group in this species. Unfortunately, we cannot tell the sexes apart by visual inspection; the sex organs themselves must be hidden in the folds of that gray hide. And this is evidently not their breeding season, for we have seen no sign of sexual activity.

"We have very little time, sirs, it seems to me. The damage they have already done will take years to repair, and the danger of upsetting the Balance irreparably grows exponentially greater with every passing work period.

"Sirs, I ask your advice and your decision."

There was a murmur of approval for his presentation as he came down from the speakers bench. Then the Keepers went into their respective committee meetings so discuss the various problems of detail that had arisen out of the one great problem.

Dodeth went into an anteroom and tried to relax and get a little sleep—though he doubted he'd get any. His nerves were too much on edge.

Ardan woke him gently. "Your breakfast, sir."

Dodeth blinked and jerked his head up. "Oh. Uhum. Ardan! Have the Keepers reached any decision yet?"

"No, sir; not yet. The data are still coming in."

It was three more work periods before the Keepers called Dodeth Pell before them again. Dodeth could almost read the decision on their faces—there was both sadness and determination there.

"It was an uncomfortable decision, Dodeth Pell," said the Eldest Keeper without preliminary, "but a necessary one. We can find no place in the Ecological Balance for this species. We have already ordered a patrol column of two hundred fully-armed pesticide robots to destroy the animals. Two are to be captured alive, if possible, but, if not, the bodies will be brought to the biological laboratories for study. Within a few hours, the species will be nearly or completely extinct.

"By the way, you may tell your assistant, Wygor, that the animal will go down in the files as *wygorex*. A unique distinction for him, in many ways, but not, I fear, a happy one."

Dodeth nodded silently. Now that the decision had been made, he felt rather bad about it. Something in him rebelled at the thought of a species becoming extinct, no matter how great the need. He wondered if it would be possible for the biologists and the geneticists to trace the evolution of the animal. He hoped so. At least they deserved that much.

Dodeth Pell delayed returning to his own city; he wanted to wait until the final results had been brought in before he returned to his duties. The delay turned out to be a little longer than he expected—much longer, in fact. The communicator in his temporary room buzzed, and when he answered, Wygor's voice came to him, a rush of excited words that didn't make any sense at all at first. And when it did make sense he didn't believe it.

"What?" he squealed. "*What?*"

"I said," Wygor repeated, "that the report has come back from the pesticide column! They've found no trace of any such animal as we've described! They're nowhere to be found, in or near the clearing!"

"I think," said Dodeth very calmly, "that I'll take a little trip over to the Brightside and take up permanent residence there. It's going to be pretty hot for me around here before long."

And he cut the connection without waiting for Wygor's answer.

The armored car jounced across the grassland at high speed. Behind it, two more cars followed, each taking care not to run exactly in the tracks of the one ahead, so that there would be as little damage as possible done to the grass.

In the lead car, Dodeth Pell watched the forest loom nearer, wondering what sort of madness he would find there this time. Beside him, the Eldest Keeper dozed gently, in the way that only the very young or the very old can doze. It was just as well; Dodeth didn't feel much like talking.

This time, as they approached the clearing, he didn't bother to tell the car to stop two miles away. If the animals were gone, there was no point in being cautious. All through the wooded area, he could see occasional members of the pesticide robots. He told the car to stop at the base of the little rise that he used before as a vantage point. Then, without further preliminaries, he got out of the car and marched up the slope to take a look at the clearing. Overhead, the burning spark of the Yellow Sun cast its pale radiance over the landscape.

At the ridge, he stopped suddenly and ducked his head. Then he grabbed his field glasses and took a good look.

The animals had built themselves a few crude-looking shelters out of the logs, but he hardly noticed that.

There were four of the animals, in plain sight, standing guard!

The others were obviously inside the rude huts, asleep!

Great galloping fungus blight! Was he out of his mind? What was going on around here? Couldn't the robots *see* the beasts?

"That's very odd," said the voice of the Eldest Keeper in puzzled tones. "I thought the robots said they'd gone away. Lend me your field glasses."

As he handed the powerful glasses over to the Keeper, who had followed him up the hill, Dodeth said: "I'm glad you can see them. I thought maybe my brain had been short-circuited."

"I can see them," said the Eldest Keeper, peering through the glasses. Then he handed them back to Dodeth. "Let's get back down to the car. I want to find out what's going on around here."

At the car, the Eldest Keeper just scowled for a moment, looking very worried. By this time, the other two cars had pulled up nearby, discharging their cargo of two more Keepers apiece. While the Eldest Keeper talked in low tones with his colleagues, Dodeth stalked over to one of the pesticide robots who was prowling nearby.

"Found anything useful?" he asked sarcastically, knowing that sarcasm was useless on a robot.

"I'm not looking for anything useful, sir. I'm looking for the animals we are supposed to destroy."

"You come over and tell the Eldest Keeper that," Dodeth said.

"Yes, sir," the robot agreed promptly, rolling along beside Dodeth as he returned to where the Keepers were waiting.

"What's going on here?" the Eldest demanded curtly of the robot. "Why haven't you destroyed the animals?"

"Because we can't find them, sir."

"What's your name?" the Eldest snapped.

"Arike, sir."

"All right, Arike," said the Eldest somewhat angrily. "Stand by for orders. You'll repeat them to the other robots, understand?"

"Yes, sir," said the robot.

"All right, then," said the Eldest. "First, you take a run up that hill and look into that clearing. You'll see those creatures in there all right."

"Yes, sir. I've seen those creatures in there."

The Eldest Keeper exploded. "Then get in there and obey your orders! Don't you realize that their very existence threatens the life of all of us? They must be eliminated before our whole culture is destroyed! Do you understand? Obey!"

"Yes, sir," said the robot. His voice sounded odd, but he spun around and went to pass the word on to the other robots. Within minutes, more and more of the pesticide robots were swarming towards and into the clearing. They could hear rumbling noises from the clearing—low grunts that were evidently made by animals who were trapped by the encircling robots.

And then there was a vast silence.

Dodeth and the Keepers waited.

Not a shot was fired.

It was as though a great, sound-proof blanket had been flung over the whole area.

"What in the Unknown Name of the Universal Motivator is going on around here?" said Dodeth in a hushed tone. He wondered how many times he had asked himself that.

"We may as well take a look," said the Eldest Keeper.

Two hundred pesticide robots were ranged around the perimeter of the clearing, their weapons facing inward. Not a one of them moved.

Inside the circle of machines, the twenty wygorex stood motionless, watching the ring of robots. Now and then, one of them gave a deep, coughing rumble, but otherwise they made no noise.

Dodeth Pell could stand it no longer. "Robots!" He shouted as loudly as he could, his voice shrill with urgency. "I order you to fire!"

It was as though he hadn't said a word. Both robots and wygorex ignored him completely.

Dodeth turned and yelled to one one of the patrol robots that was standing nearby. "You! What's your name?"

"Arvam, sir."

"Arvam, can you tell what it is those things have done to the robots?"

"They haven't done anything, sir."

"Then why don't the robots fire as they've been told?" Dodeth didn't want to admit it, even to himself, but he was badly frightened. He had never heard of a robot behaving this way before.

"They can't, sir."

"They *can't*? Don't they realize that if those things aren't killed, we may all die?"

"I didn't know that," said the patrol robot. "If we do not kill them, then you may be killed, and you have ordered us to kill them, but if we obey your orders, then we will kill them, and that will mean that you won't be killed, but they will, so we can't do that, but if we don't then you *will* be killed, and we must obey, and that means we must, but we can't, but if we don't we will, and we can't so we must but we can't but if we don't you will so we must but we can't but we—" He kept repeating it over and over again, on and on and on.

"Stop that!" snapped Dodeth.

455

But the robot didn't even seem to hear.

Dodeth was really frightened now. He looked back at the five keepers and scuttled toward them.

"What's wrong with the robots?" he asked shrilly. "They've never failed us before!"

The Elder Keeper looked at him. "What makes you think they've failed us now?" he asked softly.

Dodeth gaped speechlessly. The Eldest didn't seem to be making any more sense than the patrol robot had.

"No," the Keeper went on, "they haven't failed us. They have served us well. They have pointed out to us something which we have failed to see, and, in doing so, have saved us from making a catastrophic error."

"I don't understand," said Dodeth.

"I'll explain," the Elder Keeper said, "but first go over to that patrol robot and tell him quietly that the situation has changed. Tell him that we are no longer in any danger from the wygorex. Then bring him over here."

Dodeth did as he was told, without understanding at all.

"I still don't understand, sir," he said bewilderedly.

"Dodeth, what would happen if I told Arvam, here, to fire on you?"

"Why ... why, he'd *refuse*."

"Why should he?"

"Because I'm *human*! That's the most basic robot command."

"I don't know," the Eldest said, eying Dodeth shrewdly. "You might not be a human. You might be a snith. You *look* like a snith."

Dodeth swallowed the insult, wondering what the Eldest meant.

"Arvam," the Eldest Keeper said to the robot, "doesn't he look like a snith to you?"

"Yes, sir," Arvam agreed.

Dodeth swallowed that one, too.

"Then how do you know he *isn't* a snith, Arvam?"

"Because he behaves like a human, sir. A snith does not behave like a human."

"And if something does behave like a human, what then?"

"Anything that behaves like a human is human, sir."

Dodeth suddenly felt as though his eyes had suddenly focused after being unfocused for a long time. He gestured toward the clearing. "You mean those ... those *things* ... are ... *human*?"

"Yes sir," said Arvam solidly.

"But they don't even *talk*!"

"Pardon me for correcting you sir, but they do. I cannot understand their speech, but the pattern is clearly recognizable as speech. Most of their conversation is carried on in tones of subsonic frequency, so your ears cannot hear it. Apparently, your voices are supersonic to them."

"Well, I'll be fried," said Dodeth. He looked at the Elder Keeper. "That's why the robots reported they couldn't find any *animal* of that description in the vicinity."

"Certainly. There weren't any."

"And we were so fooled by their monstrous appearance that we didn't pay any attention to their actions," said Dodeth.

"Exactly."

"But this makes the puzzle even *worse*," said Dodeth. "How could such a creature evolve?"

"Look!" interrupted one of the other Keepers, pointing. "Up there in the sky!"

All eyes turned toward the direction the finger pointed.

It was a silvery speck in the sky that moved and became larger.

"I don't think they're from our World at all," said the Eldest Keeper. He turned to the patrol robot. "Arvam, go down and tell the pesticide robots that there is no danger to us. They're still confused, and I have a feeling that the humans in that ship up there might not like it if we are caught pointing guns at their friends."

As Arvam rolled off, Dodeth said "Another World?"

"Why not?" asked the Eldest. "The Moon, after all, is another World, smaller than ours, to be sure, and airless, but still another World. We haven't thought too much about other Worlds because we have our own World to take care of. But there was a time, back in the days of the builders of the surface cities, when our people dreamed such things. But our Moon was the only one close enough, and there was no point in going to a place which is even more hellish than our Brightside.

"But suppose the Yellow Sun also has a planet—or maybe even one of the more distant suns, which are hardly more than glimmers of light. They came, and they landed a few of their party to make a small clearing. Then the ship went somewhere else—to the dark side of our Moon, maybe, I don't know. But they were within calling range, for the ship was called as soon as trouble appeared.

"We don't know anything about them yet, but we will. And we've got to show them that we, too, are human. We have a job ahead of us—a job of communication.

"But we also have a great future if we handle things right."

Dodeth watched the ship, now grown to a silvery globe of tremendous size, drift slowly downward toward the clearing. He felt an inward glow of intense anticipation, and he fidgeted impatiently as he waited to see what would happen next.

He rippled a stomp.

THE END

What The Left Hand Was Doing

There is no lie so totally convincing as something the other fellow already knows-for-sure is the truth. And no cover-story so convincing...

The building itself was unprepossessive enough. It was an old-fashioned, six-floor, brick structure that had, over the years, served first as a private home, then as an apartment building, and finally as the headquarters for the organization it presently housed.

It stood among others of its kind in a lower-middle-class district of Arlington, Virginia, within howitzer range of the capitol of the United States, and even closer to the Pentagon. The main door was five steps up from the sidewalk, and the steps were flanked by curving balustrades of ornamental ironwork. The entrance itself was closed by a double door with glass panes, beyond which could be seen a small foyer. On both doors, an identical message was blocked out in neat gold letters: *The Society For Mystical and Metaphysical Research, Inc.*

It is possible that no more nearly perfect cover, no more misleading front for a secret organization ever existed in the history of man. It possessed two qualities which most other cover-up titles do not have. One, it was so obviously crackpot that no one paid any attention to it except crackpots, and, two, it was perfectly, literally true.

Spencer Candron had seen the building so often that the functional beauty of the whole setup no longer impressed him as it had several years before. Just as a professional actor is not impressed by being allowed backstage, or as a multimillionaire considers expensive luxuries as commonplace, so Spencer Candron thought of nothing more than his own personal work as he climbed the five steps and pushed open the glass-paned doors.

Perhaps, too, his matter-of-fact attitude was caused partially by the analogical resemblance between himself and the organization. Physically, Candron, too, was unprepossessing. He was a shade less than five eight, and his weight fluctuated between a hundred and forty and a hundred and forty-five, depending on the season and his state of mind. His face consisted of a well-formed snub nose, a pair of introspective gray eyes, a rather wide, thin-lipped mouth that tended to smile even when relaxed, a high, smooth forehead, and a firm cleft chin, plus the rest of the normal equipment that normally goes to make up a face. The skin was slightly tanned, but it was the tan of a man who goes to the beach on summer weekends, not that of an outdoorsman. His hands were strong and wide and rather large; the palms were uncalloused and the fingernails were clean and neatly trimmed. His hair was straight and light brown, with a pronounced widow's peak, and he wore it combed back and rather long to conceal the fact that a thin spot had appeared on the top rear of his scalp. His clothing was conservative and a little out of style, having been bought in 1981, and thus three years past being up-to-date.

Physically, then, Spencer Candron, was a fine analog of the Society. He looked unimportant. On the outside, he was just another average man whom no one would bother to look twice at.

The analogy between himself and the S.M.M.R. was completed by the fact that his interior resources were vastly greater than anything that showed on the outside.

The doors swung shut behind him, and he walked into the foyer, then turned left into the receptionist's office. The woman behind the desk smiled her eager smile and said, "Good morning, Mr. Candron!"

Candron smiled back. He liked the woman, in spite of her semifanatic overeagerness, which made her every declarative sentence seem to end with an exclamation point.

"Morning, Mrs. Jesser," he said, pausing at the desk for a moment. "How have things been?"

Mrs. Jesser was a stout matron in her early forties who would have been perfectly happy to work for the Society for nothing, as a hobby. That she was paid a reasonable salary made her job almost heaven for her.

"Oh, just *fine*, Mr. Candron!" she said. "Just *fine*!" Then her voice lowered, and her face took on a serious, half conspiratorial expression. "Do you know what?"

"No," said Candron, imitating her manner. "What?"

"We have a gentleman ... he came in yesterday ... a *very* nice man ... and very intelligent, too. And, you know what?"

Candron shook his head. "No," he repeated. "What?"

Mrs. Jesser's face took on the self-pleased look of one who has important inside knowledge to impart. "He has actual photographs ... three-D, full-color *pho*tographs ... of the con*trol* room of a flying saucer! And one of the Saucerites, too!"

"Really?" Candron's expression was that of a man who was both impressed and interested. "What did Mr. Balfour say?"

"Well—" Mrs. Jesser looked rather miffed. "I don't really *know*! But the gentleman is supposed to be back to*mor*row! With some *more* pictures!"

"Well," said Candron. "Well. That's really fine. I hope he has something. Is Mr. Taggert in?"

"Oh, yes, Mr. Candron! He said you should go on up!" She waved a plump hand toward the stairway. It made Mrs. Jesser happy to think that she was the sole controller of the only way, except for the fire escape, that anyone could get to the upper floors of the building. And as long as she thought that, among other things, she was useful to the Society. Someone had to handle the crackpots and lunatic-fringe fanatics that came to the Society, and one of their own kind could do the job better than anyone else. As long as Mrs. Jesser and Mr. Balfour were on duty, the Society's camouflage would remain intact.

Spencer Candron gave Mrs. Jesser a friendly gesture with one hand and then headed up the stairs. He would rather not have bothered to take the stairway all the way up to the fifth floor, but Mrs. Jesser had sharp ears, and she might wonder why his foot-steps were not heard all the way up. Nothing—but *nothing*—must ever be done to make Mrs. Jesser wonder about anything that went on here.

The door to Brian Taggert's office was open when Candron finally reached the fifth floor. Taggert, of course, was not only expecting him, but had long been aware of his approach.

Candron went in, closed the door, and said, "Hi, Brian," to the dark-haired, dark-eyed, hawk-nosed man who was sprawled on the couch that stood against one corner of the room. There was a desk at the other rear corner, but Brian Taggert wasn't a desk man. He looked like a heavy-weight boxer, but he preferred relaxation to exercise.

But he did take his feet from the couch and lift himself to a sitting position as Candron entered. And, at the same time, the one resemblance between Taggert and Candron manifested itself—a warm, truly human smile.

"Spence," he said warmly, "you look as though you were bored. Want a job?"

"No," said Candron, "but I'll take it. Who do I kill?"

"Nobody, unless you absolutely have to," said Taggert.

Spencer Candron understood. The one thing that characterized the real members of The Society for Mystical and Metaphysical Research—not the "front" members, like Balfour and Mrs. Jesser, not the hundreds of "honorable" members who constituted the crackpot portion of the membership, but the real core of the group—the thing that characterized them could be summed up in one word: *understanding*. Without that one essential property, no human mind can be completely free. Unless a human mind is capable of understanding the only forces that can be pitted against it—the forces of other human minds—that mind cannot avail itself of the power that lies within it.

Of course, it is elementary that such understanding must also apply to oneself. Understanding of self must come before understanding of others. *Total* understanding is not necessary—indeed, utter totality is very likely impossible to any human mind. But the greater the understanding, the freer the mind, and, at a point which might be called the "critical point," certain abilities inherent in the individual human mind become controllable. A change, not only in quantity, but in quality, occurs.

A cube of ice in a glass of water at zero degrees Celsius exhibits certain properties and performs certain actions at its surface. Some of the molecules drift away, to become one with the liquid. Other molecules from the liquid become attached to the crystalline ice. But, the ice cube remains essentially an entity. Over a period of time, it may change slowly, since dissolution takes place faster than crystallization at the corners of the cube. Eventually, the cube will become a sphere, or something very closely approximating it. But the change is slow, and, once it reaches that state, the situation becomes static.

But, if you add heat, more and more and more, the ice cube will change, not only its shape, but its state. What it was previously capable of doing only slightly and impermanently, it can now do completely. The critical point has been passed.

Roughly—for the analog itself is rough—the same things occurs in the human mind. The psionic abilities of the human mind are, to a greater or lesser degree, there to begin with, just as an ice cube has the *ability* to melt if the proper conditions are met with.

The analogy hardly extends beyond that. Unlike an ice cube, the human mind is capable of changing the forces outside it—as if the ice could seek out its own heat in order to melt. And, too, human minds vary in their inherent ability to absorb understanding. Some do so easily, others do so only in spotty areas, still others cannot reach the critical point before they break. And still others can never really understand at all.

No one who had not reached his own critical point could become a "core" member of the S.M.M.R. It was not snobbery on their part; they understood other human beings too well to be snobbish. It was more as though a Society for Expert Mountain Climbers met each year on the peak of Mount Everest—anyone who can get up there to attend the meeting is automatically a member.

Spencer Candron sat down in a nearby chair. "All right, so I refrain from doing any more damage than I have to. What's the objective?"

Taggert put his palms on his muscular thighs and leaned forward. "James Ch'ien is still alive."

Candron had not been expecting the statement, but he felt no surprise. His mind merely adjusted to the new data. "He's still in China, then," he said. It was not a question, but a statement of a deduction. "The whole thing was a phony. The death, the body, the funeral. What about the executions?"

"They were real," Taggert said. "Here's what happened as closely as we can tell:

"Dr. Ch'ien was kidnaped on July 10th, the second day of the conference in Peiping, at some time between two and three in the morning. He was replaced by a double, whose name we don't know. It's unimportant, anyway. The double was as perfect as the Chinese surgeons could make him. He was probably not aware that he was slated to die; it is more likely that he was hypnotized and misled. At any rate, he took Ch'ien's place on the rostrum to speak that afternoon.

"The man who shot him, and the man who threw the flame bomb, were probably as equally deluded as to what they were doing as the double was. They did a perfect job, though. The impersonator was dead, and his skin was charred and blistered clear up to the chest—no fingerprints.

"The men were tried, convicted, and executed. The Chinese government sent us abject apologies. The double's body was shipped back to the United States with full honors, but by the time it reached here, the eye-cone patterns had deteriorated to the point where they couldn't be identified any more than the fingerprints could. And there were half a hundred reputable scientists of a dozen friendly nations who were eye-witnesses to the killing and who are all absolutely certain that it was James Ch'ien who died."

Candron nodded. "So, while the whole world was mourning the fact that one of Earth's greatest physicists has died, he was being held captive in the most secret and secure prison that the Red Chinese government could put him in."

Taggert nodded. "And your job will be to get him out," he said softly.

Candron said nothing for a moment, as he thought the problem out. Taggert said nothing to interrupt him.

Neither of them worried about being overheard or spied upon. Besides being equipped with hush devices and blanketing equipment, the building was guarded by Reeves and Donahue, whose combined senses of perception could pick up any activity for miles around which might be inimical to the Society.

"How much backing do we get from the Federal Government?" Candron asked at last.

"We can swing the cover-up afterwards all the way," Taggert told him firmly. "We can arrange transportation back. That is, the Federal Government can. But getting over there and getting Ch'ien out of durance vile is strictly up to the Society. Senator Kerotski and Secretary Gonzales are giving us every opportunity they can, but there's no use approaching the President until after we've proven our case."

Candron gestured his understanding. The President of the United States was a shrewd, able, just, and ethical human being—but he was not yet a member of the Society, and perhaps would never be. As a consequence it was still impossible to convince him that the S.M.M.R. knew what it was talking about—and that applied to nearly ninety per cent of the Federal and State officials of the nation.

Only a very few knew that the Society was an *ex officio* branch of the government itself. Not until the rescue of James Ch'ien was an accomplished fact, not until there was physical, logical proof that the man was still alive would the government take official action.

"What's the outline?" Candron wanted to know.

Taggert outlined the proposed course of action rapidly. When he was finished, Spencer Candron simply said, "All right. I can take care of my end of it." He stood up. "I'll see you, Brian."

Brian Taggert lay back down on the couch, propped up his feet, and winked at Candron. "Watch and check, Spence."

Candron went back down the stairs. Mrs. Jesser smiled up at him as he entered the reception room. "Well! That didn't take long! Are you leaving, Mr. Candron?"

"Yes," he said, glancing at the wall clock. "Grab and run, you know. I'll see you soon, Mrs. Jesser. Be an angel."

He went out the door again and headed down the street. Mrs. Jesser had been right; it hadn't taken him long. He'd been in Taggert's office a little over one minute, and less than half a dozen actual words had been spoken. The rest of the conversation had been on a subtler level, one which was almost completely nonverbal. Not that Spencer Candron was a telepath; if he had been, it wouldn't have been necessary for him to come to the headquarters building. Candron's talents simply didn't lie along that line. His ability to probe the minds of normal human beings was spotty and unreliable at best. But when two human beings understand each other at the level that existed between members of the Society, there is no need for longwinded discourses.

The big stratoliner slowed rapidly as it approached the Peiping People's Airfield. The pilot, a big-boned Britisher who had two jobs to do at once, watched the airspeed indicator. As the needle dropped, he came in on a conventional landing lane, aiming for the huge field below. Then, as the needle reached a certain point, just above the landing minimum, he closed his eyes for a fraction of a second and thought, with all the mental power at his command: *NOW!*

For a large part of a second, nothing happened, but the pilot knew his message had been received.

Then a red gleam came into being on the control board.

"What the hell?" said the co-pilot.

The pilot swore. "I *told* 'em that door was weak! We've ripped the luggage door off her hinges. Feel her shake?"

The co-pilot looked grim. "Good thing it happened now instead of in mid-flight. At that speed, we'd been torn apart."

"*Blown* to bits, you mean," said the pilot. "Let's bring her in."

By that time, Spencer Candron was a long way below the ship, falling like a stone, a big suitcase clutched tightly in his arms. He knew that the Chinese radar was watching the jetliner, and that it had undoubtedly picked up two objects dropping from the craft—the door and one other. Candron had caught the pilot's mental signal—anything that powerful could hardly be missed—and had opened the door and leaped.

But those things didn't matter now. Without a parachute, he had flung himself from the plane toward the earth below, and his only thought was his loathing, his repugnance, for that too, too solid ground beneath.

He didn't hate it. That would be deadly, for hate implies as much attraction as love—the attraction of destruction. Fear, too, was out of the question; there must be no such relationship as that between the threatened and the threatener. Only loathing could save him. The earth beneath was utterly repulsive to him.

And he slowed.

His mind would not accept contact with the ground, and his body was forced to follow suit. He slowed.

Minutes later, he was drifting fifty feet above the surface, his altitude held steady by the emotional force of his mind. Not until then did he release the big suitcase he had been holding. He heard it thump as it hit, breaking open and scattering clothing around it.

In the distance, he could hear the faint moan of a siren. The Chinese radar had picked up two falling objects. And they would find two: one door and one suitcase, both of which could be accounted for by the "accident." They would know that no parachute had opened; hence, if they found no body, they would be certain that no human being could have dropped from the plane.

The only thing remaining now was to get into the city itself. In the darkness, it was a little difficult to tell exactly where he was, but the lights of Peiping weren't far away, and a breeze was carrying him toward it. He wanted to be in just the right place before he set foot on the ground.

By morning, he would be just another one of the city's millions.

Morning came three hours later. The sun came up quietly, as if its sole purpose in life were to make a liar out of Kipling. The venerable old Chinese gentleman who strolled quietly down Dragon Street looked as though he were merely out for a placid walk for his morning constitutional. His clothing was that of a middle-class office worker, but his dignified manner, his wrinkled brown face, his calm brown eyes, and his white hair brought respectful looks from the other passers-by on the Street of the Dragon. Not even the thirty-five years of Communism, which had transformed agrarian China into an industrial and technological nation that ranked with the best, had destroyed the ancient Chinese respect for age.

That respect was what Spencer Candron relied on to help him get his job done. Obvious wealth would have given him respect, too, as would the trappings of power; he could have posed as an Honorable Director or a People's Advocate. But that would have brought unwelcome attention as well as respect. His disguise would never stand up under careful examination, and trying to pass himself off as an important citizen might bring on just such an examination. But an old man had both respect and anonymity.

Candron had no difficulty in playing the part. he had known many elderly chinese, and he understood them well. even the emotional control of the oriental was simple to simulate; candron knew what "emotional control" *really* meant.

You don't control an automobile by throwing the transmission out of gear and letting the engine run wild. Suppressing an emotion is not controlling it, in the fullest sense. "Control" implies guidance and use.

Peiping contained nearly three million people in the city itself, and another three million in the suburbs; there was little chance that the People's Police would single out one venerable oldster to question, but Candron wanted an escape route just in case they did. He kept walking until he found the neighborhood he wanted, then he kept his eyes open for a small hotel. He didn't want one that was too expensive, but, on the other hand, he didn't want one so cheap that the help would be untrustworthy.

He found one that suited his purpose, but he didn't want to go in immediately. There was one more thing to do. He waited until the shops were open, and then went in search of second-hand luggage. He had enough money in his pockets to buy more brand-new expensive luggage than a man could carry, but he didn't want luggage that looked either expensive or new. When he finally found what he wanted, he went in search of clothing, buying a piece at a time, here and there, in widely scattered shops. Some of it was new, some of it was secondhand, all of it fit both the body and the personality of the old man he was supposed to be. Finally, he went to the hotel.

The clerk was a chubby, blandly happy, youngish man who bowed his head as Candron approached. There was still the flavor of the old politeness in his speech, although the flowery beauty of half a century before had disappeared.

"Good morning, venerable sir; may I be of some assistance?"

Candron kept the old usages. "This old one would be greatly honored if your excellent hostelry could find a small corner for the rest of his unworthy body," he said in excellent Cantonese.

"It is possible, aged one, that this miserable hovel may provide some space, unsuited though it may be to your honored presence," said the clerk, reverting as best he could to the language of a generation before. "For how many people would you require accommodations?"

"For my humble self only," Candron said.

"It can, I think, be done," said the clerk, giving him a pleasant smile. Then his face took on an expression of contrition. "I hope, venerable one, that you will not think this miserable creature too bold if he asks for your papers?"

"Not at all," said Candron, taking a billfold from his inside coat pocket. "Such is the law, and the law of the People of China is to be always respected."

He opened the billfold and spread the papers for the clerk's inspection. They were all there—identification, travel papers, everything. The clerk looked them over and jotted down the numbers in the register book on the desk, then turned the book around. "Your chop, venerable one."

The "chop" was a small stamp bearing the ideograph which indicated the name Candron was using. Illiteracy still ran high in China because of the difficulty in memorizing the tens of thousands of ideographs which made up the written language, so each man carried a chop to imprint his name. Officially, China used the alphabet, spelling out the Chinese words phonetically—and, significantly, they had chosen the Latin alphabet of the Western nations rather than the Cyrillic of the Soviets. But old usages die hard.

Candron imprinted the ideograph on the page, then, beside it, he wrote "Ying Lee" in Latin characters.

The clerk's respect for this old man went up a degree. He had expected to have to put down the Latin characters himself. "Our humble establishment is honored by your esteemed presence, Mr. Ying," he said. "For how long will it be your pleasure to bestow this honor upon us?"

"My poor business, unimportant though it is, will require it least one week; at the most, ten days." Candron said, knowing full well that twenty-four hours would be his maximum, if everything went well.

"It pains me to ask for money in advance from so honorable a gentleman as yourself," said the clerk, "but such are the rules. It will be seven and a half yuan per day, or fifty yuan per week."

Candron put five ten-yuan notes on the counter. Since the readjustment of the Chinese monetary system, the yuan had regained a great deal of its value.

A young man who doubled as bellhop and elevator operator took Candron up to the third floor. Candron tipped him generously, but not extravagantly, and then proceeded to unpack his suitcase. He hung the suits in the closet and put the shirts in the clothes chest. By the time he was through, it looked as though Ying Lee was prepared to stay for a considerable length of time.

Then he checked his escape routes, and found two that were satisfactory. Neither led downward to the ground floor, but upward, to the roof. The hotel was eight stories high, higher than any of the nearby buildings. No one would expect him to go up.

Then he gave his attention to the room itself. He went over it carefully, running his fingers gently over the walls and the furniture, noticing every detail with his eyes. He examined the chairs, the low bed, the floor—everything.

He was not searching for spy devices. He didn't care whether there were any there or not. He wanted to know that room. To know it, become familiar with it, make it a part of him.

Had there been any spy devices, they would have noticed nothing unusual. There was only an old man there, walking slowly around the room, muttering to himself as though he were thinking over something important or, perhaps, merely reminiscing on the past, mentally chewing over his memories.

He did not peer, or poke, or prod. He did not appear to be looking for anything. He picked up a small, cheap vase and looked at it as though it were an old friend; he rubbed his hand over the small writing desk, as though he had written many things in that familiar place; he sat down in a chair and leaned back in it and caressed the armrests with his palms as though it were an honored seat in his own home. And, finally, he undressed, put on his nightclothes, and lay down on the bed, staring at the ceiling with a soft smile on his face. After ten minutes or so, his eyes closed and remained that way for three-quarters of an hour.

Unusual? No. An old man must have his rest. There is nothing unusual about an old man taking a short nap.

When he got up again, Spencer Candron was thoroughly familiar with the room. It was home, and he loved it.

Nightfall found the honorable Mr. Ying a long way from his hotel. He had, as his papers had said, gone to do business with a certain Mr. Yee, had haggled over the price of certain goods, and had been unsuccessful in establishing a mutual price. Mr. Yee was later to be able to prove to the People's Police that he had done no business whatever with Mr. Ying, and had had no notion whatever that Mr. Ying's business connections in Nanking were totally nonexistent.

But, on that afternoon, Mr. Ying had left Mr. Yee with the impression that he would return the next day with, perhaps, a more amenable attitude toward Mr. Yee's prices. Then Mr. Ying Lee had gone to a restaurant for his evening meal.

He had eaten quietly by himself, reading the evening edition of the Peiping *Truth* as he ate his leisurely meal. Although many of the younger people had taken up the use of the knife and fork, the venerable Mr. Ying clung to the chopsticks of an earlier day, plied expertly between the thumb and forefinger of his right hand. He was not the only elderly man in the place who did so.

Having finished his meal and his newspaper in peace, Mr. Ying Lee strolled out into the gathering dusk. By the time utter darkness had come, and the widely-spaced street lamps of the city had come alive, the elderly Mr. Ying Lee was within half a mile of the most important group of buildings in China.

The Peiping Explosion, back in the sixties, had almost started World War Three. An atomic blast had leveled a hundred square miles of the city and started fires that had taken weeks to extinguish. Soviet Russia had roared in its great bear voice that the Western Powers had attacked, and was apparently on the verge of coming to the defense of its Asian comrade when the Chinese government had said irritatedly that there had been no attack, that traitorous and counterrevolutionary Chinese agents of Formosa had sabotaged an atomic plant, nothing more, and that the honorable comrades of Russia would be wise not to set off anything that would destroy civilization. The Russian Bear grumbled and sheathed its claws.

The vast intelligence system of the United States had reported that (A) the explosion had been caused by carelessness, not sabotage, but the Chinese had had to save face, and (B) the Soviet Union had no intention of actually starting an atomic war at that time. If she had, she would have shot first and made excuses afterwards. But she *had* hoped to make good propaganda usage of the blast.

The Peiping Explosion had caused widespread death and destruction, yes; but it had also ended up being the fastest slum-clearance project on record. The rebuilding had taken somewhat more time than the clearing had taken, but the results had been a new Peiping—a modern city in every respect. And nowhere else on Earth was there one hundred square miles of *completely* modern city. Alteration takes longer than starting from scratch if the techniques are available; there isn't so much dead wood to clear away.

In the middle of the city, the Chinese government had built its equivalent of the Kremlin—nearly a third of a square mile of ultra-modern buildings designed to house every function of the Communist Government of China. It had taken slave labor to do the job, but the job had been done.

A little more than half a mile on a side, the area was surrounded by a wall that had been designed after the Great Wall of China. It stood twenty-five feet high and looked very quaint and picturesque.

And somewhere inside it James Ch'ien, American-born physicist, was being held prisoner. Spencer Candron, alias Mr. Ying Lee, had to get him out.

Dr. Ch'ien was important. The government of the United States knew he was important, but they did not yet know *how* important he was.

Man had already reached the Moon and returned. The Martian expedition had landed safely, but had not yet returned. No one had heard from the Venusian expedition, and it was presumed lost. But the Moon was being jointly claimed by Russian and American suits at the United Nations, while the United Nations itself was trying to establish a claim. The Martian expedition was American, but a Russian ship was due to land in two months. The lost Venusian expedition had been Russian, and the United States was ready to send a ship there.

After nearly forty years, the Cold War was still going on, but now the scale had expanded from the global to the interplanetary.

And now, up-and-coming China, defying the Western Powers and arrogantly ignoring her Soviet allies, had decided to get into the race late and win it if she could.

And she very likely could, if she could exploit the abilities of James Ch'ien to the fullest. If Dr. Ch'ien could finish his work, travel to the stars would no longer be a wild-eyed idea; if he could finish, spatial velocities would no longer be limited to the confines of the rocket, nor even to the confines of the velocity of light. Man could go to the stars.

The United States Federal Government knew—or, at least, the most responsible officers of that government knew—that Ch'ien's equations led to interstellar travel, just as Einstein's equations had led to atomic energy. Normally, the United States would never have allowed Dr. Ch'ien to attend the International Physicists Conference in Peiping. But diplomacy has its rules, too.

Ch'ien had published his preliminary work—a series of highly abstruse and very controversial equations—back in '80. The paper had appeared in a journal that was circulated only in the United States and was not read by the majority of mathematical physicists. Like the work of Dr. Fred Hoyle, thirty years before, it had been laughed at by the majority of the men in the field. Unlike Hoyle's work, it had never received any publicity. Ch'ien's paper had remained buried.

In '81, Ch'ien had realized the importance of his work, having carried it further. He had reported his findings to the proper authorities of the United States Government, and had convinced that particular branch of the government that his work had useful validity. But it was too late to cover up the hints that he had already published.

Dr. James Ch'ien was a friendly, gregarious man. He liked to go to conventions and discuss his work with his colleagues. He was, in addition, a man who would never let anything go once he had got hold of it, unless he was convinced that he was up a blind alley. And, as far as Dr. Ch'ien was concerned, that took a devil of a lot of convincing.

The United States government was, therefore, faced with a dilemma. If they let Ch'ien go to the International Conferences, there was the chance that he would be forced, in some way, to divulge secrets that were vital to the national defense of the United States. On the other hand, if they forbade him to go, the Communist governments would suspect that Ch'ien knew something important, and they would check back on his previous work and find his publications of 1980. If they did, and realized the importance of that paper, they might be able to solve the secret of the interstellar drive.

The United States government had figuratively flipped a coin, and the result was that Ch'ien was allowed to come and go as he pleased, as though he were nothing more than just another government physicist.

And now he was in the hands of China.

How much did the Chinese know? Not much, evidently; otherwise they would never have bothered to go to the trouble of kidnaping Dr. James Ch'ien and covering the kidnaping so elaborately. They *suspected*, yes: but they couldn't *know*. They knew that the earlier papers meant something, but they didn't know what—so they had abducted Ch'ien in the hope that he would tell them.

James Ch'ien had been in their hands now for two months. How much information had they extracted by now? Personally, Spencer Candron felt that they had got nothing. You can force a man to work; you can force him to tell the truth. But you can *not* force a man to create against his will.

Still, even a man's will can be broken, given enough time. If Dr. Ch'ien weren't rescued soon...

Tonight, Candron thought with determination. *I'll get Ch'ien tonight.* That was what the S.M.M.R. had sent him to do. And that's what he would—*must*—do.

Ahead of him loomed the walls of the Palace of the Great Chinese People's Government. Getting past them and into the inner court was an act that was discouraged as much as possible by the Special Police guard which had charge of those walls. They were brilliantly lighted and heavily guarded. If Candron tried to levitate himself over, he'd most likely be shot down in midair. They might be baffled afterwards, when they tried to figure out how he had come to be flying around up there, but that wouldn't help Candron any.

Candron had a better method.

When the automobile carrying the People's Minister of Finance, the Honorable Chou Lung, went through the Gate of the Dog to enter the inner court of the Palace, none of the four men inside it had any notion that they were carrying an unwanted guest. How could they? The car was a small one; its low, streamlined body carried only four people, and there was no luggage compartment, since the powerful little vehicle was designed only for maneuvering in a crowded city or for fast, short trips to nearby towns. There was simply no room for another passenger, and both the man in the car and the guards who passed it through were so well aware of that fact that they didn't even bother to think about it. It never occurred to them that a slight, elderly-looking gentleman might be hanging beneath the car, floating a few inches off the ground, holding on with his fingertips, and allowing the car to pull him along as it moved on into the Palace of the Great Chinese People's Government.

Getting into the subterranean cell where Dr. James Ch'ien was being held was a different kind of problem. Candron knew the interior of the Palace by map only, and the map he had studied had been admittedly inadequate. It took him nearly an hour to get to the right place. Twice, he avoided a patrolling guard by taking to the air and concealing himself in the darkness of an overhead balcony. Several other times, he met men in civilian clothing walking along the narrow walks, and he merely nodded at them. He looked too old and too well-dressed to be dangerous.

The principle that made it easy was the fact that no one expects a lone man to break into a heavily guarded prison.

After he had located the building where James Ch'ien was held, he went high-flying. The building itself was one which contained the living quarters of several high-ranking officers of the People's Government. Candron knew he would be conspicuous if he tried to climb up the side of the building from the outside, but he managed to get into the second floor without being observed. Then he headed for the elevator shafts.

It took him several minutes to jimmy open the elevator door. His mind was sensitive enough to sense the nearness of others, so there was no chance of his being caught red-handed. When he got the door open, he stepped into the shaft, brought his loathing for the bottom into the fore, and floated up to the top floor. From there it was a simple matter to get to the roof, drop down the side, and enter the open window of an officer's apartment.

He entered a lighted window rather than a darkened one. He wanted to know what he was getting into. He had his gun ready, just in case, Pg 2but there was no sign of anyone in the room he entered. A quick search showed that the other two rooms were also empty. His mind had told him that there was no one awake in the apartment, but a sleeping man's mind, filled with dimmed, chaotic thoughts, blended into the background and might easily be missed.

Then Spencer Candron used the telephone, punching the first of the two code numbers he had been given. A connection was made to the room where a twenty-four-hour guard kept watch over James Ch'ien via television pickups hidden in the walls of his prison apartment in the basement.

Candron had listened to recordings of one man's voice for hours, getting the exact inflection, accent, and usage. Now, he made use of that practice.

"This is General Soong," he said sharply. "We are sending a Dr. Wan down to persuade the guest. We will want recordings of all that takes place."

"Yes, sir," said the voice at the other end.

"Dr. Wan will be there within ten minutes, so be alert."

"Yes, sir. All will be done to your satisfaction."

"Excellent," said Candron. He smiled as he hung up. Then he punched another secret number. This one connected him with the guards outside Ch'ien's apartment. As General Soong, he warned them of the coming of Dr. Wan. Then he went to the window, stepped out, and headed for the roof again.

There was no danger that the calls would be suspected. Those two phones could not be contacted except from inside the Palace, and not even then unless the number was known.

Again he dropped down Elevator Shaft Three. Only Number One was operating this late in the evening, so there was no fear of meeting it coming up. He dropped lightly to the roof of the car, where it stood empty in the basement, opened the escape hatch in the roof, dropped inside, opened the door, and emerged into the first basement. Then he started down the stairs to the subbasement.

The guards were not the least suspicious, apparently. Candron wished he were an honest-to-God telepath, so he could be absolutely sure. The officer at the end of the corridor that led to Ch'ien's apartment was a full captain, a tough-looking, swarthy Mongol with dark, hard eyes. "You are Dr. Wan?" he asked in a guttural baritone.

"I am," Candron said. This was no place for traditional politeness. "Did not General Soong call you?"

"He did, indeed, doctor. But I assumed you would be carrying—" He gestured, as though not quite sure what to say.

Candron smiled blandly. "Ah. You were expecting the little black bag, is it not so? No, my good captain; I am a psychologist, not a medical doctor."

The captain's face cleared. "So. The persuasion is to be of the more subtle type."

"Indeed. Only thus can we be assured of his co-operation. One cannot force the creative mind to create; it must be cajoled. Could one have forced the great K'ung Fu-tse to become a philosopher at the point of a sword?"

"It is so," said the captain. "Will you permit me to search you?"

The affable Dr. Wan emptied his pockets, then permitted the search. The captain casually looked at the identification in the wallet. It was, naturally, in perfect order for Dr. Wan. The identification of Ying Lee had been destroyed hours ago, since it was of no further value.

"These things must be left here until you come out, doctor," the captain said. "You may pick them up when you leave." He gestured at the pack of cigarettes. "You will be given cigarettes by the interior guard. Such are my orders."

"Very well," Candron said calmly. "And now, may I see the patient?" He had wanted to keep those cigarettes. Now he would have to find a substitute.

The captain unlocked the heavy door. At the far end, two more guards sat, complacently playing cards, while a third stood at a door a few yards away. A television screen imbedded in the door was connected to an interior camera which showed the room within.

The corridor door was closed and locked behind Candron as he walked toward the three interior guards. They were three more big, tough Mongols, all wearing the insignia of lieutenants. This was not a prisoner who could be entrusted to the care of common soldiers; the secret was too important to allow the *hoi polloi* in on it. They carried no weapons; the three of them could easily take care of Ch'ien if he tried anything foolish, and besides, it kept weapons out of Ch'ien's reach. There were other methods of taking care of the prisoner if the guards were inadequate.

The two officers who were playing cards looked up, acknowledged Dr. Wan's presence, and went back to their game. The third, after glancing at the screen, opened the door to James Ch'ien's apartment. Spencer Candron stepped inside.

It was because of those few seconds—the time during which that door was open—that Candron had called the monitors who watched Ch'ien's apartment. Otherwise, he wouldn't have bothered. He needed fifteen seconds in which to act, and he couldn't do it with that door open. If the monitors had given an alarm in these critical seconds...

But they hadn't, and they wouldn't. Not yet.

The man who was sitting in the easy-chair on the opposite side of the room looked up as Candron entered.

James Ch'ien (B.S., M.S., M.I.T., Ph. D., U.C.L.A.) was a young man, barely past thirty. His tanned face no longer wore the affable smile that Candron had seen in photographs, and the jet-black eyes beneath the well-formed brows were cold instead of friendly, but the intelligence behind the face still came through.

As the door was relocked behind him, Candron said, in Cantonese: "This unworthy one hopes that the excellent doctor is well. Permit me to introduce my unworthy self: I am Dr. Wan Feng."

Dr. Ch'ien put the book he was reading in his lap. He looked at the ceiling in exasperation, then back at Candron. "All right," he said in English, "so you don't believe me. But I'll repeat it again in the hope that I can get it through your skulls." It was obvious that he was addressing, not only his visitor, but anyone else who might be listening.

"I do not speak Chinese," he said, emphasizing each word separately. "I can say 'Good morning' and 'Good-by', and that's about it. I *do* wish I could say 'drop dead,' but that's a luxury I can't indulge. If you can speak English, then go ahead; if not, quit wasting my time and yours. Not," he added, "that it won't be a waste of time anyway, but at least it will relieve the monotony."

Candron knew that Ch'ien was only partially telling the truth. The physicist spoke the language badly, but he understood it fairly well.

"Sorry, doctor," Candron said in English, "I guess I forgot myself. I am Dr. Wan Feng."

Ch'ien's expression didn't change, but he waved to a nearby chair. "Sit down, Dr. Feng, and tell me what propaganda line you've come to deliver now."

Candron smiled and shook his head slowly. "That was unworthy of you, Dr. Ch'ien. Even though you have succumbed to the Western habit of putting the family name last, you are perfectly aware that 'Wan,' not 'Feng,' is my family name."

The physicist didn't turn a hair. "Force of habit, Dr. Wan. Or, rather, a little retaliation. I was called 'Dakta Chamis' for two days, and even those who could pronounce the name properly insisted on 'Dr. James.' But I forget myself. I am supposed to be the host here. Do sit down and tell me why I should give myself over to Communist China just because my grandfather was born here back in the days when China was a republic."

Spencer Candron knew that time was running out, but he had to force Ch'ien into the right position before he could act. He wished again that he had been able to keep the cigarettes. Ch'ien was a moderately heavy smoker, and one of those drugged cigarettes would have come in handy now. As it was, he had to handle it differently. And that meant a different approach.

"No, Dr. Ch'ien," he said, in a voice that was deliberately too smooth, "I will not sit down, thank you. I would prefer that you stand up."

The physicist's face became a frozen mask. "I see that the doctorate you claim is not for studies in the field of physics. You're not here to worm things out of me by discussing my work talking shop. What is it, *Doctor* Wan?"

"I am a psychologist." Candron said. He knew that the monitors watching the screens and listening to the conversation were recording everything. He knew that they shouldn't be suspicious yet. But if the real General Soong should decide to check on what his important guest was doing....

"A psychologist," Ch'ien repeated in a monotone. "I see."

"Yes. Now, will you stand, or do I have to ask the guards to lift you to your feet?"

James Ch'ien recognized the inevitable, so he stood. But there was a wary expression in his black eyes. He was not a tall man; he stood nearly an inch shorter than Candron himself.

"You have nothing to fear, Dr. Ch'ien," Candron said smoothly. "I merely wish to test a few of your reactions. We do not wish to hurt you." He put his hands on the other man's shoulders, and positioned him. "There," he said. "Now. Look to the left."

"Hypnosis, eh?" Ch'ien said with a grim smile. "All right. Go ahead." He looked to his left.

"Not with your head," Candron said calmly. "Face me and look to the left with your eyes."

Ch'ien did so, saying: "I'm afraid you'll have to use drugs after all, Dr. Wan. I will not be hypnotized."

"I have no intention of hypnotizing you. Now look to the right."

Ch'ien obeyed.

Candron's right hand was at his side, and his left hand was toying with a button on his coat. "Now up," he said.

Dr. James Ch'ien rolled his eyeballs upward.

Candron had already taken a deep breath. Now he acted. His right hand balled into a fist and arced upwards in a crashing uppercut to Ch'ien's jaw. At almost the same time, he jerked the button off his coat, cracked it with his fingers along the special fissure line, and threw it to the floor.

As the little bomb spewed forth unbelievable amounts of ultra-finely divided carbon in a dense black cloud of smoke, Candron threw both arms around the collapsing physicist, ignoring the pain in the knuckles of his right hand. The smoke cloud billowed around them, darkening the room and obscuring the view from the monitor screens that were watching them. Candron knew that the guards were acting now; he knew that the big Mongols outside were already inserting the key in the door and inserting their nose plugs; he knew that the men in the monitor room had hit an alarm button and had already begun to flood the room with sleep gas. But he paid no attention to these things.

Instead, he became homesick.

Home. It was a little place he knew and loved. He could no longer stand the alien environment around him; it was repugnant, repelling. All he could think of was a little room, a familiar room, a beloved room. He knew the cracks in its ceiling, the feel of the varnish on the homely little desk, the touch of the worn carpet against his feet, the very smell of the air itself. And he loved them and longed for them with all the emotional power that was in him.

And suddenly the darkness of the smoke-filled prison apartment was gone.

Spencer Candron stood in the middle of the little hotel room he had rented early that morning. In his arms, he held the unconscious figure of Dr. James Ch'ien.

He gasped for breath, then, with an effort, he stooped, allowed the limp body of the physicist to collapse over his shoulder, and stood straight again, carrying the man like a sack of potatoes. He went to the door of the room and opened it carefully. The hall was empty. Quickly, he moved outside, closing the door behind him, and headed toward the stair. This time, he dared not trust the elevator shaft. The hotel only boasted one elevator, and it might be used at any time. Instead, he allowed his dislike for the stair treads to adjust his weight to a few pounds, and then ran up them two at a time.

On the roof of the hotel, he adjusted his emotional state once more, and he and his sleeping burden drifted off into the night, toward the sea.

No mind is infinitely flexible, infinitely malleable, infinitely capable of taking punishment, just as no material substance, however constructed, is capable of absorbing the energies brought to bear against it indefinitely.

A man can hate with a virulent hatred, but unless time is allowed to dull and soothe that hatred, the mind holding it will become corroded and cease to function properly, just as a machine of the finest steel will become corroded and begin to fail if it is drenched with acid or exposed to the violence of an oxidizing atmosphere.

The human mind can insulate itself, for a time, against the destructive effects of any emotion, be it hatred, greed, despondency, contentment, happiness, pleasure, anger, fear, lust, boredom, euphoria, determination, or any other of the myriads of "ills" that man's mind—and thus his flesh—is heir to. As long as a mind is capable of changing from one to another, to rotate its crops, so to speak, the insulation will remain effective, and the mind will remain undamaged. But any single emotional element, held for too long, will break down the resistance of the natural insulation and begin to damage the mind.

Even that least virulent of emotions, love, can destroy. The hot, passionate love between new lovers must be modified or it will kill. Only when its many facets can be shifted around, now one and now the other coming into play, can love be endured for any great length of time.

Possibly the greatest difference between the sane and the unsane is that the sane know when to release a destructive force before it does more than minimal damage; to modify or eliminate an emotional condition before it becomes a deadly compulsion; to replace one set of concepts with another when it becomes necessary to do so; to recognize that point when the mind must change its outlook or die. To stop the erosion, in other words, before it becomes so great that it cannot be repaired.

For the human mind cannot contain any emotion, no matter how weak or how fleeting, without change. And the point at which that change ceases to be *con*structive and becomes, instead, *de*structive—*that* is the ultimate point beyond which no human mind can go without forcing a change—*any* change—in itself.

Spencer Candron knew that. To overuse the psionic powers of the human mind is as dangerous as overusing morphine or alcohol. There are limits to mental powers, even as there are limits to physical powers.

Psychokinesis is defined as the ability of a human mind to move, no matter how slightly, a physical object by means of psionic application alone. In theory, then, one could move planets, stars, even whole galaxies by thought alone. But, in physical terms, the limit is easily seen. Physically, it would be theoretically possible to destroy the sun if one had enough atomic energy available, but that would require the energy of another sun—or more. And, at that point, the Law of Diminishing Returns comes into operation. If you don't want a bomb to explode, but the only way to destroy that bomb is by blowing it up with another bomb of equal power, where is the gain?

And if the total mental power required to move a planet is greater than any single human mind can endure—or even greater than the total mental endurance of a thousand planetsfull of minds, is there any gain?

There is not, and can never be, a system without limits, and the human mind is a system which obeys that law.

None the less, Spencer Candron kept his mind on flight, on repulsion, on movement, as long as he could. He was perfectly willing to destroy his own mind for a purpose, but he had no intention of destroying it uselessly. He didn't know how long he kept moving eastward; he had no way of knowing how much distance he had covered nor how long it had taken him. But, somewhere out over the smoothly undulating surface of the Pacific, he realized that he was approaching his limit. And, a few seconds later, he detected the presence of men beneath the sea.

He knew they were due to rise an hour before dawn, but he had no idea how long that would be. He had lost all track of time. He had been keeping his mind on controlling his altitude and motion, and, at the same time, been careful to see whether Dr. Ch'ien came out of his unconscious state. Twice more he had had to strike the physicist to keep him out cold, and he didn't want to do it again.

So, when he sensed the presence of the American submarine beneath the waves, he sank gratefully into the water, changing the erosive power of the emotion that had carried him so far, and relaxing into the simple physical routine of keeping both himself and Ch'ien afloat.

By the time the submarine surfaced a dozen yards away, Spencer Candron was both physically and mentally exhausted. He yelled at the top of his lungs, and then held on to consciousness just long enough to be rescued.

"The official story," said Senator Kerotski, "is that an impostor had taken Dr. Ch'ien's place before he ever left the United States—" He grinned. "At least, the substitution took place before the delegates reached China. So the 'assassination' was really no assassination at all. Ch'ien was kidnaped here, and a double put in his place in Peiping. That absolves both us and the Chinese Government of any complicity. We save face for them, and they save face for us. Since he turned up here, in the States, it's obvious that he couldn't have been in China." He chuckled, but there was no mirth in it. "So the cold war still continues. We know what they did, and—in a way—they know what we did. But not how we did it."

The senator looked at the other two men who were with him on the fifth floor office of the *Society for Mystical and Metaphysical Research*. Taggert was relaxing on his couch, and Spencer Candron, just out of the hospital, looked rather pale as he sat in the big, soft chair that Taggert had provided.

The senator looked at Candron. "The thing I don't understand is, why was it necessary to knock out Ch'ien? He'll have a sore jaw for weeks. Why didn't you just tell him who you were and what you were up to?"

Candron glanced at Taggert, but Taggert just grinned and nodded.

"We couldn't allow that," said Candron, looking at Senator Kerotski. "Dr. James Ch'ien has too much of a logical, scientific mind for that. We'd have ruined him if he'd seen me in action."

The senator looked a little surprised. "Why? We've convinced other scientists that they were mistaken in their observations. Why not Ch'ien?"

"Ch'ien is too good a scientist," Candron said. "He's not the type who would refuse to believe something he saw simply because it didn't agree with his theories. Ch'ien is one of those dangerous in-betweens. He's too brilliant to be allowed to go to waste, and, at the same time, too rigid to change his manner of thinking. If he had seen me teleport or levitate, he wouldn't reject it—he'd try to explain it. And that would have effectively ruined him."

"Ruined him?" The senator looked a little puzzled.

Taggert raised his heavy head from the couch. "Sure, Leo," he said to the senator. "Don't you see? We *need* Ch'ien on this interstellar project. He absolutely *must* dope out the answer somehow, and no one else can do it as quickly."

"With the previous information," the senator said, "we would have been able to continue."

"Yeah?" Taggert said, sitting up. "Has anyone been able to dope out Fermat's Last Theorem without Fermat? No. So why ruin Ch'ien?"

"It would ruin him," Candron broke in, before the senator could speak. "If he saw, beyond any shadow of a doubt, that levitation and teleportation were possible, he would have accepted his own senses as usable data on definite phenomena. But, limited as he is by his scientific outlook, he would have tried to evolve a scientific theory to explain what he saw. What else could a scientist *do*?"

Senator Kerotski nodded, and his nod said: "I see. He would have diverted his attention from the field of the interstellar drive to the field of psionics. And he would have wasted years trying to explain an inherently nonlogical area of knowledge by logical means."

"That's right," Candron said. "We would have set him off on a wild goose chase, trying to solve the problems of psionics by the scientific, the logical, method. We would have presented him with an unsolvable problem."

Taggert patted his knees. "We would have given him a problem that he could not solve with the methodology at hand. It would be as though we had proved to an ancient Greek philosopher that the cube *could* be doubled, and then allowed him to waste his life trying to do it with a straight-edge and compass."

"We know Ch'ien's psychological pattern," Candron continued. "He's not capable of admitting that there is any other thought pattern than the logical. He would try to solve the problems of psionics by logical methods, and would waste the rest of his life trying to do the impossible."

The senator stroked his chin. "That's clear," he said at last. "Well, it was worth a cracked jaw to save him. We've given him a perfectly logical explanation of his rescue and, simultaneously, we've put the Chinese government into absolute confusion. They have no idea of how you got out of there, Candron."

"That's not as important as saving Ch'ien," Candron said.

"No," the senator said quickly, "of course not. After all, the Secretary of Research needs Dr. Ch'ien—the man's important."

Spencer Candron smiled. "I agree. He's practically indispensable—as much as a man can be."

"He's the Secretary's right hand man," said Taggert firmly.

THE END

By Proxy

It's been said that the act of creation is a solitary thing—that teams never create; only individuals. But sometimes a team may be needed to make creation effective....

R. Terrence Elshawe did not conform to the mental picture that pops into the average person's mind when he hears the words "news reporter." Automatically, one thinks of the general run of earnest, handsome, firm-jawed, level-eyed, smooth-voiced gentlemen one sees on one's TV screen. No matter which news service one subscribes to, the reporters are all pretty much of a type. And Terrence Elshawe simply wasn't the type.

The confusion arises because thirty-odd years of television has resulted in specialization. If you run up much Magnum Telenews time on your meter, you're familiar with the cultured voice and rugged good looks of Brett Maxon, "your Magnum reporter," but Maxon is a reporter only in the very literal sense of the word. He's an actor, whose sole job is to make Magnum news sound more interesting than some other telenews service, even though he's giving you exactly the same facts. But he doesn't go out and dig up those stories.

The actual leg work of getting the news into Maxon's hands so that he can report it to you is done by research reporters—men like Terrence Elshawe.

Elshawe was a small, lean man with a large, round head on which grew close-cropped, light brown hair. His mouth was wide and full-lipped, and had a distinct tendency to grin impishly, even when he was trying to look serious. His eyes were large, blue, and innocent; only when the light hit them at just the right angle was it possible to detect the contact lenses which corrected an acute myopia.

When he was deep in thought, he had a habit of relaxing in his desk chair with his head back and his eyes closed. His left arm would be across his chest, his left hand cupping his right elbow, while the right hand held the bowl of a large-bowled briar which Elshawe puffed methodically during his ruminations. He was in exactly that position when Oler Winstein put his head in the door of Elshawe's office.

"Busy?" Winstein asked conversationally.

In some offices, if the boss comes in and finds an employee in a pose like that, there would be a flurry of sudden action on the part of the employee as he tried frantically to look as though he had only paused for a moment from his busy work. Elshawe's only reaction was to open his eyes. He wasn't the kind of man who would put on a phony act like that, even if his boss fired him on the spot.

"Not particularly," he said, in his slow, easy drawl. "What's up?"

Winstein came on into the office. "I've got something that might make a good spot. See what you think."

If Elshawe didn't conform to the stereotype of a reporter, so much less did Oler Winstein conform to the stereotype of a top-flight TV magnate. He was no taller than Elshawe's five-seven, and was only slightly heavier. He wore his hair in a crew cut, and his boyish face made him look more like a graduate student at a university than the man who had put Magnum Telenews together with his own hands. He had an office, but he couldn't be found in it more than half the time; the rest of the time, he was prowling around the Magnum Building, wandering into studios and offices and workshops. He wasn't checking up on his employees, and never gave the impression that he was. He didn't throw his weight around and he didn't snoop. If he hired a man for a job, he expected the job to be done, that was all. If it was, the man could sleep at his desk or play solitaire or drink beer for all Winstein cared; if the work wasn't done, it didn't matter if the culprit looked as busy as an anteater at a picnic—he got one warning and then the sack. The only reason for Winstein's prowling around was the way his mind worked; it was forever bubbling with ideas, and he wanted to bounce those ideas off other people to see if anything new and worthwhile would come of them.

He didn't look particularly excited, but, then, he rarely did. Even the most objective of employees is likely to become biased one way or another if he thinks his boss is particularly enthusiastic about an idea. Winstein didn't want yes-men around him; he wanted men who could and would think. And he had a theory that, while the tenseness of an emergency could and did produce some very high-powered thinking indeed, an atmosphere of that kind wasn't a good thing for day-in-and-day-out work. He saved that kind of pressure for the times that he needed it, so that it was effective because of its contrast with normal procedure.

Elshawe took his heavy briar out of his mouth as Winstein sat down on the corner of the desk. "You have a gleam in your eye, Ole," he said accusingly.

"Maybe," Winstein said noncommittally. "We might be able to work something out of it. Remember a guy by the name of Malcom Porter?"

Elshawe lowered his brows in a thoughtful frown. "Name's familiar. Wait a second. Wasn't he the guy that was sent to prison back in 1979 for sending up an unauthorized rocket?"

Winstein nodded. "That's him. Served two years of a five-year sentence, got out on parole about a year ago. I just got word from a confidential source that he's going to try to send up another one."

"I didn't know things were so pleasant at Alcatraz," Elshawe said. "He seems to be trying awfully hard to get back in."

"Not according to what my informant says. This time, he's going to ask for permission. And this time, he's going to have a piloted craft, not a self-guided missile, like he did in '79."

"Ho*ho*. Well, there might be a story in it, but I can't see that it would be much of one. It isn't as if a rocket shoot were something unusual. The only thing unusual about it is that it's a private enterprise shoot instead of a Government one."

Winstein said: "Might be more to it than that. Do you remember the trial in '79?"

"Vaguely. As I remember it, he claimed he didn't send up a rocket, but the evidence showed overwhelmingly that he had. The jury wasn't out more than a few minutes, as I remember."

"There was a little more to it than that," Winstein said.

"I was in South Africa at the time," Elshawe said. "Covering the civil war down there, remember?"

"That's right. You're excused," Winstein said, grinning. "The thing was that Malcom Porter didn't claim he hadn't sent the thing up. What he did claim was that it wasn't a rocket. He claimed that he had a new kind of drive in it—something that didn't use rockets.

"The Army picked the thing up on their radar screens, going straight up at high acceleration. They bracketed it with Cobra pursuit rockets and blew it out of the sky when it didn't respond to identification signals. They could trace the thing back to its launching pad, of course, and they nabbed Malcom Porter.

"Porter was furious. Wanted to slap a suit against the Government for wanton destruction of private property. His claim was that the law forbids unauthorized rocket tests all right, but his missile wasn't illegal because it wasn't a rocket."

"What did he claim it was?" Elshawe asked.

"He said it was a secret device of his own invention. Antigravity, or something like that."

"Did he try to prove it?"

"No. The Court agreed that, according to the way the law is worded, only 'rocket-propelled missiles' come under the ban. The judge said that if Malcom Porter could prove that the missile wasn't rocket-propelled, he'd dismiss the case. But Porter wanted to prove it by building another missile. He wouldn't give the court his plans or specifications for the drive he claimed he'd invented, or say anything about it except that it operated—and I quote—'on a new principle of physics'—unquote. Said he wouldn't tell them anything because the Government was simply using this as an excuse to take his invention away from him."

Elshawe chuckled. "That's as flimsy a defense as I've heard."

"Don't laugh," said Winstein. "It almost worked."

"What? How?"

"It threw the burden of proof on the Government. They thought they had him when he admitted that he'd shot the thing off, but when he denied that it was a rocket, then, in order to prove that he'd committed a crime, they had to prove that it *was* a rocket. It wasn't up to Porter to prove that it *wasn't*."

"Hey," Elshawe said in admiration, "that's pretty neat. I'm almost sorry it didn't work."

"Yeah. Trouble was that the Army had blown up the evidence. They knew it was a rocket, but they had to prove it. They had recordings of the radar picture, of course, and they used that to show the shape and acceleration of the missile. They proved that he'd bought an old obsolete Odin rocket from one of the small colleges in the Midwest—one that the Army had sold them as a demonstration model for their rocket engineering classes. They proved that he had a small liquid air plant out there at his place in New Mexico. In other words, they proved that he had the equipment to rebuild the rocket and the fuel to run it.

"Then they got a battery of high-powered physicists up on the stands to prove that nothing else but a rocket could have driven the thing that way.

"Porter's attorney hammered at them in cross-examination, trying to get one of them to admit that it was possible that Porter had discovered a new principle of physics that could fly a missile without rockets, but the Attorney General's prosecutor had coached them pretty well. They all said that unless there was evidence to the contrary, they could not admit that there was such a principle.

"When the prosecutor presented his case to the jury, he really had himself a ball. I'll give you a transcript of the trial later; you'll have to read it for yourself to get the real flavor of it. The gist of it was that things had come to a pretty pass if a man could claim a scientific principle known only to himself as a defense against a crime.

"He gave one analogy I liked. He said, suppose that a man is found speeding in a car. The cops find him all alone, behind the wheel, when they chase him down. Then, in court, he admits that he was alone, and that the car was speeding, but he insists that the car was steering itself, and that he wasn't in control of the vehicle at all. And what was steering the car? Why, a new scientific principle, of course."

Elshawe burst out laughing. "Wow! No wonder the jury didn't stay out long! I'm going to have to dig the recordings of the newscasts out of the files; I missed a real comedy while I was in Africa."

Winstein nodded. "We got pretty good coverage on it, but our worthy competitor, whose name I will not have mentioned within these sacred halls, got Beebee Vayne to run a commentary on it, and we got beat out on the meters."

"Vayne?" Elshawe was still grinning. "That's a new twist—getting a comedian to do a news report."

"I'll have to admit that my worthy competitor, whose name et cetera, does get an idea once in a while. But I don't want him beating us out again. We're in on the ground floor this time, and I want to hog the whole thing if I can."

"Sounds like a great idea, if we can swing it," Elshawe agreed. "Do you have a new gimmick? You're not going to get a comedian to do it, are you?"

"Heaven forbid! Even if it had been my own idea three years ago, I wouldn't repeat it, and I certainly won't have it said that I copy my competitors. No, what I want you to do is go out there and find out what's going on. Get a full background on it. We'll figure out the presentation angle when we get some idea of what he's going to do this time." Winstein eased himself off the corner of Elshawe's desk and stood up. "By the way—"

"Yeah?"

"Play it straight when you go out there. You're a reporter, looking for news; you haven't made any previous judgments."

Elshawe's pipe had gone out. He fired it up again with his desk lighter. "I don't want to be," he said between puffs, "too cagey. If he's got ... any brains ... he'll know it's ... a phony act ... if I overdo it." He snapped off the lighter and looked at his employer through a cloud of blue-gray smoke. "I mean, after all, he's on the records as being a crackpot. I'd be a pretty stupid reporter if I believed everything he said. If I don't act a little skeptical, he'll think I'm either a blockhead or a phony or both."

"Maybe," Winstein said doubtfully. "Still, some of these crackpots fly off the handle if you doubt their word in the least bit."

"I'll tell you what I'll do," Elshawe said. "He used to live here in New York, didn't he?"

"Still does," Winstein said. "He has a two-floor apartment on Central Park West. He just uses that New Mexico ranch of his for relaxation."

"He's not hurting for money, is he?" Elshawe asked at random. "Anyway, what I'll do is look up some of the people he knows and get an idea of what kind of a bird he is. Then, when I get out there, I'll know more what kind of line to feed him."

"That sounds good. But whatever you do, play it on the soft side. My confidential informant tells me that the only reason we're getting this inside info is because Malcom Porter is sore about the way our competition treated him four years ago."

"Just who is this confidential informant, anyway, Ole?" Elshawe asked curiously.

Winstein grinned widely. "It's supposed to be very confidential. I don't want it to get any further than you."

"Sure not. Since when am I a blabbermouth? Who is it?"

"Malcom Porter."

Two days later, Terrence Elshawe was sitting in the front seat of a big station wagon, watching the scenery go by and listening to the driver talk as the machine tooled its way out of Silver City, New Mexico, and headed up into the Mogollon Mountains.

"Was a time, not too long back," the driver was saying, "when a man couldn't get up into this part of the country 'thout a pack mule. Still places y'can't, but the boss had t' have a road built up to the ranch so's he could bring in all that heavy equipment. Reckon one of these days the Mogollons 'll be so civilized and full a people that a fella might as well live in New York."

Elshawe, who hadn't seen another human being for fifteen minutes, felt that the predicted overcrowding was still some time off.

"'Course," the driver went on, "I reckon folks have t' live some place, but I never could see why human bein's are so all-fired determined to bunch theirselves up so thick together that they can't hardly move—like a bunch of sheep in a snowstorm. It don't make sense to me. Does it to you, Mr. Skinner?"

That last was addressed to the other passenger, an elderly man who was sitting in the seat behind Elshawe.

"I guess it's pretty much a matter of taste, Bill," Mr. Skinner said in a soft voice.

"I reckon," Bill said, in a tone that implied that anyone whose tastes were so bad that he wanted to live in the city was an object of pity who probably needed psychiatric treatment. He was silent for a moment, in obvious commiseration with his less fortunate fellows.

Elshawe took the opportunity to try to get a word in. The chunky Westerner had picked him up at the airport, along with Mr. Samuel Skinner, who had come in on the same plane with Elshawe, and, after introducing himself as Bill Rodriguez, he had kept up a steady stream of chatter ever since. Elshawe didn't feel he should take a chance on passing up the sudden silence.

"By the way; has Mr. Porter applied to the Government for permission to test his ... uh ... his ship, yet?"

Bill Rodriguez didn't take his eyes off the winding road. "Well, now, I don't rightly know, Mr. Elshawe. Y'see, I just work on the ranch up there. I don't have a doggone thing to do with the lab'r'tory at all—'cept to keep the fence in good shape so's the stock don't get into the lab'r'tory area. If Mr. Porter wants me to know somethin', he tells me, an' if he don't, why, I don't reckon it's any a my business."

"I see," said Elshawe. *And that shuts* me *up*, he thought to himself. He took out his pipe and began to fill it in silence.

"How's everything out in Los Angeles, Mr. Skinner?" Rodriguez asked the passenger in back. "Haven't seen you in quite a spell."

Elshawe listened to the conversation between the two with half an ear and smoked his pipe wordlessly.

He had spent the previous day getting all the information he could on Malcom Porter, and the information hadn't been dull by any means.

Porter had been born in New York in 1949, which made him just barely thirty-three. His father, Vanneman Porter, had been an oddball in his own way, too. The Porters of New York didn't quite date back to the time of Peter Stuyvesant, but they had been around long enough to acquire the feeling that the twenty-four dollars that had been paid for Manhattan Island had come out of the family exchequer. Just as the Vanderbilts looked upon the Rockefellers as newcomers, so the Porters looked on the Vanderbilts.

For generations, it had been tacitly conceded that a young Porter gentleman had only three courses of action open to him when it came time for him to choose his vocation in life. He could join the firm of Porter & Sons on Wall Street, or he could join some other respectable business or banking enterprise, or he could take up the Law. (Corporation law, of course—*never* criminal law.) For those few who felt that the business world was not for them, there was a fourth alternative—studying for the priesthood of the Episcopal Church. Anything else was unheard of.

So it had been somewhat of a shock to Mr. and Mrs. Hamilton Porter when their only son, Vanneman, had announced that he intended to study physics at M.I.T. But they gave their permission; they were quite certain that the dear boy would "come to his senses" and join the firm after he had been graduated. He was, after all, the only one to carry on the family name and manage the family holdings.

But Vanneman Porter not only stuck to his guns and went on to a Ph.D.; he compounded his delinquency by marrying a pretty, sweet, but not overly bright girl named Mary Kelley.

Malcom Porter was their son.

When Malcom was ten years old, both his parents were killed in a smashup on the New Jersey Turnpike, and the child went to live with his widowed grandmother, Mrs. Hamilton Porter.

Terry Elshawe had gathered that young Malcom Porter's life had not been exactly idyllic from that point on. Grandmother Porter hadn't approved of her son's marriage, and she seemed to have felt that she must do everything in her power to help her grandson overcome the handicap of having nonaristocratic blood in his veins.

Elshawe wasn't sure in his own mind whether environment or heredity had been the deciding factor in Malcom Porter's subsequent life, but he had a hunch that the two had been acting synergistically. It was likely that the radical change in his way of life after his tenth year had as much to do with his behavior as the possibility that the undeniably brilliant mental characteristics of the Porter family had been modified by the genes of the pretty but scatter-brained wife of Vanneman Porter.

Three times, only his grandmother's influence kept him from being expelled from the exclusive prep school she had enrolled him in, and his final grades were nothing to mention in polite society, much less boast about.

In her own way, the old lady was trying to do her best for him, but she had found it difficult to understand her own son, and his deviations from the Porter norm had been slight in comparison with those of his son. When the time came for Malcom to enter college, Grandmother Porter was at a total loss as to what to do. With his record, it was unlikely that any law school would take him unless he showed tremendous improvement in his pre-law courses. And unless that improvement was a general one, not only as far as his studies were concerned, but in his handling of his personal life, it would be commercial suicide to put him in any position of trust with Porter & Sons. It wasn't that he was dishonest; he simply couldn't be trusted to do anything properly. He had a tendency to follow his own whims and ignore everybody else.

The idea of his entering the clergy was never even considered.

It came almost as a relief to the old woman when Malcom announced that he was going to study physics, as his father had done.

The relief didn't last long. By the time Malcom was in his sophomore year, he was apparently convinced that his instructors were dunderheads to the last man. That, Elshawe thought, was probably not unusual among college students, but Malcom Porter made the mistake of telling them about it.

One of the professors with whom Elshawe had talked had said: "He acted as though he owned the college. That, I think, was what was his trouble in his studies; he wasn't really stupid, and he wasn't as lazy as some said, but he didn't want to be bothered with anything that he didn't enjoy. The experiments he liked, for instance, were the showy, spectacular ones. He built himself a Tesla coil, and a table with hidden AC electromagnets in it that would make a metal plate float in the air. But when it came to nucleonics, he was bored. Anything less than a thermonuclear bomb wasn't any fun."

The trouble was that he called his instructors stupid and dull for being interested in "commonplace stuff," and it infuriated him to be forced to study such "junk."

As a result, he managed to get himself booted out of college toward the end of his junior year. And that was the end of his formal education.

Six months after that, his grandmother died. Although she had married into the Porter family, she was fiercely proud of the name; she had been born a Van Courtland, so she knew what family pride was. And the realization that Malcom was the last of the Porters—and a failure—was more than she could bear. The coronary attack she suffered should have been cured in a week, but the best medico-surgical techniques on Earth can't help a woman who doesn't want to live.

Her will showed exactly what she thought of Malcom Porter. The Porter holdings were placed in trust. Malcom was to have the earnings, but he had no voice whatever in control of the principal until he was fifty years of age.

Instead of being angry, Malcom was perfectly happy. He had an income that exceeded a million dollars before taxes, and didn't need to worry about the dull details of making money. He formed a small corporation of his own, Porter Research Associates, and financed it with his own money. It ran deep in the red, but Porter didn't mind; Porter Research Associates was a hobby, not a business, and running at a deficit saved him plenty in taxes.

By the time he was twenty-five, he was known as a crackpot. He had a motley crew of technicians and scientists working for him—some with Ph.D.'s, some with a trade-school education. The personnel turnover in that little group was on a par with the turnover of patients in a maternity ward, at least as far as genuine scientists were concerned. Porter concocted theories and hypotheses out of cobwebs and became furious with anyone who tried to tear them down. If evidence came up that would tend to show that one of his pet theories was utter hogwash, he'd come up with an *ad hoc* explanation which showed that this particular bit of evidence was an exception. He insisted that "the basis of science lies in the experimental evidence, not in the pronouncements of authorities," which meant that any recourse to the theories of Einstein, Pauli, Dirac, Bohr, or Fermi was as silly as quoting Aristotle, Plato, or St. Thomas Aquinas. The only authority he would accept was Malcom Porter.

Nobody who had had any training in science could work long with a man like that, even if the pay had been high, which it wasn't. The only people who could stick with him were the skilled workers—the welders, tool-and-die men, electricians, and junior engineers, who didn't care much about theories as long as they got the work done. They listened respectfully to what Porter had to say and then built the gadgets he told them to build. If the gadgets didn't work the way Porter expected them to, Porter would fuss and fidget with them until he got tired of them, then he would junk them and try something else. He never blamed a technician who had followed orders. Since the salaries he paid were proportional to the man's "ability and loyalty"—judged, of course, by Porter's own standards—he soon had a group of technician-artisans who knew that their personal security rested with Malcom Porter, and that personal loyalty was more important than the ability to utilize the scientific method.

Not everything that Porter had done was a one-hundred-per cent failure. He had managed to come up with a few basic improvements, patented them, and licensed them out to various manufacturers. But these were purely an accidental by-product. Malcom Porter was interested in "basic research" and not much else, it seemed.

He had written papers and books, but they had been uniformly rejected by the scientific journals, and those he had had published himself were on a par with the writings of Immanuel Velikovsky and George Adamski.

And now he was going to shoot a rocket—or whatever it was—to the moon. Well, Elshawe thought, if it went off as scheduled, it would at least be worth watching. Elshawe was a rocket buff; he'd watched a dozen or more moon shots in his life—everything from the automatic supply-carriers to the three-man passenger rockets that added to the personnel of

Moon Base One—and he never tired of watching the bellowing monsters climb up skywards on their white-hot pillars of flame.

And if nothing happened, Elshawe decided, he'd at least get a laugh out of the whole episode.

After nearly two hours of driving, Bill Rodriguez finally turned off the main road onto an asphalt road that climbed steeply into the pine forest that surrounded it. A sign said: *Double Horseshoe Ranch—Private Road—No Trespassing*.

Elshawe had always thought of a ranch as a huge spread of flat prairie land full of cattle and gun-toting cowpokes on horseback; a mountainside full of sheep just didn't fit into that picture.

After a half mile or so, the station wagon came to a high metal-mesh fence that blocked the road. On the big gate, another sign proclaimed that the area beyond was private property and that trespassers would be prosecuted.

Bill Rodriguez stopped the car, got out, and walked over to the gate. He pressed a button in one of the metal gateposts and said, "Ed? This's Bill. I got Mr. Skinner and that New York reporter with me."

After a slight pause, there was a metallic click, and the gate swung open. Rodriguez came back to the car, got in, and drove on through the gate. Elshawe twisted his head to watch the big gate swing shut behind them.

After another ten minutes, Rodriguez swung off the road onto another side road, and ten minutes after that the station wagon went over a small rise and headed down into a small valley. In the middle of it, shining like bright aluminum in the sun, was a vessel.

Now I know Porter is nuts, Elshawe thought wryly.

Because the vessel, whatever it was, was parallel to the ground, looking like the fuselage of a stratojet, minus wings and tail, sitting on its landing gear. Nowhere was there any sign of a launching pad, with its gantries and cranes and jet baffles. Nor was there any sign of a rocket motor on the vessel itself.

As the station wagon approached the cluster of buildings a hundred yards this side of the machine, Elshawe realized with shock that the thing *was* a stripped-down stratojet—an old Grumman *Supernova*, circa 1970.

"Well, Elijah got there by sitting in an iron chair and throwing a magnet out in front of himself," Elshawe said, "so what the hell."

"What?" Rodriguez asked blankly.

"Nothing; just thinking out loud. Sorry."

Behind Elshawe, Mr. Skinner chuckled softly, but said nothing.

When the station wagon pulled up next to one of the cluster of white prefab buildings, Malcom Porter himself stepped out of the wide door and walked toward them.

Elshawe recognized the man from his pictures—tall, wide-shouldered, dark-haired, and almost handsome, he didn't look much like a wild-eyed crackpot. He greeted Rodriguez and Skinner rather peremptorily, but he smiled broadly and held out his hand to Elshawe.

"Mr. Elshawe? I'm Malcom Porter." His grip was firm and friendly. "I'm glad to see you. Glad you could make it."

"Glad to be here, Dr. Porter," Elshawe said in his best manner. "It's quite a privilege." He knew that Porter liked to be called "Doctor"; all his subordinates called him that.

But, surprisingly, Porter said: "Not 'Doctor,' Mr. Elshawe; just 'Mister.' My boys like to call me 'Doctor,' but it's sort of a nickname. I don't have a degree, and I don't claim one. I don't want the public thinking I'm claiming to be something I'm not."

"I understand, Mr. Porter."

Bill Rodriguez's voice broke in. "Where do you want me to put all this stuff, Doc?" He had unloaded Elshawe's baggage from the station wagon and set it carefully on the ground. Skinner picked up his single suitcase and looked at Porter inquiringly.

"My usual room, Malcom?"

"Yeah. Sure, Sam; sure." As Skinner walked off toward one of the other buildings, Porter said: "Quite a load of baggage you have there, Mr. Elshawe. Recording equipment?"

"Most of it," the reporter admitted. "Recording TV cameras, 16mm movie cameras, tape recorders, 35mm still cameras—the works. I wanted to get good coverage, and if you've got any men that you won't be using during the take-off, I'd like to borrow them to help me operate this stuff."

"Certainly; certainly. Come on, Bill, let's get this stuff over to Mr. Elshawe's suite."

The suite consisted of three rooms, all very nicely appointed for a place as far out in the wilderness as this. When Elshawe got his equipment stowed away, Porter invited him to come out and take a look at his pride and joy.

"The first real spaceship, Elshawe," he said energetically. "The first real spaceship. The rocket is no more a spaceship than a rowboat is an ocean-going vessel." He gestured toward the sleek, shining, metal ship. "Of course, it's only a pilot model, you might say. I don't have hundreds of millions of dollars to spend; I had to make do with what I could afford. That's an old Grumman *Supernova* stratojet. I got it fairly cheap because I told 'em I didn't want the engines or the wings or the tail assembly.

"But she'll do the job, all right. Isn't she a beauty?"

Elshawe had his small pocket recorder going; he might as well get all this down. "Mr. Porter," he asked carefully, "just how does this vessel propel itself? I understand that, at the trial, it was said that you claimed it was an antigravity device, but that you denied it."

"Those idiots!" Porter exploded angrily. "Nobody understood what I was talking about because they wouldn't listen! Antigravity! *Pfui!* When they learned how to harness electricity, did they call it anti-electricity? When they built the first atomic reactor, did they call it anti-atomic energy? A rocket works against gravity, but they don't call *that* antigravity, do they? My device works *with* gravity, not against it."

"What sort of device is it?" Elshawe asked.

"I call it the Gravito-Inertial Differential Polarizer," Porter said importantly.

Elshawe was trying to frame his next question when Porter said: "I know the name doesn't tell you much, but then, names never do, do they? You know what a transformer does, but what does the name by itself convey? Nothing, unless you know what it does in the first place. A cyclotron cycles something, but what? A broadcaster casts something abroad—what? And how?"

"I see. And the 'how' and 'what' is your secret, eh?"

"Partly. I can give you a little information, though. Suppose there were only one planet in all space, and you were standing on its surface. Could you tell if the planet were spinning or not? And, if so, how fast? Sure you could; you could measure the so-called centrifugal force. The same thing goes for a proton or electron or neutron or even a neutrino. But, if it *is* spinning, what is the spin relative to? To the particle itself? That's obvious nonsense. Therefore, what is commonly called 'inertia' is as much a property of so-called 'empty space' as it is a property of matter. My device simply utilizes spatial inertia by polarizing it against the matter inertia of the ship, that's all."

"Hm-m-m," said Elshawe. As far as his own knowledge of science went, that statement made no sense whatever. But the man's manner was persuasive. Talking to him, Elshawe began to have the feeling that Porter not only knew what he was talking about, but could actually do what he said he was going to do.

"What's that?" Porter asked sharply, looking up into the sky.

Elshawe followed his gaze. "That" was a Cadillac aircar coming over a ridge in the distance, its fans making an ever-louder throaty hum as it approached. It settled down to an altitude of three feet as it neared, and floated toward them on its cushion of air. On its side, Elshawe could see the words, UNITED STATES GOVERNMENT, and beneath that, in smaller letters, *Civil Aeronautics Authority*.

"Now what?" Porter muttered softly. "I haven't notified anyone of my intentions yet—not officially."

"Sometimes those boys don't wait for official notification," Elshawe said.

Porter glanced at him, his eyes narrowed. "You didn't say anything, did you?"

"Look, Mr. Porter, I don't play that way," Elshawe said tightly. "As far as I'm concerned, this is your show; I'm just here to get the story. You did us a favor by giving us advance notice; why should we louse up your show for you?"

"Sorry," Porter said brusquely. "Well, let's make a good show of it."

The CAA aircar slowed to a halt, its fans died, and it settled to its wheels.

Two neatly dressed, middle-aged men climbed out. Both were carrying briefcases. Porter walked briskly toward them, a warm smile on his face; Elshawe tagged along behind. The CAA men returned Porter's smile with smiles that could only be called polite and businesslike.

Porter performed the introductions, and the two men identified themselves as Mr. Granby and Mr. Feldstein, of the Civil Aeronautics Authority.

"Can I help you, gentlemen?" Porter asked.

Granby, who was somewhat shorter, fatter, and balder than his partner, opened his briefcase. "We're just here on a routine check, Mr. Porter. If you can give us a little information...?" He let the half-question hang in the air as he took a sheaf of papers from his briefcase.

"Anything I can do to help," Porter said.

Granby, looking at the papers, said: "In 1979, I believe you purchased a Grumman *Supernova* jet powered aircraft from Trans-American Airlines? Is that correct?"

"That is correct," Porter agreed.

Granby handed one of the papers to Porter. "That is a copy of the registration certificate. Is the registration number the same as it is on your copy?"

"I believe so," Porter said, looking at the number. "Yes, I'm sure it is."

Granby nodded briskly. "According to our records, the machine was sold as scrap. That is to say, it was not in an airworthy condition. It was, in fact, sold without the engines. Is that correct?"

"Correct."

"May I ask if you still own the machine in question?"

Porter gave the man a look that accused Granby of being stupid or blind or both. He pointed to the hulking fuselage of the giant aircraft. "There it is."

Granby and Feldstein both turned to look at it as though they had never noticed it before. "Ah, yes," Granby said, turning back. "Well, that's about all there is to it." He looked at his partner. "It's obvious that there's no violation here, eh, Feldstein?"

"Quite," said Feldstein in a staccato voice.

"Violation?" Porter asked. "What violation?"

"Well, nothing, really," Granby said, deprecatingly. "Just routine, as I said. People have been known to buy aircraft as scrap and then repair them and re-outfit them."

"Is that illegal?" Porter asked.

"No, no," said Granby hastily. "Of course not. But any ship so re-outfitted and repaired must pass CAA inspection before it can leave the ground, you understand. So we keep an eye on such transactions to make sure that the law isn't violated."

"After three years?" Porter asked blandly.

"Well ... ah ... well ... you know how it is," Granby said nervously. "These things take time. Sometimes ... due to ... clerical error, we overlook a case now and then." He glanced at his partner, then quickly looked back at Porter.

"As a matter of fact, Mr. Porter," Feldstein said in a flat, cold voice, "in view of your record, we felt that the investigation at this time was advisable. You bought a scrap missile and used it illegally. You can hardly blame us for looking into this matter."

"No," said Porter. He had transferred his level gaze to the taller of the two men, since it had suddenly become evident that Feldstein, not Granby, was the stronger of the two.

"However," Feldstein went on, "I'm glad to see that we have no cause for alarm. You're obviously not fitting that up as an aircraft. By the way—just out of curiosity—what *are* you doing with it?" He turned around to look at the big fuselage again.

Porter sighed. "I had intended to hold off on this for a few days, but I might as well let the cat out now. I intend to take off in that ship this week end."

Granby's eyes opened wide, and Feldstein spun around as though someone had jabbed him with a needle. "*What?*"

Porter simply repeated what he had said. "I had intended to make application to the Space Force for permission to test it," he added.

Feldstein looked at him blankly for a moment.

Then: "The *Space* Force? Mr. Porter, civilian aircraft come under the jurisdiction of the CAA."

"How's he going to fly it?" Granby asked. "No engines, no wings, no control surfaces. It's silly."

"Rocket motors in the rear, of course," said Feldstein. "He's converted the thing into a rocket."

"But the tail is closed," Granby objected. "There's no rocket orifice."

"Dummy cover, I imagine," Feldstein said. "Right, Mr. Porter?"

"Wrong," said Porter angrily. "The motive power is supplied by a mechanism of my own devising! It has nothing to do with rockets! It's as superior to rocket power as the electric motor is to the steam engine!"

Feldstein and Granby glanced at each other, and an almost identical expression of superior smugness grew over their features. Feldstein looked back at Porter and said, "Mr. Porter, I assure you that it doesn't matter what you're using to lift that thing. You could be using dynamite for all I care. The law says that it can't leave the ground unless it's airworthy. Without wings or control surfaces, it is obviously not airworthy. If it is not a rocket device, then it comes under the jurisdiction of the Civil Aeronautics Authority, and if you try to take off without our permission, you'll go to jail.

"If it *is* a rocket device, then it will be up to the Space Force to inspect it before take-off to make sure it is not dangerous.

"I might remind you, Mr. Porter, that you are on parole. You still have three years to serve on your last conviction. I wouldn't play around with rockets any more if I were you."

Porter blew up. "Listen, you! I'm not going to be pushed around by you or anyone else! I know better than you do what Alcatraz is like, and I'm not going back there if I can help it. This country is still Constitutionally a democracy, not a bureaucracy, and I'm going to see to it that I get to exercise my rights!

"I've invented something that's as radically new as ... as ... as the Law of Gravity was in the Seventeenth Century! And I'm going to get recognition for it, understand me?" He gestured furiously toward the fuselage of the old *Supernova*. "That ship is not only airworthy, but *space*worthy! And it's a thousand times safer and a thousand times better than any rocket will ever be!

"For your information, Mister Smug-Face, I've already flown her!"

Porter stopped, took a deep breath, compressed his lips, and then said, in a lower, somewhat calmer tone, "Know what she'll do? That baby will hang in the air just like your aircar, there—and without benefit of those outmoded, power-wasting blower fans, too.

"Now, understand me, Mr. Feldstein: I'm not going to break any laws unless I have to. You and all your bureaucrat friends will have a chance to give me an O.K. on this test. But I warn you, brother—*I'm going to take that ship up!*"

Feldstein's jaw muscles had tightened at Porter's tone when he began, but he had relaxed by the time the millionaire had finished, and was even managing to look smugly tolerant. Elshawe had thumbed the button on his minirecorder when the conversation had begun, and he was chuckling mentally at the thought of what was going down on the thin, magnetite-impregnated, plastic thread that was hissing past the recording head.

Feldstein said: "Mr. Porter, we came here to remind you of the law, nothing more. If you intend to abide by the law, fine and dandy. If not, you'll go back to prison.

"That ship is not airworthy, and—"

"How do you know it isn't?" Porter roared.

"By inspection, Mr. Porter; by inspection." Feldstein looked exasperated. "We have certain standards to go by, and an aircraft without wings or control surfaces simply doesn't come up to those standards, that's all. Even a rocket has to have stabilizing fins." He paused and zipped open his briefcase.

"In view of your attitude," he said, pulling out a paper, "I'm afraid I shall have to take official steps. This is to notify you that the aircraft in question has been inspected and found to be not airworthy. Since—"

"Wait a minute!" Porter snapped. "Who are you to say so? How would you know?"

"I happen to be an officer of the CAA," said Feldstein, obviously trying to control his temper. "I also happen to be a graduate aeronautical engineer. If you wish, I will give the ... the ... aircraft a thorough inspection, inside and out, and—"

"Oh, no!" said Porter. His voice and his manner had suddenly become very gentle. "I don't think that would do much good, do you?"

"What do you mean?"

"I mean that you'd condemn the ship, no matter what you found inside. You couldn't O.K. a ship without airfoils, could you?"

"Of course not," said Feldstein, "that's obvious, in the face of—"

"All right, then give me the notification and forget the rest of the inspection." Porter held out his hand.

Feldstein hesitated. "Well, now, without a complete inspection—"

Again Porter interrupted. "You're not going to get a complete inspection, Buster," he said with a wolfish grin. "Either serve that paper or get off my back."

Feldstein slammed the paper into Porter's hand. "That's your official notification! If necessary, Mr. Porter, we will be back with a Federal marshal! Good day, Mr. Porter. Let's go, Granby."

The two of them marched back to their aircar and climbed inside. The car lifted with a roar of blowers and headed back over the mountains toward Albuquerque.

But long before they were out of sight over the ridge, Malcom Porter had turned on his heel and started back toward the cluster of buildings. He was swearing vilely in a rumbling monotone, and had apparently forgotten all about Elshawe.

The reporter followed in silence for a dozen paces, then he asked: "What's your next step, Mr. Porter?"

Porter came to an abrupt stop, turned, and looked at Elshawe. "I'm going to phone General Fitzsimmons in Washington! I'm—" He stopped, scowling. "No, I guess I'd better phone my lawyer first. I'll find out what they can do and what they can't." Then he turned again and strode rapidly toward the nearest of the buildings.

Seventy-two hours later, Terry Elshawe was in Silver City, talking to his boss over a long-distance line.

"... And that's the way it lines up, Ole. The CAA won't clear his ship for take-off, and the Space Force won't either. And if he tries it without the O.K. of both of them, he'll be right back in Alcatraz."

"He hasn't violated his parole yet, though?" Winstein's voice came distantly.

"No." Elshawe cursed the fact that he couldn't get a vision connection with New York. "But, the way he's acting, he's likely to. He's furious."

"Why wouldn't he let the Space Force officers look over his ship?" Winstein asked. "I still don't see how that would have hurt him if he's really got something."

"It's on the recording I sent you," Elshawe said.

"I haven't played it yet," Winstein said. "Brief me."

"He wouldn't let the Space Force men look at his engine or whatever it is because he doesn't trust them," Elshawe said. "He claims to have this new drive, but he doesn't want anyone to go nosing around it. The Space Force colonel ... what's his name? ... Manetti, that's it. Manetti asked Porter why, if he had a new invention, he hadn't patented it. Porter said that he wasn't going to patent it because that would make it available to every Tom, Dick, and Harry—his very words—who wanted to build it. Porter insists that, since it's impossible to patent the discovery of a new natural law, he isn't going to give away his genius for nothing. He said that Enrico Fermi was the prime example of what happened when the Government got hold of something like that when the individual couldn't argue."

"Fermi?" Winstein asked puzzledly. "Wasn't he a physicist or something, back in the Forties?"

"Right. He's the boy who figured out how to make the atomic bomb practical. But the United States Government latched onto it, and it took him years to get any compensation. He never did get the money that he was entitled to.

"Porter says he wants to make sure that the same thing doesn't happen to him. He wants to prove that he's got something and then let the Government pay him what it's worth and give him the recognition he deserves. He says he has discovered a new natural law and devised a machine that utilizes that law. He isn't going to let go of his invention until he gets credit for everything."

There was a long silence from the other end. After a minute, Elshawe said: "Ole? You there?"

"Oh. Yeah ... sure. Just thinking. Terry, what do you think of this whole thing? Does Porter have something?"

"Damned if I know. If I were in New York, I'd say he was a complete nut, but when I talk to him, I'm halfway convinced that he knows what he's talking about."

There was another long pause. This time, Elshawe waited. Finally, Oler Winstein said: "You think Porter's likely to do something drastic?"

"Looks like it. The CAA has already forbidden him to lift that ship. The Space Force flatly told him that he couldn't take off without permission, and they said he wouldn't get permission unless he let them look over his gizmo ... whatever it is."

"And he refused?"

"Well, he did let Colonel Manetti look it over, but the colonel said that, whatever the drive principle was, it wouldn't operate a ship. He said the engines didn't make any sense. What it boils down to is that the CAA thinks Porter has rockets in the ship, and the Space Force does, too. So they've both forbidden him to take off."

"*Are* there any rocket motors in the ship?" Winstein asked.

"Not as far as I can see," Elshawe said. "He's got two big atomic-powered DC generators aboard—says they have to be DC to avoid electromagnetic effects. But the drive engines don't make any more sense to me than they do to Colonel Manetti."

Another pause. Then: "O.K., Terry; you stick with it. If Porter tries to buck the Government, we've got a hell of a story if his gadget works the way he says it does. If it doesn't—which is more likely—then we can still get a story when they haul him back to the Bastille."

"Check-check. I'll call you if anything happens."

He hung up and stepped out of the phone booth into the lobby of the Murray Hotel. Across the lobby, a glowing sign said *cocktail lounge* in lower-case script.

He decided that a tall cool one wouldn't hurt him any on a day like this and ambled over, fumbling in his pockets for pipe, tobacco pouch, and other paraphernalia as he went. He pushed open the door, spotted a stool at the bar of the dimly-lit room, went over to it and sat down.

He ordered his drink and had no sooner finished than the man to his left said, "Good afternoon, Mr. Elshawe."

The reporter turned his head toward his neighbor. "Oh, hello, Mr. Skinner. I didn't know you'd come to town."

"I came in somewhat earlier. Couple, three hours ago." His voice had the careful, measured steadiness of a man who has had a little too much to drink and is determined not to show it. That surprised Elshawe a little; Skinner had struck him as a middle-aged accountant or maybe a high school teacher—the mild kind of man who doesn't drink at all, much less take a few too many.

"I'm going to hire a 'copter and fly back," Elshawe said. "You're welcome if you want to come along."

Skinner shook his head solemnly. "No. Thank you. I'm going back to Los Angeles this afternoon. I'm just killing time, waiting for the local plane to El Paso."

"Oh? Well, I hope you have a good trip." Elshawe had been under the impression that Skinner had come to New Mexico solely to see the test of Porter's ship. He had wondered before how the man fitted into the picture, and now he was wondering why Skinner was leaving. He decided he might as well try to find out. "I guess you're disappointed because the test has been called off," he said casually.

"Called off? Hah. No such thing," Skinner said. "Not by a long shot. Not Porter. He'll take the thing up, and if the Army doesn't shoot him down, the CAA will see to it that he's taken back to prison. But that won't stop him. Malcom Porter is determined to go down in history as a great scientist, and nothing is going to stop him if he can help it."

"You think his spaceship will work, then?"

"Work? Sure it'll work. It worked in '79; it'll work now. The way that drive is built, it can't help but work. I just don't want to stick around and watch him get in trouble again, that's all."

Elshawe frowned. All the time that Porter had been in prison, his technicians had been getting together the stuff to build the so-called "spaceship," but none of them knew how it was put together or how it worked. Only Porter knew that, and he'd put it together after he'd been released on parole.

But if that was so, how come Skinner, who didn't even work for Porter, was so knowledgeable about the drive? Or was that liquor talking?

"Did you help him build it?" the reporter asked smoothly.

"*Help* him build it? Why, I—" Then Skinner stopped abruptly. "Why, no," he said after a moment. "No. I don't know anything about it, really. I just know that it worked in '79, that's all." He finished his drink and got off his stool. "Well, I've got to be going. Nice talking to you. Hope I see you again sometime."

"Sure. So long, Mr. Skinner." He watched the man leave the bar.

Then he finished his own drink and went back into the lobby and got a phone. Ten minutes later, a friend of his who was a detective on the Los Angeles police force had promised to check into Mr. Samuel Skinner. Elshawe particularly wanted to know what he had been doing in the past three years and very especially what he had been doing in the past year. The cop said he'd find out. There was probably nothing to it, Elshawe reflected, but a reporter who doesn't follow up accidentally dropped hints isn't much of a reporter.

He came out of the phone booth, fired up his pipe again, and strolled back to the bar for one more drink before he went back to Porter's ranch.

Malcom Porter took one of the darts from the half dozen he held in his left hand and hurled it viciously at the target board hung on the far wall of the room.

Thunk!

"Four ring at six o'clock," he said in a tight voice.

Thunk! Thunk! Thunk! Thunk! Thunk!

The other five darts followed in rapid succession. As he threw each one, Porter snapped out a word. "They ... can't ... stop ... Malcom ... Porter!" He glared at the board "Two bull's-eyes; three fours, and a three. Twenty-five points. You owe me a quarter, Elshawe."

The reporter handed him a coin. "Two bits it is. What can you do, Porter? They've got you sewed up tight. If you try to take off, they'll cart you right back to The Rock—if the Army doesn't shoot you down first. Do you want to spend the next ten years engrossed in the scenic beauties of San Francisco Bay?"

"No. And I won't, either."

"Not if the Army gets you. I can see the epitaph now:

Malcom Porter, with vexation, Thought he could defy the nation. He shot for space with great elation—Now he's dust and radiation.

Beneath it, they'll engrave a spaceship argent with A-bombs rampant on a field sable."

Porter didn't take offense. He grinned. "What are you griping about? It would make a great story."

"Sure it would," Elshawe agreed. "But not for me. I don't write the obituary column."

"You know what I like about you, Elshawe?"

"Sure. I lose dart games to you."

"That, yes. But you really sound worried. That means two things. One: You like me. Two: You believe that my ship actually will take off. That's more than any of those other reporters who have been prowling around and phoning in do."

Elshawe shrugged silently and puffed at his pipe. Malcom Porter's ego was showing through. He was wrong on two counts. Elshawe didn't like him; the man's arrogance and his inflated opinion of himself as a scientific genius didn't sit well with the reporter. And Elshawe didn't really believe there was anything but a rocket motor in that hull outside. A new, more powerful kind of rocket perhaps—otherwise Porter wouldn't be trying to take a one-stage rocket to the Moon. But a rocket, nonetheless.

"I don't want to go back to prison," Porter continued, "but I'll risk that if I have to. But I won't risk death just yet. Don't worry; the Army won't know I'm even gone until I'm halfway to the Moon."

"Foo!" said Elshawe. "Every radar base from Albuquerque to the Mexican border has an antenna focused on the air above this ranch. The minute you get above those mountains, they'll have a fix on you, and a minute after that, they'll have you bracketed with Cobras.

"Why don't you let the Government inspectors look it over and give you an O.K.? What makes you think they're all out to steal your invention?"

"Oh, they won't *steal* it," Porter said bitterly. "Heaven's-to-Betsy *no*! But this invention of mine will mean that the United States of America will be in complete control of the planets and the space between. When the Government wants a piece of property, they try to buy it at their price; if they can't do that, they condemn it and pay the owner what they think it's worth—not what the owner thinks it's worth. The same thing applies here; they'd give me what they thought I ought to have—in ten years or so. Look what happened to Fermi.

"No, Elshawe; when the Government comes begging to me for this invention, they can have it—on *my* terms."

"Going to keep it a secret, eh? You can't keep a thing like that secret. Look what happened with atomic energy after World War Two. We kept it a secret from the Russians, didn't we? Fine lot of good that did us. As soon as they knew it was possible, they went to work on it. Nature answers any questions you ask her if you ask her the right way. As soon as the Government sees that your spaceship works, they'll put some of their bright physicists to work on it, and you'll be in the same position as you would have been if you'd showed it to them in the first place. Why risk your neck?"

Porter shook his head. "The analogy isn't valid. Suppose someone had invented the A-bomb in 1810. It would have been a perfectly safe secret because there wasn't a scientist on Earth who included such a thing as atomic energy in his philosophy. And, believe me, this drive of mine is just as far ahead of contemporary scientific philosophy as atomic energy was ahead of Napoleon's scientists.

"Suppose I told you that the fuel my ship uses is a gas lighter than hydrogen. It isn't, but suppose I told you so. Do you think any scientist today could figure out how it worked? No. They *know* that there's no such thing as a gas with a lighter atomic weight than hydrogen. They know it so well that they wouldn't even bother to consider the idea.

"My invention is so far ahead of present-day scientific thought that no scientists except myself could have even considered the idea."

"O.K.; O.K.," Elshawe said. "So you're going to get yourself shot down to prove your point."

Porter grinned lopsidedly. "Not at all. You're still thinking in terms of a rocket. Sure—if I used a rocket, they'd knock me down fast, just as soon as I lifted above the mountains. But I don't have to do that. All I have to do is get a few feet of altitude and hug the ground all the way to the Pacific coast. Once I get out in the middle of the Pacific, I can take off straight up without being bothered at all."

"All right. If your machine will do it," the reporter said, trying to hide his skepticism.

"You still think I've got some kind of rocket, don't you?" Porter asked accusingly. He paused a moment, then, as if making a sudden decision, he said: "Look, Elshawe, I trust you. I'm going to show you the inside of that ship. I won't show you my engines, but I *will* prove to you that there are no rocket motors in her. That way, when you write up the story, you'll be able to say that you have first-hand knowledge of that fact. O.K.?"

"It's up to you," the reporter said. "I'd like to see it."

"Come along," said Malcom Porter.

Elshawe followed Porter out to the field, feeling rather grateful that he was getting something to work on. They walked across the field, past the two gun-toting men in Levis that Porter had guarding the ship. Overhead, the stars were shining brightly through the thin mountain air. Elshawe glanced at his wrist watch. It was a little after ten p.m.

He helped Porter wheel the ramp up to the door of the ship and then followed him up the steps. Porter unlocked the door and went inside. The Grumman had been built to cruise in the high stratosphere, so it was as air-tight as a submarine.

Porter switched on the lights. "Go on in."

The reporter stepped into the cabin of the ship and looked around. It had been rebuilt, all right; it didn't look anything like the inside of a normal stratojet.

"Elshawe."

"Yeah?" The reporter turned to look at Porter, who was standing a little behind him. He didn't even see the fist that arced upward and smashed into his jaw. All he saw was a blaze of light, followed by darkness.

The next thing he knew, something was stinging in his nostrils. He jerked his head aside, coughing. The smell came again. Ammonia.

"Wake up, Elshawe," Porter was saying. "Have another whiff of these smelling salts and you'll feel better."

Elshawe opened his eyes and looked at the bigger man. "I'm awake. Take that stuff away. What's the idea of slugging me?"

"I was afraid you might not come willingly," Porter said apologetically. "I needed a witness, and I figured you'd do better than anyone else."

Elshawe tried to move and found that he was tied to the seat and strapped in with a safety belt. "What's this for?" he asked angrily. His jaw still hurt.

"I'll take that stuff off in a few minutes. I know I can trust you, but I want you to remember that I'm the only one who can pilot this ship. If you try anything funny, neither one of us will get back alive. I'll let you go as soon as we get up to three hundred miles."

Elshawe stared at him. "Where are we?"

"Heading out toward mid-Pacific. I headed south, to Mexico, first. We're over open water now, headed toward Baja California, so I put on the autopilot. As soon as we get out over the ocean, we can really make time. You can watch the sun come up in the west."

"And then?" Elshawe felt dazed.

"And then we head straight up. For empty space."

Elshawe closed his eyes again. He didn't even want to think about it.

"... As you no doubt heard," Terrence Elshawe dictated into the phone, "Malcom Porter made good his threat to take a spaceship of his own devising to the Moon. Ham radios all over North America picked up his speech, which was made by spreading the beam from an eighty-foot diameter parabolic reflector and aiming it at Earth from a hundred thousand miles out. It was a collapsible reflector, made of thin foil, like the ones used on space stations. Paragraph.

"He announced that the trip was made with the co-operation of the United States Space Force, and that it represented a major breakthrough in the conquest of space. He—"

"Just a sec," Winstein's voice broke in. "Is that the truth? Was he really working with the Space Force?"

"Hell, no," said Elshawe. "But they'll have to claim he was now. Let me go on."

"Shoot."

"... He also beamed a message to the men on Moon Base One, telling them that from now on they would be able to commute back and forth from Luna to Earth, just as simply as flying from New York to Detroit. Paragraph.

"What followed was even more astounding. At tremendous acceleration, Malcom Porter and Terrence Elshawe, your reporter, headed for Mars. Inside Porter's ship, there is no feeling of acceleration except for a steady, one-gee pull which makes the passenger feel as though he is on an ordinary airplane, even though the spaceship may be accelerating at more than a hundred gravities. Paragraph.

"Porter's ship circled Mars, taking photographs of the Red Planet—the first close-ups of Mars to be seen by the human race. Then, at the same tremendous rate of speed, Porter's ship returned to Earth. The entire trip took less than thirty-six hours. According to Porter, improved ships should be able to cut that time down considerably. Paragraph."

"Have you got those pics?" Winstein cut in.

"Sure. Porter gave me an exclusive in return for socking me. It was worth it. Remember back in the Twenties, when the newspapermen talked about a scoop? Well, we've got the biggest scoop of the century."

"Maybe," said Winstein. "The Government hasn't made any announcement yet. Where's Porter?"

"Under arrest, where'd you think? After announcing that he would land on his New Mexico ranch, he did just that. As soon as he stepped out, a couple of dozen Government agents grabbed him. Violation of parole—he left the state without notifying his parole officer. But they couldn't touch me, and they knew it.

"Here's another bit of news for your personal information. A bomb went off inside the ship after it landed and blew the drive to smithereens. The only information is inside Porter's head. He's got the Government where the short hair grows."

"Looks like it. See here, Terry; you get all the information you can and be back here by Saturday. You're going to go on the Weekend Report."

"Me? I'm no actor. Let Maxon handle it."

"No. This is hot. You're an eye-witness. Maxon will interview you. Understand?"

"O.K.; you're the boss, Ole. Anything else?"

"Not right now, but if anything more comes up, call in."

"Right. 'Bye." He hung up and leaned back in his chair, cocking his feet up on the desk. It was Malcom Porter's desk and Malcom Porter's chair. He was sitting in the Big Man's office, just as though he owned it. His jaw still hurt a little, but he loved every ache of it. It was hard to remember that he had ever been angry with Porter.

Just before they had landed, Porter had said: "They'll arrest me, of course. I knew that when I left. But I think I can get out of it. There will be various kinds of Government agents all over the place, but they won't find anything. I've burned all my notebooks.

"I'll instruct my attorney that you're to have free run of the place so that you can call in your story."

The phone rang. Elshawe grabbed up the receiver and said: "Malcom Porter's residence." He wished that they had visiphones out in the country; he missed seeing the face of the person he was talking to.

"Let me talk to Mr. Terrence Elshawe, please," said the voice at the other end. "This is Detective Lieutenant Martin of the Los Angeles Police Department."

"This is me, Marty."

"Good! Boy, have I had trouble getting to you! I had to make it an official call before the phone company would put the call through. How does it feel to be notorious?"

"Great. What's new?"

"I got the dope on that Skinner fellow. I suppose you still want it? Or has success gone to your head?"

Elshawe had almost forgotten about Skinner. "Shoot," he said.

The police officer rattled off Samuel Skinner's vital statistics—age, sex, date and place of birth, and so on. Then: "He lived in New York until 1977. Taught science for fifteen years at a prep school there. He—"

"Wait a second," Elshawe interrupted. "When was he born? Repeat that."

"March fourth, nineteen-thirty."

"Fifty-three," Elshawe said, musingly. "Older than he looks. O.K.; go on."

"He retired in '77 and came to L.A. to live. He—"

"Retired at the age of forty-seven?" Elshawe asked incredulously.

"That's right. Not on a teacher's pension, though. He's got some kind of annuity from a New York life insurance company. Pays pretty good, too. He gets a check for two thousand dollars on the third of every month. I checked with his bank on that. Nice, huh?"

"Very nice. Go on."

"He lives comfortably. No police record. Quiet type. One servant, a Chinese, lives with him. Sort of combination of valet and secretary.

"As far as we can tell, he has made four trips in the past three years. One in June of '79, one in June of '80, one in June of '81, and this year he made the fourth one. In '79, he went to Silver City, New Mexico. In '80 and '81, he went to Hawaii. This year, he went to Silver City again. Mean anything to you?"

"Not yet," Elshawe said. "Are you paying for this call, or is the City of Los Angeles footing the bill?"

"Neither. You are."

"Then shut up and let me think for a minute." After less than a minute, he said: "Martin, I want some more data on that guy. I'm willing to pay for it. Should I hire a private detective?"

"That's up to you. I can't take any money for it, naturally—but I'm willing to nose around a little more for you if I can. On the other hand, I can't put full time in on it. There's a reliable detective agency here in L.A.— Drake's the guy's name. Want me to get in touch with him?"

"I'd appreciate it. Don't tell him who wants the information or that it has any connection with Porter. Get—"

"Hold it, Terry ... just a second. You know that if I uncover any indication of a crime, all bets are off. The information goes to my superiors, not to you."

"I know. But I don't think there's any crime involved. You work it from your end and send me the bills. O.K.?"

"Fair enough. What more do you want?"

Elshawe told him.

When the phone call had been completed, Elshawe sat back and made clouds of pipe smoke, which he stared at contemplatively. Then he made two calls to New York—one to his boss and another to a private detective agency he knew he could trust.

The Malcom Porter case quickly became a *cause célèbre*. Somebody goofed. Handled properly, the whole affair might have been hushed up; the Government would have gotten what it wanted, Porter would have gotten what *he* wanted, and everyone would have saved face. But some bureaucrat couldn't see beyond the outer surface of his spectacle lenses, and some other bureaucrat failed to stop the thing in time.

"Gall, gall, and bitter, bitter wormwood," said Oler Winstein, perching himself on the edge of Terry Elshawe's desk.

"You don't Gallic, bitter, wormy, or wooden. What's up?"

"Got a call from Senator Tallifero. He wants to know if you'll consent to appear before the Joint Congressional Committee for Investigating Military Affairs. I get the feeling that if you say 'no,' they'll send a formal invitation—something on the order of a subpoena."

Elshawe sighed. "Oh, well. It's news, anyway. When do they want me to be in Washington?"

"Tomorrow. Meanwhile, Porter, of course, is under arrest and in close confinement. Confusion six ways from Sunday." He shook his head. "I don't understand why they just didn't pat him on the back, say they'd been working on this thing all along, and cover it up fast."

"Too many people involved," Elshawe said, putting his cold pipe in the huge ashtray on his desk. "The Civil Aeronautics crowd must have had a spotter up in those mountains; they had a warrant out for his arrest within an hour after we took off. They also notified the parole board, who put out an all-points bulletin immediately. The Army and the Air Force were furious because he'd evaded their radar net. Porter stepped on so many toes so hard that it was inevitable that one or more would yell before they realized it would be better to keep their mouths shut."

"Well, you get up there and tell your story, and I dare say he'll come out of it."

"Sure he will. They know he's got something, and they know they have to have it. But he's going to go through hell before they give it to him."

Winstein slid off the desk and stood up. "I hope so. He deserves it. By the way, it's too bad you couldn't get a story out of that Sam Skinner character."

"Yeah. But there's nothing to it. After all, even the FBI tried to find out if there was anyone at all besides Porter who might know anything about it. No luck. Not even the technicians who worked with him knew anything useful. Skinner didn't know anything at all." He told the lie with a perfectly straight face. He didn't like lying to Winstein, but there was no other way. He hoped he wouldn't have to lie to the Congressional Committee; perjury was not something he liked doing. The trouble was, if he told the truth, he'd be worse off than if he lied.

He took the plane that night for Washington, and spent the next three days answering questions while he tried to keep his nerves under control. Not once did they even approach the area he wanted them to avoid.

On the plane back, he relaxed, closed his eyes, and, for the first time in days, allowed himself to think about Mr. Samuel Skinner.

The reports from the two detective agencies on the East and West Coasts hadn't made much sense separately, but together they added up to enough to have made it worth Elshawe's time to go to Los Angeles and tackle Samuel Skinner personally. He had called Skinner and made an appointment; Skinner had invited him out to his home.

It was a fairly big house, not too new, and it sat in the middle of a lot that was bigger than normal for land-hungry Los Angeles.

Elshawe ran through the scene mentally. He could see Skinner's mild face and hear his voice saying: "Come in, Mr. Elshawe."

They went into the living room, and Skinner waved him toward a chair. "Sit down. Want some coffee?"

"Thanks; I'd appreciate it." While Skinner made coffee, the reporter looked around the room. It wasn't overly showy, but it showed a sort of subdued wealth. It was obvious that Mr. Skinner wasn't lacking in comforts.

Skinner brought in the coffee and then sat down, facing Elshawe, in another chair. "Now," he said bluntly, "what was that remark you made on the phone about showing up Malcom Porter as a phony? I understood that you actually went to Mars on his ship. Don't you believe the evidence of your own senses?"

"I don't mean that kind of phony," Elshawe said. "And you know it. I'll come to the point. I know that Malcom Porter didn't invent the Gravito-Inertial Differential Polarizer. *You* did."

Skinner's eyes widened. "Where did you get that information?"

"I can't tell you my sources, Mr. Skinner. Not yet, anyhow. But I have enough information to tell me that you're the man. It wouldn't hold up in court, but, with the additional information you can give me, I think it will."

Skinner looked baffled, as if not knowing what to say next.

"Mr. Skinner," Elshawe went on, "a research reporter has to have a little of the crusader in him, and maybe I've got more than most. You've discovered one of the greatest things in history—or invented it, whatever you want to call it. You deserve to go down in history along with Newton, Watt, Roentgen, Edison, Einstein, Fermi, and all the rest."

"But somehow Malcom Porter stole your invention and he intends to take full credit for it. Oh, I know he's paid you plenty of money not to make any fuss, and he probably thinks you couldn't prove anything, anyway. But you don't have to be satisfied with his conscience money any more. With the backing of Magnum Telenews, you can blow Mister Glory-hound Porter's phony setup wide open and take the credit you deserve."

Skinner didn't look at all the way Elshawe had expected. Instead, he frowned a little and said: "I'm glad you came, Mr. Elshawe. I didn't realize that there was enough evidence to connect me with his project." But he didn't look exactly overjoyed.

"Well," Elshawe said tentatively, "if you'll just answer a few questions—"

"Just a minute, Mr. Elshawe. Do you mind if I ask you a few questions first?"

"Go ahead."

Skinner leaned forward earnestly. "Mr. Elshawe, who deserves credit for an invention? Who deserves the money?"

"Why ... why, the inventor, of course."

"The inventor? Or the man who gives it to humanity?"

"I ... don't quite follow you."

He leaned back in his chair again. "Mr. Elshawe, when I invented the Polarizer, I hadn't the remotest idea of what I'd invented. I taught general science in the high school Malcom Porter went to, and I had a lab in my basement. Porter was a pretty bright boy, and he liked to come around to my lab and watch me putter around. I had made this gadget—it was a toy for children as far as I was concerned. I didn't have any idea of its worth. It was just a little gadget that hopped up into the air and floated down again. Cute, but worthless, except as a novelty. And it was too expensive to build it as a novelty. So I forgot about it.

"Years later, Porter came around to me and offered to buy it. I dug it out of the junk that was in my little workshop and sold it to him.

"A couple of years after that, he came back. He said that he'd invented something. After beating all around the bush, he finally admitted that his invention was a development of my little toy. He offered me a million dollars if I'd keep my mouth shut and forget all about the thing."

"And you accepted?" Elshawe asked incredulously.

"Certainly! I made him buy me a tax-paid annuity that pays me more than enough to get by on. I don't want wealth, Mr. Elshawe—just comfort. And that's why I gave it to him."

"I don't follow you."

"Let me tell you about Malcom Porter. He is one of that vast horde of people who want to be *someone*. They want to be respected and looked up to. But they either can't, or won't, take the time to learn the basics of the field they want to excel in. The beautiful girl who wants to be an actress without bothering to learn to act; the young man who wants to be a judge without going through law school, or be a general without studying military tactics; and Malcom Porter, the boy who wanted to be a great scientist—but didn't want to take the trouble to learn science."

Elshawe nodded. He was thinking of the "artists" who splatter up clean canvas and call it "artistic self-expression." And the clodheads who write disconnected, meaningless prose and claim that it's free verse. The muddleminds who forget that Picasso learned to paint within the strict limits of classical art before he tried new methods, and that James Joyce learned to handle the English language well before he wrote "Finnegan's Wake."

"On the other hand," Skinner continued, "I am ... well, rather a shy man. As soon as Malcom told me what the device would do when it was properly powered, I knew that there would be trouble. I am not a fighter, Mr. Elshawe. I have no desire to spend time in prison or be vilified in the news or called a crackpot by orthodox scientists.

"I don't want to fight Malcom's claim, Mr. Elshawe. Don't you see, he *deserves* the credit! In the first place, he recognized it for what it was. If he hadn't, Heaven only knows how long it would have been before someone rediscovered it. In the second place, he has fought and fought hard to give it to humanity. He has suffered in prison and spent millions of dollars to get the Polarizer into the hands of the United States Government. He has, in fact, worked harder and suffered more than if he'd taken the time and trouble to get a proper education. And it got him what he wanted; I doubt that he would have made a very good scientist, anyway.

"Porter deserves every bit of credit for the Polarizer. I am perfectly happy with the way things are working out."

Elshawe said: "But what if the FBI gets hold of the evidence I have?"

"That's why I have told you the truth, Mr. Elshawe," Skinner said earnestly. "I want you to destroy that evidence. I would deny flatly that I had anything to do with the Polarizer, in any case. And that would put an end to any inquiry because no one would believe that I would deny inventing something like that. But I would just as soon that the question never came up. I would rather that there be no whisper whatever of anything like that."

He paused for a moment, then, very carefully, he said: "Mr. Elshawe, you have intimated that the inventor of the Polarizer deserves some kind of reward. I assure you that the greatest reward you could give me would be to help me destroy all traces of any connection with the device. Will you do that, Mr. Elshawe?"

Elshawe just sat silently in the chair for long minutes, thinking. Skinner didn't interrupt; he simply waited patiently.

After about ten minutes, Elshawe put his pipe carefully on a nearby table and reached down to pick up his briefcase. He handed it to Skinner.

"Here. It contains all the evidence I have. Including, I might say, the recording of our conversation here. Just take the tape out of the minirecorder. A man like you deserves whatever reward he wants. Take it, Mr. Skinner."

"Thanks," said Skinner softly, taking the briefcase.

And, on the plane winging back to New York from the Congressional investigation, Mr. Terrence Elshawe sighed softly. He was glad none of the senators had asked anything about Skinner, because he knew he would certainly have had to tell the truth.

And he knew, just as certainly, that he would have been in a great deal more hot water than Porter had been. Because Malcom Porter was going to become American Hero Number One, and Terry Elshawe would have ended up as the lying little sneak who had tried to destroy the reputation of the great Malcom Porter.

Which, all things considered, would have been a hell of a note.

THE END

Belly Laugh

You hear a lot of talk these days about secret weapons. If it's not a new wrinkle in nuclear fission, it's a gun to shoot around corners and down winding staircases. Or maybe a nice new strain of bacteria guaranteed to give you radioactive dandruff. Our own suggestion is to pipe a few of our television commercials into Russia and bore the enemy to death.

Well, it seems that Ivar Jorgensen has hit on the ultimate engine of destruction: a weapon designed to exploit man's greatest weakness. The blueprint can be found in the next few pages; and as the soldier in the story says, our only hope is to keep a sense of humor!

ME? I'm looking for my outfit. Got cut off in that Holland Tunnel attack. Mind if I sit down with you guys a while? Thanks. Coffee? Damn! This is heaven. Ain't seen a cup of coffee in a year.

What? You said it! This sure is a hell of a war. Tough on a guy's feet. Yeah, that's right. Holland Tunnel skirmish. Where the Ruskies used that new gun. Uhuh. God! It was awful. Guys popping off all around a guy and him not knowing why. No sense to it. No noise. No wound. Just popping off.

That's the trouble with this war. It won't settle down to a routine. Always something new. What the hell chance has a guy got to figure things out? And I tell you them Ruskies are coming up with new weapons just as fast as we are. Enough to make your hair stand on end.

Sugar? Christ, yes! Ain't seen sugar for a year. You see, it's like this: we were bottled up in the pits around the Tunnel for seven damn days. It was like nothing you ever saw before. Oops—sorry. Didn't mean to splash you. I was laughing about something that happened there—to a guy. Maybe you guys would get a kick out of it. After all, we got to keep our sense of humor.

You see, there was me and a Kentucky kid named Stillwell in this pit—a pretty big pit with lots of room—and we were all alone. This Stillwell was a nice kid—green and lonesome and it's pretty sad, really, but there's a yak in it, and—as I say—we got to keep a sense of humor.

Well, this Stillwell—a really green kid—is unhappy and just plain drooling for his gal back home. He talks about his mother, of course, and his old man, but it's the girl that's really on his mind as you guys can plainly understand.

He's seeing her every place—like spots in front of his eyes—nice spots doing things to him, when this Ruskie babe shows up.

My gun came up without any orders from me just as she poked her puss over the edge of the pit, and—huh? Oh, thank you kindly. It sure tastes good but I don't want to short you guys. Thank you kindly.

Well, as I was saying, this Ruskie babe pokes her nose over the edge of the pit and Stillwell dives and knocks down my gun. He says, "You son-of-a-bitch!" Just like that. Wild and desperate, like you'd say to a guy if the guy was just kicking over the last jug of water on a desert island.

It would have been long enough for her to kill us if I hadn't had good reflexes. Even then, all I had time to do was knock the pistol out of her hand and drag her into the pit.

With her play bollixed, she was confused and bewildered. She ain't a fighter, and she sits back against the wall staring at us dead pan with big expressionless eyes. She's a plenty pretty babe and I could see exactly what had happened as far as Stillwell was concerned. His spots had come to life in very adequate form so to speak.

Stillwell goes over and sits down beside her and I'm very much on the alert, because I know where his courage comes from. But I decide it's all right, because I see the babe is not belligerent, just confused kind of. And friendly.

And willing. Kind of a whipped-little-dog willing, and man oh man! She was sure what Stillwell needed.

They kind of went together like a hand and a glove—natural-like. And it followed—pretty natural—that when Stillwell got up and led her around a wing of the pit, out of sight, she went willing—like that same little dog.

Uhuh. No, you guys. Two's enough. I wouldn't rob you. Well, okay, and thanks kindly.

Well, there I was, all alone, but happy for Stillwell, cause I know it's what the kid needs, and in spots like that what difference does it make? Yank—Ruskie—Mongolian—as long as she's willing.

Then, you guys, Stillwell comes back out—wall-eyed—real wall-eyed—like being hit but not knocked out and still walking. I know what it is—some kind of shock. I get up and walk over and take a look at the babe where he'd left her—and I bust out laughing. I told you guys there was a yak in this. I laughed like a fool—it was that funny. As much as I had time to, before Stillwell cracked. It was enough to crack him—the little thing that pushes a guy over the edge.

He lets out a yell and screams, "For crisake! For crisake! Nothing but a bucket of bolts! Nothing but a couple of plastic lumps—"

That was when I hit him. I had to. He was for the birds, Stillwell was. An hour later we got relieved and a couple of medicos carried him away strapped to a stretcher—gone like a kite.

They took the robot too, and its clothes, but they forgot the brassiere, so I took it and I been carrying it ever since, but I'll leave it with you guys if you want—for the coffee. Might make you think about home. After all, like the man says, we got to keep our sense of humor.

Well, so long, you guys—and thanks.

Heist Job on Thizar

In the future, we may discover new planets; our ships may rocket to new worlds; robots may be smarter than people. But we'll still have slick characters willing and able to turn a fast buck—even though they have to be smarter than Einstein to do it.

ANSON DRAKE sat quietly in the Flamebird Room of the Royal Gandyll Hotel, listening to the alien, but soothing strains of the native orchestra and sipping a drink. He knew perfectly well that he had no business displaying himself in public on the planet Thizar; there were influential Thizarians who held no love for a certain Earthman named Anson Drake.

It didn't particularly bother Drake; life was danger and danger was life to him, and Anson Drake was known on half a hundred planets as a man who could take care of himself.

Even so, he wouldn't have bothered to come if it had not been for the fact that Viron Belgezad was a pompous braggart.

Belgezad had already suffered at the hands of Anson Drake. Some years before, a narcotics gang had been smashed high, wide, and handsome on Thizar. Three men had died from an overdose of their own thionite drug, and fifty thousand credits of illicit gain had vanished into nowhere. The Thizarian police didn't know who had done the job, and they didn't know who had financed the ring.

But Belgezad knew that Anson Drake was the former, and Drake knew that Viron Belgezad was the latter. And each one was waiting his chance to get the other.

A week before, Drake had been relaxing happily on a beach on Seladon II, twelve light-years from Thizar, reading a newsfax. He had become interested in an article which told of the sentencing of a certain lady to seven years in Seladon Prison, when his attention was attracted by another headline.

VIRON BELGEZAD BUYS ALGOL NECKLACE

Thizar (GNS)—Viron Belgezad, wealthy Thizarian financier, has purchased the fabulous Necklace of Algol, it was announced today. The necklace, made of matched Star Diamonds, is estimated to be worth more than a million credits, although the price paid by Belgezad is not known.

Such an interesting bit seemed worthy of further investigation, so Drake had immediately booked passage on the first space liner to Thizar.

And thus it was that an immaculately dressed, broad-shouldered, handsome young man sat quietly in the Flamebird Room of Thizar's flushiest hostelry surveying his surroundings with steady green eyes and wondering how he was going to get his hands on the Necklace of Algol.

The police couldn't touch Belgezad, but Anson Drake could—and would.

"Hello, Drake," said a cold voice at his elbow.

Drake turned and looked up into the sardonically smiling face of Jomis Dobigel, the heavy-set, dark-faced Thizarian who worked with Belgezad.

"Well, well," Anson said, smiling, "if it isn't Little Bo-Peep. How is the dope business? And how is the Big Dope Himself?"

Dobigel's smile soured. "You're very funny, Earthman. But we don't like Earthmen here."

"Do sit down, Dobbie, and tell me all about it. The last I heard—which was three hours ago—the government of Thizar was perfectly happy to have me here. In fact, they were good enough to stamp my passport to prove it."

Dobigel pulled out a chair and sat down, keeping his hands beneath the table. "What are you doing here, Drake?" he asked in a cold voice.

"I couldn't help it," Drake said blandly. "I was drawn back by the memory of the natural beauties of your planet. The very thought of the fat, flabby face of old Belgezad, decorated with a bulbous nose that is renowned throughout the Galaxy, was irresistible. So here I am."

Dobigel's dark face grew even darker. "I know you, Drake. And I know why you're here. Tomorrow is the date for the Coronation of His Serenity, the Shan of Thizar."

"True," Drake agreed. "And I wouldn't miss it for all the loot in Andromeda. A celebration like that is worth traveling parsecs to see."

Dobigel leaned across the table. "Belgezad is a Noble of the Realm," he said slowly. "He'll be at the Coronation. You know he's going to wear the Necklace of Algol as well as anyone, and you—"

Suddenly, he leaned forward a little farther, his right hand stabbing out toward Drake's leg beneath the table.

But Anson Drake was ready for him. Dobigel's hand was a full three inches from Drake's thigh when a set of fingers grasped his wrist in a viselike hold. Steely fingers bit in, pressing nerves against bone. With a gasp, Dobigel opened his hand. A small, metallic cylinder dropped out.

Drake caught it with his free hand and smiled. "That's impolite, Dobbie. It isn't proper to try to give your host an injection when he doesn't want it."

Casually, he put the cylinder against the arm which he still held and squeezed the little metal tube. There was a faint *pop!* Drake released the arm and handed back the cylinder. Dobigel's face was white.

"I imagine that was twelve-hour poison," Drake said kindly. "If you hurry, old Belgezad will give you the antidote. It will be painful, but—" He shrugged.

"And by the way, Brother Dobigel," he continued, "let me give you some advice. The next time you try to get near a victim with one of those things, don't do it by talking to him about things he already knows. It doesn't distract him enough."

Dobigel stood up, his fists clenched. "I'll get you for this, Drake." Then he turned and stalked off through the crowd.

No one had noticed the little by-play. Drake smiled seraphically and finished his drink. Dobigel was going to be uncomfortable for a while. Twelve-hour poison was a complex protein substance that could be varied in several thousand different ways, and only an antidote made from the right variation would work for each poison. If the antidote wasn't given, the victim died within twelve hours. And even if the antidote was given, getting over poison wasn't any fun at all.

Reflecting happily on the plight of Jomis Dobigel, Anson Drake paid his bill, tipped the waiter liberally, and strolled out of the Flamebird Room and into the lobby of the Royal Gandyll Hotel. The Coronation would begin early tomorrow, and he didn't want to miss the beginning of it. The Shan's Coronation was *the* affair of Thizar.

He went over to the robot newsvender and dropped a coin in the slot. The reproducer hummed, and a freshly-printed newsfax dropped out.

He headed for the lift tube, which whisked him up to his room on the eighty-first floor. He inserted his key in the lock and pressed the button on the tip. The electronic lock opened, and the door slid into the wall. Before entering, Drake took a look at the detector on his wrist. There was no sign of anything having entered the room since he had left it. Only then did he go inside.

With one of the most powerful financiers on Thizar out after his blood, there was no way of knowing what might happen, and therefore no reason to take chances.

There were some worlds where Anson Drake would no more have stayed in a public hotel than he would have jumped into an atomic furnace, especially if his enemy was a man as influential as Belgezad. But Thizar was a civilized and reasonably well policed planet; the police were honest and the courts were just. Even Belgezad couldn't do anything openly.

Drake locked his door, sang to himself in a pleasant baritone while he bathed, put on his pajamas, and lay down on his bed to read the paper.

It was mostly full of Coronation news. Noble So-and-So would wear such-and-such, the Archbishop would do thus-and-so. There was another item about Belgezad; his daughter was ill and would be unable to attend. *Bloody shame*, thought Drake. *Too bad Belgezad isn't sick—or dying.*

There was further mention of the Necklace of Algol; it was second only to the Crown Jewels of the Shan himself. The precautions being taken were fantastic; at a quick guess, about half the crowd would be policemen.

The door announcer chimed. Drake sat up and punched the door TV. The screen showed the face of a girl standing at his door. Drake smiled in appreciation. She had dark brown hair, brown eyes, and a smooth, tanned complexion. It was a beautiful face, and it showed promise of having a body to match.

"Who, may I ask, is calling on a gentleman at this ungodly hour, and thus compromising her reputation and fair name?"

The girl smiled, showing even, white teeth, and her eyes sparkled, showing flickers of little golden flames against the brown. "I see I've found the right room," she said. "That voice couldn't belong to anyone but Anson Drake." Then she lowered her voice and said softly: "Let me in. I'm Norma Knight."

Drake felt a tingle of psychic electricity flow over his skin; there was a promise of danger and excitement in the air. Norma Knight was known throughout this whole sector of the Galaxy as the cleverest jewel thief the human race had ever spawned. Drake had never met her, but he had definitely heard of her.

He touched the admission stud, and the door slid silently aside. There was no doubt about it, her body *did* match her face.

"Do come in, Norma," he said.

She stepped inside, and Drake touched the closing button. The door slid shut behind her.

She stood there for a moment, looking at him, and Drake took the opportunity to study the girl more closely. At last, she said: "So you're Anson Drake. You're even better looking than I'd heard you were. Congratulations."

"I have a good press agent," Drake said modestly. "What's on your mind?" He waved his hand at a nearby chair.

"The same thing that's on yours, I suspect," she said. "Do you have a drink to spare?"

Drake unlimbered himself from the bed, selected a bottle from the menu and dialed. The robot bellhop whirred, a chute opened in the wall, and a bottle slid out. Drake poured, handed the tumbler to the girl, and said: "This is your party; what do you have in mind?"

The girl took a sip of her drink before she answered. Then she looked up at Drake with her deep brown eyes. "Two things. One: I have no intention or desire to compete with Anson Drake for the Necklace of Algol. Both of us might end up in jail with nothing for our pains.

"Two: I have a foolproof method for getting the necklace, but none for getting it off the planet. I think you probably have a way."

Drake nodded. "I dare say I could swing it. How does it happen that you don't have an avenue of disposal planned?"

She looked bleak for a moment. "The man who was to help me decided to back out at the last minute. He didn't know what the job was, and I wouldn't tell him because I didn't trust him."

"And you trust me?"

Her eyes were very trustful. "I've heard a lot about you, Drake, and I happen to know you never doublecross anyone unless they doublecross you first."

"Trade about is fair play, to quote an ancient maxim," Drake said, grinning. "And I am a firm believer in fair play.

"But that's neither here nor there. The point is: what do you have to offer? Why shouldn't I just pinch the gems myself and do a quick flit across the Galaxy? That would give me all the loot."

She shook her head. "Belgezad is on to you, you know. He knows you're here. His own private police and the Shan's own Guard will be at the Coronation to protect all that jewelry." She cocked her pretty head to one side and looked at him. "What's between you and Belgezad, anyway?"

"I stole his toys when he was a child," said Drake, "and he hasn't trusted me since. How do you propose to get the Necklace of Algol if I can't?"

She smiled and shook her head slowly. "That would be telling. You let me take care of my part, and I'll let you take care of yours."

Drake shook his head—not so slowly. "Absolutely not. We either work together or we don't work at all."

The girl frowned in thought for a moment, and then reached into the belt pouch at her side and pulled out a square of electro-engraved plastic. She handed it to Drake.

Underneath all the flowery verbiage, it boiled down to an invitation to attend the post-Coronation reception. It was addressed to "Miss Caroline Smith" and was signed and sealed by the Shan of Thizar himself.

"I'm 'Caroline Smith'," she said. "I've managed to get in good with the family of Belgezad, and he wangled the invitation.

"Now, the plan is this: Right after the Invocation, while the new Shan is being prepared in his special Coronation Robes, the Nobles have to change their uniforms from red to green. Belgezad will go into his suite in the Palace to change. He'll be accompanied by two guards. One will stay on the outside, the other will help Belgezad dress. I've got the room next to his, and I've managed to get the key that unlocks the door between them. I'll use this—" She pulled a small globe of metal from her belt pouch. "It's a sleep-gas bomb. It'll knock them out for at least twenty minutes. No one will come in during that time, and I'll be able to get the necklace and get out of the palace before they wake up."

"They'll know you did it," Drake pointed out. "If you're still missing when they come to, the thief's identity will be obvious."

She nodded. "That's where you come in. I'll simply go out into the garden and throw it over the wall to you. We'll meet here afterwards."

Drake thought it over and smiled devilishly. "It sounds fine. Now let's co-ordinate everything."

They went over the whole plot again, this time with a chart of the palace to mark everything out and a time schedule was arranged. Then they toasted to success and the girl left.

When she was gone, Anson Drake smiled ruefully to himself and opened a secret compartment in his suitcase. From it, he removed a long strand of glittering jewels.

"A perfect imitation," Drake said. "And you're very pretty. It's a shame I won't be able to hang you around the neck of Belgezad in place of the real Necklace of Algol."

But his original plan had been more dangerous than the present one, and Anson Drake was always ready to desert a good plan for a better one.

Coronation Day dawned bright and clear, and the festivities began early. There were speeches and parades and dancing in the streets. A huge fleet of high-flying rockets rumbled high in the stratosphere, filling the sky with the white traceries of their exhausts. For all of Thizar, it was a holiday, a day of rejoicing and happiness. Cheers for the Shan filled the streets, and strains of music came from the speakers of the public communications system.

Anson Drake missed most of the fun; he was too busy making plans. The day passed as he worked.

Thizar's sun began to set as the hour for the actual Crowning of the Shan approached. At the proper time, Drake was waiting in the shadows outside the palace walls. There were eyes watching him, and he knew it, but he only smiled softly to himself and waited.

"*Sssssst!*"

It was the girl, on the other side of the wall.

"I'm here," whispered Drake.

Something that glittered faintly in the soft light of the twin moons of Thizar arced over the wall. Drake caught it in his hands. The Necklace of Algol!

He slipped it into a small plastic box he was carrying and then glanced at the detector on his wrist. The screen showed a pale blue pip which indicated that someone was hidden in the shadows a few yards to his right.

Drake didn't even glance toward the spy. He put the plastic box containing the necklace into his belt pouch and strode away from the palace. He had, he figured, about twenty minutes.

He headed directly for the spaceship terminal. Never once did he look back, but the detector on his wrist told him that he was being closely followed. Excellent!

Inside the terminal, he went directly to the baggage lockers. He found one that was empty, inserted a coin, and opened it. From his pouch, he took a plastic box, put it in the locker, switched on the lock with his key, and strolled away.

He glanced again at his detector. He was no longer being followed by the same man; another had taken up the trail. It figured; it figured.

He went straight to the Hotel Gandyll, making sure that his tail didn't lose him. Not until they were in the lobby did he make any attempt to shake the man who was following him. He went into the bar, ordered a drink, and took a sip. He left his change and the drink on the bar and headed out the door in the direction of the men's room. Whoever was following him wouldn't realize for a minute or two that he was leaving for good. A man doesn't usually leave change and an unfinished drink in a bar.

Drake took the lift tube up to his room, attended to some unfinished business, and waited.

Less than three minutes later, the door was opened. In walked Viron Belgezad and his lieutenant, Jomis Dobigel. Both of them looked triumphant, and they were surrounded by a squad of Royal Police.

"There he is," said Dobigel. "Arrest him!"

A police officer stepped forward. "Anson Drake, I arrest you in the name of the Shan," he said.

Drake grinned. "On what charge?"

"The theft of the Necklace of Algol."

Drake looked directly at Belgezad. "Did old Fatface here say I took it?"

"You can't talk that way," Dobigel snarled, stepping forward.

"Who says so, Ugly?"

At that, Dobigel stepped forward and threw a hard punch from his shoulder—straight at Drake's face.

It never landed. Drake side-stepped it and brought a smashing uppercut up from his knees. It lifted Dobigel off his feet and sent him crashing back against old Belgezad, toppling them both to the floor.

The policemen had all drawn their guns, but Drake was standing placidly in the middle of the room, his hands high above his head regarding the scene calmly.

"I'll go quietly," he said. "I've got no quarrel with the police."

One of the officers led him out into the hall while the others searched his room. Belgezad was sputtering incoherently. Another policeman was trying to wake up Dobigel.

"If you're looking for the Necklace of Algol," Drake said, "you won't find it there."

The captain of the police squad said: "We know that, Mr. Drake. We are merely looking for other evidence. We already have the necklace." He reached in his belt pouch and took out a small plastic box. He opened it, disclosing a glittering rope of jewels. "You were seen depositing this in a baggage locker at the spaceship terminal. We have witnesses who saw you, and we had it removed under police supervision."

Viron Belgezad smiled nastily. "This time you won't get away, Drake! Stealing anything from the palace of the Shan carries a minimum penalty of twenty years in Thizar Prison."

Drake said nothing as they took him off to the Royal Police Station and locked him in a cell.

It was late afternoon of the next day when the Prosecutor for the Shan visited Drake's cell. He was a tall, imposing man, and Drake knew him by reputation as an honest, energetic man.

"Mr. Drake," he said as he sat down in a chair in the cell, "you have refused to speak to anyone but me. I am, of course, perfectly willing to be of any assistance, but I am afraid I must warn you that any statement made to me will be used against you at the trial."

Drake leaned back in his own chair. One thing nice about Thizar, he reflected; they had comfortable jails.

"My Lord Prosecutor," he said, "I'd like to make a statement. As I understand it, Belgezad claims he was gassed, along with a police guard who was with him. When he woke up, the necklace was gone. He didn't see his assailant."

"That is correct," said the Prosecutor.

Drake grinned. That was the way it had to be. Belgezad couldn't possibly have bribed the cop, so they both had to be gassed.

"If he didn't see his assailant, how does he know who it was?"

"You were followed from the palace by Jomis Dobigel, who saw you put the necklace into the baggage locker. There are several other witnesses to that."

Drake leaned forward. "Let me point out, my Lord Prosecutor, that the only evidence you have that I was anywhere near the palace is the word of Jomis Dobigel. And he didn't see me *inside* the palace. I was outside the wall."

The Prosecutor shrugged. "We admit the possibility of an assistant inside the walls of the palace," he said. "We are investigating that now. But even if we never find your accomplice, we have proof that you were implicated, and that is enough."

"What proof do you have?" Drake asked blandly.

"Why, the necklace itself, of course!" The Prosecutor looked as though he suspected Drake of having taken leave of his senses.

Drake shook his head. "That necklace is mine. I can prove it. It was made for me by a respectable jeweler on Seladon II. It's a very good imitation, but it's a phoney. They aren't diamonds; they're simply well-cut crystals of titanium dioxide. Check them if you don't believe me."

The Lord Prosecutor looked dumbfounded. "But—what—why—"

Drake looked sad. "I brought it to give to my good friend, the Noble Belgezad. Of course it would be a gross insult to wear them at the Shan's Coronation, but he could wear them at other functions.

"And how does my good friend repay me? By having me arrested. My Lord Prosecutor, I am a wronged man."

The Prosecutor swallowed heavily and stood up. "The necklace has, naturally, been impounded by the police. I shall have the stones tested."

"You'll find they're phonies," Drake said. "And that means one of two things. Either they are not the ones stolen from Belgezad or else Belgezad has mortally insulted his Shan by wearing false jewels to the Coronation."

"Well! We shall see about this!" said the Lord Prosecutor.

Anson Drake, free as a lark, was packing his clothes in his hotel room when the announcer chimed. He punched the TV pickup and grinned. It was the girl.

When the door slid aside, she came in, smiling. "You got away with it, Drake! Wonderful! I don't know how you did it, but—"

"Did what?" Drake looked innocent.

"Get away with the necklace, of course! I don't know how it happened that Dobigel was there, but—"

"But, but, but," Drake said, smiling. "You don't seem to know very much at all, do you?"

"Wha—what do you mean?"

Drake put his last article of clothing in his suitcase and snapped it shut. "I'll probably be searched pretty thoroughly when I get to the spaceport," he said coolly, "but they won't find anything on an innocent man."

"Where is the necklace?" she asked in a throaty voice.

Drake pretended not to hear her. "It's a funny thing," he said. "Old Belgezad would never let the necklace out of his hands except to get me. He thought he'd get it back by making sure I was followed. But he made two mistakes."

The girl put her arms around his neck. "His mistakes don't matter as long as we have the necklace, do they?"

Anson Drake was never a man to turn down an invitation like that. He held her in his arms and kissed her—long and lingeringly.

When he broke away, he went on as though nothing had happened.

"Two mistakes. The first one was thinking up such an obviously silly plot. If it were as easy to steal jewels from the palace as all that, nothing would be safe on Thizar.

"The second mistake was sending his daughter to trap me."

The girl gasped and stepped back.

"It was very foolish of you, Miss Belgezad," he went on calmly. "You see, I happened to know that the real Norma Knight was sentenced to seven years in Seladon Prison over a week ago. Unfortunately, the news hadn't reached Thizar yet. I knew from the first that the whole thing was to be a frame-up. It's too bad that your father had to use the real necklace—it's a shame he lost it."

The girl's eyes blazed. "You—you *thief*! You—" She used words which no self-respecting lady is supposed to use.

Drake waited until she had finished, and then said: "Oh, no, Miss Belgezad; I'm no thief. Your father can consider the loss of that necklace as a fine for running narcotics. And you can tell him that if I catch him again, it will be worse.

"I don't like his kind of slime, and I'll do my best to get rid of them. That's all, Miss B.; it was nice knowing you."

He walked out of the room, leaving her to stand there in helpless fury.

His phony necklace had come in handy after all; the police had thought they had the real one, so they had never bothered to check the Galactic Mail Service for a small package mailed to Seladon II. All he'd had to do was drop it into the mail chute from his room and then cool his heels in jail while the Galactic Mails got rid of the loot for him.

The Necklace of Algol would be waiting for him when he got to Seladon II.

THE END

Dead Giveaway

Logic's a wonderful thing; by logical analysis, one can determine the necessary reason for the existence of a dead city of a very high order on an utterly useless planet. Obviously a shipping transfer point! Necessarily...

"Mendez?" said the young man in the blue-and-green tartan jacket. "Why, yes ... sure I've heard of it. Why?"

The clerk behind the desk looked again at the information screen. "That's the destination we have on file for Scholar Duckworth, Mr. Turnbull. That was six months ago." He looked up from the screen, waiting to see if Turnbull had any more questions.

Turnbull tapped his teeth with a thumbnail for a couple of seconds, then shrugged slightly. "Any address given for him?"

"Yes, sir. The Hotel Byron, Landing City, Mendez."

Turnbull nodded. "How much is the fare to Mendez?"

The clerk thumbed a button which wiped the information screen clean, then replaced it with another list, which flowed upward for a few seconds, then stopped. "Seven hundred and eighty-five fifty, sir," said the clerk. "Shall I make you out a ticket?"

Turnbull hesitated. "What's the route?"

The clerk touched another control, and again the information on the screen changed. "You'll take the regular shuttle from here to Luna, then take either the *Stellar Queen* or the *Oriona* to Sirius VI. From there, you will have to pick up a ship to the Central Worlds—either to Vanderlin or BenAbram—and take a ship from there to Mendez. Not complicated, really. The whole trip won't take you more than three weeks, including stopovers."

"I see," said Turnbull. "I haven't made up my mind yet. I'll let you know."

"Very well, sir. The *Stellar Queen* leaves on Wednesdays and the *Oriona* on Saturdays. We'll need three days' notice."

Turnbull thanked the clerk and headed toward the big doors that led out of Long Island Terminal, threading his way through the little clumps of people that milled around inside the big waiting room.

He hadn't learned a hell of a lot, he thought. He'd known that Duckworth had gone to Mendez, and he already had the Hotel Byron address. There was, however, some negative information there. The last address they had was on Mendez, and yet Scholar Duckworth couldn't be found on Mendez. Obviously, he had not filed a change of address there; just as obviously, he had managed to leave the planet without a trace. There was always the possibility that he'd been killed, of course. On a thinly populated world like Mendez, murder could still be committed with little chance of being caught. Even here on Earth, a murderer with the right combination of skill and luck could remain unsuspected.

But who would want to kill Scholar Duckworth?

And why?

Turnbull pushed the thought out of his mind. It was possible that Duckworth was dead, but it was highly unlikely. It was vastly more probable that the old scholar had skipped off for reasons of his own and that something had happened to prevent him from contacting Turnbull.

After all, almost the same thing had happened in reverse a year ago.

Outside the Terminal Building, Turnbull walked over to a hackstand and pressed the signal button on the top of the control column. An empty cab slid out of the traffic pattern and pulled up beside the barrier which separated the vehicular traffic from the pedestrian walkway. The gate in the barrier slid open at the same time the cab door did, and Turnbull stepped inside and sat down. He dialed his own number, dropped in the indicated number of coins, and then relaxed as the cab pulled out and sped down the freeway towards Manhattan.

He'd been back on Earth now for three days, and the problem of Scholar James Duckworth was still bothering him. He hadn't known anything about it until he'd arrived at his apartment after a year's absence.

The apartment door sighed a little as Dave Turnbull broke the electronic seal with the double key. Half the key had been in his possession for a year, jealousy guarded against loss during all the time he had been on Lobon; the other half had been kept by the manager of the Excelsior Apartments.

As the door opened, Turnbull noticed the faint musty odor that told of long-unused and poorly circulated air. The conditioners had been turned down to low power for a year now.

He went inside and allowed the door to close silently behind him. The apartment was just the same—the broad expanse of pale blue rug, the matching furniture, including the long, comfortable couch and the fat overstuffed chair—all just as he'd left them.

He ran a finger experimentally over the top of the table near the door. There was a faint patina of dust covering the glossy surface, but it was very faint, indeed. He grinned to himself. In spite of the excitement of the explorations on Lobon, it was great to be home again.

He went into the small kitchen, slid open the wall panel that concealed the apartment's power controls, and flipped the switch from "maintenance" to "normal." The lights came on, and there was a faint sigh from the air conditioners as they began to move the air at a more normal rate through the rooms.

Then he walked over to the liquor cabinet, opened it, and surveyed the contents. There, in all their glory, sat the half dozen bottles of English sherry that he'd been dreaming about for twelve solid months. He took one out and broke the seal almost reverently.

Not that there had been nothing to drink for the men on Lobon: the University had not been so blue-nosed as all that. But the choice had been limited to bourbon and Scotch. Turnbull, who was not a whisky drinker by choice, had longed for the mellow smoothness of Bristol Cream Sherry instead of the smokiness of Scotch or the heavy-bodied strength of the bourbon.

He was just pouring his first glass when the announcer chimed. Frowning, Turnbull walked over to the viewscreen that was connected to the little eye in the door. It showed the face of—what was his name? Samson? Sanders. That was it, Sanders, the building superintendent.

Turnbull punched the opener and said: "Come in. I'll be right with you, Mr. Sanders."

Sanders was a round, pleasant-faced, soft-voiced man, a good ten years older than Turnbull himself. He was standing just inside the door as Turnbull entered the living room; there was a small brief case in his hand. He extended the other hand as Turnbull approached.

"Welcome home again, Dr. Turnbull," he said warmly. "We've missed you here at the Excelsior."

Turnbull took the hand and smiled as he shook it. "Glad to be back, Mr. Sanders; the place looks good after a year of roughing it."

The superintendent lifted the brief case. "I brought up the mail that accumulated while you were gone. There's not much, since we sent cards to each return address, notifying them that you were not available and that your mail was being held until your return."

He opened the brief case and took out seven standard pneumatic mailing tubes and handed them to Turnbull.

Turnbull glanced at them. Three of them were from various friends of his scattered over Earth; one was from Standard Recording Company; the remaining three carried the return address of James M. Duckworth, Ph. Sch., U.C.L.A., Great Los Angeles, California.

"Thanks, Mr. Sanders," said Turnbull. He was wondering why the man had brought them up so promptly after his own arrival. Surely, having waited a year, they would have waited until they were called for.

Sanders blinked apologetically. "Uh ... Dr. Turnbull, I wonder if ... if any of those contain money ... checks, cash, anything like that?"

"I don't know. Why?" Turnbull asked in surprise.

Sanders looked even more apologetic. "Well, there was an attempted robbery here about six months ago. Someone broke into your mailbox downstairs. There was nothing in it, of course; we've been putting everything into the vault as it came in. But the police thought it might be someone who knew you were getting money by mail. None of the other boxes were opened, you see, and—" He let his voice trail off as Turnbull began opening the tubes.

None of them contained anything but correspondence. There was no sign of anything valuable.

"Maybe they picked my box at random," Turnbull said. "They may have been frightened off after opening the one box."

"That's very likely it," said Sanders. "The police said it seemed to be a rather amateurish job, although whoever did it certainly succeeded in neutralizing the alarms."

Satisfied, the building superintendent exchanged a few more pleasantries with Turnbull and departed. Turnbull headed back toward the kitchen, picked up his glass of sherry, and sat down in the breakfast nook to read the letters.

The one from Standard Recording had come just a few days after he'd left, thanking him for notifying them that he wanted to suspend his membership for a year. The three letters from Cairo, London, and Luna City were simply chatty little social notes, nothing more.

The three from Scholar Duckworth were from a different breed of cat.

The first was postmarked 21 August 2187, three months after Turnbull had left for Lobon. It was neatly addressed to Dave F. Turnbull, Ph.D.

Dear Dave (it read):

I know I haven't been as consistent in keeping up with my old pupils as I ought to have been. For this, I can only beat my breast violently and mutter *mea culpa, mea culpa, mea maxima culpa*. I can't even plead that I was so immersed in my own work that I hadn't the time to write, because I'm busier right now than I've been for years, and I've had to *make* time for this letter.

Of course, in another way, this is strictly a business letter, and it does pertain to my work, so the time isn't as hard to find as it might be.

But don't think I haven't been watching your work. I've read every one of your articles in the various journals, and I have copies of all four of your books nestled securely in my library. Columbia should be—and apparently is—proud to have a man of your ability on its staff. At the rate you've been going, it won't be long before you get an invitation from the Advanced Study Board to study for your Scholar's degree.

As a matter of fact, I'd like to make you an offer right now to do some original research with me. I may not be a top-flight genius like Metternick or Dahl, but my reputation does carry some weight with the Board. (*That, Turnbull thought, was a bit of needless modesty; Duckworth wasn't the showman that Metternick was, or the prolific writer that Dahl was, but he had more intelligence and down-right wisdom than either.*) So if you could manage to get a few months leave from Columbia, I'd be honored to have your assistance. (*More modesty, thought Turnbull. The honor would be just the other way round.*)

The problem, in case you're wondering, has to do with the Centaurus Mystery; I think I've uncovered a new approach that will literally kick the supports right out from under every theory that's been evolved for the existence of that city. Sound interesting?

I'm mailing this early, so it should reach you in the late afternoon mail. If you'll be at home between 1900 and 2000, I'll call you and give you the details. If you've got a pressing appointment, leave details with the operator.

All the best, Jim Duckworth

Turnbull slid the letter back into its tube and picked up the second letter, dated 22 August 2187, one day later.

Dear Dave,

I called last night, and the operator said your phone has been temporarily disconnected. I presume these letters will be forwarded, so please let me know where you are. I'm usually at home between 1800 and 2300, so call me collect within the next three or four days.

All the best, Jim

The third letter was dated 10 November 2187. Turnbull wondered why it had been sent. Obviously, the manager of the Excelsior had sent Duckworth a notice that Dr. Turnbull was off-planet and could not be reached. He must have received the notice on the afternoon of 22 August. That would account for his having sent a second letter before he got the notice. Then why the third letter?

Dear Dave,

I know you won't be reading this letter for six months or so, but at least it will tell you where I am. I guess I wasn't keeping as close tabs on your work as I thought: otherwise I would have known about the expedition to Lobon. You ought to be able to make enough credit on that trip to bring you to the attention of the Board.

And don't feel too bad about missing my first letters or the call. I was off on a wild goose chase that just didn't pan out, so you really didn't miss a devil of a lot.

As a matter of fact, it was rather disappointing to me, so I've decided to take a long-needed sabbatical leave and combine it with a little research on the half-intelligent natives of Mendez. I'll see you in a year or so.

As ever, Jim Duckworth

Well, that was that, Turnbull thought. It galled him a little to think that he'd been offered a chance to do research with Scholar Duckworth and hadn't been able to take it. But if the research hadn't panned out.... He frowned and turned back to the first letter.

A theory that would "literally kick the supports right out from under every theory that's been evolved for the existence of that city," he'd said. Odd. It was unlike Duckworth to be so positive about anything until he could support his own theory without much fear of having it pulled to pieces.

Turnbull poured himself a second glass of sherry, took a sip, and rolled it carefully over his tongue.

The Centaurus Mystery. That's what the explorers had called it back in 2041, nearly a century and a half before, when they'd found the great city on one of the planets of the Alpha Centaurus system. Man's first interstellar trip had taken nearly five years at sublight velocities, and *bing!*—right off the bat, they'd found something that made interstellar travel worthwhile, even though they'd found no planet in the Alpha Centaurus system that was really habitable for man.

They'd seen it from space—a huge domed city gleaming like a great gem from the center of the huge desert that covered most of the planet. The planet itself was Marslike—flat and arid over most of its surface, with a thin atmosphere high in CO_2 and very short on oxygen. The city showed up very well through the cloudless air.

From the very beginning, it had been obvious that whoever or whatever had built that city had not evolved on the planet where it had been built. Nothing more complex than the lichens had ever evolved there, as thousands of drillings into the crust of the planet had shown.

Certainly nothing of near-humanoid construction could ever have come into being on that planet without leaving some trace of themselves or their genetic forebears except for that single huge city.

How long the city had been there was anyone's guess. A thousand years? A million? There was no way of telling. It had been sealed tightly, so none of the sand that blew across the planet's surface could get in. It had been set on a high plateau of rock, far enough above the desert level to keep it from being buried, and the transparent dome was made of an aluminum oxide glass that was hard enough to resist the slight erosion of its surface that might have been caused by the gentle, thin winds dashing microscopic particles of sand against its smooth surface.

Inside, the dry air had preserved nearly every artifact, leaving them as they had been when the city was deserted by its inhabitants at an unknown time in the past.

That's right—deserted. There were no signs of any remains of living things. They'd all simply packed up and left, leaving everything behind.

Dating by the radiocarbon method was useless. Some of the carbon compounds in the various artifacts showed a faint trace of radiocarbon, others showed none. But since the method depends on a knowledge of the amount of nitrogen in the atmosphere of the planet of origin, the rate of bombardment of that atmosphere by high-velocity particles, and several other factors, the information on the radioactivity of the specimens meant nothing. There was also the likelihood that the carbon in the various polymer resins came from oil or coal, and fossil carbon is useless for radio-dating.

Nor did any of the more modern methods show any greater success.

It had taken Man centuries of careful comparison and cross-checking to read the evolutionary history written in the depths of his own planet's crust—to try to date the city was impossible. It was like trying to guess the time by looking at a faceless clock with no hands.

There the city stood—a hundred miles across, ten thousand square miles of complex enigma.

It had given Man his first step into the ever-widening field of Cultural Xenology.

Dave Turnbull finished his sherry, got up from the breakfast nook, and walked into the living room, where his reference books were shelved. The copy of Kleistmeistenoppolous' "City of Centaurus" hadn't been opened in years, but he took it down and flipped it open to within three pages of the section he was looking for.

"It is obvious, therefore, that every one of the indicators points in the same direction. The City was not—*could not have been*—self-supporting. There is no source of organic material on the planet great enough to support such a city; therefore, foodstuffs must have been imported. On the other hand, it is necessary to postulate *some* reason for establishing a city on an otherwise barren planet and populating it with an estimated six hundred thousand individuals.

"There can be only one answer: The race that built the City did so for the same reason that human beings built such megalopolises as New York, Los Angeles, Tokyo, and London—because it was a focal point for important trade routes. Only such trade routes could support such a city; only such trade routes give reason for the City's very existence.

"And when those trade routes changed or were supplanted by others in the course of time, the reason for the City's existence vanished."

Turnbull closed the book and shoved it back into place. Certainly the theory made sense, and had for a century. Had Duckworth come across information that would seem to smash that theory?

The planet itself seemed to be perfectly constructed for a gigantic landing field for interstellar ships. It was almost flat, and if the transhipping between the interstellar vessels had been done by air, there would be no need to build a hard surface for the field. And there were other indications. Every fact that had come to light in the ensuing century had been in support of the Greek-German xenologist's theory.

Had Duckworth come up with something new?

If so, why had he decided to discard it and forget his new theory?

If not, why had he formulated the new theory, and on what grounds?

Turnbull lit a cigarette and looked sourly at the smoke that drifted up from its tip. What the devil was eating him? He'd spent too much time away from Earth, that was the trouble. He'd been too deeply immersed in his study of Lobon for the past year. Now all he had to do was get a little hint of something connected with cultural xenology, and his mind went off on dizzy tizzies.

Forget it. Duckworth had thought he was on to something, found out that he wasn't, and discarded the whole idea. And if someone like Scholar James Duckworth had decided it wasn't worth fooling with, then why was a common Ph. D. like Turnbull worrying about it? Especially when he had no idea what had started Duckworth off in the first place.

And his thoughts came back around to that again. If Duckworth had thought enough of the idea to get excited over it, what had set him off? Even if it had later proved to be a bad lead, Turnbull felt he'd like to know what had made Duckworth think—even for a short time—that there was some other explanation for the City.

Ah, hell! He'd ask Duckworth some day. There was plenty of time.

He went over to the phone, dialed a number, and sat down comfortably in his fat blue overstuffed chair. It buzzed for half a minute, then the telltale lit up, but the screen remained dark.

"Dave!" said a feminine voice. "Are you back? Where on Earth have you been?"

"I haven't," said Turnbull. "How come no vision?"

"I was in the hammam, silly. And what do you mean 'I haven't'? You haven't what?"

"You asked me where on Earth I'd been, and I said I haven't."

"Oh! Lucky man! Gallivanting around the starways while us poor humans have to stay home."

"Yeah, great fun. Now look, Dee, get some clothes on and turn on your pickup. I don't like talking to gray screens."

"Half a sec." There was a minute's pause, then the screen came on, showing the girl's face. "Now, what do you have on your purported mind?"

"Simple. I've been off Earth for a year, staring at bearded faces and listening to baritone voices. If it isn't too short notice, I'd like to take you to dinner and a show and whatever else suggests itself afterward."

"Done!" she said. "What time?"

"Twenty hundred? At your place?"

"I'll be waiting."

Dave Turnbull cut the circuit, grinning. The Duckworth problem had almost faded from his mind. But it flared back up again when he glanced at the mail tubes on his desk.

"Damn!" he said.

He turned back to the phone, jammed a finger into the dial and spun it angrily. After a moment, the screen came to life with the features of a beautifully smiling but obviously efficient blond girl.

"Interstellar Communications. May I serve you, sir?"

"How long will it take to get a message to Mendez? And what will it cost?"

"One moment, sir." Her right hand moved off-screen, and her eyes shifted to look at a screen that Turnbull couldn't see. "Mendez," she said shortly. "The message will reach there in five hours and thirty-six minutes total transmission time. Allow an hour's delay for getting the message on the tapes for beaming.

"The cost is one seventy-five per symbol. Spaces and punctuation marks are considered symbols. *A, an, and,* and *the* are symbols."

Turnbull thought a moment. It was high—damned high. But then a man with a bona fide Ph. D. was not exactly a poor man if he worked at his specialty or taught.

"I'll call you back as soon as I've composed the message," he said.

"Very well, sir."

He cut the circuit, grabbed a pencil and started scribbling. When he'd finished reducing the thing to its bare minimum, he started to dial the number again. Then he scowled and dialed another number.

This time, a mild-faced young man in his middle twenties appeared. "University of California in Los Angeles. Personnel Office. May I serve you?"

"This is Dr. Dave Turnbull, in New York. I understand that Scholar Duckworth is on leave. I'd like his present address."

The young man looked politely firm. "I'm sorry, doctor; we can not give out that information."

"Oh, yap! Look here; I know where he is; just give me—" He stopped. "Never mind. Let me talk to Thornwald."

Thornwald was easier to deal with, since he knew both Duckworth and Turnbull. Turnbull showed him Duckworth's letter on the screen. "I know he's on Mendez; I just don't want to have to look all over the planet for him."

"I know, Dave. I'm sure it's all right. The address is Landing City, Hotel Byron, Mendez."

"Thanks, Thorn; I'll do you a favor some day."

"Sure. See you."

Turnbull cut off, dialed Interstellar Communications, sent his message, and relaxed. He was ready to make a night of it. He was going to make his first night back on Earth a night to remember.

He did.

The next morning, he was feeling almost flighty. He buzzed and flitted around his apartment as though he'd hit a high point on a manic cycle, happily burbling utter nonsense in the form of a perfectly ridiculous popular song.

My dear, the merest touch of you Has opened up my eyes; And if I get too much of you, You really paralyze! Donna, Donna, bella Donna, Clad in crimson bright, Though I'm near you, I don't wanna See the falling shades of night!

Even when the phone chimed in its urgent message, it didn't disturb his frothy mood. But three minutes later he had dropped down to earth with a heavy *clunk*.

His message to Mendez had not been delivered. There was not now, and never had been a Scholar James Duckworth registered at the Hotel Byron in Landing City. Neither was his name on the incoming passenger lists at the spaceport at Landing City.

He forced himself to forget about it; he had a date with Dee again that night, and he was not going to let something silly like this bother him. But bother him it did. Unlike the night before, the date was an utter fiasco, a complete flop. Dee sensed his mood, misinterpreted it, complained of a headache, and went home early. Turnbull slept badly that night.

Next morning, he had an appointment with one of the executives of U.C.L.I.—University of Columbia in Long Island—and, on the way back he stopped at the spaceport to see what he could find out. But all he got was purely negative information.

On his way back to Manhattan, he sat in the autocab and fumed.

When he reached home, he stalked around the apartment for an hour, smoking half a dozen cigarettes, chain fashion, and polishing off three glasses of Bristol Cream without even tasting it.

Dave Turnbull, like any really top-flight investigator, had developed intuitive thinking to a fine art. Ever since the Lancaster Method had shown the natural laws applying to intuitive reasoning, no scientist worthy of the name failed to apply it consistently in making his investigations. Only when exact measurement became both possible and necessary was there any need to apply logic to a given problem.

A logician adds two and two and gets four; an intuitionist multiplies them and gets the same answer. But a logician, faced with three twos, gets six—an intuitionist gets eight. Intuition will get higher orders of answers from a given set of facts than logic will.

Turnbull applied intuition to the facts he knew and came up with an answer. Then he phoned the New York Public Library, had his phone connected with the stacks, and spent an hour checking for data that would either prove or disprove his theory. He found plenty of the former and none of the latter.

Then he called his superiors at Columbia.

He had to write up his report on the Lobon explorations. Would it be possible for him to take a six-month leave of absence for the purpose?

It would.

The following Saturday, Dr. Dave F. Turnbull was on the interstellar liner *Oriona*, bound for Sirius.

If ever there was a Gold Mine In The Sky, it was Centaurus City. To the cultural xenologists who worked on its mysterious riches, it seemed to present an almost inexhaustible supply of new data. The former inhabitants had left everything behind, as though it were no longer of any value whatever. No other trace of them had as yet been found anywhere in the known galaxy, but they had left enough material in Centaurus City to satisfy the curiosity of Mankind for years to come, and enough mystery and complexity to whet that curiosity to an even sharper degree.

It's difficult for the average person to grasp just how much information can be packed into a city covering ten thousand square miles with a population density equal to that of Manhattan. How long would it take the hypothetical Man From Mars to investigate New York or London if he had only the City to work with, if he found them just as they stand except that the inhabitants had vanished?

The technological level of the aliens could not be said to be either "above" or "below" that of Man: it could only be said to be "different." It was as if the two cultures complemented each other; the areas of knowledge which the aliens had explored seemed to be those which Mankind had not yet touched, while, at the same time, there appeared to be many levels of common human knowledge which the aliens had never approached.

From the combination of the two, whole new fields of human thought and endeavor had been opened.

No trace of the alien spaceships had been uncovered, but the anti-gravitational devices in their aircraft, plus the basic principles of Man's own near-light-velocity drive had given Man the ultralight drive.

Their knowledge of social organization and function far exceeded that of Man, and the hints taken from the deciphered writings of the aliens had radically changed Man's notions of government. Now humanity could build a Galactic Civilization—a unity that was neither a pure democracy nor an absolute dictatorship, but resulted in optimum governmental control combined with optimum individual freedom. It was *e pluribus unum*plus. Their technological writings were few, insofar as physics and chemistry were concerned. What there were turned out to be elementary texts rather than advanced studies—which was fortunate, because it had been through these that the cultural xenologists had been able to decipher the language of the aliens, a language that was no more alien to the modern mind than, say, ancient Egyptian or Cretan.

But without any advanced texts, deciphering the workings of the thousands of devices that the aliens had left behind was a tedious job. The elementary textbooks seemed to deal with the same sort of science that human beings were used to, but, at some point beyond, the aliens had taken a slightly different course, and, at first, only the very simplest of their mechanisms could be analyzed. But the investigators learned from the simpler mechanisms, and found themselves able to take the next step forward to more complex ones. However, it still remained a fact that the majority of the devices were as incomprehensible to the investigators as would the function of a transistor have been to James Clerk Maxwell.

In the areas of the social sciences, data was deciphered at a fairly rapid rate; the aliens seemed to have concentrated all their efforts on that. Psionics, on the other hand, seemed never to have occurred to them, much less to have been investigated. And yet, there were devices in Centaurus City that bore queer generic resemblances to common Terrestrial psionic machines. But there was no hint of such things in the alien literature.

And the physical sciences were deciphered only slowly, by a process of cut-and-try and cut-and-try again.

The investigations would take time. There were only a relatively small handful of men working on the problems that the City posed. Not because there weren't plenty of men who would have sacrificed their time and efforts to further the work, but because the planet, being hostile to Man, simply would not support very many investigators. It was not economically feasible to pour more men and material into the project after the point of diminishing returns had been reached. Theoretically, it would have been possible to re-seal the City's dome and pump in an atmosphere that human beings could live with, but, aside from every other consideration, it was likely that such an atmosphere would ruin many of the artifacts within the City.

Besides, the work in the City was heady stuff. Investigation of the City took a particular type of high-level mind, and that kind of mind did not occur in vast numbers.

It was not, Turnbull thought, his particular dish of tea. The physical sciences were not his realm, and the work of translating the alien writings could be done on Earth, from 'stat copies, if he'd cared to do that kind of work.

Sirius VI was a busy planet—a planet that was as Earthlike as a planet could be without being Earth itself. It had a single moon, smaller than Earth's and somewhat nearer to the planet itself. The *Oriona* landed there, and Dave Turnbull took a shuttle ship to Sirius VI, dropping down at the spaceport near Noiberlin, the capital.

It took less than an hour to find that Scholar Duckworth had gone no farther on his journey to Mendez than Sirius VI. He hadn't cashed in his ticket; if he had, they'd have known about it on Earth. But he certainly hadn't taken a ship toward the Central Stars, either.

Turnbull got himself a hotel room and began checking through the Noiberlin city directory. There it was, big as life and fifteen times as significant. Rawlings Scientific Corporation.

Turnbull decided he might as well tackle them right off the bat; there was nothing to be gained by pussyfooting around.

He used the phone, and, after browbeating several of the employees and pulling his position on a couple of executives, he managed to get an appointment with the Assistant Director, Lawrence Drawford. The Director, Scholar Jason Rawlings, was not on Sirius VI at the time.

The appointment was scheduled for oh nine hundred the following morning, and Turnbull showed up promptly. He entered through the big main door and walked to the reception desk.

"Yes?" said the girl at the desk.

"How do you do," Turnbull said. "My name is Turnbull; I think I'm expected."

"Just a moment." She checked with the information panel on her desk, then said: "Go right on up, Dr. Turnbull. Take Number Four Lift Chute to the eighteenth floor and turn left. Dr. Drawford's office is at the end of the hall."

Turnbull followed directions.

Drawford was a heavy-set, florid-faced man with an easy smile and a rather too hearty voice.

"Come in, Dr. Turnbull; it's a pleasure to meet you. What can I do for you?" He waved Turnbull to a chair and sat down behind his desk.

Turnbull said carefully: "I'd just like to get a little information, Dr. Drawford."

Drawford selected a cigar from the humidor on his desk and offered one to Turnbull. "Cigar? No? Well, if I can be of any help to you, I'll certainly do the best I can." But there was a puzzled look on his face as he lit his cigar.

"First," said Turnbull, "am I correct in saying that Rawlings Scientific is in charge of the research program at Centaurus City?"

Drawford exhaled a cloud of blue-gray smoke. "Not precisely. We work as a liaison between the Advanced Study Board and the Centaurus group, and we supply the equipment that's needed for the work there. We build instruments to order—that sort of thing. Scholar Rawlings is a member of the Board, of course, which admits of a somewhat closer liaison than might otherwise be possible.

"But I'd hardly say we were in charge of the research. That's handled entirely by the Group leaders at the City itself."

Turnbull lit a cigarette. "What happened to Scholar Duckworth?" he said suddenly.

Drawford blinked. "I beg your pardon?"

Again Turnbull's intuitive reasoning leaped far ahead of logic; he knew that Drawford was honestly innocent of any knowledge of the whereabouts of Scholar James Duckworth.

"I was under the impression," Turnbull said easily, "that Scholar Duckworth was engaged in some sort of work with Scholar Rawlings."

Drawford smiled and spread his hands. "Well, now, that may be, Dr. Turnbull. If so, then they're engaged in something that's above my level."

"Oh?"

Drawford pursed his lips for a moment, frowning. Then he said: "I must admit that I'm not a good intuitive thinker, Dr. Turnbull. I have not the capacity for it, I suppose. That's why I'm an engineer instead of a basic research man; that's why I'll never get a Scholar's degree." Again he paused before continuing. "For that reason, Scholar Rawlings leaves the logic to me and doesn't burden me with his own business. Nominally, he is the head of the Corporation; actually, we operate in different areas—areas which, naturally, overlap in places, but which are not congruent by any means."

"In other words," said Turnbull, "if Duckworth and Rawlings were working together, you wouldn't be told about it."

"Not unless Scholar Rawlings thought it was necessary to tell me," Drawford said. He put his cigar carefully in the ashdrop. "Of course, if I *asked* him, I'm sure he'd give me the information, but it's hardly any of *my* business."

Turnbull nodded and switched his tack. "Scholar Rawlings is off-planet, I believe?"

"That's right. I'm not at liberty to disclose his whereabouts, however," Drawford said.

"I realize that. But I'd like to get a message to him, if possible."

Drawford picked up his cigar again and puffed at it a moment before saying anything. Then, "Dr. Turnbull, please don't think I'm being stuffy, but may I ask the purpose of this inquiry?"

"A fair question," said Turnbull, smiling. "I really shouldn't have come barging in here like this without explaining myself first." He had his lie already formulated in his mind. "I'm engaged in writing up a report on the cultural significance of the artifacts on the planet Lobon—you may have heard something of it?"

"I've heard the name," Drawford admitted. "That's in the Sagittarius Sector somewhere, as I recall."

"That's right. Well, as you know, the theory for the existence of Centaurus City assumes that it was, at one time, the focal point of a complex of trade routes through the galaxy, established by a race that has passed from the galactic scene."

Drawford was nodding slowly, waiting to hear what Turnbull had to say.

"I trust that you'll keep this to yourself, doctor," Turnbull said, extinguishing his cigarette. "But I am of the opinion that the artifacts on Lobon bear a distinct resemblance to those of the City." It was a bald, out-and-out lie, but he knew Drawford would have no way of knowing that it was. "I think that Lobon was actually one of the colonies of that race—one of their food-growing planets. If so, there is certainly a necessity for correlation between the data uncovered on Lobon and those which have been found in the City."

Drawford's face betrayed his excitement. "Why ... why, that's amazing! I can see why you wanted to get in touch with Scholar Rawlings, certainly! Do you really think there's something in this idea?"

"I do," said Turnbull firmly. "Will it be possible for me to send a message to him?"

"Certainly," Drawford said quickly. "I'll see that he gets it as soon as possible. What did you wish to say?"

Turnbull reached into his belt pouch, pulled out a pad and stylus, and began to write.

I have reason to believe that I have solved the connection between the two sources of data concerned in the Centaurus City problem. I would also like to discuss the Duckworth theory with you.

When he had finished, he signed his name at the bottom and handed it to Drawford.

Drawford looked at it, frowned, and looked up at Turnbull questioningly.

"He'll know what I mean," Turnbull said. "Scholar Duckworth had an idea that Lobon was a data source on the problem even before we did our digging there. Frankly, that's why I thought Duckworth might be working with Scholar Rawlings."

Drawford's face cleared. "Very well. I'll put this on the company transmitters immediately, Dr. Turnbull. And—don't worry, I won't say anything about this to anyone until Scholar Rawlings or you, yourself, give me the go-ahead."

"I'd certainly appreciate that," Turnbull said, rising from his seat. "I'll leave you to your work now, Dr. Drawford. I can be reached at the Mayfair Hotel."

The two men shook hands, and Turnbull left quickly.

Turnbull felt intuitively that he knew where Rawlings was. On the Centaurus planet—the planet of the City. But where was Duckworth? Reason said that he, too, was at the City, but under what circumstances? Was he a prisoner? Had he been killed outright?

Surely not. That didn't jibe with his leaving Earth the way he had. If someone had wanted him killed, they'd have done it on Earth; they wouldn't have left a trail to Sirius IV that anyone who was interested could have followed.

On the other hand, how could they account for Duckworth's disappearance, since the trail *was* so broad? If the police—

No. He was wrong. The trouble with intuitive thinking is that it tends to leave out whole sections of what, to a logical thinker, are pieces of absolutely necessary data.

Duckworth actually had no connection with Rawlings—no *logical* connection. The only thing the police would have to work with was the fact that Scholar Duckworth had started on a trip to Mendez and never made it any farther than Sirius IV. There, he had vanished. Why? How could they prove anything?

On the other hand, Turnbull was safe. The letters from Duckworth, plus his visit to Drawford, plus his acknowledged destination of Sirius IV, would be enough to connect up both cases if Turnbull vanished. Rawlings should know he couldn't afford to do anything to Turnbull.

Dave Turnbull felt perfectly safe.

He was in his hotel room at the Mayfair when the announcer chimed, five hours later. He glanced up from his book to look at the screen. It showed a young man in an ordinary business jumper, looking rather boredly at the screen.

"What is it?" Turnbull asked.

"Message for Dr. Turnbull from Rawlings Scientific Corporation," said the young man, in a voice that sounded even more bored than his face looked.

Turnbull sighed and got up to open the door. When it sectioned, he had only a fraction of a second to see what the message was.

It was a stungun in the hand of the young man.

It went off, and Turnbull's mind spiraled into blankness before he could react.

Out of a confused blur of color, a face sprang suddenly into focus, swam away again, and came back. The lips of the face moved.

"How do you feel, son?"

Turnbull looked at the face. It was that of a fairly old man who still retained the vitality of youth. It was lined, but still firm.

It took him a moment to recognize the face—then he recalled stereos he'd seen.

It was Scholar Jason Rawlings.

Turnbull tried to lift himself up and found he couldn't.

The scholar smiled. "Sorry we had to strap you down," he said, "but I'm not nearly as strong as you are, and I didn't have any desire to be jumped before I got a chance to talk to you."

Turnbull relaxed. There was no immediate danger here.

"Know where you are?" Rawlings asked.

"Centaurus City," Turnbull said calmly. "It's a three-day trip, so obviously you couldn't have made it in the five hours after I sent you the message. You had me kidnaped and brought here."

The old man frowned slightly. "I suppose, technically, it *was* kidnaping, but we had to get you out of circulation before you said anything that might ... ah ... give the whole show away."

Turnbull smiled slightly. "Aren't you afraid that the police will trace this to you?"

"Oh, I'm sure they would eventually," said Rawlings, "but you'll be free to make any explanations long before that time."

"I see," Turnbull said flatly. "Mind operation. Is that what you did to Scholar Duckworth?"

The expression on Scholar Rawling's face was so utterly different from what Turnbull had expected that he found himself suddenly correcting his thinking in a kaleidoscopic readjustment of his mind.

"What did you think you were on to, Dr. Turnbull?" the old man asked slowly.

Turnbull started to answer, but, at that moment the door opened.

The round, pleasant-faced gentleman who came in needed no introduction to Turnbull.

Scholar Duckworth said: "Hello, Dave. Sorry I wasn't here when you woke up, but I got—" He stopped. "What's the matter?"

"I'm just cursing myself for being a fool," Turnbull said sheepishly. "I was using your disappearance as a datum in a problem that didn't require it."

Scholar Rawlings laughed abruptly. "Then you thought—"

Duckworth chuckled and raised a hand to interrupt Rawlings. "Just a moment, Jason; let him logic it out to us."

"First take these straps off," said Turnbull. "I'm stiff enough as it is, after being out cold for three days."

Rawlings touched a button on the wall, and the restraining straps vanished. Turnbull sat up creakily, rubbing his arms.

"Well?" said Duckworth.

Turnbull looked up at the older man. "It was those first two letters of yours that started me off."

"I was afraid of that," Duckworth said wryly. "I ... ah ... tried to get them back before I left Earth, but, failing that, I sent you a letter to try to throw you off the track."

"Did you think it would?" Turnbull asked.

"I wasn't sure," Duckworth admitted. "I decided that if you had what it takes to see through it, you'd deserve to know the truth."

"I think I know it already."

"I dare say you do," Duckworth admitted. "But tell us first why you jumped to the wrong conclusion."

Turnbull nodded. "As I said, your letters got me worrying. I knew you must be on to something or you wouldn't have been so positive. So I started checking on all the data about the City—especially that which had come in just previous to the time you sent the letters.

"I found that several new artifacts had been discovered in Sector Nine of the City—in the part they call the Bank Buildings. That struck a chord in my memory, so I looked back over the previous records. That Sector was supposed to have been cleaned out nearly ninety years ago.

"The error I made was in thinking that you had been forcibly abducted somehow—that you had been forced to write that third letter. It certainly looked like it, since I couldn't see any reason for you to hide anything from me.

"I didn't think you'd be in on anything as underhanded as this looked, so I assumed that you were acting against your will."

Scholar Rawlings smiled. "But you thought I was capable of underhanded tactics? That's not very flattering, young man."

Turnbull grinned. "I thought you were capable of kidnaping a man. Was I wrong?"

Rawlings laughed heartily. "*Touché.* Go on."

"Since artifacts had been found in a part of the City from which they had previously been removed, I thought that Jim, here, had found a ... well, a cover-up. It looked as though some of the alien machines were being moved around in order to conceal the fact that someone was keeping something hidden. Like, for instance, a new weapon, or a device that would give a man more power than he should rightfully have."

"Such as?" Duckworth asked.

"Such as invisibility, or a cheap method of transmutation, or even a new and faster space drive. I wasn't sure, but it certainly looked like it might be something of that sort."

Rawlings nodded thoughtfully. "A very good intuition, considering the fact that you had a bit of erroneous data."

"Exactly. I thought that Rawlings Scientific Corporation—or else you, personally—were concealing something from the rest of us and from the Advisory Board. I thought that Scholar Duckworth had found out about it and that he'd been kidnaped to hush him up. It certainly looked that way."

"I must admit it did, at that," Duckworth said. "But tell me—how does it look now?"

Turnbull frowned. "The picture's all switched around now. You came here for a purpose—to check up on your own data. Tell me, is everything here on the level?"

Duckworth paused before he answered. "Everything *human*," he said slowly.

"That's what I thought," said Turnbull. "If the human factor is eliminated—at least partially—from the data, the intuition comes through quite clearly. We're being fed information."

Duckworth nodded silently.

Rawlings said: "That's it. Someone or something is adding new material to the City. It's like some sort of cosmic bird-feeding station that has to be refilled every so often."

Turnbull looked down at his big hands. "It never was a trade route focus," he said. "It isn't even a city, in our sense of the term, no more than a birdhouse is a nest." He looked up. "That city was built for only one purpose—to give human beings certain data. And it's evidently data that we need in a hurry, for our own good."

"How so?" Rawlings asked, a look of faint surprise on his face.

"Same analogy. Why does anyone feed birds? Two reasons—either to study and watch them, or to be kind to them. You feed birds in the winter because they might die if they didn't get enough food."

"Maybe we're being studied and watched, then," said Duckworth, probingly.

"Possibly. But we won't know for a long time—if ever."

Duckworth grinned. "Right. I've seen this City. I've looked it over carefully in the past few months. Whatever entities built it are so far ahead of us that we can't even imagine what it will take to find out anything about them. We are as incapable of understanding them as a bird is incapable of understanding us."

"Who knows about this?" Turnbull asked suddenly.

"The entire Advanced Study Board at least," said Rawlings. "We don't know how many others. But so far as we know everyone who has been able to recognize what is really going on at the City has also been able to realize that it is something that the human race *en masse* is not yet ready to accept."

"What about the technicians who are actually working there?" asked Turnbull.

Rawlings smiled. "The artifacts are very carefully replaced. The technicians—again, as far as we know—have accepted the evidence of their eyes."

Turnbull looked a little dissatisfied. "Look, there are plenty of people in the galaxy who would literally hate the idea that there is anything in the universe superior to Man. Can you imagine the storm of reaction that would hit if this got out? Whole groups would refuse to have anything to do with anything connected with the City. The Government would collapse, since the whole theory of our present government comes from City data. And the whole work of teaching intuitive reasoning would be dropped like a hot potato by just those very people who need to learn to use it.

"And it seems to me that some precautions—" He stopped, then grinned rather sheepishly. "Oh," he said, "I see."

Rawlings grinned back. "There's never any need to distort the truth. Anyone who is psychologically incapable of allowing the existence of beings more powerful than Man is also psychologically incapable of piecing together the clues which would indicate the existence of such beings."

Scholar Duckworth said: "It takes a great deal of humility—a real feeling of honest humility—to admit that one is actually inferior to someone—or something—else. Most people don't have it—they rebel because they can't admit their inferiority."

"Like the examples of the North American Amerindian tribes." Turnbull said. "They hadn't reached the state of civilization that the Aztecs or Incas had. They were incapable of allowing themselves to be beaten and enslaved—they refused to allow themselves to learn. They fought the white man to the last ditch—and look where they ended up."

"Precisely," said Duckworth. "While the Mexicans and Peruvians today are a functioning part of civilization—because they *could* and *did* learn."

"I'd just as soon the human race didn't go the way of the Amerindians," Turnbull said.

"I have a hunch it won't," Scholar Rawlings said. "The builders of the City, whoever they are, are edging us very carefully into the next level of civilization—whatever it may be. At that level, perhaps we'll be able to accept their teaching more directly."

Duckworth chuckled. "Before we can become gentlemen, we have to realize that we are *not* gentlemen."

Turnbull recognized the allusion. There is an old truism to the effect that a barbarian can never learn what a gentleman is because a barbarian cannot recognize that he isn't a gentleman. As soon as he recognizes that fact, he ceases to be a barbarian. He is *not* automatically a gentleman, but at least he has become capable of learning how to be one.

"The City itself," said Rawlings, "acts as a pretty efficient screening device for separating the humble from the merely servile. The servile man resents his position so much that he will fight anything which tries to force recognition of his position on him. The servile slave is convinced that he is equal to or superior to his masters, and that he is being held down by brute force. So he opposes them with brute force and is eventually destroyed."

Turnbull blinked. "A screening device?" Then, like a burst of sunlight, the full intuition came over him.

Duckworth's round face was positively beaming. "You're the first one ever to do it," he said. "In order to become a member of the Advanced Study Board, a scholar must solve that much of the City's secret by himself. I'm a much older man than you, and I just solved it in the past few months.

"You will be the first Ph.D. to be admitted to the Board while you're working on your scholar's degree. Congratulations."

Turnbull looked down at his big hands, a pleased look on his face. Then he looked up at Scholar Duckworth. "Got a cigarette, Jim? Thanks. You know, we've still got plenty of work ahead of us, trying to find out just what it is that the City builders want us to learn."

Duckworth smiled as he held a flame to the tip of Turnbull's cigarette.

"Who knows?" he said quietly. "Hell, maybe they want us to learn about *them*!"

Suite Mentale

Just about a year ago, two enthusiastic young men came to see me, and during the course of the visit announced that they were starting a campaign to make their living in science fiction—and also to become "names" in the best science fiction magazines. They planned to collaborate on some material, and write on their own as well, intending to make the grade both ways.

One of the pair was a well-known science fiction fan, who had appeared once or twice in the "pro mags," as fans designate journals like this one. The other was Randall Garrett, who had previously sold a respectable number of stories to various magazines in the science fiction and fantasy field.

I shall not try to insult your intelligence by stating that I told them I knew they could do it; on the contrary, I larded doubt with sympathy. However, this story, and Robert A. Madle's "Inside Science Fiction" will show how wrong I was!

Overture—Adagio Misterioso

THE NEUROSURGEON peeled the thin surgical gloves from his hands as the nurse blotted the perspiration from his forehead for the last time after the long, grueling hours.

"They're waiting outside for you, Doctor," she said quietly.

The neurosurgeon nodded wordlessly. Behind him, three assistants were still finishing up the operation, attending to the little finishing touches that did not require the brilliant hand of the specialist. Such things as suturing up a scalp, and applying bandages.

The nurse took the sterile mask—no longer sterile now—while the doctor washed and dried his hands.

"Where are they?" he asked finally. "Out in the hall, I suppose?"

She nodded. "You'll probably have to push them out of the way to get out of Surgery."

HER PREDICTION was almost perfect. The group of men in conservative business suits, wearing conservative ties, and holding conservative, soft, felt hats in their hands were standing just outside the door. Dr. Mallon glanced at the five of them, letting his eyes stop on the face of the tallest. "He may live," the doctor said briefly.

"You don't sound very optimistic, Dr. Mallon," said the FBI man.

Mallon shook his head. "Frankly, I'm not. He was shot laterally, just above the right temple, with what looks to me like a .357 magnum pistol slug. It's in there—" He gestured back toward the room he had just left. "—you can have it, if you want. It passed completely through the brain, lodging on the other side of the head, just inside the skull. What kept him alive, I'll never know, but I can guarantee that he might as well be dead; it was a rather nasty way to lobotomize a man, but it was effective, I can assure you."

The Federal agent frowned puzzledly. "Lobotomized? Like those operations they do on psychotics?"

"Similar," said Mallon. "But no psychotic was ever butchered up like this; and what I had to do to him to save his life didn't help anything."

The men looked at each other, then the big one said: "I'm sure you did the best you could, Dr. Mallon."

The neurosurgeon rubbed the back of his hand across his forehead and looked steadily into the eyes of the big man.

"You wanted him alive," he said slowly, "and I have a duty to save life. But frankly, I think we'll all eventually wish we had the common human decency to let Paul Wendell die. Excuse me, gentlemen; I don't feel well." He turned abruptly and strode off down the hall.

ONE OF the men in the conservative suits said: "Louis Pasteur lived through most of his life with only half a brain and he never even knew it, Frank; maybe—"

"Yeah. Maybe," said the big man. "But I don't know whether to hope he does or hope he doesn't." He used his right thumbnail to pick a bit of microscopic dust from beneath his left index finger, studying the operation without actually seeing it. "Meanwhile, we've got to decide what to do about the rest of those screwballs. Wendell was the only sane one, and therefore the most dangerous—but the rest of them aren't what you'd call safe, either."

The others nodded in a chorus of silent agreement.

Nocturne—Tempo di Valse

"NOW WHAT the hell's the matter with me?" thought Paul Wendell. He could feel nothing. Absolutely nothing: No taste, no sight, no hearing, no anything. "Am I breathing?" He couldn't feel any breathing. Nor, for that matter, could he feel heat, nor cold, nor pain.

"Am I dead? No. At least, I don't *feel* dead. Who am I? What am I?" No answer. *Cogito, ergo sum.* What did that mean? There was something quite definitely wrong, but he couldn't quite tell what it was. Ideas seemed to come from nowhere; fragments of concepts that seemed to have no referents. What did that mean? What is a referent? A concept? He felt he knew intuitively what they meant, but what use they were he didn't know.

There was something wrong, and he had to find out what it was. And he had to find out through the only method of investigation left open to him.

So he thought about it.

Sonata—Allegro con Brio

THE PRESIDENT of the United States finished reading the sheaf of papers before him, laid them neatly to one side, and looked up at the big man seated across the desk from him.

"Is this everything, Frank?" he asked.

"That's everything, Mr. President; everything we know. We've got eight men locked up in St. Elizabeth's, all of them absolutely psychotic, and one human vegetable named Paul Wendell. We can't get anything out of them."

The President leaned back in his chair. "I really can't quite understand it. Extra-sensory perception—why should it drive men insane? Wendell's papers don't say enough. He claims it can be mathematically worked out—that he *did* work it out—but we don't have any proof of that."

The man named Frank scowled. "Wasn't that demonstration of his proof enough?"

A small, graying, intelligent-faced man who had been sitting silently, listening to the conversation, spoke at last. "Mr. President, I'm afraid I still don't completely understand the problem. If we could go over it, and get it straightened out—" He left the sentence hanging expectantly.

"Certainly. This Paul Wendell is a—well, he called himself a psionic mathematician. Actually, he had quite a respectable reputation in the mathematical field. He did very important work in cybernetic theory, but he dropped it several years ago—said that the human mind couldn't be worked at from a mechanistic angle. He studied various branches of psychology, and eventually dropped them all. He built several of those queer psionic machines—gold detectors, and something he called a hexer. He's done a lot of different things, evidently."

"Sounds like he was unable to make up his mind," said the small man.

THE PRESIDENT shook his head firmly. "Not at all. He did new, creative work in every one of the fields he touched. He was considered something of a mystic, but not a crackpot, or a screwball.

"But, anyhow, the point is that he evidently found what he'd been looking for for years. He asked for an appointment with me; I okayed the request because of his reputation. He would only tell me that he'd stumbled across something that was vital to national defense and the future of mankind; but I felt that, in view of the work he had done, he was entitled to a hearing."

"And he proved to you, beyond any doubt, that he had this power?" the small man asked.

Frank shifted his big body uneasily in his chair. "He certainly did, Mr. Secretary."

The President nodded. "I know it might not sound too impressive when heard second-hand, but Paul Wendell could tell me more of what was going on in the world than our Central Intelligence agents have been able to dig up in twenty years. And he claimed he could teach the trick to anyone.

"I told him I'd think it over. Naturally, my first step was to make sure that he was followed twenty-four hours a day. A man with information like that simply could not be allowed to fall into enemy hands." The President scowled, as though angry with himself. "I'm sorry to say that I didn't realize the full potentialities of what he had said for several days—not until I got Frank's first report."

"YOU COULD hardly be expected to, Mr. President," Frank said. "After all, something like that is pretty heady stuff."

"I think I follow you," said the Secretary. "You found he was already teaching this trick to others."
The President glanced at the FBI man. Frank said: "That's right; he was holding meetings—classes, I suppose you'd call them—twice a week. There were eight men who came regularly."
"That's when I gave the order to have them all picked up. Can you imagine what would happen if *everybody* could be taught to use this ability? Or even a small minority?"
"They'd rule the world," said the Secretary softly.
The President shrugged that off. "That's a small item, really. The point is that *nothing* would be hidden from *anyone*.
"The way we play the Game of Life today is similar to playing poker. We keep a straight face and play the cards tight to our chest. But what would happen if everyone could see everyone else's cards? It would cease to be a game of strategy, and become a game of pure chance.

"WE'D HAVE to start playing Life another way. It would be like chess, where you can see the opponent's every move. But in all human history there has never been a social analogue for chess. That's why Paul Wendell and his group had to be stopped—for a while at least."

"But what could you have done with them?" asked the Secretary. "Imprison them summarily? Have them shot? What *would* you have done?"
The President's face became graver than ever. "I had not yet made that decision. Thank Heaven, it has been taken out of my hands."
"One of his own men shot him?"
"That's right," said the big FBI man. "We went into his apartment an instant too late. We found eight madmen and a near-corpse. We're not sure what happened, and we're not sure we want to know. Anything that can drive eight reasonably stable men off the deep end in less than an hour is nothing to meddle around with."
"I wonder what went wrong?" asked the Secretary of no one in particular.

Scherzo—Presto

PAUL WENDELL, too, was wondering what went wrong.

Slowly, over a period of immeasurable time, memory seeped back into him. Bits of memory, here and there, crept in from nowhere, sometimes to be lost again, sometimes to remain. Once he found himself mentally humming an odd, rather funeral tune:

Now, though you'd have said that the head was dead, For its owner dead was he, It stood on its neck with a smile well-bred, And bowed three times to me. It was none of your impudent, off-hand nods....

Wendell stopped and wondered what the devil seemed so important about the song.
Slowly, slowly, memory returned.
When he suddenly realized, with crashing finality, where he was and what had happened to him, Paul Wendell went violently insane. Or he would have, if he could have become violent.

Marche Funebre—Lento

"OPEN YOUR mouth, Paul," said the pretty nurse. The hulking mass of not-quite-human gazed at her with vacuous eyes and opened its mouth. Dexterously, she spooned a mouthful of baby food into it. "Now swallow it, Paul. That's it. Now another."

"In pretty bad shape, isn't he?"

Nurse Peters turned to look at the man who had walked up behind her. It was Dr. Benwick, the new interne.

"He's worthless to himself and anyone else," she said. "It's a shame, too; he'd be rather nice looking if there were any personality behind that face." She shoveled another spoonful of mashed asparagus into the gaping mouth. "Now swallow it, Paul."

"How long has he been here?" Benwick asked, eyeing the scars that showed through the dark hair on the patient's head.

"Nearly six years," Miss Peters said.

"Hmmh! But they outlawed lobotomies back in the sixties."

"Open your mouth, Paul." Then, to Benwick: "This was an accident. Bullet in the head. You can see the scar on the other side of his head."

THE DOCTOR moved around to look at the left temple. "Doesn't leave much of a human being, does it?"

"It doesn't even leave much of an animal," Miss Peters said. "He's alive, but that's the best you can say for him. (Now swallow, Paul. That's it.) Even an ameba can find food for itself."

"Yeah. Even a single cell is better off than he is. Chop out a man's forebrain and he's nothing. It's a case of the whole being *less* than the sum of its parts."

"I'm glad they outlawed the operation on mental patients," Miss Peters said, with a note of disgust in her voice.

Dr. Benwick said: "It's worse than it looks. Do you know why the anti-lobotomists managed to get the bill passed?"

"Let's drink some milk now, Paul. No, Doctor; I was only a little girl at that time."

"It was a matter of electro-encephalographic records. They showed that there was electrical activity in the prefrontal lobes even after the nerves had been severed, which could mean a lot of things; but the A-L supporters said that it indicated that the forebrain was still capable of thinking."

Miss Peters looked a little ill. "Why—that's *horrible*! I wish you'd never told me." She looked at the lump of vegetablized human sitting placidly at the table. "Do you suppose he's actually *thinking*, somewhere, deep inside?"

"Oh, I doubt it," Benwick said hastily. "There's probably no real self-awareness, none at all. There couldn't be."

"I suppose not," Miss Peters said, "but it's not pleasant to think of."

"That's why they outlawed it," said Benwick.

Rondo—Andante ma non poco

INSANITY IS a retreat from reality, an escape within the mind from the reality outside the mind. But what if there is no detectable reality outside the mind? What is there to escape from? Suicide—death in any form—is an escape from life. But if death does not come, and can not be self-inflicted, what then?

And when the pressure of nothingness becomes too great to bear, it becomes necessary to escape; a man under great enough pressure will take the easy way out. But if there is no easy way? Why, then a man must take the hard way.

For Paul Wendell, there was no escape from his dark, senseless Gehenna by way of death, and even insanity offered no retreat; insanity in itself is senseless, and senselessness was what he was trying to flee. The only insanity possible was the psychosis of regression, a fleeing into the past, into the crystallized, unchanging world of memory.

So Paul Wendell explored his past, every year, every hour, every second of it, searching to recall and savor every bit of sensation he had ever experienced. He tasted and smelled and touched and heard and analyzed each of them minutely. He searched through his own subjective thought processes, analyzing, checking and correlating them.

Know thyself. Time and time again, Wendell retreated from his own memories in confusion, or shame, or fear. But there was no retreat from himself, and eventually he had to go back and look again.

He had plenty of time—all the time in the world. How can subjective time be measured when there is no objective reality?

EVENTUALLY, there came the time when there was nothing left to look at; nothing left to see; nothing to check and remember; nothing that he had not gone over in every detail. Again, boredom began to creep in. It was not the boredom of nothingness, but the boredom of the familiar. Imagination? What could he imagine, except combinations and permutations of his own memories? He didn't know—perhaps there might be more to it than that.

So he exercised his imagination. With a wealth of material to draw upon, he would build himself worlds where he could move around, walk, talk, and make love, eat, drink and feel the caress of sunshine and wind.

It was while he was engaged in this project that he touched another mind. He touched it, fused for a blinding second, and bounced away. He ran gibbering up and down the corridors of his own memory, mentally reeling from the shock of—*identification*!

WHO WAS he? Paul Wendell? Yes, he knew with incontrovertible certainty that he was Paul Wendell. But he also knew, with almost equal certainty, that he was Captain Sir Richard Francis Burton. He was living—had lived—in the latter half of the nineteenth century. But he knew nothing of the Captain other than the certainty of identity; nothing else of that blinding mind-touch remained.

Again he scoured his memory—Paul Wendell's memory—checking and rechecking the area just before that semi-fatal bullet had crashed through his brain.

And finally, at long last, he knew with certainty where his calculations had gone astray. He knew positively why eight men had gone insane.

Then he went again in search of other minds, and this time he knew he would not bounce.

Quasi Una Fantasia Poco Andante Pianissimo

AN OLD MAN sat quietly in his lawnchair, puffing contentedly on an expensive briar pipe and making corrections with a fountain pen on a thick sheaf of typewritten manuscript. Around him stretched an expanse of green lawn, dotted here and there with squat cycads that looked like overgrown pineapples; in the distance, screening the big house from the road, stood a row of stately palms, their fronds stirring lightly in the faint, warm California breeze.

The old man raised his head as a car pulled into the curving driveway. The warm hum of the turboelectric engine stopped, and a man climbed out of the vehicle. He walked with easy strides across the grass to where the elderly gentleman sat. He was lithe, of indeterminate age, but with a look of great determination. There was something in his face that made the old man vaguely uneasy—not with fear but with a sense of deep respect.

"What can I do for you, sir?"

"I have some news for you, Mr. President," the younger one said.

The old man smiled wryly. "I haven't been President for fourteen years. Most people call me 'Senator' or just plain 'Mister'."

THE YOUNGER man smiled back. "Very well, Senator. My name is Camberton, James Camberton. I brought some information that may possibly relieve your mind—or, again, it may not."

"You sound ominous, Mr. Camberton. I hope you'll remember that I've been retired from the political field for nearly five years. What is this shattering news?"

"Paul Wendell's body was buried yesterday."

The Senator looked blank for a second, then recognition came into his face. "Wendell, eh? After all this time. Poor chap; he'd have been better off if he'd died twenty years ago." Then he paused and looked up. "But just who are you, Mr. Camberton? And what makes you think I would be particularly interested in Paul Wendell?"

"Mr. Wendell wants to tell you that he is very grateful to you for having saved his life, Senator. If it hadn't been for your orders, he would have been left to die."

The Senator felt strangely calm, although he knew he should feel shock. "That's ridiculous, sir! Mr. Wendell's brain was hopelessly damaged; he never recovered his sanity or control of his body. I know; I used to drop over to see him occasionally, until I finally realized that I was only making myself feel worse and doing him no good."

"Yes, sir. And Mr. Wendell wants you to know how much he appreciated those visits."

THE SENATOR grew red. "What the devil are you talking about? I just said that Wendell couldn't talk. How could he have said anything to you? What do you know about this?"

"I never said he *spoke* to me, Senator; he didn't. And as to what I know of this affair, evidently you don't remember my name. James Camberton."

The Senator frowned. "The name is familiar, but—" Then his eyes went wide. "Camberton! You were one of the eight men who—Why, *you're the man who shot Wendell*!"

Camberton pulled up an empty lawnchair and sat down. "That's right, Senator; but there's nothing to be afraid of. Would you like to hear about it?"

"I suppose I must." The old man's voice was so low that it was scarcely audible. "Tell me—were the other seven released, too? Have—have you all regained your sanity? Do you remember—" He stopped.

"Do we remember the extra-sensory perception formula? Yes, we do; all eight of us remember it well. It was based on faulty premises, and incomplete, of course; but in its own way it was workable enough. We have something much better now."

The old man shook his head slowly. "I failed, then. Such an idea is as fatal to society as we know it as a virus plague. I tried to keep you men quarantined, but I failed. After all those years of insanity, now the chess game begins; the poker game is over."

"It's worse than that," Camberton said, chuckling softly. "Or, actually, it's much better."

"I don't understand; explain it to me. I'm an old man, and I may not live to see my world collapse. I hope I don't."

Camberton said: "I'll try to explain in words, Senator. They're inadequate, but a fuller explanation will come later."

And he launched into the story of the two-decade search of Paul Wendell.

CODA—ANDANTINO

"TELEPATHY? Time travel?" After three hours of listening, the ex-President was still not sure he understood.

"Think of it this way," Camberton said. "Think of the mind at any given instant as being surrounded by a shield—a shield of privacy—a shield which you, yourself have erected, though unconsciously. It's a perfect insulator against telepathic prying by others. You feel you *have* to have it in order to retain your privacy—your sense of identity, even. But here's the kicker: even though no one else can get in, *you* can't get out!

"You can call this shield 'self-consciousness'—perhaps *shame* is a better word. Everyone has it, to some degree; no telepathic thought can break through it. Occasionally, some people will relax it for a fraction of a second, but the instant they receive something, the barrier goes up again."

"Then how is telepathy possible? How can you go through it?" The Senator looked puzzled as he thoughtfully tamped tobacco into his briar.

"You don't go *through* it; you go *around* it."

"NOW WAIT a minute; that sounds like some of those fourth dimension stories I've read. I recall that when I was younger, I read a murder mystery—something about a morgue, I think. At any rate, the murder was committed inside a locked room; no one could possibly have gotten in or out. One of the characters suggested that the murderer traveled through the fourth dimension in order to get at the victim. He didn't go through the walls; he went around them." The Senator puffed a match flame into the bowl of his pipe, his eyes on the younger man. "Is that what you're driving at?"

"Exactly," agreed Camberton. "The fourth dimension. Time. You must go back in time to an instant when that wall did not exist. An infant has no shame, no modesty, no shield against the world. You must travel back down your own four-dimensional tube of memory in order to get outside it, and to do that, you have to know your own mind completely, and you must be *sure* you know it.

"For only if you know your own mind can you communicate with another mind. Because, at the 'instant' of contact, you *become* that person; you must enter his own memory at the beginning and go *up* the hyper-tube. You will have all his memories, his hopes, his fears, his *sense of identity*. Unless you know—beyond any trace of doubt—who *you* are, the result is insanity."

THE SENATOR puffed his pipe for a moment, then shook his head. "It sounds like Oriental mysticism to me. If you can travel in time, you'd be able to change the past."

"Not at all," Camberton said; "that's like saying that if you read a book, the author's words will change.

"Time isn't like that. Look, suppose you had a long trough filled with supercooled water. At one end, you drop in a piece of ice. Immediately the water begins to freeze; the crystallization front moves toward the other end of the trough. Behind that front, there is ice—frozen, immovable, unchangeable. Ahead of it there is water—fluid, mobile, changeable.

"The instant we call 'the present' is like that crystallization front. The past is unchangeable; the future is flexible. But they both exist."

"I see—at least, I think I do. And you can do all this?"

"Not yet," said Camberton; "not completely. My mind isn't as strong as Wendell's, nor as capable. I'm not the—shall we say—the superman he is; perhaps I never will be. But I'm learning—I'm learning. After all, it took Paul twenty years to do the trick under the most favorable circumstances imaginable."

"I see." The Senator smoked his pipe in silence for a long time. Camberton lit a cigaret and said nothing. After a time, the Senator took the briar from his mouth and began to tap the bowl gently on the heel of his palm. "Mr. Camberton, why do you tell me all this? I still have influence with the Senate; the present President is a protégé of mine. It wouldn't be too difficult to get you men—ah—put away again. I have no desire to see our society ruined, our world destroyed. Why do you tell me?"

CAMBERTON smiled apologetically. "I'm afraid you might find it a little difficult to put us away again, sir; but that's not the point. You see, we need you. We have no desire to destroy our present culture until we have designed a better one to replace it.

"You are one of the greatest living statesmen, Senator; you have a wealth of knowledge and ability that can never be replaced; knowledge and ability that will help us to design a culture and a civilization that will be as far above this one as this one is above the wolf pack. We want you to come in with us, help us; we want you to be one of us."

"I? I'm an old man, Mr. Camberton. I will be dead before this civilization falls; how can I help build a new one? And how could I, at my age, be expected to learn this technique?"

"Paul Wendell says you can. He says you have one of the strongest minds now existing."

The Senator put his pipe in his jacket pocket. "You know, Camberton, you keep referring to Wendell in the present tense. I thought you said he was dead."

Again Camberton gave him the odd smile. "I didn't say that, Senator; I said they buried his body. That's quite a different thing. You see, before the poor, useless hulk that held his blasted brain died, Paul gave the eight of us his memories; he gave us *himself*. The mind is not the brain, Senator; we don't know what it *is* yet, but we do know what it *isn't*. Paul's poor, damaged brain is dead, but his memories, his thought processes, the very essence of all that was Paul Wendell is still very much with us.

"Do you begin to see now why we want you to come in with us? There are nine of us now, but we need the tenth—you. Will you come?"

"I—I'll have to think it over," the old statesman said in a voice that had a faint quaver. "I'll have to think it over."

But they both knew what his answer would be.

That Sweet Little Old Lady

Usually, the toughest part of the job is stating the problem clearly, and the solution is then easy. This time the FBI could state the problem easily; solving it, though was not. How do you catch a telepathic spy?

I *"What are we going to call that sweet little old lady, now that* mother *is a dirty word?"*

—Dave Foley

I

IN 1914, it was enemy aliens.

In 1930, it was Wobblies.

In 1957, it was fellow travelers.

And, in 1971....

"They could be anywhere," Andrew J. Burris said, with an expression which bordered on exasperated horror. "They could be all around us. Heaven only knows."

He pushed his chair back from his desk and stood up—a chunky little man with bright blue eyes and large hands. He paced to the window and looked out at Washington, and then he came back to the desk. A persistent office rumor held that he had become head of the FBI purely because he happened to have an initial *J* in his name, but in his case the *J* stood for Jeremiah. And, at the moment, his tone expressed all the hopelessness of that Old Testament prophet's lamentations.

"We're helpless," he said, looking at the young man with the crisp brown hair who was sitting across the desk. "That's what it is, we're helpless."

Kenneth Malone tried to look dependable. "Just tell me what to do," he said.

"You're a good agent, Kenneth," Burris said. "You're one of the best. That's why you've been picked for this job. And I want to say that I picked you personally. Believe me, there's never been anything like it before."

"I'll do my best," Malone said at random. He was twenty-eight, and he had been an FBI agent for three years. In that time, he had, among other things, managed to break up a gang of smugglers, track down a counterfeiting ring, and capture three kidnapers. For reasons which he could neither understand nor explain, no one seemed willing to attribute his record to luck.

"I know you will," Burris said. "And if anybody can crack this case, Malone, you're the man. It's just that—everything sounds so *impossible*. Even after all the conferences we've had."

"Conferences?" Malone said vaguely. He wished the chief would get to the point. Any point. He smiled gently across the desk and tried to look competent and dependable and reassuring. Burris' expression didn't change.

"You'll get the conference tapes later," Burris said. "You can study them before you leave. I suggest you study them very carefully, Malone. Don't be like me. Don't get confused." He buried his face in his hands. Malone waited patiently. After a few seconds, Burris looked up. "Did you read books when you were a child?" he asked.

Malone said: "What?"

"Books," Burris said. "When you were a child. Read them."

"Sure I did," Malone said. "'Bomba the Jungle Boy,' and 'Doolittle,' and 'Lucky Starr,' and 'Little Women'—"

"'Little Women'?"

"When Beth died," Malone said, "I wanted to cry. But I didn't. My father said big boys don't cry."

"And your father was right," Burris said. "Why, when I was a ... never mind. Forget about Beth and your father. Think about 'Lucky Starr' for a minute. Remember him?"

"Sure," Malone said. "I liked those books. You know, it's funny, but the books you read when you're a kid, they kind of stay with you. Know what I mean? I can still remember that one about Venus, for instance. Gee, that was—"

"Never mind about Venus, too," Burris said sharply. "Keep your mind on the problem."

"Yes, sir," Malone said. He paused. "What problem, sir?" he added.

"The problem we're discussing," Burris said. He gave Malone a bright, blank stare. "Just listen to me."

"Yes, sir."

"All right, then." Burris took a deep breath. He seemed nervous. Once again he stood up and went to the window. This time, he spoke without turning. "Remember how everybody used to laugh about spaceships, and orbital satellites, and life on other planets? That was just in those 'Lucky Starr' books. That was all just for kids, wasn't it?"

514

"Well, I don't know," Malone said slowly.

"Sure it was all for kids," Burris said. "It was laughable. Nobody took it seriously."

"Well, *somebody* must—"

"You just keep quiet and listen," Burris said.

"Yes, sir," Malone said.

Burris nodded. His hands were clasped behind his back. "We're not laughing any more, are we, Malone?" he said without moving.

There was silence.

"Well, are we?"

"Did you want me to answer, sir?"

"Of course I did!" Burris snapped.

"You told me to keep quiet and—"

"Never mind what I told you," Burris said. "Just do what I told you."

"Yes, sir," Malone said. "No, sir," he added after a second.

"No, sir, what?" Burris asked softly.

"No, sir, we're not laughing any more," Malone said.

"Ah," Burris said. "And why aren't we laughing any more?"

There was a little pause. Malone said, tentatively: "Because there's nothing to laugh about, sir?"

Burris whirled. "On the head!" he said happily. "You've hit the nail on the head, Kenneth. I knew I could depend on you." His voice grew serious again, and thoughtful. "We're not laughing any more because there's nothing to laugh about. We have orbital satellites, and we've landed on the Moon with an atomic rocket. The planets are the next step, and after that the stars. Man's heritage, Kenneth. The stars. And the stars, Kenneth, belong to Man—not to the Soviets!"

"Yes, sir," Malone said soberly.

"So," Burris said, "we should learn not to laugh any more. But have we?"

"I don't know, sir."

"We haven't," Burris said with decision. "Can you read my mind?"

"No, sir," Malone said.

"Can I read your mind?"

Malone hesitated. At last he said: "Not that I know of, sir."

"Well, I can't," Burris snapped. "And can any of us read each other's mind?"

Malone shook his head. "No, sir," he said.

Burris nodded. "That's the problem," he said. "That's the case I'm sending you out to crack."

This time, the silence was a long one.

At last, Malone said: "What problem, sir?"

"Mind reading," Burris said. "There's a spy at work in the Nevada plant, Kenneth. And the spy is a telepath."

The video tapes were very clear and very complete. There were a great many of them, and it was long after nine o'clock when Kenneth Malone decided to take a break and get some fresh air. Washington was a good city for walking, even at night, and Malone liked to walk. Sometimes he pretended, even to himself, that he got his best ideas while walking, but he knew perfectly well that wasn't true. His best ideas just seemed to come to him, out of nowhere, precisely as the situation demanded them.

He was just lucky, that was all. He had a talent for being lucky. But nobody would ever believe that. A record like his was spectacular, even in the annals of the FBI, and Burris himself believed that the record showed some kind of superior ability.

Malone knew that wasn't true, but what could he do about it? After all, he didn't want to resign, did he? It was kind of romantic and exciting to be an FBI agent, even after three years. A man got a chance to travel around a lot and see things, and it was interesting. The pay was pretty good, too.

The only trouble was that, if he didn't quit, he was going to have to find a telepath.

The notion of telepathic spies just didn't sound right to Malone. It bothered him in a remote sort of way. Not that the idea of telepathy itself was alien to him—after all, he was even more aware than the average citizen that research had been going on in that field for something over a quarter of a century, and that the research was even speeding up.

But the cold fact that a telepathy-detecting device had been invented somehow shocked his sense of propriety, and his notions of privacy. It wasn't decent, that was all.

There ought to be something sacred, he told himself angrily.

He stopped walking and looked up. He was on Pennsylvania Avenue, heading toward the White House.

That was no good. He went to the corner and turned off, down the block. He had, he told himself, nothing at all to see the President about.

Not yet, anyhow.

The streets were dark and very peaceful. *I get my best ideas while walking*, Malone said without convincing himself. He thought back to the video tapes.

The report on the original use of the machine itself had been on one of the first tapes, and Malone could still see and hear it. That was one thing he did have, he reflected; his memory was pretty good.

Burris had been the first speaker on the tapes, and he'd given the serial and reference number in a cold, matter-of-fact voice. His face had been perfectly blank, and he looked just like the head of the FBI people were accustomed to seeing on their TV and newsreel screens. Malone wondered what had happened to him between the time the tapes had been made and the time he'd sent for Malone.

Maybe the whole notion of telepathy was beginning to get him, Malone thought.

Burris recited the standard tape opening in a rapid mumble: "Any person or agent unauthorized for this tape please refrain from viewing further, under penalties as prescribed by law." Then he looked off, out past the screen to the left, and said: "Dr. Thomas O'Connor, of Westinghouse Laboratories. Will you come here, Dr. O'Connor?"

Dr. O'Connor came into the lighted square of screen slowly, looking all around him. "This is very fascinating," he said, blinking in the lamplight. "I hadn't realized that you people took so many precautions—"

He was, Malone thought, somewhere between fifty and sixty, tall and thin with skin so transparent that he nearly looked like a living X ray. He had pale blue eyes and pale white hair and, Malone thought, if there ever were a contest for the best-looking ghost, Dr. Thomas O'Connor would win it hands—or phalanges—down.

"This is all necessary for the national security," Burris said, a little sternly.

"Oh," Dr. O'Connor said quickly, "I realize that, of course. Naturally. I can certainly see that."

"Let's go ahead, shall we?" Burris said.

O'Connor nodded. "Certainly. Certainly."

Burris said: "Well, then," and paused. After a second he started again: "Now, Dr. O'Connor, would you please give us a sort of verbal run-down on this for our records?"

"Of course," Dr. O'Connor said. He smiled into the video cameras and cleared his throat. "I take it you don't want an explanation of how this machine works. I mean: you don't want a technical exposition, do you?"

"No," Burris said, and added: "Not by any means. Just tell us what it does."

Dr. O'Connor suddenly reminded Malone of a professor he'd had in college for one of the law courses. He had, Malone thought, the same smiling gravity of demeanor, the same condescending attitude of absolute authority. It was clear that Dr. O'Connor lived in a world of his own, a world that was not even touched by the common run of men.

"Well," he began, "to put it very simply, the device indicates whether or not a man's mental ... ah ... processes are being influenced by outside ... by outside influences." He gave the cameras another little smile. "If you will allow me, I will demonstrate on the machine itself."

He took two steps that carried him out of camera range, and returned wheeling a large heavy-looking box. Dangling from the metal covering were a number of wires and attachments. A long cord led from the box to the floor, and snaked out of sight to the left.

"Now," Dr. O'Connor said. He selected a single lead, apparently, Malone thought, at random. "This electrode—"

"Just a moment, doctor," Burris said. He was eying the machine with a combination of suspicion and awe. "A while back you mentioned something about 'outside influences.' Just what, specifically, does that mean?"

With some regret, Dr. O'Connor dropped the lead. "Telepathy," he said. "By outside influences, I meant influences on the mind, such as telepathy or mind reading of some nature."

"I see," Burris said. "You can detect a telepath with this machine."

"I'm afraid—"

"Well, some kind of a mind reader anyhow," Burris said. "We won't quarrel about terms."

"Certainly not," Dr. O'Connor said. The smile he turned on Burris was as cold and empty as the inside of Orbital Station One. "What I meant was ... if you will permit me to continue ... that we cannot detect any sort of telepath or mind reader with this device. To be frank, I very much wish that we could; it would make everything a great deal simpler. However, the laws of psionics don't seem to operate that way."

"Well, then," Burris said, "what does the thing do?" His face wore a mask of confusion. Momentarily, Malone felt sorry for his chief. He could remember how he'd felt, himself, when that law professor had come up with a particularly baffling question in class.

"This machine," Dr. O'Connor said with authority, "detects the slight variations in mental activity that occur when a person's mind is *being* read."

"You mean, if my mind were being read right now—"

"Not right now," Dr. O'Connor said. "You see, the bulk of this machine is in Nevada; the structure is both too heavy and too delicate for transport. And there are other qualifications—"

"I meant theoretically," Burris said.

"Theoretically," Dr. O'Connor began, and smiled again, "if your mind were being read, this machine would detect it, supposing that the machine were in operating condition and all of the other qualifications had been met. You see, Mr. Burris, no matter how poor a telepath a man may be, he has some slight ability—even if only very slight—to detect the fact that his mind is being read."

"You mean, if somebody were reading my mind, I'd know it?" Burris said. His face showed, Malone realized, that he plainly disbelieved this statement.

"You would know it," Dr. O'Connor said, "but you would never know you knew it. To elucidate: in a normal person—like you, for instance, or even like myself—the state of having one's mind read merely results in a vague, almost subconscious feeling of irritation, something that could easily be attributed to minor worries, or fluctuations in one's hormonal balance. The hormonal balance, Mr. Burris, is—"

"Thank you," Burris said with a trace of irritation. "I know what hormones are."

"Ah. Good," Dr. O'Connor said equably. "In any case, to continue: this machine interprets those specific feelings as indications that the mind is being ... ah ... 'eavesdropped' upon."

You could almost see the quotation marks around what Dr. O'Connor considered slang dropping into place, Malone thought.

"I see," Burris said with a disappointed air. "But what do you mean, it won't detect a telepath? Have you ever actually worked with a telepath?"

"Certainly we have," Dr. O'Connor said. "If we hadn't, how would we be able to tell that the machine was, in fact, indicating the presence of telepathy? The theoretical state of the art is not, at present, sufficiently developed to enable us to—"

"I see," Burris said hurriedly. "Only wait a minute."

"Yes?"

"You mean you've actually got a real mind reader? You've found one? One that works?"

Dr. O'Connor shook his head sadly. "I'm afraid I should have said, Mr. Burris, that we did once have one," he admitted. "He was, unfortunately, an imbecile, with a mental age between five and six, as nearly as we were able to judge."

"An imbecile?" Burris said. "But how were you able to—"

"He could repeat a person's thoughts word for word," Dr. O'Connor said. "Of course, he was utterly incapable of understanding the meaning behind them. That didn't matter; he simply repeated whatever you were thinking. Rather disconcerting."

"I'm sure," Burris said. "But he was really an imbecile? There wasn't any chance of—"

"Of curing him?" Dr. O'Connor said. "None, I'm afraid. We did at one time feel that there had been a mental breakdown early in the boy's life, and, indeed, it's perfectly possible that he was normal for the first year or so. The records we did manage to get on that period, however, were very much confused, and there was never any way of telling anything at all, for certain. It's easy to see what caused the confusion, of course: telepathy in an imbecile is rather an oddity—and any normal adult would probably be rather hesitant about admitting that he was capable of it. That's why we have not found another subject; we must merely sit back and wait for lightning to strike."

Burris sighed. "I see your problem," he said. "But what happened to this imbecile boy of yours?"

"Very sad," Dr. O'Connor said. "Six months ago, at the age of fifteen, the boy simply died. He simply—gave up, and died."

"Gave up?"

"That was as good an explanation as our medical department was able to provide, Mr. Burris. There was some malfunction, but—we like to say that he simply gave up. Living became too difficult for him."

"All right," Burris said after a pause. "This telepath of yours is dead, and there aren't any more where he came from. Or if there are, you don't know how to look for them. All right. But to get back to this machine of yours: it couldn't detect the boy's ability?"

Dr. O'Connor shook his head. "No, I'm afraid not. We've worked hard on that problem at Westinghouse, Mr. Burris, but we haven't yet been able to find a method of actually detecting telepaths."

"But you can detect—"

"That's right," Dr. O'Connor said. "We can detect the fact that a man's mind is being read." He stopped, and his face became suddenly morose. When he spoke again, he sounded guilty, as if he were making an admission that pained him. "Of course, Mr. Burris, there's nothing we can *do* about a man's mind being read. Nothing whatever." He essayed a grin that didn't look very healthy. "But at least," he said, "you know you're being spied on."

Burris grimaced. There was a little silence while Dr. O'Connor stroked the metal box meditatively, as if it were the head of his beloved.

At last, Burris said: "Dr. O'Connor, how sure can you be of all this?"

The look he received made all the previous conversation seem as warm and friendly as a Christmas party by comparison. It was a look that froze the air of the room into a solid chunk, Malone thought, a chunk you could have chipped pieces from, for souvenirs, later, when Dr. O'Connor had gone and you could get into the room without any danger of being quick-frozen by the man's unfriendly eye.

"Mr. Burris," Dr. O'Connor said in a voice that matched the temperature of his gaze, "please. Remember our slogan."

Malone sighed. He fished in his pocket for a pack of cigarettes, found one, and extracted a single cigarette. He stuck it in his mouth and started fishing in various pockets for his lighter.

He sighed again. He preferred cigars, a habit he'd acquired from the days when he'd filched them from his father's cigar case, but his mental picture of the fearless and alert young FBI agent didn't include a cigar. Somehow, remembering his father as neither fearless nor, exactly, alert—anyway, not the way the movies and the TV screens liked to picture the words—he had the impression that cigars looked out of place on FBI agents.

And it was, in any case, a small sacrifice to make. He found his lighter and shielded it from the brisk wind. He looked out over water at the Jefferson Memorial, and was surprised that he'd managed to walk as far as he had. Then he stopped thinking about walking, and took a puff of his cigarette, and forced himself to think about the job in hand.

Naturally, the Westinghouse gadget had been declared Ultra Top Secret as soon as it had been worked out. Virtually everything was, these days. And the whole group involved in the machine and its workings had been transferred without delay to the United States Laboratories out in Yucca Flats, Nevada.

Out there in the desert, there just wasn't much to do, Malone supposed, except to play with the machine. And, of course, look at the scenery. But when you've seen one desert, Malone thought confusedly, you've seen them all.

So, the scientists ran experiments on the machine, and they made a discovery of a kind they hadn't been looking for.

Somebody, they discovered, was picking the brains of the scientists there.

Not the brains of the people working with the telepathy machine.

And not the brains of the people working on the several other Earth-limited projects at Yucca Flats.

They'd been reading the minds of some of the scientists working on the new and highly classified non-rocket space drive.

In other words, the Yucca Flats plant was infested with a telepathic spy. And how do you go about finding a telepath? Malone sighed. Spies that got information in any of the usual ways were tough enough to locate. A telepathic spy was a lot tougher proposition.

Well, one thing about Andrew J. Burris—he had an answer for everything. Malone thought of what his chief had said: "It takes a thief to catch a thief. And if the Westinghouse machine won't locate a telepathic spy, I know what will."

"What?" Malone had asked.

"It's simple," Burris had said. "Another telepath. There has to be one around somewhere. Westinghouse *did* have one, after all, and the Russians *still* have one. Malone, that's your job: go out and find me a telepath."

Burris had an answer for everything, all right, Malone thought. But he couldn't see where the answer did him very much good. After all, if it takes a telepath to catch a telepath, how do you catch the telepath you're going to use to catch the first telepath?

Malone ran that through his mind again, and then gave it up. It sounded as if it should have made sense, somehow, but it just didn't, and that was all there was to that.

He dropped his cigarette to the ground and mashed it out with the toe of his shoe. Then he looked up.

Out there, over the water, was the Jefferson Memorial. It stood, white in the floodlights, beautiful and untouchable in the darkness. Malone stared at it. What would Thomas Jefferson have done in a crisis like this?

Jefferson, he told himself without much conviction, would have been just as confused as he was.

But he'd have had to find a telepath, Malone thought. Malone determined that he would do likewise. If Thomas Jefferson could do it, the least he, Malone, could do was to give it a good try.

There was only one little problem:

Where, Malone thought, *do I start looking?*

II

Early the next morning, Malone awoke on a plane, heading across the continent toward Nevada. He had gone home to sleep, and he'd had to wake up to get on the plane, and now here he was, waking up again. It seemed, somehow, like a vicious circle.

The engines hummed gently as they pushed the big ship through the middle stratosphere's thinly distributed molecules. Malone looked out at the purple-dark sky and set himself to think out his problem again.

He was still mulling things over when the ship lowered its landing gear and rolled to a stop on the big field near Yucca Flats. Malone sighed and climbed slowly out of his seat. There was a car waiting for him at the airfield, though, and that seemed to presage a smooth time; Malone remembered calling Dr. O'Connor the night before, and congratulated himself on his foresight.

Unfortunately, when he reached the main gate of the high double fence that surrounded the more than ninety square miles of United States Laboratories, he found out that entrance into that sanctum sanctorum of Security wasn't as easy as he'd imagined—not even for an FBI man. His credentials were checked with the kind of minute care Malone had always thought people reserved for disputed art masterpieces, and it was with a great show of reluctance that the Special Security guards passed him inside as far as the office of the Chief Security Officer.

There, the Chief Security Officer himself, a man who could have doubled for Torquemada, eyed Malone with ill-concealed suspicion while he called Burris at FBI headquarters back in Washington.

Burris identified Malone on the video screen and the Chief Security Officer, looking faintly disappointed, stamped the agent's pass and thanked the FBI chief. Malone had the run of the place.

Then he had to find a courier jeep. The Westinghouse division, it seemed, was a good two miles away.

As Malone knew perfectly well, the main portion of the entire Yucca Flats area was devoted solely to research on the new space drive which was expected to make the rocket as obsolete as the blunderbuss—at least as far as space travel was concerned. Not, Malone thought uneasily, that the blunderbuss had ever been used for space travel, but—

He got off the subject hurriedly. The jeep whizzed by buildings, most of them devoted to aspects of the non-rocket drive. The other projects based at Yucca Flats had to share what space was left—and that included, of course, the Westinghouse research project.

It turned out to be a single, rather small white building with a fence around it. The fence bothered Malone a little, but there was no need to worry; this time he was introduced at once into Dr. O'Connor's office. It was paneled in wallpaper manufactured to look like pine, and the telepathy expert sat behind a large black desk bigger than any Malone had ever seen in the FBI offices. There wasn't a scrap of paper on the desk; its surface was smooth and shiny, and behind it the nearly transparent Dr. Thomas O'Connor was close to invisible.

He looked, in person, just about the same as he'd looked on the FBI tapes. Malone closed the door of the office behind him, looked for a chair and didn't find one. In Dr. O'Connor's office, it was perfectly obvious, Dr. O'Connor sat down. You stood, and were uncomfortable.

Malone took off his hat. He reached across the desk to shake hands with the telepathy expert, and Dr. O'Connor gave him a limp and fragile paw. "Thanks for giving me a little time," Malone said. "I really appreciate it." He smiled across the desk. His feet were already beginning to hurt.

"Not at all," Dr. O'Connor said, returning the smile with one of his own special quick-frozen brand. "I realize how important FBI work is to all of us, Mr. Malone. What can I do to help you?"

Malone shifted his feet. "I'm afraid I wasn't very specific on the phone last night," he said. "It wasn't anything I wanted to discuss over a line that might have been tapped. You see, I'm on the telepathy case."

Dr. O'Connor's eyes widened the merest trifle. "I see," he said. "Well, I'll certainly do everything I can to help you."

"Fine," Malone said. "Let's get right down to business, then. The first thing I want to ask you about is this detector of yours. I understand it's too big to carry around—but how about making a smaller model?"

"Smaller?" Dr. O'Connor permitted himself a ghostly chuckle. "I'm afraid that isn't possible, Mr. Malone. I would be happy to let you have a small model of the machine if we had one available—more than happy. I would like to see such a machine myself, as a matter of fact. Unfortunately, Mr. Malone—"

"There just isn't one, right?" Malone said.

"Correct," Dr. O'Connor said. "And there are a few other factors. In the first place, the person being analyzed has to be in a specially shielded room, such as is used in encephalographic analysis. Otherwise, the mental activity of the other persons around him would interfere with the analysis." He frowned a little. "I wish that we knew a bit more about psionic machines. The trouble with the present device, frankly, is that it is partly psionic and partly electronic, and we can't be entirely sure where one part leaves off and the other begins. Very trying. Very trying indeed."

"I'll bet it is," Malone said sympathetically, wishing he understood what Dr. O'Connor was talking about.

The telepathy expert sighed. "However," he said, "we keep working at it." Then he looked at Malone expectantly.

Malone shrugged. "Well, if I can't carry the thing around, I guess that's that," he said. "But here's the next question: Do you happen to know the maximum range of a telepath? I mean: How far away can he get from another person and still read his mind?"

Dr. O'Connor frowned again. "We don't have definite information on that, I'm afraid," he said. "Poor little Charlie was rather difficult to work with. He was mentally incapable of co-operating in any way, you see."

"Little Charlie?"

"Charles O'Neill was the name of the telepath we worked with," Dr. O'Connor explained.

"I remember," Malone said. The name had been on one of the tapes, but he just hadn't associated "Charles O'Neill" with "Little Charlie." He felt as if he'd been caught with his homework undone. "How did you manage to find him, anyway?" he said. Maybe, if he knew how Westinghouse had found their imbecile-telepath, he'd have some kind of clue that would enable him to find one, too. Anyhow, it was worth a try.

"It wasn't difficult in Charlie's case," Dr. O'Connor said. He smiled. "The child babbled all the time, you see."

"You mean he talked about being a telepath?"

Dr. O'Connor shook his head impatiently. "No," he said. "Not at all. I mean that he babbled. Literally. Here: I've got a sample recording in my files." He got up from his chair and went to the tall gray filing cabinet that hid in a far corner of the pine-paneled room. From a drawer he extracted a spool of common audio tape, and returned to his desk.

"I'm sorry we didn't get full video on this," he said, "but we didn't feel it was necessary." He opened a panel in the upper surface of the desk, and slipped the spool in. "If you like, there are other tapes—"

"Maybe later," Malone said.

Dr. O'Connor nodded and pressed the playback switch at the side of the great desk. For a second the room was silent.

Then there was the hiss of empty tape, and a brisk masculine voice that overrode it:

"Westinghouse Laboratories," it said, "sixteen April nineteen-seventy. Dr. Walker speaking. The voice you are about to hear belongs to Charles O'Neill: chronological age fourteen years, three months; mental age, approximately five years. Further data on this case will be found in the file *O'Neill*."

There was a slight pause, filled with more tape hiss.

Then the voice began.

"... push the switch for record ... in the park last Wednesday ... and perhaps a different set of ... poor kid never makes any sense in ... trees and leaves all sunny with the ... electronic components of the reducing stage might be ... not as predictable when others are around but ... to go with Sally some night in the...."

It was a childish, alto voice, gabbling in a monotone. A phrase would be spoken, the voice would hesitate for just an instant, and then another, totally disconnected phrase would come. The enunciation and pronunciation would vary from phrase to phrase, but the tone remained essentially the same, drained of all emotional content.

"... in receiving psychocerebral impulses there isn't any ... nonsense and nothing but nonsense all the ... tomorrow or maybe Saturday with the girl ... tube might be replaceable only if ... something ought to be done for the ... Saturday would be a good time for ... work on the schematics tonight if...."

There was a click as the tape was turned off, and Dr. O'Connor looked up.

"It doesn't make much sense," Malone said. "But the kid sure has a hell of a vocabulary for an imbecile."

"Vocabulary?" Dr. O'Connor said softly.

"That's right," Malone said. "Where'd an imbecile get words like 'psychocerebral'? I don't think I know what that means, myself."

"Ah," Dr. O'Connor said. "But that's not *his* vocabulary, you see. What Charlie is doing is simply repeating the thoughts of those around him. He jumps from mind to mind, simply repeating whatever he receives." His face assumed the expression of a man remembering a bad taste in his mouth. "That's how we found him out, Mr. Malone," he said. "It's rather startling to look at a blithering idiot and have him suddenly repeat the very thought that's in your mind."

Malone nodded unhappily. It didn't seem as if O'Connor's information was going to be a lot of help as far as catching a telepath was concerned. An imbecile, apparently, would give himself away if he were a telepath. But nobody else seemed to be likely to do that. And imbeciles didn't look like very good material for catching spies with.

Then he brightened. "Is it possible that the spy we're looking for really isn't a spy?"

"Eh?"

"I mean, suppose he's an imbecile, too? I doubt whether an imbecile would really be a spy, if you see what I mean."

Dr. O'Connor appeared to consider the notion. After a little while he said: "It is, I suppose, possible. But the readings on the machine don't give us the same timing as they did in Charlie's case—or even the same sort of timing."

"I don't quite follow you," Malone said. Truthfully, he felt about three miles behind. But perhaps everything would clear up soon. He hoped so. On top of everything else, his feet were now hurting a lot more.

"Perhaps if I describe one of the tests we ran," Dr. O'Connor said, "things will be somewhat clearer." He leaned back in his chair. Malone shifted his feet again and transferred his hat from his right hand to his left hand.

"We put one of our test subjects in the insulated room," Dr. O'Connor said, "and connected him to the detector. He was to read from a book—a book that was not too common. This was, of course, to obviate the chance that some other person nearby might be reading it, or might have read it in the past. We picked 'The Blood is the Death,' by Hieronymus Melanchthon, which, as you may know, is a very rare book indeed."

"Sure," Malone said. He had never heard of the book, but he was, after all, willing to take Dr. O'Connor's word for it.

The telepathy expert went on: "Our test subject read it carefully, scanning rather than skimming. Cameras recorded the movements of his eyes in order for us to tell just what he was reading at any given moment, in order to correlate what was going on in his mind with the reactions of the machine's indicators, if you follow me."

Malone nodded helplessly.

"At the same time," Dr. O'Connor continued blithely, "we had Charlie in a nearby room, recording his babblings. Every so often, he would come out with quotations from 'The Blood is the Death,' and these quotations corresponded exactly with what our test subject was reading at the time, and also corresponded with the abnormal fluctuations of the detector."

Dr. O'Connor paused. Something, Malone realized, was expected of him. He thought of several responses and chose one. "I see," he said.

"But the important thing here," Dr. O'Connor said, "is the timing. You see, Charlie was incapable of continued concentration. He could not keep his mind focused on another mind for very long, before he hopped to still another. The actual amount of time concentrated on any given mind at any single given period varied from a minimum of one point three seconds to a maximum of two point six. The timing samples, when plotted graphically over a period of several months, formed a skewed bell curve with a mode at two point oh seconds."

"Ah," Malone said, wondering if a skewed bell curve was the same thing as a belled skew curve, and if not, why not?

"It was, in fact," Dr. O'Connor continued relentlessly, "a sudden variation in those timings which convinced us that there was another telepath somewhere in the vicinity. We were conducting a second set of reading experiments, in precisely the same manner as the first set, and, for the first part of the experiment, our figures were substantially the same. But—" He stopped.

"Yes?" Malone said, shifting his feet and trying to take some weight off his left foot by standing on his right leg. Then he stood on his left leg. It didn't seem to do any good.

"I should explain," Dr. O'Connor said, "that we were conducting this series with a new set of test subjects: some of the scientists here at Yucca Flats. We wanted to see if the intelligence quotients of the subjects affected the time of contact which Charlie was able to maintain. Naturally, we picked the men here with the highest IQ's, the two men we have who are in the top echelon of the creative genius class." He cleared his throat. "I did not include myself, of course, since I wished to remain an impartial observer, as much as possible."

"Of course," Malone said without surprise.

"The other two geniuses," Dr. O'Connor said, "happen to be connected with the project known as Project Isle—an operation whose function I neither know, nor care to know, anything at all about."

Malone nodded. Project Isle was the non-rocket spaceship. Classified. Top Secret. Ultra-Secret. And, he thought, just about anything else you could think of.

"At first," Dr. O'Connor was saying, "our detector recorded the time periods of ... ah mental invasion as being the same as before. Then, one day, anomalies began to appear. The detector showed that the minds of our subjects were being held for as long as two or three minutes. But the phrases repeated by Charlie during these periods showed that his own contact time remained the same; that is, they fell within the same skewed bell curve as before, and the mode remained constant if nothing but the phrase length were recorded."

"Hm-m-m," Malone said, feeling that he ought to be saying something.

Dr. O'Connor didn't notice him. "At first we thought of errors in the detector machine," he went on. "That worried us not somewhat, since our understanding of the detector is definitely limited at this time. We do feel that it would be possible to replace some of the electronic components with appropriate symbolization like that already used in the purely psionic sections, but we have, as yet, been unable to determine exactly which electronic components must be replaced by what symbolic components."

Malone nodded, silently this time. He had the sudden feeling that Dr. O'Connor's flow of words had broken itself up into a vast sea of alphabet soup, and that he, Malone, was occupied in drowning in it.

"However," Dr. O'Connor said, breaking what was left of Malone's train of thought, "young Charlie died soon thereafter, and we decided to go on checking the machine. It was during this period that we found someone else reading the minds of our test subjects—sometimes for a few seconds, sometimes for several minutes."

"Aha," Malone said. Things were beginning to make sense again. *Someone else.* That, of course, was the spy.

"I found," Dr. O'Connor said, "on interrogating the subjects more closely, that they were, in effect, thinking on two levels. They were reading the book mechanically, noting the words and sense, but simply shuttling the material directly into their memories without actually thinking about it. The actual thinking portions of their minds were concentrating on aspects of Project Isle."

"In other words," Malone said, "someone was spying on them for information about Project Isle?"

"Precisely," Dr. O'Connor said with a frosty, teacher-to-student smile. "And whoever it was had a much higher concentration time than Charlie had ever attained. He seems to be able to retain contact as long as he can find useful information flowing in the mind being read."

"Wait a minute," Malone said. "Wait a minute. If this spy is so clever, how come he didn't read *your* mind?"

"It is very likely that he has," O'Connor said. "What does that have to do with it?"

"Well," Malone said, "if he knows you and your group are working on telepathy and can detect what he's doing, why didn't he just hold off on the minds of those geniuses when they were being tested in your machine?"

Dr. O'Connor frowned. "I'm afraid that I can't be sure," he said, and it was clear from his tone that, if Dr. Thomas O'Connor wasn't sure, no one in the entire world was, had been, or ever would be. "I do have a theory, however," he said, brightening up a trifle.

Malone waited patiently.

"He must know our limitations," Dr. O'Connor said at last. "He must be perfectly well aware that there's not a single thing we can *do* about him. He must know that we can neither find nor stop him. Why should he worry? He can afford to ignore us—or even bait us. We're helpless, and he knows it."

That, Malone thought, was about the most cheerless thought he had heard in some time.

"You mentioned that you had an insulated room," the FBI agent said after a while. "Couldn't you let your men think in there?"

Dr. O'Connor sighed. "The room is shielded against magnetic fields and electromagnetic radiation. It is perfectly transparent to psionic phenomena, just as it is to gravitational fields."

"Oh," Malone said. He realized rapidly that his question had been a little silly to begin with, since the insulated room had been the place where all the tests had been conducted in the first place. "I don't want to take up too much of your time, doctor," he said after a pause, "but there are a couple of other questions."

"Go right ahead," Dr. O'Connor said. "I'm sure I'll be able to help you."

Malone thought of mentioning how little help the doctor had been to date, but decided against it. Why antagonize a perfectly good scientist without any reason? Instead, he selected his first question, and asked it. "Have you got any idea how we might lay our hands on another telepath? Preferably one that's not an imbecile, of course."

Dr. O Connor's expression changed from patient wisdom to irritation. "I wish we could, Mr. Malone. I wish we could. We certainly need one here to help us with our work—and I'm sure that *your* work is important, too. But I'm afraid we have no ideas at all about finding another telepath. Finding little Charlie was purely fortuitous—purely, Mr. Malone, fortuitous."

"Ah," Malone said. "Sure. Of course." He thought rapidly and discovered that he couldn't come up with one more question. As a matter of fact, he'd asked a couple of questions already, and he could barely remember the answers. "Well," he said, "I guess that's about it, then, doctor. If you come across anything else, be sure and let me know."

He leaned across the desk, extending a hand. "And thanks for your time," he added.

Dr. O'Connor stood up and shook his hand. "No trouble, I assure you," he said. "And I'll certainly give you all the information I can."

Malone turned and walked out. Surprisingly, he discovered that his feet and legs still worked. He had thought they'd turned to stone in the office long before.

It was on the plane back to Washington that Malone got his first inkling of an idea.

The only telepath that the Westinghouse boys had been able to turn up was Charles O'Neill, the youthful imbecile.

All right, then. Suppose there were another one like him. Imbeciles weren't very difficult to locate. Most of them would be in institutions, and the others would certainly be on record. It might be possible to find someone, anyway, who could be handled and used as a tool to find a telepathic spy.

And—happy thought!—maybe one of them would turn out to be a high-grade imbecile, or even a moron.

Even if they only turned up another imbecile, he thought wearily, at least Dr. O'Connor would have something to work with.

He reported back to Burris when he arrived in Washington, told him about the interview with Dr. O'Connor, and explained what had come to seem a rather feeble brainstorm.

"It doesn't seem too productive," Burris said, with a shade of disappointment in his voice, "but we'll try it."

At that, it was a better verdict than Malone had hoped for. He had nothing to do but wait, while orders went out to field agents all over the United States, and quietly, but efficiently, the FBI went to work. Agents probed and pried and poked their noses into the files and data sheets of every mental institution in the fifty states—as far, at any rate, as they were able.

It was not an easy job. The inalienable right of a physician to refuse to disclose confidences respecting a patient applied even to idiots, imbeciles, and morons. Not even the FBI could open the private files of a licensed and registered psychiatrist.

But the field agents did the best they could and, considering the circumstances, their best was pretty good.

Malone, meanwhile, put in two weeks sitting glumly at his Washington desk and checking reports as they arrived. They were uniformly depressing. The United States of America contained more subnormal minds than Malone cared to think about. There seemed to be enough of them to explain the results of any election you were unhappy over. Unfortunately, subnormal was all you could call them. Not one of them appeared to possess any abnormal psionic abilities whatever.

There were a couple who were reputed to be poltergeists—but in neither case was there a single shred of evidence to substantiate the claim.

At the end of the second week, Malone was just about convinced that his idea had been a total washout. A full fortnight had been spent on digging up imbeciles, while the spy at Yucca Flats had been going right on his merry way, scooping information out of the men at Project Isle as though he were scooping beans out of a pot. And, very likely, laughing himself silly at the feeble efforts of the FBI.

Who could he be?

Anyone, Malone told himself unhappily. *Anyone at all.* He could be the janitor that swept out the buildings, one of the guards at the gate, one of the minor technicians on another project, or even some old prospector wandering around the desert with a scintillation counter.

Is there any limit to telepathic range?

The spy could even be sitting quietly in an armchair in the Kremlin, probing through several thousand miles of solid earth to peep into the brains of the men on Project Isle.

That was, to say the very least, a depressing idea.

Malone found he had to assume that the spy was in the United States—that, in other words, there was some effective range to telepathic communication. Otherwise, there was no point in bothering to continue the search.

Therefore, he found one other thing to do. He alerted every agent to the job of discovering how the spy was getting his information out of the country.

He doubted that it would turn up anything, but it was a chance. And Malone hoped desperately for it, because he was beginning to be sure that the field agents were never going to turn up any telepathic imbeciles.

He was right.

They never did.

III

The telephone rang.

Malone rolled over on the couch and muttered under his breath. Was it absolutely necessary for someone to call him at seven in the morning?

He grabbed at the receiver with one hand, and picked up his cigar from the ashtray with the other. It was bad enough to be awakened from a sound sleep—but when a man hadn't been sleeping at all, it was even worse.

He'd been sitting up since before five that morning, worrying about the telepathic spy, and at the moment he wanted sleep more than he wanted phone calls.

"Gur?" he said, sleepily and angrily, thankful that he'd never had a visiphone installed in his apartment.

A feminine voice said: "Mr. Kenneth J. Malone?"

"Who's this?" Malone said peevishly, beginning to discover himself capable of semirational English speech.

"Long distance from San Francisco," the voice said.

"It certainly is," Malone said. "Who's calling?"

"San Francisco is calling," the voice said primly.

Malone repressed a desire to tell the voice off, and said instead: "*Who* in San Francisco?"

There was a momentary hiatus, and then the voice said: "Mr. Thomas Boyd is calling, sir. He says this is a scramble call."

Malone took a drag from his cigar and closed his eyes. Obviously the call was a scramble. If it had been clear, the man would have dialed direct, instead of going through what Malone now recognized as an operator.

"Mr. Boyd says he is the Agent-in-Charge of the San Francisco office of the FBI," the voice offered.

"And quite right, too," Malone told her. "All right. Put him on."

"One moment." There was a pause, a click, another pause and then another click. At last the operator said: "Your party is ready, sir."

Then there was still another pause. Malone stared at the audio receiver. He began to whistle "When Irish Eyes Are Smiling."

"Hello? Malone?"

"I'm here, Tom," Malone said guiltily. "This is me. What's the trouble?"

"Trouble?" Boyd said. "There isn't any trouble. Well, not really. Or maybe it is. I don't know."

Malone scowled at the audio receiver, and for the first time wished he had gone ahead and had a video circuit put in, so that Boyd could see the horrendous expression on his face.

"Look," he said. "It's seven here and that's too early. Out there, it's four, and that's practically ridiculous. What's so important?"

He knew perfectly well that Boyd wasn't calling him just for the fun of it. The man was a good agent. But why a call at this hour?

Malone muttered under his breath. Then, self-consciously, he squashed out his cigar and lit a cigarette while Boyd was saying: "Ken, I think we may have found what you've been looking for."

It wasn't safe to say too much, even over a scrambled circuit. But Malone got the message without difficulty.

"Yeah?" he said, sitting up on the edge of the couch. "You sure?"

"Well," Boyd said, "no. Not absolutely sure. Not absolutely. But it is worth your taking a personal look, I think."

"Ah," Malone said cautiously. "An imbecile?"

"No," Boyd said flatly. "Not an imbecile. Definitely not an imbecile. As a matter of fact, a hell of a fat long way from an imbecile."

Malone glanced at his watch and skimmed over the airline timetables in his mind. "I'll be there nine o'clock, your time," he said. "Have a car waiting for me at the field."

As usual, Malone managed to sleep better on the plane than he'd been able to do at home. He slept so well, in fact, that he was still groggy when he stepped into the waiting car.

"Good to see you, Ken," Boyd said briskly, as he shook Malone's hand.

"You, too, Tom," Malone said sleepily. "Now what's all this about?" He looked around apprehensively. "No bugs in this car, I hope?" he said.

Boyd gunned the motor and headed toward the San Francisco Freeway. "Better not be," he said, "or I'll fire me a technician or two."

"Well, then," Malone said, relaxing against the upholstery, "where is this guy, and who is he? And how did you find him?"

Boyd looked uncomfortable. It was, somehow, both an awe-inspiring and a slightly risible sight. Six feet one and one half inches tall in his flat feet, Boyd ported around over two hundred and twenty pounds of bone, flesh and muscle. He swung a potbelly of startling proportions under the silk shirting he wore, and his face, with its wide nose, small eyes and high forehead, was half highly mature, half startlingly childlike. In an apparent effort to erase those childlike qualities, Boyd sported a fringe of beard and a mustache which reminded Malone of somebody he couldn't quite place.

But whoever the somebody was, his hair hadn't been black, as Boyd's was—

He decided it didn't make any difference. Anyhow, Boyd was speaking.

"In the first place," he said, "it isn't a guy. In the second, I'm not exactly sure who it is. And in the third, Ken, I didn't find it."

There was a little silence.

"Don't tell me," Malone said. "It's a telepathic horse, isn't it? Tom, I just don't think I could stand a telepathic horse—"

"No," Boyd said hastily. "No. Not at all. No horse. It's a dame. I mean a lady." He looked away from the road and flashed a glance at Malone. His eyes seemed to be pleading for something—understanding, possibly, Malone thought. "Frankly," Boyd said, "I'd rather not tell you anything about her just yet. I'd rather you met her first. Then you could make up your own mind. All right?"

"All right," Malone said wearily. "Do it your own way. How far do we have to go?"

"Just about an hour's drive," Boyd said. "That's all."

Malone slumped back in the seat and pushed his hat over his eyes. "Fine," he said. "Suppose you wake me up when we get there."

But, groggy as he was, he couldn't sleep. He wished he'd had some coffee on the plane. Maybe it would have made him feel better.

Then again, coffee was only coffee. True, he had never acquired his father's taste for gin, but there was always bourbon.

He thought about bourbon for a few minutes. It was a nice thought. It warmed him and made him feel a lot better. After a while, he even felt awake enough to do some talking.

He pushed his hat back and struggled to a reasonable sitting position. "I don't suppose you have a drink hidden away in the car somewhere?" he said tentatively. "Or would the technicians have found that, too?"

"Better not have," Boyd said in the same tone as before, "or I'll fire a couple of technicians." He grinned without turning. "It's in the door compartment, next to the forty-five cartridges and the Tommy gun."

Malone opened the compartment in the thick door of the car and extracted a bottle. It was brandy instead of the bourbon he had been thinking about, but he discovered that he didn't mind at all. It went down as smoothly as milk.

Boyd glanced at it momentarily as Malone screwed the top back on.

"No," Malone said in answer to the unspoken question. "You're driving." Then he settled back again and tipped his hat forward.

He didn't sleep a wink. He was perfectly sure of that. But it wasn't over two seconds later that Boyd said: "We're here, Ken. Wake up."

"Whadyamean, wakeup," Malone said. "I wasn't asleep." He thumbed his hat back and sat up rapidly. "Where's 'here'?"

"Bayview Neuropsychiatric Hospital," Boyd said. "This is where Dr. Harman works, you know."

"No," Malone said. "As a matter of fact, I don't know. You didn't tell me—remember? And who is Dr. Harman, anyhow?"

The car was moving up a long, curving driveway toward a large, lawn-surrounded building. Boyd spoke without looking away from the road.

"Well," he said, "this Dr. Willard Harman is the man who phoned us yesterday. One of my field agents was out here asking around about imbeciles and so on. Found nothing, by the way. And then this Dr. Harman called, later. Said he had someone here I might be interested in. So I came on out myself for a look, yesterday afternoon ... after all, we had instructions to follow up every possible lead."

"I know," Malone said. "I wrote them."

"Oh," Boyd said. "Sure. Well, anyhow, I talked to this dame. Lady."

"And?"

"And I talked to her," Boyd said. "I'm not entirely sure of anything myself. But ... well, hell. You take a look at her."

He pulled the car up to a parking space, slid nonchalantly into a slot marked *Reserved—Executive Director Sutton*, and slid out from under the wheel while Malone got out the other side.

They marched up the broad steps, through the doorway and into the glass-fronted office of the receptionist.

Boyd showed her his little golden badge, and got an appropriate gasp. "FBI," he said. "Dr. Harman's expecting us."

The wait wasn't over fifteen seconds. Boyd and Malone marched down the hall and around a couple of corners, and came to the doctor's office. The door was opaqued glass with nothing but a room number stenciled on it. Without ceremony, Boyd pushed the door open. Malone followed him inside.

The office was small but sunny. Dr. Willard Harman sat behind a blond-wood desk, a chunky little man with crew-cut blond hair and rimless eyeglasses, who looked about thirty-two and couldn't possibly, Malone thought, have been anywhere near that young. On a second look, Malone noticed a better age indication in the eyes and forehead, and revised his first guess upward between ten and fifteen years.

"Come in, gentlemen," Dr. Harman boomed. His voice was that rarity, a really loud high tenor.

"Dr. Harman," Boyd said, "this is my superior, Mr. Malone. We'd like to have a talk with Miss Thompson."

"I anticipated that, sir," Dr. Harman said. "Miss Thompson is in the next room. Have you explained to Mr. Malone that—"

"I haven't explained a thing," Boyd said quickly, and added in what was obviously intended to be a casual tone: "Mr. Malone wants to get a picture of Miss Thompson directly—without any preconceptions."

"I see," Dr. Harman said. "Very well, gentlemen. Through this door."

He opened the door in the right-hand wall of the room, and Malone took one look. It was a long, long look. Standing framed in the doorway, dressed in the starched white of a nurse's uniform, was the most beautiful blonde he had ever seen.

She had curves. She definitely had curves. As a matter of fact, Malone didn't really think he had ever seen curves before. These were something new and different and truly three-dimensional. But it wasn't the curves, or the long straight lines of her legs, or the quiet beauty of her face, that made her so special. After all, Malone had seen legs and bodies and faces before.

At least, he thought he had. Off-hand, he couldn't remember where. Looking at the girl, Malone was ready to write brand-new definitions for every anatomical term. Even a term like "hands." Malone had never seen anything especially arousing in the human hand before—anyway, not when the hand was just lying around, so to speak, attached to its wrist but not doing anything in particular. But these hands, long, slender and tapering, white and cool-looking....

And yet, it wasn't just the sheer physical beauty of the girl. She had something else, something more and something different. (*Something borrowed*, Malone thought in a semi-delirious haze, *and something blue*.) Personality? Character? Soul?

Whatever it was, Malone decided, this girl had it. She had enough of it to supply the entire human race, and any others that might exist in the Universe. Malone smiled at the girl and she smiled back.

After seeing the smile, Malone wasn't sure he could still walk evenly. Somehow, though, he managed to go over to her and extend his hand. The notion that a telepath would turn out to be this mind-searing Epitome had never crossed his mind, but now, somehow, it seemed perfectly fitting and proper.

"Good morning, Miss Thompson," he said in what he hoped was a winning voice.

The smile disappeared. It was like the sun going out.

The vision appeared to be troubled. Malone was about to volunteer his help—if necessary, for the next seventy years—when she spoke.

"I'm not Miss Thompson," she said.

"This is one of our nurses," Dr. Harman put in. "Miss Wilson, Mr. Malone. And Mr. Boyd. Miss Thompson, gentlemen, is over there."

Malone turned.

There, in a corner of the room, an old lady sat. She was a small old lady, with apple-red cheeks and twinkling eyes. She held some knitting in her hands, and she smiled up at the FBI men as if they were her grandsons come for tea and cookies, of a Sunday afternoon.

She had snow-white hair that shone like a crown around her old head in the lights of the room. Malone blinked at her. She didn't disappear.

"*You're* Miss Thompson?" he said.

She smiled sweetly. "Oh, my, no," she said.

There was a long silence. Malone looked at her. Then he looked at the unbelievably beautiful Miss Wilson. Then he looked at Dr. Harman. And, at last, he looked at Boyd.

"All right," he said. "I get it. *You're* Miss Thompson."

"Now, wait a minute, Malone," Boyd began.

"Wait a minute?" Malone said. "There are four people here, not counting me. I know I'm not Miss Thompson. I never was, not even as a child. And Dr. Harman isn't, and Miss Wilson isn't, and Whistler's Great-Grandmother isn't, either. So you must be. Unless she isn't here. Or unless she's invisible. Or unless I'm crazy."

"It isn't *you*, Malone," Boyd said.

"What isn't me?"

"That's crazy," Boyd said.

"O.K.," Malone said. "I'm not crazy. Then will somebody please tell me—"

The little old lady cleared her throat. A silence fell. When it was complete she spoke, and her voice was as sweet and kindly as anything Malone had ever heard.

"You may call me Miss Thompson," she said. "For the present, at any rate. They all do here. It's a pseudonym I have to use."

"A pseudonym?" Malone said.

"You see, Mr. Malone," Miss Wilson began.

Malone stopped her. "Don't talk," he said. "I have to concentrate and if you talk I can barely think." He took off his hat suddenly, and began twisting the brim in his hands. "You understand, don't you?"

The trace of a smile appeared on her face. "I think I do," she said.

"Now," Malone said, "you're Miss Thompson, but not really, because you have to use a pseudonym." He blinked at the little old lady. "Why?"

"Well," she said, "otherwise people would find out about my little secret."

"Your little secret," Malone said.

"That's right," the little old lady said. "I'm immortal, you see."

Malone said: "Oh." Then he kept quiet for a long time. It didn't seem to him that anyone in the room was breathing.

He said: "Oh," again, but it didn't sound any better than it had the first time. He tried another phrase. "You're immortal," he said.

"That's right," the little old lady agreed sweetly.

There was only one other question to ask, and Malone set his teeth grimly and asked it. It came out just a trifle indistinct, but the little old lady nodded.

"My real name?" she said. "Elizabeth. Elizabeth Tudor, of course. I used to be Queen."

"Of England," Malone said faintly.

"Malone, look—" Boyd began.

"Let me get it all at once," Malone told him. "I'm strong. I can take it." He twisted his hat again and turned back to the little old lady.

"You're immortal, and you're not really Miss Thompson, but Queen Elizabeth I?" he said slowly.

"That's right," she said. "How clever of you. Of course, after little Jimmy—cousin Mary's boy, I mean—said I was dead and claimed the Throne, I decided to change my name and all. And that's what I did. But I am Elizabeth Regina." She smiled, and her eyes twinkled merrily. Malone stared at her for a long minute.

Burris, he thought, *is going to love this*.

"Oh, I'm so glad," the little old lady said. "Do you really think he will? Because I'm sure I'll like your Mr. Burris, too. All of you FBI men are so charming. Just like poor, poor Essex."

Well, Malone told himself, that was that. He'd found himself a telepath.

And she wasn't an imbecile.

Oh, no. That would have been simple.

Instead, she was battier than a cathedral spire.

The long silence was broken by the voice of Miss Wilson.

"Mr. Malone," she said, "you've been thinking." She stopped. "I mean, you've been so quiet."

"I like being quiet," Malone said patiently. "Besides—" He stopped and turned to the little old lady. *Can you really read my mind?* he thought deliberately. After a second he added: *... your majesty?*

"How sweet of you, Mr. Malone," she said. "Nobody's called me that for centuries. But of course I can. Although it's not reading, really. After all, that would be like asking if I can read your voice. Of course I can, Mr. Malone."

"That does it," Malone said. "I'm not a hard man to convince. And when I see the truth, I'm the first one to admit it, even if it makes me look like a nut." He turned back to the little old lady. "Begging your pardon," he said.

"Oh, my," the little old lady said. "I really don't mind at all. Sticks and stones, you know, can break my bones. But being called nuts, Mr. Malone, can never hurt me. After all, it's been so many years—so many hundreds of years—"

"Sure," Malone said easily.

Boyd broke in. "Listen, Malone," he said, "do you mind telling me what is going on?"

"It's very simple," Malone said. "Miss Thompson here ... pardon me; I mean Queen Elizabeth I ... really is a telepath. That's all. I think I want to lie down somewhere until it goes away."

"Until what goes away?" Miss Wilson said.

Malone stared at her almost without seeing her, if not quite. "Everything," he said. He closed his eyes.

"My goodness," the little old lady said after a second. "Everything's so confused. Poor Mr. Malone is terribly shaken up by everything." She stood up, still holding her knitting, and went across the room. Before the astonished eyes of the doctor and nurse, and Tom Boyd, she patted the FBI agent on the shoulder. "There, there, Mr. Malone," she said. "It will all be perfectly all right. You'll see." Then she returned to her seat.

Malone opened his eyes. He turned to Dr. Harman. "You called up Boyd here," he said, "and told him that ... er ... Miss Thompson was a telepath. Howd' you know?"

"It's all right," the little old lady put in from her chair. "I don't mind your calling me Miss Thompson, not right now, anyhow."

"Thanks," Malone said faintly.

Dr. Harman was blinking in a kind of befuddled astonishment. "You mean she really *is* a—" He stopped and brought his tenor voice to a squeaking halt, regained his professional poise, and began again. "I'd rather not discuss the patient in her presence, Mr. Malone," he said. "If you'll just come into my office—"

"Oh, *bosh*, Dr. Harman," the little old lady said primly. "I do wish you'd give your own Queen credit for some ability. Goodness knows you think *you're* smart enough."

"Now, now, Miss Thompson," he said in what was obviously his best Grade A Choice Government Inspected couchside manner. "Don't...."

"... Upset yourself," she finished for him. "Now, really, doctor. I know what you're going to tell them."

"But Miss Thompson, I—"

"You didn't honestly think I *was* a telepath," the little old lady said. "Heavens, we know that. And you're going to tell them how I used to say I could read minds ... oh, years and years ago. And because of that you thought it might be worth while to tell the FBI about me—which wasn't very kind of you, doctor, before you knew anything about why they wanted somebody like me."

"Now, now, Miss Thompson," Miss Wilson said, walking across the room to put an arm around the little old lady's shoulder. Malone wished for one brief second that he were the old little old lady. Maybe if he were a patient in the hospital he would get the same treatment.

He wondered if he could possibly work such a deal.

Then he wondered if it would be worth while, being nuts. But of course it would. He was nuts anyhow, wasn't he?

Sure, he told himself. They were all nuts.

"Nobody's going to hurt you," Miss Wilson said. She was talking to the old lady. "You'll be perfectly all right and you don't have to worry about a thing."

"Oh, yes, dear, I know that," the little old lady said. "You only want to help me, dear. You're so kind. And these FBI men really don't mean any harm. But Dr. Harman didn't know that. He just thinks I'm crazy and that's all."

"Please, Miss Thompson—" Dr. Harman began.

"Just crazy, that's all," the little old lady said. She turned away for a second and nobody said anything. Then she turned back. "Do you all know what he's thinking now?" she said. Dr. Harman turned a dull purple, but she ignored him. "He's wondering why I didn't take the trouble to prove all this to you years ago. And besides that, he's thinking about—"

"Miss Thompson," Dr. Harman said. His bedside manner had cracked through and his voice was harsh and strained. "Please."

"Oh, all right," she said, a little petulantly. "If you want to keep all that private."

Malone broke in suddenly, fascinated. "Why didn't you prove you were telepathic before now?" he said.

The little old lady smiled at him. "Why, because you wouldn't have believed me," she said. She dropped her knitting neatly in her lap and folded her hands over it. "None of you *wanted* to believe me," she said, and sniffed. Miss Wilson moved nervously and she looked up. "And don't tell me it's going to be all right. I know it's going to be all right. I'm going to make sure of that."

Malone felt a sudden chill. But it was obvious, he told himself, that the little old lady didn't mean what she was saying. She smiled at him again, and her smile was as sweet and guileless as the smile on the face of his very own sainted grandmother.

Not that Malone remembered his grandmother; she had died before he'd been born. But if he'd had a grandmother, and if he'd remembered her, he was sure she would have had the same sweet smile.

So she couldn't have meant what she'd said. Would Malone's own grandmother make things difficult for him? The very idea was ridiculous.

Dr. Harman opened his mouth, apparently changed his mind, and shut it again. The little old lady turned to him.

"Were you going to ask why I bothered to prove anything to Mr. Malone?" she said. "Of course you were, and I shall tell you. It's because Mr. Malone *wanted* to believe me. He *wants* me. He *needs* me. I'm a telepath, and that's enough for Mr. Malone. Isn't it?"

"Gur," Malone said, taken by surprise. After a second he added: "I guess so."

"You see, doctor?" the little old lady said.

"But you—" Dr. Harman began.

"I read minds," the little old lady said. "That's right, doctor. That's what makes me a telepath."

Malone's brain was whirling rapidly, like a distant galaxy. "Telepath" was a nice word, he thought. How did you telepath from a road?

Simple.

A road is paved.

Malone thought that was pretty funny, but he didn't laugh. He thought he would never laugh again. He wanted to cry, a little, but he didn't think he'd be able to manage that either.

He twisted his hat, but it didn't make him feel any better. Gradually, he became aware that the little old lady was talking to Dr. Harman again.

"But," she said, "since it will make you feel so much better, doctor, we give you our Royal permission to retire, and to speak to Mr. Malone alone."

"Malone alone," Dr. Harman muttered. "Hm-m-m. My. Well." He turned and seemed to be surprised that Malone was actually standing near him. "Yes," he said. "Well. Mr. Alone ... Malone ... please, whoever you are, just come into my office, please?"

Malone looked at the little old lady. One of her eyes closed and opened. It was an unmistakable wink.

Malone grinned at her in what he hoped was a cheerful manner. "All right," he said to the psychiatrist, "let's go." He turned with the barest trace of regret, and Boyd followed him. Leaving the little old lady and, unfortunately, the startling Miss Wilson, behind, the procession filed back into Dr. Harman's office.

The doctor closed the door, and leaned against it for a second. He looked as though someone had suddenly revealed to him that the world was square. But when he spoke his voice was almost even.

"Sit down, gentlemen," he said, and indicated chairs. "I really ... well, I don't know what to say. All this time, all these years, she's been reading my mind! My mind. She's been reading ... looking right into my mind, or whatever it is."

"Whatever what is?" Malone asked, sincerely interested. He had dropped gratefully into a chair near Boyd's, across the desk from Dr. Harman.

"Whatever my *mind* is," Dr. Harman said. "Reading it. Oh, my."

"Dr. Harman," Malone began, but the psychiatrist gave him a bright blank stare.

"Don't you understand?" he said. "She's a telepath."

"We—"

The phone on Dr. Harman's desk chimed gently. He glanced at it and said: "Excuse me. The phone." He picked up the receiver and said: "Hello?"

There was no image on the screen.

But the voice was image enough. "This is Andrew J. Burris," it said. "Is Kenneth J. Malone there?"

"Mr. Malone?" the psychiatrist said. "I mean, Mr. Burris? Mr. Malone is here. Yes. Oh, my. Do you want to talk to him?"

"No, you idiot," the voice said. "I just want to know if he's all tucked in."

"Tucked in?" Dr. Harman gave the phone a sudden smile. "A joke," he said. "It *is* a joke, isn't it? The way things have been happening, you never know whether—"

"A joke," Burris' voice said. "That's right. Yes. Am I talking to one of the patients?"

Dr. Harman gulped, got mad, and thought better of it. At last he said, very gently: "I'm not at all sure," and handed the phone to Malone.

The FBI agent said: "Hello, chief. Things are a little confused."

Burris' face appeared on the screen. "Confused, sure," he said. "I feel confused already." He took a breath. "I called the San Francisco office, and they told me you and Boyd were out there. What's going on?"

Malone said cautiously: "We've found a telepath."

Burris' eyes widened slightly. "Another one?"

"What are you talking about, another one?" Malone said. "We have one. Does anybody else have any more?"

"Well," Burris said, "we just got a report on another one—maybe. Besides yours, I mean."

"I hope the one you've got is in better shape than the one I've got," Malone said. He took a deep breath, and then spat it all out at once: "The one we've found is a little old lady. She thinks she's Queen Elizabeth I. She's a telepath, sure, but she's nuts."

"Queen Elizabeth?" Burris said. "Of England?"

"That's right," Malone said. He held his breath.

"Damn it," Burris exploded, "they've already got one."

Malone sighed. "This is another one," he said. "Or, rather, the original one. She also claims she's immortal."

"Lives forever?" Burris said. "You mean like that?"

"Immortal," Malone said. "Right."

Burris nodded. Then he looked worried. "Tell me, Malone," he said. "She *isn't*, is she?"

"Isn't immortal, you mean?" Malone said. Burris nodded. Malone said confidently: "Of course not."

There was a little pause. Malone thought things over.

Hell, maybe she was immortal. Stranger things had happened, hadn't they?

He looked over at Dr. Harman. "How about that?" he said. "Could she be immortal?"

The psychiatrist shook his head decisively. "She's been here for over forty years, Mr. Malone, ever since her late teens. Her records show all that, and her birth certificate is in perfect order. Not a chance."

Malone sighed and turned back to the phone. "Of course she isn't immortal, chief," he said. "She couldn't be. Nobody is. Just a nut."

"I was afraid of that," Burris said.

"Afraid?" Malone said.

Burris nodded. "We've got another one—if he checks out," he said. "Right here in Washington—St. Elizabeths."

"Another nut?"

"Strait-jacket case," Burris said. "Delusions of persecution. Paranoia. And a lot of other things I can't pronounce. But I'm sending him on out to Yucca Flats anyhow, under guard. You might find a use for him."

"Oh, sure," Malone said.

"We can't afford to overlook a thing," Burris said.

Malone sighed. "I know," he said. "But all the same—"

"Don't worry about a thing, Malone," Burris said with a palpably false air of confidence. "You get this Queen Elizabeth of yours out of there and take her to Yucca Flats, too."

Malone considered the possibilities. Maybe they would find more telepaths. Maybe all the telepaths would be nuts. It didn't seem unlikely. Imagine having a talent that nobody would believe you had. It might very easily drive you crazy to be faced with a situation like that.

And there they would be in Yucca Flats. Kenneth J. Malone, and a convention of looney-bin inhabitants.

Fun!

Malone began to wonder why he had gone into FBI work in the first place.

"Listen, chief," he said. "I—"

"Sure, I understand," Burris said quickly. "She's batty. But what else can we do? Malone, don't do anything you'll regret."

"What?"

"I mean, don't resign."

"Chief, how did you know—you're not telepathic too, are you?"

"Of course not," Burris said. "But that's what I would do in your place. And don't do it."

"Look, chief," Malone said. "These nuts—"

"Malone, you've done a wonderful job so far," Burris said. "You'll get a raise and a better job when all this is over. Who else would have thought of looking in the twitch-bins for telepaths? But you did, Malone, and I'm proud of you, and you're stuck with it. We've got to use them now. We have to find that spy!" He took a breath. "On to Yucca Flats!" he said.

Malone gave up. "Yes, sir," he said. "Anything else?"

"Not right now," Burris said. "If there is, I'll let you know."

Malone hung up unhappily as the image vanished. He looked at Dr. Harman. "Well," he said, "that's that. What do I have to do to get a release for Miss Thompson?"

Harman stared at him. "But, Mr. Malone," he said, "that just isn't possible. Really. Miss Thompson is a ward of the state, and we couldn't possibly allow her release without a court order."

Malone thought that over. "O.K.," he said at last. "I can see that." He turned to Boyd. "Here's a job for you, Tom," he said. "Get one of the judges on the phone. You'll know which one will do us the most good, fastest."

"Hm-m-m," Boyd said. "Say Judge Dunning," he said. "Good man. Fast worker."

"I don't care who," Malone said. "Just get going, and get us a release for Miss Thompson." He turned back to the doctor. "By the way," he said, "has she got any other name? Besides Elizabeth Tudor, I mean," he added hurriedly.

"Her full name," Dr. Harman said, "is Rose Walker Thompson. She is not Queen Elizabeth I, II, or XXVIII, and she is not immortal."

"But she is," Malone pointed out, "a telepath. And that's why I want her."

"She may," Dr. Harman said, "be a telepath." It was obvious that he had partly managed to forget the disturbing incidents that had happened a few minutes before. "I don't even want to discuss that part of it."

"O.K., never mind it," Malone said agreeably. "Tom, get us a court order for Rose Walker Thompson. Effective yesterday—day before, if possible."

Boyd nodded, but before he could get to the phone Dr. Harman spoke again.

"Now, wait a moment, gentlemen," he said. "Court order or no court order, Miss Thompson is definitely not a well woman, and I can't see my way clear to—"

"I'm not well myself," Malone said. "I need sleep and I probably have a cold. But I've got to work for the national security, and—"

"This is important," Boyd put in.

"I don't dispute that," Dr. Harman said. "Nevertheless, I—"

The door that led into the other room suddenly burst open. The three men turned to stare at Miss Wilson, who stood in the doorway for a long second and then stepped into the office, closing the door quietly behind her.

"I'm sorry to interrupt," she said.

"Not at all," Malone said. "It's a pleasure to have you. Come again soon." He smiled at her.

She didn't smile back. "Doctor," she said, "you better talk to Miss Thompson. I'm not at all sure what I can do. It's something new."

"New?" he said. The worry lines on his face were increasing, but he spoke softly.

"The poor dear thinks she's going to get out of the hospital now," Miss Wilson said. "For some reason, she's convinced that the FBI is going to get her released, and—"

As she saw the expressions on three faces, she stopped.

"What's wrong?" she said.

"Miss Wilson," Malone said, "we ... may I call you by your first name?"

"Of course, Mr. Malone," she said.

There was a little silence.

"Miss Wilson," Malone said, "what *is* your first name?"

She smiled now, very gently. Malone wanted to walk through mountains, or climb fire. He felt confused, but wonderful. "Barbara," she said.

"Lovely," he said. "Well, Barbara ... and please call me Ken. It's short for Kenneth."

The smile on her face broadened. "I thought it might be," she said.

"Well," Malone said softly, "it is. Kenneth. That's my name. And you're Barbara."

Boyd cleared his throat.

"Ah," Malone said. "Yes. Of course. Well, Barbara ... well, that's just what we intend to do. Take Miss Thompson away. We need her—badly."

Dr. Harman had said nothing at all, and had barely moved. He was staring at a point on his desk. "She couldn't possibly have heard us," he muttered. "That's a soundproof door. She couldn't have heard us."

"But you can't take Miss Thompson away," Miss Wilson said.

"We have to, Barbara," Malone said gently. "Try to understand. It's for the national security."

"She heard us thinking," Dr. Harman muttered. "That's what; she heard us thinking. Behind a soundproof door. She can see inside their minds. She can even see inside *my* mind."

"She's a sick woman," Barbara said.

"But you have to understand—"

"Vital necessity," Boyd put in. "Absolutely vital."

"Nevertheless—" Barbara said.

"She can read minds," Dr. Harman whispered in an awed tone. "She knows. Everything. She *knows*."

"It's out of the question," Barbara said. "Whether you like it or not. Miss Thompson is not going to leave this hospital. Why, what could she do outside these walls? She hasn't left in over forty years! And furthermore, Mr. Malone—"

"Kenneth," Malone put in, as the door opened again. "I mean Ken."

The little old lady put her haloed head into the room. "Now, now, Barbara," she said. "Don't you go spoiling things. Just let these nice men take me away and everything will be fine, believe me. Besides, I've been outside more often than you imagine."

"Outside?" Barbara said.

"Of course," the little old lady said. "In other people's minds. Even yours. I remember that nice young man ... what was his name?"

"Never mind his name," Barbara said, flushing furiously.

Malone felt instantly jealous of every nice young man he had ever even heard of. *He* wasn't a nice young man; he was an FBI agent, and he liked to drink and smoke cigars and carouse.

All nice young men, he decided, should be turned into ugly old men as soon as possible. That'd fix them!

He noticed the little old lady smiling at him, and tried to change his thoughts rapidly. But the little old lady said nothing at all.

"At any rate," Barbara said, "I'm afraid that we just can't—"

Dr. Harman cleared his throat imperiously. It was a most impressive noise, and everyone turned to look at him. His face was a little gray, but he looked, otherwise, like a rather pudgy, blond, crew-cut Roman emperor.

"Just a moment," he said with dignity, "I think you're doing the United States of America a grave injustice, Miss Wilson—and that you're doing an injustice to Miss Thompson, too."

"What do you mean?" she said.

"I think it would be nice for her to get away from me—I mean from here," the psychiatrist said. "Where did you say you were taking her?" he asked Malone.

"Yucca Flats," Malone said.

"Ah." The news seemed to please the psychiatrist. "That's a long distance from here, isn't it? It's quite a few hundred miles away. Perhaps even a few thousand miles away. I feel sure that will be the best thing for me ... I mean, of course, for Miss Thompson. I shall recommend that the court so order."

"Doctor—" But even Barbara saw, Malone could tell, that it was no good arguing with Dr. Harman. She tried a last attack. "Doctor, who's going to take care of her?"

A light the size and shape of North America burst in Malone's mind. He almost chortled. But he managed to keep his voice under control. "What she needs," he said, "is a trained psychiatric nurse."

Barbara Wilson gave him a look that had carloads of U_{235} stacked away in it, but Malone barely minded. She'd get over it, he told himself.

"Now, wasn't that sweet of you to think of that," the little old lady said. Malone looked at her and was rewarded with another wink.

"I'm certainly glad you thought of Barbara," the little old lady went on. "You will go with me won't you, dear? I'll make you a duchess. Wouldn't you like to be a duchess, dear?"

Barbara looked from Malone to the little old lady, and then she looked at Dr. Harman. Apparently what she saw failed to make her happy.

"We'll take good care of her, Barbara," Malone said.

She didn't even bother to give him an answer. After a second Boyd said: "Well, I guess that settles it. If you'll let me use your phone, Dr. Harman, I'll call Judge Dunning."

"Go right ahead," Dr. Harman said. "Go right ahead."

The little old lady smiled softly without looking at anybody at all. "Won't it be wonderful?" she whispered. "At last I've been recognized. My country is about to pay me for my services. My loyal subjects—" She stopped and wiped what Malone thought was a tear from one cornflower-blue eye.

"Now, now, Miss Thompson," Barbara said.

"I'm not sad," the little old lady said, smiling up at her. "I'm just so very happy. I am about to get my reward, my well-deserved reward at last, from all of my loyal subjects. You'll see." She paused and Malone felt a faint stirring of stark, chill fear.

"Won't it be wonderful?" said the little old lady.

IV

"You're *where*?" Andrew J. Burris said.

Malone looked at the surprised face on the screen and wished he hadn't called. He had to report in, of course—but, if he'd had any sense, he'd have ordered Boyd to do the job for him.

Oh, well, it was too late for that now. "I'm in Las Vegas," he said. "I tried to get you last night, but I couldn't, so I—"

"Las Vegas," Burris said. "Well, well. Las Vegas." His face darkened and his voice became very loud. "Why aren't you in Yucca Flats?" he screamed.

"Because she insisted on it," Malone said. "The old lady. Miss Thompson. She says there's another telepath here."

Burris closed his eyes. "Well, that's a relief," he said at last. "Somebody in one of the gambling houses, I suppose. Fine, Malone." He went right on without a pause: "The boys have uncovered two more in various parts of the nation. Not one of them is even close to sane." He opened his eyes. "Where's this one?" he said.

Malone sighed. "In the looney bin," he said.

Burris' eyes closed again. Malone waited in silence. At last Burris said: "All right. Get him out."

"Right," Malone said.

"Tell me," Burris said. "Why did Miss Thompson insist that you go to Las Vegas? Somebody else could have done the job. You could have sent Boyd, couldn't you?"

"Chief," Malone said slowly, "what sort of mental condition are those other telepaths in?"

"Pretty bad," Burris said. "As a matter of fact, very bad. Miss Thompson may be off her trolley, but the others haven't even got any tracks." He paused. "What's that got to do with it?" he said.

"Well," Malone said, "I figured we'd better handle Miss Thompson with kid gloves—at least until we find a better telepath to work with." He didn't mention Barbara Wilson. The chief, he told himself, didn't want to be bothered with details.

"Doggone right you'd better," Burris said. "You treat that old lady as if she were the Queen herself, understand?"

"Don't worry," Malone said unhappily. "We are." He hesitated. "She says she'll help us find our spy, all right, but we've got to do it her way—or else she won't co-operate."

"Do it her way, then," Burris said. "That spy—"

"Chief, are you sure?"

Burris blinked. "Well, then," he said, "what *is* her way?"

Malone took a deep breath. "First," he said, "we had to come here and pick this guy up. This William Logan, who's in a private sanitarium just outside of Las Vegas. That's number one. Miss Thompson wants to get all the telepaths together, so they can hold mental conversations or something."

"And all of them batty," Burris said.

"Sure," Malone said. "A convention of nuts—and me in the middle. Listen, chief—"

"Later," Burris said. "When this is over we can all resign, or go fishing, or just plain shoot ourselves. But right now the national security is primary, Malone. Remember that."

"O.K.," Malone sighed. "O.K. But she wants all the nuts here."

"Go along with her," Burris snapped. "Keep her happy. So far, Malone, she's the only lead we have on the guy who's swiping information from Yucca Flats. If she wants something, Malone, you do it."

"But, chief—"

"Don't interrupt me," Burris said. "If she wants to be treated like a queen, you treat her like one. Malone, that's an order!"

"Yes, sir," Malone said sadly. "But, chief, she wants us to buy her some new clothes."

Burris exploded: "Is that all? New clothes? Get 'em. Put 'em on the expense account. New clothes are a drop in the bucket."

"Well ... she thinks we need new clothes, too."

"Maybe you do," Burris said. "Put the whole thing on the expense account. You don't think I'm going to quibble about a few dollars, do you?"

"Well—"

"Get the clothes. Just don't bother me with details like this. Handle the job yourself, Malone—you're in charge out there. And get to Yucca Flats as soon as possible."

Malone gave up. "Yes, sir," he said.

"All right, then," Burris said. "Call me tomorrow. Meanwhile—good luck, Malone. Chin up."

Malone said: "Yes, sir," and reached for the switch. But Burris' voice stopped him.

"Just one thing," he said.

"Yes, chief?" Malone said.

Burris frowned. "Don't spend any more for the clothes than you have to," he said.

Malone nodded, and cut off.

When the director's image had vanished, he got up and went to the window of the hotel room. Outside, a huge sign told the world, and Malone, that this was the Thunderbird-Hilton-Zeckendorf Hotel, but Malone ignored it. He didn't need a sign; he knew where he was.

In hot water, he thought. *That's* where he was.

Behind him, the door opened. Malone turned as Boyd came in.

"I found a costume shop, Ken," he said.

"Great," Malone said. "The chief authorized it."

"He did?" Boyd's round face fell at the news.

"He said to buy her whatever she wants. He says to treat her like a queen."

"That," Boyd said, "we're doing now."

"I know it," Malone said. "I know it altogether too well."

"Anyhow," Boyd said, brightening, "the costume shop doesn't do us any good. They've only got cowboy stuff and bullfighters' costumes and Mexican stuff—you know, for their Helldorado Week here."

"You didn't give up, did you?" Malone said.

Boyd shook his head. "Of course not," he said. "Ken, this is on the expense account, isn't it?"

"Expense account," Malone said. "Sure it is."

Boyd looked relieved. "Good," he said. "Because I had the proprietor phone her size in, to New York."

"Better get two of 'em," Malone said. "The chief said anything she wanted, she was supposed to have."

"I'll go back right away. I told him we wanted the stuff on the afternoon plane, so—"

"And give him Bar ... Miss Wilson's size, and yours, and mine. Tell him to dig up something appropriate."

"For us?" Boyd blanched visibly.

"For us," Malone said grimly.

Boyd set his jaw. "No," he said.

"Listen, Tom," Malone said, "I don't like this any better than you do. But if I can't resign, you can't either. Costumes for everybody."

"But," Boyd said, and stopped. After a second he went on: "Malone ... Ken ... FBI agents are supposed to be inconspicuous, aren't they?"

Malone nodded.

"Well, how inconspicuous are we going to be in this stuff?"

"It's an idea," Malone said. "But it isn't a very good one. Our first job is to keep Miss Thompson happy. And that means costumes. And what's more," Malone added, "from now on she's 'Your Majesty'. Got that?"

"Ken," Boyd said, "you've gone nuts."

Malone shook his head. "No, I haven't," he said. "I just wish I had. It would be a relief."

"Me, too," Boyd said. He started for the door and turned. "I wish I could have stayed in San Francisco," he said. "Why should she insist on taking *me* along?"

"The beard," Malone said.

"*My* beard?" Boyd recoiled.

"Right," Malone said. "She says it reminds her of someone she knows. Frankly, it reminds me of someone, too. Only I don't know who."

Boyd gulped. "I'll shave it off," he said, with the air of a man who can do no more to propitiate the Gods.

"You will not," Malone said firmly. "Touch but a hair of yon black chin, and I'll peel off your entire skin."

Boyd winced.

"Now," Malone said, "go back to that costume shop and arrange things. Here." He fished in his pockets, came out with a crumpled slip of paper and handed it to Boyd. "That's a list of my clothing sizes. Get another list from B ... Miss Wilson." Boyd nodded. Malone thought he detected a strange glint in the other man's eye. "Don't measure her yourself," he said. "Just ask her."

Boyd scratched his bearded chin and nodded slowly. "All right, Ken," he said. "But if we just don't get anywhere, don't blame me."

"If you get anywhere," Malone said, "I'll snatch you baldheaded. And I'll leave the beard."

"I didn't mean with Miss Wilson, Ken," Boyd said. "I meant in general." He left, with the air of a man whose world has betrayed him. His back looked, to Malone, like the back of a man on his way to the scaffold or guillotine.

The door closed.

Now, Malone thought, who does that beard remind me of? Who do I know who knows Miss Thompson?

And what difference does it make?

Nevertheless, he told himself, Boyd's beard was really an admirable fact of nature. Ever since beards had become popular again in the mid-sixties, and FBI agents had been permitted to wear them, Malone had thought about growing one. But, somehow, it didn't seem right.

Now, looking at Boyd, he began to think about the prospect again.

He shrugged the notion away. There were things to do.

He picked up the phone and called Information.

"Can you give me," he said, "the number of the Desert Edge Sanitarium?"

The crimson blob of the setting sun was already painting the desert sky with its customary purples and oranges by the time the little caravan arrived at the Desert Edge Sanitarium, a square white building several miles out of Las Vegas. Malone, in the first car, wondered briefly about the kind of patients they catered to? People driven mad by vingt-et-un or poker-dice? Neurotic chorus ponies? Gambling czars with delusions of non-persecution?

Sitting in the front seat next to Boyd, he watched the unhappy San Francisco agent manipulating the wheel. In the back seat, Queen Elizabeth Thompson and Lady Barbara, the nurse, were located, and Her Majesty was chattering away like a magpie.

Malone eyed the rear-view mirror to get a look at the car following them and the two local FBI agents in it. They were, he thought, unbelievably lucky. He had to sit and listen to the Royal Personage in the back seat.

"Of course, as soon as Parliament convenes and recognizes me," she was saying, "I shall confer personages on all of you. Right now, the best I can do is to knight you all, and of course that's hardly enough. But I think I shall make Sir Kenneth the Duke of Columbia."

Sir Kenneth, Malone realized, was himself. He wondered how he'd like being Duke of Columbia—and wouldn't the President be surprised!

"And Sir Thomas," the queen continued, "will be the Duke of ... what? Sir Thomas?"

"Yes, Your Majesty?" Boyd said, trying to sound both eager and properly respectful.

"What would you like to be Duke of?" she said.

"Oh," Boyd said after a second's thought, "anything that pleases Your Majesty." But, apparently, his thoughts gave him away.

"You're from upstate New York?" the Queen said. "How very nice. Then you must be made the Duke of Poughkeepsie."

"Thank you, Your Majesty," Boyd said. Malone thought he detected a note of pride in the man's voice, and shot a glance at Boyd, but the agent was driving with a serene face and an economy of motion.

Duke of Poughkeepsie! Malone thought. *Hah!*

He leaned back and adjusted his fur-trimmed coat. The plume that fell from his cap kept tickling his neck, and he brushed at it without success.

All four of the inhabitants of the car were dressed in late Sixteenth Century costumes, complete with ruffs and velvet and lace filigree. Her Majesty and Lady Barbara were wearing the full skirts and small skullcaps of the era—and on Barbara, Malone thought privately, the low-cut gowns didn't look at all disappointing—and Sir Thomas and Malone—Sir Kenneth, he thought sourly—were clad in doublet, hose and long coats with fur trim and slashed sleeves. And all of them were loaded down, weighted down, staggeringly, with gems.

Naturally, the gems were fake. But then, Malone thought, the Queen was mad. It all balanced out in the end.

As they approached the sanitarium, Malone breathed a thankful prayer that he'd called up to tell the head physician how they'd all be dressed. If he hadn't—

He didn't want to think about that.

He didn't even want to pass it by hurriedly on a dark night.

The head physician, Dr. Frederic Dowson, was waiting for them on the steps of the building. He was a tall, thin, cadaverous-looking man with almost no hair and very deep-sunken eyes. He had the kind of face that a gushing female would probably describe, Malone thought, as "craggy," but it didn't look in the least attractive to Malone. Instead, it looked tough and forbidding.

He didn't turn a hair as the magnificently robed Boyd slid from the front seat, opened the rear door, doffed his plumed hat, and in one low sweep made a great bow. "We are here, Your Majesty," Boyd said.

Her Majesty got out, clutching at her voluminous skirts in a worried manner, to keep from catching them on the door jamb. "You know, Sir Thomas," she said when she was standing free of the car, "I think we must be related."

"Ah?" Boyd said worriedly.

"I'm certain of it, in fact," Her Majesty went on. "You look just exactly like my poor father. Just exactly. I dare say you come from one of the sinister branches of the family. Perhaps you are a half-brother of mine—removed, of course."

Malone grinned, and tried to hide the expression. Boyd was looking puzzled, then distantly angered. Nobody had ever called him illegitimate in just that way before.

But Her Majesty was absolutely right, Malone thought. The agent had always reminded him of someone, and now, at last, he knew exactly who. The hair hadn't been black, either, but red.

Boyd was, in Elizabethan costume, the deadest of dead ringers for Henry VIII.

Malone went up the steps to where Dr. Dowson was standing.

"I'm Malone," he said, checking a tendency to bow. "I called earlier today. Is this William Logan of yours ready to go? We can take him back with us in the second car."

Dr. Dowson compressed his lips and looked worried. "Come in, Mr. Malone," he said. He turned just as the second carload of FBI agents began emptying itself over the hospital grounds.

The entire procession filed into the hospital office, the two local agents bringing up the rear. Since they were not a part of Her Majesty's personal retinue, they had not been required to wear court costumes. In a way, Malone was beginning to feel sorry for them. He himself cut a nice figure in the outfit, he thought—rather like Errol Flynn in the old black-and-white print of "The Prince and the Pauper."

But there was no denying that the procession looked strange. File clerks and receptionists stopped their work to gape at the four bedizened walkers and their plainly dressed satellites. Malone needed no telepathic talent to tell what they were thinking.

"A whole roundup of nuts," they were thinking. "And those two fellows in the back must be bringing them in—along with Dr. Dowson."

Malone straightened his spine. Really, he didn't see why Elizabethan costumes had ever gone out of style. Elizabeth was back, wasn't she—either Elizabeth II, on the throne, or Elizabeth I, right behind him. Either way you looked at it—

When they were all inside the waiting room, Dr. Dowson said: "Now, Mr. Malone, just what is all this about?" He rubbed his long hands together. "I fail to see the humor of the situation."

"Humor?" Malone said.

"Doctor," Barbara Wilson began, "let me explain. You see—"

"These ridiculous costumes," Dr. Dowson said, waving a hand at them. "You may feel that poking fun at insanity is humorous, Mr. Malone, but let me tell you—"

"It wasn't like that at all," Boyd said.

"And," Dr. Dowson continued in a somewhat louder voice, "wanting to take Mr. Logan away from us. Mr. Logan is a very sick man, Mr. Malone. He should be properly cared for."

"I promise we'll take good care of him." Malone said earnestly. The Elizabethan clothes were fine outdoors, but in a heated room one had a tendency to sweat.

"I take leave to doubt that," Dr. Dowson said, eying their costumes pointedly.

"Miss Wilson here," Malone volunteered, "is a trained psychiatric nurse."

Barbara, in her gown, stepped forward. "Dr. Dowson," she said, "let me assure you that these costumes have their purpose. We—"

"Not only that," Malone said. "There are a group of trained men from St. Elizabeths Hospital in Washington who are going to take the best of care of him." He said nothing whatever about Yucca Flats, or about telepathy.

Why spread around information unnecessarily?

"But I don't understand," Dr. Dowson said. "What interest could the FBI have in an insane man?"

"That's none of your business," Malone said. He reached inside his fur-trimmed robe and, again suppressing a tendency to bow deeply, withdrew an impressive-looking legal document. "This," he said, "is a court order, instructing you to hand over to us the person of one William Logan, herein identified and described." He waved it at the doctor. "That's your William Logan," he said, "only now he's ours."

Dr. Dowson took the papers and put in some time frowning at them. Then he looked up again at Malone. "I assume that I have some discretion in this matter," he said. "And I wonder if you realize just how ill Mr. Logan is? We have his case histories here, and we have worked with him for some time."

Barbara Wilson said: "But—"

"I might say that we are beginning to understand his illness," Dr. Dowson said. "I honestly don't think it would be proper to transfer this work to another group of therapists. It might set his illness back—cause, as it were, a relapse. All our work could easily be nullified."

"Please, doctor," Barbara Wilson began.

"I'm afraid the court order's got to stand," Malone said. Privately, he felt sorry for Dr. Dowson, who was, obviously enough, a conscientious man trying to do the best he could for his patient. But—

"I'm sorry, Dr. Dowson," he said. "We'll expect you to send all of your data to the government psychiatrists—and, naturally, any concern for the patient's welfare will be our concern also. The FBI isn't anxious for its workers to get the reputation of careless men." He paused, wondering what other bone he could throw the man. "I have no doubt that the St. Elizabeths men will be happy to accept your co-operation," he said at last. "But, I'm afraid that our duty is clear. William Logan goes with us."

Dr. Dowson looked at them sourly. "Does he have to get dressed up like a masquerade, too?" Before Malone could answer, the psychiatrist added: "Anyhow, I don't even know you're FBI men. After all, why should I comply with orders from a group of men, dressed insanely, whom I don't even know?"

Malone didn't say anything. He just got up and walked to a phone on a small table, near the wall. Next to it was a door, and Malone wondered uncomfortably what was behind it. Maybe Dr. Dowson had a small arsenal there, to protect his patients and prevent people from pirating them.

He looked back at the set and dialed Burris' private number in Washington. When the director's face appeared on the screen, Malone said: "Mr. Burris, will you please identify me to Dr. Dowson?" He looked over at Dowson. "You recognize Mr. Andrew J. Burris, I suppose?" he said.

Dowson nodded. His grim face showed a faint shock. He walked to the phone, and Malone stepped back to let him talk with Burris.

"My name is Dowson," he said. "I'm psychiatric director here at Desert Edge Sanitarium. And your men—"

"My men have orders to take a William Logan from your care," Burris said.

"That's right," Dowson said. "But—"

While they were talking, Queen Elizabeth I sidled quietly up to Malone and tapped him on the shoulder.

"Sir Kenneth," she whispered in the faintest of voices, "I know where your telepathic spy is. And I know *who* he is."

"Who?" Malone said. "What? Why? Where?" He blinked and whirled. It couldn't be true. They couldn't solve the case so easily.

But the Queen's face was full of a majestic assurance. "He's right there," she said, and she pointed.

Malone followed her finger.

It was aimed directly at the glowing image of Andrew J. Burris, Director of the FBI.

V

ALONE opened his mouth, but nothing came out. Not even air.

He wasn't breathing.

He stared at Burris for a long moment, then took a breath and looked again at Her Majesty. "The spy?" he whispered.

"That's right," she said.

"But that's—" He had to fight for control. "That's the head of the FBI," he managed to say. "Do you mean to say he's a spy?"

Burris was saying: "... I'm afraid this is a matter of importance, Dr. Dowson. We cannot tolerate delay. You have the court order. Obey it."

"Very well, Mr. Burris," Dowson said with an obvious lack of grace. "I'll release him to Mr. Malone immediately, since you insist."

Malone stared, fascinated. Then he turned back to the little old lady. "Do you mean to tell me," he said, "that Andrew J. Burris is a telepathic spy?"

"Oh, dear me," Her Majesty said, obviously aghast. "My goodness gracious. Is that Mr. Burris on the screen?"

"It is," Malone assured her. A look out of the corner of his eye told him that neither Burris, in Washington, nor Dowson or any others in the room, had heard any of the conversation. Malone lowered his whisper some more, just in case. "That's the head of the FBI," he said.

"Well, then," Her Majesty said, "Mr. Burris couldn't possibly be a spy, then, could he? Not if he's the head of the FBI. Of course not. Mr. Burris simply isn't a spy. He isn't the type. Forget all about Mr. Burris."

"I can't," Malone said at random. "I work for him." He closed his eyes. The room, he had discovered, was spinning slightly. "Now," he said, "you're sure he's not a spy?"

"Certainly I'm sure," she said, with her most regal tones. "Do you doubt the word of your sovereign?"

"Not exactly," Malone said. Truthfully, he wasn't at all sure. Not at all. But why tell that to the Queen?

"Shame on you," she said. "You shouldn't even think such things. After all, I am the Queen, aren't I?" But there was a sweet, gentle smile on her face when she spoke; she did not seem to be really irritated.

"Sure you are," Malone said. "But—"

"Malone!" It was Burris' voice, from the phone. Malone spun around. "Take Mr. Logan," Burris said, "and get going. There's been enough delay as it is."

"Yes, sir," Malone said. "Right away, sir. Anything else?"

"That's all," Burris said. "Good night." The screen blanked.

There was a little silence.

"All right, doctor," Boyd said. He looked every inch a king, and Malone knew exactly what king. "Bring him out."

537

Dr. Dowson heaved a great sigh. "Very well," he said heavily. "But I want it known that I resent this high-handed treatment, and I shall write a letter complaining of it." He pressed a button on an instrument panel in his desk. "Bring Mr. Logan in," he said.

Malone wasn't in the least worried about the letter. Burris, he knew, would take care of anything like that. And, besides, he had other things to think about.

The door to the next room had opened almost immediately, and two husky, white-clad men were bringing in a straitjacketed figure whose arms were wrapped against his chest, while the jacket's extra-long sleeves were tied behind his back. He walked where the attendants led him, but his eyes weren't looking at anything in the room. They stared at something far away and invisible, an impalpable shifting nothingness somewhere in the infinite distances beyond the world.

For the first time, Malone felt the chill of panic. Here, he thought, was insanity of a very real and frightening kind. Queen Elizabeth Thompson was one thing—and she was almost funny, and likable, after all. But William Logan was something else, and something that sent a wave of cold shivering into the room.

What made it worse was that Logan wasn't a man, but a boy, barely nineteen. Malone had known that, of course—but seeing it was something different. The lanky, awkward figure wrapped in a hospital strait jacket was horrible, and the smooth, unconcerned face was, somehow, worse. There was no threat in that face, no terror or anger or fear. It was merely—a blank.

It was not a human face. Its complete lack of emotion or expression could have belonged to a sleeping child of ten—or to a member of a different race. Malone looked at the boy, and looked away.

Was it possible that Logan knew what he was thinking?

Answer me, he thought, directly at the still boy.

There was no reply, none at all. Malone forced himself to look away. But the air in the room seemed to have become much colder.

The attendants stood on either side of him, waiting. For one long second no one moved, and then Dr. Dowson reached into his desk drawer and produced a sheaf of papers.

"If you'll sign these for the government," he said, "you may have Mr. Logan. There seems little else that I can do, Mr. Malone—in spite of my earnest pleas—"

"I'm sorry," Malone said. After all, he *needed* Logan, didn't he? After a look at the boy, he wasn't sure any more—but the Queen had said she wanted him, and the Queen's word was law. Or what passed for law, anyhow, at least for the moment.

Malone took the papers and looked them over. There was nothing special about them; they were merely standard release forms, absolving the staff and management of Desert Edge Sanitarium from every conceivable responsibility under any conceivable circumstances, as far as William Logan was concerned. Dr. Dowson gave Malone a look that said: "Very well, Mr. Malone; I will play Pilate and wash my hands of the matter—but you needn't think I like it." It was a lot for one look to say, but Dr. Dowson's dark and sunken eyes got the message across with no loss in transmission. As a matter of fact, there seemed to be more coming—a much less printable message was apparently on the way through those glittering, sad and angry eyes.

Malone avoided them nervously, and went over the papers again instead. At last he signed them and handed them back. "Thanks for your co-operation, Dr. Dowson," he said briskly, feeling ten kinds of a traitor.

"Not at all," Dowson said bitterly. "Mr. Logan is now in your custody. I must trust you to take good care of him."

"The best care we can," Malone said. It didn't seem sufficient. He added: "The best possible care, doctor," and tried to look dependable and trustworthy, like a Boy Scout. He was aware that the effort failed miserably.

At his signal, the two plainclothes FBI men took over from the attendants. They marched Logan out to their car, and Malone led the procession back to Boyd's automobile, a procession that consisted—in order—of Sir Kenneth Malone, prospective Duke of Columbia, Queen Elizabeth I, Lady Barbara, prospective Duchess of an unspecified county, and Sir Thomas Boyd, prospective Duke of Poughkeepsie. Malone hummed a little of "Pomp and Circumstance" as they walked; somehow, he thought it was called for.

They piled into the car, Boyd at the wheel with Malone next to him, and the two ladies in back, with Queen Elizabeth sitting directly behind Sir Thomas. Boyd started the engine and they turned and roared off.

"Well," said Her Majesty with an air of great complacence, "that's that. That makes six of us."

Malone looked around the car. He counted the people. There were four. He said, puzzled: "Six?"

"That's right, Sir Kenneth," Her Majesty said. "You have it exactly. Six."

"You mean six telepaths?" Sir Thomas asked in a deferent tone of voice.

"Certainly I do," Her Majesty replied. "We telepaths, you know, must stick together. That's the reason I got poor little Willie out of that sanitarium of his, you know—and, of course, the others will be joining us."

"Don't you think it's time for your nap, dear?" Lady Barbara put in suddenly.

"My *what*?" It was obvious that Queen Elizabeth was Not Amused.

"Your nap, dear," Lady Barbara said.

"Don't call me 'dear,'" Her Majesty snapped.

"I'm sorry, Your Majesty," Barbara murmured. "But really—"

"My dear girl," Her Majesty said, "I am not a child. I am your sovereign. Do try to have a little respect. Why, I remember when Shakespeare used to say to me—but that's no matter, not now."

"About those telepaths—" Boyd began.

"Telepaths," Her Majesty said. "Ah, yes. We must all stick together. In the hospital, you know, we had a little joke—the patients for Insulin Shock Therapy used to say: 'If we don't stick together, we'll all be stuck separately.' Do you see, Sir Thomas?"

"But," Sir Kenneth Malone said, trying desperately to return to the point. "*Six?*" He had counted them up in his mind. Burris had mentioned one found in St. Elizabeths, and two more picked up later. With Queen Elizabeth, and now William Logan, that made five.

Unless the Queen was counting him in. There didn't seem any good reason why not.

"Oh, no," Her Majesty said with a little trill of laughter, "not you, Sir Kenneth. I meant Mr. Miles."

Sir Thomas Boyd asked: "Mr. Miles?"

"That's right," Her Majesty said. "His name is Barry Miles, and your FBI men found him an hour ago in New Orleans. They're bringing him to Yucca Flats to meet the rest of us; isn't that nice?"

Lady Barbara cleared her throat.

"It really isn't necessary for you to try to get my attention, dear," the Queen said. "After all, I do know what you're thinking."

Lady Barbara blinked. "I still want to suggest, respectfully, about that nap—" she began.

"My dear girl," the Queen said, with the faintest trace of impatience, "I do not feel the least bit tired, and this is such an exciting day that I just don't want to miss any of it. Besides, I've already told you I don't want a nap. It isn't polite to be insistent to your Queen—no matter how strongly you feel about a matter. I'm sure you'll learn to understand that, dear."

Lady Barbara opened her mouth, shut it again, and opened it once more. "My goodness," she said.

"That's the idea," Her Majesty said approvingly. "Think before you speak—and then don't speak. It really isn't necessary, since I know what you're thinking."

Malone said grimly: "About this new telepath ... this Barry Miles. Did they find him—"

"In a nut-house?" Her Majesty said sweetly. "Why, of course, Sir Kenneth. You were quite right when you thought that telepaths went insane because they had a sense they couldn't effectively use, and because no one believed them. How would you feel, if nobody believed you could see?"

"Strange," Malone admitted.

"There," Her Majesty said. "You see? Telepaths do go insane—it's sort of an occupational disease. Of course, not all of them are insane."

"Not all of them?" Malone felt the faint stirrings of hope. Perhaps they would turn up a telepath yet who was completely sane and rational.

"There's me, of course," Her Majesty said.

Lady Barbara gulped audibly. Boyd said nothing, but gripped the wheel of the car more tightly.

And Malone thought to himself: *That's right. There's Queen Elizabeth—who says she isn't crazy.*

And then he thought of one more sane telepath. But the knowledge did not make him feel any better.

It was, of course, the spy.

How many more are going to turn up? Malone wondered.

"Oh, that's about all of us," the Queen said. "There is one more, but she's in a hospital in Honolulu, and your men won't find her until tomorrow."

Boyd turned. "Do you mean you can foretell the future, too?" he asked in a strained voice.

Lady Barbara screamed: "Keep your eyes on the wheel and your hands on the road!"

"What?" Boyd said.

There was a terrific blast of noise, and a truck went by in the opposite direction. The driver, a big, ugly man with no hair on his head, leaned out to curse at the quartet, but his mouth remained open. He stared at the four Elizabethans and said nothing at all as he whizzed by.

"What was that?" Boyd asked faintly.

"That," Malone snapped, "was a truck. And it was due entirely to the mercy of God that we didn't hit it. Barbara's right. Keep your eyes on the wheel and your hands on the road." He paused and thought that over. Then he said: "Does that mean anything at all?"

"Lady Barbara was confused by the excitement," the Queen said calmly. "It's all right now, dear."

Lady Barbara blinked across the seat. "I was—afraid," she said.

"It's all right," the Queen said. "I'll take care of you."

"This," Malone announced to no one in particular, "is ridiculous."

Boyd swept the car around a curve and concentrated grimly on the road. After a second the Queen said: "Since you're still thinking about the question, I'll answer you."

"What question?" Malone said, thoroughly baffled.

"Sir Thomas asked me if I could foretell the future," the Queen said equably. "Of course I can't. That's silly. Just because I'm immortal and I'm a telepath, don't go hog-wild."

"Then how did you know the FBI agents were going to find the girl in Honolulu tomorrow?" Boyd said.

"Because," the Queen said, "they're thinking about looking in the hospital tomorrow, and when they look they'll certainly find her."

Boyd said: "Oh," and was silent.

But Malone had a grim question. "Why didn't you tell me about these other telepaths before?" he said. "You could have saved us a lot of work."

"Oh, heavens to Betsy, Sir Kenneth," Her Majesty exclaimed. "How could I? After all, the proper precautions had to be taken first, didn't they? I told you all the others were crazy—*really* crazy, I mean. And they just wouldn't be safe without the proper precautions."

"Perhaps you ought to go back to the hospital, too," Barbara said, and added: "Your Majesty," just in time.

"But if I did, dear," Her Majesty said, "you'd lose your chance to become a Duchess, and that wouldn't be at all nice. Besides, I'm having so much *fun*!" She trilled a laugh again. "Riding around like this is just wonderful!" she said.

And you're important for national security, Malone said to himself.

"That's right, Sir Kenneth," the Queen said. "The country needs me, and I'm happy to serve. That is the job of a sovereign."

"Fine," Malone said, hoping it was.

"Well, then," said Her Majesty, "that settles that. We have a whole night ahead of us, Sir Kenneth. What do you say we make a night *of* it?"

"Knight who?" Malone said. He felt confused again. It seemed as if he was always feeling confused lately.

"Don't be silly, Sir Kenneth," Her Majesty said. "There are times and times."

"Sure," Malone said at random. *And time and a half*, he thought. *Possibly for overtime*. "What is Your Majesty thinking of?" he asked with trepidation.

"I want to take a tour of Las Vegas," Her Majesty said primly.

Lady Barbara shook her head. "I'm afraid that's not possible, Your Majesty," she said.

"And why not, pray?" Her Majesty said. "No. I can see what you're thinking. It's not safe to let me go wandering around in a strange city, and particularly if that city is Las Vegas. Well, dear, I can assure you that it's perfectly safe."

"We've got work to do," Boyd contributed.

Malone said nothing. He stared bleakly at the hood ornament on the car.

"I have made my wishes known," the Queen said.

Lady Barbara said: "But—"

Boyd, however, knew when to give in. "Yes, Your Majesty," he said.

She smiled graciously at him, and answered Lady Barbara only by a slight lift of her regal eyebrow.

Malone had been thinking about something else. When he was sure he had a firm grip on himself he turned. "Your Majesty, tell me something," he said. "You can read my mind, right?"

"Well, of course, Sir Kenneth," Her Majesty said. "I thought I'd proved that to you. And, as for what you're about to ask—"

"No," Malone said. "Please. Let me ask the questions before you answer them. It's less confusing that way. I'll cheerfully admit that it shouldn't be—but it is. Please?"

"Certainly, Sir Kenneth, if you wish," the Queen said. She folded her hands in her lap and waited quietly.

"O.K.," Malone said. "Now, if you can read my mind, then you must know that I don't *really* believe that you are Queen Elizabeth of England. The First, I mean."

"Mr. Malone," Barbara Wilson said suddenly. "I—"

"It's all right, child," the Queen said. "He doesn't disturb me. And I do wish you'd call him Sir Kenneth. That's his title, you know."

"Now that's what I mean," Malone said. "Why do you want us to *act* as if we believe you, when you know we don't?"

"Because that's the way people do act," the Queen said calmly. "Very few people really believe that their so-called superiors *are* superior. Almost none of them do, in fact."

"Now wait a minute," Boyd began.

"No, no, it's quite true," the Queen said, "and, unpleasant as it may be, we must learn to face the truth. That's the path of sanity." Lady Barbara made a strangled noise but Her Majesty continued, unruffled. "Nearly everybody suffers from the silly delusion that he's possibly equal to, but very probably superior to, everybody else ... my goodness, where would we be if that were true?"

Malone felt that a comment was called for, and he made one. "Who knows?" he said.

"All the things people do toward their superiors," the Queen said, "are done for social reasons. For instance, Sir Kenneth: you don't realize fully how you feel about Mr. Burris."

"He's a nice guy," Malone said. "I work for him. He's a good Director of the FBI."

"Of course," the Queen said. "But you believe you could do the job just as well, or perhaps a little better."

"I do not," Malone said angrily.

Her Majesty reserved a dignified silence.

After a while Malone said: "And what if I do?"

"Why, nothing," Her Majesty said. "You don't think Mr. Burris is any smarter or better than you are—but you treat him as if you did. All I am insisting on is the same treatment."

"But if we don't believe—" Boyd began.

"Bless you," Her Majesty said, "I can't help the way you *think*, but, as Queen, I do have some control over the way you *act*."

Malone thought it over. "You have a point there," he said at last.

Barbara said: "But—"

"Yes, Sir Kenneth," the Queen said, "I do." She seemed to be ignoring Lady Barbara. Perhaps, Malone thought, she was still angry over the nap affair. "It's not that," the Queen said.

"Not what?" Boyd said, thoroughly confused.

"Not the naps," the Queen said.

"What naps?" Boyd said.

Malone said: "I was thinking—"

"Good," Boyd said. "Keep it up. I'm driving. Everything's going to hell around me, but I'm driving."

A red light appeared ahead. Boyd jammed on the brakes with somewhat more than the necessary force, and Malone was thrown forward with a grunt. Behind him there were two ladylike squeals.

Malone struggled upright. "Barbara?" he called. "Are you all right—" Then he remembered the Queen.

"It's all right," Her Majesty said. "I can understand your concern for Lady Barbara." She smiled at Malone as he turned.

Malone gaped at her. Of course she knew what he thought about Barbara; she'd been reading his mind. And, apparently, she was on his side. That was good, even though it made him slightly nervous to think about.

"Now," the Queen said suddenly, "what about tonight?"

"Tonight?"

"Yes, of course," the Queen said. She smiled, and put up a hand to pat at her white hair under the Elizabethan skullcap. "I think I should like to go to the Palace," she said. "After all, isn't that where a Queen should be?"

Boyd said, in a kind of explosion: "London? England?"

"Oh, dear me—" the Queen began, and Barbara said:

"I'm afraid that I simply can't allow anything like that. Overseas—"

"I didn't mean overseas, dear," Her Majesty said. "Sir Kenneth, please explain to these people."

The Palace, Malone knew, was more properly known as the Golden Palace. It was right in Las Vegas—convenient to all sources of money. As a matter of fact, it was one of the biggest gambling houses along the Las Vegas strip, a veritable chaos of wheels, cards, dice, chips and other such devices. Malone explained all this to the others, wondering meanwhile why Miss Thompson wanted to go there.

"*Not* Miss Thompson, *please*, Sir Kenneth," Her Majesty said.

"Not Miss Thompson what?" Boyd said. "What's going on anyhow?"

"She's reading my mind," Malone said.

"Well, then," Boyd snapped, "tell her to keep it to herself." The car started up again with a roar and Malone and the others were thrown around again, this time toward the back. There was a chorus of groans and squeals, and they were on their way once more.

"To reply to your question, Sir Kenneth," the Queen said.

Lady Barbara said, with some composure: "What question ... Your Majesty?"

The Queen nodded regally at her. "Sir Kenneth was wondering why I wished to go to the Golden Palace," she said. "And my reply is this: it is none of your business why I want to go there. After all, is my word law, or isn't it?"

There didn't seem to be a good enough answer to that, Malone thought sadly. He kept quiet and was relieved to note that the others did the same. However, after a second he thought of something else.

"Your Majesty," he began carefully, "we've got to go to Yucca Flats tomorrow. Remember?"

"Certainly," the Queen said. "My memory is quite good, thank you. But that is tomorrow morning. We have the rest of the night left. It's only a little after nine, you know."

"Heavens," Barbara said. "Is it that late?"

"It's even later," Boyd said sourly. "It's much later than you think."

"And it's getting later all the time," Malone added. "Pretty soon the sun will go out and all life on earth will end. Won't that be nice and peaceful?"

"I'm looking forward to it," Boyd said.

"I'm not," Barbara said. "But I've got to get some sleep tonight, if I'm going to be any good at all tomorrow."

You're pretty good right now, Malone thought, but he didn't say a word. He felt the Queen's eye on him but didn't turn around. After all, she was on his side—wasn't she?

At any rate, she didn't say anything.

"Perhaps it would be best," Barbara said, "if you and I ... Your Majesty ... just went home and rested up. Some other time, then, when there's nothing vital to do, we could—"

"No," the Queen said. "We couldn't. Really, Lady Barbara, how often will I have to remind you of the duties you owe your sovereign—not the least of which is obedience, as dear old Ben used to say."

"Ben?" Malone said, and immediately wished he hadn't.

"Jonson, dear boy," the Queen said. "Really a remarkable man—and such a good friend to poor Will. Why, did you ever hear the story of how he actually paid Will's rent in London once upon a time? That was while Will and that Anne of his were having one of their arguments, of course. I didn't tell you that story, did I?"

"No," Malone said truthfully, but his voice was full of foreboding. "If I might remind Your Majesty of the subject," he added tentatively, "I should like to say—"

"Remind me of the subject!" the Queen said, obviously delighted. "What a lovely pun! And how much better because purely unconscious! My, my, Sir Kenneth, I never suspected you of a pointed sense of humor—could you be a descendant of Sir Richard Greene, I wonder?"

"I doubt it," Malone said. "My ancestors were all poor but Irish." He paused. "Or, if you prefer, Irish but poor." Another pause, and then he added: "If that means anything at all. Which I doubt."

"In any case," the Queen said, her eyes twinkling, "you were about to enter a new objection to our little visit to the Palace, were you not?"

Malone admitted as much. "I really think that—"

Her eyes grew suddenly cold. "If I hear any more objections, Sir Kenneth, I shall not only rescind your knighthood and—when I regain my rightful kingdom—deny you your dukedom, but I shall refuse to co-operate any further in the business of Project Isle."

Malone turned cold. His face, he knew without glancing in the mirror, was white and pale. He thought of what Burris would do to him if he didn't follow through on his assigned job.

Even if he wasn't as good as Burris thought he was, he really liked being an FBI agent. He didn't want to be fired.

And Burris had said: "*Give her anything she wants.*"

He gulped and tried to make his face look normal. "All right," he said. "Fine. We'll go to the Palace."

He tried to ignore the pall of apprehension that fell over the car.

VI

The management of the Golden Palace had been in business for many long, dreary, profitable years, and each member of the staff thought he or she had seen just about everything there was to be seen. And those that were new felt an obligation to *look* as if they'd seen everything.

Therefore, when the entourage of Queen Elizabeth I strolled into the main salon, not a single eye was batted. Not a single gasp was heard.

Nevertheless, the staff kept a discreet eye on the crew. Drunks, rich men or Arabian millionaires were all familiar. But a group out of the Sixteenth Century was something else again.

Malone almost strutted, conscious of the sidelong glances the group was drawing. But it was obvious that Sir Thomas was the major attraction. Even if you could accept the idea of people in strange costumes, the sight of a living, breathing absolute duplicate of King Henry VIII was a little too much to take. It has been reported that two ladies named Jane, and one named Catherine, came down with sudden headaches and left the salon within five minutes of the group's arrival.

Malone felt he knew, however, why he wasn't drawing his full share of attention. He felt a little out of place. The costume was one thing, and, to tell the truth, he was beginning to enjoy it. Even with the weight of the stuff, it was going to be a wrench to go back to single-breasted suits and plain white shirts. But he did feel that he should have been carrying a sword.

Instead, he had a .44 Magnum Colt snuggled beneath his left armpit.

Somehow, a .44 Magnum Colt didn't seem as romantic as a sword. Malone pictured himself saying: "Take that, varlet." Was varlet what you called them? he wondered. Maybe it was valet.

"Take that, valet," he muttered. No, that sounded even worse. Oh, well, he could look it up later.

The truth was that he had been born in the wrong century. He could imagine himself at the Mermaid Tavern, hob-nobbing with Shakespeare and all the rest of them. He wondered if Sir Richard Greene would be there. Then he wondered who Sir Richard Greene was.

Behind Sir Kenneth, Sir Thomas Boyd strode, looking majestic, as if he were about to fling purses of gold to the citizenry. As a matter of fact, Malone thought, he was. They all were.

Purses of good old United States of America gold.

Behind Sir Thomas came Queen Elizabeth and her Lady-in-Waiting, Lady Barbara Wilson. They made a beautiful foursome.

"The roulette table," Her Majesty said with dignity. "Precede me."

They pushed their way through the crowd. Most of the customers were either excited enough, drunk enough, or both to see nothing in the least incongruous about a Royal Family of the Tudors invading the Golden Palace. Very few of them, as a matter of fact, seemed to notice the group.

They were roulette players. They noticed nothing but the table and the wheel. Malone wondered what they were thinking about, decided to ask Queen Elizabeth, and then decided against it. He felt it would make him nervous to know.

Her Majesty took a handful of chips.

The handful was worth, Malone knew, exactly five thousand dollars. That, he'd thought, ought to last them an evening, even in the Golden Palace. In the center of the strip, inside the city limits of Las Vegas itself, the five thousand would have lasted much longer—but Her Majesty wanted the Palace, and the Palace it was.

Malone began to smile. Since he couldn't avoid the evening, he was determined to enjoy it. It was sort of fun, in its way, indulging a sweet harmless old lady. And there was nothing they could do until the next morning, anyhow.

His indulgent smile faded very suddenly.

Her Majesty plunked the entire handful of chips—*five thousand dollars!* Malone thought dazedly—onto the table. "Five thousand," she said in clear, cool measured tones, "on Number One."

The croupier blinked only slightly. He bowed. "Yes, Your Majesty," he said.

Malone was briefly thankful, in the midst of his black horror, that he had called the management and told them that the Queen's plays were backed by the United States Government. Her Majesty was going to get unlimited credit—and a good deal of awed and somewhat puzzled respect.

Malone watched the spin begin with mixed feelings. There was five thousand dollars riding on the little ball. But, after all, Her Majesty was a telepath. Did that mean anything?

He hadn't decided by the time the wheel stopped, and by then he didn't have to decide.

"Thirty-four," the croupier said tonelessly. "Red, Even and High."

He raked in the chips with a nonchalant air.

Malone felt as if he had swallowed his stomach. Boyd and Lady Barbara, standing nearby, had absolutely no expressions on their faces. Malone needed no telepath to tell him what they were thinking.

They were exactly the same as he was. They were incapable of thought.

But Her Majesty never batted an eyelash. "Come, Sir Kenneth," she said. "Let's go on to the poker tables."

She swept out. Her entourage followed her, shambling a little, and blank-eyed. Malone was still thinking about the five thousand dollars. Oh, well, Burris had said to give the lady anything she wanted. *But!* he thought. *Did she have to play for royal stakes?*

"I am, after all, a Queen," she whispered back to him.

Malone thought about the National Debt. He wondered if a million more or less would make any real difference. There would be questions asked in committees about it. He tried to imagine himself explaining the evening to a group of congressmen. "Well, you see, gentlemen, there was this roulette wheel—"

He gave it up.

Then he wondered how much hotter the water was going to get, and he stopped thinking altogether in self-defense.

In the next room, there were scattered tables. At one, a poker game was in full swing. Only five were playing; one, by his white-tie-and-tails uniform, was easily recognizable as a house dealer. The other four were all men, one of them in full cowboy regalia. The Tudors descended upon them with great suddenness, and the house dealer looked up and almost lost his cigarette.

"We haven't any money, Your Majesty," Malone whispered.

She smiled up at him sweetly, and then drew him aside. "If you were a telepath," she said, "how would *you* play poker?"

Malone thought about that for a minute, and then turned to look for Boyd. But Sir Thomas didn't even have to be given instructions. "Another five hundred?" he said.

Her Majesty sniffed audibly. "Another five thousand," she said regally.

Boyd looked Malone-wards. Malone looked defeated.

Boyd turned with a small sigh and headed for the cashier's booth. Three minutes later, he was back with a fat fistful of chips.

"Five grand?" Malone whispered to him.

"Ten," Boyd said. "I know when to back a winner."

Her Majesty went over to the table. The dealer had regained control, but looked up at them with a puzzled stare.

"You know," the Queen said, with an obvious attempt to put the man at his ease, "I've always wanted to visit a gambling hall."

"Sure, lady," the dealer said. "Naturally."

"May I sit down?"

The dealer looked at the group. "How about your friends?" he said cautiously.

The Queen shook her head. "They would rather watch, I'm sure."

For once Malone blessed the woman's telepathic talent. He, Boyd and Barbara Wilson formed a kind of Guard of Honor around the chair which Her Majesty occupied. Boyd handed over the new pile of chips, and was favored with a royal smile.

"This is a poker game, ma'am," the dealer said to her, quietly.

"I know, I know," Her Majesty said with a trace of testiness. "Roll 'em."

The dealer stared at her popeyed. Next to her, the gentleman in the cowboy outfit turned. "Ma'am, are you from around these parts?" he said.

"Oh, no," the Queen said. "I'm from England."

"England?" The cowboy looked puzzled. "You don't seem to have any accent, ma'am," he said at last.

"Certainly not," the Queen said. "I've lost that; I've been over here a great many years."

Malone hoped fervently that Her Majesty wouldn't mention just how many years. He didn't think he could stand it, and he was almost grateful for the cowboy's nasal twang.

"Oil?" he said.

"Oh, no," Her Majesty said. "The Government is providing this money."

"The Government?"

"Certainly," Her Majesty said. "The FBI, you know."

There was a long silence.

At last, the dealer said: "Five-card draw your game, ma'am?"

"If you please," Her Majesty said.

The dealer shrugged and, apparently, commended his soul to a gambler's God. He passed the pasteboards around the table with the air of one who will have nothing more to do with the world.

Her Majesty picked up her hand.

"The ante's ten, ma'am," the dealer said softly.

Without looking, Her Majesty removed a ten-dollar chip from the pile before her and sent it spinning to the middle of the table.

The dealer opened his mouth, but said nothing. Malone, meanwhile, was peering over the Queen's shoulder.

She held a pair of nines, a four, a three and a Jack.

The man to the left of the dealer announced glumly: "Can't open."

The next man grinned. "Open for twenty," he said.

Malone closed his eyes. He heard the cowboy say: "I'm in," and he opened his eyes again. The Queen was pushing two ten-dollar chips toward the center of the table.

The next man dropped, and the dealer looked round the table. "How many?"

The man who couldn't open took three cards. The man who'd opened for twenty stood pat. Malone shuddered invisibly. That, he figured, meant at least a straight. And Queen Elizabeth Thompson was going in against a straight or better with a pair of nines, Jack high.

For the first time, it was borne in on Malone that being a telepath did not necessarily mean that you were a good poker player. Even if you knew what every other person at the table held, you could still make a whole lot of stupid mistakes.

He looked nervously at Queen Elizabeth, but her face was serene. Apparently she'd been following the thoughts of the poker players, and not concentrating on him at all. That was a relief. He felt, for the first time in days, as if he could think freely.

The cowboy said: "Two," and took them. It was Her Majesty's turn.

"I'll take two," she said, and threw away the three and four. It left her with the nine of spades and the nine of hearts, and the Jack of diamonds.

These were joined, in a matter of seconds, by two bright new cards: the six of clubs and the three of hearts.

Malone closed his eyes. Oh, well, he thought.

It was only thirty bucks down the drain. Practically nothing.

Of course Her Majesty dropped at once; knowing what the other players held, she knew she couldn't beat them after the draw. But she did like to take long chances, Malone thought miserably. Imagine trying to fill a full house on one pair!

Slowly, as the minutes passed, the pile of chips before Her Majesty dwindled. Once Malone saw her win with two pair against a reckless man trying to fill a straight on the other side of the table. But whatever was going on, Her Majesty's face was as calm as if she were asleep.

Malone's worked overtime. If the Queen hadn't been losing so obviously, the dealer might have mistaken the play of naked emotion across his visage for a series of particularly obvious signals.

An hour went by. Barbara left to find a ladies' lounge where she could sit down and try to relax. Fascinated in a horrible sort of way, both Malone and Boyd stood, rooted to the spot, while hand after hand went by and the ten thousand dollars dwindled to half that, to a quarter, and even less—

Her Majesty, it seemed, was a mighty poor poker player.

The ante had been raised by this time. Her Majesty was losing one hundred dollars a hand, even before the betting began. But she showed not the slightest indication to stop.

"We've got to get up in the morning," Malone announced to no one in particular, when he thought he couldn't possibly stand another half hour of the game.

"So we do," Her Majesty said with a little regretful sigh. "Very well, then. Just one more hand."

"It's a shame to lose you," the cowboy said to her, quite sincerely. He had been winning steadily ever since Her Majesty sat down, and Malone thought that the man should, by this time, be awfully grateful to the United States Government. Somehow, he doubted that this gratitude existed.

Malone wondered if she should be allowed to stay for one more hand. There was, he estimated, about two thousand dollars in front of her. Then he wondered how he was going to stop her.

The cards were dealt.

The first man said quietly: "Open for two hundred."

Malone looked at the Queen's hand. It contained the Ace, King, Queen and ten of clubs—and the seven of spades.

Oh, no, he thought. *She couldn't possibly be thinking of filling a flush.*

He knew perfectly well that she was.

The second man said: "And raise two hundred."

The Queen equably tossed—counting, Malone thought, the ante—five hundred into the pot.

The cowboy muttered to himself for a second, and finally shoved in his money.

"I think I'll raise it another five hundred," the Queen said calmly.

Malone wanted to die of shock. Unfortunately, he remained alive and watching. He was the last man, after some debate internal, to shove a total of one thousand dollars into the pot.

"Cards?" said the dealer.

The first man said: "One."

It was too much to hope for, Malone thought. If that first man were trying to fill a straight or a flush, maybe he wouldn't make it. And maybe something final would happen to all the other players. But that was the only way he could see for Her Majesty to win.

The card was dealt. The second man stood pat and Malone's green tinge became obvious to the veriest dunce. The cowboy, on Her Majesty's right, asked for a card, received it and sat back without a trace of expression.

The Queen said: "I'll try one for size." She'd picked up poker lingo, and the basic rules of the game, Malone realized, from the other players—or possibly from someone at the hospital itself, years ago.

He wished she'd picked up something less dangerous instead, like a love of big-game hunting, or stunt-flying.

But no. It had to be poker.

The Queen threw away her seven of spades, showing more sense than Malone had given her credit for at any time during the game. She let the other card fall and didn't look at it.

She smiled up at Malone and Boyd. "Live dangerously," she said gaily.

Malone gave her a hollow laugh.

The last man drew one card, too, and the betting began.

The Queen's remaining thousand was gone before an eye could notice it. She turned to Boyd.

"Sir Thomas," she said. "Another five thousand, please. At once."

Boyd said nothing at all, but marched off. Malone noticed, however, that his step was neither as springy nor as confident as it had been before. For himself, Malone was sure that he could not walk at all.

Maybe, he thought hopefully, the floor would open up and swallow them all. He tried to imagine explaining the loss of twenty thousand dollars to Burris and some congressmen, and after that he watched the floor narrowly, hoping for the smallest hint of a crack in the palazzo marble.

"May I raise the whole five thousand?" the Queen said.

"It's O.K. with me," the dealer said. "How about the rest of you?"

The four grunts he got expressed a suppressed eagerness. The Queen took the new chips Boyd had brought her and shoved them into the center of the table with a fine, careless gesture of her hand. She smiled gaily at everybody. "Seeing me?" she said.

Everybody was.

"Well, you see, it was this way," Malone muttered to himself, rehearsing. He half-thought that one of the others would raise again, but no one did. After all, each of them must be convinced that he held a great hand, and though raising had gone on throughout the hand, each must now be afraid of going the least little bit too far and scaring the others out.

"Mr. Congressman," Malone muttered, "there's this game called poker. You play it with cards and money. Chiefly money."

That wasn't any good.

"You've been called," the dealer said to the first man, who'd opened the hand a year or so before.

"Why, sure," the player said, and laid down a pair of aces, a pair of threes—and a four. One of the threes, and the four, were clubs. That reduced the already improbable chances of the Queen's coming up with a flush.

"Sorry," said the second man, and laid down a straight with a single gesture. The straight was nine-high and there were no clubs in it. Malone felt devoutly thankful for that.

The second man reached for the money but, under the popeyed gaze of the dealer, the fifth man laid down another straight—this one ten-high. The nine was a club. Malone felt the odds go down, right in his own stomach.

And now the cowboy put down his cards. The King of diamonds. The King of hearts. The Jack of diamonds. The Jack of spades. And—the Jack of hearts.

Full house. "Well," said the cowboy. "I suppose that does it."

The Queen said: "Please. One moment."

The cowboy stopped halfway in his reach for the enormous pile of chips. The Queen laid down her four clubs—Ace, King, Queen and ten—and for the first time flipped over her fifth card.

It was the Jack of clubs.

"My God," the cowboy said, and it sounded like a prayer. "A royal flush."

"Naturally," the Queen said. "What else?"

Her Majesty calmly scooped up the tremendous pile of chips. The cowboy's hands fell away. Five mouths were open around the table.

Her Majesty stood up. She smiled sweetly at the men around the table. "Thank you very much, gentlemen," she said. She handed the chips to Malone, who took them in nerveless fingers. "Sir Kenneth," she said, "I hereby appoint you temporary Chancellor of the Exchequer—at least until Parliament convenes."

There was, Malone thought, at least thirty-five thousand dollars in the pile. He could think of nothing to say.

So, instead of using up words, he went and cashed in the chips. For once, he realized, the Government had made money on an investment. It was probably the first time since 1775.

Malone thought vaguely that the Government ought to make more investments like the one he was cashing in. If it did, the National Debt could be wiped out in a matter of days.

He brought the money back. Boyd and the Queen were waiting for him, but Barbara was still in the ladies' lounge. "She's on the way out," the Queen informed him, and, sure enough, in a minute they saw the figure approaching them. Malone smiled at her, and, tentatively, she smiled back. They began the long march to the exit of the club, slowly and regally, though not by choice.

The crowd, it seemed, wouldn't let them go. Malone never found out, then or later, how the news of Her Majesty's winnings had gone through the place so fast, but everyone seemed to know about it. The Queen was the recipient of several low bows and a few drunken curtsies, and, when they reached the front door at last, the doorman said in a most respectful tone: "Good evening, Your Majesty."

The Queen positively beamed at him. So, to his own great surprise, did Sir Kenneth Malone.

Outside, it was about four in the morning. They climbed into the car and headed back toward the hotel.

Malone was the first to speak. "How did you know that was a Jack of clubs?" he said in a strangled sort of voice.

The little old lady said calmly: "He was cheating."

"The dealer?" Malone asked.

The little old lady nodded.

"In *your* favor?"

"He couldn't have been cheating," Boyd said at the same instant. "Why would he want to give you all that money?"

The little old lady shook her head. "He didn't want to give it to me," she said. "He wanted to give it to the man in the cowboy's suit. His name is Elliott, by the way—Bernard L. Elliott. And he comes from Weehawken. But he pretends to be a Westerner so nobody will be suspicious of him. He and the dealer are in cahoots ... isn't that the word?"

"Yes, Your Majesty," Boyd said. "That's the word." His tone was awed and respectful, and the little old lady gave a nod and became Queen Elizabeth I once more.

"Well," she said, "the dealer and Mr. Elliott were in cahoots, and the dealer wanted to give the hand to Mr. Elliott. But he made a mistake, and dealt the Jack of clubs to me. I watched him, and, of course, I knew what he was thinking. The rest was easy."

"My God," Malone said. "Easy."

Barbara said: "Did she win?"

"She won," Malone said with what he felt was positively magnificent understatement.

"Good," Barbara said, and lost interest at once.

Malone had seen the lights of a car in the rear-view mirror a few minutes before. When he looked now, the lights were still there—but the fact just didn't register until, a couple of blocks later, the car began to pull around them on the left. It was a Buick, while Boyd's was a new Lincoln, but the edge wasn't too apparent yet.

Malone spotted the gun barrel protruding from the Buick and yelled just before the first shot went off.

Boyd, at the wheel, didn't even bother to look. His reflexes took over and he slammed his foot down on the brake. The specially-built FBI Lincoln slowed down instantly. The shotgun blast splattered the glass of the curved windshield all over—but none of it came into the car itself.

Malone already had his hand on the butt of the .44 Magnum under his left armpit, and he even had time to be grateful, for once, that it wasn't a smallsword. The women were in the back seat, frozen, and he yelled: "Duck!" and felt, rather than saw, both of them sink down onto the floor of the car.

The Buick had slowed down, too, and the gun barrel was swiveling back for a second shot. Malone felt naked and unprotected. The Buick and the Lincoln were even on the road now.

Malone had his revolver out. He fired the first shot without even realizing fully that he'd done so, and he heard a piercing scream from Barbara in the back seat. He had no time to look back.

A .44 Magnum is not, by any means, a small gun. As hand guns go—revolvers and automatics—it is about as large as a gun can get to be. An ordinary car has absolutely no chance against it.

Much less the glass in an ordinary car.

The first slug drilled its way through the window glass as though it were not there, and slammed its way through an even more unprotected obstacle, the frontal bones of the triggerman's skull. The second slug from Malone's gun missed the hole the first slug had made by something less than an inch.

The big, apelike thug who was holding the shotgun had a chance to pull the trigger once more, but he wasn't aiming very well. The blast merely scored the paint off the top of the Lincoln.

The rear window of the Buick was open, and Malone caught sight of another glint of blued steel from the corner of his eye. There was no time to shift aim—not with bullets flying like swallows on the way to Capistrano. Malone thought faster than he had ever imagined himself capable of doing, and decided to aim for the driver.

Evidently the man in the rear seat of the Buick had had the same inspiration. Malone blasted two more high-velocity lead slugs at the driver of the big Buick, and at the same time the man in the Buick's rear seat fired at Boyd.

But Boyd had shifted tactics. He'd hit the brakes. Now he came down hard on the accelerator instead.

The chorus of shrieks from the Lincoln's back seat increased slightly in volume. Barbara, Malone knew, wasn't badly hurt; she hadn't even stopped for breath since the first shot had been fired. Anybody who could scream like that, he told himself, had to be healthy.

As the Lincoln leaped ahead, Malone pulled the trigger of his .44 twice more. The heavy, high-speed chunks of streamlined copper-coated lead leaped from the muzzle of the gun and slammed into the driver of the Buick without wasting any time. The Buick slewed across the highway.

The two shots fired by the man in the back seat went past Malone's head with a *whizz*, missing both him and Boyd by a margin too narrow to think about.

But those were the last shots. The only difference between the FBI and the Enemy seemed to be determination and practice.

The Buick spun into a flat sideskid, swiveled on its wheels and slammed into the ditch at the side of the road, turning over and over, making a horrible noise, as it broke up.

Boyd slowed the car again, just as there was a sudden blast of fire. The Buick had burst into flame and was spitting heat and smoke and fire in all directions. Malone sent one more bullet after it in a last flurry of action—saving his last one for possible later emergencies.

Boyd jammed on the brakes and the Lincoln came to a screaming halt. In silence he and Malone watched the burning Buick roll over and over into the desert beyond the shoulder.

"My God," Boyd said. "My ears!"

Malone understood at once. The blast from his own still-smoking .44 had roared past Boyd's head during the gun battle. No wonder the man's ears hurt. It was a wonder he wasn't altogether deaf.

But Boyd shook off the pain and brought out his own .44 as he stepped out of the car. Malone followed him, his gun trained.

From the rear, Her Majesty said: "It's safe to rise now, isn't it?"

"You ought to know," Malone said. "You can tell if they're still alive."

There was silence while Queen Elizabeth frowned for a moment in concentration. A look of pain crossed her face, and then, as her expression smoothed again, she said: "The traitors are dead. All except one, and he's—" She paused. "He's dying," she finished. "He can't hurt you."

There was no need for further battle. Malone reholstered his .44 and turned to Boyd. "Tom, call the State Police," he said. "Get 'em down here fast."

He waited while Boyd climbed back under the wheel and began punching buttons on the dashboard. Then Malone went toward the burning Buick.

He tried to drag the men out, but it wasn't any use. The first two, in the front seat, had the kind of holes in them people talked about throwing elephants through. Head and chest had been hit.

Malone couldn't get close enough to the fiercely blazing automobile to make even a try for the men in the back seat.

He was sitting quietly on the edge of the rear seat when the Nevada Highway Patrol cars drove up next to them. Barbara Wilson had stopped screaming, but she was still sobbing on Malone's shoulder. "It's all right," he told her, feeling ineffectual.

"I never saw anybody killed before," she said.

"It's all right," Malone said. "Nothing's going to hurt you. I'll protect you."

He wondered if he meant it, and found, to his surprise, that he did. Barbara Wilson sniffled and looked up at him. "Mr. Malone—"

"Ken," he said.

"I'm sorry," she said. "Ken—I'm so afraid. I saw the hole in one of the men's heads, when you fired ... it was—"

"Don't think about it," Malone said. To him, the job had been an unpleasant occurrence, but a job, that was all. He could see, though, how it might affect people who were new to it.

548

"You're so brave," she said.

Malone tightened his arm around the girl's shoulder. "Just depend on me," he said. "You'll be all right if you—"

The State Trooper walked up then, and looked at them. "Mr. Malone?" he said. He seemed to be taken slightly aback at the costuming.

"That's right," Malone said. He pulled out his ID card and the little golden badge. The State Patrolman looked at them, and looked back at Malone.

"What's with the getup?" he said.

"FBI," Malone said, hoping his voice carried conviction. "Official business."

"In costume?"

"Never mind about the details," Malone snapped.

"He's an FBI agent, sir," Barbara said.

"And what are you?" the Patrolman said. "Lady Jane Grey?"

"I'm a nurse," Barbara said. "A psychiatric nurse."

"For nuts?"

"For disturbed patients."

The patrolman thought that over. "You've got the identity cards and stuff," he said at last. "Maybe you've got a reason to dress up. How would I know? I'm only a State Patrolman."

"Let's cut the monologue," Malone said savagely, "and get to business."

The patrolman stared. Then he said: "All right, sir. Yes, sir. I'm Lieutenant Adams, Mr. Malone. Suppose you tell me what happened?"

Carefully and concisely, Malone told him the story of the Buick that had pulled up beside them, and what had happened afterward.

Meanwhile, the other cops had been looking over the wreck. When Malone had finished his story, Lieutenant Adams flipped his notebook shut and looked over toward them. "I guess it's O.K., sir," he said. "As far as I'm concerned, it's justifiable homicide. Self-defense. Any reason why they'd want to kill you?"

Malone thought about the Golden Palace. That might be a reason—but it might not. And why burden an innocent State Patrolman with the facts of FBI life?

"Official," he said. "Your chief will get the report."

The patrolman nodded. "I'll have to take a deposition tomorrow, but—"

"I know," Malone said. "Thanks. Can we go on to our hotel now?"

"I guess," the patrolman said. "Go ahead. We'll take care of the rest of this. You'll be getting a call later."

"Fine," Malone said. "Trace those hoods, and any connections they might have had. Get the information to me as soon as possible."

Lieutenant Adams nodded. "You won't have to leave the state, will you?" he asked. "I don't mean that you *can't*, exactly ... hell, you're FBI. But it'd be easier—"

"Call Burris in Washington," Malone said. "He can get hold of me—and if the Governor wants to know where we are, or the State's Attorney, put them in touch with Burris, too. O.K.?"

"O.K.," Lieutenant Adams said. "Sure." He blinked at Malone. "Listen," he said. "About those costumes—"

"We're trying to catch Henry VIII for the murder of Anne Boleyn," Malone said with a polite smile. "O.K.?"

"I was only asking," Lieutenant Adams said. "Can't blame a man for asking, now, can you?"

Malone climbed into his front seat. "Call me later," he said. The car started. "Back to the hotel, Sir Thomas," Malone said, and the car roared off.

VII

Yucca Flats, Malone thought, certainly deserved its name. It was about as flat as land could get, and it contained millions upon millions of useless yuccas. Perhaps they were good for something, Malone thought, but they weren't good for *him*.

The place might, of course, have been called Cactus Flats, but the cacti were neither as big nor as impressive as the yuccas.

Or was that yucci?

Possibly, Malone mused, it was simply yucks.

And whatever it was, there were millions of it. Malone felt he couldn't stand the sight of another yucca. He was grateful for only one thing.

It wasn't summer. If the Elizabethans had been forced to drive in closed cars through the Nevada desert in the summertime, they might have started a cult of nudity, Malone felt. It was bad enough now, in what was supposed to be winter.

The sun was certainly bright enough, for one thing. It glared through the cloudless sky and glanced with blinding force off the road. Sir Thomas Boyd squinted at it through the rather incongruous sunglasses he was wearing, while Malone wondered idly if it was the sunglasses, or the rest of the world, that was an anachronism. But Sir Thomas kept his eyes grimly on the road as he gunned the powerful Lincoln toward the Yucca Flats Labs at eighty miles an hour.

Malone twisted himself around and faced the women in the back seat. Past them, through the rear window of the Lincoln, he could see the second car. It followed them gamely, carrying the newest addition to Sir Kenneth Malone's Collection of Bats.

"Bats?" Her Majesty said suddenly, but gently. "Shame on you, Sir Kenneth. These are poor, sick people. We must do our best to help them—not to think up silly names for them. For shame!"

"I suppose so," Malone said wearily. He sighed and, for the fifth time that day, he asked: "Does Your Majesty have any idea where our spy is now?"

"Well, really, Sir Kenneth," the Queen said with the slightest of hesitations, "it isn't easy, you know. Telepathy has certain laws, just like everything else. After all, even a game has laws. Being telepathic did not help me to play poker—I still had to learn the rules. And telepathy has rules, too. A telepath can easily confuse another telepath by using some of those rules."

"Oh, fine," Malone said. "Well, have you got into contact with his mind yet?"

"Oh, yes," Her Majesty said happily. "And my goodness, he's certainly digging up a lot of information, isn't he?"

Malone moaned softly. "But who *is* he?" he asked after a second.

The Queen stared at the roof of the car in what looked like concentration. "He hasn't thought of his name yet," she said. "I mean, at least if he has, he hasn't mentioned it to me. Really, Sir Kenneth, you have no idea how difficult all this is."

Malone swallowed with difficulty. "*Where* is he, then?" he said. "Can you tell me that, at least? His location?"

Her Majesty looked positively desolated with sadness. "I can't be sure," she said. "I really can't be exactly sure just where he is. He does keep moving around, I know that. But you have to remember that he doesn't want me to find him. He certainly doesn't want to be found by the FBI ... would you?"

"Your Majesty," Malone said, "I *am* the FBI."

"Yes," the Queen said, "but suppose you weren't? He's doing his best to hide himself, even from me. It's sort of a game he's playing."

"A game!"

Her Majesty looked contrite. "Believe me, Sir Kenneth, the minute I know exactly where he is, I'll tell you. I promise. Cross my heart and hope to die—which I can't, of course, being immortal." Nevertheless, she made an X-mark over her left breast. "All right?"

"All right," Malone said, out of sheer necessity. "O.K. But don't waste any time telling me. Do it right away. We've *got* to find that spy and isolate him somehow."

"Please don't worry yourself, Sir Kenneth," Her Majesty said. "Your Queen is doing everything she can."

"I know that, Your Majesty," Malone said. "I'm sure of it." Privately, he wondered just how much even she could do. Then he realized—for perhaps the ten-thousandth time—that there was no such thing as wondering privately any more.

"That's quite right, Sir Kenneth," the Queen said sweetly. "And it's about time you got used to it."

"What's going on?" Boyd said. "More reading minds back there?"

"That's right, Sir Thomas," the Queen said.

"I've about gotten used to it," Boyd said almost cheerfully. "Pretty soon they'll come and take me away, but I don't mind at all." He whipped the car around a bend in the road savagely. "Pretty soon they'll put me with the other sane people and let the bats inherit the world. But I don't mind at all."

"Sir Thomas!" Her Majesty said in shocked tones.

"Please," Boyd said with a deceptive calmness. "Just Mr. Boyd. Not even Lieutenant Boyd, or Sergeant Boyd. Just Mr. Boyd. Or, if you prefer, Tom."

"Sir Thomas," Her Majesty said, "I really can't understand this sudden—"

"Then don't understand it," Boyd said. "All I know is everybody's nuts, and I'm sick and tired of it."

A pall of silence fell over the company.

"Look, Tom," Malone began at last.

"Don't you try smoothing me down," Boyd snapped.

Malone's eyebrows rose. "O.K.," he said. "I won't smooth you down. I'll just tell you to shut up, to keep driving—and to show some respect to Her Majesty."

"I—" Boyd stopped. There was a second of silence.

"*That's* better," Her Majesty said with satisfaction.

Lady Barbara stretched in the back seat, next to Her Majesty. "This is certainly a long drive," she said. "Have we got much farther to go?"

"Not too far," Malone said. "We ought to be there soon."

"I ... I'm sorry for the way I acted," Barbara said.

"What do you mean, the way you acted?"

"Crying like that," Barbara said with some hesitation. "Making an—absolute idiot of myself. When that other car—tried to get us."

"Don't worry about it," Malone said. "It was nothing."

"I just—made trouble for you," Barbara said.

Her Majesty touched the girl on the shoulder. "He's not thinking about the trouble you cause him," she said quietly.

"Of course I'm not," Malone told her.

"But I—"

"My dear girl," Her Majesty said, "I believe that Sir Kenneth is, at least partly, in love with you."

Malone blinked. It was perfectly true—even if he hadn't quite known it himself until now. Telepaths, he was discovering, were occasionally handy things to have around.

"In ... love—" Barbara said.

"And you, my dear—" Her Majesty began.

"Please, Your Majesty," Lady Barbara said. "No more. Not just now."

The Queen smiled, almost to herself. "Certainly, dear," she said.

The car sped on. In the distance, Malone could see the blot on the desert that indicated the broad expanse of Yucca Flats Labs. Just the fact that it could be seen, he knew, didn't mean an awful lot. Malone had been able to see it for the past fifteen minutes, and it didn't look as if they'd gained an inch on it. Desert distances are deceptive.

At long last, however, the main gate of the laboratories hove into view. Boyd made a left turn off the highway and drove a full seven miles along the restricted road, right up to the big gate that marked the entrance of the laboratories themselves. Once again, they were faced with the army of suspicious guards and security officers.

This time, suspicion was somewhat heightened by the dress of the visitors. Malone had to explain about six times that the costumes were part of an FBI arrangement, that he had not stolen his identity cards, that Boyd's cards were Boyd's, too, and in general that the four of them were not insane, not spies, and not jokesters out for a lark in the sunshine.

Malone had expected all of that. He went through the rigmarole wearily but without any sense of surprise. The one thing he hadn't been expecting was the man who was waiting for him on the other side of the gate.

When he'd finished identifying everybody for the fifth or sixth time, he began to climb back into the car. A familiar voice stopped him cold.

"Just a minute, Malone," Andrew J. Burris said. He erupted from the guardhouse like an avenging angel, followed closely by a thin man, about five feet ten inches in height, with brush-cut brown hair, round horn-rimmed spectacles, large hands and a small Sir Francis Drake beard. Malone looked at the two figures blankly.

"Something wrong, chief?" he said.

Burris came toward the car. The thin gentleman followed him, walking with an odd bouncing step that must have been acquired, Malone thought, over years of treading on rubber eggs. "I don't know," Burris said when he'd reached the door. "When I was in Washington, I seemed to know—but when I get out here in this desert, everything just goes haywire." He rubbed at his forehead.

Then he looked into the car. "Hello, Boyd," he said pleasantly.

"Hello, chief," Boyd said.

Burris blinked. "Boyd, you look like Henry VIII," he said with only the faintest trace of surprise.

"Doesn't he, though?" Her Majesty said from the rear seat. "I've noticed that resemblance myself."

Burris gave her a tiny smile. "Oh," he said. "Hello, Your Majesty. I'm—"

"Andrew J. Burris, Director of the FBI," the Queen finished for him. "Yes, I know. It's very nice to meet you at last. I've seen you on television, and over the video phone. You photograph badly, you know."

"I do?" Burris said pleasantly. It was obvious that he was keeping himself under very tight control.

Malone felt remotely sorry for the man—but only remotely. Burris might as well know, he thought, what they had all been going through the past several days.

Her Majesty was saying something about the honorable estate of knighthood, and the Queen's List. Malone began paying attention when she came to: "... And I hereby dub thee—" She stopped suddenly, turned and said: "Sir Kenneth, give me your weapon."

Malone hesitated for a long, long second. But Burris' eye was on him, and he could interpret the look without much trouble. There was only one thing for him to do. He pulled out his .44, ejected the remaining cartridge in his palm—and reminded himself to reload the gun as soon as he got it back—and handed the weapon to the Queen, butt foremost.

She took the butt of the revolver in her right hand, leaned out the window of the car, and said in a fine, distinct voice: "Kneel, Andrew."

Malone watched with wide, astonished eyes as Andrew J. Burris, Director of the FBI, went to one knee in a low and solemn genuflection. Queen Elizabeth Thompson nodded her satisfaction.

She tapped Burris gently on each shoulder with the muzzle of the gun. "I knight thee Sir Andrew," she said. She cleared her throat. "My, this desert air is dry—Rise, Sir Andrew, and know that you are henceforth Knight Commander of the Queen's Own FBI."

"Thank you, Your Majesty," Burris said humbly.

He rose to his feet silently. The Queen withdrew into the car again and handed the gun back to Malone. He thumbed cartridges into the chambers of the cylinder and listened dumbly.

"Your Majesty," Burris said, "this is Dr. Harry Gamble, the head of Project Isle. Dr. Gamble, this is Her Majesty the Queen; Lady Barbara Wilson, her ... uh ... her lady in waiting; Sir Kenneth Malone; and King ... I mean Sir Thomas Boyd." He gave the four a single bright impartial smile. Then he tore his eyes away from the others, and bent his gaze on Sir Kenneth Malone. "Come over here a minute, Malone," he said, jerking his thumb over his shoulder. "I want to talk to you."

Malone climbed out of the car and went around to meet Burris. He felt just a little worried as he followed the Director away from the car. True, he had sent Burris a long telegram the night before, in code. But he hadn't expected the man to show up at Yucca Flats. There didn't seem to be any reason for it.

And when there isn't any reason, Malone told himself sagely, it's a bad one.

"What's the trouble, chief?" he asked.

Burris sighed. "None so far," he said quietly. "I got a report from the Nevada State Patrol, and ran it through R&I. They identified the men you killed, all right—but it didn't do us any good. They're hired hoods."

"Who hired them?" Malone said.

Burris shrugged. "Somebody with money," he said. "Hell, men like that would kill their own grandmothers if the price were right—you know that. We can't trace them back any farther."

Malone nodded. That was, he had to admit, bad news. But then, when had he last had any good news?

"We're nowhere near our telepathic spy," Burris said. "We haven't come any closer than we were when we started. Have you got anything? Anything at all, no matter how small?"

"Not that I know of, sir," Malone said.

"What about the little old lady ... what's her name? Thompson. Anything from her?"

Malone hesitated. "She has a close fix on the spy, sir," he said slowly, "but she doesn't seem able to identify him right away."

"What else does she want?" Burris said. "We've made her Queen and given her a full retinue in costume; we've let her play roulette and poker with Government money. Does she want to hold a mass execution? If she does, I can supply some congressmen, Malone. I'm sure it could be arranged." He looked at the agent narrowly. "I might even be able to supply an FBI man or two," he added.

Malone swallowed hard. "I'm trying the best I can, sir," he said. "What about the others?"

Burris looked even unhappier than usual. "Come along," he said. "I'll show you."

When they got back to the car, Dr. Gamble was talking spiritedly with Her Majesty about Roger Bacon. "Before my time, of course," the Queen was saying, "but I'm sure he was a most interesting man. Now when dear old Marlowe wrote his 'Faust,' he and I had several long discussions about such matters. Alchemy—"

Burris interrupted with: "I beg your pardon, Your Majesty, but we must get on. Perhaps you'll be able to continue your ... ah ... audience later." He turned to Boyd. "Sir Thomas," he said with an effort, "drive directly to the Westinghouse buildings. Over that way." He pointed. "Dr. Gamble will ride with you, and the rest of us will follow in the second car. Let's move."

He stepped back as the project head got into the car, and watched it roar off. Then he and Malone went to the second car, another FBI Lincoln. Two agents were sitting in the back seat, with a still figure between them.

With a shock, Malone recognized William Logan and the agents he'd detailed to watch the telepath. Logan's face did not seem to have changed expression since Malone had seen it last, and he wondered wildly if perhaps it had to be dusted once a week.

He got in behind the wheel and Burris slid in next to him.

"Westinghouse." Burris said. "And let's get there in a hurry."

"Right," Malone said, and started the car.

"We just haven't had a single lead," Burris said. "I was hoping you'd come up with something. Your telegram detailed the fight, of course, and the rest of what's been happening—but I hoped there'd be something more."

"There isn't," Malone was forced to admit. "All we can do is try to persuade Her Majesty to tell us—"

"Oh, I know it isn't easy," Burris said. "But it seems to me—"

By the time they'd arrived at the administrative offices of Westinghouse's psionics research area, Malone found himself wishing that something would happen. Possibly, he thought, lightning might strike, or an earthquake swallow everything up. He was, suddenly, profoundly tired of the entire affair.

VIII

Four days later, he was more than tired. He was exhausted. The six psychopaths—including Her Majesty Queen Elizabeth I—had been housed in a converted dormitory in the Westinghouse area, together with four highly nervous and even more highly trained and investigated psychiatrists from St. Elizabeths in Washington. The Convention of Nuts, as Malone called it privately, was in full swing. And it was every bit as strange as he'd thought it was going to be. Unfortunately, five of the six—Her Majesty being the only exception—were completely out of contact with the world. The psychiatrists referred to them in worried tones as "unavailable for therapy," and spent most of their time brooding over possible ways of bringing them back into the real world for a while.

Malone stayed away from the five who were completely psychotic. The weird babblings of fifty-year-old Barry Miles disconcerted him. They sounded like little Charlie O'Neill's strange semi-connected jabber, but Westinghouse's Dr. O'Connor said that it seemed to represent another phenomenon entirely. William Logan's blank face was a memory of horror, but the constant tinkling giggles of Ardith Parker, the studied and concentrated way that Gordon Macklin wove meaningless patterns in the air with his waving fingers, and the rhythmless, melodyless humming that seemed to be all there was to the personality of Robert Cassiday were simply too much for Malone. Taken singly, each was frightening and remote; all together, they wove a picture of insanity that chilled him more than he wanted to admit.

When the seventh telepath was flown in from Honolulu, Malone didn't even bother to see her. He let the psychiatrists take over directly, and simply avoided their sessions.

Queen Elizabeth I, on the other hand, he found genuinely likeable. According to the psych boys, she had been—as both Malone and Her Majesty had theorized—heavily frustrated by being the possessor of a talent which no one else recognized. Beyond that, the impact of other minds was disturbing; there was a slight loss of identity which seemed to be a major factor in every case of telepathic insanity. But the Queen had compensated for her frustrations in the easiest possible way; she had simply traded her identity for another one, and had rationalized a single, over-ruling delusion: that she was Queen Elizabeth I of England, still alive and wrongfully deprived of her throne.

"It's a beautiful rationalization," one of the psychiatrists said with more than a trace of admiration in his voice. "Complete and thoroughly consistent. She's just traded identities—and everything else she does—*everything* else—stems logically out of her delusional premise. Beautiful."

She might have been crazy, Malone realized. But she was a long way from stupid.

The project was in full swing. The only trouble was that they were no nearer finding the telepath than they had been three weeks before. With five completely blank human beings to work with, and the sixth Queen Elizabeth (Malone heard privately that the last telepath, the girl from Honolulu, was no better than the first five; she had apparently regressed into what one of the psychiatrists called a "non-identity childhood syndrome." Malone didn't know what it meant, but it sounded terrible.) Malone could see why progress was their most difficult commodity.

Dr. Harry Gamble, the head of Project Isle, was losing poundage by the hour with worry. And, Malone reflected, he could ill afford it.

Burris, Malone and Boyd had set themselves up in a temporary office within the Westinghouse area. The director had left his assistant in charge in Washington. Nothing, he said over and over again, was as important as the spy in Project Isle.

Apparently Boyd had come to believe that, too. At any rate, though he was still truculent, there were no more outbursts of rebellion.

But, on the fourth day:

"What do we do now?" Burris asked.

"Shoot ourselves," Boyd said promptly.

"Now, look here—" Malone began, but he was overruled.

"Boyd," Burris said levelly, "if I hear any more of that sort of pessimism, you're going to be an exception to the beard rule. One more crack out of you, and you can go out and buy yourself a razor."

Boyd put his hand over his chin protectively, and said nothing at all.

"Wait a minute," Malone said. "Aren't there any *sane* telepaths in the world?"

"We can't find any," Burris said. "We—"

There was a knock at the office door.

"Who's there?" Burris called.

"Dr. Gamble," said the man's surprisingly baritone voice.

Burris called: "Come in, doctor," and the door opened. Dr. Gamble's lean face looked almost haggard.

"Mr. Burris," he said, extending his arms a trifle, "can't anything be done?" Malone had seen Gamble speaking before, and had wondered if it would be possible for the man to talk with his hands tied behind his back. Apparently it wouldn't be. "We feel that we are approaching a critical stage in Project Isle," the scientist said, enclosing one fist within the other hand. "If anything more gets out to the Soviets, we might as well publish our findings"—a wide, outflung gesture of both arms—"in the newspapers."

Burris stepped back. "We're doing the best we can, Dr. Gamble," he said. All things considered, his obvious try at radiating confidence was nearly successful. "After all," he went on, "we know a great deal more than we did four days ago. Miss Thompson has assured us that the spy is right here, within the compound of Yucca Flats Labs. We've bottled everything up in this compound, and I'm confident that no information is at present getting through to the Soviet Government. Miss Thompson agrees with me."

"Miss Thompson?" Gamble said, one hand at his bearded chin.

"The Queen," Burris said.

Gamble nodded and two fingers touched his forehead. "Ah," he said. "Of course." He rubbed at the back of his neck. "But we can't keep everybody who's here now locked up forever. Sooner or later we'll have to let them"—his left hand described the gesture of a man tossing away a wad of paper—"go." His hands fell to his sides. "We're lost, unless we can find that spy."

"We'll find him," Burris said with a show of great confidence.

"But—"

"Give her time," Burris said. "Give her time. Remember her mental condition."

Boyd looked up. "Rome," he said in an absent fashion, "wasn't built in a daze."

Burris glared at him, but said nothing. Malone filled the conversational hole with what he thought would be nice, and hopeful, and untrue.

"We know he's someone on the reservation, so we'll catch him eventually," he said. "And as long as his information isn't getting into Soviet hands, we're safe." He glanced at his wrist watch.

Dr. Gamble said: "But—"

"My, my," Malone said. "Almost lunchtime. I have to go over and have lunch with Her Majesty. Maybe she's dug up something more."

"I hope so," Dr. Gamble said, apparently successfully deflected. "I do hope so."

"Well," Malone said, "pardon me." He shucked off his coat and trousers. Then he proceeded to put on the doublet and hose that hung in the little office closet. He shrugged into the fur-trimmed, slash-sleeved coat, adjusted the plumed hat to his satisfaction with great care, and gave Burris and the others a small bow. "I go to an audience with Her Majesty, gentlemen," he said in a grave, well-modulated voice. "I shall return anon."

He went out the door and closed it carefully behind him. When he had gone a few steps he allowed himself the luxury of a deep sigh.

Then he went outside and across the dusty street to the barracks where Her Majesty and the other telepaths were housed. No one paid any attention to him, and he rather missed the stares he'd become used to drawing. But by now, everyone was used to seeing Elizabethan clothing. Her Majesty had arrived at a new plateau.

She would now allow no one to have audience with her unless he was properly dressed. Even the psychiatrists—whom she had, with a careful sense of meiosis, appointed Physicians to the Royal House—had to wear the stuff.

Malone went over the whole case in his mind—for about the thousandth time, he told himself bitterly.

Who could the telepathic spy be? It was like looking for a needle in a rolling stone, he thought. Or something. He did remember clearly that a stitch in time saved nine, but he didn't know nine what, and suspected it had nothing to do with his present problem.

How about Dr. Harry Gamble, Malone thought. It seemed a little unlikely that the head of Project Isle would be spying on his own men—particularly since he already had all the information. But, on the other hand, he was just as probable a spy as anybody else.

Malone moved onward. Dr. Thomas O'Connor, the Westinghouse psionics man, was the next nominee. Before Malone had actually found Her Majesty, he had had a suspicion that O'Connor had cooked the whole thing up to throw the FBI off the trail and confuse everybody, and that he'd intended merely to have the FBI chase ghosts while the real spy did his work undetected.

But what if O'Connor were the spy himself—a telepath? What if he were so confident of his ability to throw the Queen off the track that he had allowed the FBI to find all the other telepaths? There was another argument for that: he'd had to report the findings of his machine no matter what it cost him; there were too many other men on his staff who knew about it.

O'Connor was a perfectly plausible spy, too. But he didn't seem very likely. The head of a Government project is likely to be a much-investigated man. Could any tie-up with Russia—even a psionic one—stand against that kind of investigation? Malone doubted it.

Malone thought of the psychiatrists. There wasn't any evidence, that was the trouble. There wasn't any evidence either way.

Then he wondered if Boyd had been thinking of him, Malone, as the possible spy. Certainly it worked in reverse. Boyd—

No. That was silly.

Malone told himself that he might as well consider Andrew J. Burris.

Ridiculous. Absolutely ridic—

Well, Queen Elizabeth had seemed pretty certain when she'd pointed him out in Dr. Dowson's office. And even though she'd changed her mind, how much faith could be placed in Her Majesty? After all, if she'd made a mistake about Burris, she could just as easily have made a mistake about the spy's being at Yucca Flats. In that case, Malone thought sadly, they were right back where they'd started from.

Behind their own goal line.

One way or another, though, Her Majesty had made a mistake. She'd pointed Burris out as the spy, and then she'd said she'd been wrong. Either Burris was a spy or he wasn't. You couldn't have it both ways.

Why couldn't you? Malone thought suddenly. And then something Burris himself had said came back to him, something that—

I'll be damned, he thought.

He came to a dead stop in the middle of the street. In one sudden flash of insight, all the pieces of the case he'd been looking at for so long fell together and formed one consistent picture. The pattern was complete.

Malone blinked.

In that second, he knew exactly who the spy was.

A jeep honked raucously and swerved around him. The driver leaned out to curse and remained to stare. Malone was already halfway back to the offices.

On the way, he stopped in at another small office, this one inhabited by the two FBI men from Las Vegas. He gave a series of quick orders, and got the satisfaction, as he left, of seeing one of the FBI men grabbing for a phone in a hurry. It was good to be *doing* things again, important things.

Burris, Boyd and Dr. Gamble were still talking as Malone entered.

"That," Burris said, "was one hell of a quick lunch. What's Her Majesty doing now—running a diner?"

Malone ignored the bait. "Gentlemen," he said solemnly, "Her Majesty has asked that all of us attend her in audience. She has information of the utmost gravity to impart, and wishes an audience at once."

Burris looked startled. "Has she—" he began, and stopped, leaving his mouth open and the rest of the sentence unfinished.

Malone nodded gravely. "I believe, gentlemen," he said, "that Her Majesty is about to reveal the identity of the spy who has been battening on Project Isle."

The silence didn't last three seconds.

"Let's go," Burris snapped. He and the others headed for the door.

"Gentlemen!" Malone sounded properly shocked and offended. "Your dress!"

"Oh, *no*," Boyd said. "Not now."

Burris simply said: "You're quite right. Get dressed, Boyd ... I mean, of course, Sir Thomas."

While Burris, Boyd and Dr. Gamble were dressing, Malone put in a call to Dr. O'Connor and told him to be at Her Majesty's court in ten minutes—and in full panoply. O'Connor, not unnaturally, balked a little at first. But Malone talked fast and sounded as urgent as he felt. At last he got the psionicist's agreement.

Then he put in a second call to the psychiatrists from St. Elizabeths and told them the same thing. More used to the strange demands of neurotic and psychotic patients, they were readier to comply.

Everyone, Malone realized with satisfaction, was assembled. Even Burris and the others were ready to go. Beaming, he led them out.

Ten minutes later, there were nine men in Elizabethan costume standing outside the room which had been designated as the Queen's Court. Dr. Gamble's costume did not quite fit him; his sleeve ruffs were halfway up to his elbows and his doublet had an unfortunate tendency to creep. The St. Elizabeths men, all four of them, looked just a little like moth-eaten versions of old silent pictures. Malone looked them over with a somewhat sardonic eye. Not only did he have the answer to the whole problem that had been plaguing them, but *his* costume was a stunning, perfect fit.

"Now, I want you men to let me handle this," Malone said. "I know just what I want to say, and I think I can get the information without too much trouble."

One of the psychiatrists spoke up. "I trust you won't disturb the patient, Mr. Malone," he said.

"Sir Kenneth," Malone snapped.

The psychiatrist looked both abashed and worried. "I'm sorry," he said doubtfully.

Malone nodded. "That's all right," he said. "I'll try not to disturb Her Majesty unduly."

The psychiatrists conferred. When they came out of the huddle one of them—Malone was never able to tell them apart—said: "Very well, we'll let you handle it. But we will be forced to interfere if we feel you're ... ah ... going too far."

Malone said: "That's fair enough, gentlemen. Let's go."

He opened the door.

It was a magnificent room. The whole place had been done over in plastic and synthetic fibers to look like something out of the Sixteenth Century. It was as garish, and as perfect, as a Hollywood movie set—which wasn't surprising, since two stage designers had been hired away from color-TV spectaculars to set it up. At the far end of the room, past the rich hangings and the flaming chandeliers, was a great throne, and on it Her Majesty was seated. Lady Barbara reclined on the steps at her feet.

Malone saw the expression on Her Majesty's face. He wanted to talk to Barbara—but there wasn't time. Later, there might be. Now, he collected his mind and drove one thought at the Queen, one single powerful thought:

Read me! You know by this time that I have the truth—but read deeper!

The expression on her face changed suddenly. She was smiling a sad, gentle little smile. Lady Barbara, who had looked up at the approach of Sir Kenneth and his entourage, relaxed again, but her eyes remained on Malone. "You may approach, my lords," said the Queen.

Sir Kenneth led the procession, with Sir Thomas and Sir Andrew close behind him. O'Connor and Gamble came next, and bringing up the rear were the four psychiatrists. They strode slowly along the red carpet that stretched from the door to the foot of the throne. They came to a halt a few feet from the steps leading up to the throne, and bowed in unison.

"You may explain, Sir Kenneth," Her Majesty said.

"Your Majesty understands the conditions?" Malone asked.

"Perfectly," said the Queen. "Proceed."

Now the expression on Barbara's face changed, to wonder and a kind of fright. Malone didn't look at her. Instead, he turned to Dr. O'Connor.

"Dr. O'Connor, what are your plans for the telepaths who have been brought here?" He shot the question out quickly, and O'Connor was caught off-balance.

"Well ... ah ... we would like their co-operation in further research which we ... ah ... plan to do into the actual mechanisms of telepathy. Provided, of course"—he coughed gently—"provided that they become ... ah ... accessible. Miss ... I mean, of course, Her Majesty has ... already been a great deal of help." He gave Malone an odd look. It seemed to say: *what's coming next?*

Malone simply gave him a nod, and a "Thank you, doctor," and turned to Burris. He could feel Barbara's eyes on him, but he went on with his prepared questions. "Chief," he said, "what about you? After we nail our spy, what happens ... to Her Majesty, I mean? You don't intend to stop giving her the homage due her, do you?"

Burris stared, openmouthed. After a second he managed to say: "Why, no, of course not, Sir Kenneth. That is"—and he glanced over at the psychiatrists—"if the doctors think—"

There was another hurried consultation. The four psychiatrists came out of it with a somewhat shaky statement to the effect that treatments which had been proven to have some therapeutic value ought not to be discontinued, although of course there was always the chance that—

"Thank you, gentlemen," Malone said smoothly. He could see that they were nervous, and no wonder; he could imagine how difficult it was for a psychiatrist to talk about a patient in her presence. But they'd already realized that it didn't make any difference; their thoughts were an open book, anyway.

Lady Barbara said: "Sir ... I mean Ken ... are you going to—"

"What's this all about?" Burris snapped.

"Just a minute, Sir Andrew," Malone said. "I'd like to ask one of the doctors here—or all of them, for that matter—one more question." He whirled and faced them. "I'm assuming that not one of these persons is legally responsible for his or her actions. Is that correct?"

Another hurried huddle. The psych boys were beginning to remind Malone of a semi-pro football team in rather unusual uniforms.

Finally one of them said: "You are correct. According to the latest statutes, all of these persons are legally insane—including Her Majesty." He paused and gulped. "I except the FBI, of course—and ourselves." Another pause. "And Dr. O'Connor and Dr. Gamble."

"And," said Lady Barbara, "me." She smiled sweetly at them all.

"Ah," the psychiatrist said. "Certainly. Of course." He retired into his group with some confusion.

Malone was looking straight at the throne. Her Majesty's countenance was serene and unruffled.

Barbara said suddenly: "You don't mean ... but she—" and closed her mouth. Malone shot her one quick look, and then turned to the Queen.

"Well, Your Majesty?" he said. "You have seen the thoughts of every man here. How do they appear to you?"

Her voice contained both tension and relief. "They are all good men, basically—and kind men," she said. "And they believe us. That's the important thing, you know. Their belief in us— Just as you did that first day we met. We've needed belief for so long ... for so long—" Her voice trailed off; it seemed to become lost in a constellation of thoughts. Barbara had turned to look up at Her Majesty.

Malone took a step forward, but Burris interrupted him. "How about the spy?" he said.

Then his eyes widened. Boyd, standing next to him, leaned suddenly forward. "That's why you mentioned all that about legal immunity because of insanity," he whispered. "Because—"

"No," Barbara said. "No. She couldn't ... she's not—"

They were all looking at Her Majesty, now. She returned them stare for stare, her back stiff and straight and her white hair enhaloed in the room's light. "Sir Kenneth," she said—and her voice was only the least bit unsteady—"they all think *I'm* the spy."

Barbara stood up. "Listen," she said. "I didn't like Her Majesty at first ... well, she was a patient, and that was all, and when she started putting on airs ... but since I've gotten to know her I do like her. I like her because she's good and kind herself, and because ... because she wouldn't be a spy. She couldn't be. No matter what any of you think ... even you ... Sir Kenneth!"

There was a second of silence.

"Of course she's not," Malone said quietly. "She's no spy."

"Would I spy on my own subjects?" she said. "Use your reason!"

"You mean...." Burris began, and Boyd finished for him:

"... She isn't?"

"No," Malone snapped. "She isn't. Remember, you said it would take a telepath to catch a telepath?"

"Well—" Burris began.

"Well, Her Majesty remembered it," Malone said. "And acted on it."

Barbara remained standing. She went to the Queen and put an arm around the little old lady's shoulder. Her Majesty did not object. "I knew," she said. "You couldn't have been a spy."

"Listen, dear," the Queen said. "Your Kenneth has seen the truth of the matter. Listen to him."

"Her Majesty not only caught the spy," Malone said, "but she turned the spy right over to us."

He turned at once and went back down the long red carpet to the door. *I really ought to get a sword*, he thought, and didn't see Her Majesty smile. He opened the door with a great flourish and said quietly: "Bring him in, boys."

The FBI men from Las Vegas marched in. Between them was their prisoner, a boy with a vacuous face, clad in a strait jacket that seemed to make no difference at all to him. His mind was—somewhere else. But his body was trapped between the FBI agents: the body of William Logan.

"Impossible," one of the psychiatrists said.

Malone spun on his heel and led the way back to the throne. Logan and his guards followed closely.

"Your Majesty," Malone said, "may I present the prisoner?"

"Perfectly correct, Sir Kenneth," the Queen said. "Poor Willie is your spy. You won't be too hard on him, will you?"

"I don't think so. Your Majesty," Malone said. "After all—"

"Now wait a minute," Burris exploded. "How did *you* know any of this?"

Malone bowed to Her Majesty, and winked at Barbara. He turned to Burris. "Well," he said, "I had one piece of information none of the rest of you had. When we were in the Desert Edge Sanitarium, Dr. Dowson called you on the phone. Remember?"

"Sure I remember," Burris said. "So?"

"Well," Malone said, "Her Majesty said she knew just where the spy was. I asked her where—"

"Why didn't you tell me?" Burris screamed. "You knew all this time and you didn't tell me?"

"Hold on," Malone said. "I asked her where—and she said: 'He's right there.' And she was pointing right at your image on the screen."

Burris opened his mouth. Nothing came out. He closed it and tried again. At last he managed one word.

"Me?" he said.

"You," Malone said. "But that's what I realized later. She wasn't pointing at you. She was pointing at Logan, who was in the next room."

Barbara whispered: "Is that right, Your Majesty?"

"Certainly, dear," the Queen said calmly. "Would I lie to Sir Kenneth?"

Malone was still talking. "The thing that set me off this noon was something you said, Sir Andrew," he went on. "You said there weren't any sane telepaths—remember?"

Burris, incapable of speech, merely nodded.

"But according to Her Majesty," Malone said, "we had every telepath in the United States right here. She told me that—and I didn't even see it!"

"Don't blame yourself, Sir Kenneth," the Queen put in. "I did do my best to mislead you, you know."

"You sure did!" Malone said. "And later on, when we were driving here, you said the spy was 'moving around.' That's right; he was in the car behind us, going eighty miles an hour."

Barbara stared. Malone got a lot of satisfaction out of that stare. But there was still more ground to cover.

"Then," he said, "you told us he was here at Yucca Flats—after we brought him here! It had to be one of the other six telepaths."

The psychiatrist who'd muttered: "Impossible," was still muttering it. Malone ignored him.

"And when I remembered her pointing at you," Malone told Burris, "and remembered that she'd only said: 'He's right there,' I knew it had to be Logan. You weren't there. You were only an image on a TV screen. Logan was there—in the room behind the phone."

Burris had found his tongue. "All right," he said. "O.K. But what's all this about misleading us—and why didn't she tell us right away, anyhow?"

Malone turned to Her Majesty on the throne. "I think that the Queen had better explain that—if she will."

Queen Elizabeth Thompson nodded very slowly. "I ... I only wanted you to respect me," she said. "To treat me properly." Her voice sounded uneven, and her eyes were glistening with unspilled tears. Lady Barbara tightened her arm about the Queen's shoulders once more.

"It's all right," she said. "We do—respect you."

The Queen smiled up at her.

Malone waited. After a second Her Majesty continued.

"I was afraid that as soon as you found poor Willie you'd send me back to the hospital," she said. "And Willie couldn't tell the Russian agents any more once he'd been taken away. So I thought I'd just ... just let things stay the way they were as long as I could. That's ... that's all."

Malone nodded. After a second he said: "You see that we couldn't possibly send you back now, don't you?"

"I—"

"You know all the State Secrets, Your Majesty," Malone said. "We would rather that Dr. Harman in San Francisco didn't try to talk you out of them. Or anyone else."

The Queen smiled tremulously. "I know too much, do I?" she said. Then her grin faded. "Poor Dr. Harman," she said.

"Poor Dr. Harman?"

"You'll hear about him in a day or so," she said. "I ... peeked inside his mind. He's very ill."

"Ill?" Lady Barbara asked.

"Oh, yes," the Queen said. The trace of a smile appeared on her face. "He thinks that all the patients in the hospital can see inside his mind."

"Oh, my," Lady Barbara said—and began to laugh. It was the nicest sound Malone had ever heard.

"Forget Harman," Burris snapped. "What about this spy ring? How was Logan getting his information out?"

"I've already taken care of that," Malone said. "I had Desert Edge Sanitarium surrounded as soon as I knew what the score was." He looked at one of the agents holding Logan.

"They ought to be in the Las Vegas jail within half an hour," the agent said in confirmation.

"Dr. Dowson was in on it, wasn't he, Your Majesty?" Malone said.

"Certainly," the Queen said. Her eyes were suddenly very cold. "I hope he tries to escape. I hope he tries it."

Malone knew just how she felt.

One of the psychiatrists spoke up suddenly. "I don't understand it," he said. "Logan is completely catatonic. Even if he could read minds, how could he tell Dowson what he'd read? It doesn't make sense."

"In the first place," the Queen said patiently, "Willie isn't catatonic. He's just *busy*, that's all. He's only a boy, and ... well, he doesn't much like being who he is. So he visits other people's minds, and that way he becomes *them* for a while. You see?"

"Vaguely," Malone said. "But how did Dowson get his information? I had everything worked out but that."

"I know you did," the Queen said, "and I'm proud of you. I intend to award you with the Order of the Bath for this day's work."

Unaccountably, Malone's chest swelled with pride.

"As for Dr. Dowson," the Queen said, "that traitor ... *hurt* Willie. If he's hurt enough, he'll come back." Her eyes weren't hard any more. "He didn't want to be a spy, really," she said, "but he's just a boy, and it must have sounded rather exciting. He knew that if he told Dowson everything he'd found out, they'd let him go—go away again."

There was a long silence.

"Well," Malone said, "that about wraps it up. Any questions?"

He looked around at the men, but before any of them could speak up Her Majesty rose.

"I'm sure there are questions," she said, "but I'm really very tired. My lords, you are excused." She extended a hand. "Come, Lady Barbara," she said. "I think I really may need that nap, now."

Malone put the cuff links in his shirt with great care. They were great stones, and Malone thought that they gave his costume that necessary Elizabethan flair.

Not that he was wearing the costume of the Queen's Court now. Instead, he was dressed in a tailor-proud suit of dark blue, a white-on-white shirt and no tie. He selected one of a gorgeous peacock pattern from his closet rack.

Boyd yawned at him from the bed in the room they were sharing. "Stepping out?" he said.

"I am," Malone said with restraint. He whipped the tie round his neck and drew it under the collar.

"Anybody I know?"

"I am meeting Lady Barbara, if you wish to know," Malone said.

"Come down," Boyd said. "Relax. Anyhow, I've got a question for you. There was one little thing Her Everlovin' Majesty didn't explain."

"Yes?" said Malone.

"Well, about those hoods who tried to gun us down," Boyd said. "Who hired 'em? And why?"

"Dowson," Malone said. "He wanted to kill us off, and then kidnap Logan from the hotel room. But we foiled his plan—by killing his hoods. By the time he could work up something else, we were on our way to Yucca Flats."

"Great," Boyd said. "And how did you find out this startling piece of information? There haven't been any reports in from Las Vegas, have there?"

"No," Malone said.

"O.K.," Boyd said. "I give up, Mastermind."

Malone wished Boyd would stop using that nickname. The fact was—as he, and apparently nobody else, was willing to recognize—that he wasn't anything like a really terrific FBI agent. Even Barbara thought he was something special.

He wasn't, he knew.

He was just lucky.

"Her Majesty informed me," Malone said.

"Her—" Boyd stood with his mouth dropped open, like a fish waiting for some bait. "You mean she knew?"

"Well," Malone said, "she did know the guys in the Buick weren't the best in the business—and she knew all about the specially-built FBI Lincoln. She got that from our minds." He knotted his tie with an air of great aplomb, and went, slowly to the door. "And she knew we were a good team. She got that from our minds, too."

"But," Boyd said. After a second he said: "But," again, and followed it with: "Why didn't she tell us?"

Malone opened the door.

"Her Majesty wished to see the Queen's Own FBI in action," said Sir Kenneth Malone.

THE END

Viewpoint

A fearsome thing is a thing you're afraid of—and it has nothing whatever to do with whether others are afraid, nor with whether it is in fact dangerous. It's your view of the matter that counts!

There was a dizzy, sickening whirl of mental blackness—not true blackness, but a mind-enveloping darkness that was filled with the multi-colored little sparks of thoughts and memories that scattered through the darkness like tiny glowing mice, fleeing from something unknown, fleeing outwards and away toward a somewhere that was equally unknown; scurrying, moving, changing—each half recognizable as it passed, but leaving only a vague impression behind.

Memories were shattered into their component data bits in that maelstrom of not-quite-darkness, and scattered throughout infinity and eternity. Then the pseudo-dark stopped its violent motion and became still, no longer scattering the fleeing memories, but merely blanketing them. And slowly—ever so slowly—the powerful cohesive forces that existed between the data-bits began pulling them back together again as the not-blackness faded. The associative powers of the mind began putting the frightened little things together as they drifted back in from vast distances, trying to fit them together again in an ordered whole. Like a vast jigsaw puzzle in five dimensions, little clots and patches formed as the bits were snuggled into place here and there.

The process was far from complete when Broom regained consciousness.

Broom sat up abruptly and looked around him. The room was totally unfamiliar. For a moment, that seemed perfectly understandable. Why shouldn't the room look odd, after he had gone through—

What?

He rubbed his head and looked around more carefully. It was not just that the room itself was unfamiliar as a whole; the effect was greater than that. It was not the first time in his life he had regained consciousness in unfamiliar surroundings, but always before he had been aware that only the pattern was different, not the details.

He sat there on the floor and took stock of himself and his surroundings.

He was a big man—six feet tall when he stood up, and proportionately heavy, a big-boned frame covered with hard, well-trained muscles. His hair and beard were a dark blond, and rather shaggy because of the time he'd spent in prison.

Prison!

Yes, he'd been in prison. The rough clothing he was wearing was certainly nothing like the type of dress he was used to.

He tried to force his memory to give him the information he was looking for, but it wouldn't come. A face flickered in his mind for a moment, and a name. Contarini. He seemed to remember a startled look on the Italian's face, but he could neither remember the reason for it nor when it had been. But it would come back; he was sure of that.

Meanwhile, where the devil was he?

From where he was sitting, he could see that the room was fairly large, but not extraordinarily so. A door in one wall led into another room of about the same size. But they were like no other rooms he had ever seen before. He looked down at the floor. It was soft, almost as soft as a bed, covered with a thick, even, resilient layer of fine material of some kind. It was some sort of carpeting that covered the floor from wall to wall, but no carpet had ever felt like this.

He lifted himself gingerly to his feet. He wasn't hurt, at least. He felt fine, except for the gaps in his memory.

The room was well lit. The illumination came from the ceiling, which seemed to be made of some glowing, semitranslucent metal that cast a shadowless glow over everything. There was a large, bulky table near the wall away from the door; it looked almost normal, except that the objects on it were like nothing that had ever existed. Their purposes were unknown, and their shapes meaningless.

He jerked his head away, not wanting to look at the things on the table.

The walls, at least, looked familiar. They seemed to be paneled in some fine wood. He walked over and touched it.

And knew immediately that, no matter what it looked like, it wasn't wood. The illusion was there to the eye, but no wood ever had such a hard, smooth, glasslike surface as this. He jerked his fingertips away.

He recognized, then, the emotion that had made him turn away from the objects on the table and pull his hand away from the unnatural wall. It was fear.

Fear? Nonsense! He put his hand out suddenly and slapped the wall with his palm and held it there. There was nothing to be afraid of!

He laughed at himself softly. He'd faced death a hundred times during the war without showing fear; this was no time to start. What would his men think of him if they saw him getting shaky over the mere touch of a woodlike wall?

The memories were coming back. This time, he didn't try to probe for them; he just let them flow.

He turned around again and looked deliberately at the big, bulky table. There was a faint humming noise coming from it which had escaped his notice before. He walked over to it and looked at the queerly-shaped things that lay on its shining surface. He had already decided that the table was no more wood than the wall, and a touch of a finger to the surface verified the decision.

The only thing that looked at all familiar on the table was a sheaf of written material. He picked it up and glanced over the pages, noticing the neat characters, so unlike any that he knew. He couldn't read a word of it. He grinned and put the sheets back down on the smooth table top.

The humming appeared to be coming from a metal box on the other side of the table. He circled around and took a look at the thing. It had levers and knobs and other projections, but their functions were not immediately discernible. There were several rows of studs with various unrecognizable symbols on them.

This would certainly be something to tell in London—when and if he ever got back.

He reached out a tentative finger and touched one of the symbol-marked studs.

There was a loud *click!* in the stillness of the room, and he leaped back from the device. He watched it warily for a moment, but nothing more seemed to be forthcoming. Still, he decided it might be best to let things alone. There was no point in messing with things that undoubtedly controlled forces beyond his ability to cope with, or understand. After all, such a long time—

He stopped, Time? *Time?*

What had Contarini said about time? Something about its being like a river that flowed rapidly—that much he remembered. Oh, yes—and that it was almost impossible to try to swim backwards against the current or ... something else. What?

He shook his head. The more he tried to remember what his fellow prisoner had told him, the more elusive it became.

He had traveled in time, that much was certain, but how far, and in which direction? Toward the future, obviously; Contarini had made it plain that going into the past was impossible. Then could he, Broom, get back to his own time, or was he destined to stay in this—place? Wherever and whenever it was.

Evidently movement through the time-river had a tendency to disorganize a man's memories. Well, wasn't that obvious anyway? Even normal movement through time, at the rate of a day per day, made some memories fade. And some were lost entirely, while others remained clear and bright. What would a sudden jump of centuries do?

His memory was improving, though. If he just let it alone, most of it would come back, and he could orient himself. Meanwhile, he might as well explore his surroundings a little more. He resolved to keep his hands off anything that wasn't readily identifiable.

There was a single oddly-shaped chair by the bulky table, and behind the chair was a heavy curtain which apparently covered a window. He could see a gleam of light coming through the division in the curtains.

Broom decided he might as well get a good look at whatever was outside the building he was in. He stepped over, parted the curtains, and—

—And gasped!

It was night time outside, and the sky was clear. He recognized the familiar constellations up there. But they were dimmed by the light from the city that stretched below him.

And what a city! At first, it was difficult for his eyes to convey their impressions intelligently to his brain. What they were recording was so unfamiliar that his brain could not decode the messages they sent.

There were broad, well-lit streets that stretched on and on, as far as he could see, and beyond them, flittering fairy bridges rose into the air and arched into the distance. And the buildings towered over everything. He forced himself to look down, and it made him dizzy. The building he was in was so high that it would have projected through the clouds if there had been any clouds.

Broom backed away from the window and let the curtain close. He'd had all of that he could take for right now. The inside of the building, his immediate surroundings, looked almost homey after seeing that monstrous, endless city outside.

He skirted the table with its still-humming machine and walked toward the door that led to the other room. A picture hanging on a nearby wall caught his eye, and he stopped. It was a portrait of a man in unfamiliar, outlandish clothing, but Broom had seen odder clothing in his travels. But the thing that had stopped him was the amazing reality of the picture. It was almost as if there were a mirror there, reflecting the face of a man who stood invisibly before it.

It wasn't, of course; it was only a painting. But the lifelike, somber eyes of the man were focused directly on him. Broom decided he didn't like the effect at all, and hurried into the next room.

There were several rows of the bulky tables in here, each with its own chair. Broom's footsteps sounded loud in the room, the echoes rebounding from the walls. He stopped and looked down. This floor wasn't covered with the soft carpeting; it had a square, mosaic pattern, as though it might be composed of tile of some kind. And yet, though it was harder than the carpet it had a kind of queer resiliency of its own.

The room itself was larger than the one he had just quitted, and not as well lit. For the first time, he thought of the possibility that there might be someone else here besides himself. He looked around, wishing that he had a weapon of some kind. Even a knife would have made him feel better.

But there had been no chance of that, of course. Prisoners of war are hardly allowed to carry weapons with them, so none had been available.

He wondered what sort of men lived in this fantastic city. So far, he had seen no one. The streets below had been filled with moving vehicles of some kind, but it had been difficult to tell whether there had been anyone walking down there from this height.

Contarini had said that it would be ... how had he said it? "Like sleeping for hundreds of years and waking up in a strange world."

Well, it was that, all right.

Did anyone know he was here? He had the uneasy feeling that hidden, unseen eyes were watching his every move, and yet he could detect nothing. There was no sound except the faint humming from the device in the room behind him, and a deeper, almost inaudible, rushing, rumbling sound that seemed to come from far below.

His wish for a weapon came back, stronger than before. The very fact that he had seen no one set his nerves on edge even more than the sight of a known enemy would have done.

He was suddenly no longer interested in his surroundings. He felt trapped in this strange, silent room. He could see a light shining through a door at the far end of the room—perhaps it was a way out. He walked toward it, trying to keep his footsteps as silent as possible as he moved.

The door had a pane of translucent glass in it, and there were more of the unreadable characters on it. He wished fervently that he could decipher them; they might tell him where he was.

Carefully, he grasped the handle of the door, twisted it, and pulled. And, careful as he had been, the door swung inward with surprising rapidity. It was a great deal thinner and lighter than he had supposed.

He looked down at it, wondering if there were any way the door could be locked. There was a tiny vertical slit set in a small metal panel in the door, but it was much too tiny to be a keyhole. Still—

It didn't matter. If necessary, he could smash the glass to get through the door. He stepped out into what was obviously a hallway beyond the door.

The hallway stretched away to either side, lined with doors similar to the one he had just come through. How did a man get out of this place, anyway? The door behind him was pressing against his hand with a patient insistence, as though it wanted to close itself. He almost let it close, but, at the last second, he changed his mind.

Better the devil we know than the devil we don't, he thought to himself.

He went back into the office and looked around for something to prop the door open. He found a small, beautifully formed porcelain dish on one of the desks, picked it up, and went back to the door. The dish held the door open an inch or so. That was good enough. If someone locked the door, he could still smash in the glass if he wanted to, but the absence of the dish when he returned would tell him that he was not alone in this mysterious place.

He started down the hallway to his right, checking the doors as he went. They were all locked. He knew that he could break into any of them, but he had a feeling that he would find no exit through any of them. They all looked as though they concealed more of the big rooms.

None of them had any lights behind them. Only the one door that he had come through showed the telltale glow from the other side. Why?

He had the terrible feeling that he had been drawn across time to this place for a purpose, and yet he could think of no rational reason for believing so.

He stopped as another memory came back. He remembered being in the stone-walled dungeon, with its smelly straw beds, lit only by the faint shaft of sunlight that came from the barred window high overhead.

Contarini, the short, wiry little Italian who was in the next cell, looked at him through the narrow opening. "I still think it can be done, my friend. It is the mind and the mind alone that sees the flow of time. The body experiences, but does not see. Only the soul is capable of knowing eternity."

Broom outranked the little Italian, but prison can make brothers of all men. "You think it's possible then, to get out of a place like this, simply by thinking about it?"

Contarini nodded. "Why not? Did not the saints do so? And what was that? Contemplation of the Eternal, my comrade; contemplation of the Eternal."

Broom held back a grin. "Then why, my Venetian friend, have you not left this place long since?"

"I try," Contarini had said simply, "but I cannot do it. You wish to know why? It is because I am afraid."

"Afraid?" Broom raised an eyebrow. He had seen Contarini on the battlefield, dealing death in hand-to-hand combat, and the Italian hadn't impressed him as a coward.

"Yes," said the Venetian. "Afraid. Oh, I am not afraid of men. I fight. Some day, I may die—*will* die. This does not frighten me, death. I am not afraid of what men may do to me." He stopped and frowned. "But, of this, I have a great fear. Only a saint can handle such things, and I am no saint."

"I hope, my dear Contarini," Broom said dryly, "that you are not under the impression that *I* am a saint."

"No, perhaps not," Contarini said. "Perhaps not. But you are braver than I. I am not afraid of any man living. But you are afraid of neither the living nor the dead, nor of man nor devil—which is a great deal more than I can say for myself. Besides, there is the blood of kings in your veins. And has not a king protection that even a man of noble blood such as myself does not have? I think so.

"Oh, I have no doubt that you could do it, if you but would. And then, perhaps, when you are free, you would free me—for teaching you all I know to accomplish this. My fear holds me chained here, but you have no chains of fear."

Broom had thought that over for a moment, then grinned. "All right, my friend; I'll try it. What's your first lesson?"

The memory faded from Broom's mind. Had he really moved through some segment of Eternity to reach this ... this place? Had he—

He felt a chill run through him. What was he doing here? How could he have taken it all so calmly. Afraid of man or devil, no—but this was neither. He had to get back. The utter alienness of this bright, shining, lifeless wonderland was too much for him.

Instinctively, he turned and ran back toward the room he had left. If he got back to the place where he had appeared in this world, perhaps—somehow—some force would return him to where he belonged.

The door was as he had left it, the porcelain dish still in place. He scooped up the dish in one big hand and ran on into the room, letting the door shut itself behind him. He ran on, through the large room with its many tables, into the brightly lighted room beyond.

He stopped. What could he do now? He tried to remember the things that the Italian had told him to do, and he could not for the life of him remember them. His memory still had gaps in it—gaps he did not know were there because he had not yet probed for them. He closed his eyes in concentration, trying to bring back a memory that would not come.

He did not hear the intruder until the man's voice echoed in the room.

Broom's eyes opened, and instantly every muscle and nerve in his hard-trained body tensed for action. There was a man standing in the doorway of the office.

He was not a particularly impressive man, in spite of the queer cut of his clothes. He was not as tall as Broom, and he looked soft and overfed. His paunch protruded roundly from the open front of the short coat, and there was a fleshiness about his face that betrayed too much good living.

And he looked even more frightened than Broom had been a few minutes before.

He was saying something in a language that Broom did not understand, and the tenseness in his voice betrayed his fear. Broom relaxed. He had nothing to fear from this little man.

"I won't hurt you," Broom said. "I had no intention of intruding on your property, but all I ask is help."

The little man was blinking and backing away, as though he were going to turn and bolt at any moment.

Broom laughed. "You have nothing to fear from me, little man. Permit me to introduce myself. I am Richard Broom, known as—" He stopped, and his eyes widened. Total memory flooded over him as he realized fully who he was and where he belonged.

And the fear hit him again in a raging flood, sweeping over his mind and blotting it out. Again, the darkness came.

This time, the blackness faded quickly. There was a face, a worried face, looking at him through an aperture in the stone wall. The surroundings were so familiar, that the bits of memory which had been scattered again during the passage through centuries of time came back more quickly and settled back into their accustomed pattern more easily.

The face was that of the Italian, Contarini. He was looking both worried and disappointed.

"You were not gone long, my lord king," he said. "But you *were* gone. Of that there can be no doubt. Why did you return?"

Richard Broom sat up on his palette of straw. The scene in the strange building already seemed dreamlike, but the fear was still there. "I couldn't remember," he said softly. "I couldn't remember who I was nor why I had gone to that ... that place. And when I remembered, I came back."

Contarini nodded sadly. "It is as I have heard. The memory ties one too strongly to the past—to one's own time. One must return as soon as the mind had adjusted. I am sorry, my friend; I had hoped we could escape. But now it appears that we must wait until our ransoms are paid. And I much fear that mine will never be paid."

"Nor mine," said the big man dully. "My faithful Blondin found me, but he may not have returned to London. And even if he has, my brother John may be reluctant to raise the money."

"What? Would England hesitate to ransom the brave king who has fought so gallantly in the Holy Crusades? Never! You will be free, my friend."

But Richard Plantagenet just stared at the little dish that he still held in his hand, the fear still in his heart. Men would still call him "Lion-hearted," but he knew that he would never again deserve the title.

And, nearly eight centuries away in time and thousands of miles away in space, a Mr. Edward Jasperson was speaking hurriedly into the telephone that stood by the electric typewriter on his desk.

"That's right, Officer; Suite 8601, Empire State Building. I was working late, and I left the lights on in my office when I went out to get a cup of coffee. When I came back, he was here—a big, bearded man, wearing a thing that looked like a monk's robe made out of gunny sack. What? No, I locked the door when I left. What? Well, the only thing that's missing as far as I can tell is a ceramic ash tray from one of the desks; he was holding that in his hand when I saw him. What? Oh. Where did he go?" Mr. Jasperson paused in his rush of words. "Well, I must have gotten a little dizzy—I was pretty shocked, you know. To be honest, I didn't see where he went. I must have fainted.

"But I think you can pick him up if you hurry. With that getup on, he can't get very far away. All right. Thank you, Officer."

He cradled the phone, pulled a handkerchief from his pocket, and dabbed at his damp forehead. He was a very frightened little man, but he knew he'd get over it by morning.

THE END

The Penal Cluster

Tomorrow's technocracy will produce more and more things for better living. It will produce other things, also; among them, criminals too despicable to live on this earth. Too abominable to breathe our free air.

THE clipped British voice said, in David Houston's ear, *I'm quite sure he's one. He's cashing a check for a thousand pounds. Keep him under surveillance.*

Houston didn't look up immediately. He simply stood there in the lobby of the big London bank, filling out a deposit slip at one of the long, high desks. When he had finished, he picked up the slip and headed towards the teller's cage.

Ahead of him, standing at the window, was a tall, impeccably dressed, aristocratic-looking man with graying hair.

"The man in the tweeds?" Houston whispered. His voice was so low that it was inaudible a foot away, and his lips scarcely moved. But the sensitive microphone in his collar picked up the voice and relayed it to the man behind the teller's wicket.

That's him, said the tiny speaker hidden in Houston's ear. *The fine-looking chap in the tweeds and bowler.*

"Got him," whispered Houston.

He didn't go anywhere near the man in the bowler and tweeds; instead, he went to a window several feet away.

"Deposit," he said, handing the slip to the man on the other side of the partition. While the teller went through the motions of putting the deposit through the robot accounting machine, David Houston kept his ears open.

"How did you want the thousand, sir?" asked the teller in the next wicket.

"Ten pound notes, if you please," said the graying man. "I think a hundred notes will go into my brief case easily enough." He chuckled, as though he'd made a clever witticism.

"Yes, sir," said the clerk, smiling.

Houston whispered into his microphone again. "Who is the guy?"

On the other side of the partition, George Meredith, a small, unimposing-looking man, sat at a desk marked: MR. MEREDITH—ACCOUNTING DEPT. He looked as though he were paying no attention whatever to anything going on at the various windows, but he, too, had a microphone at his throat and a hidden pickup in his ear.

At Houston's question, he whispered: "That's Sir Lewis Huntley. The check's good, of course. Poor fellow."

"Yeah," whispered Houston, "if he is what we think he is."

"I'm fairly certain," Meredith replied. "Sir Lewis isn't the type of fellow to draw that much in cash. At the present rate of exchange, that's worth three thousand seven hundred and fifty dollars American. Sir Lewis might carry a hundred pounds as pocket-money, but never a thousand."

Houston and Meredith were a good thirty feet from each other, and neither looked at the other. Unless a bystander had equipment to tune in on the special scrambled wavelength they were using, that bystander would never know they were holding a conversation.

"... nine-fifty, nine-sixty, nine-seventy, nine-eighty, nine-ninety, a thousand pounds," said the clerk who was taking care of Sir Lewis's check. "Would you count that to make sure, sir?"

"Certainly. Ten, twenty, thirty, ..."

While the baronet was double-checking the amount, David Houston glanced at him. Sir Lewis looked perfectly calm and unhurried, as though he were doing something perfectly legal—which, in a way, he was. And, in another way, he most definitely was not, if George Meredith's suspicions were correct.

"Your receipt, sir." It was the teller at Houston's own window.

Houston took the receipt, thanked the teller, and walked toward the broad front doors of the bank.

"George," he whispered into the throat mike, "has Sir Lewis noticed me?"

"Hasn't so much as looked at you," Meredith answered. "Good hunting."

"Thanks."

As Houston stepped outside the bank, he casually dropped one hand into a coat pocket and turned a small knob on his radio control box. "Houston to HQ," he whispered.

"London HQ; what is it, Houston?" asked the earpiece.

"Leadenhall Street Post. Meredith thinks he's spotted one. Sir Lewis Huntley."

"Righto. We've got men in that part of the city now. We'll have a network posted within five minutes. Can you hold onto him that long?"

Houston looked around. Leadenhall Street was full of people, and the visibility was low. "I'll have to tail him pretty closely," Houston said. "Your damned English fogs don't give a man much chance to see anything."

There was a chuckle from the earphone. "Cheer up, Yank; you should have seen it back before 1968. When atomic power replaced coal and oil, our fogs became a devil of a lot cleaner."

The voice was quite clear; at the London headquarters of the UN Psychodeviant Police, there was no need to wear a throat mike, which had a tendency to make the voice sound muffled in spite of the Statistical Information-Bit Samplers which were supposed to clarify the speech coming through them.

"What do you know about 1968?" Houston asked sardonically. "Your mother was still pushing you around in a baby-carriage then."

"In a pram," corrected the Headquarters operator. "That is true, but my dear Aunt Jennifer told me all about it. She was—"

"The hell with your Aunt Jennifer," Houston interrupted suddenly. "Here comes Sir Lewis. Get me cover—fast!"

"Right. Keep us posted."

Sir Lewis Huntley stepped out of the broad door of the bank and turned left. He took a couple of steps and stopped. He didn't look around; he simply took a cigarette out of a silver case, put it in his mouth, and lit it. The glow of the lighter shone yellowly on the brass plate near the door which said: *An Affiliate of Westminster Bank, Ltd.*

Sir Lewis snapped the light out, drew on the cigarette, and strode on down the street, swinging a blue plastex brief case which contained a thousand pounds in United Nations Bank of England notes.

Houston decided the baronet had not been looking for a tail; he wished he could probe the man's mind to make sure, but he knew that would be fatal. He'd have to play the game and hope for the best.

"He's heading east," Houston whispered. "Doesn't look as if he's going to get a cab."

"Check," said the earphone.

Sir Lewis seemed in no great hurry, but he walked briskly, as though he had a definite destination in mind.

After a little way, he crossed to the south side of Leadenhall Street and kept going east. Houston stayed far enough behind to be above suspicion, but not so far that he ran a chance of losing his man.

"He's turning south on Fenchurch," Houston said a little later. "I wonder where he's going."

"Keep after him," said Headquarters. "Our net men haven't spotted either of you yet. They can hardly see across the street in this damned fog."

Houston kept going.

"What the hell?" he whispered a few minutes later. "He's still following Fenchurch Street! He's doubling back!"

Leadenhall Street, the banking center of the City of London, runs almost due east-and-west; Fenchurch Street makes a forty-five degree angle with it at the western end, running southwest for a bit and then curving toward the west, toward Lombard.

"Houston," said HQ, "touch your left ear."

Houston obediently reached up and scratched his left ear.

"Okay," said HQ. "Bogart's spotted you, but he hasn't spotted Sir Lewis. Bogart's across the street."

"He can't miss Sir Lewis," whispered Houston. "Conservatively dressed—matching coat and trousers of orange nylon tweed—royal blue half-brim bowler—carrying a blue brief case."

There was a pause, then: "Yeah. Bogart's spotted him, and so has MacGruder. Mac's on your side, a few yards ahead."

"Check. How about the rest of the net?"

"Coming, coming. Be patient, old man."

"I *am* patient," growled Houston. *I have to be*, he thought to himself, *otherwise I'd never stay alive*.

"We've got him bracketed now," HQ said. "If we lose him now, he's a magician."

Sir Lewis walked on, seemingly oblivious to the group of men who had surrounded him. He came to the end of Fenchurch Street and looked to his left, towards London Bridge. Then he glanced to his right.

"I think he's looking for a cab," Houston whispered.

"That's what MacGruder says," came the reply. "We've got Arthmore in a cab behind you; he'll pick you up. MacGruder will get another cab, and we have a private car for Bogart."

Sir Lewis flagged a cab, climbed in, and gave an address to the driver. Houston didn't hear it, but MacGruder, a heavy-set, short, balding man, was standing near enough to get the instructions Sir Lewis had given to the driver.

A cab pulled up to the curb near Houston, and he got in.

Arthmore, the driver, was a thin, tall, hawknosed individual who could have played Sherlock Holmes on TV. Once he got into character for a part, he never got out of it unless absolutely necessary. Right now, he was a Cockney cab-driver, and he would play the part to the hilt.

"Where to, guv'nor?" he asked innocently.

"Buckingham Palace," said Houston. "I've got a poker appointment with Prince Charles."

"Blimey, guv'nor," said Arthmore. "You *are* movin' in 'igh circles! 'Ow's 'Er Majesty these days?"

The turboelectric motor hummed, and the cab shot off into traffic. "According to the report I get on the blinkin' wireless," he continued, "a chap named MacGruder claims that the eminent Sir Lewis 'Untley is 'eaded for Number 37 Upper Berkeley Mews."

"One of these days," said Houston, "all those *H*'s you drop is going to bounce back and hit you in the face."

"Beg pardon, Mr. Yewston?" Arthmore asked blankly.

Houston grinned. "Nothing, cabbie; it's just that you remind me of a cultured, intelligent fellow named Jack Arthmore. The only difference is that Jack speaks the Queen's English."

"Crikey!" said Arthmore. "Wot a coincidence!" He paused, then: "The Queen's English, you say? She *'as* to be, don't she?"

"Shut up," said Houston conversationally. "And give me a cigarette," he added.

"There's a package of Players in my shirt pocket," Arthmore said, keeping his hands on the wheel.

Houston fished out a cigarette, lit it, and returned the pack.

Apropos of nothing, Arthmore said: "Reminds me of the time I was workin' for a printer, see? We 'ad to print up a bunch of 'andbills advertisin' a church charity bazaar. Down at the bottom was supposed to be printed 'Under the auspices of St. Bede's-on-Thames.' So I—"

He went on with a long, rambling tale about making a mistake in printing the handbill. Houston paid little attention. He smoked in silence, keeping his eyes on the red glow of the taillight ahead of them.

Neither man mentioned the approaching climax of the chase. Even hardened veterans of the Psychodeviant Police don't look forward to the possibility of having their minds taken over, controlled by some outside force.

It had never happened to Houston, but he knew that Arthmore had been through the experience once. It evidently wasn't pleasant.

"—and the boss was 'oppin' mad," Arthmore was saying, "but, crikey, 'ow was I to know that *auspice* was spelled A-U-S-P-I-C-E?"

Houston grinned. "Yeah, sure. How're we doing with Sir Lewis?"

"Seems to be headed in the right direction," Arthmore said, suddenly dropping the Cockney accent. "This is the route I'd take if I were headed for Upper Berkeley Mews. He probably hasn't told the driver to change addresses—maybe he won't."

"The victims never do," Houston said. "He probably is actually headed toward Number 37 Upper Berkeley Mews."

"Yeah. Nobody's perfect," said Arthmore.

Forty-five minutes of steady progress through the streets of Greater London brought Sir Lewis Huntley to Upper Berkeley and to the short dead-end street which constituted the Mews. By the time the dapper baronet stepped out of the machine and paid his driver, the whole area was surrounded by and filled with the well-armed, silent, and careful agents of the Psychodeviant Police.

Number 37 was an old concrete-and-steel structure of the George VI period, faced with a veneer of red brick. It had obviously been remodeled at least once to make the façade more modern and more fashionable; the red-violet anodized aluminum was relatively fresh and unstained. It wouldn't have taken vast wealth to rent a flat in the building, but neither would an average income have been quite enough.

Houston looked out of the window of Arthmore's cab and glanced at the tiers of windows in the building. Presumably, the man they were looking for was up there—somewhere.

So you occupy a station in the upper middle-class, thought Houston. It checked. Every bit of evidence that came his way seemed to check perfectly and fit neatly into the hypothesis which he had formed. Soon it would be time to test that theory—but the time had not yet come.

"Stand by and wait for orders, Houston," said the speaker in Houston's ear. "We've got men inside the building."

Sir Lewis Huntley opened the sparkling, translucent door of Number 37 Upper Berkeley Mews and went inside.

Arthmore pulled the cab over to the curb a few yards from the entrance and the two men waited in silence. All around them were other men, some in private cars, some walking slowly along the street. All of them were part of the net that had gathered to catch one man.

Poor fish, Houston thought wryly.

There was no noise, no excitement. Five minutes after Sir Lewis had entered the front door, it opened again. A man whom Houston had never seen before stepped out and gestured with one hand. At the same time, Houston's speaker said: "They've got him. Hit him with a stun gun when he tried to get out through the fire exit."

An ambulance which had been waiting at the entrance of the Mews pulled up in front of Number 37, and a minute or so later a little clot of men came out bearing a stretcher, which was loaded into the ambulance. Immediately after them came another man who had a firm, but polite grip on the arm of Sir Lewis Huntley.

Houston sighed and leaned back in his seat. That was that. It was all over. Simple. Nothing to it.

Another Controller had been apprehended by the Psychodeviant Police. Another deviant, already tried and found guilty, was ready to be exiled from Earth and imprisoned on one of the Penal Asteroids. All in the day's work.

There's just one thing I'd like to know, Houston thought blackly. *What in the hell's going on?*

In his hotel room near Piccadilly Circus, several hours later, David Houston sat alone, drink in hand, and put that same question to himself again.

"What's going on?"

On the face of it, it was simple. On the face of it, the answer was right in front of him, printed in black and white on the front page of the evening *Times*.

Houston lifted the paper off the bed and looked at it. The banner line said: *Controller Captured in Lambeth!*

Beneath that, in smaller type, the headline added: Robert Harris Accused of Taking Control of Barrister Sir Lewis Huntley.

The column itself told the whole story. Mr. Robert Harris, of No. 37 Upper Berkeley Mews, had, by means of mental control, taken over the mind of Sir Lewis and compelled him to draw one thousand pounds out of his bank. While Sir Lewis was returning to Harris with the money, the United Nations Psychodeviant Police had laid a trap. Sir Lewis, upon recovering his senses when Harris was rendered unconscious by a stun gun, had given evidence to the PD Police and to officials at New Scotland Yard.

Houston looked at the full-color photo of Harris that was printed alongside the column. Nice-looking chap; late twenties or early thirties, Houston guessed. Blond-red hair, blue eyes. All-in-all, a very pleasant, but ordinary sort of man.

There had been evidence that a Controller had been at work in London for some weeks now. Twelve days before, several men, following an impulse, had mailed twenty pounds to a "Richard Hempstead," General Delivery, Waterloo Station. By the time the matter had come to the authorities' attention, the envelopes had been called for and the Controller had escaped.

Robert Harris was not the first Controller to be captured, nor, Houston knew, would he be the last. The first one had shown up more than sixteen years before, in Dallas, Texas, USA.

Houston grinned as he thought of it. Projective telepathy had only been a crackpot's idea back then. In spite of the work of many intelligent, sane men, who had shown that mental powers above and beyond the ordinary did exist, the average man simply laughed off such nonsense. It was mysticism; it was magic; it was foolish superstition. It was anything but true.

But ever since "Blackjack" Donnely had practically taken control of the whole city of Dallas, the average man had changed his mind. It was still mysterious; it was still magic; but now the weird machinations of the supernormal mind were something to be feared.

In the sixteen years that had ensued since the discovery of the abnormal mental powers of "Blackjack" Donnely, rumors had spread all over the world. There were supposed to be men who could levitate—fly through the air at will. Others could walk through walls, and still others could make themselves invisible. The horrible monsters that were supposed to be walking the Earth were legion.

Actually, only one type of supernormal psychodeviant had been found—the telepath, the mindreader who could probe into the mental processes of others. Worse than that, the telepath could project his own thoughts into the mind of another, so that the victim supposed that the thoughts were his own. Actually, it was a high-powered form of hypnotism; the victim could be made to do anything the projective telepath wanted him to.

"Blackjack" Donnely had made that clear in his trial in Texas.

Donnely had been a big man—big physically, and important in city politics. He had also been as arrogant as the Devil himself.

It was the arrogance that had finally tripped up Donnely. He had thought himself impregnable. Haled into court on charges of misappropriation of public funds, he had just sat and smirked while several witnesses for the State admitted that they had aided Donnely, but they claimed he had "hypnotized" them. Donnely didn't try to interfere with the evidence—that's where he made his mistake. And that's where his arrogance tripped him up.

If he'd used telepathic projection to influence the State Attorney or the witnesses or the judge or the Grand Jury *before* the trial, he might never have been discovered as the first of the Controllers. But that wasn't Donnely's style.

"None of this namby-pamby stuff," he had once been quoted as saying; "if you got enemies, don't tease 'em—show 'em who's running things. Blackjack 'em, if you have to."

And that's exactly what "Blackjack" Donnely had done. The trial was a farce from beginning to end; each witness gave his evidence from the stand, and then Donnely took control of their minds and made them refute every bit of it, publicly and tearfully apologizing to the "wonderful Mr. Donnely" for saying such unkind things about him.

The judge and the jury knew something funny was going on, but they had no evidence, one way or another. The case, even at that point, might have ended with an acquittal or a hung jury, but Donnely wasn't through using his blackjack.

He took over the mind of the foreman of the jury. The foreman claimed later that the jury had decided that they could reach no decision. Other jurors claimed that they had decided Donnely was guilty, but that was probably an *ex post facto* switch. It didn't matter, anyway; when the foreman came out, he pronounced Donnely innocent. That should have ended it.

The other jurors began to protest, but by that time, Donnely had gained control of the judge's mind. Rapidly, the judge silenced the jurors, declared Donnely to be free, and then publicly apologized for ever daring to doubt Mr. Donnely.

The State's Attorney was equally verbose in his apology; he was almost in tears because of his "deep contrition at having cast aspersions on the spotless character of so great a man."

Donnely was released.

The next evening, "Blackjack" Donnely was shot down at the front door of his own home. There were fifteen bullets in his body; three from a .32, five from a .38, and seven from a .45.

The police investigation was far from thorough; any evidence that may have turned up somehow got lost. It was labelled as "homicide committed by person or persons unknown," and it stayed that way.

Donnely was only the first. In the next two years, four more showed up. Everyone of them, in one way or another, had attempted to gain power or money by mental projection. Everyone of them was a twisted megalomaniac.

Houston looked again at Harris's picture on the front page of the *Times*. Here was one Controller who neither looked nor acted like a megalomaniac. That wouldn't make much difference to the PD Police; as far as the officials were concerned, the ability to project telepathically and the taint of delusions of grandeur went hand in hand. Controllers were power-mad and criminal by definition.

Fear still ruled the emotional reactions against Controllers, in spite of the protection of the Psychodeviant Police.

But David Houston knew damned good and well that all telepaths were not necessarily insane.

He should know. He was a Controller, himself.

Brrrring!

David Houston tossed the paper on the bed and walked over to the phone. He cut in the circuit, and waited for the phone's TV screen to show the face of his caller. But the screen remained blank.

"Who is it?" Houston asked.

"Is this CHAring Cross 7-8161?" It was a woman's voice, soft and well-modulated.

"No, this is CHElsea 7-8161," Houston said. "You must have dialed C-H-E instead of C-H-A."

"Oh. I'm very sorry. Excuse me." There was a click, and she hung up.

Houston walked back over to the bed and picked up his paper. He looked at it, but he didn't read it. It no longer interested him.

So Dorrine was finally in London, eh? He'd recognized her voice instantly; even years of training couldn't smother the midwestern American of Chicago completely beneath the precise British of the well-educated English girl.

The signal had been agreed upon, just in case his phone was tapped. Even the Psychodeviant Police could be suspected of harboring a Controller—although Houston didn't think it too likely. Nevertheless, he wasn't one to take too many chances.

He glanced at his watch. He had an hour yet. He'd wait five minutes before he phoned headquarters.

He sat down in his chair again and forced himself to relax, smoke a cigarette, and read the paper—the sports section. Perusing the records of the season's cricket matches kept his mind off that picture on the front page. At least, he hoped they would. Let's see, now—Benton was being rated as the finest googly bowler on the Staffordshire Club ...

Everything went fine until he came across a reference to a John Harris, a top-flight batsman for Hambledon; that reminded him of Robert Harris. Houston threw down the paper in disgust and walked over to the phone.

The number was TROwbridge 5-4321, but no one ever bothered to remember it. Simply dial 8-7-6-5-4-3-2-1, and every time a voice at the other end would answer—

"Hamilton speaking."

"Houston here; will I be needed in the next hour or so?"

"Mmmm. Just a second; I'll check the roster. No; your evidence won't be needed personally. You've filed an affidavit. No, I don't think—wait a minute! Yes, there's a return here for you; reservation on the six A.M. jet to New York. Your job here is done, Houston, so you can take the rest of the evening off and relax. Going anywhere in particular?"

"I thought I'd get a bite to eat and take in a movie, maybe, but if I'm due out at six, I'll forego the cinematic diversion. When's the trial?"

"It's scheduled for eleven-thirty this evening. Going to come?"

Houston shook his head. "Not if I'm not needed to give evidence. Those Controllers always give me the creeps."

"They do everybody," said Hamilton. "Well, you caught him; there's no need for you to stick around for the windup. Have a good time."

"Thanks," said Houston shortly, and hung up.

The windup, Houston thought. *Sure. That's all it will be. A Controller's trial is a farce. Knock him out with a stun gun and then pump him full of comatol. How can he defend himself if he's unconscious all through the trial?*

Houston knew what the average man's answer to that would be: "If a Controller were allowed to remain conscious, he'd take over the judge's mind and get himself freed."

Houston said an obscene word under his breath, jammed his hat on his head, put on his coat, and left his apartment.

With the coming of darkness, the heavy fog had become still denser. The yellow beams of the sodium vapor lamps were simply golden spots hanging in an all-enveloping blackness. Walking the street was a process of moving from one little golden island of light to another, crossing seas of blankness between. The monochromatic yellow shone on the human faces that passed beneath the lamps, robbing them of all color, giving them a dead, grayish appearance beneath the yellow itself.

David Houston walked purposefully along the pavement, his hand jammed deep in his overcoat pockets. One hand held the control box for the little earpiece he wore. He kept moving the band selector, listening for any sign that the Psychodeviant Police were suspicious of a Controller in their midst.

If they were following him, of course, they would use a different scrambler circuit than the one which was plugged into his own unit, but he would be able to hear the gabble of voices, even if he couldn't understand what they were saying.

So far, there hadn't been a sound; if he was being followed, his tailers weren't using the personal intercom units.

He didn't try to elude anyone who might be following. That, in itself, would be a giveaway. Let them watch, if they *were* watching. They wouldn't see anything but a man going to get himself a bit of dinner.

The *Charles II Inn*, on Regent Street, near Piccadilly Circus, was a haven of brightness in an otherwise Stygian London. It was one of those "old-fashioned" places—Restoration style of decoration, carried out in modern plastics. The oak panelling looked authentic enough, but it was just a little too glossy to be real.

Houston pushed open the door, stepped inside, removed his hat and coat and shook the dampness from them. As he handed them to the checker, he looked casually around. Dorrine was nowhere in sight, but he hadn't expected her to be. There would be no point in their meeting physically; it might even be downright dangerous.

The headwaiter, clad in the long waistcoat and full trunk-hose of the late Seventeenth Century, bowed punctiliously.

"You're alone, sir?"

"Alone, yes," Houston said. "I'll just be wanting a light supper and a drink or two."

"This way, sir."

Houston followed the man to a small table in the rear of the huge dining room. It was set for two, but the other place was quickly cleared away. Houston ordered an Irish-and-soda from a waiter who was only slightly less elaborately dressed than the headwaiter, and then settled himself down to wait. If he knew Dorrine, she would be on time to the minute.

She came while the waiter was setting the drink on Houston's table. She stepped in through the door, her unmistakable hair glowing a rich red in the illumination of the pseudo-candlelight.

She didn't bother to look around; she knew he would be there.

After a single glance, Houston averted his eyes from her and looked back at his drink.

And in that same instant, their minds touched.

Dave, darling! I knew you'd be early!

Dorrine!

And then their minds meshed for an instant.

I—(we)—you—LOVE—you—(each other)—me!—us!

Houston looked complacently at his drink while the headwaiter led Dorrine to a table on the far side of the room. She sat down gracefully, smiled at the waiter, and ordered a cocktail. Then she took a magazine from her handbag and began—presumably—to read.

Her thought came: *Who is this Richard Harris? He's not one of our Group.*

Houston sipped at his drink. *No. An unknown, like the others. I wonder if he's even a telepath.*

What? Her thought carried astonishment. *Why, Dave—he'd* have *to be! How else could he have controlled this Sir Lewis—whatsisname—Huntley?*

Well—I've got a funny idea, Houston replied. *Look at it this way: So far as we know, there are two Groups of telepaths. There's our own Group. All we want is to be left alone. We don't read a Normal's mind unless we have to, and we don't try to control one unless our lives are threatened. We stay under cover, out of everyone's way.*

Then there are the megalomaniacs. They try, presumably, to gain wealth and power by controlling Normals. And they get caught with monotonous regularity. Right?

The girl caught an odd note in that thought. *What do you mean, "monotonous regularity"?* she asked.

I mean, Houston thought savagely, *why is it they're all so bloody stupid? Look at this Harris guy; he is supposed to have taken over Sir Lewis's mind in order to get a thousand pounds. So what did he have Sir Lewis do? Parade all around the city to pick up a PD Police net, and then give his address to a cabman in a loud voice and lead the whole net right to Harris! How stupid can a man get?*

It does look pretty silly, Dorrine agreed. *Have you got an explanation?*

Several, Houston told her. *And I don't know which one is correct.*

Let's have them, the girl thought.

Houston gave them to her. None of them, he knew, was completely satisfactory, but they all made more sense that the theory that Harris had done what the PD Police claimed he'd done.

Theory Number One: The real megalomaniac Controller had taken over Sir Lewis's mind and made him draw out the thousand pounds and head west on Leadenhall Street. Somehow, the Controller had found out that Sir Lewis was being followed, and had steered him away from the original destination, heading him toward the innocent Robert Harris. That implied that the Controller had been within a few dozen yards of the net men that afternoon. A Controller can't control a mind directly from a distance, although orders can be implanted which will cause a man to carry out a plan of action, even though he may be miles from the Controller. But in order to change those plans, the Controller would have to be within projection range.

Theory Two: Robert Harris actually was a megalomaniac Controller; with a long record of success behind him, who had finally grown careless.

At that point, Dorrine interjected a thought: *Isn't it possible that he wanted to be caught?*

Houston mulled it over for a minute. *A guilt-punishment reaction? He wanted to be punished for his crimes? I suppose that might account for part of it, yes. But if he'd been so successful, what did he do with all his money?*

Dorrine gave a mental shrug. *Who knows? What's Theory Number Three?*

Number Three was the screwiest one of all, yet it made a weird kind of sense. Suppose that Sir Lewis himself had had a grudge against Harris? The whole thing would have been ridiculously easy; all he'd have to do would be to act just as he had acted and then give evidence against Harris.

The thing that made it odd wasn't the actual frame-up (if that's what it was); these days, every crime was blamed on a Controller. A man accused of murder simply looked virtuous and said that he would never have done such a thing if he hadn't been under the power of a Controller. Ditto for robbery, rape, and any other felony you'd care to name.

An aura of fear hung over the whole Earth; each man half suspected everyone with whom he came in contact of being a Controller.

So it wasn't that the frame-up in itself was peculiar in this case; it was simply that it wasn't Sir Lewis Huntley's style. If Sir Lewis had wanted to get Harris, he'd have done it legally, without any underhanded frame-ups. Still, the theory remained as a possibility.

I suppose it does, Dorrine agreed, *but how does that tie in with our own Group? What about Jackson and Marcy? What happened to them?*

I don't know, Houston admitted, *I just don't know*.

Jackson and Marcy had been members of the Group of telepaths who had banded together for companionship and mutual protection. Both of them had been trapped by the PD Police in exactly the same way that Harris had been trapped. They were now where Harris would be in a matter of hours—in the Penal Cluster.

Their arrests didn't make sense, either; they had been accused of taking over someone's mind for the purpose of gaining money illegally—illegal, that is, according to the new UN laws that had been passed to supersede the various national laws that had previously been in effect.

But Houston had known both men well, and neither of them was the kind of man who would pull such a stunt, much less do it in such a stupid manner.

Dorrine thought: *Well, Dave, this Harris case is out of our hands now; we've got to concentrate on getting others into the Group—we've got to find the other sane ones.*

You're ready to take over here, then? he asked.

At the table, several yards away from where Houston was sitting, Dorrine, still looking at the book, smiled faintly.

I'll have to; you're being transferred back to New York at six in the morning.

Houston allowed a feeling of startled surprise to bridge the gap between their minds. *How'd you know that?* He hadn't told her, and she couldn't have forced the knowledge from his mind. A telepath can open the mind of a Normal as simply as he might open the pages of a book, but the mind of another Controller is far stronger. One telepath couldn't force anything from the mind of another; all thoughts had to be exchanged voluntarily.

She was still smiling. *We've got a few spies in the UN now*, she told him. *I got the information before you did.*

You knew before you left New York? he asked incredulously.

That's right, she thought. *The decision was made last night. Why?*

Nothing, he told her. *I was just surprised, that's all.* But deep behind the telepathic barrier he had erected against her probing mind, he was thinking something else. He had been assigned to London to capture the Controller—then unknown—who was said to be active in England. But his recall order had been decided upon *before* Harris was caught—or even suspected. Someone in the UN Psychodeviant Police Supreme Headquarters in New York must have known that Harris would be caught that day!

Something's bothering you, Dorrine stated flatly.

I was thinking about leaving London, he replied evasively. *I haven't seen you for six months, and now I have to leave again.*

I'll be back in New York within three weeks, the girl thought warmly. *I'll be—*

Her thoughts were cut off suddenly by a strident voice in Houston's ear. "Attention; all-band notice. Robert Bentley Harris, arraigned this evening on a charge of illegal use of psychodeviant powers for the purpose of compounding a felony, has been found guilty as charged. He was therefore sentenced by the Lord Justice of Her Majesty's Court of Star Chamber to be banished from Earth forever, such banishment to be carried out by the United Nations Penology Service at the Queen's pleasure."

The words that were running through Houston's brain, had been transmitted easily to Dorrine. For a moment, neither of them made any comment. Then Houston glanced at his watch.

Twenty-one minutes, he thought bitterly. *What took them so long?*

High in the thin ionosphere, seventy miles above the surface of the Earth, a fifteen-hundred-mile-an-hour rocket airliner winged its way westward across the Atlantic, pushing herself forward on the thin, whispering, white-hot jets of her atomic engine. Behind her, the outdistanced sun sank slowly below the eastern horizon.

David Houston wasn't watching the sunrise-in-reverse; he was sitting quietly in his seat, still trying to puzzle out his queer recall to New York. When Hamilton had told him about it over the phone, he'd assumed that New York, having been notified that Harris had been captured, had decided to send for Houston, now that his job was over.

But now he knew that the order had come through nearly twenty-four hours before Harris was captured.

Did someone at UN Headquarters know that Harris was going to be captured? Or did someone there suspect that there was something odd about Police Operative David Houston?

Or both?

Whatever it was, Houston would have to take his chances; to act suspiciously would be a deadly mistake.

A stewardess, clad in the chic BOAC uniform, moved down the aisle, quietly informing the passengers that they could have coffee served at their seats or take breakfast in the lounge. The atmosphere of the plane's interior was filled with the low murmur of a hundred conversations against the background of the susurrant mutter of the mighty engines.

Uhhh—uh—uh—dizzy—head hurts—uh—uh—

The sounds in the plane altered subtly as the faint thought insinuated itself on every brain inside the aircraft. None of the Normal passengers recognized it for what it was; it was too gentle, too weak, to be recognized directly by their minds.

But David Houston recognized it instantly for what it was.

Somewhere on the plane, a Controller had been unconscious. *Had* been. For now, his powerful mind was trying to swim up from the black depths of nothingness.

Uh—uhhhh—uhh—

The Normal passengers became uneasy, not knowing why they were disturbed. To them, it was like a vaguely unpleasant but totally unrecognizable nudge from their own subconscious, like some long-forgotten and deeply buried memory that had been forced down into oblivion and was now trying to obtrude itself on the conscious mind.

Uhhh—Oooohh—where?—what happened?—

A fully conscious telepath could project his thoughts along a narrow locus, focusing them on a single brain, leaving all other brains oblivious to his thoughts. Like a TV broadcasting station, he could choose his wavelength and stick to it.

But a half-conscious Controller sprayed his thoughts at random, creating mental disturbances in his vicinity. Like a thunderstorm creating radio static, there was no selectivity.

Savagely, David Houston did what he had to do. It might be a trap, but he had to avoid the carnage that might follow if this went on. He hurled a beam of thought, hard-held, at the offending mind of the awakening telepath.

DON'T THINK! RELAX!

Normally it was impossible for a Controller to take over the mind of another Controller, but these were abnormal circumstances; the half-conscious man, whoever he was, was weakened mentally by some kind of enforced unconsciousness—either a drug or a stun gun. Houston took over his mind smoothly and easily.

Robert Harris!

Houston recognized the mind as soon as he held it.

He didn't try to force anything on Harris's mind; he simply held it, cradling it, helping Harris to regain consciousness easily, bringing him up from the darkness gently.

In normal sleep, everyone's mind retains a certain amount of self-control and awareness of environment. If it didn't, noise and bright lights wouldn't awaken a sleeping person.

In normal sleep, a telepath retained enough control to keep his thoughts to himself, even when waking up.

But total anaesthesia brought on a mental blackout from which the victim recovered only with effort. And during that time, a Controller's mind was violently disturbing to the Normal minds around him, who mistook his disordered thoughts for their own.

Like pouring heavy oil on choppy waters, Houston soothed the disturbances of Harris's mind, focusing the random broadcasts on his own brain.

And while he did that, he probed gently into the weakened mind of the prisoner for information.

Harris was a Controller, all right; there was no doubt about that. But nowhere in his mind was there any trace of any knowledge of what had happened to Sir Lewis Huntley. If Sir Lewis had actually been controlled, it hadn't been done by Robert Harris.

Houston wished he'd been able to probe Sir Lewis's mind; he'd have been able to get a lot more information out of it than he had in his possession now. But that would have been dangerous; if Sir Lewis was a Controller himself, and had been acting a part, Houston would have given himself away the instant he attempted to touch the baronet's mind. If, on the other hand, Sir Lewis had actually been under the control of another telepath, any probing into the mind of the puppet would have betrayed Houston to the real Controller.

Harris knew nothing. He wasn't acquainted with any other Controllers, and had kept his nose clean ever since he'd discovered his latent powers. He knew that megalomaniac Controllers were either captured or mobbed, and he had no wish to experience either.

The Normals had long since discovered that the only way to overcome a Controller was by force of numbers. A Controller could only hold one Normal mind at a time. That was why a mob could easily kill a single Controller; that was why the Psychodeviant Police had evolved the "net" system for arresting a telepath.

Harris, then, had been framed. Or could it be called a frame-up when Harris was really guilty of the actual crime? Because the crime he had really been accused of was not that of controlling Sir Lewis, but the crime of being a telepath. That, and that alone, damned him in the eyes of the Normals; the crime of taking over a mind for gain was incidental. The stigma lies in what he *was*, not what he did.

Harris himself was in the bottom of the plane, in the baggage section near the landing gear. After his trial, still drugged, he had been secretly put aboard, to be taken to the Long Island Spaceport in New York. It had had to be secret; no Normal would knowingly ride on an aircraft which carried a Controller, even if he were drugged into total unconsciousness.

With Harris were two PD Police guards. Their low conversation impinged on Harris's ears, and was transmitted to Houston's mind.

Suddenly, one of them said: "Hey! He's moving!"

"Better give him another shot, Harry;" said the other, "when those guys wake up, they drive you crazy."

Houston could almost feel the sting of the needle as it was inserted into the arm of the helpless prisoner.

Slowly, Harris's thoughts, which had begun to become fully coherent, again became chaotic, finally sliding off into silence and darkness.

"Are you all right, sir?"

Houston looked up from his intense concentration. The stewardess was standing by his seat. He realized that there was a film of perspiration on his brow, and that he probably had looked dazed while he was concentrating on Harris's mind.

"Sure," he said quickly, "I'm all right. I'm just a little tired. Had to get up too early to catch this plane." He rubbed his forehead. "I do have a little headache; would you happen to have any aspirin aboard?"

She smiled professionally. "Certainly, sir. I'll get a couple of tablets."

As she left for the first-aid cabinet, Houston thought bleakly to himself: *Harris was framed. Possibly others have been, too. But by whom? And why?*

He could see why a Normal might do such a thing. But why would a Controller do it?

There was only one answer. Somewhere, there was a Controller, or a group of Controllers who were megalomaniacs *par excellence*. If that were so, he—or they—could make the late "Blackjack" Donnely look like a meek, harmless, little mouse.

The one part of Continental U.S.A. over which the American Government had no jurisdiction was small, areawise, in comparison with its power. The District of the United Nations occupied the small area of Manhattan Island which ran from 38th Street on the south to 49th Street on the north; its western border was Third Avenue, its eastern, the East River. From here, the UN ruled Earth.

There were no walls or fences around it; only by looking at street signs could anyone tell that they had crossed an international border. Crossing Third Avenue from west to east, one found that 45th Street had suddenly become Deutschland Strasse; 40th Street became Rue de France; 47th was the Via Italiano. 43rd Street's sign was painted in Cyrillic characters, but beneath it, in English, were the words "Avenue of Mother Russia."

Third Avenue was technically One World Drive. Second Avenue was labelled as Planetary Peace Drive, and First was United Nations Drive.

But New Yorkers are, and always have been, diehards. Just as The Avenue of the Americas had forever remained Sixth Avenue, no matter what the maps called it, so had the other streets retained their old names in conversation.

Even the International Post Office, after years of wrangling, had given up, and letters addressed to *Supreme Headquarters, United Nations Police, 45th Street at Second Avenue*, were delivered without comment, even though the IPO still firmly held that they were technically misaddressed. And, privately, even the IPO officials admitted that the numbers were easier to say and remember than the polyglot street names that had been tagged on by the General Assembly.

So when David Houston signalled a taxi at Grand Central Station and said, "Forty-fifth and Second," the driver simply set his automatic controls, leaned back in his seat, and said, "Goin' to see the cops, huh?"

When no answer was forthcoming, the driver turned around and took a good look at his passenger. "Maybe you're a UN cop yourself, huh?"

Houston shook his head. "Nope. Some kids have been scribbling dirty words on my sidewalk, and I'm going to report it to the authorities."

The driver turned back around and looked ahead again. "Jeez! That's serious. Hadn't you better take it up with the Secretary General? I wouldn't be satisfied with no underlings in a case like that."

"I'm thinking of taking it up with the Atomic Energy Control Board," Houston told him. "I think those kids are using radioactive chalk."

"That's one way for 'em to get blue jeans," said the driver cryptically.

There was silence for a moment as the taxi braked smoothly to a halt, guided and controlled by the automatic machinery in the hood.

Then, suddenly, the driver said: "Ship up!" He pointed east, along 45th Street, toward Long Island. Far in the distance was a rapidly rising vapor trail, pointing vertically toward the sky, the unmistakable sign of a spaceship takeoff. They didn't leave often, and it was still an unusual sight.

Houston said nothing as he climbed out and paid the driver, tossing in an extra tip.

"Thanks, buddy," said the driver. "Watch out for them kids."

Houston didn't answer. He was still watching the vapor trail as the cab pulled away.

There goes Harris, he was thinking. *An innocent man, guilty of nothing more than being born different. And because of that, he's labelled as an inhuman monster, not even worthy of being executed. Instead, he's taken into space, filled full of hibernene, and chained to a floating piece of rock for the rest of his life.*

Such was humanity's "humane" way of taking care of the bogey of Controllers. Capital punishment had been outlawed all over Earth; it had long since been proved that legalized murder, execution by the State, solved nothing, helped no one, prevented no crimes, and did infinitely more harm than good in the long run.

With the coming of the Controllers, a movement had arisen to bring back the old evil of judicial murder, but it had been quickly put down when the Penal Cluster plan had been put forth as a more "humane" method.

Hibernene was a drug that had been evolved from the study of animals like the bear, which spent its winters in an almost death-like sleep. A human being, given a proper dosage of the drug, lapsed into a deep coma. The bodily processes were slowed down; the heart throbbed sluggishly, once every few minutes; thought ceased. It was the ideal prison for a mental offender that ordinary prisons could not hold.

But it wasn't quite enough for the bloodthirsty desire for vengeance that the Normals held for the Controllers. There had to be more.

Following Earth in its orbit around the sun, trailing it by some ninety-three million miles, were a group of tiny asteroids, occupying what is known as the Trojan position. They were invisible from Earth, being made of dark rock and none of them being more than fifteen feet in diameter. But they had been a source of trouble in some of the early expeditions to Mars, and had been carefully charted by the Space Commission.

Now a use had been found for them. A man in a spacesuit could easily be chained to one of them. With him was a small, sun-powered engine and tanks of liquified food concentrates and oxygen. Kept under the influence of hibernene, and kept cool by the chill of space, a man could spend the rest of his life there—unmoving, unknowing, uncaring, dead as far as he and the rest of Mankind were concerned—his slight bodily needs tended automatically by machine.

It was a punishment that satisfied both sides of the life-or-death argument.

Houston shook off the bleak, black feeling of terrible chill that had crept over him and pushed his way into the UN Police building.

The thirteenth floor housed the Psychodeviant Division. As he stood in the rising elevator, Houston wondered wryly if the number 13 was good luck or bad in this case.

He stepped out of the elevator and headed for the Division Chief's office.

Division Chief Reinhardt was a heavy-set, balding man, built like a professional wrestler. His cold blue eyes gleamed from beneath shaggy, overhanging brows, and his face was almost expressionless except for a faint scowl that crossed it from time to time. In spite of the fact that a Canadian education had wiped out all but the barest trace of German accent, his Prussian training, of the old Junkers school, was still evident. He demanded—and got—precision and obedience from his subordinates, although he had no use for the strictly military viewpoint of obsequiousness towards one's superiors.

He was sitting behind his desk, scowling slightly at some papers on it when Houston stepped in.

"You wanted me to report straight to you, Mr. Reinhardt?"

Reinhardt looked up, his heavy face becoming expressionless. "Ah, Houston. Yes; sit down. You did a fine job on that London affair; that's what I call coming through at the last moment."

"How so?"

"Your orders to return," he said, "were cut before you found your man. We have a much more important case for you than some petty pilfering Controller. We are after much more dangerous game."

Houston nodded. "I see." Inwardly, he wondered. It was almost as if Reinhardt knew that Houston had found out that the recall had come early. Houston would have given his right arm at that moment to be able to probe Reinhardt's mind. But he held himself back. He had, in the past, sent tentative probes toward the Division Chief and found nothing, but he didn't know whether it would be safe now or not. It would be better to wait.

Reinhardt stood up, walked to the wall, and turned on a display screen. He twisted a knob to a certain setting, and a map of Manhattan Island sprang onto the screen in glowing color.

"As you know," Reinhardt said pedantically, "no Controller can do a perfect job of controlling a normal person. No matter how much he may want to make John Smith act naturally, some of the personality of the Controller will show up in the actions of John Smith. Am I correct?"

Houston nodded without saying anything. The question was purely rhetorical, and the statement was perfectly correct.

"Very well, then," Reinhardt continued, "by means of these peculiarities, our psychologists have found that there is widespread, but very subtle controlling going on right in the UN General Assembly itself! The amazing thing is that they all bear the—shall we say—trademark of the same Controller. Whoever he is, he seems to have a long-range plan in mind; he wants to change, ever so slightly, certain international laws so that he will profit by them. Do you follow?"

"I follow," said Houston.

"Good. It has taken painstaking research and a great deal of psychological statistical analysis, but we have found that one company—and one company only—benefits by these legal changes. Did you ever hear of Lasser & Sons?"

"Sure," said Houston. "They're in the import-export business, with a few fingers in shipping and air transport."

"That's them," said Reinhardt. "Someone in that company, presumably someone at the top, is a Controller. And he's a very subtle, very dangerous man. Unlike the others, there is nothing hasty or overt in his plans. But within a few years, if this goes on, he will have more power than the others ever dreamed of."

"And my job is to get him?" Houston asked.

Reinhardt nodded. "That's it. Get him. One way or another. You're in charge; I don't care how you do it, but this one Controller is more dangerous than any other we've come across, so get him."

Houston nodded slowly. "Okay. Can you give me all the data you have so far?"

Reinhardt patted a heavy folder on his desk. "It's all here." Then he tapped the projected map on the screen. "That's the Lasser Building—Church Street at Worth. Somewhere in there is the man we're looking for."

David Houston spent the next six weeks gathering facts, trying to determine the identity of the mysterious Controller at Lasser & Sons. Slowly, the evidence began to pile up.

At the same time, he worried over his own problem. Who was betraying non-criminal Controllers to the PD Police?

In that six-week period, two more men and a woman were arrested—one in Spain, one in India, and one in Hawaii.

There weren't very many Controllers on Earth, percentagewise. Of the three and a half billion people on Earth, less than an estimated one-thousandth of one percent were telepathic. But that made a grand total of some thirty-five thousand people.

Spread, as they were, all over the planet, it was rare that one Controller ever met another. The intelligent ones didn't use their power; they remained concealed, even from each other.

But *someone*, somewhere, was finding them and betraying them to the Psychodeviant Police.

As more and more data came in on the Lasser case, Houston began to get an idea. If there were a really clever, highly intelligent, megalomaniac Controller, wouldn't it be part of his psychological pattern to attempt to get rid of the majority of Controllers, those who simply wanted to lead normal lives?

And, if so, wasn't it possible that both his cases—the official and the unofficial—might lead to the same place: Lasser & Sons?

It began to look as though Houston could kill both his birds at once, if he could just figure out when, how, and in what direction to throw the stone.

In the middle of the seventh week, a Controller in Manchester, England, was mobbed and torn to bits by an irate crowd before the PD Police could get to him. There was no doubt in Houston's mind that this one was a real megalomaniac; he had taken over another man's brain and forced him to commit suicide. The controlled man had taken a Webley automatic, put it to his temple, and blown his brains out.

The Controller's mistake was in not realizing what the sudden shock of that bullet, transmitted to him telepathically, could do to his own mind. In the mental disorder that followed, he was spotted and killed easily.

There was still no word from Dorrine. She had flown back to the States a week after Houston had returned, but she had had to get back to England after three days. Since then, he had had three letters, nothing more. And letters are a damned unsatisfactory way for a telepath to conduct a love affair.

The one other factor that entered in was The Group, the small band of sane, reasonable telepaths who had begun to build themselves into an organization—a sort of Mutual Protective Association.

Personally, Houston didn't think much of the idea; the Group didn't have any real organization, and they refused to put one together. It was supposed to be democratic, but it sometimes bordered on the anarchic.

He stayed with them more for companionship than any other reason. When Dorrine had come back for her short stay, Houston had met with them and tried to get them to help him trace down the megalomaniac Controller who was doing so much damage, but they'd balked at the idea. Their job, they claimed, was to get enough members so that they could protect themselves from arrest by the Normals, and then just let things ride.

"After all," Dorrine had said, "things will work themselves out, darling; they always do."

"Not unless somebody helps them, they don't," Houston had snapped back. "Someone has to do something."

"But, Dave, darling—we *are* doing something! Don't you see?"

He didn't, but there was no convincing either the Group or Dorrine. She was passionately interested in the recruiting work she was doing, and she thought that the Group was the answer to every Controller's troubles.

And then she had rushed back to England. "I'll be back soon, Dave," she'd said. "I think I have a lead on a girl in Liverpool."

So far, the girl hadn't been found. Controllers didn't like to give themselves away to anyone, so they kept a tight screen up most of the time.

It seemed as though everyone on Earth was in deadly fear all the time. The Normals feared losing their identities to Controllers, and the Controllers feared death at the hands of the Normals.

And death or the Penal Cluster were their only choices if they were discovered.

Houston worried about the risks Dorrine was taking, but there was nothing he could do. She was doing what she thought was right, just as he was; how could he argue with that?

Houston went on with his job, putting together facts and rumors and statistical data analysis, searching out his quarry.

And, at the end of the eighth week, everything blew high, wide, and hellish.

It was late evening. A cool wind blew over New York, bringing with it a hint of the rain to come. Church Street, in lower Manhattan, was not crowded, as it had been in the late afternoon, but neither was it entirely deserted. The cafes and bars did a lively business, but the tall, many-colored office buildings gaped at the street with blind and darkened eyes. Only a few of the windows glowed whitely with fluorescent illumination.

In one of the small coffee shops, David Houston sat, smoking a cigarette and stirring idly at a cup of cooling coffee.

Across the street was the Lasser Building; high up on the sixtieth floor, a whole suite of offices was brightly lit. The rest of the building was clothed in blackness.

Who was up there in that suite? Houston wasn't quite sure. He had narrowed his list of suspects down to three men: John Sager, Loris Pederson, and Norcross Lasser, three top officials in the company. Sager and Pederson were both vice-presidents of the firm; Sager was in charge of the Foreign Exports department, while Pederson handled the actual shipping. Lasser, by virtue of being the grandson of the man who had founded the firm, was president of Lasser & Sons, Inc.

Lasser seemed like a poor choice as chief villain of the outfit; he was a mild, bland man, quiet and friendly. Besides, his position made him an obvious suspect; naturally, the majority stockholder of the firm would profit most by the increased power of the company. And, equally obviously, a Controller wouldn't want to put himself in such an exposed position.

Which made Lasser, in Houston's mind, a hell of a good suspect. If anything happened, Lasser could cover by claiming that he, too, had been controlled, and the chances were that he could get away with it. A Controller never did anything directly; their dirty work was done by someone else—a puppet under their mental control. At least, so ran the popular misconception. If Lasser were the man, he stood a good chance of getting away with it, even if he were caught, provided he played his cards right.

That reasoning still didn't eliminate Sager or Pederson. Either of them could be the Controller. And there still remained the possibility that some unknown, unsuspected fourth person had the company of Lasser & Sons under his thumb.

That was what Houston intended to find out tonight.

He took a sip of his coffee, found it still reasonably hot.

Damn the megalomaniacs, anyway! Houston subconsciously tightened his fists. He, personally, had more to fear from the Normals than from another Controller. Normals could kill or imprison him, while a Controller would have a hard time doing either, directly.

But Houston could understand the Normal man; he could see how fear of a Controller could drive a man without the ability into a frenzied panic. He could understand, even forgive their actions, born and bred in ignorance and fear.

No, the ones he hated were the ones who had conceived and fostered that fear—the psychologically unstable megalomaniac Controllers. There were only a handful of them—probably not more than a few hundred or a thousand. But because of them, every telepath on Earth found his life in danger, and every Normal found his life a hell of terror.

Let Dorrine and her do-nothing friends run around the globe recruiting members for their precious Group; that was all right for them. Meanwhile, David Houston would be doing something on a more basic action level.

He glanced at his watch. Almost time.

"How's the deployment?" he whispered in his throat.

"We've got the building surrounded now," said the voice in his ear. "You can go in anytime."

"How about the roof?"

"That's taken care of, sir; we've got 'copter that can be on the top of the Lasser Building at any time you call. They can land within thirty seconds of your signal."

"Okay," Houston said; "I'm going in now. Remember—no matter what I say or do, no one is to leave that building if they're conscious. And keep your eyes on me; if I act in the least peculiar, handcuff me—but don't knock me out."

"And if I'm not back on time, come in anyway."

"Right."

Houston finished his coffee, dropped a coin on the counter, and headed for the other side of the street.

The big problem was getting into the building itself. It was ringed with alarms; Lasser & Sons didn't want just anybody wandering in and out of their building.

So Houston had arranged a roundabout way. The building next to the Lasser Building was a good deal smaller, only forty-five stories high. A week before, Houston had rented an office on the eighteenth floor of the building; on the door, he had already had a sign engraved: Ajax Enterprises.

It was a shame the office would never be used.

Houston walked straight to the next-door building and opened the front door with his key. Inside, a night watchman lounged behind a desk, smoking a blackened briar. He looked up, smiled, and nodded.

"Evening, Mr. Griswold; working late tonight?"

Houston forced a smile he did not feel. "Just doing a little paper work," he said.

He took the automatic elevator to the eighteenth floor. He didn't relish the idea of walking up to the roof, but taking the elevator would make the nightwatchman suspicious.

He didn't bother going to the office; he headed directly for the stairway and began his long climb—twenty-seven floors to the roof.

All through it, he kept up a running comment through his throat mike. "I wish I weighed about fifty pounds less; carrying two hundred and twenty pounds of blubber up these stairs isn't easy."

"Blubber, hooey!" the earphone interrupted. "Any man who's six-feet-three has a right to carry that much weight. Actually, you're a skinny-looking sort of goop."

Both men were exaggerating; Houston wasn't fat, but his broad, powerful frame couldn't be called skinny, either.

When he finally reached the roof, he paused and surveyed the wall of the Lasser Building, which towered high above him, spearing an additional thirty stories in the air. Up there, the lights on the sixtieth floor gleamed in the night.

The air was growing cooler, and the beginnings of a mist were forming. Houston hoped it wouldn't start to rain before he got inside.

The forty-sixth floor of the Lasser Building had no windows on this side, but there were plenty on the forty-seventh.

Leading up to them was an inviting looking fire escape, but Houston knew he didn't dare take that. By law, every fire escape was rigged with a fire alarm, in addition to the regular burglar alarm. He'd have to use another way.

The Lasser Building was a steel structure, shelled over with a bright blue anodized aluminum sheath. Only the day before, Houston, wearing the gray coverall of a power-line workman, had checked the wall to find the big steel beams beneath the aluminum. He had also installed certain other equipment; now he was going to make use of it.

Concealed in the louvres of the air-conditioner intake of the lower building was a specially constructed suit and several hundred feet of power line which was connected to the main line of the building.

In the darkness, Houston slipped on the suit. It was constructed somewhat like a light diving suit or a spacesuit, but without the helmet. In the toes, knees, and hands, were powerful electromagnets controlled by switches in the fingers of the gloves and powered by the current in the long line.

Houston stepped over to the blue aluminum wall, reached out a hand, and lowered one finger. Instantly, the powerful magnet anchored his hand to the wall, held by the dense magnetic field to the steel beam beneath the aluminum sheath. That one magnet alone could support his full body weight, and he had six magnets to work with.

Slowly, carefully, David Houston began to crawl up the wall.

Turn on a magnet in the right hand; lift up the left hand and anchor it higher; turn on the right hand and lift it even with the left, then anchor it again; do the same with both legs; then begin the process all over again, turning the magnets off and on in rotation.

Up and up he went. Past the forty-sixth floor, past the forty-seventh, the forty-eighth, and the forty-ninth. Not until he reached the fiftieth floor did he attempt to open one of the windows.

There was a magnetic lock inside the window, but Houston had taken that, too, into account. The powerful magnet in his right glove slid it aside easily. Houston lifted the window and stepped inside.

He had ten more floors to go.

He took off the suit and rolled it up into a tight package, then dropped it out the window. It landed with a barely audible thump. Houston took a deep breath, drew his stun gun, and headed for the stairway.

On the landing of the sixtieth floor of the Lasser Building, David Houston paused for a moment.

"Sounds like you're out of breath," said the voice in his ear.

"You try climbing all that way sometime," Houston whispered. "I'm no superman, you know."

"Shucks," said the voice, "you've disillusioned me. What now?"

"I'm going to try to get a little information," Houston told him. "Hold on."

On the other side of the door, he could hear faint sound, as if someone were moving around, but he could hear no voices.

Carefully, he sent out a probing thought, trying to see if he could attune his mind with that of someone inside without betraying himself.

He couldn't detect anything. The sixtieth floor covered a lot of space; if whoever was inside was too far away, their thoughts would be too faint to pick up unless Houston stepped up his own power, and he didn't want to do that.

Cautiously, he reached out a hand and eased open the door.

The hallway was brightly lit, but there was no one in sight. The unaccustomed light made Houston blink for a moment before his eyes adjusted to it; the hallways and landings below had been pitch dark, forcing him to use a penlight to find his way up.

He stepped into the hallway, closing the door behind him.

Now he could hear voices. He stopped to listen. The conversation was coming from an office down the hall—if it could be called a conversation.

There would be long periods of silence, then a word or two: "But not that way." "Until tomorrow." "Vacillates."

There were three different voices.

Houston moved on down the hall, his stun gun ready. A few yards from the door, he stopped again, and, very gently, he sent out another thought-probe, searching for the minds of those within, carefully forging his way.

And, at that crucial instant, a voice spoke in his ear.

"Houston! What's going on? You haven't said a thing for two full minutes!"

"I'm all right!" Houston snapped. Only the force of long training and habit kept him from shouting the words aloud instead of keeping them to a subvocal whisper.

"All right or not," said the other, "we're coming in in seven minutes, as ordered. Meanwhile, there's a news bulletin for you; the British division has picked up another Controller—a woman named Dorrine Kent. Two in one night ought to be a pretty good bag."

For a moment, Houston's mind was a meaningless blur.

Dorrine!

And then another voice broke through his shock.

"Dear me, sir! Calm yourself! You're positively fizzing!"

Houston jerked. Standing in the doorway of the office was Norcross Lasser, with a benign smile on his face and a deadly-looking .38 automatic in his hand. Behind him stood John Sager and Loris Pederson, their faces wary.

"Please drop that stun gun, Mr. Cop."

In those few moments, Houston had regained control of himself. He realized what had happened. The interruption of his thought-probe had startled him just a little, but that little had been enough to warn the Controller.

He wondered which of the three men was the actual Controller.

He began to lower his weapon, then, suddenly, with all the force and hatred he could muster, he sent a blistering, shocking thought toward the man with the gun.

Lasser staggered as though he'd been struck. His gun wavered, and Houston fired quickly with his stun gun. At the same time, Lasser's automatic went off.

The bullet went wild, and the stun beam didn't do much better. It struck Lasser's hand, paralyzing it, but it didn't knock out Lasser.

The mental battle that ensued only took a half second, but at the speed of thought, a lot of things can happen in a half second.

Houston realized almost instantaneously that he had made a vast mistake. He had badly underestimated the enemy.

There was no need to worry, now, about which one of the men was a Controller—*all three of them were!*

As soon as Sager and Pederson realized what had happened, they leaped—mentally—into the battle. Lasser, already weakened by the unexpected mental blow from Houston, lost consciousness when the others let loose their blasts because his mind was still linked with Houston's, and he absorbed a great deal of the mental energy meant for Houston's brain.

Houston, fully warned by now, held up a denial wall which screened his mind from the worst that Sager and Pederson could put out, but he knew he couldn't hold out for long.

"Come in—*now!*" he said hoarsely into the microphone.

"Stupid swine!" Sager susurrated sibilantly.

Pederson said nothing aloud, but his brain was blazing with fear and hatred. His gun hand jerked towards a holster under his arm. Lasser was still crumpling towards the floor.

The entire action had taken less than a second.

Houston tried to fire again with his stun gun, but it required every bit of concentration he could sum up to hold off the combined mental assaults of Sager and Pederson.

But they, too, were at somewhat of a disadvantage. In order to keep all their efforts concentrated on the PD policeman, both Controllers had to refrain from putting too much attention on their bodily motions. Pederson was still fumbling for his gun, and Sager hadn't yet started for his.

Lasser barely touched the floor before his consciousness began to return. The resulting fraction of a second of mental static afforded Houston a brief respite; it disturbed Pederson just as he was getting his fingers on the butt of his weapon.

Both Controllers were focusing their mental energies on Houston's brain, and during the brief respite, Houston made one vital mental adjustment. He allowed both thought-probes to fuse in a small part of his consciousness. They went *through* him and lashed back at the two Controllers.

Both of them had had their minds tuned to Houston's, and in that instant they found they, were also attuned to each other.

The resultant of the energy was shocking to Houston, but it was infinitely worse for Sager and Pederson, since neither of them had been expecting it. Pederson, who had already been slightly distracted, got the major brunt of the force. He managed to jerk his gun free, but his brain was already lapsing into unconsciousness.

Houston's fingers tightened on his own weapon. It fired once at Lasser, who was trying to lift himself from the floor. Then it swept up and coughed again, dropping Pederson. His pistol barked once, sending a singing ricochet along the hall.

Sager, who had staggered to one side when he and Pederson had short-circuited each other, had time to get behind the protection of the office door. He couldn't close it because Lasser's and Pederson's inert forms blocked the doorway, but at least it afforded protection against Houston's stun gun.

His thought came through to Houston: *So the stupid Normals have a Controller working for them! Traitor!*

You're the traitor, Houston thought coldly. *You and your megalomaniac friends. It's madmen like you who have made telepaths hated and feared by the Normals.*

And so they should hate and fear us, came the snarling mental answer. *Within a few generations, we will have supplanted them. We will control Earth—not they.*

The exchange had only taken a fraction of a second. Houston was already charging toward the open door, hoping to get inside before Sager could reach a weapon.

You call me a traitor, Houston thought, *but you have been framing innocent Controllers, putting them into the hands of the PD Police.*

That's a lie! the reply came hotly. *We would never betray another telepath to the stupid Normals! If a telepath were so bullheaded as to get in our way, we'd dispose of him. But it would be Controller justice; we wouldn't turn him over to animals!*

In one blazing moment, Houston realized that the Controller was telling the truth!

No mental communication can be expressed properly in words. In, behind, and around each statement, other, dimmer nuances of thought gleam through. Each thought tells the receiver much more than can be put down in crude verbal symbols.

Thus, Houston already knew that Lasser, Sager, and Pederson were the three top men in a world-wide clique of megalomaniac Controllers. This was the top of the madmen's organization; these three were the *creme de la creme* of the Normal human's real enemies.

He knew that there were twelve others scattered over Earth, and he knew where and who they were. That brief exchange had brought all the information into Houston's own mind as it leaked from the minds of the others. He knew it without thinking about how he knew it.

And they were *not* the ones who had been turning the sane Controllers over to the Psychodeviant Police!

Then who was? And why?

Houston was right back where he had started.

But that brief instant of confusion was Houston's downfall. Sager instantly realized that he had delivered, inadvertently, a telling blow to Houston's mind.

Physically, Houston had been propelling himself toward the open door. At the instant of the revelation, he had been part way through it. And at that moment, Sager acted.

He slammed all his weight violently against his side of the door, knocking Houston off balance as the door swung and struck him. He went down, and Sager was on top of him before he struck the floor.

It was the weirdest battle ever fought, but its true worth could only have been detected by another telepath. It was intense and brutal.

The men fought both physically and mentally. They struggled for possession of the stun gun, at the same time hurling emotion-charged shafts of mental energy at each other's brains.

The struggle lasted less than a minute. Somehow, Sager managed to get one hand on the gun, twisting it. Houston, trying to keep it out of Sager's hand, jerked it up between them.

It coughed once, sending a beam of supersonic energy into the bodies of both men.

The effect was the same as if they had both been crowned with baseball bats.

Little pinpoints of light against a sea of darkness.

I'm cold, Houston thought. *And I'm sick.*

He couldn't tell whether his eyes were open or closed—and he didn't much care.

He tried to move his arms and legs, found he couldn't, and gave it up.

He blinked.

My eyes must be open, he thought, *if I can blink.*

Well, then, if his eyes were open, why couldn't he see anything? All he could see were the little pinpoints of light against a background of utter blackness.

Like stars, he thought.

Stars? STARS!

With a sudden rush, total awareness came back to him, and he realized with awful clarity where he was.

He was chained, spread-eagled, on an asteroid in the Penal Cluster, nearly a hundred million miles from Earth.

It was easy to piece together what had happened. He dimly remembered that he had started to wake up once before. It was a vague, confused recollection, but he knew what had taken place.

The PD Police, coming in response to his call, had found all four men unconscious from the effects of the stun beam. Naturally, all of them had been taken into custody; the PD Police had to find out which one of the men was the Controller and which the controlled. That could easily be tested by waiting until they began to wake up; the resulting mental disturbances would easily identify the telepath.

Houston could imagine the consternation that must have resulted when the PD men found that all three suspects—*and* their brother officer—were Controllers.

And now here he was—tried, convicted, and sentenced while he was unconscious—doomed to spend the rest of his life chained to a rock floating in space.

A sudden chill of terror came over him. Why wasn't he asleep? Why wasn't he under hibernene?

It's their way of being funny, came a bitter thought. *We're supposed to be under hibernene, but we're left to die, instead.*

For a moment, Houston did not realize that the thought was not his own, so well did it reflect his own bitterness. It was bad enough to have to live out one's life under the influence of the hibernation drug, but it was infinitely worse to be conscious. Under hibernene, he would have known nothing; his sleeping mind in his comatose body would never have realized what had happened to him. But this way, he would remain fully awake while his body used up the air too fast and his stomach became twisted with hunger pangs which no amount of intravenous feeding could quell. Oh, he'd live, all right—for a few months—but it would be absolute hell while he lasted. Insanity and catatonia would come long before death.

That's a nasty thought; I wish you hadn't brought it up.

That wasn't his own thought! There was someone else out here!

Hell, yes, my friend; we're all out here.

"Where are you?" Houston asked aloud, just to hear his own voice. He knew the other couldn't hear the words which echoed so hollowly inside the bubble of the spacesuit helmet, but the thought behind them would carry.

"You mean with relation to yourself?" came the answer. "I don't know. I can see several rocks around me, but I can't tell which one you're on."

Houston could tell now that the other person was talking aloud, too. So great was the illusion carried to his own brain that it almost seemed as though he could hear the voice with his ears.

"Then there are others around us?" Houston asked.

"Sure. There were three of us: a Hawaiian named Jerry Matsukuo; a girl from Bombay, Sonali Siddhartha; and myself, Juan Pedro de Cadiz. Jerry and Sonali are taking a little nap. You're the first of your group to wake up."

"My group?"

"Certainly, my friend. There are five of you; the other four must still be unconscious."

Four? That would be Lasser, Sager, Pederson, and—*and Dorrine!*

Juan Pedro de Cadiz picked up the whole thought-process easily.

"The girl—I'm sorry," he said. "But the other three—of us all, I think, they deserve this."

"Juan!" came another thought-voice. "Have our newcomers awakened?"

"Just one of them, my sweet," replied the Spaniard. "Sonali, may I present Mr. David Houston. Mr. Houston, the lovely Sonali Siddhartha."

"Juano has a habit of jumping to conclusions, David," said the girl. "He's never even seen me, and I'm sure that after three weeks of being locked in this prison whatever beauty I may have had has disappeared."

"Your thoughts are beautiful, Sonali," said Juan Pedro, "and with us, that is all that counts."

"It is written," said a third voice, "that he who disturbs the slumber of his betters will wake somebody up. You people are giving me dreams, with your ceaseless mental chatter."

"Ah!" the Spaniard said. "Mr. Matsukuo, may I—"

"I heard, Romeo, I heard," said the Hawaiian. "An ex-cop, eh? I wonder if I like you? I'll take a few thousand years to think it over; in the meantime, you may treat me as a friend."

"I'll try to live down my reputation," said Houston.

It was an odd feeling. Physically, he was alone. Around him, he could see nothing but the blackness of space and the glitter of the stars. He knew that the sun must be shining on the back of his own personal asteroid, but he couldn't see it. As far as his body was concerned, there was nothing else in the universe but a chunk of pitted rock and a set of chains.

But mentally, he felt snug and warm, safe in the security of good friends. He felt—

"David! David! Help me! Oh, David, David, David!"

It was Dorrine, coming up from her slumber. Like a crashing blare of static across the neural band, her wakening mind burst into sudden telepathic activity.

Gently, Houston sent out his thoughts, soothing her mind as he had soothed Harris's mind weeks before. And he noticed, as he did it, that the other three were with him, helping. By the time Dorrine was fully awake, she was no longer frightened or panicky.

"You're wonderful people," she thought simply, after several minutes.

"To one so beautiful, how else could we be?" asked Juan Pedro.

"Ignore him, Dorrine," said Sonali, "he tells me the same thing."

"But not in the same way, *amiga*!" the Spaniard protested. "Not in the same way. The beauty of your mind, Sonali, is like the beauty of a mountain lake, cool and serene; the beauty of Dorrine is like the beauty of the sun—warm, fiery, and brilliant."

"By my beard!" snorted Matsukuo. "Such blather!"

"I'll be willing to wager my beautiful *hacienda* in the lovely countryside of Aragon against your miserable palm-leaf *nipi* shack on Oahu that you have no beard," said Juan Pedro.

"Hah!" said Matsukuo; "that's all I need now—Castles in Spain."

It was suddenly dizzying for Houston. Here were five people, doomed to slow, painful death, talking as though there were nothing to worry about. Within minutes, each had learned to know the others almost perfectly.

It was more than just the words each used. Talking aloud helped focus the thoughts more, but at the same time, thousands of little, personal, fringe ideas were present with the main idea transmitted in words. Houston had talked telepathically to Dorrine hundreds of times, but never before had so much fine detail come through.

Why? Was there something different about space that made mental communication so much more complete?

"No, not that, I think," said Matsukuo. "I believe it is because we have lost our fear—not of death; we still fear death—but of betrayal."

That was it. They knew they were going to die, and soon. They had already been sentenced; nothing further could frighten them. Always before, on Earth, they had kept their thoughts to themselves, fearing to broadcast too much, lest the Normals find them out. The little, personal things that made a human being a living personality were kept hidden behind heavy mental walls. The suppression worked subconsciously, even when they actually wanted to communicate with another Controller.

But out here, there was nothing to fear on that score. Why should they, who were already facing death, be afraid of anything now?

So they opened up—wide. And they knew each other as no group of human beings had ever known each other. Every human being has little faults and foibles that he may be ashamed of, that he wants to keep hidden from others. But such things no longer mattered out here, where they had nothing but imminent death and the emptiness of space—and each other.

Physically, they were miserable. To be chained in one position, with very little room to move around, for three weeks, as Sonali had been, was torture. Sonali had been there longer than the others—for three days, there had been no one but herself out there in the loneliness of space.

But now, even physical discomfort meant little; it was easy to forget the body when the mind was free.

"What of the others?" Dorrine asked. "Where are the ones who were sentenced before us?"

Houston thought of Robert Harris. What had happened to the young Englishman?

"Space is big," said Juan Pedro. "Perhaps they are too far away for our thoughts to reach them—or perhaps they are already dead."

"Let's not talk of death." Sonali Siddhartha's thought was soft. "We have so many things to do."

"We will have a language session," said Juan Pedro. "*Si?*"

Matsukuo chuckled. "Good! Houston, until you've tried to learn Spanish, Hindustani, Arabic, Japanese, and French all at once, you don't know what a language session is. We—"

The Hawaiian's thought was suddenly broken off by a shrieking burst of mental static.

The effect was similar to someone dropping a handful of broken glass into an electric meat grinder right in the middle of a Bach cantata.

It was Sager, coming out of his coma.

Almost automatically, the five contacted his mind to relax him as he awoke. They touched his mind—and were repelled!

Stay out of my mind!

With almost savage fury, the still half-conscious Sager hurled thoughts of hatred and fear at the five minds who had tried to help him. They recoiled from the burst of insane emotion.

"Leave him alone," Houston thought sharply. "He's a tough fighter."

At first, Sager was terrified when he learned what had happened to him. Then the terror was mixed with a boiling, seething hatred. A hatred of the Normals who had done this to him, and an even more terrible hatred for Houston, the "traitor."

The very emptiness of space itself seemed to vibrate with the surging violence of his hatred.

"I know," Houston told him, "you'd kill me if you could. But you can't, so forget it."

Not even the power of that hatred could touch Houston, protected as he was by the combined strength of the other four sane telepaths. He was comparatively safe.

Sager snarled like a trapped animal. "You're all insane! Look at you! The four of you, siding with a man who has betrayed us to the Normals! He—"

What Sager thought of Houston couldn't be put into words, and if it could no sane person would want to repeat the mad foulness in those words.

"This is unbearable!" Sonali thought softly.

"That's not a mind," said Dorrine, "it's a sewer."

"I suggest," said Matsukuo, "that we do a little probing. Let's find out what makes this thing tick."

"Stay out of my mind!" Sager screamed. "You have no right!"

"You seemed to think you had the right to probe into the helpless minds of Normals," said Juan Pedro coldly. "We should show you how it feels."

"But they're just animals!" Sager retorted. "I am a Controller!"

"You're a madman," said Matsukuo. "And we must find out what makes you mad."

Synchronizing perfectly, five minds began to probe at the walls that Sager had built up around his personality. And as they probed, Sager retreated behind ever thicker walls, howling in hatred and anguish.

On and on went the five, needling, pressing at every weak spot, trying to break him down. Outnumbered and overpowered, it seemed as though Sager had no chance.

But his insanity was stronger than they suspected. The barriers he built were harder, more opaque, and more impenetrable than any they had ever seen. The five pushed on, anyway, but their advance slowed tremendously.

Then, mentally, there was a sudden silence.

Sager? they thought.

No answer.

"That's finished it," said Houston. "He's retreated so far behind those mental barriers that he's cut himself off completely."

"He's not dead, is he?" Dorrine asked.

"Dead?" said Juan Pedro. "Not in the sense you mean. But I think he is catatonic now; he has lost all touch with the outside. He is as though he were still drugged; he is physically helpless, and mentally blanked out."

"There's one difference," Matsukuo said analytically. "And that is that, although he has cut himself off from us and from the rest of the universe, he is still conscious in some little, walled-in compartment of his mind. He has no one there but himself—and that, I think, is damned poor company."

They waited then. When Pederson awoke, they were ready for him. His hatred took a slightly different form from Sager's, but the effect was the same.

And so were the results when the five bore down on him.

Again they waited. Lasser was next.

At first, it looked as though Lasser would go the way of Sager and Pederson, ending up as a hopelessly insane catatonic. Like his cohorts before him, Lasser retreated under the full pressure of the thought-probes of the five, building stronger and stronger walls.

But, quite suddenly, all his defenses crumbled. The mental barriers went down, shattered and dissolving. Lasser's whole mind lay bare. Instead of fighting and hating, Lasser was begging, pleading for help.

Lasser was not basically insane. His mind was twisted and warped, but beneath the outer shell was a personality that had enough internal strength to be able to admit that it was wrong and ask for help instead of retreating into oblivion.

"This one—I think we can do something with," Matsukuo's thought whispered.

Eight bodies, uncomfortable and pain-wracked, floated in space, chained to tiny asteroids that drifted slowly in their orbits under the constant pull of the sun. Two of them contained minds that were locked irrevocably within prisons of their own building, sealed off forever from external stimuli, but their suffering was the greater for all that.

The other six, chained though their limbs might be, had minds that were free—free, even, of any but the most necessary of internal limitations.

Eight bodies, chained to eight lumps of pitted rock, spun endlessly in endless space.

And then the ship came.

The flare of its atomic rocket could be seen for over an hour before it reached the Penal Cluster. The six eyed it speculatively. Although only two of them were facing the proper direction to see it with their physical eyes, the impressions of those two were easily transmitted to the other four.

"Another load of captives," whispered Juan Pedro de Cadiz. "How many this time, I wonder?"

"How long have we been here?" asked Houston, not expecting any answer.

"Who knows?" It was Lasser. "What we need out here is a clock to tell us when we'll die."

"Our oxygen tanks are our clocks," said Sonali. "And they'll notify us when the time comes."

"I do believe you morbid-minded people are developing a sense of humor," said Matsukuo, "but I'm not sure I care for the style too much."

The flare of the rocket grew brighter as the decelerating ship approached the small cluster of rocks. At last the ship itself took form, shining in the eternal blaze of the sun. When the whiteness of the rocket blaze died suddenly, the ship was only a few dozen yards from Houston's own asteroid.

And then a mental voice came into the minds of the six prisoners.

"How do you feel, Controllers?"

Only Houston recognized that thought-pattern, but his recognition was transmitted instantly to the others.

"*Reinhardt!*"

Hermann Reinhardt, Division Chief of the Psychodeviant Police, the one man most hated and feared by Controllers, was himself a telepath!

"Naturally," said Reinhardt. "Someone had to take control of the situation. I was the only one who was in a position to do it."

His thoughts were neither hard nor cold; it was almost as if he were one of them—except for one thing. Only the words of his thoughts came through; there were none of the fringe thoughts that the six were used to in each other.

"That's true," thought Reinhardt. "You see, we have been at this a good deal longer than you." Then he directed his thoughts at members of the crew of the spaceship, but they could still be heard by the six prisoners. "All right, men, get those people off those rocks. We have to make room for another batch."

The airlock in the side of the ship opened, and a dozen spacesuited men leaped out. The propulsion units in their hands guided them toward the prison asteroids.

"Give them all anaesthetic except Sager and Pederson," Reinhardt ordered. "They won't need it." Then, with a note of apology, "I'm sorry we'll have to anaesthetize you, but you've been in one position so long that moving you will be rather painful. We have to get you to a hospital quickly."

The minds of the six prisoners were frantically pounding questions at the PD chief, but he gave them no answer. "No; wait until you're better."

The spacesuited rescuers went to the "back" of each asteroid and injected sleep-gas into the oxygen line that ran from the tank to the spacesuit of the prisoner.

Houston could smell the sweetish, pungent odor in his helmet. Just before he blacked out, he hurled one last accusing thought at Reinhardt.

"*You're* the one who's been framing Controllers!"

"Naturally, Houston," came the answer. "How else could I get you out here?"

Houston woke up in a hospital bed. He was weak and hungry, but he felt no pain. As he came up from unconsciousness, he felt a fully awake mind guiding him out of the darkness.

It was Reinhardt.

"You're a tough man, Houston," he said mentally. "The others won't wake up for a while yet."

He was sitting on a chair next to the bed, holding a smouldering cigarette in one hand. He looked strange, somehow, and it took Houston a moment to realize that there was a smile on that broad, normally expressionless face.

Houston focussed his eyes on the man's face. "I want an explanation, Reinhardt," he said aloud. "And it better be a damned good one."

"I give you free access to my mind," Reinhardt said. "See for yourself if my method wasn't the best one."

Houston probed. The explanation, if not the best, was better than any Houston could have thought of.

When the hatred of the normal-minded people of Earth had been turned against the Controllers because of the actions of a few megalomaniacs, it had become obvious that legal steps had to be taken to prevent mob violence.

It had been Reinhardt himself who had suggested the Penal method to the UN government. At first, he had simply thought of it as a method to keep the Controllers alive until he could think of something better. But when he had discovered, by accident, what a small group of Controllers, alone in space, could do, he had set up the present machinery.

As soon as a Controller was spotted, a careful frame-up was arranged. Then, when several had been found, they were arrested in quick succession and sent to the asteroids.

Always and invariably, they had done what Houston's group had done—the sane or potentially sane ones had improved themselves tremendously, while the megalomaniacs had lapsed into catatonia.

"Why couldn't it be done on Earth?" Houston asked.

"We tried it," Reinhardt said. "It didn't work. Safe, on Earth, surrounded by Normals, a Controller still feels the hatred around him. He can't open his mind completely. Only the certain knowledge of impending death, and a complete freedom from the hatred of Normals can free the mind."

"And that's why you couldn't be told beforehand; if you knew you were going to be rescued, you wouldn't open up."

Houston nodded. It made sense. "Where are we now?" he asked.

"Antarctica," said Reinhardt. "We've built an outpost here—almost self-sufficient. When you're in better shape physically, I'll show you around."

"Do you mean that everyone who's been arrested is here, in Antarctica?"

Reinhardt laughed. "No, not by a long shot. Most of us are back out in civilization, searching for new, undiscovered Controllers, so that we can frame them. And, of course, some of us—the insane ones—have died. They will themselves to die when the going gets too tough."

"Searching for recruits? Then the Group that Dorrine was working for was—"

Reinhardt shook his head. "No. They were going about it the wrong way, just as you thought. We picked up the whole lot of them last week; they're occupying the asteroids now."

"What do you do with the insane catatonics?"

"Put them under hibernene and keep them alive. We hope, someday, to figure out a method of restoring their sanity. Until then, let them sleep."

Houston narrowed his eyes. "How long have you known I was a Controller, Reinhardt?"

The Prussian smiled. "Ever since you first tried to probe me. Fortunately, my training enabled me to put up a shield that you couldn't penetrate; I seemed like a Normal to you.

"I kept you on because I knew you'd be useful in cracking Lasser and his gang when the time came. No one else could have done what you did that night."

"Thanks," Houston said sincerely. "What's going to happen now? After I get well, I mean."

"You'll do what the others have done. A little plastic surgery to change your face a trifle, a little record-juggling to give you a new identity, and you'll be ready to go back to work for the PD Police.

"If anyone recognizes you, it's easy to take over their minds just long enough to make them forget. We allow that much Controlling."

"And then what?" Houston wanted to know. "What happens in the long run?"

"In a way," said Reinhardt, "your friend Sager was right. The Controllers will eventually become the rulers of Earth. But not by force or trickery. We must just bide our time. More and more of us are being born all the time; the Normals are becoming fewer and fewer. Within a century, we will outnumber them—we will be the Normals, not they.

"But they'll never know what's going on. The last Normal will die without ever knowing that he is in a world of telepaths.

"By the time that comes about, we'll no longer need the Penal Cluster, since Controllers will be born into a world where there is no fear of non-telepaths."

"I wonder," Houston mused, "I wonder how this ability came about. Why is the human race acquiring telepathy so suddenly?"

Reinhardt shrugged. "I can give you many explanations—atomic radiation, cosmic rays, natural evolution. But none of them really explains it. They just make it easier to live with.

"I think something similar must have happened a few hundred thousand years ago, when Cro-Magnon man, our own ancestors, first developed true intelligence instead of the pseudo-intelligence, the highly developed instincts, of the Neanderthals and other para-men.

"Within a relatively short time, the para-men had died out, leaving the Cro-Magnon, with his true intelligence, to rule Earth."

Reinhardt stood up. "Why is it happening? We don't know. Maybe we never will know, any more than we know why Man developed intelligence." He shrugged. "Perhaps the only explanation we'll ever have is to call it the Will of God and let it go at that."

"Maybe that's the best explanation, after all," Houston said.

"Perhaps. Who knows?" Reinhardt crushed his cigarette out in a tray. "I'll go now, and let you get some rest. And don't worry; I'll have you notified as soon as Dorrine starts to come out of it."

"Thanks—Chief," Houston said as Reinhardt left the room.

David Houston lay back in his bed and closed his eyes.

For the first time in his life, he felt completely at peace—with himself, and with the Universe.

THE END

Printed in Great Britain
by Amazon